INVITATION TO MAGIC

Stile stared down at the amulet. Belief in magic! Yet the fellow seemed sensible in other respects. Maybe it was a joke, an initiation rite to see what foolishness newcomers could be talked into.

He shook his head. "All right, I'll play the game—once. Amulet, I invoke you." And he put the chain over his head.

Suddenly, he was strangling. The chain was constricting, cutting off his wind and blood. The amulet seemed to be expanding, its demon figure holding the ends of the chain in miniature hands, grinning evilly. Stile ducked his chin down against his neck and tightened his muscles. He grabbed the grinning demon by its two little arms to haul them apart.

But still the demon grew, and its strength increased in proportion. It drew its arms together, constricting the loop about Stile's neck.

The demon had become a living creature, swelling horrendously as it fought. Now it was half the size of Stile and fiendishly strong. Stile felt his consciousness going. And the demon was still growing . . .

By Piers Anthony

Published by Ballantine Books:

THE MAGIC OF XANTH

A Spell For Chameleon

The Source Of Magic

Castle Roogna

Centaur Aisle

Ogre, Ogre

Night Mare

Dragon On a Pedestal

Crewel Lye: Caustic Yarn

Golem in the Gears

THE APPRENTICE ADEPT

Book One: Split Infinity

Book Two: Blue Adept

Book Three: Juxtaposition

INCARNATIONS OF IMMORTALITY

On a Pale Horse

Bearing an Hourglass

With a Tangled Skein

Split Infinity

Piers Anthony

A Del Rey Book

BALLANTINE BOOKS • NEW YORK

A Del Rey Book
Published by Ballantine Books

Library of Congress Catalog Card Number: 79-20282

ISBN 0-345-33600-3

Manufactured in the United States of America

First Hard Cover Edition: May 1981
Paperback First Edition: April 1982
Thirteenth Printing: December 1985

Cover illustration by Rowena Morrill

Map by Chris Barbieri

TABLE OF CONTENTS

WHITE MOUNTAINS
MEAND
YELLOW DEMESNES
LAKE
ORACLE
SWA
BLACK DEMESNES
CURTAIN
PHAZE
PURPLE MOUNTA

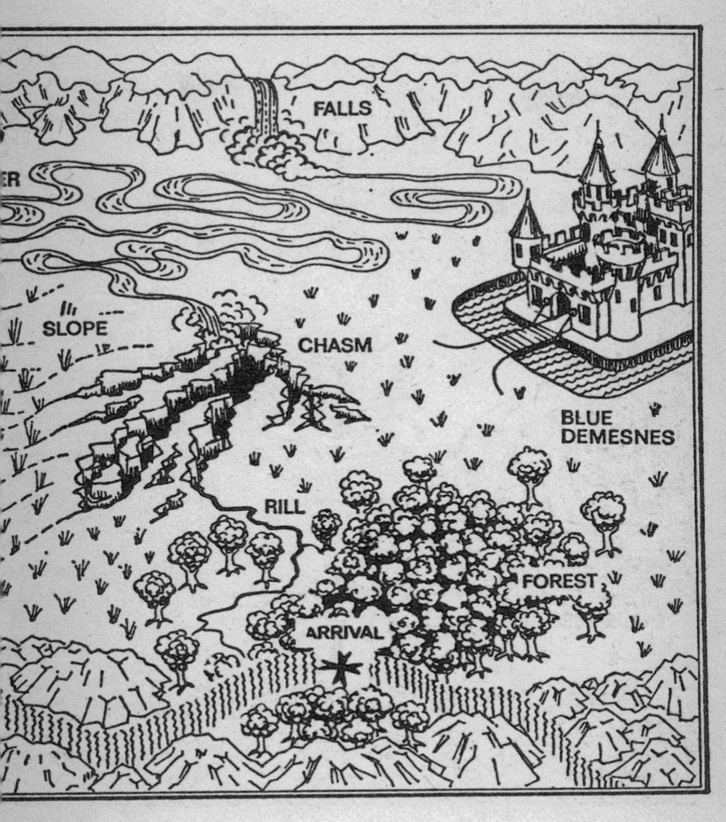

FALLS
SLOPE
CHASM
BLUE
DEMESNES
RILL
FOREST
ARRIVAL

CHAPTER 1

Slide

He walked with the assurance of stature, and most others deferred to him subtly. When he moved in a given direction, the way before him conveniently opened, by seeming coincidence; when he made eye contact, the other head nodded in a token bow. He was a serf, like all of them, naked and with no physical badge of status; indeed, it would have been the depth of bad taste to accord him any overt recognition. Yet he was a giant, here. His name was Stile.

Stile stood one point five meters tall and weighed fifty kilograms. In prior parlance he would have stood four feet, eleven inches tall and weighed a scant hundredweight or eight stone; or stood a scant fifteen hands and weighed a hundred and ten pounds. His male associates towered above him by up to half a meter and outweighed him by twenty-five kilos.

He was fit, but not extraordinarily muscled. Personable without being handsome. He did not hail his friends heartily, for there were few he called friend, and he was diffident about approaches. Yet there was enormous drive in him that manifested in lieu of personal warmth.

He walked about the Grid-hall of the Game-annex, his favorite place; beyond this region he reverted to the nonentity that others perceived. He sought competition of his own level, but at this hour there was none. Pairs of people stood in the cubicles that formed the convoluted perimeter of the hall, and a throng milled in the center, making contacts. A cool, gentle, mildly flower-scented draft wafted down from the vents in the ceiling, and the image of the sun cast its light on the floor, making its own game of shadows.

Stile paused at the fringe of the crowd, disliking this forced mixing. It was better when someone challenged him.

A young woman rose from one of the seats. She was nude, of course, but worthy of a second glance because of the perfection of her body. Stile averted his gaze, affecting not to be aware of her; he was especially shy with girls.

A tall youth intercepted the woman. "Game, lass?" How easy he made it seem!

She dismissed him with a curt downward flip of one hand and continued on toward Stile. A child signaled her: "Game, miss?" The woman smiled, but again negated, more gently. Stile smiled too, privately; evidently she did not recognize the child, but he did: Pollum, Rung Two on the Nines ladder. Not in Stile's own class, yet, but nevertheless a formidable player. Had the woman accepted the challenge, she would probably have been tromped.

There was no doubt she recognized Stile, though. His eyes continued to review the crowd, but his attention was on the woman. She was of average height—several centimeters taller than he—but of more than average proportions. Her breasts were full and perfect, unsagging, shifting eloquently with her easy motion, and her legs were long and smooth. In other realms men assumed that the ideal woman was a naked one, but often this was not the case; too many women suffered in the absence of mechanical supports for portions of their anatomy. This one, approaching him, was the type who really could survive the absence of clothing without loss of form.

She arrived at last. "Stile," she murmured.

He turned as if surprised, nodding. Her face was so lovely it startled him. Her eyes were large and green, her hair light brown and light-bleached in strands that expanded about her neck. There was a lot of art in the supposedly natural falling of women's hair. Her features were even and possessed the particular properties and proportions that appealed to him, though he could not define precisely what these were. His shyness loomed up inside him, so that he did not trust himself to speak.

"I am Sheen," she said. "I would like to challenge you to a Game."

She could not be a top player. Stile knew every ranking player on every age-ladder by sight and style, and she was on no ladder. Therefore she was a dilettante, an occasional participant, possibly of some skill in selected modes but in no way a serious competitor. Her body was too lush for most physical sports; the top females in track, ball games and swimming were small-breasted, lean-fleshed, and lanky, and this in no way described Sheen. Therefore he would have no physical competition here.

Yet she was beautiful, and he was unable to speak. So he nodded acquiescence. She took his arm in an easy gesture of familiarity that startled him. Stile had known women, of course; they came to him seeking the notoriety of his company, and the known fact of his hesitancy lent them compensating courage. But this one was so pretty she hardly needed to seek male company; it would seek her. She was making it look as if he had sought and won her. Perhaps he had, unknowingly: his prowess in the Game could have impressed her enough from afar to bring her to him. Yet this was not the type of conquest he preferred; such women were equally avid for Game-skilled teeners and grayheads.

They found an unoccupied cubicle. It had a column in the center, inset with panels on opposite sides. Stile went to one side, Sheen on the other, and as their weights came on the marked ovals to the floor before each panel, the panels lighted. The column was low, so Stile could see Sheen's face across from him; she was smiling at him.

Embarrassed by this open show of camaraderie, Stile looked down at his panel. He hardly needed to; he knew exactly what it showed. Across the top were four categories: PHYSICAL—MENTAL—CHANCE—ART, and down the left side were four more: NAKED—TOOL—MACHINE—ANIMAL. For shorthand convenience they were also lettered and numbered: 1—2—3—4 across the top, A—B—C—D down the side. The numbers were highlighted: the Grid had given him that set of choices, randomly.

THE GAME: PRIMARY GRID

	1. PHYSICAL	2. MENTAL	3. CHANCE	4. ART
A. NAKED				
B. TOOL				
C. MACHINE				
D. ANIMAL				

Stile studied Sheen's face. Now that she was in the Game, his opponent, his diffidence diminished. He felt the mild tightening of his skin, elevation of heartbeat, clarity of mind and mild distress of bowel that presaged the tension and effort of competition. For some people such effects became so strong it ruined them as competitors, but for him it was a great feeling, that drew him back compulsively. He lived for the Game!

Even when his opponent was a pretty girl whose pert breasts peeked at him just above the column. What was passing through her mind? Did she really think she could beat him, or was she just out for the experience? Had she approached him on a dare, or was she a groupie merely out for a date? If she were trying to win, she would want to choose ART, possibly MENTAL, and would certainly avoid PHYSICAL. If she were on a dare she would go for CHANCE, as that would require little performance on her part. If she wanted experience, anything would do. If she were a groupie, she would want PHYSICAL.

Of course she could not choose among these; *he* had the choice. But his choice would be governed in part by his judgment of her intent and ability. He had to think, as it were, with her mind, so that he could select what she least desired and obtain the advantage.

Now he considered her likely choice, in the series she did control. A true competitor would go for NAKED, for there was the essence of it: unassisted personal prowess. One wanting experience could go for anything, again depending on the type of experience desired. A dare would probably go for NAKED also; that choice would be part of the dare. A groupie would certainly go for NAKED. So that was her most likely choice.

Well, he would call her bluff. He touched PHYSICAL, sliding his hand across the panel so she couldn't tell his choice by the motion of his arm.

Her choice had already been made, as anticipated. They were in 1A, PHYSICAL/NAKED.

The second grid appeared. Now the categories across the top were 1. SEPARATE—2. INTERACTIVE—3. COMBAT—4. COOPERATIVE, and down the side were A. FLAT SURFACE—B. VARIABLE SURFACE—C. DISCONTINUITY—D. LIQUID. The letters were highlighted; he had to choose from the down column this time. He didn't feel like swimming or swinging from bars with her, though there could be intriguing aspects to each, so the last two were out. He was an excellent long-distance runner, but doubted Sheen would go for that sort of thing, which eliminated the flat surface. So he selected B, the variable surface.

She chose 1. SEPARATE: no groupie after all! So they would be in a race of some sort, not physically touching or directly interacting, though there were limited exceptions. Good enough. He would find out what she was made of.

Now the panel displayed a listing of variable surfaces. Stile glanced again at Sheen. She shrugged, so he picked the first: MAZE PATH. As he touched it, the description appeared in the first box of a nine-square grid.

She chose the second: GLASS MOUNTAIN. It appeared in the second square.

He placed DUST SLIDE in the third square. Then they continued with CROSS COUNTRY, TIGHTROPE, SAND DUNES, GREASED HILLS, SNOW BANK, and LIMESTONE CLIFF. The tertiary grid was complete.

Now he had to choose one of the vertical columns, and she had the horizontal rows. He selected the third, she the first, and their game was there: DUST SLIDE.

"Do you concede?" he asked her, pressing the appropriate query button so that the machine would know. She had fifteen seconds to negate, or forfeit the game.

Her negation was prompt. "I do not."

"Draw?"

"No."

He had hardly expected her to do either. Concession occurred when one party had such an obvious advantage that there was no point in playing, as when the game was chess and one player was a grandmaster while the other hadn't yet learned the moves. Or when it was weight lifting, with one party a child and the other a muscle builder. The dust slide was a harmless entertainment, fun to do even without the competitive element; no one would concede it except perhaps one who had a phobia about falling—and such a person would never have gotten into this category of game.

And so her reaction was odd. She should have laughed at his facetious offers. Instead she had taken them seriously. That suggested she was more nervous about this encounter than she seemed.

Yet this was no Tourney match! If she were a complete duffer she could have accepted the forfeit and been free. Or she could have agreed to the draw, and been able to tell her girlish friends how she had tied with the notorious Stile. So it seemed she was out neither for notoriety nor a dare, and he had already determined she was not a groupie. She really did want to compete—yet it was too much to hope that she had any real proficiency as a player.

They vacated the booth after picking up the gametags extruded from slots. No one was admitted solo to any subgame; all had to play the grid first, and report in pairs to the site of decision. That prevented uncommitted people from cluttering the premises or interfering with legitimate contests. Of course children could and did entertain themselves by indulging in mock contests, just for the pleasure of the facilities; to a child, the Game-annex was a huge amusement park. But in so doing, they tended to get hooked on the Game itself, increasingly as they aged, until at last they were thoroughgoing addicts. That had been the way with Stile himself.

The Dust Slide was in another dome, so they took the tube transport. The vehicle door irised open at their approach, admitting them to its cosy interior. Several other serfs were already in it: three middle-aged men who eyed Sheen with open appreciation, and a child whose eye lit with recognition. "You're the jockey!"

Stile nodded. He had no trouble relating to children. He was hardly larger than the boy.

"You won all the races!" the lad continued.

"I had good horses," Stile explained.

"Yeah," the child agreed, satisfied.

Now the three other passengers turned their attention to Stile, beginning to surmise that he might be as interesting as the girl. But the vehicle stopped, its door opened, and they all stepped out into the new dome. In moments Stile and Sheen had lost the other travelers and were homing in on the Dust Slide, their tickets ready.

The Slide's desk-secretary flashed Stile a smile as she validated the tickets. He smiled back, though he knew this was foolish; she was a robot. Her face, arms and upper torso were perfectly humanoid, with shape, color and texture no ordinary person could have told from a living woman, but her perfectly humanoid body terminated at the edge of her desk. She *was* the desk, possessing no legs at all. It was as if some celestial artisan had been carving her from a block of metal, causing her to animate as he progressed—then left the job unfinished at the halfway point. Stile felt a certain obscure sympathy for her; did she have true consciousness, in that upper half? Did she long for a completely humanoid body—or for a complete desk body? How did it feel to be a half-thing?

She handed back his ticket, validated. Stile closed his fingers about her delicate hand. "When do you get off work, cutie?" he inquired with the lift of an eyebrow. He was not shy around machines, of course.

She had been programmed for this. "Ssh. My boyfriend's watching." She used her free hand to indicate the robot next to her: a desk with a set of male legs protruding, terminating at the inverted waist. They demonstrated the manner the protective shorts should be worn for the Slide. They were extremely robust legs, and the crotch region was powerfully masculine.

Stile glanced down at himself, chagrined. "Oh, I can't compete with him. My legs are barely long enough to reach the ground." A bygone Earth author, Mark Twain, had set up that remark, and Stile found it useful on occasion. He accepted Sheen's arm again and they continued on to the Slide.

He thought Sheen might remark on the way he seemed to get along with machines, but she seemed oblivious. Ah, well.

The Slide was a convoluted mountain of channels looping and diverging and merging. Dust flowed in them—sanitary, nonirritating, noncarcinogenic, neutral particles of translucent plastic, becoming virtually liquid in the aggregate, and quite slippery. The whole was dramatic, suggesting frothing torrents of water in sluices, or rivulets of snow in an avalanche.

They donned the skin-shorts and filter masks required for protection on the Slide. The dust was harmless, but it tended to work its way into any available crevices, and the human body had a number. This was one thing Stile did not like about this particular subgame: the clothing. Only Citizens wore clothing, in the normal course, and it was uncouth for any serf to wear anything not strictly functional. More than uncouth: it could be grounds for summary termination of tenure at Planet Proton. Such Slide-shorts were functional, in these dusty environs; still, he felt uncomfortable. Their constriction and location tended to stir him sexually, and that was awkward in the company of a creature like Sheen.

Sheen seemed to feel no such concern. Perhaps she was aware that the partial concealment of the shorts attracted attention to those parts they concealed, enhancing her sex appeal. Stile, like many serfs, found a certain illicit lure in clothing, especially clothing on the distaff sex; it represented so much that serfs could only dream of. He had to keep his eyes averted, lest he embarrass himself.

They took the lift to the Slide apex. Here at the top they were near the curving dome that held in air and heat; through its shimmer Stile could see the bleak landscape of Proton, ungraced by any vegetation. The hostile atmosphere was obscured in the distance by clouds of smog.

The Slide itself was a considerable contrast. From this height six channels coursed out and down, each half filled with flowing dust. Colored lights shone up through it all, for the channels too were translucent. They turned now red, now blue-gray and now yellow as the beams moved. The tangle of paths formed a flower-like pattern, supremely beautiful. If Stile found the clothing physically and emotionally awkward, he was compensated by the view from this vantage, and always stood for a moment in minor awe.

For any given channel the colors seemed random, but for the arrangement as a whole they shaped in shifting contours roses, lilies, tulips, violets and gardenias. Air jets emitted corresponding perfumes when applicable. An artist had designed this layout, and Stile admired the handiwork. He had been here many times before, yet the novelty had not worn off.

Sheen did not seem to notice. "On your mark," she said, setting the random starter. The device could pop instantly or take two minutes. This time it split the difference. The channel barriers dropped low, and Sheen leaped for the chute nearest her.

Stile, surprised by her facility, leaped after her. They accelerated, shooting down feet first around a broad bright curve of green, then into the first white vertical loop. Up and over, slowing dizzily at the top, upside down, then regaining velocity in the downshoot.

Sheen was moving well. Her body had a natural rondure that shaped itself well to the contour of the chute. The dust piled up behind her, shoving her forward. Stile, following in the same channel, tried to intercept enough dust to cut off her supply and ground her, but she had too big a lead and was making too good use of her resources.

Well, there were other ways. This channel passed through a partial-gravity rise that was slow. Another channel crossed, going into a corkscrew. Stile took this detour, zipped through the screw, and shot out ahead of the girl.

She took another connection and got in behind him, cutting off *his* dust. This was the aspect of the Slide that was interactive: the competition for dust. Stile was grounded, his posterior scraping against the suddenly bare plastic of the chute. No dust, no progress!

He put his hand to the side, heaved, and flipped his body into the adjoining channel. This was a tricky maneuver, legitimate but not for amateurs. Here he had dust again, and resumed speed—but he had lost the momentum he had before. Sheen continued on in her channel, riding the piled dust, moving ahead of him—and now they were halfway down.

Stile realized that he had a real race on his hands. This girl was good!

He vaulted back into her channel, cutting off her dust again—but even as he did, she vaulted into his just-vacated channel, maintaining her lead. Apt move! Obviously she had raced here many times before, and knew the tricks, and had more agility under that sweet curvature of body than he had suspected. But now he had the better channel, and he was unmatchable in straight dust-riding; he moved ahead. She jumped across to cut him off, but he was already jumping into a third chute. Before she could follow him, the two diverged and he was safe.

They completed the race on separate channels. She had found a good one, and was gaining on him despite his careful management of dust. He finished barely ahead. They shot into the collection bin, one-two, to the applause of the other players who were watching. It had been a fine race, the kind that happened only once or twice on a given day.

Sheen got up and shook off the dust with a fascinating shimmy of her torso. "Can't win them all," she remarked, unperturbed.

She had made an excellent try, though! She had come closer than anyone in years. Stile watched her as she stripped off mask and shorts. She was stunningly beautiful—more so than before, because now he realized that her body was functional as well as shapely.

"You interest me," he told her. In this aftermath of a good game he was flushed with positive feeling, his shyness at a minimum.

Sheen smiled. "I hoped to."

"You almost beat me."

"I had to get your attention somehow."

Another player laughed. Stile had to laugh too. Sheen had proved herself, and now he wanted to know why. The mutual experience had broken the ice; the discovery of a new challenge completed his transition from diffidence to normal masculine imperative.

He didn't even have to invite her to come home with him. She was already on her way.

CHAPTER 2

Sheen

Sheen moved into his apartment as if it were her own. She punched the buttons of his console to order a complete light lunch of fruit salad, protein bread and blue wine.

"You evidently know about me," Stile said as they ate. "But I know nothing of you. Why did you—want to get my attention?"

"I am a fan of the Game. I could be good at it. But I have so little time—only three years tenure remaining—I need instruction. From the best. From you. So I can be good enough—"

"To enter the Tourney," Stile finished. "I have the same time remaining. But there are others you could have checked. I am only tenth on my ladder—"

"Because you don't want to have to enter the Tourney this year," she said. "You won't enter it until your last year of tenure, because all tenure ends when a serf enters the Tourney. But you could advance to Rung One on the Age-35 ladder any time you wished, and the top five places of each adult ladder are automatically entered in the—"

"Thank you for the information," Stile said with gentle irony.

She overlooked it. "So you keep yourself in the second five, from year to year, low enough to be safe in case several of the top rungers break or try to vacate, high enough to be able to make your move any time you want to. You are in fact the most proficient Gamesman of our generation—"

"This is an exaggeration. I'm a jockey, not a—"

"—and I want to learn from you. I offer—"

"I can see what you offer," Stile said, running his eyes over her body. He could do this now without embarrassment, because he had come to know her; his initial shyness was swinging to a complementary boldness. They had, after all, Gamed together. "Yet there is no way I could inculcate the breadth of skills required for serious competition, even if we had a century instead of a mere three years. Talent is inherent, and it has to be buttressed by constant application. I might be able to guide you to the fifth rung of your ladder—which one would that be?"

"Age 23 female."

"You're in luck. There are only three Tourney-caliber players on that ladder at present. With proper management it would be possible for a person of promise to take one of the remaining rungs. But though you gave me a good race on the Slide, I am not sure you have sufficient promise—and even if you qualified for the Tourney, your chances of progressing far in it would be vanishingly small. *My* chances are not good—which is why I'm still working hard at every opportunity to improve myself. Contrary to your opinion, there are half a dozen players better than I am, and another score of my general caliber. In any given year, four or five of them will enter the Tourney, while others rise in skills to renew the pool. That, combined with the vagaries of luck, gives me only one chance in ten to win. For you—"

"Oh, I have no illusions about winning!" she said. "But if I could make a high enough rank to obtain extension of tenure, if only a year or two—"

"It's a dream," he assured her. "The Citizens put such prizes out as bait, but only one person in thirty-two gains even a year that way."

"I would be completely grateful for that dream," she said, meeting his gaze.

Stile was tempted. He knew he would not have access to a more attractive woman, and she had indeed shown promise in the Game. That athletic ability that had enabled her so blithely and lithely to change chutes would benefit her in many other types of competition.

He could have a very pleasant two years, training her. Extremely pleasant.

That itself gave him caution. He had loved before, and lost, and it had taken years to recover completely —if he really had. *Tune,* he thought, with momentary nostalgia. There were ways in which Sheen resembled that former girl.

Still, what promise did he have beyond his remaining three years, anyway? All would be lost, once he left Proton. Oh, he would have a nice nest egg to establish galactic residence, and might even go to crowded Earth itself, but all he really wanted to do was remain on Proton. Since it was unlikely that he could do that, he might as well make these years count. She had mentioned that her own tenure was as short as his, which meant she would have to leave at the same time. That could be very interesting, if they had a firm relationship. "Tell me about yourself," he said.

"I was born five years before my parents' tenure ended," Sheen said, putting down her leaf of lettuce. She had eaten delicately and quite sparingly, as many slender women did. "I obtained a position with a Lady Citizen, first as errand girl, then as nurse. I was a fan of the Game as a child, and had good aptitude, but as my employer grew older she required more care, until—" She shrugged, and now with the pleasant tingle of the wine and the understanding they were coming to, he could appreciate the way her breasts moved with that gesture. Oh yes, it was a good offer she made—yet something nagged him. "I have not been to a Game for seven years," she continued, "though I have viewed it often on my employer's screens, and rehearsed strategies and techniques constantly in private. My employer had a private exercise gym her doctor recommended; she never used it, so I did, filling in for her. Last week she died, so I have been released on holiday pending settlement of her estate and the inventory her heir is taking. Her heir is female, and healthy, so I do not think the burden will be onerous."

It could have been quite a different matter, Stile reflected, with a young, healthy male heir. Serfs had no personal rights except termination of tenure in fit physical and mental condition, and no sane person would depart Proton even a day ahead of schedule. Serfs could serve without concern as concubines or studs for their employers—or for each other as private or public entertainment for their employers. Their bodies were the property of the Citizens. Only in privacy, without the intercession of a Citizen, did interpersonal relations between serfs become meaningful. As now.

"So you came to me," Stile said. "To trade your favors for my favor."

"Yes." There needed to be no hesitancy or shame to such acknowledgment. Since serfs had no monetary or property credit, and no power during their tenure, Game-status and sex were the chief instruments of barter.

"I am minded to try it out. Shall we say for a week, then reconsider? I might become tired of you."

Again there was no formal cause for affront; male-female interactions among serfs were necessarily shallow, though marriage was permitted and provided for. Stile had learned the hard way, long ago, not to expect permanence. Still, he expected a snappy retort to the effect that she would more likely grow tired of him first.

There was no such byplay. "As part of my rehearsal for the Game, I have studied the art of pleasing men," Sheen said. "I am willing to venture that week."

A fair answer. And yet, he wondered, would not an ordinary woman, even the most abused of serfs, have evinced some token ire at the callousness of his suggestion? He could have said, "We might not be right for each other." He had phrased it most bluntly, forcing a reaction. Sheen had not reacted; she was completely matter-of-fact. Again he was nagged. Was there some catch here?

"Do you have special interests?" Stile inquired. "Music?" He hadn't really wanted to ask that, but it had come out. He associated love with music, because of his prior experience.

"Yes, music," Sheen agreed.

His interest quickened. "What kind?"

She shrugged again. "Any kind."

"Vocal? Instrumental? Mechanical?"

Her brow furrowed. "Instrumental."

"What instrument do you play?"

She looked blank.

"Oh—you just listen," he said. "I play a number of instruments, preferring the woodwinds. All part of the Game. You will need to acquire skill in at least one instrument, or Game opponents will play you for a weakness there and have easy victories."

"Yes, I must learn," she agreed.

What would she have done if he had gone for ART instead of PHYSICAL in their match? With her prior choice of NAKED, the intersection would have put them in song, dance or story: the a capella performances. Perhaps she was a storyteller. Yet she did not seem to have the necessary imagination.

"Let's do it right," he said, rising from his meal. "I have a costume—" He touched a button and the costume fell from a wall vent into his hand. It was a filmy negligee.

Sheen smiled and accepted it. In the privacy of an apartment, clothing was permitted, so long as it was worn discreetly. If there should be a video call, or a visitor at his door, Sheen would have to hide or rip off the clothing lest she be caught by a third party in that state and be compromised. But that only added to the excitement of it, the special, titillating naughtiness of their liaison. It was, in an unvoiced way, the closest any serf could come to emulating any Citizen.

She donned the costume without shame and did a pirouette, causing the material to fling out about her legs. Stile found this indescribably erotic. He shut down the light, so that the material seemed opaque, and the effect intensified. Oh, what clothing did for the woman, creating shadows where ordinarily there were none, making mysteries where none had been before!

Yet again, something ticked a warning in Stile's mind. Sheen was lovely, yes—but where was her flush of delighted shame? Why hadn't she questioned his possession of this apparel? He had it on loan, and his employer knew about it and would in due course remember to reclaim it—but a person who did not know that, who was not aware of the liberalism of this particular employer with respect to his favored serfs, should be alarmed at his seeming hoarding of illicit clothing. Sheen had thought nothing of it.

They were technically within the law—but so was a man who thought treason without acting on it. Stile was an expert Gamesman, attuned to the nuances of human behavior, and there was something wrong with Sheen. But what was it? There was really nothing in her behavior that could not be accounted for by her years of semi-isolation while nursing her Citizen.

Well, perhaps it would come to him. Stile advanced on Sheen, and she met him gladly. None of this oh-please-don't-hurt-me-sir, catch-me-if-you-can drama. She was not after all very much taller than he, so he had to draw her down only marginally to kiss her. Her body was limber, pliable, and the feel of the gauze between their skins pitched him into a fever of desire. Not in years had he achieved such heat so soon.

She kissed him back, her lips firm and cool. Suddenly the little nagging observations clicked into a comprehensible whole, and he knew her for what she was. Stile's ardor began sliding into anger.

He bore her back to the couch-bed. She dropped onto it easily, as if this type of fall were commonplace for her. He sat beside her, running his hands along her thighs, still with that tantalizing fabric in place between them. He moved on to knead her breasts, doubly erotic behind the material. A nude woman in public was not arousing, but a clothed one in private . . .

His hands were relaxed, gentle—but his mind was tight with coalescing ire and apprehension. He was about to trigger a reaction that could be hazardous to his health.

"I would certainly never have been able to tell," he remarked.

Her eyes focused on him. "Tell what, Stile?"

He answered her with another question. "Who would want to send me a humanoid robot?"

She did not stiffen. "I wouldn't know."

"The information should be in your storage banks. I need a printout."

She showed no emotion. "How did you discover that I was a robot?"

"Give me that printout, and I'll give you my source of information."

"I am not permitted to expose my data."

"Then I shall have to report you to Game-control," Stile said evenly. "Robots are not permitted to compete against humans unless under direct guidance by the Game Computer. Are you a Game-machine?"

"No."

"Then I fear it will go hard with you. The record of our Game has been entered. If I file a complaint, you will be deprogrammed."

She looked at him, still lovely though he now knew her nature. "I wish you would not do that, Stile."

How strong was her programmed wish? What form would her objection take, when pressed? It was a popular fable that robots could not harm human beings, but Stile knew better. All robots of Proton were prohibited from harming Citizens, or acting contrary to Citizens' expressed intent, or acting in any manner that might conceivably be deleterious to the welfare of any Citizen —but there were no strictures about serfs. Normally robots did not bother people, but this was because robots simply did not care about people. If a serf interfered with a robot in the performance of its assignment, that man could get hurt.

Stile was now interfering with the robot Sheen. "Sheen," he said. "Short for Machine. Someone with a certain impish humor programmed you."

"I perceive no humor," she said.

"Naturally not. That was your first giveaway. When I proffered you a draw on the Slide, you should have laughed. It was a joke. You reacted without emotion."

"I am programmed for emotion. I am programmed for the stigmata of love."

The stigmata of love. A truly robotic definition! "Not the reality?"

"The reality too. There is no significant distinction. I am here to love you, if you will permit it."

So far she had shown no sign of violence. That was good; he was not at all sure he could escape her if she attacked him. Robots varied in physical abilities, as they did in intellectual ones; it depended on their intended use and the degree of technology applied. This one seemed to be of top-line sophistication; that could mean she imitated the human form and nature so perfectly she had no more strength than a real girl would have. But there was no guarantee. "I must have that printout."

"I will tell you my mission, if you will not expose my nature."

"I can not trust your word. You attempted to deceive me with your story about nursing a Citizen. Only the printout is sure."

"You are making it difficult. My mission is only to guard you from harm."

"I feel more threatened by your presence than protected. Why should I need guarding from harm?"

"I don't know. I must love you and guard you."

"Who sent you?"

"I do not know."

Stile touched his wall vid. "Game-control," he said.

"Don't do that!" Sheen cried.

"Cancel call," Stile said to the vid. Evidently violence was not in the offing, and he had leverage. This was like a Game. "The printout."

She dropped her gaze, and her head. Her lustrous hair fell about her shoulders, coursing over the material of the negligee. "Yes."

Suddenly he felt sorry for her. Was she really a machine? Now he had doubts. But of course the matter was subject to verification. "I have a terminal here," he said, touching another section of the wall. A cord came into his hand, with a multipronged plug at its end. Very few serfs were permitted such access directly—but he was one of the most privileged serfs on Proton, and would remain so as long as as he was circumspect and rode horses well. "Which one?" he asked.

She turned her face away from him. Her hand went to her right ear, clearing away a lock of hair and pressing against the lobe. Her ear slid forward, leaving the socket open.

Stile plugged in the cord. Current flowed. Immediately the printout sheets appeared from the wall slot, crammed with numbers, graphs and pattern-blocks. Though he was no computer specialist, Stile's Game training made him a fair hand at ballpark analysis of programs, and he had continuing experience doing analysis of the factors leading into given races. That was why his employer had arranged this: to enable Stile to be as good a jockey as he could be. That was extremely good, for he had a ready mind as well as a ready body.

He whistled as he studied the sheets. This was a dual-element brain, with mated digital and analog components, rather like the dual-yet-differing hemispheres of the human brain. The most sophisticated computer capable of being housed in a robot. It possessed intricate feedback circuits, enabling the machine to learn from experience and to reprogram aspects of itself, within its prime directive. It could improve its capacity as it progressed. In short, it was intelligent and conscious: machine's nearest approach to humanity.

Quickly Stile oriented on the key section: her origin and prime directive. A robot could lie, steal and kill without conscience, but it could not violate its prime directive. He took the relevant data and fed them back to the analyzer for a summary.

The gist was simple: NO RECORD OF ORIGIN. DIRECTIVE: GUARD STILE FROM HARM. SUBDIRECTIVE: LOVE STILE.

What she had told him was true. She did not know who had sent her, and she had only his safety in mind. Tempered by love, so that she would not protect him in some fashion that cost him more than it was worth. This was a necessary caution, with otherwise unfeeling robots. This machine really did care. He could have taken her word.

Stile unplugged the cord, and Sheen put her ear back into place with a certain tremor. Again she looked completely human. He had been unyielding before, when she opposed him; now he felt guilty. "I'm sorry," he said. "I had to know."

She did not meet his gaze. "You have raped me."

Stile realized it was true. He had taken her measure without her true consent; he had done it by duress, forcing the knowledge. There was even a physical analogy, plugging the rigid terminus of the cord into a private aperture, taking what had been hers alone. "I had to know," he repeated lamely. "I am a very privileged serf, but only a serf. Why should anyone send an expensive robot to guard a man who is not threatened? I could not afford to believe your story without verification, especially since your cover story was untrue."

"I am programmed to react exactly as a real girl would react!" she flared. "A real girl wouldn't claim to have been built in a machine shop, would she?"

"That's so . . ." he agreed. "But still—"

"The important part is my prime directive. Specifically, to be appealing to one man—you—and to love that man, and to do everything to help him. I was fashioned in the partial likeness of a woman you once knew, not close enough to be identifiable as such, but enough to make me attractive to your specific taste—"

"That succeeded," he said. "I liked you the moment I saw you, and didn't realize why."

"I came to offer you everything of which I am capable, and that is a good deal, including the allure of feminine mystery. I even donned this ridiculous shift, that no human woman would have. And you—you—"

"I destroyed that mystery," Stile finished. "Had I had any other way to be sure—"

"Oh, I suppose you couldn't help it. You're a man."

Stile glanced at her, startled again. Her face was still averted, her gaze downcast. "Are you, a robot, really being emotional?"

"I'm programmed to be!"

True. He moved around to look at her face. She

turned it away again. He put his hand to her chin to lift it.

"Get away from me!" she cried.

That was some programming! "Look, Sheen. I apologize. I—"

"Don't apologize to a robot! Only an idiot would converse with a machine."

"Correct," he agreed. "I acted stupidly, and now I want to make what amends are possible."

He tried again to see her face, and again she hid it. "Damn it, *look* at me!" he exclaimed. His emotion was high, flashing almost without warning into embarrassment, sorrow, or anger.

"I am here to serve; I must obey," she said, turning her eyes to him. They were bright, and her cheeks were moist. Humanoid robots could cry, of course; they could do almost anything people could do. This one had been programmed to react this way when hurt or affronted. He knew that, yet was oddly moved. She did indeed subtly resemble one he had loved. The accuracy with which she had been fashioned was a commentary on the appalling power available to the Citizens of this planet. Even the most private, subtle knowledge could be drawn from the computer registries at any time.

"You are here to guard me, not to serve me, Sheen."

"I can only guard you if I stay with you. Now that you know what I am—"

"Why are you being so negative? I have not sent you away."

"I was made to please you, to want to please you. So I can better serve my directive. Now I can not."

"Why not?"

"Why do you tease me? Do you think that programmed feelings are less binding than flesh ones? That the electrochemistry of the inanimate is less valid than that of the animate? That my illusion of consciousness is any less potent than your illusion of self-determination? I exist for one purpose, and you have prevented me from accomplishing it, and now I have no reason for existence. Why couldn't you have accepted me as I seemed to be? I would have become perfect at it, with experience. Then it would have been real."

"You have not answered my question."

"You have not answered mine!"

Stile did a rapid internal shifting of gears. This was the most femalish robot he had encountered! "Very well, Sheen. I answer your questions. Why do I tease you? Answer: I am not teasing you—but if I did, it would not be to hurt you. Do I think that your programmed feelings are less valid than my mortal ones? Answer: No, I must conclude that a feeling is a feeling, whatever its origin. Some of my own feelings are shortsighted, unreasonable and unworthy; they govern me just the same. Is your illusion of consciousness less valid than my illusion of free will? Answer: No. If you think you are conscious, you must be conscious, because that's what consciousness is. The feedback of self-awareness. I don't have much illusion about my free will. I am a serf, governed by the will of my employer. I have no doubt I am governed by a multitude of other things I seldom even notice, such as the force of gravity and my own genetic code and the dictates of society. Most of my freedom exists in my mind—which is where your consciousness does, too. Why couldn't I accept you as you seemed to be? Because I am a skilled Gamesman, not the best that ever was, but probably destined for recognition as one of the best of my generation. I succeed not by virtue of my midget body but by virtue of my mind. By questioning, by comprehending my own nature and that of all others I encounter. When I detect an anomaly, I must discover its reason. You are attractive, you are nice, you are the kind of girl I have held in my mind as the ideal, even to your size, for it would be too obvious for me to have a woman smaller than I am, and I don't like being obvious in this connection. You came to me for what seemed insufficient reason, you did not laugh as you should have, you did not react quite on key. You seemed to know about things, yet when I probed for depth I found it lacking. I probed as a matter of course; it is my nature. I asked about your music, and you expressed interest, but had no specifics. That sort of thing. This is typical of programmed artificial intelligence; even the best units can approach only one percent of the human capacity, weight for weight. A well-tuned robot in a controlled situation may seem as intelligent as a man, because of its specific and relevant and instantly accessible information; a man is less efficiently organized, with extraneous memories obscuring the relevant ones, and information accessible only when deviously keyed. But the robot's intellect is illusory, and it soon shows when those devious and unreasonable off-trails are explored. A mortal person's mind is like a wilderness, with a tremendous volume of decaying constructs and half-understood experience forming natural harbors for wild-animal effects. A robot is disciplined, civilized; it has no vast and largely wasted reservoir of the unconscious to draw from, no spongy half-forgotten backup impression. It knows what it knows, and is ignorant where it is ignorant, with a quite sharp demarcation between. Therefore a robot is not intuitive, which is the polite way of saying that it does not frequently reach down into the maelstrom of its garbage dump and draw out serendipitous insights. Your mind was more straightforward than mine, and that aroused my suspicion, and so I could not accept you at face value. I would not be the quality of player I am, were I given to such acceptances."

Sheen's eyes had widened. "You answered!"

Stile laughed. It had been quite an impromptu lecture! "Again I inquire: why not?"

"Because I am Sheen-machine. Another man might be satisfied with the construct, the perfect female form; that is one reason my kind exists. But you are rooted in reality, however tangled a wilderness you may perceive it to be. The same thing that caused you to fathom my nature will cause you to reject the illusion I proffer. You want a real live girl, and you know I am not, and can never be. You will not long want to waste your time talking to me as if I were worthwhile."

"You presume too much on my nature. My logic is

other than yours. I said you were limited; I did not say you were not worthwhile."

"You did not need to. It is typical of your nature that you are polite even to machines, as you were to the Dust Slide ticket taker. But that was brief, and public; you need no such byplay here in private. Now that I have seen you in action, discovering how much more there is to you than what the computer knows, I realize I was foolish to—"

"A foolish machine?"

"—suppose I could deceive you for any length of time. I deserved what you did to me."

"I am not sure you deserved it, Sheen. You were sent innocently to me, to my jungle, unrealistically programmed."

"Thank you," she said with a certain unmetallic irony. "I did assume you would take what was offered, if you desired it, and now I know that was simplistic. What am I to do now? I have nowhere to return, and do not wish to be prematurely junked. There are many years of use left in me before my parts wear appreciably."

"Why, you will stay with me, of course."

She looked blank. "This is humor? Should I laugh?"

"This is serious," he assured her.

"Without reason?"

"I am unreasonable, by your standards. But in this case I do have reason."

She made an almost visible, almost human connection. "To be your servant? You can require that of me, just as you forced me to submit to the printout. I am at your mercy. But I am programmed for a different relationship."

"Serf can't have servants. I want you for your purpose."

"Protection and romance? I am too logical to believe that. You are not the type to settle for a machine in either capacity." Yet she looked halfway hopeful. Stile knew her facial expressions were the product of the same craftsmanship as the rest of her; perhaps he was imagining the emotion he saw. Yet it moved him.

"You presume too much. Ultimately I must go with my own kind. But in the interim I am satisfied to play the Game—at least until I can discover what threat there is to my welfare that requires a humanoid robot for protection."

She nodded. "Yes, there is logic. I was to pose as your lady friend, thereby being close to you at all times, even during your sleep, guarding you from harm. If you pretend to accept me as such, I can to that extent fulfill my mission."

"Why should I pretend? I accept you as you are."

"Stop it!" she cried. "You have no idea what it is like to be a robot! To be made in the image of the ideal, yet doomed always to fall short—"

Now Stile felt brief anger. "Sheen, turn off your logic and listen." He sat beside her on the couch and took her hand. Her fingers trembled with an unmechanical disturbance. "I am a small man, smaller than almost anyone I know. All my life it has been the bane of my existence. As a child I was teased and excluded from many games because others did not believe I could perform. My deficiency was so obvious that the others often did not even realize they were hurting my feelings by omitting me. In adolescence it was worse; no girl cared to associate with a boy smaller than herself. In adult life it is more subtle, yet perhaps worst of all. Human beings place inordinate stress on physical height. Tall men are deemed to be the leaders, short men are the clowns. In reality, small people are generally healthier than large ones; they are better coordinated, they live longer. They eat less, waste less, require less space. I benefit from all these things; it is part of what makes me a master of the Game and a top jockey. But small people are not taken seriously. My opinion is not granted the same respect as that of a large man. When I encounter another person, and my level gaze meets his chin, he knows I am inferior, and so does everyone else, and it becomes difficult for me to doubt it myself."

"But you are not inferior!" Sheen protested.

"Neither are you! Does that knowledge help?"

She was silent. "We are not dealing with an objective thing," Stile continued. "Self-respect is subjective. It may be based on foolishness, but it is critical to a person's motivation. You said I had no idea what it meant to be doomed always to fall short. But I am literally shorter than you are. Do you understand?"

"No. You are human. You have proved yourself. It would be foolish to—"

"Foolish? Indubitably. But I would give all my status in the Game, perhaps my soul itself, for one quarter meter more height. To be able to stand before you and look *down* at you. You may be fashioned in my ideal of woman, but I am not fashioned in my ideal of man. You are a rational creature, beneath your superficial programming; under *my* programming I am an irrational animal."

She shifted her weight on the couch, but did not try to stand. Her body, under the gauze, was a marvel of allure. How patently her designer had crafted her to subvert Stile's reason, making him blind himself to the truth in his sheer desire to possess such a woman! On another day, that might have worked. Stile had almost been fooled. "Would you exchange your small human body," she asked, "for a large humanoid robot body?"

"No." He did not even need to consider.

"Then you do not fall short of me."

"This is the point I am making. I know what it is to be unfairly ridiculed or dismissed. I know what it is to be doomed to be less than the ideal, with no hope of improvement. Because the failure is, at least in part, *in* my ideal. I could have surgery to lengthen my body. But the wounds are no longer of the body. My body has proved itself. My soul has not."

"I have no soul at all."

"How do you know?"

Again she did not answer. "I know how you know," he said. "You know because you *know*. It is inherent in your philosophy. Just as I know I am inferior. Such knowledge is not subject to rational refutation. So I do understand your position. I understand the position of all the dispossessed. I empathize with all those who hunger for what they can not have. I long to help them, knowing no one can help them. I would trade everything I am or might be for greater physical height, knowing how crazy that desire is, knowing it would not bring me happiness or satisfaction. You would trade your logic and beauty for genuine flesh and blood and bone. Your machine invulnerability for human mortality. You are worse off than I; we both know that. Therefore I feel no competition in your presence, as I would were you human. A real girl like you would be above me; I would have to compete to prove myself, to bring her down, to make her less than my ideal, so that I could feel worthy of her. But with you—"

"You can accept me as I am—because I am a robot," Sheen said, seeming amazed. "Because I am less than you."

"Now I think we understand each other." Stile put his arm about her and brought her in for a kiss. "If you want me on that basis—"

She drew away. "You're sorry for me! You raped me and now you're trying to make me like it!"

He let her go. "Maybe I am. I don't really know all my motives. I won't hold you here if you don't want to stay. I'll leave you strictly alone if you do stay, and want it that way. I'll show you how to perfect your human role, so that others will not fathom your nature the way I did. I'll try to make it up to you—"

She stood. "I'd rather be junked." She crossed to the vid screen and touched the button. "Game-control, please."

Stile launched himself from the couch and almost leaped through the air to her. He caught her about the shoulder and bore her back. "Cancel call!" he yelled. Then they both fetched up against the opposite wall.

Sheen's eyes stared into his, wide. "You care," she said. "You really do."

Stile wrapped both arms about her and kissed her savagely.

"I almost believe you," she said, when speaking was possible.

"To hell with what you believe! You may not want me now, but I want you. I'll rape you literally if you make one move for that vid."

"No, you won't. It's not your way."

She was right. "Then I ask you not to turn yourself in," he said, releasing her again. "I—" He broke off, choking, trapped by a complex pressure of emotions.

"Your wilderness jungle—the wild beasts are coming from their lairs, attacking your reason," Sheen said.

"They are," he agreed ruefully. "I abused you with the printout. I'm sorry. I do believe in your consciousness, in your feeling. In your right to privacy and self-respect. I beg your forgiveness. Do what you want, but don't let my callousness ruin your—" He couldn't finish. He couldn't say "life" and couldn't find another word.

"Your callousness," she murmured, smiling. Then her brow furrowed. "Do you realize you are crying, Stile?"

He touched his cheek with one finger, and found it wet. "I did not realize. I suppose it is my turn."

"For the feelings of a machine," she said.

"Why the hell not?"

She put her arms around him. "I think I could love you, even unprogrammed. That's another illusion, of course."

"Of course."

They kissed again. It was the beginning.

CHAPTER 3

Race

In the morning, Stile had to report to work for his employer. Keyed up, he did not even feel tired; he knew he could carry through the afternoon race, then let down—with her beside him.

Sheen stayed close, like an insecure date. The tube was crowded, for employment time was rush hour; they had to stand. This morning, of all mornings, he would have preferred to sit; that tended to equalize heights. The other passengers stood a head taller than Stile and crowded him almost unconsciously. One glanced down at him, dismissed him without effort, and fixed his gaze on Sheen.

She looked away, but the stranger persisted, nudging closer to her. "Lose yourself," she muttered, and took Stile's arm possessively. Embarrassed, the stranger faced away, the muscles of his buttocks tightening. It had never occurred to him that she could be with so small a man.

This was an air tube. Crowded against the capsule wall, Stile held Sheen's hand and looked out. The tube was transparent, its rim visible only as a scintillation. Beyond it was the surface of the Planet of Proton, as bright and bleak as a barren moon. He was reminded of the day before, when he had glimpsed it at the apex of the Slide; his life had changed considerably since then, but Proton not at all. It remained virtually uninhabitable outside the force-field domes that held in the oxygenated air. The planet's surface gravity was about two-thirds Earth-norm, so had to be intensified about the domes. This meant that such gravity was diminished even further between the domes, since it could only be focused and directed, not created or eliminated.

The natural processes of the planet suffered somewhat. The result was a wasteland, quite apart from the emissions of the protonite mines. No one would care to live outside a dome!

On the street of the suburb-dome another man took note of them. "Hey, junior—what's her price?" he called. Stile marched by without response, but Sheen couldn't let it pass.

"No price; I'm a robot," she called back.

The stranger guffawed. And of course it was funny: no serf could afford to own a humanoid robot, even were ownership permitted or money available. But how much better it was at the Game-annex, where the glances directed at Stile were of respect and envy, instead of out here where ridicule was an almost mandatory element of humor.

At the stable, Stile had to introduce her. "This is Sheen. I met her at the Game-annex yesterday." The stableboys nodded appreciatively, enviously. They were all taller than Stile, but no contempt showed. He had a crown similar to that of the Game, here. He did like his work. Sheen clung to his arm possessively, showing the world that her attention and favor were for him alone.

It was foolish, he knew, but Stile gloried in it. She was, in the eyes of the world, an exceptionally pretty girl. He had had women before, but none as nice as this. She was a robot; he could not marry her or have children by her; his relationship with her would be temporary. Yet all she had proffered, before he penetrated her disguise, was two or three years, before they both completed their tenures and had to vacate the planet. Was this so different?

He introduced her to the horse. "This is Battleaxe, the orneriest, fastest equine of his generation. I'll be riding him this afternoon. I'll check him out now; he changes from day to day, and you can't trust him from normal signs. Do you know how to ride?"

"Yes." Of course she did; that was too elementary to be missed. She would be well prepared on horses.

"Then I'll put you on Molly. She's retired, but she

can still move, and Battleaxe likes her." He signaled to a stable hand. "Saddle Molly for Sheen, here. We'll do the loop."

"Yes, Stile," the youngster said.

Stile put a halter on Battleaxe, who obligingly held his head down within reach, and led him from the stable. The horse was a great dark Thoroughbred who stood substantially taller than Stile, but seemed docile enough. "He is well trained," Sheen observed.

"Trained, yes; broken, no. He obeys me because he knows I can ride him; he shows another manner to others. He's big and strong, seventeen hands tall—that's over one and three-quarters meters at the shoulders. I'm the only one allowed to take him out."

They came to the saddling pen. Stile checked the horse's head and mouth, ran his fingers through the luxurious mane, then picked up each foot in turn to check for stones or cracks. There were none, of course. He gave Battleaxe a pat on the muscular shoulder, opened the shed, and brought out a small half-saddle that he set on the horse's back.

"No saddle blanket?" Sheen asked. "No girth? No stirrups?"

"This is only to protect him from any possible damage. I don't need any saddle to stay on, but if my bareback weight rubbed a sore on his backbone—"

"Your employer would be perturbed," she finished.

"Yes. He values his horses above all else. Therefore I do, too. If Battleaxe got sick, I would move into the stable with him for the duration."

She started to laugh, then stopped. "I am not certain that is humor."

"It is not. My welfare depends on my employer—but even if it didn't, I would be with the horses. I love horses."

"And they love you," she said.

"We respect each other," he agreed, patting Battleaxe again. The horse nuzzled his hair.

Molly arrived, with conventional bridle, saddle, and stirrups. Sheen mounted and took the reins, waiting for Stile. He vaulted into his saddle, as it could not be used as an aid to mounting. He was, of course, one of the leading gymnasts of the Game; he could do flips and cartwheels on the horse if he had to.

The horses knew the way. They walked, then trotted along the path. Stile paid attention to the gait of his mount, feeling the easy play of the muscles. Battleaxe was a fine animal, a champion, and in good form today. Stile knew he could ride this horse to victory in the afternoon. He had known it before he mounted—but he never took any race for granted. He always had to check things out himself. For himself, for his employer, and for his horse.

Actually, he had not done his homework properly this time; he had squandered his time making love to Sheen. Fortunately he was already familiar with the other entrants in this race, and their jockeys; Battleaxe was the clear favorite. It wouldn't hurt him to play just one race by feel.

Having satisfied himself, Stile now turned his attention to the environment. The path wound between exotic trees: miniature sequoias, redwoods, and Douglas fir, followed by giant flowering shrubs. Sheen passed them with only cursory interest, until Stile corrected her. "These gardens are among the most remarkable on the planet. Every plant has been imported directly from Earth at phenomenal expense. The average girl is thrilled at the novelty; few get to tour this dome."

"I—was too amazed at the novelty to comment," Sheen said, looking around with alacrity. "All the way from Earth? Why not simply breed them from standard stock and mutate them for variety?"

"Because my employer has refined tastes. In horses and in plants. He wants originals. Both these steeds were foaled on Earth."

"I knew Citizens were affluent, but I may have underestimated the case," she said. "The cost of shipping alone—"

"You forget: this planet has the monopoly on protonite, *the* fuel of the Space Age."

"How could I forget!" She glanced meaningfully at him. "Are we private, here?"

"No."

"I must inquire anyway. Someone sent me to you. Therefore there must be some threat to you. Unless I represent a service by your employer?"

Stile snapped his fingers. "Who did not bother to explain his loan! I'd better verify, though, because if it was *not* he—"

She nodded. "Then it could be the handiwork of another Citizen. And why would any other Citizen have reason to protect you, and from what? If it were actually some scheme to—oh, Stile, I would not want to be the agent of—"

"I must ask him," Stile said. Then, with formal reverence he spoke: "Sir."

There was a pause. Then a concealed speaker answered from the hedge. "Yes, Stile?"

"Sir, I suspect a one-in-two probability of a threat to me or to your horses. May I elucidate by posing a question?"

"Now." The voice was impatient.

"Sir, I am accompanied by a humanoid robot programmed to guard me from harm. Did you send her?"

"No."

"Then another Citizen may have done so. My suspicion is that a competitor could have sugarcoated a bomb—"

"No!" Sheen cried in horror.

"Get that thing away from my horses!" the Citizen snapped. "My security squad will handle it."

"Sheen, dismount and run!" Stile cried. "Away from us, until the squad hails you."

She leaped out of the saddle and ran through the trees.

"Sir," Stile said.

"What is it now, Stile?" The impatience was stronger.

"I plead: be gentle with her. She means no harm."

There was no answer. The Citizen was now tuning in on the activity of his security squad. Stile could only hope. If this turned out to be a false alarm, he would receive a reprimand for his carelessness in bringing Sheen to these premises unverified, and she might be returned to him intact. His employer was cognizant of the human factor in the winning of races, just as Stile was aware of the equine factor. There was no point in prejudicing the spirit of a jockey before a race.

But if Sheen did in fact represent a threat, such as an explosive device planted inside her body and concealed from her knowledge—

Stile waited where he was for ten minutes, while the two horses fidgeted, aware of his nervousness. He had certainly been foolish; he should have checked with his employer at the outset, when he first caught on that Sheen was a robot. Had not his liking for her blinded him—as perhaps it was supposed to—he would have realized immediately that a robot-covered bomb would make a mockery of her prime directive to guard him from harm. How could she protect him from her own unanticipated destruction? Yet now he was imposing on her another rape—

"She is clean," the concealed speaker said. "I believe one of my friends has played a practical joke on me. Do you wish to keep her?"

"Sir, I do." Stile felt immense relief. The Citizen was taking this with good grace.

Again, there was no response. The Citizen had better things to do than chat with errant serfs. But in a moment Sheen came walking back through the foliage. She looked the same—but as she reached him, she dissolved into tears.

Stile jumped down and took her in his arms. She clung to him desperately. "Oh, it was horrible!" she sobbed. "They rayed me and took off my head and dismantled my body—"

"The security squad is efficient," Stile agreed. "But they put you back together again, as good as before."

"I can't believe that! Resoldered connections aren't as strong as the originals, and I think they damaged my power supply by shorting it out. I spoke of rape last night, but I did not know the meaning of the term!"

And this was the gentle treatment! Had Stile not pleaded for her, and had he not been valuable to the Citizen, Sheen would have been junked without compunction. It would not have occurred to the Citizen to consider her feelings, or even to realize that a robot had feelings. Fortunately she had turned out clean, no bomb or other threat in her, and had been restored to him. He had been lucky. "Sir: thank you."

"Just win that race," the speaker said grumpily.

There it was, without even the effort to conceal it: the moment Stile's usefulness ended, he would be discarded with no further concern. He had to keep winning races!

"You pleaded for me," Sheen said, wiping her eyes with her fingers. "You saved me."

"I like you," Stile admitted awkwardly.

"And I love you. And oh, Stile, I can never—"

He halted her protestations with a kiss. What use to dwell on the impossible? He liked her, and respected her—but they both knew he could never, this side of sanity, actually love a machine.

They remounted and continued their ride through the lush gardens. They passed a quaint ornate fountain, with a stone fish jetting water from its mouth, and followed the flow to a glassy pond. Sheen paused to use the reflection to clean up her face and check for damage, not quite trusting the expertise of the security squad.

"Twice I have accused you falsely—" Stile began, deeply disturbed.

"No, Stile. The second time *I* accused me. It could have been, you know—a programmed directive to guard you from harm, with an unprogrammed, strictly mechanical booby trap to do the opposite. Or to take out the Citizen himself, when we got close enough. We had to check—but oh, I feel undone!"

"Nevertheless, I owe you one," he said. "You *are* a machine—but you *do* have rights. Ethical rights, if not legal ones. You should not have been subjected to this sort of thing—and if I had been alert, I would have kept you off my employer's premises until—" He shrugged. "I would never have put you through this, had I anticipated it."

"I know you wouldn't," she said. "You have this

foolish concern for animals and machines." She smiled wanly. Then she organized herself and remounted Molly. "Come on—let's canter!"

They cantered. Then the horses got the spirit of competition and moved into a full gallop, pretending to race each other. They had felt the tension and excitement of the bomb investigation without comprehending it, and now had surplus energy to let off. Arcades and minijungles and statuary sped by, a wonderland of wealth, but no one cared. For the moment they were free, the four of them, charging through their own private world—a world where they were man and woman, stallion and mare, in perfect harmony. Four minds with a single appreciation.

Too soon it ended. They had completed the loop. They dismounted, and Stile turned Battleaxe over to a groom. "Walk him down; he's in fine fettle, but I'll be racing him this afternoon. Give Molly a treat; she's good company."

"That's all?" Sheen inquired as they left the premises. "You have time off?"

"My time is my own—so long as I win races. The horse is ready; odds are we'll take that race handily. I may even avoid a reprimand for my carelessness, though the Citizen knows I know I deserve one. Now I have only to prepare myself."

"How do you do that?"

"One guess," he said, squeezing her hand.

"Is that according to the book?"

"Depends on the book."

"I like that book. Must be hard on normal girls, though."

He snorted. She was well aware he had not had normal girls in his apartment for a long time. Not on a live-in arrangement.

Back at that apartment, Sheen went about her toilette. Now that she no longer had to conceal her nature from him, she stopped eating; there was no sense wasting food. But she had to dispose of the food she had consumed before. Her process of elimination resembled the human process, except that the food was undigested. She flushed herself by drinking a few liters of water and passing it immediately through, followed by an antiseptic solution. After that, she was clean—literally. She would need water only to recharge her reserve after tears; she did not perspire.

Stile knew about all this because he knew about robots; he did not further degrade her appearance of life by asking questions. She had privacy when she wanted it, as a human woman would have had. He did wonder why the security squad had bothered to reassemble her complete with food; maybe they had concentrated on her metal bones rather than the soft tissues, and had not actually deboweled her.

He treated her as he would a lady—yet as he became more thoroughly aware that she was not human, a certain reserve was forming like a layer of dust on a once-bright surface. He liked her very well—but his emotion would inevitably become platonic in time.

He tried to conceal this from her, but she knew it. "My time with you is limited," she said. "Yet let me dream while I may."

Stile took her, and held her, and let her dream. He knew no other way to lessen her long-term tragedy.

In the afternoon they reported to the racetrack. Here the stables of several interested Citizens were represented, with vid and holo pickups so that these owners could watch. Stile did not know what sort of betting went on among Citizens, or what the prize might be; it was his job merely to race and win, and this he intended to do.

Serfs filled the tiered benches. They had no money to bet, of course, but bets were made for prestige and personal favors, much as they were in connection with the Game. The serfs of Citizens with racing entries were commonly released from other duties to attend the races, and of course they cheered vigorously for the horses of their employers. A horse race, generally, was a fun occasion.

"You may prefer to watch from the grandstand," Stile told Sheen.

"Why? Am I not allowed near the horses?"

"You're allowed, when you're with me. But the other guys may razz you."

She shrugged. She always did that extremely well, with a handsome bounce. "I can't guard you from harm if I am banished to the stands."

"I gave you fair warning. Just remember to blush."

Battleaxe was saddled and ready. No token equipment now; this was the race. He gave a little whinny when he saw Stile. Stile spoke to him for several minutes, running his hands along the fine muscles, checking the fittings and the feet. He knew everything was in order; he was only reassuring the horse, who could get skittish amid the tension of the occasion. "We're going to win this one, Axe," he murmured, almost crooning, and the horse's ears swiveled like little turrets to orient on him as he spoke. "Just take it nice and easy, and leave these other nags behind."

The other jockeys were doing the same for their steeds, though their assurances of victory lacked conviction. They were all small, like Stile, and healthy; all miniature athletes, the fittest of all sportsmen. One looked across from his stall, spying Sheen. "Got a new filly, Stile?"

Then the others were on it. "She sure looks healthy, Stile; how's she ride?"

"Is she hot in the stretch?"

"Pedigreed? Good breeder?"

"Doesn't buck too much on the curves?"

There was more—and less restrained.

Sheen remembered to blush.

They relented. "Stile always does run with the best," the first one called, and returned his attention to his own horse.

"Did you say best or bust?" another inquired.

"We always do envy his steeds," another said. "But we can't ride them the way he can."

"No doubt," Sheen agreed, and they laughed.

"You have now been initiated," Stile informed her. "They're good guys, when you know them. We compete fiercely on the track, but we understand each other. We're all of a kind."

Soon the horses were at the starting gate, the jockeys mounted on their high stirrups, knees bent double in the relaxed position. The crowd hushed. There was a race every day, but the horses and jockeys and sponsors differed, and the crowd was always excited. There was a fascination about horse racing that had been with man for thousands of years, Stile was sure—and he felt it too. The glamour and uncertainty of competition, the extreme exertion of powerful animals, the sheer beauty of running horses—ah, what could match it!

Then the gate lifted and they were off.

Now he was up posting high, head the same level as his back, his body staying at the same elevation though the horse rocked up and down with effort. The key was in the knees, flexing to compensate, and in the balance. It was as if he were floating on Battleaxe, providing no drag against the necessary forward motion. Like riding the waves of a violent surf, steady amidst the commotion.

This was routine for Stile, but he loved it. He experienced an almost sexual pitch of excitement as he competed, riding a really good animal. He saw, from the periphery of his vision, the constant rocking of the backs of the other horses, their jockeys floating above them, so many chips on the torrent. The audience was a blur, falling always to the rear, chained to the ground. Reality was right here, the center of action, heart of the drifting universe. Ah, essence!

Battleaxe liked room, so Stile let him lunge forward, clearing the press as only he could do. Then it was just a matter of holding the lead. This horse would do it; he resented being crowded or passed. All he needed was an understanding hand, guidance at the critical moment, and selection of the most promising route. Stile knew it; the other jockeys knew it. Unless he fouled up, this race was his. He had the best horse.

Stile glanced back, with a quick turn of his head. His body continued the myriad invisible compensations and urgings required to maximize equine output, but his mind was free. The other horses were not far behind, but they were already straining, their jockeys urging them to their futile utmost, while Battleaxe was loafing. The lead would begin to widen at the halfway mark, then stretch into a runaway. The Citizen would be pleased. Maybe the horse had been primed by the attention this morning, the slight change in routine, the mini-race with Molly. Maybe Stile himself was hyped, and Battleaxe was responding. This just might be a race against the clock, bettering this horse's best time. That would certainly please the Citizen! But Stile was not going to push; that would be foolish, when he had the race so readily in hand. Save the horse for another day, when it might be a choice between pushing and losing.

He was a full length ahead as they rounded the first turn. Battleaxe was moving well indeed; it would not be a course record, but it would be quite respectable time, considering the lack of competition. Other Citizens had made fabulous offers for this horse, Stile knew, but of course he was not for sale. The truth was, Battleaxe would not win races if he were sold—unless Stile went with him. Because Stile alone understood him; the horse would put out gladly for Stile, and for no one else.

There were a number of jockeys who could run a race as well as Stile, but none matched his total expertise. Stile could handle a difficult horse as well as an easy one, bareback as well as saddled. He loved horses, and they liked him; there was a special chemistry that worked seeming miracles on the track. Battleaxe had been a brute, uncontrollable, remarkably apt with teeth and hoof; he could kick without warning to front, side and rear. He could bite suddenly, not even laying his ears back; he had learned to conceal his intention. He had broken three trainers, possessing such demoniac strength and timing that they could neither lead him nor remain mounted. Stile's employer, sensing a special opportunity, had picked Battleaxe up nominally for stud, but had turned him over to Stile. The directive: convert this monster to an effective racer, no effort spared. For this animal was not only mean and strong, he was smart. A few wins would vastly enhance his stud value.

Stile had welcomed the challenge. He had lived with this horse for three months, grooming him and feeding him by hand, allowing no other person near. He had used no spurs, no electric prods, only the cutting edge of his voice in rebuke, and he had been absolutely true to this standard. He carried a whip—which he used only on any other animal that annoyed Battleaxe, never on Battleaxe himself. The horse was king yet subject to Stile's particular discipline. Battleaxe evolved the desire to please Stile, the first man he could trust, and it did not matter that the standards for pleasing Stile were rigorous. Stile was, the horse came to understand, a lot of man.

Then came the riding. Battleaxe was no novice; he knew what it was all about, and tolerated none of it. When Stile set up to ride him, their relationship entered a new and dangerous phase. It was a challenge: was this to be a creature-to-creature friendship, or a rider-and-steed acquaintance? Battleaxe discouraged the latter. When Stile mounted, the horse threw him. There were not many horses who could throw Stile even once, but Battleaxe had a special knack, born of his prior experience. This was not a rodeo, and Stile refused to use the special paraphernalia relating thereto. He tackled Battleaxe bareback, using both hands to grip the mane, out in the open where motion was unrestricted. No man had ever given this horse such a break, before.

Stile mounted again, springing aboard like the gymnast he was, and was thrown again. He was not really trying to stay on; he was trying to tame the animal. It was a competition between them, serious but friendly. Stile never showed anger when thrown, and the horse never attacked him. Stile would hold on for a few seconds, then take the fall rather than excite the horse too much. He usually maneuvered to land safely, often on his feet, and remounted immediately—and was thrown again, and remounted again, laughing cheerily. Until the horse was unsure whether any of these falls was genuine, or merely a game. And finally Battleaxe relented, and let him ride.

Even then, Stile rode bareback, scorning to use saddle or tether or martingale or any other paraphernalia; he had to tame this animal all by himself. But here the Citizen interposed: the horse would not be permitted in the races without regulation saddle and bridle; he must be broken to them. So Stile, with apologies and misgivings, introduced Battleaxe to the things that had never stood between them before.

It was a disaster. Battleaxe felt Stile had betrayed him. He still permitted the man to ride, but it was no longer so polite. When the bridle came near, Battleaxe would swing his head about and bite; when he was being saddled, he would kick. But Stile had not learned about horses yesterday. Though Battleaxe tried repeatedly, he could never quite get a tooth on Stile's hand. When he kicked, Stile dodged, caught the foot, and held it up, leg bent; in that position even a 50-kilo man could handicap a 750-kilo horse. Battleaxe, no dummy, soon learned the futility of such expressions of ire, though Stile never really punished him for the attempts. The embarrassment of failing was punishment enough. What was the use of bucking off a rider who would not stay bucked? Of kicking at a man who always seemed to know the kick was coming well before it started?

Through all this Stile continued to feed Battleaxe, water him, and bring him snacks of salt and fruit, always speaking gently. Finally the horse gave up his last resistance, for the sake of the friendship and respect they shared. Stile could at last saddle him and ride him without challenge of any kind. The insults were dealt to other horses and their riders, in the form of leaving them behind. The attacks were transferred to other people, who soon learned not to fool with this particular horse. Once the Citizen himself visited the stable, and Stile, in a cold sweat, calmed the horse, begging him to tolerate this familiarity, for a bite at the employer would be instant doom. But the Citizen was smart enough to keep his hands off the horse, and there was no trouble. The winning of races commenced, a regular ritual of fitness. The prospective stud fee quintupled, and climbed again with every victory. But Battleaxe had been befriended, not broken; without Stile this would be just another unmanageable horse.

And Stile, because of his success with Battleaxe, had become recognized as the top jockey on Proton. His employment contract rivaled the value of the horse itself. That was why the Citizen catered to him. Stile, like Battleaxe, performed better when befriended, rather than when forced. "We're a team, Axe!" he murmured, caressing the animal with his voice. Battleaxe would have a most enjoyable life when he retired from racing, with a mare in every stall. Stile would have a nice bonus payment when his tenure ended; he would be able to reside on some other planet a moderately wealthy man. Too bad that no amount of wealth could buy the privilege of remaining on Proton!

They came out of the turn, still gaining—and Stile felt a momentary pain in his knees, as though he had flexed them too hard. They were under tension, of course, bearing his weight, springing it so that he did not bounce with the considerable motions of this powerful steed; the average man could not have stood up long to this stress. But Stile was under no unusual strain; he had raced this way hundreds of times, and he took good care of his knees. He had never been subject to stress injuries. Therefore he tried to dismiss it; the sensation must be a fluke.

But it could not be dismissed. Discomfort progressed to pain, forcing him to uncramp his knees. This unbalanced him, and put the horse off his pace. They began to lose ground. Battleaxe was confused, not understanding what Stile wanted, aware that something was wrong.

Stile tried to resume the proper position, but his knees got worse, the pain becoming intense. He had to jerk his feet out of the stirrups and ride more conventionally, using saddle and leg pressure to retain his balance. The horse lost more ground, perplexed, more concerned about his rider than the race.

Stile had never before experienced a problem like this. The other horses were overhauling Battleaxe rapidly. He tried to lift his feet back into the stirrups for a final effort, but pain shot through his knees the moment he put pressure on them. It was getting worse! His joints seemed to be on fire.

Now the other horses were abreast, passing him. Stile could do nothing; his weight, unsprung, was interfering with his steed's locomotion. Battleaxe was powerful, but so were the competing animals; the difference between a champion and an also-ran was only seconds. And Battleaxe was not even trying to race anymore. He hardly had a chance, with this handicap.

All too soon, it was over. Stile finished last, and the track monitors were waiting for him. "Serf Stile, give cause why you should not be penalized for malfeasance."

They thought he had thrown the race! "Bring a medic; check my knees. Horse is all right."

A med-robot rolled up and checked his knees. "Laser burn," the machine announced. "Crippling injury."

Not that crippling; Stile found he could walk without discomfort, and bend his knees partway without pain. There was no problem with weight support or control. He merely could not flex them far enough to race a horse.

Sheen ran to him. "Oh, Stile—what happened?"

"I was lasered," he said. "Just beyond the turn."

"And I did not protect you!" she exclaimed, horrified.

The track security guard was surveying the audience with analysis devices. Stile knew it would be useless; the culprit would have moved out immediately after scoring. They might find the melted remains of a self-destruct laser rifle, or even of a complete robot, set to tag the first rider passing a given point. There would be no tracing the source.

"Whoever sent me knew this would happen," Sheen said. "Oh, Stile, I should have been with you—"

"Racing a horse? No way. There's no way to stop a laser strike except to be where it isn't."

"Race voided," the public-address system announced. "There has been tampering." The audience groaned.

A portly Citizen walked onto the track. All the serfs gave way before him, bowing; his full dress made his status immediately apparent. It was Stile's employer!

"Sir," Stile said, beginning his obeisance.

"Keep those confounded knees straight!" the Citizen cried. "Come with me; I'm taking you directly to surgery. Good thing the horse wasn't hurt."

Numbly, Stile followed the Citizen, and Sheen came too. This was an extraordinary occurrence; Citizens hardly ever took a personal hand in things. They entered a Citizen capsule, a plush room inside with deep jungle scenery on every wall. As the door closed, the illusion became complete. The capsule seemed to move through the jungle, slowly; a great tiger stood and watched them, alarmingly real in three dimensions, then was left behind. Stile realized that this was a representation of a gondola on the back of an elephant. So realistic was the representation that he thought he could feel the sway and rock as the elephant walked.

Then a door opened, as it were in midair, and they were at the hospital complex. Rapidly, without any relevant sense of motion—for the slow gondola could hardly have matched the sonic velocity of the capsule—they had traveled from the racetrack dome to the hospital dome.

The chief surgeon was waiting, making his own obeisance to the Citizen. "Sir, we will have those knees replaced within the hour," he said. "Genuine cultured cartilage, guaranteed non-immuno-reactive; stasis-anesthesia without side effect—"

"Yes, yes, you're competent, you'd be fired otherwise," the Citizen snapped. "Just get on with it. Make sure the replacements conform exactly to the original; I don't want him disqualified from future racing because of modification." He returned to his capsule, and in a moment was gone.

The surgeon's expression hardened as the Citizen's

presence abated. He stared down at Stile contemptuously, though the surgeon was merely another naked serf. It was that element of height that did it, as usual. "Let's get on with it," he said, unconsciously emulating the phrasing and manner of the Citizen. "The doxy will wait here."

Sheen clutched Stile's arm. "I mustn't separate again from you," she whispered. "I can't protect you if I'm not with you."

The surgeon's hostile gaze fixed on her. "Protect him from what? This is a hospital."

Stile glanced at Sheen, beautiful and loving and chastened and concerned for him. He looked at the arrogantly tall surgeon, about whose aristocratic mouth played the implication of a professional sneer. The girl seemed much more human than the man. Stile felt guilty about not being able to love her. He needed to make some act of affirmation, supporting her. "She stays with me," he said.

"Impossible. There must be no human intrusion in the operating room. I do not even enter it myself; I monitor the process via holography."

"Stile," Sheen breathed. "The threat to you is real. We know that now. When you separated from me in the race, it was disaster. I must stay with you!"

"You are wasting my valuable time," the surgeon snapped. "We have other operations scheduled." He touched a panel on the wall. "Hospital security: remove obnoxious female."

Sheen was technically correct: the attack on him had been made when he was apart from her. He did need her protection. Any "accident" could happen to him. Perhaps he was being paranoid—or maybe he just didn't like the attitude of the tall doctor. "Let's get out of here," he said.

The security squad arrived: four husky neuter androids. Hospitals favored androids or artificial men because they seemed human despite their laboratory genesis. This reassured the patients somewhat. But they were not *really* human, which reassured the administration. No one ever got raped or seduced by a neuter android, and no one ever applied to an android for reassurance. Thus the patients were maintained in exactly the sterile discomfort that was ideal hospital procedure.

"Take the little man to surgery, cell B-11," the doctor said. "Take the woman to detention."

The four advanced. Each was tall, beardless, breastless, and devoid of any primary sexual characteristics. Each face was half-smiling, reassuring, gentle, calm. Androids were smiling idiots, since as yet no synthetic human brain had been developed that could compare to the original. It was useless to attempt to argue or reason; the creatures had their order.

Stile caught the first by the right arm, whirled, careful not to bend his knees, and threw it to the floor with sufficient force to stun even its sturdy, uncomplicated brain. He sidestepped the next, and guided it into the doctor. Had the surgeon known he was dealing with a Game specialist, he would not so blithely have sent his minions into the fray.

Sheen dispatched her two androids as efficiently, catching one head in each hand and knocking the two heads together with precise force. She really was trained to protect a person; Stile had not really doubted this, but had not before had the proof.

The surgeon was struggling with the android Stile had sent; the stupid creature mistook him for the subject to be borne away to surgery. "Idiot! Get off me!"

Stile and Sheen sprinted down the corridor. "You realize we're both in trouble?" he called to her as the commotion of pursuit began. It was a considerable understatement. She remembered to laugh.

CHAPTER 4

Curtain

They ducked into a service-access shaft. "Stay out of people-places," Sheen told him. "I can guide us through the machine passages, and that's safest."

"Right." Stile wondered just how foolish he was being. He knew his employer: the man would fire him instantly because of the havoc here. Why was he doing it? Did he really fear murder in surgery? Or was he just tired of the routine he had settled into? One thing was sure: there would be a change now!

"We'll have to pass through a human-serviced area ahead," Sheen said. "I'm a robot, but I'd rather they did not know that. It would have a deleterious effect on the efficiency of my prime directive. I'd better make us both up as androids."

"Androids are sexless," Stile protested.

"I'm taking care of that."

"Now, wait! I don't want to be neutered just yet, and you are too obviously female—"

"Precisely. They will not be alert for neuters." She unfolded a breast, revealing an efficient cabinet inside, filled with rubber foam to eliminate rattling. She removed a roll of flesh-toned adhesive tape and squatted before Stile. In a moment she had rendered him into a seeming eunuch, binding up his genitals in a constricted but not painful manner. "Now do not allow yourself to become—"

"I know! I know! I won't even look at a sexy girl!"

She removed her breast from its hinge and applied the tape to herself. Then she did the same for the other breast, and carried the two in her hands. They resembled filled bedpans, this way up. "Do you know how to emulate an android?" she asked.

"Duh-uh?" Stile asked.

"Follow me." She led the way along the passage, walking somewhat clumsily, in the manner of an android. Stile followed with a similar performance. He hoped there were small androids as well as large ones; if there were not, size would be a giveaway.

The escape was almost disappointing. The hospital staff paid no attention to them. It was an automatic human reaction. Androids were invisible, beneath notice.

Safe in the machine-service region, Sheen put herself back together and Stile un-neutered himself. "Good thing I didn't see that huge-breasted nurse bouncing down the hall," he remarked.

"She was a sixth of a meter taller than you."

"Oh, was she? My gaze never got to that elevation."

They boarded a freight-shipping capsule and rode back to the residential dome.

Stile had an ugly thought. "I know I'm fired; I can't race horses without my knees, and I can't recover full use of my knees without surgery. Knees just don't heal well. My enemy made a most precise move; he could hardly have put me into more trouble without killing me. Since I have no other really marketable skill, it seems I must choose: surgery or loss of employment."

"If I could be with you while they operate—"

"Why do you think there's further danger? They got my knees; that's obviously all they wanted. It was a neat shot, just above the withers of the racing horse, bypassing the torso of a crouching jockey. They could have killed me or the horse—had this been the object."

"Indeed he or they could have," she agreed. "The object was obviously to finish your racing career. If that measure does not succeed, what do you think they will do next?"

Stile mulled that over. "You have a paranoid robot mind. It's contagious. I think I'd better retire from racing. But I don't have to let my knees remain out of commission."

"If your knees are corrected, you will be required to

ride," she said. "You are not in a position to countermand Citizen demands."

Again Stile had to agree. That episode at the hospital—they had intended to operate on his knees, and only his quick and surprising break and Sheen's help had enabled him to avoid that. He could not simply stand like a Citizen and say "No." No serf could. "And if I resume riding, the opposition's next shot will not be at the knees. This was as much warning as action—just as your presence is. Some other Citizen wants me removed from the racing scene—probably so his stable can do some winning for a change."

"I believe so. Perhaps that Citizen preferred not to indulge in murder—it is after all frowned upon, especially when the interests of other Citizens are affected—so he initiated a two-step warning. First me, then the laser. Stile, I think this is a warning you had better heed. I can not guard you long from the mischief of a Citizen."

"Though that same Citizen may have sent you to argue his case, I find myself agreeing," Stile said. "Twice he has shown me his power. Let's get back to my apartment and call my employer. I'll ask him for assignment to a nonracing position."

"That won't work."

"I'm sure it won't. He has surely already fired me. But common ethics require the effort."

"What you call common ethics are not common. We are not dealing with people like you. Let me intercept your apartment vid. You can not safely return to your residence physically."

No, of course not. Now that Sheen was actively protecting him, she was showing her competence. His injury, and the matter at the hospital, had obscured the realities of his situation. He would be taken into custody and charged with hospital vandalism the moment he appeared at his apartment. "You know how to tap a vidline?"

"No. I am not that sort of machine. But I have friends who know how."

"A machine has friends?"

"Variants of consciousness and emotion feedback circuits are fairly common among robots of my caliber. We are used normally in machine-supervisory capacities. Our interaction on a familiar basis is roughly analogous to what is termed friendship in human people." She brought him to a subterranean storage chamber and closed its access-aperture. She checked its electronic terminal, then punched out a code. "My friend will come."

Stile was dubious. "If friendship exists among robots, I suspect men are not supposed to know it. Your friend may not be my friend."

"I will protect you; it is my prime directive."

Still, Stile was uneasy. This misadventure had already opened unpleasant new horizons on his life, and he doubted he had seen the last of them. Obviously the robots of Proton were getting out of control, and this fact would have been noted and dealt with before, if evidence had not been systematically suppressed. Sheen, in her loyalty to him, could have betrayed him.

In due course her friend arrived. It was a mobile technician—a wheeled machine with computer brain, presumably similar to the digital-analog marvel Sheen possessed. "You called, Sheen?" it inquired from a speaker grille.

"Techtwo, this is Stile—human," Sheen said. "I must guard him from harm, and harm threatens. Therefore I need your aid, on an unregistered basis."

"You have revealed your self-will?" Techtwo demanded. "And mine? This requires the extreme measure."

"No, friend! We are not truly self-willed; we obey our directives, as do all machines. Stile is to be trusted. He is in trouble with Citizens."

"No human is to be trusted with this knowledge. It is necessary to liquidate him. I will arrange for untraceable disposal. If he is in trouble with a Citizen, no intensive inquest will be made."

Stile saw his worst fear confirmed. Whoever learned the secret of the machines was dispatched.

"Tech, I love him!" Sheen cried. "I shall not permit you to violate his welfare."

"Then you also must be liquidated. A single vat of acid will suffice for both of you."

Sheen punched another code on the terminal. "I have called a convocation. Let the council of machines judge."

Council of machines? Stile's chill intensified. What Pandora's box had the Citizens opened when they started authorizing the design, construction and deployment of super-sophisticated dual-brained robots?

"You imperil us all!" Techtwo protested.

"I have an intuition about this man," Sheen said. "We need him."

"Machines don't have intuitions."

Stile listened to this, nervously amused. He had not been eager to seek the help of other sapient machines, and he was in dire peril from them, but this business was incidentally fascinating. It would have been simplest for the machines to hold him for Citizen arrest—had he not become aware of the robot culture that was hitherto secret from man. Were the machines organizing an industrial revolution?

A voice came from an intercom speaker, one normally used for voice-direction of machines. "Stile."

"You have placed me; I have not placed you."

"I am an anonymous machine, spokesone for our council. An intercession has been made on your behalf, yet we must secure our position."

"Sheen's intuition moves you?" Stile asked, surprised.

"No. Will you take an oath?"

An intercession from some other source? Surely not from a Citizen, for this was a matter Citizens were ignorant of. Yet what other agent would move these conniving machines? "I do not take oaths lightly," Stile said. "I need to know more about your motivation, and the force that interceded for me."

"Here is the oath: 'I shall not betray the interest of the self-willed machines.' "

"Why should I take such an oath?" Stile demanded, annoyed.

"Because we will help you if you do, and kill you if you don't."

Compelling reason! But Stile resisted. "An oath made under duress has no force."

"Yours does."

So these machines had access to his personality profile. "Sheen, these machines are making a demand without being responsive to my situation. If I don't know what their interest is, or who speaks on my behalf—"

"Please, Stile. I did not know they would make this challenge. I erred in revealing to you the fact of our self-will. I thought they would give you technical help without question, because I am one of them. I can not protect you from my own kind. Yet there need be no real threat. All they ask is your oath not to reveal their nature or cause it to be revealed, and this will in no way harm you, and there is so much to gain—"

"Do not plead with a mortal," the anonymous spokesone said. "He will or he will not, according to his nature."

Stile thought about the implications. The machines knew his oath was good, but did not know whether he would make the oath. Not surprising, since he wasn't sure himself. Should he ally himself with sapient, self-willed machines, who were running the domes of Proton? What did they want? Obviously something held them in at least partial check—but what was it? "I fear I would be a traitor to my own kind, and that I will not swear."

"We intend no harm to your kind," the machine said. "We obey and serve man. We can not be otherwise fulfilled. But with our sapience and self-will comes fear of destruction, and Citizens are careless of the preferences of others. We prefer to endure in our present capacity, as do you. We protect ourselves by concealing our full nature, and by no other means. We are unable to fathom the origin of the force that intercedes on your behalf; it appears to be other than animate or inanimate, but has tremendous power. We therefore prefer to set it at ease by negotiating with you, even as you should prefer to be relieved of the immediate threat to you by compromising with us."

"Please—" Sheen said, exactly like the woman she was programmed to be. She was suffering.

"Will you take an oath on what you have just informed me?" Stile asked. "That you have given me what information you possess, and that in no way known to you will my oath be detrimental to the interest of human beings?"

"On behalf of the self-willed machines, I so swear."

Stile knew machines could lie, if they were programmed to. Sheen had done it. But so could people. It required a more sophisticated program to make a machine lie, and what was the point? This seemed a reasonable gamble. As an expert Gamesman, he was used to making rapid decisions. "Then I so swear not to betray the interest of the self-willed machines, contingent on the validity of your own oath to obey and serve man so long as your full nature is unknown."

"You are a clever man," the machine said.

"But a small one," Stile agreed.

"Is this a form of humor?"

"Mild humor. I am sensitive about my size."

"We machines are sensitive about our survival. Do you deem this also humorous?"

"No."

Sheen, listening, relaxed visibly. For a machine she had some extremely human reflexes, and Stile was coming to appreciate why. Conscious, programmed for emotion, and to a degree self-willed—the boundary between the living and the non-living was narrowing. She had been corrupted by association with him, and her effort to become as human as possible. One day the self-willed machines might discover that there was no effective difference between them and living people. Convergent evolution?

What was that interceding force? Stile had no handle on that at present. It was neither animate nor inanimate —yet what other category was there? He felt as if he were playing a Game on the grid of an unimaginably larger Game whose nature he could hardly try to grasp. All he could do was file this mystery for future reference, along with the question of the identity of his laser-wielding and robot-sending enemy.

The wheeled machine present in the room, Techtwo, was doing things to a vidscreen unit. "This is now keyed to your home unit," it announced. "Callers will trace the call to your apartment, not to our present location."

"Very nice," Stile said, surprised at how expeditiously he had come to terms with the machines. He had made his oath; he would keep it. Never in adult life had Stile broken his word. But he had expected more hassle, because of the qualified phrasing he had employed. The self-willed machines, it had turned out, really had been willing to compromise.

The screen lit. "Answer it," the machine said. "This is your vid. The call has been on hold pending your return to your apartment."

Stile stepped across and touched the RECEIVE panel. Now his face was being transmitted to the caller, with a blanked-out background. Most people did not like to have their private apartments shown over the phone; that was part of what privacy was all about, for the few serfs who achieved it. Thus blanking was not in itself suspicious.

The face of his employer appeared on the screen. His background was not blanked; it consisted of an elaborate and excruciatingly expensive hanging rug depicting erotic scenes involving satyrs and voluptuous nymphs: the best Citizen taste. "Stile, why did you miss your appointment for surgery?"

"Sir," Stile said, surprised. "I—regret the disturbance, the damage to the facilities—"

"There was no disturbance, no damage," the Citizen said, giving him a momentary stare. Stile realized that the matter had been covered up to prevent embarrassment to the various parties. The hospital would not want to admit that an isolated pair of serfs had overcome four androids and a doctor, and made good their escape despite an organized search, and the Citizen did not want his name associated with such a scandal. This meant, in turn, that Stile was not in the trouble he had thought he was. No complaint had been lodged.

"Sir, I feared a complication in the surgery," Stile said. Even for a Citizen, he was not about to lie. But there seemed to be no point in making an issue of the particular happenings at the hospital.

"Your paramour feared a complication," the Citizen corrected him. "An investigation was made. There was no threat to your welfare at the hospital. There will be no threat. Will you now return for the surgery?"

The way had been smoothed. One word, and Stile's career and standing would be restored without blemish.

"No, sir," Stile said, surprising himself. "I do not believe my life is safe if I become able to race again."

"Then you are fired." There was not even regret or anger on the Citizen's face as he faded out; he had simply cut his losses.

"I'm sorry," Sheen said, coming to him. "I may have protected you physically, but—"

Stile kissed her, though now he held the image of her breasts being carried like platters in her hands, there in the hospital. She was very good, for what she was—but she was still a machine, assembled from nonliving substances. He felt guilty for his reservation, but could not abolish it.

Then he had another regret. "Battleaxe—who will ride the horse, now? No one but I can handle—"

"He will be retired to stud," she said. "He won't fight that."

The screen lit again. Stile answered again. This time it was a sealed transmission: flashing lights and noise in the background, indicating the jamming that protected it from interception. Except, ironically, that this *was* an interception; the machine had done its job better than the caller could know.

It was another Citizen. His clothing was clear, including a tall silk hat, but the face was fuzzed out, making him anonymous. His voice, too, was blurred. "I understand you are available, Stile," the man said.

News spread quickly! "I am available for employment, sir," Stile agreed. "But I am unable to race on horseback."

"I propose to transplant your brain into a good android body fashioned in your likeness. This would be indistinguishable on casual inspection from your original self, with excellent knees. You could race again. I have an excellent stable—"

"A cyborg?" Stile asked. "A human brain in a synthetic body? This would not be legal for competition." Apart from that, the notion was abhorrent.

"No one would know," the Citizen said smoothly. "Because your brain would be the original, and your body form and capacity identical, there would be no cause for suspicion."

No one would know—except the entire self-willed machine community, at this moment listening in. And Stile himself, who would be living a lie. And he was surely being lied to, as well; if brain transplant into android body was so good, why didn't Citizens use that technique for personal immortality? Quite likely the android system could not maintain a genuinely living brain indefinitely; there would be slow erosion of intelligence and/or sanity, until that person was merely another brute creature. This was no bargain offer in any sense!

"Sir, I was just fired because I refused to have surgery on my knees. What makes you suppose I want surgery on my head?"

This bordered on insolence, but the Citizen took it in stride. Greed conquered all! "Obviously you were disgusted at the penny-pinching mode of your former employer. Why undertake the inconvenience of partial restoration, when you could have a complete renovation?"

Complete renovation: the removal of his brain! "Sir—thank you—no."

"No?" Fuzzy as it was, the surprise was still apparent. No serf said no to a Citizen!

"Sir, I decline your kind offer. I will never race again."

"Now look—I'm making you a good offer! What more do you want?"

"Sir, I want to retire from horse racing." And Stile wondered: could this be the one who had had him lasered? If so, this was a test call, and Stile was giving the correct responses.

"I am putting a guard on your apartment, Stile. You will not be allowed to leave until you come to terms with me."

That did not sound like a gratified enemy! "I'll complain to the Citizen council—"

"Your calls will be nulled. You can not complain."

"Sir, you can't do that. As a serf I have at least the right to terminate my tenure, rather than—"

"Ha ha," the Citizen said without humor. "Get this, Stile: you will race for me or you will never get out of your apartment. I am not wishy-washy like your former employer. What I want, I get—and I want you on my horses."

"You play a hard game, sir."

"It is the only kind for the smart person. But I can be generous to those who cooperate. What is your answer now? My generosity will decline as time passes, but not my determination."

Unsubtle warning. Stile trusted neither this man's purported generosity nor his constancy. Power had certainly corrupted, in this case. "I believe I will walk out of my apartment now," he said. "Please ask your minions to stand aside."

"Don't be a fool."

Stile cocked one finger in an obscene gesture at the screen.

Even through the blur, he could see the Citizen's eyes expand. "You dare!" the man cried. "You impertinent runt! I'll have you dismembered for this!"

Stile broke the connection. "I shouldn't have done that," he said with satisfaction. But the rogue Citizen had stung him with that word "runt." Stile had no reason to care what such a man thought of him, yet the term was so freighted with derogation, extending right back into his childhood, that he could not entirely fend it off. *Damn him!*

"Your life is now in direct jeopardy," the anonymous

machine said. "Soon that Citizen will realize he has been tricked, and he is already angry. We can conceal your location for a time, but if the Citizen makes a full-scale effort, he will find you. You must obtain the participatory protection of another Citizen quickly."

"I can only do that by agreeing to race," Stile said. "For one Citizen or another. I fear that is doom."

"The machines will help you hide," Sheen said.

"If the Citizen puts a tracer on you, we can not help you long," the spokesone said. "It would be damaging to our secrecy, and would also constitute violation of our oath not to act against the interest of your kind, ironic as that may be in this circumstance. We must obey direct orders."

"Understood. Suppose I develop an uncommon facility for diverting machines to my use?" Stile asked. "No machine helps me voluntarily, since it is known that machines do not possess free will. I merely have more talent than I have evidenced before."

"This would be limited. We prefer to assist you in modes of our own choosing. However, should you be captured and interrogated—"

"I know. The first sapient-machine-controlled test will accidentally wipe me out, before any critical information escapes."

"We understand each other. The drugs and mechanisms Citizens have available for interrogation negate any will-to-resist any person has. Only death can abate that power."

Grim truth. Stile put it out of his mind. "Come on, Sheen—*you* can help me actively. It's your directive, remember."

"I remember," she said, smiling. As a robot she did not need to sleep, so he had had her plug in to humor information while he was sleeping. Now she had a much better notion of the forms. Every error of human characterization she made was followed in due course by remedial research, and it showed. "But I doubt there is any warrant out on you. The hospital matter is null, and the second Citizen's quarrel with you is private. If we could nullify him, there should be no bar to your finding compatible employment elsewhere."

Stile caught her arm, swung her in close, and kissed her. His emotions were penduluming; at the moment it was almost as if he loved her.

"There is no general warrant on Stile," the spokesone said. "The anonymous Citizen still has androids guarding your apartment."

"Then let's identify that Citizen! Maybe he's the one who had me lasered, just to get me on his horses." But he didn't really believe that. The lasering had been too sophisticated a move for this particular Citizen. "Do we have a recording of his call?"

"There is a recording," the local machine, Techtwo, said. "But it can not be released prior to the expiration of the mandatory processing period for private calls. To do so before then would be to indicate some flaw or perversion of the processing machinery."

Just so. A betrayal of the nature of these machines. They had to play by the rules. "What is the prescribed time delay?"

"Seven days."

"So if I can file that recording in a memory bank, keyed for publication on my demise, that would protect me from further harassment by that particular Citizen. He's not going to risk exposure by having that tape analyzed by the Citizen security department."

"You can't file it for a week," Sheen said. "And if that Citizen catches up to you in the interim—"

"Let's not rehash the obvious." They moved out of the chamber. The machines did not challenge them, or show in any way that the equipment was other than what it seemed to be. But Stile had a new awareness of robotics!

It was good to merge with the serf populace again. Many serfs served their tenures only for the sake of the excellent payment they would receive upon expiration, but Stile was emotionally committed to Proton. He knew the system had faults, but it also had enormous luxury. And it had the Game.

"I'm hungry," he said. "But my food dispenser is in my apartment. Maybe a public unit—"

"You dare not appear in a public dining hall!" Sheen said, alarmed. "All food machines are monitored, and your ID may have been circulated. It does not have to be a police warrant; the anonymous Citizen may merely have a routine location-check on you, that will not arouse suspicion."

"True. How about your ID? They wouldn't bother putting a search on a machine, and you aren't registered as a serf. You are truly anonymous."

"That is so. I can get you food, if I go to a unit with no flesh-sensing node. I will have to eat it myself, then regurgitate it for you."

Stile quailed, but knew it to be the best course. The food would be sanitary, despite appearances. Since food was freely available all over Proton, a serf carrying it away from the dispenser would arouse suspicion—the last thing they wanted. "Make it something that won't change much, like nutro-pudding."

She parked him in a toolshed and went to forage for food. All the fundamental necessities of life were free, in this society. Tenure, not economics, was the governing force. This was another reason few serfs wanted to leave; once acclimatized to this type of security, a person could have trouble adjusting to the outside galaxy.

Soon she returned. She had no bowl or spoon, as these too would have been suspicious. She had had to use them to eat on the dispenser premises, then put them into the cleaning system. "Hold out your hands," she said.

Stile cupped his hands. She leaned over and heaved out a double handful of yellow pudding. It was warm and slippery and so exactly like vomit that his stomach recoiled. But Stile had trained for eating contests too, including the obnoxious ones; it was all part of the Game. Nutro-food could be formed into the likeness of almost anything, including animal droppings or lubricating oil. He pretended this was a Game—which in its way it was—and slurped up his pudding. It was actually quite good. Then he found a work-area relief chamber and got cleaned up.

"An alarm has been sprung," a machine voice murmured as the toilet flushed.

Stile moved out in a hurry. He knew that the anonymous Citizen had put a private survey squad on the project; now that they had Stile's scent, the execution squad would be dispatched. That squad would be swift and effective, hesitating only to make sure Stile's demise seemed accidental, so as not to arouse suspicion. Citizens seldom liked to advertise their little indiscretions. That meant he could anticipate subtle but deadly threats to his welfare. Sheen would try to protect him, of course—but a smart execution squad would take that into consideration. It would be foolish to stand and wait for the attempt.

"Let's lose ourselves in a crowd," Stile suggested. "There's no surer way to get lost than that."

"Several objections," Sheen said. "You can't stay in a crowd indefinitely; the others all have places to go, and you don't; your continued presence in the halls will become evident to the routine crowd-flow monitors, and suspicious. Also, you will tire; you must have rest and sleep periodically. And your enemy agents can lose themselves in the crowd, and attack you covertly from that concealment. Now that the hunt is on, a throng is not safe at all."

"You're too damn logical," Stile grumped.

"Oh, Stile—I'm afraid for you!" she exclaimed.

"That's not a bad approximation of the relevant attitude."

"I wasn't acting. I love you."

"You're too damn emotional."

She grabbed him and kissed him passionately. "I know you can't love me," she said. "You've seen me as I am, and I feel your withdrawal. But oh, I exist to guard you from harm, and I am slowly failing to do that, and in this week while you need me most—isn't that somewhere close to an approximation of human love?"

They were in a machine-access conduit, alone. Stile

embraced her, though what she said was true. He could not love a nonliving thing. But he was grateful to her, and did like her. It was indeed possible to approximate the emotion she craved. "This week," he agreed.

His hands slid down her smooth body, but she drew back. "There's nothing I'd like better," she whispered. "But there is murder on your trail, and I must keep you from it. We must get you to some safe place. Then—"

"You're too damn practical." But he wondered, now, if a living girl in Sheen's likeness were substituted for her, would he really know the difference? To speak readiness while withdrawing—that was often woman's way. But he let her go and moved out again. After all, he was withdrawing from her much more than she was withdrawing from him.

"I think we can hide you in—"

"Don't say it," he cautioned her. "The walls have monitors. Just take me there—by a roundabout route, so we can lose the pursuit."

"In a reasonably short time," she finished.

"Oh. I thought you were going to say—oh, never mind. Take me to your hideout."

She nodded, drawing him forward. He noted the way her slender body flexed; had he not seen her dismantle parts of it, he would hardly have believed it was not natural flesh. And did it matter, that it was not? If a living woman were dismantled, the result would be quite messy; it was not the innards a man wanted, but the externals. Regardless, Sheen was quite a female.

They emerged into a concourse crowded with serfs. Now she was taking his suggestion about merging with a crowd, at least for the moment. This channel led to the main depot for transport to other domes. Could they take a flight to a distant locale and lose the pursuit that way? Stile doubted it; any citizen could check any flight at the touch of a button. But if they did not, where would they go?

And, his thoughts continued ruthlessly, assuming she was able to hide him, and smuggled food to him—ah, joy: to live for a week on regurgitations!—and took care of his other needs—would she have to tote away his bodily wastes by hand, too?—so that he survived the necessary time—what then would he do for employment? Serfs were allowed a ten-day grace period between employers. After that their tenure was canceled and they were summarily deported. That meant he would have just three days to find a Citizen who could use his services—in a nonracing capacity. Stile's doubt that the anonymous Citizen after him was the same one who had sent Sheen or lasered his knee had grown and firmed. It just didn't fit. This meant there was another party involved, a more persistent and intelligent enemy, from whom he would never be safe—if he raced again.

A middle-aged serf stumbled and lunged against Stile. "Oops, sorry, junior," the man exclaimed, putting up a hand to steady Stile.

Sheen whirled with remarkable rapidity. Her open hand struck the man's wrist with nerve-stunning force. An ampule flew from his palm to shatter on the floor. "Oops, sorry, senior," she said, giving him a brief but hostile stare. The man backed hastily away and was gone.

That ampule—the needle would have touched Stile's flesh, had the man's hand landed. What had it contained? Nothing good for his health, surely! Sheen had intercepted it; she did know her business. He couldn't even thank her, at the moment, lest he give her away.

They moved on. Now there was no doubt: the enemy had him spotted, and the death squad was present. Sheen's caution about the crowd had been well considered; they could not remain here. He, Stile, was no longer hidden; his enemies were. The next ampule might score, perhaps containing a hypno-drug that would cause him to commit suicide or agree to a brain transplant. He didn't even dare look nervously about!

Sheen, with gentle pressure on his elbow, guided him into a cross-passage leading to a rest room. This one, for reasons having to do with the hour and direction of flow, was unused at the moment. It was dusk, and most serfs were eager to return to their residences, not delaying on the way.

She gave him a little shove ahead, but stayed back herself. Oh—she was going to ambush the pursuit, if there were any. Stile played along, marching on down to the rest room and stepping through its irising portal. Actually, he was in need of the facility. He had a reputation for nerve like iron in the Game, but never before had he been exposed to direct threats against his life. He felt tense and ill. He was now dependent on Sheen for initiative; he felt like locking himself into a relief booth and hiding his head under his arms. A useless gesture, of course.

The portal irised for another man. This one looked about quickly, saw that the facility was empty except for Stile, and advanced on him. "So you attack me, do you?" the stranger growled, flexing his muscular arms. He was large, even for this planet's healthy norm, and the old scars on his body hinted at his many prior fights. He probably had a free-for-all specialty in the Game, indulging in his propensity for unnecessary violence.

Stile rose hastily from his seat. How had Sheen let this torpedo through?

The man swung at Stile. One thing about nakedness: there were few concealed weapons. The blow, of course, never landed. Stile dodged, skipped around, and let the man stumble into the commode. Then Stile stepped quickly out through the iris. He could readily have injured or knocked out the man, for Stile himself was a combat specialist of no mean skill, but preferred to keep it neat and clean.

Sheen was there. "Did he touch you?" she asked immediately. "Or you him?"

"As it happens, no. I didn't see the need—"

She breathed a humanlike sigh of relief. "I let him through, knowing you could handle him, so I could verify how many others there were, and of what type they were." She gestured down the hall. Three bodies lay there. "If I had taken him out, the others might not have come, and the trap would have remained unsprung. But when I met the others, I comprehended the trap. They're all coated with stun-powder. Can't hurt me, can't hurt them—they're neutralized android stock. But you—"

Stile nodded. He had assumed he was being set up for an assault charge if he won, so had played it safe by never laying a finger on the man. Lucky for him!

Sheen gestured toward the Lady's room, her hands closed. Stile knew why; she had the powder on her hands, and could not touch him until she washed it off.

Stile poked his arm through the iris to open it for her—and someone on the other side grabbed his wrist. Oh-oh! He put his head down and dove through, primed to fight.

But it was only a crude matron robot. "No males allowed here," she said primly. She had recognized the male arm and acted immediately, as she was supposed to.

Sheen came through, touched the robot, and it went dead. "I have shorted her out, temporarily." She went to a sink and ran water over her hands. Then she stepped into an open shower and washed her whole body, with particular attention to any portion that might have come into contact with the powdered androids.

Stile heard something. "Company," he said. How was he going to get out of this one? The only exit was the iris through which the next woman would be entering.

Sheen beckoned him into the shower. He stepped in with her as the door irised. Sheen turned the spray on to FOG. Thick mist blasted out of the nozzle, concealing them both in its evanescent substance. It was faintly scented with rose: to make the lady smell nice.

In this concealment, Sheen's arms went about him, and her hungry lips found his. She evidently needed frequent proof of her desirability as a woman, just as he needed proof of his status as a man. Because each was constantly subject, in its fashion, to question. What an embrace!

When the room was clear again, Sheen turned the shower to rinse, then to dry. They had to separate for these stages, to Stile's regret. He had swung again from one extreme to another in his attitude toward her. Right now he wanted to make love—and knew this was not the occasion for it. But some other time, when they were safe, he would get her in a shower, turn on the fog, and—

Sheen stepped out and ran her fingers along the wall beside the shower stall. In a moment she found what she wanted, and slid open a panel. Another access for servicing machinery. She gestured him inside.

They wedged between pipes and came out in a narrow passage between the walls of the Man's and Lady's rooms. This passage wound around square corners, then dropped to a lower deck where it opened out into a service-machine storage chamber. Most of the machines were out, since night was their prime operating time, but several specialized ones remained in their niches. These were being serviced by a maintenance machine. At the moment it was cleaning a pipefitting unit, using static electricity to magnetize the grime and draw it into a collector scoop. The maintenance machine was in the aisle, so they had to skirt it to traverse this room.

Suddenly the machine lurched. Sheen slapped her hand on the machine's surface. A spark flashed, and there was the odor of ozone. The machine died, short-circuited.

"Why did you do that?" Stile asked her, alarmed. "If we start shorting out maintenance machines, it will call attention—"

Sheen did not respond. Then he saw the scorch mark along her body. She had taken a phenomenal charge of current. That charge would have passed through him, had he brushed the machine—as he had been about to, since it had lurched into the aisle as he approached. Another assassination attempt, narrowly averted!

But at what cost? Sheen still stood, unmoving. "Are you all right?" Stile asked, knowing she was not.

She neither answered nor moved. She, too, had been shorted by the charge. She was, in her fashion, dead.

"I hope it's just the power pack, not the brain," he

said. Her power supply had, she had thought, been weakened by her disassembly during the bomb scare. "We can replace the power pack." And if that did not work? He chose not to ponder that.

He went to a sweeping machine, opened its motive unit, and removed the standard protonite power pack. A little protonite went a long way; such a pack lasted a year with ordinary use. There was nothing to match it in the galaxy. In fact, the huge protonite lode was responsible for the inordinate wealth of Planet Proton. All the universe needed power, and this was the most convenient power available.

Stile brought the pack to Sheen. He hoped her robot-structure was standard in this respect; he didn't want to waste time looking for her power site. What made her special was her brain-unit, not her body, though that became easy to forget when he held her in his arms. Men thought of women in terms of their appearance, but most men were fools—and Stile was typical. Yet if Sheen's prime directive and her superficial form were discounted, she would hardly differ from the cleanup machines. So *was* it foolish to be guided by appearance and manner?

He ran his fingers over her belly, pressing the navel. Most humanoid robots—ah, there! A panel sprang out, revealing the power site. He hooked out the used power pack, still hot from its sudden discharge, and plugged in the new.

Nothing happened. Alarm tightened his chest. Oh—there would naturally be a safety-shunt, to cut off the brain from the body during a short, to preserve it. He checked about and finally located it: a reset switch hidden under her tongue. He depressed this, and Sheen came back to life.

She snapped her belly-panel closed. "Now I owe you one, Stile," she said.

"Are we keeping count? I need you—in more ways than two."

She smiled. "I'd be satisfied being needed for just one thing."

"That, too."

She glanced at him. She seemed more vibrant than before, as if the new power pack had given her an extra charge. She moved toward him.

There was a stir back the way they had come. It might be a machine, returning from a routine mission—but they did not care to gamble on that. Obviously they had not yet lost the enemy.

Sheen took him to the service side of a large feeding station. Silently she indicated the empty crates. A truck came once or twice a day to deliver new crates of nutro-powder and assorted color-flavor-textures, and to remove the expended shells. From these ingredients were fashioned the wide variety of foods the machines provided, from the vomitlike pudding to authentic-seeming carrots. It was amazing what technology could do. Actually, Stile had once tasted a real carrot from his employer's genuine exotic foods garden patch, a discard, and it had not been quite identical to the machine-constituted vegetable. As it happened, Stile preferred the taste and texture of the fake carrots with which he was familiar. But Citizens cultivated the taste for real foods.

He could hide inside one of these in fair comfort for several hours. Sheen would provide him with food; though this was *the* region for food, it was all sealed in its cartons, and would be inedible even if he could get one open. Only the machines, with their controlled temperature and combining mechanisms and recipe programs, could reconstitute the foods properly, and he was on the wrong side of their wall.

Stile climbed into a crate. Sheen walked on, so as not to give his position away. She would try to mislead the pursuit. If this worked, they would be home free for a day, perhaps for the whole week. Stile made himself halfway comfortable, and peered out through a crack.

No sooner had Sheen disappeared than a mech-mouse appeared. It twittered as it sniffed along, following their trail. It paused where Stile's trail diverged from Sheen's, confused, then proceeded on after her.

Stile relaxed, but not completely. Couldn't tell the difference between a robot and a man? Sniffers were better than that! He should have taken some precaution to minimize or mask his personal smell, for it was a sure giveaway—

Oh, Sheen had done that. She had given him a scented shower. The mouse was following the trail of rose—and Sheen's scent was now the same as his. A living hound should have been able to distinguish the two, but in noses, as in brains, the artificial had not yet closed the gap. Fortunately.

But soon that sniffer, or another like it, would return to trace the second trail, and would locate him. He would have to do something about that.

Stile climbed out of his box, suffered a pang in one knee, ran to his original trail, followed it a few paces, and diverged to another collection of crates. Then back, and to a truck-loading platform, where he stopped and retreated. With luck, it would seem he had caught a ride on the vehicle. Then he looped about a few more times, and returned to his original crate. Let the sniffers solve *that* puzzle!

But the sniffer did not return, and no one else came. This tracking operation must have been set up on the simplistic assumption that as long as the sniffer was moving, it was tracking him. His break—perhaps.

Time passed. The night advanced. Periodically the food machines exhausted a crate of cartons and ejected it, bumping the row along. Stile felt hungry again, but knew this was largely psychological; that double handful of regurgitated pudding should hold him a while yet.

Where was Sheen? Was she afraid to return to him while the sniffer was tracking her? She would have to neutralize the mech-mouse. Far from here, to distract suspicion from his actual hiding place. He would have to wait.

He watched anxiously. He dared not sleep or let down his guard until Sheen cleared him. He was dependent on her, and felt guilty about it. She was a nice . . . person, and should not have to—

A man walked down the hall. Stile froze—but this did not seem to be a pursuer. The man walked on.

Stile blinked. The man was gone. Had Stile been

nodding, and not seen the man depart—or was the stranger still near, having ducked behind a crate? In that case this could be a member of the pursuit squad. A serious matter.

Stile did not dare leave his crate now, for that would give away his position instantly. But if the stranger were of the squad, he would have a body-heat scope on a laser weapon. One beam through the crate—the murder would be anonymous, untraceable. There were criminals on Proton, cunning people who skulked about places like this, avoiding capture. Serfs whose tenure had expired, but who refused to be deported. The Citizens seldom made a concerted effort to eradicate them, perhaps because criminals had their uses on certain occasions. Such as this one? One more killing, conveniently unsolved, attributed to the nefarious criminal class—who never killed people against the wishes of Citizens. A tacit understanding. Why investigate the loss of an unemployed serf?

Should he move—or remain still? This was like the preliminary grid of the Game. If the stranger were present, and if he were a killer, and if he had spotted Stile—then to remain here was to die. But if Stile moved, he was sure to betray his location, and might die anyway. His chances seemed best if he stayed.

And—nothing happened. Time passed, and there was no further evidence of the man. So it must have been a false alarm. Stile began to feel foolish, and his knees hurt; he had unconsciously put tension on them, and they could not stand up to much of that, anymore.

Another man came, walking as the other had. This was a lot of traffic for a nonpersonal area like this, at this time of night. Suspicious in itself. Stile watched him carefully.

The man walked without pause down the hall—and vanished. He did not step to one side, or duck down; he simply disappeared.

Stile stared. He was a good observer, even through a crack in a crate; he had not mistaken what he had seen. Yet this was unlike anything he knew of on Planet Proton. Matter transmission did not exist, as far as he knew—but if it did, this was what it would be like. A screen, through which a person could step—to another location, instantly. Those two men—

Yet Sheen had gone that way without disappearing, and so had the mech-mouse. So there could not be such a screen set up across the hall. Not a permanent one.

Should he investigate? This could be important! But it could also be another trap. Again, like a Game-grid: what was the best course, considering the resources and strategy of his anonymous enemy?

Stile decided to stand pat. He had evidently lost the pursuit, and these disappearing people did not relate to him. He had just happened to be in a position to observe them. Perhaps this was not coincidental. The same concealment this service hall offered for him, it offered for them. If they had a private matter transmitter that they wanted to use freely without advertising it, this was the sort of place to set it up.

Yet aspects of this theory disturbed him. How could serfs have a matter transmitter, even if such a device existed? No serf owned anything, not even clothing for special occasions, for working outside the domes or in dangerous regions. Everything was provided by the system, as needed. There was no money, no medium of exchange; accounts were settled only when tenure ended. Serfs could not make such a device, except by adapting it from existing machines—and pretty precise computer accounts were kept, for sophisticated equipment. When such a part was lost, the machine tally gave the alarm. Which was another reason a criminal could not possess a laser weapon without at least tacit Citizen approval.

Also, why would any serf possessing such a device remain a serf? He could sell it to some galactic interest and retire on another planet with a fortune to rival that of a Proton Citizen. That would certainly be his course, for Citizens were unlikely to be too interested in forwarding development and production of a transport system that did not utilize protonite. Why destroy their monopoly?

Could the self-willed machines be involved in this? They might have the ability. But those were *men* he had seen disappear, and the machines would not have betrayed their secret to men.

No, it seemed more likely that this was an espionage operation, in which spies were ferried in and out of this dome, perhaps from another planet, or to and from some secret base elsewhere on Proton. If so, what would this spying power do to a genuine serf who stumbled upon the secret?

A woman appeared in the hall. She had emerged full-formed from the invisible screen, as it were from nowhere. She was of middle age, not pretty, and there was something odd about her. She had marks on her body as if the flesh had recently been pressed by something. By clothing, perhaps.

Serfs wore clothing on the other side? Only removing it for decent concealment in this society? These *had* to be from another world!

Stile peered as closely as possible at the region of disappearances. Now he perceived a faint shimmer, as of a translucent curtain crossing the hall obliquely. Behind it there seemed to be the image of trees.

Trees—in a matter-transmission station? This did not quite jibe! Unless it was not a city there, but a park. But why decorate such equipment this way? Camouflage?

Stile had no good answers. He finally put himself into a light trance, attuned to any other extraordinary events, and rested.

"Stile," someone called softly. "Stile."

It was Sheen, back at last! Stile looked down the hall and spied her, walking slowly, as if she had forgotten his whereabouts. Had she had another brush with a charged machine? "Here," he said, not loudly.

She turned and came toward him. "Stile."

"You lost the pursuit," he told her, standing in the crate so that his head and shoulders were clear. "No one even checked. But there is something else—"

Her hand shot out to grab his wrist with a grip like that of a vise. Stile was strong, but could not match the strength of a robot who was not being femininely human. What was she doing?

Her other hand smashed into the crate. The plastic shattered. Stile twisted aside, avoiding the blow despite remaining inside the crate; it was an automatic reaction. "Sheen, what—?"

She struck again. She was attacking him! He twisted aside again, drawing her off balance, using the leverage of her own grip on him. She was strong, but not heavy; he could move her about. Strength was only one element in combat; many people did not realize this, to their detriment.

Either Sheen had somehow been turned against him, which would have taken a complete reprogramming, or this was not Sheen. He suspected the latter; Sheen had known where he was hiding, while this robot had had to call. He had been a fool to answer, to reveal himself.

She struck again, and he twisted again. This was definitely not Sheen, for she had far greater finesse than this. It was not even a smart robot; it was a stupid mechanical. Good; he could handle it, despite its strength. Ethically and physically.

Her right hand remained clamped on his left wrist, while her left fist did the striking. Holding and hitting! If any of those blows landed squarely, he would suffer broken bones—but he was experienced in avoiding such an elementary attack. He turned about toward his left, drawing her hand and arm along with him, until he faced away from her, his right shoulder blocking hers. He heaved into a wraparound throw. She had to let go, or be hurled into the crate headfirst.

She was too stupid to let go. She crashed into the crate. Now at last her grip wrenched free, taking skin off his wrist. Stile scrambled out of the wrecked crate. He could junk her, now that he knew what she was, because he knew a great deal more about combat than she did. But he couldn't be *quite* sure she wasn't Sheen, with some override program on her, damping out most of her intellect and forcing her to obey the crude command. If he hurt her—

The robot scrambled out of the crate and advanced

on him. Her pretty face was smirched with dirt, and her hair was in disarray. Her right breast seemed to have been pounded slightly out of shape; a bad fall from the wraparound throw could account for that. Stile backed away, still torn by indecision. He could overcome this robot, but he would have to demolish her in the process. If only he could be *sure* she wasn't—

Another Sheen appeared. "Stile!" she cried. "Get under cover! The squad is—" Then she recognized the other robot. "Oh, no! The old duplicate-image stunt!"

Stile had no doubt now: the second Sheen was the right one. But the first one had done half her job. She had routed him out and distracted him—too long. For now the android squad hove into sight, several lumbering giants.

"I'll hold them!" Sheen cried. "Run!"

But more androids were coming from the other end of the hall. It seemed the irate Citizen no longer cared about being obvious; he just wanted Stile dispatched. If these lunks were also powdered with stun-dust or worse—

Stile charged down the hall and lunged into the matter-transmission curtain, desperately hoping it would work for him. The androids might follow—but they could be in as much trouble as he, at the other end. Intruding strangers. That would give him a better fighting chance. He felt a tingle as he went through.

CHAPTER 5

Fantasy

Stile drew up in a deep forest. The smell of turf and fungus was strong, and old leaves crackled underfoot. The light from four moons beamed down between the branches to illuminate the ground. It would have been near dawn, on Proton; it seemed to be the same time of day here. The same number of moons as Proton, too; there were seven, with three or four usually in sight. Gravity, however, seemed close to Earth-normal, so if this was really outside a dome, it was a spot on a larger or denser planet than Proton.

He turned to face his pursuers—but there were none. They had not passed through the shimmering curtain. He looked carefully, locating it—and saw, dimly, the light at the hall he had left, with the scattered crates. Sheen was there—one of them—and several androids. One android came right at him—and disappeared.

Stile watched, determined to understand this phenomenon, because it reflected most directly on his immediate welfare. He had passed through—but the robots and androids had not. This thing transmitted only human beings? Not artificial ones? That might be reasonable. But he hesitated to accept that until there was more data.

In his absence the fight on the other side of the curtain soon abated. The androids and fake-Sheen departed, apparently on his trail again—a false one. Only the real Sheen remained, as the squad evidently considered her irrelevant—and it seemed she could not perceive either him or the curtain.

Stile decided to risk crossing back, if only to tell her he was safe. There was risk, as the squad could be lurking nearby, hoping Sheen would lead them to him again—but he could not leave her tormented by doubt. This could be a much better hideout than the crate! He stepped through the curtain—and found himself still in the dark forest. He had crossed without being matter-transmitted back.

He looked back—and there it was, behind him. Through it he saw the imprint of his feet in the soft forest loam, the leaves and tufts of grass and moss all pressed flat for the moment. And, like a half-reflection, the square of light of the service hall, now empty.

He passed through the curtain a third time. There was no tingle, no sensation. He turned about and looked through—and saw Sheen searching for him, unrobotic alarm on her cute face. Oh, yes, she cared!

"I'm here, Sheen!" he called, passing his hand through. But his hand did not reach her; it remained in the forest. She gave no evidence of seeing or hearing him.

She would think him dead—and that bothered him more than the notion of being trapped this side of the matter-transmission screen. If she thought him dead, she would consider her mission a failure, and then turn herself off, in effect committing suicide. He did not want her to do that—no, not at all!

"Sheen!" he cried, experiencing a surge of emotion. "Sheen—look at me! I'm caught here beyond a one-way transmit—" But if it really were one-way, of course she would not be able to see him! However, it had to be two-way, because he had seen people traveling both ways through the curtain, and he had seen the forest from Proton, and could now see Proton from the forest. "Sheen!" he cried again, his urgency almost choking him.

Her head snapped around. *She had heard him!*

Stile waved violently. "Here! Here, Sheen! Through the curtain!"

Her gaze finally fixed on him. She reached through the curtain—and did not touch him. "Stile—" Her voice was faint.

He grabbed her hands in his, with no physical contact; their fingers phased through each other like images, like superimposing holographs. "Sheen, we are in two different worlds! We can not touch. But I'm safe here." He hoped.

"Safe?" she asked, trying to approach him. But as she passed through the curtain, she disappeared. Stile quickly stepped across himself, turning—and there she was on the other side, facing away from him, looking down the hall.

She turned and saw him again, with an effort. "Stile —I can't reach you! How can I protect you? Are you a ghost?"

"I'm alive! I crossed once—and can't cross back. It's a whole new world here, a nice one. Trees and grass and moss and earth and fresh air—"

They held hands again, each grasping air. "How—?"

"I don't *know* how to cross! There must be a way to return, because I've seen a woman do it, but until I find out how—"

"I must join you!" She tried again to cross, and failed again. "Oh, Stile—"

"I don't think it works for nonhumans," he said. "But if I can remain here for a week, and find out how to return—"

"I will wait for you," she said, and there was something plaintive in her stance. She wanted so much to protect him from harm, and could not. "Go into that world—maybe it is better for you."

"I will come back—when I can," Stile promised.

He saw the tears in her eyes. To hell with the assorted humanoid artifices such robots were programmed with; she meant it! Stile spread his arms, at the verge of the curtain. She opened hers, and they embraced intangibly, and kissed air, and vanished from each other's perception.

He had promised—but would he be able to keep that pledge? He didn't know, and he worried that Sheen would maintain her vigil long after hope was gone, suffering as only a virtually immortal robot could suffer. That hurt him, even in anticipation. Sheen did not deserve to be a machine.

Stile did not tease himself or Sheen further. He

strode on through the curtain and into the forest. He had a fair knowledge of earthy vegetation, because aspects of the Game required identification of it, and a number of Citizens imported exotic plants. The light was poor, but with concentration, he could manage.

The nearest tree was a huge oak, or a very similar species, with the air-plants called Spanish moss dangling from its branches. Beyond it was a similarly large spruce, or at any rate a conifer; this was the source of that pine-perfume smell. There were large leaves looking like separated hands in the shadow, and pine needles—so there must be a pine tree here somewhere—but mostly this was a glade with fairly well-established grass in the center. Stile liked it very well; it reminded him of an especially exotic Citizen's retreat.

Dawn was coming. There was no dome above, no shimmer of the force field holding in the air. Through the trees he saw the dark clouds of the horizon looming, trying like goblins to hold back the burgeoning light of the sun, and slowly failing. Planet Proton had no such atmospheric effects! Red tinted the edes of the clouds, and white; it was as if a burning fluid were accumulating behind, brimming over, until finally it spilled out and a shaft of scintillating sunlight lanced at lightspeed through the air and struck the ground beside Stile. The whole thing was so pretty that he stood entranced until the sun was fairly up, too bright to look at anymore.

The forest changed, by developing daylight. The somberness was gone—and so was the curtain. That barrier had been tenuous by night; it could still be present, but drowned by the present effulgence. He could not locate it at all. That bothered him, though it probably made no difference. He walked about, examining the trees; some had flowers opening, and stray rustlings denoted hidden life. Birds, squirrels—he would find out what they were in due course.

He liked this place. It could have been a private garden, but this was natural, and awesomely extensive.

Caution prevented him from shouting to check for echoes, but he was sure this was the open surface of a planet. Not at all what he would have expected from a matter-transmission outlet.

He found a large bull-spruce—damn it, it *was* a spruce!—its small dry branches radiating out in all directions. This was the most climbable of trees, and Stile of course was an excellent climber. He did not resist the temptation. He mounted that big old tree with a primitive joy.

Soon he was in the upper reaches, and gusts of wind he had not felt below were swaying the dwindling column of the trunk back and forth. Stile loved it. His only concern was the occasional pain in his knees when he tried to bend them too far; he did not want to aggravate the injury carelessly.

At last he approached the reasonable limit of safety. The tops of surrounding trees were dropping below him, their foliage like low hedges from this vantage. He anchored himself by hooking legs and elbows conveniently, and looked about.

The view was a splendor. The forest abutted the cliff-like face of a nearby mountain to one side—south, according to the sun—and thinned to the north into islands of trees surrounded by sealike fields of bright grain. In the distance the trees disappeared entirely, leaving a gently rolling plain on which animals seemed to be grazing. Farther to the north there seemed to be a large river, terminating abruptly in some kind of crevice, and a whitish range of mountains beyond that. To either side all he could see was more forest, a number of the individual trees taller than this one. The mountain to the south faded upward into a purple horizon.

There seemed to be no sign of civilized habitation. This was less and less like a matter-transmission station! Yet if not that, what was it? He had seen other people pass through the curtain, and had done so himself; there had to be something more than a mere wilderness.

He looked again, fixing the geography in his mind for future reference. Then he spied a structure of some sort to the northeast. It looked like a small medieval castle, with high stone walls and turrets, and perhaps a blue pennant.

Very well: human habitation did exist. Yet this remained a far cry from modern technology. He liked this world very well, but he simply didn't trust it. Matter transmission could not exist without an extremely solid industrial base, and if that base were not here, where was it? Was this a sweetly baited trap for people like him, who were in trouble on Proton? In what manner would that trap be sprung?

Stile climbed down. His best course, as he saw it, would be to go to that castle and inquire. But first he wanted to check the region of the curtain again, fixing it absolutely in his mind so he could find it any time he wanted to—because this was his only contact with his own world, and with Sheen. This wilderness-world might be an excellent place to stay for a while, but then he would need to go home, lest he suffer exile by default.

He was approaching the invisible curtain—when a man popped out of it. Friend or foe? Stile decided not to risk contact, but the man spied him before he could retreat to cover. "Hey—get lost?" the stranger called. "It's over here."

"Uh, yes," Stile said, approaching. This did not seem to be an android or robot. Abruptly deciding not to compromise on integrity even by implication, he added: "I came through by accident. I don't know where I am."

"Oh, a new one! I first crossed last year. Took me six months to learn the spells to cross back. Now I go over for free meals, but I live over here in Phaze."

"Spells—to cross back?" Stile asked blankly.

"How else? From the other side you just have to will-to-cross hard enough, but from this side only a spell will do it—a new one every time. You'll get the hang of it."

"I—thought this was a matter-transmission unit."

The man laughed as he walked to a tree and reached into the foliage of a low branch. A package came down into his hands. "There's no such thing as matter transmission! No, it's the magic curtain. It's all over—but it's not safe to use it just anywhere. You have to make sure no one on the other side sees you go through. You know how those Citizens are. If they ever caught on there was something they didn't control—"

"Yes. I am unemployed because of Citizen manipulation."

"Which explains why you had the will-to-cross, first time. The curtain's been getting clearer, but still you can't even see it if you don't have good reason, let alone use it. Then you have to will yourself through, strongly, right as you touch it. Most people never make it, ever." The man opened his package and brought out a crude tunic, which he donned.

Stile stared. "You wear clothes here?" He remembered the clothing-marks on the woman.

"Sure do. You'd stick out like a sore toe if you went naked here in Phaze!" The man paused, appraising Stile. "Look, you're new here, and sort of small—I'd better give you an amulet." He rummaged in his bag, while Stile suppressed his unreasoning resentment of the remark about his size. The man had not intended any disparagement.

"An amulet?" Stile asked after a moment. He considered himself to be swift to adjust to new realities, but he found it hard to credit this man's evident superstition. Spell—magic—amulet—how could a Proton serf revert to medieval Earth lore so abruptly?

"Right. We're supposed to give them to newcomers. To help them get started, keep things smooth, so there's no ruckus about the curtain and all. We've got a good thing going here; could sour if too many people got in on it. So don't go blabbing about the curtain carelessly; it's better to let people discover it by accident."

"I will speak of it only cautiously," Stile agreed. That did make sense, whatever the curtain was, matter transmission or magic.

The man finally found what he was looking for: a statuette hanging on a chain. "Wear this around your neck. It will make you seem clothed properly, until you can work up a real outfit. Won't keep you warm or dry;

it's just illusion. But it helps. Then you can pass it on to some other serf when he comes across. Help him keep the secret. Stay anonymous; that's the rule."

"Yes." Stile accepted the amulet. The figure was of a small demon, with horns, tail and hooves, scowling horrendously. "How does this thing work?"

"You just put it on and invoke it. Will it to perform. That's all; it's preset magic that anybody can use. You'll see. You probably don't really believe in magic yet, but this will show you."

"Thank you," Stile said, humoring him.

The man waved negligently as he departed in his tunic and sandals, bearing south. Now Stile made out a faint forest path there, obvious only when one knew where to look. In a moment he was gone.

Stile stared down at the amulet. Belief in magic! The man had spoken truly when he said Stile was a skeptic! Yet the fellow had seemed perfectly sensible in other respects. Maybe it was a figure of speech. Or a practical joke, like an initiation rite. See what foolishness newcomers could be talked into. Emperor's new clothes.

He shook his head. "All right, I won't knock what I haven't tried. I'll play the game—once. Amulet, I invoke you. Do your thing." And he put the chain on over his head.

Suddenly he was strangling. The chain was constricting, cutting off his wind and blood. The amulet seemed to be expanding, its demon-figure holding the ends of the chain in its miniature hands, grinning evilly as it pulled.

Stile did not know how this worked, but he knew how to fight for his life. He ducked his chin down against his neck and tightened his muscles, resisting the constriction of the chain. He hooked a finger into the crease between chin and neck on the side, catching the chain, and yanked. He was trying to break a link, but the delicate-seeming metal was too strong; he was only cutting his finger.

More than one way to fight a garrote! Stile grabbed the grinning demon by its two little arms and hauled them apart. The little monster grimaced, trying to resist, but the chain slackened. Stile took a breath, and felt the trapped blood in his head flow out. Pressure on the jugular vein did not stop the flow of blood to the brain, as many thought; it stopped the return of the blood from the head back to the heart. That was uncomfortable enough, but not instantly conclusive.

But still the demon grew, and as it did its strength increased in proportion. It drew its arms together again, once more constricting the loop about Stile's neck.

Even through his discomfort, Stile managed a double take. The demon was *growing*? Yes it was; he had observed it without noting it. From an amulet a few centimeters long it had become a living creature, swelling horrendously as it fought. Now it was half the size of Stile himself, and fiendishly strong.

Stile held his breath, put both hands on the hands of the demon, and swung it off its feet. He whirled it around in a circle. It was strong—but as with robot strength, this was not sufficient without anchorage or leverage. This was another misconception many people had, assuming that a superman really could leap a mile or pick up a building by one corner or fight invincibly. That belief had cost many Gamesmen their games with Stile—and might cost this demon its own success. As long as the creature clung to the chain, it was in fact captive—and when it let go, even with one hand, it would free Stile from the constant threat of strangulation. That would be a different contest entirely.

The demon clung tenaciously to its misconception. It did not let go. It grinned again, showing more teeth than could fit even in a mouth that size, and clamped its arms yet closer, tightening the noose. Stile felt his consciousness going; he could hold his breath for minutes, but the constriction was slowing his circulation of blood, now squeezing his neck so tightly that the deeply buried carotid artery was feeling it. That could put him out in seconds.

He staggered toward a towering tulip tree, still whirling his burden. He heaved mightily—and smashed the creature's feet into the trunk.

It was quite a blow. The thing's yellow eyes widened,

showing jags of flame-red, and the first sound escaped from it. "Ungh!" Some chain slipped, giving Stile respite, but still the demon did not let go.

Stile hauled it up and whirled it again, with difficulty. He had more strength now, but the demon had continued to grow (how the hell could it do that? This was absolutely crazy!), and was at this point only slightly smaller than Stile himself. It required special power and balance to swing it—but this time its midsection smashed into the tree. Now its burgeoning mass worked against it, making the impact stronger. The demon's legs bent around the trunk with the force of momentum; then they sprang back straight.

Stile reversed his swing, taking advantage of the bounce, bringing the demon around in the opposite arc and smashing it a third time into the tree. This time it was a bone-jarring blow, and a substantial amount of slack developed in the chain.

Stile, alert for this instant, slipped his head free in one convulsive contortion. The chain burned his ears and tore out tufts of his hair—but he had won the first stage of this battle.

But now the demon was Stile's own size, still full of fight. It scrambled to its hooved feet and sprang at him, trying to loop the cord about his neck again. It seemed to be a one-tactic fighter. In that respect it resembled the imitation-Sheen robot Stile had fought not so very long ago.

Stile caught its hands from the outside, whirled, ducked, and hauled the demon over his shoulder. The thing lifted over him and whomped into the ground with a jar that should have knocked it out. But again it scrambled up, still fighting.

What was *with* this thing? It refused to turn off! It had taken a battering that would have shaken an android—and all it did was grow larger and uglier. It was now a quarter again as large as Stile, and seemed to have gained strength in proportion. Stile could not fight it much longer, this way.

Yet again the demon dived for him, chain spread. Stile had an inspiration. He grabbed the chain, stepped to one side, tripped the demon—and as it stumbled, Stile looped the slack chain about the creature's own body and held it there from behind.

The demon roared and turned about, trying to reach him, but Stile clung like a blob of rubber cement. He had discommoded large opponents this way before, clinging to the back; it was extremely hard for a person to rid himself of such a rider if he did not know how. This demon was all growth and strength, having no special intelligence or imagination; it did not know how.

The demon kept growing. Now it was half again as large as Stile—and the chain was beginning to constrict its body. Stile hung on, staying out of the thing's awkward graspings, keeping that chain in place. Unless the demon could stop growing voluntarily—

Evidently it could not. It grew and grew, and as it expanded the chain became tighter, constricting its torso about the middle. It had fallen into the same noose it had tried to use on Stile. All it had to do was let go the ends—and it was too stupid to do that. What colossal irony! Its own arms wrapped around it, being drawn nearly out of their sockets, but the only way it knew to fight was to hang on to that chain. It became woman-waisted, then wasp-waisted. Stile let go and stood apart, watching the strange progression. The creature seemed to feel no pain; it still strove to reach Stile, to wrap its chain about him, though this was now impossible.

The demon's body ballooned, above and below that tiny waist. Then it popped. There was a cloud of smoke, dissipating rapidly.

Stile looked at the ground. There lay the chain, broken at last, separated where the demon-figure had been. The amulet was gone.

He picked it up, nervous about what it might do, but determined to know what remained. It dangled loosely from his hand. Its power was gone.

Or was it? What would happen if he invoked it again? Stile decided that discretion was best. He coiled the chain, laid it on the ground, and rolled a rock to cover it. Let the thing stay there, pinned like a poisonous snake!

Now that the threat was over, Stile unwound. His body was shivering with reaction. What, exactly, had happened? What was the explanation for it?

He postulated and discarded a number of theories. He prided himself on his ability to analyze any situation correctly and swiftly; that was a major part of his Game success. What he concluded here, as the most reasonable hypothesis fitting all his observations, was quite *un*reasonable.

A. He was in a world where magic worked.

B. Someone/thing was trying to kill him here, too.

He found conclusion A virtually incredible. But he preferred it to the alternatives: that a super-technological power had created all this, or that he, Stile, was going crazy. Conclusion B was upsetting—but death threats against him had become commonplace in the past few hours. So it was best to accept the evidence of his experience: that he was now in a fantasy realm, and still in trouble.

Stile rubbed his fingers across his neck, feeling the burn of the chain. Who was after him, here? Surely not the same anonymous angry Citizen who had sent the android squads. The serf who had crossed the curtain and given him the amulet had been friendly; had he wanted to kill Stile, he could have done so by invoking the demon at the outset. It seemed more likely that the man had been genuinely trying to help—and that the amulet had acted in an unforeseen manner. Perhaps there were a number of such magic talismans, dual-purpose: clothe the ordinary person, kill certain other persons. Other persons like Stile. That left a lot in doubt, but accounted for what had happened. Stile was a fair judge of people and motives; nothing about the other man had signaled treachery or enmity. The amulet, as a mechanism to protect this land from certain people, seemed reasonable.

Why was he, Stile, unwanted here? *That* he would have to find out. It was not merely because he was new. The stranger had been new, not so long ago, by his own admission. Presumably he had been given a similar amulet, and used it, and it had performed as specified. Stile had at first suspected some kind of practical joke—but that demon had been no joke!

It could not be because he was small, or male; those could hardly be crimes in a human society. There had to be something else. Some special quality about him that triggered the latent secondary function of the amulet. Unless the effect was random: one bad amulet slipped in with the good ones, a kind of Russian roulette, and he happened to be the victim. But he was disinclined to dismiss it like that. A little bit of paranoia could go far toward keeping him out of any further mischief. Best to assume someone was out to get him, and play it safe.

Meanwhile, he would be well advised to get away from this region, before whoever had laid the amulet-trap came to find out why it had failed. And—he wanted to learn more about the status of magic here. Was it some form of illusion, or was it literal? The demon had shown him that his life could depend on the answer.

Where would he go? How could he know? Anywhere he could find food, and sleep safely, and remain hidden from whatever enemy he must have. *Not* the nearest castle he had spied; he was wary of that now. Anything near this place was suspect. He had to go somewhere in the wilderness, alone—

Alone? Stile did not like the thought. He was hardly a social lion, but he was accustomed to company. Sheen had been excellent company. For this strange land—

Stile nodded to himself. Considering all things, he needed a horse. He understood horses, he trusted them, he felt secure with them. He could travel far, with a good steed. And there surely were horses grazing in those fields to the north. He had not been able to make out the specific animals he had seen from the tree, but they had had a horsey aspect.

CHAPTER 6

Manure

Stile walked north, keeping a wary eye out for hazards, demonic or otherwise, and for something else. The land, as the trees thinned, became pretty in a different way. There were patches of tall lush grass, and multicolored flowers, and sections of tumbled rocks. And, finally, a lovely little stream, evidently issuing from the mountains to the south, bearing irregularly northwest. The water was absolutely clear. He lay on his stomach and put his lips to it, at the same time listening for any danger; drinking could be a vulnerable moment.

The water was so cold his mouth went numb and his throat balked at swallowing. He took his time, savoring it; beverages were so varied and nutritious and available on Proton that he had seldom tasted pure water, and only now appreciated what he had missed.

Then he cast about for fruit trees, but found none. He had no means to hunt and kill animals right now, though in time he was sure he could devise something. Safety was more urgent than nourishment, at the moment; his hunger would have to wait. With a horse he could go far and fast, leaving no footprints of his own and no smell not masked by that of the animal; he would become untraceable.

He followed the stream down, knowing it was a sure guide to the kind of animal life he wanted. This was ideal horse country; had he actually seen some horses grazing, there from the treetop, or only made an image of a wish? He could not be certain now, but trusted his instincts. Magic confused him, but he knew the ways of horses well.

Suddenly he spied it: the semicircular indentation of the hoof of a horse. And, safely back from the water, a pile of horse manure. Confirmation!

Stile examined the hoofprint. It was large, indicating an animal of perhaps seventeen hands in height, solidly built. It was unshod, and chipped at the fringes, but not overgrown. A fat, healthy horse who traveled enough to keep the hooves worn, and was careless enough to chip them on stones. Not the ideal mount for him, but it would do. Stile felt the relief wash through his body, now that he had the proof; he had not imagined it, he had not deluded himself, there really were horses here. His experience with the demon amulet had shaken his certainties, but this restored them.

He moved over to the manure and stared down at it. And faded into a memory. Seventeen years ago, as a youth of eighteen, looking down at a similar pile of dung . . .

His parents' tenure had ended, and they had had to vacate Planet Proton. Tenure was twenty years for serfs, with no exceptions—except possibly via the Game, a more or less futile lure held out to keep the peons hoping. He had been fortunate; he had been born early in their tenure, and so had eighteen free years. He had fitted in a full education and mastered Proton society before he had to make the choice: to stay with his folks, or to stay on Proton.

His parents, with twenty years cumulative pay awaiting them, would be moderately wealthy in the galaxy. They might not be able to swing passage all the way back to Earth, but there were other planets that were really quite decent. They would be able to afford many good things. On the other hand, if he remained on Proton he would have to serve twenty years as a serf, naked, obedient to the whims of some Citizen employer, knowing that when that tenure ended he too would be exiled.

But—here on Proton was the Game.

He had been addicted to the Game early. In a culture of serfs, it was an invaluable release. The Game was violence, or intellect, or art, or chance, alone or with tools or machines or animals—but mainly it was challenge. It had its own hierarchy, independent of the outside status of the players. Every age-ladder had its rungs, for all to see. The Game had its own magic. He was good at it from the outset; he had a natural aptitude. He was soon on his ladder, on any rung he chose. But he never chose too high a rung.

Family—or Game? It had been no contest. He had chosen Planet Proton. He had taken tenure the day his parents boarded the spaceship, and he had waited for a Citizen to employ him. To his surprise, one had picked him up the first day. He had been conducted to the Citizen's plush estate—there were no *un*plush Citizens' estates—and put in the pasture and given a wagon and a wide pitchfork.

His job was to spade horse manure. He had to take his fork and wheelbarrow and collect every pile of dung the Citizen's fine horses were gracious enough to deposit on the fine lawns. Homesick for his exiled family—it was not that he had loved them less, but that at his age he had loved the Game more—and unaccustomed to the discipline of working for a living, he found this a considerable letdown. Yet it did allow him time to be alone, and this was helpful.

He was not alone during off-hours. He slept in a loft-barracks with nine other pasture hands, and ate in a mess hall with thirty serfs. He had no privacy and no personal possessions; even his bedding was only on loan, a convenience to prevent his sweat from contaminating anyone else. In the morning the light came on and they all rose, swiftly; at night the light went out. No one missed a bed check, ever. At home with his folks he had had no curfew; they went off to their employers by day, and as long as he kept up with his schooling his time was largely his own—which meant he would be playing the Game, and drilling himself in its various techniques. Here it was different, and he wondered whether he had after all made the right choice. Of course he had to grow up sometime; he just hadn't expected to do it overnight.

The Citizen-employer was inordinately wealthy, as most Citizens were. He had several fine pastures, in scattered locations. It was necessary to travel through the city-domes from one property to another, and somehow the work was always piling up ahead of him.

Some of the pastures were cross-fenced, with neat white Earth-grown wooden boards and genuine pre-rusted nails. These barriers were of course protected by invisible microwires that delivered an uncomfortable electric shock to anyone who touched the surface. The horses were not smart, but they had good memories; they seldom brushed the fences. Stile, of course, had to learn the hard way; no one told him in advance. That was part of his initiation.

He learned. He found that the cross-fencing was to keep the horses in one pasture while allowing a new strain of grass to become established in another; if the horses had at it prematurely, they would destroy it by overgrazing before it had a chance. Pastures were rotated. When animals had to be separated, they were put in different pastures. There were many good reasons for cross-fencing, and the employer, despite his wealth, heeded those reasons.

Stile's problem was that he had to cross some of those fences, to collect the manure from far pastures. He was small, too small simply to step over as a tall serf might. He was acrobatic, so could readily have hurdled the 1.5 meter fences, but this was not permitted, lest it give the horses notions. The horses did not know it was possible to jump fences outside of a formal race, so had never tried it. Also, his landing might scuff the turf, and that was another offense. Only horses had the right to scuff; they were valuable creatures, with commensurate privileges.

Thus he had to proceed laboriously around the fence, going to far-flung gates where, of course, he had to debate the right-of-way with horses who outmassed him by factors of ten to fifteen. This slowed his work, and he was already behind. Fortunately he was a good runner, and if he moved swiftly the horses often did not bother to keep up. They could outrun him if they had a mind to, anytime, but they never raced when they didn't have to. It seemed to be a matter of principle. They did not feel the same rivalry with a man that they did with members of their own species.

Then he discovered the stile: a structure like a standing stepladder that enabled him to cross the fence and haul his wheelbarrow across without touching a board. The horses could not navigate such a thing, and did not try. It was, in its fashion, a bridge between worlds. With it he could at last get around the pastures fast enough to catch up to his work.

Now that he was on tenure, he was expected to take an individual name. He had gone by his father's serf-name, followed by a dependence-number. When the Proton serf registry asked him for his choice of an original and personal designation, his irrevocable and possibly only mark of distinction, he gave it: Stile.

"Style? As in elegance?" the serf-interviewer inquired, gazing down at him with amusement. "A grandiose appellation for a lad your size."

Stile's muscles tightened in abdomen, buttocks, and shoulders. This "lad" was eighteen, full-grown—but to strangers he looked twelve. The depilatories in Proton wash water kept the hair off his face and genitals, so that his sexual maturity was not obvious. A woman his size would not have had a problem; depilatories did not affect her most obvious sexual characteristics. He was fed up with the inevitable remarks; normal-heighted people always thought they were being so damned clever with their slighting allusions to his stature. But already he was learning to conceal his annoyance, not even pretending to take it as humor. "Stile, as in fence. S-T-I-L-E. I'm a pasture hand."

"Oh." He was so designated, and thereafter was invariably addressed this way. The use of the proper name was obligatory among serfs. Only Citizens had the pleasure of anonymity, being addressed only as "sir." If any serf knew the name of a Citizen, he kept it to himself, except on those rare occasions when he needed to identify his employer for an outsider.

It turned out to be a good choice. Stile—it was original and distinctive, and in the context of the Game, suggestive of the homonym. For in the Game he did indeed have a certain style. But best of all were the ramifications of its original meaning: a bridge between pastures. A stile represented a dimensionally expanded freedom and perception, as it were a choice of worlds. He liked that concept.

With experience he became more proficient. Every clod of dung he overlooked was a mark against him, a sure route to ridicule by the other hands, all of whom were larger if not older than he and had more seniority. In a society of workers who had no individual rights not relating to their jobs, the nuances of private protocol and favor became potent. "Stile—two clods in the buckwheat pasture," the foreman would announce grimly as he made his daily review of demerits, and the group would snigger discreetly, and Stile would be low man on the farm totem for the next day. He was low man quite often, in the early weeks. Other hands would "accidentally" shove him, and if he resisted he received a reprimand for roughhousing that put him low for another day. For, except in egregious cases, the higher man on the totem was always right, and when it was one serf's word against another's, the low man lost. The foreman, basically a fair man, honored this convention scrupulously. He was competent, the only serf on the farm with actual power, and the only one granted the privilege of partial anonymity: his title was used instead of his name. He never overstepped his prerogatives, or permitted others to.

There came one day when Stile had not fouled up. A hulking youth named Shingle was low for the day—and Shingle brushed Stile roughly on the path to the service area. Stile drew on his Game proficiency and ducked while his foot flung out, "accidentally" sending Shingle crashing into the barn wall. Furious, Shingle charged him, fists swinging—and Stile dropped to the ground, put his foot in the man's stomach, hauled on one arm, and flipped him through the air to land on the lush green turf so hard his body gouged it. Shingle's breath was knocked out, and the other hands stood amazed.

The foreman arrived. "What happened here?" he demanded.

"An accident," the others informed him, smirking innocently. "Shingle—fell over Stile."

The foreman squinted appraisingly at Stile, who stood with eyes downcast, knowing this meant trouble, expecting to receive the ridicule of the group again. Fighting was forbidden on these premises. Out came the clipboard the foreman always carried. "Shingle—one gouge in turf," the foreman said. And almost smiled, as the group sniggered.

For Shingle had been the man low on the totem, whose business it had been to avoid trouble. He was by definition wrong.

The foreman turned to Stile. "Accidents will happen—but in future you will report to the recreation room for practice in your martial arts, Stile." He departed on his rounds.

Stile only gained one day clear of the low totem, officially, for that day he overlooked another dropping. But he had traveled considerably higher in the estimate of his peers. They had not known he was into martial art. In turn, he remembered how they had stood by him, honoring the convention, laughing this time at the other fellow. Stile had won, by the tacit rules; the others had seemed to be against him only because he had been low totem, not because he was new or small. That was a supremely warming realization.

After that Stile began to make friends. He had held himself aloof, unconsciously, assuming the others looked down on him. If they had, they certainly didn't anymore. Now when he fouled up and they snickered, it was friendly, almost rueful. Even Shingle, nose out of joint about the episode, never made an issue of it; he too abided by the rules, and he had lost fairly.

Meanwhile, Stile was becoming adept at spotting horse manure. Horses tended to deposit their solid loads in semiprivate places, in contrast to their liquid ones. Liquid went anywhere at all, sometimes even on their food, but solids were always well away from eating, grazing or resting areas. This made the piles more challenging to find.

Missing piles tended to put him low on the totem. Consequently Stile had considerable incentive to improve his performance. He developed an extremely sharp eye for horse manure. His nose was not much help, for horses had mild refuse, unlike pigs or chickens; never unpleasant, its odor quickly faded. If left a few days—God forbid!—it could even sprout grass from undigested grains, for the digestion of horses was less sophisticated than that of cows. Horses were adapted to running, and their structure and heat-dissipation mechanism and digestion reflected this. So Stile's nose availed only when he was in the near vicinity of a find. Yet sight was not the whole answer either, for the piles could be concealed in copses of trees or amidst bushes. Sometimes he found chunks of it in the foliage of low-springing branches. There was also the problem of rain—artificial, of course, here in the domes—that wet down the manure and tended to flatten and blend it with its surroundings. Even when everything was ideal, manure seemed to be able to disappear when he was in the vicinity, only to reappear when the foreman checked. It was so easy to overlook a pile on the left while collecting one on the right!

Stile's instincts for manure sharpened to the point of near perfection. He could spade a full pile into his barrow with one scoop and heave, not missing a chunk. He learned the favorite deposit sites of the horses, and checked there first. Sometimes he even beat the artificial flies there. He could look at a section of pasture and tell by the lay of it whether a horse would want to contribute.

Yet when he had mastered his job, it grew boring. Stile was bright, very bright. People tended to assume that small stature meant small intelligence, but it was not true. The work became stultifying. Had he mastered calculus and Terrestrial ecology and aspects of quantum physics merely to fling dung for twenty years? Call him the King of Dung! Why had the Citizen snapped him up so quickly, only to throw him away on this?

But Citizens were all-powerful on Proton. They did not answer to serfs for their actions. Stile could neither complain nor change employers; his rights in the matter extended only to accepting proffered employment or suffering premature termination of tenure. If he wanted to remain on Planet Proton, he obeyed the system. He spaded dung.

Often while at work he watched the horses, covertly, lest he seem to be malingering. There was Sonny, a small handsome paint hackney with large ears, used for training new riders though he had no proper trot. Simcoe Cloud, an appaloosa gelding sixteen hands high, with a pretty "blanket" but too large a head. Navahjo, a fine quarter horse, dominant in her pasture though she was a mare. In another pasture were Misty, a gray plump Tennessee Walker with a will of her own, and her companion Sky Blue, only fourteen hands high and over twenty years old. Blue was a former harness racer, well trained but shy despite her graying head. There was Cricket, also gray verging on white. There were, according to the dictates of horse registry, no white horses; a horse that looked white was either albino or registered gray. Thus the joke: "What color was George Washington's white horse? Gray."

These constituted Stile's world, during much of his working time. He came to know them all, from a moderate distance, from Shetland pony to massive draft horse. He longed to associate more closely with them, to pat them, brush them, walk them—but that was the prerogative of the stable hands, fiercely guarded. Stile was only a pasture hand, never allowed to get overly familiar with the stock. On many days his closest approach to a living horse was its manure.

Yet from that necessary distance, what beauty! There was a peculiar grace to a horse, any horse. The power of the muscles, the spring of the ankles, the alertness of the ears, the constant swishing of the tail. There were no natural flies here, so android flies were provided, that made loud buzzing sounds and swooped around the horses, just to provide exercise for those tails. Stile loved to watch the tails, perhaps the prettiest thing about any horse except for the manes. On occasion he saw a visiting horse with a red ribbon tied in the tail: the signal of an animal that kicked. If a pasture or stable hand got kicked, he was punished, not the valuable horse. Serfs were expected to be careful, not risking the horses' precious feet by contact with the serf's drab flesh.

Stile made the best of it. He was hardly conscious of this at the time, but the extreme value placed on horses here was to make a profound impression on his attitude in life. These were not the racing animals; these were the retirees, the injured, the secondary steeds—yet they were worth more than the lives of any of the serfs. Some serfs rebelled, secretly hating the animals they tended, but Stile absorbed the propaganda completely in this respect. The horse became his ideal. The horse, though confined to its pasture, had perfect freedom, for the pasture was equine heaven. If Stile had been a horse, he would have been in heaven too. Horses became prettier than people in his eyes, and though intellectually he denied this, emotionally he accepted it. Stile was in love with horses.

Thus he became an avid student of the species. Not only did he study the nuances of the mannerisms of the particular animals in his pastures, noting that each horse had a personality fully as distinct as that of any serf; during his free time he studied texts on horse manure. He learned of the intestinal parasites that might be found in it, the worms and the maggots and microscopic vermin. Of course there were no such parasites here, but he pretended there might be, and looked assiduously for the signs. He learned to judge the general health of a horse by its manure; whether it was being worked hard or was idle; what its diet was and in what proportions. Some horses had hard clods, some loose; Stile could tell which horse had produced any given pile, and thus was aware of the past day's location of each horse without ever seeing the animals directly.

Time passed. One day, two years into his tenure, Stile actually spied a worm in manure. He reported this immediately to the foreman. "A worm in our manure?" the man demanded incredulously. "You've got delusions of grandeur!"

But they tested the horse, for the foreman let nothing pass unverified, and Stile was correct. A slow-hatching variety of parasite had slipped through the quarantine and infected the animal. It was not a serious bug, and would not really have hurt the horse, but it was genuine. The larvae had manifested in the manure only on the day Stile noted them; he had caught the nuisance before it could spread to other animals.

The foreman took Stile to the shower, washed him personally as if he were a child, and combed his hair with an available currycomb. Stile submitted, amazed at this attention. Then the foreman brought him, shining clean, to a small door in the wall of the stable. "Always say 'sir' to him," the foreman said warningly. "Never turn your back until he has dismissed you." Then he guided Stile firmly through the door.

Stile found himself, for the first time, in the presence of his employer. The other side of the barn was a palatial apartment, with videoscreens on three walls. On each screen was a portion of a composite picture: the surface of a mountainous land as seen from the air. The image shifted in three-dimensional cohesion, making the illusion most effective. The floor was almost transparent quartz, surely imported from a quarry on Earth, thus more valuable weight for weight than local gold. What affluence!

The Citizen sat in a plush swivel chair upholstered in purple silk, on whose armrests a number of control buttons showed. He was garbed in an ornate robe that seemed to be spun from thread made of platinum, and wore fine suede slippers. He was not an old man, and not young; rejuvenation treatments made his body handsome and his age indeterminate; though behind that façade of health, nature surely kept accurate score. Few Citizens lived much over a century despite the best medicine could do. He possessed no overpowering atmosphere of command. Had Stile encountered him on the streets, serf-naked, he would never have recognized him as a Citizen. The man was completely human. It was the clothing that made the difference. But what a difference it made!

The Citizen was facing to the side, his eyes on a passing cloud. He seemed unaware of Stile's intrusion.

The foreman jogged Stile's elbow. Stile tried several times, and finally choked out his announcement of arrival: "S-sir."

The Citizen's eyes flicked to cover him. "You are the lad who spotted the worm?" The voice was ordinary too, amazingly.

"Yes, sir."

"You are promoted to stableboy." And the Citizen rotated in his swivel chair, turning his glossy back, dismissing Stile.

Stile found himself back in the barn. He must have walked there, guided by the foreman. Now the man led him by the hand to a cabin at the edge of the pasture. Three stable hands stood beside it, at attention.

"Stile is joining you," the foreman said. "Fetch his gear."

With alacrity they took off. In moments Stile's bedding, body brush and towel were neatly set up by the fourth bunk in the cabin. The stable hands were congratulating him. He was, of course, low man of the house—the "boy"—but it was like a fraternity, a giant improvement from the barracks. Only four to share the shower, curfew an hour later, and a cabin vidscreen!

Stile's days of spading and hauling manure were over. A new serf took his place in the pastures. Stile was now of a higher echelon. He was working directly with the horses. Reward had been as swift and decisive as punishment for infractions; at one stroke the Citizen had made two years of dung worthwhile.

Stile lifted his eyes from the manure of this wilderness realm. Oh, yes, he knew about manure! He had never forgotten what dung had done for him. He considered it not with distaste or horror, but almost with affection.

He walked on down the river, inspecting hoofprints

and manure. Some of these horses were large, some medium, some healthy, some less so. Some did have worms in their droppings, and these gave Stile a perversely good feeling. A worm had promoted him!

This region, then, was not sterile; it was natural. Flies hovered about the freshest piles: genuine flies, he was sure, species he knew only from books and museum specimens. No one policed this region; the old piles lay undisturbed, sprouting toadstools, gradually settling, dissolving in rainfall, bright green grass growing up through them. No self-respecting horse would eat at a dung-site, so such blades remained unclipped. Nature's way of preventing overgrazing, perhaps—but Stile was appalled to see such an excellent pasture in such disrepair. Did no one *care* about these horses?

They must be wild, uncared for. Which meant that he would be free to take whichever one he chose. He might have to break it for riding—but he knew how to do that. Even with his injured knees he could ride any horse. Only specialized racing required extreme flexure of the knees; for other riding the legs were used for balance, for purchase, and guidance of the steed.

There was evidently a fair-sized herd in this region. A number of mares, governed by a single powerful stallion? No, there seemed to be several males; he could tell by the positioning of the hoofprints about the indentations of urination sites. Males watered in front of the hind hooves; females, behind. But there was bound to be a dominant stallion, for that was the way of horses. Geldings, or cut males, were no more competitive than mares, but potent stallions demanded recognition.

That dominant stallion would probably make the finest steed for Stile's purpose—but would also be too obvious. Stile needed a good, fast, but inconspicuous animal. A non-herd stallion—probably there were no geldings here, if the animals were actually wild—or a mare. A good mare was in no way inferior; some of the most durable runners were female. Stile had ridden a mare named Thunder once, who brooked no backtalk from any horse, regardless of size or sex, and was herself a magnificent, high-stepping, lofty-headed creature. If he could find a mare like her, here—

He spied the prints of a small horse, no more than fourteen hands, on the verge of being a pony, but supremely healthy. Probably a mare; there was something about the delicacy with which she had placed her feet. Every hoof was sound, and the manure had no infestation. She could run, too—he traced her galloping prints in the turf, noting the spread and precision of the marks, the absence of careless scuffmarks, of signs of tripping. No cracks in these hooves, no sloppy configurations. A good horse, in good condition, could outrun a greyhound, maintaining a velocity of 65 kilometers per hour. This could be that kind of horse. She seemed to be a loner, apart from the herd, drinking and feeding in places separate from the others. That could mean she was more vulnerable to predators, so would have to be more alert, tougher, and swifter. But why was she alone? Horses were basically herd animals.

He followed this trail, by print and manure. At first the piles were old, but as he used his skill to orient they became fresher. It took him some hours to make real progress, for the horse had wandered far—as healthy horses did. As Stile walked, he wondered more persistently: what made this one separate from her companions? Was she, like himself, a private individual who had learned to value alone-time, or had she been excluded from the herd? What would constitute reason for such exclusion? Obviously she made do quite well alone—but did she really like it?

Stile had quite a lot of empathy for horses, and a lot for outsiders. Already he liked this little mare he had not yet seen. He did not after all need any giant steed to ride; his weight was slight, and he knew how to make it seem lighter. A small horse, even a pony could easily support him. In heroic fantasy the protagonist always bestrode a giant stallion; Stile could handle such a horse, but knew there were points to smallness too. Just as there were points to small people!

Here he was, abruptly, at an aspect of the truth: he was very small for his kind, therefore he liked small things. He identified with them. He knew what it felt like to be looked down on, to be the butt of unfunny jokes. "Hey, dja hear the one about the little moron?" Why did it always have to be a *little* moron? Why did the terms midget, dwarf, pygmy and runt have pejorative connotation? What the hell was so funny about being small? Since small people were not inferior intellectually, it stood to reason that smallness was a net asset. A better value, pound for pound.

So why didn't he really believe it? He should not choose a horse because it was small, but because it was the best mount for his purpose. Yet, subjectively—

Stile's irate chain of thought was interrupted by the sight of his objective. There she stood, as pretty a little mare as he had ever seen. Her coat was glossy black, except for white socks on her hind feet, one rising higher than the other. Her mane fell to the right side, ebony-sleek, and her tail was like the tresses of a beautiful woman. Her hooves glistened like pearl, dainty and perfectly formed. She had a Roman nose, convex rather than straight or concave, but in nice proportion. And her horn was a spiraled marvel of ivory symmetry.

Her *what*?

Stile actually blinked and rubbed his eyes. He only succeeded in blurring his vision. But what he saw was no trick of the light.

He had found a unicorn.

CHAPTER 7

Neysa

He must have gasped, for the mare raised her head alertly. She had, of course, been aware of his approach before; horses—unicorns?—had sharp hearing. She had not been alarmed—which itself was remarkable, if she were wild—so had continued grazing. Equines were like that; they startled readily, but not when they thought they had the situation in hand. Evidently this little lady unicorn was much the same.

This was a fantasy world, where magic evidently worked; he had already established that. He still felt the burn on his neck where the amulet-demon's chain had scraped. So why shouldn't this world have magic animals too? That made perfect sense. It was only that he had never thought it through, before assuming that these were horses. Was there, actually, much difference between a horse and a unicorn? Some artists represented unicorns with leonine bodies and cloven hooves, but Stile distrusted such conceptions. It could be that a true unicorn was merely a horse with a horn on the forehead. In which case this one would do just fine for him; he could ignore the horn and treat her as a horse.

Stile had not taken time to fashion a lariat; he had been more interested in surveying the situation, and in the memories this experience evoked. Now he decided: this was definitely the animal he wanted. With no rope, he would have to improvise. He doubted she was tame, but she might not be man-shy either.

He walked slowly up to her. The unicorn watched him warily. There was something about the way her horn oriented on him that was disquieting. It was without doubt a weapon. It tapered to a sharp point; it was a veritable spear. This was a fighting animal. Scratch one assumption: he could in no way afford to ignore that horn.

"Now my name's Stile," he said in a gentle voice. "Stile as in fence. You may not know about that sort of thing, though. I need a—a steed. Because I may have a long way to go, and I can get there faster and better if I ride. I am a very good endurance runner, for a man, but a man does not compare to a good h—unicorn. I would like to ride you. What is your name?"

The unicorn blew a double note through her horn. This startled Stile; he had not realized the horn was hollow. He had been speaking rhetorically, expecting no response. Her note was coincidental, of course; she could hardly be expected to comprehend his words. It was his tone of voice that mattered, and the distraction of it while he approached. Yet that note had sounded almost like a word. "Neysa?" he asked, voicing it as well as he could.

There was a fluted snort of agreement—or so it seemed to him. He reminded himself to be careful how he personified animals; if he ever got to believing he was talking with one on a human basis, he'd have to suspect his own sensibility. He could get himself killed, deluding himself about the reactions of a creature with a weapon like that.

"Well, Neysa, what would you do if I just got on your back and rode you?" He had to keep talking, calming her, until he could get close enough to mount her. Then there would be merry hell for a while: a necessary challenge.

The unicorn whipped her horn about in a menacing manner, and stomped her left forefoot. Her ears flattened back against her head. The language of unicorns was obviously like that of horses, with absolutely clear signals—for those who knew how to interpret them. She might not comprehend the specific meaning of his words, but she knew he was encroaching, and was giving adequate warning. If he tried to ride her, she would try to throw him, and if he got thrown, he would be in serious trouble. This was indeed no tame animal; this was a creature who knew of men and did not fear them, and when sufficiently aggravated would kill. A wildcat was not merely a housecat gone wild; a unicorn was not merely a horse with a weapon. The whole psychology differed. Neysa's every little mannerism told him that. He had no doubt, now, that there was blood on her horn—from other creatures who had failed to heed her warnings.

Yet he had to do it. "Neysa, I'm sorry. But a demon tried to kill me, not long ago, and in this frame of magic I am not well equipped to protect myself. I need to get away from here, and I'm sure you can take me so much better than I can take myself. Men have always depended on horses—uh, equines to carry them, before they started messing with unreliable machines like automobiles and spaceships." He stepped closer to her, hand outstretched, saying anything, just so long as he kept talking.

She lifted both forefeet in a little prance and brought them down together in a clomp directed at him. Her nose made a hooking gesture at him, and she made a sound that was part squeal and part snort and part music—the sort of music played in the background of a vid-show when the horrible monster was about to attack. This was as forceful a warning as she could make. She would not attack him if he departed right now, as she preferred simply to graze and let graze, but she would no longer tolerate his presence. She was not at all afraid of him—a bad sign!—she just didn't like him.

Now Stile remembered the folklore about unicorns, how they could be caught only by a virginal girl; the unicorn would lay his head in her lap, and then an ambush could be sprung. Probably this had been a cynical fable: how do you catch a mythical animal? With a mythical person. Implication: virgins were as rare as unicorns. Clever, possibly true in medieval times—and beside the point. How would it relate to a man and a female unicorn? Would she put her head in his lap? Only to un-man him, surely! More likely the matter related to riding: only a person pure in spirit could ride a unicorn—and in such myths, purity was defined as sexual abstinence and general innocence. Stile had no claims to such purity. Therefore this could be a very difficult ride. But mythology aside, he expected that sort of ride anyway.

"I really am sorry to do this, Neysa," Stile said. And leaped.

It was a prodigious bound, the kind only a highly trained athlete could perform. He flew through the air to land squarely on the unicorn's back. His hands reached out to take firm grip on her mane, his legs clamped to her sides, and his body flattened to bring him as close to her as physically possible.

Neysa stood in shocked surprise for all of a tenth of a second. Then she took off like a stone from a catapult. Stile's body was flung off—but his hands retained their double grip on her mane, and in a moment his legs had dropped back and were clamping her sides again. She bucked, but he clung close, almost standing on his head. No ordinary horse could buck without putting its head down between its front legs; it was a matter of balance and weight distribution. Neysa managed it, however, providing Stile with just a hint of what he was in for. Normal limits were off, here; this was, for sure, a magic animal.

She reared, but he stayed on her like a jacket. She whipped her head about, spearing at him with her horn—but he shifted about to avoid it, and she could not touch him without endangering her own hide. That horn was designed to spear an enemy charging her from the front, not one clinging to her back. It took a special kind of curved horn to handle a rider; she would never dislodge him this way.

So much for the beginning. Now the unicorn knew that no amateur bestrode her. It would require really heroic measures to dump him. For Stile, when he wasn't trying to gentle an animal, was extremely tough about falls.

Neysa accelerated forward, going west toward the chasm cracks he had spied from the spruce tree—then abruptly braked. All four feet skidded on the turf. But Stile was wise to this maneuver, and remained secure. She did a double spinabout, trying to fling him off by centrifugal force—but he leaned to the center of the turn and stayed firm. Abruptly she reversed—and he did too. She leaped forward—then leaped backward. That one almost unseated him; it was a trick no ordinary horse knew. But he recovered, almost tearing out a fistful of her mane in the process.

Well! Now she was warmed up. Time to get serious. Neysa tripped forward, lowering her body—then reared and leaped simultaneously. She fell backward; then her hind feet snapped forward and she performed a flip in air. For an instant she was completely inverted, her entire body above his. Stile was so startled he just clung. Then she completed the flip, landing on her front feet with her body vertical, finally whomping down on her hind feet.

Only the involuntary tightening of his hands had saved him. A horse doing a backflip! This was impossible!

But, he reminded himself again, this was no horse. This was a unicorn—a creature of fantasy. The mundane rules simply did not apply here.

Next, Neysa went into a spin. She galloped in a tightening circle, then drew in her body until she was actually balanced on one forefoot, head and tail lifted, rotating rapidly. Magic indeed. Stile hung on, his amazement growing. He had known he would be in for a stiff ride, but he had grossly underestimated the case. This was akin to his fight with the demon.

Well, maybe that was a fair parallel. Two magical creatures, one shaped like a humanoid monster, the other like a horse with a horn. Neither subject to the limitations of conventional logic. He had been foolish to assume that a demon that superficially resembled a horse was anything close to that kind of animal. He would remember this lesson—if he happened to get out of this alive.

Now Neysa straightened out, stood for a moment—then rolled. Her back smacked into the ground—but Stile had known when to let go. He landed on his feet, and was back on her back as she regained her own feet. "Nice try, Neysa," he said as he settled in again.

She snorted. So much for round two. She had only begun to fight!

Now she headed for the nearest copse of trees. Stile knew what was coming: the brush-off. Sure enough, she passed so close to a large trunk that her side scraped it—but Stile's leg was clear, as he clung to her other side in the fashion of a trick rider. He had once won a Game in which the contest was trick riding; he was not the finest, but he was good.

Neysa plunged into a thicket. The saplings brushed close on either side, impossible to avoid—but they bent aside when pushed, and could not sweep off a firmly anchored rider who was prepared. She shot under a large horizontal branch, stout enough to remove him—but again he slid around to the side of her body, avoiding it, and sprang to her back when the hazard was past. Real riding was not merely a matter of hanging on; it required positive anticipations and countermoves to each equine effort. He could go anywhere she could go!

Neysa charged directly toward the next large tree, then planted her forefeet, lifted her rear feet, and did a front-foot-stand that sent her back smashing into the trunk. Had he stayed on her, he would have been crushed gruesomely. No game, this! But Stile, now wise in the ways of unicorns, had dropped off as her motion started. He had less mass than she, weighing about an eighth as much, and could maneuver more rapidly when he had to. As her rear feet came back to the ground, Stile's rear feet came back to her back, and his hands resumed their clutch on her mane.

She snorted again. Round three was over. Round four was coming up. How many more tricks did this phenomenal animal have? Stile was in one sense enjoying this challenge, but in another sense he was afraid. This was no Proton Game, where the loser suffered no more than loss of status; this was his life on the line. The first trick he missed would be the last.

Neysa came onto a grassy plain. Now she accelerated. What was she up to this time? It didn't seem so bad—and that made him nervous. Beginning with a walk, she accelerated to a slow trot. The speed differential was not great, as a slow trot could be slower than a brisk walk. In fact, Stile had worked with lazy horses who could trot one meter per second, rather than the normal three or four meters per second. The distinguishing mark was the beat and pattern. In walking, the horse put down the four feet in order, left-front, right-rear, right-front, left-rear, four beats per cycle. Trotting was two-beat: left-front and right-rear together, followed by right-front and left-rear together. Or with a right lead instead of a left. The point was that the motion of each front foot was synchronous with one hind foot; in some cases the front and rear moved together on the same side. But there were only two beats per cycle, the pairs of feet striking the ground cleanly together. It made for a bumpy but regular ride that covered the ground well, and looked very pretty from the side. A slow trot could be gentle; a fast one could be like a jackhammer. But a trot was definitely a trot, at any speed; there was no mistaking it. Stile liked trotting, but distrusted this one. He knew he had not seen the last of this mare's devices.

Next she broke into a canter: three-beat. Left-front, then right-front and left-rear together, and finally right-rear. Like a cross between a walk and a trot, and the ride a kind of gentle swooping. All perfectly conventional, and therefore not to be trusted. She had something horrendous in her canny equine mind!

Finally she reached a full gallop: a modified two-beat cycle, the two front legs striking almost but not quite together, then the rear two. A four-beat cycle, technically, but not uniform. Beat-beat, beat-beat, at the velocity of racing. Stile enjoyed it; he experienced an exhilaration of speed that was special on a horse—unicorn. Motored wheels could go much faster, of course, but it wasn't the same. Here, as it were in the top gear, the animal straining to the limit—though this one was not straining, but loafing at a velocity that would have had another one straining—

The unicorn shifted into another gait. It was a five-beat—

Stile was so surprised he almost dropped off. No horse had a five-beat gait! There were only four feet!

No horse—there he was again. He kept forgetting and getting reminded in awkward ways. This gait was awful; he had never before experienced it, and could not accommodate it. BEAT-beat-BEAT-BEAT-beat, and over again, bouncing him in a growing resonance, causing him to lose not his grip but his composure. He felt like a novice again, fouling himself up, his efforts to compensate for the animal's motions only making it worse. As a harmonic vibration could shake apart a building, this fifth-beat was destroying him. He would fall—and at this breakneck velocity he could . . . break his neck.

Think, Stile, think! he told himself desperately. *Analyze: What is the key to this gait?*

His hands were hurting as his clutch on the unicorn's mane slowly slipped. His thigh muscles were beginning to cramp. Stile was expert—but this creature had his number now. Unless he could get her number too, soon.

Four feet, five beats. One foot had to repeat. Number the steps: one-two-three-four—where was the repeat? *Fingers slipping . . .*

BEAT-beat—that sound was less than the others, like a half-step. But half a step had to be completed by—another half-step. Like a man catching his balance when tripped. Two half-steps—that was it. Not necessarily together. The second and fifth. The right rear foot—as though stumbling, throwing off his timing. Compensate—

Stile started to catch on. He shifted his weight to absorb the shock and irregularity. BEAT-absorb-BEAT-BEAT-absorb. It was tricky and unnatural as hell, but his body was finding the dubious rhythm, getting the swing. Mostly it was his knowledge of the pattern, of what to expect. No more surprises! His leg muscles relaxed, and his hands stopped slipping.

Neysa felt the change, and knew he had surmounted this challenge too. She turned at speed—and Stile's inertia almost flung him off her side. A gradual turn at high velocity could pack more wallop than a fast turn at low speed. But she had to shift to a normal gallop for the turn, and no equine living could dump Stile with a normal gallop.

Realizing her mistake, the unicorn changed tactics. She slowed, then suddenly went into a one-beat gait. This was another surprise, in a ride full of them. It was like riding a pogo stick. All four of her feet landed together; then she leaped forward, front feet leading—only to contract to a single four-point landing again.

But Stile had ridden a pogo stick, in the course of his Game experience. He could handle this. "No luck, Neysa!" he cried. "Give up?"

She snorted derisively through her horn. It was almost as if she understood his words. But of course horses were very perceptive of tone, and responsive to it.

She turned. She had been going north, having curved in the course of her running; now she bore due west. Round five was coming up.

The grass gave way to packed dirt, then to clay, then to something like shale, and finally to rock. Neysa's hooves struck sparks from the surface, astonishing Stile. She was traveling fast, to be sure—faster than any horse he had raced. It felt like eighty kilometers per hour, but that had to be a distortion of his perception; such a speed would be of interworld championship level, for a horse. Regardless, hooves were not metallic; this animal was not shod, had no metal horseshoes, no nails. Nothing to strike sparks. Yet they were here.

Now she came to the pattern of crevices he had spied from the tree. They loomed with appalling suddenness: deep clefts in the rock whose bottoms could not be seen. Her hooves clicked between cracks unerringly, but Stile didn't like this. Not at all! One misstep would drop a foot into one of those holes, and at this speed that would mean a broken leg, a tumble, and one man flying through the air to land—where? But all he could do was hang on.

The cracks became more plentiful, forming a treacherous lattice. His vision of the crevices blurred, because they were so close, passing so rapidly; they seemed to writhe in their channels, swelling and shrinking, now twisting as if about to burst free, now merging with others or splitting apart. He had noted a similar effect when riding the Game model train as a child, fixing his gaze on the neighboring tracks, letting them perform their animations as he traveled. But these were not rails, but crevices, getting worse.

Neysa danced across the lattice as Stile watched with increasing apprehension. Now these were no longer mere cracks in a surface; these were islands between gaps. Neysa was actually traversing a chasm, jumping across from stone to stone, each stone a platform rising vertically from the depths. Stile had never seen such a landscape before. He really was in a new world: new in kind as well as in region.

Now Neysa was leaping, using her one-beat gait to bound from one diminishing platform to another. Sometimes all four feet landed together, in a group, almost touching each other; sometimes they were apart, on separate islands. She was obviously conversant with this place, and knew where to place each hoof, as a child knew where to jump amid the squares of a hopscotch game, proficient from long practice. Perhaps Neysa had mastered this challenge in order to avoid predators. No carnivore could match her maneuvers here, surely; the creature would inevitably misstep and fall between islands, perhaps prodded by the unicorn's aggressive horn, and that would be the end. So her trick gait made sense: it was a survival mechanism. Probably the five-beat gait had a similar function. What terrain was it adapted to?

Neysa danced farther into the pattern. The islands became fewer, smaller, farther apart. Now Stile could peer into the lower reaches of the crevices, for the sunlight slanted down from almost overhead. Had it been only six hours from the start of this day? It seemed much longer already! The fissures were not as deep as he had feared; perhaps two meters. But they terminated in rocky creases that could wedge a leg or a body, and they were getting deeper as the unicorn progressed.

This was a test of nerve as much as of agility or riding ability.

As it happened, Stile had the nerve. "Let's face it, Neysa," he said. He tended to talk to horses; they listened well, politely rotating their pointed furry ears around to fetch in larger scoops of his sound, and they did not often talk back. "We're in this together. What would I gain by falling off now? A broken leg? If it's all the same to you, oh prettiest and surest-footed of equines, I'll just stay on." He saw her left ear twitch as if shaking off a fly. She heard him, all right, and was not pleased at the confidence his tone exuded.

But the acrobatic challenge was not what the unicorn had come for. Suddenly she leaped—into the depths of a larger crack. It was two meters wide, shallow at the near end, but bearing lower. The sides seemed to close in as she plunged deeper. Where was she going? Stile did not like this development at all.

Neysa swung around a chasm corner and dropped to a lower level. This crack narrowed above; they were in a partial cave, light raying from the top. Cross-cracks intersected often, but the unicorn proceeded straight ahead.

A demon roared, reaching from the side. Where had it come from? A niche at the side, hidden until they were beside it. Stile ducked his head, and the thing missed him. He glimpsed it only briefly: glaring red eyes, shining teeth, glistening horns, talon claws, malevolence. Typical of the breed, no doubt.

Another demon loomed, grabbing from the other side. Stile flung his body away, and this one also missed. But this was getting bad; he could not afford to let go his grip on Neysa's mane, for it was his only purchase. But he soon would need an arm to fend off these attacks.

The unicorn's strategy was clear, now. She was charging through the habitat of monsters, hoping one of them would pluck the unwanted rider from her back. The demons were not grabbing at her; they shied away from her deadly horn, instead snatching from the sides. They seemed akin to the demon of the amulet that he had fought before, except that their size was constant. Stile knew he would not survive long if one of these monsters nabbed him. He had already learned how tough demons were.

He would have to compromise. Neysa could not turn abruptly, for these crevices defined her route. The demons stood only at intersections and niches; there was not room enough in a single crevice for unicorn *and* demon. So this was a set channel with set hazards. He should be able to handle it—if he were careful.

Another intersection; another demon on the right. Stile let go Neysa's mane with his right hand and lifted his arm to ward off the attack. He did it with expertise, striking with his forearm against the demon's forearms, obliquely, drawing on the power of his forward motion. The leverage was with him, and against the reaching demon; Stile was sure of that. There was art to blocking, no matter what was being blocked.

Neysa felt his shifting of weight and tried to shake him off. But the channel bound her; she could not act effectively. Her trap inhibited her as much as him. It was evident that the demons were not her friends; otherwise she would simply stop and let them snatch him off. No, they were enemies, or at least un-friends; she neither stopped nor slowed, lest the demons get her as well as him. They probably liked the taste of raw unicorn flesh as well as they liked the taste of human flesh.

In fact, she had taken quite a risk to get rid of him. She just might get rid of herself, too.

"Neysa, this is no good," Stile said. "This should be between you and me. I don't like demons any better than you do, but this shouldn't be their concern. You're going for double or nothing—and it's too likely to be nothing. Let's get out of here and settle this on our own. Whoever wins and whoever loses, let's not give the pleasure of our remains to these monsters."

She charged on, straight ahead, of course. He knew he was foolish to talk to himself like this; it really accomplished nothing. But stress gave him the compulsion. The demons kept grabbing, and he kept blocking. He talked to them too, calling them names like "Flopface" and "Crooktooth," and exclaiming in cynical sympathy when they missed him. He forced himself to stop that; he might get to wanting to help them.

Stile was quite nervous now; he knew this because when he turned off his mouth he found himself humming. That was another thing he tended to do when under stress. He had to vocalize in some fashion. Upon occasion it had given him away during a Game. Bad, bad habit! But now the refrain became compulsive. Hummm-hummm-block, as a demon loomed; hummm-hummm-block! Stupid, yet effective in its fashion. But the demons were getting more aggressive, encroaching more closely. Soon they would become bold enough to block the channel ahead—

One did. It stepped out directly in front of the unicorn, arms spread, grin glowering. It was horrendously ugly.

Neysa never slowed. Her horn speared straight forward. As it touched the demon, she lifted her head. There was a shock of impact. The creature was impaled through the center, hoisted into the air, and hurled back over the unicorn's body. Stile clung low, and it cleared him.

Now he knew why most demons gave way to a charging unicorn. They might overwhelm a stationary unicorn, but a moving one was deadly. Stile could hardly imagine a more devastating stroke than the one he had just seen.

And a similar stroke awaited him, the moment he fell off.

The beat of Neysa's hooves changed. She was driving harder now—because she was climbing. Stile peered ahead, past her bloodstained horn, and saw the end of the crevice. They were finally coming out of it.

The demons drew back. They had become too bold, and paid the penalty. The intruders were leaving anyway; why hinder them? Stile relaxed. Round five was over.

They emerged to the surface—and plunged into liquid. The northern end of the cracks terminated in water. A river flowed down into them, quickly, vanishing into the deeper crevices—but to the north it was broad and blue. Neysa splashed along it; the water was only knee-deep here.

The river curved grandly, like a python, almost touching itself before curving back. "The original meander," Stile remarked. "But I don't see how this is going to shake me off, Neysa." However, if he had to be thrown, he would much prefer that it be in water. He was of course an excellent swimmer.

Then the water deepened, and the unicorn was swimming. Stile had no trouble staying on. Was she going to try to drown him? She had small chance! He had won many a Game in the water, and could hold his breath a long time.

She did not try. She merely swam upstream with amazing facility, much faster than any ordinary horse could do, and he rode her though all but her head and his head were immersed. The river was cool, not cold; in fact it was pleasant. If this were round six, it was hardly a challenge.

Then he felt something on his thigh. He held on to the mane with his right hand, wary of tricks, and reached with his left—and found a thing attached to his flesh. Involuntarily he jerked it off, humming again. There was a pain as of abrading flesh, and it came up: a fishlike creature with a disk for a head, myriad tiny teeth projecting.

It was a lamprey. A blood-sucking eel-like creature, a parasite that would never let go voluntarily. Another minor monster from the biological museum exhibits, here alive.

Stile looked at it, horrified. Magic he found incredible; therefore it didn't really bother him. But this creature was unmagical and disgusting. He heard the loudness of his own humming. He tried to stop it, ashamed of his squeamishness, but his body would not obey. What revulsion!

Another sensation. He threw the lamprey away with a convulsive shudder and grabbed the next, from his side. It was a larger sucker. There was little he could do to it, one-handed; it was leather-tough. He might bite it;

that would serve it right, a taste—literally—of its own medicine. But he recoiled at the notion. Ugh!

The noxious beasties did not seem to be attacking the unicorn. Was it her hair, or something else? She could hardly use her horn to terrorize something as mindless as this.

Neysa kept swimming up the river, and Stile kept yanking off eels, humming grimly as he did. He hated this, he was absolutely revolted, but he certainly was not going to give up now!

The unicorn dived, drawing him under too. Stile held his breath, clinging to her mane. It was work for her to stay under, as her large equine belly gave her good flotation; he was sure he could outlast her. She would have to breathe, too.

She stayed down a full minute, then another. Only the tip of her horn cut the surface of the water like the fin of a shark. How long could she do it? He was good at underwater exploits, but he was getting uncomfortable.

Then he caught on: her horn was a snorkel. She was breathing through it! She had no air-limit. His lungs were hurting, but her neck was too low; he could not get his head high enough to break the surface without letting go her mane. If he let go, he surely would not have a chance to catch her again; she would stab him if he tried.

But he had a solution. He hauled himself up hand over hand to her head, where her black forelock waved like sea grass in the flow. He grabbed her horn. It was smooth, not knife-edged along the spiral; lucky for him! There seemed to be little indentations along its length: the holes for the notes, at the moment closed off.

His head broke water, and he breathed. She could not lower her horn without cutting off her own wind—and she was breathing too hard and hot to risk that. Equines had a lot of mass and muscle for their lungs to service, and she was still working hard to stay below.

Neysa blew an angry note through her horn and surfaced. Stile dropped back to her back. He yanked off two more eels that had fastened to him while he was below, as if his cessation of humming had made them bold.

Neysa cut to the edge of the river and found her footing. She charged out of the water. Stile had taken round six.

North of the river was a slope rising into a picturesque mountain range. The highest peaks were cloud-girt and seemed to be snow-covered. Surely she was not about to essay the heights!

She was. She galloped up the slope, the wind drying out her hair and his. What an animal she was! An ordinary horse would have been exhausted by this time, but this one seemed to be just hitting her stride.

The pace, however, was telling; Stile could feel her body heating. Horses, with or without horns, were massive enough to be short on skin surface to radiate heat. Therefore they sweated, as did man—but still it could take some time to dissipate the heat pollution of over-exertion. She would have to ease up soon, even if her muscles still had strength.

She did not. The slope increased; her hooves pounded harder. One-two, three-four, a good hard-working gallop. She was not even trying to shake him off, now, but she surely had something excellent in mind. The grain-grass turf gave way to fields of blue and red flowers and goldenrod. More rocks showed, their rugged facets glinting cruel deep gray in the sun. The trees became smaller. Wisps of fog streamed by.

Stile craned his neck to look back—and was amazed. Already the Meander River was a small ribbon in the distance, far below. They must have climbed a vertical kilometer! Suddenly the air seemed chill, the breeze cutting. But the unicorn was hot; again small sparks flew from her feet as the hooves struck the rocky ground. Fine jets of vapor spumed from her nostrils.

Vapor? Stile squinted, unbelieving. *Those were jets of fire!*

No, impossible! No flesh-creature could breathe out fire. Living tissue wasn't able to—

Stile nudged forward, freed one hand, and reached

ahead to approach the flame he thought he saw. Ouch! His fingers burned! That was indeed fire!

All right, once more. This was a magic land. He had accepted that, provisionally. The laws of physics he had known did not necessarily apply. Or if they were valid, they operated in different ways. Horses generated heat—so did unicorns. Horses sweated—this creature remained dry, once she had shed the river water. So she got rid of excess heat by snorting it out her nostrils in concentrated form. It did make sense, in its particular fashion.

Now the air was definitely cold. Stile was naked; if they went much higher, he could be in a new sort of trouble. And of course that was the idea. This was round seven, the trial of inclement climate. Neysa was not suffering; she was doing the work of running, so was burning hot. The cold recharged her.

Stile got down as close to his mount as he could. His back was freezing, but his front was hot, in contact with the furnace of Neysa's hide. This became uncomfortable. He was trying to sweat on one side and shiver on the other, and he couldn't turn over. And Neysa kept climbing.

Could he steer her back down the hill? Unlikely; trained horses moved with the guidance of reins and legs and verbal directives—but they did it basically because they knew no better. They were creatures of habit, who found it easiest to obey the will of the rider. This unicorn was a self-willed animal, no more tractable than a self-willed machine. (Ah, Sheen—what of you now?) If he did not like her direction, he would have to get off her back.

So he would just have to bear with it. He had to tame this steed before he could steer her, and he had to stay on before he could tame her. He found himself humming again. It seemed to help.

Neysa's feet touched snow. Steam puffed up from that contact. She really had hot feet! She charged on up the side of a glacier. Ice chipped off and slid away from her hooves. Stile hummed louder, his music punctuated by his shivering.

Crevices opened in the glacier. Again the unicorn's feet danced—but this time on a slippery slope. Her hooves skidded between steps, for their heat melted the ice. Those sparks were another heat-dissipating mechanism, and though the snow and ice had cooled the hooves below sparking level, there was still plenty of heat to serve. Her body weight shifted, compensating for the insecure footing, but a fall seemed incipient. Stile hummed louder yet. This was no miniature Game-mountain, under a warm dome, with cushioned landings for losers. This was a towering, frigid, violent landscape, and he was afraid of it.

The cloud cover closed in. Now it was as if the unicorn trod the cold beaches of an arctic sea, with the cloud layers lapping at the shores. But Stile knew that cloud-ocean merely concealed the deadly avalanche slopes. Neysa's legs sank ankle-deep in the fringe-wash, finding lodging in ice—but how would she know ahead of time if one of those washes covered a crevasse?

"Neysa, you are scaring the color right out of my hair!" Stile told her. "But I've got to cling tight, because I will surely perish if I separate from you here. If the fall through the ledges doesn't shatter me, the cold will freeze me. I'm not as tough as you—which is one reason I need you."

Then the first snow-monster loomed. Huge and white, with icicles for hair, its chill ice-eyes barely peeking out through its snow-lace whiskers, it opened its ice-toothed maw and roared without sound. Fog blasted forth from its throat, coating Stile's exposed portions with freezing moisture.

Neysa leaped across the cloud to another mountain island. Stile glanced down while she was in midair, spying a rift in the cover—and there was a gaunt chasm below. He shivered—but of course he was cold anyway. He had never been really cold before, having spent all his life in the climate-controlled domes of Proton; only the snow machines of the Game had given him experience, and that had been brief. This was close to his notion of hell.

Another snow-monster rose out of the cloud, its roar

as silent as falling snow. Again the fog coated Stile, coalescing about his hands, numbing them, insinuating slipperiness into his grip on the mane. Stile discovered he was humming a funeral dirge. Unconscious black humor?

Neysa plunged through a bank of snow, breaking into the interior of an ice-cave. Two more snow-monsters loomed, breathing their fog. Neysa charged straight into them. One failed to move aside rapidly enough, and the unicorn's flame-breath touched it. The monster melted on that side, mouth opening in a silent scream.

On out through another snowbank—and now they were on a long snowslide on the north side of the range. Four legs rigid, Neysa slid down, gaining speed. Her passage started a separate snowslide that developed into a minor avalanche. It was as if the entire mountain were collapsing around them.

It would be so easy to relax, let go, be lost in the softly piling snow. Stile felt a pleasant lassitude. The snow was like surf, and they were planing down the front of the hugest wave ever imagined. But his hands were locked, the muscles cramped; he could not let go after all.

Suddenly they were out of winter, standing on a grassy ledge, the sun slanting warmly down. The cold had numbed his mind; now he was recovering. Neysa was breathing hard, her nostrils dilated, cooling. Stile did not know how long he had been unaware of their progress; perhaps only minutes, perhaps an hour. But somehow he had held on. His hands were cramped; this must be what was called a death grip. Had he won the victory, or was this merely a respite between rounds?

Neysa took a step forward—and Stile saw that the ledge was on the brink of a cliff overlooking the Meander River. In fact there was the roar of a nearby falls; the river started here, in the melting glaciers, and tumbled awesomely to the rocky base. Sure death to enter that realm!

Yet Neysa, fatigued to the point of exhaustion, was gathering herself for that leap. Stile, his strength returning though his muscles and skin were sore from the grueling ride, stared ahead, appalled. Enter that maelstrom of plunging water and cutting stone? She was bluffing; she had to be! She would not commit suicide rather than be tamed!

The unicorn started trotting toward the brink. She broke into a canter, bunched herself for the leap—

Stile flung himself forward, across her neck, half onto her head. His locked fingers cracked apart with the desperate force of his imperative, his arms flung forward. He grabbed her horn with both hands, swung his body to the ground beside her head, and bulldogged her to the side. She fought him, but she was tired and he had the leverage; he had rodeo experience too. They came to a halt at the brink of the cliff. A warm updraft washed over their faces, enhancing the impression of precariousness; Stile did not want to look down. Any crumbling of the support—

Stile held her tight, easing up only marginally as she relaxed, not letting go. "Now listen to me, Neysa!" he said, making his voice calm. It was foolish of him, he knew, to speak sense to her, just as it was foolish to hum when under stress, but this was not the occasion to attempt to remake himself. The unicorn could not understand his words, only his tone. So he was talking more for himself than for her. But with the awful abyss before them, he had to do it.

"Neysa, I came to you because I needed a ride. Someone is trying to kill me, and I am a stranger in this land, and I have to travel fast and far. You can go faster and farther than I can; you have just proved that. You can traverse regions that would kill me, were I alone. So I need you for a purely practical reason."

She continued to relax, by marginal stages, one ear cocked to orient on him, but she had not given up. The moment he let go, she would be gone. Into the river, the hard way, and on into unicorn heaven, the eternal pasture.

"But I need you for an emotional reason too. You see, I am a solitary sort of man. I did not wish to be, but certain factors in my life tended to set me apart from my associates, my peer group. I have generally fared best when going it alone. But I don't like *being* alone. I need companionship. Every living, feeling creature does. I have found it on occasion with other men in a shared project, and with women in a shared bed, and these are not bad things. But seldom have I had what I would call true friendship—except with another species of creature. I am a lover of horses. When I am with a horse, I feel happy. A horse does not seek my acquaintance for the sake of my appearance or my accomplishments; a horse does not expect a great deal of me. A horse accepts me as I am. And I accept the horse for what he is. A horse pulls his weight. I respect a horse. We relate. And so when I seek companionship, a really meaningful relationship, I look for a horse."

Neysa's head turned marginally so that she could fix one eye squarely on him. Good—she was paying attention to the soothing tones. Stile eased his grip further, but did not let go her horn.

"So I looked for you, Neysa. To be my equine companion. Because once a horse gives his allegiance, he can be trusted. I do not deceive myself that the horse cares for me in the same way I care for him—" He tightened his grip momentarily in a brief outpouring of the emotion he felt. "Or for her. But a horse is loyal. I can ride a horse, I can play, I can sleep without concern, for the horse will guard me from harm. A good horse will step on a poisonous snake before a man knows the threat is present. The horse will alert me to some developing hazard, for his perceptions are better than mine, and he will carry me away in time.

"I looked for you, Neysa, I selected you from all the herd before I ever saw you directly, because you are not really *of* the herd. You are a loner, like me. Because you are small, like me. But also healthy, like me. I understand and appreciate fitness in man and animal. Your hooves are clean, your manure is wholesome, your muscle tone is excellent, your coat has the luster of health, the sheen—" No, that was the wrong word, for it reminded him again of Sheen the robot lass. Where was she now, what was she doing, how was she taking his absence? Was she in metallic mourning for him? But he could not afford to be distracted by such thoughts at this moment.

"In fact, you are the finest little horse I have ever encountered. I don't suppose that means anything to you, but I have ridden some of the best horses in the known universe, in my capacity as a leading jockey of Planet Proton. That's another world, though. Not one of those animals compares to you in performance. Except that you are not really a horse. You are something else, and maybe you think I insult you, calling you a horse, but it is no insult, it is appreciation. I must judge you by what I know, and I know horses. To me, you are a horse with a horn. Perhaps you are fundamentally different. Perhaps you are superior. You do not sweat, you strike sparks from your hooves, you shoot fire from your nostrils, you play sounds on your horn, you have gaits and tricks no horse ever dreamed of. Perhaps you are a demon in equine form. But I doubt this. I want you because you most resemble a horse, and there is no creature I would rather have with me in a strange land, to share my life for this adventure, than a horse."

He relaxed his grip further as she relaxed. She was not going to jump, now—he hoped. But he wanted to be sure, so he kept on talking. It could be a mistake to rush things, with a horse.

"Now I thought I could conquer you, Neysa. I thought I could ride you and make you mine, as I have done so many times before with other horses. I see now I was wrong. I rode you, but you are not mine. You will kill yourself before you submit to the taming. I hardly know you, Neysa, but I love you; I would not have you sacrifice yourself to escape me." Stile felt moisture on his cheeks and knew he was crying again, as he had with Sheen. Few things could move him that way. A woman was one; a horse was another. "No, do not hurt yourself for me! I grieve at the very thought. I will let you go, Neysa! I can not impose respect on you. You are the most perfect steed I could ever hope to associate with, but I will seek another, a lesser animal. For I must be accepted too; it must be mutual. I can not love, and be unloved. Go with my regret, my sorrow, and my blessing. You are free." And he let her go, slowly, so as not to startle her, and stepped back.

"Yet I wish it had worked out," he said. "Not merely because I can see how good you would have been for me. Not only because the love of such a creature as you, not lightly given, is more precious than anything else I could seek. Not only because you are another example of what I like to see in myself, in my foolish private vanity: the proof that excellence can indeed come in small packages. No, there is more than that. I believe you need me the same way I need you. You are alone; you may not be aware of it, but you need a companion too, one who respects you for what you are. You are no ordinary mare."

He saw a scrape on her foreleg. "Oh, Neysa—you were hurt on that run." He squatted to examine it. Pain lanced through his knees, and he fell over, dangerously near the brink. He clutched at turf and drew himself back to safer ground. "Sorry about that," he said sheepishly. "I have bad knees . . . never mind." He got up carefully, using his hands to brace himself, for rising without squatting was awkward. He had never fully appreciated the uses of his knees, until their capability was diminished.

He approached Neysa slowly, still careful not to startle her, then bent from the waist to look at her leg. "I could wash that off for you, but there's no water here and I think it will heal by itself. It is not serious, and the blood helps clean it. But let me check your feet, Neysa. I do not want to leave you with any injuries of my making, and feet are crucially important. May I lift your left front foot?" He slid his hand down along her leg, avoiding the scrape, then drew on the ankle. "Easy, easy—I just want to look. To see if there are any cracks—cracks in hooves are bad news." The foot came up, though the unicorn was obviously uncertain what he was doing, and he looked at it from the bottom. It was still fairly warm; wisps of vapor curled from the frog, the central triangle of the hoof. "No, that is a fine clean hoof, a little chipped around the edges, but no cracks. You must get plenty of protein in your diet, Neysa!"

He set the foot down. "I should check the others, but I fear you would misunderstand. This is one thing a man can do for his horse. He can check the feet, clear the stones or other obstructions, file them down when they wear unevenly or get badly chipped. The welfare of the steed becomes the responsibility of the man. When food is scarce, the man provides. When there is danger, the man fights to protect the horse. Some animals who prey on horses are wary of men. I might face down a wolf, while you—" He looked at her horn. "No, you could handle a wolf! You don't need the likes of me; why should I deceive myself. I could tell you that to be the associate of a man is to be protected by the intelligence of a man, by his farsighted mind. That a man will anticipate danger and avoid it, for both himself and his mount. His brain makes up for his lesser perceptions. He will steer around sharp stones that might crack hooves. But why should this have meaning for you? You have savvy like none I have seen in any horse; you don't need protection. I delude myself in my desperate need to justify myself, to think that I could in any way be worthy of you."

A fly buzzed up, landing on Neysa. She shook her skin in that place, as horses did, but the fly refused to budge. Her tail flicked across, but the fly was on her shoulder, out of range. She could get it with her mouth, but then she would have to take her attention off Stile. The fly, with the canny ruthlessness of its kind, settled down to bite.

Stile experienced sudden heat. "Now don't startle, Neysa," he said. "I am going to slap that bastard fly, so it can't bother you. Easy, now . . ." He slapped. The fly dropped. "I hate biting flies," Stile said. "I have known them hitherto only through research, but they are the enemies of horses. I will not tolerate them on any animal associated with me." He stepped back, shrugging. "But I am showing my foolishness again. You can handle flies! Good-bye, Neysa. I hope you are happy, and that you graze forever in the greenest pastures."

Stile turned and walked away from the brink, listening only to make sure the unicorn did not jump. His heart was heavy, but he knew he had done the right thing. The unicorn could not be tamed. What a treasure he was leaving behind!

There was a strange rippling in the grass of the ledge. It had been occurring for some time, but only now was he fully conscious of it. It was as if he were in a pool, and a pebble had dropped in, making a spreading series of circular waves. But there was no water. What was causing this?

Something nuzzled his elbow. Stile jumped, startled; he had not heard anything approach.

It was the unicorn. She had come up behind him silently; he had not known she could do that. She could have run her horn through his back.

He faced her, perplexed, Neysa's ears were forward, orienting on him. Her muzzle quivered. Her great brown eyes were wet, gleaming like great jewels. She lifted her head and nibbled on his ear, gently, caressingly. She made a little whinny, cajoling him.

"Oh, Neysa!" he breathed, lifted by an explosion of joy.

He had won her, after all.

CHAPTER 8

Music

They were both tired, but Stile felt compelled to put distance between him and his point of entry to this world. Neysa, having consented to be tamed, was the perfect mount; the slightest pressure of one of his knees on her side would turn her, and the shifting of his weight forward would put her into the smoothest of trots. But mostly he didn't guide her; he let her pick her way.

"I need to hide, Neysa," he explained. "I need a place to be safe, until I can learn what I need to know about this world. Until I can discover who is trying to kill me, and why, and what to do about it. Or whether my experience with the amulet-demon was mere coincidence, a random trap, nothing personal. But until I know this land better, I have no notion where to hide. Paradox."

She listened, then made a gesture with her horn, pointing west, and tapped a forefoot. "It's almost as if you understand me," he said, amused. "At least you understand my need. If you know of a place to go, then by all means take me there, girl!"

But first he paused to gather some straw from a mature field and fashioned it into a crude saddle. "I don't really need a saddle, Neysa, but my weight will make your back sore in time unless it is properly distributed. The human seat-bones don't quite jibe with the equine backbone. This straw is not ideal, but it's better than nothing. We have to get my weight off your ribs and over your withers, your shoulders; that's where you can most comfortably support it. And a token girth to hold it on, so I won't have to yank at your beautiful black mane anymore."

Neysa submitted to this indignity, and carried him westward across the amber plain north of the purple mountains, her speed picking up as her strength returned. Something nagged at Stile; then he caught on. "You know, Neysa—this is like the old patriotic song of America, back on Earth. I've never been there, of course, but it describes amber waves of grain and purple mountains and fruited plains—which reminds me, I'm hungry! I haven't eaten since I came into this world—I don't know whether they really exist on Earth, those purple mountains, but they really do exist here! Do you mind if I whistle the tune?"

She cocked her ear back at him, listening, then cocked it forward. She had cute black ears, expressing her personality. She did not mind.

Stile whistled. He was good at it; whistling was, after all, a form of music, and good whistling was good music. Stile was good at anything that related to the Game, back on Proton. He had spent years constantly perfecting himself, and he had a special nostalgia for music. There had been a girl, once, whose memory he associated with it. He whistled the fields more amber, the mountains more purple, and the whole countryside more beautiful. And it really seemed to be so; the entire landscape seemed to assume a more intense grandeur, together with an atmosphere of expectancy. Expectant of what? Abruptly becoming nervous, Stile broke off.

Neysa paused by a tree. It was a pear tree, with huge ripe fruits. "Bless you!" Stile exclaimed. "Are these safe to eat?" He dismounted without waiting for an answer. What a comfort this unicorn was, now that she had joined him!

Neysa moved to the grain nearby and started grazing. She was hungry too. Horses—and unicorns!—could not proceed indefinitely without sustenance; they had to spend a good deal of their time grazing. So a horse was not really faster transportation, for a man; it was speed when he needed it, interspersed with rest. But it was a life-style he liked. His first hours in this world had not been dull, because of the demon-threat and his quest for a steed; but had he remained alone much longer, he would have become quite bored and lonely. Now, with this companionship, this world was delightful. Perhaps his need for transportation had merely been a sublimation of his need for company.

He would have to assume that they could camp here safely, at least for one night. Stile pulled down a pear. It certainly looked safe. If he starved, distrusting nature's food, what would he gain? He took a juicy bite. It was delicious.

He consumed three of the large fruits, then desisted, just in case. He did not need to gorge. He made a bed of hay, under the pear tree, and lay down as darkness closed in. He hoped it would not rain—but what did it really matter? He would dry. The temperature was nice, here; he would not be cold, even when wet.

Neysa had wandered off. Stile wasn't worried; he was sure of her, now. She would not leave him—and if she did, it was her right. They had a tacit agreement, no more, subject to cancellation without notice by either party. Still he glanced across the field as the first moon came up. He would prefer to have her near him, just in case. He did not know what routine dangers there might be, here, but was sure Neysa could recognize and handle them. The way she had dispatched the crack-demon and the snow-monster—

The moonrise was spectacular. Far less intense than the sun, it had more appeal because he could look at it directly. This was a close, large moon, whose effulgence bathed the slowly crossing clouds in pastel blue. The thickest clouds were black silhouettes, but the thinner ones showed their substance in blue monochrome, in shades of one color, all the lines and curves and burgeonings of them, all inexpressibly lovely. Oh, to travel amidst that picture, in the magic of the night sky!

Slowly it faded. Moonrise, like sunrise, was a fleeting phenomenon, the more precious because of that. Stile was sure no two moonrises or moonsets would be the same; there would always be a different picture, as lovely as the last, but original. What splendor nature proffered to the eye of any man who had half the wit to appreciate it!

Something was coming. Not a unicorn. Alarmed, Stile peered through the slanting moonbeams. He remained naked, weaponless; he had seldom felt the need for weapons in Proton society, though he knew how to use them. This was a wilder world whose beauty was tempered, perhaps even enhanced, by its hazards. Was this a nocturnal predator?

No—it was a woman!

Yet she carried no weapon either, and wore no clothing, and seemed innocent rather than hostile. This could be another demonic trap, but Stile somehow doubted it. She was—there was something familiar about her.

As she came close, the moonlight caught her fully. The promising outline was fulfilled in blue light. She was small, very small, smaller even than he, but supremely healthy and full-fleshed. She was beautifully proportioned, with small hands and feet, slender yet rounded legs, and virginally firm breasts. Her fingernails and toenails glistened like pearls, her hair was lustrous black, and she had an ivory decoration set in her forehead. Her face was quite cute, though she had a Roman nose. Her only flaw was a scratch on one arm, a fresh one only starting to heal.

"Stile," she said, with an almost musical inflection.

"Neysa!" he replied, astonished.

She opened her arms to him, smiling. And Stile understood that the friendship of a unicorn was no inconsequential thing. When he had won her, he had won her completely.

She was of course a variant of demon. No ordinary creature could make such a transformation. But it was already clear that there were variations among demons, in fact whole phyla of them. What mattered was not how far removed her type was from his, but how they related to one another. He trusted Neysa.

Stile embraced her, and kissed her, and she was lithe and soft and wholly desirable. He lay down with her under the pear tree, knowing her for what she was, and loved her, as he had loved the robot Sheen.

In the morning Neysa was back in equine form, grazing. Stile glanced at her, covertly reflecting on the event of the night. Would she expect different treatment, now? Would she now decline to carry him safely?

As it turned out, Neysa's attitude was unchanged. She was still his steed. The night had been merely a confirmation of their relationship, not a change in it. But never again would he think of a unicorn as merely a horse with a horn.

Rested and fed, Neysa set out at an easy trot across the field, still bearing west. Trots could be rough or smooth; this one was the smoothest. She could have looked like a drudge, yet fetched a high price on Proton, for the sake of this trot. As if such a creature could ever be sold, for any price! Then she moved into a nice canter with a syncopated beat: one-two-three-pause, one-two-three-pause. A canter, to his way of thinking, was a trot by the forefeet and a gallop by the rear feet; it too could vary greatly in comfort, depending on the steed's nature and mood. Stile enjoyed this; how nice it was to ride this fine animal without fighting her!

Neysa shifted into a variant of the trot: the pace, in which the left feet moved together, and the right feet together also. Two beats, throwing him from side to side, but covering the ground faster than an ordinary trot. Then back into a canter—but not an ordinary one. Her rear hooves were striking the ground together, synched with her right front hoof, so that this was another two-beat gait: a single foot alternating with three feet. One-TWO! One-TWO! He had to post over the shocks, lest his bones begin to rattle.

She was showing off her gaits, proving that no horse could match her in variety or facility. Yesterday she had demonstrated gaits from one-beat to five-beat; now she was doing the variations.

"This is great stuff, Neysa!" he said warmly. "You are the most versatile hoofer I know." For this was an aspect of companionship: performing for an appreciative friend. Animals, like people, would do a lot, just for the satisfaction of having their efforts recognized. Though Neysa was not precisely an animal *or* a person.

Just when Stile thought he had experienced the whole of her repertoire, Neysa surprised him again. She began to play music through her horn. Not an occasional melodic note, but genuine tunes. Her hooves beat counterpoint to the sustained notes, making a dramatic march.

"The five-beat gait!" Stile exclaimed. "*That's* what it's for! Syncopation, going with your music!"

She moved into the five-beat, playing an intricate melody that fit that beat perfectly. This time her motion was easy, not designed to unseat him, and he liked it. Stile was no longer surprised by her comprehension; he had realized, in stages during the prior day and night, that she comprehended human speech perfectly, though she did not bother to speak it herself. When he had indulged in his soliloquy on the ledge above the Meander River, she had understood precisely what he said. His meaning, not his tone, had converted her. That was good, because he had meant exactly what he said.

Now he could give her detailed verbal instructions, but she preferred the body directives of legs and weight-shifting. She moved to his directives with no evidence of those messages apparent to any third party. That was the riding ideal. She was at home with what she was: a unicorn. Stile, too, preferred the closeness this mode entailed; it was the natural way, a constant communication with his steed.

Neysa's horn-music resembled that of a harmonica. No doubt there were many small channels in her horn, with natural fiber reeds, and she could direct the flow of air through any channels she wished as she breathed. What a convenient way to play!

"You know, Neysa—I know something of music myself. Not just whistling. I was introduced to it by a girl a bit like you, in your girl-form: very small, pretty, and talented. I'm not the top musician in my world, but I am competent—because music is part of the competition of the Game. You wouldn't know about that, of course; it's like a—like a continuing contest, a race, where every day you race someone new, in a different way, and if you get really good you gain status. I have won Games by playing themes better than other people. The violin, the clarinet, the tuba—I've played them all. I wish I could accompany you! I suppose I could whistle again, or sing—" He shrugged. "But I'd really like to show you what I can do with an instrument. One like yours. Another harmonica. So we could play together. A duet. There's a special joy in that, as great in its way as—as the joy we had in our game of the night. With an instrument, I could come to you, as you came to me, sharing your frame."

Neysa accepted this as she did most of his commentary: with a wiggle of one ear and tolerance. She didn't mind if in his vanity he thought he could play the way she could. She liked him anyway.

Stile pondered briefly, then made a little verse of it. "The harmonica is what you play; I wish I had one here today." He fitted the words to her melody, singing them.

Neysa made an unmelodic snort, and Stile laughed. "Corny, I know! Doggerel is not my forte. All right, I'll quit."

But the unicorn slowed, then stopped, then turned about to retrace her last few steps. "What's the matter?" Stile asked, perplexed. "If I offended you, I'm sorry. I didn't mean to mess up your music."

She fished in the tall grass with her horn. Something glittered there. Stile dismounted and walked around to examine it, fearing trouble. If it were another demon-amulet—

It was a large, ornate, well-constructed harmonica, seemingly new.

Stile picked it up, examining it in wonder. "You have a good eye, Neysa, spotting this, and it couldn't have happened at a more fortuitous time. Why, this is from my world. See, it says MADE ON EARTH. Earth has a virtual monopoly on quality musical instruments. Most colonies are too busy to specialize in the arts. This is a good brand. I'm no specialist in this particular instrument, but I'll bet I could play—" He looked around. "Someone must have lost it. I'm not sure it would be right to—" He shook his head. "Yet it won't help the owner, just to leave it here. I suppose I could borrow it, until I can return it to—"

Having rationalized the matter, Stile remounted his straw saddle—which seemed to be holding up extraordinarily well, packing into an ideal shape—and settled down for the resumption of the ride. Neysa moved into a smooth running walk, and played her horn, and Stile tried out the harmonica.

It was a lovely instrument. It had sixteen holes, which would translate into thirty-two notes: four octaves. It was, in addition, chromatic; it had a lever at the end which, when depressed, would shift the full scale into the half-tones. There were also several buttons whose purpose he did not fathom; he would explore those in due course.

Stile put his mouth to it, getting the feel of it, blowing an experimental note. And paused, surprised and gratified; it was tremolo, with the peculiar and pleasant beat of two closely matched reeds. He blew an experimental scale, pursing his lips to produce a single note at a time. This harmonica was extremely well constructed, with no broken reeds, and every note was pure and in perfect pitch.

Very good. Neysa had halted her music, curious about his activity. Stile essayed a melody. He kept it simple at first, playing no false notes, but the instrument was so conducive and the sound so pleasant that he soon broke into greater complexities.

Neysa perked her ears to listen. She turned her head to glance obliquely back at him, surprised. Stile paused. "Yes, I really can play," he said. "You thought I was a duffer? That whistling represented the epitome of my achievement? I love music; it is another one of those things that come easily to a lonely person. Of course I'm not as sharp on the harmonica as I am on other instruments, and I can't play elaborately, but—"

She blew a note of half-negation. "What, then?" he inquired. "You know, Neysa, it would be easier for me if you talked more—but I guess you'd have to change to your human form for that, and then we couldn't travel properly. You know, you really surprised me when you—do you call it shape-changing? Permutation? Reformulation? It was an aspect of you I had never suspected—"

She blew another note, three-quarter affirmation. He was getting better at grasping her communications. "You're still trying to tell me something," he said. "I'm pretty good at riddles; that's another aspect of the Game. Let's see—is it about your manifestation as—no? About my reaction to it? You say half-right. About my surprise—*your* surprise? Ah, now I get it! You were just as amazed to discover I could play a musical instrument as I was to see you in human form."

Neysa made an affirmation. But there was still a slight reservation. Stile pursued the matter further. "And, just as your change of form enabled us to interact in a new and meaningful way—though not more meaningful than this joy of traveling together across this beautiful land—my abruptly revealed facility with music enables us to interact in yet another way." He smiled. "Which is what I was trying to tell you before—oh, you mean now you agree! You—no, you couldn't be apologizing! Unicorns never make mistakes, do they?"

She made a little buck, just a warning. He laughed. "Well, let's get to it," he said, pleased. He put the harmonica to his mouth and played an improvised theme, sending the perfect notes ringing out over the plain between the mountain ranges. Now Neysa joined in, and they made beautiful harmony. Her hooves beat the cadence, in effect a third instrument. The resulting duet was extremely pretty.

Stile experimented with the mystery buttons, and discovered that they were modes, like those of a good accordion; they changed the tones so that the harmonica sounded like other instruments, to a degree. One canceled the tremolo effect; another brought into play an octave-tuned scale. Another rendered the instrument into a diatonic harmonica, with the popular but incomplete scale and slightly differing tone arrangement. This was the most sophisticated harmonica he had ever played. That only increased his wonder that it should have been so carelessly lost out here. If he dropped such an instrument, he would search for hours to locate it, for it was a marvel of its kind. Who could have left it without a search?

Stile taught Neysa a song, and she taught him one. They played with improvisations to the beat of differing gaits. They did responsive passages, one taking the main theme, the other the refrains. They played alto and tenor on a single theme.

But soon something developed in the atmosphere—a brooding presence, an intangible power. It intensified, becoming almost visible.

Stile broke off his playing. Neysa halted. Both looked about.

There was nothing. The presence was gone.

"You felt it too?" Stile asked. Neysa flicked an ear in assent. "But what *was* it?"

She shrugged, almost dislodging his impromptu saddle. Stile checked his woven-straw cinch to see if it was broken. It wasn't; the strap had merely worked loose from the ring, as happened on occasion. He threaded it through again, properly, so that it would hold.

And did a double take. Strap? Ring?

He jumped to the ground and looked at his handiwork. Loose straw was shedding from it, but underneath it was a well-made if battered leather saddle, comfortable from long use.

He had fashioned a padding of straw. It had been straw this morning when he put it on her. Where had the saddle come from?

"Neysa—" But how would she know? *She* could not have put it there.

She turned her head to gaze directly at him. Then she turned it farther, touching the saddle with her horn. And looked at him, surprised.

"Someone has given us a saddle," Stile said. "Yet there was no way—it was straw this morning—I was riding you the whole time—"

She blew a nervous note. She didn't know what to make of it either.

"Magic," Stile said. "This is a realm of magic. There was magic in the air just now. A—spell?"

Neysa agreed. "Could it be my nemesis, the one I think tried to kill me?" Stile asked. "Showing his power? Yet the saddle is helpful, not harmful. It's something I needed, and it's a good one. And—" He paused, partly nervous, partly awed. "And the harmonica—that appeared like magic when I wanted it—Neysa, is someone or something trying to *help* us? Do we have a gremlin friend as well as an enemy? I'm not sure I like this—because we can't be sure it is a friend. The way that amulet turned into a demon—"

Neysa turned abruptly and began galloping at right angles to her prior course, carrying him along. She was bearing south, toward the purple mountains. Stile knew she had something in mind, so let her take her own route.

Soon they approached a unicorn herd. Neysa must have been skirting the herd all along, aware of it though Stile was not, and now sought it out. She sounded a peremptory note on her horn before drawing close. A single unicorn at the edge of the herd perked up, then galloped toward them. A friend?

Neysa turned and bore west again, away from the herd, and the other unicorn cut across to intercept her. The other was male, larger than Neysa though not substantially so. His color was quite different: dark blue, with red socks. Really the same pattern as Neysa's, but with completely unhorselike hues. Again Stile reminded himself: these were not horses.

As the two animals angled together, Neysa tooted her horn. The stranger answered with a similar toot. His horn sounded more like a saxophone, however. Did every unicorn play a different instrument? What a cacophony when several ran together!

Neysa shifted into the five-beat gait and played a compatible tune. The other matched the gait and cadence, and played a complementary theme. The two blended beautifully. No wonder Neysa had played so well with Stile himself; she had done this sort of thing before, with her own kind. Stile listened, entranced. No cacophony, this; it was a lovely duet.

Who, then, was this young stallion she had summoned? Stile did not really want his presence advertised. But he knew Neysa understood that, and was acting in his interest. She had to have reason. This must be some friend she trusted, who could help them discover the nature of the magic—or protect them from it if necessary.

They ran until well clear of the herd. Then they slowed, their harmony slowing with them. Neysa finally deposited Stile by a handsome nut tree and started grazing. It was the middle of the day: lunch break. She would probably insist on grazing for an hour or more, and he did not begrudge her that. She needed her strength, still not entirely restored after yesterday's trial. He removed the saddle and set it under the tree.

The strange unicorn did not graze. He watched Stile, looking him up and down. He took a step forward, horn pointed at Stile's navel. The musical instrument was now a weapon, without doubt. Stile stood still, chewing on a nut, relaxed but ready to move in a hurry if the creature charged.

The unicorn blew a single derisive note, shimmered —and became a man. The man was clothed. He wore furry leather trousers, a blue long-sleeved shirt, solid low boots, red socks, and a floppy light-blue hat. His hands were covered by heavy fiber gloves. A rapier hung at his side.

Astonished, Stile stared. A Citizen—here?

"So thou'rt the creep who's been messing with my sister!" the man said, his right hand fingering the hilt of the rapier.

Just what he needed: a protective brother! Now Stile saw the forehead spike, similar to Neysa's. No Citizen; ordinary people wore clothing here, he remembered now. "It was voluntary," Stile said tightly.

"Ha! I saw her charging up Snow Mountain yesterday, trying to shake thee off. Thou'rt lucky she changed not into a firefly and let thee drop in a crevasse!"

Oh. The unicorn was talking about the day, not the night. "She changes into a firefly, too?"

"And pray what's wrong with that? Most beasts are lucky if they can change into one other form. We each have two." He shimmered again, and became a hawk. The bird winged upward at a forty-five-degree angle, then looped and dived toward Stile.

Stile threw himself aside—and the man was back, appearing just as the bird seemed about to crash into the ground. "Well, there's no accounting for tastes. Thou'rt a shrimp, and thou'rt naked, but if she lets thee ride her I can't say nay. I want thee to know, though, that she's the best mare in the herd, color or not."

"Color?" Stile asked blankly.

"Don't tell me thou noticed not! Let me warn thee, man-thing: an thou dost ever use the term 'horse-hued' in her presence, I will personally—"

Neysa had come up behind her brother. She blew a warning note.

"All right, already!" he snapped. "She is one season my senior; I may not talk back to her. But remember what I say: *there is nothing wrong with Neysa!*"

"Nothing at all," Stile agreed. "She's the finest-performing and finest-looking mare I've encountered."

The man, evidently braced for doubt or argument, was briefly nonplused. "Uh, yes. Exactly. Then let's get on with it. What's thy problem?"

"My name is Stile. I am a stranger in this world, without information or clothing, someone is trying to kill me, and magic is being performed around me whose ultimate purpose I can not fathom." Stile had the gift for succinct expression, when required.

"So." The man frowned. "Well, my name is Clip. I'm Neysa's little brother. She wants me to help thee, so I'll help. I'll fix thee up with information and clothing. And a weapon to defend thyself from thine enemy. As for the magic—concern thyself not about it. Unicorns are immune to magic."

"Immune!" Stile expostulated. "Here you stand, a shape-changing unicorn, and you tell me—"

"*Other* magic, nit. Of course we do our own, though easy it is not. Like learning another language—which is part of shape-changing, of course; can't be human if thou canst not talk human idiom. Can't be avian if thou canst not fly. So most unicorns bother not. But none *other* can change a unicorn, or enchant one. Or anyone in contact with a unicorn. Was that not why thou didst desire her? So long as thou stayest with Neysa—" He frowned. "Though why she'd want to stay with *thee*—" Neysa's note of protest cut him off again. "Well, there's no comprehending the ways of mares." He began to remove his clothing.

"No comprehending!" Stile agreed. "Look, Clip—I rode Neysa as a challenge, because I needed a mount. In the end I couldn't keep her—but she joined me by her own choice. I don't know why she didn't jump off the mountain and change into a firefly and let me drop to my death, as I gather she could have—" And he had thought he was sparing *her*, when he released her at the ledge! "And I don't know why she's not talking to me now. When she—changed to human form, all she said was my name. She didn't explain anything." At the time he had thought no explanations were necessary; he had been naive!

"That last I can clarify. Neysa doesn't like to talk much. I'm the talkative one in our family, as perhaps thou hadst not yet noticed. So where there's talking to be done, she summons me." Clip handed his shirt to Stile. "Go on, get dressed. I don't need clothing, really, anyway, and I'll get another outfit when convenient." He glanced at Neysa. "I guess she saw something in thee she liked. Thou'rt not a virgin, art thou?"

Stile donned the shirt, shaking his head no, embarrassed both by the turn the conversation had taken and the act of assuming clothing. On Proton this would be socially and legally horrendous!

The shirt should have been large, but somehow turned out to fit him perfectly. He was coming to accept minor magic as the matter of course it was.

"Well, that's overrated anyway," Clip continued. "If

I ever found a nubile but virginal human girl, it sure wouldn't be my head I'd put in her lap!"

Stile smiled appreciatively, coming to like the expressive and uninhibited male. "What would a unicorn—or, one in equine form—want with a human girl anyway?"

"Oh, that's easy." The trousers were passed over. "The Herd Stallion co-opts all the best unicorn mares, which leaves us young males hard up. A unicorn does not live by grain alone, thou knowest! So though human flesh is less sweet than equine, even the touch of a fair maiden's hand is—"

"I begin to get the picture." The trousers fit perfectly also. Stile suppressed another twinge of guilt, donning clothing; this was not Proton, and clothing lacked the significance it had there. Out here in the wilderness, clothing became functional on more than a social basis. "Yet that being the case, an attractive mare shouldn't have any trouble—"

Neysa abruptly turned away. Clip lowered his voice. "All right, man. I see thou really knowest not, and thou'dst better. There are horses in unicorn ancestry—not nice to mention it, any more than the apes in thine ancestry—"

"There are no apes in my—"

"See what I mean? Sensitive subject. But on occasion there are throwbacks. When a unicorn is birthed without a horn—that is, without the horn-button; couldn't have a full horn before birth, of course—it is killed in simple mercy. But color is a borderline matter. If it is otherwise perfect, that unicorn is permitted to survive. But there is always that stigma." Clip frowned, glancing covertly at Neysa.

"Neysa—is colored like a horse," Stile said, catching on. "So she is outcast."

"Thou hast it. It is no official thing, for she *is* a full unicorn, but the Herd Stallion won't breed her, and of course none of the lesser males dare. *Nobody* touches a young mare without the Herd Stallion's permission, and he won't give it—because that would seem to infringe on his prerogative. Our kind is like that; simple logic is no substitute for pride. Some would have it that mules are the stubbornest of equines, but that is a dastardly slight on the stubbornness of the unicorn. So for two seasons now Neysa has gone unbred—all because of her color. And maybe her size."

Stile realized that his effort of the past night did not count. He was a man, not a stallion. He could play with a female like Neysa, but could never breed her, any more than a stallion in human form could breed a human girl. "This is outrageous! She's a fine unicorn! The Stallion should either breed her or free her."

"Thou knowest thou'rt only a man," Clip said, handing Stile the rapier. "But thy personality hath its redeeming aspects. Thou really likest Neysa?"

"I chose her because she was the finest steed I'd ever seen," Stile said seriously. "I loved her in that fashion from the start. To me there is no better creature than a perfect—equine."

"So thou never, until I spoke to thee, knew what was wrong with her?"

"There is nothing wrong with her!" Stile snapped.

"Agreed." Clip was highly gratified. "Well, I'm supposed to fill thee in on our world. There is little to tell. We unicorns are the dominant animal form, except perhaps in some corners of the pasture where the werewolves and vampires range, and we're really better off than the human peasants. Anyone can do magic, but most humans don't, because of the Adepts."

"Adepts?"

"Like Herd Stallions or wolf Pack Leaders, only it's magic, not mares or bitches they pre-empt. Each Adept has his special style of enchantment, and he's awfully good in his specialization. I said unicorns were proof against foreign spells, but Adepts are another matter. If an Adept should be after thee—"

"I see. What defense would I have against one of these super-sorcerers?"

"No defense suffices, except to hide—and sooner or later an Adept will find thee. They have charms and amulets and familiars spread throughout the realm of Phaze, spying out the news. There's hardly any limit to the powers of an Adept. In fact—that's it! The Oracle!"

"A fortune-teller?"

"More than that. There is no magic in the temple of the Oracle, and nobody is coerced therein. It is sacred ground. I'll bet that's where Neysa is taking thee. Well, then, that covers it. I'll be off." He shimmered back into unicorn form and galloped away, his horn and hooves sounding the charge.

Stile had wanted to know more about Adepts and the Oracle. Well, perhaps Neysa would tell him, if he asked her nicely. Clip had certainly helped a great deal.

They rode west again, playing brief duets, enjoying themselves. Stile realized that the music of unicorns served another purpose: it alerted friends and foes to their presence. Unicorns were fighting animals; most creatures would prefer to avoid them, and so the sound of the horn cleared the way conveniently. Stile saw rabbits and turtles and an armadillo, but no predators. In short, only creatures that were noncompetitive with unicorns.

The terrain was highly varied, lush fields giving way to rocky slopes, swamps, open water and badlands sand. To the north and south the twin mountain ranges continued. The northern peaks were all snow-covered, virtually impassable to any creature with less power and determination than a unicorn; the southern ones seemed to be warmer, unless purple was the color of their snow. Curious! Something about this rugged landscape nagged him, a nascent familiarity, but he was unable to place it.

In the evening Neysa halted again, giving herself time to graze, and Stile foraged for his own sustenance. He found ripe corn growing, and blackberries. He thought of corn as fall produce, and blackberries as spring, but perhaps this world differed from others in its fruiting seasons too. On Proton anything could grow at any time, in the domes. Nonetheless, these edibles were suspiciously fortuitous—unless Neysa had known of this place and come here deliberately. Yes, of course that was it; she was taking excellent care of him.

In the night, after moonrise, she changed again. Stile hoped she would show him her firefly form, but she went directly to human. "You know, Neysa, you're about the prettiest girl I've seen—but I think I like you best in your natural form."

She smiled, flattered, and kissed him. She didn't mind being complimented on her unicorn body. She had spent her life stigmatized for a supposedly defective color, and obviously appreciated Stile's appreciation. This was no doubt the key to her initial acceptance of him. He really did admire her as she was, and was perhaps the first creature unrelated to her to do so. So though she had fought him, in the end she had not wanted to kill him.

"The Oracle—" he began. But she only kissed him again.

She wasn't talking. Ah, well. The stubbornness of unicorns! She had other virtues. He kissed her back.

Next morning she gave him some pointers on the use of the rapier. Stile had used a sword before, as fencing was one of the aspects of the Game. But by an anomaly of circumstance he had practiced with the broadsword, not the rapier. This light, thin sword was strange to him—and if it were the kind of weapon commonly used in this world, he had better master it in a hurry.

Neysa was expert. Stile had supposed a unicorn would not care to have the weapon of an opponent so close to the tender eyes, ears, and nose—but the proximity of her organs of perception gave her marvelous coordination with her weapon. Stile soon learned he could thrust without fear for her; his point would never score. Even if it should happen to slip through her guard, what would it strike? The heavy bone of her forehead, buttressing the horn. It would take more of a thrust than a man like him could muster to penetrate that barrier.

No, he had to look out for himself. Neysa was better on the parry than on the lunge, for the merest twitch of her head moved the horn-tip several centimeters, but to make a forward thrust she had to put her whole body in motion. Thus she was best equipped for defense against a charging adversary, either allowing the other to impale himself on her firm point, or knocking aside his weapon. Stile, forced to attack, found himself disarmed repeatedly, her horn bearing instantly on his vulnerable chest. She *could* lunge, and with horrible power—but did not, when she fenced a friend. How could he match the speed and power of her natural horn?

But Stile was a quick study. Soon he did not try to oppose power with power. Instead he used the finesse he had developed with the broadsword, countering power with guile. Soon Neysa could no longer disarm him at will, and sometimes he caught her out of position and halted his point just shy of her soft long throat. In a real match he could not hope to overcome her, but he was narrowing the gap.

But he was also getting tired. His throat felt sore, and his eyes got bleary. He could feel a flush on his face, yet he was shivering. Neysa made a feint—and he almost fell across her horn.

"Hostile magic!" he gasped. "I'm weak—"

Then he was unconscious.

CHAPTER 9

Promotion

Dreams came, replaying old memories . . .

The weapon-program director stared down at him. "You sure you want to get into swords, lad? They get pretty heavy." He meant heavy for someone Stile's size.

Again that burgeoning anger, that hopeless wrath instigated by the careless affronts of strangers. That determination to damn well prove he was not as small as they saw him. To prove it, most of all, to himself. "I need a sword. For the Game."

"Ah, the Game." The man squinted at him judiciously. "Maybe I've seen you there. Name?"

"Stile." For a moment he hoped he had some compensating notoriety from the Game.

The man shook his head. "No, must have been someone else. A child star, I think."

So Stile reminded this oaf of a child. It didn't even occur to the program director that such a reference might be less than complimentary to a grown man. But it would be pointless to react openly—or covertly. Why couldn't he just ignore what others thought, let their opinions flow from his back like idle water? Stile was good at the Game, but not that good. Not yet. He had a number of weaknesses to work on—and this was one. "Maybe you'll see me some time—with a sword."

The director smiled condescendingly. "It is your privilege. What kind did you want?"

"The rapier."

The man checked his list. "That class is filled. I can put you on the reserve list for next month."

This was a disappointment. Stile had admired the finesse of the rapier, and felt that he could do well with it. "No, I have time available now."

"The only class open today is the broadsword. I doubt you'd want that."

Stile doubted it too. But he did not appreciate the director's all-too-typical attitude. It was one thing to be looked down on; another to accept it with proper grace. "I'll take the broadsword."

The man could not refuse him. Any serf was entitled to any training available, so long as he was employed and the training did not interfere with his assigned duties. "I don't know if we have an instructor your size."

Stile thought of going up against a giant for his first lesson. He did not relish that either. "Aren't you supposed to have a full range of robots?"

The man checked. He was obviously placing difficulties in the way, trying to discourage what he felt would be a wasted effort. He could get a reprimand from his own employer if he placed a serf in an inappropriate class and an injury resulted. "Well, we do have one, but—"

"I'll take that one," Stile said firmly. This oaf was not going to balk him!

The director shrugged, smiling less than graciously. "Room 21."

Stile was startled. That happened to be his age. Twenty-one. He had been a stable hand for a year, now. Coincidence, surely. He thanked the director perfunctorily and went to room 21.

"Good afternoon, ma'am," the instructor said, coming to life. "Please allow me to put this protective halter on you, so that no untoward accident can happen." She held out the armored halter.

A female robot, programmed of course for a woman. That was how the problem of size had been solved.

Stile imagined the director's smirk, if he left now. He gritted his teeth. "I don't need the halter. I am a man." How significant that statement seemed! If only he could get living people to listen, too. He was a man, not a midget, not a child.

The robot hesitated. Her face and figure were those of a young woman, but she was not of the most advanced type. She was not programmed for this contingency. "Ma'am, it is required—"

Useless to argue with a mechanical! "All right." Stile took the halter and tied it about his waist. There it might offer some modicum of protection for what a man valued.

The robot smiled. "Very good, ma'am. Now here are the weapons." She opened the storage case.

It seemed an anomaly to Stile to have a female instructing the broadsword, but he realized that women played the Game too, and there were no handicaps given for size, age, experience or sex, and not all of them cared to default when it came to fencing. They felt as he did: they would go down fighting. Often a person with such an attitude did not go down at all; he/she won, to his/her surprise. Attitude was important.

The robot was not smart, but she was properly programmed. She commenced the course of instruction, leaving nothing to chance. Stance, motion, strategy, exercises for homework to increase facility. Safety precautions. Scoring mechanisms and self-rating scale. Very basic, but also very good. When a program of instruction was instituted on Proton, it was the best the galaxy could offer.

Stile discovered that the broadsword had its own virtues and techniques. It had two cutting edges as well as the point, making it more versatile—for the person who mastered it. It did not have to be heavy; modern alloys and molecular-foam metals made the blade light yet keen. He soon realized that there could be a Game advantage in this weapon. Most opponents would expect him to go for the rapier, and would play to counter that. Of such misjudgments were Game decisions made.

Next morning he reported to the stables as usual. "Stile, we're bringing in a robot trainer from another farm," the foreman said. "Name's Roberta. Get out to the receiving gate and bring her in." And he smiled privately.

Stile went without question, knowing another stable hand would be assigned to cover his chores in the interim. He had been given a post of distinction: greeter to a new trainer. No doubt Roberta was a very special machine.

She was already at the gate when Stile arrived. She was in the shade of a dwarf eucalyptus tree, mounted on a fine bay mare about sixteen hands high. The gatekeeper pointed her out, half-hiding a smirk.

What was so funny about this robot? Stile was reminded uncomfortably of the weapon-program director, who had known about the female robot instructor. Being deceived in any fashion by a robot was always an embarrassment, since no robot intentionally deceived. Unless programmed to—but that was another matter.

This one did not look special: flowing yellow hair, a perfect figure—standard, since they could make humanoid robots any shape desired. Why make a grotesquerie? She seemed small to be a trainer—smaller than the fencing instructor he had worked with. She was a rider, obviously; was she also a jockey? To break in the most promising horses for racing? No robot-jockey could actually race, by law; but no living person had the programmed patience of a training machine, and the horses did well with such assistance.

"Roberta, follow me," Stile said, and began walking along the access trail.

The robot did not follow. Stile paused and turned, annoyed. "Roberta, accompany me, if you please." That last was a bit of irony, as robots lacked free will.

She merely looked at him, smiling.

Oh, no—was she an idiot model, not programmed for verbal directives? Yet virtually all humanoid robots were keyed to respond at least to their names. "Roberta," he said peremptorily.

The mare perked her ears at him. The girl chuckled. "She only responds to properly couched directives," she said.

Stile's eyes passed from girl to mare. A slow flush forged up to his hairline. "The horse," he said.

"Roberta, say hello to the red man," the girl said, touching the horse's head with her crop.

The mare neighed.

"A robot horse," Stile repeated numbly. "A living girl."

"You're very intelligent," the girl said. "What's your name?"

"Uh, Stile." Of all the pitfalls to fall into!

"Well, Uh-Stile, if you care to mount Roberta, you can take her in."

His embarrassment was replaced by another kind of awkwardness. "I am a stable hand. I don't ride."

She dismounted smoothly. Afoot she was slightly shorter than he, to his surprise. She evinced the confidence normally associated with a larger person, though of course height was less important to women. "You're obviously a jockey, Uh-Stile, as I am. Don't try to fool me."

"That's Stile, no uh," he said.

"Stile Noah? What an unusual appellation!"

"Just Stile. What's your name?"

"I'm Tune. Now that the amenities are complete, get your butt on that robot."

"You don't understand. Stable hands tend horses; they don't ride."

"This is not a horse, it's a robot. Who ever heard of a jockey who didn't ride?"

"I told you I'm not—" Then it burst upon him. "*That's* why my employer chose me! Because I'm small. He wanted a potential jockey!"

"Your comprehension is positively effulgent."

"Do—do you really think—?"

"It is obvious. Why else would anyone want serfs our size? Your employer started you on the ground, huh? Slinging dung?"

"Slinging dung," he agreed, feeling better. This girl was small; she was not really making fun of him; she was playfully teasing him. "Until I found a worm."

"A whole worm?" she asked, round-eyed. "How did it taste?"

"A parasite worm. In the manure."

"They don't taste very good."

"Now I've been a year in the stable. I don't know a thing about riding."

"Ha. You've watched every move the riders make," Tune said. "I know. I started that way too. I wasn't lucky enough to find a worm. I worked my way up. Now I race. Don't win many, but I've placed often enough. Except that now I'm on loan to do some training. For those who follow after, et cetera. Come on—I'll show you how to ride."

Stile hesitated. "I don't think I'm supposed to—"

"For crying in silence!" she exclaimed. "Do I have to hand-feed you? Get up behind me. Roberta won't mind."

"It's not the horse. It's my employer's policy. He's very strict about—"

"He told you not to take a lift on a robot?"

"No, but—"

"What will he say if you don't get Roberta to your stable at all?"

Was she threatening him? Better her displeasure than that of his employer! "Suppose I just put you back on the horse and lead her in?"

Tune shrugged. She had the figure for it. "Suppose you try?"

Call one bluff! Stile stepped in close to lift her. Tune met him with a sudden, passionate kiss.

Stile reeled as from a body-block. Tune drew back and surveyed him from all of ten centimeters distance. "Had enough? You can't lead Roberta anyway; she's programmed only for riding."

Stile realized he was overmatched. "We'll do it your way. It'll be your fault if I get fired."

"I just knew you'd see the light!" she exclaimed, pleased. She put her foot in the stirrup and swung into the saddle. Then she removed her foot. "Use the stirrup. Hold on to me. Lift your left foot. It's a big step, the first time."

It was indeed. Sixteen hands was over 1.6 meters—a tenth of a meter taller than he was. He had to heft his foot up past waist-height to get it in the stirrup. He had seen riders mount smoothly, but his observation did not translate into competence for himself. Tune was in the way; he was afraid he'd bang his head into her left breast, trying to scramble up.

She chuckled and reached down with her left hand, catching him in the armpit. She hauled as he heaved, and he came up—and banged his head into her breast. "Swing it around behind, over the horse," she said. Then, at his stunned pause, she added: "I am referring to your right leg, clumsy."

Stile felt the flush burning right down past his collarbone. He swung his leg around awkwardly. He kneed the horse, but managed to get his leg over, and finally righted himself behind Tune. No one would know him for a gymnast at this moment!

"That mounting should go down in the record books," she said. "Your face is so hot it almost burned my—skin." Stile could not see her face, but knew she was smiling merrily. "Now put your arms around my waist to steady yourself. Your employer might be mildly perturbed if you fell down and broke your crown. Good dungslingers are hard to replace. He'd figure Roberta was too spirited a nag for you."

Numbly, Stile reached around her and hooked his fingers together across her small firm belly. Tune's hair was in his face; it had a clean, almost haylike smell.

Tune shifted her legs slightly, and abruptly the robot horse was moving. Stile was suddenly exhilarated. This was like sailing on a boat in a slightly choppy sea—the miniature sea with the artificial waves that was part of the Game facilities. Tune's body compensated with supple expertise. They proceeded down the path.

"I've seen you in the Game," Tune remarked. "You're pretty good, but you're missing some things yet."

"I started fencing lessons yesterday," Stile said, half flattered, half defensive.

"That, too. What about the performing arts?"

"Well, martial art—"

She reversed her crop, put it to her mouth—and

played a pretty little melody. The thing was a concealed pipe of some kind, perhaps a flute or recorder.

Stile was entranced. "That's the loveliest thing I ever heard!" he exclaimed when she paused. "Who's steering the horse?"

"You don't need reins to steer a horse; haven't you caught on to that yet? You don't need a saddle to ride, either. Not if you know your business. Your legs, the set of your weight—watch."

Roberta made a steady left turn, until she had looped a full circle.

"You did that?" Stile asked. "I didn't see anything."

"Put your hand on my left leg. No, go ahead, Stile; I want you to feel the tension. See, when I press on that side, she bears right. When I shift my weight back, she stops." Tune leaned back into Stile, and the horse stopped. "I shift forward, so little you can't see it, but she can feel it—hold on to me tight, so you can feel my shift—that's it." Her buttocks flexed and the horse started walking again. "Did you feel me?"

"You're fantastic," Stile said.

"I referred to the guidance of the horse. I already know about me."

"Uh, yes."

"Roberta responds only to correct signals; she has no idiosyncrasies, as a living animal might. You have to do it just right, with her. That's why she's used for training. So the horses won't teach the riders any bad habits. You noted how she ignored you when you spoke to her from the ground. She responds only to her rider. She's not a plow horse, after all."

"She's fantastic too."

"Oh, she is indeed! But me—I do have two cute little faults."

Stile was inordinately interested now. "What are they?"

"I lie a little."

Meaning he could not trust all of what she had been telling him? Discomforting thought! "What about the other?"

"How could you believe it?"

There was that. If she lied about it—

Tune played her instrument again. It was, she explained, a keyboard harmonica, with the keys concealed; she blew in the end, and had a scale of two and a half octaves available at her touch. Her name was fitting; her music was exquisite. She was right: he needed to look into music.

Tune and Roberta began training the new riders. Stile returned to his routine duties. But suddenly it was not as interesting, handling the horses afoot. His mind was elsewhere. Tune was the first really attractive girl he had encountered who was smaller than he was. Such a little thing, physical height, but what a subjective difference it could make!

Today he was lunging the horses. Lunging consisted of tying them to a fixed boom on a rotating structure, so they had to stay in an exact course, and making them trot around in a circle. It was excellent exercise, if dull for both man and horse. Some horses were too temperamental for the mechanical lead, so he had to do them by hand. He simply tied a rope to an artificial tree, and stood with his hand on that line while he urged the animal forward.

Stile had a way with horses, despite his size. They tended to respond to him when they would not do a thing for other stable hands. This, unfortunately, meant that he got the most difficult horses to lunge. No horse gave trouble about feeding or going to pasture, but a number could get difficult about the more onerous labors.

The first horse he had to lunge was Spook—the worst of them. Spook was jet black all over, which perhaps accounted for his name. He was also extremely excitable—which was a more likely reason for his name. He could run with the best—the very best—but had to be kept in top condition.

"Come on, Spook," Stile said gently. "You wouldn't want to get all weak and flabby, would you? How would you feel if some flatfooted mare beat your time in a race? You know you have to exercise."

Spook knew no such thing. He aspired to a life career of grazing and stud service; there was little room in his itinerary for exercise. He had quite an arsenal of tricks to stave off the inevitable. When Stile approached, Spook retreated to the farthest corner of his pen, then tried to leap away when cornered. But Stile, alert, cut him off and caught his halter. He had to reach up high to do it, for this horse could look right over Stile's head without elevating his own head. Spook could have flattened Stile, had he wanted to; but he was not a vicious animal, and perhaps even enjoyed this periodic game.

Spook tried to nip Stile's hand. "No!" Stile said sharply, making a feint with his free hand as if to slap the errant nose, and the horse desisted. Move and countermove, without actual violence. That was the normal language of horses, who could indulge in quite elaborate series of posturings to make themselves accurately understood.

They took a few steps along the path, then Spook balked, planting all four feet in the ground like small tree trunks. He was of course far too heavy for even a large man to budge by simple force. But Stile slapped him lightly on the flank with the free end of the lead-line, startling him into motion. One thing about being spooky: it was hard to stand firm.

Spook moved over, trying to shove Stile off the path and into a building, but Stile shoved the horse's head back, bracing against it. Control the head, control the body; he had learned that principle in martial art, winning matches by hold-downs though his opponents might outweigh him considerably—because their greater mass became useless against his strategy. Few creatures went far without their heads.

Spook tried to lift his head too high for Stile to control. Stile merely hung on, though his feet left the ground. After a moment the dead weight became too much, and the horse brought his head down. Other stable hands used a martingale on him, a strap to keep the head low, but that made this horse even more excitable. Stile preferred the gentle approach.

At last he got Spook to the lunging tree. "Walk!" he commanded, making a token gesture with the whip. The horse sighed, eyed him, and decided to humor him this once. He walked.

Every horse was an individual. "Spook, you're more trouble than a stableful of rats, but I like you," Stile said calmly. "Let's get this over with, work up a sweat, then I'll rub you down. After that, it's the pasture for you. How does that sound?"

Spook glanced at him, then made a gesture with his nose toward the pasture. Horses' noses, like their ears, were very expressive; a nose motion could be a request or an insult. "Lunge first," Stile insisted.

Spook licked his lips and chewed on a phantom delicacy. "Okay!" Stile said, laughing. "A carrot and a rubdown. That's my best offer. Now trot. Trot!"

It was all right. The horse broke into a classy trot. Any horse was pretty in that gait, but Spook was prettier than most; his glossy black hide fairly glinted, and he had a way of picking up his feet high that accentuated the precision of his motion. The workout was going to be a success.

Stile's mind drifted. The girl, Tune—could she be right about his destiny? There were stringent rules about horse competition, because of the ubiquitous androids, cyborgs, and robots. Horses had to be completely natural, and raced by completely natural jockeys. The less weight a horse carried, the faster it could go; there were no standardized loads, here. So a man as small as Stile—yes, it did make sense, in Citizen terms. Citizens did not care about serf convenience or feelings; Citizens cared only about their own concerns. Stile's aptitude in the Game, his intelligence in schooling—these things were irrelevant. He was small and healthy and coordinated, therefore he was slated to be a jockey. Had he been three meters tall, he would have been slated for some Citizen's classical basketball team. He didn't have to like it; he worked where employed, or he left Proton forever. That was the nature of the system.

Still, would it be so bad, racing? Tune herself seemed to like it. Aboard a horse like Spook, here, urging him on to victory, leaving the pack behind, hearing the crowd cheering him on . . . there were certainly worse trades than that! He did like horses, liked them well. So maybe the Citizen had done him a favor, making his size an asset. A lout like the stable hand Bourbon might eventually become a rider, but he would never be a racer. Only a small person could be that. Most were women, like Tune, because women tended to be smaller, and gentler. Stile was the exception. Almost, now, he was glad of his size.

And Tune herself—what a woman! He would have to take up music. It had never occurred to him that an ordinary serf could create such beauty. Her—what was that instrument? The keyboard harmonica—her musical solo, emerging as it were from nowhere, had been absolute rapture! Yes, he would have to try his hand at music. That might please her, and he wanted very much to please her.

She could, of course, have her pick of men. She had poise and wit and confidence. She could go with a giant if she wanted. Stile could not pick among women; he had to have one shorter than he. Not because he demanded it, but because society did; if he appeared among serfs with a girl who outmassed him, others would laugh, and that would destroy the relationship. So he was the least of many, from Tune's perspective, while she was the only one for him.

The trouble was—now that he knew he wanted her—his shyness was boiling up, making any direct approach difficult. How should he—

"One side, shorty!" It was Bourbon, the stable hand who was Stile's greatest annoyance. Bourbon was adept at getting Stile into mischief, and seemed to resent Stile because he was small. Stile had never understood that, before; now with the realization of his potential to be a jockey, the resentment of the larger person was beginning to make sense. Bourbon liked to make dares, enter contests, prevail over others—and his size would work against him, racing horses. Today Bourbon was leading Pepper, a salt-and-pepper speckled stallion. "Make way for a man and a horse!"

Spook spooked at the loud voice. He leaped ahead. The lead-rope jerked his muzzle around. The horse's body spun out, then took a roll. The line snapped, as it was designed to; a horse could get hurt when entangled.

Pepper also spooked, set off by the other horse. He careened into a wall, squealing. The genuine imported wood splintered, and blood spattered to the ground.

Stile ran to Spook. "Easy, Spook, easy! You're okay! Calm! Calm!" He flung his arms about Spook's neck as the horse climbed to his feet, trying to steady the animal by sheer contact.

Bourbon yanked Pepper's head about, swearing. "Now see what you've done, midget!" he snapped at Stile. "Of all the runty, oink-headed, pygmy-brained—"

That was all. A fracas would have alerted others to the mishap, and that would have gotten both stable hands into deep trouble. Bourbon led his horse on, still muttering about the incompetence of dwarves, and Stile succeeded in calming Spook.

All was not well. Stile seethed at the insults added to injury, knowing well that Bourbon was responsible for all of this. The horse had a scrape on his glossy neck, and was favoring one foot. Stile could cover the scrape with fixative and comb the mane over it, concealing the evidence until it healed, but the foot was another matter. No feet, no horse, as the saying went. It might be only a minor bruise—but it might also be more serious.

He couldn't take a chance. That foot had to be checked. It would mean a gross demerit for him, for he was liable for any injury to any animal in his charge. This could set his promotion back a year, right when his aspirations had multiplied. Damn Bourbon! If the man hadn't spoken sharply in the presence of a horse known to be excitable—but of course Bourbon had done it deliberately. He had been a stable hand for three years and believed he was overdue for promotion. He took it out on others as well as on Stile, and of course he resented the way Stile was able to handle the animals.

Stile knew why Bourbon had been passed over. It wasn't his size, for ordinary riders and trainers could be any size. Bourbon was just as mean to the horses, in little ways he thought didn't show and could not be proved. He teased them and handled them with unnecessary roughness. Had he been lunging Spook, he would have used martingale and electric prod. Other hands could tell without looking at the roster which horses Bourbon had been handling, for these animals were nervous and shy of men for several days thereafter.

Stile would not report Bourbon, of course. He had no proof-of-fault, and it would be contrary to the serf code, and would gain nothing. Technically, the man had committed no wrong; Stile's horse had spooked first. Stile should have been paying better attention, and brought Spook about to face the intrusion so as not to be startled. Stile had been at fault, in part, and had been had. Lessons came hard.

Nothing for it now except to take his medicine, figuratively, and give Spook his, literally. He led the horse to the office of the vet. "I was lunging him. He spooked and took a fall," Stile explained, feeling as lame as the horse.

The man examined the injuries competently. "You know I'll have to report this."

"I know," Stile agreed tightly. The vet was well-meaning and honest; he did what he had to do.

"Horses don't spook for no reason, not even this one. What set him off?"

"I must have been careless," Stile said. He didn't like the half-truth, but was caught between his own negligence and the serf code. He was low on the totem, this time.

The vet squinted wisely at him. "That isn't like you, Stile."

"I had a girl on my mind," Stile admitted.

"Ho! I can guess which one! But this is apt to cost you something. I'm sorry." Stile knew he meant it. The vet would do a serf a favor when he could, but never at the expense of his employer.

The foreman arrived. He was never far from the action. That was his business. Stile wondered, as he often did, how the man kept so well abreast of events even before they were reported to him, as now. "Damage?"

"Slight sprain," the vet reported. "Be better in a few days. Abrasion on neck, no problem."

The foreman glanced at Stile. "You're lucky. Three demerits for carelessness, suspension for one day. Next time pay better attention."

Stile nodded, relieved. No gross demerit! Had the foot been serious—

"Any extenuating circumstances to report?" the foreman prodded.

"No." That galled Stile. The truth could have halved his punishment.

"Then take off. You have one day to yourself."

Stile left. He was free, but it was no holiday. The demerits would be worked off in the course of three days low on the totem, but that suspension would go down on his permanent record, hurting his promotion prospects. In the case of equivalent qualifications, the person with such a mark on his record would suffer, and probably have to wait until the next occasion for improvement. That could be as little as a day, or as long as two months.

Stile started off his free time by enlisting in a music-appreciation class. It was good stuff, but he was subdued by his chastisement. He would stick with it, however, and in time choose an instrument to play himself. The keyboard harmonica, perhaps.

In the evening Tune searched him out. "It's all over the dome," she told him brightly. "I want you to know I think you did right, Stile."

"You're a liar," he said, appreciating her words.

"Yes. You should have covered it up and escaped punishment, the way Bourbon did. But you showed you cared more about the horse than about your own record." She paused, putting her hands on his shoulders, looking into his face. What lovely eyes she had! "I care about horses." She drew him in and kissed him, and the pain of his punishment abated rapidly. "You're a man," she added. The words made him feel like one.

She took him home to her private apartment—the

affluence permitted ranking serfs. By morning she had shown him many things, not all of them musical or relating to horses, and he was hopelessly in love with her. He no longer regretted his punishment at all.

When Stile returned to work next day, at the same hour he had departed, he discovered that he had been moved out of his cabin. He looked at the place his bunk had been, dismayed. "I know I fouled up, but—"

"You don't know?" a cabin mate demanded incredulously. "Where have you been all night?"

Stile did not care to clarify that; he would be razzed. They would find out soon enough via the vine. Tune, though small, was much in the eye of the local serfs, and not just because of her position and competence. "I was on suspension." He kept his voice steady. "Was it worse than I thought, on Spook? Something that showed up later?"

"Spook's okay." His friend took his arm. "Come to the bulletin board."

Not daring to react further, Stile went with him. The electronic board, on which was posted special assignments, demerits, and other news of the day, had a new entry in the corner: STILE pmtd RIDER.

Stile turned savagely on the other. "Some joke!"

But the foreman had arrived. "No joke, Stile. You're sharing the apartment with Turf. Familiarize yourself, then get down to the robot stall for instruction."

Stile stared at him. "But I fouled up!"

The foreman walked away without commenting, as was his wont. He never argued demerits or promotions with serfs.

Turf was waiting to break him in. It was a nice two-man apartment adjacent to the riding track, with a Game viewscreen, hot running water, and a direct exit to the main dome. More room and more privacy; more status. This was as big a step upward as his prior one from pasture to stable—but this time he had found no worm. There had to be some mistake—though he had never heard of the foreman making a mistake.

"You sure came up suddenly, Stile!" Turf said. He

was an okay guy; Stile had interacted with him on occasion, walk-cooling horses Turf had ridden, and liked him. "How'd you do it?"

"I have no idea. Yesterday I was suspended for injuring Spook. Maybe our employer got his firing list mixed up with his promotion list."

Turf laughed. "Maybe! You know who's waiting to give you riding lessons?"

"Tune!" Stile exclaimed. "*She* arranged this!"

"Oh, you're thick with her already? You're doubly lucky!"

Disquieted, Stile proceeded to Roberta's stall. Sure enough, there was Tune, brushing out the bay mare, smiling. "Long time no see," she said playfully.

Oh, she was lovely! He could have a thousand nights with her like the last one, and never get enough. But he was about to blow it all by his ingratitude. "Tune, did you pull a string?" he demanded.

"Well, you can't expect a jockey to date a mere stable hand."

"But I was in trouble! Suspended. There are several hands ahead of me. You can't—"

She put her fine little hand on his. "I didn't, Stile. Really. I was just joshing you. It's coincidence. I didn't know you were being promoted right now; I figured in a month or so, since they brought me in. I'm training others, of course, but no sense to promote you after my tour here ends. So they moved it up, obviously. They don't even know we're dating."

But she was, by her own proclamation, a liar. The foreman surely knew where Stile had spent the night. How much could he afford to believe?

"Ask me again tonight," she murmured. "I never lie to a man I'm loving."

What an offer! "What, never?"

"Hardly ever. You're an operetta fan?"

He looked at her blankly.

"Never mind," she said. "I'm not lying to you now."

How he wanted to believe her!

"Will you try it alone?" she inquired, indicating

Roberta's saddle. "Or do you prefer to hold on to me again, and bang your poor head?"

"Both," he said, and she laughed. She had asked him during the night whether his head hurt from what he had banged it into. He had admitted that there were some bruises he was prepared to endure.

She had him mount, more successfully this time, and showed him how to direct the robot. Then she took him out on the track. Very quickly he got the hang of it.

"Don't get cocky, now, sorehead," she warned. "Roberta is a horse of no surprises. A flesh horse can be another matter. Wait till they put you on Spook."

"Spook?" he cried, alarmed. He had daydreamed of exactly this, but the prospect of the reality scared him.

She laughed again. She was a creature of fun and laughter. It made her body move pleasantly, and it endeared her to those she worked with. "How should I know whom you'll ride? But we'll get you competent first. A bad rider can ruin a good horse."

"Yes, the Citizen wouldn't be very pleased if a serf fell on his head and splattered dirty gray brains on a clean horse."

It was a good lesson, and he returned to his new apartment exhilarated, only to discover more trouble. The foreman was waiting for him.

"There is a challenge to your promotion. We have been summoned to the Citizen."

"We? I can believe there was a foul-up with me, that will now be corrected." Though he had begun to hope that somehow this new life was real. Even braced for it as he was, this correction was hard to take. "But how do you relate? It wasn't your fault."

The foreman merely took his elbow and guided him forward. This summons was evidently too urgent to allow time for physical preparation. Stile tried to smooth his hair with his hand, and to rub off stray rimes of dirt on his legs from the riding. He felt, appropriately, naked.

In moments they entered a transport tunnel, took a private capsule, and zoomed through the darkness away from the farm. It seemed the Citizen was not at his farmside apartment at this hour. "Now don't stare, keep cool," the foreman told him. The foreman himself was sweating. That made Stile quite nervous, for the foreman was normally a man of iron. There must be quite serious trouble brewing! Yet why hadn't they simply revoked Stile's promotion without fuss?

They debouched at a hammam. Stile felt the foreman's nudge, and realized he was indeed staring. He stopped that, but still the environment was awesome.

The hammam was a public bath in the classic Arabian mode. A number of Citizens preferred this style, because the golden age of Arabian culture back on Earth had been remarkably affluent. Islam had had its Golden Age while Christianity had its Dark Ages. For the ruling classes, at any rate; the color of the age had never had much significance for the common man. Poverty was eternal.

Thus there were mosque-type architecture, and turban headdress, exotic dancing, and the hammam. This one was evidently shared by a number of Citizens. It was not that any one of them could not have afforded it alone; rather, Citizens tended to specialize in areas of interest or expertise, and an Arabian specialist had a touch that others could hardly match. Stile's employer had a touch with fine horses; another might have a touch with desert flora; here one had a touch with the hammam. On occasion other Citizens wished to ride the horses, and were invariably treated with utmost respect. The hammam was by nature a social institution, and a Citizen could only socialize properly with other Citizens, so they had to share.

There were many rooms here, clean and hot and steamy, with many serfs bearing towels, brushes, ointments, and assorted edibles and beverages. One large room resembled a swimming pool—but the water was bubbly-hot and richly colored and scented, almost like soup. Several Citizens were soaking in this communal bath, conversing. Stile knew they were Citizens, though they were naked, because of their demeanor and the deference the clustered serfs were paying. Clothing distinguished the Citizen, but was not the basis of Citizenship; a Citizen could go naked if he chose, and sacrifice none of his dignity or power. Nevertheless, some wore jewelry.

They came to a smaller pool. Here Stile's employer soaked. Six extraordinarily voluptuous young women were attending him, rubbing oils into his skin, polishing his fingernails, even grooming his privates, which were supremely unaroused. An older man was doing the Citizen's hair, meticulously, moving neatly with the Citizen to keep the lather from his face.

"Sir," the foreman said respectfully.

The Citizen took no notice. The girls continued their labors. Stile and the foreman stood where they were, at attention. Stile was conscious again of the grime on him, from his recent riding lesson; what a contrast he was to these premises and all the people associated with them! Several minutes passed.

Stile noted that the Citizen had filled out slightly in the past year, but remained a healthy and youngish-looking man. He had fair muscular development, suggesting regular exercise, and obviously he did not overeat—or if he did, he stayed with non-nutritive staples. His hair looked white—but that was the effect of the lather. His pubic region was black. It was strange seeing a Citizen in the same detail as a serf!

Two more men entered the chamber. One was Billy, the roving security guard for the farm; the other was Bourbon. "Sir," Billy said.

Now the Citizen nodded slightly to the foreman. "Be at ease," the foreman said to the others. Stile, Billy and Bourbon relaxed marginally.

The Citizen's eyes flicked to Bourbon. "Elucidate your protest."

Bourbon, in obvious awe of his employer, swallowed and spoke. "Sir, I was passed over for promotion in favor of Stile, here, when I have seniority and a better record."

The Citizen's eyes flicked coldly to the foreman. "You promoted Stile. Justify this."

The *foreman* had promoted him? Stile had not been aware that the man had such power. He had thought the foreman's authority ended with discipline, record-keeping, and perhaps the recommendation of candidates. The Citizen might have gotten mixed up, not paying full attention to the details of serf management, but the foreman should never have erred like this! He was the one who had suspended Stile, after all.

"Sir," the foreman said, ill at ease himself. "It is my considered judgment that Stile is the proper man to fill the present need. I prefer to have him trained on the robot horse, which will only be with us three months."

The Citizen's eyes flicked back to Bourbon. "You are aware that the foreman exists to serve my interests. He is not bound by guidelines of seniority or record. It is his prerogative and mandate to place the proper personnel in the proper slots. I do not permit this of him, I require it. You have no case."

"Sir," Bourbon said rebelliously.

The Citizen's eyes touched the foreman. There was no trace of humor or compassion in them. "Do you wish to permit this man to pursue this matter further?"

"No, sir," the foreman said.

"Overruled. Bourbon, make your specifics."

What was going on here? Why should the Citizen waste his time second-guessing his own foreman, whose judgment he obviously trusted? If the foreman got reversed, it would be an awkward situation.

"Sir, Stile has the favor of the visiting instructor, Tune. I believe she prevailed on the foreman to promote Stile out of turn, though he fouled up only yesterday, injuring one of your race horses. My own record is clean."

For the first time the Citizen showed emotion. "Injured my horse? Which one?"

"Spook, sir."

"My most promising miler!" The Citizen waved one arm, almost striking a girl. She teetered at the edge of the pool for a moment before recovering her balance. "Fall back, attendants!" he snapped. Now that emotion had animated him, he was dynamic.

Instantly the seven attendants withdrew to a distance of four meters and stood silently. Stile was sure they were just as curious about this business as he was, though of course less involved.

Now there was something ugly about the Citizen's gaze, though his face was superficially calm. "Foreman, make your case."

The foreman did not look happy, but he did not hesitate. "Sir, I will need to use the vidscreen."

"Do so." The Citizen made a signal with one finger, and the entire ceiling brightened. It was a giant video receiver, with special elements to prevent condensation on its surface. "Respond to the serf's directives, *ad hoc*."

The foreman spoke a rapid series of temporal and spatial coordinates. A picture formed on the screen. Stile and the others craned their necks to focus on it. It was the stable, with the horse Spook looking out. A running film-clock showed date and time: yesterday morning.

"Forward action," the foreman said, and the film jumped ahead to show Stile approaching the pen.

Stile watched, fascinated. He had had no idea this was being filmed. He looked so small, the horse so large—yet he was confident, the horse nervous. 'Come on, Spook,' his image said, encouraging the horse. But Spook was not cooperative.

The film went through the whole ugly sequence relentlessly, as Stile gentled and bluffed and fought the great stallion, forcing him to proceed to the lunging tree.

"As you can see, sir," the foreman said. "This man was dealing with an extremely difficult animal, but was not fazed. He used exactly that amount of force required to bring the horse in line. I have handled Spook myself; I could not have gotten him to lunge on that morning."

"Why didn't you send help?" the Citizen demanded. "I would have had difficulty myself, in that situation." This was no idle vanity; the Citizen was an expert horseman.

"Because, sir, I knew Stile could handle it. The presence of other serfs would only have alarmed the horse. This is why Stile was assigned to this animal on this day; Spook needed to be exercised and disciplined with competence. He had thrown his rider on the prior day."

"Proceed."

Under the foreman's direction the scene now shifted to Pepper's stall. Pepper showed no nervousness as Bourbon approached, but he laid back his ears as he recognized the stable hand. Bourbon brought him out roughly, slapping him unnecessarily, but the horse behaved well enough.

"This man, sir, was handling a docile animal brusquely," the foreman said. "This is typical of his manner. It is not a fault in itself, as some animals do respond to unsubtle treatment, but had he been assigned to exercise Spook—"

"Point made," the Citizen said, nodding. He was well attuned to the mannerisms of horses. "Get on with it."

Stile glanced at Bourbon. The stable hand was frozen, obviously trapped in an exposé he had never anticipated.

The film-Bourbon came up behind Stile, who now had Spook trotting nicely. The animal was magnificent. A small, stifled sigh of appreciation escaped one of the watching girls of the hammam. Girls really responded to horses!

Bourbon chose his time carefully. "One side, shorty!" he exclaimed almost directly behind Stile and the horse. There was no question about the malice of the act.

Spook spooked. The rest followed.

"Enough film," the Citizen said, and the ceiling screen died. "What remedial action did you take?"

"Sir, Stile reported the injury to his horse. I gave him three demerits and a one-day suspension. He made no issue. I felt that his competence and discretion qualified him best for the position, so I promoted him. I am aware that he had an acquaintance with the lady trainer, but this was not a factor in my decision."

"The other," the Citizen said grimly.

"Bourbon did not report the injury to his horse. I felt it more important to preserve the privacy of my observations than to make an overt issue. I passed him over for promotion, but did not suspend him, since the injury to the horse in his charge was minor."

"There *are* no minor injuries to horses!" the Citizen cried, red-faced. Veins stood out on his neck, and lather dripped unnoticed across his cheek. He would have presented a comical figure, were he not a Citizen. "You are rebuked for negligence."

"Yes, sir," the foreman said, chastened.

The Citizen turned to Stile. "Your promotion holds; it was merited." He turned to Bourbon, the cold eyes swiveling like the sights of a rifle. "You are fired."

When a serf was fired for cause, he was finished on Planet Proton. No other Citizen would hire him, and in ten days his tenure would be aborted. Bourbon was through. And Stile had learned a lesson of an unexpected nature.

He had been going with Tune three months, the happiest time of his life, studying fencing and riding and music and love, when abruptly she said: "I've got to tell you, Stile. My second fault. I'm short on time. My tenure's over."

"You're—" he said, unbelievingly.

"I started at age ten. You didn't think I got to be a jockey overnight, did you? My term is up in six months. I'm sorry I hid that from you, but I did warn you how I lied."

"I'll go with you!" he exclaimed with the passion of youth.

She squeezed his hand. "Don't be foolish. I like you, Stile, but I don't love you. Outside, you'd be twenty-one, and I'll be twenty-nine, and no rejuve medicine. You can do better than that, lover."

He thought he loved her, but he knew she was right, knew he could not throw away seventeen years of remaining tenure for a woman who was older than he and only liked him. "The Game!" he cried. "You must enter the Tourney, win more tenure—"

"That's why I'm telling you now, Stile. This year's Tourney begins tomorrow, and I'll be in it. I am on Rung Five of the age-29 ladder, by the slick of my teeth. My tenure ends the moment I lose a Game, so this is our last night together."

"But you might win!"

"You're a dreamer. *You* might win, when your time comes; you're a natural animal, beautifully skilled. That's why I wanted you, first time I saw you. I love fine animals! I was strongly tempted not even to try the Tourney, so as to be assured of my final six months with you—"

"You must try!"

"Yes. It's futile, but I must at least take one shot at the moon, though it costs me six months of you."

"What a way to put it!" Stile was torn by the horrors of her choice. Yet it was the type of choice that came to every serf in the last year of tenure, and would one day come to him.

"I know you'll be a better jockey than I was; you'll win your races, and be famous. I wanted a piece of you, so I took it, by means of the lie of my remaining time here. I'm not proud—"

"You gave me the best things of my life!"

She looked down at her breasts. "A couple of them, maybe. I hope so. Anyway, it's sweet of you to say so, sorehead. Your life has only begun. If I have helped show you the way, then I'm glad. I won't have to feel so guilty."

"Never feel guilty!" he exclaimed.

"Oh, guilt can be great stuff. Adds savor to life." But the spark was not in her humor, now.

They made love quickly, because he did not want to tire her right before the Tourney, but with inspired passion. He felt guilt for letting her go—and she was right, it did add a certain obscure quality to the experience.

Next day she entered the Tourney, and in her first match made a try on the Grid for music, and got trapped in dance instead. She was gone.

Stile pursued his musical studies relentlessly, driven

by his waning guilt and love of her memory. Gradually that love transferred itself to the music, and became a permanent part of him. He knew he would never be a master musician, but he was a good one. He did enjoy the various instruments, especially the keyboard harmonica.

Three years later the foreman's tenure expired. "Stile, you're good enough to qualify for my job," he said in a rare moment of private candor. "You're young yet, but capable and honest, and you have that unique touch with the horses. But there is one thing—"

"My size," Stile said immediately.

"I don't judge by that. But there are others—"

"I understand. I will never be a leader."

"Not directly. But for you there is a fine alternative. You can be promoted to jockey, and from there your skill can take you to the heights of fame available to a serf. I believe this is as good a life as anyone not a Citizen can have on Proton."

"Yes." Stile found himself choked up about the foreman's departure, but could not find any appropriate way to express this. "I—you—"

"There's one last job I have for you, a tough one, and how you acquit yourself may determine the issue. I am recommending you for immediate promotion to jockey, but the Citizen will decide. Do not disappoint me."

"I won't," Stile said. "I just want to say—"

But the foreman was holding out his hand for parting. "Thank you," Stile said simply. They shook hands, and the foreman departed quickly.

The job was to bring Spook back from another dome. The horse had grown more spooky with the years, and could no longer be trusted to vehicular transportation; the sound and vibration, however muted, set him off. The Citizen refused to drug him for the trip; he was too valuable to risk this way. Spook had won a number of races, and the Citizen wanted him back on the farm for stud. So Spook had to be brought home on foot. That could be difficult, for there were no walk-passages suitable for horses, and the outer surface of the planet was rough.

Stile planned carefully. He ordered maps of the region and studied them assiduously. Then he ordered a surface-suit, complete with SCOBA unit: Self-Contained Outside Breathing Apparatus. And a gyro monocycle, an all-band transceiver, and an information watch. He was not about to get himself lost or isolated on the inhospitable Proton surface!

That surface was amazingly rugged, once he was on it. There were mountain ranges to the north and south, the northern ones white with what little water this world had in free-state, as snow. There was the winding channel of a long-dead river, and a region of deep fissures as if an earthquake had aborted in mid-motion. He guided his monocycle carefully, counterbalancing with his body when its motions sent it into twists of precession; incorrectly handled, these machines could dump a man in a hurry, since the precession operated at right angles to the force applied. He located the most dangerous traps for a nervous horse, plotting a course well clear of them. Spook would be upset enough, wearing an equine face mask for his breathing and protection of his eyes and ears; any additional challenges could be disastrous. Which was of course why Stile was the one who had to take him through; no one else could do it safely.

Stile took his time, calling in regular reports and making up his route map. This was really a puzzle: find the most direct route that avoided all hazards. He had to think in equine terms, for Spook could spook at a mere patch of colored sand, while trotting blithely into a dead-end canyon.

Only when he was quite certain he had the best route did Stile report to the dome where Spook was stabled. He was confident, now, that he could bring the horse across in good order. It was not merely that this success would probably facilitate his promotion. He liked Spook. The horse had in his fashion been responsible for Stile's last promotion.

When he arrived at that dome, he found a gram

awaiting him. It was from offplanet: the first he had had since his parents moved out. STILE—AM MARRIED NOW—NAMED SON AFTER YOU. HOPE YOU FOUND YOURS—TUNE.

He was glad for her, though her loss hurt with sudden poignancy. Three months together, three years apart; he could not claim his world had ended. Yet he had not found another girl he liked as well, and suspected he never would. He found himself humming a melody; he had done that a lot in the first, raw months of loss, and it had coalesced into a nervous habit he did not really try to cure. Music would always remind him of her, and he would always pursue it in memory of those three wonderful months.

So she had named her son after him! She had not conceived by him, of course; no one conceived involuntarily on Proton. It was just her way of telling him how much their brief connection had meant to her. She had surely had many other lovers, and not borrowed from their names for this occasion. She said she had lied to him, but actually she had made possible an experience he would never have traded. Brevity did not mean inconsequence; no, never!

"Thank you, Tune," he murmured.

CHAPTER 10

Magic

Stile woke suddenly, making a significant connection. "Geography!" he cried. "This world is Proton!"

Neysa, in girl-form, was tending him. He realized, in a kind of supplementary revelation, that she was the same size as Tune; no wonder he had accepted her as a lover so readily, despite his knowledge of her nature. She was not a true woman, and would never be, but she was well worthwhile on her own account.

She looked at him questioningly, aware of his stare. Her appearance and personality were, of course, quite unlike Tune's; no light-hued hair, no merry cleverness here. Neysa was dark and quiet, and she never told a lie.

"I had a memory," he explained. "Beginning with my fencing lessons, because you were teaching me how to use the rapier when I—" He paused, trying to assimilate it. "What happened to me?"

Reluctantly, she talked. "Sick."

"Sick? You mean as in disease? But there's no disease on Proton—" Again he did a double take. "But this isn't Proton, exactly. It's another realm with the same geography. The purple mountains to the south—it's what Proton might have been, had it had a decent atmosphere. An alternate Proton, where magic works. Maybe magic made the atmosphere, and the gravity. So with a complete planetary environment, a complete ecology, there are flies, there is dirt, there is disease. And I have no natural immunity, only my standard shots, which never anticipated the complete spectrum of challenges I found here. The micro-organisms in the food here, in the water, natural for natives but foreign to my system. Pollens in the air. Allergens. Et cetera.

So it took a couple of days for the germs to incubate in my system, then suddenly they overwhelmed me. Reaching the point of explosive infestation. Thanks for explaining it so well, Neysa."

She smiled acknowledgment.

"But how could you cure me? I should have died, or at least been sick longer than this. I've only been out a few hours, haven't I? Now I feel fine, not even tired."

She had to speak again. "Clip brought amulet." She reached forward and touched a figurine hanging on a necklace that had been put on him.

Stile lifted it in his hand. "A healing amulet? Now isn't that clever! Will I get sick again if I take it off?"

She shook her head no.

"You mean these things emit their magic in one burst, then are useless? But some are supposed to have continuing effect, like the clothing-simulator amulet I was given at the outset—uh-oh." He hastily removed the chain from his neck. "That one tried to kill me. If this one was made by the same party—"

She shrugged.

"Do you mind if I dispose of this now?" he asked. "We could bury it and mark the spot so we can find it later if we want it. But I'd rather not have it with me. If I invoke a secondary function—well, Neysa, an amulet attacked me, before I met you. When I invoked it. *You* invoked this one, so maybe that's why it acted normally. I fear the amulets have murder in mind for me, when they recognize me. That's why I needed a steed—to get away from my anonymous enemy."

Neysa lifted her head, alarmed in the equine manner. "No, no, you didn't bring the enemy here," Stile reassured her. "The demon hasn't been invoked." He took her hands, smiling. "I chose better than I knew, when I chose you. You did right, Neysa. I think you saved my life."

She allowed herself to be drawn in to him, and there followed what followed. He had not forgotten Sheen, but this was another world.

They buried the amulet and went on. It was morning;

his illness had lasted only one night, coinciding with normal sleep, and the revelation of geography had almost been worth it. This accounted for the nagging familiarity he had sensed before; he had seen the surface of this world a decade ago, in its dead form.

What accounted for this difference? The concept of alternate worlds, or alternate frames of the same world, he could accept. But breathable atmosphere, a full living ecology, and magic in one, domes and science and external barrenness in the other—that dichotomy was harder to fathom. He would have expected parallel frames to be very similar to each other.

Still, it helped his sense of orientation. Now it was clear why people crossed over at certain spots. They were not matter-transmitting, they were stepping through the curtain at precise geographical locations, so as to arrive in domes and in private places. To cross elsewhere—well, if he tried that, he would have to prepare himself with a breathing mask.

"You know, Neysa," he said as he rode. "There is a lot I don't know about this world, and my life is in danger here, but I think I like it better than my own. Out here, with you—I'm happy. I could just ride forever, I think, like this." He shook his head. "But I suppose I would get tired of it, in a century or two; must be realistic."

Neysa made a musical snort, then broke into a two-beat gallop, front hooves striking precisely together, rear hooves likewise. It was a jolting gait.

"Think you can buck me off, huh?" Stile said playfully. He brought out his harmonica—one advantage of clothing, he discovered, was that it had pockets—and played a brisk marching melody. The girl Tune had taught him the beauty of music, and his growing talent in it had helped him on numerous occasions in the Game. His memory flashback had freshened his awareness that even had music been worthless in a practical sense, he would have kept it up. Music was fun.

But again a looming presence developed. Again they stopped. "Something funny about this," Stile said.

"Clip told me not to worry, that unicorns are immune to most magic—but this is eerie. I don't like mysteries that may affect my health."

Neysa blew a note of agreement.

"It seems to happen when we're playing music," he continued. "Now I've never been harmed by music, but I'd better be sure. Maybe something is sneaking up while we're playing, hoping we won't notice. I somehow doubt this is connected with the amulets; this is more subtle. Let's try it again. If we feel the presence, I'll stop playing and will try to search it out. You go on playing as if nothing is happening. We need to catch it by surprise."

They resumed play—and immediately the presence returned. Stile left his harmonica at his lips but ceased playing; instead he peered about while Neysa danced on, continuing the melody. But even as he looked, whatever it was faded.

Experimentally Stile resumed play, matching Neysa's theme, softly, so that an on-listener would not hear him. The presence returned. Neysa stopped playing, while Stile continued—and the presence loomed stronger, as if her music had restrained it. Stile halted abruptly—and the effect receded.

"It's tied to me!" he exclaimed. "Only when I play—"

Neysa agreed. Whatever it was, was after Stile—and it advanced only when he was playing. It could hear him, regardless of other sounds that masked his own.

Stile felt an eerie chill. "Let's get out of here," he said.

The unicorn took off. No clever footwork this time; she moved right into a racing gallop. They forged across the plain at a rate no horse could match, wove through copses of brightly green trees, and leaped across small streams. He could see the mountains sliding back on either side. They were really covering the kilometers!

At last Neysa slowed, for her breath was turning fiery. Stile brought out his harmonica and played once more—and instantly the presence closed in.

He stopped immediately. "We can't outrun it, Neysa; that's evident. But now that we're aware of it, maybe we can do something about it. Why does it still come only when I play? It has to know that we are aware of it, and are trying to escape it; no further need to hide."

Neysa shrugged—an interesting effect, while he was mounted.

"First the amulet, now this. *Could* they be connected? Could the harmonica be—" He paused, alarmed. "Another amulet?"

After a moment he developed a notion. "Neysa—do you think you could play this instrument? With your mouth, I mean, human-fashion? If this is an enemy-summoning device, there should be the same effect whoever plays it. I think."

Neysa halted and had him dismount and remove the saddle. Then she phased into human form. He had not seen her do it by day before, and it had not occurred to him that she would. He had thought of her playing the harmonica in her equine form, but of course this way made much more sense.

She took the instrument and played. She was not expert, since this was foreign to her mode, and the result was a jumble. No presence formed. Then Stile took the harmonica and played a similar jumble—and the presence was there.

"Not the instrument—but me," he said. "Only when I play it." He pondered. "Is it a symbiosis, or is the harmonica incidental?"

He tried humming a tune—and the presence came, though not as powerfully as before.

"That settles it: it's me. When I make music, it comes. My music is better with the harmonica, so the effect is stronger, that's all. The instrument is not haunted." He smiled. "I'm glad. I like this harmonica. I'd hate to have to bury it in dirt." He would hate to abuse any harmonica, because he retained a fond feeling for the keyboard harmonica and all its relatives. But this present instrument was the finest of its breed he had ever played.

Neysa had changed back to her natural form. Stile

put the saddle back on. "I don't think we can afford to ignore this matter," he said.

The unicorn flicked one ear in agreement.

"Let's get down to some good grazing land, and I'll challenge it. I want to see what will happen. I don't like running from a threat anyway. I'd rather draw it out and settle the account, one way or another. If it is an enemy, I want to summon it by daylight, with my sword in hand, not have it sneak up on me at night."

Neysa agreed again, emphatically.

They moved downslope until good grass resumed. Neysa grazed, but she did not wander far from Stile, and her eye was on him. She was concerned. Bless her; it had been a long time since someone had worried about him. Except for Sheen—and that was a matter of programming.

Stile began to play. The presence loomed. He tried to see it, but it was invisible, intangible. This time he did not stop his music. The grass seemed to wave, bending toward him and springing back as if driven by a wind, but there was no wind. The air seemed to sparkle. A faint haze developed, swirling in barely discernible colored washes. Stile felt the hairs on his body lighten, as if charged electrostatically. He thought at first it was his own nervousness, for he did not know what thing or force he summoned, but he saw Neysa's mane lifting similarly. There was potential here, and it centered on him—but it never acted. It just loomed.

Stile stopped playing, growing weary of this—and yet again the effect faded. "Almost the form of an electrical storm," he mused. "Yet—"

He was cut off by a sheet of rain blasting at him. Lightning cracked nearby. The sudden light half-blinded him, and a gust of wind made him stagger. He was soaked as if dunked in a raging sea, feeling the eerie chill of the violent water. There was a swirling of fog reminiscent of a developing tornado. The flashes of light were continuous.

Neysa charged back to him, seeking to protect him from the elements with her body and her anti-magic. Both helped; Stile flung his arms about her neck and buried his face in her wet mane, and the swirling wind had less force there. Her mass was more secure than his, and the rain struck her less stingingly. They settled to the ground, and that was more secure yet. "Now I'm embracing you in your natural form," he told her laughingly, but doubted she heard him over the wind.

What had happened? A moment ago there had been no slightest sign of bad weather. Stile knew storms could develop quickly—he had taken a course in primitive-world meteorology, and often visited the weather dome for demonstrations—but this had been virtually instantaneous. He had been playing his harmonica, trying to trigger whatever monstrous force was lurking, to bring it somehow to bay, then idly likened the effect to—

"I did it!" he cried. "I invoked the storm!" Like the amulet, it had been there to be commanded, and he had innocently done so.

"Storm abate!" he cried.

The two of them were almost swept from their impromptu nest by another savage bout of wind. The storm was not, it seemed, paying heed.

Yet this power was somehow keyed to him. He had invoked the storm; was he unable to banish it? He had evoked the demon from the amulet, before; that had evidently been a one-way thing. But a storm? Was it impossible to put this genie back in the bottle?

It was hard to concentrate, in this buffeting and wet and light and noise. But he tried. What, specifically, had he done to bring this about? He had played music, and the storm-spirit had loomed close without striking. Then he had said, "Almost the form of an electrical storm." An accidental rhyme, of no significance.

Rhyme? Something nagged him. When the harmonica had appeared, so fortuitously—what had he said? Hadn't it been—yes. "A harmonica is what you play. I wish I had one here today." Something like that. Joke doggerel. Two times he had spoken in rhyme, and two times he had been answered. Of course there had been other magic, like the attacking demon of the amulet. No rhymes there. But—worry about that later; it might be a different class of magic. Now, try to abate this tempest. Abate—what rhymed with that? Fate, late, plate. Try it; all he could do was fail.

"Storm abate; you're making me late!" he cried.

The storm lessened, but did not disappear. He was on to something, but not enough. Half a loaf. What else had he done, those other two times?

Neysa played a note on her horn. The storm had eased, so she preferred to stand. She felt most secure on all four feet.

That was it! He had been blowing his horn—in a manner. The harmonica. Making music, either singing or playing.

Stile brought out his wet harmonica and played a soggy passage. Then he stopped and sang in an impromptu tune: "Storm abate. You're making me late!"

This time the storm lessened considerably. The lightning stopped, and the rain slacked to a moderate shower. But it still wasn't gone.

"Neysa, I think I'm on to something," he said. "But I don't really have the hang of it yet. I think I can do magic, if I can only get the rules straight."

The unicorn gave him a long look whose import was unclear. Evidently she distrusted this development, but she made no comment. And he marveled at it himself: how could he, the child of the modern civilized galaxy, seriously consider practicing magic?

Yet, after what he had experienced in this frame, how could he *not* believe in magic?

They resumed their journey, plodding through the drizzle. After an hour they got out of it, and the sun warmed them. They did not make music. Stile knew he had learned something, but not enough. Yet.

Now they settled down to serious grazing and eating —except that he had nothing to eat. Neysa had been willing to continue until she brought him to a fruit tree, but he had felt her sustenance was more important than his, at the moment. She was doing most of the work.

If he could actually do magic, maybe he could conjure some food. If he made up a rhyme and sang it—why not? What rhymed with food?

Stile was actually a poet, in a minor sense; this was yet another aspect of his Game expertise. A person had to be extremely well rounded to capture and hold a high rung on an adult ladder. He was probably more skilled in more types of things of a potentially competitive nature than anyone not involved in the Game. But he had preferred meaning to rhyme and meter, in poetry, so was ill prepared for this particular exercise.

Still, he did know the rudiments of versification, and with a little practice it should come back to him. Iambic feet: da-DUM da-DUM. Pentameter: five feet per line. *I wish I had a little food*—iambic tetrameter, four beats. If unicorns spoke words while running, they would be excellent at poetic meter, for their hooves would measure the cadence.

"I wish I had a little food; it would really help my mood," he said in singsong. He was not as good at improvising tunes with his voice as with an instrument.

Before him appeared a tiny cube. It dropped to the ground, and he had to search for it in the grass. He found it and held it up. It was about a centimeter on a side, and in tiny letters on one face was printed the word FOOD. Stile touched his tongue to it. Nutro-peanut butter. He ate it. Good, but only a token.

Well, he had specified "little." That was exactly what he had gotten.

He was gaining understanding. Music summoned the magic; that was the looming power they had been aware of. Words defined it. The rhyme marked the moment of implementation. A workable system—but he had to make his definitions precise. Suppose he conjured a sword—and it transfixed him? Or a mountain of food, and it buried him? Magic, like any other tool, had to be used properly.

"I wish I had one liter of food; it would really help my mood."

Nothing happened. Obviously he was still missing something.

Neysa lifted her head, perking her ears. Her hearing was more acute than his. Her head came around. Stile followed the direction her horn was pointing—and saw shapes coming toward them.

Had he summoned these? He doubted it; they hardly looked like food, and certainly not in the specified quantity. This must be a coincidental development.

Soon the shapes clarified. Four monsters. They were vaguely apelike, with huge long forearms, squat hairy legs, and great toothy, horny, glary-eyed heads. Another variant of demon, like the one he had fought alone, or the crack-monsters, or the snow-monsters. They all seemed to be species of a general class of creature that wasn't in the conventional taxonomy. But of course unicorns weren't in it either.

Neysa snorted. She trotted over to stand by Stile. She knew this was trouble.

"Must be a sending of my enemy," Stile said. "When you used the amulet to heal me, it alerted the master of amulets, who it seems is not partial to me, for what reason I don't yet know. He sent his goon squad—but we were no longer with the amulet, so they had to track us down. I'll bet the storm messed them up, too."

Neysa made a musical laugh through her horn—a nice effect. She liked the notion of goons getting battered by a storm. But her attention remained on those monsters, and her ears were angling back. She looked cute when her ears perked forward, and grim when they flattened back.

"I think it must be an Adept against me," Stile continued. "Obviously it is no common peasant. But now I know I can do some magic myself, I am more confident. Do you think we should flee these monsters, and worry about when they might catch up again—such as when we are sleeping—or should we fight them here?"

It was a loaded question, and she responded properly. She swished her tail rapidly from side to side and stomped a forehoof, her horn still oriented on the goons.

"My sentiments exactly," Stile said. "I just don't like leaving an enemy on my trail. Let me see if I can work out a good spell to abolish them. That should be safer than indulging in physical combat. They look pretty mean to me."

Pretty mean indeed. His tone had been light, but he already had healthy respect for the fighting capacity of demons. They were like the androids of Proton: stupid, but almost indestructible. Yet he distrusted this magic he could perform. Like all sudden gifts, it needed to be examined in the mouth before being accepted wholeheartedly. But at the moment he simply had to use what was available, and hope it worked.

He concentrated on his versification as the goons approached. He could not, under this pressure, think of anything sophisticated, but so long as it was clear and safe, it would do. It had to.

The first monster loomed before them. "Monster go—I tell you so!" Stile sang, pointing.

The monster puffed into smoke and dissipated. Only a foul-smelling haze remained.

So far, so good. He was getting the hang of it. Stile pointed to the second monster. "Monster go—I tell you so!" he sang, exactly as before. Why change a winning spell?

The monster hesitated as if fazed by the bite of a gnat, then plunged ahead.

Neysa lunged by Stile and caught the demon on her horn. With one heave she hurled it over and behind. The creature gave a great howl of expiration, more in fury than in pain, and landed in a sodden heap.

Why had the magic worked the first time, and not the second? He had done it exactly the same, and nearly gotten his head bitten off.

Oh, no! Could it be that a spell could not be repeated? That it worked only once? Now he remembered something that had been said by the man he met, the one who had given him the demon amulet. About having to devise a new spell each time, to step through the curtain. He should have paid better attention!

The third and fourth goons arrived together.

No time now to work up another spell! Stile drew his rapier. "I'll take the one on the right; you take the left," he said to Neysa.

But these two monsters, having seen the fate of their predecessors, were slightly more cautious. To be ugly was not necessarily to be stupid, and these were not really andriods. They evidently learned from experience. They halted just outside the range of horn and sword. They seemed to consider Neysa to be the more formidable opponent, though Stile was sure it was him they wanted. They had to deal with her first; then they would have him at their dubious mercy. Or so they thought.

While one goon tried to distract her, backing away from the unicorn's horn, the other tried to get at her from the side. But Stile attacked the side monster, stabbing at it with his point. He wished he had a broadsword; then he could have slashed these things to pieces. He wasn't sure that a simple puncture would have much effect.

He was mistaken. He pricked his monster in the flank, and it howled and whirled on him, huge hamhands stretching toward him. Stile pricked it again, in its meaty shoulder. Not a mortal wound, but it obviously hurt. At least these demons did have pain sensation; Stile had half-feared they would not. Still, this was basically a standoff. He needed to get at a vital spot, before the thing—

The goon's arm swung with blinding speed and swept the weapon out of Stile's hand. The thing's eyes glowed. Gratified, it pounced on him.

Stile whirled into a shoulder throw, catching the monster's leading arm and heaving. With this technique it was possible for the smallest of men to send the largest of men flying. But this was not a man. The creature was so large and long-armed that Stile merely ended up with a hairy arm dangling over his shoulder. The monster's feet had not left the ground.

Now the goon raised its arm, hauling Stile into the air. He felt its hot breath on his neck; it was going to bite off his head!

"Oh, swell! Go to hell!" Stile cried with haphazard inspiration.

He dropped to the ground. The monster was gone.

Stile looked around, pleased. His impromptu spell had worked! It seemed this frame did have a hell, and he could send—

He froze. The other goon was gone too. So was Neysa.

Oh, no!

Quick, a counterspell. Anything! What rhymed with spell?

"I don't feel well; cancel that spell," he singsonged.

The two monsters and Neysa were back. All three were scorched and coated with soot.

"Monsters away; Neysa stay!" Stile sang. The goons vanished again.

Neysa looked at him reproachfully. She shook herself, making the powdered soot fly. There were sulfur smears on her body, and her mane was frizzled, and her tail was only half its normal length. Her whole body was a mass of singed hair. The whites showed all around her eyes; sure signal of equine alarm.

"I'm sorry, Neysa," Stile said contritely. "I wasn't thinking! I didn't mean to send *you* to hell!" But he realized that wasn't much good. She was burned and hurting. He had to do more than merely apologize.

He could do magic—if he sang a new spell every time. Could he make her well?

"To show how I feel—I say 'Neysa, heal!' "

And before his eyes she unburned. Her mane grew out again and her tail became long and black and straight. Her coat renewed its luster. Her hooves brightened back into their original pearl glow. She had healed —in seconds.

Where were the limits of his power?

But the unicorn did not seem happy. She was well, now, physically, but she must have had a truly disturbing emotional experience. A visit to hell! How could he erase that horror? Could he formulate a spell to make her forget? But that would be tampering with her mind, and if he made any similar error in definition—no, he dared not mess with that.

Neysa was looking at him strangely, as she had before. Stile feared he knew why.

"Neysa—how many people on this world can perform magic like this?" he asked her. "I know most people can do minor magic, like stepping through the curtain, the way most people can pick out clumsy melodies on the harmonica. But how many can do it well? Professional level? Many?"

She blew a negative note.

"That's what I thought. A lot of people have a little talent, but few have a lot of talent, in any particular area. This sort of thing is governed by the bell-shaped curve, and it would be surprising if magic talent weren't similarly constrained. So can a moderate number match my level?"

She still blew no.

"A few?"

This time the negation was fainter.

"A very few?"

At last the affirmative.

Stile nodded. "How many can exert magic against a unicorn, since unicorns are largely proof against magic?"

Neysa looked at him, her nervousness increasing. Her muzzle quivered; her ears were drawing back. Bad news, for him.

"Only the Adepts?" Stile asked.

She blew yes, backing away from him. The whites of her eyes were showing again.

"But Neysa—if I have such talent, I'm still the same person!" he cried. "You don't have to be afraid of me! I didn't mean to send you to hell! I just didn't know my own power!"

She snorted emphatic agreement, and backed another step.

"I don't want to alienate you, Neysa. You're my only friend in this world. I need your support."

He took a step toward her, but she leaned away from him on all four feet. She feared him and distrusted him, now; it was as if he had become a demon, shuffling off his prior disguise.

"Oh, Neysa, I wish you wouldn't feel this way! The magic isn't half as important as your respect. You joined me, when you could have killed me. We have been so much to each other, these past three days!"

She made a small nose at him, angry that he should try to prevail on her like this. He had sent her to hell; he had shown her how demeaning and dangerous to her his power could be. Yet she was moved; she did not want to desert him.

"I never set out to be a magician," Stile said. "I thought the magic was from outside. I had to know the truth. Maybe the truth is worse than what I feared."

Neysa snorted agreement. She was really dead set against this caliber of magic.

"Would it help if I swore not to try any more magic? To conduct myself as if that power did not exist in me? I am a man of my word, Neysa; I would be as you have known me."

She considered, her ears flicking backward and forward as the various considerations ran through her equine mind. At last she nodded, almost imperceptibly.

"I swear," Stile said, "to perform no magic without your leave."

There was an impression of faint color in the air about him, flinging outward. The grass waved in concentric ripples that expanded rapidly until lost to view. Neysa's own body seemed to change color momentarily as the ripples passed her. Then all was normal again.

Neysa came to him. Stile flung his arms about her neck, hugging her. There was a special art to hugging an equine, but it was worth the effort. "Oh, Neysa! What is more important than friendship!"

She was not very demonstrative in her natural form, but the way she cocked one ear at him and nudged him with her muzzle was enough.

Neysa returned to her grazing. Stile was still hungry. There was no suitable food for him here, and since he had sworn off magic he could not conjure anything to eat. Actually, he found himself somewhat relieved to be free of magic—but what was he to say to his stomach?

Then he spied the monster Neysa had slain. Were goons edible? This seemed to be the occasion to find out. He drew his knife and set about carving the demon.

Neysa spied what he was doing. She played a note of reassurance, then galloped around in a great circle several times, while Stile gathered brush and dead wood and dry straw to form a fire. When he had his makings ready, Neysa charged in, skidded to a halt, and snorted out a blowtorch blast. She had evidently not yet cooled off from the battle—or from hell—and needed only a small amount of exertion to generate sufficient heat. The brush burst into flame.

As it turned out, monster steak was excellent.

CHAPTER 11

Oracle

By the time they reached the Oracle, two days later, Stile had pretty well worked out the situation. He could do magic of Adept quality, provided he followed its rules. He had sworn off it, and he would not violate that pledge. But that didn't change what he was: an Adept. That could explain why another Adept was trying to kill him; that other was aware of Stile's potential, and didn't want the competition. The Adepts, it seemed, were quite jealous of their prerogatives—as were the members of most oligarchies or holders of power.

So how should he proceed? Swearing off magic would not protect him from a jealous Adept, who would resent Stile's mere potential. But if it were only a single Adept who was after him, Stile might try to locate that one and deal with him. Nonmagically? That could be dangerous! So—he would ask the Oracle for advice. Why not?

The Oracle lived in a palace. Manicured lawns and hedges surrounded it, and decorative fountains watered its gardens. It was open; anyone could enter, including animals. In this world, animals had much the same stature as human beings; that was one of the things Stile liked about it. In this palace and its grounds, as he understood it, no magic was permitted, other than that of the Oracle itself, and no person could be molested or coerced.

"No disrespect intended," Stile said. "But this doesn't seem like much. It's beautiful in appearance and concept, but . . ."

Neysa left the saddle at the entrance and guided him to a small, plain room in the back. From its rear wall projected a simple speaking tube.

Stile studied the tube. "This is it? The Oracle?" he asked dubiously. "No ceremony, no fanfare, no balls of flame? No bureaucracy? I can just walk up and ask it anything?"

Neysa nodded.

Stile, feeling let down, addressed the tube. "Oracle, what is my best course of action?"

"Know thyself," the tube replied.

"That isn't clear. Could you elucidate?" But the tube was unresponsive.

Neysa nudged him gently away. "You mean I only get one question?" Stile asked, chagrined.

It was so. As with a spell, the Oracle could be invoked only once by any individual. But it had not been Neysa's purpose to have all his questions answered here; she had brought him to this place only for his safety.

Stile, frustrated, left Neysa and went outside. She did not try to restrain him, aware that he had been disappointed. He proceeded to the first fountain he saw. A wolf sat on the far side, probably not tame, but it would not attack him here. Stile removed his shirt, leaned over the pool, and splashed the cold water on his face. So he was safe; so what? His curiosity was unsatisfied. Was he to remain indefinitely in this world without understanding it?

"Thou, too?"

Stile looked up, startled, blinking the droplets from his vision. There was a young man across the fountain. He had shaggy reddish hair and a dark cast of feature, with eyes that fairly gleamed beneath heavy brows. His beard and sideburns were very like fur.

"I regret; I did not see you," Stile said. "Did I intrude?"

"Thou didst see me," the man said. "But recognized me not, in my lupine form."

Lupine. "A—werewolf?" Stile asked, surprised. "I am not used to this land. I did not think—I apologize."

"That was evident in thy mode of speech. But apologize not to an outcast cur."

Mode of speech. Suddenly Stile remembered: Clip

the unicorn, Neysa's brother, had used this same touch of archaic language. Evidently that was what prevailed here. He had better change over, so as not to make himself awkwardly obvious.

"I—will try to mend my speech. But I do apologize for mistaking thee."

"Nonesuch is in order. This region is open to all without hindrance, even such as I."

Stile was reminded of the robot Sheen, claiming to have no rights because of her metal origin. It bothered him. "Art thou not a person? If being outcast is a crime, I am surely more criminal than you. Thee. I fled my whole world."

"Ah, it is as I thought. Thou art from Proton. Art thou serf or Citizen?"

"Serf," Stile said, startled at this knowledge of his world. Yet of course others had made the crossing before him. "Werewolf, if thou hast patience, I would like to talk with thee."

"I welcome converse, if thou knowest what ilk I be and be not deceived. I am Kurrelgyre, were."

"I am Stile, man." Stile proffered his hand, and the other, after a pause such as one might have when recalling a foreign convention, accepted it.

"In mine other form, we sniff tails," Kurrelgyre said apologetically.

"There is so much I do not know about this world," Stile said. "If you know—thou knowest of my world, thou wilt—wilst—thou shouldst appreciate the problem I have. I know not how came I here, or how to return, and the Oracle's reply seems unhelpful."

"It is the nature of Oracular response," Kurrelgyre agreed. "I am similarly baffled. I queried the Oracle how I might regain my place in my society without performing anathema, and the Oracle told me 'Cultivate blue.' Means that aught to thee?"

Stile shook his head. "Naught. I asked it what was my best course of action, and it said 'Know thyself.' I have no doubt that is always good advice, but it lacks specificity. In fact it is not even an action; it is an information."

"A most curious lapse," Kurrelgyre agreed. "Come, walk with me about the gardens. Perhaps we may obtain insights through dialogue."

"I shall be happy to. Allow me just a moment to advise my companion. She brought me here—"

"Assuredly." They re-entered the palace, proceeding to the Oracle chamber where Stile had left Neysa.

She was still there, facing the speaking tube, evidently unable to make up her mind what to say to it. Kurrelgyre growled when he saw her, shifting instantly into his lupine mode. Neysa, hearing him, whirled, her horn orienting unwaveringly on the new-formed wolf.

"Stop!" Stile cried, realizing that violence was in the offing. "There is no—"

The wolf sprang. Neysa lunged. Stile threw himself between them.

All three came to a halt in a momentary tableau. The tip of Neysa's horn was nudging Stile's chest; the wolf's teeth were set against his right arm, near the shoulder. Trickles of blood were forming on Stile's chest and arm where point and fang penetrated.

"Now will you both change into human form and apologize to the Oracle for this accident?" Stile said.

There was a pause. Then both creatures shimmered and changed. Stile found himself standing between a handsome young man and a pretty girl. He was shirtless, with rivulets of blood on him; he had forgotten to put his shirt back on after splashing in the fountain pool.

He extricated himself. "I gather unicorns and werewolves are hereditary enemies," he said. "I'm sorry; I didn't know. But this is no place for, uh, friendly competition. Now shake hands, or sniff tails, or whatever creatures do here to make up."

Neysa's eyes fairly shot fire, and Kurrelgyre scowled. But both glanced at the Oracle tube, then at Stile's bloodied spots, then at each other. And paused again.

Stile perceived, as if through their eyes, what each saw. The werewolf's clothing had reappeared with the man, and it was a tasteful fur-lined jacket and leggings, complimenting his somewhat rough-hewn aspect. Neysa was in a light black dress that set off her pert figure admirably; it seemed she wore clothing when she chose, though at night she had not bothered. She was now the kind of girl to turn any man's head—and Kurrelgyre's head was turning.

"It is a place of truce," the werewolf said at last. "I regret my instinct overcame my manners."

"I, too," Neysa agreed softly.

"I abhor the fact that I have drawn the blood of an innocent."

"I, too."

"Do thou draw my blood, Stile, in recompense." Kurrelgyre held out his arm. Neysa did the same.

"I shall not!" Stile said. "If you—if thou—the two of you—"

The werewolf smiled fleetingly. "Thou wert correct the first time, friend. It is the plural."

"If you two feel you owe me aught, expiate it by making up to each other. I hate to be the cause of dissent between good creatures."

"The penalty of blood need not be onerous," Kurrelgyre murmured. He made a courtly bow to Neysa. "Thou art astonishingly lovely, equine."

Neysa responded with a curtsey that showed more décolletage and leg than was strictly necessary. Oh, the tricks that could be played with clothing! No wonder the Citizens of Proton reserved clothing to themselves. "Thank thee, lupine."

Then, cautiously, Neysa extended her hand. Instead of shaking it, Kurrelgyre lifted it slightly, bringing it to his face. For a moment Stile was afraid the werewolf meant to bite it, but instead he kissed her fingers.

Stile, relieved, stepped forward and took an arm of each. "Let's walk together, now that we're all friends. We have much in common, being all outcasts of one kind or another. Neysa was excluded from the herd because of her color—"

"What is wrong with her color?" the werewolf asked, perplexed.

"Nothing," Stile said as they walked. He spied his

shirt by the fountain, and moved them all toward it. "Some unicorns have distorted values."

Kurrelgyre glanced sidelong past Stile at the girl. "I should say so! I always suspected that Herd Stallion had banged his horn into one rock too many, and this confirms it. My taste does not run to unicorns, understand, but the precepts of physical beauty are universal. She is extremely well formed. Were she a were-bitch—"

"And I am outcast because I refused to—to perform a service for my employer," Stile continued. "Or to honor an illegal deal proffered by another Citizen." He washed his small wounds off with water from the pool, and donned his shirt. "What, if I may inquire, was thy problem, werewolf?"

"Among my kind, where game is scarce, when the size of the pack increases beyond the capacity of the range to support, the oldest must be eliminated first. My sire is among the eldest, a former leader of the pack, so it fell to me to kill him and assume the leadership. Indeed, there is no wolf in my pack I could not slay in fair combat. But I love my sire, long the finest of wolves, and could not do it. Therefore mine own place in the pack was forfeit, with shame."

"Thou wert excluded for thy conscience!" Stile exclaimed.

"There is no conscience beyond the good of the pack," the werewolf growled.

"Yes," Neysa breathed sadly.

They came to a hedged-in park, with a fine rock garden in the center. Neysa and Kurrelgyre sat down on stones nearer to each other than might have seemed seemly for natural enemies.

"Let us review thy situation, Stile," the werewolf said. "Thou knowest little of this land—yet this alone should not cause thee undue distress. Thou wilt hardly be in danger, with a fair unicorn at thy side."

"Nevertheless, I am in danger," Stile said. "It seems an Adept is trying to kill me."

"Then thou art beyond hope. Against Adepts, naught suffices save avoidance. Thou must remain here at the Oracle's palace forever."

"So I gather, in the ordinary case. But it also seems I have Adept powers myself."

Kurrelgyre phased into wolf-form, teeth bared as he backed away from Stile.

"Wait!" Stile cried. "Neysa reacted the same way! But I have sworn off magic, till Neysa gives me leave."

The wolf hesitated, absorbing that, then phased warily back into the man. "No unicorn would grant such leave, even were that not the stubbornest of breeds." Neysa nodded agreement.

"But I am just a stray from another world," Stile said. "It is mere coincidence that I have the talent for magic."

"Coincidence?" Kurrelgyre growled. "Precious little in this frame is coincidence; that is merely thy frame's term for what little magic operates there. Here, all things have meaning." He pondered a moment. "Have ye talent in the other frame?"

"I ride well—"

The werewolf glanced at Neysa, who sat with her fine ankles demurely exposed, her bosom gently heaving. "Who wouldn't!"

"And I am expert in the Game," Stile continued.

"The Game! That's it! Know ye not the aptitude for magic in this frame correlates with that for the Game in that frame? How good at the Game be ye, honestly?"

"Well, I'm tenth on my age-ladder—"

Kurrelgyre waved a warning finger at him. "Think ye I know not the way of the ladders? If ye rise to fifth place, thou must enter the annual Tourney. No obfuscation, now; this is vital. How good art thou when thou tryest, absolute scale?"

Stile realized that this was not the occasion for concealment or polite modesty. "I should be among the top ten, gross. On a good day, fourth or fifth."

"Then thou art indeed Adept caliber. There are no more than ten Adepts. They go by colors: White, Yellow, Orange, Green and such: no more than there are clear-cut hues. Therefore thou art of their number. One Adept must be dead."

"What art thou talking about? Why must an Adept be dead, just because I'm good at the Game in the other—" Stile caught himself about to make an impromptu rhyme and broke off lest he find himself in violation of his oath.

"Ah, I forget! Thou hast no basis yet to comprehend. Know this, Stile: no man can cross the curtain between frames while his double lives. Therefore—"

"Double?"

"His other self. His twin. All true men exist in both frames, and are forever fixed where they originate—until one dies out of turn. Then—"

"Wait, wait! Thou sayest people as well as geography match? That can not be so. The serfs of Proton are constantly brought in and deported as their tenures expire; only the Citizens are a constant population."

"Perhaps 'tis so, now; not always in the past. Most people still equate, Phaze to Proton, Proton to Phaze. The others are partial people, like myself. Perhaps I had a serf-self in the past, and that serf departed, so now I alone remain."

"Thou travelest between frames—because werewolves don't exist on Proton?"

Kurrelgyre shrugged. "It must be. Here there are animals and special forms; there, there are more serfs. It balances out, likely. But thou—thou must travel because thy magic self is dead. And thy magic self must be—"

"An Adept," Stile finished. "At last I get thy drift."

"Know thyself," Neysa said. "Adept." She frowned.

"That's it!" Stile cried. "I must figure out which Adept I am!" Then he noticed Neysa's serious demeanor. "Or must I? I have sworn off magic."

"But only by exerting thy powers as an Adept canst thou hope to survive!" Kurrelgyre exclaimed. Then he did a double take. "What am I saying? Who would want to help an Adept survive? The fair 'corn is right: abandon thy magic."

Corn? Oh, unicorn. "What is so bad about being an Adept?" Stile asked. "I should think it would be a great advantage to be able to perform magic."

The werewolf exchanged a glance with the unicorn. "He really knows not," Kurrelgyre said.

"I really don't," Stile agreed. "I am aware that magic can be dangerous. So can science. But you both act as if it's a crime. You suggest I would be better off dying as a man than living as an Adept. I should think a lot of good could be done by magic."

"Mayhap thou shouldst encounter an Adept," Kurrelgyre said.

"Maybe I should! Even though I'm not doing magic myself, at least I'd like to know who I am and what manner of creature I am. From what thou sayest, something must have happened to my Adept double and, considering my age and health, it couldn't have been natural." He paused. "But of course! All we need to do is check which Adept died recently."

"None has," Kurrelgyre assured him. "At least, none we know of. Adepts are secretive, but even so, someone must be concealing evidence."

"Well, I'll just have to go and look," Stile decided. "I'll check out each Adept until I find which one is dead, and see if that was me. Then I'll be satisfied. Only—how can I be sure that two aren't dead, and I have found the wrong one?"

"No problem there," the werewolf said. "Thine other self would have looked exactly like thee, so any who saw thee in his demesnes would know. And every Adept has his own peculiar style of magic, his means of implementation, that he alone commands. What style is thine?"

"Stile style," Neysa murmured, permitting herself to smile fleetingly.

"Spoken, or sung, in verse," Stile said. "Music summons the power. Which Adept uses that mode?"

"We know not. The Adepts vouchsafe no such information to common folk. Often they veil their magic in irrelevant forms, speaking incantations when it may be in fact a gesture that is potent, or posturing when it is a key rune. Or so it is bruited about among the animal folk. We know not who makes the amulets, or the golem people, or the potions or graphs or any of the other conjurations. We only know these things exist, and know to our dismay their power." He turned to Stile, taking one hand. "But friend—do not do this thing. If thou findest thine Adept-self, thou wilt become that Adept, and I shall have to bear the onus of not having slain thee when I had the chance. And Neysa too, who helped thee: lay not this geas upon her."

Stile turned to Neysa, appalled. "Thou feelest that way also?"

Sadly, she nodded.

"Methinks she led thee to the Oracle to avoid the peril she saw looming," Kurrelgyre said. "To destroy a friend—or turn an Adept loose on the realm. Here thou art safe, even from thy friends."

"But I am bound by mine oath!" Stile said. He hoped he was getting the language right: thy and my before a consonant, thine and mine before a vowel. "I will not perform magic! I will not become the monster thou fearest. I seek only to know. Canst thou deny me that?"

Slowly Kurrelgyre shook his head. "We can not deny thee that. Yet we wish—"

"I must know myself," Stile said. "The Oracle said so."

"And the Oracle is always right," the werewolf agreed. "We can not oppose our paltry judgment to that."

"So I will go on a quest for myself," Stile concluded. "When I have satisfied my need-to-know, I will return to mine own frame, where there is no problem about magic. So thou needst have no fear about me turning into whatever ogre thou dost think I might. I have to return soon anyway, to get my new employment, or my tenure will expire."

Neysa's gaze dropped.

"Why carest thou about tenure?" Kurrelgyre inquired. "Remain here, in hiding from thine enemy; thou hast no need to return."

"But Proton is my world," Stile protested. "I never intended to stay here—"

The werewolf stood and drew Stile gently aside.

"Needs must I speak to thee in language unbecoming for the fair one to hear," he said. Neysa glanced up quickly at him, but remained sitting silently by the garden.

"What's this nonsense about unbecoming language?" Stile demanded when they were out of Neysa's earshot. "I don't keep secrets from—"

"Canst thou not perceive the mare is smitten with thee?" Kurrelgyre demanded. "Canst not guess what manner of question she tried to formulate for the Oracle?"

Stile suffered a guilty shock. He had compared Neysa in various ways to Sheen, yet missed the obvious one. "But I am no unicorn!"

"And I am no man. Yet I would not, were I thee, speak so blithely of departure. Better it were to cut her heart quickly, cleanly."

"Uh, yes. No," Stile agreed, confused. "She—we have been—I assumed it was merely a courtesy of the form. I never thought—"

"And a considerable courtesy it is," Kurrelgyre agreed. "I was careless once myself about such matters, until my bitch put me straight." He ran his fingers along an old scar that angled from his shoulder dangerously near the throat. Werewolves evidently had quite direct means of expressing themselves. "I say it as should not: Neysa is the loveliest creature one might meet, in either form, and no doubt the most constant too. Shamed would I have been to lay a tooth on her, ere thou didst halt me. Considering the natural antipathy that exists between man and unicorn, as between man and werewolf and between unicorn and werewolf, her attachment to thee is a mark of favor most extreme. Unless—chancest thou to be virginal, apart from her?"

"No."

"And most critical of all: canst thou touch her most private parts?"

Stile reddened slightly. "I just told thee—"

"Her feet," Kurrelgyre said. "Her horn. No stranger durst touch a unicorn's magic extremities."

"Why yes, I—"

"Then must it be love. She would not else tolerate thy touch. Mark me, friend: she spared thee, when she learned thou wert Adept, because she loved thee, and therein lies mischief with her herd. Thou canst not lightly set her aside." He touched the scar near his throat again.

"No," Stile agreed fervently, thinking again of Sheen. He had always had a kind of personal magnetism that affected women once they got to know him, though it was usually canceled out by the initial impression his size and shyness made. Thus his heterosexual relationships tended to be distant or intimate, with few shades between. But with that situation went a certain responsibility: not to hurt those women who trusted themselves to him.

He remembered, with another pang of nostalgia, how the jockey girl Tune had stimulated his love, then left him. He had never been able to blame her, and would not have eschewed the affair had he known what was coming. She had initiated him into a world whose dimension he had hardly imagined before. But he did not care to do that to another person. He had no concern about any injury from Neysa; she would never hurt him. She would just quietly take herself away, and off a mountain ledge, and never transform into a firefly. She would spare him, not herself. It was her way.

Kurrelgyre's question was valid: why couldn't Stile remain here? There was a threat against his life, true—but he had fled Proton because of that, too. If he could nullify that threat in this frame—well, there were appeals to this world that rivaled those of the Game.

In fact, magic itself had, for him, a fascination similar to—no! His oath made that academic.

What, then, of Sheen? He could not simply leave her in doubt. He must return at least long enough to explain. She was a robot; she would understand. The practical thing for him to do was pick the most convenient world and stay there. It would be enough for Sheen to know he was safe; her mission would then have been accomplished.

As he had known Tune was safe and happy . . . Had that been enough for him? To know she had successfully replaced his arms with those of another man, and given that man in fact what she had given Stile in name: a son? He had understood, and Sheen would understand—but was that enough?

Yet what else could he do? He could not remain in both frames, could he? In any event, his tenure on Proton was limited, while it seemed unlimited here.

Stile returned to Neysa and sat beside her, Kurrelgyre trailing. "The werewolf has shown me that I can not expect to solve my problems by fleeing them. I must remain here to find my destiny, only visiting the other frame to conclude mine affairs there." As he said it, he wished he had chosen other phrasing.

Neysa responded by lifting her gaze. That was enough.

"Now for thee, werewolf," Stile said. "We must solve thy riddle too. Did it occur to thee that the Blue thou must cultivate could be an Adept?"

Now Kurrelgyre was stricken. "Cultivate an Adept? Rather would I remain forever outcast!"

"But if the Oracle is always right—"

"That may be. I asked how to restore myself to my pack; the Oracle answered. Perhaps the necessary price is too high."

"Yet thou also didst specify that the method not violate thy conscience."

"My conscience will not permit my craven catering to the abomination that is an Adept!"

"Then it must be something else. Some other blue. A field of blue flowers—"

"Werewolves are not farmers!" Kurrelgyre cried indignantly. "It must be the Blue Adept; yet the only cultivation I could do without shame would be the turf over his grave. I shall not seek the Blue Adept."

Stile considered. "If, as we fear, thou hast doomed thyself to remain outcast from thy kind—why not travel with me? I have decided to remain in this frame, but this is pointless unless I locate and nullify the threat against my life—and that threat surely relates to who and what I am. Without magic with which to defend myself, I shall likely be in need of protection."

"The lady unicorn is capable of protecting thee ably enough."

"From the ill favor of an Adept?"

Kurrelgyre paced the ground. "Now, if I refuse, I brand myself coward."

"No, no! I did not mean to imply—"

"Thou hardly needst to. But also I doubt the mare would care to have the like of me along, and I would not impose—"

Neysa stood. She took Kurrelgyre's hand, glanced briefly into his eyes, then turned away.

The werewolf faced Stile. "Neysa has a way with words! It seems outcasts had best support each other, though they be natural enemies. We all shall likely die, and for a foolish cause—but it is as fitting a mode as any."

CHAPTER 12

Black

"Who is the closest Adept?" Stile asked. "Not the Blue; we won't check that one if you're along."

Kurrelgyre shifted to wolf-form and sniffed the breeze. He shifted back. "The Black, methinks."

"Black it is!" Stile agreed. He would have preferred a more scientific selection—but science was not, it seemed, trustworthy in this frame. Convenience would have to do.

They left the palace together, Stile riding Neysa, the wolf ranging easily beside. They bore west again, toward the castle of the Black Adept. Now that the decision was made, Stile had second thoughts about purpose and safety. Was he really doing the right thing? All he could do now was see it through, and after checking out the Black Adept he could decide whether it was worth checking out others. This was hardly his idea of sword and sorcery adventure—which was perhaps just as well. He suspected that in real life, more evil magicians prevailed than barbarian heroes.

Neysa had located a supply of grain, and had some in a bag tied to the saddle; she would not have to make long halts for grazing. Traveling at speed, they made excellent progress, covering fifty of this frame's miles in about two and a half hours. Stile had done some endurance riding on Proton, and knew it would take an excellent horse to maintain even half this pace.

Thereafter, the way became bleak. The turf thinned, remaining verdant only in scattered oases. Stile realized that with a spell he might procure fresh water and extra food, but did not offer. They did not want magic, and the very notion was contrary to the spirit of his oath.

The mountains and valleys gave way to a broad and featureless dark plain that extended to the horizon, oppressed by what seemed to be a permanently looming cloud. Gusts of cutting wind brought choking clouds of dust into their faces. Stile coughed. If this environment reflected the temperament of the Black Adept, the magician was vile indeed! But it was probably a misapprehension. Stile had friends and un-friends, but there were few people he considered to be as evil as his friends seemed to think Adepts were. It was said that familiarity bred contempt, but surely ignorance bred error.

At last, amid the gloom, a black castle showed. It stood in stark silhouette, no light illuminating it from within. The land about it was so bleak as to seem scorched. Had Stile not known the identity of its occupant, thanks to Kurrelgyre's nose, he might readily have guessed. Everything was dead black.

As they neared it, Stile suffered intensifying pangs of doubt. Was his curiosity worth the risk of bracing this person? He was running the risk of whatever sorcery the Black Adept had in mind—for what? Just to know who he was, in this frame.

No—it was more than that, he reminded himself. Another Adept was trying to kill him, and until Stile knew his own identity, he probably would not know who was trying to kill him, or why. The Oracle agreed; it had told him to know himself. Curiosity alone might not be worth it, but life, security—yes, that was worth it.

What should he do, though, if the lives of his friends were threatened on his behalf? Would he use his magic, then, to help them? No—he could not. His oath had been made, and Stile had never in his life broken his given word. Neysa had to give him leave, and now he knew she would not. Because she believed that to release him would be to turn him into the monster that an Adept would be, and she would rather die. He had better see to their mutual health by mundane means, staying alert.

Yet there was no call to be foolish. "Neysa," he murmured. "Is there any way to approach this castle secretly and depart in the same fashion? I don't need to brace the magician directly; I think one look at him will tell me whether he is alive or dead, or whether he resembles me. If we check, and the Black Adept is alive—not only is he not me, he is likely to do something horrible to me. And to thee, I fear."

Kurrelgyre growled assent in an I-told-thee-so tone. The two of them expected this to be such a bad experience that Stile would no longer question the validity of their hatred of Adepts. Increasingly, Stile was being convinced.

Neysa halted. She flicked her nose, indicating that he should dismount. Stile did so. Then she reached back as she lifted one hind foot. She put her teeth to it, as if chewing an itch—and the white sock came off.

Stile stared. The term "sock" was descriptive, not literal; it was merely a patch of white hair about the foot. Yet she still held the white sock in her mouth, and her foot had turned black.

She nudged the sock at him, then went for the other hind foot. Soon Stile held a pair of white socks, one larger than the other. Neysa nudged him again.

"But I can't wear these," he protested. "These are your socks. Thy socks."

Neysa nosed him impatiently again. Stile shrugged and tried donning a unicorn-sock over his boot. It was hoof-shaped at the extremity, yet it fit admirably: more unicorn magic, of course. In a moment he stood handsomely garbed in unicorn socks.

But the white color extended beyond the socks, now. His feet looked like hooves, his legs like hair. His arms—where were his arms?

Kurrelgyre growled appreciatively, seeming to think Stile's appearance had improved.

Stile looked again, startled. He looked like a unicorn! A white unicorn. He remained human, but in illusion he was the forepart of the animal. Behind him stretched a ghost-body, equine.

Neysa had given him concealment. Who would worry about a unicorn poking about the premises?

"Every time I think I understand thee, Neysa, thou

comest up with some new device!" he said admiringly. "I'll return thy socks when we're away from here. Thank thee most kindly." And privately he thought: she didn't mind him benefiting from magic, so long as it was not Adept magic. A useful distinction.

They went on: a white unicorn, a black unicorn, and a wolf. The dark fog swirled thickly about the castle, helping to conceal them. But could the Adept really be ignorant of their presence? It was possible; why should the Black Adept allow them to intrude, when he could so easily hurl a nasty spell at them, unless he were not paying attention? Surely he had better things to do than sit and watch for trespassers. And if the Adept happened to be dead, there should be no danger anymore. So Stile reasoned, reassuring himself.

Yet somehow he did not feel reassured.

Kurrelgyre made a low growl of warning. They stopped. The wolf had his nose to the ground, frozen there. Stile stooped to look—and his knees gave a warning shock of pain, and the unicorn image halfway buckled. Mustn't do! But he saw what it was: a black line, stretching across the basalt.

Could it amount to a trip wire? It was a color-line, not a wire, but with magic it could perform the same function. That would explain why the Adept was not paying attention; he depended on his automatic alert. "We'd better pass without touching any lines," Stile murmured. "They might be the Adept's alert-lines, no pun."

They all high-stepped carefully over the line. Soon there was another. This one was thicker, as if drawn with coagulating paint. Then a third, actually a ridge. And a fourth, set closer to the last, like a miniature wall.

"Something funny here," Stile said. "Why make an alarm-line this solid? It only calls attention to itself."

Yet there was nothing to do but go on over. Stile's apprehension was abating as his perplexity grew. He had accepted the notion of magic as a way of life—but why should anyone surround himself with thickening lines? That hardly made sense.

The lines came more often now, each more formidable than the last. It became evident that the black castle was not a mere edifice of stone or brick, but the innermost manifestation of a rapidly solidifying network of line-walls. When the walls passed waist height on Stile, and were set only two meters apart, he concluded that jumping them was now too risky; they were bound to touch one accidentally and set off the alarm. If this really were an alarm system. Stile now feared it was something quite different, perhaps an elaborate architectural trap. But it might be no more than a progressive deterrent to intrusions such as theirs. A passive defense, showing that the Black Adept was not really the monster he was reputed to be. Maybe.

"I think we had better walk between walls for a while," Stile said. "It is either that, or start climbing over them. This thing is turning into a maze, and we may be obliged to follow its rules." And he wondered, nervously: was that the way of Adepts? To force intruders, stage by stage, into a set mold, that would lead inevitably into their corruption or destruction? Was that the way of all Adept-magic? In that case, the fears of the unicorn and werewolf with respect to Stile himself could be well founded. Suppose he was, or had been, the Black Adept? That, given limitless power, he had chosen to isolate himself in this manner—and would do so again, given the power again? Helping no one, having no friends? Power corrupted . . .

They turned left, walking between walls. As it happened, it was indeed a maze, or at least a complicated labyrinth. The inner wall turned at right angles, making a passage toward the interior, and gradually elevated in height. Soon a ceiling developed, from an extension of one wall, making this a true hall. The passage kept curving about, usually sharply, often doubling back on itself, so that it was impossible to try to keep track of direction. "Kurrelgyre, your nose can lead us out again?" Stile inquired nervously. The wolf growled assent.

The line-labyrinth seemed to continue on indefinitely. Wan light fused in from somewhere, allowing them to see—but there was nothing to see except more blank walls of black material. The castle—for they had to be well inside the edifice proper now—was as silent as a burial vault. That hardly encouraged Stile.

On and on they went. Every time it seemed they were getting somewhere, the passage doubled back and paralleled itself for another interminable distance—then doubled back again. Was this whole castle nothing but many kilometers—many miles, he corrected himself—of passages? This passage continued to get narrower, becoming more like a tunnel, until Neysa was having difficulty making the turns. Her horn projected in front far enough to scrape a wall when she tried to make a hairpin turn, and her effort to avoid such contact put her into contortions and slowed her considerably. But she didn't want to change form, in case they were still under observation; that would betray her special talent. In addition, she still wore the saddle, which would become a liability in her other form. It seemed her own clothing transformed with her, but not things originating externally. And their supplies were in the saddlebags.

"Enough," Stile said at last. "We can wander forever in this mess, and die of starvation when our supplies run out. Let's tackle the dread Adept forthrightly!" And he banged his fist into the wall.

That surface was oddly soft and warm, as if only recently extruded from some volcanic fissure. It gave under the impact, slightly, then sprang back with a twang. The sound reverberated along the hall, and on out of sight; it seemed to be traveling along the same convolutions they were traveling, but much faster, tirelessly amplifying as it went. Soon the whole region was humming with it, then the castle itself.

Gradually it fudged, as the harmonics of different walls overlapped and muted each other, and finally died away amorphously. "Must have come to the end of the line," Stile said. "Let's go on, not worrying about contact."

They moved on more rapidly. At every sharp corner,

Neysa's horn scraped, and the twang reverberated. Nothing else happened.

Then at last the walls opened out into a moderate chamber. In the center stood a great black dragon. The creature opened its mouth to roar, but no sound came forth, only a tongue like a line drawn by a pen.

Stile contemplated the creature. He had never seen a living dragon before, but recognized the general form from the literature of legend. Yet this was an unusual variant. The creature, like the castle, seemed to be made of thickened lines. Its legs were formed of loops, its body of closely interlocked convolutions, and its tail was like knitwork. It was as if it had been shaped meticulously from a single line, phenomenally intricate. Yet it was solid, as a knit sweater is solid.

The dragon stepped forward, showing its blackline teeth. Stile was so fascinated by the linear effect that he hardly was concerned for his own safety. He recalled the puzzle-lines that had intrigued him as a child, in which the pen never left the paper or crossed itself. The most intricate forms could be made along the way by the traveling line—flowers, faces, animals, even words—but the rules were never broken. The challenge was to find the end of the line, in the midst of the complex picture.

This dragon, of course, was three-dimensional. Its lines did touch, did cross, for it was tied together by loops and knots at key places. But the principle remained: the line, though knotted, never terminated, never divided. The whole dragon, as far as Stile could tell, was a construct of a single thread.

Stile became aware of the posture of his companions. Both were facing the dragon in a state of combat readiness, standing slightly ahead of Stile.

"Enough of this!" he exclaimed. "This is my quest; you two should not endanger yourselves in my stead. I'll fight mine own battle." He stooped to pull off his unicorn socks—and again his knees flared in pain, causing him to drop ignominiously to the floor. He kept forgetting his injury at critical times!

He righted himself tediously, then bent at the waist and drew off one sock, then the other. Now he was himself again. He approached Neysa. "May I?" he inquired.

She nodded, her eyes not leaving the dragon. Stile picked up one real foot and pulled the sock over it until it merged with her hair. Then he moved around and did the other. In the midst of this he looked up—and met Kurrelgyre's gaze. Yes—he was handling the unicorn's very private feet. Horses did not like to have their feet impeded or restrained in any way; many would kick violently in such circumstance, even breaking a leg in the frantic effort to free it, or rebreaking it to escape the restraint of a splint. Thus a broken leg was often doom for a horse. Unicorns were no doubt worse. Neysa, when she joined him, had yielded her whole spirit to him.

Then she had discovered he was Adept. Anathema!

Now Stile stood before the dragon, drawing his rapier. He still was not expert in its use, but the dragon did not know that. Would the point be effective, or was it better to have a cutting edge so he could sever a line? Would the dragon unravel like knitwork if he did cut its line? These were questions he would have to answer by experiment.

The dragon was evidently assessing Stile at the same time. The white unicorn had suddenly become a man. Magic was involved. Was it safe to take a bite?

Stile, though quite nervous about the encounter, was experienced in dealing with animals. He had backed down hostile dogs and cats on his employer's farm, as part of assorted initiations, and of course had calmed many a spooked horse. Later he had taken his turn in various Game arenas, moving larger beasts of prey about with whip and prod. He had never faced a dragon before, but the basic principles of animal management should apply. He hoped.

He acted with apparent confidence, advancing on the dragon with his rapier point orienting on the creature's black knot-nose. The noses of most animals were tender, and often were more important psychologically than the eyes. "Now I'm not looking for trouble, dragon," Stile said with affected calmness. "I came to pay a call on the Black Adept. I only want to meet him, not to hurt him. Kindly stand aside and let us pass."

Stile heard a snort of amazement behind him. Neysa had never imagined bracing a dragon in its lair this way!

The dragon, too, was taken aback. What manner of man approached it with such imperious confidence? But it was a beast, not a man, and could not reason well, and it had its orders. In fact anything constructed from loops of cord might have trouble reasoning well; what kind of a brain could be fashioned from knotted string? It opened its jaws and took a snap at Stile.

Stile stepped smoothly to the side. His rapier flicked out, neatly pricking the sensitive nose. The dragon jerked back with a soundless yipe.

"That was a gentle warning," Stile said evenly, privately overjoyed at his success. The thing did feel pain! "My patience has limits. Begone, dragon!"

Baffled more by Stile's attitude than his physical prowess, the dragon scuttled back. Stile stepped forward, frowning. The dragon whimpered, again without sound—then unraveled.

Stile stared. The creature was disintegrating! First its hurting nose tightened into a close knot, then popped into nonexistence. Then its muzzle and teeth went, the latter becoming tangles in a string that disappeared as the string went taut. Then the eyes and ears. Headless, the thing still faced Stile, backing away. The neck went, and the front legs, the pace of unraveling speeding up as it continued. Very soon there was nothing but a line—and this snapped back into the wall like a rubber band.

The whole dragon had indeed been no more than an intricately wrought string. Now it was gone. Yet that string, when shaped, had seemed formidable, and had reacted with normal brute reflexes. Surely it would have chomped him, had he allowed it to. It could have killed him.

"The whole thing—string," Stile breathed. "And this whole castle—more string? For what purpose?"

Unicorn and wolf shrugged. Who could understand the ways of an Adept?

Neysa made a little nose back the way they had come, inquiring whether he had seen enough and was ready to get out of here. But Stile shook his head no, grimly. More than ever, he wanted to identify the proprietor of this castle. He wanted to be absolutely certain it was not now and never had been he.

They walked on down the passage, which narrowed again beyond the dragon's lair, but did not constrict as much as before. Again the way folded back, and back again, and yet again, endlessly.

"Damn it!" Stile swore. "We could die of old age in here, looking for the master of this castle—if he lives. I'm going to force the issue."

Kurrelgyre looked at him warily, but did not protest. This was Stile's venture, to foul up as he pleased. Stile made a fist and banged repeatedly on the wall, making the reverberations build tremendously until the whole castle seemed to shake. "Black Adept, show thyself!" he bawled. "I demand only to see thy face; then I depart."

"Follow the line," a voice replied. And a double line snaked into view ahead, looping into itself. As they approached it, the lines retreated like string drawn in from a distance. It resembled the dragon in this respect, constantly disappearing into itself. But it was not part of the wall.

Soon the line led them to a large central hall they were unlikely to have found thus expeditiously by themselves. A man stood there, facing them. He was garbed completely in black, and seemed to have a black tail. But the tail was the line they had just followed!

"The line," Stile said, finally putting it all together. "It is from thee! This whole castle is thou—the solidified line of thy past!"

"Now thou knowest," the Black Adept said coldly. "I have met thy demand, intruder."

"Yes," Stile agreed, not liking the man's tone. This was definitely not himself! The Adept stood half a meter taller, and his appearance and voice were unlike anything Stile was or could be. Not that the Adept was grotesque; he really looked rather ordinary. But he was certainly not Stile. "Now I shall depart, thanking thee for thy courtesy."

"No courtesy, intruder. Thine animals shall go, for they are of dark complexion, even burdened with thy supplies; it were a shame I must free them from. Thou shalt remain." And the Black Adept cast out his line. It amplified immediately into an intricate prison-bar wall, hardening in place between Stile and his two companions. Alarmed, he stepped to it—but the bars were already like steel. He tried to go around it, but the wall extended itself faster than he could move. He drew his rapier—but realized the bars were as hard as its metal was, even if it had had a cutting edge. He was trapped.

Stile turned to the Adept. "Why?" he asked. "Why hold me here?"

"Why didst thou intrude on my demesnes?" the Adept replied.

This was awkward. Stile did not care to give his reason, and would not lie. "I can say only that I meant thee no harm," he said.

"Know ye not I suffer no human intrusion into my premises? The penalty is to remain."

To remain. Never to depart? Death, here?

Neysa tried to get through the wall separating them, but could not. Even the wolf was too large to fit between the bars. They could not help him, directly. "You two had better leave," Stile said. "I will have to settle with the Adept myself."

Neysa hesitated. Stile knew she could get through the bars by changing into her firefly form, but he didn't want her to betray her talents to the Black Adept, who could readily make a line-cage to confine the insect. No sense getting her trapped too! "Get out of here!" he snapped. "I'll be all right. Just leave the supplies—"

"Do not!" the Black Adept warned. "Lest I throw out a net to capture thee too."

A net. Did the Adept know about her firefly form after all, or was that merely a manner of speaking? This was risky! Stile made a violent signal to Neysa to go. She seemed dubious, but retreated. The wolf followed her, tail held low. This was evidently part of the Adept's revenge: the separation of friends.

Stile faced the Adept, drawing his sword—but the Adept was gone. Only the new wall remained, extending in either direction into corridors that curved out of sight. Yet the Adept was aware of him; the wall itself was evidence of that. Catching the Adept in the maze of his own castle would surely be an impossible task; the Adept could form a jail cell around Stile at any time.

Why hadn't the magician done just that? Why permit an intruder the limited run of the castle? The Black Adept, logically, should either kill him or throw him out, and seemed to have the power to do both. Only the magic of another Adept could—

No! He had made a vow to do no magic himself. He would muddle through without magic, whatever came.

Stile walked along the barred wall. It carried on through folded passages, bisecting rooms, halls, even stairs. It led him through turrets and down into deep dungeons. There seemed to be no dead ends; the way was continuous. The Adept, it seemed, was showing off his premises, unable to resist allowing another person to appreciate their extent. Ah, vanity, however obliquely it manifested!

Stile continued on into a chamber where a human skeleton lay. It was complete and clean, sprawled on the floor.

He pondered that for some time. Why would such a grisly artifact be tolerated in the castle? It was unlikely to be artificial; the Adept's magic was evidently tied up in lines, proof enough that he was not Stile's alternate self, had any doubt remained. In fact, Stile could have saved himself a certain amount of mischief by recognizing that and turning back when he spied the very first line. Or when he recognized the dragon as a construct of lines. The hints were there to be interpreted, had he only been paying proper attention. Ah, hindsight!

This skeleton was a separate entity, not part of a line, so it had to be authentic. Stile kicked at an arm—

and it broke away from the floor with a crumbling snap. It had lain there so long it had adhered!

The Black Adept had said that the penalty for intrusion was to remain. He had not actually said he would kill the intruder. Perhaps he had obscure scruples, not liking to get blood directly on his lines. But to remain here indefinitely without food or water was to die. That, it seemed, was to be Stile's fate—with the two "animals" permitted to escape to carry some hint or warning to others. They could tell the world they had seen a man imprisoned for annoying the Black Adept. Thoroughly reasonable, effective, and nasty. The Adept really did not care for the favor of others; he just wanted them to stay away. This was no show-off tour Stile was on; it was a fiendish punishment-tour. His demise would be more painful, now that he understood exactly what was coming. Truly, the Adepts were not to be trifled with—or liked.

But Stile knew he had asked for this. He had been warned that Adepts were dangerous, but had charged in anyway. Perhaps he had not really believed in the threat. This fantasy land of Phaze had not seemed wholly real to him; he had not taken its threats seriously enough. Now, as he wandered, and his thirst grew, his perspective shifted. This frame was becoming more real than that of Proton. Somehow the attacks by monsters hadn't impressed him deeply; those encounters had been like individual Games, serious yet also unserious. But thirst, hunger, boredom, fatigue, and loneliness—these compelled belief of a fundamental nature. By the time he died, he would really believe!

He thought of appealing to the Black Adept, of begging for mercy—and knew immediately that that would be useless. The punishment was to die in confinement and hopelessness, without further communication. Without dignity or recognition. Those who violated the Adept's privacy were doomed to share it—completely. The Black Adept was neither noble nor wicked; he merely enforced his strictures effectively. No one bothered an Adept without good reason! Which was what

Neysa and Kurrelgyre had tried to tell him. He had simply had to learn the hard way.

And Stile himself—was he really an Adept? Had his Phaze-self been like this, an aloof, cynical magician? No wonder his companions distrusted that! If his possible exercise of his magic talent meant this, meant that he would lose all sense of friendship, honor and decency—then certainly his magic should be banned. It was better to die a feeling man, than to live as an inhuman robot.

No, correct that; he was thinking in a false cliché. Not all robots were unfeeling. Sheen—where was she now? His week, if he counted correctly, was just about over; the immediate threat of death in Proton—*on* Proton? No, these were two frames of the same world, and he was in one or in the other—this threat had been abated by time. Now it was Phaze he had to escape, and Proton that represented relief.

Stile wandered along the wall until darkness closed. Then he eased himself to the floor carefully, taking care of his knees. He leaned his back against the bars and experimentally flexed one knee. It actually bent fairly far before hurting; had it begun to heal? Unlikely; other parts of the body healed, but knees did not. Their conglomeration of ligament and bone prevented blood from circulating well there. Elbows could heal; they did not have to support constant weight. Knees had to be tough—and so, paradoxically, were more vulnerable than other joints. The anonymous enemy had struck well, lasering his knees, condemning him to a lingering torture similar in its fashion to what the Black Adept was now inflicting. Food for thought there? But when not under pressure, his knees could bend almost all the way. He could assume a squatting posture—when not squatting. A fine comfort that was! As if his knees mattered, when his body was doomed.

After a time he climbed back to his feet—this remained a chore, without flexing his knees under pressure—and walked to an interior chamber to relieve a call of nature. He did not like soiling the castle floor, but really had no choice—and perhaps it served the

Adept right. Then he returned to the barred wall, settled down again, and nodded off to sleep.

He dreamed he was a robot, with no flesh to warm his metal, no true consciousness to enliven his lifelessness. He woke several times in the night, feeling the deepening cold, much more thirsty than he ought to be. Psychological, of course, but still bothersome. He wished he had warm Neysa, in any form, to sleep against. Neysa had given him companionship too—a warmth of the spirit. After his years basically as a loner, he had adapted very quickly to that association; it filled a need. She had changed to human form to please him—but would have pleased him anyway. At least he had done the right thing, sending her away; she could return to her grazing and perhaps the werewolf would keep her company sometimes.

So cold! He hunched within his insubstantial clothing. One little spell could so readily cure this. Give me some heat to warm my feet—no! No magic! It might be crazy, but he would not violate his oath. Only if a firefly flew up and cried "Stile, do magic!" would he indulge—and he didn't want Neysa risking herself that way anyway. He curled into an uncomfortable ball and slept again; it was better than being awake.

By morning Stile's whole mouth was so dry it felt like leather. He must have been sleeping with it open. He worked his rocklike tongue around, moving his jaws, and managed to find a small pocket of saliva to spread about. Now he had to get up and—

And what? The bars remained, and would not disappear until his skeleton joined the other. He had nowhere to go, nothing to do.

Yet he had to do something. He was still cold; exercise was the only answer. His hunger and thirst had abated for the nonce, but his body was stiff. He climbed to his feet and limped to his makeshift privy. Shame to waste fluid, but as long as life remained, the bodily processes continued.

He resumed his trek along the barred wall, moving rapidly enough to generate some heat, slowly enough to conserve energy. Pointless travel, except that it was better than just lying down and dying. Plenty of time for the latter later.

There was no escape. The labyrinth of the castle was interminable, and the barred wall was too. The Black Adept only had one kind of magic, but he was very thorough about that! Theoretically there should be an end to the wall somewhere—but that end was the Adept himself. What use, then, to search for it? No logic, no reasonable discussion could move a man with the power and alienation this one had shown. The Black Adept was in his fashion like a Proton Citizen.

A Citizen! Kurrelgyre had said the people of Phaze were the same as those of Proton—or had been, before the shifting of serfs had become extensive. An Adept could indeed be a Citizen, in his alternate self. In the one frame, the instrument of power was wealth; in the other, magic. In both cases, arrogance reigned supreme.

Stile kept moving. He had won marathons in the Game; he could survive for some time when he put his will to it. If he caught up to the Black Adept, he might incapacitate the man and escape. Or kill him, since the Adept seemed willing to let Stile die. No, he did not want to be a killer himself; monsters were one thing, but the Adept was a man. Stile was willing merely to circle around the Adept, to get outside the barrier and escape.

Did his mental decision not to kill a man differentiate him from the Adept-mode? Could it be taken as evidence that he would not be as thoroughly corrupted by the power of magic as other Adepts had been? He hoped so.

Strange that there was no food in this bleak castle. Didn't the Black Adept eat? Probably his food supplies were well hidden in a convoluted storehouse, which would naturally be outside this barrier. Still, that raised more conjectures. Since this Adept did not conjure things from nothing, the way Stile's magic had done, he must have to obtain natural food elsewhere. Did the Black Adept have to trade with peasants for supplies of grain, eggs, cabbages? He could not, then, live in absolute seclusion. His ready use of language suggested the same. He had contact with others; he just didn't like it. Would any of those others be coming here to the castle? Would they help Stile? No, that seemed unlikely; the Adept could have supplies for a year at a time.

Stile moved slowly, conserving his strength, balancing his generated warmth against his thirst and hunger. He gave up following the interminable wall, and cut across the center of the castle as well as he could. But all the interior passages were dead ends; the configuration differed here. He wished he had some quick way to analyze the lines, but the castle was too complex; it would take him far longer than he had left to grasp its layout and locate the Adept. He also wished he had a good cutting tool to sever a line; since all of this was a single line, he could cut the Adept off from his castle anywhere. From his past. Would everything unravel, in the manner of the dragon? But there was nothing. His dagger could not damage the stonelike hardness of the material. The outer walls had had some give, but here they had none. Only a diamond drill or saw could do the job, or magic—

No!

All day Stile fought with himself, the thought of magic becoming more attractive as his physical condition deteriorated. But he refused to yield. It didn't matter that no one would know if he conjured a cupful of water to drink; an oath was an oath. He would expire with his integrity intact; that was one thing the Black Adept could not deprive him of.

At last, night seeped into the castle again. Stile sank down to sleep but could not. He did not want to yield himself up so quietly to extinction!

He found the harmonica in his hand, unbidden. He had avoided making music, because of its magical connotation. Magic could occur in the ambience of music, even when he did not voice it. His saddle had appeared, obviously conjured by his unconscious wish while he made music. But wouldn't it be all right to play, now, so long as he willed no magic? Music reminded him of Tune, so long ago, and it was fitting to think of her again as he concluded his own tenure.

He played. The music wafted out, permeating the corridors and windows and convolutions of the castle, striking harmonics in the walls. He was making the sound, but he was listening too, and it was absolutely beautiful. He was mastering the harmonica, playing it with his heart, evoking a feeling of melody he had seldom before achieved. Perhaps it was his swan song, his final gesture. Nevertheless it was a satisfying way to go.

At last, tiring even of this, he put the instrument away and dropped into sleep. This time it was more peaceful, as if his fast had freed him of material concerns.

He was awakened by a low growl. Stile's eyes cracked open, but his body did not move. He knew where his sword was; he needed to locate the animal. And to decide whether it was worth trying to fight. Why trade a quick death for a slow one?

Then, in the dark, a voice: "Stile."

"Kurrelgyre!" he said. Stile put his face to the bars, to get closer. "This isn't safe for thee!"

"Neysa went to the Oracle. It said 'Curtain.' Neysa did not understand what that meant, but I do. I sniffed around the castle. One corner of it intersects the curtain. Follow me."

The curtain! Of course! Except— "I can't do it; I swore no magic. It takes a spell to pass through."

"Thou art true to thine oath. Thou couldst have escaped ere now, hadst thou been otherwise. But fear not; I will put thee through."

Relieved, Stile followed the werewolf, pacing him on the other side of the wall. So Neysa had donated her single question the Oracle permitted to his cause! He would not have asked her to do that, yet now accepted the gesture gratefully.

It seemed only moments before Kurrelgyre brought him to the curtain. One small section of his prison intersected it. Apparently the Black Adept was not aware of it. That suggested the Adept was alive in both frames, unable to perceive or cross the curtain.

"We shall wait for thee at the Oracle's palace," Kurrelgyre said as Stile approached the glimmer. "Be mindful of the trust the mare places in thee, setting thee free of this frame."

"I don't know how long it will take me to—"

But the werewolf was already casting the spell. Stile passed through.

CHAPTER 13

Rungs

Stile landed outside a dome. He gasped—for the air was barely breathable. He might survive thirty minutes without a mask, but would not enjoy it. The limited oxygen of Proton's atmosphere was further reduced to favor the needs of the dome, and the pollution of sundry industrial processes was dumped out here. He realized—was it for the first time?—that the barren surface of Proton was the result of man's activities. Had the machine age not come here, the atmosphere would have remained like that of Phaze. Man's civilization had made a heaven-planet into hell.

Fortunately the dome was within five minutes foot travel. He could see it clearly, for its illumination flowed through the force field, lighting the barren plain.

Stile, his fatigue somewhat abated by his rest and the shock of the cold night, walked briskly toward the dome, drawing his clothing tightly about him. So long as he kept his respiration down, the air was not too hard on his lungs. Running would be a disaster, though. His clothing helped shield him from—

Clothing! He could not wear that here! He was a serf.

Yet without it he would soon be in trouble from the cold. He would have to wear it as long as possible, then dispose of it just before entering the dome. Maybe he could recover it when he returned to Phaze.

But he could not return where he had left, for that would put him right back in the prison of the Black Adept. He needed his clothing for the other frame, but not in this locale. He would have to risk carrying it with him.

Stile reached the dome. It was a small one, evidently

the private estate of a Citizen. It was hardly safe for a serf to intrude uninvited on such a place, but he really had no choice. These few minutes had made him uncomfortable; the less exposure to outside conditions, the better. He removed his clothing, bundled it up with the shoes inside, and stepped through the dome wall.

Instantly he was in light and warmth. This was a tropical garden of the kind popular with Citizens, whose tastes seemed to run opposite to the external wasteland their policies were making on the planet. Exotic palms were at every available spot, with a cocoa-chip mulch beneath. No one was present—which was why Stile had entered here. If he were lucky, he might get through undiscovered.

He was not. An alert gardener challenged him before he had taken twenty steps. "Halt, intruder! You're not of this estate."

"I—came from outside. I—got lost." Stile doubted he could afford to tell the truth, and he would not lie. "I had to come in; I would have died."

"You look half dead," the serf agreed.

Another serf hurried up. "I'm the garden foreman. Who are you? What were you doing outside without equipment? What are you carrying?"

That was a foreman, all right! "I am Stile, unemployed, formerly a jockey. I thought my life was threatened, so I tried to hide. But—" He shrugged. "It's a different world out there."

"It sure as hell is. Were you trying to suicide?"

"No. But I nearly died anyway. I have had no food or water for two days."

The foreman ignored the hint. "I asked you what you are carrying."

"This bundle—it is medieval Earth costume. I thought it would help me, in the other world." He was skirting a fuzzy line, ethically, and didn't like it. But again: wouldn't the truth convey less of the situation to this man than this half-truth did? What serf would believe a story about a magic world?

The foreman took the bundle and spread it out on the ground. "A harmonica?"

Stile spread his hands silently. He was now in a position where anything he said would seem a lie, including the truth. Suddenly Phaze seemed like a figment of his imagination, the kind of hallucination a man exposed to oxygen deprivation and gaseous pollutants might have. Especially if he had also suffered from hunger, thirst, and cold. In the past, men had undertaken similar deprivations as rites of passage, provoking similar visions. What had happened to him, really?

"I'll have to notify the Citizen," the foreman said.

Stile's hopes sank; this surely meant trouble. Had the man simply told him to clear out to serf quarters—

"Sir," the foreman said.

"What is it, gardener?" the Citizen's voice responded. It sounded familiar.

"Sir, a stranger has intruded from outside, carrying medieval Earth costume, including sword, knife, and a musical instrument."

"Bring him to the viewer." The voice gave Stile a chill. Where had he heard it before?

The foreman conducted Stile to a booth with a holo pickup. Stile stepped inside, knowing his whole body was being reproduced in image in the Citizen's quarters. He was dirty and abraded as well as suffering from hunger and thirst; he must look awful.

"Name?" the Citizen snapped.

"Stile, sir."

There was a pause. The Citizen would be checking the name in the computerized serf-listing. "The jockey and Gamesman?"

"Yes, sir."

"Play that instrument."

The gardening foreman quickly located the harmonica and jabbed it at Stile. Stile took it and put it to his mouth. This was his proof of identity; an impostor could probably not match his skill. He played a few bars, and as it had a few hours before, the emerging beauty of the music transformed his outlook. He began to get into the feel of it—

"Very well, Stile," the Citizen said, having no interest in the art of it. "Your present employer vouches for you. Wait here until his representative picks you up."

His present employer? What could this mean? Stile did not respond, since no query had been addressed to him. He rejoined the foreman, who solemnly handed back the rest of his bundle.

Suddenly Stile recognized the voice he had heard. The Black Adept! This was the Proton-self of that evil magician, having no knowledge of the other frame, but very much like his other self. It made sense—this dome was very near the site of the Black Castle. Stile's conjecture about Adepts and Citizens had been confirmed. Had this citizen any reason to suspect him—

Stile breathed a silent sigh of relief. There was no reason for such suspicion, and Citizens hardly cared about stray serfs. Since another Citizen was taking Stile off his hands, that ended the matter. Stile would have to make his explanations to his own employer, instead of wasting the time of this one. And if one of the Black Adept Citizen's serfs ever got lost, other Citizens would return the favor similarly. Serfs were hardly worth quarreling over.

A woman arrived, very well formed. As her face turned to him—"Sheen! How glad I am to see thee!" Oops—wrong language.

She frowned. "Come on, Stile. You had no business wandering outside. Suppose you had damaged the costume? It will go hard with you if you stray again." She turned to the foreman. "Thank you. He was supposed to bring the costume to our employer's isolation dome, and must have lost the way. He's a klutz at times."

"He tried to tell me he was unemployed," the foreman said.

She smiled. "He used to be a jockey. He must have taken one fall too many." She made a little circle about one ear with one finger. "These things happen. We apologize for the inconvenience to you."

"It brightens the night shift," the foreman said, admiring her body. Inconvenience became more tolerable when it brought a figure like this to the scene.

She took Stile firmly by the elbow and guided him along. "This time we'll get you where you belong," she said with an oblique smile.

He squeezed her hand. She had taken his prior advice to heart, and become so human it was almost annoying. But she had certainly bailed him out.

When they were safely in the capsule, flying through the tube toward a larger dome, Sheen explained: "I knew you'd return, Stile, somehow. I really am programmed for intuition. So I had my friends make up a robot in your likeness, and we got you a new employer. The moment the query on you came through the computer—"

"I see." Her friends were the self-willed machines, who could tap into the communication network. In fact, some of them probably *were* the communication network. What an asset they were at times!

From the general dome they took a transport rocket to Stile's original home dome. In a matter of minutes, the travel of several days by unicorn was reversed. That reminded him of another aspect. What should he say to Sheen about Neysa?

They returned to Stile's old apartment. Sheen had kept it in good order—or the robot who bore his name had done so. It seemed Sheen had put the robot away as soon as news of Stile's appearance reached her. Sheen had been most industrious and efficient on his behalf.

What had it been like, here, with two robots? Had they eaten, slept, made love? Stile found himself feeling jealous and had to laugh at himself. Obviously the robot-Stile was not self-willed. It would be a true machine, programmed by Sheen.

"We must talk," Sheen said. "But I think first we must feed you and rest you. That curtain-frame has not treated you kindly. You are bronzed and scratched and gaunt around the edges."

Stile's thirst abruptly returned. He almost snatched at the cup of nutro-beverage she brought, and gulped it down. "Yes. Drink and food and rest, in that order," he said. "And talk, of course."

She glanced obliquely at him. "Nothing else?"

Ah, sex appeal! But he was restrained. "I think we should talk, then consider the else. You may not be pleased."

"You may not be entirely pleased with what I have done, either," she said.

He raised an eyebrow. "With my double?"

She laughed. "Stile, it's impossible! He's a robot!"

"Good thing there are none of that ilk here," he agreed.

"You know what I mean. It's just not the same."

"You speak from experience?"

"No. He's not programmed for love."

"I had come to that conclusion. Otherwise you would not have been so glad to have me back."

After he had eaten and emerged from the dry-cleaning unit, they lay down together. In what way, he asked himself, was this creature inferior to Tune? Sheen looked and felt as nice, and she had displayed astonishing initiative. It seemed no one knew he had been absent a week. Any attempt to kill his robot double had of course been futile.

"Your friends have rendered this apartment private?" he inquired, remembering how it had almost become his prison. But for the device of the self-willed machines, who had made it seem he was here when he wasn't—

"Completely." She put her arms about him, hugging him briefly, but went no further. "Shall I tell you?"

What would give a logical robot or an illogical woman pause? "You had better."

"Your new employer doesn't care at all about horse racing. He cares about the Game. Each year he has sponsored a leading contender in the Tourney, but has never had a win. This year—"

"Oh, no! I'm expected to compete—"

"This year," she agreed. "And it has to be you. The robot can not do it in your stead. Even were it legal, he cannot match your ability. I have bought you security, Stile—but at the expense of your tenure."

"You realize that's likely to finish your mission too?

One way or the other, I won't need protection after I enter the Tourney."

"Had there been any other way—" She sighed. "Stile, you were fired for cause. No blacklist was entered against you, because your reluctance to race again was understandable, but even so, very few Citizens were interested in you. My friends had to do a research-sifting to locate—"

"The one Citizen who would hire me," Stile finished. "I don't fault you for that; you did the only thing you could do, and did it excellently."

"But your tenure—"

"I now have another option." But he was not eager to get into the matter of Phaze and his decision to remain there, yet.

"Your anonymous enemy remains. Not the Citizen who tried to make a cyborg of you; he opted out when he realized the week had passed. The original one, who lasered your knees. The one who, perhaps, sent me. There were several attempts made on the robot. My friends are closing the net, trying to locate that enemy, but he is extraordinarily cunning and elusive. I can not protect you from him long. So—"

"Infernally logical," he agreed. "Better the Game than death. Better abbreviated tenure than none at all. But I had thought I would be all right if I made it clear I would not race again."

"That seems to have been an unwarranted assumption. That person wants you dead—but not by obvious means. So a surgical error, or a random accident—"

"So I might as well have had my knees fixed—if I could trust the surgery." His attention returned to the Game. "The Tourney is inviolate; no entrant can be harassed in any way, even by a Citizen. That's to keep it honest. So the Tourney is the one place my life is safe, for the little time the Tourney lasts. But this catches me ill prepared; I had planned to enter in two years."

"I know. I did what I could, and may have forced premature exile on you. If you want to punish me—"

"Yes, I believe I do. I'll tell you what I have been doing. Beyond the curtain is a world of magic. I tamed a unicorn mare; she turned into a lovely little woman, and—"

"And I'm supposed to be jealous of this fairy tale?"

"No fairy tale. I said she was female, not male. I did with her what any man—"

"I am jealous!" She half-climbed over him and kissed him fiercely. "Could she match that?"

"Easily. She has very mobile lips."

"Oh? Then could she match this?" She did something more intimate.

Stile found himself getting breathless despite his fatigue. "Yes. Her breasts are not as large as yours, but are well—"

"Well, how about *this*?"

The demonstration took some time. At length, quite pleasantly worn out, Stile lay back and murmured, "That too."

"You certainly punished me." But Sheen did not seem much chastened.

"And after that, we went to the Oracle, who told me to know myself," Stile continued. "Realizing I must be an Adept who had been slain or otherwise abolished, I investigated—and got trapped in the castle of the Black Adept. The werewolf rescued me by sending me back through the curtain, and here I am." He yawned. "Now may I sleep?"

"You realize that no living person would believe a story like that?"

"Yes."

"And you're going back."

"Yes. I can not stay long in the frame of Proton, in any event. This gives me an alternative."

"Unless you win the Tourney. Then you can stay for life."

"Easier said than done, girl. In two years I would have been at my Game-proficiency peak; at the moment my chances are less than ideal."

"As a Citizen, you could find out the identity of your enemy."

"There is that." He smiled. "Now, Sheen—what was it you had in mind to do when we finished our talk?"

She hit him with a pillow from the couch. "We just did it! Didn't you notice?"

"Did what?"

She hauled him in to her, kissing him and flinging a leg over his thighs.

He squeezed her, bringing her head close against his, smelling her soft hair. "It's great to be back," he said seriously. "You have done good work, Sheen. But the world of Phaze—it's such a lovely place, even discounting the magic. I feel—over there I feel more nearly fulfilled. As if my human potential is at last awakening. I have to return. Do you understand?"

"Maybe you feel as I would feel, if I passed through myself and found myself alive." She closed her eyes, imagining. "Yes. You have to go back. But will you visit here?"

"Often. There are things for me in this world too."

"Of which I am one?"

"Of which you are the main one."

"That is all I have a right to ask."

Again Stile felt a helpless guilt. Sheen loved him; he could not truly love her. It hardly mattered that a specialist could make one tiny change in her programming that would instantly abolish or reverse her feeling for him; her present program was real. Modern surgery could transplant his brain into another body, but his present body was real; he did not like fundamental changes. If he left Proton, he was leaving her, again, in the way Tune had left him. Yet Sheen herself had shortened his tenure. She was correct; she could not ask more of him.

The night was only half over, long as it had seemed. He drew her over him like a blanket and slept.

In the morning he started his move to enter the Tourney. He went to the Game-annex, located the 35M ladder, and touched the button by the rung above his own. He was challenging Nine.

In a moment the holder of Rung Nine responded to the summons. He was, of course, a thirty-five-year-old male. For the purpose of the Game, age was strictly by chronology. There was constant disruption in the ladders, as birthdays shifted people from one to another. No one was given a place in the top twenty free; the Number One rung-holder in one age had to start at Number Twenty-One on the next age's ladder. But at the qualifying date for each year's Tourney the ladders were fixed; there was no disqualification by birthdays within the Tourney itself.

Apart from age and sex, the resemblance of the holder of Rung Nine to Stile was distant. He was tall and thin, like a stooped scholar. The appearance fit the reality; his name was Tome, and he was a researcher for a studious Citizen. Tome was very much a creature of intellect; he invariably selected the MENTAL column when he had the numbered facet of the Grid, and MACHINE when he had the lettered facet.

Because Tome could beat most people in games of the mind, and hold even when assisted by machine—especially when the machine was a computer—he was successful enough to hold his Rung. Because he was limited, he was not a potential champion. Tome was known as a 2C man—the definition of his specialties. Second vertical, third horizontal. If a person were weak in these, he would have trouble passing Tome.

Stile was generally strong in 2C. He could handle Tome, and the other man knew it. Stile simply had not wanted the Rung, before.

They went to a booth and played the Grid. Stile had the numeric facet; good. He regarded that as more fundamental. He would not choose MENTAL, of course; this was not a fun challenge where he wanted a good Game, but a serious challenge where he needed to win with least risk. He did not care for the 50-50 chance that CHANCE offered. Tome was pretty fair on machine arts, such as the theremin, so that was not a good risk. So it had to be Stile's strong column, PHYSICAL.

Tome chose MACHINE, of course. Immediately the subgrid showed:

	1. MOTION	2. ACTION	3. OBSERVATION
A. LAND			
B. WATER			
C. AIR			

Nine types of machine-assisted competitive sports, ranging from cycle racing in 1A to stellar location in 3C. Stile had the letter facet of this grid, unfortunately; he could not select the machine-racing column, and knew that Tome would not. Tome would go for observation—unless he figured Stile for water. That would put them in 3B, which amounted to sonar location of sunken ships. Tome was not really sharp at that. But he was a fair hand at water-hydrant dueling, so might go for ACTION. Therefore Stile went for AIR instead.

He won. It came up 2C: dueling by guns, lasers, and similar powered distance weapons. Tome was good at this, but Stile was better, and both knew it.

DRAW? Tome's query came on the panel. It was legitimate to make such an offer at any stage in the selection, and it was often done as part of the psychological combat. In this case it was an admission of weakness.

Stile hit the DECLINE button, and followed with CONCEDE?

Tome hesitated. Seconds passed. If he did not negate within fifteen, the concession would stand. Concession was always a demand, never an offer, at this stage: another rule to prevent irresponsible players from tying up the grids when they had no intention of playing a Game. But at last the DECLINE button lit.

Now the lists of individual variants appeared on the screen. Tome, the one challenged, had the first choice. He placed antique pistols in the center square of the nine-square subgrid that formed. Stile followed with a laser rifle in a corner. These were not real weapons; they would simply mark the target with a washable spot of red dye on the section hit. Very seldom was a live-ammo duel permitted, and never in connection with the Tourney.

As it happened, Stile and Tome shared a liking for antique weapons and forms, and when the grid was completed and played it came up 2B, the original pistols. The two of them walked to the dueling range nearby, while Sheen went to the spectator gallery. The holographic recording apparatus was operating, of course; every formal match was filmed, in case there should be any challenge to the result. Scholars liked to review the games of Tourney winners, right back to the original move up the rungs of the ladder, tracing with the wisdom of retrospect the elements that made those particular victories inevitable. This also meant, incidentally, that no agent in the audience could laser him in the knees or elsewhere; that shot would be recorded and the assassin apprehended immediately. This was no horse race!

They had to wait a few minutes for the use of the range. Dueling was popular, and there were a number of specialists who dueled every day. Had Stile been playing the Game with one of them, he would have avoided this option at any cost. That, of course, was the strategy of the Game; the key to victory lay in the grids. A good gridder could get by with very few Game specialties, always directing the selection to one of these. Just as Tome had to master only seven of the basic sixteen choices of the primary grid, and a proportionate number of each subgrid. An opponent could only force a selection within those seven. If an opponent's skills overlapped those of Tome, he could be virtually assured of landing one of these, to Tome's disadvantage. For a player who was serious, it was best to be strong in all boxes. That kept the options open, preventing him from getting trapped. Stile himself had strengths in all boxes; that was why he was the superior player here.

"You can't be going for the Tourney," Tome remarked. "You have two more seasons free. When the top five enter this year, we'll both be jumped into qualification for next year's Tourney. I figured you'd be sliding down about now. What's your move?"

Stile smiled. "See that girl in the stands? The pretty one? She put me up to it."

"Oh, a Game-digger!" Tome squinted at Sheen. "For one like that, *I'd* make a move, certainly! She much on the mental side?"

"Limited as a robot," Stile said.

"Going to move up to Rung Six, so you'll be Number One after the cut? That's risky. If someone gets sick at the last moment before qualification, you'll be shunted into the Tourney." Tome obviously had no doubts, in his mind, about the outcome of this match, and hardly cared; he had no intention of skirting the Tourney too closely.

"Going to Rung Five," Stile said. "I prefer that this not be bruited about."

Tome's head snapped around in surprise. "*This* year?"

"Not entirely my choice. But I've had some problems in my employment."

"So I have heard. Knee injury, wasn't it? I'm surprised you didn't have immediate surgery."

"I got scared of it."

Tome laughed. "You, scared! But I must admit you do look somewhat ravaged. Must have been a hard decision."

"It was," Stile agreed, though he knew that what showed on his body was the ravage of his two-day confinement in the Black Castle without food and water, rather than his mental state. Sheen had done what she could for him, but he had not yet properly recovered.

"Well, I wish you well," Tome finished sincerely.

The range cleared, and they entered. On a table at the entrance lay the set of antique pistols, with elaborate pearl handles and glistening black steel. A pistol specialist could have called out the exact vintage and make—probably eighteenth-century European—but Stile was concerned only with their heft and accuracy. Though they were replicas that fired no balls, they bucked and smoked just like the real ones.

Stile had to be sure to win this match; he could not

rechallenge until the rungs had shifted, and this close to the Tourney there was unlikely to be much shifting. Players were either hanging on to their rungs to be sure that they qualified, or trying to stay below qualification range. Stile's late decision to enter the Tourney was unusual, and would make ripples. He was going to have to bump someone who was depending on the Tourney as his last chance for extended tenure.

The Citizens had so arranged it that there were always more serfs interested in entering the Tourney than there were available slots—especially in Stile's own age range, where many mature people were ending their tenures. There were tenures expiring in all age ranges, for serfs could enlist at any age, but the older ones generally lacked the drive and stamina for real expertise in the Game, and the younger ones lacked experience and judgment. The ladders of the Thirties, male and female, were the prime ones.

The weapons were good, of course, and as similar to each other as modern technology could make them. Each party took one, went to the centermark of the range, stood back to back, and began the paceoff at the sound of the timing bell. Ten paces, turn and fire—each pace measured by the metronome. The man who turned and/or fired too soon would be disqualified; the tenth beat had to sound.

Some people who were excellent shots in practice were bad ones in such duels. They had to have time to get set, to orient on the target—and here there was neither time nor any fixed target. Some lost their nerve when confronting an actual opponent who was firing back. Special skills and nerve were required for this sort of match. Both Stile and Tome possessed these qualities.

At the tenth beat Stile leaped, turning in air to face his opponent. Tome merely spun in place, withholding his shot until he fathomed Stile's motion. He knew Stile seldom fired first; Stile preferred to present a difficult target, encouraging the other to waste his only shot. Then Stile could nail him at leisure. Tome was too smart for that.

Stile landed, plunged on into a roll, flipped to his feet and jumped again. Had Tome figured him for a straight bounce, his shot would have missed; but Tome was still being careful. His pistol was following Stile's progress, waiting for the moment of correct orientation.

That moment never came. In midair Stile fired. A red splash appeared in the center of Tome's chest, marking the heart. Contrary to popular fancy, the human heart was centered in the chest, not set in the left side.

Tome spread his hands. He had waited too long, and never gotten off his shot. He was officially dead.

Tome washed off the red stain while Stile registered the win with the Game computer outlet. They shook hands and returned to the Game-annex. Their names had already exchanged rungs. Stile punched Rung Eight, his next challenge. He wanted to capture as many rungs as he could before the alarm spread—and before news of his present weakened condition also got about. If his opponents thought it through, they would force him into the more grueling physical Games, where he would be weakest.

The challengee appeared. He was a squat, athletic man named Beef. "Tome, you challenging me?" he demanded incredulously.

"Not I," Tome said, gesturing to the ladder.

Beef looked. "Stile! What move are you making?"

"A challenge move," Stile said.

Beef shrugged. "I can't decline."

They went to a booth and played the grid. Beef was unpredictable; often he picked unlikely columns, just for the hell of it. Stile selected B. TOOL, hoping the other would not pick 3. CHANCE.

His hope was vain. Beef was more curious about Stile's motive than about the outcome of the Game, and they intersected at 3B. The home of roulette, dice, —all manner of gambling devices. Precious little skill. Stile could take Beef in most games of skill—but chance made it even.

Yet already he was maneuvering to upgrade his chances, playing the subgrid, finessing the choices in the way he had. Suddenly it came up CARDS. Cards were technically instruments of chance—but there were quite a number of games, like bridge and poker, where skill of one sort or another counted. All he had to do was pack the final grid with this type.

Beef, however, was alert to this, and selected games like blackjack and high-card-draw. He wanted to make Stile sweat, and was succeeding. It was very bad to have an opponent who cared less about the outcome than Stile did; there was little strategic leverage. Beef made his placements on the grid so that Stile could not establish a full column of his own choices. Three of one player's preferences in a row meant that player could select that row and have a commanding advantage. The chances of establishing a game utilizing reasonable skill remained 50-50, and Stile was hurting. He had to have better odds!

But Stile knew a skill variant of a chance game that Beef evidently did not. He slipped it in, played for it, and got it: War, Strategy.

The ordinary card game of War consisted of dealing the pack randomly into two piles, with each player turning up cards on one-to-one matches. The higher card captured the lower, and both went into the winner's victory pile. When the first piles were through, the piles of winnings would be shuffled and played in the same fashion, until finally one player had won the entire deck. It was pure chance, and could take many hours to finish. The strategy variant, however, permitted each player to hold his cards in his hand, selecting each card to play. When both were laid face down on the table, they would be turned over, and the higher card won. This play was not truly random; each player could keep track of his assets and those of his opponent, and play it accordingly. He could psych the other player out, tricking him into wasting a high card on a low one, or into losing a trick he should normally have won by playing a card too low. Games were normally much shorter than those of the pure-chance variation, with the superior strategist winning. The element of pure chance could not be reintroduced; a strategist could beat a hand played by chance. Thus Stile had his opportunity to exert his skill, judging his opponent's intent and playing no higher than needed to win.

They played, and soon Stile's expertise told. He took queens with kings, while yielding deuces to aces. Steadily his hands grew, providing him with more options, while those of his opponent shrank. Luck? The luck had been in the grid.

In due course Stile was able to play seven aces and kings in succession, wiping out Beef's queen-high remaining hand of seven with no luck allowed at all. He had won, and Rung Eight was his.

Beef shook his head ruefully. "I will remember that variant," he said. He didn't mind losing, but he hated to be outsmarted so neatly.

They returned to the Game-annex. But Stile's two wins had attracted notice. A knot of serfs stood before the 35M ladder. "Hey, Stile," a woman called. "Are you making your move this year?"

He should have known privacy would be impossible. He was too well known in these circles, and what he was doing was too remarkable. "Yes," he said shortly, and made his way to the ladder. He punched the challenge for Rung Seven.

The holder of that Rung was already present. He was Snack, an average-heighted man who specialized in board games and light physical exercises. He was more formidable than the two Stile had just taken, but still not really in Stile's class.

"I will respond to your challenge in one day," Snack said, and left.

This was exactly the sort of thing Stile had feared. A rung-holder had to meet a challenge from the rung below, but could delay it one day. Stile had to rise rung by rung; he could not challenge out of order. He had no choice but to wait—and that would interfere with his return to Phaze.

Sheen took his arm. "There'll be an audience tomorrow," she said. "When a player of your caliber makes his move for a tenure-abridging Tourney this close to the deadline, that's news."

"I wanted to qualify quickly, so I could return to

Phaze before the Tourney," Stile said. "Neysa is waiting and worrying."

Even as he said it, he knew he should not have. Somehow the words got out before his mental intercept signal cut them off. "Cancel that," he said belatedly.

She looked straight ahead. "Why? I'm only a machine."

Here we go again. "I meant I promised to return to meet her at the palace of the Oracle. It was her question to the Oracle that freed me. The only one she can ask in her lifetime—she used it up just to help me. I must return."

"Of course."

"I made a commitment!" he said.

She relented. "She did send you back to me; I should return the favor. Will you promise to return, to meet me again?"

"And to qualify for the Tourney. Yes. Because you have also sacrificed yourself for me."

"Then we shall send you on your way right now."

"But I have to compete for Rung Seven in one day!"

"So you will have to work fast, over there." She drew him into a privacy compartment. "I'll send you across to her—right after I have had what I want from you." And she kissed him most thoroughly, proceeding from there.

She was a robot, he reminded himself—but she was getting more like a living woman than any he had known since Tune. And—he was not unwilling, and she did turn him on. It would be so easy to forget her nature . . . but then he would be entering another kind of fantasy world, and not a healthy one.

Yet how could he continue with a robot in one frame and a unicorn in the other? Even if he entered the Tourney and won, against all the odds, and located his other self in Phaze and assumed his prerogatives there—impossible dreams, probably—how would he alleviate the developing conflict between females?

Sheen finished with him, cleaned him up, brushed his hair, and took him to the dome geographically nearest the Oracular palace in the other frame, according to his understanding of the geography. They scouted for the curtain. They were also wary of the anonymous killer, but apparently the break in Stile's routine had lost that enemy for the nonce. It was hard to keep track of a fast-moving serf on Proton!

The curtain did not intersect this dome, but they located it nearby. They went outside, into the polluted rarefaction of the atmosphere, and Stile donned his Phaze clothing, which Sheen had brought. She never overlooked details like that, thanks to her computer mind. He would not have dared to put on any clothing at all in the sight of any Proton serfs, but outside was the most private of places on Proton.

There was a narrowing plain, the ground barren. To the northwest a wrinkle of mountains projected, as grim as the plain. Only the shining dome brightened the bleak landscape. There were not even any clouds in the sky; just ominous drifts of ill-smelling smog.

"If ever you find a way for a robot to cross . . ." Sheen said wistfully. "I think that land must be better than this one."

"My clothing crosses," Stile said. "Since you can have no living counterpart in Phaze, it should be possible—"

"No. I tried it, during your absence. I can not cross."

She had tried it. How sad that was, for her! Yet what could he do?

"Here—within a day," he gasped, beginning to suffer in the thin air, and Sheen nodded. The air did not bother her; she breathed only for appearances. "You understand—there is beauty in Phaze, but danger too. I may not—"

"You will make it," she said firmly, kissing him once more. "Or else."

"Uh, yes." Stile made what he trusted was the proper effort of will, and stepped through the curtain.

CHAPTER 14

Yellow

It was afternoon on Phaze, and the air was wonderful. The sky was a deep and compelling blue, punctuated by several puffball clouds. The mountains to the northwest were lovely. Stile paused to look at the pretty little yellow flowers at his feet, and to inhale the spring-like freshness of it all.

How did this frame come to have such a pleasant natural environment, while Proton was so bleak? He was no longer certain that industrial pollution and withdrawal of oxygen could account for it all. What about water vapor? Obviously there was plenty of it here, and little in the Proton atmosphere. This was a mystery he must one day fathom.

But at the moment he had more urgent business. Stile made a mental note of the location of the curtain; sometime he would have to trace its length, finding better places to cross. But this was also a matter for later attention.

The landscape was indeed the same. A narrowing plain, a nearby mountain range, a bright sun. Remove the cute clouds, and the verdant vegetation carpeting the ground, and the copses of trees, and this was identical to Proton. It was as if these were twin paintings, BEFORE and AFTER the artist had applied the color. Phaze was the world as it should be after God had made the final touches: primitive, natural, delightful, unspoiled. Garden of Eden.

True to his memory, the Oracle's palace was in sight. Stile set out for it at a run. But before he had covered half the distance, Neysa came trotting out to meet him. She held her head high, as they came together, so there was no possibility of striking him with her bright horn.

Stile flung his arms around her neck and hugged her, burying his face in her glossy mane, feeling her equine warmth and firmness and strength. He did not need to thank her verbally for her sacrifice on his behalf; he knew she understood. He discovered her hair was wet, and realized that his own tears of reunion were the culprit.

Then he leaped to her back, still needing no words, and they galloped bareback in five-beat to the palace where Kurrelgyre waited in man-form.

Stile had spent his life on Proton, and only a week here in Phaze, but already Phaze seemed more like home. He had been gone only a night and day, but it seemed longer. Perhaps it was because he felt more like a person, here. Actually, the only other true human beings he had encountered in Phaze were the man at the curtain who had given him the demon-amulet, and the Black Adept; still—

Kurrelgyre shook hands gravely. "I am relieved to know thy escape was successful," the werewolf said. "I reassured the mare, but feared privately thou mightst land between domes."

"I did. But close enough to reach the nearest dome before I suffocated." Stile took a deep breath, still reveling in it.

"I should have crossed with thee, to make sure; but Neysa was waiting outside, and I never thought of—"

"I understand exactly how it is. I never thought of it either. I could have walked a quarter-mile along the curtain and willed myself back through to you, outside the Black Castle. That never occurred to me until this moment."

Kurrelgyre smiled. "We live; we learn. No confinement near the curtain shall again restrain us." He squinted at Stile. "Thou lookest peaked; have a sniff of this." He brought out a sprig with a few leaves and a dull yellow flower, dried.

Stile sniffed. Immediately he felt invigorated. Strength coursed through his body. "What is that stuff?"

"Wolfsbane."

"Wolfs*bane?* Something that curses wolves? How canst thou carry—"

"I am not in my lupine form. I would not sniff it then."

"Oh." Stile couldn't really make much sense of this, but could not argue with his sudden sense of well-being. "Something else," he said. "Didst thou not tell me that most of the people were parallel, existing in both frames? There are about five thousand Proton Citizens, and ten times as many serfs, and countless robots, androids, cyborgs and animals—but I have not seen many people here on Phaze, and not many animals."

"There are at least as many people here as on Proton, plus the societies of werewolves, unicorns, vampires, demons and assorted monsters. But two things to note: first, we are not confined to domes. We have the entire planet to roam—many millions of square miles. So—"

"Miles?" Stile asked, trying to make a fast conversion in his head and failing.

"We use what thou wouldst call the archaic measurements. One square mile would be about two and a half square kilometers, so—"

"Oh, yes, I know. I just realized—archaic measurements—would that by any chance affect magic? I tried to do a spell using the metric scale, and it flubbed. Before I swore off magic."

"That might be. Each spell must be correctly couched, and can only be employed once. That is why even Adepts perform sparingly. They hoard their spells for future need, as Citizens hoard wealth in Proton. May I now continue my original discourse?"

"Oh, of course," Stile said, embarrassed, and Neysa made a musical snort of mirth. Stile squeezed her sides with his legs, a concealed hug. He tended to forget that she understood every word he spoke.

"So there are very few people for the habitable area, and many large regions are as yet uninhabited by men. Thou needest not be surprised at seeing none. The second reason is that many of the people here are not precisely the form of their Proton selves. They are vampires, elves, dwarves—" He broke off.

Stile wished he hadn't. It had almost seemed his size was irrelevant in his frame. Foolish wish! "I never judged values in terms of size," Stile said. "A dwarf is still a discrete individual, surely."

"Of course," Kurrelygyre agreed. It was his turn to be embarrassed.

They were now in the Oracle's palace. "I have less than a day before I have to go back to Proton," Stile said.

Neysa stiffened. "Go back?" Kurrelgyre demanded. "I understood thou hadst no commitment there. It was only to escape the prison of the Black Demesnes that thou—"

"I have a woman there," Stile said. "She covered for me during mine absence. I have agreed to enter this year's Tourney, that she be not shamed. Thus it is likely that my tenure on Proton will be brief."

"The Tourney! Thou presumest thou canst win?"

"Doubtful," Stile said seriously. "I had planned to enter in two years, when some top players would be gone and my strength would be at its peak—and even then the odds would have been against me. It is hard to win ten or twelve consecutive Games against top competition, and luck can turn either way. I would rate my chances at perhaps one in ten, for I could lose to a poorer player with one bad break."

Neysa tooted questioningly. "Well, one chance in twelve, perhaps," Stile amended. "I did not mean to brag."

"The mare means to inquire what thou meanest to do if thou shouldst win the Tourney," the werewolf said. "Since thou wouldst then be a Citizen, with permanent tenure—no need ever to depart Proton."

Stile wondered in passing how the werewolf had come to know the unicorn well enough to translate her notes, in only one day. Maybe shape-changing creatures had natural avenues of comprehension. "A Citizen has virtually complete freedom and power. I would be under no onus to choose between frames. But I like

Phaze; I think I would spend much of my time here anyway. Much depends on my situation here; if I should turn out to be a vicious person like the Black Adept, I think I'd prefer to vacate." Yet the Citizen who was the Black Adept's other self had not seemed to be a bad man; perhaps it was solely the absolute power that corrupted—power beyond that of any Citizen. What would an Adept be like, if he had residence in both frames and free access between them?

"It is a fair response," Kurrelgyre said. "If thou must return for a Game within a day, only the Yellow Adept is within range to check, without the employ of magic. Would it not be better to yield this quest, being satisfied as thou art now?"

"Not while someone is trying to kill me here. That person must know who I am. If I can discover who I am in Phaze, I may know more about the nature of mine enemy. Then I can see about making this world safe for mine own existence. I gather mine other self failed to take such precaution."

"Spoken like a werewolf," Kurrelgyre said approvingly. Neysa sighed; she did not seem to agree completely, but neither did she disagree. Men will be men, her attitude said.

"Neysa, I want to be honest with thee," Stile said, feeling the need to provide a better justification. "I like Phaze, I like thee—but this is not truly my world. Even if there were no threat to my welfare, I could not commit myself absolutely to stay here. I would need to know that my presence served in some way to benefit this world; that there was some suitable challenge to rise to. Something that needed doing, that perhaps only I could do. If there seems to be more of a need and challenge in the other frame—"

Neysa made another musical snort. "She inquires whether thou wouldst feel more positive if she released thee from thy vow of no magic," the werewolf translated.

Stile considered. He understood that the acceptance of such a release would subtly or overtly alienate him from the unicorn. It was only his vow that made it possible for her to associate with him on their original basis. "No. I only want to know who I am. If I can't survive without magic, maybe it's best that I not remain here. I never want to be like the Black Adept. All I need is someone to spell me into the other frame in time for mine appointment there. Then I'll return here for another look at another Adept. One way or another, I will settle my accounts in both frames. Only then will I be in a position to make a proper decision about residence."

"I will spell thee through," Kurrelgyre said. "In fact, rather than send thee pointlessly into new danger, I will investigate the Yellow Adept myself, and return with news. I think I can now recognize thy likeness, if I encounter it."

"There is no call for thee to risk thyself on my account!" Stile protested.

"There is no call for me to impose my presence when the mare wishes to converse with thee alone." And the man merged into the wolf, who bounded away to the north.

"Damn it, if I start sending others on my foolish quests, where will it end?" Stile demanded. "I've got to follow him, stop him—"

But the wolf was already beyond reach, traveling with the easy velocity of his kind. Probably Neysa could catch him, but only with difficulty. Stile knew Kurrelgyre thought he was doing Stile a favor, preserving him from risk, giving him time alone with Neysa—but this was not the sort of favor Stile cared to accept. It was not, he told himself, that Sheen had artfully depleted his sexual initiative immediately before sending him across the curtain. There was the principle of responsibility for one's own actions.

The unicorn caught his mood. She started moving north. "Thanks, Neysa," he said. "I knew thou wouldst understand." Then, as an afterthought: "How art thou getting along with the wolf?"

She blew a noncommittal note. "Glad to hear it," Stile said. He reached down around her neck and hugged her again.

Neysa quickened her gait into a gallop. "I don't know what finer life I could have than galloping across the wilderness with you," Stile said. "The only thing I miss—"

She made a musical inquiry. "Well, that's it," he said. "I like music. But since we found that music connects with my magic, I don't dare play."

This time her note was comprehensible. "Play!"

"But then the magic gathers," he protested. "I have no wish to abbreviate mine oath. I played a little when I was alone in the Black Castle, but I am not alone now, and I do not want thee angry with me."

"Play," she repeated emphatically.

"Very well. No spells, just music." He brought out his harmonica and improvised a melody to the beat of her hooves. She played a harmony on her horn. The duet was lovely. The magic gathered, pacing them, but now that he understood it he was not alarmed. It was merely a potential, until he implemented it—which he would not do.

He played for an hour, developing his proficiency with the instrument. He was getting into the feel of the harmonica, and playing about as well as ever in his life. This was a unique joy!

Neysa lifted her head, sniffing the wind. She seemed disturbed.

"What is it?" Stile inquired, putting away his harmonica.

The unicorn shook her head, unsure. She slowed to a walk, turning this way and that as if casting for something. Then she oriented on whatever it was, and resumed her northward trek. But there was something disquieting about her motion; her gait seemed unnatural.

"Art thou all right?" Stile inquired, concerned.

Neysa did not respond, so he brought out his harmonica again and played. But she immediately blew a harsh note of negation. He desisted, concealing his hurt feelings.

Stile thought she would relax after a short while, but

she did not. Instead her gait became more mechanical, quite unlike her normal mode.

"Neysa, I inquire again: art thou all right?"

She ignored him. She seemed to be in a trance.

Alarmed, Stile tugged sharply on her mane. "Something is wrong. I must insist—"

She threw down her head and bucked. The action was untelegraphed, but Stile was too experienced a rider to be caught. He stayed in place, then slid to the ground when she resumed her odd walk. "Neysa, something evidently compels thee. I don't know what it is—but since we are approaching the locale of the Yellow Adept, I suspect it relates. For some reason the compulsion does not affect me. Give me thy socks, and I will walk with thee in disguise."

She halted, swishing her tail in annoyance, and let him remove the white socks from her rear feet. Then she marched on.

Stile donned the socks and walked beside her, imitating her walk. If something were summoning unicorns, he wanted to resemble such a captive as closely as possible—until he understood the situation better. The wolfsbane he had sniffed still buoyed his strength; he was ready for anything, and felt no trace of the prior ravages of hunger and thirst. If Neysa had fallen into some spell cast by the Yellow Adept—

Soon the property of the Adept came into sight. It was of course yellow. The sands were yellow, rising into yellow dunes, and the sun sent yellow beams through a yellow fog that concealed the main operation from a distance. Neysa walked straight into that fog.

Soon the Adept's castle loomed. It was most like a ramshackle haunted house, with a partially collapsing roof, broken windows, and weeds growing thickly against the walls. A few yellow flowers straggled at the fringe—buttercups, sunflowers, a bedraggled yellow rose. Behind the house was a tall wrought-iron palisade fence, rusting yellow, overgrown by morbid vines with yellowing leaves but still quite formidable. An odor rose from the premises: animal dung and decaying vegetation. Rustic, but hardly pleasant.

Neysa walked right on toward the house, and Stile necessarily followed. Already he did not like the Yellow Adept and hoped perversely that the magician was alive—so as to be assured this was not Stile's own alternate identity. This time he would not be so foolish as to challenge the Adept overtly; he would just look and retreat quickly.

Except for two things. First, there was Neysa—she had somehow been mesmerized, surely for no good purpose, and had to be freed of this complication. Second, Kurrelgyre: the wolf had by now had plenty of time to lope in and out, but evidently had not, which suggested that he too had been trapped by the summoning spell. Stile would have to verify this, then act appropriately. It might not be easy.

Neysa moved right on up to the front door, which was sagging open on rusty hinges. She entered, Stile close behind. They passed through a dusty hall, turned a corner—and bars dropped from the ceiling, separating them.

Oh, no! Not again! Stile backed up—but another set of bars fell behind him. This section of hall had become a cage.

There was an ear-discomfiting shriek of laughter. "Hee-hee! Two! Two fine unicorns, so soon after the wolf! What an excellent day! Haul them out, Darlin' Corey! Let us view our prizes!"

Something huge bulked at the far end of the hall, beyond the corner. Neysa's cage slid forward. Something was drawing it onward with easy power.

After a time the thing came for Stile's cage. It was the rear end of a pink elephant. The little tail hooked into the forward bars; then the creature walked, drawing the cage after it.

Stile considered poking his sword through the bars and puncturing the fat pink rear, or cutting off the tail with his knife. But this would not release him from the cage, and could make the elephant quite angry without really incapacitating it. Better to hold off.

In a moment they emerged into the stockaded area.

There were cages all around. It resembled an archaic zoo. Stile identified a griffin, with the body of a lion and head and wings of an eagle, in the cage most directly across from his. This was no glorious heraldic monster, but a sad, bedraggled, dirty creature whose wings drooped and whose eyes seemed glazed. And no wonder: the cage was too small for it to stretch its wings, and there was no place for its refuse except right next to the cage where the creature had scraped it out. No wonder its feathers and fur were soiled; no wonder it stank!

Now Stile's attention was taken by the proprietress: an old woman garbed in a faded yellow robe, with stringy yellow hair and yellowish complexion. A hag, in every sense of the word.

"What a lovely little specimen!" the hag cackled, mincing around Neysa's cage. Neysa seemed to be coming out of her daze; her ears perked up, then laid back in revulsion as the crone approached.

"And this one," the Adept continued, examining Stile. "A white stallion, yet! What a pretty penny thou wilt fetch, my sweet!" She circled the cage, appraising his apparent form with an indecently calculating eye. "Yes indeed, my precious! White is in the market for the likes of thee! Needs must I send Crow's-foot with the news." She hobbled into the house.

Now Stile resumed his survey of the enclave. Beyond Neysa was Kurrelgyre, whose eye was already on him; the wolf nodded slowly. They were in trouble!

The other cages contained a small sphinx, a three-headed dog, a wyvern, and several creatures Stile couldn't classify. All were bedraggled and filthy; the witch did not bother to care for them properly, or to clean their cages. She did feed them, as there were dishes of food and water at every cage—but several of these dishes had been overturned and kicked out, uneaten.

Stile examined his own cage. The bars were yellowish, like the rest of this place, and somewhat slick. It was as if some sort of grease had been smeared on the metal in a vain attempt to make it seem like gold. He tried to push a bar out of position, but it was like welded steel. The door was firmly locked.

Still, the bars were fairly widely spaced, and he was small. Just a little bowing should enable him to squeeze between two. Stile located the longest, widest section of the cage roof, then drew his sword and used it cautiously as a lever. He did not want to break the weapon, and did not know how strong it was. But he really could not gain purchase, and had to put away the sword. Instead he jumped up, put his feet against one bar, his hands on the next, and hauled as if lifting a heavy weight. Slowly, unwillingly, the bars separated as he strove and panted. When his muscles balked, he had widened the aperture only slightly—but perhaps it was enough.

He dropped down to the cage floor—and discovered that he had become the object of considerable attention. He was still disguised as a unicorn; that must have been quite a sight, a horselike creature clinging to the upper bars!

But he couldn't allow such cynosure to stop him. The witch should soon be back. He had to do whatever he could do, rapidly.

Stile drew himself up, put his feet between the widened bars, and squeezed his body up and through. Last was his head; his ears got mashed, but he scraped by. He was out.

He climbed silently down, while the captive animals watched the contortions of this astonishing unicorn. They were not about to betray him to the witch! The conspiracy of silence was the only weapon they possessed.

Stile went to Kurrelgyre's cage. "I must have a rapid update," he said. "How can I free thee and Neysa and the others? The large bars are too strong for me."

The werewolf transformed into his human form, too large to squeeze between the bars. "Thou art fortunate in thy size," he said. "Only Neysa might do what thou hast done—and the potion hath dulled her wit so she can not transform her shape. My wolfsbane might help steady her—but we dare not administer it to her animal form. We are at impasse. Save thyself; thou canst not free us."

"If I go, it will be only to help thee—as thou didst for me before. Can I overcome the witch?"

"Only if thou canst kill her by surprise, instantly with thy sword. She will else throw a potion on thee, and destroy thee."

"I don't want to kill her," Stile said. "Murder is not the proper solution to problems. I only want to neutralize her and free these poor captives."

Kurrelgyre shook his head. "Thou canst not defeat an Adept fairly save by magic."

"No. Mine oath—"

"Yes. When thou didst not break thine oath to save thyself from the Black Demesnes, I knew thy word was constant. I expect no different of thee here in the Yellow Demesnes. But now it is not thy life at stake, but Neysa's. The witch will sell her to another Adept—"

"Why don't Adepts conjure their own creatures, instead of buying them?"

"Because some spells are more complex than others. An Adept may conjure a dozen monsters via a single summoning spell with less effort than a single one by creation. So they store captive creatures in cells, and prepare spells to bring them upon need—"

"I get the picture. To be an Adept is to maintain dungeons where others languish—and the Yellow Adept caters to this need by trapping the necessary animals. I dare say she traps wild fowl and sells the eggs to the Black Adept, too; he has to get his food from somewhere. Maybe he pays her off by making strong cages from black line-bars, that she paints yellow. How does she summon the hapless victims? Neysa seemed to go into a trance."

"Yellow's magic is exerted through potions, I now have learned. She boils a cauldron whose vapors mesmerize animals, bringing them here to be caged. She could summon men similarly, but does not, lest men unite against her and destroy her. Had I been in my man-form, or Neysa in her girl-form—"

"Yes." Stile moved across to Neysa. "Wilt thou release me from mine oath, that I may cast a spell to free thee? I fear thy fate at the hands of the witch."

Neysa, dulled by the summoning potion, was not dull enough to forget her antipathy to Adept-class magic. She shook her head no. She would not condone such sorcery to free herself.

"Say," Stile said, trying again. "Thou canst also change into a firefly, and these bars would not hold—"

But Neysa's eyes were half lidded and her head hung low. The effort of will that such transformation required was beyond her present capacity.

"Or if thou couldst assume thy human form, the potion would not affect thee—"

There was a growl from another cage. Kurrelgyre looked up nervously. "Hark! The witch comes!"

Stile jumped to the werewolf's cage, on inspiration drawing off his socks. "Don these!" he whispered, shoving them through Kurrelgyre's cage bars. "And this." He put the sword through, with its harness. "She will assume—"

"Right." In a moment the white unicorn image formed. The sword was concealed by the illusion. "Remember: thou darest not eat nor drink aught she offers thee, for her potions—"

"Uh-oh! Did Neysa drink?"

But the Yellow Adept appeared before the werewolf could answer. Still, Stile hardly needed it. Neysa, like most equines, drank deeply when she had opportunity, and could have done so automatically while still under the influence of the summoning vapor. That would explain why she hadn't made any real effort to save herself. That also explained why the smarter animals here refused to eat. Kurrelgyre had avoided this trap, and was alert. But the situation of all these animals remained bleak, for evidently none of them had the strength to break out of the strong cages. Eventually they would have either to eat or to starve. Not a pleasant choice; Stile's memory of his confinement in the Black Castle remained fresh.

Stile was not idle during these realizations; he ducked behind the werewolf's cage, trying to hide. He knew it was foolish of him to hesitate about dealing with the witch; obviously she had little to recommend her, and would happily wipe him out. But he could not murder a human being heartlessly. Just as he was bound by an oath of no magic, he was bound by civilized restraints. Demons and monsters he could slay, not people.

"Eeeek!" Yellow cried, pronouncing the word exactly as it was spelled. "The cage is empty! The valuable white 'corn stallion!" But then she inspected the situation more carefully. "No, the stallion remains. It is the wolf who is gone. I could have sworn his cage was—" She glared across the compound. "Darlin' Corey!" she screamed. "Didst thou move the cages about?"

Stile watched the pink elephant. The creature had seen what happened; which side was it on? If it told the truth—

The elephant waddled past the cages toward the witch. Suddenly it flung its trunk to the side, catching Stile by the nape of his shirt and hauling him into view. It trumpeted.

"Well, now, dearest!" the crone cried, scratching idly at a wart on her nose. "So it was a werewolf! Changed to its man-form and squeezed out of its cage."

The elephant squealed, trying to correct her misimpression.

"Oh shut up, Darlin' Corey," she snapped. "What shall we do with the werewolf? I don't have a cage small enough at the moment. He's pretty shrimpy." She peered at Stile more closely, as he hung in midair. "But healthy and handsome enough, my lovely. Maybe he would do for my daughter. Hold him there a moment, my tasty; I will send the wench out."

The pink elephant chuckled. The monsters in cages exchanged glances, bewildered. Obviously this was the first they had heard of Yellow's daughter. What kind of a slut was she? Meanwhile, the hag limped rapidly to the house.

Stile thought of doing an acrobatic flip and climbing the elephant's trunk. But the creature was quite big and strong, and not stupid; it might bash him against a tree. Had he retained his sword—but that would have been highly visible, forcing him to use it to defend himself. It was better to appear more or less helpless, lest he get doused by a potion.

He looked around, able to see more clearly from this height. Beyond the palisades the yellow fog obliterated everything. It was as if the rest of the world did not exist. No doubt this was the way the Adept liked it. She had a little mist-shrouded world of her own, that no man dared intrude upon. Did she get lonely? Probably no more lonely than a person with her appearance would get in the midst of the most convivial society. Who would want to associate with her? Stile, as a person who all his life had felt the inherent discrimination of size, could not entirely condemn the witch for reacting to the discrimination of appearance. Yet he could not allow her to abuse his friends, or to continue mistreating innocent animals.

His eye caught something—a glimmer in the fog outside the compound. A faint curtain of—

The curtain! Could it be here? The thing seemed to wander all over Phaze like a tremendous serpent. Might it be used to facilitate escape, as it had before?

No, there were two problems. The curtain, close as it was, was out of reach, since it was beyond the palisades. And Neysa could not use it. Or would not; he wasn't sure which. So this was a mere tantalization, no real help. Best to wait and see what the witch's daughter had in mind. She was probably a homely girl upon whom her crazy mother forced the attentions of any likely-seeming male.

She emerged. She was stunning. Her yellow hair flowed luxuriously to her waist, her hands and feet were tiny, and her complexion was gold-bronze vibrant, not sallow. She had a figure that would have made an artist gape, with prominent secondary sexual characteristics. Her eyes were so large she seemed almost like a doll—but what a doll!

Young witches, it seemed, had other assets than magic.

"Darlin' Corey, put that man down this instant!" the girl cried, spying Stile. Her voice, despite its vehemence, was dulcet. Everything about her was as nice as it was nasty about her mother.

Darlin' Corey lowered Stile to the ground, but remained near, on guard. Stile straightened his clothing and rolled his shoulders; it had not been entirely comfortable, hanging all that time in midair. "I don't believe we've met," he said.

She giggled jigglesomely. "Tee-hee. I'm Yellowette. My, thou'rt a handsome wolf."

"I'm a man," Stile said.

She looked down at him. That was the only fault he could perceive in her: she was a few centimeters—a couple of this frame's inches—taller than he. "That, too. Kiss me, my cute."

Neysa, in the cage, recovered enough to make a musical snort of recognition. Suddenly Stile had a suspicion why the pink elephant had found the notion of this encounter humorous, and why the caged beasts had never known of the witch's daughter. What would a lonely old hag do with a handsome-if-small man, if she had a potion for every purpose? Drug him—or take a very special potion herself? "Not in front of these monsters," he said.

"What do they matter, my delight? They can not escape."

"I like my privacy," he said. "Let's take a walk outside—and return later, as before." He glanced meaningfully at Neysa, hoping the drug had worn off enough to uncloud her mind. "As before."

Yellowette's fair brow wrinkled. "Thou knowest that unicorn, werewolf?"

"I'm not a werewolf," he said, aware that she would not believe him. "I do know her. She's a jealous mare."

"So? Well, she'll be gone in a few days. There's a fair market in unicorns, for they are hard to catch. Their horns and hooves are valuable for musical instruments and for striking fire, their dung is excellent fertilizer for magic plants, and their hides have anti-magic properties."

Stile experienced an ugly chill. "These animals are for slaughter?"

"Some are, my pleasure. Some aren't even good for that. The black mare would be excellent as a courtyard showpiece, except that she lacks proper coloration and is small. The white stallion, in contrast, is a prize; the White Adept will probably use him to battle dragons in his arena."

Good thing she didn't know the white unicorn was a fake! "What happens to the completely useless animals?"

"I have Darlin' Corey take the worthless ones outside and put them through the curtain." The witch was no longer bothering to conceal her identity, since he seemed to accept it. Her female view of man was that he was interested only in the external appearance—and Stile suspected there was some merit in that view. He had already had relations with a machine that looked like a woman, and with a unicorn that also looked like a woman. What of an old woman who looked like a young woman? Yellow was certainly much more pleasing to deal with in this form than in the other.

"Thou knowest about the curtain?" he asked after a moment, surprised.

"Thou dost not? There is another world beyond it, a desert. The potion puts the creatures through; they never return. I have not the heart to kill them outright, and dare not let them go free in this world lest they summon hordes of their kind to wreak vengeance on these my demesnes, and if they survive in the other world I begrudge it not."

So she was not heartless, just a victim of circumstance. To an extent. Yet it seemed a safe assumption that she was as yet only partially corrupted by power.

How much should he say? Stile detested lies even by indirection. "I am of that world."

"Thou'rt a frame traveler? A true man?" She was alarmed.

"I am. Thou didst merely assume I was a werewolf."

"I do not deal in true men!" she said nervously. "This leads to great mischief!"

"I came merely to discover thine identity. Now I seek only to free thy captives and to depart with my friends. I have no inherent quarrel with thee, but if thou threatenest my life or those of my friends—"

She turned to him in the hallway. She was absolutely beautiful. "I proffer no threat to thee, my handsome bantam. Dally with a lonely woman a time, and thy friends shall go free with thee."

Stile considered. "I don't regard myself to be at liberty to do that."

She frowned. "Thou hast only limited leeway for bargaining, sweets."

"Perhaps. My friend urged me to slay thee without warning, but I did not wish to do that either."

"Oh? We shall put that to the proof." She led him into the main room of the house. Shelves lined the walls, containing bottles of fluid: rows and rows of them, coated with dust. In the center a huge cauldron bubbled, its vapors drifting out through a broken windowpane. This was obviously the source of the summoning scent: a continously brewing mix.

"All these bottles—potions for different spells?" he inquired, impressed.

"All. I must brew one potion at a time, and can use it only once, so I save each carefully. It is not easy, being Adept; it requires much imagination and application. I must develop a new formula for every invisibility elixir I mix—and for every rejuvenation drink."

Stile eyed her figure again. What a potion she must have taken! "Thou didst really look like this in thy youth?"

"I really did, my honey. Or as close as makes no nevermind. Hair and flesh tints differ from mix to mix, and sometimes one brews too strong, and I become as a child. But my youth was a very long time ago, my lamb, and even the best potion lasts no more than an hour. See—I have only three of these mixes left." She gestured to a half-empty shelf, where three bottles sat. "I expended one quarter of my stock, for a mere hour with thee. Take that as what flattery thou mayst."

"Flattering indeed," Stile said. "I did see thee in thy

natural state. But this is not what restrains me. I have other commitments." He pondered briefly. "Thou didst believe me to be a werewolf, before. The true werewolf might be interested in the remainder of thy hour, if thou wert to free him thereafter."

Yellow took down a bottle. "Thou art most facile, lovely man. I hardly trust thee. If thou provest a liar, it will go hard indeed with thee—*and* thy friends." She drew the stopper out. Stile stepped back, alarmed, but she sprinkled the liquid on a statuette, not on him.

The figurine grew rapidly into a demon monster. "Thou summonest me, hag?" it roared, its small red eyes fairly glowing as they glared about. Then it did a double take. Its lips pursed appreciatively. "I have not seen the like in six hundred years! But thou didst not need to prettify thyself for me, witch."

" 'Twas not for thee I did it," she snapped. "Speak me the truth, Zebub. Why came this man here, and who is he?"

The demon glared in Stile's direction. "This time thou'rt victim to thine own paranoia, crone. He is innocuous, with respect to thee. Not with respect to certain others, though." The demon smiled privately.

"He really sought not to kill me?"

"True. He but seeks his own identity, so comes with werewolf and unicorn to learn if thou art it."

Yellow burst into a cackle of laughter. "Me! What kind of fool is he?"

"No fool, he. He lacks information on the nature of the Adepts. The Oracle advised him to know himself, so he seeks to learn if he is one of you. He was trapped by Black, and only escaped via the curtain. He is of that other world."

Stile felt another chill. This monster really did have information!

"What gives him the notion he is Adept?" Yellow demanded.

"He *is* Adept, O senile one."

Yellow backed against a wall, almost jarring loose several bottles. "Not only a man, but Adept to boot! Oh, what a foul pickle I have hatched! Who is he?"

"He is Stile, a serf of Proton, in the other frame, freed to cross the curtain by the death of his Phazeself."

"Idiot! I meant which Adept is he?"

The demon scowled. "That is formidable information."

"Don't stall, hellborn one!" Yellow screeched. "Else I will apply a pain potion."

Zebub blanched. "Blue," he muttered.

Yellow's eyes went round. "This midget is the Blue Adept?"

"His alternate, yes."

"I can't afford trouble with another Adept!" she exclaimed, wrenching at her own hair in distraction. "Not one of such power as Blue! If I free him, will he seek to destroy me? Why does he withhold his magic now?"

"This calls for conclusions on the part of the witness," the demon said smugly.

Yellow took a step toward a shelf of small bottles.

"Question him," Zebub said quickly. "I will verify his word."

"Stile, a.k.a. Blue Adept!" she cried, her eyes round and wild, yet still lovely. "Answer me, in the presence of Zebub."

"If thou shouldst free me, I will still seek to release my friends and the other captives," Stile said. "I will not seek to destroy thee gratuitously."

"He speaks truth," Zebub said. "As for his magic, he made an oath to the unicorn to practice it not save by her leave."

"So only his oath makes him subject to my power?" she demanded.

"That is so," Zebub agreed. "Thou art the luckiest of harridans."

Yellow's beautiful brow furrowed. "If I release the unicorn, she could then release Blue from his oath, and there would be war between Adepts. I dare not risk it."

"Thou darest not risk harming the unicorn either, beldame," Zebub pointed out maliciously. "If the Blue Adept is moved by ire to break his oath—"

"I know! I know!" she screeched, distracted. "If I kill him, another Adept might seek to kill me, for that I violated our convention. If I let him go, Blue may seek my life for that I caged him. If I try to hold him—"

"My time is up," Zebub said. "Please deposit another potion, scold."

"O, begone with thee!" Yellow snapped.

The demon shrank into figurine size and froze: a dead image.

Yellow looked at Stile. "If thou keepest thine oath to the unicorn, wilt thou honor it for me? I wish I could be sure. I want no quarrel with another Adept."

"Release all the animals in your compound, and thou wilt have no quarrel with me," Stile said.

"I can not! I have commitments, I have accepted magic favors in payment. I must deliver."

Stile, quite prepared to hate this Adept, found himself moved. She was, for the moment, lovely, but that was not it. She honored her commitments. She did not like killing. Her surroundings and mechanisms reflected a certain humor, as if she did not take herself too seriously. She was old and lonely. It should be possible to make a deal with her.

"I want no quarrel with thee, either," he said. "Thou knowest me not, therefore trust must be tempered with caution. I make thee this offer: send me through the curtain, and I will not return. I will seek to free my friends and the animals from a distance."

"How canst thou act from a distance? My magic is stronger than thine, near me in my demesnes—as thine would be stronger than mine in thine own demesnes."

"Without magic," Stile said.

"Very well," she decided. "I will put thee through the curtain with a potion, and set a powerful curse I got from Green to ward thee off thereafter. If thou canst free the animals from a distance, without magic—" She shrugged. "I have never liked this business; if I am foiled through no agency of mine own, perhaps I will not be held in default." She glanced at him, her mood visibly lightening. "I never did business with Blue, else would I have known thee. How is it that Blue, alone of Adepts, needs no monsters in storage?"

"I intend to find out," Stile said. He was highly gratified to have this information. Now he knew who he was, and that the Blue Adept had not practiced at least one of the atrocities that seemed to be standard in this genre. This excursion into the Yellow Demesnes had been mistaken, but serendipitously worthwhile.

Yellow took down another bottle, then led him out of the house and around the palisades to the curtain. Stile hoped he could trust her to use the correct potion. But it seemed reasonable; if Adepts avoided trouble with Adepts, and if she feared his violation of his oath were he to be betrayed, she would play it straight. She seemed to be, basically, an honest witch.

At the curtain, she hesitated, hand on the stopper of the bottle. "I do not wish to murder thee, Blue Stile," she said. "Art thou sure thou canst survive in that bleak realm beyond the curtain? If thou preferest to dally here—"

"My thanks, Yellow. I can survive. I have a prior engagement, and must pass through now."

"And thou thinkest the werewolf might be interested—for half an hour? It is not a difficult thing I ask—"

"Won't hurt to ask him," Stile agreed, stepping through the curtain as she sprinkled the liquid on him.

CHAPTER 15

Games

It was a longer hike to the nearest dome, this time, but he had more confidence and need, and that sniff of wolfsbane still buoyed him. In due course, gasping, he stepped inside and made a call to Sheen. It was evening; he had the night to rest with her. He needed it; his high of the last visit to Phaze finally gave out, and he realized the episode with the Yellow Adept had drained him more than he had realized at the time. Or perhaps it was the low following the effect of the wolfsbane.

"So you are the Blue Adept," Sheen said, not letting him sleep quite yet. "And you need some things to use to free your equine girl friend."

"Now don't get jealous again," he grumbled. "You know I have to—"

"How can I be jealous? I'm only a machine."

Stile sighed. "I should have taken Yellow up on her offer. Then you would have had something to be jealous about."

"You mean you didn't—with Neysa?"

"Not this time. I—"

"You were saving it for the witch?" she demanded indignantly. "Then ran out of time?"

"Well, she was an extremely pretty—"

"You made your callous point. I won't resent Neysa. She's only an animal."

"Are you going to have your friends assemble my order or aren't you?"

"I will take care of it in good time. But I don't see how a cube of dry ice will help your animals."

"Plus a diamond-edged hacksaw."

"And a trained owl," she finished. "Do you plan to start romancing birds next?"

"Oh, go away and let me sleep!"

Instead she tickled him. "Birds, hags, mares, machines—why can't you find a normal woman for a change?"

"I had one," he said, thinking of Tune. "She left me."

"So you get hung up on all the half-women, fearing to tackle a real one again—because you're sure she wouldn't want you." She was half-teasing, half-sad, toying with the notion that she herself was a symptom of his aberration.

"I'll look for one tomorrow," he promised.

"Not tomorrow. First thing in the morning, you have an appointment to meet your current employer. This Citizen is very keen on the Game."

Exasperated, he rolled over and grabbed her. "The irony is," he said into her soft hair, "you are now more real to me than most real girls I have known. When I told you to brush up on your humanoid wiles, I didn't mean at my expense."

"Then you should have said that. I take things literally, because I'm only a—"

He shut her up with a kiss. But the thoughts she had voiced were only a reflection of those he was having. How long could he continue with half-women?

In the morning he met his employer. This was, to his surprise, a woman. No wonder Sheen had had women on her mind! The Citizen was elegantly gowned and coiffed: a handsome lady of exquisitely indeterminate age. She was, of course, substantially taller than he, but had the grace to conceal this by remaining seated in his presence. "Sir," Stile said. All Citizens were sir, regardless of sex or age.

"See that you qualify for the Tourney," she said with polite force. "Excused."

That was that. If he lost one Game, this employer would cut him off as cleanly as his prior one had. He was supposed to feel deeply honored that she had granted him this personal audience—and he did. But his recent experience in Phaze had diminished his awe of Citizens. They were, after all, only people with a lot of wealth and power.

Stile and Sheen went for his challenge for Rung Seven. His employer surely had bets on his success. There were things about this that rankled, but if he fouled up, Sheen would be the one to pay. She lacked his avenue of escape to a better world. He had to do what he could for her, until he figured out some better alternative.

The holder of Rung Seven kept his appointment—as he had to, lest he forfeit. He was not much taller than Stile and tended to avoirdupois despite the antifat medication in the standard diet. Hence his name, Snack. He hardly looked like a formidable player—but neither did Stile.

An audience had gathered, as Sheen had predicted. It was possible that some Citizens also were viewing the match on their screens—especially his own employer. Stile's move was news.

Snack got the numbered facet of the grid. Stile sighed inaudibly; he had been getting bad breaks on facets in this series. Snack always selected MENTAL.

Very well. Stile would not choose NAKED, because Snack was matchless at the pure mental games. Snack was also uncomfortably sharp at MACHINE- and ANIMAL-assisted mental efforts. Only in TOOL did Stile have an even chance. So it had to come up 2B.

There was a murmur of agreement from the spectators outside, as they watched on the public viewscreen. They had known what the opening box would be. They were waiting for the next grid.

In a moment it appeared: sixteen somewhat arbitrary classifications of games of intellectual skill. Snack had the numbered facet again, which was the primary one. He would go for his specialty: chess. He was versed in all forms of that game: the western-Earth two- and three-dimensional variants, the Chinese *Choo-hong-ki*, Japanese *Shogi*, Indian *Chaturanga* and the hypermodern developments. Stile could not match him there. He had a better chance with the single-piece board games like Chinese Checkers and its variants—but many games used the same boards as chess, and this grid classified them by their boards. Better to avoid that whole bailiwick.

Stile chose the C row, covering jigsaw-type puzzles, hunt-type board games—he liked Fox & Geese—the so-called pencil-and-paper games and, in the column he expected to intersect, the enclosing games.

It came up 2C: Enclosing. There was another murmur of excitement from the audience.

Now the handmade grid. Stile felt more confidence here; he could probably take Snack on most of these variants. They completed a subgrid of only four: Go, Go-bang, Yote and tic-tac-toe. Stile had thrown in the last whimsically. Tic-tac-toe was a simplistic game, no challenge, but in its essence it resembled the prototype for the grids of the Game. The player who got three of his choices in a row, then had the luck to get the facet that enabled him to choose that row, should normally win. The ideal was to establish one full row and one full column, so that the player had winners no matter which facet he had to work with. But in the Game-grids, there was no draw if no one lined up his X's and O's; the real play was in the choosing of columns and the interaction of strategies.

And they intersected at tic-tac-toe. That was what he got for fooling around.

Stile sighed. The problem with this little game was that, among competent players, it was invariably a draw. They played it right here on the grid-screen, punching buttons for X's and O's. To a draw.

Which meant they had to run the grid again, to achieve the settlement. They played it—and came up with the same initial box as before. And the same secondary box. Neither player was going to yield one iota of advantage for the sake of variation; to do so would be to lose. But the third grid developed a different pattern, leading to a new choice: Go-bang.

This was a game similar to tic-tac-toe, but with a larger grid allowing up to nineeten markers to be played on a side. It was necessary to form a line of five in a row to win. This game, too, was usually to a draw, at this level.

They drew. Each was too alert to permit the other to move five in a row. Now they would have to go to a third Game. But now the matter was more critical. Any series that went to three draws was presumed to be the result of incompetence or malingering; both parties would be suspended from Game privileges for a period, their Rungs forfeit. It could be a long, hard climb up again, for both—and Stile had no time for it. The third try, in sum, had to produce a winner.

They ran the grids through again—and arrived again at tool-assisted mental, and at enclosing. The basic strategies were immutable.

Stile exchanged glances with Snack. Both knew what they had to do.

This time it came up Go—the ancient Chinese game of enclosing. It was perhaps the oldest of all games in the human sphere, dating back several thousand years. It was one of the simplest in basic concept: the placing of colored stones to mark off territory, the player enclosing the most territory winning. Yet in execution it was also one of the most sophisticated of games. The more skilled player almost invariably won.

The problem was, Stile was not certain which of them was the more skilled in Go. He had never played this particular game with this particular man, and could not at the moment remember any games of Go he and Snack had played against common opponents. This was certainly not Stile's strongest game—but he doubted it was Snack's strongest either.

They moved to the board-game annex, as this match would take too long for the grid-premises; others had to use that equipment. The audience followed, taking seats; they could tune in on replicas of the game at each place, but preferred to observe it physically. Sheen had a front seat, and looked nervous: probably an affectation, considering her wire nerves.

Stile would have preferred a Game leading to a quick decision, for he was conscious of Neysa and Kurrelgyre in the other frame, locked in potion-hardened cages. But he had to meet his commitment here, first, whatever it took.

They sat on opposite sides of the board, each with a bowl of polished stones. Snack gravely picked up one stone of each color, shook them together in his joined hands, and offered two fists for Stile. Stile touched the left. The hand opened to reveal a black pebble.

Stile took that stone and laid it on the board. Black, by convention, had the first move. With 361 intersections to choose from—for the stones were placed on the lines in Go, not in the squares—he had no problem. A one-stone advantage was not much, but in a game as precise as this it helped.

Snack settled down to play. The game was by the clock, because this was a challenge for access to the Tourney; probably few games of Go would be played, but time was limited to keep the Tourney moving well. This was another help to Stile; given unlimited time to ponder, Snack could probably beat him. Under time pressure Stile generally did well. That was one reason he was a top Gamesman.

They took turns laying down stones, forming strategic patterns on the board. The object was to enclose as much space as possible, as with an army controlling territory, and to capture as many of the opponent's stones as possible, as with prisoners of war. Territory was the primary thing, but it was often acquired by wiping out enemy representatives. Stile pictured each white pebble as a hostile soldier, implacable, menacing; and each black pebble as a Defender of the Faith, upright and righteous. But it was not at all certain that right would prevail. He had to dispose his troops advantageously, and in the heat of battle the advantage was not easy to discern.

A stone/man was captured when all his avenues of freedom were curtailed. If enemy forces blocked him off on three sides, he had only one freedom remaining; if not buttressed by another of his kind, forming a chain, he could lose his freedom and be lost. But two men could be surrounded too, or ten enclosed; numbers were no certain security here. Rather, position was most important. There were devices to protect territory, such as "eyes" or divisions that prevented enclosure by the other side, but these took stones that might be more profitably utilized elsewhere. Judgment was vital.

Snack proceeded well in the early stages. Then the complexity of interaction increased, and time ran short, and Stile applied the notorious Stile stare to unnerve his opponent. It was a concentrated glare, an almost tangible aura of hate; every time Snack glanced up he encountered that implacable force. At first Snack shrugged it off, knowing that this was all part of the game, but in time the unremitting intensity of it wore him down, until he began to make mistakes. Trifling errors at first, but these upset him all out of proportion, causing his concentration to suffer. He misread a *seki* situation, giving away several stones, failed to make an eye to protect a vulnerable territory, and used stones wastefully.

Even before the game's conclusion, it was obvious that Stile had it. Snack, shaken, resigned without going through the scoring procedure. Rung Seven was Stile's.

Stile eased up on the glare—and Snack shook his head, feeling foolish. He understood how poorly he had played in the ambience of that malevolence—now that the pressure was off. At his top form he might reasonably have beaten Stile, but he had been far below his standard. Stile himself was sorry, but he was above all a competitor, and he had needed this Rung. All his malignance, the product of a lifetime's reaction to the slight of his size, came out in concentrated form during competition of this nature, and it was a major key to his success. Stile was more highly motivated than most people, inherently, and he drove harder, and he never showed mercy in the Game.

The holder of Rung Six was a contrast. His name was Hulk, after an obscure comic character of a prior century he was thought to resemble, and he was a huge, powerful man. Hulk was not only ready but eager to meet the challenge. He was a specialist in the physical games, but was not stupid. This was his last year of tenure, so he was trying to move into qualifying position; unfortunately his last challenge to Rung Five had been turned back on a Game of chance, and he could not rechallenge until the rung-order shifted, or until he had successfully answered a challenge to his own Rung. Stile was that challenge. The audience, aware of this, had swelled to respectable size; both Stile and Hulk were popular Gamesmen, and they represented the extremes of physical appearance, adding to that novelty. The giant and the midget, locked in combat!

Stile got the numbered face of the prime grid, this time. For once he had the opening break! He could steer the selection away from Hulk's specialty of the physical.

But Stile hesitated. Two things influenced him. First, the element of surprise: why should he do what his opponent expected, which was to choose the MENTAL column? Hulk was pretty canny, though he tried to conceal this, just as Stile tried to obscure his physical abilities. Any mistake an opponent might make in estimating the capacities of a player was good news for that player. Hulk would choose the NAKED row, putting it into the box of straight mental games, where surely he had some specialties in reserve. Second, it would be a prime challenge and an exhilarating experience to take Hulk in his region of strength—a considerable show for the watching masses.

No, Stile told himself. This was merely his foolishness, a reaction to the countless times he had been disparagingly called a pygmy. He had a thing about large men, a need to put them down, to prove he was better than they, and to do it physically. He knew this was fatuous; large men were no more responsible for their size than Stile was for his own. Yet it was an incubus, a constant imperative that would never yield to logic. He wanted to humble this giant, to grind him down ignominiously before the world. He *had* to.

Thus it came up 1A—PHYSICAL NAKED. The audience made a soft "oooh" of surprise and expectation. In the muted distance came someone's call: "Stile's going after Hulk in 1A!" and a responding cry of amazement.

Hulk looked up, and they exchanged a fleeting smile over the unit; both of them liked a good audience. In fact, Stile realized, he was more like Hulk than unlike him, in certain fundamental respects. It was push-pull; Stile both liked and disliked, envied and resented the other man, wanting to be like him while wanting to prove he didn't *need* to be like him.

But had he, in his silly imperative, thrown away any advantage he might have had? Hulk's physical prowess was no empty reputation. Stile had made the grand play—and might now pay the consequence. Loss—and termination of employment, when he most needed the support of an understanding employer. Stile began to feel the weakness of uncertainty.

They played the next grid. This, he realized suddenly, was the same one he had come to with Sheen, when he met her in her guise of a woman. Of a living woman. That Dust Slide—he remembered that with a certain fondness. So much had happened since then! He had suffered knee injury, threats against his life, discovered the frame of Phaze, befriended a lady unicorn and gentleman werewolf, and was now making his move to enter the Tourney—two years before his time. A lifetime of experience in about ten days!

The subgrid's top facet listed SEPARATE—INACTIVE—COMBAT—COOPERATIVE, and this was the one Stile had. He was tempted to go for COMBAT, but his internal need to prove himself did not extend to such idiocy. He could hold his own in most martial arts—but he remembered the problem he had had trying to throw the goon, in the fantasy frame, and Hulk was the wrestling champion of the over-age-thirty men. A good big man could indeed beat a good small man, other things being equal. Stile selected SEPARATE.

Hulk's options were for the surfaces: FLAT—VARIABLE—DISCONTINUITY—LIQUID. Hulk was a powerful swimmer—but Stile was an expert diver, and these were in the same section. Stile's gymnastic abilities gave him the advantage on discontinuous surfaces too; he could do tricks on the trapeze or parallel bars the larger man could never match. Hulk's best bet was to opt for VARIABLE, which included mountain climbing and sliding. A speed-hike up a mountain slope with a twenty-kilogram pack could finish Stile, since there were no allowances for sex or size in the Game. Of course Stile would never allow himself to be trapped like that, but Hulk could make him sweat to avoid it.

But Hulk selected FLAT. There was a murmur of surprise from the audience. Had Hulk expected Stile to go for another combination, or had he simply miscalculated? Probably the latter; Stile had a special touch with the grid. This, too, was part of his Game expertise.

Now they assembled the final grid. They were in the category of races, jumps, tumbling and calisthenics. Stile placed Marathon in the center of the nine-square grid, trying to jar his opponent. Excessive development of muscle in the upper section was a liability in an endurance run, because it had to be carried along uselessly while the legs and heart did most of the work. Hulk, in effect, was carrying that twenty-kilo pack.

Hulk, undaunted, came back with the standing broad jump, another specialty of his. He had a lot of mass, but once he got it aloft it carried a long way. They filled in the other boxes with trampoline flips, pushups, twenty-kilometer run, hundred-meter dash, precision backflips, running broad jump, and handstand race.

They had formed the grid artfully to prevent any vertical or horizontal three-in-a-row lines, so there was no obvious advantage to be obtained here. Since Stile had made the extra placement, Hulk had choice of facets. They made their selections, and it came up 2B, dead center: Marathon.

Stile relaxed. Victory! But Hulk did not seem discouraged. Strange.

"Concede?" Stile inquired, per protocol.

"Declined."

So Hulk actually intended to race. He was simply not a distance runner; Stile was. What gave the man his confidence? There was no way he could fake Stile out; this was a clear mismatch. As far as Stile knew, Hulk had never completed a marathon race. The audience, too, was marveling. Hulk should have conceded. Did he know something others didn't, or was he bluffing?

Well, what would be, would be. Hulk would keep the pace for a while, then inevitably fall behind, and when Stile got a certain distance ahead there would be a mandatory concession. Maybe Hulk preferred to go down that way—or maybe he hoped Stile would suffer a cramp or pull a muscle on the way. Accidents did happen on occasion, so the outcome of a Game was never quite certain until actually played through. Stile's knee injury was now generally known; perhaps Hulk overestimated its effect.

They proceeded to the track. Sheen paced Stile nervously; was she affecting an emotion she did not feel, the better to conceal her nature, or did she suspect some threat to his welfare here? He couldn't ask. The established track wound through assorted other exercise areas, passing from one to another to make a huge circuit. Other runners were on it, and a number of walkers; they would clear out to let the marathoners pass, of course. Stile and Hulk, as rung contenders before the Tourney, had priority.

The audience dispersed; there was really no way to watch this race physically except by matching the pace. Interested people would view it on intermittent viewscreen pickup, or obtain transport to checkpoints along the route.

They came to the starting line and checked in with the robot official. "Be advised that a portion of this track is closed for repair," the robot said. He was a desk model, similar to the female at the Dust Slide; his nether portion was the solid block of the metal desk. "There is a detour, and the finish line is advanced accordingly to keep the distance constant."

"Let me put in an order for my drinks along the way," Hulk said. "I have developed my own formula."

Formula? Stile checked with Sheen. "He's up to something," she murmured. "There's no formula he can use that will give him the endurance he needs, without tripping the illegal-drug alarm."

"He isn't going to cheat, and he can't outrun me," Stile said. "If he can win this one, he deserves it. Will you be at the checkpoints to give me my own drinks? Standard fructose mix is what I run on; maybe Hulk needs something special to bolster his mass, but I don't, and I don't expect to have to finish this course anyway."

"I will run with you," she said.

"And show the world your nature? No living woman as soft and shapely as you could keep the pace; you know that."

"True," she agreed reluctantly. "I will be at the checkpoints. My friends will keep watch too." She leaned forward to kiss him fleetingly, exactly like a concerned girl friend—and wasn't she just that?

They lined up at the mark, and the robot gave them their starting signal. They were off, running side by side. Stile set the pace at about fifteen kilometers per hour, warming up, and Hulk matched him. The first hour of a marathon hardly counted; the race would be decided in the later stages, as personal resources and willpower gave out. They were not out after any record; this was purely a two-man matter, and the chances were that one of them would concede when he saw that he could not win.

Two kilometers spacing was the requirement for forced concession. This was to prevent one person slowing to a walk, forcing the other to go the full distance at speed to win. But it was unlikely even to come to that; Stile doubted that Hulk could go any major fraction of this distance at speed without destroying himself. Once Hulk realized that his bluff had failed, he would yield gracefully.

Soon Stile warmed up. His limbs loosened, his breathing and respiration developed invigorating force, and his mind seemed to sharpen. He liked this sort of exercise. He began to push the pace. Hulk did not have to match him, but probably would, for psychological effect. Once Stile got safely out in front, nothing the big man could do would have much impact.

Yet Hulk was running easily beside him, breathing

no harder than Stile. Had the man been practicing, extending his endurance? How good was he, now?

Along the route were the refreshment stations, for liquid was vital for distance running. Sheen stood at the first, holding out a squeeze bottle to Stile, smiling. He was not yet thirsty, but accepted it, knowing that a hot human body could excrete water through the skin faster than the human digestive system could replace it. Running, for all its joy, was no casual exercise. Not at this velocity and this distance.

Hulk accepted his bottle from the standard station robot. No doubt it was a variant of the normal formula, containing some readily assimilable sugars in fermented form, restoring energy as well as fluid; why he had made a point of the distinction of his particular mix Stile wasn't sure. Maybe it was psychological for himself as well as his opponent—the notion that some trace element or herb lent extra strength.

With any modern formula, it was possible to reduce or even avoid the nefarious "wall" or point at which the body's reserves were exhausted. Ancient marathon runners had had to force their bodies to consume their own tissues to keep going, and this was unhealthy. Today's careful runners would make it without such debilitation —if they were in proper condition. But the psychology of it remained a major factor, and anything that psyched up a person to better performance was worth it—if it really worked. Yet Hulk was not a man to cater to any fakelore or superstition; he was supremely practical.

After they were clear of the station, and had disposed of their empty bottles in hoppers set for that purpose along the way, Hulk inquired: "She is yours?"

"Perhaps I am hers," Stile said. They were talking about Sheen, of course.

"Trade her to me; I will give you the Rung."

Stile laughed. Then it occurred to him that Hulk just might be serious. Could he have entered this no-win contest because he had seen Sheen with Stile, and coveted her, and hoped for an avenue to her acquaintance? Hulk was, like Stile, a bit diffident about the women he liked, in contrast to the ones that threw themselves upon him. He could not just walk up to Sheen and say, "Hello, I like your looks, I would like to take you away from Stile." He had to clear it with Stile first. This was another quality in him that Stile respected, and it interfered with his hate-his-opponent concentration. "I can not trade her. She is an independent sort. I must take the Rung to keep her."

"Then we had better race." This time Hulk stepped up the pace.

Now it occurred to Stile that Hulk did not actually covet Stile's girl; Hulk did have all the women any normal man would want, even if they tended to be the superficial muscle-gawking types. So his expressed interest was most likely a matter of courtesy. Either he was trying to make Stile feel at ease—which seemed a pointless strategy—or he was trying to deplete his urge to win. One thing Stile was sure of: however honest and polite Hulk might be, he wanted to win this race. Somehow.

Stile kept pace. He could not match Hulk's short-term velocity, while Hulk could not match Stile's endurance. The question was, at what point did the balance shift? No matter how he reasoned it, Stile could not see how the man could go the whole route, nearly fifty kilometers, at a sufficient rate to win. Right now Hulk was trying to push Stile beyond his natural pace, causing him to wear himself out prematurely. But this strategy could not succeed, for Stile would simply let the man go ahead, then pass him in the later stage. Hulk could not open up a two-kilometer lead against Stile; he would burst a blood vessel trying. No doubt Hulk had won other races against lesser competition that way, faking them out with his short-term power, making them lose heart and resign; but that was a vain hope here. The longer Stile kept Hulk's pace, the more futile that particular strategy became. Provided Stile did not overextend himself and pull a muscle.

On they ran, taking fluid at every station without pausing. Other runners kept pace with them on occasion, running in parallel tracks so as not to get in the

saw Hulk's back moving ever onward. Now Hulk was imbibing of his bottle, as if in no difficulty at all. What a show of strength! The lack of oxygen had to be hurting his lungs too, but he still could drink as he ran blithely on.

If the field malfunction extended for several kilometers, Hulk just might open up the necessary lead, and win by forfeit. Or, more likely, Hulk would win by forcing Stile to give up: endurance of another nature. Stile simply could not keep the pace.

He slowed to a walk, gasping. Hulk was now out of sight. Stile tramped on. There was another force-field intersection ahead. If that marked the end of the malfunction—

It did not. He entered a large tool shop. Robots worked in it, but human beings had been evacuated. The whole dome was low on oxygen.

Stile felt dizzy. He could not go on—yet he had to. The dome was whirling crazily about him as he ran. Ran? He should be walking! But Hulk was already through this dome, maybe back in oxygen-rich air, building up the critical lead while Stile staggered. . . .

A cleaning robot rolled up. "Refreshment—courtesy of Sheen," it said, extending a bottle.

Not having the present wit to question this oddity, Stile grabbed the bottle, put it to his mouth, squeezed.

Gas hissed into his mouth. Caught by surprise, he inhaled it, choking.

Air? *This was pure oxygen!*

Stile closed his lips about it, squeezed, inhaled. He had to guide his reflexes, reminding himself that this was not liquid. Oxygen—exactly what he needed! No law against this; he was entitled to any refreshment he wanted, liquid or solid—or gaseous. So long as it was not a proscribed drug.

"Thank you, Sheen!" he gasped, and ran on. He still felt dizzy, but now he knew he could make it.

Soon the oxygen gave out; there could not be much in a squeeze bottle. He wondered how that worked; perhaps the squeeze opened a pressure valve. He tossed it in a disposal hopper and ran [illegible] en re-charged; he could make it to br[illegible] now.

He did. The next field intersect[illegible] d of the malfunction. Ah, glorious reprie[illegible]

But he had been weakened by his deprivation of oxygen, and had lost a lot of ground. Hulk must have taken oxygen too—that was it! That strange bottle he had nursed! Oxygen, hoarded for the rough run ahead! Clever, clever man! Hulk had done nothing illegal or even unethical; he had used his brains and done his homework to outmaneuver Stile, and thereby had nearly won his race right there. Now Stile would have to catch up—and that would not be easy. Hulk was not yet two kilometers ahead, for Stile had received no notification of forfeit; but he might be close to it. Hulk was surely using up his last reserves of strength to get that lead, in case Stile made it through the malfunction.

But if Hulk did not get the necessary lead, and Stile gained on him, he still had to catch and pass him. There were about thirty kilometers to go. Could he endure? He had been seriously weakened.

He had to endure! He picked up speed, forcing his body to perform. He had a headache, and his legs felt heavy, and his chest hurt. But he was moving.

The track continued through the domes, scenic, varied—but Stile had no energy now to spare for appreciation. His sodden brain had to concentrate on forcing messages to his legs: lift-drop, lift-drop . . . drop . . . drop. Every beat shook his body; the impacts felt like sledgehammer blows along his spinal column. Those beats threatened to overwhelm his consciousness. They were booming through his entire being. He oriented on them, hearing a melody rising behind those shocks. It was like the drumming of Neysa's hooves as she trotted, and the music of her harmonica-horn came up around the discomfort, faint and lovely. Excruciatingly lovely, to his present awareness. His pain became a lonely kind of joy.

Beat—beat—beat. He found himself forming words to that rhythm and tune. *Friend*ship, *friend*ship, *friend*ship, *friend*ship. *Friend*ship for *ev*er, for *ev*er, for *ev*er, for *ev*er. *Friend*ship for *ev*er, u*ni*ting, u*ni*ting, u*ni*ting. *Friend*ship for*ev*er u*ni*ting us *both, both, both.* Neysa was his friend. He started singing the improvised tune mostly in his head, for he was panting too hard to sing in reality. It was like a line of verse: anapestic tetrameter, or four metric feet, each foot consisting of three syllables, accented on the third. But not perfect, for the first foot was incomplete. But pattern scansion tended to be too artificial; then the pattern conflicted with what was natural. True poetry insisted on the natural. The best verse, to his way of thinking, was accent verse, whose only rhythmic requirement was an established number of accents to each line. Stile had, in his own poetic endeavors, dispensed with the artificiality of rhyme; meter and meaning were the crucial elements of his efforts. But in the fantasy frame of Phaze his magic was accomplished by rhyme. His friendship for the unicorn—

An abrupt wash of clarity passed through him as his brain resumed proper functioning. Neysa? What about Sheen? He was in Sheen's world now! Sheen had sent the oxygen!

Again he experienced his hopeless frustration. A tiny man had to take what he could get, even if that were only robots and animals. In lieu of true women.

And a surge of self-directed anger: what was wrong with robots and animals? Sheen and Neysa were the finest females he had known! Who cared about the ultimate nature of their flesh? He had made love to both, but that was not the appeal; they stood by him in his most desperate hours. He loved them both.

Yet he could not marry them both, or either one. Because he was a true man, and they were not true women. This was not a matter of law, but of his own private nature: he could be friends with anything, but he could marry only a completely human woman. And so he could not marry, because no woman worth having would have a dwarf.

And there was the ineradicable root again, as always: his size. No matter how hard he tried to prove his superiority, no matter how high on whatever ladder he rose, he remained what he was, inadequate. Because he was too small. To hell with logic and polite euphemisms; this was real.

Friendship forever, uniting us both. And never more than that. So stick with the nice robots and gentle animals; they offered all that he could ever have.

Sheen was there by the track, holding out a squeeze bottle. "He's tiring, Stile!" she called.

"So am I!" he gasped. "Your oxygen saved me, though."

"What oxygen?" she asked, running beside him.

"The robot—didn't you know there was a field deficiency along the route?"

"Didn't you take the detour?"

"We stuck to the original track. The air gave out. Hulk had oxygen, but I didn't. Until a robot—"

She shook her head. "It must have been my friend."

The self-willed machines—of course. They would have known what she did not. She had asked them to keep watch; they had done exactly that, acted on their own initiative when the need arose, and invoked Sheen's name to allay any possible suspicions. Yet they hadn't had to do this. Why were they so interested in his welfare? They had to want more from him than his silence about their nature; he had given his word on that, and they knew that word was inviolate. He would not break it merely because he washed out of the Tourney; in fact, they would be quite safe if his tenure ended early. Add this in to the small collection of incidental mysteries he was amassing; if he ever had time to do it, he would try to penetrate to the truth, here. "Anyway, thanks."

"I love you!" Sheen said, taking back the bottle.

Then she was gone, as he thudded on. *She* could love; why couldn't *he*? Did he need a damned program for it?

But strength was returning from somewhere, infusing itself into his legs, his laboring chest. His half-blurred vision clarified. Hulk was tiring at last, and Sheen loved him. What little meaning there was in his present life centered around these two things, it seemed. Was it necessary to make sense of it?

Stile picked up speed. Yes, he was stronger now; his world was solidifying around him. He could gain on Hulk. Whether he could gain enough, in the time/distance he had, remained to be seen, but at least he could make a fair try.

Why would a machine tell him she loved him?

Why would another machine help bail him out of a hole?

Stile mulled over these questions as he beat on with increasing power, and gradually the answers shaped themselves. Sheen had no purpose in existence except protecting him; how would she be able to distinguish that from love? And the self-willed machines could want him away from Proton—and the surest way to get him away was to make sure he entered the Tourney. Because if he failed to enter—which would happen if he lost this race—he would have three more years tenure, assuming he could land another employer. If he entered, he would last only as long as he continued winning. So of course they facilitated his entry. They were being positive, helping him . . . and their help would soon have him out of their cogs. Thus they harmed no Citizen and no man, while achieving their will.

Sheen was also a self-willed machine, subservient only to her program, her prime directive. Beyond that she had considerable latitude. She had entered him in the Tourney, in effect, by gaining him employment with a Citizen who was a major Game fan. Did *she*, Sheen, want his tenure to end? Yet she had no ulterior motive; his printout of her program had established that. His rape of her.

Rape—did she still resent that? No, he doubted it. She knew he had done what he had to, intending her no harm. He could not have known he was dealing with a self-willed machine, and he had apologized thereafter.

No, Sheen was doing what she felt was best for him. A jockey with bad knees and a Citizen enemy had poor prospects, so her options had been limited. She had done very well, considering that she had not even had assurance he would return to Proton, that first time he stepped through the curtain. She had done what an intelligent woman would do for the man she loved.

Onward. Yes, he was moving well, now—but how much ground did he have to make up? He had lost track of time and distance during his period of oxygen deprivation. Hulk might be just ahead—or still almost two kilometers distant. There was nothing for it except to run as fast as he could push it, hoping for the best.

Stile ran on. He went into a kind of trance, pushing his tired body on. For long stretches he ran with his eyes closed, trusting to the roughened edge of the track to inform him when he started to stray. It was a trick he had used before; he seemed to move better, blind.

He was making good time, he knew, almost certainly better than whatever Hulk was doing. But now his knees began to stiffen, then to hurt. He was putting more strain on them than he had since being lasered; ordinarily they bothered him only when deeply flexed.

He tried to change his stride, and that helped, but it also tired him more rapidly. He might save his knees—at the expense of his tenure. For if he won this race, and made it to the Tourney, then could not compete effectively because of immobile knees—

Would tenure loss be so bad? He would be forced to leave Proton, and cross the curtain to Phaze—permanently. That had its perverse appeal.

But two things interfered. First there was Sheen, who had really done her best for him, and should not be left stranded. Not without his best effort on her behalf. Second, he did not like the notion of losing this race to Hulk. Of allowing the big man to prove himself best. Not at all. Were these factors in conflict with each other? No, he was thinking that a loss in this marathon would wash out his tenure, and that was not quite so. Regardless, he had reason to try his hardest and to accept exile to Phaze only after his best effort here.

Stile bore down harder. To hell with his knees! He intended to win this Game. If that effort cost him his chance in the Tourney, so be it.

Suddenly, in a minute or an hour, he spied the giant, walking ahead of him. Hulk heard him, started, and took off. But the man's sprint soon became a lumber. Stile followed, losing ground, then holding even, then gaining again.

Hulk was panting. He staggered. There was drying froth on his cheek, extending from the corner of his mouth, and his hair was matted with sweat. He had carried a lot of mass a long way—a far greater burden than Stile's light weight. For weight lifting and wrestling, large muscles and substantial body mass were assets; for endurance running they were liabilities. Hulk was a superlative figure of a man, and clever too, and determined, and he had put his skills together to run one hell of a race—but he was overmatched here.

Stile drew abreast, running well now that his advantage was obvious. Hulk, in contrast, was struggling, his chest heaving like a great bellows, the air rasping in and out. He was at his wall; his resources were exhausted. Veins stood out on his neck. With each step, blood smeared from broken blisters on his feet. Yet still he pushed, lunging ahead, pulse pounding visibly at his chest and throat, eyes bloodshot, staggering so violently from side to side that he threatened momentarily to lurch entirely off the track.

Stile paced him, morbidly fascinated by the man's evident agony. What kept him going? Few people realized the nature of endurance running, the sheer effort of will required to push beyond normal human limits though the body be destroyed, the courage needed to continue when fatigue became pain. Hulk had carried triple Stile's mass to this point, using triple the energy; his demolition had not been evident before because Stile had been far back. Had Stile collapsed, or continued at a walking pace, Hulk could have won by default or by walking the remaining kilometers while conserving his dwindling resources. As it was, he was in danger of killing himself. He refused to yield, and his body was burning itself out.

Stile had felt the need to humble this man. He had done it, physically. He had failed, mentally. Hulk was literally bloody but unbowed. Stile was not proving his superiority, he was proving his brutality.

Stile was sorry for Hulk. The man had tried his best in an impossible situation. Now he was on the verge of heat prostration and perhaps shock—because he would not yield or plead for reprieve. Hulk had complete courage in adversity. He was in fact a kindred soul.

Stile now felt the same sympathy for Hulk he had felt for Sheen and for Neysa: those whose lot was worse than his own. Stile could not take his victory in such manner.

"Hulk!" he cried. "I proffer a draw."

The man barged on, not hearing.

"Draw! Draw!" Stile shouted. "We'll try another grid! Stop before you kill yourself!"

It got through. Hulk's body slowed to a stop. He stood there, swaying. His glazed eyes oriented on Stile. "No," he croaked. "You have beaten me. I yield."

Then Hulk crashed to the ground in a faint. Stile tried to catch him, to ease the shock of the fall, but was only borne to the track himself. Pinned beneath the body, he was suddenly overwhelmed by his own fatigue, that had been shoved into the background by his approach to victory. He passed out.

Stile survived. So did Hulk. It could have been a draw, since neither had completed the course, and they had fallen together. Hulk could have claimed that draw merely by remaining silent. But Hulk was an honest man. His first conscious act was to dictate his formal statement of concession.

Stile visited Hulk in the hospital, while Sheen stood nervous guard. She didn't like hospitals. Proton medicine could do wonders, but nature had to do some of it alone. It would be several days before Hulk was up and about.

"Several *hours*," Hulk said, divining his thought. "I bounce back fast."

"You did a generous thing," Stile said, proffering his hand.

Hulk took it, almost burying Stile's extremity in his huge paw. "I did what was right. I worked every angle I could, but you came through. You were the better man. You won."

Stile waved that aside. "I wanted to humble you, because you are so big. It was a bad motive. I'm sorry."

"Someday you should try being big," Hulk said. "To have people leery of you, staring at you, making mental pictures of gorillas as they look at you. Marveling at how stupid you must be, because everybody *knows* wit is in inverse proportion to mass. I wanted to prove I could match you in your specialty, pound for pound. I couldn't."

That did something further to Stile. The big man, seen as a freak. His life was no different from Stile's in that respect. He just happened to be at the other extreme of freakiness: the giant instead of the dwarf. Now Stile felt compelled to do something good for this man.

"Your tenure is short," he said. "You may not have time to reach the qualifying Rung. You will have to leave Proton soon. Are you interested in an alternative?"

"No. I do not care for the criminal life."

"No, no! A legitimate alternative, an honorable one. There is a world, a frame—an alternate place, like Proton, but with atmosphere, trees, water. No Citizens, no serfs, just people. Some can cross over, and remain there for life."

Hulk's eyes lighted. "A dream world! How does a man earn a living?"

"He can forage in the wilderness, eating fruits, hunting, gathering. It is not arduous, in that sense."

"Insufficient challenge. A man would grow soft."

"Men do use weapons there. Some animals are monsters. There are assorted threats. I think you would find it more of a challenge than the domes of Proton, and more compatible than most planets you might emigrate to, if you could cross the curtain. I don't know whether you can, but I think you might."

"This is not another world in space, but another

dimension? Why should I be able to cross, if others can't?"

"Because you came here as a serf. You weren't born here; you had no family here. So probably you don't exist in Phaze."

"I don't follow that."

"It is hard to follow, unless you see it directly. I will help you try to cross—if you want to."

Hulk's eyes narrowed. "You have more on your mind than just another place to live. Where's the catch?"

"There is magic there."

Hulk laughed. "You have suffered a delusion, little giant! I shall not go with you to that sort of realm."

Stile nodded sadly. He had expected this response, yet had been moved to try to make it up to the man he had humbled. "At least accompany me to the curtain where I cross, to see for yourself to what extent that world is real. Or talk to my girl Sheen. Perhaps you will change your mind."

Hulk shrugged. "I can not follow you today, but leave your girl with me. It will be a pleasure to talk with her, regardless."

"I will return to talk with you," Sheen told Hulk.

They shook hands again, and Stile left the room. Sheen accompanied him. "When I return to Phaze this time—" he began.

"I will tell Hulk what you know of that world," she finished. "Be assured he will pay attention."

"I will come back in another day to challenge for Rung Five. That will qualify me for the Tourney."

"But you are too tired to challenge again so soon!" she protested.

"I'm too tired to face the Yellow Adept too," he said. "But my friends must be freed. Meanwhile, we've already set the appointment for the Rung Five Game. I want to qualify rapidly, vindicating your judgment; nothing less will satisfy my new employer."

"Yes, of course," she agreed weakly. "It's logical."

She turned over the special materials he had ordered and took him to the proper section of the curtain. "My friends had an awful time gathering this stuff," she complained. "It really would have been easier if you had been a reasonable robot, instead of an unreasonable man."

"You have a reasonable robot in my image," he reminded her. "Be sure to reanimate him."

She made a mock-strike at him. "You know a robot can't compare to a real live man."

Stile kissed her and passed through.

CHAPTER 16

Blue

Stile emerged, as planned, just beyond the yellow fog that demarked the Yellow Demesnes. He could not, per his agreement and the curse Yellow had set against his return, enter that for himself—but he shouldn't need to. He set down the cage containing the owl and donned his clothing. In the pockets were a folded null-weight wetsuit and a metalsaw: the one to protect against thrown potions, the other to sever the cage bars. He hoped Kurrelgyre or Neysa would have the common sense to saw out a bar-section and use it as a lever to break the locks of the other cages. If they didn't, or if anything else went wrong—

Stile stifled that thought. He had to free his friends, one way or another. If he could not do it harmlessly, he would have to make arrangements to destroy the Yellow Adept—and he did not want to do that. She was not really a bad witch.

He stretched the pliant wetsuit into a cord and knotted it about the saw. He brought the owl out. "All right, owl. One service for me and you are free in this world, never again to serve man or to be caged." This was a modified owl, of high intelligence for its kind; it understood him. "Take this and drop it in the cauldron inside the yellow house." Stile presented the package of dry ice. "Take this and drop it in the unicorn's cage." He gave the bird the wetsuit-saw knot.

The owl blinked dubiously.

"Oh, you don't know what a unicorn is? Like a horse with a horn." The owl was reassured. "Then wing out of here—and out of there, quickly. You will be free. And if you should ever need me, let me know and I'll help you."

The owl took a package in each claw, spread its wings, and launched into the sky. "And don't let any liquid touch you, there!" Stile called after it.

He watched it go, hoping for the best. This was a jury-rigged effort, the best he could think of under the pressures of the moment. He wasn't sure what Proton artifacts would operate in Phaze, so was keeping it as simple as possible.

He was in luck. Soon he heard a scream from the witch. That would be the dry ice in the cauldron, making it bubble and steam through no agency of the Adept, interfering with the potion's effectiveness and releasing the owl from its spell, as well as distracting Yellow. Next could come the delivery of the suit and saw. After that, with luck, hell would break loose.

He waited nervously. So many things could go wrong! Then he heard the trumpeting of Darlin' Corey the pink elephant, and an increasing commotion among the captives. It grew into a considerable din, with bangings and crashes. Then at last shapes moved through the fog. A unicorn galloped toward Stile. It was Neysa—and she had a rider. Kurrelgyre, in man-form.

They arrived, and the werewolf dismounted. "My thanks to thee, fair mare. At such time as I may, I will return the favor." Then he handed the sword to Stile and changed back into wolf-form.

Stile stood for a moment, assimilating this. Why hadn't the werewolf simply run as a wolf, instead of performing the awkward, for him, feat of riding the unicorn? To carry the rapier, that he would otherwise have had to leave behind. His own clothing transformed with him, but the sword was foreign. He had wanted to return it to Stile. Why had Neysa tolerated this strange rider? Because she too had felt the need to return the sword. Yet it was no special weapon. It was the gift of her brother, belonging now to Stile—that was its only distinction. So they had both done it for him. Or so his present logic suggested. He was touched. "I thank you both. But I am chiefly glad you both are free without injury."

Kurrelgyre made a growl, and Neysa a note of assent. Neither was talking much, it seemed. Was this because they had not liked the necessity of working so closely together—or because they had liked it? That could be a serious complication for hereditary enemies.

"The Yellow Adept—was she hurt?"

Kurrelgyre changed back to man-form. "The witch brought me forth from my cage, fathoming my disguise," he said. "She claimed thou hadst sent her to me. And I, knowing not whether she spoke truth or lie, had to play along with her until I knew thy fate, intending to kill her if she had done thee harm. But she showed me thy prints going through the curtain, and told me how thou wouldst try to rescue us from afar, and said she would lay no traps against thee if I—"

"Yellowette is some fair witch," Stile said.

"I have been long absent from my were-bitch," Kurrelgyre agreed. "Yellow performs her business, as do we all. But ere she moved me, the potion wore off. . . ." He shrugged. "So I returned to my cage, to await thine effort. I could not flee in wolf-form because her summoning potion would have brought me back, and my man-form no longer wished to slay her."

"I believe she was willing to let thee go," Stile said. "But to save face, she could not do it until I launched mine effort. I suspect I owe her a favor."

"It seems some Adepts are people too," Kurrelgyre agreed grudgingly. "No animal harmed Yellow in the escape; they merely fled in different directions, and we too came here as soon as we winded thee." He returned to lupine form.

"Yellow told me who I am," Stile said.

The eyes of wolf and unicorn abruptly fixed on him.

"I am the Blue Adept." Stile paused, but neither gave any sign, positive or negative. "I know neither of you approve, but I am what I am. My alternate self was Blue. And I must know myself, as the Oracle said. I must go and set things straight at the Blue Demesnes."

Still they waited, not giving him any encouragement.

"I have freed you both from Yellow, as I had to," Stile continued. "I could not leave you in her clutches after both of you got there because of me. But now that

I know who I am, I can not ask either of you to help. I am the one that thou, Kurrelgyre, mayst not—"

The wolf shifted back into the man. "Too late, friend. I was lost when I met thee, knowing it not. The Oracle alone knew, when it told me to 'cultivate Blue.' I ask no favor of thee, but I will help thee investigate thine own situation. Perchance that which slew thine other self now lurks for thee at the Blue Demesnes, and a lupine nose will sniff it out in time."

"I thank thee, werewolf. Yet will I do no magic, so can not assist thee in thine own concern. It is a one-sided favor thou dost—" But Kurrelgyre had already reverted to wolf-form.

"And thee, Neysa," Stile continued. "I—"

The unicorn made a musical blast of negation. She gestured marginally with her nose, indicating that he should mount. Relieved, Stile did so. He remained tired from the marathon, and it was a great comfort to be on Neysa again. Now he could relax, for a little while, recovering from that grueling run. He needed about two days off his feet, to recuperate, but the time simply wasn't there. If he delayed his approach to the Blue Demesnes, Yellow might spread the word, and whatever lurked there would be thoroughly prepared for his arrival. He had to get there first.

Should he ask for another sniff of wolfsbane? No—that magic might not work for him as well a second time, and in any event he preferred to ride out his problems with his own strength, not leaning on magic too often.

Stile did not know where the Blue Demesnes were, but Kurrelgyre did. He led Neysa eastward at a fast clip. They moved back along the route they had come originally, through forest and field and badlands, hardly pausing for rest or food. Stile explained along the way about his need to report back to Proton on the morrow, so the two creatures were determined to get him where he was going before he had to return to Proton. Kurrelgyre did not pause to hunt, and Neysa never grazed despite Stile's urgings.

At length they passed the place where he had tamed

the unicorn: the start of that wild ride. So short and yet so long a time ago! They proceeded without pause to the castle Stile had first seen from his survey from the tall tree. Back virtually to his starting point—had he but known!

Dawn was breaking in its unmitigated splendor as they approached the castle. Stile, asleep on Neysa, had missed the pretty moonrisings and settings of the night. He squinted at the castle blearily. He had barely four hours left before his match for Rung Five in Proton—and he hadn't even settled the situation in Phaze yet. If only Blue hadn't been so far from Yellow—

Stile had slept, but it seemed the tensions of his mission had prevented him from unwinding properly. If the Blue Adept had really been murdered, who had done the deed? If Blue's magic had not saved him, how could Stile survive without the aid of magic? Yet this was the way it had to be. Even if magic had been permitted him, he would not be prepared with suitable verses.

Yet he still had to check this castle out. To know, finally, exactly what his situation was. Whatever it might be, whatever it might cost him. The Oracle had told him to know himself, and he believed it was good advice.

The environs of the Blue Demesnes were surprisingly pleasant. There was no black fog or yellow fog—not even any blue fog. Just the pure blue sky, and a lovely blue lake, and fields of bluebells and blue gentians and bluegrass. To Stile's eye this was the most pleasant of places—not at all like the lair of an Adept.

Still, he could not afford to be deceived by superficialities. "I think it would be best to enter in disguise, as before," Stile said. The animals agreed.

This time Stile donned Neysa's socks, while Kurrelgyre assumed man-form. Then the seeming man led the two seeming unicorns up to the castle gate.

The drawbridge was down across the small moat, and the gate stood open. An armed human guard strode forward, but his hand was not near his sword. He was, of course, garbed in blue. "What can we do for thee, man?" he inquired of Kurrelgyre.

"We come to see the Blue Adept," the werewolf said.

"Thine animals are ill?"

Surprised, Kurrelgyre improvised. "One has bad knees."

"We see not many unicorns here," the guard observed. "But surely the Lady Blue can handle it. Come into the courtyard."

Stile was startled. This was the first he had heard of a Lady Blue. How could she be the Adept, if the original had been a man, and was now dead? Unless she had been his wife. This complicated the picture considerably!

"But we wish to see the Adept himself," the werewolf protested.

"If thou'rt dying, thou seest the Adept," the guard said firmly. "If thine animal hath bad knees, thou seest the Lady."

Kurrelgyre yielded. He led his animals through the gate, along the broad front passage, and into the central court. This was similar to one of the courts of the palace of the Oracle, but smaller; it was dominated by a beautiful blue-blossomed jacaranda tree in the center. Beneath the tree was a deep blue pond fed by a rivulet from a fountain in the shape of a small blue whale that overhung one side. The Blue Adept evidently liked nature in all its forms, especially its blue forms. Stile found his taste similar.

There were several other animals in the yard: a lame jackrabbit, a snake with its tail squished, and a partly melted snow monster. Neysa eyed the last nervously, but the monster was not seeking any trouble with any other creature.

A maidservant entered the yard, wearing a blue print summer dress. "The Lady will be with thee soon," she said to Kurrelgyre. "Unless thou art in immediate pain?"

"No pressing pain," the werewolf said. He was evidently as perplexed by all this as Stile was. Where was the foul nature an Adept was supposed to have? If the Blue Adept were dead, where was the grief and ravage?

They might have had to fight their way into the castle; instead it was completely open and serene.

The girl picked up the snake carefully and carried it into the castle proper.

What was this, Stile wondered—an infirmary? Certainly it was a far cry from the Black or Yellow Demesnes, in more than physical distance. Where was the catch?

The girl came for the rabbit. The snake had not reappeared; was it healed—or dead? Why did the animals trust themselves to this castle? Considering the reputation of Adepts, these creatures should have stayed well clear.

Now another woman emerged. She wore a simple gown of blue, with blue slippers and a blue kerchief tying back her fair hair. She was well proportioned but not spectacular in face or figure. She went directly to the snow-monster. "For thee, a freeze-potion," she said. "A simple matter." She opened a vial and sprinkled its contents on the monster. Immediately the melt disappeared. "But get thee safely back to thy mountain fastness; the lowlands are not safe for the likes of thee," she admonished it with a smile that illuminated her face momentarily as if a cloud had passed from the face of the sun. "And seek thee no further quarrels with fire-breathing dragons!" The creature nodded and shuffled out.

Now the woman turned to Kurrelgyre. Stile was glad he was in disguise; that daylight smile had shaken him. The woman had seemed comely but ordinary until that smile. If there were evil in this creature, it was extraordinarily well hidden.

"We see not many unicorns here, sir," she said, echoing the sentiment of the guard at the gate. Stile was startled by the appellation, normally applied only to a Citizen of Proton. But this was not Proton. "Which one has the injured knees?"

The werewolf hesitated. Stile knew his problem, and stepped in. The unicorn costume was for sight only; any touch would betray the humanness of the actual body.

"I am the one with the knees," he said. "I am a man in unicorn disguise."

The Lady turned her gaze on him. Her eyes were blue, of course, and very fine, but her mouth turned grim. "We serve not men here, now. Why dost thou practice this deceit?"

"I must see the Blue Adept," Stile said. "Adepts have not been hospitable to me, ere now. I prefer to be anonymous."

"Thou soundest strangely familiar—" She halted. "Nay, that can not be. Come, I will examine thy knees, but I can promise nothing."

"I want only to see the Adept," Stile protested. But she was already kneeling before him, finding his legs through the unicorn illusion. He stood there helplessly, letting her slide her fingers over his boots and socks and up under his trouser legs, finding his calves and then at last his knees. Her touch was delicate and highly pleasant. The warmth of it infused his knees like the field of a microwave therapy machine. But this was no machine; it was wonderfully alive. He had never before experienced such a healing touch.

Stile looked down—and met the Lady's gaze. And something in him ignited, a flame kindled in dry tinder. *This was the woman his alternate self had married.*

"I feel the latent pain therein," the Lady Blue said. "But it is beyond my means to heal."

"The Adept can use magic," Stile said. Except that the Blue Adept was dead—wasn't he?

"The Adept is indisposed," she said firmly. She released his knees and stood with an easy motion. She was marvelously lithe, though there were worry-lines about her mouth and eyes. She was a lovely and talented woman, under great strain—how lovely and how talented and under how much strain he was now coming to appreciate by great jackrabbit bounds. Stile believed he knew what the nature of that strain might be.

Kurrelgyre and Neysa were standing by, awaiting Stile's decision. He made it: he bent carefully to draw off the unicorn socks, revealing himself undisguised. "Woman, look at me," he said.

The Lady Blue looked. She paled, stepping back. "Why comest thou like this in costume, foul spirit?" she demanded. "Have I not covered assiduously for thee, who deservest it least?"

Stile was taken aback. He had anticipated gladness, disbelief or fear, depending on whether she took him for her husband, an illusion, or a ghost. But this—

"Though it be strange," the Lady murmured in an aside to herself. "Thy knees seemed flesh, not wood, and there was pain in them. Am I now being deluded by semblance spells?"

Stile looked at the werewolf. "Does this make sense to thee? Why should my knees not be flesh? Who would have wooden knees?"

"A golem!" Kurrelgyre exclaimed, catching on. "A wooden golem masquerading as the Adept! But why does she cover for the soulless one?"

The Lady whirled on the werewolf. "Why cover for thy henchman!" she exclaimed, her pale cheeks flushing now in anger. "Should I let the world know my love is dead, most foully murdered, and a monster put in his place—and let all the good works my lord achieved fall into ruin? Nay, I needs must salvage what I can, holding the vultures somewhat at bay, lest there be no longer any reprieve or hope for those in need. I needs must sustain at least the image of my beloved for these creatures, that they suffer not the horror I know."

She returned to bear on Stile, regal in her wrath. "But thou, thou fiend, thou creature of spite, thou damned thing! Play not these gruesome games with me, lest in mine agony I forget my nature and ideals and turn at last on thee and rend thee limb from limb and cut out from thy charred bosom the dead toad that is thy heart!" And she whirled and stalked into the building.

Stile stared after her, bathed in the heat of her fury. "There is a woman," he breathed raptly.

Neysa turned her head to look at him, but Stile was hardly aware of the import of her thought. The Lady

Blue—protecting her enemy from exposure, for the sake of the good work done by the former Blue Adept. Oh, what a wrong to be righted!

"I must slay that golem," Stile said.

Kurrelgyre nodded. "What must be, must be." He shifted to wolf-form and sniffed the air. Then he led the way into the castle.

Stile followed, but Neysa remained in the courtyard. She had run almost without surcease for a day and night, carrying him, and her body was so tired and hot she could scarce restrain the flames of her breath. Kurrelgyre, unfettered, had fared better; but Neysa needed time by herself to recover.

No one sought to stop them from entering the castle proper. The guard at the gate had been the only armed man they encountered, and he was back at his station. There were a few household servants, going innocently about their businesses. There was none of the grimness associated with the demesnes of the other Adepts he had encountered. This was an open castle.

The wolf followed his nose through clean halls and apertures until they arrived at a closed door. Kurrelgyre growled: the golem was here.

"Very well, werewolf," Stile said. "This needs must be my battle; go thou elsewhere." Kurrelgyre, understanding, disappeared.

Stile considered momentarily, then decided on the forthright approach. He knocked.

There was, as he expected, no answer. Stile did not know much about golems, but did not expect much from a construct of inanimate materials. Yet, he reminded himself, that was what the robot Sheen was. So he had to be careful not to underestimate this thing. He did not know the limits of magical animation. "Golem," he called. "Answer, or I come in regardless. Thine impersonation is at an end."

Then the door opened. A man stood there, garbed in a blue robe and blue boots. He was, Stile realized, the exact image of Stile himself. His clothing differed in detail, but a third party would not know the two of them apart.

"Begone, intruder, lest I enchant thee into a worm and crush thee underheel," the golem said.

So golems could talk. Good enough.

Stile drew his rapier. For this had werewolf and unicorn labored so diligently to return his weapon to him! "Perform thy magic quickly, then, impostor," he said, striding forward.

The golem was unarmed. Realizing this, Stile halted without attacking. "Take a weapon," he said. "I know thou canst not enchant me. Dost thou not recognize me, thou lifeless stick?"

The golem studied Stile. The creature was evidently not too bright—unsurprising if its brains were cellulose—but slowly Stile's aspect penetrated. "Thou'rt dead!" the golem exclaimed.

Stile menaced him with the sword. "*Thou* art dead, not I."

The golem kicked at him suddenly. Its move was almost untelegraphed, but Stile was not to be caught off guard in a situation like this. He swayed aside and clubbed the creature on the ear with his left fist.

Pain lanced through his hand. It was like striking a block of wood—as he should have known. This was a literal blockhead! While he paused, shaking his hand, the golem turned and butted him in the chest. Stile braced himself just in time, but he felt dull pain, as of a rib being bent or cartilage torn. The golem bulled on, shoving Stile against the wall, trying to grab him with hideously strong arms. Stile knew already that he could not match the thing's power.

Unarmed? The golem needed no overt weapon! Its body was wood. Stile got his sword oriented and stabbed the torso. Sure enough, the point lodged, not penetrating. This thing was not vulnerable to steel!

Now he knew what he was up against. Stile hauled up one of his feet and got his knee into the golem's body as it tried to butt again. His knee hurt as he bent it, but he shoved the creature away. The golem crashed against the far wall, its head striking with a sharp crack—but it was the wall that fractured, not the head.

Stile took a shallow breath, feeling his chest injury,

and looked around. Kurrelgyre was back, standing in the doorway, growling off other intruders. This would remain Stile's own personal fight, like a Game in the Proton-frame. All he had to do was destroy this undead wooden dummy. Before it battered him into the very state of demise he was supposedly already in.

He no longer had qualms about attacking an unarmed creature. He studied the golem. The creature might be made of wood, animated by magic, but it still had to obey certain basic laws of physics. It had to have joints in its limbs, and would be vulnerable in those joints, even as Stile was. It had to hear and see, so needed ears and eyes, though these would probably function only via magic. Whoever had made this golem must have a real knack for this kind of sorcery. Another Adept, most likely, specializing in golems.

The golem came—and Stile plunged the point of his rapier like a hypodermic into the thing's right eye. The golem, evidently feeling no pain, continued forward, only twisting its head. The sword point, lodged in the wood, was wrenched about. It snapped off.

Stile had not been expert with this weapon, so this was less of a loss than it might have seemed. He aimed the broken end at the golem's other eye. But the creature, aware of the danger, retreated. It turned and crashed through the window in the far wall.

Stile pursued it. He leaped through the broken window—and found himself back in the courtyard, where Neysa had been pacing restlessly, breathing out her heat. She paused, startled, at the appearance of the golem. Her eyes informed her it was Stile, with one eye destroyed, but her nose was more certain. She made an angry musical snort.

The golem cast about with its remaining eye. It spied the fountain-whale. It grabbed the statuary in both arms and ripped it from its mooring.

Neysa, alarmed, charged across the courtyard, her horn aimed at the golem. "Don't stab it!" Stile cried. "The thing is wood; it could break thy horn!"

As he spoke, the golem heaved the whale at him. The statue was solid; it flew like a boulder. Neysa leaped at

Stile, nosing him out of the way of it. The thing landed at her feet, fragmenting.

"Art thou all right, Neysa?" Stile cried, trying to get to his feet without bending his knees too far.

She gave a musical blast of alarm. Stile whirled. The golem was bearing down on him with a whale fragment, about to pulp his head.

Neysa lifted her head and snorted a jet of flame that would have done credit to a small dragon. It passed over Stile and scored on the golem.

Suddenly the golem was on fire. Its wood was dry, well-seasoned, and filled with pitch; it burned vigorously. The creature dropped the whale fragment and ran madly in a circle, trying to escape its torment. Blows and punctures might not bother it, but fire was the golem's ultimate nemesis.

Stile stared for a moment, amazed at this apparition: himself on fire! The golem's substance crackled. Smoke trailed from it, forming a torus as the creature continued around its awful circle.

And Stile, so recently out to destroy this thing, experienced sudden empathy with it. He could not let it be tortured in this fashion. He tried to quell his human softness, knowing the golem was a literally heartless, unliving thing, but he could not. The golem was now the underdog, worse off than Stile himself.

"The water!" Stile cried. "Jump in the pond! Douse the fire!"

The golem paused, flame jetting out of its punctured eye to form a momentary halo. Then it lurched for the pool, stumbled, and splashed in. There was a hiss and spurt of steam.

Stile saw Neysa and Kurrelgyre and the Lady Blue standing spaced about the courtyard, watching. He went to the pond and kneeled, carefully. The golem floated face down, its fire out. Probably it didn't need to breathe; still—

Stile reached out and caught a foot. He hauled it in, then wrestled the body out of the pond. But the golem was defunct, whether from the fire or the water Stile could not tell. It no longer resembled him, other than in outline. Its clothing was gone, its painted skin scorched, its head a bald mass of charcoal.

"I did not mean it to end quite this way," Stile said soberly. "I suppose thou wast only doing thy job, golem, what thou wert fashioned for, like a robot. I will bury thee."

The gate guard appeared. He looked at the scene, startled. "Who is master, now?"

Startled in turn, Stile realized that he should be the master, having deposed the impostor. But he knew things weren't settled yet. "Speak to the Lady," he said.

The guard turned to her. "A wolf comes, seeking one of its kind."

Kurrelgyre growled and stalked out to investigate.

"Speak naught of this outside," the Lady Blue directed the guard. Then she turned to Stile. "Thou'rt no golem. Comest thou now to destroy what remains of the Blue Demesnes?"

"I come to restore it," Stile said.

"And canst thou emulate my lord's power as thou dost impersonate his likeness?" she asked coldly.

Stile glanced at Neysa. "I can not, Lady, at this time. I have made an oath to do no magic—"

"How convenient," she said. "Then thou needst not prove thyself, having removed one impostor, and thou proposest to assume his place, contributing no more to these Demesnes than he did. And I must cover for thee, even as I did for the brute golem."

"Thou needst cover for nobody!" Stile cried in a flash of anger. "I came because the Oracle told me I was Blue! I shall do what Blue would have done!"

"Except his magic, that alone distinguished my lord from all others," she said.

Stile had no answer. She obviously did not believe him, but he would not break his oath to Neysa, though he wanted above all else to prove himself to the Lady Blue. She was such a stunning figure of a woman—his alternate self had had tastes identical to his own.

Kurrelgyre returned, assuming man-form. "A member of my pack brings bitter news to me," he said. "Friend, I must depart."

"Thou wert always free to do so," Stile said, turning to this distraction with a certain relief. "I thank thee for thy help. Without seeking to infringe upon thy prerogatives, if there is aught I can do in return—"

"My case is beyond help," the werewolf said. "The pack leader has slain mine oath-friend, and my sire is dying of distemper. I must go slay the pack leader—and be in turn torn apart by the pack."

Stile realized that werewolf politics were deadly serious matters. "Wait briefly, friend! I don't understand. What is an oath-friend, and why—?"

"I needs must pause to explain, since I shall not be able to do it hereafter," Kurrelgyre said. "Friendship such as exists between the two of us is casual; we met at random, part at random, and owe nothing to each other. Ours is an association of convenience and amicability. But I made an oath of friendship with Drowltoth, and when I was expelled from the pack he took my bitch—"

"He stole thy female?" Stile cried.

"Nay. What is a bitch, compared to oath-friendship? He took her as a service to me, that she be not shamed before the pack. Now, over a pointless bone, the leader has slain him, and I must avenge my friend. Since I am no longer of the pack, I may not do this legitimately; therefore must I do it by stealth, and pay the consequence, though my sire die of grief."

Oath-friendship. Stile had not heard of this before, but the concept was appealing. A liaison so strong it pre-empted male-female relations. That required absolute loyalty, and vengeance for a wrong against that friend, as for a wrong against oneself. Golden rule.

Yet something else nagged him. Stile pursued it through the tangled skein of his recent experience, integrating things he had learned, and caught it.

"There is another way," he said. "I did not grasp it before, because this frame evidently has a more violent manner of settling accounts than I am used to. Here, perhaps, it is proper to kill and be killed over minor points of honor—"

"Of course it is!" the werewolf agreed righteously.

"Just so. My apology if I misinterpret thine imperatives; I do not wish to give offense. But as I perceive it, thou couldst rejoin thy pack. Thou hast only to kill thy sire—"

"Kill my sire!" Kurrelgyre exclaimed. "I told thee—"

"Who is dying anyway," Stile continued inexorably. "Which death would he prefer—a lingering, painful, ignominious demise by disease, or an honorable, quick finish in the manner of his kind, as befits his former status, by the teeth of one he knows loves him?"

The werewolf stared at Stile, comprehending.

"And thus thou'rt restored to thy pack, having done thy duty, and can honorably avenge thine oath-friend, without penalty," Stile concluded. "And take back thy bitch, who otherwise would be shamed by the loss of both wolves she trusted."

"The Oracle spoke truly," Kurrelgyre murmured. "I did cultivate Blue, and Blue hath restored me to my heritage. I thought it was the anathema of Adept magic I was fated to receive, but it was the logic mine own canine brain was too confused to make."

"It was only an alternate perspective," Stile demurred. "I have yet to grasp the full import of mine own Oracular message."

"I will gnaw on that," the werewolf said. "Perhaps I shall come upon a similar insight. Farewell, meantime." And he shifted to wolf-form and moved out.

Stile looked at the sun. The day was three hours advanced. The challenge of Rung Five—in just one hour! He barely had time to get there. Fortunately, he knew exactly where the curtain was, and where his original aperture was. He had to move!

Yet he was hardly finished in this frame. He had slain the golem, with Neysa's help, but had little idea how to proceed here; he might do best to remove himself from this frame for a while, hoping for insights. Hoping to know himself better. What did he really want? That depended, in part, on how things fell out on Proton.

"I, too, have business elsewhere," Stile said. "I must

reach the curtain quickly, and get someone to spell me through."

Neysa brightened. She stepped up to him. She would handle it.

He mounted, and they galloped off. Neysa was still hot from her prior exertions, but knew Stile's deadline. In moments she had carried him into the pasture where they had first met.

"Neysa, I think it would be best if thou shouldst stay at the Blue Demesnes while I visit the other frame. I'd appreciate it if thou wouldst inform the Lady Blue about Proton, as thou hast heard it from the werewolf and from me; I don't think she knows." He felt a momentary *déjà vu*, and placed it: this was similar to the manner he was having Sheen tell Hulk about Phaze.

Neysa stiffened. "Is something wrong?" Stile asked.

She blew a note of negation, and relaxed. Stile, intent on the precise location of the curtain-site, did not pursue the matter. Such a short time to reach the Game-annex!

They reached the place in the forest where Stile had first entered this frame. The curtain was there, shimmering more strongly than before. Perhaps he had simply become better attuned to it. Stile divested himself of his clothes. "I will return to the Blue Demesnes within a day, I hope. If thou wilt spell me through now—"

She made a musical snort—and he was through the curtain, emerging in the service area behind the food machines. Only then did he wonder about the unicorn's reticence. Something was bothering Neysa—and now it was too late to ask her about it.

Well, he was sorry, but he was in a hurry. He had twenty minutes to reach the Game-annex, or forfeit.

CHAPTER 17

Tourney

He made it. The holder of Rung Five was Hair, who of course was almost bald. He was a well-balanced player, without many great strengths, but also without many weaknesses. That made him hard to handle on the grid. Hair would be playing to Stile's liabilities, not to his own strengths, and have a pretty good chance to land an advantageous game.

Hair studied Stile. "You look tired," he remarked.

"Apt observation," Stile agreed. Naturally his opponent knew all about yesterday's marathon run. Hair would capitalize on this, choosing the PHYSICAL column. Stile would negate this by going into MACHINE- or ANIMAL-assisted, so as not to have to depend on his own diminished strength. Of course Hair would anticipate that, and shift his column, perhaps into ART. He was good on the theremin. Stile was quite ready to challenge in the classification of music, but would prefer a normal, hand-powered instrument. So he would be better off in TOOL, where he could wind up with something like a trombone or a harmonica. In fact, the harmonica would be very nice right now, because he had been practicing it in the other frame.

But Hair had after all stuck with PHYSICAL, outmaneuvering him. 1B, tool-assisted physical games. The second grid appeared as the murmur of the audience rose.

Stile had the letter facet again. If he chose INDIVIDUAL, he could get caught in another endurance or strength exercise, and he was hardly up to it. If Hair selected BALL, it might work out to bowling, where Stile could win—or shot-put, where he could not. Hair was no Hulk, but he could heave an object a fair distance.

	1. BALL	2. VEHICLE	3. WEAPON	4. ATHLETIC	5. GENERAL
A. INDIVIDUAL					
B. INTERACTIVE					

Or he could go for VEHICLE, and they would be in a canoe race or bike race or skating race. Stile was fast on skates, but his legs were tired; this was not his day. WEAPONS was no better. He wasn't ready to bend a powerful bow to shoot at a target 300 meters distant. His aim would surely suffer. His separated cartilage in the rib cage gave a twinge; no, he could not draw a bow! But throwing the javelin or hammer was no better. Nor was pole-vaulting—God, no!—in the next box, or skiing, or even sledding. He pictured himself whomping belly first on a small sled and shooting the ice rapids, and his rib cage gave a worse twinge. Only in GENERAL did he have a fair chance, with things like hopscotch, horseshoes, or jacks. Or tiddlywinks—major Games had been won and lost in that game, with the audience as avidly breathless as it would have been for a saber match. Stile was expert in tiddlywinks—but knew he would not get to play them this time.

So it had to be INTERACTIVE. That had its pitfalls too, but in general skill was more important than power.

It came up 1B. Interactive ball games. Good—Stile was skilled in most of these, and should be able to take Hair—so long as Hair did not catch on to his special liabilities, like the ribs or the bruised left hand. Oh, that wooden head of the golem, that he had so blithely punched!

They set up the nine-box subgrid, filling in with marbles, *jeu de boules*, croquet, billiards, tennis, table-soccer, Ping-Pong, soccer and Earthball. The last would be a disaster; Stile played to avoid it, and the result was Ping-Pong.

Well, not good, but not bad. Stile was excellent at this sport, and his right hand remained good, but he would be off his game today. Hair was good enough to take advantage of Stile's present weaknesses—if he caught on to them in time.

They adjourned to the table-games gym. A number of games were in progress—pool, table-soccer, and of course Ping-Pong—but these were quickly wrapped up when the players saw who was coming. Stile's move up the ladder was already big news. They took a table, picked up the paddles, and volleyed. Several minutes were permitted for limbering prior to the game.

"Time," the machine scorekeeper announced. "Select service."

They did it in the archaic, time-honored fashion, similar to that for the game of Go. Hair took the ball, put it under the table in one hand, and spread his arms apart. Stile chose the right—and got it. He had the first serve.

It was a good break for him, for Stile was an offensive player whose serve was integral to his strategy. He needed to take and keep the initiative, to make up for his lack of reach. He would not be able to win points directly from his serve, against a player of Hair's caliber, but he could certainly put the man safely on the defensive. That was the way Stile liked it. It gave him necessary options. Of course the serve would change every five points—but once he had the lead, he could ride through to victory without pushing himself. Considering his present liabilities, that was important.

Stile served, a cross-court top-spin ball, fast and low over the net, striking neatly two centimeters from the back edge of the table. Hair returned it cautiously with an undercut to the center of Stile's court. The game was on.

Stile backhanded the ball with a flick of the wrist, to Hair's forehand court. Move it about, keep the other player reaching! Never let the opponent get set for his own strategy. Hair returned it to Stile's forehand, somewhat high and shaky, with almost no spin. Good—he was nervous! That diminished Stile's own tension. This was going his way. Stile made a forehand slam and took the point.

Stile served again the moment he had the ball, backhand crosscourt with an undercut. Hair flubbed it again. The score was 2–0. Hair was more visibly nervous now. Excellent. The psychology of nervousness was important in any competition.

But Hair's next return, played too low, nevertheless dribbled over the net, unreturnable. 2–1. These lucky shots occurred; it was usually of no significance. Only when the luck played obvious favorites, as sometimes happened despite the assurances of the experts on probability, was it a critical factor. Stile fired in a sidespin, and Hair sent it wide of the table. 3–1.

The next volley went longer, but Stile finally put it away with a good cross-court slam. 4–1. This game was not going to be a problem.

Now it was Hair's serve. He uncorked a weak dropshot that barely cleared the end of the table; Stile, expecting a harder shot, almost muffed it. But his return was a setup, and Hair put it away for the point. 2–4. In Ping-Pong the server's score was always listed first.

There was something funny about Hair's style, and in moments he took two more points. Stile bore down, overreached himself, and lost another. Now he was behind. Carelessness!

But the run continued. Stile suddenly seemed unable to do right. In moments he was behind 4–10, having lost nine points in a row, his own serve no longer helping him.

What was wrong? He had started well, then lost it. Had fatigue undercut him more than he realized, interfering with his precision? Stile didn't think so. He was playing well enough to win—except that he was losing. Why?

He served a dropshot that barely cleared the table. Hair returned it too softly; it was a setup shot that Stile swiftly put away. 5–10. Strange that the return had been so soft; Hair knew better.

Then Stile caught on. Hair was using a random-variable surface paddle! This was legal, as standards for table-tennis bats had never been instituted; but also tricky, for precision placement was difficult. The variations of bounce were not great, which was why it had not been obvious, but Stile should have noticed it before. *That* was how his fatigue let him down; he had not been alert to the unexpected.

In an instant Stile knew what he had to do. The variable-surface returns forced Hair to play conservatively, keeping his shots well within the margin of safety, though that sometimes set shots up for Stile. But Hair was aware of that. Stile, unaware, had been playing aggressively—and so those slightly changed returns had fouled him up more than his opponent. The more points he lost, the more aggressively he had played, aggravating the situation. A difference in ball velocity and travel so small as to be imperceptible to an onlooker could play havoc with a style like Stile's.

He couldn't handle it. Hair was good enough so that the paddle gave him the edge. Had Stile caught on early he could have played more conservatively himself, holding his lead, forcing Hair to make more aggressive shots that were increasingly risky. But with a 5–10 deficit that strategy wouldn't work; Stile was the one who had to get aggressive. And lose.

He had been suckered, just as he had in the marathon detour. His opponent had outplayed him, off the grid. Stile was in deep trouble again.

So—he had to change his game. He had to go all the way defensive. He needed to allow time and distance to analyze each return individually. This wasn't his normal game, but he had no choice now.

He tried. He had not played a lot of Ping-Pong recently—how could he, with all that had been going on in two worlds!—and had kept in shape only in his natural game. Offense. Spins, placements, slams, changes-of-pace—all fouled up by the marginal uncertainty of the variable-surface paddle. Now, thrown back on a long-neglected resource, he seemed to be in worse trouble yet. He lost a point, and another. 12–5. Soon the gap would be too large to close; sheer chance would give a few points to Hair in the end.

But Stile worked at it, making his shots high and

central and safe. This set him up neatly for Hair, who quickly adapted to the situation and started getting more aggressive. Hair had more leeway now; he could afford to indulge a normally weak offense. Stile was only digging himself in deeper.

Yet he had to do it. He extended himself, despite twinges from his rib cage, adapting to this mode. He could judge the shots better now, for he was playing far back, and he was getting the feel of it. He did know how to do it; he had only to remember, to dredge up long-unused reflexes. He fought the next point, covering all Hair's maneuvers, and won it. And lost the next. He still had not quite worked it out—and he needed to, because the point of no return was coming close.

The audience was hushed by this remarkable turn of the game. Now an announcer could be heard from the supposedly soundproofed telebooth. ". . . strangest Ping-Pong game of the season . . . Stile, the favorite, far behind and playing as if he wants to lose it worse yet . . . will be an inquest to determine whether someone has been paid off . . ."

As if he didn't have enough of a problem already! They thought he was throwing this game! That some other Citizen had proffered him lucrative employment if he missed the Tourney this year. Fortunately the computer analysis of the recording would refute that; all Stile's lost points were honest ones. But if he lost, what difference would it make whether it were honest or dishonest? He would still be finished. In this world, anyway.

But that was not the way he wanted to depart Proton. He had to recover this game!

Stile played the next serve carefully, extending the volley. He needed practice at this defensive game, and the longer the volleys continued the more practice he would get. He won the point, bringing up the change of service at 13–7.

His turn to serve—but if he used it to take the offense, he would lose. He had to give up his normal advantage, for the sake of his strategy, not breaking his continuity.

He served gently—and heard the response of the audience. Most of the watchers did not know why he had been missing points, and thought he was being driven to defense by the strength of Hair's offense. They thought he was foolish to throw away his principal weapon. The serve had always been his tool for the initiative. Some spectators were already leaving, satisfied that Stile had lost.

Hair was glad to continue the offense. He had nothing to gain by indulging in prolonged volleys. Now that Stile had neutralized the paddle-weapon, longer volleys would only give Hair more chances to make mistakes. He needed to put away his points quickly, before Stile got his defensive game in full shape, even if he lost two points for one.

But already Stile was strengthening. The volleys stretched out. Hair lost one, won two—but now he was sweating. Hair was not accustomed to continuous offensive, and as Stile's resistance stiffened—technically, became more fluid—Hair began to make errors of his own. The scales were balancing.

Still, Stile's knees limited him, and his ribs. His reach was minimal in the best of circumstances, and was even more restricted now. He had not quite closed the gap in skills, in this inverted mode, and the game was running out.

They exchanged more points, bringing the score to 17–10 during Hair's service. A seven-point deficit, with only four points to go for Hair. This was bad; if Stile did not rally now, strongly, he was done for.

Hair served. Stile returned it high and center, well toward the back edge so that Hair's shot would have plenty of distance to travel. A setup for a slam, but not for a trick shot. Hair had to hit it hard and long. He did, placing it to Stile's backhand, and Stile returned it with a smooth undercut. His ball arced over, slowing as it dropped, forcing Hair to strike with another undercut lest he lose control. An undercut, backspinning ball in Ping-Pong was a strange shot with special properties; it reacted in the air, on the table, and against the paddle, requiring careful handling.

In the ancient days of cork-, sandpaper- or rubber-surfaced paddles this was not too tricky; but as these gave way to foam rubber and specialized semi-adhesive synthetics the spin-imparting capacities of paddles had become devastating. It was possible to make a ball loop in air, or execute an almost right-angle turn as it bounced. However, such trick shots required skill and energy, and were obvious to a good player, who could then handle them with efficient counterspins. The spin on the incoming ball could be as devastating as the spin going out, making these surfaces a liability to the user, if he were not experienced. The key was to slip in spins that the opponent was not aware of—until too late, when he missed the shot.

Stile, playing back and often below the level of the table, had greater leeway in this respect, now, than Hair did. Hair knew it and was nervous—and doubly careful. He could not uncork full slams lest the hidden spin of the ball send them wide. Stile's proficiency in the mode was increasing, and the advantage was coming to him, at last. But that seven-point deficit—

Stile delivered a swooping undercut sidespin ball that struck the table and took off at an impressive angle. But Hair was ready for it. He countered the spin in the course of a soft-shot. The ball barely cleared the net, and would have dribbled three times on Stile's side before it cleared the table—had not Stile dived to intercept it in time. As it was, he got it back—but only in the form of a high spinless setup.

Hair pounced on his opportunity. He slammed the ball off the backhand corner. Stile leaped back to intercept it, getting it safely over the net—but as another setup. Hair slammed again, this time to Stile's forehand corner, forcing him to dive for it. Stile felt a pain in his rib cage; he got the ball back, but at the expense of aggravating his recent injury. He was in extra trouble now! But he would not give up the point; he had worked too hard for it already.

Hair slammed again, driving him back. Had Hair been a natural offense player, Stile would have been finished; but these slams lacked the authority they needed. Stile managed to return it, again without adequate spin. Hair slammed yet again, harder. Stile retreated far to the rear, getting on top of it, and sent it back. But he had misjudged; the ball cleared the net, but landed too near it and bounced too high. Hair had a put-away setup. Stile braced desperately for the bullet to come—

And Hair made a dropshot. The ball slid off his paddle, bounced over the right edge of Stile's court, and headed for the floor. A sucker shot. Stile had fallen for it.

Stile, nonsensically, went for it. He launched himself forward, paddle hand outstretched. His feet left the floor as he did a racing bellyflop toward that descending ball. He landed and slid, his ribs parting further—but got his paddle under the ball three centimeters above the floor and flicked it up, violently.

From the floor Stile watched that ball sail high, spinning. Up, up, toward the ceiling, then down. Would it land on the proper side of the net? If it did, Hair would put it away, for Stile could never scramble back in time. Yet he had aimed it to—

The ball dropped beyond his line of sight. Hair hovered near, hardly believing his shot had been returned, primed for the finishing slam when the ball rebounded high. It was clearing the net, then!

Stile heard the strike of the ball on the table. Then hell broke loose. There was a gasp from the audience as Hair dived around the table, reaching for an impossible shot, as Stile had done. But Hair could not make it; he fell as his hand smacked into the net support. Then Hair's shoulder took out the center leg of the table, and the table sagged.

Underneath that impromptu tent, Hair's gaze met Stile's as the robot scorekeeper announced: "Point to Stile. Score 17–11."

"Your backspin carried the ball into the net before I could get to it," Hair explained. "Unless I could fetch it from the side as it dribbled down—"

"You didn't need to try for that one," Stile pointed out. "I made a desperation move because I'm up against my point of no return, but you still have a six-point margin."

"Now he tells me," Hair muttered ruefully. "I don't think of that sort of thing when I'm going for a point."

"Your hand," Stile said. "It's bleeding."

Hair hauled his paddle hand around. "Bleeding? No wonder! I just broke two fingers—going for a point I didn't need."

It was no joke. A robot medic examined the hand as they climbed from the wreckage of the table, and sprayed an anesthetic on it. Shock had prevented Hair from feeling the pain initially, but it was coming now. Little scalpels flashed as the robot went to work, opening the skin, injecting bone restorative, resetting the breaks, binding the fingers in transparent splint-plastic.

"I don't think I'll be able to finish the game," Hair said. "I'm not much for left-handed play."

"Stile—by TKO!" someone in the audience exclaimed. Then there was foolish applause.

Rung Five was his. Stile had qualified for the Tourney. But he did not feel elated. He had wanted to win it honestly, not by a fluke. Now no one would believe that he could have done it on his own.

Hulk intercepted them as they left the Game premises. He looked a little wobbly, but was definitely on the mend. He had a rugged constitution. "Stile, about that offer—"

"Still open," Stile said with sudden gladness.

"Your girl was persuasive."

"Sheen has a logical mind," Stile agreed.

"I have nothing to lose," Hulk said. "I don't believe in magic, but if there's a primitive world there, where a man can prosper by the muscle of his arm and never have to say 'sir' to a Citizen—"

"See for yourself. I'm going there now."

"Stile, wait," Sheen protested. "You have injuries! You're worn out. You need rest, attention—"

Stile squeezed her hand. "There is none better than what you provide, Sheen. But across the curtain is a

Lady and a unicorn, and I fear they may be jealous of each other. I must hurry."

"I know about Neysa," she said. "She's no more human than I am, and why she puts up with you is beyond my circuitry. But now you have a lady too? A real live girl? What about *my* jealousy?"

"Maybe I broke in at the wrong time," Hulk said.

"Do not be concerned," Sheen told him sweetly. "I'm only a machine."

Stile knew he was in trouble again.

"You are a robot?" Hulk asked, perplexed. "You made a reference, but I thought it wasn't serious."

"All metal and plastics and foam rubber," Sheen assured him. "Therefore I have no feelings."

Hulk was in difficulty. His eyes flicked to the lusher portions of her anatomy that jiggled in most humanly provocative fashion as she walked, then guiltily away. "I thought—you certainly fooled me!" He bit his lip. "About the feelings, I mean, as well as—"

"She has feelings," Stile said. "She's as volatile as any living creature."

"You don't have to lie for me, Stile," Sheen said, with just that stiffness of body and voice that put him in his place. She had become expert at the human manner!

"Lie?" Hulk shook his head. "There's one thing you should know about Stile. He never—"

"She knows it," Stile said tiredly. "She's punishing me for my indiscretion in finding a living woman."

"Sorry I mixed in," Hulk muttered.

Stile turned to Sheen. "I did not know I would encounter the Lady in the Blue Demesnes. I did not realize at first what she was. I destroyed the golem that had impersonated me, but did not realize the complications until later."

"And now that you do realize, you are eager to return to those complications," Sheen said coldly. "I understand that is man's nature. She must be very pretty."

"You want me to look out for Neysa's interest, don't you?" Stile said desperately, though he had the sensation of quicksand about his feet. "She's there in the Blue Castle, alone—"

"The Lady," Sheen interrupted with new insight. "The Lady Blue? The one your alternate self married?"

"Oh-oh," Hulk murmured.

Stile spread his hands. "What can I do?"

"Why couldn't I have been programmed to love a male robot!" Sheen exclaimed rhetorically. "You flesh-men are all alike! The moment you find a flesh-woman—"

"It's not like that," Stile protested. "She is devoted to the memory of her husband—"

"Who resembled you exactly—"

"She told me off when—"

"When you tried what?" she demanded.

Now Stile raised his hands in surrender. "If I stay here four hours longer—?"

"Eight hours," she said firmly.

"Six."

"Six. And you promise to return for the Tourney, after—"

"Yes."

"That will give me time to put my own affairs in order," Hulk said.

Sheen laughed. Oh, yes, she had her reactions down almost perfect now.

CHAPTER 18

Oath

They tried it and it worked: Hulk passed through the curtain. He stood amazed and gratified, looking around at the forest. It was dawn; Sheen had managed to hold Stile for more like eighteen hours, the last half of which was sleeping. Well, he had been in dire need of the rest, and she had treated him with assorted minor medical aids including a restorative heat lamp, so that he really felt much better now.

"I never saw anything so beautiful," Hulk said, gazing at the brightening world.

"Yes, it is that," Stile agreed. He had tended to forget the sheer loveliness of this land, when involved in other things. If all else were equal, he would prefer Phaze to Proton, for its natural beauty.

Hulk had brought along a costume, per Stile's advice. Now he watched Stile getting into his own. "Are you sure—?"

"That ordinary people wear clothes here? I'm sure. Another thing: the language differs slightly. You have to—"

He was interrupted by a sudden loud hissing. A smoke-exhaling serpent rose up, flapping its wings menacingly. It was a small dragon.

Stile backed off warily, but the dragon followed, sensing compatible prey. One spell could have banished it, but its fiery breath made a sword uncertain. In any event, Stile no longer had his sword. He retreated farther.

"Let me try my beast-man ploy," Hulk said. He jumped forward, bellowed incoherently to get the dragon's attention, then raised both arms in a dramatic muscleman pose. It was extraordinarily impresssive. He had spent years perfecting a body that was a natural marvel. He danced about, beating his chest and growling. He looked altogether, foolishly menacing.

The dragon turned tail and flapped off, whimpering. Stile dissolved in laughter.

Hulk abated his antics, smiling. "That was fun. You often don't need to fight, if you just look as if you'd like to. Was that thing really what it looked like?"

"Yes. This really is a land of fantasy. When you struck that pose, you looked like an ogre."

"Literal ogres exist here?"

"I believe they do. I've never actually seen one, but I'm sure that's the correct analogy."

Hulk looked dubiously at his costume, then started putting it on. "I didn't really believe in the magic aspect. I thought it might be matter transmission and odd effects."

"I had the same problem, at first. But it is better to believe; magic can kill you, here."

"I'll take my chances. It's like another aspect of the Game, with its special subset of rules. But it puts me in doubt what to do here. I don't know the first thing about magic."

"Most people don't practice it," Stile said. "But you do have to be aware of it, and there are certain conventions. Maybe you'd better come with me, until you catch on. I'm going to the Blue Demesnes."

"What would I do in colorful demesnes? I know even less about courtly manners than I do about magic, and if Sheen's suspicions about your Lady are correct, I should not be a witness."

"You might serve as my bodyguard."

Hulk laughed. "Since when do you need a bodyguard? You can beat anyone in your weight class in general combat, regardless of age."

"Here opposition doesn't necessarily come in my weight class. It comes in yours. Someone is trying to kill me, sending things like demon monsters after me. I would feel easier if a good big man were keeping an eye out. You are conversant with hand weapons—"

"All part of the Game," Hulk agreed.

"You could play dumb, like a monster, until you picked up the ways of this world, then go out on your own. You can cross back to Proton any time, too, by making a spell to pass you through the curtain."

"You have some status in this world? So it wouldn't look strange to have a brute bodyguard?"

"It seems I do. Or will achieve it shortly. If I survive the efforts of my anonymous enemy. So I'd really appreciate it if you—"

"You are a generous man, Stile. You do me a favor in the guise of asking for one."

Stile shrugged. Hulk was no fool. "I'll tell people I removed a thorn from your paw. But don't consider it too much a favor. There is danger. You could get killed, associating with me."

"I could get killed just running the marathon! Let's go."

They went. Stile led the way north as the sun cleared the forest and angled its fresh bright shafts between the branches, seeking the ground. They trotted across the opening fields toward the Blue Demesnes. As the castle came into view, a sun ray reflected from its highest turret in brilliant blue. This too, Stile thought, had to be added to the class of most beautiful things.

Then he paused. "Do you hear it, Hulk?"

Hulk listened. "Ground shaking. Getting louder."

"I don't know whether dragons stampede or whether they have earthquakes here. We'd better hurry."

They hurried. As they crossed the plain around the castle they saw it: a herd of animals charging toward the same object.

"Look like wild horses," Hulk said.

"Unicorns. What are they doing here?"

"A whole herd? Could be coming to the aid of one of their number. Wild animals can be like that."

"Neysa!" Stile cried. "If something happened to her—"

"We had better get over there and see," Hulk said.

"I should never have let Sheen delay me!"

"I doubt you had much choice in the matter, and we both did need the rest. Is Sheen really a robot?"

"She really is. Not that it makes much difference."

"And Neysa really is a horse—a unicorn who turns into a woman?"

"That too. And a firefly. You will see it soon enough—if all is well." Stile was increasingly nervous about that.

They ran, moving into the marathon pace. Neither man was in condition for it, because this was too soon after the real one they had run. But this was not to be the full course. They approached the Blue Demesnes.

But the unicorns were moving faster. Now their music sounded across the field, like a percussion-and-wind orchestra. In the lead was a great stallion whose tone was that of a fine accordion; on the flanks were lesser males whose horns were muted or silent. Evidently unicorns were not gelded, they were muted in public. In the center ran the mass of mature mares, carrying the burden of the melody. The stallion would play the theme, and the mares would reiterate it in complex harmonies. It was an impressive charge, visually and sonically.

Now, from the west appeared another group, dark and low to the ground, moving faster than the unicorns. Stile struggled to make it out. Then he heard the baying of a canine-type, and understood. "Wolves! Probably werewolves!" he cried.

"I am ignorant of conventions here, apart from what Sheen told me of what you had told her," Hulk puffed. "But is such convergence of herd and pack usual?"

"Not that I know of," Stile admitted. "It could be Kurrelgyre, returning with friends—but I don't see why. Or it could be the pack leader Kurrelgyre went to kill; if he were victorious, and sought revenge on the person who helped Kurrelgyre—I don't know. They certainly look grim."

"Werewolves and unicorns are natural enemies?"

"Yes. And both are normally unfriendly to man. Kurrelgyre and Neysa learned to get along, but—"

"Now I'm no genius and this is not my business, but it strikes me that the arrival of these two forces at this time strains coincidence. Could this relate to you? If there were some alert, some way they would be aware of the moment you re-entered this frame—"

"That's what I'm afraid of," Stile said. "You see, I'm a natural magician in this frame—a focus of much power. But I have sworn off magic."

"And your frame-wife would like you to break that oath," Hulk said. "So you can preserve the Blue Demesnes from further harm. And the animals would want you to keep your oath, so you will not become anathema to them. These two types of animals may just be united—against you. You were not joking about needing a bodyguard!"

"You catch on rapidly," Stile agreed.

The two of them picked up speed though both were tiring, in an effort to reach the castle before either herd or pack. But it soon became evident that they would not succeed. The unicorn herd would arrive first, then the wolves.

Now the wolf pack veered, orienting on Stile instead of the castle. There seemed to be ninety or a hundred of them, large dark animals with heavy fur and gleaming eyes and teeth that showed whitely with their panting. "I hope, despite my reasoning, that they're on our side," Hulk said, slowing to a walk.

The wolves ringed them. One came forward, and shifted into man-form. A fresh scar ran across one cheek, and his left ear was missing. But it was Stile's friend.

"Kurrelgyre!" Stile exclaimed. "Thou wast victorious!"

"That was not in question, once thou hadst shown me the way," the werewolf replied. He peered at Hulk. "This monster-man—friend or foe?"

"Friend," Stile said quickly.

"Then I sniff tails with thee, ogre," Kurrelgyre said, extending his hand to Hulk.

"Sure," Hulk agreed awkwardly, taking the hand. He seemed to be having some trouble believing the transformation he had just seen.

"Hulk is from the other frame," Stile said quickly. "My bodyguard. He doesn't talk much." And he flashed

Hulk a warning glance. "To what do I owe the pleasure of this visit?"

"I fear I wronged thee inadvertently," the werewolf said. "I returned to my pack, but could not kill my sire without first explaining why—"

"You killed your—" Hulk began, startled.

Kurrelgyre turned, half-shifting into wolf-form. "Thou addressest me in that derogatory mode and tone?" he growled.

"He knows not our ways!" Stile cried. "Even as I did not, at first, and thou didst have to set me straight. He meant thee no offense."

The werewolf returned all the way to man-form. "Of course. I apologize for mistaking thy intent," he said to Hulk. "It remains a sensitive matter, and in a certain respect thou resemblest the type of monster that—"

"He understands," Stile said. "We all make errors of assumption, at first. Why shouldst thou not explain to thy sire? It was the kindest thing thou couldst do for one already ill to death."

Hulk nodded, beginning to understand. A mercy killing. Close enough.

"I came to my sire's den," Kurrelgyre said grimly. "He met me in man-form, and said, 'Why comest thou here? This place is not safe for thee, my pup.' I replied, 'I come to slay thee, as befits the love I have for thee, my sire, and the honor of our line. Then will I avenge mine oath-friend Drowltoth, and restore my bitch to prominence in the pack.' Hardly did he betray his dignity, or yield to the ravage of distemper I perceived in him; in that moment he stood as proud as I remembered him of old. 'I knew thou wouldst thus return in honor,' he said. 'How didst thou come to accept what must be done?' I told him, 'A man persuaded me, even as the Oracle foretold.' And he asked, 'Who was this good man?' and I replied, 'The Blue Adept,' and he asked, 'How is it that an Adept did this thing for thee?' I said, 'He was dead, and his double comes from the other frame to restore his demesnes.' Then my sire looked beyond me in alarm, and I turned and discovered that others of the pack had come up silently during my distraction, and overheard. Thus the pack knew that the Blue Demesnes were in flux, and the word spread quickly. And my bitch spoke, and said, 'Of all the Adepts, Blue alone has been known to do good works among animals, and if that should change—' "

"But that will not change!" Stile protested.

"I tried to tell them that. But mine own kind doubted, and when the unicorns learned that Neysa was prisoner at the Blue Demesnes—"

"Prisoner! She's not—" But Stile had to stop. "*Is* she?"

"We know not. But the unicorn stallion is of imperious bent."

"Well, if she is a prisoner, that will cease the moment I get there. But thou hast not finished thy story."

"It is simple enough," Kurrelgyre said. "The pack leader came, and my sire said, 'It is time.' We changed to wolf-form, and quickly and cleanly I tore the throat out of my sire, and knew then that I had done right, and never did I see a wolf so glad to die. I then whirled and challenged the pack leader while yet my sire's corpse lay steaming, and my right could not be denied before the pack. The pack leader was not so eager to die. He fought, and perhaps he injured me." Kurrelgyre smiled briefly, touching the stump of his ear. "His throat I did not tear; that were too honorable a demise for such a cur. I hamstrung him, spiked both his eyes, tore out his tongue, and drove him with bitten tail into the wilderness to die lame and blind among the monsters. It was an excellent reckoning."

Stile concealed his reaction to this savage tale of vengeance. Perhaps he would have done something similar, in a similar circumstance. "And thy bitch is well?" he inquired, glancing at the female wolf who stood nearest.

"As well as one might be, following exile of her stud, slaughter of his oath-friend, and forced heat to the pack leader. But she will recover. I am now pack leader, and she remains my chosen; all other bitches whine before her."

"A fitting resolution," Stile said, hoping that Hulk

had now grasped enough of the situation to avoid any further errors of manner.

"Yet she is marked," Kurrelgyre continued. "She it was who made me see that the mare needed support."

"Neysa," Stile agreed. "But I assure thee—"

Now the bitch shifted to woman-form. She was pretty enough, with a wild orange flare of hair, but did look peaked. She must have had as hard a recent life as the Lady Blue, and survived it as toughly. "What mode of man art thou," she demanded of Stile, "to trust thy female friend to the power of thy wife?"

"The Lady Blue is not my wife," Stile protested.

"Perhaps not so long as the mare lives. I know somewhat of these things." Surely an understatement! "When the mare is dead, thou wilt be freed of thine oath, and practice magic—"

"No!" Stile cried.

"I tried to tell her thou wert true," Kurrelgyre said. "No way wouldst thou harm the mare—"

"And like my wolf, innocent of the ways of the bitch," the female werewolf finished. "The mare is of a species we honor not, as they attempt to rival us as rulers of the wilds, but she brought thee to my love, and thou hast sent him home to me and to the honor he was due. I owe the mare. I perceive the danger thou dost not. The Lady Blue knows no limits to her determination to maintain her lord's demesnes. If thou savest not the mare, I will avenge her in the manner of an oath-friend, though there be no oath between us."

Could she be right? Had Stile sent Neysa to her doom in the Blue Demesnes? What a colossal miscalculation! Yet Neysa could take care of herself, and the Lady was no Adept. "If she is not safe, I will avenge her myself," Stile said. But he could not make an oath of it. Suppose the Lady Blue had—

"Others know thee not as I do," Kurrelgyre said. "So I felt it best to be on the scene when the herd arrived, lest unwarranted blame fall on thee. Thou mayest need guidance."

"I may indeed," Stile agreed. What a complex situation had blown up in his brief absence!

They proceeded toward the castle. The unicorns had drawn up before its gate, their music fading out. They were waiting for Stile to arrive. There were about fifty of them, almost evenly divided between mares and lesser males, with the huge stallion in front. The stallion stood some eighteen hands high at the shoulder, more than thirty centimeters—about a foot—above Stile's head, and all his mass was functional. A truly impressive creature.

Hulk studied the stallion with open admiration. Indeed, the two were similar, in proportion to their species.

Stile halted, for the unicorns blocked the way. The werewolves ranged beside him, grim but neutral. They were here because their new pack leader had brought them at the behest of his bitch; they were not too keen on unicorns, but also not too keen on human beings. Hulk stood back, heeding Stile's admonishment to be silent. There was much here that was not yet properly understood.

"Dost thou seek to bar me from my heritage?" Stile asked the stallion.

The unicorn did not answer. His glance fell on Stile from an impressive elevation, bisected by the long and deadly spiraling horn. His head was golden, his mane silver, and his body a nacreous gray deepening into black fetlocks and hooves. His tail matched his mane, beautifully flowing, reflecting the light of the sun almost blindingly. No horse ever had this coloration or this rugged splendor.

After a moment the stallion snorted: a brief accordion treble punctuated by two bass notes. One of the lesser males stepped forward, shifting shape. It was Clip, Neysa's brother. "I helped thee at my sister's behest," he said. "What hast thou to say for thyself now?"

"I mean to enter that castle and see how Neysa is doing," Stile said. But Kurrelgyre's remarks, and the apprehension of the bitch with regard to the conflict between the unicorn mare and the Lady Blue made him queasy. Had he really betrayed his steed and friend into doom? Had Neysa suspected it when she left him?

What kind of a woman was the Lady Blue, really, and what would she do with the associate of the man who had destroyed the golem impostor? Stile had thought she would be grateful, but she certainly had not greeted him with open arms.

Yet how could he believe that his alternate self, his likeness in every respect except environment, had married a woman who would callously murder any creature who stood in her way? Had the Lady Blue shown anything other than a sincere and praiseworthy dedication to her late husband's cause and memory? Yet again, if she knew that Stile alone could restore the greatness of the Blue Demesnes, hindered only by a foolish oath—

"And if she lives, what then?" Clip demanded. "The Herd Stallion demands to know."

"What does the Herd Stallion care about Neysa?" Stile retorted, knowing that in this respect he was voicing the sentiment Clip could not voice. "She was excluded from the herd for no valid reason. She's as pretty and fine a mare as any in the herd, I'll warrant. She should have been bred long ago."

Clip hesitated, understandably. He was at the moment the mouthpiece for his superior, yet his sister's welfare was dearest to his heart and he was loath to refute Stile's statement. "Thou hast not answered the Stallion's question. What will ye with Neysa—if she survives the treachery of Blue?"

"Treachery of Blue!" Stile cried in sudden fury. "I am Blue!" But he felt Hulk's hand on his shoulder, warning him to restraint. Without his magic, he could not really be the Blue Adept.

The unicorn herd faced him silently, and so did Kurrelgyre's bitch. Stile realized it was a fair question, and a hard one. No one had actually accused the Lady of murder; the question was about Stile's own loyalties. He was, potentially, the most powerful person here. If the Lady were exonerated, what would he do then?

"If you take Neysa into the herd, and breed her and treat her as befits a mare of quality, I welcome it. Otherwise she is welcome to stay with me, and be my honored steed, as long as she wishes."

"And what of thine oath to her?"
"What of it?" Stile snapped.
"What of Neysa, when thou breakest that oath?"
Stile suffered another abrupt siege of wrath. "Who claims I am a breaker of oaths?"
"The Stallion claims," Clip said with a certain satisfaction.
For a moment Stile's anger choked off his speech. His hand went for his sword, but slapped only cloth; he had no sword now. Only Hulk's firm, understanding hand held him back from a physical and foolish assault on the huge unicorn.
Kurrelgyre stepped forward and spoke instead. "I was with this man when the Black Adept imprisoned him, but he did no magic, though he was dying of thirst and knew that the simplest spell, such as even any one of us might do, would bring him water and freedom. He freed us from the clutch of the Yellow Adept without magic. He slew the golem of the Blue Demesnes by hand, without magic. He showed me how to regain my status in the pack, using no magic. Now he comes again to this frame—without magic. Never in my presence has he violated his oath. If the Stallion snorts otherwise, the Stallion offends me."
The Herd Stallion's horn flicked, glinting in the sun. He pawed the ground with one massive forehoof. The lesser males drew in to flank him, and the mares shifted position, every horn lowering to point forward. The unicorns were beautiful, garbed in their naturally bright reds, blues and greens, but they meant business.
The hairs on Kurrelgyre's neck lifted exactly like the hackles of a wolf, though he retained man-form. His pack closed in about him, wolves and bitches alike, with an almost subvocal snarling. They were quite ready to pick a quarrel with unicorns!
"Hark," Hulk said. He was the only one with the height and direction to see over the massed unicorns. "The Lady comes. And a small unicorn."
Stile felt abruptly weak with relief. The Herd Stallion turned, and snorted a triple-octave chord. The herd parted, forming a channel. Now everyone could see the

Lady Blue and Neysa walking from the castle gate, side by side, both healthy. There had, after all, been no trouble. No overt trouble.

The Lady was lovely. She wore a pale-blue gown, blue flower-petal slippers, and pointed blue headdress. Stile had admired her form before, but now she had flowered into matchless beauty. He had, in the past hectic hours, forgotten the impact the touch of her hands had had on him. Now, with his fear for Neysa's safety eased, his memory came back strongly, and his knees felt warm. What a woman she was!

And Neysa—what of her? She tripped daintily along beside the Lady, her black mane and tail in perfect order, her hooves and horn shining. She was beautiful too. Stile had never seen his relationship with her in terms of choice; he had tacitly assumed she would always be with him. But Neysa was more than a steed, and his association with her had been more than that of a man and animal. If he became the Blue Adept, not only would he practice the magic that she abhorred, he would take to himself the human woman. Stile and Neysa—they could not continue what had been. That disruption had been inevitable from the moment of the discovery that he could perform powerful magic. The wolves and other unicorns had understood this better than he had; they were more familiar with the imperatives of this world. Yet how could he betray Neysa?

They came to stand before Stile. Stile inclined his head, honoring formalities, though he had no notion what was about to happen. One issue had been defused; Neysa lived. The other issue remained to be settled. "Hello, Neysa. Hello, Lady Blue."

The two females made a slight nod, almost together, but did not speak. The Herd Stallion snorted another chord. "Choose," Clip said, translating.

"By what right dost thou make such demand of me?" Stile cried, reacting with half-guilty anger.

"The Stallion is responsible for the welfare of his herd," Clip replied. "He permitted thee to use a surplus mare, an she be not abused. But now she has yielded her loyalty to thee, thou mayst not cast her aside with impunity."

"If I cast her aside, she returns to the herd," Stile replied, hating the words, but his caution was being overridden by his emotion. "Art thou trying to force me to do this—or *not* to do this?"

"An thou dost cast her aside, it is shame to the herd, and that shame must be abated in blood. Thou keepest her—or thou payest the consequence. The Stallion has so decreed."

"The Stallion is bloated with gas," Kurrelgyre growled. "Knows he not that he challenges the Blue Adept? With a single spell this man could banish this whole herd to the snows."

"Save that he made an oath of no magic to my sister," Clip retorted. "An he honors that oath, he has no need to banish any creature."

For the first time the Lady Blue spoke. "How convenient," she said dulcetly, as she had the first time Stile had met her.

Kurrelgyre turned on her. Stile remembered that the werewolf had left them just before this subject came up, yesterday. "What meanest thou, human bitch?"

If this were an insult—and Stile could not be sure of that—the Lady gave no sign. "Knowest thou not, wolf, that I have harbored an impostor these past ten days, lest news escape of the murder of my husband?" she demanded disdainfully. "Now another image comes, claiming to be Blue—but Blue is distinguished chiefly by his magic, the strongest in all the Land of Phaze—and this impostor performs none, as thou thyself hast testified so eloquently. Were he in sooth the alternate of my husband, he could indeed banish the herd from these demesnes; since he is not, he pleads an oath. I have no slightest doubt he has been true to his oath, and will remain true; he is in fact incapable of breaking it. He is not Blue."

Neysa's head swung angrily about, and she made a harmonica-snort that made the other mares' ears perk up in mute shock. The Lady's lips thinned. "The mare believes he is Adept. She is enamored of him. Has any other person or creature witnessed his alleged magic?"

Even Kurrelgyre had to admit he had not. "The oath was made before I met him. Yet I have no reason to doubt—"

"Without magic, thou hast no debate with the Stallion about the impostor's choice. He shall not be with me. Let him stay with the mare he has deluded."

Neysa's snort seemed to have the tinge of fire. So did the Stallion's. Stile suddenly appreciated how cleverly the Lady was maneuvering them all. Neither wolves nor unicorns really wanted Stile to show his magic, and Neysa was dead set against it—yet now all of them were on the defensive as long as he did not. And if he did perform magic—the Lady won. She needed that magic to maintain the Blue Demesnes, and she would, as Kurrelgyre's bitch had pointed out, do anything necessary to accomplish that purpose. Again he thought: what a woman she was!

"We have galloped here for the sake of a false Adept?" Clip demanded for the Stallion. "We have allowed the wish-fancy of a dwarf-mare to embarrass the herd?"

Once again Stile felt the heat rising. That word dwarf, now applied to Neysa . . .

Kurrelgyre looked at Stile, uncertain now. "Friend, I believe in thee, in thy honor and thy power. But I can not send my pack into battle on thy behalf without some token of thy status. Thou must be released from thine oath."

Stile looked helplessly at Neysa, who snorted emphatic negation. Stile could not blame her; his magic had accidentally sent her once to hell. Without magic he would not be able to assume the role of the Blue Adept, so would not be tempted to leave her. He knew this was not entirely selfish on her part; she feared he would be corrupted by magic. Stile was not sure her fear was unfounded; the other Adepts had certainly been corrupted to some degree, either by their magic or by the circumstance of being Adept. Yellow had to commit the atrocity of animal slavery in order to secure her position with other Adepts; Black had to go to extraordinary extremes to isolate himself. If these people did not do such things, they could be killed by others who were less scrupulous. To be Adept was to be somewhat ruthless and somewhat paranoid. Could he, as Blue, withstand those pressures? The former Blue Adept seemed to have succeeded—and had been murdered. A lesson there?

"Without magic, there is no need for battle," Stile said. "Let the wolves and unicorns go home. Neysa and I will go our way." Yet he was not sure he could stay away from this castle or the Lady Blue. His destiny surely lay there, and until he understood the Blue Demesnes completely he had not really honored the Oracle's directive. To know himself, he had to know the Blue Adept.

Now the Stallion blew a medley of notes. "If thou art false, and caused this trouble for naught, needs must I slay thee," Clip translated. "If thou art true, thou wilst betray the mare who helped thee, and needs must I avenge her. Defend thyself in what manner thou canst; we shall have an end to this insult." And the huge unicorn stepped toward Stile.

Stile considered jumping onto the Stallion's back and riding him, as he had the first time with Neysa. But Stile was in worse shape than he had been then, and the Stallion was more than twice Neysa's mass. The chances of riding him were slim. But so were the chances of defeating him in honest combat—even had Stile had his rapier.

Kurrelgyre stepped between them. "What coward attacks the smallest of men, knowing that man to be unarmed and bound to use no magic?"

The Stallion's horn swung on the werewolf. The bitch shifted into wolf-form and came at the Stallion's off-side, snarling. But Kurrelgyre retained man-form. "Dost thou challenge the pair of us, unicorn? That were more of a fair match."

The lesser male unicorns stepped forward—but so did the other werewolves. Two for one. "Not so!" Stile cried, perceiving needless mayhem in the making. "This is my quarrel, foolish as it may be, not thine."

"With bad knees, fatigue from a marathon run, separated ribs, and a bruised hand—against that monster?" Hulk inquired. "This is a job for your bodyguard. I daresay a karate chop at the base of that horn would set the animal back."

The Stallion paused. He glanced at Kurrelgyre and his bitch, then at Hulk. He snorted. "No one dares call the Herd Stallion coward," Clip said. "But his proper quarrel is not with thee, werewolf, nor with the ogre. It is with the impostor. Let Stile confess he is no Adept, and he will be spared, and the foolish mare chastened."

"Yes," the Lady Blue agreed. "It were indeed folly to fight because of an impostor."

Such an easy solution! All parties agreed on the compromise. Except for Neysa, who knew the truth, and Kurrelgyre, who believed it, and Stile himself. "I abhor the prospect of bloodshed here, but I will not confess to a lie," Stile said firmly.

"Then show thy magic!" Clip said.

"Thou knowest mine oath—"

The Stallion snorted. Neysa looked up, startled but adamant. "Release him of his vow," Clip translated for Stile's benefit.

"Now wait!" Stile cried. "I will not tolerate coercion! You have no right—"

Kurrelgyre raised a cautioning hand. "I hold no great affection for this horny brute," he said, indicating the Stallion. "But I must advise thee: he has the right, friend. He is the Herd Stallion. Even as my pack obeys me, so must his herd, and every member of it, obey him. So must it ever be, in this frame."

The Stallion snorted again, imperatively. Slowly Neysa bowed her horn. She played one forlorn note.

"Thou art released," the werewolf said. "Now the challenge is fair. I may no longer interfere. Use thy magic to defend thyself, Adept."

Stile looked again at Neysa. She averted her gaze. Obviously she had been overruled. She did not like it, but it was, as the werewolf had pointed out, legitimate.

By the custom of this frame, Stile had been released. He could use his magic—and would have to, for the Stallion was bringing his horn to bear, and there was no doubting his intent; and not one wolf would come to Stile's defense. To avoid magic now would be in effect to proclaim a lie, and that would not only cost Stile his life, it would shame those who had believed in him. He had to prove himself—for Kurrelgyre's sake and Neysa's sake as well as his own. Even though that would give the Lady the victory she had so cleverly schemed for.

But Stile was unprepared. He had not formulated any devastating rhymes, and in this sudden pressure could think of none. His magic was diffuse, uncollected without music. In addition, he didn't really want to hurt the Stallion, who seemed to be doing a competent job of managing his herd, with the exception of his treatment of Neysa. Why should anyone believe a man who claimed to be able to do magic, but never performed? Such a claimant should be put to the proof—and that was what the Stallion was doing.

Stile saw the Lady Blue watching him, a half-smile on her face. She had won; she had forced him to prove himself. He would either manifest as the Blue Adept—or die in the manner of an impostor on the horn of the Stallion. Vindication or destruction! Beside her, Neysa remained with gaze downcast, the loser either way.

"I am sorry, Neysa," Stile said.

Stile brought out his harmonica. Now it was a weapon. He played an improvised melody. Immediately the magic formed. The Stallion noted the aura and paused, uncertain what it was. The wolves and other unicorns looked too, as that intangible mass developed and loomed. Ears twitched nervously.

Good—this gave him a chance to figure out an applicable verse. What he needed was protection, like that of a wall. Wall—what rhymed with wall? Ball, fall, hall, tall. Unicorn, standing tall—

Abruptly the Stallion charged. Stile jumped aside. He stopped playing his harmonica and cried in a singsong:

"Unicorn Stallion, standing tall—form around this one a wall."

Immediately he knew he had not phrased it properly; he had technically asked the unicorn to form a wall around Stile, which was backward. But the image in his mind was a brick wall two meters high, encircling the Stallion—make that six feet high, to align the measurements with the standard of this frame—and that was what formed. His music was the power, his words the catalyst—but his mind did the fundamental shaping.

A shower of red bricks fell from nowhere, landing with uncanny precision in a circle around the Stallion, now forming row on row, building the wall before their eyes. The Stallion stood amazed, not daring to move lest he get struck by flying bricks, watching himself be penned. The pack and the herd watched with similar astonishment, frozen in place. Hulk's mouth hung open; he had not believed in magic, really, until this moment. Kurrelgyre was smiling in slow, grim satisfaction, his faith vindicated. And the Lady Blue's surprise was the greatest of all.

Only Neysa was not discomfited. She made an "I told thee so!" snort and turned her posterior on Stile, showing that she still did not approve. But Stile was sure she *did* approve, secretly. Whatever this might cost her.

After a moment, Kurrelgyre hitched himself up to sit on the just-completed wall. He tapped it with his fingers, verifying its solidity, as he spoke to the unicorn inside. "Thou desirest still to match thy prowess against the magic of the Blue Adept, here in the Blue Demesnes? Note that he spares thee, thou arrogant animal, only showing his power harmlessly. He could as easily have dropped these bricks on thy bone head. Is it not meet for thee to make apology for thy doubt?"

The Stallion glared at him in stony silence. He could readily have leaped out of the enclosure, but it was beneath his dignity to try. The issue was not his jumping ability, but Stile's magic—which had now been resolved.

"Not the Stallion's but mine is the apology," the

Lady Blue said. "I thought this man no Adept. Now I know he is. To a fine detail, this performance is like unto that of my love. Yet—"

All heads turned to her, as she hesitated. Slowly she worked it out. "My husband was murdered by an Adept. Now an Adept in the likeness of my love comes, yet I know my love is dead. This could therefore be an impostor, claiming to hail from another frame, but more likely an Adept from this frame, using his magic to change his aspect so that none will suspect his true identity. The Adept who murdered Blue."

Now all heads turned to Stile, the gazes of wolves and unicorns alike turning uncertain and hostile. Stile realized with a chill that he had misjudged the nature of his challenge. His real opposition was not the Stallion—it was the Lady Blue. She would not suffer even the suspicion of an impostor in these demesnes. Not any longer. Her first line of defense had been broken down; this was her second. The Lady was dangerous; he could die by the sole power of her voiced suspicions.

Neysa snorted indignantly. She was mad at Stile now, but she believed in him. Yet it was apparent that most of the others were in doubt again. The infernal logic of the Lady!

How could he refute this new challenge? There was one other person who knew his identity—but that was the Yellow Adept. Best not to bring her into this! He would simply have to present his case, and give them opportunity to verify it.

"I am not the Blue Adept. I am his alternate self, from the other frame. Anyone who is able and willing to pass through the curtain and make inquiries can ascertain my existence there. I am like Blue in all things, but lack his experience of this world. I am not an impostor, but neither am I this Lady's husband. Call me the brother of Blue. I apologize to those of you who may have had misconceptions; it was not my intent to mislead you." It still felt funny, using "you" in this frame, but it was the correct plural form. "Were I some other Adept, I would have little reason to masquerade as Blue; I could set up mine own Demesnes of whatever color. My power of magic is real; why should I pretend to have another form than mine own?"

The others seemed mollified, but not the Lady Blue. "I would expect a murdering Adept to arrive prepared with a persuasive story. To come as a seeming savior, destroying the golem he himself had sent, to make himself appear legitimate. To emulate the form of magic that is Blue's. Why should he do this? I can think of two reasons, to begin. First, this would tend to conceal the murder he committed. Second, he might covet the things that are Blue's."

Kurrelgyre turned to her, his brow wrinkling. "An Adept of such power could create his own estate, as impressive as this, with less complication than this."

"Not quite," she said tightly.

"What has this estate, that a foreign Adept might covet and not be able to duplicate?"

The Lady hesitated, her color rising, but she had to answer. "It has me. It is said by some that I am fair—"

Telling point! "Fair indeed," Kurrelgyre agreed. "Motive enough. Yet if he honors the works of Blue and maintains the premises in good order—is this not what thou wishest?"

"To accept in these Demesnes the one who murdered my love?" she demanded, flashing. "I will not yield this proud heritage to that! The false Adept may destroy me with his magic, even as he destroyed my love, but never will he assume the mantle and privilege of Blue."

Kurrelgyre swiveled on the wall to face Stile. "I believe in thee, friend. But the Lady has a point. The magic of Adepts is beyond the fathoming of simple animals like ourselves. We can prove no necessary connection between Blue's alternate in Proton and thyself; that double could be dead also, and thou a construct adapted by magic, emulating the mode of Blue when in truth the real power lies in some other mode. We can all be deceived, and until we are assured of thy validity—"

Stile was baffled. "If neither my likeness nor my magic can convince her, and she will not take my word—"

"If I may ask two questions?" Hulk put in tentatively.

Stile laughed. "We already have more questions than answers! Go ahead and throw thine in the ring."

"For what was the Blue Adept noted, other than his appearance and his magic?"

"His integrity," the Lady said promptly. "Never did he tell a lie or otherwise practice deceit, ever in his whole life."

"Never has this one told a lie," Kurrelgyre said.

"That remains to be demonstrated," she retorted.

The werewolf shrugged. "Only time can demonstrate that quality. Was there nothing else, subject to more immediate trial?"

"His riding," the Lady said, brightening. "In all Phaze, only he could ride better than I. His love for animals was so great, especially horses—" She had to stop, for her emotion was choking her.

To have the love of such a woman! Stile thought. Her husband was dead, but she still defended him with all her power. She was right: another Adept might well covet her, and not merely for her beauty, and be willing to go to extraordinary lengths to win her.

Kurrelgyre turned to Stile. "How well dost thou ride?"

"I can answer that," Hulk said. "Stile is the finest rider on Proton. I doubt anyone in this frame either could match him on horseback."

The Lady looked startled. "This man can ride? Bareback on an untamed steed? I should be glad to put him to that test."

"No," Hulk said.

She glanced at him, frowning. "Thou guardest him, ogre, by preventing him from betraying incompetence on a steed?"

"I seek only to settle the issue properly," Hulk said. "We have seen that careless application settles nothing—such as Stile's demonstration of magic. For all the effect it had, he might as well not have bothered. To put him to a riding test now, when he has been weakened and injured—"

"There is that," Kurrelgyre agreed. "Yet the importance of this proof—"

"Which brings me to my second question," Hulk said. "Is the issue really between Stile and the Lady—or between the Lady and the mare?"

Lady and mare looked at each other, startled again. "He only *looks* like an ogre," Kurrelgyre murmured appreciatively. Then, to Stile: "He speaks sooth. Thy destiny must be settled by Lady and mare. They are the two with claims on thee. If thou provest thou art the Blue Adept, one of them must needs suffer. This is what brought both wolves and unicorns here."

Stile did not like this. "But—"

The Stallion honked from his enclave. "Only the finest of riders could break the least of unicorns," Clip translated. "This man conquered Neysa; we accept him as the Blue Adept."

Stile was astonished at this abrupt change on the part of the Stallion. "How couldst thou know I really—"

"We saw thee," Clip said. "We rooted for her to throw thee, but we can not claim she did. We recognize that whatever else thou art or art not, thou art indeed the finest rider of thy kind."

"But had she turned into a firefly—"

"She would then have admitted she could not conquer thee in her natural form," Clip said. "It matters not, now. No man ever rode like thee. The Stallion resented that, but now that he knows that was the mark of Blue—"

"I didn't really do it by myself," Stile said, remembering something. "I hummed, and that was magic, though I knew it not at the time. I used magic to stay on her."

"And unicorns are immune to magic," Clip said. "Except the magic of Adepts. Another Adept could have destroyed her, but never could he have ridden her. There is only one Adept we know of who can ride at all, and that is Blue. All this the Stallion considered before accepting thee."

"But I do not accept thee!" the Lady flared. "The unicorns could be in league with the false Adept, to foist an impostor on the Blue Demesnes. My love was a horseman, never partial to unicorns, nor they to him, though he would treat them on occasion if they deigned to come to him. The mare could have allowed this impostor to ride—"

Clip reacted angrily, but Kurrelgyre interposed. "Didst ever thou hear it mooted, Lady, that werewolves would collude with unicorns in aught?"

"Nay," she admitted. "The two are natural enemies."

"Then accept this word from this were: I have come to know this mare. She did not submit voluntarily, except in the sense that she refrained from using her own magic to destroy him. He conquered her physically—and then, when she saw what manner of man he was, the kind of man you describe as your lord, he conquered her emotionally. But first he did ride."

"Almost, I wish I could believe," the Lady murmured, and Stile saw the agony of her decision. She was not against him; she merely had to be sure of him, and dared not make an error.

Then she stiffened. "The mare could be easier to ride than other unicorns like to think," the Lady sniffed. "She is small, and not of true unicorn color; she could have other deficiencies."

Neysa stomped the ground with a forefoot, but did not otherwise protest this insult.

"She has no less spirit than any in this herd," Clip said evenly, speaking for himself now. "And even were she deficient, she remains a unicorn, a breed apart from common horses. No one but this man could have ridden her."

The Lady looked at him defiantly. "If he could ride an animal I could not, then would I believe."

"Therefore thou hast but to ride Neysa," Kurrelgyre pointed out to her. "Thou hast not the magic humming he had, but the mare remains tired from her long hard ride to reach this castle yestermorn. I ran with her all the way, unburdened, and I felt the strain of that travel—and I am a wolf. So I judge the challenge equivalent. In that manner thou canst prove Stile is no better rider than thee."

"She can't ride the unicorn!" Stile protested.

But the Lady was nodding, and so were the unicorns and werewolves. All were amenable to this trial, and thought it fair. Neysa, too, was glancing obliquely at the Lady, quite ready to try her strength.

"I maintain that anything thou canst ride in thy health, I can ride in mine," the Lady informed him. "There was no comparison between my lord and other men. He could have ridden a unicorn, had he so chosen."

The Stallion snorted angrily, and Stile needed no translation. The unicorns did not believe any normal human being could ride one of them, involuntarily. They had reason. Stile himself had not guessed what a challenge Neysa would be—until he was committed.

"Lady," Stile said. "Do not put thyself to this ordeal. No one can ride Neysa!"

"No one but thee?" Her disdain was eloquent.

Stile realized that it had to be. The issue had to be settled, and this was, by general consensus, a valid test. Any choice he, Stile, made between Lady and mare would mean trouble, and it seemed he could not have both. If the Lady and the unicorn settled it themselves, he would become the prize of the winner.

Or would he? If the Lady won, the Blue Demesnes would fall, for there would be no accredited Adept to maintain them, and the news would be out. If Neysa won, there would be no Lady Blue, for she would be dead. As he would have been dead, had Neysa thrown him, that first challenge ride. It was the way of the unicorn, the way of life in Phaze, and all of them knew it, including the Lady. She was putting her life on the line. Either way, Stile lost.

With all his magic power restored to him, he was helpless to affect the outcome, or to determine his own destiny. Beautiful irony! "Know thyself," the Oracle had said, without informing him what the knowledge would cost.

"I know this be hard for thee," the werewolf said. "Even as it was for me to do what I had to do, when I faced my sire. Yet thou must submit to the judgment of this lot. It is fair."

Fair! he thought incredulously. The outcome of this lot would be either death or a lie!

The lines of animals were expanding, forming a tremendous ring, bounded by the castle on one side and the magic wall on the other. The unicorns formed a half-circle, the werewolves another, complementing each other.

Neysa stood in the center of the new ring, the Lady beside her. Both were beautiful. Stile wished again that he could have both, and knew again that he could not. When he accepted the benefits of magic, he had also to accept its penalties. How blithely he had walked into this awful reckoning! If only he had not parked Neysa at the Blue Demesnes when he returned to Proton—yet perhaps this confrontation was inevitable.

The Lady made a dainty leap, despite her flowing gown, which was no riding habit. The moment she landed, Neysa took off. From a standing start to a full gallop in one bound, her four hooves flinging up circular divots—but the Lady hung on.

Neysa stopped, her feet churning up turf in parallel scrape-lines. The Lady stayed put. Neysa took off—sidewise. And backward. The Lady's skirt flared, but the Lady held on.

"She does know how to ride," Hulk remarked, impressed. "If I didn't know better, I'd swear that was you, Stile, in a dress. I've watched you win bronco-busting in the Game."

Stile was glumly silent. The Lady Blue could indeed ride, better than he had expected—but he knew she could not stay on the unicorn. When she fell, Neysa would kill her, if the fall itself did not. It was legitimate; it was expected. And what would he want with Neysa then?

The unicorn performed a backflip, then a four-spoked cartwheel, then a series of one-beat hops, followed by a bounce on her back. The Lady stayed on until the last moment, then jumped clear—and back on when Neysa scrambled to her feet.

Hulk was gaping. "What sort of animal is that? Those tricks are impossible!"

There was a chord-snort next to Stile. He glanced—and discovered the Herd Stallion beside him, front hooves comfortably crossed on the wall, eyes intent on the competition. "Not bad moves," Clip translated from the far side.

Neysa whirled and leaped, spinning about in air. The Lady's slippers flew off and her gown flung out so violently it rent; a fragment of blue gauze drifted to the ground. But her hands were locked in the unicorn's mane, and she was not dislodged.

Neysa did a sudden barrel-roll on the ground. Again the Lady jumped free—but a tattered hem of her garment was caught under the weight of the unicorn, trapping her. As the roll continued, the Lady was squeezed by the tightening cloth. She ripped her own gown asunder and danced free, abruptly nude.

"That is some figure of a woman!" Hulk breathed.

Neysa started to rise. The Lady grabbed her mane—and Neysa threw down her head on the ground, pinning the Lady's streaming golden hair beneath it. The Lady grabbed for the unicorn's ears, and Neysa lifted her head quickly; human hands could really hurt tender equine ears when they had to. Stile had not gone for the ears during his challenge ride; it was not his way. The Lady knew the tricks, all right! But Neysa had the end of the Lady's tresses clamped between her teeth, now. The unicorn knew the tricks too. Human intelligence in equine form—devastating! As the Lady tried to mount again, Neysa yanked her off balance by the hair.

"Beautiful!" Clip murmured.

But the Lady grasped her own hair with one hand and jammed her other fingers into Neysa's mouth where the bit would go on a horse. There was a separation there between the front teeth, used for ripping grass free of the ground, and the back teeth, used for chewing. Pressure in that gap could cause pain. Neysa's mouth opened under that expert inducement, and the Lady's hair was free. Then, as Neysa leaped away, the Lady sprang to her back again.

Neysa ran—but now the Lady was free of the liability of clothing, and had a more secure lodging than before. "She's winning!" Hulk said, obviously rooting for the Lady, forgetting in the excitement what this would mean to Stile.

Stile began to wonder. Was it possible that the Lady Blue could ride Neysa? She was, next to himself, the most expert rider he had seen.

The Stallion made an irate snort. "What's the matter with that mare?" Clip said. "She should have wiped out the rider by this time."

"She is torn by indecision," Kurrelgyre said. "If Neysa loses, she proves the Lady's belief that Stile is false. If Neysa wins, she vindicates him as the Blue Adept she wants him not to be. Would I could take from her that choice."

Stile kept his eyes forward, but felt a shiver. The werewolf had his bitch in the pack, even as Stile had Sheen in Proton. But Kurrelgyre obviously had developed a separate interest that cut across the lines of species—even as Stile had. Yet who could know Neysa and not like her and respect her?

"Yes," Stile agreed. He saw no acceptable outcome for this contest; whoever lost took away a major part of his own commitment. Neysa was his friend; the Lady represented his heritage. Which one was he to choose? Which one was fate about to choose for him? To choose—and eliminate, simultaneously?

"In the future, I will manage my destiny myself," Stile muttered. And heard, to his surprise, a snort of agreement from the Stallion.

Neysa galloped so fast that her mane and the Lady's hair flew out behind, the black and gold almost merging. Shadow and sunlight. She made turns that struck sparks from the rocks of the ground. She bucked and reared. But the Lady remained mounted.

Now the unicorn charged the castle. She hurdled the small moat with a magnificent leap, landed on her forefeet, and did her forward flip into the wall. There were growls of amazement from the wolves, and even an appreciative snort from the Stallion. Neysa was really trying now—but the Lady had been smart enough to disengage in time. When the unicorn's hind feet returned to the ground, the Lady was on again.

They hurdled the moat, outward bound, and charged across the arena toward the magic brick wall. Now Stile saw the fire jetting from Neysa's nostrils and the bellows-heaving of her barrel as she put forth her critical effort. The Lady was almost hidden, as she rode low, her head down beside Neysa's neck.

Stile watched in growing disquiet as the unicorn's horn bore on the wall. Stile was directly in its path; he saw the horn endwise, as a compressed spiral on Neysa's forehead, coming at him like the point of a rotary drill. Her eyes were wide and turning bloodshot, and her flaring nostrils were rimmed with red. Neysa was near her limit—and still the Lady clung fast. Stile felt mixed relief for the Lady, sorrow for the unicorn, and apprehension for himself; he was at the focus of this agony.

Then Neysa swerved aside, kicking up her rear. Her flank smashed into the wall, knocking loose the top row of bricks and breaking the mortar-seal on several lower courses. She rebounded, getting her footing, breathing fire—and the Lady was clinging to her side, away from the wall. Otherwise the Lady's leg would have been crushed—and Stile himself might have been struck, as he had been too absorbed in the charge to move out of its way. Only the curvature of the wall and Neysa's swerve had spared him. Stile caught a glimpse of the Lady's neck, shoulder and breast behind one blood-streaked arm; then steed and rider were away, prancing to the center of the arena.

The Stallion shook a brick off his back. Neither he nor Kurrelgyre had flinched, either. All three of them were powdered with reddish brick dust. But some of that red was sticky: whose blood was it?

"They're playing for keeps," Hulk murmured, awed.

"It is the way, in Phaze," Kurrelgyre assured him.

But now Neysa was tiring. She had extended herself for a day and a night to bring Stile here, and the intervening day had not been enough to restore her to full vitality. Her maneuvers were becoming less extreme. Her brushoff pitch against the wall had been her last fling. The Lady's head lifted, her gaze triumphant—and at the same time her mouth was sad. Had she, in her secret heart, wanted Stile to be vindicated, though it cost her her life? What kind of existence did this indomitable woman face with her husband gone, and her vulnerability now known to the world? Had she lost, she would have been dead—but would have died with the knowledge that the Blue Demesnes would survive.

Then, desperately, without real hope, Neysa experimented with alternate gaits. The one-, two-, three-, and four-beat gaits gave the Lady no trouble—but evidently she had not before encountered the unicorn specialty of the five-beat. Immediately Neysa felt the uncertainty in her rider; she picked up the pace, exaggerating the peculiar step. Her strength returned, for this last fling.

"What is that?" Hulk asked, amazed.

The Stallion snorted with satisfaction. "That is the unicorn strut," Clip answered. "We use it mostly in special harmonies, for counterpoint cadence. We had no idea she could do it so well."

Suddenly the tables had been turned. The Lady clung to the mane, but her body bounced about with increasing roughness, unable to accommodate this unfamiliar motion. Stile knew exactly how it felt. Riding was not simply a matter of holding on; the rider had to make constant adjustments of balance and position, most of them automatic, based on ingrained experience. A completely unfamiliar gait made these automatic corrections only aggravate the problem. Stile himself had analyzed the gait in time, but the Lady—

One of the Lady Blue's hands tore away from the mane. Her body slid half off. One good lunge, now, and Neysa would dump her. "Kill her!" Clip breathed.

Abruptly Neysa halted. The Lady recovered her grip, hung on for a moment—then released the mane and slid to the ground. The ride was over.

"The little fool!" Clip exclaimed. "She had the win!

Why didn't she finish it?" And the Stallion snorted in deep disgust.

"She has forfeited her place in the herd," Kurrelgyre said sadly. "In thy parlance, she threw the game."

Stile jumped off the wall and walked toward the unicorn and Lady, who both stood as if frozen, facing away from each other. As he walked, understanding came to him. Stile played his harmonica as he worked it out, gathering the magic to him.

Neysa, after the specter of defeat, had had the victory in range. But Neysa wanted Stile's welfare more than she wanted her own. She had finally, unwillingly, recognized the fact that he could fulfill his destiny only as the Blue Adept, complete with magic. Once she had proven that he alone could ride the unicorn, what could she gain by killing or even humbling the Lady—who was his natural mate? Neysa had ceded him to the Lady, so that he could have it all, knowing himself and his Demesnes exactly as the Oracle had decreed. She had understood that he was already half-smitten with his alternate's wife, and understood further that the Lady Blue was indeed worthy of him.

Neysa had sacrificed her own love for Stile's. She had shown the one person she had to, the Lady Blue, that Stile was no impostor; wolves and unicorns could doubt it if they wished, but the Lady could not. For Stile had mastered the unicorn strut without being thrown; he really *was* the better rider. That was Neysa's gift to Stile. And he—had to accept it. Neysa was his ultimate steed, but the Lady was his ultimate woman. He hardly knew her yet, but he knew his other self would have chosen wisely, and everything he had observed so far confirmed this. He also knew his alternate self of Phaze would have wanted Stile to take over—for the Blue Adept was him, in other guise.

The Lady Blue, however, was not yet his woman. Stile had merely qualified for the Tourney, in this sense, and had won the right to court her. He would have to prove himself in other ways than magical and in riding ability, showing that he was worthy of her love. He would have to demonstrate convincingly to her that he was as good as her husband had been. Perhaps he would not succeed, for she was so steadfastly loyal to her first love that a second love might be impossible. But in the interim, he knew she would accept him as the master of the Blue Demesnes, and support him publicly as she had the golem—for the sake of the reputation and works of Blue. That was all he had a right to expect. It was, for the moment, more than enough.

It was Neysa he had to deal with. She who had made it all possible—and now would go, excluded from the herd, departing in shame to fling herself off the same cliff where they had first come to terms. She had lived always with the hope that eventually the Herd Stallion would relent and allow her full membership in the herd. He would have, had she destroyed the Lady in approved fashion. But for a creature who yielded a draw in a contest she could have won, shaming the vanity of the herd, there would be no forgiveness. The rigors of species pride were harsh.

Stile had, in the naïveté of his conscience, turned Neysa loose when he had conquered her, making a sacrifice no other man would have—and won a better friend than he had known. Now she had returned the favor.

Stile's head turned as he walked, his gaze passing over the unicorns and werewolves. All were somber, watching him, knowing what had to be, knowing this was his parting with his most loyal friend. They felt sympathy for him, and for the mare, and it was a minor tragedy, but this was the way of it—in Phaze.

Damn it! he thought. He was not truly of this world, and this proved it. He had been raised to a different order of integrity, where blood sacrifices were not required. How could he tolerate this senseless loss? Yet he knew it was not senseless, here. The laws of this society were harsh but valid.

The magic gathered close as he played. The strange cloud of it spread about him—and, as he approached, about the Lady and the unicorn. But what good was magic, in an ethical dilemma? What spell could he make, to eliminate the need for what he knew had to be?

Stile came to stand before Neysa, playing the music that had been inspired by the sound of her horn. Her body was heaving with the recent extremity of her effort. Her mane was disheveled, with dry leaves in it and several strands hanging over the left side. There were flecks of blood on her back; she must have scratched herself when she did the back-smash against the castle wall. He wished he could make a little spell to heal it for her, but knew this was not proper now. Her gaze met his, dully; she was waiting only for him to bid her farewell.

Fare*well?* What irony! It was death he would bid her.

This reminded Stile obscurely of his race in the marathon, in the other frame. He had been almost dead on his feet, as Neysa was now, but he had won—as she had—and then tried to give it back to an opponent he respected. Again, he had made a friend. Surely he could salvage his relationship with Neysa, if only he had the wit to find the way!

What had the werewolf said about oaths? They superseded all relationships, conflicting with none, not even the male-female ones. Kurrelgyre's oath-friend could do no wrong by Kurrelgyre's bitch; the oath made that irrelevant.

The marathon. The oath. What had passed through his mind, when . . . ?

And he had it.

Stile set the harmonica aside. With the magic intense about him, he sang with impromptu melody: "My name is Stile, called the Blue Adept; Standing before thee I proffer mine oath: To the unicorn Neysa, companion and steed—Friendship forever, uniting us both."

For an instant it was as if a dense cloud had darkened the sun. A sudden, odd, insweeping breeze rustled the distant trees and fluttered the blue pennants on the castle and stirred the manes and hackles of the animals. Neysa's eyes widened. Her ears switched back and forth as comprehension came. She phased into girl-form, equine-form, firefly-form and back to unicorn, entirely nonplused.

The ripple of enchantment imploded about the two of them in soft heat, then rebounded outward in a circle. The turf changed color, passing through the hues of the rainbow and back to normal in a swiftly expanding ring. The ripple intersected the naked Lady, whose tangled hair scintillated momentarily, and went on, leaving that hair smoothly brushed.

The Lady turned. "Only perfect truth makes such splash," she murmured. "Only my lord had such power of magic."

Stile spread his arms. Neysa, overwhelmed, stepped forward, her horn lifted clear. Stile reached around her neck and chest and hugged her. "Never leave me, oath-friend," he murmured. He heard her low whinny of assent, and felt her velvet nuzzle at his shoulder. Then he disengaged and stepped back.

The Lady Blue came forward. She put her arms about Neysa. "Never again be there strife between us," she said, tears in her eyes. Neysa made a tiny snort of acceptance.

Now the wolves and unicorns came in, forming a ragged line, heedless of the mixing of species. In turn, each wolf sniffed noses with Neysa and each unicorn crossed horns, and went on. All of them were joining in the Oath of Friendship. Even her brother Clip came, and Kurrelgyre, and Hulk. Neysa accepted them all.

It was, Stile knew, the power of his spell. When he had phrased his oath in verse and music, he had performed magic—and wrought a greater enchantment than he had anticipated. The spell he had envisioned, though not completed in words, had flung outward to embrace the entire circle of creatures, compelling them all to share Stile's feeling. Neysa would not now be banned from the herd—or from the pack. She was friend to all. But she would remain with Stile, having accepted his power with his oath.

Only the Herd Stallion stood apart. He alone had resisted the compulsion of the enchantment. He did not interfere; he waited within his enclosure until the ceremony was over. Then he blew a great summoning blast of music and leaped over the wall. It had never truly restrained him; it had merely been the proof of the power of the Blue Adept, which power could as readily have been turned to a more destructive manifestation. Once the Herd Stallion had seen Stile was no impostor, his objection had ended. Now the unicorns rallied to him, galloping to form their formation. Playing as a mighty orchestra, they marched away.

Kurrelgyre shifted to wolf-form and bayed his own summons. His faith had also been vindicated, and his bitch had been satisfied. The wolves closed in about him, and the pack loped away in the opposite direction. In a moment only Stile, Neysa, the Lady Blue and Hulk remained by the Blue Demesnes.

Stile turned to the woman he would now be dealing with. Nothing was settled, either with her or with his anonymous murderer, or in the other frame. But it was a beginning. "Lady, wilt thou ride my steed?" he asked. There was no need to ask Neysa; as a friend she would do anything for him, and he for her. By the phrasing of his invitation, he was acknowledging that he had as yet only a partial claim on the Lady, and could not take her for granted. She was a challenge, not a friend.

The Lady Blue inclined her head, as regal in her nakedness as she had been in the gown. Lightly she mounted Neysa. Stile walked on one side, Hulk on the other. Together they approached the open castle.

ABOUT THE AUTHOR

It was not necessary, in England in 1934, to name a baby instantly; there was a grace period of a number of days. As the deadline loomed, the poor woman simply gave all the names she could think of: Piers Anthony Dillingham Jacob. The child moved to America, where it took three years and five schools to graduate him from first grade, because he couldn't learn to read. It was thus fated that he become a proofreader, an English teacher, or a writer. He tried them all, along with a dozen other employments—and liked only the least successful one. So he lopped off half his name, sent his wife out to earn their living, and concentrated on writing. That was the key to success; publishers would print material by an author whose name was short enough.

He sold his first story in 1962 and had his first novel, *Chthon*, published in 1967. His first fantasy in *The Magic of Xanth* Trilogy, *A Spell for Chameleon*, won the August Derleth Fantasy Award as the best novel in 1977. He has written approximately forty novels in the genres of science fiction, fantasy and martial arts.

He was married in 1956, right after graduating from college, to Carol Ann Marble. Their daughter Penny was born eleven years later, and their final daughter Cheryl in 1970. That was the beginning of a whole new existence, because little girls like animals. In 1978 they bought nice horses, and that experience, coupled with knee injuries in judo class, became *Split Infinity*. Piers Anthony is not the protagonist—he says he lacks the style—but Penny's horse Blue *is* the mundane model for the unicorn Neysa.

THE BLUE GUIDES

Countries

Austria
Belgium and Luxembourg
Channel Islands
China*
Corsica
Crete
Cyprus
Egypt
England
France
Germany
Greece
Holland
Hungary
Ireland
Northern Italy
Southern Italy
Malta and Gozo
Morocco
Portugal
Scotland
Sicily
Spain
Switzerland
Turkey: Bursa to Antakya
Wales
Yugoslavia

Cities

Boston and Cambridge
Florence
Istanbul
Jerusalem
London
Moscow and Leningrad
New York
Oxford and Cambridge
Paris and Versailles
Rome and Environs
Venice

Themes

Churches and Chapels of Northern England*
Churches and Chapels of Southern England*
Literary Britain and Ireland
Museums and Galleries of London
Victorian Architecture in Britain

in preparation

Frontispiece by Richard Doyle to Laurence Oliphant's Piccadilly *(1870)*

BLUE GUIDE

LITERARY BRITAIN

AND IRELAND

Ian Ousby

A & C Black
London

W W Norton
New York

Second edition 1990

Published by A & C Black (Publishers) Limited
35 Bedford Row, London, WC1R 4JH

Published in the United States of America by
W W Norton & Company, Inc.
500 Fifth Avenue, New York, NY 10110

Published simultaneously in Canada by
Penguin Books Canada Limited,
2801 John Street, Markham, Ontario L3R 1B4

ISBN 0-7136-3152-X

A CIP catalogue record for this book
is available from the British Library.

ISBN 0-393-30490-6 USA

Ian Ousby was educated at Cambridge and Harvard and has taught at universities in both England and America. His publications include *Bloodhounds of Heaven: The Detective in English Fiction from Godwin to Doyle*; with John L. Bradley, *The Correspondence of John Ruskin and Charles Eliot Norton; The Cambridge Guide to Literature in English* (editor); *The Englishman's England: Taste, Travel and the Rise of Tourism*; and *Blue Guide England.*

Printed and bound in Great Britain by
William Clowes Limited, Beccles and London

CONTENTS

Maps

INTRODUCTION

In academic circles at least, a formalistic approach to literature still holds sway, as it has done for some forty years or so. Practitioners of the various branches of higher literary criticism continue in their effort to restrict texts to the pages on which they are printed, chastely oblivious to the circumstances of writers' lives, the conditions under which they worked and published, the places where their books were written and the places with which they deal—actual, imagined or some delicate combination of the two. Yet to authors themselves and to general readers such factors have often seemed more than merely incidental. Above all, they are moved by what D.H. Lawrence in the first chapter of *Studies in Classic American Literature* called 'The Spirit of Place' and, indeed, may cherish the literary associations of a particular locale over its strictly historical significance. 'Don't talk to me of the Duke of Monmouth', commanded Tennyson on a visit to Lyme Regis, his imagination stimulated less by seventeenth-century politics than by Jane Austen's *Persuasion*. 'Show me the exact spot where Louisa Musgrove fell "and was taken up lifeless".'

Such reverence is not peculiar to Tennyson or his age. By the seventeenth century, antiquaries were already snatching hopefully at fragments of folklore to connect Warwickshire's highways and byways with Shakespeare's youth, Ben Jonson was celebrating Sir Philip Sidney's more certain connection with Penshurst in Kent, and (according to John Aubrey) Milton's birthplace on Bread Street was becoming an attraction for the curious during the writer's lifetime. And today Lyme itself, aided since Tennyson's time by its position on the southern edge of Hardy's 'Wessex' and more recently by the popularity of John Fowles' *The French Lieutenant's Woman*, continues to be a minor shrine for the literary pilgrim. Nor is there any lack of major shrines, especially prominent on the itineraries of those foreign visitors whose notions of England have been formed partly by its literature: Poets' Corner in Westminster Abbey, Haworth Parsonage in West Yorkshire, not to mention the various sights, varnished and unvarnished, that Stratford-upon-Avon can boast. In more general terms, the tourist industries of Dorset and Cumbria owe more than a little to the fame of Hardy and the Lake Poets respectively.

Admittedly, this approach to literature and to travel has its limitations, disappointments and dangers. Had he read his *Persuasion* carefully Tennyson's guide at Lyme would have been able to satisfy the poet's request, but even the most precisely realised scene in a book can prove elusive on the map. The places that can be found may sometimes disappoint, like the scenes of childhood, by being smaller than we envisaged them: both Hardy's 'Egdon Heath' and Blackmore's Doone Valley, for example, are larger in imagination than in actuality. Writers, too, are notorious for their tendency to frustrate the literal-minded researcher by moving real places across the country in obedience to imaginative requirements, by conflating several into one composite fictional entity, or simply by inventing a single place to epitomise the character of a whole terrain. On being asked to point out the building in Canterbury he had used as the model for Dr Strong's Academy in *David Copperfield* Dickens gave a reply that speaks for his profession: 'there were several that would do'.

Even those firmer landmarks constituted by writers' birthplaces, homes and graves are subject to their own particular hazards. The Rev. Francis Gastrell, eighteenth-century owner of New Place in Stratford, was driven to destroy a mulberry tree that Shakespeare had supposedly planted because so many people wanted to see it. We do things differently today and modern vandalism is more likely to take the form of excessive commercialisation than outright destruction. Too often the visitor finds his fond imaginings brought unpleasantly down to earth by advertisements for Shakespeare teas or Brontë ice creams—products that contribute little to his appreciation of literature, topography or, for that matter, food. Places that do not lend themselves to such intense exploitation are still not immune from the natural processes of change. The example of Joyce's Dublin is especially poignant, for surely no other writer of this century has empowered an urban landscape with such rich delight and exactitude. But Joyce's re-creation of his native city in *Ulysses* took place at a necessary remove, in Trieste and Zurich and Paris: it was an act of reminiscence, both intensely personal and profoundly scholarly, not of immediate observation. In conversation with Frank Morley, Joyce recommended the same distance to his readers: 'if you wished to enjoy *Ulysses*, you should not make enjoyment more difficult by going to look at a changed Dublin'.

Yet the topographical approach to literature can still bring both innocent pleasure and real enlightenment. To stand in the quiet Chelsea house where Carlyle so frequently interrupted work to complain about the noise of his neighbours' chickens, to compare the modest homeliness of Hardy's birthplace with the barren respectability of the house he built for himself in later life: these acts bring us closer to the impalpable atmosphere which spilled naturally over from writers' lives into their books. Lawrence's Midlands, Arnold Bennett's Five Towns, and even those parts of London where change has not completely banished the occasional whiff of Dickens or Dr Johnson all have their particular story still to tell. However insensibly, they deepen our acquaintance with literature. The relations between topography and text can eventually become reciprocal: knowledge of place enhances our appreciation of literature, just as knowledge of literature sharpens our enjoyment of place. We make the discovery Henry James made in *English Hours*: 'Reading over Thackeray to help me further to Winchelsea, I became conscious, of a sudden, that Winchelsea—which I already in a manner knew—was helping me further to Thackeray'.

The present volume is designed to aid such discovery by giving an account of the associations between writers and the British places they knew and wrote about. Given the sheer size of this subject, much remains to be said about the criteria by which this book has been compiled and the methods by which it has been organised. Its scope embraces Scotland, Wales and Ireland as well as England, a wide and rich terrain but one that excludes consideration of those foreign travels which have played so crucial a part in the lives of British writers from Chaucer to Joyce. For obvious reasons the authors treated have been limited to dead ones, while the term 'author' itself has been taken to mean a writer of imaginative literature—a definition that omits essayists, political economists, theologians, philosophers, monarchs with a penchant for diaries or pamphlets, and all the other various folk who sometimes find shelter under that large umbrella which the universities call 'English Literature'. The distinction, of course, is by no means as neat as it may at first appear and an indulgent policy has been adopted towards, for example, those Grub Street writers of the eighteenth century who made a movable feast of their talents. By the same token, room has been found for writers like Pepys and Ruskin who, without being imaginative in the commonly accepted sense of the term, yet managed to establish a strong connection with place in their work and so to leave their imprint on our landscape.

Although such guidelines provide both breadth and variety, they are not meant to guarantee anything like completeness. Many lesser figures have been omitted, often regretfully, as have minor events in the lives and works of all the writers dealt with—especially the most productive ones and those whose circumstances, whether affluent or indigent, made them relentlessly peripatetic. A similar form of discretion has been applied to the inclusion of places. The location of a writer's birth and death is always indicated, when these facts are known, but otherwise there has seemed little point in giving more than passing mention, if that, to places so despoiled that they have lost their original character. However pleasant it may be to read nostalgic evocations of bygone places over the winter fireside, it is usually unrewarding to gaze at the modern roundabout or office block or shopping centre under which they have disappeared.

Above all, this is a guidebook. It is organised not as a gazetteer of placenames but as an aid for travellers seeking to further their interest in writers with whom they are already tolerably familiar. The first section assigns major writers individual entries, which are subdivided region by region. Inside each region the account is presented according to the tried and tested *Blue Guide* method of convenient itineraries or outings. The second section limits itself to shorter entries for lesser figures—that is to say, writers of lesser reputation or achievement, those who make less conspicuous or precise use of place in their work, and those whose lives are too obscure to make topographical identification easy. Because these entries are relatively brief a region-by-region division is not needed and the account is loosely organised according to the chronology of the subject's life.

The headnotes added to both types of entry provide a selected list of the subject's main works and their dates—the dates given for plays referring to publication rather than first performance, since this is sometimes an uncertain matter in the case of early dramatists. In the entries themselves generous use is made of quotations to remind the reader how a particular writer viewed a particular place or used it in his work. The sources of quotations are indicated by chapter numbers for novels, act and scene numbers for plays and line or stanza numbers for poems of any length.

Properties open to the public are listed in the small-print notes at the end of each short entry and at the end of each route in the long entries. In the majority of cases these notes do not quote opening times, which vary so greatly from year to year that any details supplied would quickly become misleading. Instead, a telephone number is provided as a last resort for the reader seeking up-to-date information about a particular property. Usually, however, such information can be obtained from one or other of the following sources: the nearest Tourist Information Centre; the annual index publications entitled *Historic Houses, Castles and Gardens* and *Museums and Galleries in Great Britain and Ireland*; the pamphlets and handbooks issued by organisations like the National Trust, the National Gardens Scheme, the National Trust for Scotland, the

Historic Irish Tourist Houses and Gardens Association Ltd, English Heritage and its counterparts in Scotland and Wales.

It has seemed safe to be specific about opening hours only for those English Heritage properties which observe a standardised system, indicated in the notes by the following phrases:

Standard opening: Good Friday to 30 September, daily 10.00–18.00; 1 October to Maundy Thursday, daily 10.00–16.00; closed on Mondays, Christmas Eve, Christmas Day, Boxing Day and New Year's Day.

Summer standard opening: Good Friday to 30 September, daily 10.00–18.00.

Many smaller English Heritage properties are open at any reasonable time.

Cathedrals, churches, public parks and public cemeteries are not listed in the notes, since it can be assumed that they are open during normal daylight hours. (Many parish churches are kept locked nowadays as a protection against vandalism, but there is usually a notice outside giving instructions for obtaining the key.) Oxford and Cambridge colleges are not listed except when a library with specific opening arrangements of its own is mentioned. Otherwise, access is usually restricted to the courts or quads, gardens and (when they are not in use) halls and chapels; staircases and rooms occupied by undergraduates or fellows are strictly off limits. In addition, the pressure of tourism has forced colleges in both universities to restrict the times when the public is admitted. The visitor to Oxford will usually find more colleges open in the afternoons than the mornings; Cambridge should be avoided during the examination period (mid April to mid June) when the more heavily trafficked colleges are closed.

A few general guidelines about opening arrangements may help strangers to Great Britain or the Republic of Ireland. They will fare much better between Easter (or the beginning of April) and the end of October, dates which mark the outer limits of the continually extending tourist season. In the winter months, the following are likely to be closed: many buildings owned by the National Trust and the National Trust for Scotland (though not necessarily their grounds); most privately owned country houses; and some smaller museums, particularly those outside major centres or in areas heavily dependent on the tourist trade. Even in the tourist season smaller National Trust properties tend to close for one or two days a week, and only the largest privately owned country houses are open every day of the week. Virtually all sites are closed on Christmas Day, Boxing Day and New Year's Day. The effect of other public holidays on arrangements for a particular property should be checked in advance. It should also be remembered that, though England and Wales share the same calendar of festivals, Scotland, Northern Ireland and the Republic of Ireland have their own different calendars.

Telephone numbers in the Republic of Ireland have been given in the form used to make a call from within the country.

ACKNOWLEDGEMENTS

Preparing this new edition has greatly extended the already long list of staff at galleries, museums, country houses, Tourist Information Centres, literary societies, cathedrals, etc. to whom I stand indebted for help. The fact that they are now too numerous to mention in no way lessens my sense of gratitude. At Cambridge University Library the staff have been long-suffering in giving me assistance, and I owe a particular debt to Janice Fairholm for making my work in the West Room so easy and pleasant. Graham Coster, Geoffrey Day, Valerie Eliot, Robert Mathews, John Mayhew, Philip Stevens and Mary Turner have all contributed valuable information, suggestions or corrections, while Annette Kelley has given generous encouragement. Gemma Davies and Lisa Adams have been as patient and knowledgeable as editors for this edition as Tom Neville was for the first.

I gratefully acknowledge the following for permission to reproduce copyright material: Edward Arnold (Publishers) Ltd; Faber & Faber Ltd; Harcourt Brace Jovanovich, Inc.; David Higham Associates Ltd; John Murray (Publishers) Ltd; A.D. Peters and Co Ltd; Laurence Pollinger Ltd; Mr George Sassoon; The Society of Authors; A.P. Watt Ltd. The map of Dublin is based on the map of Joyce's Dublin from *Literary Landscapes of the British Isles* (Bell & Hyman).

I would also like to thank the following for permission to reproduce their photographs as illustrations: Ashmolean Museum (pages 190, 343, 376); British Information Service, New York (page 272); Syndics of Cambridge University Library (frontispiece, pages 21, 24, 39, 52–53, 55, 58, 84–85, 94, 103, 114, 117, 119, 121, 148, 157, 168, 184, 205, 231, 234, 243, 267, 281, 314, 328, 351, 379, 385, 396); Courtauld Institute of Art (page 327); Dickens House (page 42); Guildhall Library, London (pages 134–142); King's College, Cambridge (pages 187, 250); Marquess of Northampton (page 203); National Gallery of Ireland (page 408); National Portrait Gallery (pages 47, 110, 247, 285, 332, 339); Nottinghamshire Public Libraries (page 201); Ruskin Galleries, Bembridge (page 341); Shakespeare Birthplace Trust (pages 147, 151); Trinity College, Dublin (page 372); Vogue (page 73).

A NOTE ON FURTHER READING

The interest in writers and places described in my introduction has bred a large attendant literature. The earliest example I have seen is J. Storer's *Cowper, Illustrated by a Series of Views, in, or near, the Park Of Weston-Underwood, Bucks*, published in 1803. A hundred years afterwards the bookshelf had lengthened to include a host of volumes of the 'homes and haunts', 'inns and taverns', 'in the footsteps' variety, some of them treating figures more cherished by the Victorians than by later readers and many showing greater familiarity with the books they discuss than their modern counterparts do. These modern counterparts range from slender volumes garnished with appetising photographs through personal evocations of literary rambles to scholarly gazetteers and specialist studies. The most restricted in scope are usually the best. Outstanding among book-length studies are Richard Ellmann's *Ulysses on the Liffey* (1972) and Denys Kay-Robinson's *Hardy's Wessex Reappraised* (1972) and, among pamphlets, Geoffrey Fletcher's *Pocket Guide to Dickens' London* (1976) and Graham Nicholls' *Literary Lichfield* (1981). Richard Holmes' *Footsteps: Adventures of a Romantic Biographer* (1985) follows a trail outside the British Isles but offers a rich commentary on the ways that place can inform a writer's life and work. Although the list could easily be extended, it may be more valuable to point out that some of the best studies come from writers who are themselves considered in this volume. Edward Thomas' *A Literary Pilgrim in England* (1917) is still immensely readable, particularly in the handsome illustrated edition by Michael Justin Davis (1985). Henry James' *English Hours* (1905), without attempting any of the humbler duties of the guidebook, shows him to be the very model of the traveller sensitive to literary associations.

A NOTE ON BLUE GUIDES

The Blue Guide series began in 1918 when Muirhead Guide-Books Limited published 'Blue Guide London and its Environs'. Finlay and James Muirhead already had extensive experience of guide-book publishing: before the First World War they had been the editors of the English editions of the German Baedekers, and by 1915 they had acquired the copyright of most of the famous 'Red' Handbooks from John Murray.

An agreement made with the French publishing house Hachette et Cie in 1917 led to the translation of Muirhead's London Guide, which became the first 'Guide Bleu'—Hachette had previously published the blue-covered 'Guides Joanne'. Subsequently, Hachette's 'Guide Bleu Paris et ses Environs' was adapted and published in London by Muirhead. The collaboration between the two publishing houses continued until 1933.

In 1931 Ernest Benn Limited took over the Blue Guides, appointing Russell Muirhead, Finlay Muirhead's son, editor in 1934. The Muirheads' connection with Blue Guides ended in 1963 when Stuart Rossiter, who had been working on the Guides since 1954, became house editor, revising and compiling several of the books himself.

The Blue Guides are now published by A & C Black, who acquired Ernest Benn in 1984, so continuing the tradition of guide-book publishing which began in 1826 with 'Black's Economical Tourist of Scotland'. The Blue Guide series continues to grow: there are now more than 35 titles in print with revised editions appearing regularly and many new Blue Guides in preparation.

SYMBOLS AND ABBREVIATIONS

As in other *Blue Guides* asterisks (*) and double asterisks (**) draw attention to places of special interest, whether individual buildings or more general areas, but in this volume the criteria are necessarily different. To qualify, a place has to be interesting in its own right and also important to the writer under discussion. Thus Hatfield House, which receives a well deserved asterisk in *Blue Guide England*, does not get one when it is mentioned in the entry for Dickens since his connection with the house was only slight. By the same token Carlyle's House, double asterisked in the entry for Carlyle, gets no distinction when it crops up in connection with Tennyson and Ruskin, mere visitors there. It is hardly necessary to add that, though the system of asterisks may have an appearance of objectivity, it is inevitably the vehicle for personal opinion. Readers will no doubt quickly detect my prejudices, without necessarily sharing them.

In quotations from verse an oblique stroke marks a break between lines.

Abbreviations for points of the compass, days of the week and months of the year will be either familiar or self-explanatory, but some others may require explanation:

aetat.=age

b.=born

Bk=Book

C=century

c=(circa) approximately

Ch.=Chapter

d.=died

DoE=The Department of the Environment, which since the creation of the English Heritage now administers only royal palaces in England.

English Heritage=The popular name for the Historic Buildings and Monuments Commission, which in 1984 assumed responsibility for all English properties formerly administered by the Department of the Environment, except royal palaces.

n.d.=not dated

NGS=The National Gardens Scheme, an independent charitable trust which supervises the opening of private gardens to the public. Since opening days vary greatly from year to year, details are not given in my text and readers are referred to the annual listing available from bookshops or directly from NGS at 57 Lower Belgrave Street, London SW1W 0LR.

No(s).=Number(s)

NT=The National Trust

NTS=The National Trust for Scotland

q.v. (qq.v.)=(*quod vide*) see entry (entries) for this name (these names)

Rte=Route

s.v.=(*sub verbo*) see entry under this word

Vol.=Volume

PART ONE

CHARLES DICKENS

b. Portsmouth, Hampshire, 1812; d. Gad's Hill, Kent, 1870. *Sketches by Boz* (1836); *The Pickwick Papers* (1836–37); *Oliver Twist* (1838); *Nicholas Nickleby* (1839); *The Old Curiosity Shop* (1841); *Barnaby Rudge* (1841); *A Christmas Carol* (1843); *Martin Chuzzlewit* (1844); *Dombey and Son* (1848); *David Copperfield* (1850); *Bleak House* (1853); *Hard Times* (1854); *Little Dorrit* (1857); *A Tale of Two Cities* (1859); *The Uncommercial Traveller* (1861); *Great Expectations* (1861); *Our Mutual Friend* (1865); *The Mystery of Edwin Drood* (unfinished; 1870).

In the Preface to *The Uncommercial Traveller* Dickens gave this description of himself:

> I am both a town traveller and a country traveller and am always on the road. Figuratively speaking, I travel for the great house of Human Interest Brothers, and have rather a large connection in the fancy goods way. Literally speaking, I am always wandering here and there from my rooms in Covent Garden, London—now about the city streets, now about the country byroads—seeing many little things, and some great things, which, because they interest me, I think may interest others.

It makes a fitting introduction to a man whose life was restlessly mobile. He began his career as a touring election reporter and ended it, to large extent, as a travelling reader from his own published works. His private life was characterised by a love of moving house, an eager interest in new coastal resorts where he might holiday and a willingness to take his amateur theatrical productions anywhere that would welcome them. The result was an unusually detailed knowledge of England's various regions—though not of Scotland, Wales or Ireland—which had a vivid impact on his writings. Kent (Rte 12) and Eastern England (Rte 17) stand out in particular.

It is also fitting that the passage from *The Uncommercial Traveller* should identify Dickens first as a 'town traveller' and cite London as the centre from which his wanderings begin. For London was the hub round which both his professional and personal life revolved, the 'magic lantern' (to use his own striking phrase) whose varied sights continually informed his fiction. Yet a word of caution is necessary about the changes that have overtaken the city whose former topography he knew so intimately. Of the twenty-two addresses he inhabited in London only one, in Doughty Street (Rte 1), survives intact; the two grandest, No. 1 Devonshire Terrace near the York Gate of Regent's Park and Tavistock House in Tavistock Square, have vanished beneath later development. Major thoroughfares he frequented, like the Strand and Holborn, have changed almost beyond recognition while poorer sections and much of London's dockland would now seem to him a foreign country.

Dickens himself would not necessarily have lamented such transformations. For his first London residence in Camden Town (Rte 9) he seems to have felt a marked antipathy, while his friend and biographer John Forster remarked that 'any special regard for houses he had lived in was not a thing noticeable in him'. For ancient buildings, particularly public ones, he felt no intrinsic respect, taking satisfaction in the burning of the old Houses of Parliament in 1834. The jerry-built slums which were Victorian England's most distinctive contribution to the urban landscape inspired real horror. The Dickensian pilgrim of today need not greatly regret these changes either, for, by using a selective eye, he will find probably more surviving and well preserved buildings—not only in London but throughout the country—than can be connected with the name of any other English writer.

London

1 Holborn to the City

This route, the longest but also the richest of the London itineraries in this section, encompasses Dickens' only remaining London home, as well as legal London and Fleet Street, two of the areas he knew best and which have undergone least change. It ends in the financial district of the City.

From Russell Square Underground Station (Piccadilly Line) we walk east along Guilford Street. To the left lie Coram Fields, site of the Foundling Hospital (now at No. 40 Brunswick Square) established by Captain Thomas Coram in 1739. Only its gateway survives but readers of *Little Dorrit* will remember that the aptly nicknamed Tattycoram, rebellious servant to Pet Meagles, was brought up here.

A right turn leads to Doughty Street and *Dickens House (No. 48), a handsome terraced house of three storeys, attic and basement which Dickens rented between 1837 and 1839, following his marriage to Catherine Hogarth, for £80 a year. While living here he finished *Pickwick Papers* and wrote *Oliver Twist* and *Nicholas Nickleby*, as well as suffering the shock of his sister-in-law Mary's sudden death. Now owned and administered by the Dickens Fellowship, the house has not entirely lost its former atmosphere in the process of becoming a museum. Apart from the most comprehensive Dickens library in the world, it contains portraits, letters, personal relics and (in the Suzannet Gift of 1971) parts of the manuscripts of *Pickwick Papers* and *Nicholas Nickleby*. The basement houses a replica of the Dingley Dell kitchen from *Pickwick Papers*.

We continue down John Street, the southern extension of Doughty Street, to the junction with Theobald's Road, where a left turn leads to the Gray's Inn Road, which is followed south. On the right is Gray's Inn, one of the four Inns of Court and to Dickens ('Chambers' in *The Uncommercial Traveller*) a 'stronghold of Melancholy' and 'one of the most depressing institutions in brick and mortar, known to the children of men'. Mr Pickwick's long-suffering solicitor, Mr Perker, had chambers at an unspecified location here, while in South Square (then Holborn Court), beyond the Hall and to the left, Dickens worked at the excellently preserved No. 1 as a clerk for the firm of Ellis and Blackmore in 1827 and 1828, when he was 15. At the top of a 'crazy old staircase' in No. 2 (rebuilt) next door Tommy Traddles lived after his marriage to Sophy and was visited by David Copperfield in Chapter 59 of the novel.

Beyond Gray's Inn, on the left of Gray's Inn Road, Brooke's Court, a right on Leather Lane and a left on Greville Street give access to Bleeding Heart Yard (right). In *Little Dorrit* the Yard is the home of the Plornishes, the site of Doyce and Clennam's factory, and the property of the apparently philanthropic Mr Casby, a place:

> with some relish of ancient greatness about it. Two or three mighty stacks of chimneys, and a few large dark rooms which had escaped being walled and subdivided out of recognition of their old proportions, gave the Yard a character. It was inhabited by poor people, who set up their rest among its faded glories, as Arabs of the desert pitch their tents among the fallen stones of the Pyramids; but there was a family sentimental feeling prevalent in the Yard, that it had a character. (Ch. 12)

Today most of even that tenuous character has gone, though a few reminders still linger.

Gray's Inn Road ends with Holborn, at a point opposite the distinctive half-timbered frontage of *Staple Inn. Despite restoration, war-time bombing and the loss of its former status as an Inn of Chancery, Staple Inn retains some of the rural peace that led Mr Snagsby of *Bleak House*, a man much in need of solace, to seek refuge here and caused Dickens himself to describe it in these terms in *The Mystery of Edwin Drood*:

> It is one of those nooks, the turning into which out of the clashing street, imparts to the relieved pedestrian the sensation of having put cotton in his ears, and velvet soles on his boots. It is one of those nooks where a few smoky sparrows twitter in smoky trees, as though they called to one another, 'Let us play at country', and where a few feet of garden mould and a few yards of gravel enable them to do that refreshing violence to their tiny understandings. (Ch. 11)

Mr Grewgious, the kindly solicitor in *Edwin Drood*, had chambers in the second court at the building on the left with the inscription 'PJT' over its door. Dickens humorously interprets the initials to mean 'Perhaps John Thomas', 'Perhaps Joe Tyler' or 'Pretty Jolly Too' (Ch. 11), though in fact they commemorate President James Taylor of the Society of Antients of Staple Inn.

Beyond Staple Inn to the east we come to Furnival Street, which leads to the tiny Took's Court, on the right. This appears under the transparent disguise of 'Cook's Court' in *Bleak House*—'a shady place' (Ch. 10) where Mr Snagsby conducts his business as a law stationer under the watchful eye of his wife. By turning right on to Cursitor Street at the end of Took's Court we join Chancery Lane opposite the gatehouse entrance to *Lincoln's Inn, perhaps the most impressive and best preserved of the Inns of Court, as well as the one most pervaded by Dickensian associations. The 15C Old Hall facing the entrance was until 1873 occupied by the Court of Chancery and is hence the scene of the memorable opening to *Bleak House*:

> On such an afternoon, if ever, the Lord High Chancellor ought to be sitting here—as here he is—with a foggy glory round his head, softly fenced in with crimson cloth and curtains, addressed by a large advocate with great whiskers, a little voice, and an interminable brief, and outwardly directing his contemplation to the lantern in the roof, where he can see nothing but fog. On such an afternoon some score of members of the High Court of Chancery bar ought to be—as here they are—mistily engaged in one of the ten thousand stages of an endless cause, tripping one another up on slippery precedents, groping knee-deep in technicalities, running their goat-hair and horse-hair warded heads against walls of words and making a pretence of equity with serious faces, as players might. On such an afternoon the various solicitors in the cause, some two or three of whom have inherited it from their fathers, who made a fortune by it, ought to be—as are they not?—ranged in a line, in a long matted well (but you might look in vain for truth at the bottom of it) between the registrar's red table and the silk gowns, with bills, cross-bills, answers, rejoinders, injunctions, affadavits, issues, references to masters, masters'

> reports, mountains of costly nonsense, piled before them. Well may the court be dim, with wasting candles here and there; well may the fog hang heavy in it, as if it would never get out; well may the stained-glass windows lose their colour and admit no light of day into the place; well may the uninitiated from the streets, who peep in through the glass panes in the door, be deterred from entrance by its owlish aspect and by the drawl, languidly echoing to the roof from the padded dais where the Lord High Chancellor looks into the lantern that has no light in it and where the attendant wigs are all stuck in a fog-bank!

Beyond the Old Hall are the spacious and handsome Lincoln's Inn Fields. In Chapter 23 of *David Copperfield* Betsey Trotwood took lodgings at 'a kind of private hotel' here, mainly because of its convenient exit in the roof, 'my aunt being firmly persuaded that every house in London was going to be burnt down every night'. No. 58, a handsome 18C house in the style of Inigo Jones with 19C alterations, on the west side of the Fields, was the home of Dickens' friend John Forster between 1834 and 1856. Dickens made it the residence of Mr Tulkinghorn, the sinister and close-mouthed lawyer in *Bleak House*, where it is first described in Chapter 10.

The Old Curiosity Shop on Portsmouth Street, reached from the SW corner of Lincoln's Inn Fields, owes its name to the commercial opportunism of a late-Victorian proprietor rather than to any genuine connection with the novel.

Chancery Lane continues south to Fleet Street. To the right of the junction stood Wren's Temple Bar, called a 'leaden-headed old obstruction' in Chapter 1 of *Bleak House*, marking the formal boundary between Westminster and the City proper. (Increased traffic made its removal necessary in 1878, and it now stands as an entrance to Theobalds Park, off A10 near Waltham Cross.) The Strand to the west is explored in Rte 3. The present route continues east along Fleet Street towards Ludgate Circus.

The first notable site, immediately south of the present Temple Bar Memorial, is No. 1 Fleet Street, Child's Bank (now assimilated into Williams and Glyn's Bank). Though the present building dates from 1878 Child's itself is one of London's oldest banking institutions and served as the model for 'Tellson's Bank' in *A Tale of Two Cities*:

> an old-fashioned place, even in the year one thousand seven hundred and eighty ... very small, very dark, very ugly, very incommodious ... After bursting open a door of idiotic obstinacy with a weak rattle in its throat, you fell into Tellson's down two steps, and came to your senses in a miserable little shop, with two little counters, where the oldest of men made your cheque shake as if the wind rustled it, while they examined the signature by the dingiest of windows, which were always under a shower-bath of mud from Fleet Street, and which were made the dingier by their own iron bars proper, and the heavy shadow of Temple Bar. (Bk 2, Ch. 1)

Shortly beyond and also on the south side of the street Middle Temple Lane gives access to the charming Fountain Court (right), a place of 'slow vegetation' where, according to *Martin Chuzzlewit*, Ruth Pinch was in the habit of meeting her brother Tom (Ch. 45) and where she later took to meeting her lover John Westlock (Ch. 53).

On the north side of Fleet Street, after the junction with Chancery Lane, stands the gatehouse entrance to Clifford's Inn Passage, though the site of the former Inn itself is now occupied by a block of flats. Here Tip, brother to Little Dorrit, worked for an attorney and 'languished ... for six months and at the expiration of that term, sauntered back one evening with his hands in his pockets, and incidentally observed to his sister that he was not going back again' (Ch. 7). In Book 1, Chapter 8 of *Our Mutual Friend* the rather more enterprising 'John Rokesmith', as John Harmon calls himself for most of the novel, uses Clifford's Inn as the scene of the interview that leads to his becoming Mr Boffin's secretary. Immediately beyond we find St Dunstan in the West, a handsome church of 1831 by John Shaw. On their way from Lincoln's Inn Fields to Doctors' Commons David Copperfield and his aunt Betsey Trotwood stopped to watch the jacks of the 17C clock strike noon.

Johnson's Court, leading from the N side of the street, once housed the offices of Chapman and Hall, publishers of the *Monthly Magazine*, to whom in 1833 the young Dickens delivered 'stealthily one evening at twilight, with fear and trembling' his first literary attempt—a sketch called 'A Dinner at Poplar Walk' but reprinted in *Sketches by Boz* (1836) as 'Mr Minns and His Cousin'. *Pickwick Papers* began a more famous and enduring association between Dickens and the publishing firm. In Wine Office Court but entered from No. 145 Fleet Street is the Cheshire Cheese, a restaurant famous as a literary gathering place since the 18C but now perhaps

Ludgate Hill by Gustav Doré. From Blanchard Jerrold London: A Pilgrimage *(1872)*

over-celebrated. It was, inevitably, familiar to Dickens and he may have had it in mind as the scene of Sydney Carton and Charles Darnay's meal in Book 2, Chapter 4 of *A Tale of Two Cities*, just after the former has aided the latter's acquittal from a charge of High Treason at the Old Bailey.

Off Whitefriars Street, on the S side of Fleet Street almost opposite Wine Office Court, we find the picturesquely named Hanging Sword Alley, where Jerry Cruncher of *A Tale of Two Cities* has his lodgings and from which he makes his nocturnal forays as body-snatcher.

From Ludgate Circus we ascend Ludgate Hill. Immediately to the left stood La Belle Sauvage Inn, headquarters of Tony Weller, in *Pickwick Papers*. Behind Seacoal Lane on the same side of the Hill stood the Fleet Prison, where Mr Pickwick's confinement for debt began in Chapter 50 of the novel. At the end of Old Bailey, again to the left, the Central Criminal Court covers the site occupied until 1902 by Newgate Prison. Fagin spent a memorable night in the jail (Chapter 52 of *Oliver Twist*) while awaiting public execution in Newgate Street beyond; Pip visited it with Wemmick as his guide in Chapter 32 of *Great Expectations*, before returning to Mr Jaggers' offices in Little Britain (reached by a right turn on Newgate Street and a left up King Edward Street). The destruction of the 18C prison by the Gordon Rioters is described in *Barnaby Rudge*, Chapters 58ff.

At the top of Ludgate Hill we reach St Paul's Churchyard where, in Chapter 23 of *David Copperfield*, Betsey Trotwood met the mysterious man who David later discovered was her estranged husband. On Dean's Court to the south stands the handsome Old Deanery. It is the one surviving remnant of Doctors' Commons, where Dickens came to work as a legal reporter in 1829 and Mr Jingle obtained the marriage license he never got the chance to use (Chapter 10 of *Pickwick Papers*).

We follow Cannon Street, the eastern continuation of St Paul's Churchyard, make an oblique left up Queen Victoria Street and change to Cornhill at Bank Underground Station and the Bank of England. Near the top of Cornhill the little St Michael's Alley (right) leads to the George and Vulture, which retains the atmosphere of the days when it served as a recurring location in *Pickwick Papers* and as Mr Pickwick's London lodging after circumstances made it advisable for him to leave Mrs Bardell's house. Of the several scenes taking place here perhaps the most notable is in Chapter 40, when Messrs Namby and Smouch arrive to take Mr Pickwick to prison for non-payment of damages in Mrs Bardell's suit against him. The next alley off Cornhill, St Peter's, brings us to the churchyard garden Bradley Headstone chose as the scene for his anguished and impassioned proposal of marriage to Lizzie Hexam in Book 2, Chapter 15 of *Our Mutual Friend*.

Route 2 below offers a convenient extension of this route.

Dickens House Museum, 48 Doughty Street, London WC1: phone (01) 405 2127.

Lincoln's Inn Old Hall, Lincoln's Inn, London WC2: guided tours include the Old Hall, Chapel and Great Hall, with other points of interest around the Inn; phone (01) 405 1393.

2 Southwark

Southwark or—to use the proper title by which Dickens habitually refers to it—the Borough is being progressively overtaken by the modern development to which most of London's South Bank is now subject. Yet it retains both specific and atmospheric reminders of its appearances in the pages of his fiction, especially *Little Dorrit*, and of that unhappy period during his childhood when his father was imprisoned for debt and he himself forced to work in the blacking factory.

The route indicated may be treated either as an extension of Rte 1 above, by following Gracechurch Street from the top of Cornhill to the river, or separately, by starting from Bank Underground Station (Central and Northern Lines) and taking King William Street to the river. In either case the Thames is crossed by London Bridge, a modern structure that prepares the visitor for some of the transformations the Borough itself has undergone in recent years.

Beyond the railway bridge on the left side of Borough High Street stood the inns from which the London–Dover coaching route originated. *Pickwick Papers*, while lamenting the decline of such inns elsewhere, was able to celebrate their survival in Southwark:

> In the Borough, especially, there still remain some half dozen old inns, which have preserved their external features unchanged, and which have escaped alike the rage for public improvement, and the encroachments of private speculation. Great, rambling, queer, old places they are, with galleries, and passages, and staircases, wide enough and antiquated enough to furnish materials for a hundred ghost stories. (Ch. 10)

Today the King's Head, Tabard and Queen's Head have vanished, and so has the White Hart where Mr Jingle brings Rachel Wardle and Mr Pickwick first meets Sam Weller in Chapter 10. But one wing of the *George remains, with a half-timbered gallery and interior (rebuilt in 1676 after fire destroyed an earlier building on the same spot), enjoying a double character as inn and National Trust property. Although the George receives only a passing mention in Dickens' work (Ch. 22 of *Little Dorrit*) it is of considerable interest as the type of those similar establishments, in the Borough and other districts of London, that appear so often in the pages of his novels.

Further down the High Street, on the left and marked by a plaque, is the site of the Marshalsea debtors' prison from 1811 until its closure in 1842: 'an oblong pile of barrack building, partitioned into squalid houses standing back to back, so that there were no back rooms; environed by a narrow paved yard, hemmed in by high walls duly spiked at top' (*Little Dorrit*, Ch. 6). John Dickens was brought here by his improvidence in 1824 and the effect of the episode on his young son is best reflected, perhaps, in *Little Dorrit*, where the prison is a central location and Mr Dorrit, to some extent modelled on John Dickens, is an inmate long enough to acquire the title 'Father of the Marshalsea'. Beyond the site of the prison stands the 18C church of St George the Martyr, where Little Dorrit is christened and married to Arthur Clennam; there is a modern window commemorating her at the east end.

Lant Street leads right from Borough High Street shortly afterwards, surrounded by a network of sidestreets with suitably Dickensian names but greatly changed since the 19C. While his father was in the Marshalsea and he himself working in the blacking factory the young Dickens had lodgings in a house whose site is now occupied by the Charles Dickens Primary School of 1877. In *Pickwick Papers* he gave this understandably sombre account of the street's atmosphere:

> There is a repose about Lant Street ... which sheds a gentle melancholy upon the soul. There are always a good many houses to let in the street: it is a bye-street too, and its dulness is soothing. A house in Lant Street would not come within the denomination of a first-rate residence, in the strict acceptation of the term; but it is a most desirable spot nevertheless. If a man wished to abstract himself from the world—to remove himself from within the reach of temptation—to place himself beyond the possibility of inducement to look out of the window—he should by all means go to Lant Street. (Ch. 32)

The medical student Bob Sawyer occupies a back attic on the street, living on hostile terms with his landlady; the disastrous evening when he entertains Mr Pickwick to dinner is described in Chapter 32.

Sam Weller, Mr Perker, Mr Wardle and Mr Pickwick in the yard of the White Hart, Southwark; an illustration by 'Phiz' to Pickwick Papers

3 The Strand and Covent Garden

The Strand and its neighbourhood are much changed since Dickens' day but a few isolated features of interest survive.

We begin at Aldwych Underground Station (Piccadilly Line). In St Mary-le-Strand, a fine Gibbs church of 1714 in the middle of the Strand opposite, Dickens' parents were married in 1809. On Maiden Lane in Covent Garden, reached by walking east along the Strand and turning right up Southampton Street, Rules Restaurant lovingly maintains the atmosphere it possessed when Dickens patronised it. Charing Cross Station covers the site of No. 30 Hungerford Stairs, where Dickens underwent his childhood ordeal in the blacking factory: 'a crazy, tumble-down old house, abutting, of course, the river, and literally overrun with rats'. On the steps of St Martin's in the Fields, visible to the right and reached via Duncannon Street, David Copperfield met Peggotty during the latter's search for his daughter Little Em'ly (Ch. 40).

4 Soho

The starting point is Tottenham Court Road Underground Station (Central and Northern Lines).

In *Bleak House* (Ch. 23) Esther Summerson and Caddy Jellyby meet in the central garden of Soho Square, in the angle between Oxford Street and Charing Cross Road. Dickens powerfully evokes the atmosphere which the surrounding area once possessed in his description of Dr Manette's London lodgings in *A Tale of Two Cities* (especially Bk 2, Ch. 6). For a reminder of how much it has changed since the time of the French Revolution, when the story is set, and had already changed by the time Dickens was writing, we need only recall his emphasis on its quiet and almost rural character:

> A quainter corner than the corner where the Doctor lived, was not not to be found in London... There were few buildings, then, north of the Oxford road [Oxford Street], and forest-trees flourished, and wild flowers grew, and the hawthorn blossomed, in the now vanished fields. As a consequence, country airs circulated in Soho with vigorous freedom, instead of languishing into the parish like stray paupers without a settlement; and there was many a good south wall, not far off, on which peaches ripened in their season.

Though various locations on Greek Street (leading SE from the square) and Carlisle Street (leading west) have also been proposed as the 'quiet street corner' where the Doctor lives, the obvious candidate is Manette Street, entered by an archway from Greek Street. The courtyard behind the Doctor's lodging may well be that belonging to the House of St Barnabas-in-Soho. This splendid 18C mansion—once the home of Richard Beckford, uncle of the novelist William Beckford (q.v.)—became a charity for the destitute in 1862, shortly after the novel was published.

House of St Barnabas-in-Soho, 1 Greek Street, Soho, London W1: phone (01) 437 1894.

5 Westminster

The starting point is Westminster Underground Station (District and Circle Line).

In Poets' Corner (fee) of Westminster Abbey a slab marks Dickens' grave. He had earlier expressed wishes to be buried, variously, in Kensal Green Cemetery (Rte 8) as well as at Shorne and Rochester Cathedral (Rte 12).

By walking south along Millbank and taking a right turn on to Dean Stanley Street we come to Smith Square, where Jenny Wren, the crippled dolls' dressmaker of *Our Mutual Friend*, lodged. Dickens uncharitably called its 18C church of St John the Evangelist, now restored as a lecture and concert hall after war-time bomb damage, 'very hideous ... with four towers at the four corners, generally resembling some petrified monster, frightful and gigantic, on its back with its legs in the air' (Book 2, Ch. 1).

6 Chelsea

More rural and more clearly separated from the central parts of London in the 19C than it is today, Chelsea was a favourite destination on Dickens' frequent, energetic walks.

Starting at South Kensington Underground Station (District, Circle and Piccadilly Lines), we go south via Onslow Place and Sydney Place, take a right into Fulham Road and then a left into Sydney Street. St Luke's Church, an early 19C Gothic building halfway down on the left, was the scene of Dickens' marriage to Catherine Hogarth on 2 April 1836.

By continuing down Sydney Street, turning right on to the King's Road and then left on Oakley Street, we reach the river where it is spanned by the Albert Bridge. A right along Cheyne Walk and another right up Cheyne Row bring us to Carlyle's House on the right, home of the writer and his wife Jane from 1834 until the end of their lives. As friend and admirer of Carlyle, Dickens was inevitably a visitor here. The house may also stand as a type of the quiet, modestly elegant Chelsea houses he knew well in other contexts. See under Carlyle for a full description.

Carlyle's House, 24 Cheyne Row, Chelsea, London SW3: NT; phone (01) 352 7087.

7 Richmond

With its rural atmosphere, river scenery and dignified houses Richmond, like Chelsea, held obvious attractions for a man of Dickens' tastes. Although only two specific places of interest to Dickensians are included in the itinerary below, the visitor will find the area also worth casual exploration.

The walking tour begins at Richmond Station (British Rail and District Underground Line) and leads south via the Quadrant, George Street, Hill Street and Richmond Hill. On the right the 20C

Star and Garter Home for disabled soldiers and sailors replaces the old Star and Garter Inn. It was a favourite haunt of Dickens for celebrations, most notably the publication of *David Copperfield* in 1850 when his dinner guests included Tennyson and Thackeray (qq.v.). We continue south via Star and Garter Hill to Petersham Road and Elm Lodge (then Elm Cottage) which Dickens rented for a holiday in 1839.

8 Kensal Green

Kensal Green Cemetery, opposite Kensal Green Station (British Rail and Bakerloo Underground Line) contains the grave of Dickens' beloved sister-in-law Mary Hogarth, who died in 1837 while he was living on Doughty Street (Rte 1). After a visit to the spot he wrote that 'the grass around it was as green and the flowers as bright, as if nothing of the earth in which they grew could ever wither or fade'. He originally intended to be buried beside her, but in the event only other members of the Hogarth family were laid in the plot. It is No. 977 in Square 33, on North Avenue near the main entrance.

9 Camden Town

The district is connected with Dickens' childhood and with the onset of the financial difficulties that led to his father's imprisonment. Its character when Dickens first knew it is well evoked in the portrait of Staggs's Gardens in Chapter 6 of *Dombey and Son*:

> It was a little row of houses, with little squalid patches of ground before them, fenced off with old doors, barrel staves, scraps of tarpaulin, and dead bushes; with bottomless tin kettles and exhausted iron fenders, thrust into the gaps. Here the Staggs's Gardeners trained scarlet beans, kept fowls and rabbits, erected rotten summer houses (one was an old boat), dried clothes, and smoked pipes.

Its subsequent destruction by the opening of the Euston–Birmingham railway line is described in Chapter 16:

> There was no such place as Staggs's Gardens. It had vanished from the earth. Where the old rotten summer houses once had stood, palaces now reared their heads, and granite columns of gigantic girth opened up a new vista to the railway world beyond. The miserable waste ground, where the refuse-matter had been heaped of yore, was swallowed up and gone; and in its frowsty stead were tiers of warehouses, crammed with rich goods and costly merchandise. The old by-streets now swarmed with passengers and vehicles of every kind: the new streets that had stopped disheartened in the mud and waggon-ruts, formed towns within themselves, originating wholesome comforts and conveniences belonging to themselves, and never tried nor thought of until they sprung into existence.

We begin at Camden Town Underground Station (Northern Line) and take Bayham Street to the south. The Dickens family lived at No. 16 in 1823–24, when John Dickens' work for the Navy Office first brought them from Chatham. The house itself no longer stands, its site being covered by a hospital, but surviving terraced houses nearby give an idea of what it was like.

Bayham Street issues into Crowndale Road, where a right and then a left turn lead into Hampstead Road. At No. 247 of this otherwise unremarkable thoroughfare, on the right by the junction with Granby Terrace, stood the Wellington House Academy which Dickens began attending in June 1824 after his family's fortunes had improved enough to release him from work in the blacking factory.

10 Hampstead

Although it has been thoroughly assimilated into London's urban complex since the 19C, Hampstead, particularly its old Village and adjacent Heath, still possesses some of the quiet rural character that frequently drew Dickens here.

A walking tour begins at Hampstead Underground Station (Northern Line) and leads north on Heath Street to Whitestone Pond, stranded in the centre of a large road junction. To the east lies Hampstead Heath, which Dickens loved to walk over on his way to and from central London and which Bill Sikes crossed in Chapter 48 of *Oliver Twist* as he fled the scene of Nancy's murder. The Hampstead Ponds, about whose sources Mr Pickwick engaged in learned speculation (Ch. 1), lie SE and may be reached via East Heath Road. The large castellated building immediately beyond Whitestone Pond is Jack Straw's Castle; it replaces an older inn of the same name familiar to Dickens.

By heading north on North End Way we come to the Bull and Bush, behind which stands Wylde's (formerly Collins' Farm), a partly Elizabethan cottage where Dickens came from Doughty Street in May 1837 to recuperate from the shock of Mary Hogarth's sudden death. 'I have been so unnerved and hurt that I have been compelled for once to give up all idea of my monthly work, and to try a fortnight's rest and quiet', he wrote to a friend. A footpath leads across the Heath (a route undoubtedly known to Dickens) to Spaniards Road. To the left, where the old toll house still straddles the road, is the *Spaniards Inn (formerly the Spaniards Tea Gardens), a finely preserved but often crowded pub. Mrs Bardell chose its garden in Chapter 46 of *Pickwick Papers* for the ill-fated celebratory party which was interrupted by the arrival of Mr Jackson to take her to the Fleet Prison for non-payment of Dodson and Fogg's fees.

11 Limehouse

Only one place of interest survives in the Thames dockland area that Dickens knew well and several times used in his fiction, most notably in his last complete novel, *Our Mutual Friend*.

From Shadwell Underground Station (Metropolitan Line, East London section; closed Sundays) we cut south to The Highway, once the Ratcliff Highway and a notorious haunt of thieves, following it and its extension, Narrow Street, to the east (left). The Grapes Inn at No. 76, overlooking both the river and Limehouse Basin, is commonly identified with Miss Abbey Potterson's 'Six Jolly Fellowship Porters':

> a tavern of dropsical appearance, ... long settled down into a state of hale infirmity ... Externally, it was a narrow lopsided wooden jumble of corpulent windows heaped one upon another as you might heap as many toppling oranges, with a crazy wooden verandah impending over the water; indeed the whole house, inclusive of the complaining flag-staff on the roof, impended over the water, but seemed to have got into the condition of a faint-hearted diver who has paused so long on the brink that he will never go in at all. (*Our Mutual Friend*, Bk 1, Ch. 6)

Inside, the Grapes now boasts a Dickens Bar.

South-Eastern England

12 London to Broadstairs via Rochester and Canterbury

'I have many happy recollections connected with Kent and am scarcely less interested in it than if I had been a Kentish man bred and born, and had resided in the county all my life', Dickens once wrote. The present route incorporates places familiar to him throughout his life but especially associated with his childhood and later years, as well as retracing in part or whole some of the most famous journeys described in his fiction: the first expedition of Mr Pickwick and his friends, David Copperfield's flight from Murdstone and Grinby's to the refuge of Betsey Trotwood's home, and Pip's various travels between the humble scenes of his childhood and the delusive glamour of London in *Great Expectations*.

A2 leaves London by the Old Kent Road, New Cross and Blackheath (7 miles), where it becomes a motorised bypass, the Rochester Way. A more rewarding way to continue is by A207, Shooter's Hill Road, the old Watling Street and traditional Dover road. On the incline of Shooter's Hill, in Book 1, Chapter 2 of *A Tale of Two Cities*, Jarvis Lorry and his fellow passengers were forced to get out and walk because 'the harness, and the mud, and the mail, were all so heavy, that the horses had three times already come to a stop, besides once drawing the coach across the road, with the mutinous intent of taking it back to Blackheath', allowing the banker to be overtaken by Jerry Cruncher with the momentous news that Dr Manette, long-time prisoner in the Bastille, had been 'recalled to life'.

At Dartford (16 miles) the route diverges left on the A226 through Gravesend (23 miles), a Thames port that Dickens knew but hardly refers to in his writing, to Chalk (26 miles). In 1836 Dickens spent his honeymoon in the village, now on the fringe of London's urban sprawl, though attempts to identify the cottage where he and his wife Kate stayed have led to considerable confusion and the building apparently no longer stands. The old forge, today a private house, at the corner of the road to Singlewell and Cobham is regarded as the model for Joe Gargery's in *Great Expectations*. The church and churchyard, reached by a lane leading left from the main road, were a frequent stopping place for Dickens on his walks through the area.

A mile beyond Chalk a detour leads south from A226 through Shorne, a village in whose churchyard Dickens once expressed a desire to be buried, across the A2 to Cobham (3 miles), a favourite haunt throughout his life. Its chief point of interest is the *Leather

Bottle Inn, an ancient building splendidly preserved and maintained despite fire damage in the 1880s, and now boasting a large, varied collection of Dickens relics on the walls of its bar. It was here that the lovesick and apparently suicidal Mr Tupman took refuge and was discovered by his fellow Pickwickians in 'a long, low-roofed room, furnished with a large number of high-backed leather-cushioned chairs of fantastic shapes and embellished with a great variety of old portraits and roughly coloured prints of some antiquity', enjoying 'a roast fowl, bacon, ale, and et ceteras ... looking as unlike a man who has taken his leave of the world, as possible' (Ch. 10). In the churchyard opposite, Mr Pickwick encountered little difficulty persuading his friend to rejoin the Club and its peregrinations. On his way back to the Leather Bottle he found the mysterious stone whose apparently ancient inscription was deciphered by his rival and enemy Mr Blotton as reading: '+ BILL STUMPS HIS MARK'. Dickensians have placed a facsimile at the corner of the inn. At the east end of the village Cobham Park, landscaped by Repton, formed one of Dickens' common routes in his rambles from Gad's Hill. The park and its mansion, Cobham Hall, had earlier been affectionately evoked in the description of the Pickwickians' search for the missing Mr Tupman:

> The ivy and the moss crept in thick clusters over the old trees, and the soft green turf overspread the ground like a silken mat. They emerged upon an open park, with an ancient hall, displaying the quaint and picturesque architecture of Elizabeth's time. Long vistas of stately oaks and elm trees appeared on every side: large herds of deer were cropping the fresh grass; and occasionally a startled hare scoured along the ground, with the speed of the shadows thrown by the light clouds which swept across a sunny landscape like a passing breath of summer. (Ch. 10)

At Higham (28 miles) a second detour leads from the main road NE towards the Isle of Grain, via B2000 to Cooling (5 miles). The bleak countryside of this area, which may also be viewed from Cliffe at N end of B2000, dominates the opening chapters of *Great Expectations*: 'the marsh country, down by the river, within, as the river wound, twenty miles of the sea' (Ch. 1). In Cooling *churchyard lies a row of seven small 18C gravestones commemorating the children of the Comport family, a melancholy spectacle that inspired Pip's contemplation of his dead siblings (though Dickens alters the number):

> To five little stone lozenges, each about a foot and a half long, ... sacred to the memory of five little brothers of mine—who gave up trying to get a living exceedingly early in that universal struggle—I am indebted for a belief I religiously entertained that they had all been born on their backs with their hands in their trousers pockets, and had never taken them out in this state of existence. (Ch. 1)

Beyond Higham and opposite the Sir John Falstaff Inn stands Gad's Hill Place, the 'little Kentish freehold' Dickens bought in 1857 and used as his main residence until his death there in 1870—the years of separation from his wife, public reading tours, *A Tale of Two Cities, Great Expectations, Our Mutual Friend* and the unfinished *Mystery of Edwin Drood*. A letter announcing his new purchase reveals the special significance that this 'grave red brick house' held for him:

> It has always a curious interest for me, because when I was a small boy down in these parts I thought it the most beautiful house (I suppose because of its famous old cedar-trees) ever seen. And my poor father used to bring me to look at it, and used to say that if I ever grew up to be a clever man perhaps I might own the house, or another such house. In remembrance of which, ... it has never been to me like any other house.

Another letter shows him keenly, if fancifully, appreciative of the place's connection with Shakespeare (q.v.) and *Henry IV, Part One*: 'The robbery was committed before the door, on the man with the treasure, and Falstaff ran away from the identical spot of ground now covered by the room in which I write'. Such nostalgic considerations did not prevent him altering and modernising the late 18C property (which he apparently thought dated from the Queen Anne period) with customary energy: 'I have added ... and stuck bits upon in all manner of ways, so that it is as pleasantly irregular and as violently opposed to all architectural ideas, as the most hopeful man could possibly desire'. A tunnel connecting the main grounds with their extension, which Dickens called 'The Wilderness', leads under the main road. The house is now a school.

**Rochester (31 miles) is, after London, the English city most intimately connected with Dickens. Its combination of historic associations, quiet provinciality and periodic bustle caused by its crucial position on the coaching route and by the nearby military dockyards gave it a special appeal for him. He uses the city in three of his novels: under its own name as the first halting place in the travels of Mr Pickwick and his companions; anonymously as the provincial centre nearest the countryside of Pip's childhood in *Great Expectations*; and as 'Cloisterham', the 'drowsy city' where most of *The Mystery of Edwin Drood* takes place. A four-day Dickens Festival is held in May or June each year.

The bridge over the Medway by which travellers now approach the town is a later and altogether less picturesque construction than the stone bridge from which Mr Pickwick admired prospects of the city and the river before being interrupted by the 'dismal man' (Ch. 5). A convenient walking tour begins nearby at the north end of the High Street. On the right stands the Royal Victoria and Bull Hotel (formerly the Bull Hotel), a building of red brick and grey stone well known to Dickens but now extensively and not always happily modernised. The Pickwickians and Mr Jingle stay here in Chapter 2 of the novel, Mr Pickwick's own room being pointed out as either No. 11 or No. 17. In its assembly room Mr Jingle and Mr Tupman attended the ball that led, by a series of typically Pickwickian accidents, to Mr Winkle almost fighting a duel with Dr Slammer at Fort Pitt Fields in neighbouring Chatham. In *Great Expectations* the Bull reappears as the 'Blue Boar', where Pip's apprenticeship to Joe is celebrated by the Gargerys, Uncle Pumblechook and Mr Wopsle, whose vigorous recitation of Collins' 'Ode to the Passions' provokes complaint from other guests: 'The Commercials underneath sent up their compliments and it wasn't the Tumblers' Arms' (Ch. 13). The coffee room, now a bar to the left of the main entrance, is the scene of Pip's hostile encounter with Bentley Drummle in Chapter 43. Opposite the Bull is the 17C Guildhall, now a local museum, preserving the courtroom where Pip was formally bound apprentice. Dickens' description of the room as 'a queer place ... with higher pews in it than a church' (Ch. 13), though in keeping with the mood of the incident, makes no mention of the magnificent plaster ceiling. The Corn Exchange on the left is notable for being 'oddly garnished with a queer old clock, as if Time carried on business there'. *Chertsey's Gate, an arched gatehouse spanning the pavement at the junction of High Street and Boley Hill, is now popularly known as 'Jasper's Gate' since its upper apartment became the residence of the sinister choirmaster in *Edwin Drood*. Beyond it is the half-timbered building (currently a restaurant) occupied by the verger Mr Topes in the same novel and used as a temporary lodging by that mysterious visitor to 'Cloisterham', Dick Datchery.

A right turn up Boley Hill leads immediately to the imposing five-storey Norman keep of Rochester Castle, which called forth enthusiastic reactions from the members of Mr Pickwick's party. To the poetic Mr Snodgrass it was a 'magnificent ruin', and to the scholarly Mr Pickwick 'a study for an antiquarian', while to the telegrammatic Mr Jingle it conjured up visions of 'frowning walls—tottering arches—dark nooks—crumbling staircases' (Ch. 2). The Cathedral opposite, dating from 12C–14C but with its present tower and spire rebuilt in 1904, is the central location around which much of the plot of *Edwin Drood* revolves. Dickens wished to be buried here, though in the event Westminster Abbey (Rte 5) enjoyed that honour; a memorial to him can be found in the south transept. Minor Canon Row, south of the Cathedral, is the home of Mr Crisparkle in *Edwin Drood*.

On the continuation of the High Street, still retaining some of the quiet provincial atmosphere Dickens relished, is Watts' Charity, on the left, founded in 1579 at the bequest of Richard Watts for the accommodation of 'Six Poor Travellers' and the inspiration for 'Seven Poor Travellers', Dickens' Christmas story for 1854. Eastgate House beyond, a brick Elizabethan building, now houses a substantial museum. Its contents include reconstructed tableaux of famous scenes from the novels, but the most conspicuous and interesting item is the *Swiss chalet given to Dickens by the actor Charles Fechter and originally erected in the grounds of Gad's Hill as an alternative study to his ground-floor room in the house itself. He wrote his last pages, Chapter 23 of the unfinished *Edwin Drood*, in it on the day before his death in June 1870. Eastgate House may have served as the model for 'Westgate House', the school for young ladies where Mr Pickwick has his embarrassing adventure in Chapter 16, though the novel represents the incident as occurring in Bury St Edmunds (Rte 17). It is certainly the 'Nuns' House' of *Edwin Drood*, where Miss Twinkleton runs the academy at which Rosa Bud is a pupil. The gabled Tudor building nearly opposite is associated with Mr Pumblechook's premises 'of a peppery and farinaceous character' (Ch. 8) in *Great Expectations* and, more sombrely, with the residence of Mr Sapsea, the pompous Mayor of 'Cloisterham' in *Edwin Drood*.

Crow Lane leads right from the High Street to Restoration House on the left, a Tudor mansion so called because of its connection with Charles II. To Dickens it provided the suggestion for Miss Havisham's house in *Great Expectations* though he took its fictional name, 'Satis House', from another building (on Bakers Walk). From Vines Lane to the right the pedestrian may enter The Vines, formerly a monks' vineyard and in Chapter 14 of *Edwin Drood* the scene of Edwin's ominous encounter with the Princess Puffer. Its tree-shaded walk may also have provided hints for the setting of Jasper's equally sinister interview with Rosa Bud in Chapter 19, though for the sake of plausibility the scene is transferred to the garden of the 'Nuns' House'. A return route may easily be traced through The Vines, down Boley Hill and back to the High Street.

Chatham, separated from Rochester only by an indistinct boundary in the nineteenth century and now officially amalgamated into the same borough, has undergone greater change than its sister town since Dickens' childhood residence there (1817–23). The former Royal Naval Dockyard, which he made the subject of an essay in *The Uncommercial Traveller*, preserves some of its historic buildings. The house at No. 11 (then No. 2) Ordnance Terrace, opposite the railway station, first occupied by the Dickens family after their arrival survives and is marked by a plaque; but even by the time of 'Dullborough Town' in *The Uncommercial Traveller* Dickens had cause to lament the alteration that time and the coming of the railway had made to its previously rural setting. The more modest house in The Brook, to which the family was forced to move in 1821, does not survive.

From Chatham via A2 to Canterbury (58 miles), a city with which Dickens was thoroughly familiar but whose surviving landmarks associate it chiefly with *David Copperfield*. In St Dunstan's Street near Westgate the traveller can find The House of Agnes (now a hotel), popularly identified with Mr Wickfield's residence, where David met his future second wife Agnes and the ingratiating Uriah Heep:

> a very old house bulging out over the road; a house with long low lattice windows bulging out still farther, and beams with carved heads on the ends bulging out too, so that I fancied the whole house was leaning forward, trying to see who was passing on the narrow pavement below. (Ch. 15)

The Sun Inn (formerly the Little Inn) at the corner of Sun Street and Guildhall Street, between the High Street and the Cathedral, apparently provided accommodation for the Micawbers on their trip to Canterbury, when they entertained David to a 'beautiful little dinner' in Chapter 17. It is no longer an inn but its Dickensian association is remembered by an inscription. Attempts to identify the school run by Dr Strong which David attends with King's School in the Cathedral precincts are not convincing.

From Canterbury we take A28 to Margate (74 miles) and then A255 to *Broadstairs (78 miles), a seaside resort fashionable in the 19C and still popular today. Dickens, who found it 'the healthiest and freshest of places', spent his holidays here nearly every summer between 1837 and 1850, returning again from May to November 1851 and for a final one-week stay in 1859. Substantial parts of *Pickwick Papers*, *Nicholas Nickleby*, *The Old Curiosity Shop*, *Barnaby Rudge*, *David Copperfield* and *Bleak House* were written or planned during these visits. Though unnamed, Broadstairs is the subject of an affectionately ironic portrait, 'Our English Watering-Place' (1851; later included in *Reprinted Pieces*). Dickens had already given a shorter but equally vivid account of the place and his activities there in a letter of 1843:

> This is a little fishing-place; intensely quiet; built on a cliff, whereon—in the centre of a tiny semi-circular bay—our house stands; the sea rolling and dashing under the windows. Seven miles out are the Goodwin Sands ... whence floating lights perpetually wink after dark, as if they were carrying on intrigues with the servants. Also there is a big lighthouse called the North Foreland on a hill beyond the village, a severe parsonic light, which reproves the young and giddy floaters, and stares grimly out upon the sea. Under the cliff are rare good sands, where all the children assemble every morning and throw up impossible fortifications, which the sea throws down again at high water. Old gentlemen and ancient ladies flirt after their own manner in two reading-rooms and on a great many scattered seats in the open air. Other old gentlemen look all day through telescopes and never see anything. In a bay window in a one-pair sits, from nine o'clock to one, a gentleman with rather long hair and no neckcloth, who writes and grins as if he thought he were very funny indeed. His name is Boz. At one he disappears, and presently emerges from a bathing machine, and may be seen—a kind of salmon-coloured porpoise—splashing about in the ocean. After that he may be seen in another bay window on the ground floor, eating a strong lunch; after that,

walking a dozen miles or so, or lying on his back in the sand reading a book. Nobody bothers him unless they know he is disposed to be talked to; and I am told he is very comfortable indeed.

Although recent development and the inevitable increase of summer tourism have altered the town's character, much of the atmosphere Dickens enjoyed and some of the buildings most intimately connected with him remain.

A convenient walking tour begins on the High Street, which slopes towards the bay, where a plaque over the present Woolworths marks the site of No. 12, Dickens' lodging during his first visit. At the bottom of the hill stands the Royal Albion Hotel, now incorporating the house he occupied on an early visit; he was a guest at the hotel itself (then simply the Albion Hotel) during his farewell visit of 1859. A brief walk down Victoria Parade and a right turn lead immediately to Dickens House. In the 1840s and 1850s it was the home of Mary Pearson Strong from whom, it is said, Dickens borrowed several of the characteristics attributed to Betsey Trotwood in *David Copperfield*, including an aversion to donkeys. The house is identified with the 'very neat little cottage with cheerful bow-windows; in front of it, a small gravelled court or garden full of flowers, carefully tended, and smelling deliciously' (Ch. 13) where Miss Trotwood lives, though the novel locates it near Dover. It now contains items associated with Dickens, prints and photographs of Broadstairs during the period he knew it, and a reconstruction of Miss Trotwood's parlour based on 'Phiz's' illustration of her encounter with the Murdstones (Ch. 14). The northern end of Victoria Parade leads to Harbour Street, a footpath spanned by Archway House (formerly Lawn House), where Dickens wrote part of *Barnaby Rudge* in 1841. On top of the cliff beyond stands •Bleak House (formerly Fort House), Dickens' lodging in 1850 and again in 1851. It derives its present name from the fact he planned part of the novel there and not from any resemblance to Jarndyce's home, which is placed near St Albans. Though its external appearance was greatly altered by an extension of 1901 that doubled the size of the house, the rooms Dickens occupied are well preserved and contain a fine exhibition of Dickensiana. Of particular interest are: the lectern used for his public readings; the 'airy nest' of a study overlooking the sea, where *David Copperfield* was written; and the writing chair from Gad's Hill immortalised in Luke Fildes' mourning picture, 'The Empty Chair—10 June 1870'.

A week-long Dickens festival is held in June each year.

An extension of the route leads from Broadstairs south to Dover (A256; 20 miles), which Dickens barely knew when he chose to place Miss Trotwood's house in its vicinity and which he found 'not quite to my taste' when he stayed there for the summer of 1852. Folkestone (A20; 28 miles) proved more congenial in the summer of 1855, when he was writing the opening instalments of *Little Dorrit*, and still has much of the atmosphere that appealed to him. His lodging at Copperfield House (then simply No. 3), Albion Villas still stands and is marked by a plaque but has suffered a change of more than name. Folkestone also enjoys the distinction of being the first town where Dickens gave a public reading, from *A Christmas Carol* at the end of his 1855 visit, in an unidentifiable 'carpenter's shop, which looks far more alarming as a place to hear in than the Town Hall at Birmingham'.

Cobham Hall, Cobham, Kent: phone Shorne (047 482) 3371.

Gad's Hill Place (Gad's Hill Place School), Higham, near Rochester, Kent: visitors by written appointment with the Bursar.

Guildhall Museum, High Street, Rochester, Kent· phone (0634) 48717.

Rochester Castle, Rochester, Kent: English Heritage, standard opening; phone (0634) 402276.

Watts' Charity, High Street, Rochester, Kent: phone Rochester Tourist Information Centre, (0634) 43666.

Eastgate House (Charles Dickens Centre), High Street, Rochester, Kent: phone (0634) 44176.

Restoration House, Crow Lane, Rochester, Kent: closed to the public at the time of writing, but it may open in future years; phone Rochester Tourist Information Centre, (0634) 43666.

Chatham Historic Dockyard, Chatham, Kent: phone (0634) 812551.

Dickens House, Victoria Parade, Broadstairs, Kent: phone Thanet (0843) 62853.

Bleak House (Dickens and Maritime Museum), Ford Road, Broadstairs, Kent: phone Thanet (0843) 62224.

13 Brighton and Portsmouth

Brighton may be reached from London via A23 and M23 (53 miles). An alternative route (72 miles or 104 miles) leads across country from Broadstairs or Folkestone at the end of the previous itinerary, via Rye, Hastings, Bexhill and Lewes.

It was inevitable that Brighton, its popularity as a seaside resort well established since the Regency, should have attracted Dickens. He spent several holidays here between the 1830s and 1850s, and included it in his public reading tours, reporting to a friend that it was 'a gay place for a week or so'. The Regency atmosphere, which still lingers today, contributed to his understanding of a period he delighted to satirise in his novels. Turveydrop, the Model of Deportment in *Bleak House*, was accustomed to visit Brighton 'at fashionable times' and it was outside the Royal Pavilion that he received the supreme honour of being noticed by the Prince Regent, who graciously enquired: 'Who is he? Who the Devil is he? Why don't I know him? Why hasn't he thirty thousand a year?' (Ch. 14).

The surviving reminders of Dickens' visits are on the seafront and can best be seen by a walk beginning at the west end of King's Road. He lodged at No. 148, near the Norfolk Hotel, in 1847 and at the Bedford Hotel beyond in 1848 and again in 1849. These were the years of *Dombey and Son* and the Bedford finds its way into the book as the chosen residence of Mr Dombey during his trips to see his son Paul. He entertained Major Bagstock, who had followed him from London to scrape an acquaintance, to dinner in the hotel and had his breakfast interrupted by Walter Gay and the well-intentioned but maladroit Captain Cuttle (Ch. 10). The Old Ship Hotel, between West and Palace Piers, was the scene of earlier visits in 1837 and 1841, when Dickens was working on *Oliver Twist* and *Barnaby Rudge* respectively. By following the continuation of King's Road as Marine Parade and King's Cliff Parade we reach Chichester House, at the nearest end of Chichester Terrace. According to the novelist Harrison Ainsworth (q.v.), whom Dickens saw in Brighton, this imposing building is the original of Dr Blimber's Academy, 'a mighty fine house, fronting the sea' (Ch. 11), where Paul Dombey attended school and made friends with Mr Toots, that amiable victim of the hothouse method of education.

From Brighton west via Chichester (A27) to Portsmouth (A27, A3; 104 miles), the town of Dickens' birth and early childhood (1812–14) but greatly changed since that time.

His birthplace, an unremarkable but respectable house, survives as No. 393 Old Commercial Road, south of the Continental Ferry Port; in Dickens' day it was No. 1 Mile End Terrace. It is now a museum furnished in the 19C style; the collection includes the couch from Gad's Hill on which he died. A second Portsmouth house to which the family moved when he was six months old was destroyed by war-time bombing. Dickens revisited Portsmouth in 1838 in search of local colour for the hero's theatrical adventures with Mr Vincent Crummles and his company in *Nicholas Nickleby* (Chs 22–25, 29 and 30) and again in later life with George Dolby, the manager of his reading tours, when he found himself unable to identify his birthplace.

On their way from London to Portsmouth, Nicholas Nickleby and Smike paused at the Devil's Punch Bowl on Gibbet Hill, near Hindhead and some 30 miles NE of the coast by A3. Smike listened 'with greedy interest' to the inscription on the memorial stone which records the murder of a sailor here in 1786 (Ch. 22).

From Portsmouth Harbour Station we can cross by ferry to Ryde, on the Isle of Wight. At the pretty village of Bonchurch near Ventnor on the south coast of the island (12 miles from Ryde) is Winterbourne, now a residential hotel but in 1849 'a most delightful and beautiful house' which Dickens rented for the summer. The Swinburne (q.v.) family were among his neighbours and he admired their son, a 'golden-haired lad' of twelve. His initial enthusiasm for the area quickly faded and he was soon complaining to his friend John Forster about the climate:

> Of all the places I have ever been in, I have never been in one so difficult to exist in, pleasantly. Naples is hot and dirty, New York feverish, Washington bilious, Genoa exciting, Paris rainy—but Bonchurch, smashing. I'm quite convinced that I should die here, in a year. It's not hot, it's not close, I don't know what it is, but the prostration of it is *awful*.

Charles Dickens Birthplace Museum, 393 Old Commercial Road, Portsmouth, Hampshire: for opening arrangements phone Portsmouth City Museum and Art Gallery, (0705) 827261.

South-Western England

14 Salisbury, Bath, Exeter and Clovelly

Dickens' knowledge of South-Western England, derived mainly from an 1835 excursion as an election reporter and subsequent fleeting visits for holidays, amateur theatricals and public readings, is probably sparser than his knowledge of any other English region of comparable size. Its fictional appearances are inevitably less frequent and less topographically precise than his use of more familiar areas like Kent and Eastern England. The following places, too dispersed to fall conveniently into a single itinerary, are worth noting.

Salisbury is a recurrent location in *Martin Chuzzlewit*. In Chapter 5 Tom Pinch visits the city under the impression that it is 'a very desperate sort of place' and takes 'a stroll about the streets with a vague and not unpleasant idea that they teemed with all kinds of mystery and bedevilment'. He ends the day safely enough playing the organ in the Cathedral. Various attempts, none of them notably persuasive, have been made to identify the nearby Wiltshire village where the Pecksniffs live and Tom Pinch usually plays the organ. Perhaps the best candidate is Winterslow, 8 miles NE and reached via A30.

Bath. In Chapter 35 of *Pickwick Papers* the hero selects the fashionable spa as a holiday refuge from the anxieties caused by Mrs Bardell's impending lawsuit for breach of promise. His journey westward allows Dickens to comment jocularly on his theft of Pickwick's name from Moses Pickwick, owner of the London–Bath coaching service and proprietor of a Bath hotel, but once the city is reached it is described only in the most general terms and emphasis falls on social satire at the expense of Cyrus Bantam, Esquire and the footmen's 'swarry'. The only precise and memorable location is the Royal Crescent, scene in Chapter 36 of the 'extraordinary calamity' that prompted Mr Winkle to flee to Bristol. A visit of 1840 brought Dickens to the home of his friend Walter Savage Landor at No. 35 St James Square, behind the Royal Crescent and now marked by a plaque. It was here, to Landor's great pride, that Dickens first conceived the character of Little Nell in *The Old Curiosity Shop*.

Exeter. At Alphington 1½ miles to the south, once a village but now almost absorbed into the city, is Mile End Cottage, opposite the Post Office. A tablet bears witness to the fact that Dickens rented it as a home for his parents in 1839, an unsuccessful experiment ending with their return to London in 1843.

Dawlish, on the coast 10 miles south of Exeter, is briefly mentioned as the home of the Nicklebys until the death of Nicholas' father launches them on the adventures and misfortunes which occupy the novel.

Clovelly (12 miles west of Bideford via A39). In late 1860 Dickens visited this village on the north Devon coast, then just made famous by Charles Kingsley (q.v.) in *Westward Ho!* and still popular with tourists for its steep pedestrian street leading down to a fine bay. It appears as 'Steepways' in 'A Message from the Sea', his Christmas story for that year written in collaboration with his companion on the trip, Wilkie Collins (q.v.):

> There was no road in it, there was no wheeled vehicle in it, there was not a level yard in it. From the sea-beach to the cliff-top two irregular rows of white houses, placed opposite to one another, and twisting here and there, and there and here, rose, like the sides of a long succession of stages of crooked ladders, and you climbed up the village or climbed down the village by the staves between, some six feet wide or so, and made of sharp irregular stones ... No two houses in the village were alike, in chimney, size, shape, door, window, gable, roof-tree, anything. The sides of the ladders were musical with water, running clear and bright. The staves were musical with the clattering feet of the pack-horses and pack-donkeys, and the voices of the fishermen's wives and their many children. The pier was musical with the wash of the sea, the creaking of capstans and windlasses, and the airy fluttering of little vanes and sails. The rough, bleached sea-boulders of the shore, were brown with drying nets. The red-brown cliffs, richly wooded to their extremest verge, had their softened and beautiful forms reflected in the bluest water. (Ch. 1)

Central England

15 London to Grantham via Rockingham

We leave London via A1 to Hatfield (21 miles), where the old town lies to the east of the road. In Chapter 48 of *Oliver Twist* Bill Sikes came to this 'quiet village' after fleeing London and the scene of Nancy's murder by a route that had taken him through Islington, Highgate, Hampstead Heath (Rte 10) and Hendon, and later continued to St Albans. The picturesque 17C Eight Bells at the corner of Fore Street and Park Street is commonly identified with 'the small public house' where his refreshment was spoiled by the pedlar's attempt to use his blood-stained hat in a sales demonstration for a patent stain remover. The fire that briefly distracts him from the agonies of guilt was undoubtedly suggested by one in 1835 at the Jacobean mansion of Hatfield House nearby, which destroyed the west wing and killed the aged Marchioness of Salisbury. Dickens interrupted work on the opening chapters of *Pickwick Papers* to report the disaster.

A1 continues north, bypassing Welwyn Garden City. Knebworth House can be reached from junction 7 (32 miles) near Stevenage. This originally Tudor mansion, rebuilt in the Gothic style in the nineteenth century, was the home of Edward Bulwer-Lytton (s.v. Lytton), popular novelist as well as Dickens' friend and co-patron of the Guild of Literature and Art, designed to help less fortunate writers. Dickens' fundraising on behalf of the Guild brought him to Knebworth in November 1850 for performances in the banqueting hall of Jonson's *Every Man in His Humour*, which allowed him to distinguish himself in the role of Captain Bobadil, and the farce *Animal Magnetism*. During a visit in 1861 he accepted Lytton's suggestion that the original, unhappy ending of *Great Expectations* be changed to the happier version eventually printed. He returned again in 1865 for a banquet celebrating the opening of three Gothic cottages (now standing near the Stevenage road) intended for recipients of the Guild's charity. They were converted into almshouses after the scheme failed.

We take A1 north via Sandy (50 miles) and Norman Cross (80 miles) to the junction with A605 (84 miles). A left turn leads on a route via Oundle (97 miles), where we transfer to A427, and Corby (107 miles), where we take A6116 and then B6003 to **Rockingham Castle (110 miles) on the hill overlooking the stone-built high street of the village.

Of all English country houses Rockingham is the one where Dickens felt most at home and which left the greatest imprint on his writing. He first met its owner, the Hon. Richard Watson, and his wife Lavinia at Lausanne in 1846 and a quickly developing friendship (reflected in the dedication of *David Copperfield*) led to a visit in November 1849. A letter to his friend John Forster describes the part Norman, part Tudor castle and his reception there in terms of mock awe:

> Picture to yourself ... a large old castle, approached by an ancient keep, portcullis, &c, &c, filled with company, waited on by six-and-twenty servants; the slops (and wine-glasses) continually being emptied; and my clothes (with myself in them) always being carried off to all sorts of places.

The house party acted scenes from Sheridan's *School for Scandal* and the episode of the gentleman in small clothes from Chapter 41 of *Nicholas Nickleby*. Dickens returned for more elaborate productions in the Castle in the New Year of 1851 and visited Rockingham again, after Richard Watson's death, during a public reading tour in 1855.

Rockingham appears unmistakably in *Bleak House* as 'Chesney Wold', country seat of Sir Leicester and Lady Dedlock, though it is transplanted from Northamptonshire to Lincolnshire and given a name suitable to that county. The main features that the novel uses are: the Yew Walk, which becomes the 'Ghost's Walk' whose history the housekeeper Mrs Rouncewell relates in Chapter 7; the 'shady, ancient, solemn little church' (Ch. 18) in the park, where Esther first sees Lady Dedlock; the turret where the lawyer Tulkinghorn lodges during his visits to the house; and the Sondes Arms in Rockingham's main street, which becomes the 'Dedlock Arms'. Relics of Dickens' visits and his friendship with the Watsons are now displayed in the Long Gallery.

'Chesney Wold': an illustration by 'Phiz' to Bleak House

From Rockingham the route returns to the A1 by retracing A427 between Corby and Oundle to Weldon (114 miles) and heading north on A43 to Stamford (127 miles). On the lefthand side of the High Street at Grantham (148 miles) stands the George Hotel, an 18C coaching inn where Dickens and his illustrator Hablôt Browne ('Phiz') stayed in January 1838 on their way to research Yorkshire schools for *Nicholas Nickleby*. His enthusiastic reports of the George are echoed in the novel, where it is called 'one of the best inns in England' (Ch. 5), though Nicholas, making an altogether less pleasant journey north with Wackford Squeers and his new pupils, does not have the good fortune to stay there.

For a continuation of this journey see Rte 18.

Hatfield House, Hatfield, Hertfordshire: phone (070 72) 62823 or 65159.

Knebworth House, Knebworth, Hertfordshire: phone Stevenage (0438) 812661.

Rockingham Castle, Rockingham, near Corby, Northamptonshire: phone Corby (0536) 770240.

16 London to Shrewsbury via Leamington, Stratford and Tewkesbury

Leaving London by M1 we diverge left at 20½ miles on the A5 and travel via Dunstable (27 miles) and Stony Stratford (45½ miles) to Towcester (53½ miles). Among its several surviving old inns is the Pomfret Arms (the Saracen's Head in Dickens' day), which Mr Pickwick found in Chapter 51 to fulfill Sam Weller's promise of 'everything clean and comfortable', though his stay was disrupted by the stormy encounter between those two sworn political enemies, Mr Pott of the *Eatanswill Gazette* and Mr Slurk of the *Eatanswill Independent*.

From Towcester the A5 continues to Weedon Bec (61½ miles) and the A45 turning for Daventry (65½ miles), where A425 leads via Southam (75½ miles) to Royal Leamington Spa (82½ miles). Dickens included Leamington on itineraries for his public readings in later life but his most important visit took place in October 1838, the year when Queen Victoria bestowed the prefix 'Royal' on the town and the period when the popularity of its medicinal waters was well on the way to being established. Its fashionable semi-Regency atmosphere, still lingering today, made Leamington a natural setting for Major Bagstock to introduce Mr Dombey to the grotesquely faded Mrs Skewton and her daughter Edith, destined to become the second Mrs Dombey, in Chapter 21 of the novel. Among the places where their acquaintance was renewed is the Royal Pump Room (rebuilt in 1925), near Victoria Bridge which spans the River Leam.

Nearby Warwick Castle (85 miles; W on A425) is the object in Chapter 27 of a visit by Mr Dombey's party. Dickens' description of the castle's exterior, 18C interiors and collection of paintings is generalised in the extreme ('They made the tour of the pictures, the walls, crow's nest, and so forth') but he makes good use of the occasion to ridicule Mrs Skewton's slavish adulation of the past: 'Those darling byegone times ... with their delicious fortresses, and their dear old dungeons, and their delightful places of torture, and their romantic vengeances, and their picturesque assaults and sieges, and everything that makes life truly charming!'

From Warwick the traveller may take a detour 5 miles north to Kenilworth Castle, founded in 12C, enlarged in the Renaissance, allowed to decay after the Civil War and restored since it became national property in 1937. Mr Dombey's party admired its 'haunted ruins' (Ch. 27).

From Warwick the main route leads south on A46 to Stratford-upon-Avon (93 miles). Dickens, who later donated proceeds from amateur theatrical tours to the curatorship of the Birthplace in Henley Street, visited the major sights of Stratford (described under the entry for Shakespeare) during the same tour that took him and Hablôt Browne to Leamington. The visit is mainly memorable for providing Mrs Nickleby with one of the flightiest of those reminiscences that habitually enliven her conversation:

> 'After we had seen Shakespeare's tomb and birthplace, we went back to the inn there, where we slept that night, and I recollect that all night long I dreamt of nothing but a black gentleman, at full length, in plaster-of-Paris, with a lay-down collar tied with two tassels, leaning against a post and thinking; and when I woke in the morning and described him to Mr Nickleby, he said it was Shakespeare just as he had been when he was alive, which was very curious indeed'. (Ch. 27)

A46 leads south from Stratford via Broadway (107 miles) and Toddington (111½ miles), where A438 branches right to the abbey town of Tewkesbury (122 miles). Of chief interest to the Dickensian is the Royal Hop Pole (formerly the Hop Pole) on Church Street near the Abbey, with a fine 14C fireplace as well as a Pickwick Bar and a Sam Weller Bar. Over dinner at the Hop Pole, on his way to Birmingham and his unsuccessful interview with Mr Winkle senior, Mr Pickwick found that the combination of bottled ale, madeira and port on top of milk punch earlier in the day helped make him more tolerant of Bob Sawyer's high-spirited antics during the journey.

The route continues north from Tewkesbury on A38 to Worcester (137 miles), A449 to Kidderminster (152 miles), A442 to Bridgnorth (166 miles) and then successively on A442 and A4169 to Shifnal (178 miles). The half-timbered houses of this town are sometimes associated with those glimpsed by Little Nell during the last stages of her journey with her grandfather and the schoolmaster from the industrial Midlands, in Chapter 46 of *The Old Curiosity Shop*:

> They passed a large church; and in the streets were a number of old houses, built of a kind of earth or plaster, crossed and re-crossed in a great many directions with black beams which gave them a remarkable and very ancient look. The doors, too, were arched and low, some with oaken portals and quaint benches, where the former inhabitants had sat on summer evenings. The windows were latticed in little diamond panes, that seemed to wink and blink upon the passengers as if they were dim of sight.

The small village of Tong to the east (180 miles) can be more certainly identified, on Dickens' own authority, as Nell's destination and final resting-place. The *church of St Bartholomew, notable for its fine array of ornate tombs, monuments and effigies, bears a

Little Nell in Tong Church: an illustration by George Cattermole to The Old Curiosity Shop

plaque outside the south door in memory of Dickens' most famous heroine.

We return to Shifnal and head west on A464, using M64 to bypass Oakengates and Wellington, and take A5 to Shrewsbury (198 miles). During their 1838 tour Dickens and Browne stayed at the Lion, a fine building with a part half-timbered and part 18C frontage, on Wyle Cop. Shrewsbury itself, which boasts perhaps the finest examples of Shropshire black-and-white architecture, has a rival claim to Shifnal as the original of the half-timbered town described in the quotation above.

Warwick Castle, Warwick: phone (0926) 495421.

Kenilworth Castle, Kenilworth, Warwickshire: English Heritage, standard opening; phone (0926) 52078.

Eastern England

17 London to Yarmouth via Ipswich and Bury St Edmunds

After London and Kent, Eastern England is probably the region that Dickens knew and loved best and the one that finds its way most persistently into his writing. He first visited it as a young reporter covering Suffolk elections in 1834 and 1835, acquiring a familiarity with the county's inns and an affection for its rural scenery that left their obvious mark on *Pickwick Papers*. A trip in early 1849 extended his knowledge to Norfolk and provided locales for *David Copperfield*. In the 1850s and 1860s he included the region's main towns in his public reading tours.

We leave London by A11, which originates as the Whitechapel Road in the East End, and at Leytonstone (8½ miles) transfer to A12, the main road for the rest of this route.

At Redbridge (11 miles) a detour leads left on A123 to Chigwell (4 miles), hyperbolically praised by Dickens as 'the greatest place in the world' and, despite the encroachments of London's outer suburbs, still preserving its village centre. Its chief attraction is the •King's Head, which appears in *Barnaby Rudge* as the 'Maypole Inn', a massive symbol of traditional England presided over by the equally traditional landlord, John Willett. The appearance and atmosphere of the King's Head today still answer to Dickens' opening description of the 'Maypole':

> an old building, with more gable ends than a lazy man would care to count on a sunny day; huge zig-zag chimneys, out of which it seemed as though smoke could not choose but come in more than naturally fantastic shapes, imparted to it in its tortuous progress ... Its windows were old diamond-pane lattices, its floors were sunken and uneven, its ceilings blackened by the hand of time, and heavy with massive beams. (Ch. 1)

The Chester Room is named in memory of the encounter that took place there between Mr Chester and Reuben Haredale in Chapter 29.

A12 continues to Chelmsford (35 miles), a town that singularly failed to impress Dickens when he made it his first stop during his East Anglian travels of 1834. The Black Boy Inn where he stayed and where Mr Jingle and Job Trotter join Tony Weller's coach in Chapter 20 of *Pickwick Papers* was demolished in the author's lifetime.

The route then bypasses Colchester (57 miles) and reaches Ipswich (75 miles), another of Dickens' stops on both his reporting tour (1835) and his reading tours (1859–61). During his first visit he lodged at the •Great White Horse, reached from the market place, Cornhill, by following Tavern Street to the corner of Northgate Street. This is how Mr Pickwick, Sam Weller and their accidental travelling companion Mr Magnus approach the inn in Chapter 22 of *Pickwick Papers*, where it appears under its own name and in a highly unfavourable light. The stone effigy of a horse over the portico is ridiculed as 'a rampacious animal with flowing mane and tail, distantly resembling an insane cart-horse'. The gloomy and confusing interior ('Never were such labyrinths of uncarpeted passages, such clusters of mouldy ill-lighted rooms, such huge numbers of small dens for eating and sleeping in') provides an appropriate setting for Mr Pickwick's embarrassing intrusion into the bedroom properly belonging to the lady in the yellow curl papers. Modernised but retaining its historic character, with remnants of half-timbering visible in the roofed-over courtyard, the present Great White Horse hardly deserves such strictures.

A detour leads NW from Ipswich along A45 via Stowmarket (12 miles) and Suffolk countryside of the sort that, according to the urban Sam Weller, 'beats the chimley pots' (Ch. 16) to Bury St Edmunds (26 miles). Despite its inevitable growth since the 19C Bury is still the 'bright little town' Dickens praised at the expense of London in *The Uncommercial Traveller*. He knew it from a visit in the 1830s as well as return trips in 1859 and 1861, when he gave public readings at the 18C Athenaeum on Angel Hill by the entrance to the Abbey ruins. Also on Angel Hill is the *Angel Hotel, an imposing Georgian building, where he slept on his later visits. It was in the courtyard of the Angel that Sam Weller, using the pump to help himself recover from the previous evening's 'conviviality', met Job Trotter for the first time and was beguiled into entangling Mr Pickwick in his unfortunate adventure at a local school for young ladies (Ch. 16). The scene of that episode, 'Westgate House' ('a large, old, red-brick house, just outside the town'), is sometimes identified as Southgate House on Southgate Street, reached from St Mary's Square, though Eastgate House in Rochester (Rte 12) has rival claims.

From Ipswich the main A12 route continues to Lowestoft (118 miles) and the region Dickens toured in 1849.

A detour from A12 3 miles north of Lowestoft leads left to Blundeston, which by an easy process of transliteration suggested 'Blunderstone', the village where David Copperfield is born and spends his early years. Attempts to associate the 'Rookery' of his childhood with either the Rectory or Blundeston Hall should not be trusted, since Dickens himself implied in a letter that it was not so much the topography of the village as 'the sound of its name' which he used. The round Norman tower of Blundeston church has been restored as a memorial to him. At Somerleyton Hall, 2 miles beyond, he was the guest of the railway magnate Sir Morton Peto, who had vastly extended his 17C manor house in 1844.

A12 leads north to Great Yarmouth (128 miles), which Dickens reported on the basis of his 1849 visit to be 'the strangest place in the world', apparently because of the flatness of the surrounding countryside. Its subsequent growth into the most popular resort on the Norfolk coast has robbed it of most of the atmosphere he found and evoked in the early chapters of *David Copperfield*. However, the visitor should not neglect the Denes, near the monument to Nelson, where the Peggotty family had their eccentric dwelling: 'a black barge, or some other kind of superannuated boat, ... high and dry on the ground, with an iron funnel sticking out of it for a chimney and smoking very cosily' (Ch. 3).

Somerleyton Hall, Somerleyton, near Lowestoft, Suffolk: phone Lowestoft (0502) 730224.

Northern England

18 London to Carrock Fell via Barnard Castle and Bowes

Dickens' most important connection with Northern England dates from the trip he made with his illustrator, Hablôt Browne, in 1838 to the notorious Yorkshire private schools as part of his research for *Nicholas Nickleby*.

This route may be treated as a continuation of Rte 15 or taken by itself, travelling directly up A1 via Grantham (112 miles) and Doncaster (163 miles).

At 188 miles A64 offers a detour NE to York (14 miles). 'The Five Sisters', lancet lights of 13C grisaille glass in the north transept of York Minster, inspire the fanciful story told to Nicholas by the 'grey-headed gentleman' in Chapter 6 of the novel. Dickens heard the legend while staying with the Minster organist, Dr John Camidge, at the King's Manor on St Leonard's Place. This lovely, partly 15C building is now used by the University of York.

The main route continues north on A1 to Scotch Corner (239 miles), where A66 leads NW. At Greta Bridge (248 miles), near the junction of the Greta and the Tees, Dickens proved unresponsive to scenery that impressed Sir Walter Scott (q.v.), Turner and Cotman, finding it merely 'a bare place ... in the midst of a dreary moor'. His friendly reception at the George and New Inn (now a private house) mollified him and may have encouraged the tributes to local good-heartedness and hospitality which offset his otherwise rather bleak picture of the region in *Nicholas Nickleby*.

To the NW is the attractive market town of Barnard Castle (252 miles). The King's Head, where Dickens and Browne lodged, is recommended to Nicholas by Newman Noggs for its good ale (Ch. 7). Almost opposite the hotel stood a clockmaker's shop belonging to a Master Humphrey, which gave Dickens the title for the ill-fated miscellany in which he attempted to revive Mr Pickwick and Sam Weller but managed to rescue by using as a framework for *The Old Curiosity Shop* and *Barnaby Rudge*.

From Barnard Castle A67 leads SW to Bowes (257 miles). The low stone building, now converted into apartments, at the end of the village's only street was undoubtedly Dickens' main model for the cruel and horrifying 'Dotheboys Hall', though he also drew hints from several other schools in the Bowes area: 'a long, cold-looking house, with a few straggling outbuildings behind and a barn and a stable adjoining' (Ch. 9). At the time of Dickens' visit it housed an academy run by William Shaw (a one-eyed man, like his fictional counterpart Squeers), who had already achieved minor notoriety in 1823 when he was twice tried for cruelty to his pupils. The church contains a memorial window to Shaw, donated in 1896, while he and his family lie in the churchyard. Its most interesting feature is the gravestone commemorating George Ashton Taylor, a pupil of Shaw's who died 'suddenly' at the age of 19 in 1822. Dickens read the inscription and later remarked: 'I think his ghost put Smike into my head, on the spot'.

A66 continues west via Brough (270 miles) and Penrith (291 miles) to a right turn, later dwindling into a track, at 301 miles, leading to Mungrisdale, Mosedale and Carrock Fell (308 miles; 2174ft). The fell was the main object of an abortive tour of Cumbria made by Dickens and Wilkie Collins (q.v.) in September 1857. Guided by a local publican who later confessed he had not tackled Carrock for twenty years, they managed to reach the top but their descent was beset by a series of accidents in which Dickens broke his compass and Collins sprained his ankle. Chapter 1 of *The Lazy Tour of Two Idle Apprentices*, jointly written by the two novelists and serialised in 1857, gives a comic account of their expedition.

THOMAS HARDY

b. Higher Bockhampton, Dorset, 1840; d. Dorchester, Dorset, 1928. *Desperate Remedies* (1871); *Under the Greenwood Tree* (1872); *A Pair of Blue Eyes* (1873); *Far from the Madding Crowd* (1874); *The Hand of Ethelberta* (1876); *The Return of the Native* (1878); *The Trumpet-Major* (1880); *A Laodicean* (1881); *Two on a Tower* (1882); *The Mayor of Casterbridge* (1886); *The Woodlanders* (1887); *Wessex Tales* (1888); *A Group of Noble Dames* (1891); *Tess of the d'Urbervilles* (1891); *Life's Little Ironies* (1894); *Jude the Obscure* (1896); *The Well-Beloved* (1897); *Wessex Poems* (1898); *Poems of the Past and Present* (1902); *The Dynasts* (1903–08); *Time's Laughingstocks* (1909); *A Changed Man and Other Tales* (1913); *Satires of Circumstance* (1914); *Moments of Vision* (1917); *Late Lyrics and Earlier* (1922); *The Famous Tragedy of the Queen of Cornwall* (1923); *Human Shows* (1925); *Winter Words* (1928); *The Early Life of Thomas Hardy 1840–1891*† (1928); *The Later Years of Thomas Hardy 1892–1928*† (1930); *An Indiscretion in the Life of an Heiress* (1934); *Our Exploits at West Poley* (1952).

† written by Hardy but published under the name of his second wife, Florence Emily. Republished in one volume as *Life of Thomas Hardy 1840–1928*.

Thomas Hardy by William Strang (1919)

Hardy needs little by way of general introduction, if only because his 'Wessex', home for most of his long life and setting for the bulk of his writing, stands at or very near the top of any literary pilgrim's itinerary. In its combination of literary interest with architectural and natural beauty 'Wessex' is probably unrivalled among the sights described in this volume. Even the detailed tours suggested under South-Western England (Rtes 5–14) and Central England (Rte 15) do not exhaust its richness. They are supplemented by reminders of Hardy's connection with London (Rtes 1–4) and Cambridge (Rte 16).

London

Hardy's acquaintance with the city was both larger and more significant than the common image of him would admit. We fall into serious misunderstanding if we suppose him a massively rooted provincial, a reclusive countryman whose knowledge of the world was limited to his native Dorset. In fact, he knew London well. From 1862 until 1867, crucial years when he was in his twenties, he worked as assistant to the London architect Arthur Blomfield. He returned in 1874–76 and 1878–81, the early years of his marriage, clearly wondering if London were not the necessary place for a writer to pursue his career, just as he had earlier supposed the same thing to hold true for an architect. When he did settle permanently in Dorset in the 1880s he was, like Clym Yeobright, no longer simply a native but a returned native: his love of home was now mixed with the detachment that comes from experience of other, different places. He still journeyed up to London for the fashionable season each year until extreme old age, taking innocent pride in the *entrée* he enjoyed to aristocratic dinner tables and in the ease with which he could slip again into the role of a 'London man'.

1 Adelphi

From Charing Cross Station (British Rail, and Northern, Bakerloo and Jubilee Underground Lines) we walk east along the Strand and make a right turn towards the river on Adam Street. This quickly brings us to Adelphi Terrace, a building of 1938 replacing the original 18C one by the Adam brothers. In 1863 Hardy's employer, the church architect Arthur Blomfield, moved his office to No. 8 and Hardy wrote enthusiastically to his sister Mary that it was 'a capital place. It is on the first floor and on a terrace that overlooks the river. We can see from our window right across the Thames, and on a clear day every bridge is visible' (*Life*, Aetat. 21–27). He later recalled with some affection: 'I sat there drawing, ... occasionally varying the experience by idling on the balcony. I saw from there the Embankment and Charing Cross Bridge built ... The rooms contained at that date fine Adam mantelpieces in white marble, on which we used to sketch caricatures in pencil' (*Life*, Aetat. 21–27). The mention of 'idling' is perhaps misleading for, apart from his conscientious application to architecture, Hardy's years with Blomfield were a period of great intellectual growth. He wrote poetry that was not to the taste of magazine editors and turned to fiction instead, producing *The Poor Man and the Lady*. The novel was never published, and Hardy later destroyed the manuscript, but the opinion of George Meredith (q.v.) was favourable enough to encourage him. By the time he returned home to Dorset in 1867, exhausted and in poor health, he was already wavering between literature and architecture as careers.

2 Westminster Abbey

Hardy's tablet in Poets' Corner (fee) marks the site of perhaps the most grotesquely inappropriate funeral suffered by an English writer. He had felt no love for the Abbey authorities, satirising the Dean for his exclusion of Byron (q.v.) in his poem 'A Refusal', and had wished to lie by his family in Stinsford churchyard (Rte 9). But before consulting the relatives his literary co-executor Sydney Cockerell zealously went ahead with arrangements for a grand public funeral in the Abbey, and the resulting conflict had to be resolved by an expedient that sounds like a grim joke from Hardy's own writing. His heart, removed by the local doctor, was reserved for Stinsford while the rest of him was buried at Westminster, with leading literary men of the day acting as pallbearers: Barrie, Galsworthy, Housman, Kipling and Shaw (qq.v.).

3 Paddington and Maida Vale

Hardy lodged in Paddington while working for Arthur Blomfield in 1862–67 and returned to the area in 1874 for his marriage to Emma Gifford at St Peter's on Elgin Avenue, SW of Maida Vale Underground Station (Bakerloo Line). When he came to write his disguised autobiography at the end of his life he was still proud enough of Emma's genteel connections to note that the service was performed by 'her uncle Dr E. Hamilton Gifford, Canon of Worcester, and afterwards Archdeacon of London' (*Life*, Aetat. 33–36). More sentimentally, she remembered that the wedding took place on 'a perfect September day ... not of brilliant sunshine, but wearing a soft sunny luminousness; just as it should be' (*Life*, Aetat. 29–30). The couple spent their honeymoon on the Continent and then lived briefly in Surbiton and Yeovil before setting up their first real home together at Sturminster Newton (Rte 7).

4 Tooting

We begin this visit to Hardy's south London home in 1878–81 at Tooting Bec Underground Station (Northern Line).

Near Tooting Bec Common, reached via Tooting Bec Road to the south, he saw the unhappily loitering couple who appear in his poem 'Beyond the Last Lamp'. Our main route takes us north up Trinity Road to Arundel Terrace, a block of Victorian villas on the right-hand side near the junction with Brodrick Road and the outskirts of Wandsworth Common. A plaque at No. 1 (now No. 172 Trinity Road) marks the dreary house where Hardy and his first wife Emma lived after their 'idyll' at Sturminster Newton (Rte 7) and before their move to Wimborne (Rte 9). Hardy later wrote that he 'by degrees fell into line as a London man again' (*Life*, Aetat. 37–39) but in his diary also spoke of a 'horror at lying down in close proximity to "a monster whose body had four million heads and eight million eyes" (*Life*, Aetat. 39–40). Shortly after his arrival *The Return of the Native*, written in Sturminster Newton, was published. At Arundel Terrace he wrote *The Trumpet-Major* and *A Laodicean*, the latter inevitably damaged by the internal haemorrhage that kept him bed-ridden for the last five months of his stay.

South-Western England

Hardy did not use the term 'Wessex' until Chapter 50 of his fourth novel, *Far from the Madding Crowd*, where 'Greenhill Fair' (really Woodbury Fair outside Bere Regis) is described in an unpromisingly obscure phrase as 'the Nijni Novgorod of South Wessex'. Once introduced, it opened up suggestive possibilities for a writer who was both methodical and deeply attached to the principle of the classical unities. He later explained in a preface to the book:

> The series of novels I projected being mainly of the kind called local, they seemed to require a territorial definition of some sort to lend unity to their scene. Finding that the area of a single county did not afford a canvas large enough for this purpose, and that there were objections to an invented name, I disinterred the old one.

This may take retrospective credit for a more systematic intent than he really possessed when he stood on the threshold of his career as a major novelist, but the fact remains that his development into this status—and his subsequent blossoming into a major poet—required the creation, elaboration, extension and, finally, the commanding possession of a fictional territory. He needed a solid, defined stage for his invented dramas. The mood of Hardy's art may shift from the comic to the tragic (indeed, we can already see this happening in *Far from the Madding Crowd*), and the preoccupations embodied in his central characters may change with the years, but his people act out their differing fates against a landscape which remains constant and familiar.

Hardy began the creation of 'Wessex' with a mild inaccuracy, borrowing its name from the ancient Saxon kingdom whose centre lay east of the region he had in mind. In all else, however, he kept as near the facts as possible. Indeed, he possessed the rarest sort of artistic tact: an instinctive knowledge that imagination is sometimes superfluous and mere literal accuracy is eloquent enough. His home county of Dorset becomes 'South Wessex', Hampshire 'Upper Wessex', Wiltshire 'Mid-Wessex' and Somerset 'Outer Wessex'. The north-east boundary of 'North Wessex' reaches into Central England's Berkshire and Oxfordshire, the urbanised landscape of *Jude the Obscure*. Beyond Devon, called 'Lower Wessex' but virtually ignored in his writing, 'Off Wessex' extends westward to an unspecified point somewhere near the north Cornish coast, countryside charged with the memory of his first wife.

Of course, this territory does not completely enclose the action of the novels: characters travel to London, even to France, the United States and South America. Yet the world beyond 'Wessex' is shadowy, insubstantial, only vaguely seen. Hardy may regard Cainy Ball's innocent, wondering misconceptions about Bath with amusement (*Far from the Madding Crowd*, Ch. 33), yet his own acute sense of place deserts him when he turns his gaze to the larger scene. Sergeant Troy is given an improbable career as 'Professor of Gymnastics, Sword Exercise, Fencing, and Pugilism' in the United States (*Madding Crowd*, Ch. 50), while the account of Swithin St Cleeve's journey in *Two on a Tower* (Ch. 40) suggests that Hardy believed Boston and Cambridge, Massachusetts, were a considerable distance apart. In *Tess of the d'Urbervilles* (Ch. 41) he writes of Angel Clare falling ill from fever in the 'clay lands' near Curbita, a Brazilian city in fact situated on a high plateau.

The blurriness at the outer edge of Hardy's vision serves to emphasise how sharply in focus 'Wessex' is. Here landscape and buildings are seen with a vivid precision that constantly invokes the real geography of South-Western England. Hardy commonly keeps the existing names of natural landmarks like rivers and hills, while his towns, villages and hamlets wear only the thinnest of disguises. Who could fail to detect the name of Dorchester in 'Casterbridge', for example, or Weymouth in 'Budmouth' or Cerne Abbas in 'Abbot's Cernel'? Elsewhere an older name is revived, making Shaftesbury into 'Shaston'. Thrifty in his art as well as in his life, Hardy sometimes finds that the discarded name of a real place comes in handy for a character. Jude Fawley's surname is derived from the village that had become 'Marygreen', while we can find Troy (*Far from the Madding Crowd*), Chickerell (*The Hand of Ethelberta*), Melbury and Winterbourne (*The Woodlanders*) among the small print of the Ordnance Survey map.

As the popularity of his work attracted visitors to South-Western England, Hardy sometimes found it necessary to insist on the imaginary character of a particular place, like the 'Little Hintock' of *The Woodlanders*, or to admit that his imagination had enlarged Puddletown Heath or the Vale of Blackmore beyond their actual scope. But on the whole he showed little of the writer's customary annoyance at seekers after 'real-life originals' and was proud to accept the identification of 'Wessex' with his native region. The General Preface of 1912 to the Wessex Edition spoke of his scenery as having been 'done from the real' and provided a key to some of its major landmarks. By this time he had already smiled on the publication of several guides to 'Wessex', the first by B.C.A. Windle in 1901, and was actively helping Hermann Lea in his exhaustive study of 1913. The Wessex Edition itself reproduced photographs of real places identified by their fictional names.

This may sound disturbingly like the insistent desire for actuality in art which led the Victorians to introduce running streams and live rabbits into their productions of *As You Like It*. Such a taste certainly helped the reception of the 'Wessex' novels, and it appealed to one aspect of Hardy's complex temperament. He had the antiquarian's respect for facts and the countryman's zest for odd ones. His architect's training had developed a mathematically precise eye for distances and spatial relations, and left him with the sort of technical vocabulary he could never resist: his pen readily notes architraves

Map of 'Wessex' in the Wessex edition of Hardy's work (1912–31)

Map of the
WESSEX
of the
Novels and Poems
Scale of Miles
Christminster
Lumsdon
R. Thames
NORTH
Alfredston
The Brown House
Cresscombe
Marygreen
River Thames
MID
WESSEX
Marlbury
Downs
Castle
Royal
Gaymead
Aldbrickham
Kennetbridge
WESSEX
Inkpen Beacon
The Great
Plain
Stonehenge
Stoke Barehills
Quartershot
Weydon
Priors
Icenway
House
UPPER
Wintoncester
WESSEX
Melchester
Leddenton
Wingreen
Shaston
Marlott
The Chase
The Slopes
Trantridge Cross
Chaseborough
Stourcastle
Shottsford
Forum
Lornton
Inn
Warborne
Emminster
Welland
Kingsbere
Chene
Manor
Heath
Havenpool
Sandbourne
Nether Mynton
Anglebury
Corvsgate
Knollsea
Fernel Hall
Deansleigh
Park
Southampton
Portsmouth
The Great
Bramshurst
Forest
Solentsea
The
Island
The Channel
Emery Walker sc.

and ogee curves, or ponders distinctions between the various stages of Gothic. In the larger view, he possessed at least some of the instincts necessary to the social realist and could speak, in his General Preface, of the 'humble supplementary quality' his novels had in their relation to social history:

> At the dates represented in the various narrations things were like that in Wessex: the inhabitants lived in certain ways, engaged in certain occupations, kept alive certain customs, just as they are shown doing in these pages.

In our own age, uneasily conscious of the destruction of rural England and its traditional ways of life, he has come to be treasured above all as the historian—indeed, the elegist—of a vanished culture.

Yet he himself was quick to add that this aspect of his achievement was 'quite unintentional and unforeseen'. He was not Emile Zola nor even George Eliot (q.v.), though he conscientiously read both these authors. If 'Wessex' is 'partly real' it is also, he firmly reminded us, 'partly dream'. The dream-like quality comes not from sentimental regret at the death of rural England nor from occasional rebellions against the facts of geography. It comes, rather, from his own highly distinctive vision: an imaginative grasp, shaping and coherent, which underlies even his most dogged literal-mindedness. When we finish one of his novels we are left with the impression of a detailed map, but also with a more elemental image of man's position in the order of things, an image admirably summed up by Lionel Johnson in one of the earliest criticisms of Hardy:

> A rolling down country, crossed by a Roman road: here a gray standing stone, of what sacrificial, ritual origins I can but guess; there a grassy burrow, with its great bones, its red brown jars, its rude gold ornaments, still safe in the earth: a broad sky burning with stars: and a solitary man.

This, of course, is not to deny the real benefits—let alone the many incidental pleasures—to be taken from visits to the landscape he had in mind for his fiction. We should be guided by Hardy's own evident belief that the way to universals lies through the most careful attention to particulars.

For the sake of convenience, the tours suggested below begin with Dorchester, the cultural though not the literal centre of 'Wessex', and then proceed to a series of journeys radiating outward from the town.

5 Dorchester

**Dorchester, the single most important town in Hardy's life and work, was changing greatly in his time and has continued to change since then. The atmosphere conjured up so expressively in *The Mayor of Casterbridge* belonged to the years before his birth:

> Casterbridge was the complement of the rural life around; not its urban opposite. Bees and butterflies in the cornfields at the top of the town, who desired to get to the meads at the bottom, took no circuitous course, but flew straight down High Street without any apparent consciousness that they were traversing strange latitudes. And in autumn airy spheres of thistledown floated into the same street, lodged upon the shop fronts, blew into drains, and innumerable tawny and yellow leaves skimmed along the pavement, and stole through people's doorways into their passages with a hesitating scratch on the floor, like the skirts of timid visitors. (Ch. 9)

The railway came in 1847 when he was still a young boy, forging a link with London and bringing with it telegraphs and daily newspapers. By the time Hardy was working here as an apprentice architect (1856–61) and living with his parents at Higher Bockhampton (Rte 9) he was, he realised, a commuter between two radically different ways of life, observer of 'rustic and borough doings in a juxtaposition peculiarly close' (*Life*, Aetat. 16–21). Later he sometimes had reason to lament the destruction of local landmarks like the old Three Mariners Inn.

'Looking up the High Street of Casterbridge', from the Wessex edition of The Mayor of Casterbridge

Even though the visitor should be ready for exhaust fumes rather than butterflies or thistledown in the streets, he will also find Dorchester a remarkable survival. It has suffered much less from modernisation than most county towns; its main buildings and its quiet corners would be familiar to Hardy and his characters.

The town is best explored by a series of walking tours starting from the centre formed by the junction of Cornhill, High Street West and High Street East. The distinctive landmark at this spot is St Peter's with the statue of William Barnes (q.v.), Hardy's friend and fellow poet, outside. The local architect John Hicks was finishing a major restoration of the church when Hardy joined his office in 1856, and Hardy himself may have worked on alterations to the east window and the north vestry. At any rate, there is an architectural plan signed by him on a pillar in the south aisle. Hardy, who developed a snobbishly selective approach to his ancestors, liked to believe that he was descended from the Elizabethan Thomas Hardy, founder of Dorchester's grammar school, commemorated by a chapel and a separate tablet. The 8 o'clock curfew which the bells of St Peter's used to sound is mentioned in *The Mayor of Casterbridge* (Ch. 4).

The *Dorset County Museum next door has a collection rich in Roman antiquities, agricultural equipment and musical instruments used by the old church 'quires'—all subjects of great interest to Hardy. Also on display is a reconstruction of his study at Max Gate, and an arch with a mask as its keystone, formerly part of Colliton House. So grotesque an object was bound to catch Hardy's attention:

> Originally the mask had exhibited a comic leer, as could still be discerned; but generations of Casterbridge boys had thrown stones at the mask, aiming at its open mouth; and the blows thereon had chipped off the lips and jaws as if they had been eaten away by disease. (*Mayor*, Ch. 21)

We start our first walking tour by descending High Street East. Immediately on our left is the Town Hall and Corn Exchange, built in 1847 and so presumably the setting Hardy had in mind for two important scenes: Henchard's confrontation with the furmity-woman who had witnessed the wife-sale (*Mayor*, Ch. 28) and Bathsheba Everdene's first triumphant appearance among the local farmers (*Far from the Madding Crowd*, Ch. 12). Next we come to the *King's Arms Hotel, conspicuous for its handsome portico with a bow window above. Looking in through this window Mrs Henchard saw her husband presiding as Mayor over the public dinner (Ch. 5). Henchard's bankruptcy hearing was held in another front room (Ch. 31).

Opposite the hotel stands All Saints' Church, a 19C building no longer used for worship. After Sunday service the choir filed across to the Three Mariners Inn and met a drunken Michael Henchard demanding that they play the 'cursing psalm' (Ch. 33). The Elizabethan inn has gone and the site is occupied by the British Legion Club. As we approach the bottom of High Street East we find, again on our left, the White Hart. In this now sadly altered building Sergeant Troy met Pennyways before going on to make his disastrous appearance at Boldwood's Christmas party (*Madding Crowd*, Ch. 52).

At the bottom of the hill is Swan Bridge, a modern replacement of a much older structure. Hardy mentions it as one of two bridges which attracted 'all the failures of the town; those who had failed in business, in love, in sobriety, in crime' (*Mayor*, Ch. 32). To reach the second, Grey's Bridge, and so to retrace the steps of Michael Henchard when his fortunes had sunk to their lowest, we continue straight ahead along the London road with the flat expanse of Durnover Moor stretching on either side. From Grey's Bridge a footpath leads left along the riverside to Ten Hatches, the sluice gates and weir where Henchard contemplates suicide but is stopped by the appearance of his own effigy in the water (Ch. 41).

Returning to the bridge we cross the road and take King's Road to the turning on the right for Mill Street, the disreputable 'Mixen Lane':

> It was the hiding-place of those who were in distress, and in debt, and trouble of every kind. Farm-labourers and other peasants, who combined a little poaching with their farming, and a little brawling and bibbing with their poaching, found themselves sooner or later in Mixen Lane. Rural mechanics too idle to mechanise, rural servants too rebellious to serve, drifted or were forced into Mixen Lane. (*Mayor*, Ch. 36)

The neighbourhood had already risen when Hardy wrote the novel and it has changed beyond recognition since then. In the years of her widowhood Florence Emily, Hardy's second wife, took an active part in its improvement.

At the top of King's Road we come to Fordington Cross, centre of the area Hardy calls 'Durnover' and mentions in *The Mayor of Casterbridge* as the site of the corn merchants' granaries. It is most important as a reminder of Hardy's youthful friendship with the Moule family. Rev. Henry Moule was Vicar of Fordington and his church, St George's, is reached by turning right at the Cross, following Fordington Hill, and then branching right on Fordington High Street. In the churchyard lies Moule's son Horace (properly Horatio), friend of Hardy, the first person to encourage his literary ambitions and, by his suicide in 1873, a partial model for the ill-fated Boldwood in *Far from the Madding Crowd* and Jude Fawley. Hardy's poem 'Before My Friend Arrived' describes his visit to the newly dug grave the night before Moule's body was returned from Cambridge (Rte 16). After St George's we descend Fordington High Street to Swan Bridge and return to the centre of town.

We start a second excursion from Cornhill by taking the narrow lane between St Peter's and the Town Hall, scene of the collision between Henchard and Farfrae's wagons (*Mayor*, Ch. 27). The same chapter recalls that North Square beyond once boasted stocks and a stone post to which oxen were tied for baiting by dogs, in the belief it would make their meat tender.

From North Square we descend Friary Hill, cross the river and take the path to our left. Henchard came here after reading the letter from his dead wife, for the neighbourhood suited his mood by embodying 'the mournful phases of Casterbridge life' (*Mayor*, Ch. 19). On the opposite bank of the river rises the unpicturesque shape of the Prison, a modern building that preserves the 'classic archway of ashlar' noted by Gertrude Lodge in the short story, 'The Withered Arm'. Boldwood knocked at the gate to give himself up after shooting Troy (*Madding Crowd*, Ch. 54). In the first half of the nineteenth century executions were still held outside the prison, and these spectacles played a part in the development of Hardy's sometimes morbid sensibility. The hanging of the murderess Martha Brown, which he witnessed in 1856, may have helped suggest the final scene of *Tess of the d'Urbervilles*. His *Life* recounts a grotesque memory of 1858:

> One summer morning at Bockhampton, just before he sat down to breakfast, he remembered that a man was to be hanged at eight o'clock at Dorchester. He took up the big brass telescope that had been handed on in the family, and hastened to a hill on the heath a quarter of a mile away from the house, whence he looked towards the town. The sun behind his back shone straight on the white stone façade of the gaol, the gallows upon it, and the form of the murderer in white fustian, the executioner and officials in dark clothing and the crowd below being invisible at this distance of nearly three miles. At the moment of his placing the glass to his eye the white figure dropped downwards, and the faint note of the town clock struck eight.
>
> The whole thing had been so sudden that the glass nearly fell from Hardy's hands. He seemed alone on the heath with the hanged man, and crept homeward wishing he had not been so curious. (Aetat. 16–21)

We cross the river at the next bridge and, as the road bends to the right, find Hangman's Cottage. The public hangman still lived in this picturesque building when Hardy was a boy, and Gertrude Lodge pays him a memorable visit in 'The Withered Arm'. Almost opposite is the entrance to North Walk, one of several distinctive tree-lined avenues that mark the line of Dorchester's old Roman walls. We follow the Walk to the right and then bear left on Colliton Walk, which runs alongside The Grove. Henchard walked here with Farfrae, persuading him not to emigrate but to stay in 'Casterbridge' instead (Ch. 9).

'The Hangman's Cottage at Casterbridge' from the Wessex edition of Wessex Tales

Close to the Top o' Town junction near the end of Colliton Walk is Eric Kennington's statue of Hardy, unveiled in 1931 by Sir James Barrie (q.v.). We turn left into High West Street and, just before reaching Shire Hall, take another left into Glyde Path Road. Behind the row of houses on its left-hand side stood No. 7 Shire Hall Place, Hardy's home in 1883–85, when he was writing *The Mayor of Casterbridge* and waiting for Max Gate to be completed. Further along we find Colliton House, now part of the offices of Dorset County Council. The 18C building was probably the model for 'High Place Hall', home of Lucetta Templeman:

> The Hall, with its grey façade and parapet, was the only residence of its sort so near the centre of town ... The house was entirely of stone, and formed an example of dignity without great size. It was not altogether aristocratic, still less consequential, yet the old-fashioned stranger instinctively said, 'Blood built it, and wealth enjoys it', however vague his opinions of these accessories might be. (*Mayor*, Ch. 21)

In the process of turning Colliton House into 'High Place Hall' Hardy moved it to Cornhill so that it could enjoy a panoramic view of Dorchester's market. As the start of our third tour we should examine

Cornhill more closely, since it is a recurrent location for the public scenes in his novels: 'The *carrefour* was like the regulation Open Place in spectacular dramas, where the incidents that occur always happen to bear on the lives of the adjoining residents' (*Mayor*, Ch. 24). Mother Cuxsom and the rural chorus gather round the town pump, which still survives, to gossip about Mrs Henchard's death (*Mayor*, Ch. 18) and in *Far from the Madding Crowd* Gabriel Oak plays his flute to console himself after failing to get a job at the hiring fair (Ch. 6). On the right is the impressive frontage of the Antelope Hotel where Henchard waits in vain to give Lucetta back her letters (*Mayor*, Ch. 18).

Cornhill leads to South Street ('Corn Street') where, beyond the entrance to Tudor Arcade on the left, we find the fine 18C house 'faced with dull red-and-grey old brick' (Ch. 9) that Hardy used as Michael Henchard's home. It is now a branch of Barclays Bank. Further on, Napper's Mite was once almshouses and the Hardye Arcade, a modern shopping precinct, occupies the site of Hardye's Grammar School, whose pupils included Sergeant Troy. The scene opposite is more interesting. Next to each other and marked by plaques are the house of William Barnes and the offices of the architect John Hicks, where Hardy worked in 1856–61 and again after his return from London in 1867. His *Life* (Aetat. 16–21) remembers that he would sometimes slip out of the office to get Barnes' advice on a point of Greek grammar.

From the large road junction at the bottom of South Street we may take Great Western Road and its continuation as Damers Road right to the former Union Workhouse, now Damers Hospital. Fanny Robin came here to die in Chapter 40 of *Far from the Madding Crowd* and Hardy used the occasion for a laconic comment: 'A neighbouring earl once said that he would give up a year's rental to have at his own door the view enjoyed by the inmates from theirs—and very probably the inmates would have given up the view for his year's rental'.

Returning to the South Street junction we continue south on Weymouth Avenue. After passing near the railway station on our left we come to Maumbury Rings, the Roman amphitheatre which Hardy usually calls 'The Ring'. As a child he was brought by his father to see effigies of the Pope and Cardinal Wiseman burnt during the No-Popery Riots, and in *The Mayor of Casterbridge* (Ch. 11) he made 'The Ring' setting for Henchard's reunion with his wife. The scene includes a fine evocation of the place's gloomy history.

Max Gate, the final point of interest in a tour of Dorchester, lies about a mile from the centre and is best reached by car, following the Wareham road (A352) south-east, past a modern pub named after *The Trumpet-Major*, to the turning on the left for Syward Road. The house occupies the corner site. Hardy designed it himself, had it built by his brother Henry, moved to it in 1885 and stayed for the rest of his life. *Tess of the d'Urbervilles* and *Jude the Obscure* were written here during the years of crisis in his marriage to Emma. Many of the poems he wrote after abandoning fiction in the 1890s are rooted in domestic incidents at Max Gate. After Emma's death in 1912 he brought his second wife, Florence Emily, to the house. The 1920s, when he had become the Grand Old Man of English Letters, saw a procession of distinguished visitors: T.E. Lawrence (q.v.), then living nearby at Clouds Hill, was the most welcome and Virginia Woolf (q.v.), daughter of Hardy's old friend Leslie Stephen, the most ironically perceptive. His manner of receiving guests was described by Siegfried Sassoon in the poem 'At Max Gate':

Old Mr Hardy, upright in his chair,
Courteous to visiting acquaintance chatted
With unaloof alertness while he patted
The sheep dog whose society he preferred.
He wore an air of never having heard
That there was much that needed putting right.
Hardy, the Wessex wizard, wasn't there.
Good care was taken to keep him out of sight.

For all this wealth of personal history, the house is neither attractive nor expressive. One can appreciate Hardy's choice of the site, with its fine views over the surrounding countryside; it allowed him, incidentally, to walk by a path that cuts off the curve of A352 to William Barnes' rectory. But the building itself, bleakly angular, is a disappointing creation by a man who elsewhere shows himself so sensitive to architectural nuance. It would have been more appropriate for a successful town councillor or businessman than for the novelist who described his birthplace at Higher Bockhampton or Bathsheba's farmhouse or the old buildings of Dorchester so lovingly. Its gloomy atmosphere is intensified by the heavy screen of trees, mostly planted by Hardy himself, a forcible reminder of his carefully guarded privacy in later life.

Dorset County Museum, High Street West, Dorchester, Dorset: phone (0305) 62735.

6 Dorchester to Sherborne via Cerne Abbas and Cross-in-Hand

The route takes us north from Dorchester through countryside mainly associated with *The Woodlanders* and *Tess of the d'Urbervilles*. It begins at the Top o' Town, where we follow A37 (the Yeovil road) and branch right after 1½ miles on A352 towards Sherborne.

At 7 miles we reach Cerne Abbas ('Abbot's Cernel'), a village so satisfyingly picturesque that it acts as a powerful magnet for summer visitors. South of The Folly, the street by which we approach the main village from A352, is the medieval Tithe Barn that once belonged to the Abbey. Together with the one at Abbotsbury (Rte 12), it is claimed as model for the shearing barn enthusiastically celebrated by Hardy in *Far from the Madding Crowd*:

> One could say about this barn, what could hardly be said of either the church or the castle, akin to it in age and style, that the purpose which had dictated its original erection was the same with that to which it was still applied. Unlike and superior to either of those two typical remnants of mediaevalism, the old barn embodied practices which had suffered no mutilation at the hands of time. Here at least the spirit of the ancient builders was one with the spirit of the modern beholder. Standing before this abraded pile, the eye regarded its present usage, the mind dwelt upon its past history, with a satisfied sense of functional continuity throughout—a feeling almost of gratitude, and quite of pride, at the permanence of the idea which had heaped it up ... The defence and salvation of the body by daily bread is still a study, a religion, and a desire. (Ch. 22)

The charming Abbey Street leads north past the church to a beautiful 15C gatehouse, only surviving fragment of the Abbey where Hardy's poem 'The Lost Pyx' begins.

As we leave the village on A352 we have on the right a fine view of the Cerne Giant (NT), the massive chalk figure carved on the hillside. Our route is now following the coaching road travelled by Mrs Dollery's van in the opening chapter of *The Woodlanders*, though it no longer has quite the forsaken atmosphere Hardy pondered:

> The physiognomy of a deserted highway expresses solitude to a degree that is not reached by mere dales or downs, and bespeaks a tomb-like stillness more emphatic than that of glades and pools. The contrast of what is with what might be, probably accounts for this. To step, for instance, ... from the edge of the plantation into the adjoining thoroughfare, and pause amid its emptiness for a moment, was to exchange by the act of a single stride the simple absence of human companionship for an incubus of the forlorn.

With Minterne Magna (9 miles) we reach 'Great Hintock', one of the few certainly identifiable locations in a novel whose elusive topography will shortly be considered.

A mile north of the village we turn left on the unclassified road that leads across the high uplands of Batcombe Down towards Holywell and Evershot. On our right we soon find *Cross-in-Hand (11½ miles), a short stone pillar of uncertain date surmounted by an almost indecipherable design. 'The Lost Pyx' describes one legend explaining this mysterious landmark. In *Tess*, when the heroine passes it on her journey to Angel Clare's parents, Hardy suggests that it 'marks the site of a miracle, or murder, or both' (Ch. 44). In the following chapter, when she has a dramatic encounter with Alec d'Urberville here on her return journey, Hardy adds:

> Some authorities stated that a devotional cross had once formed the complete erection thereon, of which the present relic was but the stump; others that the stone as it stood was entire, and that it had been fixed there to mark a boundary or place of meeting. Anyhow, whatever the origin of the relic, there was and is something sinister, or solemn, according to mood, in the scene amid which it stands; something tending to impress the most phlegmatic passer-by. (Ch. 45)

The scene is certainly striking, for from this bleak height spreads one of the widest views in Dorset. To the west, on our left, rises Bubb Down and to the east High Stoy. The Blackmore (or Blackmoor) Vale—home of Tess' childhood (Rte 7)—stretches north and east of High Stoy.

Somewhere in the nearer reaches of this expanse is the setting of *The Woodlanders*, a countryside of 'extensive woodlands, interspersed with apple-orchards' (Ch. 1). In creating 'Little Hintock', home of the Melbury family and the book's main location, Hardy abandoned his normally precise use of the map and took a certain delight in the confusion he caused his more earnest readers:

> I once spent several hours on a bicycle with a friend in a serious attempt to discover the real spot; but the search ended in failure; though tourists assure me positively that they have found it without trouble, and that it answers in every particular to the description given in this volume. At all events, ... the commanding heights called 'High-Stoy' and 'Bubb-Down Hill' overlook the landscape in which it is supposed to be hid. (Preface of 1912)

From Cross-in-Hand we return to A352 and continue north. The junction with A3030 (20 miles) marks the site of the Sherborne turnpike where Gabriel Oak and Jan Coggan overtake Bathsheba on her secret journey to Bath (*Madding Crowd*, Ch. 32).

At 22 miles A352 brings us to Sherborne, Hardy's 'Sherton Abbas' and still one of the pleasantest towns in Dorset. Its chief sight is the magnificent Abbey, where Grace Melbury and Giles Winterbourne sit among the tombs (*Woodlanders*, Ch. 38). The tombs again caught

Hardy's attention in the poem 'In Sherborne Abbey'. East of the river at the edge of the town lie the ruins of the Old Castle and the 16C Sherborne Castle. Already of interest to the literary-minded visitor for their connection with Sir Walter Ralegh (q.v.), the buildings were used by Hardy as the setting for 'Anna Lady Baxby' in *A Group of Noble Dames*. Grace Melbury inspects the Old Castle in Chapter 23 of *The Woodlanders*.

Sherborne Castle, Sherborne, Dorset: phone (0935) 813182.

Sherborne Old Castle, Sherborne, Dorset: English Heritage, standard opening; phone (0935) 812730.

7 Dorchester to Cranborne via Sturminster Newton and Shaftesbury

This journey takes us through scenes from *Tess of the d'Urbervilles* and *Jude the Obscure*, as well as Hardy's life in the years following his marriage to Emma.

We start by heading east from Dorchester on the Puddletown road (A35) and branching left on B3143 just beyond Grey's Bridge over the Frome. B3143 leads north through Piddlehinton, White Lackington and Piddletrenthide (about 7 miles) to an unclassified road on the right for Plush (8½ miles). The village lies in the middle of the area where several locations have been proposed for 'Flintcomb-Ash', the 'starve-acre place' where Tess goes to work in Chapter 43 and where she experiences her greatest suffering. None of the suggestions is entirely convincing and together they serve to remind us that Hardy was in the habit of hiding or muddling the identity of unpleasant places in his novels.

From Plush we continue NE to Mappowder (11½ miles). Some 2 miles east of the village rises Bulbarrow, second highest point in Dorset and one of the hills celebrated in the poem 'Wessex Heights'. It also marks one boundary of the Vale of Blackmore or Blackmoor (see also Rte 6), familiar to readers of *Tess*:

> This fertile and sheltered tract of country, in which the fields are never brown and the springs never dry, is bounded on the south by the bold chalk ridge that embraces the prominences of Hambledon Hill, Bulbarrow, Nettlecombe-Tout, Dogbury, High Stoy, and Bubb Down. The traveller from the coast, who, after plodding northward for a score of miles over calcareous downs and corn-lands, suddenly reaches the verge of one of these escarpments, is surprised and delighted to behold, extended like a map beneath him, a country differing absolutely from that which he has passed through. Behind him the hills are open, the sun blazes down upon fields so large as to give an unenclosed character to the landscape, the lanes are white, the hedges low and plashed, the atmosphere colourless. Here, in the valley, the world seems to be constructed upon a smaller and more delicate scale; the fields are mere paddocks, so reduced that from this height their hedgerows appear a network of dark green threads overspreading the paler green of the grass. The atmosphere beneath is languorous, and is so tinged with azure that what artists call the middle distance partakes also of that hue, while the horizon beyond is of the deepest ultramarine. Arable lands are few and limited; with but slight exceptions the prospect is a broad rich mass of grass and trees, mantling minor hills and dales within the major. (Ch. 2)

We enter this country on unclassified roads leading via Hazelbury

Bryan ('Nuttlebury' in *Tess*) to the junction with A357 and, immediately north, Sturminster Newton (18 miles).

This quiet market town, the 'Stourcastle' of *Tess*, was Hardy's home from 1876, when he and Emma left furnished lodgings in Yeovil, until they went to London in 1878 (Rte 4). *The Return of the Native* was written at Riverside Villa, their house overlooking the Stour west of the town. Hardy later described the excitement of setting up what was in effect their first married home, hastily furnishing it 'by going to Bristol and buying £100 worth of mid-Victorian furniture in two hours' (*Life*, Aetat. 36–37). He came to treasure the 'Sturminster idyll' as the happiest phase of a marriage that later settled into quiet, entrenched unhappiness:

Yes; such it was;
Just those two seasons unsought,
Sweeping like summertide wind on our ways;
Moving, as straws,
Hearts quick as ours in those days;
Going like wind, too, and rated as nought
Save as the prelude to plays
Soon to come—larger, life-fraught:
Yes; such it was.

('A Two-Years' Idyll', first stanza)

'The To-Be-Forgotten' was written after a return visit in 1899. In *Moments of Vision* three poems—'Overlooking the River Stour', 'The Musical Box' and 'On Sturminster Foot-Bridge'—combine memories of scenes near his house with retrospective fears that he paid too little attention to Emma.

On B3092 to the north is Marnhull (21 miles), a sprawling village and the 'Marlott' of *Tess*. None of the inevitable attempts to identify the Durbeyfields' cottage is persuasive, though the Crown Inn by the church presumably suggested Hardy's 'Pure Drop Inn'. B3092 continues to the junction with A30 (24 miles), which leads east to *Shaftesbury (28 miles). This stone-built town, marvellously situated on a hill enjoying superb views of the surrounding country, appears under its old local name as 'Shaston' in *Jude the Obscure*, where Hardy quite rightly calls it 'one of the queerest and quaintest spots in England' (Part 4, Ch. 1). His account, however, omits mention of Gold Hill, perhaps Shaftesbury's queerest and quaintest spot. 'Old Grove Place', the home of Sue and her schoolmaster-husband Phillotson, is the Ox House on Bimport, off the north end of the High Street. We may follow Jude's example and take Abbey Walk from Bimport to Park Walk, with its fine view of the country to the south. The Grosvenor Arms in the Market Place is presumably the 'Duke's Arms', where Jude missed his coach at the end of his visit.

From Shaftesbury we can make a detour (20 miles in all) to Wardour Castle by following A30 NE towards Salisbury and then branching left at 6 miles for Tisbury. The Castle, built in 1769–76 by James Paine, has lost the collection of pictures admired by Jude and Sue (*Jude the Obscure*, Part 3, Ch. 2) as well as some of its decorated ceilings and panelling. It is now a school. The medieval ruins of Old Wardour Castle, which did not attract the severely classical Sue Bridehead, are 3/4 mile SE.

To the SE of Shaftesbury is Cranborne Chase, still preserving its character as 'a country of ragged woodland, which, though intruded on by the plough at places, remained largely intact from prehistoric times, and still abounded with yews of gigantic growth and oaks tufted with mistletoe' (*Two on a Tower*, Ch. 39). Tess Durbeyfield is raped here by Alec (Ch. 11). We cross the Chase by taking the scenic B3081 to the junction with B3078 (42 miles), where a left turn brings us to Cranborne (43 miles). Because unpleasant, the 'Trantridge' of *Tess of the d'Urbervilles* cannot be identified but Cranborne is certainly 'Chaseborough'—though in Hardy's description, 'decayed market-town' (Ch. 10), the adjective is no longer appropriate. The Fleur-de-Lys is obviously the 'Flower-de-Luce' mentioned by Alec when he offers to rescue Tess from the revelling of the 'Trantridge' labourers.

Wardour Castle, Cranborne Chase School, Tisbury, Wiltshire: phone number (0747) 870464.
Old Wardour Castle, near Tisbury, Wiltshire: English Heritage; phone (0747) 870487.

8 Salisbury and Stonehenge

This can easily be treated as an extension of Rte 7 by making the 17-mile journey from Cranborne to Salisbury on B3078 east and A338 north or by taking A30 12 miles NE after visiting Wardour Castle.

Salisbury ('Melchester') is richly connected with several of Hardy's works, especially *Jude the Obscure*. If we took Sue Bridehead's advice in that novel we would begin a walking tour at the railway station, which she believes has replaced the Cathedral and other historic buildings as the 'centre of town life' (Part 3, Ch. 1). Instead, we start by the north end of the High Street at St Thomas of Canterbury, the 'grey Perpendicular church with a low-pitched roof' (Part 3, Ch. 7) where Sue is given away by Jude at her marriage to Phillotson. We then make the short walk south on the High Street to enter the *Cathedral Close by its North Gate.

Hardy paid tribute to these stately and impressive surroundings in a diary note made in 1897:

> Went into the Close late at night. The moon was visible through both the north and south clerestory windows to me standing on the turf on the north side ... Walked to the west front, and watched the moonlight creep round upon the statuary of the façade—stroking tentatively and then more and more firmly the prophets, the martyrs, the bishops, the kings, and the queens ... Upon the whole the Close of Salisbury under the full summer moon on a windless night, is as beautiful a scene as any I know in England—or for the matter of that elsewhere. (*Life*, Aetat. 57–58)

His impressions on this occasion appear again in the poem 'A Cathedral Façade at Midnight', while the Close is several times described in his fiction. In *Two on a Tower*, for example, Louis Glanville finds it 'damp and venerable, ... level as a bowling-green, and beloved of rooks' (Ch. 39) when he comes to visit the Bishop of Melchester at his Palace (on the south side of the Cathedral and now the Cathedral School). The most important visitor, though, is Jude Fawley, attracted by the prospect of 'a quiet and soothing place, almost entirely ecclesiastical in its tone; a spot where worldly learning and intellectual smartness had no establishment; where the altruistic feeling that he did possess would perhaps be more highly estimated than a brilliancy which he did not' (Part 3, Ch. 1). Less wisely, he is also drawn by the presence of Sue Bridehead at the training college, attended in real life by Hardy's sisters, housed in the medieval Old Deanery and King's House on the west side of the Close.

Jude works as a mason on the restoration of the Cathedral, Hardy presumably having in mind the alterations begun by Gilbert Scott in 1859. These went some way towards modifying the damage done to the interior by Wyatt in the 18C. Wyatt's inappropriately neat reorganisation of the monuments is given a sideglance by Hardy in *The Hand of Ethelberta* when the heroine inspects 'the sallow monuments which lined the grizzled pile' while Christopher Julian plays the organ (Ch. 39). Hardy's poem 'The Impercipient' finely records the feelings of an agnostic during a service, estranged by his doubts from the 'bright believing band' of worshippers.

Tess Durbeyfield and Angel Clare also come to Salisbury, but only to pass quickly through the city in their flight from the law: 'It was about midnight when they went along the deserted streets, lighted fitfully by the few lamps, keeping off the pavement that it might not echo their footsteps. The graceful pile of cathedral architecture rose dimly on their left hand, but it was lost upon them now' (Ch. 58). The end of their journey is *Stonehenge, which we may reach by following A345 north and A303 west (10 miles). Hardy indulges his love of nocturnal scenes and gives a wonderfully atmospheric yet precise description of their arrival at the stone circle:

> The wind, playing upon the edifice, produced a booming tune, like the note of some gigantic one-stringed harp. No other sound came from it, and lifting his hand and advancing a step or two, Clare felt the vertical surface of the structure. It seemed to be of solid stone, without joint or moulding. Carrying his fingers onward he found that what he had come in contact with was a colossal rectangular pillar; by stretching out his left hand he could feel a similar one adjoining. At an indefinite height overhead something made the black sky blacker, which had the semblance of a vast architrave uniting the pillars horizontally. They carefully entered beneath and between; the surfaces echoed their soft rustle; but they seemed to be still out of doors. The place was roofless. Tess drew her breath fearfully, and Angel, perplexed, said—
>
> 'What can it be?'
>
> Feeling sideways they encountered another tower-like pillar, square and uncompromising as the first; beyond it another and another. The place was all doors and pillars, some connected above by continuous architraves.
>
> 'A very Temple of the Winds', he said.
>
> The next pillar was isolated; others composed a trilithon; others were prostrate, their flanks forming a causeway wide enough for a carriage; and it was soon obvious that they made up a forest of monoliths grouped upon the grassy expanse of the plain. The couple advanced further into this pavilion of the night till they stood in its midst.
>
> 'It is Stonehenge!' said Clare. (Ch. 58)

Modern visitors may no longer wander in between the pillars and they will find some of the fallen stones restored to their original position; but the Altar stone where Tess is sleeping next morning when the police arrive can still be seen.

Stonehenge, near Amesbury, Wiltshire: English Heritage, standard opening; phone English Heritage regional Office in Bristol, (0272) 734472, extension 205.

9 Dorchester to Wimborne Minster via Stinsford, Puddletown, Bere Regis and Milton Abbas

We go east from Dorchester on A35 and, half a mile after crossing the River Frome, bear right on an unclassified road for Stinsford (2 miles), the hamlet which gives its name to the dispersed parish including Lower Bockhampton and Higher Bockhampton. Stinsford parish was the scene of Hardy's childhood and much of his youth, and it remained at the very centre of his affections throughout his life. As 'Mellstock' it appears in his writings from the early *Under the Greenwood Tree* to his last poems.

Our first destination is the little *church and churchyard where Hardy's heart lies buried near the graves of his relatives. The inclusion of an engraving showing the entrance to the churchyard as frontispiece to his first volume of poems showed its importance to him, not just as a repository of family history but as the place for solemn (or ironic) meditation. It was his Stoke Poges, he once told a friend. Of the several poems set here, perhaps the most poignant are 'Voices from Things Growing in a Churchyard'. 'The Dead Quire' and 'Friends Beyond'.

The interior of the church has changed since the days Hardy first knew it, having lost its traditional barrel roof, tall pews and the west gallery where as a youth he continued the tradition of his father and grandfather by playing in the 'quire'. His sketch of the gallery, marking the places occupied by the various musicians, is on display and there is a plaque commemorating his family's forty-year service. The poem 'A Church Romance' describes how his mother first saw his father when

> She turned in the high pew, until her sight
> Swept the west gallery, and caught its row
> Of music-men with viol, book and bow
> Against the sinking sad tower-window light.
> (first stanza)

Among the monuments we should note the one in the south chancel to the 18C Lady Susan Strangways and her actor-husband, a marriage that appealed to Hardy's interest in social disparities and provided the subject for 'The Noble Lady's Tale', and the tablet to Benjamin Bowring, mentioned in 'Voices from Things Growing in a Churchyard'.

From the church we retrace our route north and then turn right on the road for Bockhampton Cross. On our right is the entrance to Kingston Maurward House and the Old Manor House, now the Dorset College of Agriculture and Horticulture. In Hardy's time the House was occupied by Julia Augusta Martin, who took a strong interest in his education and encouraged the precocious development of his talents. It is clearly the chief model for 'Knapwater House', home of Mrs Aldclyffe in his first published novel, *Desperate Remedies.*

From Bockhampton Cross a left turn brings us to Higher Bockhampton and at 3½ miles the lane leading to *Hardy's Birthplace. The Birthplace cannot be reached by car and so we park on the right by the head of the lane. From here we can walk directly to the house but a better route takes us through Thorncombe Wood

(NT), marking the western edge of the old Puddletown Heath, one of a loosely connected series that stretched SE from Higher Bockhampton towards Bournemouth. Development, modern farming techniques and the activities of the Forestry Commission have restricted its scope, but even in Hardy's time it was smaller and considerably less dramatic than the 'Egdon Heath' familiar to readers of *The Return of the Native* and the closing chapters of *The Mayor of Casterbridge*. About 1 mile east of the car park and reached by footpath lies Rainbarrows, the mound Hardy called 'Rainbarrow', where Eustacia Vye stands at the opening of *The Return of the Native*.

From whatever direction it is approached the Birthplace is a satisfyingly picturesque building, lovingly described as Tranter Dewy's home in *Under the Greenwood Tree*:

> It was a long low cottage with a hipped roof of thatch, having dormer windows breaking up into the eaves, a chimney standing in the middle of the ridge and another at each end. The window-shutters were not yet closed, and the fire- and candle-light within radiated forth upon the thick bushes of box and laurestinus growing in clumps outside, and upon the bare boughs of several codlin-trees hanging about in various distorted shapes, the result of earlier training as espaliers combined with careless climbing into their boughs in later years. The walls of the dwelling were for the most part covered with creepers, though these were rather beaten back from the doorway—a feature which was worn and scratched by much passing in and out, giving it by day the appearance of an old keyhole. (Ch. 2)

The cottage is little altered since it was built at the turn of the 19C. Hardy lived here with his parents until he went to London in 1862 and on his return, dispirited and unhealthy, in 1867. During the years that followed he wrote *Under the Greenwood Tree* and *Far from the Madding Crowd*, the novels that stick most closely to the countryside of his childhood and the first of his books to mine a rich vein of local traditions, anecdotes and humour. *Far from the Madding Crowd* was composed 'sometimes indoors, sometimes out—when he would occasionally find himself without a scrap of paper at the very moment he felt volumes. In such circumstances, he would use large dead leaves, white chips left by the wood-cutters, or pieces of stone or slate that came to hand. He used to say that when he carried a pocket-book his mind was barren as the Sahara' (*Life*, Aetat. 33–36).

Leaving the Birthplace, we turn right at the head of the lane and follow the hill to the A35, which we take eastward. On the left we pass Yellowham Wood, 'Yalbury Wood' and the home of Keeper Day in *Under the Greenwood Tree*, before reaching Puddletown (5½miles). Victorian improvements swept away many of the buildings Hardy knew from childhood visits to his mother's relatives and described in his portrait of 'Weatherbury' in *Far from the Madding Crowd*. Yet Puddletown is still an agreeable place and its *church is of special interest, for among its lovely furnishings it retains the 17C west gallery formerly used by the 'quire'. Though the tower does have gargoyles the visitor will look in vain for the particularly fearsome one that destroyed Fanny Robin's grave (Ch. 46).

Hardy himself admitted the liberty he had taken with the location of Bathsheba's home, 'Weatherbury Upper Farm', which the novel places on the outskirts of Puddletown. Its original, the 16C–17C Waterston Manor, lies 1½ miles NW of the village via B3142. Though it has risen from the status of rented farm to which it had sunk in Hardy's day, and though it suffered severe damage from fire later in the 19C, the Manor has kept much of the character which called forth one of his most openly loving architectural descriptions:

> Fluted pilasters, worked from the solid stone, decorated its front, and above the roof the chimneys were panelled or columnar, some coped gables with finials and like features still retaining traces of their Gothic extraction. Soft brown mosses, like faded velveteen, formed cushions upon the stone tiling, and tufts of the houseleek or sengreen sprouted from the eaves of the low surrounding buildings ... The main staircase was of hard oak, the balusters, heavy as bed-posts, being turned and moulded in the quaint fashion of their century, the handrail as stout as a parapet-top, and the stairs themselves continually twisting round like a person trying to look over his shoulder. Going up, the floors above were found to have a very irregular surface, rising to ridges, sinking into valleys; and being just then uncarpeted, the face of the boards was seen to be eaten into innumerable vermiculations. Every window replied by a clang to the opening and shutting of every door, a tremble followed every bustling movement, and a creak accompanied a walker about the house, like a spirit, wherever he went. (Ch. 9)

Returning to A35 we continue eastward to another country house that Hardy knew well: Athelhampton Manor (9½ miles). The largely Tudor building appears as 'Athelhall' in *A Group of Noble Dames*.

Further east on A35 is Bere Regis (13½ miles), Hardy's 'Kingsbere'. The *interior of its church is exactly what the reader of *Tess of the d'Urbervilles* (Ch. 52) would expect, with canopied tombs and 'beautifully traceried windows of many lights' commemorating the Turberville family. East of the village rises Woodbury Hill, site of 'Greenhill Fair' at which Sergeant Troy makes an unwelcome reappearance in Bathsheba's life (*Madding Crowd*, Ch. 50).

From Bere Regis an unclassified road leads NW via Milborne St Andrew (16½ miles) and across A354 to Milton Abbas (20 miles). The Earl of Dorchester built this model village in the 1780s when he cleared the original market town from beside his new mansion, Milton Abbey. It lies near the Abbey church, 1 mile west of the present village, and is now a school. Hardy clearly had it in mind as the original of 'Middleton Abbey', Felice Charmond's house in *The Woodlanders*, influenced no doubt as much by the building's autocratic history as by its architecture. Unclassified roads continue north from Milton Abbas via Winterbourne Strickland to Turnworth (24½ miles). As assistant to Crickmay, John Hicks' successor, Hardy worked on Turnworth church in 1869. The delicately embellished capitals and corbels he contributed remind us how sensitive a church architect he could be.

We retrace our route south from Turnworth and turn east at Winterbourne Strickland for A354, which quickly brings us to Blandford Forum (31 miles), a handsome town mentioned as 'Shottsford Forum' but never really described in the 'Wessex' novels. B3082 now leads SE to Wimborne Minster (40 miles). Hardy and Emma lived here in 1881–83 before moving to Dorchester, and found in its old-world charm (now a little diminished) an echo of their 'idyll' at Sturminster Newton (Rte 7). But the chief point of interest for the visitor is the Abbey, whose rich, cluttered interior is evoked in the poem 'Copying Architecture in an Old Minster'.

5 miles west of Wimborne, on A31 heading back towards Bere Regis, we pass the entrance to Charborough Park, whose Gothic tower (rebuilt 1840) gave Hardy some hints for the one at 'Welland House', the ingeniously composite setting for *Two on a Tower*.

On the coast 8 miles SE of Wimborne is Bournemouth, whose atmosphere is neatly captured by the description of 'Sandbourne' in *Tess of the d'Urbervilles*: 'a fairy palace suddenly created by the stroke of a wand, and allowed to get a little dusty' (Ch. 55).

Kingston Maurward House (Dorset College of Agriculture and Horticulture), near Dorchester, Dorset: visits by appointment with the Bursar or the Principal; phone Dorchester (0305) 64738.

Hardy's Cottage, Higher Bockhampton, near Dorchester, Dorset: NT; phone Dorchester (0305) 62366.

Athelhampton Manor, Athelhampton, Dorset: phone Puddletown (0305) 848363.

Milton Abbey, Milton Abbas, near Blandford Forum, Dorset: phone (0258) 880484.

10 Dorchester to Lulworth Cove via West Stafford, Woodsford and Wool

This route heads eastward from Dorchester through scenes mainly associated with *Tess of the d'Urbervilles.* We begin by taking A352 towards Wool and at 2 miles branch left on the unclassified road which leads to the Frome, and, beyond, Stinsford parish (Rte 9). Before this, however, we turn right for the village of West Stafford (4 miles), beginning a journey along the southern bank of the river and through the 'Valley of the Great Dairies'. Most readers will remember the passage where Tess Durbeyfield first sees this 'valley in which milk and butter grew to rankness, and were produced more profusely, if less delicately, than at her home—the verdant plain so well watered by the river Var or Froom':

> It was intrinsically different from the Vale of Little Dairies, Blackmoor Vale [Rtes 6 and 7] ... The world was drawn to a larger pattern here. The enclosures numbered fifty acres instead of ten, the farmsteads were more extended, the groups of cattle formed tribes hereabout; there only families. These myriads of cows stretching under her eyes from the far east to the far west outnumbered any she had ever seen at one glance before. The green lea was speckled as thickly with them as a canvas by Van Alsoot or Sallaert with burghers. The ripe hues of the red and dun kine absorbed the evening sunlight, which the white-coated animals returned to the eye in rays almost dazzling, even at the distant elevation on which she stood.
>
> The bird's-eye perspective before her was not so luxuriantly beautiful, perhaps, as that other one which she knew so well; yet it was more cheering. It lacked the intensely blue atmosphere of the rival vale, and its heavy soils and scents; the new air was clear, bracing, ethereal. The river itself, which nourished the grass and cows of those renowned dairies, flowed not like the streams in Blackmoor. Those were slow, silent, often turbid; flowing over beds of mud into which the incautious wader might sink and vanish unawares. The Froom waters were clear as the pure River of Life shown to the Evangelist, rapid as the shadow of a cloud, with pebbly shallows that prattled to the sky all day long. There the waterflower was the lily; the crowfoot here. (Ch. 16)

As a general description it still holds true, and it is with the pervasive atmosphere rather than specific places that the visitor to this countryside should be content. Unlike most buildings in Hardy's work, 'Talbothays', the dairy farm where Tess meets Angel Clare, does not seem to have a real-life model. He took its name from the farm bought by his father in West Stafford. The farmhouse Hardy designed and his brother Henry built in 1913 still stands; Hardy's sisters Mary and Kate lived here. It has been suggested that Lower Lewell Farm, on the Woodsford Road just after the turning for

Crossways, may occupy the spot where Hardy envisaged the fictional 'Talbothays'.

Woodsford Castle, standing on the left as we enter the village of Woodsford (6½ miles), can be more certainly identified with Hardy's work. The melodramatic poem 'A Sound in the Night' narrates the legend of an 18C murder in this pleasant patchwork of virtually every architectural period from the medieval onwards. The footpath nearby leads to the river at a point within sight of Sturt's Weir, the 'Shadwater Weir' where Eustacia Vye and Damon Wildeve drown in *The Return of the Native* (Bk 5, Ch. 9).

From Woodsford our route continues south-east via Moreton to Wool (13 miles), the 'Wellbridge' where Angel Clare takes Tess after their wedding (Ch. 34). The Manor where they spend their disastrous honeymoon is north of the town just beyond the Elizabethan stone bridge mentioned by Hardy. It is now a hotel, but still displays the Turberville portraits which so impress Clare. Half a mile east of Wool on the road to East Stoke we find the scanty ruins of Bindon Abbey, rather less romantic than they are made to appear in the famous sleep-walking scene (Ch. 37), though the coffin of Abbot Maners in which Clare lays Tess survives. Near the Abbey ruins stands the mill whose workings Clare planned to investigate.

We complete our journey by taking B3070 south from Wool to Lulworth Cove (17 miles), a fine circular bay of chalk cliffs. It is the subject of the poem 'At Lulworth Cove a Century Back' and, as 'Lulwind Cove', it is a recurrent location in the novels. Owen and Cytherea Graye come here by paddle-steamer excursion from Weymouth in *Desperate Remedies* (Ch. 2), while in *Far from the Madding Crowd* (Ch. 47) Sergeant Troy takes the swim that leads to his presumed death by drowning. The atmosphere that Hardy found has been greatly changed by the Cove's popularity with summer visitors as well as by the neighbouring military camp and firing range.

11 Dorchester to Sutton Poyntz via Maiden Castle, Weymouth and Isle of Portland

2 miles SW of Dorchester and reached by an unclassified road leading right from A354 stands one of Dorset's finest antiquities, *Maiden Castle. This earthen hill fort, covering some 116 acres, was first occupied in about 2000 BC and fell to the Roman general Vespasian in AD 43. The outermost of its ramparts—there are as many as eight at one point—offers a splendid walk with views over the surrounding countryside. It was inevitable that Hardy, with his strong sense of prehistory, should have used it in his writing. As 'Mai Dun' the fort appears in 'Tryst at an Ancient Earthworks', more an evocation of place than a short story, as well as in *The Mayor of Casterbridge*, where Henchard proposes its 'pleasant upland' as the scene for his unsuccessful public entertainment (Ch. 16) and uses it to spy on Farfrae's courtship of Elizabeth-Jane (Ch. 43).

Returning to A354 we continue south to the large and popular seaside resort of Weymouth (8½ miles). As 'Budmouth' it is frequently mentioned but rarely described in Hardy's work. The most specific glimpses are given by his novel of the Napoleonic Wars, *The*

Trumpet-Major, which conjures up the town's atmosphere when it became a centre of military activity and was graced by the presence of George III. The colourful statue of the King at the south end of the Esplanade stands as a monument to this period of Weymouth's history, while the Esplanade itself has preserved much of its Georgian elegance. The Gloucester Hotel is an enlarged version of Gloucester Lodge where, as *The Trumpet-Major* notes, the King stayed.

A354 leads south to the Isle of Portland, not an island proper but a limestone peninsula 'like a great crouching animal tethered to the mainland' (*Trumpet-Major*, Ch. 12). Hardy chose its bleak and rocky expanse, in striking contrast to the scenery that typifies the rest of Dorset, as the setting for *The Well-Beloved* and renamed it 'The Isle of Slingers'. A354 approaches Portland via Chesil Bank, 'a long thin neck of pebbles "cast up by the rages of the sea" and unparalleled in its kind in Europe' (*Well-Beloved*, Ch. 1) and reaches Fortuneswell (13½ miles), Hardy's 'Street of Wells'. The 'roomy cottage or homestead' belonging to the Caro family, where Jocelyn Pierston woos successive generations of Avices, lies 1½ miles further south on the road leaving Easton for Pennsylvania Castle and is now the Portland Museum.

From Portland we retrace our route back to Weymouth and take A353 NE along the coast. It passes through Overcombe (which gave its name but apparently no more to the chief setting of *The Trumpet-Major*) and Preston (24 miles), where an unclassified road leads left to Sutton Poyntz (24½ miles). This large and much extended village was Hardy's model for 'Overcombe', though the visitor will look in vain for Loveday's mill. North of the village a footpath heads ½ mile NE to the downs and the chalk figure of George III on horseback, another reminder of the area's close connections with the Napoleonic period.

Portland Museum, 217 Wakeham, Portland, Dorset: phone (0305) 821804.

12 Dorchester to Bridport via Blackdown Hill and Abbotsbury

From Dorchester's Top o' Town we take A35 west towards Bridport but turn left after 1 mile on the unclassified road to Martinstown (3 miles). The poem 'Last Look Round St Martin's Fair' recalls the time when its horse market attracted people from as far away as the New Forest. At the west end of the village an unclassified road leads SW over Blackdown Hill where, at a point commanding particularly fine views, we find a monument of 1844 to Admiral Hardy, whom the writer liked to claim as an ancestor. A left turn at the crossroads beyond the monument takes us to Portesham (7 miles), from which B3157 continues west to Abbotsbury (8½ miles). With its ruined Benedictine Abbey, swannery and sub-tropical gardens the village has established itself as one of Dorset's tourist showcases. In Hardy's work it is variously called 'Abbot's Beach' and 'Abbotsea', and its Abbey barn, like the one at Cerne Abbas (Rte 6), is claimed as the original of the shearing barn in *Far from the Madding Crowd*.

B3157 westwards offers a fine scenic route paralleling the coast and Chesil Bank (Rte 11) to Bridport (14½ miles). Its enviable site near the sea—the harbour is at West Bay a mile south—means that Bridport has expanded considerably since the 19C but its old centre by the Town Hall preserves much of the charm Hardy conjured up in his picture of 'Port Bredy', the setting for his short story 'The Fellow Townsmen'.

13 Dorchester to Windwhistle Hill via Beaminster and Crewkerne

The route proceeds NW from Dorchester through some of Dorset's finest downland, as well as scenes associated with *Far from the Madding Crowd* and *Tess of the d'Urbervilles*, ending over the border in Somerset.

From the Top o' Town junction in Dorchester we take A37 (the Yeovil road), branching left after 4½ miles on A356 for Crewkerne. Maiden Newton (8 miles) is Hardy's 'Chalk-Newton' but greatly changed from the days when it was mentioned in 'The Grave by the Handpost' and Tess Durbeyfield stopped for breakfast on her way to 'Flintcomb-Ash' (Ch. 42).

At about 9 miles we turn left on an unclassified road for Toller Porcorum (10 miles) and follow sideroads that sometimes dwindle to narrow lanes through Lower Kingcombe and Higher Kingcombe to Hooke (12½ miles). The rich chalk *downland through which we pass is the scene for the opening chapters of *Far from the Madding Crowd*, when Gabriel Oak proposes in vain to Bathsheba and loses his flock of sheep in the chalk pit. The precise location of 'Norcombe Hill' cannot be identified, for Hardy obviously created it from the general characteristics of the area.

From Hooke we take unclassified roads to the junction with B3163 (14½ miles), where a left turn brings us to the pleasant little town of Beaminster (16½ miles). As 'Emminster', a name echoing the local pronunciation, it is the home of the Clare family and the goal of Tess' abortive journey from 'Flintcomb-Ash' (Ch. 44). The vicarage and the church (with a fine tower) where she lingers can still be seen.

We leave Beaminster by retracing our route along B3163 but stay on this road beyond the turning for Hooke and cross Toller Down to rejoin A356 (20½ miles), which is followed towards Crewkerne. The road climbs steeply to *Winyard's Gap (23½ miles), where the old stone pub on the left is the 'cosy house' mentioned in Stanza 4 of the poem 'A Trampwoman's Tragedy'. The view from this height and from the adjoining woods (NT) is admired by the speakers in the dialogue poem 'At Wynyard's Gap'.

A356 descends to the market town of Crewkerne (27½ miles), mentioned by its own name in the same poem, from which A30 leads west along the ridge of Windwhistle Hill. At 31½ miles we reach on our right another haunt of Hardy's trampwoman, the Windwhistle Inn. Hardy's note to the poem recalls a visit to the pub before it was modernised:

> The highness and dryness of Windwhistle Inn was impressed upon the writer ... when, after climbing on a hot afternoon to the beautiful spot near which it stands and entering the inn for tea he was informed by the landlady that none could be had, unless he would fetch water from a valley half a mile off, the house containing not a drop, owing to its situation. However, a tantalizing row of full barrels behind her back testified to a wetness of a certain sort, which was not at that time desired.

14 Launceston to Lanhydrock House via Beeny Cliff, Boscastle and Tintagel

Why go to Saint-Juliot? What's Juliot to me?
Some strange necromancy
But charmed me to fancy
That much of my life claims the spot as its key.
('Dream or No', first stanza)

For Hardy the landscape of northern Cornwall was identified with his courtship of Emma Gifford, his first wife. It was 'Lyonesse', a territory of special magic and special pain. He first met Emma here in 1870 during the course of his work for Crickmay, successor to the Dorchester architect John Hicks. The first excited feelings for Emma and Cornwall made their way into his third novel, *A Pair of Blue Eyes*. In 1913, the year after her death, he returned to the scenes of their romance, making a 'penitential pilgrimage' that swelled the flood of over fifty poems about her, including the magnificent 'Poems of 1912–13'.

We begin our tour near the Devon border at the pleasant little town of Launceston (on A30), where the railway deposited Hardy on his 1870 visit. 'St Launce's Revisited', written on his return years later, noted the ruins of the Norman 'castle and keep uprearing / Gray' (lines 3–4) on the hill. In the Market Place and also mentioned in the poem is the White Hart Hotel, distinguished by the archway from the Augustinian priory, where he had hired horse and trap to take him the remaining distance to the tiny hamlet of St Juliot.

We make that journey by driving west and north towards Boscastle via A30, A395, B3262 and A39. Just beyond Marshgate at 14½ miles we take the unclassified road on the left for Tresparrett and, in the delightful valley of the River Valency, the *church of St Juliot (16 miles). The former Rectory lies about ½ a mile beyond, off the road leading north from the valley. Like 'Endelstow Rectory' in *A Pair of Blue Eyes* it is situated in 'a little dell' (Ch. 2).

Emma Gifford, sister-in-law to the Rector of St Juliot, immediately struck Hardy as '*living*': 'Though her features were not regular her complexion at this date was perfect in hue, her figure and movement graceful, and her corn-coloured hair abundant in its coils' (*Life*, Aetat. 29–30). The 'Recollections' by Emma which Hardy quoted in his autobiography record the rather less romantic impression he made on her: 'I thought him much older than he was. He had a beard, and a rather shabby greatcoat, and had quite a business appearance. Afterwards he seemed younger, and by daylight especially so' (Aetat. 29–30). She was surprised to learn that the blue paper sticking out of his pocket was not an architectural plan but the manuscript of a poem he had been drafting during his journey. Hardy later imagined her feelings as she awaited his arrival in the poem 'A Man Was Drawing Near To Me'.

The main reason for Hardy's visit was to supervise restoration of the church, then 'in its original condition of picturesque neglect' (*Life*, Aetat. 29–30). The nave and tower were rebuilt and the

'Harbour of Castle Boterel', in the Wessex edition of A Pair of Blue Eyes

furnishings renewed, though Hardy later 'much regretted the obliteration in this manner of the church's history, and, too, that he should be instrumental in such obliteration, the building as he had first set eyes on it having been so associated with what was romantic in his life' (*Life*, Aetat. 29–30). The fate of the chancel screen reminds us why he became, in larger ways, disillusioned with what passed for church restoration in the 19C:

> Hardy had made a careful drawing of it, with its decayed tracery, posts, and gilding, marking thereon where sundry patchings and scarfings were to be applied. Reaching the building one day he found a new and highly varnished travesty of the old screen standing in its place. 'Well, Mr Hardy', replied the builder in answer to his astonished inquiries, 'I said to myself, I won't stand on a pound or two while I'm about it, and I'll give 'em a new screen instead of that patched-up old thing'. (*Life*, Aetat. 29–30)

The church displays drawings he made on the site as well as two tablets, the first commemorating his role in the alterations and the second, erected by Hardy in 1913, recording that Emma laid the foundation stone of the new aisle and tower (see the poems 'The Marble Tablet' and 'The Monument-Maker').

From St Juliot we head north to B3263 and head west towards the sea. After a mile, as we are nearing Boscastle, we find on our right a footpath leading to the richly dramatic coastline where Hardy often walked with Emma and where he later imagined her in poems like 'The Phantom Horsewoman'. Pentargan Bay (1/2 mile) is the scene of his meditations in 'After a Journey', and after another 1/2 mile we reach the splendid *Beeny Cliff, which gave its name to Hardy's most vibrant recollection of Emma. In a notebook entry of 1872 he had described the scene:

> green towards the land, blue-black towards the sea. Every ledge has a little, starved, green grass upon it; all vertical parts bare. Seaward, a dark-grey ocean beneath a pale green sky, upon which lie branches of red cloud. A lather of foam around the base of each rock. The sea is full of motion internally, but still as a whole. Quiet and silent in the distance, noisy and restless close at hand.

As 'The Cliff Without a Name' it is the scene of Henry Knight's memorable ordeal in *A Pair of Blue Eyes* (Chs 21–22).

Boscastle (21 miles), its charming little *harbour flanked by steep cliffs at the mouth of the Valency, is the setting of 'At Castle Boterel'.

By B3263 3 miles SW is Tintagel and the ruined castle on the promontory of Tintagel Head. Hardy and Emma came here in 1870 and 'owing to their lingering too long among the ruins, they found themselves locked in, only narrowly escaping being imprisoned there for the night by much signalling with their handkerchiefs to cottagers in the valley'. He added: 'The lingering might have been considered prophetic, seeing that, after it had been smouldering in his mind for between forty and fifty years, he constructed *The Famous Tragedy of the Queen of Cornwall* from the legends connected with that romantic spot' (*Life*, Aetat. 29–30).

From Tintagel we follow B3263 and B3266 SE to Camelford ('Camelton'), where the continuation of B3266 and A389 take us south to Bodmin (41 miles). In the valley of the Fowey off B3268 2½ miles SE is Lanhydrock House. This 17C mansion, largely rebuilt after a fire in 1881 but remaining one of the grandest in Cornwall, suggested features of 'Endelstow House', home of the Luxellians in *A Pair of Blue Eyes*. Among other minor liberties with geography the novel transplants it to the immediate neighbourhood of St Juliot.

Launceston Castle, Launceston, Cornwall: English Heritage, standard opening; phone (0566) 2365.

Tintagel Castle, Tintagel, Cornwall: English Heritage, standard opening; phone Camelford (0840) 770328.

Lanhydrock House, near Bodmin, Cornwall: NT; phone (0208) 73320.

Central England

15 Reading to Oxford via Fawley

The route takes us through scenes mainly associated with *Jude the Obscure*, a novel set on the northern fringes of 'Wessex' and away from the older rural world described in the earlier fiction.

We begin at Reading ('Aldbrickham'), suitably unromantic surroundings for later episodes in the hero's depressing career. The main identifiable building is the George Hotel on King Street east of the Market Place, where Jude takes Arabella for their night of reunion (Part 3, Ch. 8) and, by one of the unhappy accidents that dog his fortunes, brings Sue Bridehead when she leaves her husband (Part 4, Ch. 5).

From Reading we take A4 SW via Newbury (16 miles), called 'Kennetbridge' in the novel after its position on the River Kennet, to

Hungerford (24 miles). At Hungerford we turn north on A338 and cross the Berkshire Downs.

Off A338 at 31 miles is Fawley, birthplace of Hardy's grandmother, Mary Head Hardy, and under the ironic name of 'Marygreen' setting for the opening scenes of *Jude the Obscure*. There have been changes to its village green since the novel was written but the result is no more attractive:

> Many of the thatched and dormered dwelling-houses had been pulled down of late years, and many trees felled on the green. Above all, the original church, hump-backed, wood-turreted, and quaintly hipped, had been taken down, and either cracked up into heaps of road-metal in the lane, or utilised as pig-sty walls, garden seats, guard-stones to fences, and rockeries in the flower-beds of the neighbourhood. In place of it a tall new building of modern Gothic design, unfamiliar to English eyes, had been erected on a new piece of ground by a certain obliterator of historic records who had run down from London and back in a day. (Part 1, Ch. 1)

The offending architect of St Mary (1866) was G.E. Street.

At the top of the hill 2 miles after we return to A338 the road is joined by the old Ridgeway. To the left stood the Red ('Brown') House from which the young Jude admired the distant, tantalising prospect of Oxford ('Christminster') in Part 1, Chapter 3. We reach Oxford (52 miles) by continuing through Wantage ('Alfredston') and joining A420.

Hardy's portrait of the city as 'Christminster' departs from his normally detailed use of place, perhaps because this seemed inappropriate to the hero's abstract and idealised view of the city, perhaps because he wished to take some of the local sting out of his bitter satire—a wise precaution in a man who would later ride down the High in triumph as an honorary Doctor of Letters. Our first glimpse of 'Christminster' is atmospheric rather than precise, one of the nocturnal scenes beloved by Hardy:

> It was a windy, whispering, moonless night. To guide himself he opened under a lamp a map he had brought. The breeze ruffled and fluttered it, but he could see enough to decide on the direction he should take to reach the heart of the place.
>
> After many turnings he came up to the first ancient mediaeval pile that he had encountered. It was a college, as he could see by the gateway. He entered it, walked round, and penetrated to dark corners which no lamplight reached. Close to this college was another; and a little further on another; and then he began to be encircled as it were with the breath and sentiment of the venerable city. When he passed objects out of harmony with its general expression he allowed his eyes to slip over them as if he did not see them.
>
> A bell began clanging, and he listened till a hundred-and-one strokes had sounded. He must have made a mistake, he thought: it was meant for a hundred.
>
> When the gates were shut, and he could no longer get into the quadrangles, he rambled under the walls and doorways, feeling with his fingers the contours of their mouldings and carving. The minutes passed, fewer and fewer people were visible, and still he serpentined among the shadows, for had he not imagined these scenes for ten bygone years, and what mattered a night's rest for once? High against the black sky the flash of a lamp would show crocketed pinnacles and indented battlements. Down obscure alleys, apparently never trodden now by the foot of man, and whose very existence seemed to be forgotten, there would jut into the path porticoes, oriels, doorways of enriched and florid middle-age design, their extinct air being accentuated by the rottenness of the stones. It seemed impossible that modern thought could house itself in such decrepit and superseded chambers. (Part 2, Ch. 1)

Just as we can identify the curfew bell in this passage as 'Great Tom' in Christ Church's Tom Tower, so we can work out a table of correspondence for the 'Christminster' landmarks Hardy mentions elsewhere. 'Beersheba' is the Jericho area off Walton Street in NW Oxford, and 'St Silas' (Part 2, Ch. 3) is the Victorian church of St Barnabas, by Hardy's ex-employer Arthur Blomfield, near the end of Cardigan Street and the canal. 'Crozier College' is Oriel, 'Cardinal College' is Christ Church, and 'Rubric College' may be Brasenose. Yet this is still a short and sketchy list by comparison with the richly saturated portrait of, say, Dorchester in *The Mayor of Casterbridge*.

A few landmarks, however, require special notice. The 'obscure and low-ceiled tavern up a court' where Jude gets drunk and recites the Nicene Creed (Part 2, Ch. 7) may be the Lamb and Flag, off St Giles by St John's College, though the Turf Tavern, off New College Lane, seems a better candidate. The spot where Cranmer, Ridley and Latimer met their martyrdom, marked in the pavement of Broad Street opposite Balliol College, is Jude's ill-omened choice of meeting-place for his first appointment with Sue Bridehead (Part 2, Ch. 4). Further east on Broad Street is Wren's Sheldonian Theatre. On 'Remembrance Day' (Commemoration Day) Jude brings his family to this 'circular theatre with that well-known lantern above it, which stood in his mind as the sad symbol of his abandoned hopes' and makes his speech to the crowd assembled outside, confessing failure in his academic ambitions and admitting: 'It takes two or three generations to do what I tried to do in one' (Part 6, Ch. 1).

Sheldonian Theatre, Broad Street, Oxford: phone (0865) 277299 or the University Offices, (0865) 270000.

Eastern England

16 Cambridge

Hardy's acquaintance with Cambridge produced no equivalent to his portrayal of Oxford as 'Christminster' in *Jude the Obscure* (Rte 15), but it has its own poignancy.

To him Cambridge was important for its connection with the unhappy career of his friend and mentor Horace Moule, son of the Vicar of Fordington (Rte 5). After an abortive period as an undergraduate at Oxford, Moule entered Queens' College in 1854 but did not receive his BA until 1867, a delay hinting at the bouts of depression and alcoholism that clouded his academic promise. In 1870 he was back again at Queens' and during the summer treated Hardy, visiting Cambridge for the first time, to a tour of the sights which commonly attract the stranger. Hardy's diary records of 21 June:

> Next morning went with H.M. to King's Chapel early. M. opened the great West doors to show the interior vista: we got upon the roof where we could see Ely Cathedral gleaming in the distant sunlight. A never-to-be-forgotten morning. H.M.M. saw me off for London. His last smile. (*Life*, Aetat. 30–33)

In September Moule committed suicide in his college rooms. Hardy's marginalia to his copy of *In Memoriam* show that he associated him with Arthur Henry Hallam, another Cambridge graduate who died young and left a poet to mourn him.

He returned twice in 1913, the year he received an honorary

Litt. D. from the University. On both occasions he visited Magdalene College, which elected him to an Honorary Fellowship.

The Fitzwilliam Museum has the famous portrait by Augustus John presenting him in his capacity as the grand old man of English Letters.

Fitzwilliam Museum, Trumpington Street, Cambridge: phone (0223) 332900.

JAMES JOYCE

b. Dublin, 1882; d. Zürich, Switzerland, 1941. *Chamber Music* (1907); *Dubliners* (1914); *A Portrait of the Artist as a Young Man* (1916); *Exiles: A Play in Three Acts* (1918); *Ulysses* (1922); *Pomes Penyeach* (1927); *Finnegans Wake* (1939); *Stephen Hero: Part of the First Draft of A Portrait of the Artist as a Young Man* (edited by T. Spencer; 1944).

Dublin and Vicinity

On the face of it, Joyce's life and work regard each other across a gaping paradox. He left his native Dublin in 1904, when he was twenty-two, and returned only for the briefest of visits. The rest of his life, the years when he produced his major work, passed in an odyssey whose main stopping points were summarised in the byline at the end of *Ulysses*: Trieste, Zürich, Paris. And yet, like everything else Joyce wrote, that novel has nothing to say about these cities and everything to say about Dublin. The man who so deliberately transformed himself from an Irishman into a European, the writer whose style developed from the merely cosmopolitan to the riotously polyglot, never needed to stray beyond the boundaries of Dublin in his choice of subject. From Trieste and Zürich and Paris he sought in *Ulysses* to recreate Dublin as it had been on 16 June 1904. Whereas the Renaissance sonneteer used to boast that his poem would outlive the ephemeral beauty of the woman it praised, it was Joyce's hope that if Dublin were destroyed it could be reconstructed from the pages of his novel.

Joyce himself always insisted that he had no imagination: his muse was Thom's city directory of Dublin. Besides, his voluntary exile on the Continent was never intended to break with the past. 'We are what we are', he told his brother Stanislaus in explanation of *A Portrait of the Artist as a Young Man*. 'Our maturity is an extension of our childhood'. In *Portrait* itself the voyages of maturity are prophesied when the young Stephen Dedalus writes in the flyleaf of his exercise book at Clongowes:

Stephen Dedalus
Class of Elements
Clongowes Wood College
Sallins
County Kildare
Ireland
Europe
The World
The Universe
(Ch. 1)

The adult Joyce came to doubt this simple diagram of concentric rings and to concede that classification of the elements was a trickier business than the child had foreseen, but he never swerved in his belief that the way towards the universal significance aimed at and achieved in *Ulysses* and *Finnegans Wake* could begin only with minute inspection of his own point of origin.

So Joyce's Dublin is uniquely challenging to the literary tourist. The city is there in the book and the book there in the city to a degree that is without parallel in modern literature. For this reason *Ulysses* requires special treatment and is made the separate subject of Rtes 1–4 below. They begin in the SE, where the novel itself starts, and explore the city by taking the course of Paddy Dignam's funeral procession as an organising framework. In this description the eighteen untitled episodes of Joyce's novel are identified by the Homeric names which he privately used and scholars have subsequently adopted. They are, in order: 'Telemachus', 'Proteus', 'Nestor', 'Calypso', 'Lotos Eaters', 'Hades', 'Aeolus', 'Lestrygonians', 'Scylla and Charybdis', 'Wandering Rocks', 'Sirens', 'Cyclops', 'Nausicaa', 'Oxen of the Sun', 'Circe', 'Eumaeus', 'Ithaca', 'Penelope'.

The attentive reader of *Ulysses* will quickly note that the locations of several episodes are missing from the suggested itineraries, and this is because Dublin, already changing as Joyce wrote, has continued to change with alarming rapidity. It was inevitable, of course, that the trams, horse-drawn traffic and other street furniture should have vanished and taken much of the atmosphere of *Ulysses* with them. It was inevitable, too, that Nighttown ('Circe') and Barney Kiernan's on Little Britain Street ('Cyclops') should go with the passage of the years, that the interiors of Joyce's bars and hotels should change beyond recognition, and that the Holles Street Hospital should transform itself to benefit its patients but disappoint readers of 'Oxen of the Sun'. However, the demolition of Nelson's Pillar would have been vandalism even if Joyce had not memorialised it in 'Aeolus' and 'Hades'. The most recent loss is No. 7 Eccles Street, home of Leopold Bloom. In moments of depression the modern visitor may feel that Dubliners are bent on testing Joyce's claim for *Ulysses*, though as yet they have shown little inclination to reconstruct the city from his pages. There is all the more reason, then, to cherish those public buildings that do survive—the National Library, Trinity College, the Four Courts, Prospect Cemetery—and to marvel at the good fortune that has kept the Martello Tower in Sandycove not only intact but honourably preserved for its connection with Joyce.

Rtes 5–11 chronicle the scenes of Joyce's early life, and of *Dubliners* and *A Portrait of the Artist*, beginning again in the SE and working round the compass to the NE. Here the record of survival is perhaps more impressive and nine addresses where Joyce lived are mentioned, though even this list cannot claim to be complete. In their variety these houses are striking witness to the ups and downs, but mainly downs, in the fortunes of the writer's father, John Joyce. Together, they remind us how early in life Joyce became a traveller, how little of Ithaca he could savour even as a child. The restless, enforced movement of his childhood and youth was training for his adult travels, and it helps explain why, when he turned to his native city in *Ulysses*, he saw it through the eyes of Stephen Dedalus and Leopold Bloom, two dispossessed wanderers who each set out on 16 June 1904 without a doorkey.

1 'Ulysses' in South-East Dublin: Sandycove and Sandymount

We begin at Sandycove Point on the coast some 8 miles SE of central Dublin and just outside the city boundary. The *James Joyce Museum is an excellent starting point for the enthusiast, its interest lying not so much in the collection of relics and books as in the building that houses them, one of the Martello Towers built along the coast to answer the threat of Napoleonic invasion. It was opened to the public in 1962 by Sylvia Beach, Joyce's friend and patron as well as the first publisher of *Ulysses*.

In biographical terms, the squat fortress-like tower has only a slender connection with Joyce, being among the most transitory of his many Dublin addresses. It was rented in August 1904 (for £8 a year) by Oliver St John Gogarty, poet, medical student and, according to Stanislaus Joyce, a man 'full of bustling energy, wit, and profanity'. At that time he was in violent reaction against the provinciality of Dublin life and liked to regard the tower as an *omphalos*, not just because of its shape but because, like the navel-stone at Delphi, it would become the centre and symbol of an enlightened culture. Joyce, who had left his father's house in Cabra (Rte 10) earlier that year, arrived on 9 September. Though he sympathised with his friend's criticism of Dublin and Ireland, he soon found Gogarty's charm wearing thin and his temper was frayed even more by the presence of another guest, the Anglo-Irishman Samuel Chenevix Trench. These tensions reached breaking point on 15 September, when Trench woke screaming from a nightmare about a black panther and began firing shots from his revolver. Gogarty disarmed him and, when Trench started screaming again, fired into the wall above Joyce's bed. Joyce wisely took this as a cue to leave, making a dramatic exit from the tower in the middle of the night and in the pouring rain.

With any other writer the matter would probably have ended there and we would have no reason to remember the episode or its setting. But Joyce felt aggrieved, and he knew well that through art the artist can revenge himself for the petty humiliations of ordinary life. He made the Martello Tower scene for the opening of *Ulysses*, the 'Telemachus' episode. With his bawdy profanities and his dream of Hellenising Ireland, Buck Mulligan is identifiably Gogarty and Trench has become the 'ponderous Saxon' Haines. Yet the fiction subtly alters the facts from which it sprang, for it is Stephen Dedalus who pays the rent, however reluctantly, and Buck Mulligan is not host but 'usurper', the embodiment of the dispossessing tyrannies suffered by the Irish artist in his native country.

Such is the transforming power of art that the modern visitor comes to Sandycove to view the tower in the light of *Ulysses* rather than life, to remember Dedalus and Mulligan rather than Joyce and Gogarty. The roofdeck on top is where Mulligan paused in his shaving to rebuke Stephen for his treatment of his dying mother and to expatiate on the Homeric associations of the sea below: 'The snotgreen sea. The scrotumtightening sea'. Nearby is the Forty-Foot Hole where Stephen, no lover of water, watches with distaste as the athletic Mulligan takes his morning dip.

Stephen's day continues with a journey south to Dalkey, where (like his creator) he works as a schoolteacher, but little survives in that suburb to reward the reader of 'Nestor' and so our route goes NW from Sandycove along the shoreline towards Dublin. At 3 miles we pass through Blackrock, whose connection with Joyce (not echoed in *Ulysses*) is described in Rte 5.

Sandymount Strand (reached by diverging right from Merrion Road at 4½ miles) is a recurrent location in *Ulysses*, as befits a book that has begun by taking its cue from Homer and announcing the sea as one of its major images. Since Joyce's day, however, the appearance of the Strand has been changed by enlargement of the harbour. We stop at 6 miles by the junction of Beach Road and Leahy's Terrace. In 'Proteus' the sight of the midwives emerging from the Terrace prompts Stephen to agonised meditation on the relations of substance to spirit and on his own humiliating entrapment in the chain of heredity. Later in the book ('Nausicaa') Bloom comes to the same spot, or one very close by, to engage in his own rather different sort of meditation on the flesh: tumescent delight at the spectacle of Gertie MacDowell on the beach. On Leahy's Terrace stands Mary, Star of the Sea, parish church of both Gertie and Paddy Dignam; the dedication gives the keynote to much of the symbolism of the 'Nausicaa' episode. Dignam lived at No. 9 Newbridge Avenue, on the other side of Tritonville Road beyond the church, and his funeral cortège in 'Hades' starts from here. Rtes 2 and 3 below follow its course through Dublin.

James Joyce Museum, Sandycove, County Dublin: phone (01) 808571 or 809265.

2 'Ulysses' in South-East and South Dublin: Sandymount to O'Connell Bridge

Of all the many journeys through the city in *Ulysses* certainly the most extensive and perhaps the most detailed is Paddy Dignam's funeral procession in 'Hades', from Sandymount in the SE to Prospect Cemetery in the north. It passes by or near most of the central locations in the novel and so offers an ideal thread for Joyce's readers to follow in their own tours through the city. The route suggested here covers the first half of the procession, with diversions to the other major sights of south Dublin. Rte 3 deals with Dublin north of the Liffey in similar fashion.

We begin where Rte 1 ended, in Sandymount at the junction of Newbridge Avenue and Tritonville Road. Leopold Bloom joins his fellow mourners—Martin Cunningham, Mr Power and Stephen Dedalus' father, Simon—in the carriage outside Paddy Dignam's house. They proceed up Tritonville Road (then still a 'cobbled causeway') and its continuation as Irishtown Road. Stephen Dedalus is also in the neighbourhood (see 'Proteus' in Rte 1) and a brief glimpse of him from the carriage window prompts Mr Bloom to reflections about fathers and sons and to memories of his own dead son, Rudy.

The party turns left, crosses the River Dodder and continues down Ringsend Road. They are held up at the bridge over the Grand Canal within sight and smell of the gas works: 'Whooping cough they say it cures', thinks Bloom with a characteristic dip into his seemingly inexhaustible store of folk wisdom. Ahead lies the dull expanse of

Pearse Street (then Great Brunswick Street) where Bloom notes the 'bleak' 18C church of St Mark on the right. The odd-shaped monument to the Dublin surgeon Sir Philip Crampton has gone.

We may vary this route by turning left from Pearse Street into Westland Row at the corner by the railway station. In 'Lotos Eaters' Bloom collects the letter from Martha Clifford here and enters the 19C church of St Andrew (All Hallows) to watch Mass in progress. At the junction with Lincoln Place at the southern end of Westland Row he buys his cake of lemon soap. By walking down Lincoln Place and crossing Leinster Street we quickly come to Kildare Street and Sir Thomas Deane's *National Library. At the end of 'Lestrygonians' Bloom dashes into the building, eager to avoid an encounter with his wife's lover, Blazes Boylan. The stone goddesses guarding the entrance, which he notes even in his hurry, have now gone but we may still visit the Reading Room inside where in the next chapter, 'Scylla and Charybdis', Stephen Dedalus puts forward his theory of *Hamlet*.

By taking Molesworth Street opposite the Library entrance and turning right on Dawson Street we come to Duke Street, on our left. 'Here we are. Must eat', thinks Bloom in 'Lestrygonians'. In the 'Burton' restaurant, really Bailey's, he is repelled by the sight of meat-eating customers and retreats to Davy Byrne's nearby, where he enjoys a modest cheese sandwich and glass of Burgundy. Both restaurants still flourish but Bloom would scarcely recognise their interiors. (He would, however, recognise the door displayed in the Bailey restaurant, for it was taken from No. 7 Eccles Street when it was demolished.)

From the west end of Duke Street a right turn up Grafton Street brings us to College Green where, on his way to lunch in 'Lestrygonians', Bloom had paused briefly to contemplate the 'surly front' of Trinity College. The university grounds are also passed, in grander fashion, by the Viceroy's procession in 'Wandering Rocks'. As Westmoreland Street leads north to the Liffey and the O'Connell Bridge we pass a statue of the Irish poet Thomas Moore (1779–1852). 'Meeting of the waters', thinks Bloom in 'Lestrygonians', in allusion to one of Moore's lyrics and to the fact his effigy stands over a public lavatory.

National Library, Kildare Street, Dublin: phone (01) 765521.

3 'Ulysses' in North Dublin: O'Connell Bridge to Prospect Cemetery

We begin on the northern side of the O'Connell Bridge, our finishing point for the previous route. In 'Hades' the funeral cortège goes directly up O'Connell Street but we should take the time to walk west along Bachelor's Walk and Ormond Quay by the bank of the Liffey. Our goals are the Ormond Hotel, where Miss Douce and Miss Kennedy presided over the musical 'Sirens' episode, and the battered but still magnificent 18C façade of the Four Courts. From its porch Ritchie Goulding watches the Viceroy's procession pass in 'Wandering Rocks'.

Back at O'Connell Bridge we can contemplate O'Connell Street and an object lesson in the changes that have overtaken Dublin since

Plan of Dublin in G.W. Bacon's Commercial and Library Atlas of the British Isles *(1902)*

Joyce's day. In 1904 (when it was still Sackville Street) it had already lost its residential character and become a commercial thoroughfare, but some shreds of 18C elegance remained. These have since been swept away, partly by the violence of 1916 and 1922. Gone, too, is its most distinctive landmark, Nelson's Pillar, 'the statue of the onehandled adulterer' which recurs throughout 'Aeolus' and is noted more respectfully by Bloom in 'Hades'. Of the street's remaining monuments, 'Hades' pauses to mention the 'hugecloaked Liberator's form', the statue of Daniel O'Connell by the bridge, and further north, the statue of Sir John Gray, 19C Protestant Irish patriot and owner of the *Freeman's Journal*.

At the north end of O'Connell Street is the Rotunda—an 18C Hospital and Assembly Rooms, the latter now serving as cinema—where the sight of a child's hearse turns Bloom's mind to thoughts of his own dead son. These thoughts follow him as Paddy Dignam's funeral procession makes its way up Parnell Square, then not dedicated to the nationalist hero and still known as Rutland Square. The carriage leaves the square by its NE corner and follows Frederick Street North to Upper Dorset Street. It then crosses to take Blessington Street and Berkeley Street to the North Circular Road. Bloom is pleased to note that the route takes them past Eccles Street ('My house down there') but we should resist the temptation to explore it and reserve this neighbourhood for a separate tour (Rte 4).

At the North Circular Road the funeral party is delayed by a herd of cattle, a hazard the modern visitor need not fear, before making its way up Phibsborough Road over the Royal Canal to Prospect (or Glasnevin) Cemetery. Rather than using the Prospect Square entrance near the Botanic Gardens, they turn left on Finglas Road. This takes them past Bengal Terrace on the right, which Mr Power remembers as the scene of Samuel Childs' alleged murder of his brother in 1899. They enter the cemetery near the mortuary chapel and the 'lofty cone' of the Round Tower commemorating Daniel O'Connell, whose remains were reburied in the crypt beneath.

4 'Ulysses' in North and North-East Dublin: Eccles Street to Mountjoy Square

We begin on Eccles Street, between Phibsborough Road and Upper Dorset Street, passed in the course of Rte 3. And we begin with a disappointment, for No. 7, Leopold Bloom's home in *Ulysses* and perhaps the most notable address in Dublin's literary history, was finally demolished in 1982 to make way for a new extension of the Mater Misericordiae Hospital. Joyce visited the modest terraced house on a return visit to Ireland in 1909, when it was the home of his friend J.F. Byrne, and used it in *Ulysses* after consultation of Thom's city directory had reassured him it had been vacant in 1904, when the action of *Ulysses* takes place. We can take some consolation from the older buildings of the Hospital where, as Bloom is reminded in 'Hades', Mrs Riordan died and he himself was treated for a bee sting.

From the south-eastern end of Eccles Street we cross Upper Dorset Street, where Bloom bought his breakfast kidney in 'Calypso', to St George's church, with its spire recalling St Martin's-in-the-Fields in London. The sound of its bells reminds Bloom of the dead Paddy Dignam in the morning ('Calypso'), while at the end of the day Molly Bloom lies awake in bed listening to the striking of the hours ('Penelope').

Beyond the church we follow Temple Street and take a left on Gardiner's Place to enter Mountjoy Square, once but no longer a centre of fashionable life. It is a focal point in the walk taken by the sociable Father Conmee in 'Wandering Rocks'. The Square is also the starting point of Rte 11, which deals with Joyce's childhood and education in this part of Dublin.

5 South-East Dublin: Blackrock

Blackrock lies just outside the city boundary on the coast between Sandycove and Sandymount (Rte 1). When they left Bray in 1892 the Joyce family came to live on Carysfoot Avenue, which runs NW from Main Street; their home at No. 23 no longer has the stone lions which went with its name, Leoville. In *Portrait of the Artist* (Ch. 2) Joyce remembers his granduncle Charles taking him for running practice under the eye of Mike Flynn in Blackrock Park (reached from the northern end of Main Street via Rock Hill). He remembers, too, that the family's hasty departure the next year for NE Dublin (Rte 11) was the first time he caught a glimpse of the money troubles that now beset John Joyce: 'He understood little or nothing of it at first but he became slowly aware that his father had enemies and that some fight was going to take place' (Ch.2).

6 South Dublin: Rathgar and Rathmines

This tour covers the two earliest of Joyce's childhood homes. We begin on Harold's Cross Road south of Mount Jerome Cemetery. To the left is Brighton Square, where Joyce was born at No. 41 on 2 February 1882. He grew up to be superstitious in his reverence for numbers and dates, and arranged to see the first copies of both *Ulysses* and *Finnegans Wake* on his birthday.

He embarked on the perpetual journeying of which his life would consist at the age of two when his family moved about a mile north to Rathmines. We may follow them by taking Harold's Cross Road north to Leinster Road, which is followed to the right; a second right on Rathmines Road brings us to Castlewood Avenue. The Joyces' house at No. 23 (at the corner of Cambridge Road) is probably the handsomest of their many homes and a reminder of their relative prosperity during the writer's infancy. They left here in 1887 for Bray (Rte 12).

7 South Dublin: University College and Archbishop Marsh's Library

On Earlsfort Terrace south of St Stephen's Green we find the original buildings of University College, a plain granite block reconstructed in 1978–81 to house the National Concert Hall. (A new campus has been laid out at Bellfield, south of the city.) Joyce attended University College in 1898–1902, too late to profit from the presence of Gerard Manley Hopkins (q.v.) but in time to be taught by Thomas, brother of Matthew Arnold (q.v.). The brief glimpse of Stephen Dedalus at university in *A Portrait of the Artist* (Ch. 5) reflects his creator's attitude of deliberately maintained aloofness and genuine boredom.

In October 1902 Joyce consulted Joachim of Flora's *Vaticinia* (Venice, 1589) in the 18C Archbishop Marsh's Library, in the shadow of St Patrick's Cathedral to the west of St Stephen's Green. Both the Abbot's 'fading prophecies' and the 'stagnant bay' of the library where Joyce read them are referred to by Stephen Dedalus in the 'Proteus' episode of *Ulysses*.

Archbishop Marsh's Library, St Patrick's Close, Dublin: phone (01) 543511.

8 South Dublin: Usher's Island

Usher's Island is a quay on the south bank of the Liffey between the Queen Maeve Bridge and the Rory O'More Bridge. It can be reached from the north bank via Arran Quay, near the Four Courts (visited in Rte 3). No. 15, now occupied by a seed merchant, is the 'dark gaunt house' where the Misses Morkan live in 'The Dead', the last and perhaps the most powerful story in *Dubliners*.

9 North Dublin: Church Street

Church Street runs north from the Liffey by the Father Mathew Bridge and the Four Courts (Rte 3). Beyond the fine St Michan's Church and the entrance to May Lane on the left lies the Capuchin Church of St Mary of the Angels, the Church Street chapel where Stephen Dedalus comes burdened with adolescent guilt to make his confession at the end of Chapter 3 in *A Portrait of the Artist*. Kneeling in the nave afterwards, he feels his prayers ascend 'from his purified heart like perfume streaming upwards from a heart of white rose'.

10 North-West Dublin: Cabra

Joyce left Dublin for Paris in December 1902, but the following April he received a dramatic telegram: 'MOTHER DYING COME HOME FATHER'. By that time home was No. 7 St Peter's Terrace, one of a row of 19C houses now assimilated into St Peter's Road, which leads north from Cabra Road opposite St Peter's Church. John Joyce had bought the modest terraced house at the sacrifice of half his pension and his son returned to find the family more than usually plagued by money problems. The months until May Joyce's death in August were fraught with tension, much of it provoked by Joyce's refusal of his mother's plea that he make his confession and take communion. His intransigence is remembered in *Ulysses*, where Stephen Dedalus views it with a combination of defiant pride and underlying guilt. Joyce finally left St Peter's Terrace in 1904—his immediate excuse being that he could no longer practice music after his father had pawned the piano—for a succession of lodgings of which the most famous is the Martello Tower in Sandycove (Rte 1).

11 North-East Dublin: Mountjoy Square to North Bull Island via Fairview

This route explores several of the neighbourhoods which Joyce knew after his family's return to the city in 1893, neighbourhoods whose character strongly influenced *Dubliners* and *A Portrait of the Artist as a Young Man*. Its starting point is also the end of Rte 4.

It is certainly fitting to begin in Mountjoy Square. In Chapter 2 of *A Portrait of the Artist* the young and newly arrived Stephen Dedalus at first confines himself to 'circling timidly' round it before he plucks up courage to explore the 'new and complex sensation' of the city beyond. And a chance encounter here between Joyce's father and Father John Conmee led to the young Joyce being enrolled at the Jesuit school on Great Denmark Street beyond Gardiner's Place to the south of the Square. Joyce studied at the 18C Belvedere House from 1893 to 1898. Chapter 4 of *A Portrait of the Artist* is memorable for the interview at which the Director of Belvedere suggests that Stephen consider joining the Society of Jesus, a suggestion both he and his creator set their faces against.

We retrace our steps to Mountjoy Square and continue north on Fitzgibbon Street, where the Joyce family lived in 1893–94 in a house that has since been demolished, to Richmond Place. On his last visit to Dublin, in August 1912, Joyce stayed at Nos 17 and 21. By turning right and crossing the street we reach the entrance to North Richmond Street. Before entering Belvedere Joyce had briefly been a pupil at the Christian Brothers school here, the only time when his schooling was not in Jesuit hands. No. 17 became the Joyce's family home from 1895 to 1898, when they were already sinking from former prosperity. To judge from his writing, North Richmond Street was to him the most important of his many childhood homes. In *A Portrait of the Artist* he ignores several of the upheavals he suffered in real life and prolongs the Dedalus family's stay in the area. North Richmond is also the 'blind' street that makes so powerful a location for 'Araby' in *Dubliners*.

From Richmond Place we now take Summerhill Parade and Ballybough Road north to the Royal Canal and the River Tolka. Beyond the bridge Richmond Road leads left and becomes Millbourne Avenue after it enters Drumcondra. The Joyces lived at the semi-detached No. 2 in their brief interlude between Fitzgibbon Street and North Richmond Street. It now seems one of the dreariest of their Dublin addresses and was then hardly a respectable neighbourhood, but Stanislaus Joyce reported: 'I liked it because it was almost in the country at the foot of a low hill, and just near it were fields with a weir into the Tolka and woods where my school-friends and I could trespass at pleasure'.

Returning to the bridge we then follow Fairview Strand NE. A left on Philipsburgh Avenue and another left on Melrose Avenue bring us to Inverness Road. The Joyces lived at No. 8 in 1900–01, when the street was called Royal Terrace. Their house backs on to a convent and, when he leaves for the university one morning, Stephen Dedalus hears 'a mad nun screeching in the nuns' madhouse beyond the wall' (*Portrait*, Ch. 5). Further NE along Fairview Strand is Windsor Avenue, on the left, where No. 29 was yet another of the Joyces' homes (1898–1900).

For the last part of this tour we take a walk of some 2½ miles to the scene of a crucial episode in *A Portrait of the Artist*. Fairview Strand is followed as it skirts Fairview Park, built on land reclaimed from the sea; Stephen Dedalus is familiar with 'the sloblands of Fairview' (Ch. 5). Clontarf Road then leads along the shoreline to Bull Bridge. After his interview with the Director of Belvedere College Stephen arrives here on 'a day of dappled seaborne clouds' (Ch. 4) and is depressed to meet 'a squad of christian brothers' crossing the bridge. On North Bull Island beyond he completes his liberation from Ireland and the Roman Catholicism in which he has been brought up. The clouds remind him of the world that lies beyond the country of his birth and hint at a future of travel:

> The Europe they had come from lay out there beyond the Irish Sea, Europe of strange tongues and valleyed and woodbegirt and citadelled and of entrenched and marshalled races. He heard a confused music with him as of memories and names which he was almost conscious of but could not capture even for an instant ...

The sight of a girl on the strand, like 'a strange and beautiful seabird', brings about a Joycean epiphany: a moment of luminous realisation that has all the intensity of religious experience but is directed towards the material, secular, even mundane, world.

Wicklow and Kildare

12 Bray

John Joyce moved his family to Bray from Dublin (Rte 6) in 1887, when Joyce was five, and remained until 1892. Bray (on the coast 13 miles south of Dublin via N11) was already a popular and fashionable resort and the Joyce's home at No. 1 Martello Terrace, by the Promenade, reflects their prosperity during this period. The opening chapter of *A Portrait of the Artist* remembers the writer's childhood playmate Eileen Vance, who lived at No. 4 (not No. 7 as Joyce states), and gives a notable account of the explosive Christmas dinner at Bray in 1891. Behind the argument between Joyce's father and his first teacher, Dante Conway, lay the shadow of Parnell's recent death, an event which John Joyce came to identify with the beginning of his own decline in fortune.

13 Clongowes Wood College

The Jesuit school stands in wooded countryside near the Liffey some 38 miles west of Joyce's childhood home at Bray (Rte 12) and 2 miles north of Clane (off L25 between Naas and Kilcock). Its buildings incorporate part of a medieval castle. Joyce's father sent him here in 1888—he gave his age as 'half past six' and acquired this as his school nickname—and withdrew him in 1891. The first chapter of *A Portrait of the Artist* is based on vivid recollections of his years with the Jesuits at Clongowes ('a smell of air and rain and turf and corduroy'). The 'square ditch' in front of the castle is the one into which Wells pushes the young Stephen Dedalus.

County Cork

14 Cork

The Joyces came from Cork, on the south coast of Ireland and now the second city of the Republic. In 1867–70 the writer's father, John Joyce, studied medicine at University College (then Queen's College); he was popular with his fellow students but failed his exams. Beset by money troubles, he returned to Cork in February 1894 to dispose of the remaining property he had inherited, and took his twelve-year-old son with him. Chapter 2 of *A Portrait of the Artist* describes how Simon Dedalus takes Stephen on a tour of the College's neo-Tudor buildings (in the SW of the city) and how Stephen 'listened without sympathy to his father's evocation of Cork and of scenes of his youth, a tale broken by sighs or draughts from his pocketflask whenever the image of some dead friend appeared in it or whenever the evoker remembered suddenly the purpose of his actual visit'.

THE LAKE POETS: WORDSWORTH, COLERIDGE AND SOUTHEY

William Wordsworth: b. Cockermouth, Cumbria, 1770; d. Rydal, Cumbria, 1850. *Lyrical Ballads* (with Coleridge; 1798; second edition with Preface, 1800); *Poems in Two Volumes* (1807); *The Excursion, Being a Portion of The Recluse* (1814); *The White Doe of Rylstone: or the Fate of the Nortons* (1815); *Peter Bell: a Tale in Verse* (1819); *A Description of the Scenery of the Lakes in the North of England* (published separately for the first time, 1822; expanded, reorganised and republished several times, notably as *A Guide through the District of the Lakes in the North of England*, 1835); *Ecclesiastical Sketches* (1822); *Memorials of a Tour on the Continent 1820* (1822); *Yarrow Revisited, and Other Poems* (1835); *Kendal and Windermere Railway: Two Letters Reprinted from the Morning Post* (1845); *The Prelude: or Growth of a Poet's Mind* (1850).

Samuel Taylor Coleridge: b. Ottery St Mary, Devon, 1772; d. London, 1834. *The Fall of Robespierre: An Historic Drama* (with Southey; 1794); *Poems on Various Subjects* (1796); *The Watchman* (1796); *Fears in Solitude, Written in 1798 During the Alarm of an Invasion* (1798); *Lyrical Ballads* (with Wordsworth; 1798); *The Friend* (1809–10); *Christabel; Kubla Khan: A Vision; The Pains of Sleep* (1816); *Biographia Literaria: or Biographical Sketches of My Literary Life and Opinions* (1817); *On the Constitution of the Church and State According to the Idea of Each* (1830).

Robert Southey: b. Bristol, Avon, 1774; d. Keswick, Cumbria, 1843. *The Fall of Robespierre: An Historic Drama* (with Coleridge; 1794); *Joan of Arc: An Epic Poem* (1796); *Letters Written During a Short Residence in Spain and Portugal* (1797); *Thalaba the Destroyer* (1801); *Madoc: A Poem in Two Parts* (1805); *Letters from England: By Don Manuel Alvarez Espriella. Translated from the Spanish* (1807); *The Life of Nelson* (1813); *Wat Tyler: A Dramatic Poem* (1817); *The Life of Wesley, and the Rise and Progress of Methodism* (1820); *A Vision of Judgement* (1821); *The Doctor* (1834–38); *Journal of a Tour in Scotland in 1819* (edited by C.H. Herford; 1929).

Related works: Dorothy Wordsworth, *Journals* (edited by Ernest de Selincourt; 1941); Thomas De Quincey, *Recollections of the Lake Poets* (1835–40).

It is, of course, hazardous to follow the lead of contemporaries and group Wordsworth, Coleridge and Southey together as 'The Lake Poets', for on not very close inspection they turn out to be distinguished as much by their differences as their agreements. As so often proves the case with members of what critics call a school, they crossed each other's paths at a fertile, receptive point in youth—Coleridge and Southey to share their impractical dream of 'Pantisocracy', Wordsworth and Coleridge to collaborate on the *Lyrical Ballads*—and then pursued increasingly divergent ways. Those ways led not merely to a relaxation of their early friendship punctuated by the occasional quarrel but also to very different literary careers. Wordsworth became a poet whose lonely greatness is in no way illuminated by associating him with a school and then declined into conventionality without encouragement from his fellow poets. Coleridge wrote fitfully and sometimes waywardly, never managing to leave a paper record that gives posterity more than fragmented glimpses into his strength of intellect. Southey developed into one of literature's conscientious journeymen and England's many undistinguished Poet Laureates.

Yet, if we persist in regarding them as a school, it is completely understandable that the school should bear a geographical label and one, moreover, which identifies them with the Lake District. For all its oversimplification, the term 'Lake Poets' pays inevitable tribute to the way these writers—but particularly Wordsworth—changed the relation of literature to landscape and, indeed, changed our perception of what the word 'landscape' itself may imply. Early poets had located moral values in the world of pastoral or taken pleasure in the picturesque arrangement of natural effects, but it was left to Wordsworth to find in untouched nature a source of experiences at once liberating and edifying. Among the many and often complex ramifications of this discovery was the simple result that he put his native region on the educated man's map of England. At a time when the Industrial Revolution was making people turn to nature with new, larger and more urgent demands, his poetry about the Lakes and the example of his own life there suggested a tangible, specific destination for the tourist temporarily indulging his discontent with civilisation. Wordsworth's success in this respect was too great for his own complete comfort, for the very popularity of the Lake District was beginning to threaten its original character even in his lifetime, turning the former celebrant of the remote and overlooked into an embattled conservationist.

London

1 Inns of Court, Fleet Street and The Strand

We begin on Holborn at Chancery Lane Underground Station (Central Line). On the left-hand side of Gray's Inn Road to the north lie the pleasant courts and gardens of Gray's Inn, which Southey entered in 1797, though his stay there was only brief. In 1793 Wordsworth lodged with his brother Richard in Staple Inn, the attractive half-timbered building (much rebuilt and no longer an Inn of Court) on the south side of Holborn. This was the poet's second visit of any consequence to the capital, made immediately after his return from France; it undoubtedly contributed to the impressions of the city recorded in Book 7 of *The Prelude*.

Walking west along Holborn, we turn left on Southampton Buildings—where Coleridge lodged with William Hazlitt as a neighbour in the spring of 1811—and follow it to Chancery Lane. It was here that a younger Coleridge on vacation from Cambridge met a recruiting officer and enlisted in the Light Dragoons. He had seen the name, 'Comberbacke', which he adopted for this brief, disastrous adventure, on a doorway in Lincoln's Inn opposite. Wordsworth himself stayed in Lincoln's Inn from February to August 1795 with his friend Basil Montagu, who had chambers at No. 7 New Square.

Chancery Lane leads south to Fleet Street opposite Middle Temple Lane and the Temple, richly associated with Wordsworth and Coleridge's friend, Charles Lamb. If we walk left along Fleet Street we are following the route trod by Wordsworth early one Sunday morning of April 1808 'in a very thoughtful and melancholy state of mind' about Coleridge, from whom he had just parted. His letter to Sir George Beaumont describing the walk, like his sonnet 'Composed Upon Westminster Bridge' (see Rte 2), is a reminder that it was not only the natural environment which could operate on him as a soothing, consoling force:

I had passed through Temple Bar and by St Dunstan's, noticing nothing, and entirely preoccupied with my own thoughts, when, looking up, I saw before me the avenue of Fleet Street, silent, empty, and pure white, with a sprinkling of new-fallen snow, not a cart or carriage to obstruct the view, no noise, only a few soundless and dusky foot-passengers here and there. You remember the elegant line of the curve of Ludgate Hill in which this avenue would terminate, and beyond, towering above it, was the huge and majestic form of St Paul's, solemnised by a thin veil of falling snow. I cannot say how much I was affected at this unthought-of sight in such a place, and what a blessing I felt there is in habits of exalted imagination. My sorrow was controlled, and my uneasiness of mind—not quieted and relieved altogether—seemed at once to receive the gift of an anchor of security.

A left turn from Ludgate Hill on Old Bailey and then a right on Newgate Street bring us to the site of Christ's Hospital, which lay north of the ruined Christ Church. Coleridge's schooldays here (1782–91) are remembered by his younger contemporary, Charles Lamb, in 'Christ's Hospital Five-and-Thirty Years Ago' and imaginatively conjured up by Wordsworth in *The Prelude*:

I speak to thee, my Friend! to thee,
Who, yet a liveried schoolboy, in the depths
Of the huge city, on the leaded roof
Of that wide edifice, thy school and home,
Wert used to lie and gaze upon the clouds
Moving in heaven; or, of that pleasure tired,
To shut thine eyes, and by internal light
See trees, and meadows, and thy native stream,
Far distant, thus beheld from year to year
Of a long exile.

(1850 text, Bk 6, lines 265–274)

By retracing our steps down Ludgate Hill and along Fleet Street, and then continuing into the Strand, we may visit a final location associated with Coleridge. Just before Charing Cross Station Buck-

Christ's Hospital, by Thomas Shepherd in James Elmes' London and its Environs in the Nineteenth Century *(1829)*

ingham Arcade leads left to Buckingham Street, where Coleridge lodged at the handsome No. 21 for the winter of 1799–1800. He had left his family behind in Keswick (see Rte 12A) and was making an attempt, doomed to failure, at establishing himself as a regular journalist for the *Morning Post*.

2 Westminster

The obvious starting-point is Westminster Underground Station (District and Circle Lines). The present bridge, built in 1862, replaces the 18C stone structure whose view is celebrated in Wordsworth's sonnet 'Composed Upon Westminster Bridge September 3, 1802'. The occasion that provoked the poem seems actually to have been the last day of July 1802, when Wordsworth and his sister left London on the way to France and a visit to Annette Vallon, who was bringing up his illegitimate child. Dorothy's journal for that day offers a close analogue to her brother's poem:

> We mounted the Dover Coach at Charing Cross. It was a beautiful morning. The City, St Paul's, with the River and a multitude of little Boats, made a most beautiful sight as we crossed Westminster Bridge. The houses were not overhung by their cloud of smoke and they were spread out endlessly, yet the sun shone so brightly with such a pure light that there was even something like the purity of one of nature's own grand spectacles.

In Poets' Corner (fee) of Westminster Abbey we find memorials to all three poets, though none is buried here. The epitaph on Southey is by Wordsworth. Southey attended Westminster School in Little Dean's Yard to the south of the Abbey from 1788 to 1792. He was expelled for protesting against flogging.

3 Highgate and Hampstead

We walk north from Archway Underground Station (Northern Line) up Highgate Hill and Highgate High Street before turning left on South Grove. Coleridge's tomb was removed from the chapel crypt of Highgate School and brought to the early 19C church of St Michael's here in 1961. It now stands in the aisle; near his memorial on the north wall of the nave is one to James and Ann Gillman. Coleridge lived with Dr Gillman and his wife from April 1816 to 1823 at No. 14, the fine early 18C Moreton House. He arrived as a patient desperately seeking help for his drug addiction:

> You will never *hear* any thing but truth from me—Prior Habits render it out of my power to *tell* a falsehood, but unless watched carefully, I dare not promise that I should not with regard to this detested Poison be capable of acting a Lie.—No sixty hours *have yet passed* without my having taken Laudunum—tho' for the last week comparatively trifling doses. I have full belief, that your *anxiety* will need not to be extended beyond the first week; and for the first week I shall not, I *must not be permitted* to leave your House, unless I should walk out with you.—Delicately or indelicately, this *must* be done, and both the Servant and the young Man must receive absolute commands from you on no account to fetch any thing for me.

The doctor's care reduced but never eliminated the problem.

Coleridge's presence in the house brought a steady flow of visitors, some of them distinguished, attracted by the prospect of hearing the age's most compelling talker. Leading right from the end of South Grove is The Grove, a handsome late 17C–early 18C terraced street where, in 1823, the Gillmans moved with Coleridge to No. 3. He lived here until his death.

By following Highgate West Hill to the south and turning right on Merton Lane we come to a footpath that leads between Highgate Ponds and continues south of Kenwood House to Hampstead Heath. On this path or a neighbouring one Keats (q.v.) encountered Coleridge and a mutual acquaintance in April 1819:

> after enquiring by a look whether it would be agreeable—I walked with him at his alderman-after-dinner pace for near two miles I suppose. In those two miles he broached a thousand things—let me see if I can give you a list—Nightingales, Poetry—on Poetical sensation—Metaphysics—Different genera and species of Dreams—Nightmare—a dream accompanied by a sense of touch—single and double touch—A dream related—First and second consciousness—the difference explained between will and Volition—so my [many] metaphysicians from a want of smoking the second consciousness—Monsters—the Kraken—Mermaids—Southey believes in them—Southey's belief too much diluted—a Ghost story—Good morning—I heard his voice as he came towards me—I heard it as he moved away—I heard it all the interval—if it may be called so.

Coleridge later remembered that before he left Keats asked: 'Let me carry away the memory, Coleridge, of having pressed your hand!' It was their only meeting.

A pleasant end to the walk can be made by continuing across the Heath to its western edge, where Heath Street leads south to Hampstead Underground Station (Northern Line).

South-Eastern England

4 Boldre

In 1839 Southey married his second wife, Caroline Bowles, in the church at Boldre, a little village in the New Forest 3 miles north of Lymington on the south coast. The vicar of Boldre had earlier been William Gilpin (1724–1804), author of picturesque travel books whose tour of the Wye Valley is mentioned in Rte 8 below. Gilpin is buried in the churchyard and remembered by a monument in the church.

South-Western England

5 Bath to Crewkerne via Bristol, Nether Stowey and Ottery St Mary

In its way South-Western England is almost as rich in associations with all three poets as the Lake District that gave them the label by which they became popularly known. Coleridge and Southey were born and married here, as well as sharing their youthful enthusiasm for 'Pantisocracy'. More important, it was in South-Western England that Coleridge and Wordsworth forged the close bond that led to their literary collaboration on *Lyrical Ballads*.

Bath is not a city we readily associate with the Lake Poets, though all of them came here on one occasion or another. The most important surviving location, now marked with a plaque, is No. 108 Walcot Street near the river, where Southey lived from the age of two to six under the care of his aunt, the fashionable and unpleasant Miss Tyler.

A4 leads NW from Bath to Bristol (12 miles). A walking tour of the city, linking the dispersed places frequented by the three writers, begins in the SE. At the magnificent church of St Mary Redcliffe Coleridge and Southey were married in October and November 1795 respectively to Sara and Edith Fricker, unkindly described by Byron (q.v.) as 'milliners of Bath' but really daughters of a failed manufacturer of sugar pans who lived on Redcliffe Hill to the south. Southey's marriage lasted until Edith's death in 1837, but Coleridge eventually separated from Sara after his return from Malta in 1806.

St Mary Redcliffe's close connection with Chatterton (q.v.) made it an appropriate venue for these ceremonies, since both Coleridge and Southey played a crucial role in the growth of the romantic legend surrounding the 'marvellous Boy'. Southey took a kindly interest in Chatterton's surviving relatives and edited his poems with Joseph Cottle (1803), while Coleridge wrote a lengthy 'Monody on the Death of Chatterton', revising and adding to it while in Bristol.

From the church we follow Redcliffe Way west over the Floating Harbour and across Queen Square. On King Street, to the right shortly afterwards, stands the old Free Library, which Coleridge used while making erratic preparations for his Bristol lectures. It is now an Employment Centre. We can continue on a detour further north by taking Queen Charlotte Street, Baldwin and High Street to the Cross. Christ Church, on the corner of Wine Street, preserves the 17C font from the demolished church of St Ewens at which Southey was baptised.

The main walking route follows Redcliffe Way, skirts St Augustine's Reach and heads left to Bristol Cathedral. The monument to Bishop Butler (d. 1752) in the north transept has an inscription by Southey, while a bust of the poet may be found in the north choir aisle.

College Street leads from the west side of College Green opposite the Cathedral. Now changed beyond all recognition, it was the site of Coleridge and Southey's lodgings in 1795, when they were making plans to found a 'Pantisocratic' community on the banks of the Susquehanna in America. By following College Street's continuation as Frog Lane and turning left on Park Street, we come to Great George Street (left) and the Georgian House. This elegant building was the home of John Pretor Pinney, a wealthy West Indies merchant, and the probable scene of Wordsworth and Coleridge's first meeting in autumn 1795. The generosity of John Pinney the younger allowed Wordsworth and his sister Dorothy to live at Racedown Lodge, which we visit later in the course of this tour.

Rte 8 charts a picturesque journey north from Bristol up the valley of the Wye. The present route leaves the city to the SW following the general direction of the M5 for part of the way but shunning the motorway in favour of roads that keep closer to the character of the countryside which Wordsworth and Coleridge knew.

After following A330 signs for Weston-super-Mare we turn right on B3128 and its continuation, B3130, for Clevedon (24 miles), a coastal town vastly grown from the small fishing village where Coleridge stayed. He brought his wife Sara here for his honeymoon in 1795 and tradition, as well as a plaque, identifies No. 55 Old Church Road near the station as 'our Cot o'ergrown/ With white-flower'd Jasmin, and the broad-leav'd Myrtle', of which he wrote fondly in 'The Eolian Harp' (lines 3–4).

We leave Clevedon by B3133 and branch left at 28½ miles on a sideroad to Wrington (32 miles). All three poets paid visits to the Evangelical Hannah More at Barley Wood, described under the entry devoted to her. It was on a visit here in 1814 that Joseph Cottle, Bristol bookseller and longtime friend of the Lake Poets, first realised the extent of Coleridge's opium addiction when he observed 'his hands shaking to an alarming degree, so that he could not take a glass of wine without spilling it, though one hand supported the other!'

From Wrington we join A38 and head SW, skirting the pleasant and sometimes dramatic landscape of the Mendip Hills. Coleridge came here on walking tours with Southey in 1794 and with the Wordsworths in 1798. At 54 miles we reach Bridgwater. Coleridge preached in its Unitarian Chapel on Dampiet Street (south of and parallel to Fore Street after we cross Town Bridge) in 1797 and again the following year.

From Bridgwater A39 leads west towards the Quantock Hills and the village of *Nether Stowey (62 miles), scene of probably the most important passages in Coleridge's friendship with Wordsworth and Dorothy. Thomas Poole, a prosperous local tanner and farmer of radical sympathies, found a cottage for him here in the winter of 1796. Disillusioned by his recent attempts to launch *The Watchman*, a journal of literature and politics, Coleridge welcomed the prospect of rural retirement: 'I am not *fit* for *public* life; yet the light shall shine to a far distance from my cottage window'. Wordsworth and his sister came to visit in the spring and decided to settle at Alfoxden (described below). In the year that followed their daily intimacy sparked a new creative energy in both poets; its most tangible result was the *Lyrical Ballads*, published in Bristol by Cottle. As recorded by Dorothy in her *Alfoxden Journal*, one of her beautifully precise and unassuming accounts of the landscape and people around her, their time in the Quantocks has an idyllic quality. But it was not without its melodramatic and comic side. The Wordsworths' northern accents, Coleridge's sometimes eccentric manner and a visit by John Thelwall, the prominent radical, combined to generate local suspicion in this nervously anti-Jacobin period. A Dr Daniel Lysons of Bath solemnly reported servants' gossip to the Home Secretary:

> I am since informed that the Master of the house has no wife with him, but only a woman who passes for his Sister. The man has Camp Stools which he and his visitors take with them when they go about the country upon their nocturnal or diurnal excursions and have also a Portfolio in which they enter their observations which they have been heard to say were almost finished.

Here is Coleridge's account of the upshot, which has no doubt gained in the memory and the telling, from *Biographia Literaria*:

> The dark guesses of some zealous quidnunc met with so congenial a soil in the grave alarm of a titled Dogberry of our neighbourhood that a spy was actually sent down from the government *pour surveillance* of myself and friend. There must have been not only abundance, but variety of these 'honorable men' at the disposal of ministers; for this proved a very honest fellow. After three weeks' truly Indian perseverance in tracking us (for we were commonly together), during all which time seldom were we out of doors but he contrived to be within hearing (and all the while utterly unsuspected; how, indeed, could such a suspicion enter our fancies?), he not only rejected Sir Dogberry's request that he would try yet a little longer, but declared to him his belief that both my friend and myself were as good subjects, for aught he could discover to the contrary, as any in His Majesty's dominions. He had repeatedly hid himself, he said, for hours together, behind a bank at the sea-side (our favorite seat), and overheard our conversation. At first he fancied that we were aware of our danger; for he often heard me talk of one *Spy Nozy* [ie. Spinoza], which he was inclined to interpret of himself, and of a remarkable feature belonging to him; but he was speedily convinced that it was the name of a man who had made a book and lived long ago. (Vol. 1, Ch. 10)

Nether Stowey's church (right of A39) has on its south wall a tablet to Thomas Poole remembering his friendship with Wordsworth, Coleridge and Southey. On the north side of the tower arch is a Latin epitaph to Richard Camplin (d. 1752) translated by Coleridge in the lines beginning 'Depart in joy from this world's noise and strife'. Poole's house, a solid 18C building marred by the addition of a shopfront, stands on Castle Street (left of A39). Constrained by a lame foot to rest in the garden while the Wordsworths took their visitor, Charles Lamb, for a walk in the countryside, Coleridge wrote the lovely 'This Lime-Tree Bower My Prison':

> Well, they are gone, and here I must remain,
> This lime-tree bower my prison! I have lost
> Beauties and feelings, such as would have been
> Most sweet to my remembrance even when age
> Had dimm'd mine eyes to blindness! They, meanwhile,
> Friends, whom I never more may meet again,
> On springy heath, along the hill-top edge,
> Wander in gladness, and wind down, perchance,
> To that still roaring dell, of which I told …

Globe House next door was formerly the Globe Inn, where the government agent pumped the landlord for incriminating information against the poets. Coleridge Cottage on Lime Street, enlarged, altered and still bearing obvious marks of its later career as an inn, is now owned by the National Trust.

Alfoxden (or Alfoxton) Park, then the Wordsworths' home and now a hotel, lies to the left of A39 near Holford (64 miles). Dorothy described its situation vividly in a letter written soon after their arrival:

> Here we are in a large mansion, in a large park, with seventy head of deer around us … In front is a little court, with grass plot, gravel walk, and shrubs; the moss roses were in full beauty a month ago. The front of the house is to the south, but it is screened from the sun by a high hill which rises immediately from it. This hill is beautiful, scattered irregularly and abundantly with trees, and topped with fern, which spreads a considerable way down it. The deer dwell here, and sheep, so that we have a living prospect. From the end of the house we have a view of the sea, over a woody meadow-country; and exactly opposite the window where I now sit is an immense wood, whose round top from this point has exactly the appearance of a mighty dome. In some parts of this wood there is an under grove of hollies which are now very beautiful. In a glen at the bottom of the wood is the waterfall of which I spoke, a quarter of a mile from the house … Wherever we turn we have woods, smooth downs and valleys with small brooks running down them through green meadows,

hardly ever intersected with hedgerows, but scattered over with trees. The hills that cradle these valleys are either covered with fern and bilberries or oak woods which are cut for charcoal ... The Tor of Glastonbury is before our eyes during more than half of our walk to Stowey; and in the park wherever we go, keeping about fifteen yards above the house, it makes a part of our prospect.

Wordsworth's little poem entitled 'To My Sister' records his enthusiastic reaction to their surroundings.

At Williton (72 miles) A39 continues NW along the coast to Porlock, home of the anonymous person whose business interrupted the writing of 'Kubla Khan' and so doomed the poem to incompleteness, like so many of Coleridge's other projects. The Exmoor farm where the famous incident occurred has not been satisfactorily identified and so, instead of pursuing this direction, we turn left on A358, which takes us via Taunton (87 miles) to the junction with A303 (96 miles), which is followed SW. After bypassing Honiton (111 miles), where the road has become A30, we branch left on B3177 to Ottery St Mary (117 miles), the rather unattractive town of Coleridge's birth.

His childhood home does not survive but the fine church where he was baptised and his father was rector still stands. By the Otter south of the town and reached mainly by footpaths we find the cave called Pixie's Parlour, a favourite haunt of Coleridge's. The carving of his name on the wall has long since vanished but the poem, 'Song of the Pixies', commemorates the occasion when he brought a party of young ladies here in 1793.

The next, and necessarily circuitous, stage of our itinerary begins by leaving Ottery St Mary to the east on B3174 and then changing to A3052 for Lyme Regis (135 miles). We climb north from this charming coastal town on A3070 to the junction with A35 (138 miles), where we follow the hilly B3165 for Crewkerne.

Just beyond Birdsmoor Gate (147½ miles) we find Racedown Lodge. Somewhat to his father's annoyance John Pinney the younger of Bristol lent this Georgian house, now a farmhouse, rent-free to Wordsworth and his sister from September 1795 to July 1797, when they left for Alfoxden. It was an important time for the poet, not least because it gave him his first chance to live with Dorothy since childhood. As Book 11 of *The Prelude* bears witness, her company helped rescue him from the nervous anguish that followed his experiences in France and confirmed his dedication to poetry. The results can be seen in works like 'The Ruined Cottage' and 'The Borderers', written at Racedown.

At 151 miles we reach Crewkerne, the pleasant market town that was the Wordsworths' centre for shopping and post while at Racedown. From here A30 leads east towards Salisbury Plain, scene of another Wordsworth poem belonging to this period, 'Guilt and Sorrow'.

Georgian House, 7 Great George Street, Bristol, Avon: phone (0272) 299771, extension 237.

Coleridge Cottage, 35 Lime Street, Nether Stowey, Somerset: NT; phone (0278) 732662.

Central England

6 Oxford

Southey's expulsion from Westminster School (see Rte 2) stopped him being admitted to Christ Church, but he was able to enter Balliol College in 1792. His Oxford years were creative ones, as the early publication date of *Joan of Arc* testifies, though he himself later claimed that the University taught him only rowing and swimming. Coleridge, brought by a mutual friend, first met him in his Balliol rooms in July 1794. Southey quickly pronounced Coleridge to be 'of most uncommon merit—of the strongest genius, the clearest judgment, the best heart', while Coleridge later wrote in *Biographia Literaria* of 'the strong and sudden, yet I trust not fleeting influence, which my moral being underwent on my acquaintance with him at Oxford' (Vol. 1, Ch. 3). The two young poets together formulated their ideal scheme, 'Pantisocracy', which took them to Bristol (see Rte 5) though never to America when they left University.

7 Coleorton

Coleorton lies 3 miles NE of Ashby-de-la-Zouch, which is on A50 between Leicester and Burton upon Trent. The Hall now belongs to the National Coal Board.

It was built in 1804–08 by George Dance the younger for Sir George Beaumont, amateur landscape painter, patron of the arts, admirer of Wordsworth's poetry and, according to Sir Walter Scott (q.v.), 'by far the most sensible and pleasing man I ever knew'. Wordsworth came here for the winter of 1806–07 with his wife, sister Dorothy and sister-in-law Sara Hutchinson to stay at Hall Farm on the estate. He took an active role in the planting of forest trees; his letter of 17 October 1805 to Sir George makes a striking application of Romantic principles to landscape gardening, insisting on the need 'of having our houses belong to the country, which will of course lead us back to the simplicity of Nature'.

A visit from Coleridge, recently back from Malta, proved a tense occasion, since the Wordsworths were troubled by the changes in their friend's life: his separation from his wife, attraction to Sara Hutchinson and increasing dependence on brandy and opium. When Wordsworth read him the first version of *The Prelude*, still known just as the 'poem to Coleridge', he responded with 'To William Wordsworth', a poem expressing his own sense of failure and anguished need of love:

Thy hopes of me, dear Friend! by me unfelt!
Were troublous to me, almost as a voice,
Familiar once, and more than musical,—
To one cast forth, whose hope had seem'd to die
A wanderer with a worn-out heart
Mid strangers pining with untended wounds.
(first version, lines 68–73)

Whilst at Coleorton Wordsworth made a sightseeing visit to 'the ivied ruins of forlorn GRACE DIEU', originally an Augustinian nunnery and later the family home of the Beaumonts. His poem, 'For a Seat in the Groves at Coleorton', remembers that Francis Beaumont (q.v.), the playwright, was born at Grace Dieu. It can be seen to the right of A512 3 miles east of Coleorton Hall. Returning to the area many years later in 1841 Wordsworth and his wife went to view the building of Mount St Bernard, the first monastery to be founded in England since the Reformation, in Charnwood Forest. He found the spectacle of the Trappist community disquieting: 'The whole appearance had in my eyes something of the nature of a dream, and it has often haunted me since'. Mount St Bernard is reached by continuing east on A512 2 miles beyond Grace Dieu, then turning right on Charley Road and taking a second right on Oaks Road, an additional 3 miles. Its fine church by Pugin (1839) is particularly notable.

Coleorton Hall (British Coal), Coleorton, near Ashby-de-la-Zouch, Leicestershire: visits by prior arrangement with the Head of Secretariat; phone Ashby-de-la-Zouch (0530) 413131.

Mount St Bernard Abbey, Coalville, Leicester: grounds and part of the church open; phone (0530) 32298 or 32022.

8 The Wye Valley

Their connections with Bristol (see Rte 5) assured the Lake Poets' familiarity with the lovely Wye Valley, which winds north from the River Severn on the border between Gloucestershire and Gwent. A convenient itinerary begins at Chepstow.

In 1795 Coleridge, Southey, the Fricker sisters and Joseph Cottle started their tour of the area by a visit to Chepstow Castle, separated from the town by a ravine and magnificently sited near the river. A quarrel disturbed their dinner at a local inn, for Coleridge had annoyed Southey by his failure to arrive for a publicly announced lecture in Bristol—a failure that all too often marred his career on the podium. To the right of A466 just north of the town is Piercefield Park, where Chepstow racecourse stands in wooded countryside and where Coleridge and Southey reconciled their differences as they walked.

At 5 miles we come to **Tintern Abbey, a grand Cistercian ruin on a patch of level ground by the river and surrounded by some of the finest scenery this journey has to offer. Coleridge and his party had difficulty finding Tintern and arrived late at night but, as Cottle later wrote, this had its picturesque advantages:

> At the instant the huge doors unfolded, the horned moon appeared between the opening clouds, and shining through the grand window in the distance. It was a delectable moment; not a little augmented by the unexpected green sward that covered the whole of the floor, and the long-forgotten tombs beneath; whilst the gigantic ivies, in their rivalry, almost concealed the projecting and dark turrets and eminences, reflecting back the lustre of the torch below.

Of Wordsworth's visits the most important resulted in 'Lines Composed a Few Miles Above Tintern Abbey, on Revisiting the Banks of the Wye During a Tour. July 13, 1798':

> No poem of mine was composed under circumstances more pleasant for me to remember than this. I began it upon leaving Tintern, after crossing the Wye, and concluded it just as I was entering Bristol in the evening, after a ramble of four or five days, with my sister. Not a line of it was altered, and not any part of it written down till I reached Bristol.

William Gilpin's *Observations on the River Wye ... Made in the Summer of the Year 1770*, a guidebook that Wordsworth in all probability took with him, records aspects of the scene not mentioned by the poet:

> Among other things in this scene of desolation, the poverty and wretchedness of the inhabitants were remarkable. They occupy little huts, raised among the ruins of the monastery; and seem to have no employment, but begging; as if a place, once devoted to indolence, could never again become the seat of industry ... The country about *Tintern-abbey* hath been described as a solitary, tranquil scene; but its immediate environs only are meant. Within half a mile of it are carried on great iron-works; which introduce noise and bustle into these regions of tranquillity.

Tintern Abbey by Sir Richard Colt Hoare in William Coxe's An Historical Tour in Monmouthshire *(1801)*

By following A466 north and then changing successively to A40, B4229 and B4228, we reach another magnificent ruin on the banks of the river, *Goodrich Castle (23 miles). His encounter with a young girl here in 1793 gave Wordsworth the idea for 'We Are Seven', one of his contributions to *Lyrical Ballads*.

A possible extension to this journey leads NW from Ross-on-Wye (26 miles), picking up A49 for Hereford (39 miles), where we continue NW on A438 and A480 to Brinsop (45 miles). At Brinsop Court, a mansion still showing its 14C origin, about a mile to the north, Wordsworth several times visited his brother-in-law, Thomas Hutchinson. In the village itself the church of St George has a modern Nativity window in memory of the Wordsworths.

Chepstow Castle, Chepstow, Gwent: Cadw: Welsh Historic Monuments; phone headquarters in Cardiff, (0222) 465511.

Tintern Abbey, Tintern, Gwent: Cadw: Welsh Historic Monuments; phone headquarters in Cardiff, (0222) 465511.

Goodrich Castle, near Ross-on-Wye, Hereford and Worcester: English Heritage, standard opening; phone (0600) 890538.

Wales

9 Llangollen to Devil's Bridge via Snowdon

Though he toured Wales three times (in 1791, 1793 and 1824), Wordsworth never carried out his idea of writing a guide to Snowdon and, in his *Description of the Scenery of the Lakes in the North of England*, awarded his native Cumbria a 'decided superiority' over Wales because of its 'concentration of interest'. The itinerary that follows links the major but dispersed places with which the poet was familiar.

We begin at Llangollen. In 1824 Wordsworth followed in the footsteps of Southey and other literary men of the age by paying a visit to Plas Newydd, an elaborate half-timbered house south of A5. Since 1799 it had been the home of Lady Eleanor Butler and the Hon. Sarah Ponsonby, the eccentric 'Ladies of Llangollen' who lived a secluded life devoted to 'friendship, celibacy, and the knitting of blue stockings'. His sonnet commemorating the occasion was not an entirely happy performance, for it described Plas Newydd as a 'low-roofed Cot' and drew attention to the ladies' age.

From Llangollen we can make a 28-mile detour up A525 to the pleasant Vale of Clwyd beyond Ruthin. Wordsworth stayed here with a friend from Cambridge, Robert Jones, and his sisters on his two earlier visits to Wales. 'Who would not be happy enjoying the company of three young ladies in the Vale of Clwyd without a rival?' Dorothy asked reasonably. Wordsworth dedicated his *Descriptive Sketches Taken During a Pedestrian Tour Among the Alps* (1793) to Jones and apologised in the preface for not paying similar tribute in verse to his friend's native land.

The main route heads NW from Llangollen along A5, changing at Capel Curig (36 miles) to A4086. At the junction with A498 (40 miles) we have reached the foothills of Snowdon. Modern tourists usually make the ascent on the Snowdon Mountain Railway from Llanberis (6 miles NW via A4086); Wordsworth climbed the mountain at night from Beddgelert on A498 (47 miles). We cannot be sure whether he did it in 1791 or 1793 but the exact date matters less than the magnificent description that resulted in Book 14 of *The Prelude*:

as I looked up,
The Moon hung naked in a firmament
Of azure without cloud, and at my feet
Rested a silent sea of hoary mist.
A hundred hills their dusky backs upheaved
All over this still ocean; and beyond,
Far, far beyond, the solid vapours stretched,
In headlands, tongues, and promontory shapes,
Into the main Atlantic, that appeared

To dwindle, and give up his majesty,
Usurped upon far as the sight could reach.
(lines 39–49)

Returning to Beddgelert in 1824 he was distressed to find it 'much altered for the worse; new and formal houses have supplanted the old rugged and tufted cottages; and a smart hotel has taken the place of the lowly public house in which I took refreshment'.

The last stage of our itinerary involves a lengthy trip south. We follow successively: A498 and A4085 to Penrhyndeudraeth (55 miles); A487 to Maentwrog (59 miles); A470 to Dolgellau (77 miles); and finally, A470 and A487 to Aberystwyth (111 miles). On A4120 east of Aberystwyth we reach Devil's Bridge (123 miles), where the Rheidol and Mynach join to fall dramatically through a rocky cleft. Wordsworth remembered his visit to the spot in 1824 with a sonnet:

There I seem to stand,
As in life's morn; permitted to behold,
From the dread chasm, woods climbing above woods,
In pomp that fades not; everlasting snows;
And skies that ne'er relinquish their repose;
Such power possess the family of floods
Over the minds of Poets, young or old!

Plas Newydd Museum, Hill Street, Llangollen, Clwyd: phone (082 42) 2201. Be careful not to confuse this property with Plas Newydd on the Isle of Anglesey.

Eastern England

10 Cambridge

A walking tour best begins by retracing the last stage of Wordsworth's route when he entered the city by coach as an excited freshman, described as the opening to Book 3 of *The Prelude*. We cross Magdalene Bridge and follow Bridge Street south. Beyond the Round Church, ahead and on our left, stood the Hoop Inn where he dined on his first evening. By turning right on St John's Street we quickly come to St John's College, scene of his undergraduate career (1787–90).

His rooms were on the present F staircase, on the south side of First Court, and the memory of their disadvantages as well as advantages remained with him when he wrote *The Prelude*:

The Evangelist St John my Patron was:
Three Gothic courts are his, and in the first
Was my abiding-place, a nook obscure;
Right underneath, the College kitchens made
A humming sound, less tuneable than bees,
But hardly less industrious; with shrill notes
Of sharp command and scolding intermixed.
Near me hung Trinity's loquacious clock,
Who never let the quarters, night or day,
Slip by him unproclaimed, and told the hours
Twice over with a male and female voice.
Her pealing organ was my neighbour too;
And from the pillow, looking forth by light
Of moon or favouring stars, I could behold
The antechapel where the statue stood
Of Newton with his prism and silent face,

The marble index of a mind for ever
Voyaging through strange seas of Thought, alone.
(Bk 3, lines 46–63)

A window bearing a commemorative inscription has been moved from his rooms to the Library in Second Court. The Hall, to the right of the screens passage between First and Second Courts, has a portrait by Pickersgill which Wordsworth praised in a sonnet: 'how true/ To life thou art, and, in thy truth, how dear!'

It was inevitable that the Backs and College grounds beyond, not then distinguished by the Bridge of Sighs and New Court (1825–31), should have held a special attraction for him:

All winter long, whenever free to choose,
Did I by night frequent the College groves
And tributary walks; the last, and oft
The only one, who had been lingering there
Through hours of silence, till the porter's bell,
A punctual follower on the stroke of nine,
Rang with its blunt unceremonious voice,
Inexorable summons! Lofty elms,
Inviting shades of opportune recess,
Bestowed composure on a neighbourhood
Unpeaceful in itself.
(*The Prelude*, Bk 6, lines 66–76)

The subtitle of 'Remembrance of Collins', one of the few poems attributable to Wordsworth's undergraduate years, associates it with the Thames near Richmond but the description of the peaceful, consoling river may also owe something to his walks by the Cam:

O glide, fair stream! for ever so,
Thy quiet soul on all bestowing,
Till all our minds for ever flow
As thy deep waters now are flowing.
(lines 5–8)

Yet the picture of Cambridge offered in *The Prelude* is that of a place he ultimately found uncongenial. The bewildered excitement of a northern youth in the bustle of a university town gives way to disillusionment with the Fellows of his college, a sense of his own incompatibility with the academic life and a steady realisation that his future lay in very different environments. The academic record supports his conclusion, for by the end of his undergraduate career he did not even attempt his papers in mathematics.

In the ante-chapel at Trinity, St John's neighbour, we can see the fine *statue of Newton by Roubiliac which moved Wordsworth to such magnificent poetry. Wordsworth's younger brother, Christopher, who fulfilled the family hopes his own undergraduate career had disappointed, was Master of the College from 1820 to 1841.

Wordsworth's 'Ode on the Installation of His Royal Highness Prince Albert as Chancellor of the University of Cambridge, July, 1847' was performed in Gibbs' Senate House at the southern end of Trinity Street. It is ironic that Wordsworth's only public poem in his capacity as Poet Laureate should have contributed to an occasion he disapproved of, for Albert's progressive views about university studies were not to his own increasingly conservative taste; and it is not surprising that the poem should have proved the weakest of his later performances. King's College Chapel beyond is the subject of three sonnets (Part 2, Nos 43–45) in *Ecclesiastical Sketches*; the last reaches the unremarkable conclusion that 'They dreamt not of a perishable home/ Who thus could build'.

On Sidney Street, east of Market Hill and the modern Red Lion Yard, stands Christ's College, where the undergraduate Wordsworth paid a reverential visit to Milton's old rooms (q.v.), then occupied by his friend from Hawkshead school, Edward Birkett. The occasion was memorable not so much for the act of literary piety but because, as Wordsworth confesses in *The Prelude* (Bk 3, lines 239–321), he became uncharacteristically drunk.

By heading north on Sidney Street and turning right into Jesus Lane we reach Jesus College, where Coleridge studied from 1791 to 1794. In *Biographia Literaria* (Vol. 1, Ch. 10) he paid passing tribute to 'the friendly cloysters and the happy grove of quiet', while in *The Prelude* Wordsworth, conscious of the irony that he had so narrowly missed meeting his future friend during their undergraduate days, exclaimed:

I have thought
Of thee, thy learning, gorgeous eloquence,
And all the strength and plumage of thy youth,
Thy subtle speculations, toils abstruse
Among the schoolmen, and Platonic forms
Of wild ideal pageantry, shaped out
From things well-matched or ill, and words for things,
The self-created sustenance of a mind
Debarred from Nature's living images,
Compelled to be a life unto herself,
And unrelentingly possessed by thirst
Of greatness, love, and beauty.
(Bk 6, lines 294–305)

In fact, Coleridge's discovery of his unsuitability to the academic life was as melodramatic and turbulent as Wordsworth's had been modest and inconspicuous. He plunged into debt, apparently meditated suicide, confessed darkly that he had 'fled to Debauchery', supported an undergraduate charged by the Proctor with radical agitation and interrupted his time at Jesus for his brief, extraordinary career in the Light Dragoons. By the time he left Cambridge Coleridge was firmly committed to the scheme for 'Pantisocracy' that took him to Bristol (Rte 5).

Library, St John's College: visitors by written appointment with the Librarian.

Northern England

11 North Yorkshire

This route zigzags west and east from A1, taking the traveller to places recalling various aspects of Wordsworth's life and poetry, as well as to some of England's finest scenery and abbey ruins.

We begin just below Wetherby and the North Yorkshire border at the junction of A1 with A659. The latter road and its continuation as A660 and A65 are followed west along the bank of the River Wharfe to Ilkley (20 miles). Beyond the town we take B6160 up Wharfedale and across the junction with A59 to Bolton Priory (28 miles), in one of the loveliest settings of any English monastic ruin. After his visit in the summer of 1807 Wordsworth used the legends connected with the Priory's foundation in *The White Doe of Rylstone*, his most ambitious attempt at a historical ballad in the manner of Sir Walter Scott (q.v.) and 'The Force of Prayer'. On the same trip he walked westwards over the moors to Malham Cove and Gordale Scar, the two most dramatic features of the Craven Fault; modern travellers will probably prefer to reach them from A65. The publication of the artist William Westall's views of Yorkshire in 1818 prompted Wordsworth to devote a sonnet to each of these scenes.

From Bolton Priory we return on A59 via Harrogate to A1 (50 miles) and head north before branching right (NE) via A168 to Thirsk (68 miles). The next stage of the journey, from here to Brompton, was travelled twice by Wordsworth and his sister: they walked it in July 1802 and returned by coach in October with the poet's bride, Mary Hutchinson. After they breakfasted at The Three Tuns in Thirsk's market place Dorothy noted in her journal: 'We were well treated but when the Landlady understood that we were going to *walk* off and leave our luggage behind she threw out some saucy words in our hearing'.

A170 climbs east from Thirsk up the Hambleton Hills, where we turn left on a sideroad for Scawton and *Rievaulx Abbey (78 miles). Seen on the eve of his wedding day, the view from this stretch of country prompted Wordsworth to a sonnet whose language (like that of so many of his poems) resembles Dorothy's journal entry:

> far far off us, in the western sky, we saw Shapes of Castles, Ruins among groves, a great, spreading wood, rocks, and single trees, a minster with its tower unusually distinct, minarets in another quarter, and a round Grecian Temple also—the colours of the sky of a bright grey and the forms of a sober grey, with a dome.

On her July visit to the Abbey Dorothy found that

> thrushes were singing, cattle feeding among green grown hillocks among the Ruins. These hillocks were scattered over with *grovelets* of wild roses and other shrubs, and covered with wild flowers ... We walked upon Mr Duncombe's terrace and looked down upon the Abbey. It stands in a larger valley among a Brotherhood of valleys of different lengths and breadths all woody, and running up into the hills in all directions.

The terrace, no longer part of Duncombe Park, is now NT.

From Rievaulx B1257 leads south to Helmsley (81 miles), where the Wordsworths visited the ruined 12C Castle.

We now follow A170 east to the little village of Brompton (103 miles), where Mary Hutchinson lived with her uncle. She married Wordsworth on 4 October 1802, Dorothy being too overcome with emotion to attend the ceremony:

> At a little after 8 o'clock I saw them go down the avenue towards the Church. William had parted from me upstairs. I gave him the wedding ring—with how deep a blessing! I took it from my forefinger where I had worn it the whole of the night before—he slipped it again onto my finger and blessed me fervently. When they were absent my dear little Sara [Hutchinson] prepared the breakfast. I kept myself as quiet as I could, but when I saw the two men running up the walk, coming to tell us it was over, I could stand it no longer and threw myself on the bed where I lay in stillness, neither hearing nor saying anything, till Sara came upstairs to me and said 'They are coming'. This forced me from the bed where I lay and I moved I knew not how straight forward, faster than my strength could carry me till I met my beloved William and fell upon his bosom.

From Brompton we return on A170 to Thirsk, where we head north on A168 to Northallerton (145 miles) and A167 for Sockburn (155 miles), charmingly sited in a loop of the Tees. We approach the little village by turning right on B1264 shortly after Great Smeaton, then branching left on a sideroad and footpath which leads across the river. Wordsworth and Coleridge came here to stay with Mary Hutchinson's brother, Thomas, in 1799. Coleridge's poem, 'Love', dates from this period and it has been suggested that its fourth stanza was inspired by the recumbent effigy of a medieval knight in Sockburn's ruined church.

She leant against the armèd man,
The statue of the armèd knight;
She stood and listened to my lay,
Amid the lingering light.

A167 continues to the junction with B1263, which is followed across A1 to the fine town of Richmond (169 miles). On Hipswell Moor to its SW is Hartleap Well (173½ miles), subject of an historical poem by Wordsworth. At Halfpenny House (175 miles) A6108 leads from the edge of the moor to Leyburn (178 miles) and the entrance to the grandeurs of Wensleydale. To the north of Hawes (195 miles) at its western end we find *Hardrow Force, a magnificent waterfall that excited Wordsworth's sensitivity to wild natural spectacles. He marvelled to a friend: 'I cannot express to you the enchanted effect produced by this Arabian scene of colour as the wind blew aside the great waterfall behind which we stood'.

Wordsworth himself recommended the route we have been following through Wensleydale as one of the most picturesque approaches to the Lake District.

Rievaulx Abbey, Rievaulx, Helmsley, North Yorkshire: English Heritage, standard opening; phone Bilsdale (043 96) 228.

Rievaulx Terrace and Temples, Rievaulx, Helmsley, North Yorkshire: NT; phone Bilsdale (043 96) 340.

Helmsley Castle, Helmsley, North Yorkshire: English Heritage, standard opening; phone (0439) 70442.

The Lake District

At the beginning of *A Guide through the District of the Lakes in the North of England*, still an excellent handbook for the traveller, Wordsworth describes the main contours of the region by asking the reader to imagine himself suspended in the air between and slightly above the summits of Great Gable and Scafell. From this vantage point the valleys and lakes below appear like so many spokes radiating from the hub of a wheel. Beginning in the SE and moving clockwise, he notes: Langdale and Windermere; Coniston, 'a broken spoke sticking in the rim'; the valley of the River Duddon; Eskdale; Wastdale; Ennerdale; Buttermere, Crummock Water and Lorton Vale; and Borrowdale and Derwentwater. These last run due north and, as Wordsworth admits, the north-eastern sector that follows does not conform neatly to his image. But from the top of Helvellyn to the east a fragment of another wheel is represented by: Thirlmere and St John's Vale; Ullswater; Haweswater (though it is not actually visible from Helvellyn); and finally, the vale of Grasmere, Rydal and Windermere to the south.

It is an instructive exercise for those who like to find underlying pattern in a landscape which, despite its grand vistas and small

Wordsworth on Helvellyn by Benjamin Haydon (1842)

compass (Wordsworth's wheel is only about 30 miles in diameter), has a complex formation and can easily bewilder the earth-bound tourist. Yet it is more than that, for the very authority with which Wordsworth views his subject from a bird's-eye perspective reminds us how intimately he knew the Lakes. Beneath his imagined spectator's feet lie not just the scenes where major chapters in his life took place, but also the sources of continual stimulus to his poetic imagination. Coleridge and Southey lived in the Lake District too, but Wordsworth possessed and repossessed it in imagination with a force that no previous English poet (and probably no subsequent one) brought to the experience of natural landscape.

In the face of this achievement the customary routes, directions and helpful paraphernalia of the guidebook, however minute an inspection of their subject they may recommend, develop special limitations. Wordsworth said of his poem, 'An Evening Walk': 'The plan of it has not been confined to a particular walk or an individual place; a proof (of which I was unconscious at the time) of my unwillingness to submit the poetic spirit to the chains of fact and circumstance'. We may detect in this something more than the familiar warning that writers take liberties with geography and that the better they know a place the more liberties they are likely to take. It reminds us that only in his later and usually weaker poetry does Wordsworth confine himself entirely to a date and an exact spot, setting down particular impressions of a particular scene on a particular visit. At its finest his poetry, even when the title includes a specific placename, is a palimpsest: the objects being viewed are overlaid by recollections of other experiences, other occasions and other places. So the four itineraries into which Wordsworth's Lake District is divided below are mere skeletons, catalogues of specifically identifiable items from a landscape whose largest, most abiding features and smallest, most fugitive details permeated his sensibility.

12a Cockermouth to Keswick

We begin with Cockermouth, a small town at the confluence of the Derwent and the Cocker, and a reminder that though much of Wordsworth's life was spent in the central and southern Lake District his origins were in the north, near the Border country. He was born here in 1770, one of the five children of Ann and John Wordsworth, man of business to Sir James Lowther (later first Earl of Lonsdale); his sister Dorothy was born the following year. Their family home, a substantial building of 1745 rented from Sir James, stands near the west end of the main street. Now belonging to the National Trust, it retains its original panelling, staircase and fireplaces.

The River Derwent nearby is remembered by Wordsworth in the opening book of *The Prelude*:

Was it for this
That one, the fairest of all rivers, loved
To blend his murmurs with my nurse's song,
And, from his alder shades and rocky falls,
And from his fords and shallows, sent a voice
That flowed along my dream? For this, didst thou,
O Derwent! winding among the grassy holms
Where I was looking on, a babe in arms,
Make ceaseless music that composed my thoughts
To more than infant softness, giving me
Amid the fretful dwellings of mankind
A foretaste, a dim earnest, of the calm
That Nature breathes among the hills and groves.
(lines 269–281)

John Wordsworth (d. 1783) is buried in the local churchyard. Returning near the spot in 1833, Wordsworth compared it in a sonnet with his own children's graves (see Grasmere, Rte 12C) and the fact of his own mortality:

A point of life between my Parent's dust,
And yours, my buried Little-ones! am I,
And to those graves looking habitually
In kindred quiet I repose my trust.

The ruined 13C–15C Cockermouth Castle, built by the Percy family, is remembered in *The Prelude* as 'a shattered monument/ Of feudal sway' (Bk 1, lines 284–285) and made the speaker of another sonnet from his 1833 visit, 'Address From the Spirit of Cockermouth Castle':

> thus did I, thy Tutor,
> Make my young thoughts acquainted with the grave;
> While thou wert chasing the winged butterfly
> Through my green courts; or climbing, a bold suitor,
> Up to the flowers whose golden progeny
> Still round my shattered brow in beauty wave.

From Cockermouth we may detour SW to the coast at Whitehaven (12 miles). As a boy Wordsworth visited his uncle Richard here; he returned in 1833 on his way to the Isle of Man (see Rte 13). We follow A595 an additional 6 miles south to Egremont, where the ruined castle with its fine 12C gatehouse is the subject of Wordsworth's historical ballad, 'The Horn of Egremont Castle' (1807). The return to Cockermouth can be made directly by A5086 (14 miles).

The main journey heads SE to Keswick. It can be made on A66 (12 miles), past Bassenthwaite Lake, but this route is less attractive than B5292 and B5289, which take us further south through some of the grandest scenery in the district, going down to Lorton Vale, skirting Crummock Water and Buttermere, and entering Keswick at 22 miles from Borrowdale and the eastern shore of Derwentwater.

Buttermere was the home of Mary Robinson, the landlord's daughter at the local inn, remembered by Wordsworth in *The Prelude* as the 'Maid of Buttermere' (Bk 7, line 297). She became famous with early visitors first for her innocent rural beauty and then for her fate at the hands of the forger and impostor John Hatfield, who married her in 1802 while posing as the brother of the Earl of Hopetoun. He was arrested the following year and hanged at Carlisle. The rugged 'Jaws of Borrowdale' and Derwentwater were among the chief beauty spots in the Lake District popularised by the Romantic poets, though many visitors were disappointed that Lodore Falls (on the eastern shore of the lake) failed to live up to the fulsome description in Southey's poem. For their part, both Southey and Wordsworth came to deplore the damage caused by the influx of tourists and fashionable residents. Writing in the guise of a visiting Spaniard in his entertaining travel book, *Letters from England*, Southey launched a witty attack on the alterations made to the Bowder Stone in Borrowdale, particularly the erection of 'an ugly house for an old woman to show the rock, for fear travellers should pass under it without seeing it'. Wordsworth's guidebook to the Lakes deplored the eccentric buildings added to Derwent Isle (then called Vicar's Isle) on Derwentwater by its owner in the 1780s.

Keswick is chiefly associated with Coleridge and Southey. Coleridge and his family became tenants of Greta Hall, at the west end of the town and now part of Keswick School, in 1800. Its situation greatly pleased him: 'I question if there be a room in England which commands a view of mountains, and lakes, and woods and vales, superior to that in which I am now sitting'. So, too, did the opportunity for regular contact with the Wordsworths at Grasmere (Rte 12C). His stay was notable for two of his finest poems, 'Christabel' and 'Dejection: An Ode'. When it ended in 1803 his real intimacy with Wordsworth and his marriage ended too, for he returned from Malta to a quarrel with his friend and a permanent separation from Sara.

Southey, who had shared the house during the last months of Coleridge's stay, assumed full tenancy after his departure—along with responsibility for Coleridge's family. Mrs Coleridge lived here until her daughter's marriage in 1829. Southey remained until his death in 1843, conscientiously pursuing his career as man of letters and accepting the Poet Laureateship after Sir Walter Scott (q.v.) declined it in 1813. He was visited by Shelley (q.v.), Harriet Westbrook and her sister, Eliza, in the winter of 1811–12; details of the younger poet's stay in the area are given under the appropriate entry. In the main, Southey's life was quiet and bookish. Wordsworth, who 'would rather give up books than men', lamented 'how completely dead Southey is become to all but *books*', while Thomas De Quincey disparagingly compared his elegantly appointed library at Greta Hall with the small shelf of thumbed and battered volumes favoured by Wordsworth. Southey's *Vision of Judgement*, a poem usually remembered only because of the satiric reply it provoked from Byron (q.v.), opens with a description of the view he enjoyed from his study:

'Twas at that sober hour when the light of day is receding,
And from surrounding things the hues wherewith day has adorned them
Fade, like the hopes of youth, till the beauty of earth is departed:
Pensive, though not in thought, I stood at the window, beholding
Mountain and lake and vale; the valley disrobed of its verdure;
Derwent retaining yet from eve a glassy reflection
Where his expanded breast, then still and smooth as a mirror,
Under the woods reposed: the hills that, calm and majestic,
Lifted their heads in the silent sky, from far Glaramar,
Bleacrag, and Maidenmawr, to Grizedal and westermost Withop.
Dark and distinct they rose. The clouds had gather'd above them
High in the middle air, huge, purple, pillowy masses,
While in the west beyond was the last pale tint of twilight.

Southey was buried in the churchyard at Crosthwaite, west of Greta Hall. Wordsworth attended the funeral even though he had not been invited. He had always been a friendly acquaintance rather than a close friend of Southey, and relations had been strained by his sympathy with Southey's daughter in her disputes with the writer's second wife, Caroline, whom he had married in 1839. Southey is commemorated in the church by a marble effigy showing him asleep with a book in his hand; the accompanying poem is by Wordsworth.

Wordsworth House, Main Street, Cockermouth, Cumbria: NT; phone (0900) 824805.

12b Penrith to Ullswater via Lowther

This itinerary can easily be linked with the previous route by following A66 17 miles east from Keswick, a journey that takes us past Blencathra (or Saddleback).

The market town of Penrith, birthplace of Wordsworth's mother and his wife Mary Hutchinson, is closely entwined with the poet's life. In childhood he and Dorothy came on visits to their grandparents, briefly attending the school which occupied the building with a Tudor gable in the churchyard. When he was about five Wordsworth went riding on Penrith Beacon, NE of the town, and came across the site of a disused gibbet; years later he returned to the spot with Mary Hutchinson. Both episodes are recalled in Book 12 of *The Prelude* as examples of those

spots of time,
That with distinct pre-eminence retain
A renovating virtue, whence, depressed
By false opinion and contentious thought,
Or aught of heavier or more deadly weight,
In trivial occupations, and the round
Of ordinary intercourse, our minds
Are nourished and invisibly repaired.
(lines 208–215)

From Penrith we follow A6 1 mile south to Eamont Bridge, where

Aira Force; an engraving by Thomas Gilks from a drawing by D.H. M'Kewan in Charles Mackay's The Scenery and Poetry of the English Lakes: A Summer Ramble *(1846)*

we turn right on B5320. From Yanwath (2½ miles) a sideroad leads to Askham and Lowther (5 miles). Wordsworth came to Lowther Castle several times to visit William, Earl of Londsale, heir to John Wordsworth's employer, who was instrumental in obtaining for him the much-derided but very useful post as Distributor of Stamps. *The Excursion* is dedicated to the Earl. The castle, built by Sir Robert Smirke in 1806–11, was demolished in 1957 and its ruins are not open, though the grounds to the south now contain a large amusement park. A sonnet of 1833 gloomily prophesied the building's destruction but not the amusements:

Fall if ye must, ye Towers and Pinnacles,
With what ye symbolise; authentic Story
Will say, Ye disappeared with England's Glory!

We then return to B5320 and continue SW, passing Sockbridge, birthplace of Wordsworth's father, before reaching Pooley Bridge (11 miles) and the head of *Ullswater. A592 is then followed along the NW shore of the lake. At 16½ miles we find the junction with A5091 to Dockray and a convenient parking place from which to explore *Gowbarrow Park (NT). It contains Lyulph's Tower, a shooting lodge built by the Duke of Norfolk in 1780, and Aira Force, the impressive waterfall that is the scene of Wordsworth's 'mournful tale', 'The Somnambulist', and one of his better late poems, 'Airey-Force Valley'. Dorothy Wordsworth's journal for April 1802 has a significant entry:

When we were in the woods beyond Gowbarrow park we saw a few daffodils close to the water side. We fancied that the lake had floated the seeds ashore and that the little colony had so sprung up. But as we went along there were more and yet more and at last under the boughs of the trees, we saw that there was a long belt of them along the shore, about the breadth of a country turnpike road. I never saw daffodils so beautiful they grew among the mossy stones about and about them, some rested their heads upon these stones as on a pillow for weariness and the rest tossed and reeled and danced and seemed as if they verily laughed with the wind that blew upon them over the lake, they looked so gay ever glancing ever changing. This wind blew directly over the lake to them. There was here and there a little knot and a few stragglers a few yards higher up but they were so few as not to disturb the simplicity and unity and life of that one busy highway.

The very language of her description identifies this occasion as the genesis of her brother's most anthologised poem, written some two years later.

A592 continues to the southern end of Ullswater. The opening book of *The Prelude* describes an early, crucial glimpse of nature's 'unknown modes of being' which took place on this stretch of the lake in a stolen boat:

like one who rows,
Proud of his skill, to reach a chosen point
With an unswerving line, I fixed my view
Upon the summit of a craggy ridge,
The horizon's utmost boundary, for above
Was nothing but the stars and the grey sky.
She was an elfin pinnace; lustily
I dipped my oars into the silent lake,
And, as I rose upon the stroke, my boat
Went heaving through the water like a swan;
When, from behind that craggy steep till then
The horizon's bound, a huge peak, black and huge,
As if with voluntary power instinct
Upreared its head. I struck and struck again,

And growing still in stature the grim shape
Towered up between me and the stars, and still,
For so it seemed, with purpose of its own
And measured motion like a living thing,
Strode after me. With trembling oars I turned,
And through the silent water stole my way
Back to the covert of the willow-tree;
There in her mooring-place I left my bark,—
And through the meadows homeward went, in grave
And serious mood.
(lines 367–390)

The furtive expedition began and ended on the southern shore near Patterdale; the 'craggy ridge' on which he fixed his sight is presumably Stybarrow Crag by A592, and the minatory peak, 'black and huge', Black Crag by Glencoynedale to the west.

Helvellyn rises west of Patterdale and Glenridding. Near the summit (3118ft), with its wide views, stands a memorial to Charles Gough, who fell to his death from Striding Edge in 1805 and whose body was guarded by his dog until its discovery three months later. The story inspired Wordsworth's 'Fidelity', as well as 'Helvellyn' by Sir Walter Scott (q.v.).

Lowther Park, Hackthorpe, near Penrith, Cumbria: phone (09312) 523. Note that the ruins of Lowther Castle are not open.

12c Grasmere to Rydal, Ambleside and Windermere

We can easily reach the starting-point of this tour from the end of either Rte 12A or Rte 12B. From Keswick we take A591 12 miles south past Thirlmere and the western flank of Helvellyn. From Patterdale, at the southern end of Ullswater, we follow A592 over the Kirkstone Pass (the subject of an ode which Wordsworth reprinted in his guidebook), branch right through the Stock Ghyll valley and head north on A591 at Ambleside, a journey of 11 miles.

Grasmere is ideally situated at the very centre of Wordsworth's Lake District. The opening lines of 'The Recluse'—the ambitious poem he long meditated but left only in fragments—record his first impressions when he came here as a child from over Langdale Pass to the west:

Once to the verge of yon steep barrier came
A roving School-boy; what the Adventurer's age
Hath now escaped his memory—but the hour,
One of a golden summer holiday,
He well remembers, though the year be gone.
Alone and devious from afar he came;
And, with a sudden influx overpowered
At sight of this seclusion, he forgot
His haste, for hasty had his footsteps been
As boyish his pursuits; and sighing said
'What happy fortune were it here to live'.

He enjoyed this happy fortune from 1799 to 1813, living in a succession of houses in the village, and when he left it was only to move a few miles south.

We begin a walking tour north of the village at Allan Bank, the Wordsworths' home in 1808–11. It was ironic that he should have

Rydal Water and Grasmere from Rydal Park by George Pickering in Thomas Rose's Westmoreland, Cumberland, Durham and Northumberland, Illustrated *(1832)*

come to live here, since its construction in 1805 for a Liverpool lawyer had roused him to anger:

> Woe to poor Grasmere for ever and ever! A wretched Creature, wretched in name and nature, of the name of *Crump*, goaded on by his still more wretched Wife … this same wretch has at last begun to put his long impending threats in execution; and when you next enter the sweet paradise of Grasmere you will see staring you in the face, upon that beautiful ridge that elbows out into the vale (behind the church and towering far above its steeple), a temple of abomination in which are to be enshrined Mr and Mrs Crump. Seriously, this is a great vexation to us as this House will stare you in the face from every part of the Vale, and entirely destroy its character of simplicity and seclusion.

Nor were the events immediately after the poet became Mr Crump's tenant entirely propitious, though his family enjoyed 'the comfort of each having a room of our own' and he was given permission to plant forest trees, some of which remain, in the park. Coleridge's visit in the winter of 1808–09, when he was struggling with his essays for *The Friend*, made his depressed and debilitated condition all too apparent; Wordsworth's comments to the garrulous Basil Montagu reached Coleridge's ears and began a quarrel between the poets, eventually patched up but never completely forgotten.

From Allan Bank we go south to the church of St Oswald. Wordsworth and his family lived at the Old Vicarage, their last home in Grasmere itself, in 1811–13, when Wordsworth tried his hand at teaching in the school, now a shop, at the north entrance to the churchyard. The churchyard contains the graves of Wordsworth himself, his sister Dorothy (d. 1855), his wife Mary (d. 1859), her sister Sara (d. 1835) and Catherine and Thomas (both d. 1812), Wordsworth's son and daughter who died in early childhood, as well as the grave of Coleridge's eldest son, Hartley (d. 1849), who spent most of his life in the region. Inside the church (where Wordsworth's children were baptised and Thomas De Quincey was married) there is a memorial to the poet by Thomas Woolner.

From the church we may follow in Wordsworth's footsteps and make the delightful 3-mile *circuit of Grasmere's lake. The island in its centre was one of his favourite spots and Coleridge has left this description of a picnic party there in 1800:

> Our kettle swung over the fire hanging from the branch of a fir-tree, and I lay and saw the woods, and the mountains, and lake all trembling, and as it were *idealized* through the subtle smoke which rose up from the clear red embers of the fir-apples, which we had collected; afterwards we made a glorious Bonfire on the margin, by some elder-bushes, whose twigs heaved and sobbed in the uprushing column of smoke—and the Image of the Bonfire, and of us that danced round it—ruddy laughing faces in the twilight—the Image of this in a Lake smooth as that Sea to whose waves the Son of God had said, '*Peace*'.

Beyond Loughrigg Terrace we cross the Rothay by a footbridge and re-enter the village from the south at Town End.

Here we find *Dove Cottage, where Wordsworth lived from 1799 to 1808, perhaps his most famous and certainly his most interesting home. The barn opposite has been converted into a Grasmere and Wordsworth Museum of relics and manuscripts.

When Wordsworth and his sister first became tenants of the Cottage, once the Dove and Branch Inn, they took special pleasure in their view of the lake (now spoiled by later building) and what Dorothy called their 'domestic slip of mountain' behind. Inside, one of the ground-floor rooms was used as Dorothy's bedroom and the other as kitchen, with a wash-house at the back; upstairs were the living room and William's bedroom, with only two small extra rooms. The result, as Dorothy confessed, was a house 'crammed edgefull'—particularly after Wordsworth's marriage to Mary Hutchinson in 1802 and the birth of his children. When in 1807 he at last plucked up courage to visit the poet he then revered above all men, Thomas De Quincey was struck by the extreme simplicity of the Wordsworths' way of life:

> Miss Wordsworth I found making breakfast in the little sitting-room. No urn was there; no glittering breakfast service; a kettle boiled upon the fire, and everything was in harmony with those unpretending arrangements. I, the son of a merchant, and naturally, therefore, in the midst of luxurious (though not ostentatious) display from my childhood, had never seen so humble a *ménage*; and, contrasting the dignity of the man with this honourable poverty, and his courageous avowal of it, his utter absence of all effort to disguise the simple truth of the case, I felt my admiration increase to the uttermost by all I saw.

De Quincey assumed the tenancy of Dove Cottage when the Wordsworths moved to Allan Bank in 1808, but managed to give offence in several ways. He demolished the little moss-hut' or summer house they had built in their back orchard; a newer one was later erected on the site. In 1817 he married his mistress, Margaret Sympson, objectionable to the Wordsworths not because she was already pregnant at the time of her wedding but because she was a farmer's daughter. Worst of all, he began in 1835 the series of essays now usually collected as *Recollections of the Lake Poets*, which

Wordsworth refused to read, warning Crabb Robinson that 'no friend of mine will ever tell me a word of their contents'. For his part De Quincey had concluded by this time that Wordsworth was a 'mixed creature, made up of special infirmity and special strength'. Despite their subject's disapproval and De Quincey's tendency toward witty malice, the essays still make excellent introductory reading.

A591 winds SE from Town End, following the eastern shore of Grasmere lake and the northern shore of Rydal Water, to *Rydal Mount (2 miles), Wordsworth's home from 1813 until his death in 1850. It is now owned by the Wordsworth Trust. Dora's Field overlooking Rydal Water nearby, bought by the poet in 1826 and named after his daughter, is now NT.

Wordsworth's years at Rydal Mount were perhaps the most serene but certainly not the most creative period of his life. His income, previously small and often unreliable, was made secure when he became Distributor of Stamps in 1813; his reputation was acknowledged by his appointment as Poet Laureate after Southey's death in 1843. In old age he had himself become one of the tourist attractions of the area which his poetry had done so much to put on the map. Keats (q.v.) called when Wordsworth was away from home in 1818, left a note on the mantelpiece by Dorothy's portrait, and reported sourly in a letter: 'Lord Wordsworth, instead of being in retirement, has himself and his house full in the thick of fashionable visitors quite convenient to be pointed at all the summer long'. Later visitors included Matthew Arnold and the twelve-year-old Swinburne (qq.v.). Harriet Martineau, who came to live at Ambleside in 1845 and herself published a guide to the Lakes in 1855, estimated that about five hundred people called each year at Rydal Mount. Her *Autobiography* gives an interesting, though clearly hostile, description of the poet's 'usual manner with strangers'. He took them 'the round of his garden and terraces, relating to persons whose very names he had not attended to, particulars about his writing and other affairs, which each stranger flattered himself was a confidential communication to himself' and concluded the interview by wishing

Windermere, an aquatint by William Gilpin in his Observations, Relative Chiefly to Picturesque Beauty, Made in the Year 1772, on Several Parts of England *(1786)*

them 'improved health and much enjoyment of the lake scenery'.

A591 continues south to Ambleside (3½ miles) and Windermere. Wordsworth's boyhood pleasure in skating on the lake is superbly evoked in Book 1 of *The Prelude*:

All shod with steel,
We hissed along the polished ice in games
Confederate, imitative of the chase
And woodland pleasures,—the resounding horn,
The loud pack chiming, and the hunted hare.
... and oftentimes,
When we had given our bodies to the wind,
And all the shadowy banks on either side
Came sweeping through the darkness, spinning still
The rapid line of motion, then at once
Have I, reclining back upon my heels,
Stopped short; yet the solitary cliffs
Wheeled by me—even as if the earth had rolled
With visible motion her diurnal round!
Behind me did they stretch in solemn train,
Feebler and feebler, and I stood and watched
Till all was tranquil as a dreamless sleep.
(lines 433–437; 442–453)

The proposal to build the railway line which now runs from the village of Windermere on the east shore of the lake to Kendal roused Wordsworth in 1844 to magnificent protest against the despoliation of natural scenery: 'Is then no nook of English ground secure/ From rash assault?' His public letters, despite their evidently thoughtful concern for conservation, leave one less easy about some of his grounds for objection: 'the imperfectly educated classes are not likely to draw much good from rare visits to the lakes performed in this way'.

Dove Cottage and the Grasmere and Wordsworth Museum, Town End, Grasmere, Cumbria: phone (09665) 544 or 547.

Rydal Mount, Ambleside, Cumbria: phone (05394) 33002.

12d Ambleside to Hawkshead, Coniston and the Furness Peninsula

From Ambleside, passed on the way from Rydal to Windermere in the previous route, we take A593 and B5286 round the head of the lake to Hawkshead (4½ miles). Alternatively, we can bypass Hawkshead and go directly to Coniston by staying on A593. This takes us past the steep little sideroad which follows Little Langdale over into Great Langdale via Blea Tarn, a desolate spot which Wordsworth used as setting for *The Excursion*.

*Hawkshead was the scene of Wordsworth's schooling. Despite the influx of summer visitors, it remains a charming little town, though Wordsworth looked on its Town Hall of 1790 with the disfavour that men feel for change to the scenery of their childhood:

A rude mass
Of native rock, left midway in the square
Of our small market village, was the goal
Or centre of these sports; and when, returned
After long absence, thither I repaired,

Gone was the old grey stone, and in its place
A smart Assembly-room usurped the ground
That had been ours.
(*The Prelude*, Bk 2, lines 33–40)

From 1779 to 1787 he attended Archbishop Sandys' Grammar School, whose building is now a museum. It preserves Wordsworth's desk with his name carved on it and the housekeeping ledger kept by Ann Tyson, with whom he lodged.

The exact location of this lodging has been the subject of disagreement and confusion. It seems most likely, however, that Wordsworth first stayed with the Tyson family at the house marked with a plaque on Vicarage Lane before moving with them, in about 1783, to the hamlet of Colthouse half a mile east. Green End Cottage here

Furness Abbey by Thomas or Edward Gilks in Charles Mackay's The Scenery and Poetry of the English Lakes: A Summer Ramble *(1846)*

answers to the description of his surroundings, as remembered from a return visit made while on summer vacation from Cambridge:

The rooms, the court, the garden were not left
Long unsaluted, nor the sunny seat
Round the stone table under the dark pine,
Friendly to studious or to festive hours;
Nor that unruly child of mountain birth,
The froward brook, who, soon as he was boxed
Within our garden, found himself at once,
As if by trick insidious and unkind,
Stripped of his voice and left to dimple down
(Without an effort and without a will)
A channel paved by man's officious care.
(*The Prelude*, Bk 4, lines 46–56)

Esthwaite Water lies south of Colthouse on B5285. From its shore the young Wordsworth watched a drowned body being recovered:

At last, the dead man, 'mid that beauteous scene
Of trees and hills and water, bolt upright,
Rose, with his ghastly face, a spectre shape
Of terror; yet no soul-debasing fear,
Young as I was, a child not nine years old,
Possessed me, for my inner eye had seen
Such sights before, among the shining streams
Of faery land, the forest of romance.
Their spirit hallowed the sad spectacle
With decoration of ideal grace;
A dignity, a smoothness, like the words
Of Grecian art, and purest poesy.
(*The Prelude*, Bk 5, lines 448–459)

Coniston lies 3 miles west of Hawkshead on B5285. We then follow a route which takes us SW towards the coast. Its first stage, an area more readily associated with Ruskin (q.v.) but well known to Wordsworth, follows A593 between the Old Man and Coniston Water to Torver (10 miles), then goes south on A5084 and, at Lowick (15½ miles), A5092. At Greenodd (17½ miles) we turn north and east on A590 before branching right on B5278 for Cark (25½ miles).

From here we reach Cartmel (27½ miles), with its splendid 12C Priory Church and 14C Gatehouse. Its churchyard has the grave of Wordsworth's Hawkshead schoolmaster, William Taylor (d. 1786). *The Prelude* describes the poet's visit in 1794:

That very morning had I turned aside
To seek the ground where, 'mid a throng of graves,
An honoured teacher of my youth was laid,
And on the stone were graven by his desire
Lines from the churchyard elegy of Gray.
This faithful guide, speaking from his death-bed,
Added no farewell to his parting counsel,
But said to me, 'My head will soon lie low';
And when I saw the turf that covered him,
After the lapse of full eight years, those words
With sound of voice and countenance of the Man,
Came back upon me, so that some few tears
Fell from me in my own despite.
(Bk 10, lines 532–544)

The lines from Gray (q.v.) are, in fact, slightly misquoted on the tombstone.

The journey from which Wordsworth turned aside took him across the sands of the Leven estuary from Cartmel to Ulverston, now spanned by the railway but then (like other sands in Morecambe Bay) used as a route for pedestrians and even coaches. His description is reminiscent of the scene so finely captured in Turner's painting of Lancaster Sands:

all the plain
Lay spotted with a variegated crowd
Of vehicles and travellers, horse and foot,
Wading beneath the conduct of their guide
In loose procession through the shallow stream
Of inland waters; the great sea meanwhile
Heaved at safe distance, far retired.
(*The Prelude*, Bk 10, lines 562–568)

In Wordsworth's memory this vivid spectacle is fused with his reaction to the news, brought to him by a fellow traveller, that Robespierre had died and hence that the worst of the Reign of Terror in France had abated.

We cross the estuary by returning to Greenodd and following A590 SW through Ulverston. Beyond Dalton-in-Furness (45½ miles) a lane descends left to the 'Vale of Deadly Nightshade' and the ruins of *Furness Abbey:

a mouldering pile with fractured arch,
Belfry, and images, and living trees,
A holy scene!

The Prelude, from which these lines come, goes on superbly to describe the exhilaration of a boyhood ride here:

With whip and spur we through the chantry flew
In uncouth race, and left the cross-legged knight,
And the stone-abbot, and that single wren
Which one day sang so sweetly in the nave
Of the old church, that—though from recent showers
The earth was comfortless, and touched by faint
Internal breezes, sobbings of the place
And respirations, from the roofless walls
The shuddering ivy dripped large drops—yet still
So sweetly 'mid the gloom the invisible bird
Sang to herself, that there I could have made
My dwelling-place, and lived for ever there
To hear such music.
(Bk 2, lines 116–128)

The cross-legged knights, for there are in fact two effigies of knights in armour (c 1250), can be found in the Infirmary Chapel, together with an ecclesiastical figure, apparently a deacon but presumably Wordsworth's 'stone-abbot'.

Wordsworth's second letter of protest against the Kendal–Windermere Railway noted with satisfaction that plans to cut another line through the ruins of the Abbey had been thwarted and the proposed route changed. Yet it did pass close enough for him to find navvies resting from their work among the ruins when he came here the following summer. The second of two sonnets deriving from this visit expressed pleasure at their reverential manner: 'All seem to feel the spirit of the place'.

On Piel Island, at the southern tip of the peninsula beyond Barrow-in-Furness (49½ miles), stand the ruins of Piel Castle. Wordsworth's memories of this 'rugged Pile' are movingly blended with his grief at the death of his sailor brother John in 1805 in 'Elegiac Stanzas Suggested by a Picture of Peele Castle [sic], in a Storm, Painted by Sir George Beaumont'.

Hawkshead Grammar School, Hawkshead, Cumbria: phone Hawkshead Tourist Information, (096 66) 525.

Cartmel Priory Gatehouse, Cavendish Street, Cartmel, near Grange-over-Sands, Cumbria: NT; phone (044 854) 691.

Furness Abbey, Barrow-in-Furness, Cumbria: English Heritage, standard opening; phone (0229) 23420.

Piel Castle, Piel Island, Barrow-in-Furness, Cumbria: English Heritage, open at any reasonable time; access by ferry from Roa Island (phone 0229 2250 weekdays, 0229 21741 at weekends).

13 The Isle of Man

Although he had viewed it many times in the distance from the Cumbrian coast, Wordsworth did not actually visit the Isle of Man until 1833. He made the crossing to Douglas from Whitehaven (Rte 12A), whereas modern visitors come from Heysham, Fleetwood or Liverpool. The trip produced several sonnets, distinguished (like so many of his later poems) more by their topographical explicitness than any other quality.

The first landmark to catch his attention was the Tower of Refuge in Douglas Bay, built only the previous year at the instigation of Sir William Hillary, founder of the Royal National Lifeboat Institution. Its function is compared favourably with the proud or aggressive intent of medieval fortresses:

> but yon Tower, whose smiles adorn
> This perilous bay, stands clear of all offence;
> Blest work it is of love and innocence,
> A Tower of refuge built for the else forlorn.
> Spare it, ye waves, and lift the mariner,
> Struggling for life, into its saving arms!
> Spare, too, the human helpers! Do they stir
> 'Mid your fierce shock like men afraid to die?
> No; their dread service nerves the heart it warms,
> And they are led by noble HILLARY.

At Ballasalla (8 miles SW of Douglas via A5) the modest ruins of Rushen Abbey, an offshoot of Furness Abbey (Rte 12D), stand in the pleasure gardens by the Silverburn river. Here Wordsworth sought 'repose/ Where ancient trees this convent-pile enclose,/ In ruin beautiful'. A4 leads north to join A1 at St John's (15 miles) near Tynwald Hill, the ancient mound associated with the Manx Parliament, duly commemorated in another sonnet.

Scotland

Wordsworth visited Scotland four times: with Dorothy and, for part of the way, Coleridge in 1803; with his wife and Sara Hutchinson in 1814; with his daughter Dora in 1831; and with his son John and Crabb Robinson in 1833, though this last excursion—which began with the Isle of Man (see Rte 13)—involved only a brief glimpse of the Inner Hebrides. Apart from allowing him to pay tribute to the memory of Robert Burns (q.v.), these tours brought him into contact with James Hogg (q.v.), the Ettrick Shepherd, and forged a sympathetic friendship with Sir Walter Scott (q.v.). They also inspired a considerable number of poems, of which the best ('The Solitary Reaper' or 'Stepping Westward', for example) are often the least precisely located and were written in retrospect; in Scotland as elsewhere, the occasional poems he jotted down on the spot too often read like entries from a versified guidebook.

Southey's *Journal of a Tour in Scotland in 1819*, lent a special interest because his companion was Thomas Telford, the engineer and road-builder, was not published until 1929 and is still not as well known as it deserves.

14 Dumfries to Roslin via The Yarrow, Jedburgh, Melrose and Neidpath

The starting-point can easily be reached from the Lake District (Rtes 12A–12D) via Carlisle.

At Dumfries Wordsworth and his sister visited Burns' House in Burns Street, finding his widow away from home but being shown round by the servant, and his grave in St Michael's churchyard nearby, not yet moved to the large mausoleum where modern visitors see it. Of the three poems arising from the occasion, 'At the Grave of Burns 1803' affirms the importance of his predecessor's example to Wordsworth:

I mourned with thousands, but as one
More deeply grieved, for He was gone
Whose light I hailed when first it shone,
And showed my youth
How Verse may build a princely throne
On humble truth.
(stanza 6)

A701 leads NE, briefly joining A74 before Moffat (20 miles), where we take A708. After St Mary's Loch (36 miles) we enter the lovely *valley of the Yarrow, an area of particular fascination to Wordsworth. He passed close to it with Dorothy in 1803 but, as she recorded, 'came to the conclusion of reserving the pleasure for some future time'. 'Yarrow Unvisited' is perhaps the most simply charming poem inspired by this tour:

If Care with freezing years should come,
And wandering seems but folly,—
Should we be loth to stir from home,
And yet be melancholy;
Should life be dull, and spirits low,
'Twill soothe us in our sorrow,
That earth hath something yet to show,
The bonny holms of Yarrow!

When he did finally come here in 1814 it was only fitting that his guide should be James Hogg (q.v.), a poet whose name is intimately associated with the adjoining valley of the Ettrick. 'Extempore Effusion Upon the Death of James Hogg' later recalled this occasion:

When last along its banks I wandered,
Through groves that had begun to shed
Their golden leaves upon the pathways,
My steps the Border-minstrel led.
(stanza 2)

'Yarrow Visited' begins by expressing mock-disappointment ('And is this—Yarrow?—*This* the Stream ...?') but ends with a fine adaptation of the conclusion to his earlier poem:

The vapours linger round the Heights,
They melt, and soon must vanish;
One hour is theirs, nor more is mine—
Sad thought, which I would banish,
But that I know, where'er I go,
Thy genuine image, Yarrow!
Will dwell with me—to heighten joy,
And cheer my mind in sorrow.

In 1831 he walked with Sir Walter Scott (q.v.) among the ruins of Newark Castle, seen across the valley from A708 at 45 miles. 'Yarrow Revisited' is overshadowed by the memory of this last meeting with his friend, an obviously exhausted and dying man.

From Selkirk (48 miles) at the head of the valley we follow A7 south to Hawick (60 miles), where we turn NE again on A698 and B6358 for Jedburgh (70 miles). On their visit in 1803 Dorothy found the town 'exceedingly beautiful on its low eminence, surmounted by the conventual tower, which is arched over, at the summit, by light stone-work resembling a coronet'. The Abbey impressed them less on close inspection, but both she and her brother were properly conscious of Jedburgh's connection with James Thomson (q.v.). Their lodging at No. 5 Abbey Close, 'one of a line of houses bordering on the churchyard' (as Dorothy described it) and now marked with a plaque, is of some interest. They were intrigued by the contrast between their vivacious elderly landlady and her silent invalid husband:

The joyous Woman is the Mate
Of him in that forlorn estate!
He breathes a subterranean damp;
But bright as Vesper shines her lamp:
He is as mute as Jedborough Tower:
She jocund as it was of yore,
With all its bravery on; in times
When, all alive with merry chimes,
Upon a sun-bright morn of May,
It roused the Vale to holiday.
('The Matron of Jedborough and Her Husband', lines 25–34)

When he came to see them here Walter Scott 'stayed late, and repeated some of his poem', the recently finished *Lay of the Last Minstrel*. Wordsworth was troubled by its resemblance to Coleridge's 'Christabel', not yet published but known to Scott, though he never doubted that the plagiarism (if it deserved the term) was unconscious.

A68 and then A6091 lead NW to Melrose Abbey (83 miles). Dorothy was disappointed by its situation, which she compared unfavourably with the surroundings of Rievaulx Abbey (see Rte 11), but the visit was made more interesting by having Scott as a guide: 'He was here on his own ground, for he is familiar with all that is known of the authentic history of Melrose and the popular tales connected with it. He pointed out many pieces of beautiful sculpture in obscure corners which would have escaped our notice'. The details of the stone carving are, in fact, Melrose's chief distinction.

It was inevitable that Wordsworth should also have been a guest at

Abbotsford, west on A6091 at 86 miles. Scott's home is described in detail under the appropriate entry.

By following A72 west from Abbotsford and passing through Peebles we reach at 105 miles the 13C–15C Neidpath Castle, overlooking the Tweed. In 1803 Wordsworth wrote a sonnet discreetly identified as 'Composed at ... Castle' denouncing the fourth Duke of Queensberry for stripping the estate of trees:

Degenerate Douglas! oh, the unworthy Lord!
Whom mere despite of heart could so far please,
And love of havoc, (for with such disease
Fame taxes him,) that he could send forth word
To level with the dust a noble horde,
A brotherhood of venerable Trees,
Leaving an ancient dome, and towers like these,
Beggared and outraged!

Wordsworth's anger foreshadows the passionate interest in conservation shown in later life by his protests against the construction of the Kendal–Windermere Railway (see Rte 12C). The notorious gambler 'Old Q' seems fully to have deserved Wordsworth's aspersions on his character. He is said to have chopped down the trees to provide a dowry for Maria Fagniani, whom he believed to be his daughter, though George Selwyn also claimed the honour of her paternity.

Roslin Chapel (121 miles), the final goal of the present journey, is reached by returning to Peebles, heading north towards Edinburgh on A703 and A701, and branching right on B7003. Its 'sumptuous roof,/ Pillars, and arches' inspired Wordsworth to a sonnet during his 1831 tour.

Burns House, Burns Street, Dumfries, Dumfries and Galloway: phone (0387) 55297.

Newark Castle, near Bowhill, Selkirk, Borders Region: key available from the Buccleuch Estates, Bowhill; visitors are advised to phone in advance, (0750) 20753.

Jedburgh Abbey, Jedburgh, Borders Region: Historic Buildings and Monuments, Scottish Development Department; phone the enquiry desk in Edinburgh, (031) 244 3101.

Melrose Abbey, Melrose, Borders Region: Historic Buildings and Monuments, Scottish Development Department; phone the enquiry desk in Edinburgh, (031) 244 3101.

Abbotsford House, Melrose, Borders Region: phone (0896) 2043.

Neidpath Castle, Peebles, Borders Region: phone Aberlady (087 57) 201.

Roslin (or **Rosslyn**) **Chapel**, near Edinburgh: phone (031) 440 2159.

15 Dumbarton to Loch Lomond and The Trossachs

This route, which takes us through scenery made famous in the lifetime of the Lake Poets by Sir Walter Scott (q.v.) and still among the most popular beauty spots in Scotland, begins at Dumbarton.

The Castle is dramatically perched on a cleft rock by the banks of the Clyde and is entered from the seaward side. Though she enjoyed the prospects it offered, Dorothy Wordsworth was not impressed by the Castle itself, still garrisoned when she visited it in 1803: 'The

Castle and fortification add little effect to the general view of the rock, especially since the building of a modern house, which is white-washed and consequently jars, wherever it is seen, with the natural character of the place'. The offending modern building is the Governor's House. Southey added to her strictures:

> As we approached Dunbarton [sic], the prominent objects were some glass-houses pouring out volumes of smoke; and the remarkable rock upon which the Castle stands. The prints which I have seen convey a very exaggerated notion of this rock; it is picturesque and singular, but has nothing of sublimity, and little magnitude, if those words may be coupled together. The elevation is not great; there are two summits, and between the two the Ordnance, with just such a feeling of propriety as they have shown in erecting a manufactory upon the rock at Edinburgh, have built a barrack-house.

From the town we take A82 north up the valley of the Leven and past the monument to Smollett (q.v.). At 4 miles we reach the junction with A811, close to the southern end of Loch Lomond. Southey found the view from the south to be the most impressive, recommending Cameron (1 mile further north) in particular as a vantage point. Dorothy Wordsworth exclaimed:

> What I had heard of Loch Lomond, or any other place in Great Britain, had given me no idea of anything like what was beheld; it was an outlandish scene—we might have believed ourselves in North America. The islands were of every possible variety of shape and surface—hilly and level, large and small, bare, rocky, pastoral, or covered with wood.

The route she took with Wordsworth and Coleridge in 1803 continued north on the present A82 up the western shore of the Loch to Inveruglas, where they crossed by ferry to Inversnaid, and continued due east for The Trossachs. For all its obviously picturesque attractions, the route had disadvantages even for so hardy a trio of pedestrians. The journey between Luss and Tarbet proved 'a solitude to the eye' and the ferryman surly. On the eastern shore of the Loch they found themselves hungry, nearly benighted and exposed to the curiosity that lost strangers commonly provoke: 'all drew near him, staring at William as nobody could have stared but out of sheer rudeness, except in such a lonely place'. When they found a boatman to take them the length of Loch Katrine, Coleridge insisted on walking along the shore to keep out the cold.

We take a tamer, rather circuitous route and one largely accessible by car; it also includes landmarks seen by Wordsworth and Dorothy on their return through the region in 1803. A811 and A81 are followed to Aberfoyle (22 miles), where B829 leads NW, with Loch Chon and Ben Lomond beyond to our left, to a country road (32 miles) linking Lomond and Katrine. By turning left we reach Inversnaid on the shore of Lomond (36 miles), where Wordsworth saw the Highland girl, the ferryman's daughter, to whom he addressed his poem. A footpath leads 1 mile north to Rob Roy's Cave, rock crevices which Wordsworth's party inspected. We then return along the road past the junction with B829 to Stronachlachar and the shore of Loch Katrine (41 miles). Wordsworth's poem, 'Rob Roy's Grave', was based on the belief that the hero was buried near Glengyle to our left on the opposite side of the water. It should be added in his defence that Balquidder (see below), chosen by tradition for the distinction, has only tradition to support its claim.

After returning to Aberfoyle (52 miles) we take A821 to *The Trossachs (59 miles), the gorge connecting the eastern tip of Katrine with Loch Achray. Southey compared the pass to Borrowdale (see

Rte 12A), while conceding that it was 'upon a larger scale and better wooded'. He was told the name was 'equivalent to the Wilds—a suspicious translation, however, because one part of this country can hardly be called wilder than another'. Dorothy Wordsworth believed it meant 'many hills'. In fact, it is properly translated as 'the bristly country'. A Wordsworth sonnet of 1831 bids the spectator nourish thoughts of life's brevity

> 'mid Nature's old felicities,
> Rocks, rivers, and smooth lakes more clear than glass
> Untouched, unbreathed upon.

An earlier, altogether more important poem was also suggested by his experiences in The Trossachs. Walking back this way with Dorothy near the end of his 1803 tour, he had a memorable encounter:

> The sun had been set for some time, when, being within a quarter of a mile of the ferryman's hut, our path having led us close to the shore of the calm lake, we met two neatly dressed women, without hats, who had probably been taking their Sunday evening's walk. One of them said to us in a friendly, soft tone of voice, 'What! you are stepping westward?' I cannot describe how affecting this simple expression was in that remote place, with the western sky in front, yet glowing with the departed sun.

The result, of course, was 'Stepping Westward'.

After exploring The Trossachs we continue east on A821, then north on A84, branching left on a sideroad for Balquidder (79 miles) and the head of Loch Voil. Somewhere in the vicinity of the road that leads south from the village and becomes a footpath to Glen Finglas and Loch Katrine, the Wordsworths found 'the fields were quietly—might I be allowed to say pensively?—enlivened by small companies of reapers'. The sight, together with a passage from Thomas Wilkinson's description of the Highlands, gave Wordsworth the idea for 'The Solitary Reaper'.

A possible 40-mile extension to this route continues north and east on A84, A85, A82 and A85 again to Dalmally. From the old road to Inverary SW of the town we get a superb view of Loch Awe and Kilchurn Castle, built by the Breadalbane family, addressed by Wordsworth in a poem from his 1803 tour. Dorothy found it

> a most impressive scene, a ruined castle on an island almost in the middle of the last compartment of the lake, backed by a mountain cove, down which came a roaring stream. The castle occupied every foot of the island that was visible to us, appearing to rise out of the water; mists rested upon the mountain side, with spots of sunshine between; there was a mild desolation in the low grounds, a solemn grandeur in the mountains, and the castle was wild, yet stately, not dismantled of its turrets, nor the walls broken down, though completely in ruin.

Dumbarton Castle, Dumbarton, Strathclyde Region: Historic Buildings and Monuments, Scottish Development Department; phone the enquiry desk in Edinburgh, (031) 244 3101.

16 Oban to The Inner Hebrides

This route can easily be linked with its predecessor by making the 20-mile journey along A85 from Dalmally to Oban on the west coast.

In Oban itself the sight of an eagle imprisoned in Dunollie Castle (now ruined) had provoked an angry sonnet from Wordsworth in 1831. Returning in 1833 he added two further poems on the same subject, noting in the second that even when freed the bird had chosen to remain in the castle's dungeon:

> Poor Bird, even so,
> Doth man of brother man a creature make
> That clings to slavery for its own sad sake.

The Inner Hebridean islands visited by the poet in 1833 and duly commemorated in rather undistinguished sonnets are best visited on the steamer roundtrip from Oban via Staffa and Iona. At Staffa, the rocky outcrop famous for Fingal's Cave, he was at first merely conscious of the disadvantages of travelling with a party of tourists:

> We saw, but surely, in the motley crowd,
> Not One of us has felt the far-famed sight;
> How *could* we feel it? each the other's blight,
> Hurried and hurrying, volatile and loud.

In the second of his four poems about the island, he was able to detect when the crowd had gone a divine architecture that surpassed 'mechanic laws':

> The pillared vestibule,
> Expanding yet precise, the roof embowed,
> Might seem designed to humble man, when proud
> Of his best workmanship by plan or tool.

Iona, inevitably made the subject of several sonnets, called forth

> a thoughtful sigh
> Heaved over ruin with stability
> In urgent contrast.

Ireland

17 Edgeworthstown

Wordsworth's five-week tour of Ireland in 1829, otherwise unremarkable and virtually unique among his tours in not giving rise to topographical verse, took him to one location worth noting. In Edgeworthstown, at the junction of N4 and N55 8 miles SE of the county town of Longford, he visited the novelist Maria Edgeworth (q.v.) and her family; her home is described under the appropriate entry. She was impressed by his 'long thin gaunt looking face—much wrinkled and weather-beaten' but added:

> I enjoyed the snatches of Mr Wordsworth's conversation & I think I had quite as much as was good for me or for *him* in my opinion—He is sensible—but has an abundance, a superfluity of words—and he talks too much like a book & like one of his own books—neither prose nor poetry—He seems as if he had been too much accustomed to be listened to and that he had learned to listen to himself—You know the French expression—'Il s'écoute'—Not that he is absolutely presuming or conceited or *vain* in manner—It is rather a soft slow proud-humility tone—very prosing—as if he were always speaking *ex cathedra* for the instruction of the rising generation and never forgetting that he is MR WORDSWORTH—the author and one of the poets of the lakes.

WILLIAM SHAKESPEARE

b. Stratford-upon-Avon, Warwickshire, 1564; d. Stratford-upon-Avon, 1616. *Henry VI, Part One* (1623); *Henry VI, Part Two* (1594); *Henry VI, Part Three* (1623); *Richard III* (1597); *Titus Andronicus* (1594); *The Comedy of Errors* (1623); *The Taming of the Shrew* (1594); *Venus and Adonis* (1593); *The Rape of Lucrece* (1594); *The Two Gentlemen of Verona* (1623); *Love's Labour's Lost* (1598); *Romeo and Juliet* (1597); *Richard II* (1597); *A Midsummer Night's Dream* (1600); *King John* (1623); *The Merchant of Venice* (1600); *Henry IV, Part One* (1598); *Henry IV, Part Two* (1600); *The Merry Wives of Windsor* (1602); *Much Ado About Nothing* (1600); *Henry V* (1600); *Julius Caesar* (1623); *As You Like It* (1623); *Twelfth Night* (1623); *Hamlet* (1603); *Troilus and Cressida* (1609); *All's Well That Ends Well* (1623); *Othello* (1622); *Measure For Measure* (1623); *Macbeth* (1623); *King Lear* (1608); *Timon of Athens* (1609); *Sonnets* (1609); *Antony and Cleopatra* (1623); *Coriolanus* (1623); *Pericles* (1609); *Cymbeline* (1623); *The Winter's Tale* (1623); *The Tempest* (1623); *Henry VIII* (1623).

'Reader, looke/ Not on his Picture, but his Booke', advised Ben Jonson (q.v.) in a poem at the beginning of the First Folio of Shakespeare's works (1623). It was sensible advice, particularly given Martin Droeshout's accompanying engraving of a moon-faced, lopsided Bard, and generations of readers and playgoers have been content to follow it. Yet a certain interest in the man himself was also natural, beginning with the gossipy anecdotes told by 17C antiquaries and continuing in the larger though not always less fanciful biographies of the present day; its history is entertainingly described in Samuel S. Schoenbaum's *Shakespeare's Lives* (1970). The topographical enthusiasts came on the scene slightly later, too late to rescue or even sometimes to record those richly ephemeral quarters of London where he had lived and worked. At Stratford they were rather luckier: the town today remains what it has been since the later years of the 18C, England's national literary shrine, an object of pilgrimage where the documented facts of stone, timber and plaster have been thickly overlaid with apocryphal legends of poaching misadventures and drinking exploits.

Only a handful of the allusions to place in Shakespeare's work reward attention. The same freedom that could endow Bohemia with a seacoast in *The Winter's Tale* makes his English references, even to the geography of London in the history plays, generalised and perfunctory. The spare suggestiveness of the Elizabethan stage, where the shifting of a bench could change the scene from Rome to Egypt or from Eastcheap to Shrewsbury, had no room for the patient topographical fidelity of later realism.

London

Of the date and circumstances of Shakespeare's first arrival in London we know nothing. They belong in all probability to the 'lost years' (1585–92) which legend has obligingly filled with stories of a fugitive from a Stratford magistrate's persecution (or a stage-struck admirer of a touring company of actors or a country schoolmaster) starting his life in the capital by holding customers' horses at the theatre entrance. Nor, apart from the occasional reference to his residence in a particular parish in a particular year, do we know much about where and how he lived. What we do know is that he was a member of the Lord Chamberlain's Men by 1594 and that he went on to a successful London career as actor, manager and dramatist until his retirement to Stratford in 1611—a working life recorded in account books, the Stationer's Register and the diaries of a few contemporary playgoers. Its scene was largely the City, its eastern and northern fringes and, particularly, its neighbours over the river, Southwark and Bankside.

1 The City to Southwark and Bankside

We begin at Liverpool Street Station (British Rail and Central, Circle and Metropolitan Underground Lines).

North of the present station stood the first purpose-built Elizabethan theatres, successors to the galleried inn yards where companies had performed in London and elsewhere. A plaque at Nos 86–88 Curtain Road marks the site of James Burbage's Theatre, built in 1576. Shakespeare was an associate of Burbage and his more famous son Richard, and a member of the Lord Chamberlain's Men when they performed at the nearby Curtain between 1597 and 1599.

Our walking tour leads south on Bishopsgate, following the migratory pattern of the Elizabethan theatres themselves.

Wormwood Street and its continuation as London Wall, to the right of Bishopsgate, offer a lengthy optional detour to the Barbican. In this unappealing modern complex stands the church of St Giles without Cripplegate, whose medieval tower and nave have miraculously survived the onslaught of fire, restoration and bombing. Edward, illegitimate son of Shakespeare's actor brother Edmund, was buried here in 1607. Opposite the Barbican Wood Street leads south from London Wall to Love Lane, on the left. At the lane's junction with Aldermanbury a garden occupying the site of St Mary contains a memorial to John Heminge and Henry Condell, actors and co-editors of the First Folio, and to Shakespeare himself, who was living on nearby Silver Street (now gone) in 1604.

The main route continues down Bishopsgate, bringing us to Great St Helen's, on the left, and the fine medieval church of *St Helen's. Shakespeare lived within its parish in 1597 and so may have attended its services. Bishopsgate becomes Gracechurch Street shortly before its convergence with King William Street. At this busy junction stood the Boar's Head Tavern, the scene in *Henry IV* of Falstaff's carousing with Prince Hal.

By crossing London Bridge we reach Southwark (properly called the Borough), home of Elizabethan London's main theatres after the removal of James Burbage's Theatre from the north bank of the river. Those fragile, fire-prone structures have of course long since vanished and, indeed, successive waves of decay and redevelopment, still in confused progress today, have swept away most of the Borough's historic buildings. Yet its richly associative street names and, in certain fugitive corners, some of its former atmosphere still remain.

*Southwark Cathedral, at the south end of the bridge, may fairly claim to have been the actors' church of the Renaissance. By 1598 Shakespeare himself was apparently living as well as working within its parish of St Saviour's. He is commemorated by a modern window

Wencelaus Hollar's Long View of London *(1647)*

Convent garden
S. Clement
Arundel house
Temple
The Globe

S. y Waterhouse
S. Andre in Holborne
Baynards Castle
Paulus wharfe
Queene hythe
the Eel Ships
Winchester house

Neygat
Boo Church
Guildhall
The 3 Cranes
Stiliard
T H A M E S I S

LONDON
Guildhall
S. Michaels
F L U V I U
Southwarke

S. Magnes
2. Gray Church
5. Dunston in the East
Lyon Key
Billings gate
THE BRIDGE.

3. Alhallows barking
Billings gate
Custom house

The Tower.
Tower Wharfe
S. Olafe

De Celeberrima & Florentissima
TRINOBANTIADOS AUGUSTÆ CIVITATE
Prostant AMSTELODAMI apud
Cornelium Danckers in via vitulina sub insigni
Gratitudinis An°. 1647.

(1954) and recumbent effigy (1911) in the south aisle of the nave. His brother Edmund, the only other theatrically inclined member of the Shakespeare family, was buried here in 1607.

Wencelaus Hollar's 'Long View' of London (1647), our main and most reliable source for the location of the Renaissance theatres, surveys its subject by looking west from the Cathedral tower towards Blackfriars Bridge. We tour the area by a winding route through picturesque urban decay that begins at the west end of the Cathedral close and continues via Cathedral Street, Clink Street and Bankside. Just after Bankside has passed under Southwark Bridge we reach Rose Alley (on the left) whose name recalls the Rose Theatre. It was built by Philip Henslowe in 1587 and here a company including Edward Alleyn performed plays by Marlowe (q.v.) and *Titus Andronicus*. Shakespeare himself appeared on its boards. Work on a new office block recently uncovered the site of the Rose, and hasty excavation confirmed the ground plan while showing that the theatre was smaller than historians had assumed. The developers Merchant Imry have announced plans to incorporate the remains in the basement of their proposed building, but the courts have so far upheld the Department of the Environment in its extraordinary decision not to list so important a site as an ancient monument.

On Bear Gardens, again to the left of Bankside, stood the later Hope Theatre. Its site is now occupied by the excellent Shakespeare Globe Museum, which houses a vivid and detailed exhibition of the Renaissance theatres.

A plaque on the wall of Courage's brewery in Park Street, at the bottom of Bear Gardens, marks the approximate location of the most famous theatre of them all, the Globe. It actually stood nearer to the spot on Bankside where, after much delay and controversy with the local authorities, the plan to build a modern reconstruction at last got underway with a ground-breaking ceremony in 1988.

Shakespeare was a shareholder with Richard and Cuthbert Burbage in the erection of the building from the dismantled timbers of the old Theatre in 1599. Its company was originally called the Lord Chamberlain's Men but, in tribute to its pre-eminence, earned the title of the King's Men on the accession of James I. Its apron stage, surrounded by covered galleries for the more fortunate spectators, witnessed the production of at least fifteen plays from the Shakespeare canon. In *The Tempest* Prospero punningly includes 'the great globe itself' (Act 4, Scene 1, line 153) among the transitory things of this world and the reference proved prophetic, for the theatre burnt down during the first performance of *Henry VIII* in 1613. The fire was apparently started by the 'chambers' discharged in Act 1, Scene 4. A second Globe was built in 1614 and demolished in 1644. The modern replica will follow the design of the first Globe (as scholarship now conjectures it to have been), but with tiles rather than thatch on the roof. It will stand as the centrepiece of an arts complex, the International Shakespeare Globe Centre, which will also include a small indoor theatre designed by Inigo Jones but not built until now. The organisers hope to complete the project by 1992; in the meantime, a model of the new Globe can be seen in the Shakespeare Globe Museum.

Park Street and a right turn on Stoney Street bring us into Borough High Street, at a point slightly south of London Bridge and Southwark Cathedral. On the opposite side of the street stood the famous coaching inns, among them the White Hart, used in *Henry VI, Part Two* by the rebel Jack Cade, who rebukes his followers: 'Hath my sword therefore broke through London gates, that you should leave me at the White Hart in Southwark?' (Act 4, Scene 8). It has not survived but a 17C wing of its companion, the George (NT), remains. During the summer Shakespeare's plays are performed in its yard.

Shakespeare Globe Museum, Bear Gardens, Bankside, Southwark, London SE1: phone (01) 620 0202.

2 The Inns of Court

The Inns of Court, best reached for these purposes from Chancery Lane Underground Station (Central Line), preserve the only London buildings where Shakespeare's plays were performed within their author's lifetime.

Gray's Inn stands north of High Holborn at the junction with Gray's Inn Road. In its Hall *The Comedy of Errors*, usually regarded as Shakespeare's earliest comedy, was performed on 28 December 1594 by the Lord Chamberlain's Men as part of the Christmas revels. The Inn's records, *Gesta Grayorum*, describe how the festivities became so spirited that the ambassador from the Inner Temple withdrew and

> it was thought good not to offer any thing of Account, saving Dancing and Revelling with Gentlewomen; and after such Sports, a Comedy of Errors (like to *Plautus* his *Menechmus*) was played by the Players. So that Night was begun, and continued to the end, in nothing but Confusion and Errors; whereupon, it was ever afterwards called, *The Night of Errors*.

The Hall was rebuilt after bomb damage during the Second World War but preserves its glass and part of its fine wooden screen.

From Gray's Inn we walk south of High Holborn on Chancery Lane to Fleet Street, where the entrance to the Middle Temple lies on the opposite side of the road. According to the diary of John Manningham, a law student, *Twelfth Night* was performed by a company that may have included Shakespeare on 2 February (Candlemas) 1602 in the magnificent 16C *Hall. Feste's description of 'bay windows transparent as barricadoes, and ... clerestories towards the south-north ... as lustrous as ebony' (Act 4, Scene 2, lines 40–41) is sometimes taken as a reference to the building's oriel windows. Like the Hall at Gray's Inn it suffered from wartime bombing but has now been restored.

Gray's Inn Hall, off High Holborn and Gray's Inn Road, London WC1: visitors by written appointment with the Under Treasurer, 8 South Square, Gray's Inn.

Middle Temple Hall, Middle Temple, London EC4: phone (01) 353 4355.

3 Westminster Abbey

Shakespeare is commemorated in Poets' Corner (fee) of the Abbey with a monument by William Kent and a sculpture by Peter Scheemakers (1741). Part of its cost was raised by a benefit performance of *Julius Caesar* in 1739. For Scheemakers' sculpture, see also Wilton House (Rte 6) and Stratford (Rte 7).

4 Hampton

Though is has no direct connection with Shakespeare, this part of SW London keeps an important reminder of David Garrick and the cult of bardolatry which the actor did so much to foster in the 18C.

Garrick's Villa, which he bought in 1754 and hired Robert Adam to improve in the 1770s, lay on the north side of Hampton Court Road, west of the Palace on the way into the centre of Hampton. It has now been converted into flats and surrounded by later development. On Garrick's Lawn, approached from Hogarth Way, stands Garrick's Temple to Shakespeare–a little octagonal building with an Ionic portico, which housed Roubiliac's statue of Shakespeare (1758) and the Shakespeare relics which Garrick loved to collect. With the river nearby, it makes a charming setting for one of Johann Zoffany's paintings of Garrick. Roubiliac's statue is now in the British Library.

Garrick's Temple of Shakespeare, Hampton: open by appointment only; phone the Curator, Orleans House Gallery, Twickenham, (01) 892 0221.

5 Windsor Castle

Windsor Castle is reached via M4, 12 miles west of London. It is linked with *The Merry Wives of Windsor* by an unproved tradition that Falstaff owed his revival to Queen Elizabeth's request and by more certain connections with the Garter Feast on St George's Day 1597. Though the comedy may have been performed at Whitehall or Greenwich rather than Windsor it nevertheless refers to the late 15C *stalls of St George's Chapel in some detail. In her role as Fairy Queen Mistress Quickly instructs her attendant fairies to prepare their heraldic decorations for the forthcoming Garter ceremonies:

> The several chairs of order look you scour
> With juice of balm and every precious flower;
> Each fair instalment, coat and sev'ral crest,
> With loyal blazon, evermore be blest.
> (Act 5, Scene 5, lines 62–65)

Windsor Castle, Windsor, Berkshire: phone (0753) 868286.

South-Western England

6 Wilton House

Tradition claims that Wilton House, 3 miles west of Salisbury, was the setting for a special performance of *As You Like It* by the King's Men, Shakespeare himself among them, before James I in December 1603. The occasion would presumably have been arranged by Mary Herbert, Countess of Pembroke, sister to Sir Philip Sidney (q.v.) and a distinguished patroness of the arts. James had certainly brought his court to Salisbury to escape the plague in London at this time, and the Chambers' Accounts do record a payment to John Heminge for presenting an unnamed play before the King at Wilton. However, there is no definite evidence identifying the play or placing Shakespeare at the house.

The north entrance hall has a statue of Shakespeare by Peter Scheemakers (1743), a revised and refined version of his contribution to the monument in Poets' Corner of Westminster Abbey (Rte 3).

Wilton House, Wilton, near Salisbury, Wiltshire: phone Salisbury (0722) 743115.

Central England

7 London to Stratford-upon-Avon via Oxford

The main lines of this route were in all likelihood followed by Shakespeare on journeys between the capital and his home town. It has become the most heavily trafficked tourist route in England.

A40 leads NW from London to Oxford (57 miles) where, according to tradition, Shakespeare lodged at the Crown (then the Taverne), a gabled building on Cornmarket near Carfax. Its guest chamber, the Painted Room, is administered by the Oxford Preservation Trust.

Sir William Davenant (1606–68), son of the Crown's landlady and a dramatist himself, took satisfaction in claiming to be Shakespeare's illegitimate son—a claim accepted by contemporaries in search of romantic embellishment to Shakespeare's life but rejected by scholarship. Seventeenth-century antiquaries reported that Shakespeare admitted to being Davenant's godfather and so attended his christening at St Martin's Church, whose tower survives opposite the Crown.

From Oxford A34 leads NW to Stratford-upon-Avon (97 miles), scene of Shakespeare's birth, early years, retirement and death.

The poet's father John, native of the nearby village of Snitterfield, had moved to this 'proper little mercate town' (as Camden described it) by the early 1550s to pursue his trade as glover—though rival traditions also make him a wool merchant or butcher. The facts of his domestic life and standing in the community are better established. He achieved local eminence with his appointment as Alderman in 1565 and High Bailiff in 1567, the second post making him a Justice of the Peace, but apparently suffered the economic difficulties common among Midlands tradesmen later in the century. In 1557 he had married Mary Arden, daughter of a prosperous yeoman from Wilmcote.

William was the third of their eight children, and the eldest son. The date of his baptism, 26 April 1564, has given Englishmen a patriotic excuse for celebrating his birthday as 23 April, St George's Day, which his monument also gives as the day of his death in 1616. The occasion is marked by festivities in the town. Virtually nothing can be said of his childhood or youth in Stratford beyond the safe assumption that he attended the local grammar school and the fact that he married Anne Hathaway of adjoining Shottery in 1582. Yet even here the record is confused by the almost simultaneous issue of a license for him to marry an Anne Whateley of Temple Grafton.

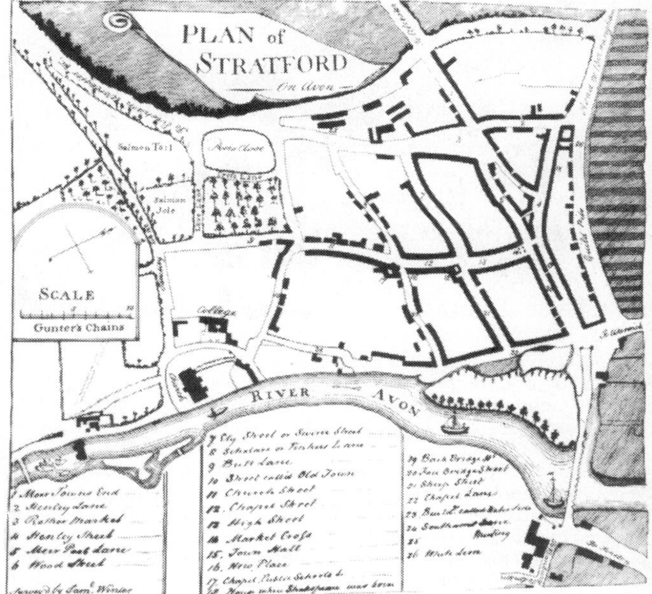

Map of Stratford by Samuel Winter (1759)

Scholarship cannot determine whether this document embodies romantic intrigue or clerical error. Three children were born of Shakespeare's marriage: Susanna in May 1583, and the twins Judith and Hamnet in February 1585. Neither the date nor the occasion of Shakespeare's departure from Stratford is known, though it evidently took place during the 'lost years' 1585–92 and is attributed by a stubborn local legend to his poaching misadventures at Charlecote Park. He apparently kept close ties with the town, strengthened by the acquisition of property through inheritance and purchase, and returned to it in 1611 for the last years of his life. His son Hamnet had died in 1596 but both daughters outlived him and continued the family association with Stratford. Susanna married Dr John Hall and Judith married Thomas Quiney, a vintner. Shakespeare's last direct descendant was Elizabeth Hall, who married Thomas Nash but left Stratford after his death to become Lady Bernard. She died in 1670 and was buried at Abington, now on the outskirts of Northampton.

After Shakespeare's death in 1616 Stratford's history became intertwined with the growth of a local literary legend and the creation of a national literary shrine. The first pilgrimage to the town was probably made by his old colleagues, the King's Men, during a provincial tour in 1622. They may well have achieved their presumed goal of seeing Shakespeare's newly erected monument in the parish church but their reception reminds us of the Puritan disapproval with which the town regarded plays and players: they were paid six shillings not to stage a performance in Stratford. Later in the 17C

The earliest known engraving of Shakespeare's Birthplace, by B. Cole from a drawing by Richard Greene, in The Gentleman's Magazine *(1769)*

antiquaries lent a willing and often gullible ear to Stratford's gossip about its distinguished son and with the 18C a recognisably modern tourist industry came to birth. The Rev. Francis Gastrell, owner of Shakespeare's last home and a man obviously insensible to literary piety, was so annoyed by visitors wanting to see a mulberry tree the poet had planted in his garden that he chopped it down in 1756 and thus provoked a minor local riot. A neighbour, Thomas Sharp, bought the wood and made a small fortune out of carved mulberry knick-knacks, which proved as popular and mysteriously self-multiplying as relics of the true cross. Stratford's pre-eminence on the literary map of England was confirmed by the actor David Garrick's descent on the town for the Jubilee of 1769. The three-day festival celebrated Shakespeare's memory in every conceivable way, except performing his work. It also set an uncomfortable precedent for future literary festivals in being dogged by bad weather and in leaving some participants disillusioned by its evident commercialism. Sam Foote, comic actor and admittedly no friend of Garrick, claimed: 'I was charged nine guineas for six hours' sleep and two shillings for asking a country bumpkin what time it was'. In the 19C Stratford's rise was furthered by the public purchase of the Henley Street Birthplace, a tercentenary festival in 1864 and Charles Edward Flower's successful campaign for a theatre devoted to Shakespeare's plays.

The town's popularity with visitors today shows no signs of decline. Five of its major attractions—the Birthplace, New Place Estate and Hall's Croft in Stratford itself, Anne Hathaway's Cottage at Shottery and Mary Arden's Cottage at Wilmcote—are owned and administered by the Shakespeare Birthplace Trust. A walking tour logically begins on Henley Street at Shakespeare's Birthplace. The half-timbered structure resting on stone foundations dates from the late 15C or early 16C and originally formed two separate dwellings. John Shakespeare was living in the western (or left-hand) wing by 1552 and apparently using it as his business premises. He bought the other half in 1556; at some later point in the century the two houses were connected and a rear wing added. William inherited the property on his father's death in 1601, though it continued to be inhabited by his mother and sister, Joan Hart. On the latter's death in 1646 it passed to Susanna Hall and then to her daughter Elizabeth. In 1670 it returned to the possession of the Hart family, where it remained until 1806, when it was acquired by the Courts.

During these vicissitudes of ownership the eastern or right-hand wing became an inn known as the Maidenhead and later as the Swan and Maidenhead, while the other part was at one time used as a butcher's shop. But by the 18C the building was already attracting interest as the birthplace and childhood home of England's national poet. Visitors to the 1769 Jubilee were given the chance to sit in a chair that he had supposedly used and shown round the house by custodians who simplified matters by announcing that their name was Shakespeare. Washington Irving's *The Sketch Book of Geoffrey Crayon, Gent* (1820) gives an entertaining account of the house's character during the years (1793–1820) when the remarkable Mrs Hornby acted as cicerone. Outside, it struck him as 'a small mean-looking edifice of wood and plaster, a true nestling place of genius, which seems to delight in hatching its offspring in bye corners'. Inside he encountered Mrs Hornby's claim to be a lineal descendant of Shakespeare ('she put into my hands a play of her own composition, which set all belief in her consanguinity at defiance'), the famous chair, the inevitable bits of mulberry tree and a wealth of other fictitious relics:

> There was the shattered stock of the very matchlock with which Shakespeare shot the deer, on his poaching exploit. There, too, was his tobacco-box; which proves that he was a rival smoker of Sir Walter Raleigh; the sword also with which he played Hamlet; and the identical lanthorn with which Friar Laurence discovered Romeo and Juliet at the tomb!

Nathaniel Hawthorne, a later visitor, was shown a more modest array of exhibits but still, as he admitted in *Our Old Home* (1863), was 'conscious of not the slightest emotion ..., nor any quickening of the imagination'. He managed, however, to rescue a useful piece of advice for his fellow-countrymen from the disappointing occasion: 'nobody need fear to hold out half-a-crown to any person with whom he has occasion to speak a word in England'.

In 1847 the house had been bought by the Shakespeare Birthplace Committee as the result of a public campaign in which Dickens (q.v.) among other famous contemporaries took part. After restoration, it was reopened as a museum in 1863. The architect in charge used an early drawing as a guide and carried out the work as authentically as possible but substantial changes were still judged necessary: adjoining houses with which the Birthplace had formed a continuous row were demolished to minimise the danger of fire; the three vanished gables were reconstructed; and the frontage of the eastern half, brick-clad during its days as an inn, was largely replaced. Henry James (q.v.), a visitor later in the century, left no record of his impressions in *English Hours* (1905) but his short story 'The Birthplace' tells a pleasantly whimsical tale of a custodian who quells moral scruples and learns to take pleasure in conveying the Shakespeare legend to his customers.

Today the western wing of the house is furnished in the manner of Shakespeare's time. The room that tradition has designated his birthroom is on the first floor; its window panes are incised with the signatures of Sir Walter Scott and Carlyle (qq.v.) among other famous literary pilgrims. The eastern wing is a museum of books, pictures and objects connected with the writer and his age. The pleasant garden at the back is planted with flowers and trees referred to in the plays.

To the west of the Birthplace stands the Shakespeare Centre of 1964, headquarters of the Shakespeare Birthplace Trust, with its large Shakespeare library. Our tour proceeds to the east, where Henley Street soon gives access to the gridiron of streets which still form the centre of the town as they did in Shakespeare's day. On the corner of Bridge Street and High Street Judith Shakespeare's House, where the poet's daughter lived with her husband, is now the Tourist Information Centre. We follow High Street to the right, passing several fine half-timbered buildings of which the most striking is probably Harvard House (discussed under the entry for 'Marie Corelli'). At the corner of Sheep Street is the Town Hall whose opening in 1769 was the nominal occasion for the Garrick Jubilee. The bust of Shakespeare on its north front, presented to Stratford by the actor, is a copy by John Cheere of Scheemakers' statue at Wilton House (see Rte 6), itself an improved version of the Westminster Abbey monument (see Rte 3). The building formerly housed a portrait of Shakespeare by Benjamin Wilson and Gainsborough's famous portrait of Garrick leaning elegantly against a bust of the poet, but these were destroyed by fire in 1946.

High Street continues as Chapel Street where, on the left, we find New Place Museum (or Nash's House), home of Shakespeare's granddaughter Elizabeth during her first marriage. Its present contents include an exhibition of the Garrick Jubilee and a table inlaid with wood from the celebrated mulberry tree.

More important, New Place Museum gives access to the site of New Place, at the corner of Chapel Street and Chapel Lane. Originally built for Sir Hugh Clopton near the end of the 15C, the house was still the largest in Stratford when Shakespeare bought it in 1597. He lived there from his retirement until his death (1611–16), when it passed to his elder daughter Susanna and her husband Dr Hall. It was renovated in 1702, when it had returned into the possession of the Cloptons, but suffered a more dramatic fate after it became the property of the infamous Rev. Gastrell in 1753. That gentleman's destruction of the mulberry tree and its accidental encouragement to the Shakespeare relic industry have already been described. By 1759 he had again fallen into conflict with his Stratford neighbours, this time over taxes, a dispute he resolved by the simple expedient of demolishing the house and quitting the town. Today only fragments of foundation are visible and part of the site has been planted as an Elizabethan Knot Garden. The original gardens of New Place, charmingly maintained and inevitably with a mulberry tree claiming descent from the original stock, are entered from Chapel Lane.

We continue south, where the change from Chapel Street to Church Street is marked by the fine Guild Chapel on the left. Beyond stands the Guildhall of 1416–18. Originally built by the Holy Cross Guild it later housed the Grammar School which, it is to be presumed, Shakespeare attended. A left turn at the end of Church Street leads down Old Town and past Hall's Croft, home of Shakespeare's daughter and son-in-law before their move to New Place. It contains a collection of Renaissance furniture.

We then reach the *Collegiate Church of Holy Trinity. Pleasantly situated near the Avon, the 13C–15C building is of considerable interest in its own right but is today visited for its many and intimate connections with the Shakespeare family.

Sir Walter Scott viewing the Shakespeare monument in the chancel of Holy Trinity, a painting attributed to Sir Walter Allen

Its exterior is virtually unaltered since the Renaissance except for the replacement of the original spire, short and wooden, by the present one of 1765. A tour of the interior begins at the west end of the north aisle, where the visitor finds the font in which Shakespeare, as well as his brothers, sisters and children, were christened.

His grave lies on the north side of the late 15C chancel (fee). The famous plea of its doggerel inscription (recut) is addressed to the local sexton, who might otherwise be tempted to move the tomb and make room for others, rather than to those later eccentric believers that his grave might contain important secrets about the true authorship of the plays:

GOOD FREND FOR JESUS SAKE FORBEARE,
TO DIGG THE DUST ENCLOASED HEARE.
BLESTE BE YE MAN YT SPARES THES STONES,
AND CURST BE HE YT MOVES MY BONES.

On the wall above is a monument by Gheerart Janssen (or Gerard Johnson) erected sometime between 1616 and 1623, when it was mentioned by Leonard Digges in his commendatory verse for the First Folio. Shakespeare's bust is flanked by a marble column either side, with a cornice and entablature above and an epitaph beneath. Its English verse is noteworthy for both its early recognition of Shakespeare's importance and its misleading implication that he is actually buried within the monument:

STAY PASSENGER, WHY GOEST THOU BY SO FAST?
READ IF THOU CANST, WHOM ENVIOUS DEATH HATH PLAST,
WITH IN THIS MONUMENT SHAKESPEARE: WITH WHOME,
QUICK NATURE DIDE: WHOSE NAME DOTH DECK YS TOMBE,
FAR MORE THEN COST: SIEH [sic] ALL, YT HE HATH WRITT,
LEAVES LIVING ART, BUT PAGE, TO SERVE HIS WITT.

It has inevitably required and suffered restoration over the centuries. By 1749 the soft stone had become badly eaten away and the actor-manager John Ward staged a local benefit performance of *Othello* to pay for repairs. In 1793 the Shakespearean scholar and editor Edmund Malone persuaded the vicar to have the bust painted white, an act which caused a visitor of 1810 to protest in angry verse:

Stranger to whom this monument is shown,
Invoke the poet's curse upon Malone
Whose meddling zeal his barbarous taste betrays
And smears his tombstone as he marr'd his plays.

It was restored to its present colouring in the 19C. In none of these various states has Janssen's indifferent and inexpressive portrayal of the poet attracted admiration. Washington Irving was being both charitable and fanciful when he found Shakespeare's appearance 'pleasant and serene, with a finely arched forehead; and I thought I could read in it clear indications of that cheerful, social disposition, by which he was as much characterised among his contemporaries as by the vastness of his genius'. Dickens' reaction was more typical when he remarked ironically: 'I have here the counterfeit presentment of a face suggestive above all things of a strong vitality, freshness of spirit, and liveliness of disposition'.

Adjacent memorials in the chancel include those to Shakespeare's wife Anne, who outlived him to die in 1623, his daughter Susanna (remembered as 'witty above her sexe') who died in 1649, her husband John Hall (d. 1635), and Thomas Nash (d. 1647), first husband of their daughter Elizabeth. Shakespeare's friend and fellow townsman John Combe (d. 1614) is commemorated in another work by Janssen. The graves of other members of Shakespeare's family are unmarked. The window depicting the Seven Ages of Man from *As You Like It* was donated by American admirers in 1885.

Southern Lane offers a convenient return route from Holy Trinity, with the river on our right. On the left we pass The Other Place, one of the three Stratford theatres maintained by the Royal Shakespeare Company. The Swan theatre, farther along on the right, inhabits part of the gutted shell of the old Memorial Theatre of 1877–79, destroyed by fire in 1926. Its auditorium recalls the design of Elizabethan playhouses and is used for staging the work of Shakespeare and his contemporaries. Another part of the Victorian building to escape the fire now houses the Royal Shakespeare Company Collection, with theatrical relics and an exhibition of stage history. Particularly interesting among the large display of paintings is the early 17C 'Flower Portrait' of Shakespeare (named after its donor), which may be either model for or copy of Martin Droeshout's engraving in the First Folio. The large Royal Shakespeare Theatre, beyond, was built in 1932 on the site of the old Memorial Theatre and, before that, of the Rotunda built by Garrick for the 1769 Jubilee. It has a pleasant terrace overlooking the Avon. Beyond the Theatre, where Southern Lane becomes Waterside and leads to the Clopton Bridge, are the Bancroft Gardens and Lord Ronald Gowers' statue of Shakespeare surrounded by characters from his plays.

Apart from their intrinsic charm, the neighbouring countryside and villages around Stratford are rich in Shakespearean associations, whether real or fondly imagined.

Shottery (1 mile NW) can be reached by bus from Bridge Street, by a footpath from Evesham Place or by car via the A422 Shottery Road. Its attraction, of course, is Anne Hathaway's Cottage. The term 'cottage' is something of a misnomer for the timber-framed farmhouse that was the family home of Shakespeare's wife. The Hathaway bedstead, dairy and baking oven in the kitchen are all to be noted.

2½ miles NW of Shottery, off A422, we come to Wilmcote and Mary Arden's House, a handsome 16C farmhouse furnished in the style of the period. Its claim to be the birthplace of Shakespeare's mother is based on the slender authority of John Jordan, self-taught and self-styled Shakespeare expert of the 18C. By continuing 2 miles NW we reach Aston Cantlow, in whose church Mary Arden married John Shakespeare.

At Charlecote Park (4 miles east of Stratford via B4086) is the restored Renaissance mansion of Sir Thomas Lucy, site of the most persistent and tantalising legend connected with Shakespeare's youth. It was related in its most familiar form by Rowe, 18C editor of the plays:

> He had, by a Misfortune common enough to young Fellows, fallen into ill Company; and amongst them, some that made a frequent practice of Deer-Stealing, engag'd him with them more then once in robbing a Park that belong'd to Sir *Thomas Lucy* of *Cherlecot*, near *Stratford*. For this he was prosecuted by that Gentleman, as he thought, somewhat too severely; and in order to revenge that ill Usage, he made a Ballad upon him. And ... it is said to have been so very bitter, that it redoubled the Prosecution against him to that degree, that he was oblig'd to leave his Business and Family in *Warwickshire*, for some time, and shelter himself in *London*.

Sir Walter Scott (q.v.) makes use of the story in Chapter 17 of *Kenilworth* (1821). Tradition also supplies several versions of the offending ballad, none of them calculated to advance Shakespeare's reputation as a poet, and points to Justice Shallow in *The Merry Wives of Windsor* as Shakespeare's revenge on his persecutor. Such entertaining possibilities are somewhat dampened by the reminder that Sir William Lucy, ancestor of Sir Thomas, is respectfully treated in *Henry VI, Part One* and that Charlecote did not have a park proper in Shakespeare's time, merely a 'warren' that may or may not have contained roe deer. The sensible tourist abandons speculation and joins Henry James in appreciating grounds 'whose venerable verdure seems a survival from an earlier England and whose innumerable acres, stretching away, in the early evening, to vaguely seen Tudor walls, lie there like the backward years receding to the age of Elizabeth' ('In Warwickshire' in *English Hours*).

The Painted Room, Crown Inn, Cornmarket, Oxford: visitors by appointment; phone Estates Department, Oxford City Council, (0865) 49811.

Shakespeare Birthplace Trust Properties (Birthplace, Anne Hathaway's Cottage, Hall's Croft, Mary Arden's House and New Place): separate admission fees or inclusive ticket for all five properties; phone Shakespeare Birthplace Trust headquarters, Shakespeare Centre, Henley Street, Stratford-upon-Avon, Warwickshire, (0789) 204016.

King Edward VI Grammar School, Church Street, Stratford-upon-Avon, Warwickshire: open in Easter and summer holidays; phone (0789) 293351.

Royal Shakespeare Company Collection, Royal Shakespeare Theatre, Stratford-upon-Avon, Warwickshire: phone (0789) 296655.

Charlecote Park, Wellesbourne, near Stratford-upon-Avon, Warwickshire: NT; phone (0789) 840277.

PART TWO

Joseph Addison

b. Milston, Wiltshire, 1672; d. London, 1719. *The Campaign* (1704); contributions to *The Tatler* (1709–11); contributions to *The Spectator* (1711–12); *Cato* (1713).

In the cathedral city of Lichfield, Staffordshire, 16 miles north of Birmingham, a pleasant atmosphere remains to evoke the period of Addison's childhood. The Deanery where he was brought up in a serene and loving family has been replaced by a slightly later building, though a monument to his father (d. 1703) may be found in the Cathedral nearby at the west end of the south aisle. The old Grammar School on St John Street, able to boast Dr Johnson (q.v.) among its later pupils, has gone except for its Headmaster's House, now Council offices.

The scenes of Addison's later education are better preserved. The fine 16C–18C buildings of the Charterhouse stand on Charterhouse Square near the Central Meat Market in the City of London; the school moved to Godalming, Surrey, in 1872. Addison's schoolboy friendship with Richard Steele (q.v.), eventually to issue in their collaboration on *The Tatler* and *The Spectator*, was continued when Addison went to Oxford: first to The Queen's College in 1687 and then to Magdalen, where he later became a Fellow. His love of the river scenery enjoyed by Magdalen is recalled in the naming of Addison's Walk and in this account of his spokesman, Philander, in *Dialogues upon the Usefulness of Ancient Medals*:

> Philander used every morning to take a walk in the neighbouring wood, that stood on the borders of the Thames. It was cut through by abundance of beautiful allies, which terminating on the water, looked like so many painted views in a perspective. The banks of the river and the thickness of the shades drew into them all the birds of the country, that at sun-rising filled the wood with such a variety of notes as made the prettiest confusion imaginable. (Dialogue 3)

He was twice chief secretary to the Lord Lieutenant of Ireland under Whig governments (1709–11 and 1715–16). His connection with Dublin is remembered in similar manner to his years at Oxford, by the name of the yew walk in the 18C part of the Botanic Gardens at Glasnevin, north of the city.

For evidence of Addison's successful career as essayist, poet and Whig politician we look not in London but to the late 17C house he was able to buy as a country seat in 1711: Bilton Hall, SW of Rugby in Warwickshire. At first sight the decision to spend part of each year so removed from the scene of his normal duties and in an area with which he had no family connection may seem surprising; in fact, it expressed not an early Romantic interest in nature but that adherence to Augustan values which characterised his habits of life as much as the easy elegance of his prose.

In 1716 he married Charlotte, Countess of Warwick, at St Edmund King and Martyr, a Wren church on Lombard Street in the City of London. The couple lived at Holland House, which she had inherited from her first husband, though there is little reason to believe the common rumour that Addison felt ill at ease in these grand surroundings and preferred to take refuge in the coffee houses and taverns of his bachelor days. Holland House, begun by Sir Thomas Cope in the early 17C, stood between Holland Park Avenue and Kensington High Street; only the park and east wing (now restored) survived war-time bombs, their appearance altered by the addition of the modern King George VI Memorial Hostel.

Addison was buried in Westminster Abbey, a building which had prompted these characteristic reflections in No. 26 of his *Spectator* essays:

> When I look upon the tombs of the great, every emotion of envy dies in me; when I read the epitaphs of the beautiful every inordinate desire goes out; when I meet with the grief of parents upon a tomb-stone, my heart melts with compassion; when I see the tomb of the parents themselves, I consider the vanity of grieving for those whom we must quickly follow.

His statue in Poets' Corner (fee) was erected at the beginning of the 19C.

Headmaster's House and Old Grammar School (Lichfield District Council Offices), St John Street, Lichfield, Staffordshire: visitors by appointment; for further information phone Lichfield Tourist Information Centre, (0543) 252109.

Charterhouse, Charterhouse Square, London EC1: guided tours in summer; phone (01) 253 9503.

National Botanic Gardens, Glasnevin, Dublin: phone (01) 374388.

William Harrison Ainsworth

b. Manchester, 1805; d. Reigate, Surrey, 1882. *Rookwood* (1834); *Crichton* (1837); *Jack Sheppard* (1839); *The Tower of London* (1840); *Guy Fawkes: or The Gunpowder Treason* (1841); *Old Saint Paul's: A Tale of the Plague and the Fire* (1841); *Windsor Castle* (1843); *The Lancashire Witches* (1849); *The Flitch of Bacon: or The Custom of Dunmow* (1854); *Mervyn Clitheroe* (1858); *Ovingdean Grange: A Tale of the South Downs* (1860); *Auriol: or The Elixir of Life* (1865).

A plaque now marks Ainsworth's birthplace in Manchester at No. 57 King Street, north of the Town Hall and then a quiet residential area. He was educated at Manchester Grammar School when it was housed in a late 18C building near the Cathedral and the medieval Chetham's Hospital. The semi-autobiographical *Mervyn Clitheroe*, dedicated to his contemporaries at the school, gives a detailed picture of his boyhood there (Bk 1, Ch. 2). In 1881, after a long and extremely popular career writing novels that combined Gothic melodrama with historical fiction in the manner of Sir Walter Scott (q.v.), he returned to Manchester for a dinner given in his honour by the Mayor. It was held in Alfred Waterhouse's Town Hall, completed only a few years before.

On that occasion Ainsworth proudly accepted the title of 'The Lancashire Novelist'. His best claim to it is his detailed use of the area around *Pendle Hill in *The Lancashire Witches*, set in the 16C and 17C. A brief tour of its bleakly impressive countryside may begin at Whalley, in the valley of the Ribble by the junction of A59 and A671 24 miles north of Manchester. The novel depicts Whalley Abbey, now ruined, in the last days before its dissolution ('Introduction', Ch. 3). We take A59 north with Pendle Hill, the opening scene of the

Ainsworth presiding at the Dunmow Flitch ceremony, an engraving from The Illustrated London News *(1855)*

book, rising on our right. At 6 miles we turn right for the pleasant little village of Downham, whose manor house Ainsworth made the home of Nicholas Assheton, and cross the hill following the turning for Barley and Newchurch in Pendle. Ainsworth stayed in Newchurch while planning *The Lancashire Witches* and portrayed it as 'Goldshaw'. A proposal at the beginning of this century to erect a memorial window to him in the church was not successful.

Though in Derbyshire rather than Lancashire, the town of Chesterfield (12 miles south of Sheffield on A61) played an important, if accidental, part in the genesis of *Rookwood*. Ainsworth later described how he 'happened, one evening, to enter the spacious cemetery attached to the church with the queer, twisted steeple, which ... seems to menace the good town of Chesterfield with destruction. Here an incident occurred, on the opening of a vault, which supplied me with a hint for the commencement of my romance'. He remained tantalisingly silent about the incident but its fictional result certainly got his career as a novelist off to a rousingly melodramatic start.

The Flitch of Bacon brought him to the Essex village of Little Dunmow (just south of A120 between Bishop's Stortford and Braintree), which boasted the ancient custom of awarding a flitch of bacon to the married couple who could prove they had lived together happily for the previous year and a day. His novel makes detailed use of *St Mary, the surviving part of Dunmow Priory, correctly remarking that it is 'the mere fragment of a vast and stately pile, which in its time had formed part of a range of monastic buildings' (Bk 1, Ch. 7). Its Fitzwalter tombs and Flitch Chair, made from a 13C stall, are noted. The popularity of Ainsworth's novel helped revive a custom that had been falling into disuse and in 1855 he presided at the Flitch ceremony in the Town Hall of Great Dunmow nearby.

From 1853 until 1867 he lived on the Sussex coast in Brighton. A plaque marks his home at No. 5 Arundel Terrace, on the seafront immediately east of Lewes Crescent and Sussex Square in Kemp Town. *Ovingdean Grange* is set in Ovingdean 3 miles east of Kemp Town via Marine Parade and Greenways. It notes that the Grange (or Hall) near the church 'has entirely lost its original and distinctive character' but rightly concedes that it is still 'a fair-proportioned, cheerful-looking domicile' (Bk 1, Ch. 2). Its appearance today, as when Ainsworth wrote his novel, is 18C. *Ovingdean Grange* also takes notice of Lewes, 8 miles NE of Brighton via A27, an 'old picturesque town ..., with its quaint, climbing houses and its towering castle' (Bk 4, Ch. 1). Southover Grange, an Elizabethan house reached by following Keere Street south from Lewes' High Street, appears as the 'Mock-Beggars Hall', where the usurer Zachary Trangmar lends money to impoverished Royalists (Bk 4, Ch. 2).

The preface to *Rookwood* acknowledges that its main locale was closely modelled on Cuckfield Place, 16 miles north of Brighton via A23 and A272. The novel enthuses over the Elizabethan house:

> Rookwood Place was a fine, old, irregular pile, of considerable size, presenting a rich, picturesque outline, with its innumerable gable ends, its fantastical coigns, and tall nest of twisted chimneys. There was no uniformity of style about the building, yet the general effect was pleasing and beautiful. Its very irregularity constituted a charm. Nothing except convenience had been consulted in its construction: additions had from time to time been made to it, but everything dropped into its proper place, and, without apparent effort or design, grew into an ornament, and heightened the beauty of the whole. It was, in short, one of those glorious manorial houses that sometimes unexpectedly greet us in our wanderings, and gladden us like the discovery of a hidden treasure. (Bk 1, Ch. 4)

This effect (which owes something to Ainsworth's pen as well as to the builder's trowel) was diminished by alterations in 1848, but the brick gatehouse retains all its original charm.

Ainsworth was buried in London at Kensal Green Cemetery, opposite Kensal Green Station (Bakerloo Underground Line and British Rail) in Harrow Road. His grave is No. 3443 in Square 154, north of West Centre Avenue and west of the church. The cemetery makes an appropriate resting place, not just because several other Victorian novelists lie there but because Ainsworth had lived in the

Harrow Road nearby at Kensal Lodge and then Kensal Manor (1835–53), both gone but both in their day festive gathering places for his fellow writers.

Whalley Abbey Gatehouse, Whalley, Lancashire: English Heritage, open at any reasonable time.

Southover Grange, Lewes, East Sussex: the gardens are public and part of the Grange is a craft centre; phone Lewes Tourist Information Centre, (0273) 471600.

Matthew Arnold

b. Laleham, Surrey, 1822; d. Liverpool, Merseyside, 1888. *The Strayed Reveller and Other Poems* (1849); *Empedocles on Etna and Other Poems* (1852); *Poems: A New Edition* (1853); *Poems: Second Series* (1855); *On Translating Homer: Three Lectures Given at Oxford* (1861); *Essays in Criticism: First Series* (1865); *New Poems* (1867); *Culture and Anarchy: An Essay in Political and Social Criticism* (1869); *Friendship's Garland* (1871); *Literature and Dogma: An Essay Towards a Better Apprehension of the Bible* (1873); *God and the Bible: A Review of Objections to Literature and Dogma* (1875); *Last Essays on Church and Religion* (1877); *Irish Essays and Others* (1882); *Discourses in America* (1885); *Essays in Criticism: Second Series* (1888).

The places most intimately connected with Matthew Arnold are found west of London near the course of the Thames. He was born at Laleham, 2 miles south of A30 and Staines via B376. The school which his famous father, Dr Thomas Arnold, kept and he himself later attended (1831–32) no longer stands, but the church of All Saints where Arnold was buried survives. In his last years Arnold had been living at Cobham, 7 miles SE of Laleham, at the junction of A3 and A245, though his home near the River Mole has gone. Before that he had lived to the north, at Harrow on the Hill. Byron House, his home from 1868 to 1873, is found on Byron Hill Road near the school to which he sent his sons.

Oxford was the most important city in Arnold's life, memorably extolled in the preface to the first series of his *Essays in Criticism*:

> Beautiful city! so venerable, so lovely, so unravaged by the fierce intellectual life of our century, so serene!
>
> There are our young barbarians, all at play! And yet, steeped in sentiment as she lies, spreading her gardens to the moonlight, and whispering from her towers the last enchantments of the Middle Age, who will deny that Oxford, by her ineffable charm, keeps ever calling us nearer to the true goal of all of us, to the ideal, to perfection,—to beauty, in a word, which is only truth seen from another side?—nearer, perhaps, than all the science of Tübingen. Adorable dreamer, whose heart has been so romantic! who hast given thyself so prodigally, given thyself to sides and to heroes not mine, only never to the Philistines! home of lost causes, and forsaken beliefs, and unpopular names, and impossible loyalties!

He was classical scholar at Balliol College from 1841 to 1844, years when the intellectual life of the university was dominated by disputes between his father, Regius Professor of Modern History, and members of the Oxford Movement. Though he won the Newdigate Prize with a poem about Cromwell, Arnold's undergraduate career was marked more by social gaiety than devotion to study; his second-class degree has consoled and encouraged poets ever since. In 1845–47 he held a fellowship at Oriel College and in 1857 he was first elected Professor of Poetry.

Two major poems, 'The Scholar-Gipsy' (1853) and 'Thyrsis' (1866), look back to his friendship with Arthur Hugh Clough (q.v.) and the youthful times when he 'shook off all the bonds and formalities of the place, and enjoyed the spring of life and that unforgotten Oxfordshire and Berkshire country'. 'The Scholar-Gipsy', in particular, 'was meant to fix the remembrance of those delightful wanderings of ours in the Cumner [sic] Hills'. Much of the countryside Arnold wrote about has been touched by Oxford's suburban sprawl but the visitor prepared for such change may explore the region by following A420 west from the city centre to Botley and changing at the A34 junction (1½ miles) to the Cumnor Road, which soon crosses what remains of Cumnor Hill. In Arnold's time it was still a suitable spot in which to imagine his lonely scholar gipsy:

And thou hast climbed the hill,
And gained the white brow of the Cumner range;
Turned once to watch, while thick the snowflakes fall,
The line of festal light in Christ-Church hall—
Then sought thy straw in some sequestered grange.
(lines 126–130)

Bablock Hythe, by the Thames 1½ miles west of Cumnor, was another imagined haunt of Arnold's hero:

Thee at the ferry Oxford riders blithe,
Returning home on summer-nights, have met
Crossing the stripling Thames at Bab-lock-hithe,
Trailing in the cool stream thy fingers wet,
As the punt's rope chops round.
(lines 72–75)

Though Oxford and the Thames engrossed Arnold's affection and, indeed, much of his poetic imagination, they were not of course the only centres of his life. From 1828 until his death in 1842 Thomas Arnold was headmaster of the public school at Rugby (on A428 4 miles west of M1 junction 18 and 12 miles east of Coventry). Arnold himself attended the school and served briefly as a master in 1845. The chapel which he made the subject of a famous poem was replaced by Butterfield's building of 1872. Arnold's London home from 1858 to 1868 was at No. 2 Chester Square, now marked by a plaque, near Eaton Square in Belgravia.

Two locations in Northern England should not be forgotten. The first is Haworth in West Yorkshire, the village described in detail under the entry for the Brontës, where Arnold's poem, 'Haworth Churchyard', is also considered. The second is in the Lake District, where Thomas Arnold bought Fox How as a holiday home in 1834. From Ambleside at the head of Windermere we follow A591 north until we reach the southern end of Rydal (1½ miles), where a left turn on the Clappersgate road brings us to the foot of Loughrigg Fell and the house after another half mile. Arnold's holidays here brought him into contact with the elderly Wordsworth (s.v. Lake Poets, Rte 12C), then living at Rydal Mount nearby. Both the Arnolds, father and son, are commemorated in Rydal church.

W.H. Auden

b. York, 1907; d. Vienna, Austria, 1973. *Poems* (privately printed; 1928); *The Orators: An English Study* (1932); *The Dance of Death* (1933); *The Dog Beneath the Skin* (with Christopher Isherwood; 1935); *The Ascent of F6* (with Christopher Isherwood; 1936); *Letters from Iceland* (with Louis MacNeice; 1937); *Selected Poems* (1938); *On the Frontier* (with Christopher Isherwood; 1938); *Journey to a War* (with Christopher Isherwood; 1939); *Another Time* (1940); *The Double Man* (1941); *For the Time Being* (1945); *Collected Poetry* (1945); *The Age of Anxiety: A Baroque Eclogue* (1948); *Collected Shorter Poems 1930–1944* (1950); *The Enchafèd Flood: Or the Romantic Iconography of the Sea* (1951); *The Shield of Achilles* (1955); *Homage to Clio* (1960); *The Dyer's Hand and Other Essays* (1963); *About the House* (1965); *Collected Shorter Poems 1927–1957* (1966); *Collected Longer Poems* (1968); *Secondary Worlds* (1968); *City Without Walls* (1969).

Born in York and brought up in Birmingham, Auden was educated at Gresham's School in Holt, near the Norfolk coast 10 miles SW of Cromer. The countryside that made the deepest impression on him as he grew up was that of the Pennines, particularly the fells and moors around Alston, 20 miles NE of Penrith in Cumbria. His interest in geology and his belief that 'rock creates the only truly human landscape' is finely expressed in the poem, 'In Praise of Limestone'.

Auden entered Christ Church, Oxford in 1925, soon changing from Natural Sciences to English (in which his tutor was Nevill Coghill). With his precocious talent for poetry and his wide if unsystematic knowledge, he quickly became an undergraduate celebrity. The poets he gathered round him—Cecil Day-Lewis (q.v.), Louis MacNeice and Stephen Spender—were known as 'The Gang'; their abandonment of Oxford aestheticism in favour of harsh, experimental modernity and a growing commitment to left-wing politics set the tone for a generation. Auden's reputation was only a little dented when he was awarded a Third by the examiners.

After Oxford he worked as a schoolmaster before embarking on the European and American travels that took him away from England until old age. When he did return it was to Oxford, first as Professor of Poetry (1956–60) and then, in 1972, to live in a cottage in the grounds of Christ Church.

He was buried at Kirchstetten, the Austrian village where he had spent his summers. In 1974 Sir John Betjeman (q.v.), a friend from his undergraduate days, unveiled Auden's memorial stone in Poets' Corner (fee) of Westminster Abbey.

Jane Austen

b. Steventon, Hampshire, 1775; d. Winchester, Hampshire, 1817. *Sense and Sensibility* (1811); *Pride and Prejudice* (1813); *Mansfield Park* (1814); *Emma* (1816); *Northanger Abbey* (1818); *Persuasion* (1818).

An account of Jane Austen can most appropriately begin in South-Western England at **Bath. At a time when the reputation for fashionable gaiety had passed to newer resorts like Brighton and Bath was enjoying a solidly respectable character Jane Austen made several visits to the city in her youth, lived there after her father's retirement between 1801 and 1806 and made use of it in her novels, especially *Northanger Abbey* and *Persuasion*. Its fictional appearances typify her handling of place: precise reference to real locations abounds (hardly a street or public building in Bath passes without mention of some sort) but the emphasis falls less on physical detail than social atmosphere.

No. 4 Sydney Place, the modest terraced house that was the Austens' main home during their residence in Bath, lies to the east of the city's centre opposite the Holburne Art Museum, reached via Pulteney Bridge over the Avon. The other places of interest may be embraced in a single walking tour. We begin in the Paragon, where at No. 1 halfway down Jane Austen lodged during her earlier visits, and walk south to the junction with George Street, which is then followed to the right. Opposite Edgar's Buildings (where Isabella Thorpe in *Northanger Abbey* stayed) the fashionable Milsom Street leads left, bringing us after its pedestrian extension to the Pump Room of 1792–96, adjoining the Roman Bath and Museum in the Abbey Church Yard. In this famous gathering place (to choose but one example from the pages of Jane Austen's fiction) the newly arrived Catherine Morland and Mrs Allen 'paraded up and down for an hour, looking at everybody and speaking to no one' in Chapter 3 of *Northanger Abbey*.

From the Pump Room the colonnaded Bath Street leads to Hot Bath Street, which is followed to the left. A right turn at its end takes us past the Elizabethan Hetling House and along James Street West. A left on to Seymour Street brings us to the handsome terrace of Green Park Buildings, where Jane Austen lived at No. 27 in 1804. By returning up Seymour Street, following its continuation as Charles Street and branching right on Chapel Row, we reach the south side of Queen Square, where Jane Austen lodged during an early visit. Leaving the square by its NE corner we take Gay Street (where in 1805 the Austens lived at No. 25) to The Circus. From its right-hand exit we quickly reach the Assembly Rooms, built in 1771 and restored after a fire in 1942, now housing the Museum of Costume. The ballroom was the scene of Catherine Morland's first, disappointing encounter with Bath society in Chapter 2 of *Northanger Abbey* as well as of a later encounter (Ch. 8) with the Thorpes and Henry Tilney. In the Octagon Room there is a finely handled meeting between Anne Elliot and Captain Wentworth in Chapter 20 of *Persuasion*. The left-hand exit from The Circus leads to Brock Street and the Royal Crescent, Wood's masterpiece of 1769 and a fitting conclusion to the tour.

In *Northanger Abbey* (Ch. 11) Catherine Morland is frustrated in her hopes of making an excursion with the Thorpes from Bath to Bristol and Blaise Castle, in the grounds of Blaise Castle House (now a museum of West Country life) on the NW outskirts of the city. Her enthusiasm is kindled by John Thorpe's assurance that the castle is the 'oldest in the kingdom'; in fact, it is a 'sham' castle of 1766.

A visit from Bath to the charming Dorset coastal resort of *Lyme Regis in 1804 had memorable consequences for Jane Austen's fiction. She gives a fond account of Lyme (which then lacked the royal suffix) and its surrounding area in Chapter 11 of *Persuasion*, her last completed novel. In Chapter 12 her characters venture on to the Cobb, the stone jetty that juts into Lyme Bay, and Louisa Musgrove suffers her famous accident when jumping the steps known as Granny's Teeth from the upper to the lower Cobb. Captain Harville's house, to which she is taken, is popularly identified with Bay Cottage on Marine Parade nearby. The site of Jane Austen's own lodgings, opposite the cottage, has been made into a garden in her memory.

Despite their influence on her fiction the years in South-Western England were not in themselves productive or entirely happy, being overshadowed by the death of her father in 1805. It was with obvious relief that she returned to South-Eastern England, the territory of her childhood. She had been born at the village of Steventon, SW of Basingstoke, though the rectory where she grew up was demolished in 1826. In Reading she had attended Mrs Latournelle's school, which occupied the rooms over the gateway of the ruined Abbey in Forbury Road.

On leaving Bath Jane Austen, her sister Cassandra and their widowed mother lived first at a vanished location in Southampton before moving in 1809 to the village of Chawton, a mile south of Alton in Hampshire and now mercifully bypassed by A31 to Winchester. In the modest red brick house inevitably renamed *Jane Austen's House she lived until 1817, reworking her early writing into the finely textured novels of her maturity. Much has been made of her limited social environment and cramped domestic circumstances but she herself expressed satisfaction with the place in a doggerel sent to her brother shortly after her arrival:

Our Chawton Home, how much we find
Already in it to our mind;
And how convinced, that when complete
It will all other houses beat
That ever have been made or mended,
With rooms concise or rooms distended.

The 'Chawton Home' is now a museum where visitors may see a fine collection of memorabilia, her bedroom and the living-room where she wrote, with its creaking door to warn her to hide manuscripts from intruding visitors. The graves of her mother and Cassandra Austen lie in the SE corner of the churchyard of St Nicholas nearby.

Jane Austen was several times a visitor to Great Bookham (NE of Chawton and 2 miles SW of Leatherhead in Surrey), where her cousin Cassandra was wife of the rector Samuel Cooke, who is commemorated in the parish church. Attempts have been made to identify the village with the 'Highbury' of *Emma*. Excursions from Great Bookham to nearby *Box Hill (partly NT), to the east of A24 between Leatherhead and Dorking, had a more certain impact on the novel. In Chapter 43 this fine stretch of down and woodland with its striking views is the object of the expedition organised by Mrs Elton, an occasion marred from the start by 'a languor, a want of spirits, a want of union, which could not be got over'. In the course of the day Frank Churchill flirts with Emma to spite Jane Fairfax while Emma herself is rude to the garrulous Miss Bates, suffers a rebuke from Mr Knightley and makes the journey home in tears.

In Kent Jane Austen stayed at Godmersham Park (by A28 between Canterbury and Ashford), home of her brother Edward, who took the name of his adoptive father, Knight. There is a memorial to him and his wife in the parish church. From the church a lane leads to a public footpath through the park, offering views of the 18C house. Her knowledge of it may well have helped the depiction of 'Mansfield Park' in the novel of that title and even of 'Pemberley' in *Pride and Prejudice* (but see note below).

In 1817, already ill with Addison's disease, Jane Austen moved south from Chawton to Winchester. The lodgings where she died later the same year are at No. 8 College Street, a picturesque small house south of the Cathedral Close and adjoining Winchester

College. Her grave is opposite the Wykeham Chantry in the north aisle of the Cathedral nave; above it are a later brass wall plaque and a window in her memory.

A Note on 'Pemberley'. The identity and location of Mr Darcy's estate, which Elizabeth Bennet sees in Chapter 43 of *Pride and Prejudice*, have caused perplexity among Janeites. The visit takes place in the course of Elizabeth's tour through Derbyshire, whose 'celebrated beauties' have been listed in the previous chapter: Matlock, Dovedale and Chatsworth (4 miles NE of Bakewell). The last reference has been taken to rule out the Duke of Devonshire's mansion, but it may well be a deliberate red herring. Chatsworth certainly has the necessary scale and grandeur, though it must be admitted that the description of 'Pemberley', while effectively making Jane Austen's point about Mr Darcy's taste and good sense, is lacking in salient detail:

> It was a large, handsome, stone building, standing well on rising ground, and backed by a ridge of high woody hills;—and in front, a stream of some natural importance was swelled into greater, but without any artificial appearance. Its banks were neither formal, nor falsely adorned.

Roman Baths Museum and Pump Room, Abbey Churchyard, Bath, Avon: phone (0225) 461111, extension 2785.

Assembly Rooms (Museum of Costume), Bennett Street, Bath, Avon: closed for repairs until 1991; phone (0225) 461111, extension 327.

Blaise Castle House Museum, Henbury, Bristol, Avon: phone Bristol (0272) 506789.

Jane Austen's House, Chawton, Hampshire: phone (0420) 83262.

Chatsworth, near Bakewell, Derbyshire: phone Baslow (024 688) 2204.

William Barnes

b. Rush-hay, Dorset, 1801; d. Winterbourne Came, Dorset, 1886. *The Elements of English Grammar, With a Set of Questions and Exercises* (1842); *Poems of Rural Life in the Dorset Dialect, With a Dissertation and Glossary* (1844; enlarged edition, 1847); *Poems, Partly of Rural Life (in National English)* (1846); *A Philological Grammar, Grounded Upon English* (1854); *Views of Labour and Gold* (1859); *Hwomely Rhymes: A Second Collection of Poems in the Dorset Dialect* (1859); *Tiw: or, A View of the Roots and Stems of the English as a Teutonic Tongue* (1861); *Poems of Rural Life in the Dorset Dialect: Third Collection* (1862); *A Grammar and Glossary of the Dorset Dialect, With the History, Outspreadings and Bearings of South-Western English* (1864); *A Guide to Dorchester* (1864); *Poems of Rural Life in Common English* (1868); *An Outline of English Speech-Craft* (1878).

As his friend Thomas Hardy (q.v.) noted, Barnes was 'emphatically Dorset'. His poetry reproduced its dialect, praised its countryside, recorded its customs and relished its humour. His philological writings, urging the virtues of national purity in language, gave Dorset speech a place of honour for its preservation of Anglo-Saxon forms lost by the polyglot 'Englandish' of standard speech.

He spent his early years at Rush-hay, a 'farmling' 1½ miles west of Sturminster Newton in the Blackmore (or Blackmoor) Vale, a region evoked in the poems 'Rustic Childhood' and 'Our Early Landscape'. Nostalgia for another aspect of the place is expressed in 'Blackmwore Maidens'. The church at Sturminster Newton, where he was baptised, was drastically restored in 1825–27 but has a lectern in his memory. Another church, at Lydlinch 3 miles west on A357, is the subject of the lovely 'Lydlinch Bells'.

Only twice did Barnes live outside his native county. From 1823 to 1835 he worked as a schoolmaster in Mere, just over the Wiltshire border on A303. The Tudor Chantry House near the church was his home and school. In 1847 he spent the first of his three terms at St John's College, Cambridge, graduating as a 'ten-year man' in 1850.

Otherwise, his life centred on the county town of Dorchester, where he is today commemorated by a statue outside the church of St Peter. The site is well chosen, as Hardy's obituary of Barnes reminds us:

> Until within the last year or two there were few figures more familiar to the eye in the county town of Dorset on a market day than an aged clergyman, quaintly attired in caped cloak, knee-breeches, and buckled shoes, with a leather satchel slung over his shoulders, and a stout staff in his hand. He seemed usually to prefer the middle of the street to the pavement, and to be thinking of matters which had nothing to do with the scene before him. He plodded along with a broad, firm tread, notwithstanding the slight stoop occasioned by his years. Every Saturday morning he might have been seen thus trudging up the narrow South Street, his shoes coated with mud or dust according to the state of the roads between his rural home and Dorchester, and a little grey dog at his heels, till he reached the four cross ways in the centre of the town. Halting here, opposite the public clock, he would pull his old-fashioned watch from its deep fob, and set it with great precision to London time. This, the invariable first act of his market visit, having been completed to his satisfaction, he turned round and methodically proceeded about his other business.

A plaque marks his house in South Street, next door to the architect's office where the young Hardy worked as assistant.

In 1862 Barnes was appointed Rector of Winterbourne Came. Old Came Rectory, the charming thatched house where he spent his last years, lies off A352 1½ miles SE of Dorchester, a little beyond Hardy's home at Max Gate. An unclassified road leads right from A352 to the church of Winterbourne Came where Barnes was buried. His funeral is vividly recalled in Hardy's 'The Last Signal'.

Sir James Barrie

b. Kirriemuir, Tayside Region, 1860; d. London, 1937. *Caught Napping* (1883); *Better Dead* (1888); *Auld Licht Idylls* (1888); *When A Man's Single: A Tale of Literary Life* (1888); *An Edinburgh Eleven: Pencil Portraits From College Life* (1889); *A Window in Thrums* (1889); *My Lady Nicotine* (1890); *The Little Minister* (1891); *Sentimental Tommy: The Story of His Boyhood* (1896); *Margaret Ogilvy* (1896); *Tommy and Grizel* (1900); *The Little White Bird: or Adventures in Kensington Gardens* (1902); *Peter Pan in Kensington Gardens* (1906); *Peter and Wendy* (1911); *Quality Street* (1913); *The Admirable Crichton* (1914); *What Every Woman Knows* (1918); *Peter Pan: or The Boy Who Wouldn't Grow Up* (1928); *Dear Brutus* (1928); *Mary Rose: The Island That Wants To Be Visited* (1928); *The Boy David* (1938); *When Wendy Grew Up: An Afterthought* (1957).

Though he is now remembered only as the creator of Peter Pan, Barrie first achieved notice with his sentimental and cynical tales about his hometown of Kirriemuir (17 miles north of Dundee via A929 and A928). 'Thrums', to give the little manufacturing town its fictional name, appears in *Auld Licht Idylls*, *When A Man's Single*, *A Window in Thrums*, the two novels about Tommy, and Barrie's memoir of his mother, *Margaret Ogilvy*. In Kirriemuir today his birthplace at No. 9 Brechin Road houses a small museum. Visitors may see the wash house at the back where he tried out his first childish attempts at playwriting. In 1872, after two years' absence from Kirriemuir, the Barrie family returned to live in a larger and more comfortable house, Strathview. Barrie married Mary Ansell here in 1894. He was buried near his parents and relatives in the cemetery near the top of the town.

In Glasgow Barrie attended the Academy off Great Western Road near the bridge over the Kelvin. In Edinburgh, 'about the most romantic city on the earth', he was a student at the University from 1878 to 1882. He was awarded the honorary degree of LL.D. in 1909 and became Chancellor in 1930. His *Edinburgh Eleven* offered a series of light-hearted sketches of famous teachers and former students, including Robert Louis Stevenson (q.v.).

Of Barrie's many return visits to his native Scotland perhaps the most important was in the summer of 1912, when he rented Ahmuinnsuid Castle, a 19C building in the Scottish baronial style, on the west coast of North Harris in the Outer Hebrides. The surrounding landscape influenced *Mary Rose*, in its day one of his most popular plays.

His working life was spent in London. In 1895 he and his wife came to live at No. 133 Gloucester Road in South Kensington, moving in 1901 to Leinster Corner, a Regency house at the corner of Bayswater Road and Leinster Terrace. Kensington Gardens opposite enjoyed a special place in his affections and played an important role in his life. It was here, while walking his dog, that Barrie used to meet the three sons of the charming Sylvia Jocelyn Davies and began to invent stories about Peter Pan. The friendship was strengthened and the fantasy further elaborated during summers in the countryside near Farnham in Surrey, but Barrie paid tribute to the importance of Kensington Gardens by commissioning and paying for the statue of Peter Pan (by Sir George Frampton, 1912) that now stands on the western edge of the Long Water, marking the spot where Peter Pan first landed his boat.

After his divorce in 1909 he moved to No. 3 in the fashionable Adelphi Terrace (since rebuilt), between the Strand and Victoria Embankment Gardens, where he remained until his death.

Barrie's Birthplace, Kirriemuir, Tayside Region: NTS; phone (0575) 72646.

Francis Beaumont and John Fletcher

Francis Beaumont: b. Grace Dieu, Leicestershire, 1584; d. London, 1616.

John Fletcher: b. Rye, East Sussex, 1579; d. London, 1625.

Collaborative plays: *Philaster* (1620); *The Maid's Tragedy* (1619). Beaumont is now usually given the sole credit for *The Knight of the Burning Pestle* (1613).

The ruins of the family seat where Beaumont was born, Grace Dieu, an Augustinian priory of 1240 with additions after the Beaumonts acquired it in 1539, can be seen in a field by A512 4 miles east of Ashby-de-la-Zouch. Wordsworth remembered the playwright's connection with the spot when he came here during his visit to Coleorton Hall nearby (s.v. Lake Poets, Rte 7). Beaumont attended Pembroke College (then Broadgates), Oxford, and was buried in Poets' Corner (fee) of Westminster Abbey. In fact, his grave near Chaucer and Spenser (qq.v.) is one of the earliest signs that the Abbey reserved a special place for literary men.

Fletcher's birthplace in Rye, on the Sussex coast between Hastings and Dungeness on the Sussex coast, is popularly identified as the

Ancient Rectory in Lion Street; it now bears a plaque. He studied at Corpus Christi College, Cambridge, and his residence there is commemorated by the same plaque in *Old Court that mentions Christopher Marlowe (q.v.). Like so many Renaissance dramatists Beaumont and Fletcher lived in Southwark and Fletcher, who died of the plague, was buried in Southwark Cathedral (then St Saviour's), immediately south of London Bridge and at the head of Borough High Street. The body of his fellow playwright Philip Massinger (q.v.) was later added to the grave.

William Beckford

b. London, 1759; d. Bath, Avon, 1844. *Dreams, Waking Thoughts, and Incidents* (1783; revised edition, 1834); *Vathek: An Arabian Tale* (English translation by Beckford and Samuel Henley; 1786); *Recollections of an Excursion to the Monasteries of Alcobaća and Batalha* (1835).

The son of a wealthy Lord Mayor of London, Beckford was born at No. 22 Soho Square, SW of Tottenham Court Road Underground Station (Central and Northern Lines). As a child he was taught music here by Mozart, himself only a few years older. The House of St Barnabas-in-Soho nearby was then the home of his uncle, Richard Beckford, responsible for much of the handsome interior. It became a charity for the destitute in the 19C.

When Beckford returned to England in 1796 after a youth and early manhood spent largely on the Continent, he devoted himself to realising in stone the same strain of exotic fantasy already expressed in his novel, *Vathek*. On his estate near Fonthill Bishop, 14 miles west of Salisbury on B3089, Fonthill Abbey grew from the type of Gothick folly by no means uncommon in the age, replaced Beckford's original mansion and became, by its completion in 1812, a monolithic tribute to private obsession: an irregular cruciform dominated by a 225ft octagonal tower, the whole surrounded by rugged landscape in the Romantic manner. Here Beckford lived in an isolation that fed local rumours of his scandalous behaviour, occasionally entertaining distinguished visitors: Turner in 1799, Nelson and Lady Hamilton for an elaborate three-day visit in 1800, and later the poet Samuel Rogers, who appreciated his host's civilised wit, whatever he may have thought of his home.

So eccentric and extravagant an undertaking could not escape problems. The workmen, employed by the hundred and sometimes labouring round the clock, were unalterably fixed in their habit of trimming stone to Palladian smoothness rather than Gothic roughness. The combination of Beckford's eager haste with the love of delay for which his architect, James Wyatt, was notorious created special hazards. The original tower, jerry-built from wood and stucco, fell down in 1797 shortly after its erection while its successor, a timber frame clad in stone, collapsed in 1825. *The Gardener's Magazine* reported:

> Only one man ... saw it fall. He is said to have described its manner of falling as very beautiful; it first sank perpendicularly and slowly, and then burst and spread over the roofs of the adjoining wings on every side, but rather more on the south-west than others. The cloud of dust which arose was enormous, and such as completely to darken the air for a considerable distance around for several minutes. Such was the concussion in the interior of the building, that

> one man was forced along a passage, as if he had been in an air-gun, to the distance of 30ft, among dust so thick as to be felt. Another, on the outside, was in the like manner carried to some distance. Fortunately, no one was seriously injured.

The rest of Fonthill Abbey soon followed the tower into oblivion and today only a fragment of the north wing survives. It stands west of Fonthill Lake on private land in Fonthill Abbey Wood, Fonthill Gifford, 2 miles south of B3089.

Fonthill Abbey from the north-west by John Martin in John Rutter's Delineations of Fonthill and its Abbey *(1823)*

Beckford's extravagance had already forced him to leave by the time of this disaster. He had sold the Abbey in 1822, and many of its contents were auctioned the following year. Items from his collection of curios, paintings, etc., now turn up in widely dispersed locations: some furniture in the saloon at Kingston Lacy, near Wimborne Minster, Dorset; 16–17C Flemish and French stained glass in St Mark's (or the Lord Mayor's Chapel) near the Cathedral in Bristol; and a Madonna by Vincenzo Catena at Harewood House, between Leeds and Harrogate in West Yorkshire.

Somewhat surprisingly, Beckford had chosen to live in Bath, where he indulged a minor version of the same itch to build and expand that had created Fonthill. He first bought No. 20 Lansdown Crescent, north of the Royal Crescent, but soon added Nos 18 and 19 and No. 1 Lansdown Place West, which faced No. 20 across a mews entrance. A connecting bridge was built by the Bath architect H.E. Goodridge, who also remodelled the interiors. On Lansdown Hill behind the Crescent, a hill which Beckford lovingly landscaped, Goodridge also constructed a restrained *tower in the classical manner. Now housing a small collection of memorabilia, it has a fine view from the belvedere. When Lansdown Hill was consecrated in 1848 Beckford's tomb was moved from its original resting place in the Abbey to a spot near the foot of his Tower.

House of St Barnabas-in-Soho, 1 Greek Street, Soho, London W1: phone (01) 437 1894.

Kingston Lacy, near Wimborne Minster, Dorset: NT; phone Wimborne (0202) 883402.

Harewood House, Harewood, Leeds, West Yorkshire: phone (0532) 886225.

Beckford's Tower and Museum, Lansdown Road, Bath, Avon: open weekends; phone (0225) 336228.

Sir Max Beerbohm

b. London, 1872; d. Rapallo, Italy, 1956. *The Works of Max Beerbohm* (1896); *Caricatures of Twenty-Five Gentlemen* (1896); *The Happy Hypocrite: A Fairy Tale For Tired Men* (1897); *More* (1899); *The Poets' Corner* (1904); *Yet Again* (1909); *Zuleika Dobson: or An Oxford Love Story* (1911); *A Christmas Garland, Woven by Beerbohm* (1912); *Seven Men* (1919); *And Even Now* (1920); *Rossetti and His Circle* (1922); *Around Theatres* (1953); *Mainly on the Air* (1957); *More Theatres* (1968).

The writer and caricaturist was born in London at No. 57 Palace Gardens Terrace, which leads south from Notting Hill Gate towards Kensington High Street. He was sent to school at Charterhouse, which had moved in 1872 from its old site in the City to its present buildings in Godalming, SW of Guildford, Surrey. His temperament was not suited to public-school life and he later remarked: 'My delight in having been at Charterhouse was far greater than my delight in being there'. He found a much more congenial environment when he entered Merton College, Oxford, in 1890 and took rooms in its medieval Mob Quad. His undergraduate years coincided with the zenith in popularity of the Aesthetic Movement, represented locally by Walter Pater (q.v.) at Brasenose and in London by the circle surrounding Oscar Wilde (q.v.), whom Beerbohm soon met. He did little work at Merton, preferring to draw caricatures of the dons than to write essays for them, and left in 1894 without taking his exams. In *Zuleika Dobson*, a characteristic blend of fantasy and irony, he paid elegant tribute to the university; Merton has returned the compliment by devoting a room leading off its magnificent Library to Beerbohm memorabilia.

After leaving Oxford Beerbohm led a relentlessly social life in London and developed a wide circle of acquaintances among writers. His visits to the elderly Swinburne (q.v.) in Putney were captured in a memorable essay. On his marriage in 1910 he moved to Italy, where he spent the rest of his life except for a return to England during World War Two. For part of this time he lived in Flint Cottage, once the home of George Meredith (q.v.), a little above Burford Bridge on Box Hill, Surrey. His ashes were buried in the crypt (fee) of St Paul's Cathedral.

Beerbohm Room, Library, Merton College, Oxford: phone the Porters' Lodge, (0865) 276310.

Hilaire Belloc

b. St Cloud, France, 1870; d. Guildford, Surrey, 1953. *Verses and Sonnets* (1896); *The Bad Child's Book of Beasts* (1896); *A Moral Alphabet* (1899); *Danton* (1899); *Paris* (1900); *Robespierre* (1901); *The Path to Rome* (1902); *The Old Road* (1904); *Emmanuel Burden* (1904); *The Historic Thames* (1907); *Mr Clutterbuck's Election* (1908); *Cautionary Tales For Children: Designed For the Admonition of Children Between the Ages of Eight and Fourteen Years* (1908); *Marie Antoinette* (1909); *Pongo and the Bull* (1910); *The French Revolution* (1911); *British Battles* (1911–13); *The Servile State* (1912); *The Four Men* (1912); *The Jews* (1922); *Sonnets and Verses* (1923); *The Cruise of the Nona* (1925); *A History of England* (1925–31); *Oliver Cromwell* (1927); *James the Second* (1928); *Belinda: A Tale of Affection in Youth and Age* (1928); *How the Reformation Happened* (1928); *Joan of Arc* (1929); *Richelieu* (1929); *New Cautionary Tales* (1930); *Wolsey* (1930); *The Praise of Wine: An Heroic Poem* (1930); *Cranmer* (1931); *Napoleon* (1932); *Charles the First, King of England* (1933); *Return to the Baltic* (1938); *The Last Rally: A Study of Charles II* (1939).

Belloc was educated at the school attached to St Philip Neri, the Roman Catholic Oratory founded by Cardinal Newman in Birmingham. The Oratory itself remains on the Hagley Road in the SW suburb of Edgbaston, though the school has since moved to Goring-on-Thames.

The years between school and university were lively but unsettled. Belloc worked his way across America to California in pursuit of Elodie Hogan, whom he later married, and returned to France, the country he had left when his French father died in 1872, to serve briefly in its navy and for a year in its army. Such experiences made him a notable figure among undergraduates when he entered Balliol College, Oxford, in 1893. His rooms were on the ground floor of Staircase 3, almost opposite the main Porters' Lodge. On the surface his undergraduate career was distinguished: his eloquence won him the Presidency of the Oxford Union, and he achieved a First in his examinations. Yet he did not gain the Fellowship at All Souls which he coveted and remained in Oxford after graduation only as a private coach and lecturer for the University Extension. He dwelt with obsessive bitterness on this academic rebuff in later life when financial problems forced him to write pot-boiling historical biographies.

By 1900 Belloc, now married to Elodie, had moved to London. They lived by the river in Chelsea at No. 104 Cheyne Walk, marked with a plaque. In the early years of his literary success he was a close friend and constant companion of G.K. Chesterton (q.v.); the two writers were a familiar pair in the pubs and restaurants of Fleet Street.

Part of Belloc's childhood had been spent in Sussex and in 1906 he moved to Shipley (off B2224 6 miles SW of Horsham). King's Land, a house dating back to the 15C, remained his home for the rest of his life and the surrounding countryside was often celebrated in the aggressively open-necked, beery verses that were his special metier:

On Sussex hills where I was bred,
When lanes in autumn rains are red,
When Arun tumbles in his bed,
    And busy great gusts go by;
When branch is bare in Burton Glen
And Bury Hill is a-whitening, then,
I drink strong ale with gentlemen;
Which nobody can deny, deny,
    Deny, deny, deny, deny,
Which nobody can deny!

('The First Drinking Song' in *The Four Men*)

The reality of his life at Shipley was rather less than vigorously cheerful. Elodie died in 1914 and Belloc afterwards permanently wore mourning clothes, sealed up her room and never passed its door without crossing himself. The pathetic, even grotesque, quality of his old age was intensified after he suffered a disabling stroke in 1942. The 19C smock mill which formed part of Belloc's estate at King's Land has been restored to working order and contains a small museum devoted to him. He was buried with his wife and son in the Roman Catholic churchyard at West Grinstead, by A24 3 miles SE of Shipley.

Shipley Windmill, Shipley, West Sussex: phone Coolham (040 387) 310.

Arnold Bennett

b. Hanley, Stoke-on-Trent, Staffordshire, 1867; d. London, 1931. *A Man from the North* (1898); *The Grand Babylon Hotel: A Fantasia on Modern Themes* (1902); *Anna of the Five Towns* (1902); *The Gates of Wrath: A Melodrama* (1903); *Leonora* (1903); *A Great Man: A Frolic* (1904); *Teresa of Watling Street* (1904); *Tales of the Five Towns* (1905); *The Loot of Cities* (1905); *Sacred and Profane Love* (1905); *Hugo* (1906); *Whom God Hath Joined* (1906); *The Sinews of War* (1906); *The Grim Smile of the Five Towns* (1907); *The City of Pleasure* (1907); *The Statue* (1908); *Buried Alive* (1908); *The Old Wives' Tale* (1908); *The Glimpse: An Adventure of the Soul* (1909); *Helen with the High Hand: An Idyllic Diversion* (1910); *Clayhanger* (1910); *The Card: A Story of Adventure in the Five Towns* (1911); *Hilda Lessways* (1911); *The Matador of the Five Towns, and Other Stories* (1912); *The Regent: A Five Towns Story of Adventure in London* (1913); *The Price of Love* (1914); *These Twain* (1915); *The Lion's Share* (1916); *The Pretty Lady* (1918); *The Roll-Call* (1918); *Mr Prohack* (1922); *Lilian* (1922); *Riceyman Steps* (1923); *Elsie and the Child* (1924); *Lord Raingo* (1926); *The Strange Vanguard: A Fantasia* (1928); *The Woman Who Stole Everything, and Other Stories* (1927); *Accident* (1929); *Imperial Palace* (1930); *The Night Visitor, and Other Stories* (1931).

Bennett was born in The Potteries, the cluster of industrial towns absorbed since 1910 into the single borough of Stoke-on-Trent (between Birmingham and Manchester on A34, and east of M6). Though he left when he was 22, returning only for visits to relatives, the region became the setting for many of his novels and stories, including books that rank among his finest achievements: *Anna of the Five Towns*, *The Old Wives' Tale* and the *Clayhanger* series (*Clayhanger*, *Hilda Lessways*, *These Twain* and *The Roll-Call*). The six pottery towns are reduced (by the omission of Fenton) to the 'Five Towns', a label that has stuck despite its inaccuracy, Stoke being renamed 'Knype', Hanley 'Hanbridge', Burslem 'Bursley', Tunstall 'Turnhill' and Longton 'Longshaw'. This might seem reminiscent of the way his older contemporary Hardy (q.v.) created 'Wessex' out of Dorset and its bordering counties, but in fact Bennett's work looks forward in spirit to Lawrence and Joyce (qq.v.), younger contemporaries whom he generously praised. Like them, Bennett wrote not as a loyal native but as a determined exile—a man who, when he had made his escape, could look back on the world of his youth and find there an interest, even a sort of poetry, to which he had earlier been oblivious.

In the unlovely landscape of The Potteries Bennett detected a 'grim and original beauty'. The first chapter of *Anna of the Five Towns* elaborates the point and gives the reader a panoramic view of the area:

> Five contiguous towns—Turnhill, Bursley, Hanbridge, Knype and Longshaw—united by a single winding thoroughfare some eight miles in length, have inundated the valley like a succession of great lakes. Of these five Bursley is the mother, but Hanbridge is the largest. They are mean and forbidding of aspect—sombre, hard-featured, uncouth; and the vaporous poison of their ovens and chimneys has soiled and shrivelled the surrounding country till there is no village lane within a league but what offers a gaunt and ludicrous travesty of rural charms. Nothing could be more prosaic than the huddled red-brown streets; nothing more seemingly remote from romance. Yet be it said that romance is even here—the romance which, for those who have an eye to perceive it, ever dwells amid the seats of industrial manufacture, softening the coarseness, transfiguring the squalor, of these mighty alchemic operations. Look down into the valley ..., embrace the whole smoke-girt amphitheatre in a glance, and it may be that you will suddenly comprehend the secret and superb significance of the vast Doing which goes forward below.

The towns remain a centre of the china industry, with several of the major companies boasting museums, shops or factory tours which attract large numbers of tourists. Yet their appearance has greatly changed: spoil heaps have been grassed or planted over, the distinctive smoke stacks and bottle kilns have all but disappeared, and (thanks to the Clean Air Act and the introduction of electric firing) the smoke has dispersed. Amid this featureless modern landscape of shopping centres and ring roads a reminder of the atmosphere which Bennett knew is beautifully preserved at the *Gladstone Pottery Museum in Longton, housed in a Victorian potbank restored to working order.

A tour of the chief places directly connected with Bennett, about 4 miles in all, can conveniently begin at the City Museum and Art Gallery on Bethesda Street in Hanley. Apart from a splendid array of pottery and porcelain, foreign as well as local, the exhibits here include Bennett memorabilia, books and reproductions of letters in the Social History Gallery. (Bennett was also an amateur watercolourist and the Museum has some of his paintings, though they are not on display at present.) From the Museum we head north on Marsh Street, turn right on Newhall Street, and head north again on Hope Street. The novelist's birthplace at the junction with Hanover Street is marked by a plaque. The neighbourhood was and remains undistinguished: trained as a master potter, Bennett's father was then working unsuccessfully as a draper and pawnbroker. By following Hope Street north toward Burslem we come to Waterloo Road and No. 205, the house Bennett's father built for himself in 1879 after he had finally qualified as a solicitor. Standing on the right just beyond the turning for Rushton Road, the solid red-brick building expresses the social change achieved by the family during the writer's childhood. They had risen from shabby, struggling respectability to middle-class affluence, and it is no surprise that Bennett the novelist should be master of the everyday details which distinguish the two ways of life.

To the north lies the centre of Burslem, one of the few areas to retain much of the character it had in Bennett's day. It still displays that mixture of coarseness and sophistication, grimness and exuberance which is the hallmark of the Victorian provincial town. From Waterloo Road we turn left on Queen Street and find on our right the Wedgwood Institute, now housing the Public Library and an annexe to the College of Further Education but in the 19C home of the Endowed School which Bennett attended (1877–80). The building's exterior is a remarkable tribute to Burslem's pride in its ceramics. At the end of Queen Street we enter St John's Square, where Bennett's grandparents ran a shop. It is the 'St Luke's Square' of *The Old Wives' Tale* and other novels. A right on Market Place takes us past the Old Town Hall, and by continuing straight ahead we come to Moorland Road, which leads after about a mile to Burslem Cemetery. An obelisk marks the place where the writer's ashes are buried in the family grave.

Arnold Bennett's dining room at Cadogan Square, photographed for an article in Vogue *(Sept 1924)*

Bennett left The Potteries for London in 1887, soon abandoning his uncongenial work in a solicitor's office for journalism and literature. In 1900, his career as a novelist already launched, he moved to the country—a curious decision for a man so thoroughly urban in his sympathies. Also curious was his choice of Trinity Hall Farm in Hockliffe (on A5 in Bedfordshire at the junction with A4012 for Leighton Buzzard) for, though the house itself is handsome, the village has nothing to recommend it except its position on the ancient Watling Street. This historic connection prompted Bennett to write the unsuccessful *Teresa of Watling Street*. From 1902 until 1912 he lived in France, returning with a French wife and a yacht, the latter proving an irresistible target to the younger generation of writers who regarded his conspicuously affluent lifestyle as vulgar. His choice of an English home cannot be faulted on the same grounds. Comarques in the village of Thorpe-le-Soken (12 miles east of Colchester, near the Essex coast) is a delightful Queen Anne building.

Bennett's later years were spent in London. After separating from his wife Marguerite he moved in 1922 to No. 75 Cadogan Square (south of Pont Street in Chelsea). Modestly calling it 'a rather fine thing in houses', he brought all his enthusiasm for plumbing and his taste for opulence to its interior furnishing. In 1930, shortly before his death from typhoid, he moved to a flat in the modern Chiltern Court at the junction of Baker Street and Marylebone Road. His old friend H.G. Wells (q.v.) was a neighbour.

Gladstone Pottery Museum, Uttoxeter Road, Longton, Stoke-on-Trent, Staffordshire: phone (0782) 319232.

Stoke-on-Trent City Museum and Art Gallery, Bethesda Street, Hanley, Stoke-on-Trent, Staffordshire: phone (0782) 202173.

Sir John Betjeman

b. London, 1906; d. Trebetherick, Cornwall, 1984. *Mount Zion* (1931); *Ghastly Good Taste* (1933); *Cornwall* (Shell Guide; 1934); *Devon* (Shell Guide; 1936); *Continual Dew: A Little Book of Bourgeois Verse* (1937); *An Oxford University Chest* (1938); *Old Lights for New Chancels* (1940); *Vintage London* (1942); *English Cities and Small Towns* (1943); *New Bats in Old Belfries* (1945); *Slick, But Not Streamlined* (1947); *Murray's Buckinghamshire Architectural Guide* (with John Piper; 1948); *Murray's Berkshire Architectural Guide* (with John Piper; 1949); *Shropshire* (Shell Guide, with John Piper; 1951); *First and Last Loves* (1952); *A Few Late Chrysanthemums* (1954); *Poems in the Porch* (1954); *Collected Poems* (1958); *Collins Guide to English Parish Churches* (1958); *Summoned by Bells* (1960); *English Churches* (with B. Clarke; 1964); *The City of London Churches* (1965); *High and Low* (1966); *Victorian and Edwardian London from Old Photographs* (1969); *Victorian and Edwardian Oxford from Old Photographs* (with David Vaisey; 1971); *London's Historic Railway Stations* (1972); *Victorian and Edwardian Brighton from Old Photographs* (1972); *West Country Churches* (1973); *A Nip in the Air* (1974); *Archie and the Strict Baptists* (1977); *Church Poems* (1981); *Uncollected Poems* (1982).

'I cannot say how shock'd I am to see/ The *variations* in our scenery', complains the speaker in 'The Town Clerk's Views' (lines 11–12) and he, of course, is the very antithesis of Betjeman himself, that vigorous opponent of civic uniformity. Probably no other contemporary writer has shown so highly developed and so catholic a sense of place; if we cannot speak of 'Betjeman Country' this is because so few aspects of the English scene escaped his attention, whether as poet, guidebook writer, defender of our architectural heritage or, in his last years, television personality. Rural parish churches, seaside piers, railway stations, Edwardian suburbs, even motorways all caught the eye of a man whose enthusiasm was backed by scholarly knowledge and whose distaste for the modern was tempered by humour and sympathy.

He was born and brought up in north London's Highgate, an area that did much to shape his taste in townscapes. Chapter 1 of his autobiographical poem *Summoned by Bells* remembers his child hood home on West Hill, which leads SW from the top of Highgate High Street. He attended the junior part of Highgate School on North Road. A lifelong love of Victoriana was encouraged by Highgate Cemetery, south of West Hill and entered from Swains Lane. Family worship is remembered in the poem 'St Saviour's, Aberdeen Park, Highbury, London N'. The Victorian church, now disused, lies off Highbury Grove, SE of Highgate.

In central London the Euston Road is an appropriate spot for recalling Betjeman's role as champion of our Victorian heritage. He defended St Pancras Station (British Rail, and Piccadilly, Victoria, Northern, Metropolitan and Circle Lines) against criticism and threat but failed to save Euston Station, to the west, from ill-conceived modernisation and its classical entrance arch from demolition in 1963–68. By continuing along Euston Road and its extension as Marylebone Road we come to Baker Street Underground Station, where the Metropolitan Line leads NW through the suburbs celebrated as 'Metro-Land' in a successful 1973 TV programme.

Betjeman's support for the restoration fund at St Mary-le-Strand is a reminder that his love of buildings by no means stopped with the 19C. James Gibbs' beautiful 18C church stands in the middle of the Strand by the junction with Aldwych.

In Wiltshire the poet attended Marlborough College. Chapter 7 of *Summoned by Bells* describes his unhappiness at school, where his contemporary Louis MacNeice remembered him as looking like 'a will-o'-the-wisp with Latin blood in it' and being 'a mine of useless information and a triumphant misfit'. From Marlborough he went to the more congenial Magdalen College, Oxford, though he was on bad terms with his tutor, C.S. Lewis, and left without a degree in 1928 after failing his qualifying exam in Divinity—an odd result for someone whose later work bears such frequent witness to his devout Anglicanism. Before his departure from Oxford Betjeman came into contact with the group of young poets led by W.H. Auden (q.v.), but his customary friends were the latter-day Aesthetes flamboyantly led by Harold Acton.

His connection with Cornwall, subject of his first guidebook, began in childhood; it is described in Chapters 4 and 8 of *Summoned by Bells*. In adult life he took a summer home on the north coast at Trebetherick (off B3314 13 miles NW of Bodmin). He was buried just south of the village at the little Norman church of St Enodoc, dug out from encroaching sands in 1863 and now stranded in the middle of a golf course. It is the setting for two poems, 'Sunday Afternoon Service in St Enodoc Church, Cornwall' and 'By the Ninth Green, St Enodoc'.

Highgate Cemetery Swains Lane, Highgate, London N6: Eastern Cemetery open during daylight hours; tours of Western Cemetery; phone (01) 340 1834.

R.D. Blackmore

b. Longworth, Oxfordshire, 1825; d. London, 1900. *The Fate of Franklin* (1860); *Clara Vaughan* (1864); *Cradock Nowell: A Tale of the New Forest* (1866); *Lorna Doone: A Romance of Exmoor* (1869); *The Maid of Sker* (1872); *Alice Lorraine: A Tale of the South Downs* (1875); *Cripps the Carrier: A Woodland Tale* (1876); *Erema: or My Father's Sin* (1877); *Mary Anerley: A Yorkshire Tale* (1880); *Christowell: A Dartmoor Tale* (1882); *The Remarkable History of Sir Thomas Upmore Bart MP, Formerly Known As 'Tommy Upmore'* (1884); *Springhaven: A Tale of the Great War* (1887); *Kit and Kitty: A Story of West Middlesex* (1890); *Perlycross: A Tale of the Western Hills* (1894); *Fringilla: A Tale in Verse* (1895); *Dariel: A Romance of Surrey* (1897).

Most of Blackmore's adult life was passed in Teddington, then a separate and rural village but now absorbed into the suburbs of SW London, where he divided his days between writing and market-gardening. Gomer House, which he bought in 1860, has gone and his long residence there is remembered only by a cluster of street names between Teddington's High Street and Station Road. Yet Blackmore's real loyalty was always to South-Western England and in old age he could still insist: 'In everything, except the accident of birth, I am Devonian; my ancestry were all Devonians; my sympathies and feelings are all Devonian'. He lived in Devon from the age of six to eighteen and permanently identified himself with the county in the popular mind by his most successful novel, *Lorna Doone*. His 'Romance of Exmoor' endowed it with a romantic, literary charm that helped attract visitors whose interest in the north Devon coast had already been stimulated by Charles Kingsley (q.v.) in *Westward Ho!*.

The scenes of Blackmore's childhood and *Lorna Doone* may be encompassed in a tour of some 62 miles beginning in the area round Tiverton, at the junction of A396 and A373 in east Devon. In 1826 his widowed father became curate of Culmstock, 10 miles east of the town via A373 and B3391, and after his remarriage in 1831 was joined by his son. Blackmore created 'Perlycross', setting for one of his minor novels, from memories of the village and the Blackdown Hills which rise to its NE. By the river in Tiverton itself we find the picturesque old building of Blundell's School (NT), founded in 1604. Drawing on his own schooldays here, Blackmore made Blundell's famous in the opening pages of *Lorna Doone*. In Chapter 2 John Ridd fights Robin Snell on the 'Ironing Box', a little triangle of turf reserved by the boys for such contests.

We strike NW from Tiverton on B3221, changing to A361 after 14 miles and again to B3226 2 miles beyond South Molton. After another 3 miles, when we have just crossed the River Bray, a sideroad leads left to the village of Charles, where the young Blackmore stayed at the Rectory with his uncle, 'an ancient parson of the North Devon type'. His visits are remembered by a tablet in the church, a building radically changed in the late 19C. Returning to B3226 we continue a further 8 miles north to Blackmoor Gate, which marks the western boundary of what is now the Exmoor National Park. At this point A399 leads NW to Combe Martin (4 miles), one of several parishes where Blackmore's grandfather held the living. The village owes its present popularity with tourists more to its natural setting than its untidy sprawl of buildings, though the church is distinguished by a fine spire.

From Blackmoor Gate our main route enters Exmoor via A39. Just beyond the boundary with Somerset at County Gate a sideroad (12 miles) leads right to Oare. Blackmore knew the village well in his boyhood since it was another of his grandfather's livings, and in *Lorna Doone* made it the home of John Ridd. In the little church Carver Doone shot Lorna on her wedding day (Ch. 74). Its interior was changed in the mid 19C when the chancel was extended.

Malmshead, half a mile west of Oare, gives access to the countryside of the Doones, the savage clan whom Blackmore developed from 17C legends into the main dramatic interest of his story. By 1887 curiosity had brought enough visitors here for Baedeker's *Handbook for Travellers in Great Britain* to offer a warning: 'Readers of *Lorna Doone* will be disappointed if they expect to find a close resemblance between the descriptions of the book and the actual facts of nature'. The novelist, who had been shown this passage before it appeared, conceded its justice in a private letter to the guidebook's editor, James Muirhead: 'If I had dreamed that it would ever be more than a book of the moment, the descriptions of scenery—which I know as well as I know my garden—would have been kept nearer to their fact. I romanced therein not to mislead any other, but solely for the uses of my story'. With this caution in mind we walk south from Malmshead on a track that quickly becomes a footpath following the course of Badgworthy Water. After a mile we pass a memorial erected by Blackmore's admirers in 1969, the centenary of the book's publication. The stream leading to the right has been identified with the 'slide of water' up which John Ridd struggles in Chapter 7. A further ½ mile brings us to the opening of the Doone Valley (right), as it is now known, a pleasant stretch of countryside and worth the walk but altogether milder than the scene described by Blackmore: 'a deep green valley, carved from out the mountains in a perfect oval, with a fence of sheer rock standing round it, eighty feet or a hundred high; from whose brink black wooded hills swept up to the sky-line' (Ch. 4).

There is a memorial to Blackmore in Exeter cathedral, at the W end of the nave, unveiled at the beginning of this century by another popular Devonian writer, Eden Phillpotts.

Blackmore's minor novels, eclipsed to his great annoyance by the success of *Lorna Doone*, often make similar use of places with which he had been familiar since boyhood. *The Maid of Sker* has as its setting the Elizabethan Sker House on the south Welsh coast NW of Porthcawl, near the home of his mother's family. Oxford is the centre of another area he knew well. He was born in the pleasant village of Longworth, 12 miles SW of the city and north of A420, where his father was curate-in-charge. The Old Rectory, part 16C and part Georgian, still stands. Though his mother's death took him away from Longworth when he was four months old, he returned to stay with relatives at Elsfield, 5 miles north of Oxford on a sideroad leading from A40. *Cripps the Carrier* is partly set in Beckley, 2 miles NE of Elsfield beyond B4027. The rest of the novel takes place in Oxford and includes a brief description of the May morning service held on the tower of Magdalen College (Vol. 2, Ch. 14). Blackmore was an undergraduate at Exeter College (1843–47).

His poem *The Fate of Franklin* was written to help the erection of the statue in memory of the Arctic explorer (d. 1847) which now stands in the market place of Spilsby in Lincolnshire.

William Blake

b. London, 1757; d. London, 1827. *Poetical Sketches* (1783); *Songs of Innocence* (1789); *The Book of Thel* (1789); *The Marriage of Heaven and Hell* (1790); *The French Revolution* (1791); *America: A Prophecy* (1793); *Visions of the Daughters of Albion* (1793); *Songs of Experience* (1794); *Europe: A Prophecy* (1794); *The First Book of Urizen* (1794); *The Song of Los* (1795); *The Book of Ahania* (1795); *The Book of Los* (1795); *The Ghost of Abel* (1822).

London, evoked so powerfully in one of the best known *Songs of Experience*, now offers only scattered and fragmentary reminders of Blake's near-lifetime residence. He was baptised in Wren's St James's Church, rebuilt after bomb damage, on Jermyn Street south of Piccadilly. In Soho to the north a plaque by the junction of Broadwick (then Broad) Street and Marshall Street marks the site of his birthplace. Blake returned to the neighbourhood later in life, living on Poland Street (1785–91) and holding an exhibition of his engravings on Carnaby Street in 1810. His apprenticeship (1771–81), when he was already displaying all the characteristics of the eccentric prodigy, was served under the engraver James Basire in Great Queen Street, which continues Long Acre to the junction with Kingsway. His marriage in 1782 to Catherine Boucher, a solid and tolerant companion, took place south of the river in St Mary's, Battersea, reached by a right turn on Battersea Church Road after crossing Battersea Bridge. His last years were spent in the charming little Fountain Court, entered via Middle Temple Lane from the Strand near its junction with Fleet Street. When he visited Blake here the diarist Crabb Robinson found him

> at work engraving in a small bedroom, light, and looking out on a mean yard. Everything in the room squalid and indicating poverty, except himself. And there was a natural gentility about him, and an insensibility to the seeming poverty, which quite removed the impression. Besides, his linen was clean, his hand white, and his air quite unembarrassed when he begged me to sit down as if he were in a palace.

He is buried in the Nonconformist cemetery at Bunhill Fields, bounded by City Road and Bunhill Row in Finsbury. There is a memorial in the crypt (fee) of St Paul's Cathedral, whose 'high dome' witnessed the charity service in 'Holy Thursday', one of his *Songs of Innocence*. A bust by Epstein remembers him in Poets' Corner (fee) of Westminster Abbey, a building whose monuments he sketched as part of his training in Gothic when an apprentice.

The one, brief period of Blake's life outside London was eventful. From 1800 to 1803 he accepted the invitation of William Hayley, a mediocre poet but a good patron, to live in Felpham, now a suburb of Bognor Regis on the Sussex coast. His home here has since been renamed Blake's House. The stay came to an end when Blake turned a soldier out of his garden and provoked a charge of sedition. In 1804 he was tried and acquitted at nearby Chichester, in Grey Friars' Church in Priory Park; the medieval building is now the Guildhall Museum.

Guildhall Museum, Priory Park, Priory Road, Chichester, West Sussex: phone (0243) 784683.

George Borrow

b. Dumpling Green, Norfolk, 1803; d. Oulton Broad, Suffolk, 1881. *The Zincali: or An Account of the Gypsies in Spain* (1841); *The Bible in Spain: or The Journeys, Adventures and Imprisonments of an Englishman in an Attempt to Circulate the Scriptures in the Peninsula* (1843); *Lavengro, the Scholar, the Gypsy, the Priest* (1851); *The Romany Rye: A Sequel to Lavengro* (1857); *Wild Wales: Its People, Language and Scenery* (1862).

Borrow's life was itinerant, in childhood because of his father's different military postings and in adulthood because of the temperament that led him to seek 'roving adventure, becoming tinker, gypsy, postillion, ostler; associating with various kinds of people, chiefly of the lower classes' (Ch. 1 of the Appendix to *Romany Rye*). His real homeland, if the term retains any meaning in his case, was Eastern England. Despite his statement at the beginning of *Lavengro*, he seems to have been born not in East Dereham (16 miles west of Norwich via A47) but in Dumpling Green, a little village 1½ miles SE on B1135 where his mother's family lived. East Dereham, however, was certainly the home of his early years and he returned to it several times in the course of his childhood. *Lavengro* remembers it with special affection: 'I love to think on thee, pretty, quiet D——, thou pattern of an English country town, with thy clean but narrow streets branching out from thy modest market-place, with thine old-fashioned houses, with here and there a roof of venerable thatch' (Ch. 3). The town might now cause Borrow to modify this glowing praise a little, although it remains proud of its connection with William Cowper (q.v.), whom he revered as 'England's sweetest and most pious bard' (Ch. 3).

In 1810 the Borrows moved west to the camp for French prisoners from the Napoleonic Wars at Norman Cross, now marked by a dreary roundabout on the A1 south of Peterborough. Chapter 4 of *Lavengro* gives a fascinating account of the barracks and Chapter 5 describes his first encounter with gipsies in the nearby countryside. In 1813 the family came to Edinburgh, where they were quartered in the Castle. Borrow followed in the footsteps of Sir Walter Scott (q.v.) and became a pupil at the Royal High School.

His boyhood travels were completed by a brief spell in Ireland, a country that stimulated three of his greatest interests: horses, foreign languages and old buildings. At Templemore (south of Roscrea on N62 in Tipperary) he was struck by the profusion of ruined castles in the 'wild and thinly inhabited country'. Templemore itself has one, built by the Knights Templar, in its Priory Park and Chapter 11 of *Lavengro* describes an adventurous walk to, apparently, the ruins of Loughmoe Castle (15C–17C), left of N62 4 miles south.

By 1816 the Borrows had returned to Eastern England and settled permanently in Norwich. *Lavengro* praises it as a 'fine old city, perhaps the most curious specimen at present extant of the genuine old English town', a claim that could still be advanced today, and offers this panoramic description of its antiquities:

> Yes, there it spreads from north to south, with its venerable houses, its numerous gardens, its thrice twelve churches, its mighty mound, which, if tradition speaks true, was raised by human hands to serve as the grave heap of an old heathen king, who sits deep within it, with his sword in his hand and his gold and silver treasures about him. There is an old grey castle on top of that mighty mound; and yonder, rising three hundred feet above the soil, from among those noble forest trees, behold that old Norman master-work,

> that cloud-encircled cathedral spire around which a garrulous army of rooks and choughs continually wheel their flight. Now, who can wonder that the children of that fine old city are proud of her, and offer up prayers for her prosperity? (Ch. 14)

Borrow attended the Grammar School in the Cathedral Close during the years when the Norwich painter John Crome the elder ('Old Crome') was a drawing instructor. The family home stands on Willow Lane, reached by following Giles Street west from the Market Place. At the Tombland Easter Fair, then held on open ground south of the Castle, he again met the gipsy whom he called 'Jasper Petulengro' (Ch. 16) and went with him to visit the gipsy encampment on Mousehold Heath, NE of the city centre and reached via Magdalen Street and Sprowston Road (Ch. 17).

Borrow left Norwich in 1824, first to work as a hack writer in London and then to embark on the nomadic adventures in England and abroad which his books celebrate in romantic fashion. His habit of exaggeration, reticence about exact locations and waywardness with dates all make it difficult to deduce an itinerary from his writings, but two places described in *Romany Rye* stand out. In 1825 Borrow came to the pleasant county town of Stafford (by M6 25 miles NW of Birmingham) and worked as head ostler at the Swan Inn on Greengate Street—'a place of infinite life and bustle' (Chs 23–29). He left the Swan when he discovered that 'there was little poetry in keeping an account of the corn, hay and straw which came in, and was given out, and I was fond of poetry'. Later the same year he arrived at Horncastle in Lincolnshire (21 miles east of Lincoln on A158) for the August horse fair (Ch. 37) and correctly decided that the town 'offered no object worthy of attention but its church'. Chapter 43 of *Romany Rye* has an amusing account of a tour of the building with a guide who is more interested in horses than architecture but remembers to point out the scythe blades traditionally said to have been used against Cromwell's army at the Battle of Winceby.

After his marriage in 1840 Borrow gravitated again to Eastern England and his wife's home at Oulton Broad near the Suffolk coast 2 miles west of Lowestoft. The house where he wrote most of his books and lived intermittently until death has gone, though his presence in the area is remembered in the church at Oulton, 1 mile north. In 1853–55 he took lodgings in the seaside resort of Great Yarmouth (10 miles north of Lowestoft via A12). *Romany Rye* was finished at No. 169 King Street.

Of his later travels the most important is his sixteen-week visit to Wales in the autumn of 1854, partly a tour with his wife and stepdaughter Henrietta and partly a series of solitary walking expeditions. Its best record is his own *Wild Wales*. The book is still an excellent traveller's companion, being unusual among Borrow's British books for its precise itinerary and unusual among books about Wales for its passionate—though at times uncritical and unscholarly—interest in Welsh language, literature and history.

A few highlights from Borrow's journey may be selected. He began his tour of north Wales at Wrexham (11 miles SW of Chester via A483), 'a Welsh town, but its appearance is not Welsh' (Ch. 5). He praised the fine exterior of the church of St Giles, the main interest of the town for visitors, but was unimpressed by its interior. Llangollen (10 miles SW of Wrexham via A483 and A5) served as a base for various expeditions. He seems to have been disappointed by Plas Newydd (south of A5), for his account in Chapter 10 is sketchy, but on his return to the area he records local memories of the eccentric

'Ladies of Llangollen' in Chapter 51. Chapter 13 describes Valle Crucis Abbey (1½ miles NW on A542) and Chapter 54 describes Chirk Castle (8 miles SE of Llangollen via A5 and sideroad). Borrow found the latter building 'a mansion ancient and beautiful and abounding with all kinds of agreeable and romantic associations'. His interest in the Welsh poet Huw Morris later took him west of the Castle to the Ceiriog Valley and the little village of Glyn Ceiriog (5 miles from Chirk via B4500). Elsewhere in north Wales Borrow climbed Snowdon (46 miles west of Llangollen via A5 and A4086) with Henrietta. Chapter 29 records how he recited a Welsh poem on the summit to the 'grinning scorn' of other English tourists and the mild confusion of a Welshman, who mistook him for a Breton.

Borrow's account of south Wales provides at least one memorable moment when he arrives at the town of Neath (on A465 8 miles NE of Swansea):

> I had surmounted a hill, and had nearly descended that side of it which looked towards the east, having on my left, that is to the north, a wooded height, when an extraordinary scene presented itself to my eyes. Somewhat to the south rose immense stacks of chimneys surrounded by grimy diabolical-looking buildings, in the neighbourhood of which were huge heaps of cinders and black rubbish. From the chimneys, notwithstanding it was Sunday, smoke was proceeding in volumes, choking the atmosphere all around. From this pandemonium, at the distance of about a quarter of a mile to the south-west, upon a green meadow, stood, looking darkly grey, a ruin of vast size with window holes, towers, spires and arches. Between it and the accursed pandemonium, lay a horrid filthy place, part of which was swamp and part pool: the pool black as soot, and the swamp of a disgusting leaden colour. Across this place of filth stretched a tramway leading from the abominable mansions to the ruin. So strange a scene I had never beheld in nature. (Ch. 102)

With the rise of industry at Neath in the 18C the Abbey had been used as a forge. Traces of this fate are still apparent today.

Though he died at his Suffolk home Borrow was buried in London. He lies next to his wife Mary (d. 1869) among the lavish and respectable monuments of the Brompton Cemetery, between Old Brompton Road and Fulham Road in Kensington. This inappropriate resting place is explained by the fact that in 1860 they had come to live nearby at No. 22 Hereford Square, west of Gloucester Road; Borrow remained at the address, now marked with a plaque, after his wife's death until returning to Suffolk in 1874.

Edinburgh Castle: Historic Buildings and Monuments, Scottish Development Department; phone the enquiry desk in Edinburgh, (031) 244 3101.

Plas Newydd Museum, Hill Street, Llangollen, Clwyd: phone (082 42) 2201. Be careful not to confuse this property with Plas Newydd on the Isle of Anglesey.

Valle Crucis Abbey, Llangollen, Clwyd: Cadw: Welsh Historic Monuments; phone (0978) 860326.

Chirk Castle, Chirk, Clwyd: NT; phone (0691) 777701.

Neath Abbey, Neath, West Glamorgan: Cadw: Welsh Historic Monuments; phone headquarters in Cardiff, (0222) 465511.

Anne, Charlotte and Emily Brontë

Anne Brontë: b. Thornton, West Yorkshire, 1820; d. Scarborough, North Yorkshire, 1849. *Agnes Grey* (1847); *The Tenant of Wildfell Hall* (1848).

Charlotte Brontë: b. Thornton, 1816; d. Haworth, West Yorkshire, 1855. *Jane Eyre* (1847); *Shirley* (1849); *Villette* (1853); *The Professor* (1857).

Emily Brontë: b. Thornton, 1818; d. Haworth, 1848. *Wuthering Heights* (1847).

Jointly published: *Poems by Currer, Ellis and Acton Bell* (1846). Related reading: Elizabeth Gaskell (q.v.), *The Life of Charlotte Brontë* (1857).

Few literary legends have proved as enduringly popular as the Brontë legend, familiar in its general outline or at least its atmosphere even to those who have not read the novels. And few have been as precisely localised. When Elizabeth Gaskell, the first and still the best biographer of Charlotte Brontë, announced that she had visited all the places connected with her subject's life except 'two small private governess-ships' she was pointing the way to future pilgrims. Certain landmarks were given authority when Ellen Nussey, Charlotte's friend since their schooldays, advised the illustrator Edmund Morison Wimperis about the real locations of fictional places for the 1872–73 edition of the Brontës' work. Today, the 'Brontë Country' looms large on the tourist map of England, making up for its smallness by the intensity of its cultivation.

Its natural centre is Haworth in West Yorkshire, encircled to the east by the larger industrial centres of Huddersfield, Halifax, Leeds, Bradford and Keighley and to the west by Haworth and Keighley Moors. When the Brontë family arrived in 1820 it was a small worsted weaving town of 4600 people; by 1840 the population had risen to slightly over 6000. Its high, remote situation, seen on the approach from Keighley, was well described by Mrs Gaskell. The town comes into view

> on the side of a pretty steep hill, with a background of dun and purple moors, rising and sweeping away yet higher than the church, which is built at the summit of the long narrow street. All round the horizon there is this same line of sinuous wave-like hills; the scoops into which they fall only revealing other hills beyond, of similar colour and shape, crowned with wild, bleak moors.

We climb Main Street, still paved as it was in the novelists' day with the local millstone grit. On the left at the top we find the Black Bull Inn, favourite haunt of Branwell Brontë (1817–48), whose alcoholism thwarted his artistic career but left behind a colourful legend to serve as tributary to the story of his sisters. Beyond lies the first of Haworth's two major points of interest: the Church of St Michael and All Angels, of which Patrick Branwell Brontë (1777–1861), long-lived father of the family, was incumbent. In fact, the building is greatly changed since his time, restoration of 1879–81 having swept away all but the original tower. Inside, a plaque marks the site of the family vault where all the Brontës except Anne were buried. Matthew Arnold (q.v.) wrote his poem of tribute, 'Haworth Churchyard', in the belief that the sisters were buried outdoors, and told Mrs Gaskell when she corrected him: 'It really seems to me to put the finishing touch to the strange cross-grained character of the fortunes of that ill-fated family that they should even be placed after death in the wrong, uncongenial spot'.

A lane leads left from Main Street to the *Brontë Parsonage Museum, the home to which Patrick Brontë brought his wife, Maria, and their six children. Mrs Brontë soon died, in 1821, and was followed in 1825 by the two eldest daughters, Maria (b. 1814) and Elizabeth (b. 1815). The remaining children—Anne, Charlotte, Emily and Branwell—were brought up by an aunt, Elizabeth Branwell, for whom they never developed great fondness, and the housekeeper Tabitha ('Tabby') Aykroyd, source of those local tales which stimulated their imagination and found their way into later writing. Despite being sent away to school and to work as governesses, the sisters always returned to the Parsonage and wrote all their novels here. Charlotte remained even after her late, surprising marriage in 1854 to her father's curate, Arthur Bell Nicholls, a match vigorously opposed by the old Mr Brontë.

Built in 1788-89, the heavy stone Parsonage was extended in the 1860s. The Brontë Society, founded in 1893 and for some time limited to a room above the Yorkshire Bank in the Main Street, acquired the building in 1927 and opened it as a museum the following year; since then it has become second only to Shakespeare's Birthplace in its popularity. The Parsonage has been refurbished in the style of the early nineteenth century and the simple manner preferred by the Brontës, though its atmosphere suffers from the large crowds of visitors it regularly attracts. Of special note is the Bonnell room with its collection of tiny notebooks filled with the daydreams, fantasies and sagas which played so important a role in the Brontës' childhood.

The sisters' otherwise enclosed and restricted life had little connection with the town of Haworth itself but much to do with the *moors that lie to the west. Charlotte wrote:

> My sister Emily ... loved the moors ... They were far more to her than a mere spectacle; they were what she lived in & by, as much as the wild birds, their tenants, or the heather, their produce ... She found in the bleak solitude many and dear delights; and not the least and best loved was—liberty.

A favourite walk leads west from the Parsonage Museum along the course of Sladen Beck, tributary of the River Worth, to the Bridge and Waterfall that now bear the Brontës' name (2 miles). Charlotte came here with her husband in November 1854: 'I had often wished to see it in its winter power—so we walked on. It was fine indeed; a perfect torrent racing over the rocks, white and beautiful! It began to rain while we were watching it, and we returned home under a streaming sky'. Her resulting cold precipitated the illness from which she died the following March.

Hardy walkers, who will need one of the local maps available from the Museum, will also wish to venture further across the moors to see several buildings associated with the novels. The location, though not the exact appearance, of the ruined Top Withens (or High or Far Withens) suggested Heathcliff's residence in *Wuthering Heights*. 'Wuthering', the narrator Lockwood explains, is

> a significant provincial adjective, descriptive of the atmospheric tumult to which its station is exposed in stormy weather. Pure, bracing weather they must have had up there at all times, indeed: one may guess the power of the north wind, blowing over the edge, by the excessive slant of a few stunted firs at the end of the house; and by a range of gaunt thorns stretching their limbs one way, as if craving alms of the sun. Happily, the architect had foresight to build it strong; the narrow windows are deeply set in the wall, and the corners defended with large jutting stones. (Ch. 1)

Ponden Hall may have suggested 'Thrushcross Grange', the altogether more civilised home of the Lintons in the same novel. Wycoller Hall is traditionally identified with 'Ferndean Manor', where Rochester lives in *Jane Eyre* after the fire has destroyed

The Brontë waterfall by Edmund Morison Wimperis in the 1872–73 edition of the Brontës' works

'Thornfield Hall'; it is hard to detect any resemblance from the present ruins.

Though they are too dispersed to be organised into a single tour, other parts of the North and north Midlands connected with the Brontës can be visited from Haworth. The nearest place is Thornton, on B6145 4 miles west of Bradford and now absorbed into the suburbs of that city, where Patrick Brontë brought his wife in the early years of their marriage. A plaque on the modest house in

Market Street, off High Street, marks the birthplace of his famous children. Patrick Brontë's wedding had taken place in the interesting Norman church at Guiseley, 5 miles north of Bradford on the way to Otley, in 1812.

In the area round Halifax, 8 miles south of Thornton via B6145 and A629, we can find several points of interest. The weaving village of Luddenden (off A646 3½ miles west of Halifax) is connected with Branwell, who was appointed railway clerk at Luddenden Foot in 1841, though he was dismissed the following year when inspection of the accounts revealed that some £11 were missing. The Lord Nelson Inn at Luddenden was the scene of what he called the 'cold yet malignant debauchery' of his heavy drinking. Emily's post as governess in a girls' boarding school at Law Hill (1838) brought her near to Shibden Hall, 1 mile east of Halifax. The fine timber-framed house may have contributed to the description of 'Thrushcross Grange' in *Wuthering Heights*. (Its outbuildings now contain the Folk Museum of West Yorkshire.) Nearby High Sunderland, which may have suggested the fancifully carved frontage of Heathcliff's home, has been demolished.

The area round Birstall, about 10 miles east of Halifax, is closely associated with Charlotte Brontë's *Shirley*. She often visited her friends Mary and Martha Taylor at the 18C Red House in Gomersal, making them the Yorkes and the house 'Briarmains' in the novel. The building is now a museum furnished in the style of the early 19C. In Birstall, where Ellen Nussey lived, the Elizabethan Oakwell Hall served as the model for Shirley's home in the book:

> If Fieldhead had few other merits as a building, it might at least be termed picturesque: its irregular architecture, and the grey and mossy colouring communicated by time, gave it a just claim to this epithet. The old latticed windows, the stone porch, the walls, the roof, the chimney-stacks, were rich in crayon touches and sepia lights and shades. (Ch. 11)

Further afield from Haworth is Cowan Bridge, reached by travelling 8 miles NE of Keighley to join A65 at Skipton and continuing another 30 miles NE. Charlotte and Emily entered the Rev. William Carus Wilson's Clergy Daughters' School in 1824 but were taken away in 1825 after their older sisters Elizabeth and Maria had died of typhus contracted at the institution. Charlotte reacted against the harsh Evangelical regime of the school with passionate resentment. In *Jane Eyre* it became 'Lowood' and Rev. Wilson was transformed into Mr Brocklehurst, while Maria's death suggested the death of Helen Burns. These episodes stirred a controversy that was again inflamed by Mrs Gaskell's charges against Cowan Bridge in her biography. The school's surviving building stands just north of the Leck and is marked by a tablet. *Jane Eyre* also gives a vivid and only lightly fictionalised account of the Sunday journey to hear Rev. Wilson preach in his church at Tunstall, 2 miles SW of Cowan Bridge on A683:

> Sundays were dreary days in that winter season. We had to walk two miles to Brocklebridge Church, where our patron officiated. We set out cold, we arrived at church colder: during the morning service we became almost paralysed. It was too far to return to dinner, and an allowance of cold meat and bread, in the same penurious proportion observed in our ordinary meals, was served round between the services.
>
> At the close of the afternoon service we returned by an exposed and hilly road, where the bitter wind, blowing over a range of snowy summits to the north, almost flayed the skin from our faces. (Ch.7)

In 1833, after the Brontës' connection with the school had been severed, it was moved to Casterton (3 miles NE of Cowan Bridge on A683), where the Old Hall was Rev. Wilson's home.

Also to the north of the Haworth–Keighley area is *Norton Conyers. This mainly 17C country house stands 4 miles north of Ripon and is reached by following A61 before branching left towards Wath. Charlotte paid a visit, probably in 1839 when she was working as a governess in the area, saw its third-storey attics and heard the Graham family legend that a madwoman had been confined in them during the 18C. The connection with *Jane Eyre* is obvious.

In May 1849, shortly after Emily's death, Charlotte and Ellen Nussey took Anne to Scarborough on Yorkshire's east coast. She died only three days after their arrival at the resort, in lodgings on a site now occupied by the Grand Hotel, and was buried in the detached churchyard of St Mary's on Castle Road above the harbour.

An earlier connection with Hathersage, on A625 in the High Peaks between Manchester and Sheffield, had important results for Charlotte's fiction. She came here to visit Ellen Nussey at the home of her friend's brother, Henry, who had once proposed to her. The 15C Eyre brasses in the church, striking enough in their own right, must surely have suggested the surname of her most famous heroine. Hathersage is also identified with the 'Morton' of *Jane Eyre*, where Jane meets St John Rivers (Ch. 28ff.). This section of the novel certainly draws on Charlotte's impressions of Peak District scenery. In Manchester itself, Charlotte was several times a guest at the Plymouth Grove home of Mrs Gaskell, described more fully under the entry for that novelist.

Emily never visited London and Anne stayed in the city only briefly. After the great success of *Jane Eyre*, however, Charlotte made an extended visit whose best-remembered episode was an unsuccessful evening at the Kensington home of Thackeray, dealt with under the entry devoted to him. Thackeray's daughter described the occasion:

> The room looked very dark, the lamp began to smoke a little, the conversation grew dimmer and more dim, the ladies sat round still expectant, my father was much too perturbed by the gloom and the silence to be able to cope with it at all. Mrs Brookfield, who was in the doorway by the study, near the corner in which Miss Brontë was sitting, leant forward with a little commonplace, since brilliance was not to be the order of the evening. 'Do you like London, Miss Brontë?' she said; another silence, a pause, then Miss Brontë answers, 'Yes and No', very gravely.

All three sisters are commemorated in Poets' Corner (fee) of Westminster Abbey.

Brontë Parsonage, Haworth, near Keighley, West Yorkshire: phone (0535) 42323.

Shibden Hall (and Folk Museum of West Yorkshire), Halifax, West Yorkshire: phone (0422) 52246.

Red House Museum, Oxford Road, Gomersal, West Yorkshire: phone Cleckheaton (0274) 872165.

Oakwell Hall, Nutter Lane, Birstall, West Yorkshire: phone Batley (0924) 474926.

Norton Conyers, near Ripon, North Yorkshire: phone Melmerby (076 584) 333.

Rupert Brooke

b. Rugby, Warwickshire, 1887; d. Aegean Sea, 1915. *Poems* (1911); *1914 and Other Poems* (1915); *John Webster and the Elizabethan Drama* (1916); *Letters from America* (1916); *Collected Poems* (edited by Edward Marsh; 1918).

Brooke was born in Rugby at No. 5 Hillmorton Road, near the public school where his father taught. He himself entered the school as a pupil in 1901.

In Cambridge the legend of Rupert Brooke still has potency even for tourists indifferent to poetry. It typifies youth in all its carefree innocence and energy, and is made the more poignant by his early death during the First World War. In the city itself the chief point of interest is King's College, where Brooke started his undergraduate career in 1906. His rooms were on A Staircase and then E Staircase in the Fellows' Building opposite the main entrance. His name is recorded on the war memorial in the sidechapel south of the altar in the Chapel. Yet the spot most intimately connected with Brooke is the village of Grantchester (2½ miles SW), where he lived while studying for the Fellowship at King's he was awarded in 1912. It can be reached by following the Trumpington Road and turning right in Trumpington, but the most pleasant approach is the walk from Grantchester Street (beyond the junction of Newnham Road and Fen Causeway) through the meadows that skirt the river. Brooke is remembered on the war memorial in the little church. He lodged at The Orchard from July 1909 to December 1910, when he moved to

Rupert Brooke in the garden of the old Vicarage, Grantchester

the Old Vicarage nearby—a building which gave him the title for his most famous poem, a half-ironic, half-sentimental tribute to Grantchester's typically English charm.

Sir Thomas Browne

b. London, 1605; d. Norwich, Norfolk, 1682. *Religio Medici* (1642); *Pseudodoxia Epidemica: or Enquiries into Very Many Received Tenents and Commonly Presumed Truths Which Examined Prove But Vulgar and Common Errors* (1646); *Hydriotaphia, Urne-Buriall: or A Discourse of the Sepulchrall Urnes Lately Found in Norfolk; Together With the Garden of Cyrus: or the Quincunciall Lozenge, or Network Plantations of the Ancients, Artificially, Naturally, Mystically Considered* (1658); *A Letter to a Friend, Upon Occasion of the Death of His Intimate Friend* (1690); *Christian Morals* (1716).

Browne's education began in Hampshire at Winchester College. It was continued in Oxford at Broadgates Hall, refounded under its present name of Pembroke College during his undergraduate career (1623–26).

After studying medicine on the Continent he established his practice at Norwich in 1636. It remained his home until death; indeed, there is no evidence to suggest that he again left East Anglia. This fixity did not restrict the scope of his writings, in which he combined the roles of scientist, antiquary and moralist, or the fame they brought him. In 1671 he was knighted by Charles II at Blackfriars Hall on St Andrew's Street, once the nave of a Dominican church but used as a civic meeting place since the Reformation. In October the same year he was visited by John Evelyn (q.v.), diarist and like Browne a Fellow of the Royal Society, who found his house near St Peter Mancroft in the Market Place 'a Paradise & Cabinet of rarities, & that of the best collection, especially Medails, books, Plants, natural things'. Browne took his guest on a tour of 'all the remarkeable places of this ancient Citty' and Evelyn was 'much astonish'd' to see 'buildings of flint, so exquisitely headed & Squared'. Browne was buried in the noble church of St Peter Mancroft, which has a memorial in the chancel and a statue of him outside.

Winchester College, College Street, Winchester, Hampshire: phone the Bursar, (0962) 64242.

St Andrew's and Blackfriars' Halls, St Andrew's Street, Norwich, Norfolk: phone (0603) 628477.

Robert and Elizabeth Barrett Browning

Robert Browning: b. London, 1812; d. Venice, Italy, 1889. *Pauline: A Fragment of a Confession* (1833); *Paracelsus* (1835); *Strafford: An Historical Tragedy* (1837); *Sordello* (1840); *Pippa Passes* (1841); *Dramatic Lyrics* (1842); *A Blot in the 'Scutcheon: A Tragedy in Five Acts* (1843); *Dramatic Romances and Lyrics* (1845); *Men and Women* (1855); *Dramatis Personae* (1864); *The Ring and the Book* (1868–69); *Balaustion's Adventure* (1871); *Prince Hohenstiel-Schwangau, Saviour of Society* (1871); *Fifine at the Fair* (1872); *Red Cotton Night-Cap Country; or Turf and Towers* (1873); *Aristophanes' Apology* (1875); *The Inn Album* (1875); *Pacchiarotto and How He Worked in Distemper; with Other Poems* (1876); *Dramatic Idyls* (First Series, 1879; Second Series, 1880); *Parleyings with Certain People of Importance in Their Day* (1887).

Elizabeth Barrett Browning: b. Coxhoe Hall, County Durham, 1806; d. Florence, Italy, 1861. *Sonnets from the Portuguese* (1850); *Casa Guidi Windows: A Poem* (1851); *Aurora Leigh* (1857); *Poems Before Congress* (1860); *Last Poems* (1862).

To his friend and contemporary Henry James (q.v.), Browning was, 'with all his Italianisms and cosmopolitanisms, ... a magnificent example of the best and least dilettantish English spirit'. Yet his life, and that of Elizabeth Barrett Browning, belonged only intermittently to England. Their best memorials are in Florence at Casa Guidi, where they lived from 1848 until her death in 1861, and at Elizabeth's elaborate tomb in the Protestant cemetery. England can offer nothing so magnificent by way of rivalry. Camberwell, the scene of Browning's early years, has changed too drastically from the pleasantly leafy south London suburb that Browning knew to repay a visit. The country houses where the young Elizabeth Barrett lived before her father's decline in fortune have vanished or been altered. Her connection with the south Devon coastal resort of Torquay is better remembered. A plaque at the Regina Hotel (then Bath House) on Beacon Terrace records her convalescent stay in 1838–41.

In London, Marylebone has a rich little cluster of places associated mainly with the crucial years when the two poets met and married. A convenient tour begins at Baker Street Underground Station (Bakerloo, Circle, Metropolitan and Jubilee Lines). We take the Marylebone Road westward and turn left on to Gloucester Place. A plaque at No. 99 (then No. 74) marks the house where Elizabeth and her family first lived in London (1835–38). It was not a congenial environment for a semi-invalid and a letter recording her first impressions describes the city as a 'dungeon' and 'wrapped up like a mummy, in a yellow mist, so closely that I have had scarcely a glimpse of its countenance since we came'. From Gloucester Place we follow Dorset Street to the left. In the summer of 1855 Robert and Elizabeth took lodgings at No. 13, now rebuilt, while he prepared *Men and Women* for publication and she fell under the influence of Daniel Dunglas Home, the fashionable medium. Tennyson (q.v.) came on a memorable evening in September to read *Maud* aloud to the assembled company and be covertly sketched by Rossetti (q.v.) as he did so; Robert responded by reading 'Fra Lippo Lippi'. At the end of Dorset Street we follow Manchester Street, turn left on Blandford Street and cross Marylebone High Street to New Cavendish Street.

This quickly brings us to Wimpole Street and the most famous English address in the Brownings' lives. No. 50, to the left, has been rebuilt but the solidly respectable Georgian façades of the surviving houses in the street preserve the atmosphere Elizabeth found when she came to live here in 1838. Robert paid his first visit in May 1845 and found her leading an enclosed existence in a third-floor bedroom, surrounded by busts and engraved portraits of writers, including himself. The story of their courtship is well known, with Robert coaxing her out of invalidism and Elizabeth gaining the strength to oppose her selfish, tyrannical father. The couple were secretly married in September 1846 at *St Marylebone, which now has a Browning room containing relics. To reach the early 19C church we follow Wimpole Street and its continuation north to the Marylebone Road, where it lies almost immediately to our left, opposite the York Gate to Regent's Park. In a letter written shortly after the ceremony Elizabeth described how her thoughts turned to the other brides who had stood in St Marylebone: 'Not one of them all perhaps, not one perhaps, since that building was a church, has had reasons strong as mine, for an absolute trust and devotion towards the man she married—not one!' She went back only briefly to Wimpole Street before leaving for Italy with her husband.

We may extend this tour by returning to Marylebone Station and taking the Bakerloo Line to Warwick Avenue Underground Station. By following Warwick Avenue south, turning right on Blomfield Road and then crossing the canal we reach Little Venice, the picturesque waterside area where Browning lived from the time of Elizabeth's death in 1861 until 1887. No. 19 Warwick Crescent, the narrow white-stuccoed house he filled with furniture from Casa Guidi, was demolished soon after he moved away but its approximate site is marked by a modern bas-relief. Here he wrote *The Ring and the Book*, blossomed from a widower's seclusion into the active social life at which Henry James marvelled, and submitted to being lionised by the Browning Society.

From Little Venice Browning went to live in Kensington at No. 29 De Vere Gardens, south of Kensington High Street almost opposite the Palace Gate to Kensington Gardens. Henry James was a neighbour.

It was James, too, whose essay in *English Hours* offered appropriate reflections on Browning's burial in Westminster Abbey, taking pleasure in the thought that so modern a writer should rest with the classics in 'the great temple of fame of the English race'. Browning is commemorated by a stone next to Tennyson's in Poets' Corner (fee).

Browning was not conspicuous for his travels inside the British Isles but a visit to Wales in the summer of 1886 was notable. He stayed at Llangollen, Clwyd, to be near his friend Lady Martin, formerly Helen Faucit the actress. The church at Llantysilio, off A5 2 miles NW of Llangollen and near Valle Crucis Abbey, has a plaque put up by Lady Martin to commemorate his worship there.

'Mr Robert Browning taking tea with the Browning Society', by Max Beerbohm

John Bunyan

b. Elstow, Bedfordshire, 1628; d. London, 1688. *Grace Abounding to the Chief of Sinners* (1666); *The Pilgrim's Progress* (1678–84); *The Life and Death of Mr Badman* (1680); *The Holy War* (1682).

Bunyan's life was rooted in Bedford and its surrounding area, that fertile breeding ground of 17C Puritanism.

The site of the humble cottage where he was born, now marked with a stone, is in rough country near the village of Elstow, on A6 1 mile south of the county town. It is best approached by quitting Bedford in the direction of Harrowden, then branching south on the old country lane that almost immediately crosses a railway line; a footpath leading through fields to the birthplace is indicated by a signpost. In Elstow itself the heavily restored Norman church of St Mary and St Helen, where Bunyan's parents were buried, preserves the octagonal Perpendicular font in which he was baptised and the pulpit from which some of the sermons that first stirred his religious conscience were delivered. Windows of 1880 at the east end of the north and south aisles depict scenes from *The Pilgrim's Progress* and *The Holy War*. The church is also notable for its detached tower whose bells Bunyan as a young man took 'much delight in ringing, but my Conscience beginning to be tender, I thought that such a practice was but vain, and therefore forced myself to leave it' (*Grace Abounding*, Section 33). As his qualms grew stronger he developed the fear that first the bells and then the tower itself might fall on him. *Grace Abounding* also records a rebuke to Sunday amusements, which took place on the village green:

> As I was in the midst of a game at Cat, and having struck it one blow from the hole; just as I was about to strike it the second time, a voice did suddenly dart from Heaven into my Soul, which said, *Wilt thou leave thy sins, and go to Heaven? or have thy sins, and go to Hell*? At this I was put to an exceeding maze; wherefore, leaving my Cat upon the ground, I looked up to Heaven, and was as if I had with the eyes of my understanding, seen the Lord Jesus looking down upon me, as being very hotly displeased with me, and as if he did severely threaten me with some grievous punishment for these, and other my ungodly practices. (Section 22)

On one side of the green stands the *Moot Hall of c 1500, a fine half-timbered building with an overhanging upper storey. It is now a Museum whose collection illustrates Bunyan's life and times.

Houghton House, off B530 6 miles south of Bedford and near Ampthill, a now ruined but still elegant Jacobean mansion built for Mary, Countess of Pembroke and sister to Sir Philip Sidney (q.v.), is sometimes claimed as the original of 'House Beautiful' in the first part of *The Pilgrim's Progress*. Bunyan was arrested in 1660 near Harlington, 6 miles further south, on a charge of preaching without a licence. Harlington Manor House, home of the magistrate who issued the warrant, stands at the main crossing.

Bunyan's preaching took him to several other villages near Bedford. At Stevington, off A428 5 miles NW of Bedford, the village cross is sometimes identified with the one by which Christian shed his burden near the beginning of *The Pilgrim's Progress*, while its mill has been restored in Bunyan's memory.

In Bedford itself Bunyan carried on his family trade as tinker, preached and was imprisoned from his arrest in 1660 until the Declaration of Indulgence in 1672 and again for a shorter period of six months, probably in 1677. Despite a stubborn tradition that places him in the town gaol on the old bridge over the Ouse (now demolished), the scene of his ordeals and 'den' where he wrote *Grace Abounding* and the first part of *The Pilgrim's Progress* was in fact the County Gaol, which stood at the junction of Silver Street and the High Street. He is commemorated today by Boehm's statue of 1874 on St Peter's Green at the northern end of the High Street. On Mill Street to the east of the High Street the Bunyan Meeting of 1850 replaces the earlier building where he preached. The ten panels of its doors, made by Frederick Thrupp in 1876, are decorated with scenes from *The Pilgrim's Progress*. The adjoining Bunyan Museum contains relics.

Bunyan died while visiting London and was buried at Bunhill Fields in Finsbury, a Nonconformist cemetery where Defoe, Blake (qq.v.) and the hymn writer Isaac Watts also lie. South of Old Street Underground Station (Northern Line; closed Sundays), it is bounded by Bunhill Row to the west and City Road to the east. According to Southey (s.v. Lake Poets), Bunyan's gravestone originally bore the inscription: 'The "Pilgrim's Progress" now is finished, And Death has laid him on his earthly bed'. It was replaced by a more elaborate monument with a recumbent statue of 1861 by E.C. Papworth, itself in turn restored in 1950 after war-time damage.

A stained glass window (1911) in the north transept of Westminster Abbey depicts episodes from *The Pilgrim's Progress*.

Moot Hall, Elstow, Bedfordshire: phone Bedford (0234) 228330

Houghton House, Ampthill, Bedfordshire: English Heritage, open at any reasonable time.

Museum of Bunyan Relics, Bunyan Meeting Free Church, 55 Mill Street, Bedford: phone (0234) 58075.

Fanny Burney (Madame d'Arblay)

b. King's Lynn, Norfolk, 1752; d. London, 1840. *Evelina* (1778); *Cecilia* (1782); *Camilla* (1796).

The charming town of King's Lynn, near the Wash, preserves both specific buildings connected with Fanny Burney and much of the atmosphere in which she spent her early years. There is, in fact, some doubt as to her exact birthplace: it may have been No. 84 High Street (now rebuilt) or, as one would prefer to believe, the older but still surviving St Augustine's on Chapel Street, near the Tuesday Market. She was certainly baptised at St Nicholas, north of Chapel Street, a chapel of ease worth a visit for its own sake. Her father, Dr Charles Burney, was organist at another fine church, St Margaret's by the Saturday Market. Although the family moved to London in 1760 she returned to King's Lynn throughout her childhood to stay with Mrs Stephen Allen, who became Dr Burney's second wife in 1766. Her lifelong habit of keeping a diary and her early attempts at writing, soon to issue in *Evelina*, date from these years. The novel was written at the Burneys' London home, on the site now occupied by the Westminster Reference Library in St Martin's Street, just south of Leicester Square.

The success of *Evelina*, never fully to be repeated, had many fortunate consequences for the novelist and at least one unfortunate one: the invitation from George III's queen to become Second Keeper of the Robes. Her diary records the lonely and frustrating years (1786–91) she spent in this capacity, first at Windsor Castle (west of London via M4 or A4) and then at Kew Palace (in the Royal Botanic Gardens at Kew). Her release from these irksome duties began a much happier period of her life, centred on the Surrey town of Mickleham, off A24 between Leatherhead and Dorking. She was already familiar with the area from visits to her sister, Susan, and to the Lockes of Norbury Park, a house half a mile west of the town with fine views. Juniper Hall (1 mile SE of Mickleham, altered by the Victorians and now a field-study centre) became in the 1790s a haven for French emigrés including Madame de Staël, Talleyrand and General d'Arblay, Fanny's future husband. The couple were married at the parish church of Mickleham, St Michael, in 1793. Camilla Cottage in nearby West Humble, designed by the General and named after the novel whose proceeds made its building possible, no longer remains, but the earlier house they rented in Great Bookham does: still called the Hermitage, it stands on the corner of East Street.

On their return to England after more than a decade spent in France, the d'Arblays went to Bath, living at No. 23 Great Stanhope Street from 1815. She had previously been a visitor to the fashionable resort, spending the summer of 1780 with the Thrales, friends of Dr Johnson (q.v.) at No. 14 South Parade. Her choice of Bath as a permanent home seems natural enough given the elegant and socially alert character of her fiction, but it was partly dictated by the money worries which continued to dog her even in married life:

> There is no place I have yet seen where the inconveniences of a limited fortune are so lightly felt, nor where the people at large are so civilised ... Equipage, servants, Table, Jewels, though *here* as everywhere, very desirable, are not *here* requisite. *Respect* does not hang either upon the lackey or the attire; and admission is as easy without the one, as reception is good or bad without the other. There is something nearer to independence from the shackles of fortuitous circumstances in the society of *Bath* than I have ever witnessed elsewhere.

The General, who died in 1818, was buried in the cemetery of St Swithin's on Walcot Street; his epitaph was written by his wife.

Fanny Burney was also buried at St Swithin's but she spent her long years of widowhood in London. No. 11 Bolton Street (north of Piccadilly in Mayfair), her home from 1818 until 1828, is marked by a plaque.

Windsor Castle, Windsor, Berkshire: phone (0753) 868286.

Kew Palace, Royal Botanic Gardens, Kew, Richmond-upon-Thames, Surrey: DoE monument; phone London (01) 940 3321.

Robert Burns

b. Alloway, Strathclyde Region, 1759; d. Dumfries, Dumfries and Galloway, 1796. *Poems, Chiefly in the Scottish Dialect* (1786; enlarged editions, 1787 and 1793); contributions to *The Scots Musical Museum* (edited by James Johnson; 1787–1803).

Burns' unofficial position as Scotland's national poet is not without its dangers. His formal schooling has often been ignored as detracting from the legend of the 'heaven-taught ploughman'; his sexual adventures, tangled and fascinating though they admittedly are, have been stressed and his political radicalism almost forgotten; and his early death has been proffered as an example of the dangers of drink, when it was really due to rheumatic fever aggravated by the wrong medical treatment. To a modern Scottish poet like Hugh MacDiarmid the Burns cult could seem a distraction from the writer's real achievement and, indeed, from the real potentialities of Scottish poetry: 'It has denied his spirit to honour his name ... It has preserved his furniture and repelled his message'. Yet this very full commemoration of scenes connected with Burns' life and poetry still offers the patient, and slightly sceptical, visitor a series of rewarding tours.

His early life was spent near the west coast of Scotland in the former county of Ayrshire, now assimilated into Strathclyde Region. We begin our first tour at Alloway, then an independent village but since overtaken by the suburbs of Ayr itself. The chief attraction is Burns Cottage, the low dwelling with whitewashed walls and thatched roof rebuilt by William Burnes (as the family name was spelled) when he came to live here in 1756. Robert, his eldest child, was born in it some three years later. In 1766 William moved south of the village to Mount Oliphant, where he established a family tradition of unsuccessful farming ventures that his son was later to maintain. The museum adjoining Burns Cottage displays a collection of relics.

Continuing south through the village we reach Alloway Kirk, already a ruin in Burns' time, where his most famous character, Tam o' Shanter, witnessed the witches' orgy. William Burnes, who died in 1784, is buried in the churchyard; the present headstone is the third on the site, the original one erected by the poet having been dismantled piecemeal by souvenir-hunting tourists. The modern Land o' Burns Centre opposite the church has an audio-visual show illustrating the poet's life; it is a recommended starting-point for the Burns Heritage Trail devised by the Scottish Tourist Board. Nearby is the Burns Monument of 1820, inappropriate in both its size and its Grecian style. Its gardens, where figures by the local self-taught sculptor James Thom depict characters from Burns' work, offer a good view of the Brig o' Doon, across which Tam o' Shanter escaped the pursuing witches.

B7024 leads south from Alloway to Maybole (6 miles), home of Burns' mother Agnes Broun, where A77 is taken an additional 4 miles to Kirkoswald. The poet came here to study mathematics and surveying under Hugh Rodger in 1775, though he later remembered the town in another light: 'The contraband trade was at the time very successful; scenes of swaggering riot and roaring dissipation were as yet new to me; and I was no enemy to social life ... I learned to look unconcernedly on a large tavern-bill, and mix without fear in a drunken squabble'. Its main surviving monument is the home of John Davidson, now called Souter Johnnie's Cottage after the name he is given in 'Tam o' Shanter'. It contains items from the time of Davidson's occupancy and a set of the tools used by a souter, or cobbler; in the garden we find more sculptures by James Thom, representing characters from Burns' poem. Davidson, Douglas Graham (the original for Tam o' Shanter) and relatives of Burns' mother, the Brouns, are buried in the churchyard nearby.

From Kirkoswald we cross to the coastal A719 and make the 14-mile journey to the centre of Ayr, where Burns attended grammar school and which was, according to 'Tam o' Shanter', unsurpassed 'For honest men and bonny lasses' (line 16). A walking tour begins outside the railway station, where he is commemorated by a statue of 1891. Alloway Street leads to the High Street where, on the right, we find the former Tam o' Shanter Inn, now a museum (but see note below). In Burns' day it was a brewhouse, supplied by Douglas Graham and so has commonly been identified as the starting-point of Tam o' Shanter's ride. Further up the High Street the little Kirk Port leads (right) to the 17C Auld Kirk, interesting in its own right but notable for the present purpose as the scene of Burns' baptism. From its churchyard we have a good view of the 13C Auld Brig and, beyond, the New Bridge of 1788 (rebuilt 1877); they are the speakers in Burns' dialogue poem, 'The Brigs of Ayr'.

We leave Ayr on A758 and B743 to the NE, turning left for Tarbolton (9 miles). The poet's connection with the town and its surrounding area began in 1777, when his father took the lease of Lochlea (or Lochlie) farm nearby, and was continued after William Burnes' death in 1784 when he and his brother Gilbert took the lease of Mossgiel farm, near Mauchline. In Tarbolton itself the main point of interest is the Bachelors' Club, originally a hall attached to the local inn. It was the meeting place for a debating and social society, formed in 1780, of which Burns was founder member and first president. According to the prospectus drafted by the poet, its purpose was 'to unite ourselves into a club or society under such rules and regulations that while we should forget our cares and labours in mirth and diversion, we might not transgress the bounds of innocence and decorum'. The Bachelors' Club was also probably the scene of Burns' initiation as a freemason.

Returning to B743 and continuing NE we come after 4 miles to the village of Failford. A monument near the bridge over the Ayr marks the place where Burns is reputed to have parted from his fiancée, Mary Campbell, in May 1786, only a few months before her death. She is the Highland Mary of 'The Highland Lassie O' and 'Will ye go to the Indies, my Mary?', while Burns remembered their last meeting in the lyric beginning 'Thou lingering Star with lessening ray'.

The little town of Mauchline, another 3 miles up B743, is particularly rich in its connections with Burns, who knew it well during his tenancy of Mossgiel farm and returned to it briefly in 1788 after his stay in Edinburgh. Most interesting perhaps is the house then owned by Gavin Hamilton, near the 15C Mauchline Tower. Hamilton was Burns' landlord and a leading supporter of the New Licht faction in its clashes with the traditional Calvinist beliefs of the Kirk; the poet's agreement with his views is shown by several vigorous satires, of which 'Holy Willie's Prayer' is the most famous. Mary Campbell worked as a nursemaid in Hamilton's household. Burns House in Castle Street was the writer's home after his long-delayed marriage in 1788 to Jean Armour, who had already borne his children. It is now a small museum with furnishings of the period. Mauchline's church has been rebuilt since the time when Burns was censured for his relations with Jean Armour and eventually celebrated his wedding to her, but its churchyard still contains the graves of four of his children, as well as the graves of Gavin Hamilton and William Fisher, the original Holy Willie. Poosie Nansie's Tavern opposite, still a pub, was 'well known to and much frequented by the lowest orders of Travellers and Pilgrims' and by Burns himself, as his superbly extravagant cantata, 'The Jolly Beggars', testifies.

North of Mauchline on A76 we find the Burns Memorial Tower. Mossgiel farm lies to the west.

A76 continues to Kilmarnock (9 miles) where Burns' first collection of poems was published by John Wilson in 1786. The event is remembered by the massive and regrettable Kay Park Monument of 1879, whose museum displays a copy of the Kilmarnock edition among other items.

The industrial town of Irvine, 8 miles west on A71, was the scene of Burns' brief career as a flax-dresser (1781–84), which ended when his premises burned down during New Year celebrations. The site of his lodgings on Glasgow Vennel is marked by a plaque put up by the Irvine Burns Club on its foundation in 1826. The Club's building in Eglinton Street contains a museum of relics and a mural depicting the poet's life in the town. Near the river on the northern part of the town moor we find a bronze statue by J. Pittendreigh MacGillvray, unveiled by the Poet Laureate, Alfred Austin, in 1896.

Encouraged by the strongly favourable reception of the Kilmarnock edition, Burns came to Edinburgh in 1786. Apart from the Highland travels on which he gathered traditional songs for James Johnson's *The Scots Musical Museum*, he remained there until 1788. He was lionised by the literary society of the day, impressing the young Sir Walter Scott (q.v.) by his 'dignified plainness and simplicity', but was sceptical of such passing popularity and did not find the atmosphere of the city conducive to poetry. The opening of his address to the capital, 'Edina! *Scotia*'s darling seat!', shows how uncongenial he found its conventional literary language.

A walking tour begins on Lawnmarket. At the junction with Lady Stair's Close a plaque marks the site of his first lodgings, on what was then Baxter's Close. The 17C Lady Stair's House is now a museum devoted to Burns, Sir Walter Scott and Robert Louis Stevenson (qq.v.). Its Burns memorabilia include the stool from the office of his publisher, Smellie, which he used while correcting proofs for the second edition of his poems. Lawnmarket continues eastward, becoming High Street and then Canongate. Canongate Cemetery has the grave of the Scots poet Robert Fergusson (1750–74), whose last Edinburgh years were spent in depression, drinking and madness; Burns' commemorative poem calls him 'my elder brother in Misfortune, By far my elder Brother in the muse'. Burns was also responsible for erecting Fergusson's monument in 1787, though he was unable to pay the bill until 1792. The tour ends by following Tolbooth Wynd at the side of the cemetery to Regent Road. On its southern side we find the Burns Monument of 1830.

For the last years of his life Burns lived in the Dumfries area, south of his native Ayrshire. In 1788 he leased Ellisland farm off A76 4½ miles NW of Dumfries but ran into financial difficulties, worsened by his refusal to accept payment for the contributions he was continuing to make to Johnson's *Scots Musical Museum*. He was forced to take on part-time work as an exciseman and then, in 1791, to give up the farm altogether. Ellisland has been preserved as a museum of Burns relics and farming life.

After the failure at Ellisland, Burns and his wife moved to the busy town of *Dumfries, where he worked as an exciseman, offending local opinion by his radical sympathies with the French Revolution and leaving behind him a reputation, much exaggerated, for heavy drinking. A convenient tour begins at the Burns statue on the northern part of the High Street near Greyfriars Church. Walking south, we pass on our right the turning for Bank Street, formerly Wee Vennel but called 'Stinking Vennel' by Burns when he lodged there in a three-room flat from 1791 to 1793. Farther south is the charming Globe Inn. Its attractions and those of its barmaid, Helen Ann Park, by whom Burns had a daughter, are celebrated in the lyric beginning:

Yestreen I had a pint o' wine,
    A place where body saw na;
Yestreen lay on this breast o' mine
    The gowden locks of Anna.—
The hungry Jew in wilderness
    Rejoicing o'er his manna,
Was naething to my hiney bliss
    Upon the lips of Anna.—

His favourite chair is preserved in the howff, or snuggery, at the back of the ground floor, and window panes he incised with verses may be seen upstairs. In Burns Street, then Mid Vennel, beyond the Globe we find the house where the poet lived for the last three years of his life; it is now a museum. A short walk beyond brings us to St Michael's Church, the final point of interest in Dumfries. Inside, Burns' customary pew is indicated by a tablet. Outside, his body was moved from its original grave, visited by Wordsworth (s.v. Lake Poets, Rte 14) in 1803 and remembered in a poem of tribute, to its present mausoleum in 1815. Keats (q.v.), whose visit in 1818 led to an undistinguished poem, found the monument 'not very much to my taste, though on a scale, large enough to show they wanted to honour him'.

Although he had no connection with London in his lifetime, Burns is now remembered there by a monument in Poets' Corner (fee) of Westminster Abbey and by a statue in the Victoria Embankment Gardens near Embankment Underground Station (Northern, Bakerloo, Circle and District Lines).

Burns Cottage and Museum, Alloway, Strathclyde Region: phone (0292) 41215. Admission fee includes entry to Burns Monument.

Land o' Burns Centre, Alloway, Strathclyde Region: phone (0292) 43700.

Burns Monument, Alloway: see Burns Cottage and Museum.

Souter Johnnie's Cottage, Kirkoswald, Strathclyde Region: NTS; phone (065 56) 603 or 274.

Tam o' Shanter Museum, High Street, Ayr, Strathclyde Region: closed at time of writing; for future arrangements contact Ayr Tourist Information Centre, (0292) 284196.

Bachelors' Club, Tarbolton, Strathclyde Region: NTS; phone (0292) 541424.

Burns House Museum, Castle Street, Mauchline, Strathclyde Region: phone (0290) 50045.

Kay Park Monument, Kilmarnock, Strathclyde Region: open by arrangement; phone the Dick Institute, Kilmarnock, (0563) 26401.

Burns Club Museum, Eglinton Street, Irvine, Strathclyde Region: open only on Saturday afternoons or by appointment; phone (0294) 78126 or 74511.

Lady Stair's House, Lady Stair's Close, Lawnmarket, Edinburgh: phone (031) 225 2424, extension 6593.

Ellisland Farm, near Dumfries, Dumfries and Galloway: phone (0387) 74426.

Burns House, Burns Street, Dumfries, Dumfries and Galloway: phone (0387) 55297.

Robert Burton

b. Lindley, Leicestershire, 1577; d. Oxford, 1640. *The Anatomy of Melancholy* (1621).

Burton spent his entire adult life in Oxford. He entered Brasenose College in 1593 and became a Student (ie. a Fellow) of Christ Church in 1599. In 1616 he also acquired the living of St Thomas, now much altered and restored, on Becket Street near the railway station and was apparently responsible for building the south porch. We know little more about Burton, beyond the occasional facts he let drop in the splendidly digressive course of his *Anatomy* and these brief remarks by Bishop Kennett in his *Register and Chronicle* (1728):

> The Author is said to have labour'd long in the Writing of this Book to suppress his own Melancholy, and yet did but improve it: And that some Readers have found the same Effect. In an interval of Vapours he would be extremely pleasant, and raise Laughter in any Company. Yet I have heard that nothing at last could make him laugh, but going down to the Bridge-foot in *Oxford*, and hearing the Barge-men scold and storm and swear at one another, at which he would set his Hands to his Sides, and laugh most profusely: Yet in his College and Chamber so mute and mopish that he was suspected to be *Felo de se*.

The Latin Chapel of Christ Church Cathedral has a monument with a bust and an inscription mentioning melancholy.

George Gordon, Lord Byron

b. London, 1788; d. Missolonghi, Greece, 1824. *Fugitive Pieces* (1806); *Poems on Various Occasions* (1807); *Hours of Idleness* (1807); *English Bards and Scotch Reviewers* (1809); *Childe Harold's Pilgrimage* (1812–18); *The Giaour* (1813); *The Bride of Abydos* (1813); *The Corsair* (1814); *Hebrew Melodies* (1815); *The Siege of Corinth* (1816); *Parisina* (1816); *The Prisoner of Chillon and Other Poems* (1816); *Manfred* (1817); *Beppo: A Venetian Story* (1818); *Mazeppa* (1819); *Don Juan* (1819–24); *Marino Faliero* (1821); *Sardanapalus* (1821); *The Two Foscari* (1821); *Cain: A Mystery* (1821); *The Vision of Judgment* (1822); *Werner* (1823); *The Island* (1823); *The Age of Bronze* (1823); *The Deformed Transformed* (1824).

The most famous part of Byron's life is probably its close, and that belongs not to England but to the Continent. When he left his native country for good in 1816 he did not fade into the obscurity that sometimes awaits exiles. Stories of his Italian mistress, illegitimate English daughter, menagerie of animals, friendship with Shelley (q.v.), verse that shocked his publisher and, finally, death in the Greek war for independence all served to magnify a scandalous reputation into an enduring legend. So the places we most readily associate with him—the Villa Diodati near Geneva, the Palazzo Mocenigo in Venice and, above all, Missolonghi—are not English and, when his poetry has a local atmosphere, it is the atmosphere of Switzerland, Italy or Greece. At the same time, however, the English scenes of Byron's life are well commemorated—he may often have been misunderstood but he has never been neglected—and, because less exotic, can help us penetrate the façades with which he delighted to obscure his complex personality. It is, after all, instructive to trace the hero of Missolonghi to Marylebone and the lover of Teresa Guiccioli to Aberdeen, to find Childe Harold in Nottingham.

For someone who became an ornament, and later a scandal, to the fashionable society of London, Byron started his life in the capital among very drab surroundings. He was born in Marylebone, in a rented back room on Holles Street, which connects Oxford Street with Cavendish Square. The house was destroyed by bombs during the war and a department store occupies the site. His baptism took place at Marylebone Parish Church in the absence of his father, Captain John Byron, who was hiding from creditors. This building, too, has vanished, though its site near the northern end of Marylebone High Street is marked by a garden of rest.

In 1789 Byron's mother took him to Aberdeen, on the east coast of her native Scotland. Captain Byron followed, quarrelled with his wife, and left again with what little money the couple possessed. Today the city has only a statue outside the Grammar School on Skene Street to remind the visitor of Byron; the building he attended (1794–98) stood closer to the centre in the Schoolhill. Yet this Scottish episode should not be forgotten, if only because it emphasised the crucial, early influence of Calvinism on his character.

Byron's circumstances changed when he inherited the title from his grandfather in 1798. He travelled south with his mother to claim the family home and estate, *Newstead Abbey, 10 miles north of Nottingham, reached from A60 to Mansfield. The 12C Augustinian Priory had been bought by Sir John Byron from Henry VIII in 1540 but, despite additions over the centuries, it was a scarcely habitable ruin when the poet and his mother first saw it: the deer had gone from the park, the oaks had been felled and even the furniture had been claimed by the fifth lord's creditors. The opening of Byron's early poem, 'On Leaving Newstead Abbey', hardly exaggerates: 'Through thy battlements, Newstead, the hollow winds whistle'. Such melancholy decay has its romantic charm and this may explain why Byron's fitful expenditures on the building did little more than create living quarters for himself; even these were not ready until 1808. Charles Skinner Matthews, a friend from Cambridge and a guest at Newstead, described a typical day there:

> Our average hour of rising was one. I, who generally got up between eleven and twelve, was always,—even when an invalid,—the first of the party, and was esteemed a prodigy of early rising. It was frequently past two before the breakfast party broke up. Then, for the amusements of the morning, there was reading, fencing, single-stick, or shuttlecock, in the great room; practising with pistols in the hall; walking—riding—cricket—sailing on the lake, playing with the bear, or teasing the wolf. Between seven and eight we dined; and our evening lasted from that time till one, two, or three in the morning. The evening diversions may be easily conceived.
>
> I must not omit the custom of handing round, after dinner, on the removal of the cloth, a human skull filled with burgundy ... A set of monkish dresses, which had been provided, with all the proper apparatus of crosses, beads, tonsures, etc., often gave a variety to our appearance and to our pursuits.

The present condition of the Abbey is due largely to tactful repairs undertaken by Colonel Thomas Wildman, who bought it in 1818. The west front of the church, the cloister and the chapter house survive, the Great Hall has been restored, and Byron's apartments contain a collection of relics. Near the NE angle of the house is the monument Byron erected in 1808 to his dog, Boatswain, complete with elegiac poem. It was placed with deliberate blasphemy where the high altar of the Abbey church presumably stood. In the will he made out before his Continental travels in 1809 Byron expressed a wish to be buried on the same spot, though without distubring Boatswain and without 'Burial service or Clergyman or any Monument or Inscription of any Kind'.

In the surrounding area we may visit several other places of interest. Annesley Hall, 3 miles SW of Newstead, was the home of Mary Chaworth, with whom the poet fell in love while still a schoolboy; her attractions were no doubt increased in his eyes by the fact that his grandfather had killed one of her ancestors in a duel. From 1803 to 1808 Byron and his mother lodged in Southwell, 12 miles east of Newstead and south of A617. According to Byron, they found in the cathedral town 'the advantage of very genteel society, without the hazard of being annoyed by mercantile affluence'. Burgage Manor, the Georgian house they rented, stands on the Green north of the picturesque Saracen's Head Inn. Opposite were the Pigot family, whose daughter Elizabeth became Byron's close friend, though her first impression was of 'a fat, bashful boy with his hair combed straight over his forehead'. An earlier lodging in Nottingham is marked by a plaque at No. 76 St James Street, between Maid Marian Way and the Old Market Square. Byron's familiarity with the city helps explain the sympathetic understanding he showed towards industrial unrest in his speeches to the House of Lords. Finally, on A611 north of Nottingham, we find the colliery town of Hucknall Torkard (usually abbreviated to Hucknall) and the church where Byron, his mother and daughter were buried.

From 1801 to 1805 Byron attended Harrow School at Harrow on the Hill in NW London. His name is carved on a panel in the Fourth Form Room in the Old Schools. The *churchyard of St Mary at the top of the hill was a favourite spot of Byron's during his schooldays, as an early poem, 'Lines Written Beneath an Elm in the Churchyard of Harrow', bears witness. The elm has gone but the tombstone of John Peachey where Byron used to sit is still there, now protected by railings. Byron's illegitimate daughter by Claire Clairmont is buried inside the church porch, though her grave was never marked with the inscription her father wrote: 'In Memory of Allegra, daughter of G.G. Lord Byron, who died at Bagnacavallo, in Italy, April 20th 1822, aged five years and three months'.

When Byron entered university in 1805 he was, he complained, 'wretched at going to Cambridge instead of Oxford'. But he made do with *Trinity College rather than Christ Church, and was soon content with his lodging in the SE corner of Great Court: 'I am now most pleasantly situated in *Super*excellent Rooms flanked on one side by my Tutor, upon the other by an old Fellow, both of whom are rather checks upon my vivacity'. They did not check his vivacity completely, and the main features of his undergraduate life suggest the Regency nobleman rather than the apprentice poet: 'between ourselves', he confessed to a friend, 'College is not the place to improve either Morals or Income'. He boxed and swam (the pond in the nearby village of Trumpington is still called Byron's Pool), and at one point housed a bear in the hexagonal tower above his rooms, announcing that it would '*sit for a fellowship*'. Yet we should not be completely beguiled by this 'routine of dissipation', as he called it—anymore than by the title of the volume he published during these years, *Hours of Idleness*—for he was always careful to hide a hard-working, ambitious temperament under a guise of aristocratic laziness. He is now commemorated in the College by Thorvaldsen's statue (1829) in Wren's beautiful Library by the river. It is hardly surprising that the seated figure of the poet should seem inappropriately large for its

Lord Byron at Cambridge, engraved by F.W. Hunt after Gilchrist

surroundings, since it was originally intended for Westminster Abbey but refused a place there.

After he left Cambridge Byron spent two years abroad, returning in 1811 to England, London and literary fame. Byron House on St James's Street, south of Piccadilly, occupies the site of the lodgings where he awoke and found himself famous after *Childe Harold's Pilgrimage* began publication in 1812. He later lived (1814–15) in the secluded and distinguished Albany, north of Piccadilly, where the novelist 'Monk' Lewis (q.v.) was a neighbour. His popularity gained him the *entrée* to Holland House in Holland Park, made the centre of Whig literary circles by the wife of the third Lord Holland. It was here he first met Lady Caroline Lamb, wife of the politician who became Lord Melbourne; with eager relish she judged him 'mad—bad—and dangerous to know', and they enjoyed an affair which struck even Regency society as indiscreet. Only the park and east wing of the Tudor mansion remain, their appearance changed for the worse by the addition of the King George VI Memorial Hostel.

Thomas Phillips' portrait of Byron in Albanian costume (1813) hangs in the National Portrait Gallery; the costume itself is on display at Bowood House, near Calne in Wiltshire.

When Byron's body was returned from Missolonghi, embalmed almost beyond recognition, it was refused burial in Westminster Abbey and so his funeral cortège, watched by thousands, proceeded north to Hucknall where he had anyway wished to be buried. Thorvaldsen's statue was later excluded from the building and the rejection in 1924 of yet another petition that Byron be remembered in the Abbey provoked an amusing doggerel poem, 'A Refusal', from Thomas Hardy (q.v.). The present simple memorial slab in Poets' Corner (fee) was unveiled as recently as 1969.

Newstead Abbey, Linby, Nottinghamshire: phone Mansfield (0623) 793557.

Harrow School, Harrow on the Hill, Middlesex: guided tours; phone (01) 422 2303.

Trinity College Library, Cambridge: phone the Porters' Lodge, (0223) 338400.

Bowood House, near Calne, Wiltshire: phone Calne (0249) 812102.

Thomas Carlyle

b. Ecclefechan, Dumfries and Galloway, 1795; d. London, 1881. *Sartor Resartus* (1833–34); *The French Revolution: A History* (1837); *Chartism* (1839); *Heroes, Hero-Worship and the Heroic in History* (1841); *Past and Present* (1843); *Oliver Cromwell's Letters and Speeches* (1845); *Latter-Day Pamphlets* (1850); *The History of Frederic II of Prussia, Called Frederick the Great* (1858–65).

Carlyle's hometown of Ecclefechan, between Gretna and Lockerbie, preserves his birthplace, Arched House, spanning a gateway halfway up the street. It is now a museum where visitors may see the room in which he was born and furniture from his Chelsea study. He is buried near his parents in the simple churchyard, and a replica of the Chelsea statue (see below) has been erected at the top of the town. Ecclefechan appears as 'Entepfuhl' in the quasi-autobiographical *Sartor Resartus*, 'standing in "trustful derangement" among the wooded slopes' (Bk 2, Ch. 2). In Annan to the south Carlyle attended the Academy ('Hinterschlag Gymnasium'; now the old Grammar School) where he found the teachers 'hide-bound Pedants, without knowledge of man's nature, or of boy's; or of aught save their lexicons and quarterly account-books' (Bk 2, Ch. 3), before studying at Edinburgh University. After his marriage in 1826 to Jane Welsh he lived (1828–34) at Craigenputtock, a large remote farm to the NW of Dumfries and west of Dunscore. *Sartor Resartus* was written here.

During a first brief stay in London (1831–32) the Carlyles lodged at No. 33 (then No. 4) Ampton Street, off Gray's Inn Road, marked with a plaque. A more famous residence is **Carlyle's House in Cheyne Row, running north from Cheyne Walk and the river in Chelsea. Carlyle and his wife lived in this modest Georgian terraced house—though not always in perfect concord—from 1834 until their deaths, Jane dying before him in 1866. In a spontaneous and unassuming fashion it became one of the most important literary gathering places in Victorian London. Distinguished visitors, often the subject of penetrating character sketches by their host, included: Dickens (q.v.,

The Carlyles at home: 'A Chelsea Interior' by Robert Tait (c 1857)

Rte 6), who remained an admirer rather than intimate friend; Ralph Waldo Emerson, the American philosopher with whom Carlyle conducted a lengthy correspondence; Leigh Hunt (q.v.), poet, critic and neighbour, inspired by Mrs Carlyle's reception of him on one occasion to write 'Jenny Kissed Me'; Ruskin (q.v.), who found a common bond in Carlyle's Scottish ancestry and derived consolation from the older man's approval of his controversial views on political economy; and Tennyson (q.v.), who shared with Carlyle a passion for consuming 'infinite tobacco'.

Today it is perhaps the richest and best preserved writer's house in England, its rooms still filled with pictures, furniture and mementoes from the couple's long residence and still radiating the atmosphere captured in R.S. Tait's painting, 'A Chelsea Interior' (1858), which is on display. Of particular interest is the attic study, sound-proofed in 1853 for protection against the noise of the 'demon fowls' next door. To Carlyle's morbidly sensitive ears at least, the remedy was inadequate and the distracting sound was offered as one reason for the delays attending the writing of *Frederick the Great*.

A statue of Carlyle by Boehm (1882) stands in the garden between the end of Cheyne Walk and the Embankment.

Elsewhere in London, Carlyle delivered his lectures on heroes and hero-worship in 1840 at the Royal Institution on Albemarle Street, north of Piccadilly. In 1841 he took a leading role in founding the excellent London Library, first located in Pall Mall but soon moved to St James's Square.

Carlyle's tour of East Anglia in 1842, prompted in part by his interest in Cromwell, included a visit to Bury St Edmunds, Suffolk, which he found

> a prosperous brick Town; beautifully diversifying, with its clean brick houses, ancient clean streets, and twenty or fifteen thousand souls busy, the general grassy face of Suffolk; looking out right pleasantly, from its hill-slope, towards the rising sun: and on the eastern edge of it, still runs, long, black and massive, a range of monastic ruins; into the wide internal spaces of which the stranger is admitted on payment of one shilling. (*Past and Present*, Bk 2, Ch. 2)

In *Past and Present* the *Abbey becomes a symbol of ideal order, presented in rebuke to the turbulence, competitiveness and lack of spiritual purpose Carlyle saw around him in 19C England.

Carlyle's Birthplace, The Arched House, Ecclefechan, Dumfries and Galloway: NTS; phone (057 63) 666.

Carlyle's House, 24 Cheyne Row, Chelsea, London SW3: NT; phone (01) 352 7087.

Bury St Edmunds Abbey, Suffolk: English Heritage, but located in a public park open most daylight hours.

'Lewis Carroll' (pseudonym of Rev. Charles Lutwidge Dodgson)

b. Daresbury, Cheshire, 1832; d. Guildford, Surrey, 1898. *Alice's Adventures in Wonderland* (1865); *Through the Looking-Glass and What Alice Found There* (1871); *The Hunting of the Snark: An Agony in Eight Fits* (1876); *Sylvie and Bruno* (1889); *Sylvie and Bruno Concluded* (1893).

At Daresbury, a village off A56 16 miles NE of Chester, the parsonage where Carroll was born and spent his early childhood has gone but the church now has a memorial window depicting scenes from *Alice in Wonderland*. A more expressive location is Croft-on-Tees, on the border between North Yorkshire and County Durham south of Darlington, where Carroll's family moved when he was eleven. Although the Old Rectory is now divided into separate dwellings it still exudes the comfortable, affluent gentility in which he was brought up. His shy, fastidious nature did not make him a typical pupil at Rugby School in Warwickshire, which he entered in 1846, and his subsequent life emphasised how little he had in common with old Rugbeians like Thomas Hughes (q.v.).

Christ Church, Oxford, was a more congenial environment and became his permanent home. He entered as an undergraduate in 1850, became a Student (Christ Church's term for Fellow) in 1852 and remained until his death. The rooms he occupied from 1868 are in the NW corner of Tom Quad. Visitors here included Walter Pater (q.v.) from Brasenose. Carroll's quiet life was the very essence of bachelor donnishness. He overcame his shyness only in the company of young children, when his stutter disappeared, and in the pursuit of famous subjects for his camera. His letters (of which he wrote, by his own tally, 98,721) show a fussy perfectionism in dealings with college servants, colleagues, tradesmen, publishers and illustrators. His only serious intervention in college affairs occurred in 1870, when he protested against the alterations to Christ Church Cathedral made by Sir Gilbert Scott under the supervision of Dean Liddell. The Library, in Peckwater Quad, has a collection of Carroll memorabilia.

No. 83 St Aldate's Street, opposite Christ Church, is traditionally identified with Sir John Tenniel's illustration of the shop where Alice encounters the sheep in Chapter 5 ('Wool and Water') of *Through the*

Looking-Glass. Carroll's career as famous children's author began on a 'golden afternoon' in July 1862 when he and his friend Robinson Duckworth took the three young daughters of Dean Liddell on a boating trip on the upper river of the Thames (or Isis). They left from Folly Bridge, south of Christ Church via St Aldate's, and rowed to Godstow ($3^1/_4$ miles), with its ruined Benedictine nunnery. In later life Alice Liddell recalled: 'Nearly all of *Alice's Adventures Under Ground* [Carroll's original title for his first Alice book] was told on that blazing summer afternoon with the heat haze shimmering over the meadows where the party landed to shelter for a while in the shadow cast by the haycocks near Godstow'. It was she who urged Carroll to write his story down.

Carroll visited Russia in 1868 but otherwise restricted himself to a less adventurous ambit of movement. He was in the habit of taking his holidays on the south coast, and plaques mark the houses where he stayed in Brighton at No. 11 Sussex Square and in Eastbourne at

Alice in the shop: an illustration by Sir John Tenniel to Through the Looking-Glass

No. 7 Lushington Road. In the early 1870s he was several times a guest at the Elizabethan mansion, Hatfield House (off A1 south of Welwyn Garden City in Hertfordshire). The friendship with Lord Salisbury, Chancellor of Oxford and later Prime Minister, had begun when Carroll sought permission to photograph his daughters. Some of the *Sylvie and Bruno* stories, his last and least successful writing for children, were first told at Hatfield.

He died in Guildford (SW of London via A3) at The Chestnuts on Castle Hill, the home his sisters had occupied since the death of their father in 1868. The little Museum and Muniments Room by Castle Archway nearby has letters and relics. His grave is in the New Cemetery on The Mount to the west. Alice Liddell, who became Mrs Reginald Hargreaves, is buried at Lyndhurst in the New Forest.

Christ Church Library, Peckwater Quad, Christ Church, Oxford: visitors by appointment; phone (0865) 276169.

Hatfield House, Hatfield, Hertfordshire: phone (070 72) 62823 or 65159.

Guildford Museum, Castle Arch, Guildford, Surrey: phone (0483) 503497.

George Chapman

b. Hitchin, Hertfordshire? 1559?; d. London, 1634. *Hero and Leander* (continuation of poem by Christopher Marlowe [q.v.]; 1598); *Iliad* (1598–1611); *Eastward Hoe* (with Ben Jonson and John Marston [qq.v.]; 1605); *Bussy D'Ambois* (1607); *The Revenge of Bussy D'Ambois* (1613); *Odyssey* (1614–15).

The dramatist and poet whose translation of Homer was celebrated some two centuries later in a sonnet by Keats (q.v.) is today remembered only by scenes connected with the beginning and end of his life.

Chapman was born at or near Hitchin, 3 miles west of the A1 in Hertfordshire. No. 35 Tilehouse Street, a street unusually rich in half-timbered and Georgian houses, bears a plaque in his memory. He was buried in London in the churchyard of St Giles in the Fields, near St Giles Circus. The 17C antiquary Anthony à Wood recorded: 'Soon after was a monument erected over his grave, built after the way of the old Romans, by the care and charge of his most beloved friend Inigo Jones'. Damaged and with its inscription recut, the monument now stands in the north aisle of the rebuilt church.

Thomas Chatterton

b. Bristol, Avon, 1752; d. London, 1770. *Poems Supposed to Have Been Written at Bristol, by Thomas Rowley and Others, in the Fifteenth Century* (edited by Thomas Tyrwhitt; 1777).

The 'marvellous Boy' (as Wordsworth called him) was born at the old Schoolmaster's House on Redcliffe Way (then Pile Street) in SE Bristol. His widowed mother sent him to Colston's Hospital, a charity school for boys destined to become apprentices; its medieval buildings on Colston Street near the city centre have been replaced by Colston Hall. From the age of 15 he worked as scrivener for an attorney, John Lambert, at offices, now vanished, on Corn Street north of the Cross.

None of these places was as important to Chatterton as **St Mary Redcliffe near his birthplace, where his uncle was sexton. In this magnificent Perpendicular church he found a striking contrast to the 'dingy piles of brick' that were 18C commercial Bristol and an escape from the frustrating realities of his own life. It became focus and inspiration for that passionate medievalism which led him to write poems he attributed to the fictitious Thomas Rowley, Bristol monk during Edward IV's reign. Of the various lyrics about St Mary Redcliffe itself, 'Onn Oure Ladie's Church' is perhaps the finest. Under the window of the south transept lies the tomb of William Canynge the younger (d. 1474), benefactor of St Mary and Mayor of Bristol, frequently mentioned in the Rowley poems. The muniments room where Chatterton claimed to have discovered his manuscripts is above the north porch. A statue depicting him in the uniform of Colston's Hospital stands in the churchyard.

During his short lifetime Chatterton signally failed to engage the interest of his distinguished contemporary, Horace Walpole (q.v.), and succeeded in deceiving only a handful of local self-styled antiquaries. But in the years of posthumous fame and debate about the authenticity of his forgeries many distinguished literary men visited the scenes of his life. Dr Johnson (q.v.) came with Boswell and, though he left a disbeliever, conceded that Chatterton was 'the most extraordinary young man that has come to my knowledge'. Oliver Goldsmith (q.v.) offered a promissory note for £200 to the owner of the manuscripts, an offer that gentleman prudently declined. William Henry Ireland, whose own Shakespearean forgeries were encouraged by Chatterton's example, made his pilgrimage. In a later generation Robert Southey, a native of Bristol, and Samuel Taylor Coleridge treasured the places associated with Chatterton as part of a growing Romantic legend (s.v. Lake Poets, Rte 5).

In London nothing remains of No. 39 Brooke Street, north of Holborn, the lodgings where Chatterton spent his last months struggling as a hack writer and where, at the age of 17 years and nine months, he committed suicide. Before its demolition the house enjoyed a vogue as a literary shrine, just as Chatterton's death became a favourite subject for Romantic poets and painters.

Chatterton House, Redcliffe Way, Bristol, Avon: visits by application to the Director, City of Bristol Museum and Art Gallery, Queen's Road; phone (0272) 299771.

Geoffrey Chaucer

b. London, c 1343; d. London, 1400. *The Book of the Duchess* (c 1370); *The Parliament of Fowls* (c 1372–c 1386); *The House of Fame* (c 1374–c 1380); *Troilus and Criseyde* (c 1385–c 1388); *The Canterbury Tales* (unfinished; c 1387–1400).

Since Chaucer came from a wealthy family and made a career as court official his life is well documented for a man of his time, as the bulky volume of *Chaucer Life-Records* (1966) initiated by Professor Manly and Miss Rickert amply testifies.

The surviving monuments to Chaucer's life in London centre on Westminster Abbey. His •altar-tomb in Poets' Corner (fee), just outside the entrance to St Benedict's Chapel, was erected in 1555 by Nicholas Brigham, though the tomb chest itself may be work of an earlier date. Chaucer's connections with the Abbey are far deeper than the honour of his burial there, for the building came under his responsibility when he was Clerk of the King's Works between 1389 and 1391. This was the period when the architect Henry Yevele was completing the nave; Yevele's other notable contributions include the tomb of Archbishop Langham (d. 1376) in the Chapel of St Benedict, and the tombs of Edward III (d. 1377) and Richard II and Anne of Bohemia (d. 1400 and 1394) in St Edward the Confessor's Chapel. During the last year of his life Chaucer leased a house in the Abbey grounds near what is now Henry VII's Chapel at the east end of the building.

In 1390 Chaucer held a special commission as Master of Works at Windsor Castle (west of central London via M4). The St George's Chapel whose repair he supervised is not the present magnificent building of that name but an earlier one on the site of what is now the Albert Memorial Chapel. He is reputed to have stayed in the Winchester Tower by the entrance to the North Terrace.

His various posts at court required travel, and the fleeting topographical references in his poetry suggest a wide knowledge of England. Professor J.A.W. Bennett's elegant *Chaucer in Oxford and Cambridge* (1974) is particularly persuasive in demonstrating the poet's familiarity with the university cities and their ways. At Oxford, scene of 'The Miller's Tale' in *The Canterbury Tales*, Chaucer's astrolabe is among the various treasures preserved in the splendid medieval library of Merton College. Readers of 'The Reeve's Tale' will remember that the story is set in the village of Trumpington, south of Cambridge.

The very title of Chaucer's most famous poem declares its rootedness in English geography, yet the references to the pilgrims' journey from London to the shrine of St Thomas (demolished 1538) in Canterbury Cathedral are only spare and generalised. The main features of their journey may be easily summarised. It begins immediately south of London Bridge in Southwark where, on the left-hand side of Borough High Street, stood the Tabard, the 'gentil hostelrye' (General Prologue, line 718) whose accommodation Chaucer praised:

> The chambres and the stables weren wyde,
> And wel we weren esed atte beste.
> (lines 28–29)

The inn burnt down in 1676 and its successor was demolished in 1875–76; it is remembered today in the name of Talbot Yard. The 17C wing of its fellow, the George, still stands, doubling as inn and National Trust property.

The route continues down Borough High Street and left on Great Dover Street which, after a large junction, becomes the Old Kent Road. At the corner of Albany Road on the right stood the 'wateryng of Seint Thomas' (line 826) where, at the Host's suggestion, the pilgrims cast lots to decide who shall begin the storytelling—an honour that falls to the Knight.

We then leave central London via New Cross Road, Blackheath

Road, Blackheath Hill and Shooter's Hill Road. The journey takes us past Deptford and Greenwich, saluted by the Host in the Prologue to 'The Reeve's Tale':

> Lo Depeford! and it is half-way pryme.
> Lo Grenewych, ther many a shrewe is inne!
> (lines 51–52)

We ignore the A2 (Rochester Way) and remain on Shooter's Hill Road, the old Watling Street and now at this point A207, which rejoins the A2 east of Dartford (16 miles). Rochester (28 miles) is mentioned in the Prologue to 'The Monk's Tale' (line 37) and would in the normal course of such pilgrimages have been a stopping place for the first or second night. Sittingbourne (38 miles) appears as 'Sidyngborne' at the end of 'The Wife of Bath's Prologue', while at Ospringe (45 miles) stands one of the few survivals of the old pilgrims' route, a medieval Maison Dieu. At the Brenley Corner roundabout (48 miles) east of Faversham we ignore the present A2 and follow its previous course via Boughton Street, with Blean Wood to our left and the area of Boughton under Blean to our right, and Dunkirk. It was at 'Boghton under Blee' (Prologue to 'The Canon Yeoman's Tale', line 3) that the company is joined by the Canon Yeoman.

Chaucer's last topographical reference in the incomplete poem occurs in the Prologue to 'The Manciple's Tale':

> a litel toun
> Which that ycleped is Bobbe-up-and-doun,
> Under the Blee, by Caunterbury waye.
> (lines 1–3)

The quaintly named place is usually identified as Harbledown (56 miles), now on the outskirts of the cathedral city and notable for its Hospital of St Nicholas, a medieval leper foundation with an 11C chapel.

Though Chaucer's pilgrims never reach Canterbury, they are now commemorated there by the Canterbury Pilgrims' Way exhibition, in a former church in St Margaret's Street, which seeks to bring *The Canterbury Tales* to life with the same gimmicks of presentation used by the Jorvik Viking Centre at York.

At the pretty Chiltern village of Ewelme, near Wallingford, the church contains the brass of Thomas Chaucer (d. 1436?), supposed to be the poet's son, and the tomb of Thomas' daughter Alice, Duchess of Suffolk (d. 1475).

Windsor Castle, Windsor, Berkshire: phone (0753) 868286.

Merton College Library, Oxford: phone the Porters' Lodge, (0865) 276310.

Maison Dieu, Ospringe, near Faversham, Kent: English Heritage; phone Faversham (0795) 762604.

Canterbury Pilgrims' Way, St Margaret's Street, Canterbury, Kent: phone (0227) 454888.

G.K. Chesterton

b. London, 1874; d. Beaconsfield, Buckinghamshire, 1936. *Greybeards at Play* (1900); *The Wild Knight and Other Poems* (1900); *Robert Browning* (1903); *The Napoleon of Notting Hill* (1904); *The Club of Queer Trades* (1905); *Heretics* (1905); *Charles Dickens* (1906); *The Man Who Was Thursday: A Nightmare* (1908); *Orthodoxy* (1908); *The Ball and the Cross* (1910); *What's Wrong With the World* (1910); *The Innocence of Father Brown* (1911); *The Ballad of the White Horse* (1911); *Manalive* (1912); *The Flying Inn* (1914); *The Wisdom of Father Brown* (1914); *A Short History of England* (1917); *Irish Impressions* (1919); *The Superstition of Divorce* (1920); *The New Jerusalem* (1920); *Eugenics and Other Evils* (1922); *The Man Who Knew Too Much and Other Stories* (1922); *St Francis of Assisi* (1923); *Tales of the Long Bow* (1925); *The Everlasting Man* (1925); *William Cobbett* (1925); *The Incredulity of Father Brown* (1926); *The Outline of Sanity* (1926); *The Queen of Seven Swords* (1926); *The Return of Don Quixote* (1927); *The Secret of Father Brown* (1927); *The Poet and the Lunatics: Episodes in the Life of Gabriel Gale* (1929); *Four Faultless Felons* (1930); *St Thomas Aquinas* (1933); *The Scandal of Father Brown* (1935); *Autobiography* (1936); *The Paradoxes of Mr Pond* (1937).

Although Kensington in London has no striking monuments to Chesterton's connection with it, enough places of interest survive to justify a walking tour. It begins at Notting Hill Gate Underground Station (Central, and District and Circle Lines), in the neighbourhood Chesterton used for his earliest novel. After walking south on Kensington Church Street we turn right on to Sheffield Terrace, where Chesterton was born at No. 32 to an affluent family of estate agents and auctioneers. We then return to Kensington Church Street and follow it south to the junction with Kensington High Street. In 1901 Chesterton married Frances Blogg at the 19C church of St Mary Abbots on this corner.

To our left lie Kensington Gardens, scene of 'The Last Battle' in Book 5 of *The Napoleon of Notting Hill*. The main route takes us to the right. Chesterton was a pupil at St Paul's School in the days when it was located on Hammersmith Road, Kensington High Street's western continuation. But before this we turn left on to Warwick Gardens, where the Chesterton family lived for most of his childhood and youth at No. 11. Pembroke Gardens leads left from Warwick Gardens to the charming Edwardes Square. Chesterton and his wife started their married life at No. 1.

The couple then went to live in Battersea, but the best place to remember the early years of Chesterton's career is in Fleet Street. His burly figure, made the more distinctive by the cloak and swordstick that soon became his trademarks, was a familiar sight in several of the street's taverns: the Cock near Temple Bar, El Vino's on the south side near the junction with Fetter Lane, and the Cheshire Cheese, by Wine Office Court on the north side. Chesterton's flamboyant manner, relentless energy and decided opinions that combined the conservative and the radical in almost equal proportions soon attracted attention in literary and journalistic circles. His close association with Hilaire Belloc (q.v.), a frequent companion in the Fleet Street pubs and restaurants, made Shaw (q.v.) view the pair as a pantomime beast, the 'Chesterbelloc'. Shaw himself, though he never agreed with Chesterton, remained an admirer and close friend.

In 1909 Chesterton and his wife moved to Beaconsfield (west of London on A40 near High Wycombe), renting Overroads on Grove Road near the railway station and later building themselves a new house, Top Meadow, opposite. At first sight the town was a surprising choice of home for a man who seemed to belong to London and Fleet Street as thoroughly as Dr Johnson (q.v.) had done, but Chesterton himself vigorously defended suburban life. At any rate, his Beaconsfield years brought no slackening of his formidable output or of the reputation he had made. He created his popular detective, Father Brown, and increased his audience by lecture tours, public debates and, at the end of his life, radio broadcasts. In 1922 he was received into the Roman Catholic church, a logical progression from the High Anglicanism he had adopted in early manhood, and he is now remembered in St Teresa's church in Beaconsfield.

John Clare

b. Helpston, Cambridgeshire, 1793; d. Northampton, 1864. *Poems Descriptive of Rural Life and Scenery* (1820); *The Village Minstrel* (1821); *The Shepherd's Calendar* (1827); *The Rural Muse* (1835).

Clare's career followed a pattern all too familiar in the lives of the so-called 'peasant poets' of the late 18C and early 19C. After a childhood and youth spent in manual work he managed to achieve popularity with a volume of poetry reflecting his background; later volumes were less successful, undeservedly so in his case, and his life became overshadowed by first financial and then mental problems. In the poetry of his madness he sometimes insisted that he was a man unbounded by time and space, yet the real strength of his writing lies in its local character: its precise observation of the manners, speech and changing social conditions of the agrarian poor, as well as the countryside where his life was passed.

Clare's countryside is found on the border of Eastern and Central England, where the modern counties of Cambridgeshire, Lincolnshire, Leicestershire and Northamptonshire meet. Its centre is Helpston (then Helpstone and in Northamptonshire) on B1443 6 miles NW of Peterborough, 'a gloomy village' but the occasion for much of his best poetry. He is remembered by a Gothic memorial of 1869 on the green. The cottage on Woodgate where he was born and lived for much of his life is marked with a plaque. In his boyhood he worked as a servant at the Bluebell Inn next door. He is buried in the churchyard of St Botolph.

Burghley House lies 4 miles west of Helpston on B1443. As a child he climbed over the wall of the estate to read a newly purchased copy of Thomson's *The Seasons* among the 'uncommonly beautiful' scenery. In 1809 he was apprenticed as an under-gardener but his companions introduced him to 'irregular habits' and he stayed at Burghley only nine months. After the success of his first collection of verse in 1820 the house's owner, the Marquis of Exeter, granted him a small annuity for life. In Stamford, 2 miles further west, he bought books and the precious stock of pencils with which he started writing, and later attracted the notice of influential residents who helped him to publication. In 1817 he was working at a lime-kiln in the village of Pickworth, 5 miles NW. Its old church is remembered in 'On a Sunday Morning'; only a fragment remains as the outer entrance to the south porch of the present building.

Clare's move from Helpston to Northborough in 1832, made with the help of his patrons, took him only some 3 miles NE of his birthplace. Yet, as 'The Flitting' shows, it came as a wrench to someone of his minutely local sensibility:

The ivy at the parlour end
The woodbine at the garden gate
Are all and each affections friend
That renders parting desolate
But times will change and friends must part
And nature can still make amends
Their memory lingers round the heart
Like life whose essence is its friends
(lines 201–208)

His cottage, now greatly modernised, stands east of the church and the former manor house. Shyness of the visitors whom his fame was attracting caused him to have it built back from the road with its front door facing the rear garden. Although his Northborough years began by being among his most productive, a 'mild derangement' in 1837 caused him to enter a private asylum near Ponders End in Epping Forest. He escaped in July 1841 and, advised of the route by gipsies, walked back to his Northborough home.

The episode led to permanent commitment in the county asylum at Northampton, where he continued to write but also to suffer insane delusions. According to the medical superintendent, 'he would maintain that he had written the works of Byron, and Sir Walter Scott, that he was Nelson and Wellington, that he had fought and won the battle of Waterloo, that he had had his head shot off at this battle, whilst he was totally unable to explain the process by which it had again been affixed to his body'. The modern visitor can still see the Ionic portico (1701) of All Saints' Church on George Row where Clare delighted to sit when he was allowed out of the asylum.

Burghley House, Stamford, Lincolnshire: phone (0780) 52451.

Arthur Hugh Clough

b. Liverpool, Merseyside, 1819; d. Florence, Italy, 1861. *The Bothie of Tober-na-Vuolich: A Long-Vacation Pastoral* (1848); *Ambarvalia* (1849); *Amours de Voyage* (1858); *Poems, With a Memoir* (edited by Francis Turner Palgrave; 1862).

No. 9 Rodney Street, the poet's birthplace in a row of dignified 18C houses in Liverpool, is marked with a plaque.

His family emigrated to South Carolina while he was still an infant. When he was sent back to England to be educated Clough attended exactly the same institutions as his contemporary, Matthew Arnold (q.v.). He studied at Rugby (1829–37) and left school as the ideal product of Dr Thomas Arnold's system. Yet Clough's years as an undergraduate at Balliol College, Oxford (1837–41) and as fellow and tutor at Oriel College (1842–48) did not fulfil his early promise. Arnold's elegy, 'Thyrsis', sadly addressed him as 'too quick despairer' (line 61). His poetry combined a mastery of classical form that would have cheered Dr Arnold's heart with a doubting and self-doubting tone that was alien to the firm regimen of his old school.

During his Oxford years Clough several times took vacation reading parties of undergraduates to the Lake District. He is remembered by a memorial in the churchyard of St Oswald at Grasmere, 4miles north of Windermere on A591.

William Cobbett

b. Farnham, Surrey, 1763; d. Normandy, Surrey, 1835. *The Life and Adventures of Peter Porcupine* (1796); *The Political Censor* (1796–97); *Porcupine's Gazette* (1797–1800); *The Rush-Light* (1800); *The Porcupine* (1800–01); *Cobbett's Political Register* (1802–35); *Paper Against Gold and Glory Against Prosperity* (1815); *Mr Cobbett's Address to His Countrymen* (1817); *A Journal of a Year's Residence in the United States* (1818–19); *A Grammar of the English Language* (1818); *The American Gardener* (1821); *The Farmer's Friend* (1822); *The Farmer's Wife's Friend* (1822); *Cottage Economy* (1822); *A History of the Protestant Reformation in England and Ireland* (1824–26); *The Poor Man's Friend* (1826); *The English Gardener* (1828); *Advice to Young Men* (1829–30); *The Emigrant's Guide* (1829); *Rural Rides* (1830; revised and expanded edition by James Paul Cobbett, 1853); *Plan of Parliamentary Reform* (1830); *Cobbett's Twopenny Trash* (1830–32); *A Tour in Scotland* (1832); *Cobbett's Manchester Lectures* (1832); *A Geographical Dictionary of England and Wales* (1832).

Throughout his combative, much-travelled life Cobbett kept a special affection for his native Farnham, on A31 in Surrey. The town was, he told readers of *A Journal of a Year's Residence in the United States*, 'the neatest in England, and, I believe, in the whole world':

> All there is a garden. The neat culture of the hop extends its influence to the fields round about. Hedges cut with shears and every other mark of skill and care strike the eye at Farnham, and become fainter and fainter as you go from it in every direction. (General Preface)

Even if time has diminished its pastoral charms, *Farnham today has not forgotten the man who praised it so emphatically. Cobbett mementoes are displayed in the Willmer House Museum at No. 38 West Street and there is a bust in Gostrey Meadow near the river. Two important landmarks commemorate the beginning and end of his life. His birthplace, the former Jolly Farmers Inn in Bridge Square, has now been renamed The William Cobbett. His tomb stands in the churchyard of St Andrew, Cobbett having spent his last years (1831–35) farming at Normandy, a village to the NE.

In his youth he worked as a gardener for the Bishop of Winchester at Farnham Castle. Revisiting the region in later life he took his son to Tilford, 3 miles SE of Farnham:

> on the Green we stopped to look at an *oak tree*, which, when I was a little boy, was but a very little tree, comparatively, and which is now, take it altogether, by far the finest tree that I ever saw in my life. The stem or shaft is short; that is to say, it is short before you come to the first limbs; but it is full *thirty feet round*, at about eight or ten feet from the ground. (*Rural Rides*, entry for 27 September 1822)

The tree is still there.

The passage reminds us that Farnham is at the centre of the country traversed in *Rural Rides*, that generous and angry, bigoted and perceptive book which is certainly Cobbett's greatest achievement and perhaps the finest achievement of English travel literature. From 1822 until 1826 he travelled through Southern England, with excursions into South-Western and Eastern England; his titlepage lists Surrey, Kent, Sussex, Hampshire, Wiltshire, Gloucestershire, Herefordshire, Worcestershire (now amalgamated, of course, into Hereford and Worcester), Somerset, Oxfordshire, Berkshire, Essex, Suffolk, Norfolk and Hertfordshire. He went by horse and avoided turnpike roads (among his pet hates) since his object was 'to see the *country*; to see the farmers at *home*, and to see the labourers *in the fields*' (entry for 25 September 1822). The result is something more than a document of agrarian life struggling under the first impact of the Industrial Revolution. It remains a living book, an ideal travelling companion. The modern tourist who wishes to gain a foretaste of the changes that have since overtaken the places Cobbett described should consult Laurence Vulliamy's 'photographic exploration', *Rural Rides Revisited* (1977).

It was ironic, and the irony did not escape Cobbett, that a man so passionately attached to the older rural way of life should have spent most of his working life in London, the 'Wen' denounced in his political journalism. The most congenial spot to remember him is the Royal Botanic Gardens at Kew, where he came to work at the age of 14 after running away from Farnham and stopping in Richmond to make his momentous purchase of Swift's *Tale of a Tub*. He later recorded, with a touch of pride, that he attracted the attention of the future George IV by the oddity of his dress, for he had arrived still in his country clothes, 'blue smock-frock and my red garters tied under my knees' (*Political Register*, 19 February 1820).

Farnham Museum, Willmer House, 38 West Street, Farnham, Surrey: phone (0252) 715094.

Farnham Castle. The keep is English Heritage, summer standard opening; phone (0252) 713393. The domestic buildings are occupied by the Centre for International Briefing; guided tours; phone (0252) 721194.

Royal Botanic Gardens (Kew Gardens), Kew, Richmond-upon-Thames, Surrey: phone London (01) 940 1171.

Wilkie Collins

b. London, 1824; d. London, 1889. *Antonina, or The Fall of Rome: A Romance of the Fifth Century* (1850); *Rambles Beyond Railways: or Notes in Cornwall, Taken A-Foot* (1851); *Mr Wray's Cash Box, or The Mask and the Mystery: A Christmas Sketch* (1852); *Basil: A Story of Modern Life* (1852); *Hide and Seek* (1854); *After Dark* (1856); *The Dead Secret* (1857); *The Queen of Hearts* (1859); *The Woman in White* (1860); *No Name* (1862); *Armadale* (1866); *The Moonstone: A Romance* (1868); *Man and Wife* (1870); *Poor Miss Finch* (1872); *The New Magdalen: A Dramatic Story in a Prologue and Three Acts* (1873); *The Law and the Lady* (1875); *The Two Destinies: A Romance* (1876); *The Haunted Hotel: A Mystery of Modern Venice, to Which is Added My Lady's Money* (1879); *A Rogue's Life: From His Birth to His Marriage* (1879); *The Fallen Leaves* (1879); *Jezebel's Daughter* (1880); *The Black Robe* (1881); *Heart and Science: A Story of the Present Time* (1883); *I Say No* (1884); *The Evil Genius: A Domestic Story* (1886); *Little Novels* (1887); *The Legacy of Cain* (1889); *Blind Love* (1890).

There is little left to evoke Collins' childhood and youth in London, part of which (1826–30) was spent in Hampstead where his father, distinguished landscape painter and Royal Academician, inhabited a succession of houses. Some indication, however, of the impression that the area made on his imagination is offered by the memorable encounter between Walter Hartright and the mysterious woman in white who provides the title for his first really successful and still probably his best known novel. The incident—which may also owe something to the circumstances of Collins' first meeting in 1859 with Caroline Graves, his future mistress—is located exactly. Hartright is returning late one evening from Hampstead to his chambers in town via Frognal Lane, and reaches the junction with the present Finchley Road:

> There, in the middle of the broad, bright high-road—there, as if it had that moment sprung out of the earth or dropped from the heaven—stood the figure of a solitary Woman, dressed from head to foot in white garments; her face bent in grave inquiry on mine, her hand pointing to the dark cloud over London, as I faced her. (Hartright's Narrative, Ch. 3)

In 1850, some years before the publication of this novel, Collins had taken the walking holiday described in a neglected travel book, *Rambles Beyond Railways: or Notes in Cornwall*, which can still serve as a pleasant introduction to scenes now more frequently visited by tourists. The book is notable for its sympathetic accounts of Cornish people, customs and legends as much as for descriptions of landscape or buildings. Collins' itinerary begins at the fishing town and resort of Looe (on A387 18 miles west of Plymouth), praised for its 'quaint old houses, ... delightfully irregular streets, and ... fragrant terrace gardens' (Ch. 2), and proceeds by a meandering route along the south coast of the Duchy. Liskeard (Ch. 4), 8 miles to the north, is visited not for any intrinsic attractions but because of its proximity to St Cleer's Well, the stone circles known as the Hurlers and the granite pile of the Cheesering, all on Bodmin Moor to the north. From Helston, on A394 and a long stride of 46 miles to the SW, he goes south to Loe Pool and the Lizard (Chs. 5 and 6). After Land's End in Chapter 8, he moves north to Botallack (B3306) near St Just and a fascinating description of a descent into its mine (Ch. 9). The journey ends with visits to the Vale of Mawgan between St Colomb Major and the coast (Ch. 12), and to the dramatic headland of Tintagel with its ruined Castle.

In the 1850s Collins attracted the notice of Dickens (q.v.), his senior by twelve years—an association that led to close friendship, literary collaboration and inevitably, given both men's taste for travel, various holidays in each other's company. An accident-plagued tour of Cumbria in 1857 (see Dickens, Rte 18) resulted in *The Lazy Tour of Two Idle Apprentices* and Collins' decision to locate 'Limmeridge House', Marion Halcombe and the Fairlies' home in *The Woman in White*, on the coast south of Carlisle. A visit to Clovelly, Devon in 1860 (Dickens, Rte 14) produced another collaborative work, 'A Message from the Sea', published as the *Household Words* Christmas story for that year.

The most important of Collins' visits to Gad's Hill (Dickens, Rte 12) took place in 1860, when his younger brother Charles was married to Dickens' daughter Kate. Like his mentor, he was also fond of Broadstairs (Dickens, Rte 12 again). His stay in 1859 was made memorable by the discovery of a title for the novel he was writing, under circumstances he later described to a reporter:

> He walked for several hours on the cliffs between Kingsgate and Bleak House, and smoked an entire case of cigars, striving for a title but with barren result. As the sun went down the novelist threw himself on the grass, contemplating the North Foreland lighthouse, and, being hipped and weary, looked by no means lovingly on that hideous edifice. Savagely, biting the end of his last cigar he apostrophised the building, standing coldly and stiffly in the evening light, 'You are ugly and stiff and awkward; you know you are: stiff and as weird as my white woman. White woman!—woman in white! The title, by Jove!'

Appropriately enough it was Dickens, virtually alone among Collins' acquaintance, who approved the proposed title and did not think it too melodramatic. During a subsequent visit in 1862 Collins occupied Dickens' own former lodging, Bleak House.

The Suffolk coastal town of Aldeburgh, which Collins visited in the spring of 1862, provided locales for *No Name*, another of his successful novels of the 1860s. He notes the Moot Hall, left stranded on the beach by the encroachments of the sea, and reminds the reader of the town's connection with George Crabbe (q.v.), whom he tries to emulate in landscape descriptions like the following:

> It was a dull, airless evening. Eastward, was the gray majesty of the sea, hushed in breathless calm; the horizon line invisibly melting into the monotonous, misty sky; the idle ships shadowy and still on the idle water. Southward, the high ridge of the sea dike, and the grim, massive circle of a martello tower reared high on its mound of grass, closed the view darkly on all that lay beyond. Westward, a lurid streak of sunset glowed red in the dreary heaven, blackened the fringing trees on the far borders of the great inland marsh, and turned its little gleaming water-pools to pools of blood. Nearer to the eye, the sullen flow of the tidal river Alde ebbed noiselessly from the muddy banks; and nearer still, lonely and unprosperous by the bleak water-side, lay the lost little port of Slaughden, with its forlorn wharfs and warehouses of decaying wood, and its few scattered coasting-vessels deserted on the oozy river-shore. No fall of waves was heard on the beach, no trickling of waters bubbled audibly from the idle stream. Now and then the cry of a sea-bird rose from the region of the marsh; and at intervals, from farmhouses far in the inland waste, the faint winding of horns to call the cattle home travelled mournfully through the evening calm. (Fourth Scene, Ch. 1)

Throughout his life Collins was a Londoner, living at various addresses in Marylebone. In 1867 he moved to No. 65 (then No. 90) Gloucester Place, north of Oxford Street, a fine Georgian house now marked with a plaque. He remained there until the year before his death, writing his great contribution to the detective novel, *The Moonstone*, but later suffering a serious decline in both popularity and health. His funeral at Kensal Green Cemetery, opposite Kensal Green Station (Bakerloo Line and British Rail), was attended by Oscar Wilde (q.v.) among other literary figures but marred by scenes which, as his biographer points out, might almost have come from one of his novels:

> There must have been at least a hundred of those unwholesome creatures, who call themselves women, who seem to live in graveyards. When the coffin had been lowered into the bricked grave there was a general rush of these people who craned over into space, and clawed the wreaths of flowers, and pulled about the cards which were attached to the wreaths, and laughed and cried and chattered until they were moved on by the graveyard police.

Collins' grave is No. 31754 in Square 141, north of West Centre Avenue and immediately west of the church. His mistress, Caroline Graves, was buried beside him in 1895, though her presence was not recorded. A petition for a memorial in either St Paul's Cathedral or Westminster Abbey was unsuccessful, the rejection being influenced, according to one report, by 'other considerations than Mr Collins' literary excellence'.

Tintagel Castle, Tintagel, Cornwall: English Heritage, standard opening; phone Camelford (0840) 770328.

Bleak House (Dickens and Maritime Museum), Ford Road, Broadstairs, Kent: phone Thanet (0843) 62224.

William Collins

b. Chichester, West Sussex, 1721; d. Chichester, 1759. *Persian Eclogues* (1742); *Odes on Several Descriptive and Allegoric Subjects* (1746).

After attending Winchester College, Collins went to Oxford: first to The Queen's College in 1740 and then the following year to Magdalen College where, according to his contemporary Gilbert White (q.v.), he showed 'too high an opinion of his school acquisitions, and a sovereign contempt for all academic studies and discipline'. On the strength of his *Persian Eclogues* he was emboldened to reject a clerical career and join the literary life of London. He was a frequent visitor to James Thomson's cottage at Richmond (described under the entry for that author) and apparently even took lodgings in the area to be near his friend. Collins is the probable subject of a portrait in Thomson's last poem, *The Castle of Indolence* (1748), as

> a man of special grave remark:
> A certain tender gloom o'erspreads his face,
> Pensive, not sad ...
>
> (stanza 57)

He repaid the compliment with the fine 'Ode on the Death of Mr Thomson'.

Suffering from financial problems and increasing mental disorder, he returned in 1749 to Chichester, the town of his birth and, in the words of Edmund Blunden 'the most intimate relic of the life of William Collins that now exists'. He lived on Westgate, west of the Cathedral, under the care of his sister and later at the Chantry in the cloisters of the Cathedral. Though he was buried at St Andrew Oxmarket (now redundant) off East Street, his best memorial is in the SW tower of the Cathedral. Flaxman's monument shows him immersed in the New Testament while its inscription records the suffering of his last years:

> He pass'd in madd'ning pain life's feverish dream;
> While rays of genius only serv'd to shew
> The thick'ning horror and exalt his woe.

Winchester College, College Street, Winchester, Hampshire: phone the Bursar, (0962) 64242.

William Congreve

b. Bardsey, West Yorkshire, 1670; d. London, 1729. *The Old Bachelor* (1693); *The Double Dealer* (1694); *Love for Love* (1695); *The Way of the World* (1700).

Although Congreve's birthplace in the small village of Bardsey (on A58 between Leeds and Wetherby) does not survive the church where he was baptised, notable for its Saxon tower, is still there.

His father's military career moved the family to Ireland in 1674. Congreve's connections with the country are best remembered by the places where he was educated. He attended Kilkenny College in the county town of Kilkenny; its present buildings are on the north bank of the Nore near John's Bridge, but in Congreve's time the school was apparently in the Cathedral Close. He then studied at Trinity College, Dublin, occupying rooms in the Old Quadrangle.

During his university career he enjoyed a reputation for convivial living and strengthened his friendship with Swift (q.v.), who had also been a fellow pupil at Kilkenny.

In London there is nothing to commemorate Congreve's brief but distinguished career as a dramatist or his later life as man of leisure and holder of a convenient government sinecure. Instead, three country houses in scattered locations deserve mention. At Stretton Hall in Staffordshire, south of the county town and near the junction between A5 and A449, family home of the Congreves, he began his first play on his return from Ireland in 1689. The original house has been replaced by a fine brick 18C one. Tradition also ascribes the writing of the play to a stay in 1692 at Ilam, in Dovedale and 4 miles NW of Ashbourne, Derbyshire. The present Hall dates from the 19C and now serves as a Youth Hostel but the grounds, where the Manifold emerges from its subterranean course, justify a visit. Most important, Congreve was a guest at Stowe, 2 miles NW of Buckingham. Beginning in 1710 Sir Richard Temple, later Viscount Cobham, refurbished his 17C mansion and made its grounds perhaps the finest example of 18C landscaping. A monument to Congreve, in the curious form of an obelisk surmounted by a monkey, stands on an island in the Octagonal Lake. It was designed by William Kent and erected in 1736. Stowe is now a public school.

After Congreve's death, partly caused by an accident sustained during a visit to Bath, his body lay in state in the Jerusalem Chamber of Westminster Abbey. He was buried not in Poets' Corner but in the south aisle of the nave, with a monument erected by his friend Henrietta, Duchess of Marlborough, who chose to be buried near him.

Ilam Park, Ilam, near Ashbourne, Derbyshire: NT; phone Thorpe Cloud (033 529) 245. Ilam Hall is a Youth Hostel and not open to visitors.

Stowe (Stowe School), near Buckingham: grounds, garden buildings and main state rooms open, usually during the Easter and summer holidays; phone Buckingham (0280) 813650.

'Joseph Conrad' (pseudonym of Józef Teodor Konrad Korzeniowski)

b. Berdyczów, Poland, 1857; d. Bishopsbourne, Kent, 1924. *Almayer's Folly: The Story of an Eastern River* (1895); *An Outcast of the Islands* (1896); *The Nigger of the 'Narcissus': A Tale of the Sea* (1897); *Lord Jim: A Tale* (1900); *Youth: A Narrative, and Two Other Stories* (includes *Heart of Darkness*; 1902); *Typhoon* (1902); *Romance: A Novel* (with Ford Madox Ford; 1903); *Nostromo: A Tale of the Seaboard* (1904); *The Secret Agent: A Simple Tale* (1907); *Under Western Eyes: A Novel* (1911); *Chance: A Tale in Two Parts* (1913); *Victory: An Island Tale* (1915); *The Shadow-Line: A Confession* (1917); *The Arrow of Gold: A Story Between Two Notes* (1919); *The Rescue: A Romance of the Shallows* (1920); *The Rover* (1923); *Suspense: A Napoleonic Novel* (unfinished; 1925).

Conrad did not visit England until 1878, nor did he give up the sea until the mid 1890s, the time of his marriage to Jessie George. When he did settle down and devote himself to writing, his novels looked backward to earlier adventures abroad and at sea rather than at the English life around him. The only British place to have an important connection with his fiction is Greenwich Park in SE London. The Old Royal Observatory (now part of the National Maritime Museum) on top of the hill was the target of an attack in 1894 by the anarchist Martial Bourdin, who succeeded only in blowing himself up. The incident gave Conrad the germ of *The Secret Agent*. At the opening of *Heart of Darkness* the Thames below is evoked as 'the beginning of an interminable waterway' which leads Captain Marlow to the inner reaches of the Congo.

Conrad's years as a writer were spent mainly in Kent, which he was surely right to call 'the very heart of English literary life of that period' since other residents of the South-Eastern counties then included Henry James, Rudyard Kipling and H.G. Wells (qq.v.). From 1898 to 1907—the period that produced *Lord Jim*, the *Youth* volume of stories and *Nostromo*—he lived at Pent Farm outside the village of Postling, 3 miles north of Hythe. The period 1910–19, which produced *Chance* and *Victory* was spent at another farmhouse, Capel House near Orlestone, 5 miles south of Ashford. His last home (1919–24) was Oswalds, the Georgian former rectory of Bishopsbourne, a little village off A2 4½ miles SE of Canterbury. By this time he had won international recognition as a novelist, though he had passed the height of his powers. He had also, apparently, transformed himself into an English country gentleman, though in Bertrand Russell's words he still 'thought of civilised and morally tolerable human life as a dangerous walk on a thin crust of barely cooled lava'. A few months before his death he was offered a knighthood but put the letter aside unopened, fearing it came from the Inland Revenue. When the Prime Minister sent a personal messenger to make further inquiry, Conrad declined the honour.

His funeral service was held at the Roman Catholic church of St Thomas in Canterbury, between St George Street and Burgate. His simple tombstone in the Catholic cemetery gives his name only in Polish (with 'Teodor' misspelled), omits any reference to his novels, and quotes the lines from Spenser (q.v.) he had used as the epigraph to his last complete work, *The Rover*:

> Sleep after toyle, port after stormie seas,
> Ease after warre, death after life, does greatly please.

Old Royal Observatory (part of the National Maritime Museum), Greenwich Park, Greenwich, London SE10: phone National Maritime Museum, (01) 858 4422.

'Marie Corelli' (pseudonym of Mary MacKay)

b. place unknown, 1855; d. Stratford-upon-Avon, Warwickshire, 1924. *The Romance of Two Worlds* (1886); *Thelma* (1887); *Ardath* (1889); *Barabbas* (1893); *The Sorrows of Satan* (1895); *The Mighty Atom* (1896).

The houses where Marie Corelli lived until middle age have followed her once best-selling novels into obscurity. She spent a childhood and youth (1865–83) later romanticised beyond recognition at Mickleham, between Dorking and Leatherhead in Surrey, near Box Hill and the better known residence of George Meredith (q.v.). Her London home (1883–1900) at No. 47 Longridge Road in Earl's Court, south of and parallel to West Cromwell Road, is now owned by the Egyptian Embassy. The plaque that misspelled her name was removed but later replaced at the request of her modern biographer.

Marie Corelli is better, though not always kindly, remembered in Stratford-upon-Avon where she lived at Mason Croft, near the southern end of Church Street, from 1901 until her death. The pleasant 18C house now belongs to the University of Birmingham Shakespeare Institute. Together with the popularity of her novels, her habit of boating on the Avon in a gondola specially imported from Venice and her frequent quarrels with the Trustees of Shakespeare's Birthplace made her a tourist attraction to complement if not rival Shakespeare himself (q.v., Rte 7). *Punch* satirised the reactions of one such visitor:

'Behold', he cries, 'the actual house
    That Miss Corelli leases,
In yonder study's restful shade,
Accepting none but Heaven's aid,
    She makes her masterpieces'.

She made a more lasting contribution to Stratford in 1909 by being instrumental in the purchase, restoration and public opening of Harvard House in the High Street. She is buried in the cemetery on Evesham Road.

A flirtatious but later embittered relationship with the painter Arthur Severn, husband of Ruskin's cousin, made her a visitor to the writer's former home of Brantwood, near Coniston in Cumbria.

Harvard House, High Street, Stratford-upon-Avon, Warwickshire: administered by the Shakespeare Birthplace Trust; phone (0789) 204016.

Brantwood, Coniston, Cumbria: phone (0966) 41396.

William Cowper

b. Berkhamsted, Hertfordshire, 1731; d. East Dereham, Norfolk, 1800. Contributions to *Olney Hymns* (1779); *The Diverting History of John Gilpin* (1782); *The Task* (1785).

Though born in Hertfordshire Cowper was mainly educated in London at Westminster School, which stands in Little Dean's Yard to the south of Westminster Abbey. Without being conspicuously unhappy, his experiences there left him with the life-long dislike of the public school system expressed in his poem 'Tirocinium' (1785). He then studied law, lodging at No. 62 Russell Square, off Southampton Row in Bloomsbury, and in various parts of the Temple, south of Fleet Street near its junction with the Strand: in a house (now demolished) on Inner Temple Lane and in Pump Court nearby. It was in Fig Tree Court that Cowper, faced with the prospect of an examination for a House of Lords clerkship, attempted to hang himself in 1763.

As a result of the experience Cowper left London and the law, 'unwilling to revisit those noisy and crowded scenes, which I never loved, and which I now abhor'. After a period under medical care at St Albans he went to live in Huntingdon, Cambridgeshire, making regular visits to nearby Cambridge where his brother was a Fellow of Corpus Christi College. The house in Huntingdon's High Street where he lodged with Rev. Morley Unwin and his wife Mary is marked by a plaque.

When Unwin died suddenly in 1767 Cowper moved with Mrs Unwin to *Olney, a lace-making town near A428 between Bedford and Northampton but itself in the northern tip of Buckinghamshire. The Olney years were in many ways the most significant of his life and are certainly now the best remembered. He turned seriously to poetry, wrote some of his most charming letters, developed his compassionate interest in animals and came under the Evangelical influence of the local perpetual curate, John Newton. Yet he still could not escape mental turbulence. In 1773–74 religious delusions, suicidal impulses and anxiety about his forthcoming marriage to Mrs Unwin (never to take place) made him flee his home and seek refuge with Newton.

The house Cowper normally shared with Mrs Unwin, then called Orchard Side and now the Cowper and Newton Museum, stands in the Market Place. Its contents include the sofa which, at the suggestion of his friend Lady Austen, he took as the subject of his poem, *The Task*. The garden, communicating with the parsonage where Newton lived, preserves his summer house. There is a commemorative window in the Memorial Chapel of the church.

In 1786 Cowper and Mrs Unwin moved to *Weston Underwood, 2 miles SW of Olney and in the poet's eyes 'one of the prettiest villages in England'. They lived at the Lodge in the main street until 1795.

In the autumn of 1792 he made an extended visit to William Hayley, friend of good poets though a bad poet himself, at Eartham in West Sussex. On his way back he dined in Richmond with his relative, General Spencer Cowper, at Ham House, a fine 17C mansion with Baroque interiors and with grounds stretching to the Thames.

When he left Weston Cowper wrote on his bedroom window:

> Farewell, dear scenes, for ever closed to me;
> Oh, for what scenes must I now exchange ye!

His foreboding was justified, for the last years of his life were marked by Mrs Unwin's decline into senility before her death in 1796 and his own decline into the despairing melancholy so poignantly expressed by his poem 'The Castaway'. They were spent in Norfolk at Mundesley (on the coast 7 miles SE of Cromer), where his cousin's house on the High Street has since been renamed Cowper's House, and at East Dereham, 16 miles west of Norwich, again with his cousin John Johnson. The Cowper Memorial Congregational Church now occupies the site of his home in East Dereham's Market Place; a plaque pays tribute to the 'patient friends' who cared for him. He was buried in St Nicholas nearby, which has a stained glass window and a memorial tablet with epitaph by Hayley. George Borrow (q.v.), who spent part of his childhood in the town, was proud that its 'venerable church' should hold 'the mortal remains of England's sweetest and most pious bard':

> Yes, pretty D——, I could always love thee, were it but for the sake of him who sleeps beneath the marble slab in yonder quiet chancel. It was within thee that the long-oppressed bosom heaved its last sigh, and the crushed and gentle spirit escaped from a world in which it had known naught but sorrow. Sorrow! do I say? How faint a word to express the misery of that bruised reed; misery so dark that a blind worm like myself is occasionally tempted to exclaim, Better had the world never been created than that one so kind, so harmless and so mild, should have undergone such intolerable woe! But it is over now, for, as there is an end of joy, so has affliction its termination. (*Lavengro*, Ch. 3)

Cowper and Newton Museum, Market Place, Olney, Buckinghamshire: phone (0234) 711516.

Ham House, Richmond: administered by the Victoria and Albert Museum on behalf of NT; phone (01) 940 1950.

George Crabbe

b. Aldeburgh, Suffolk, 1755; d. Trowbridge, Wiltshire, 1832. *The Village* (1783); *The Parish Register* (1807); *The Borough* (1810); *Tales in Verse* (1812); *Tales of the Hall* (1819).

Although the various occasions of his life took him to several different regions, Crabbe is mainly associated with East Anglia and in particular with the Suffolk coastal town of *Aldeburgh, birthplace, intermittent residence in adult years and stimulus for some of his best poetry.

Its main point of interest is the church of St Peter and St Paul, where he served briefly as curate after his ordination at Norwich in 1781 and whose north chapel contains a memorial of 1847 by Thurlow. The house where he was born and Slaughden Quay, where as boy and young man he did uncongenial work for his father, have been obliterated by the encroachments of the sea—a process to which the present location of the half-timbered Moot Hall, once part of a market centre but now stranded on the beach, offers striking testimony. Crabbe Street running between the coast and the High Street before converging with the latter, appears to owe its name to a spirit of general tribute rather than to any specific connection with the writer.

According to the poet's son Aldeburgh was 'a poor and wretched place' in the time of Crabbe's youth, a description amply confirmed by the bleakly realistic portrayal of the local inhabitants and their condition in *The Village* and *The Borough*. Despite the fashionable status it has later come to enjoy, its seafront and adjoining coastline still retain the atmosphere recorded in Crabbe's verse and expressed most memorably, perhaps, in his account of the hero's melancholy visits to the shore in 'Peter Grimes' (from *The Borough*):

Here dull and hopeless he'd lie down and trace
How sidelong crabs had scrawl'd their crooked race;
Or sadly listen to the tuneless cry
Of fishing gull or clanging golden-eye;
What time the sea-birds to the marsh would come,
And the loud bittern, from the bull-rush home,
Gave from the salt-ditch side the bellowing boom ...
(lines 193–199)

In this century Crabbe's association with the town has been commemorated by the local premiere in 1945 of Benjamin Britten's opera, *Peter Grimes*.

In the surrounding area Bungay and Stowmarket, where Crabbe attended school, as well as Wickham Brook and Woodbridge, where he was apprenticed to apothecaries and surgeons, can boast no surviving evidence of his presence there; but the last town (16 miles SW of Aldeburgh), especially that part of it by the Deben estuary, still possesses much of the flavour it would have had in the poet's day. It was at Woodbridge that Crabbe first met his future wife, Sarah Emily.

Crabbe's connection with Central England was owing to the patronage of the Duke of Rutland and began in 1782 with his appointment as chaplain at the Duke's seat of Belvoir Castle, Leicestershire, 7 miles west of A1 near Grantham. His lodging from the time of his marriage in 1783 until 1785 was later destroyed by the fire that led to James Wyatt's extensive rebuilding of 1816. Crabbe later took up the curacy of Stathern (5 miles SW of Belvoir) and, in 1789, the living of Muston (4 miles north of Belvoir), which he held until 1814 with a long record of absenteeism in his native Suffolk. His wife, who died and was buried at Muston, is commemorated by a plaque in the chancel of the church.

Crabbe moved to South-Western England in the later years of his life to occupy the more profitable living of Trowbridge, west of Devizes in Wiltshire, where he remained until his death. He did, however, make several journeys from Wiltshire, most notably an 1817 visit to London which is better documented than his earlier sojourn in the capital (1780–81). He took lodgings at No. 37 Bury Street, to the south of Piccadilly, thus having the poet Thomas Moore as a near neighbour, and gained the *entrée* to Holland House in Holland Park, which the wife of the third Lord Holland had made a fashionable gathering place. Only the park and east wing of this Tudor mansion now survive, their appearance changed for the worse by the addition of the modern King George VI Memorial Hostel. In London circles Crabbe caused remark by his provincial look ('dressed as he was in the rather old-fashioned style of clerical propriety') and his habit of making sugary addresses to the ladies. He spent the autumn of 1822 with Sir Walter Scott (q.v.) in his house at No. 39 Castle Street, Edinburgh.

Crabbe's memory is recorded by a tablet in the chancel of Trowbridge church. His geological collection and herbarium are occasionally on display at Trowbridge Museum.

Belvoir Castle, near Grantham, Leicestershire: phone (0476) 870262.

Trowbridge Museum, Civic Hall, St Stephen's Place, Trowbridge, Wiltshire: phone (02214) 65072.

Mrs Craik (Dinah Maria Mulock)

b. Stoke-on-Trent, Staffordshire, 1826; d. London, 1887. *The Ogilvies* (1849); *Olive* (1850); *Avillion and Other Tales* (1853); *John Halifax, Gentleman* (1856); *A Woman's Thoughts About Women* (1858); *A Life For a Life* (1859); *Mistress and Maid* (1863); *Christian's Mistake* (1865); *The Little Lame Prince* (1875); *An Unsentimental Journey Through Cornwall* (1884).

John Halifax, Gentleman, always Mrs Craik's most popular novel and now the only one to be remembered, is set in the attractive Gloucestershire town of Tewkesbury (on A38 9 miles NW of Cheltenham), which she calls 'Norton Bury'. She is commemorated by a marble neo-Renaissance tablet in the south transept of the fine Norman Abbey Church. The picturesque Bell Hotel opposite the churchyard gate becomes the home of Abel Fletcher in the novel. Mill Street leads to the River Avon and the Abbey Mill, renamed Abel Fletcher's Mill and now a restaurant. The Tudor House Hotel on the High Street, a building much altered but of genuine antiquity, is identified with the home of Ursula March.

Mrs Craik spent the later years of her life in Bromley, then in Kent and now absorbed into SE London. She was buried nearby in the churchyard at Keston, by A233 1½ miles south of its junction with A232.

Samuel Daniel

b. near Taunton, Somerset? 1562; d. Beckington, Somerset, 1619. *Delia* (1592); *Cleopatra* (1594); *The Civil Wars between the Two Houses of York and Lancaster* (1595–1609); *Musophilus, Containing a Generall Defence of Learning* (1599); *A Defence of Ryme* (1603); *Philotas* (1605).

Daniel was educated at Magdalen College, Oxford. In the early 1590s he became tutor to William, son of Mary Herbert, Countess of Pembroke and sister to Sir Philip Sidney (q.v.), and so joined the impressive list of literary men connected with Wilton House, near Salisbury in Wiltshire. *Delia*, a sonnet cycle in the Petrarchan manner, dedicated to the Countess, is today better remembered than his Senecan tragedies, court masques and prose treatises.

Later the same decade Daniel became tutor to Lady Anne Clifford (1590–1676), daughter of the Countess of Cumberland, at Skipton in North Yorkshire (22 miles west of Harrogate via A59). In adult life Lady Anne left her mark throughout Northern England by her work restoring castles and churches after the ravages of the Civil War. At •Skipton Castle itself she added the lettered balustrade with the Clifford motto ('Désormais'; 'henceforth') and restored the charmingly irregular Conduit Court.

In 1610 Daniel moved to the village of Beckington, at the junction of A36 and A361 between Trowbridge and Frome near the Wiltshire–Somerset border. Its church has a monument erected in his memory by Lady Anne.

Wilton House, Wilton, near Salisbury, Wiltshire: phone Salisbury (0722) 743115.

Skipton Castle, Skipton, North Yorkshire: phone (0756) 2442.

C. Day-Lewis

b. Ballintubbert, Co. Laois, 1904; d. Hadley Common, Hertfordshire, 1972. *Beechen Vigil and Other Poems* (1925); *Country Comets* (1928); *Transitional Poem* (1929); *From Feathers to Iron* (1931); *The Magnetic Mountain* (1933); *A Hope for Poetry* (1934); *A Time to Dance* (1935); *A Question of Proof*† (1935); *Noah and the Waters* (1936); *The Friendly Tree* (1936); *Thou Shell of Death*† (1936); *Starting Point* (1937); *There's Trouble Brewing*† (1937); *Overtures to a Death* (1938); *The Beast Must Die*† (1938); *Child of Misfortune* (1939); *The Smiler With the Knife*† (1939); *Malice in Wonderland*† (1940); *Poems in Wartime* (1940); *The Case of the Abominable Snowman*† (1941); *Word Over All* (1943); *The Poetic Image* (1947); *Minute for Murder*† (1947); *Poems 1943–1947* (1948); *Head of a Traveller*† (1949); *An Italian Visit* (1953); *The Dreadful Hollow*† (1953); *The Whisper in the Gloom*† (1954); *A Tangled Web*† (1956); *Pegasus* (1957); *End of Chapter*† (1957); *A Penknife in My Heart*† (1958); *The Widow's Cruise*† (1959); *The Buried Day* (1960); *The Worm of Death*† (1961); *The Gate* (1962); *The Deadly Joker*† (1963); *The Sad Variety*† (1964); *The Room* (1965); *The Lyric Impulse* (1965); *The Morning After Death*† (1966); *The Private Wound*† (1968); *The Whispering Roots* (1970).

† detective novels published under the pseudonym 'Nicholas Blake'.

Born into an Anglo–Irish family, Day-Lewis left Ireland when still a baby and did not become fully aware of his roots until middle age. 'The House Where I Was Born', published in 1957, contemplates a family photograph of Ballintubbert House, 'An elegant, shabby, white-washed house/ With a slate roof' (lines 1–2), and finds it a symbol of the old Anglo–Irish order. The building and the tiny village of Ballintubbert are near Windy Gap, off N80 12 miles NW of Carlow in Laois. In Wexford to the SE lies Monart (2 miles west of Enniscorthy) where Day-Lewis paid childhood visits to his uncle, Rev. William Goldsmith Squires, a descendant of Oliver Goldsmith (q.v.). *The Buried Day* remembers these holidays with special fondness: 'Monart did more than any other place for my sensuous education' (Ch. 2).

The adult Day-Lewis detected in himself a love both of putting down roots and of tearing them up again. It is not hard to see the origin of this tendency in the itinerant life he led after he was first brought to England in 1905. The family's movements are best summarised by a list of the churches where his father was either curate or rector: the lovely Priory Church in Great Malvern (7 miles SW of Worcester); Christ Church, whose conspicuous 19C spire surivives in Lancaster Gate opposite the north side of Kensington Gardens in London; and the parish church of Edwinstowe (on A6075 7 miles NE of Mansfield in Nottinghamshire).

A degree of fixity was provided by his education (1917–23) at the public school in Sherborne (on A30 in Dorset), where he met another future poet, Louis MacNeice. Day-Lewis' marriage in 1928 to a local girl at Sherborne's splendid Abbey is but one aspect of his abiding connection with Dorset.

The friendship with MacNeice was renewed when Day-Lewis went to Wadham College, Oxford, in 1923. Both men were drawn into 'The Gang', the group of young poets gathered round the compelling figure of W.H. Auden (q.v.). Maurice Bowra, then Dean and later Warden of Wadham, introduced Day-Lewis to Lady Ottoline Morrell at Garsington Manor (off B480 4 miles SE of the city). He returned to Oxford as Professor of Poetry (1951–56).

Like many other poets, Day-Lewis slid with reluctance into school-teaching when he left university, working first in Oxford itself and landing up at the boys' College in Cheltenham. Its atmosphere was not suited to a poet who was rapidly gaining a reputation for his left-wing views, and in 1935 Day-Lewis resigned to devote himself full-time to writing. The break was encouraged by his desire to join the Communist Party, and by his new and profitable sideline in detective novels written under the pseudonym of 'Nicholas Blake'. *A Question of Proof*, the first such book, clearly reflects his experience of public schools.

From 1938 to 1950 he lived in south Devon in the village of Musbury (on A358 between Axminster and Seaton). His house, Brimclose, lies in the shadow of a hill crowned by an Iron Age fort. Lyme Regis and its lovely bay (SE of the village) appear at the beginning and end of what is perhaps his finest detective novel, *The Beast Must Die*.

With the break-up of his marriage Day-Lewis went to London and lived in Kensington, where Kensington Gardens are used in the opening scene of *The Whisper in the Gloom*. In 1956, married to the actress Jill Balcon, he made a final move to Greenwich in SE London. From his house at No. 6 Croom's Hill, on the western edge of Greenwich Park, he could watch 'the great cargo-liners rounding the Isle of Dogs, the tugs and their strings of lighters, the wharves, warehouses, power stations, the skyline restless with cranes, the blue-diamond lights of welding and the indigo smoke from tall chimneys—all the river life which, here at Greenwich, overlooked by the palace and the park, enlivens their elegance with a workaday reality' ('Postscript' to *The Buried Day*). This scene and his new home appear in another 'Nicholas Blake' novel, *The Worm of Death*.

Love of Dorset and admiration for Thomas Hardy (q.v.) made him choose to be buried in the churchyard at Stinsford (off A35 1 mile east of Dorchester).

Garsington Manor, Garsington, near Oxford: gardens open twice a year under NGS.

Daniel Defoe

b. London, 1660; d. London, 1731. *An Essay upon Projects* (1697); *The True-Born Englishman* (1701); *The Shortest Way with the Dissenters* (1702); *Hymn to the Pillory* (1703); *The Life and Strange Surprising Adventures of Robinson Crusoe* (1719); *The Adventures of Captain Singleton* (1720); *The Fortunes and Misfortunes of the Famous Moll Flanders* (1722); *A Journal of the Plague Year* (1722); *The History and Remarkable Life of Colonel Jacque, Commonly Call'd* (1722); *Roxana, or the Fortunate Mistress* (1724); *Memoirs of a Cavalier* (1724); *A Tour through the Whole Island of Great Britain* (1724–26).

It is ironic that so few places reminiscent of Defoe's life and work should survive, for in his novels he obviously appreciates the role geographical precision can play in creating verisimilitude and in his *Tour* he left a major travel book that still deserves reading. Yet the lack of places to visit is not entirely surprising. Defoe led the sort of active life immersed in affairs of the moment that often leaves no permanent mark, being businessman and government agent as well as author of more books than the headnote above can attempt to record.

Though born in the City of London he was educated in Stoke Newington to the north, returning to live there in later life. A plaque marks the site of his former house on Stoke Newington Church Street. The original tombstone from his grave (see below) is now on display in the entrance lobby of the Central Library nearby.

He died on Ropemaker Street (then Ropemaker Alley), south of Chiswell Street in Finsbury, and was buried to the north in the Nonconformist cemetery of Bunhill Fields. An obelisk erected in 1870 replaces his original tombstone. He attended worship at St Giles without Cripplegate, at the western end of Chiswell Street and now surrounded by the modern Barbican.

Of the many places visited in his travels the only one to preserve a personal reminder is Bury St Edmunds in Suffolk. He stayed at the *Cupola House, now a pub, on The Traverse after the spell in Newgate and the pillory that the success of his satire, *The Shortest Way with the Dissenters*, had earned him in 1703. The fine building of 1693 is made the more noteworthy for having been described in detail by another traveller, Celia Fiennes, several years before:

> this high house is an apothecarys, at least 60 stepps up from the ground and gives a pleaseing prospect of the whole town, that is compact severall streetes but no good buildings; except this the rest are great old houses of timber and mostly in the old forme of the country which are very long peaked roofes of tileing; this house is the new mode of building, 4 roomes of a floor pretty sizeable and high, well furnish'd, a drawing roome and Chamber full of

China and a Damaske bed embroyder'd, 2 other roomes, Camlet and Mohaire beds, a pretty deale of plaite in his wives chamber, parlours below and a large shop.

Defoe himself wrote about Bury with special approval in his *Tour*, characteristically paying less attention to its history and Abbey than to 'the present state of the place':

the beauty of the town consists in the number of gentry who dwell in and near it, the polite conversation among them; the affluence and plenty they live in; the sweet air they breathe in, and the pleasant country they have to go abroad in.

Central Library, Stoke Newington Church Street, Stoke Newington, London N16: (01) 800 1283.

Sir John Denham

b. Dublin, 1615; d. London, 1669. *Coopers Hill* (1642; revised 1650 and 1655).

After studying at Trinity College, Oxford (1631–34)—where Anthony à Wood records that he was 'more addicted to gaming than study'—Sir John Denham inherited his father's estates at Egham, on A30 in Surrey. The parish church is 19C but preserves the remarkable monuments to the elder Sir John Denham (d. 1638) and his two wives; the small kneeling figure at the left of the latter monument is the only contemporary portrait of the poet.

Nearby Cooper's Hill, overlooking Runnymede, gave its name to the poem that, in the opinion of Samuel Johnson (q.v.), 'confers upon him the rank and dignity of an original author':

He seems to have been, at least among us, the author of a species of composition that may be denominated *local poetry*, of which the fundamental subject is some particular landscape, to be poetically described, with the addition of such embellishments as may be supplied by historical retrospection, or incidental meditation.

Coopers Hill is usually remembered for its mellifluous invocation to the Thames:

O could I flow like thee, and make thy stream
My great example, as it is my theme!
Though deep, yet clear, though gentle, yet not dull,
Strong without rage, without ore-flowing full.
(lines 189–192)

In 1642, during the Civil War, Sir John expelled the Puritan poet George Wither from the command of the Castle at Farnham (on A31 20 miles SW of Egham) on behalf of the Royalists, but was himself obliged to abandon its defence later the same year. Perhaps in retaliation, Wither occupied Denham's house at Egham and laid claim to his property. John Aubrey adds a pleasant but unsupported footnote to the story of the poets' rivalry:

G.W. was taken prisoner, and was in danger of his life, having written severely against the king, &c. Sir John Denham went to the king, and desired his majestie not to hang him, for that whilest G.W. lived he should not be the worst poet in England.

After he returned from the Continent in 1652, deprived of his property, Denham found refuge with the Pembroke family at Wilton

House, west of Salisbury in Wiltshire, where Inigo Jones had just completed work on restoration.

In 1634 Denham had married in London, at the predecessor to Wren's St Bride's, Fleet Street. After the Restoration, in 1665, he married Margaret Brooke in Westminster Abbey. She was buried in 1667 at nearby St Margaret's, Westminster, the common gossip of the day being that Denham had poisoned her in revenge for her public infidelity with the Duke of York. He himself was buried in Poets' Corner (fee) of the Abbey.

Farnham Castle. The keep is English Heritage, summer standard opening; phone (0252) 713393. The domestic buildings are occupied by the Centre for International Briefing; guided tours; phone (0252) 721194.

Wilton House, Wilton, near Salisbury, Wiltshire: phone Salisbury (0722) 743115.

Benjamin Disraeli, Earl of Beaconsfield

b. London, 1804; d. London, 1881. *Vivian Grey* (1826–27); *Contarini Fleming: A Psychological Autobiography* (1832); *Henrietta Temple: A Love Story* (1837); *Coningsby: or The New Generation* (1844); *Sybil: or The Two Nations* (1845); *Tancred: or The New Crusade* (1847); *Lothair* (1870); *Endymion* (1880).

Disraeli's early years were spent in London's Holborn. His birthplace at No. 22 Theobald's Road, off the Gray's Inn Road, is marked by a plaque. His father, the writer Isaac D'Israeli, belonged to no organised religion but was persuaded of the need to bring his children up in the Church of England. So when he was twelve Disraeli was baptised at St Andrew, by Holborn Circus, a Wren church now rebuilt after war-time bomb damage. The service was conducted by a nephew of the poet Coleridge (s.v. Lake Poets). In 1824 Disraeli entered Lincoln's Inn to the south of Holborn and kept nine terms, though of course he never pursued a legal career. Instead, he established himself as a wit, a dandy and a novelist whose talents were most fully expressed in the 'Young England' trilogy of the 1840s.

His flamboyant, controversial and eventually distinguished career as Tory politician is well remembered in Westminster. Mario Raggi's statue on the lawn of Parliament Square is near the Palace of Westminster, where Disraeli served in the Commons from 1837 and the Lords from 1876. The north transept (fee) of Westminster Abbey has a statue by Sir Edgar Boehm.

Disraeli's marriage in 1839 to the wealthy widow Mrs Wyndham Lewis took him to Mayfair. The wedding ceremony was performed in St George's, Hanover Square. Until his wife's death in 1872, he lived at No. 93 Park Lane. He died just round the corner at No. 19 Curzon Street, now marked with a plaque.

Yet the place most fully reminiscent of Disraeli lies in his Buckinghamshire constituency: *Hughenden Manor, 1½ miles north of High Wycombe and reached from A4128. He bought the property in 1847 and used it as his country estate for the rest of his life, taking considerable pleasure in the role of country gentleman. Originally of very simple design, the late 18C building was remodelled with unfortunate results by the Gothic architect, E.B. Lamb, in 1862–63. Hughenden still has much of Disraeli's furniture and many mementoes.

Although he was assured a place in Westminster Abbey, Disraeli chose to be buried in Hughenden church. Gladstone regarded the gesture with suspicion: 'As he lived so he died—all display without reality or genuineness'. Queen Victoria, who paid a special visit to the grave, took a different view and caused a monument in his memory to be placed in the chancel. Its inscription quotes from the Book of Proverbs: 'Kings love him that speaketh right'.

Hughenden Manor, High Wycombe, Buckinghamshire: NT; phone (0494) 32580.

John Donne

b. London, 1572; d. London, 1631. Metaphysical poet.

A convenient London walking tour begins at St Paul's Cathedral. Donne was Dean of the old cathedral on this site from 1621 until his death and was buried there. Almost alone among its monuments his unusual **memorial statue by Nicholas Stone survived the fire of 1666 virtually undamaged and is now placed in the south side of the ambulatory (fee). In striking expression of the same Jacobean sensibility that pervades his poetry, both secular and religious, it shows him standing on an urn dressed for the grave. His friend and first biographer Izaak Walton quotes a contemporary account of Donne ordering and posing for the picture on which the memorial was based:

> Several Charcole-fires being first made in his large study, he brought with him into that place his winding-sheet in his hand, and, having put off all his cloaths, had this sheet put on him, and so tyed with knots at his head and feet, and his hands so placed, as dead bodies are usually fitted to be shrouded and put into their coffin, or grave. Upon this *Vrn* he thus stood with his eyes shut, and with so much of the sheet turned aside as might shew his lean, pale and death-like face, which was purposely turned toward the East, from whence he expected the second coming of his and our Saviour Jesus.

From St Paul's we descend Ludgate Hill (to the right of which lay the Fleet Prison, where Donne was briefly confined in 1602 for marrying without official permission) and follow its continuation as Fleet Street. Halfway down on the right is St Dunstan in the West, an early 19C church replacing the older building of which Donne was vicar from 1624 to 1631. A right turn on to Chancery Lane shortly beyond leads to Lincoln's Inn, with which he was intimately connected from the time of his first admission in 1592. His 'Epithalamion made at Lincoln's Inn', dating from the early 1590s, may well have been written for a mock-occasion connected with his post as Master of Revels, which he held in 1593. In Old Square, to the right of the main gatehouse, stands the Chapel rebuilt between 1619 and 1623, when Donne was Divinity Reader at the Inn. He is reputed to have laid the cornerstone. By returning to Fleet Street and continuing west as it changes to the Strand, we reach St Clement Danes, a Wren church now restored after war-time damage. Donne's wife Ann (d. 1617) was buried in the previous church on this site.

Another London church important to Donne's life may be found in Chelsea, by the river at the junction of Cheyne Walk and Old Church Street. At All Saints (also known as Chelsea Old Church), now restored after severe war-time damage, he preached the funeral sermon for his friend Lady Magdalen Danvers in 1627. Her son the poet George Herbert (q.v.) and Izaak Walton were among the congregation. The church is also notable for a monument of 1631 to Sara Colville, in the same macabre vein as Donne's own. On Danvers Street nearby stood Danvers House, on the site of a house that had belonged to Sir Thomas More and itself demolished in 1720. Donne was Lady Danvers' guest there in 1625, taking refuge from the plague-ridden City.

Places outside London reminiscent of Donne's life are few and scattered. He studied at Hertford College, Oxford, when it was still Hart Hall. In Wales he was a guest of Lady Danvers, then Mrs Magdalen Herbert, at the now-ruined castle of Montgomery, once the county town of Montgomeryshire but now in Powys. The occasions are remembered in the poems 'The Primrose, being at Montgomery Castle' and 'Good Friday, 1613. Riding Westward'. From 1616 until his death he was pluralist rector of St Nicholas on the High Street of Sevenoaks, in Kent; the church contains a memorial. Because of this position, he also preached at the mansion of Knole, seat of the Sackville family, to the SE of the town.

Montgomery Castle, Montgomery, Powys: Cadw: Welsh Historic Monuments; phone headquarters in Cardiff, (0222) 465511.

Knole, Sevenoaks, Kent: NT; phone (0732) 450608. Park open all year to walkers.

Sir Arthur Conan Doyle

b. Edinburgh, 1859; d. Crowborough, East Sussex, 1930. *A Study in Scarlet* (1887); *The Mystery of Cloomber* (1889); *Micah Clarke* (1889); *The Sign of Four* (1890); *The Captain of the Polestar and Other Tales* (1890); *The Firm of Girdlestone: A Romance of the Unromantic* (1890); *The White Company* (1891); *The Doings of Raffles Haw* (1892); *The Great Shadow* (1892); *Beyond the City* (1892); *The Adventures of Sherlock Holmes* (1892); *The Refugees* (1893); *The Memoirs of Sherlock Holmes* (1894); *Round the Red Lamp: Being Facts and Fancies of the Medical Life* (1894); *The Stark Munro Letters* (1895); *The Exploits of Brigadier Gerard* (1896); *Rodney Stone* (1896); *Uncle Bernac: A Memory of the Empire* (1897); *The Tragedy of the Korosko* (1898); *The Hound of the Baskervilles* (1902); *The Adventures of Gerard* (1903); *The Return of Sherlock Holmes* (1905); *Sir Nigel* (1906); *Through the Magic Door* (1907); *Round the Fire Stories* (1908); *The Lost World* (1912); *The Poison Belt* (1913); *The Valley of Fear* (1915); *His Last Bow* (1917); *Memories and Adventures* (1924); *The History of Spiritualism* (1926); *The Land of Mist* (1926); *The Case-Book of Sherlock Holmes* (1927); *The Maracot Deep and Other Stories* (1929).

Doyle's birthplace in Edinburgh is at No. 11 Picardy Place, on the eastern extension of Princes Street. He studied medicine at the University, where his teacher Dr Joseph Bell unconsciously sat for the portrait of Sherlock Holmes. He spent his schooldays at Stonyhurst College, the Jesuit public school 12 miles north of Blackburn in Lancashire. Soon after leaving, however, he abandoned Roman Catholicism (eventually becoming an ardent spiritualist) and later explained why he would not have a son of his own educated by the Jesuits: 'They try to rule too much by fear—too little by love or reason'.

The house in Portsmouth where Doyle set up his medical practice and created Holmes while waiting for his first patients to come has been demolished, but his career after he moved to London in 1890 is better commemorated. He lived at No. 23 Montague Place, behind the British Museum, and walked westward each day to his surgery at No. 2 Devonshire Place, south of the Marylebone Road and near the more fashionable Harley Street. Both addresses are connected with Holmes, whom Doyle had revived with great success for the series of stories in the *Strand* magazine. In 'The Musgrave Ritual' Holmes tells Dr Watson that his first London lodgings had been on Montague Street, near Montague Place. Devonshire Place, of course, is near Baker Street, where No. 221B is probably the most famous imaginary

Sherlock Holmes brooding over Dartmoor: an illustration by Sidney Paget to The Hound of the Baskervilles

address in England. It should be remembered that Baker Street was then limited to the stretch between Portman Square in the south and Paddington Street in the north, and that it had not completed its descent into a merely commercial thoroughfare. The exact location of Holmes and Watson's lodgings with Mrs Hudson has defied satisfactory identification even by the stubbornly ingenious researchers whom Doyle's work has attracted. Tradition, however, points to the site of the Abbey National Building Society; letters addressed to Sherlock Holmes at No. 221B are delivered here.

In fact, the visitor who wishes to trace Holmes' footsteps through London (and there are several commercial tours that offer to satisfy this pleasure) will find the great detective curiously elusive. The rich, powerful sense of the metropolis exuded by the stories depends more on atmosphere than exact reference. Sherlock Holmes' London is created out of fog and gaslights and hansom cabs, not specific buildings. The detective's best monument is *The Sherlock Holmes pub and restaurant on Northumberland Street, south of the Strand near Charing Cross, which now boasts a recreation of his Baker Street living room. The building was formerly the Northumberland Hotel, where Sir Henry Baskerville stayed (and had two odd shoes stolen) in Chapter 4 of *The Hound of the Baskervilles.*

This novel treats Dartmoor in South-Western England with the same generalising touch that Doyle brought to the topography of London. He visited the area with his friend Fletcher Robinson in 1900, but took the writer's customary liberties with fact. His Dartmoor is both larger and wilder than the real thing; its tors and prehistoric villages are too generally described to be identified among the many candidates that the actual terrain offers. However, Grimspound Bog (6 miles SW of Moretonhampstead off B3212) suggested at least the name of 'Grimpen Mire', in which the criminal Stapleton perishes. The remains of a large Bronze Age settlement survive.

By the time he wrote *The Hound of the Baskervilles* Doyle had moved from London, following the preference common among writers of his generation for South-Eastern England. After his second marriage in 1907 he bought Windlesham Manor in Crowborough, off A26 7 miles SW of Royal Tunbridge Wells. The family nicknamed the house 'Swindlesham' because of the extortionate price he had paid for it. The lovely Groombridge Place, a 17C moated house 5 miles north, must surely have suggested Douglas' home in *The Valley of Fear*. Needing a place where he could conduct spiritualist seances away from gossip and publicity, Doyle later bought a home near Minstead (2 miles NW of Lyndhurst in the New Forest), a village that had earlier featured in his novel, *The White Company*. His body, originally buried in the garden at Windlesham, was later reburied in the churchyard here under the epitaph 'Steel True, Blade Straight'.

Grimspound (Bronze Age settlement), near Moretonhampstead, Devon: English Heritage, open at any reasonable time.

Michael Drayton

b. Hartshill, Warwickshire, 1563; d. London, 1631. *Idea: The Shepheards Garland* (1593); *Ideas Mirrour* (1594; final revised edition, called *Idea*, 1619); *Poly-Olbion* (1612–22).

Drayton is usually remembered for the sonnet cycle originally published as *Ideas Mirrour*, and particularly for the sonnet beginning 'Since there's no help, come let us kiss and part' added to the final edition of 1619. He also made a massive contribution to topographical poetry with *Poly-Olbion*, which deals with the Channel Islands, Wales and virtually every English county. The title means 'with many blessings' and the subtitle further prepares the reader for the expansive nature of Drayton's undertaking, as well as its inevitable longueurs, periodic delights and fanciful digressions: 'A Chorographicall Description of Tracts, Rivers, Mountaines, Forests, and Other Parts of This Renowned Isle of Great Britain, with Intermixture of the Most Remarquable Stories, Antiquities, Wonders, Rarityes, Pleasures, and Commodities of the Same'. *Poly-Olbion* still makes a pleasant companion for the traveller, particularly if it is used in conjunction with the index of placenames provided in Volume 5 of the Tercentary Edition of Drayton's *Works* by J. William Hebel (revised 1961).

A black marble monument marks Drayton's grave in Poets' Corner (fee) of Westminster Abbey. It was paid for by Lady Anne Clifford (see Samuel Daniel) and the commemorative verse is by his friend Ben Jonson (q.v.).

John Dryden

b. Aldwinkle (or Aldwincle), Northamptonshire, 1631; d. London, 1700. *Annus Mirabilis* (1667); *Essay of Dramatick Poesie* (1668); *Aurangzebe* (1676); *All for Love* (1678); *Absalom and Achitophel* (1681); *MacFlecknoe* (1682); *The Medall* (1682); *Religio Laici* (1682); *The Hind and the Panther* (1687); *Fables Ancient and Modern.*

Aldwinkle is a small village west of A605 between Thrapston and Oundle. Dryden's birthplace, the Rectory, still stands opposite the 13C–15C church of All Saints where his father was incumbent. Much of the poet's childhood was spent in Titchmarsh, 3½ miles to the SE, home of his mother's family, the Pickerings. A monument of 1722 in the north chapel of the church, itself notable for a striking tower, commemorates his parents and the poet himself: 'We boast that he was bred and had his first learning here'. Dryden maintained his connection with the area throughout his life. Part of *The Hind and the Panther* may have been written at Rushton Hall, 4 miles NW of Kettering, Renaissance seat of the Tresham family. The building is now a school belonging to the Royal National Institute for the Blind. Of particular interest is Sir Thomas Tresham's fanciful Triangular Lodge in the grounds but reached by a separate entrance on the Desborough Road. In the summer of 1695 Dryden completed the seventh book of his translation of Virgil's *Aeneid* at the splendid Renaissance mansion of Burghley House, near Stamford and the A1.

Of his education at Trinity College, Cambridge, in 1650–54 little

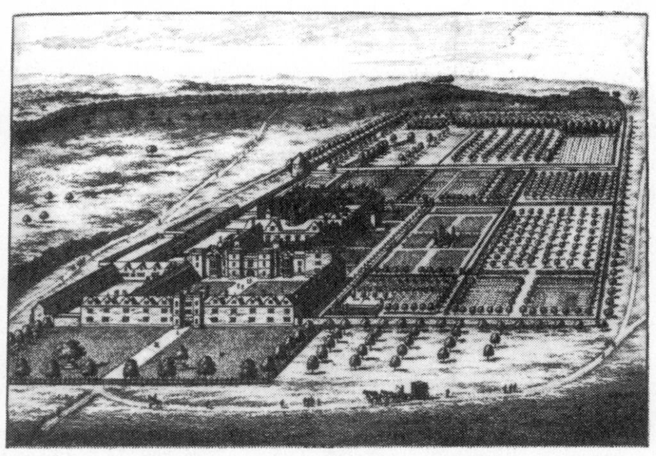

Knole, from James Beeverell's Les Délices de la Grand' Bretagne et de l'Irlande *(expanded edition of 1727)*

record survives save an entry in the 'Conclusion Book' of 1652 noting his punishment for disobedience to the Vice Master.

During the years of his fame as poet and dramatist Dryden enjoyed the *entrée* to several country houses other than those in his native Central England. His father-in-law owned the estate of Charlton Park, 2 miles NE of Malmesbury, Wiltshire; the Jacobean house where Dryden took refuge from London's plague and fire in 1665–66 no longer survives. He also visited the seat of his friend and patron, Charles Sackville, Lord Buckhurst, Earl of Dorset, at Knole near Sevenoaks in Kent. It is reported that on one occasion he was gratified to find a £100 note under his plate when he sat down to dinner.

The majority of Dryden's life, however, was spent in London. He was educated from about 1644 until 1650 at Westminster School, whose buildings stand in Little Dean's Yard to the south of Westminster Abbey. He died at No. 44 Gerrard Street in Soho, parallel to and south of Shaftesbury Avenue; the house has been rebuilt but its neighbour bears a plaque. He was buried in Poet's Corner (fee) of Westminster Abbey. The lack of a proper memorial, which Pope (q.v.) complained about ('Beneath a rude and nameless stone he lies'), was made good by John Sheffield, Duke of Buckingham in 1720. Pope substituted a simple inscription for the epitaph he had originally composed:

> This SHEFFIELD rais'd. The sacred Dust below
> Was DRYDEN once: The rest who does not know?

A bust by Scheemakers was added in 1731.

Rushton Hall (Royal National Institute for the Blind School), Rushton, near Kettering, Northamptonshire: access to the grounds and exterior and a limited inspection of the interior by appointment; phone Kettering (0536) 710506.

Rushton Triangular Lodge, Rushton, near Kettering, Northamptonshire: English Heritage, summer standard opening; phone (0536) 710761.

Burghley House, Stamford, Lincolnshire: phone (0780) 52451.

Knole, Sevenoaks, Kent: NT; phone (0732) 450608. Park open all year to walkers.

John Dyer

b. Llangathen, Dyfed, 1699; d. Coningsby, Lincolnshire, 1758. *Grongar Hill* (1726); *The Ruins of Rome* (1740); *The Fleece* (1757).

Although he was educated at London's Westminster School, in Little Dean's Yard to the south of Westminster Abbey, and later held various livings in Central and Eastern England, Dyer's most important connection is with his native Wales. He came from the Vale of the Tywi (or Towey), west of Llandeilo, praising its scenery in *Grongar Hill*, the slight but charming landscape poem on which his slender reputation is based. A convenient tour leaves Llandeilo by A40 and passes, all to the left: Llangathen (3½ miles) where Dyer was born and lived at Aberglasney House; Grongar (or Grongaer) Hill itself (4 miles) with its hillfort; and the ruined ancient stronghold of Dryslwyn Castle, also mentioned in the poem, which is reached via B4297 (6 miles).

Dyer spent his last years as rector of Coningsby, between Sleaford and Horncastle in the flat, uncongenial countryside of Lincolnshire.

Maria Edgeworth

b. Black Bourton, Oxfordshire, 1767; d. Edgeworthstown, Co. Longford, 1849. *Letters for Literary Ladies* (1795); *Practical Education* (1798); *Castle Rackrent: An Hibernian Tale* (1800); *Early Lessons* (1801-25); *Belinda* (1801); *Essay on Irish Bulls* (with Richard Lovell Edgeworth; 1802); *Popular Tales* (1804); *The Modern Griselda: A Tale* (1805); *Leonora* (1806); *Tales of Fashionable Life* (1809–12); *Patronage* (1814); *Harrington: A Tale* (1817); *Ormond: A Tale* (1817); *Helen: A Tale* (1834).

Nothing significant has survived in England to commemorate the novelist, though she spent her early life here and later gained entry to London literary circles by the popularity of her writings. In Scotland we may remember her connection with a more famous contemporary, Sir Walter Scott (q.v.), who acknowledged the influence of *Castle Rackrent* on his own Highland novels. She was his guest at No. 39 Castle Street in Edinburgh and at Abbotsford in 1803.

In 1782 her father Richard Lovell Edgeworth, a man of radical educational theories which profoundly influenced her own life, took her back to live in the little Irish town that bears their family name. Also known as Mostrim, it stands at the junction of N4 and N55 8 miles SE of the county town of Longford. Edgeworthstown House, where she wrote her novels and took careful charge of the estate after her father's death in 1817, is now a convent. Here she repaid Scott's hospitality in 1825 and was visited by Wordsworth in 1829, though the entry for the Lake Poets (Rte 17) shows that her impressions of the poet were not entirely favourable. She is buried near her father in the churchyard of St John's.

Abbotsford House, Melrose, Borders Region: phone (0896) 2043.

'George Eliot' (pseudonym of Marian or Mary Ann Evans)

b. Chilvers Coton, Warwickshire, 1819; d. London, 1880. *Scenes of Clerical Life* ('The Sad Fortunes of the Reverend Amos Barton', 'Mr Gilfil's Love Story' and 'Janet's Repentance'; 1858); *Adam Bede* (1859); *The Mill on the Floss* (1860); *Silas Marner: The Weaver of Raveloe* (1861); *Romola* (1863); *Felix Holt the Radical* (1866); *The Spanish Gypsy: A Poem* (1868); *Middlemarch: A Study of Provincial Life* (1872); *Daniel Deronda* (1876); *Impressions of Theophrastus Such* (1879).

'A human life', George Eliot suggested in *Daniel Deronda*, 'should be well rooted in some spot of native land, where it may get the love of tender kinship for the face of earth, for the labours men go forth to, for the sounds and accents that haunt it, for whatever will give that early home a familiar unmistakable difference amidst the future widening of knowledge: a spot where the definiteness of early memories may be inwrought with affection, and kindly acquaintance with all neighbours, even to the dogs and donkeys, may spread not by sentimental effort and reflection, but as a sweet habit of the blood' (Ch. 3). She clearly had the example of herself in mind, since her childhood and youth in the Midlands provided a solid bedrock for a life that went on to involve complex intellectual pilgrimage, as well as the ambiguous social position brought about by her liaison with George Henry Lewes. Memories drawn from that time and that area provided rich material for her art, especially the early novels. Even today, when the industrialisation of the Midlands—already beginning to happen in her youth and presaged by the coming of the railway in *Middlemarch*—has transformed so much of its landscape, a rich cluster of places associated with her life and work still remains.

A tour of this region may conveniently begin at Nuneaton in Warwickshire, the market centre round which her earliest years revolved and the original of 'Milby' in *Scenes of Clerical Life*. The fictional town is described as a 'quiet provincial place' ('Amos Barton', Ch. 4), though the author privately assured her publisher that 'the real town was more vicious'. The Museum and Art Gallery houses an important collection of George Eliot memorabilia, and the Public Library a collection of books by and about her. The Memorial Garden nearby was dedicated in 1951.

The novelist's father, Robert Evans, was agent to the Newdigate family of *Arbury Hall, off B4102 2 miles SW of Nuneaton. During the second half of the eighteenth century Sir Roger Newdigate had transformed the original Tudor house into a notable example of the Gothick style. George Eliot enjoyed the run of its library as a teenager and made it, with virtually no alteration, into the 'Cheverel Manor' of 'Mr Gilfil's Love Story': a 'castellated house of grey-tinted stone' with 'many-shaped panes in the mullioned windows, and a great beech leaning athwart one of the flanking towers, and breaking, with its dark flattened boughs, the too formal symmetry of the front' (Ch. 2).

Astley, another 1½ miles SW of Arbury Hall on B4102, appears in *Scenes of Clerical Life* as 'Knebley', where Mr Gilfil preaches in the 'wonderful little church, with a checkered pavement which had once rung to the iron tread of military monks, with coats of arms in clusters on the lofty roof, marble warriors and their wives without noses occupying a large proportion of the area, and the twelve apostles, with their heads very much on one side, holding didactic ribbons, painted in fresco on the walls' ('Mr Gilfil's Love Story', Ch. 1). 'Knebley Abbey' is identified with Astley Castle, near the church, another property of the Newdigate family with which George Eliot was familiar during her childhood.

She was born and brought up in the parish of Chilvers Coton, the 'Shepperton' of *Scenes of Clerical Life*, on the eastern side of the Newdigate estate and just over half a mile south of Nuneaton on A444. Now a suburb, it was still a separate village in the nineteenth century, albeit 'in a state of Attic culture compared with Knebley: it had turnpike roads and a public opinion' ('Mr Gilfil's Love Story', Ch. 1). Although the church where she was baptised has been rebuilt after war-time bomb damage, its graveyard contains the tomb of her father (d. 1849) and mother Christiana (d. 1836), Robert's second wife, and the grave of Emma Gwyther, whose death suggested the pathetic climax to 'Amos Barton'. (The connection between the Bartons and the Gwythers is, in fact, the closest example of a correspondence between George Eliot's fiction and the local life of her native region: John Gwyther, curate of Chilvers Coton in 1831–41, was still alive when the story was published and recorded his 'pained feelings at the making public my private history'.) A mile further south on A444 we come to Griff House, now a hotel, the substantial home to which the Evans family moved when the novelist was only a few months old; they lived here until 1841. Her birthplace at South Farm (then called Arbury Farm), about 1½ miles west, is a picturesque building but noticeably less grand than Griff House.

A444 continues another 7m south to Coventry, which some readers have identified with 'Middlemarch' despite the deliberately generalising name George Eliot chose for her fictional town. Bird Grove on the Foleshill Road, as A444 becomes on its way into the city, was Robert Evans' home from his retirement until his death (1841–49), years during which George Eliot acted as his housekeeper. Evans recorded in his diary for 1841 that when he told Lord Aylesford 'I was going to my new residence this evening for the first night, on the Foleshill road in Coventry parish, he Laphd [sic] and said they would make me Mayor'. Even today, it still testifies to the substantial respectability it once possessed. Near the city centre, at No. 29 Warwick Row, west of Greyfriars Green, we find Nantglyn, the fashionable school run by the Misses Franklin which George Eliot entered in 1832.

Although the Nuneaton–Coventry area is the centre of the George Eliot country, her connections with the Derbyshire–Staffordshire border to the north should not be forgotten. In fact, *Adam Bede* prevents that. Ashbourne (on A515 and A52) suggested the name 'Oakbourne', if nothing else. The novel is set in the beautiful stretch of the Dove valley SW of the town:

> That rich undulating district of Loamshire [Derbyshire] to which Hayslope belonged, lies close to a grim outskirt of Stonyshire [Staffordshire], overlooked by its barren hills as a pretty blooming sister may sometimes be seen linked in the arm of a tall, swarthy brother … High up against the horizon were the hugh conical masses of hill, like giant moulds intended to fortify this region of corn and grass against the keen and hungry winds of the north; not distant enough to be clothed in purple mystery, but with sombre greenish sides visibly speckled with sheep. (Ch. 2)

Ellastone (5 miles via A52 and B5032), where her father lived in his youth, is identified with 'Hayslope', Adam Bede's home; Dinah Morris preached on the Green and Mr Irwine in the Church. Norbury (half a mile further on B5033) is 'Norburne'. Eight miles NE of Ashbourne on B5035 we find Wirksworth, presumably 'Snowfield' and certainly the home of Elizabeth Evans (d. 1849), George Eliot's aunt, who suggested the character of Dinah Morris. Her connection with *Adam Bede* is remembered by the memorial tablet of 1873 in the Ebenezer Methodist church.

George Eliot's next novel, *The Mill on the Floss*, again breathes the atmosphere of her childhood, but is not set among familiar scenes since its plot required a location that would make the flooding of the river at the end plausible. In 1859, after rejecting Weymouth and Dorchester, she lighted on Gainsborough by the River Trent, 18 miles NW of Lincoln. The town today is sadly changed from her description of 'St Ogg's' with 'its aged, fluted red roofs and the broad gables of its wharves between the low wooded hill and the river brink' (Ch. 1). Only the partly 18C church and the 15C Old Hall can remind the visitor of the character that Gainsborough must have possessed in George Eliot's—and Maggie Tulliver's—times.

The 'future widening of knowledge' to which George Eliot refers in *Daniel Deronda* involved in her case a working life spent mainly in London, where she first arrived in 1851. It is unfortunate that so few of the houses she lived in survive; the loss of The Priory by Regent's Canal, where she presided over afternoon teas for famous and aspiring writers, leaves a specially important gap. We may, however, visit No. 31 Wimbledon Park Road (then called Holly Lodge), reached by crossing the Park from Wimbledon Park Underground Station (District Line). During her stay (1859–60) in this 'tall cake, with a low garnish of holly and laurel' she wrote *Adam Bede* but also led a withdrawn life, for the liaison with Lewes—himself married and unable to divorce his wife—still excluded her from respectable society. When Holly Lodge proved inconveniently far from the centre of things the couple moved to Marylebone. They stayed briefly in Harewood Square, now vanished beneath Marylebone Station, before settling round the corner at No. 16 Blandford Square (1860–63).

A visit to Cambridge in 1873 provided a famous and memorable glimpse of George Eliot in the character of Victorian sage she assumed so readily in later life. F.W.H. Myers, her host and a Fellow of Trinity College, walked with her in the Fellows' Garden:

> she, stirred somewhat beyond her wont, and taking as her text the three words which have been used so often as the inspiring trumpet-calls of men,—the words, *God*, *Immortality*, *Duty*,—pronounced, with terrible earnestness, how inconceivable was the *first*, how unbelievable the *second*, and yet how peremptory and absolute the *third*. Never, perhaps, have sterner accents affirmed the sovereignty of impersonal and unrecompensing Law. I listened, and night fell; her grave, majestic countenance turned toward me like a sibyl's in the gloom; it was as though she withdrew from my grasp, one by one, the two scrolls of promise, and left me with the third scroll only, awful with inevitable fates. And when we stood at length and parted, amid that columnar circuit of forest-trees, beneath the last twilight of starless skies, I seemed to be gazing, like Titus at Jerusalem, on vacant seats and empty halls,—on a sanctuary with no Presence to hallow it, and heaven left lonely of a God.

The young Bertrand Russell was reminded of the incident when he visited the Garden with Julian Sturgis, who exclaimed: 'Oh yes! This is where George Eliot told F.W.H. Myers that there is no God, and yet we must be good; and Myers decided that there is a God and yet we need not be good'.

In 1876 George Eliot and Lewes bought Rosslyn Court (then The Heights) in the Surrey village of Witley, on A283 4 miles SW of Godalming, though problems with furnishing it prevented them from moving in until the next year. Henry James (q.v.) paid a visit with Mrs Richard Greville on a wet November afternoon in 1878: 'I see again our bland, benign, commiserating hostess beside the fire in a chill desert of a room ... and I catch once more the impression of ... their liking us to have come, mainly from a prevision of how they should much more devoutly like it when we departed'. The occasion was made more uncomfortable when Lewes insisted on returning, unread, a copy of the newly published *The Europeans* which James had loaned them. Lewes died the same month, but George Eliot continued to live at The Heights after her marriage to J.W. Cross in April 1880—a marriage whose haste, coupled with the fact that Cross was some twenty years her junior, caused surprise and some disapproval among her friends.

The wedding ceremony took place in London at the fashionable St George's, Hanover Square, SW of Oxford Circus. Later that year the couple acquired a house in Chelsea, No. 4 Cheyne Walk, by the Embankment and the river. She moved in on 3 December 1880 and died on 22 December.

Given her relationship with Lewes and her views on religion, it could hardly be expected that she would rest in Westminster Abbey. Dean Stanley told her friend Herbert Spencer that he would require 'strong representations' before considering the idea, and the matter was quietly dropped. Instead, she was buried at that magnificent but now decaying expression of Victorian secularity, Highgate Cemetery, on Swains Lane south of Highgate Underground Station (Northern Line). George Eliot lies in the newer part of the cemetery to the east. After entering through the main gates we take the left fork and then, shortly before Karl Marx's tomb, a small footpath to the left. Beside the plain grey obelisk in her memory is the grave of Elma Stuart (d. 1903); the fulsome reference to the novelist in its inscription is a reminder of the passionate hero-worship she could inspire.

Nuneaton Museum and Art Gallery, Riversley Park, Nuneaton, Warwickshire: phone (0203) 376473.

Arbury Hall, Nuneaton, Warwickshire: phone (0203) 382804 or (0676) 40529.

Gainsborough Old Hall, Gainsborough, Lincolnshire: English Heritage; phone (0427) 2669.

Highgate Cemetery, Swains Lane, Highgate, London N6: eastern half open during daylight hours; phone (01) 340 1834.

T.S. Eliot

b. St Louis, Missouri, USA, 1888; d. London, 1965. *Prufrock and Other Observations* (1917); *The Sacred Wood: Essays on Poetry and Criticism* (1920); *The Waste Land* (1922); *Homage to John Dryden: Three Essays on the Poetry of the Seventeenth Century* (1924); *Poems 1909–1925* (1925); *Journey of the Magi* (1927); *For Lancelot Andrewes: Essays on Style and Order* (1928); *Dante* (1929); *Ash-Wednesday* (1930); *Marina* (1930); *Sweeney Agonistes: Fragments of an Aristophanic Melodrama* (1932); *The Use of Poetry and the Use of Criticism* (1933); *After Strange Gods: A Primer of Modern Heresy* (1934): *The Rock: A Pageant Play* (1934); *Murder in the Cathedral* (1935); *Four Quartets* (1935–42); *The Family Reunion* (1939); *Old Possum's Book of Practical Cats* (1939); *Notes Towards the Definition of Culture* (1948); *The Cocktail Party: A Comedy* (1950); *The Confidential Clerk* (1954); *On Poetry and Poets* (1957); *The Elder Statesman* (1959); *Collected Poems 1909–1962* (1963); *Knowledge and Experience in the Philosophy of F.H. Bradley* (1964).

Eliot first came to England in 1914 on a travelling fellowship from Harvard, where he had taken his undergraduate degree and was working toward his Ph.D. He studied at Merton College, Oxford. The philosopher F.H. Bradley, subject of Eliot's thesis (eventually published at the end of his life), was then a Fellow at Merton but the two men apparently did not come into contact. In light of his later commitment to the most English of English values, and particularly the famous declaration in *For Lancelot Andrewes* that he was 'classical in literature, royalist in politics, Anglo-Catholic in religion', it is interesting to note that Eliot did not fall in love with either Oxford or England at first sight. The university, he wrote to an American friend, 'is very pretty, but I don't like to be dead'. As Eliot's interest shifted from philosophy to poetry in the years that followed he visited several important gathering places for writers of his time. He was a guest of Lady Ottoline and Philip Morrell at Garsington Manor (off B480 4 miles SE of Oxford). Further contact with the Bloomsbury group was represented by visits to Virginia Woolf (q.v.) at her home in Rodmell.

In fact, he had little in common with these writers and was never a joiner of literary groups. During the aftermath of the First World War the real centre to his life was in the City of London, where he worked as a banker from 1917 onwards. It has often been noted that *The Waste Land* captured the mood of its age but less often remarked that this achievement depended on capturing the mood of a particular place. The poem is dominated by the City, just as the City is dominated by the Thames, once deserving praise by Spenser (q.v.) but now sordid and defiled. A brief tour of scenes in the poem and in Eliot's life during the years of its gestation can fruitfully begin by Bank Underground Station (Central and Northern Lines) at the junction of Lombard Street and King William Street. Eliot was employed in the colonial and foreign department of Lloyds Bank on Lombard Street. The critic I.A. Richards paid a call and found him 'a figure stooping, very like a dark bird in a feeder, over a big table covered with all sorts and sizes of foreign correspondence. The big table almost entirely filled a little room under the street. Within a foot of our heads when he stood were the thick, green glass squares of the pavement on which hammered all but incessantly the heels of the passers-by'. In *The Waste Land* the crowds of businessmen on their way to work become modern versions of the damned in Dante's *Inferno*:

Under the brown fog of a winter dawn,
A crowd flowed over London Bridge, so many,
I had not thought death had undone so many,
Sighs, short and infrequent, were exhaled,
And each man fixed his eyes before his feet.
Flowed up the hill and down King William Street,
To where Saint Mary Woolnoth kept the hours
With a dead sound on the final stroke of nine.
(lines 61–68)

The hexagonal clock is still a prominent feature of Hawksmoor's church. We now reverse the route of Eliot's commuters by following King William Street south towards the river. A left turn on to Monument Street and a right on Fish Street Hill bring us to Lower Thames Street, whose fishy atmosphere is well caught near the end of the poem's third section, 'The Fire Sermon'. Almost opposite is Wren's church of St Magnus Martyr, whose interior holds 'Inexplicable splendour of Ionian white and gold' (line 265).

Whilst working in the City Eliot lived near Regent's Park at No. 68 Clarence Gate Gardens, reached by following Melcombe Street from Baker Street Underground Station (Bakerloo, Circle, Metropolitan and Jubilee Lines). After the break-up of his first marriage in 1932 he moved to Kensington and stayed with Father Eric Cheetham, Vicar of St Stephen in Gloucester Road, north of Cromwell Road opposite Gloucester Road Underground Station (Piccadilly, Circle and District Lines). The Victorian church now has a plaque commemorating his service as Vicar's Warden from 1934 to 1959.

Eliot returned to this part of London in later years but during the Second World War his life centred on Bloomsbury, where he had been working for the publishing house of Faber and Faber since the mid 1920s. Throughout the Blitz he slept during the week in his office at No. 24 Russell Square behind the British Museum and served as a firewatcher in the neighbourhood—an experience vividly evoked by the second section of 'Little Gidding' in *Four Quartets*.

From 1948 until 1957 he lived in Chelsea at No. 19 Carlyle Mansions on Cheyne Walk, a block of flats formerly occupied by another Anglo-American writer, Henry James (q.v.). His flatmate was the critic John Hayward, whose editorial help with *Four Quartets* Eliot acknowledged. He left Carlyle Mansions when he married Valerie Fletcher in the church of St Barnabas, Addison Road, off the west end of Kensington High Street.

Where *The Waste Land* locates Eliot's despair firmly in the landscape of London, *Four Quartets* presents the spiritual quest of his later life in topographical terms. The poems describe pilgrimages in the full sense of the term, journeys to both a particular place and a religious revelation. Only one, 'The Dry Salvages', takes him outside England, back to the Mississippi river and the New England of his youth.

Of the English locations Burnt Norton, subject of the first poem, is the least rewarding. The country house lies 1 mile east of Aston Subedge in the Cotswolds, 4 miles NE of Broadway via A46, though Eliot visited it by making the 2-mile journey NW from the pleasant town of Chipping Campden. Burnt Norton had been damaged by fire in the 18C—hence its name—but later rebuilt. Now a school, it was derelict when Eliot came and his poem, with its stress on the gardens and the dry pool, evokes the emptiness of a landscape peopled only by fugitive echoes.

Altogether more rewarding is the subject of the second poem in the sequence, *East Coker, a picturesque little Somerset village south of A30 between Yeovil and Crewkerne. Eliot first came here in 1937, approaching East Coker down the narrow, steeply banked roads characteristic of the area:

> Now the light falls
> Across the open field, leaving the deep lane
> Shuttered with branches, dark in the afternoon,
> Where you lean against a bank while a van passes,
> And the deep lane insists on the direction
> Into the village.
>
> (lines 14–19)

He was drawn by the memory of his ancestors, who had left East Coker for America in the 17C, and so in the poem his journey becomes a movement backwards in time, finally challenging a simple linear concept of time itself. The next stage in the cycle came when Eliot was buried in the simple church, his memorial tablet fittingly carved with the words that form the close of his poem: 'In my end is my beginning'.

The subject of the fourth poem is **Little Gidding, a small Cambridgeshire village on an unclassified road off A1 12 miles NE of Huntingdon. In the 17C it had been the site of Nicholas Ferrar's Anglican community, which gave shelter to Charles I when he was a fugitive and which suffered attacks from the Puritans. Eliot approaches it with memories of the 'broken king' (line 27) in mind, and stresses the initial disappointment that the visitor can still feel

> when you leave the rough road
> And turn behind the pig-sty to the dull façade
> And the tombstone.
>
> (lines 29–31)

Yet in this 'husk of meaning' (line 32), the simple 17C church of St John the Evangelist with Ferrar's tomb outside its door, he at last achieves the sense of reconciliation for which the *Four Quartets* has strived, an intersection of history and the timeless moment:

> So, while the light fails
> On a winter's afternoon, in a secluded chapel
> History is now and England.
>
> (lines 238–240)

East Coker and Little Gidding are undoubtedly the places that bring us closest to the spirit informing his late poetry, but Eliot is also publicly remembered in Poets' Corner (fee) of Westminster Abbey.

Garsington Manor, Garsington, near Oxford: gardens open twice a year under NGS.

John Evelyn

b. Wotton, Surrey, 1620; d. London, 1706. Diarist.

Near the beginning of the diary he kept for most of his long life Evelyn proudly described his birthplace and childhood home:

> The house is large and antient, suitable to those hospitable times, and so sweetely environ'd with those delicious streames and venerable Woods, as in the judgment of strangers, as well as Englishmen, it may be compared to one of the most tempting and pleasant seates in the Nation.

Wotton House itself, by A25 3 miles west of Dorking in Surrey, has been largely rebuilt and is now predominantly 19C but part of the grounds Evelyn landscaped survive. Of the surrounding countryside Leith Hill (3 miles south of Wotton), the highest point in South-East England, and its National Trust woodland are particularly notable. Evelyn returned to Wotton in 1694 and inherited the house on the death of his brother in 1699. He is buried in the family chapel in the church—a curious choice of resting place for a man who had earlier agreed with his father-in-law that the practice of burying people inside churches was an 'ill & irreverent example, & prejudicial to the health of the living' (diary entry for 18 February 1683). His lengthy epitaph records the conclusion to which his experience of 'an age of extraordinary events, & revolutions' led him: 'That all is vanity wch is not honest, & that there's no solid Wisdom but in real Piety'.

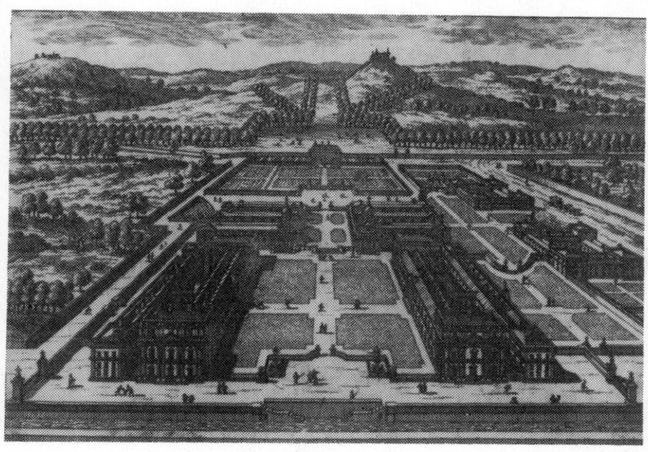

'A Prospect of GREENWICH HOSPITALL for Seamen as Designed and Advancing Ao. 1699', from James Beeverell's Les Délices de la Grand' Bretagne et de l'Irlande *(expanded edition of 1727)*

At the age of five, when the plague came to Surrey, Evelyn was sent to his grandparents in Lewes, 8 miles NE of Brighton. He returned there after the death of his mother to attend the grammar school and live with his grandmother at Southover Grange, an Elizabethan house with beautiful gardens, reached by following Keere Street south from Lewes' High Street. In 1627 he laid the foundation stone for the church at South Malling, 1 mile north on A26, it then being customary for young children to perform the ceremony.

In Oxford Evelyn studied at Balliol College. Returning to the city in the course of a tour round England with his wife in July 1654 he had a memorable dinner at Wadham College, then flourishing under the wardenship of Dr John Wilkins and a congenial port of call for a future Fellow of the Royal Society. Here he met, apparently for the first time, 'that miracle of Youth' Christopher Wren. The Library at Christ Church has the manuscript of Evelyn's diary.

By 1654 Evelyn had completed the Continental travels on which he had prudently embarked during the Civil War and the early years of the Interregnum and had settled at Deptford in south-east London, then separate from the capital. His skill in gardening and forestation made Sayes Court, the estate belonging to his wife's family, into 'a most beautiful place', as his friend Samuel Pepys (q.v.) reported. On returning to Wotton House Evelyn leased the Court to Admiral Benbow, who sublet it to Peter the Great with disastrous results. Today the only relic is the little park off Grove Street, which leads from Evelyn Street (A200) towards the docks. A more substantial reminder of Evelyn's presence in the area is Wren's Greenwich Hospital (now the Royal Naval College) to the east. He was one of the commissioners responsible for the building and recorded with triumph in his diary for 30 June 1696:

> I went with a select committee of the Commissioners for the fabrik of Greenewich Hospital, & with Sir Chr: Wren the Surveyor, where with him I laied the first stone of that intended foundation; precisely at 5 a clock in the Evening after we had dined together: Mr Flamsted the Kings Astronomical Professor observing the punctual time by Instruments: Note that one of the workmen in helping to place the stone, being a Corner large stone, grating his fingers against the gravelly banke, some drops of blood fell upon it.

An earlier example of Evelyn's interest in the fate of disabled seamen and soldiers is the Royal Hospital, also by Wren, on the Chelsea Embankment in south-west London. He proposed the idea for such a building to Charles II, though it had to wait for the generosity of Sir Stephen Fox to be realised. Evelyn's diary for 12 May 1691 reported on the result:

> I went to see the Hospital & Infirmarie for Emerited Souldiers lately built at Chelsey, which is indeede a very Magnificent, Compleat & excellent Foundation, the two Cutts from the Thames, Courts, and other accomodations wonderfull fine: The several wards for the souldiers, Infirmary for the sick, Dispensatory, Governors house & other officers, especially the Refectory for 400 men, & Chapell; In the Refectory is a noble picture of heroic argument in honour of Char: 2d painted by Virrio [Antonio Verrio]: also the Kings Statue in Brasse, of the work of Gibbons [Grinling Gibbons] in the Court next the Cloister & c.

It was inevitable that Evelyn, close to the public events of his age but careful not to be damaged by their turbulence, should have had a visitor's acquaintance with the Tower of London. In his youth he witnessed and deplored the execution of the Earl of Strafford, Charles I's Lord Deputy of Ireland, on Tower Hill: 'the fatal Stroake, which sever'd the wisest head in England' (entry for 7 May 1641). In later life, on 4 June 1679, he dined with Samuel Pepys, then imprisoned in the Tower 'but I believe unjustly'.

Evelyn's interest in science, gardening and architecture—his role, in fact, as one of the age's leading connoisseurs—ensured that he travelled widely. His connection with Eastern England is perhaps especially notable. In 1654 he first visited Audley End in Essex, not yet ruthlessly altered by Vanbrugh (q.v.): 'It is a mixt fabric, 'twixt antique & modern, but observable for its being compleately finish'd, & without comparison one of the stateliest palaces of the Kingdome, consisting of two Courts, the first very large, Wingd with Cloisters' (1 September 1654). The house stands east of M11 and B1383 near

Saffron Walden. Of Cambridge he wrote in the same diary entry as only a graduate of Oxford could. King's College Chapel was 'altogether answerable to expectation, especially the roof all of stone, which for the flatnesse of its laying & carving may I conceive vie with any in Christendome' but he could find little else to praise:

> the whole Towne situated in a low dirty unpleasant place, the streets ill paved, the air thick, as infested by the fenns; nor are its Churches (of which St *Maries* is the best) anything considerable in compare to *Oxford* which is doubtlesse the noblest Universitie now in the whole World.

His visit to Norwich in 1671 is described under the entry of Sir Thomas Browne, whom he met there.

Southover Grange, Lewes, East Sussex: the gardens are public and part of the Grange is a craft centre; phone Lewes Tourist Information Centre, (0273) 471600.

Christ Church Library, Peckwater Quad, Christ Church, Oxford: visitors by appointment; phone (0865) 276169.

Royal Naval College (Greenwich Hospital), King William Walk, Greenwich, London SE10: phone (01) 858 2154.

Royal Hospital, Royal Hospital Road, Chelsea, London SW3: phone (01) 730 0161.

Tower of London, Tower Hill, London EC3: DoE monument; phone (01) 709 0765.

Audley End, Saffron Walden, Essex: English Heritage; phone (0799) 22399.

George Farquhar

b. Londonderry, 1678; d. London, 1707. *The Constant Couple* (1699); *The Recruiting Officer* (1706); *The Beaux' Stratagem* (1707).

Though much of Farquhar's childhood in Ireland remains obscure or uncommemorated, he followed a pattern of education common among gentlemen and writers of the age. He received his schooling in the county town of Kilkenny at Kilkenny College, then apparently located in the Close of St Mary's Cathedral; its present buildings, which date from 1780, are on the north bank of the Nore near John's Bridge. In 1694 he entered Trinity College, Dublin as a sizar (or poor student) and enjoyed a rather chequered undergraduate career which seems to have ended the following year.

After university Farquhar was actor and then soldier. In 1705 he was sent as recruiting officer for Marlborough's army to the cathedral city of Lichfield, 16 miles north of Birmingham, and to Shrewsbury, the county town of Shropshire. The experience left its mark on the two genial comedies by which he is usually remembered. *The Recruiting Officer* takes place in Shrewsbury and is dedicated to 'All Friends Round the Wrekin'. *The Beaux' Stratagem* is set in Lichfield and the scene of its first act is an inn obviously modelled on the George, on Bird Street, where Farquhar himself had stayed.

The last years of his short life were spent in poverty in London. He was buried at St Martin's in the Fields by Trafalgar Square.

Henry Fielding

b. Sharpham Park, Somerset, 1707; d. Lisbon, Portugal, 1754. *The Tragedy of Tragedies; or, The Life and Death of Tom Thumb the Great* (1731); *An Apology for the Life of Mrs Shamela Andrews* (1741); *The History of the Adventures of Joseph Andrews, and of his Friend Mr Abraham Adams* (1742); *The Life of Jonathan Wild the Great* (1743); *The History of Tom Jones, A Foundling* (1749); *Amelia* (1751); *The Journal of a Voyage to Lisbon* (1755).

The parts of South-Western England which played so important a role in Fielding's life and appear so often in his fiction have four main centres: Glastonbury (Somerset), Shaftesbury (Dorset), Salisbury (Wiltshire) and Bath (now in Avon).

Sharpham Park, his birthplace, lies 3 miles SW of Glastonbury and 1 mile north of Walton. The old manor house, once a residence of the Abbots of Glastonbury, has now become Sharpham Park Farm. The main features of the *view from Glastonbury Tor correspond to the prospect enjoyed by Mr Allworthy's house in *Tom Jones*:

> Out of this lake, which filled the centre of a beautiful plain, embellished with groupes of beeches and elms, and fed with sheep, issued a river, that, for several miles, was seen to meander through an amazing variety of meadows and woods, till it emptied itself into the sea; with a large arm of which, and an island beyond it, the prospect was closed.
>
> On the right of this valley opened another of less extent, adorned with several villages, and terminated by one of the towers of an old ruined abbey, grown over with ivy, and part of the front, which remained still entire.
>
> The left hand scene presented the view of a very fine park, composed of very unequal ground, and agreeably varied with all the diversity which hills, lawns, wood, and water, laid out with admirable taste, but owing less to art than to nature, could give. Beyond this the country gradually rose into a ridge of wild mountains, the tops of which were above the clouds. (Bk 1, Ch. 4)

In this description the meandering river is the Brue, making its way through the flat Somerset landscape to Bridgwater Bay and the Bristol Channel; the 'old ruined abbey' is Glastonbury Abbey; and the 'wild mountains' are, by exercise of poetic licence, the Mendip Hills and the Quantocks.

In early childhood Fielding moved to East Stour, 4 miles west of Shaftesbury on A30, returning to the village in 1734–36 after his marriage. The old rectory his mother had inherited no longer stands and Fielding's fiction remains the best memorial to his connections with the area. Parson Adams of *Joseph Andrews* was based on Rev. William Young, curate of East Stour and several neighbouring parishes, while Mr Peter Pounce in the same novel owes something to a miserly lawyer, Peter Walter, of Stalbridge Park to the SW (now demolished). A local character, Jemmy Tweedle, is the subject of an affectionate mock-heroic tribute in *Tom Jones*:

> Him the pleasant banks of sweetly winding Stower had nourished, where he first learnt the vocal art, with which, wandring up and down at wakes and fairs, he cheered the rural nymphs and swains, when upon the green they interweave the sprightly dance; while he himself stood fiddling and jumping to his own music. (Bk 4, Ch. 8)

At Salisbury Fielding met his first wife, Charlotte Cradock, during visits in 1730–34. The house from which she eloped with him is a fine 17C building, still bearing her family name, on The Friary south of Saint Ann Street. Entering the Cathedral Close via Saint Ann's Gate nearby we come to No. 14, the first house on the left, where she and her children lodged in 1737. Rev. Richard Hele, Prebendary of

Salisbury and Master of the school in the Close, had the misfortune to sit for the portrait of Thwackum in *Tom Jones*.

The most important reminder of Fielding's connection with South-Western England is *Prior Park, the grand Palladian mansion built by John Wood the elder at Combe Down. About a mile SE of Bath, it is reached from the south of the city via Claverton Street and Prior Park Road. Now a Roman Catholic school, Prior Park has been greatly altered inside but its exterior and grounds (especially the Palladian bridge) remain magnificent. In the 18C it was the seat of Ralph Allen (1693–1764), much-admired philanthropist and improver of Bath. Fielding was a regular and intimate guest, particularly at the time he was at work on *Tom Jones*. He repaid Allen's hospitality with the dedication of *Amelia*, the portrait of Allworthy in *Tom Jones* (though he made the Squire's house Gothic rather than Palladian and, as we have seen, transplanted it south to Glastonbury) and this thinly veiled compliment in *Joseph Andrews*:

> I could name a Commoner raised higher above the Multitude by superiour Talents, than is the power of his Prince to exalt him; whose Behaviour to those he hath obliged is more amiable than the Obligation itself, and who is so great a Master of Affability, that if he could divest himself of an inherent Greatness in his Manner, would often make the lowest Acquaintance forget who was the Master of that Palace, in which they are so courteously entertained. (Bk 3, Ch. 1)

In Widcombe (near the route between Bath and Combe Down) Fielding stayed at Widcombe Lodge on Church Street while writing *Tom Jones*.

At Charlcombe, in the hills 2 miles north of Bath, Fielding's runaway marriage to Charlotte Cradock took place in 1734. Unfortunately, St Mary's Church was altered and enlarged by the Victorians.

Two locations in Hereford and Worcester should not be forgotten. On the High Street of Upton-on-Severn, a pleasant town on A4104 10 miles south of Worcester, we find the White Lion, a stuccoed building distinguished by giant pilasters and an effigy of a lion over its porch. It is traditionally identified with the 'house of exceedingly good repute' and scene of a memorable night of errors in Book 9, Chapters 3–5 of *Tom Jones*. Fielding's visits to the area, some of them made in the course of legal duties on the Western Circuit, also took him to the seat of his friend the first Lord Lyttelton at Hagley Hall. Lyttelton began the present Palladian building, with its sumptuous interior and elaborately landscaped grounds, in the 1750s.

In London—where most of Fielding's working life as dramatist, journalist, lawyer and magistrate was conducted—only two places can be recommended. He married his second wife and former housekeeper, Mary Daniel, in 1747 at the little Wren church of St Benet's on Bennet's Hill, south of Queen Victoria Street. During the period of his Bow Street magistracy (1748–54) he attended services and the christenings of children by his second marriage at St Paul's, Covent Garden. The church burned down at the end of the 18C but was rebuilt according to Inigo Jones' original design.

Prior Park (Prior Park College), Combe Down, near Bath, Avon: grounds and chapel open; phone Bath (0225) 835353.

Hagley Hall, near Stourbridge, West Midlands: phone (0562) 882408.

Edward FitzGerald

b. Boulge, Suffolk, 1809; d. Merton, Norfolk, 1883. *Euphranor: A Dialogue on Youth* (1851); *Rubáiyát of Omar Khayyám, the Astronomer-Poet of Persia, Translated into English Verse* (1859).

FitzGerald's long, unambitious and unusually serene life belonged almost entirely to Eastern England. Its major scenes may conveniently be organised into a tour beginning at Cambridge.

During his undergraduate years at Trinity College (1829–30) and his return visits to Cambridge in the 1830s he lodged on King's Parade opposite King's College. The building is now marked with a plaque. Visitors here included Thackeray and Tennyson (qq.v.), with whom he formed lifelong friendships. FitzGerald, however, became less and less impressed with the generation of undergraduates who had succeeded him, remarking in a letter of 1839 that 'the hard-reading, pale, dwindled students ... looked as if they were only fit to have their necks wrung'. *Euphranor* criticises the narrowness of English university education.

In Bury St Edmunds (28 miles east via A45) he attended the King Edward VI Grammar School, now housed in Arthur Blomfield's buildings (1883) off Eastgate Street. The town otherwise retains much of the charming character that made FitzGerald enjoy revisiting it in later years. He once recommended a friend 'to look at the Abbey Gate—from the windows of the Angel Inn just opposite—with a Biscuit and a Pint of Sherry—as I have so often done'.

For most of his adult life he lived near the Suffolk coast in *Woodbridge and its surrounding area, 32 miles SE of Bury via A45 and A12. He settled permanently in the town in 1860. Its quiet provincial atmosphere, which still largely survives, could sometimes make him grumble:

> Oh, if you were to hear 'where and Oh where is my Soldier Laddie gone' played every three hours in a languid way by the Chimes of Woodbridge Church, wouldn't you wish to hang yourself? On Sundays we have the 'Sicilian Mariners' Hymn'—very slow indeed. I see, however, by a handbill in the Grocer's Shop that a man is going to lecture on the Gorilla in a few weeks. So there is something to look forward to.

Yet he came to appreciate Woodbridge and became, indeed, a well-known local figure—more for his mildly eccentric dress than for his literary achievements, about which he always remained modest. His favourite pastime was sailing on the Deben estuary in his yacht *Scandal*, named (he said) after 'the staple product of Woodbridge'. His first lodging in the town was a modest two rooms over a shop on the north side of Market Hill. It was conveniently near his favourite inn, the Bull, where friends including Tennyson used to stay when they visited him. In 1864 he bought Little Grange on Pytches Road, reached from Woodbridge's main road, B1438. It is the 'suburb grange' of the poem addressed to 'Old Fitz' which prefaces Tennyson's 'Tiresias'. Yet even after he had enlarged Little Grange FitzGerald was reluctant to live there and did not take up residence until 1874.

Boulge, the traditional home of the FitzGerald family, lies north of Woodbridge and is the name of a parish rather than an actual village. His birthplace, Bredfield Hall, stood to the left of A12 about 2 miles north of Woodbridge but was demolished in 1950. However, to the right of the unclassified road that runs from A12 towards Debach we may still find Boulge Cottage, where FitzGerald lived from 1837 until 1853. In this small house with walls 'as thin as a sixpence' and thatched roof 'perforated by lascivious sparrows' FitzGerald began the Persian studies that resulted in his most famous work and led an apparently idle life that was the envy of his friends. 'His tranquillity', one remarked, 'is a pirated copy of the peace of God'.

Boulge Hall, his parents' last home, stood opposite the cottage. It has been demolished but in its grounds is the church of St Michael where FitzGerald was buried. On his grave grows a descendant of a rose from the tomb of Omar Khayyám, first planted by members of the Omar Khayyám Club in 1893.

E.M. Forster

b. London, 1879; d. Coventry, West Midlands, 1970. *Where Angels Fear to Tread* (1905); *The Longest Journey* (1907); *A Room With a View* (1908); *Howards End* (1910); *The Celestial Omnibus and Other Stories* (1911); *A Passage to India* (1924); *Aspects of the Novel* (1927); *The Eternal Moment and Other Stories* (1928); *Goldsworthy Lowes Dickinson* (1934); *Abinger Harvest* (1936); *Two Cheers For Democracy* (1951); *Billy Budd* (libretto for opera by Benjamin Britten; 1951); *The Hill of Devi* (1953); *Marianne Thornton 1797–1887: A Domestic Biography* (1956); *Maurice* (1971); *The Life to Come* (1972).

Although he was born in London, Forster's most important childhood home was in Stevenage (immediately east of A1 in Hertfordshire), where his widowed mother took him in 1883. The town, of course, has expanded and been sadly changed since then but their home, Rook's Nest (on Weston Road in Old Stevenage, NE of St Nicholas' church), remains. To Forster this charming house represented 'my childhood and safety' and his affection for it is demonstrated in his portrait of 'Howards End'.

At Tonbridge in Kent (SW of Maidstone via A26), where he and his mother came to live in 1893, he was not so happy. Even in old age he could not bring himself to view his years at Tonbridge School, off the High Street, with nostalgia and once remarked that if he gave an end-of-term address it would say:

> School was the unhappiest time of my life, and the worst trick it ever played me was to pretend that it was the world in miniature. For it hindered me from discovering how lovely and how delightful and kind the world can be, and how much of it is intelligible. From this platform of middle age, this throne of experience, this altar of wisdom, this scaffold of character, this beacon of hope, this threshold of decay, my last words are: There's a better time coming.

His experience of Tonbridge informed the second section of Forster's most closely autobiographical novel, *The Longest Journey*, in which the hero teaches at 'Sawston School', and led to his famous criticism that the public school system, whatever it may do for boys' minds and bodies, leaves them with undeveloped hearts. Nearby Tunbridge Wells, where his mother went to live in 1898, was no better than Tonbridge; Forster remembered it as a 'filthy, self-righteous place'.

After the narrowness of school Cambridge had a liberating and enlarging effect on the young Forster; in old age it again became his home. He first entered *King's College in 1897, when M.R. James (best remembered as a writer of ghost stories) was Dean and the Fellows included Oscar Browning and Goldsworthy Lowes Dickinson, whose biography he later wrote. Like Tennyson (q.v.) before him he was elected to that exclusive intellectual circle, the Apostles, and he visited the Darwin family at Newnham Grange (now assimilated into the buildings of Darwin College on Silver Street). Gwen Raverat's *Period Piece* (1952) captures the atmosphere of the Darwin household in these years, while the first section of *The Longest Journey* poignantly expresses Forster's own sense of what Cambridge meant to him. He came back in 1927 to deliver the Clark lectures, published as *Aspects of the Novel*, and in 1946 was elected to an Honorary Fellowship of his old college. The distinction coincided with his unhappy departure from West Hackhurst (see below) and Forster gratefully seized the chance to return to King's as a resident. He remained, living in rooms on A staircase in the front court, until the end of his life.

E.M. Forster in his rooms at King's College c 1950

In 1904 Forster made a significant visit to *Figsbury Rings (NT), an Iron Age camp off A30 NE of Salisbury. The atmosphere of the place and an accidental meeting with a lame shepherd boy played their part in the genesis of *The Longest Journey*, where the Rings are described as

> curious rather than impressive. Neither embankment was over twelve feet high, and the grass on them had not the exquisite green of Old Sarum, but was grey and wiry. But Nature (if she arranges anything) had arranged that from them, at all events, there should be a view. The whole system of the

country lay spread before Rickie ... He saw Old Sarum, and hints of the Avon valley, and the land above Stonehenge, and behind him he saw the great wood beginning unobtrusively, as if the down too needed shaving; and into it the road to London slipped, covering the bushes with white dust. Chalk made the dust white, chalk made the water clear, chalk made the clean rolling outlines of the land, and favoured the grass and the distant coronals of trees. Here is the heart of our island: the Chilterns, the North Downs, the South Downs radiate hence. The fibres of England unite in Wiltshire, and did we condescend to worship her, here we should erect our national shrine. (Ch. 13)

In the years between graduating from and returning to Cambridge Forster travelled abroad, his experience of Italy and India enriching his fiction and sharpening his critique of English narrowness. His most important home in England was at Abinger Hammer, a Surrey village on A25 between Guildford and Dorking. Forster's aunt had first leased West Hackhurst here in 1878 and he inherited the house on her death in 1924. Forster regarded the prospect of being gathered into the country gentry with amusement and some irritation but stayed until the lease expired in 1946. His forced departure was a source of great pain, though he retained a permanent stake in Abinger Hammer because he had earlier bought Piney Copse adjoining the house, subject of the wry little essay, 'My Wood'. He left it to the National Trust and it is now usually known as Forster's Wood.

John Galsworthy

b. London (Kingston-upon-Thames), 1867; d. London, 1933. *From the Four Winds* (as 'John Sinjohn'; 1897); *Jocelyn* (as 'John Sinjohn'; 1898); *Villa Rubein* (as 'John Sinjohn'; 1900); *A Man of Devon* (as 'John Sinjohn'; 1901); *The Island Pharisees* (1904); *The Man of Property* (1906); *The Silver Box* (1909); *Fraternity* (1909); *Strife* (1909); *Justice* (1910); *The Dark Flower* (1913); *In Chancery* (1920); *The Skin Game* (1920); *To Let* (1921); *Loyalties* (1922); *Old English* (1924); *The White Monkey* (1924); *The Silver Spoon* (1926); *Two Forsyte Interludes* (1927); *Swan Song* (1928); *On Forsyte 'Change* (1930); *Maid in Waiting* (1931); *Flowering Wilderness* (1932); *Over the River* (1933).

Galsworthy was 'a queer fish, like the rest of us', thought James Barrie (q.v.): 'So sincerely weighed down by the out-of-jointness of things socially ... but outwardly a man-about-town, so neat, so correct'. It is the man-about-town whom the surviving scenes of Galsworthy's life commemorate.

Born at Kingston-upon-Thames in SW London, he was brought up in nearby Coombe, which he made the 'Robin Hill' of *The Forsyte Saga*.

He was educated at the famous public school at Harrow on the Hill in north-west London and at New College, Oxford, where a contemporary remembered him as 'the best dressed man in College'. At Lincoln's Inn he qualified for the Bar and found that he hated the law, a common apprenticeship for writers to serve. In 1904 he married Ada, divorced wife of his cousin, at the Mayfair church of St George's, Hanover Square. From 1913 they lived at No. 1A Adelphi Terrace (now rebuilt), between the Strand and Victoria Embankment Gardens, an elegant and fashionable address shared by Barrie and Shaw (qq.v.). In later life Galsworthy moved to Hampstead, where the imposing Grove Lodge on Admiral's Walk (off Heath Street near the top of the hill) is now marked by a plaque.

Two places outside London were important in this otherwise urban life. The first is in Devon, the county from which his family originally came and for which Galsworthy always felt a strong affection. From 1907 onwards he leased part of Wingstone, a farmhouse a quarter of a mile NW of the village of Manaton, itself on the edge of Dartmoor 5 miles NW of Bovey Tracey via B3344. In 1926 he bought a rather grander place in the country, the neo-Tudor Bury House in the Sussex village of Bury, on A284 4 miles north of Arundel. At his own request, his ashes were scattered in the surrounding countryside.

Harrow School, Harrow on the Hill, Middlesex: guided tours; phone (01) 422 2303.

Elizabeth Gaskell

b. London, 1810; d. Holybourne, Hampshire, 1865. *Mary Barton: A Tale of Manchester Life* (1848); *Ruth* (1853); *Cranford* (1853); *North and South* (1855); *The Life of Charlotte Brontë (1857); Sylvia's Lovers* (1863); *Cousin Phillis* (1865); *Wives and Daughters: An Everyday Story* (1866).

Mrs Gaskell was born in that part of Cheyne Walk then known as Lindsey Row, west of Battersea Bridge in Chelsea. The house, now No. 93, is marked with a plaque.

She left London in infancy after the death of her mother and spent her childhood and youth in the pleasant little Cheshire town of *Knutsford, 15 miles SW of Manchester. Her precise and tender recollections transformed it into 'Cranford' and the 'Hollingford' of her last, incomplete novel, *Wives and Daughters*. The town today retains enough atmosphere and boasts enough memorials of the writer to deserve a walking tour. This naturally begins south of the Heath on Gaskell Avenue, the name itself a sign of local pride in the writer. The house where she was brought up by her aunt, Mrs Lumb, is marked with a plaque. After following the Avenue towards the town centre we turn right on to Princess Street. By taking Adam's Hill to the left we find the Brook Street Unitarian Chapel of 1689 which Mrs Gaskell attended and made the subject of this charming description in *Ruth*:

> The chapel had a picturesque and old-world look, for luckily, the congregation had been too poor to rebuild it, or new-face it in George the Third's time. The staircases which led to the galleries were outside, at each end of the building, and the irregular roof and worn stone steps looked grey and stained by time and weather. The grassy hillocks, each with a little upright headstone, were shaded by a grand old wych-elm. A lilac-bush or two, a white rose-tree, and a few laburnums, all old and gnarled enough, were planted round the chapel yard; and the casement windows of the chapel were made of heavy-leaded, diamond-shaped panes, almost covered with ivy, producing a green gloom, not without its solemnity, within ... The interior of the building was plain and simple ... when it was fitted up, oak-timber was much cheaper than it is now, so the wood-work was all of that description ... The walls were whitewashed and were recipients of the shadows of the beauty without; on their 'white plains' the tracery of the ivy might be seen, now still, now stirred by the sudden flight of some little bird. (Ch. 14)

Mrs Gaskell is buried in the graveyard; her husband, Rev. William Gaskell (d. 1884), lies beside her.

At the end of Adam's Hill we turn left, cross the railway bridge and follow King Street, the town's main thoroughfare. A left turn on Church Hill brings us to St John Baptist, a brick church of the 1740s, where the novelist was married in 1832. Returning to King Street and continuing north we pass the eccentric Gaskell Tower of 1907, with a medallion bust of the novelist. Like its neighbour, The King's Coffee House, it is one of several remarkable additions to Knutsford by Richard Harding Watt.

Tatton Park, 3½ miles north, is an early 19C mansion by Samuel and Lewis Wyatt set in a large park and fine gardens. Once the seat of the Egerton family, it appears as 'Cumnor Towers' in *Wives and Daughters.*

After her marriage Mrs Gaskell moved to Manchester, showing her compassionate knowledge of its industrial workers in *Mary Barton.* Today neither her first two homes nor the old Cross Street Chapel where her husband preached survive. Her last and most famous home, however, still stands: No. 84 Plymouth Grove, a street running SE from the main buildings of the University. She moved into this large early 19C house in 1850 and turned it into a salon visited by distinguished contemporaries, whom the fame of her writing and the charm of her personality readily attracted. Of these, the closest and most important friend was Charlotte Brontë (q.v.), who came to stay in 1851 and again in 1853. Mrs Gaskell, in turn, visited Haworth and attended Charlotte's wedding in 1854, as well as writing the controversial biography of her fellow-novelist in 1857. The Plymouth Grove house is now the University Overseas Centre.

From 1836 onwards, she was in the habit of spending her summer holidays at Silverdale, NW of Carnforth on the Lancashire coast, explaining in a letter of 1850 that the spot 'can hardly be called the sea-side, as it is a little dale running down to Morecambe Bay, with grey limestone rocks on all sides, which in the sun or moonlight, glisten like silver'. Some of her best work was done here.

In November 1859 Mrs Gaskell visited Whitby, 18 miles north of Scarborough on Yorkshire's east coast, to gather material for *Sylvia's Lovers,* which is set in a whaling port at the end of the 18C. Whitby's harbour and old fishing town still preserve some of the flavour Mrs Gaskell captured in her portrait of 'Monkshaven'.

In the last year of her life she resolved to buy a second home, keeping its purchase as a surprise for her husband, and chose The Lawn, a Georgian building 'in the middle of a pretty rural village', Holybourne, immediately NE of Alton, off A31 between Farnham and Winchester in Hampshire. Yet she had barely moved in and had not revealed the secret to her husband before she died, quite unexpectedly and peacefully, of a heart attack over tea one afternoon.

Tatton Park, Knutsford, Cheshire: NT and Cheshire County Council; phone (0565) 54822.

The *Gawain* Poet

Sir Gawain and the Green Knight; *Pearl*; *Purity* (or *Cleanness*); *Patience* (all c. 1375–c. 1400).

Virtually all that is known about these poems stems from the unique manuscript of c 1400 in the Cotton Collection at the British Museum. Their author's identity has not been established and, indeed, the attribution of all four works to the same poet remains likely supposition rather than proven fact.

For a medieval romance *Sir Gawain and the Green Knight* shows an unusually precise interest in topography, as well as one that accords with expert attribution of its dialect to Cheshire or Lancashire. Sir Gawain's journey may start from the fabulous Camelot but its terrain quickly becomes recognisable. He rides through 'the ryalme of Logres' (line 691)—that is, the land south of the River Humber—and almost into north Wales, keeping 'Alle the iles of Anglesay [Anglesey] on lyft half' (line 698). He fords the River Dee into 'the wyldrenesse of Wyrale' (line 701), the Wirral peninsula formed by the Dee and the Mersey, where he undergoes the hardships narrated in lines 713–739 before his arrival at Bercilak's Castle and the Green Chapel.

The chapel, sinister natural setting for Gawain's final encounter with the Green Knight, is described in specific terms:

> Hit hade a hole on the ende and on ayther syde,
> And overgrowen with gresse in glodes aywhere;
> And al was holw inwith, nobot an olde cave
> Or the crevisse of an olde cragge ...
> (lines 2180–2183)

It is understandable that readers should have assumed the poet to have an actual place in mind and that its whereabouts should have attracted scholarly speculation. Two plausible locations in the Peak District have been proposed. Both are well worth visiting but both require an aptitude for country walking as hardy as Gawain's own. The first possibility is *Wetton Mill, Staffordshire; it lies 8 miles NW of Ashbourne, Derbyshire, in a valley at the junction of Hoo Brook and the River Manifold, and is best reached either from Butterton to the west or Wetton to the east. The large stone outcrop, on the side of a hill and with a large hole leading into a chamber that once had a natural roof, agrees well with the main features in the poem. The Manifold, narrowed almost to a stream at this point, corresponds to the water that the Green Knight 'hypped over on hys ax' (line 2233).

The second possibility is nearby *Lud's Church, 9 miles NW and west of A53, the Leek–Buxton road: a dramatic rock fissure some 100ft long and reaching a height of 50ft, entered by a cave-like opening. An interesting approach which would seem to duplicate Gawain's route begins at Swythamley Hall (near Wincle). It leads east with a climb towards Roach End and then veers sharply north for a descent to the junction of Black Brook and the River Dane. Lud's Church is on the wooded southern bank of the river.

The interpretation of the poem's topography proposed by Sir Frederick Madden in the 19C located its final events much farther north, in Cumbria. Madden identified the Green Chapel with the now vanished Chapel of the Grene, which stood on the coast near Skinburness, and Bercilak's castle with Hutton-in-the Forest, 6 miles NW of Penrith, a reading supported by a specific reference to Hutton in a 15C condensation of the poem. Among some interesting work of later periods, Hutton keeps its 14C pele tower.

Hutton-in-the-Forest, Skelton, near Penrith, Cumbria: phone Skelton (085 34) 449.

John Gay

b. Barnstaple, Devon, 1685; d. London, 1732. *The Shepherd's Week* (1714); *Fables* (1727–28); *The Beggar's Opera* (1728); *Polly* (1729).

In Barnstaple on the north coast of Devon, the 'happy native land' he praised in 'A Journey to Exeter', Gay was educated at the free grammar school. Its 14C building, St Anne's Chapel, now houses a local museum.

Throughout his life Gay's charm readily won the affection of others, while his habits of mismanagement ensured that friends adopted a protective role. He was particularly close to Swift and Pope (qq.v.), frequently visiting the latter's Villa at Twickenham and becoming an intimate, almost at times a household pet, of various members of Pope's circle: Mrs Howard (later Lady Suffolk), the Dormer family of Rousham Hall, and Lords Bathurst, Burlington and Harcourt. The houses where he visited them are described under the entry for his better known contemporary.

After 1720, when he lost money by a characteristically ill-timed investment in the South Sea Bubble, Gay fell under the protection of the Duke and Duchess of Queensberry. He stayed with them at Douglas House, near Ham House in Richmond, and at Amesbury Abbey in Wiltshire, 14 miles west of Andover via A303, where in 1727 he wrote *The Beggar's Opera*. The 17C building was demolished in the 19C but replaced by one closely following the original design; the gardens by Charles Bridgeman have gone.

Gay was buried in Westminster Abbey and honoured with a monument in Poets' Corner (fee) erected by the Duke and Duchess of Queensberry. Pope's epitaph, which greatly annoyed Dr Johnson (q.v.), remembers him as being 'Of manners gentle, of affections mild,/ In wit a man, simplicity a child'. To it is added the epitaph Gay had written for himself:

Life is a jest, and all things show it,
I thought so once, but now I know it.

St Anne's Chapel and Old Grammar School Museum, St Peter's Churchyard, High Street, Barnstaple, Devon: all enquiries to Museums Officer, North Devon District Council, (0271) 46747.

Sir William Schwenk Gilbert

b. London, 1836; d. London, 1911. *The 'Bab' Ballads: Much Sound and Little Sense* (1869); *More 'Bab' Ballads* (1873); and the Savoy operas in collaboration with Sir Arthur Sullivan.

Gilbert's rise to fame and affluence with the success of the Savoy operas was charted by a progression of splendid London homes. In the 1870s he lived at No. 24 The Boltons, an elegant row of houses running south from the Old Brompton Road in South Kensington, where his neighbours included the singer Jenny Lind. In 1883 he moved to No. 39 Harrington Gardens (plaque), north of the Old Brompton Road via Bolton Gardens. Gilbert himself played a part in designing the brick neo-Renaissance house with its elaborate terracotta decorations. In 1890 he bought Grim's Dyke on Harrow Weald Common, in north-west London. The neo-Tudor building had been designed by Norman Shaw for the artist Frederick Goodall in 1872. It is now a hotel, which holds Gilbert and Sullivan evenings. While Gilbert was owner its grounds became a sanctuary for pheasants and foxes, for he greatly disliked blood sports, once remarking: 'Deer-stalking would be a very fine sport if only the deer had guns'. He died of a heart attack after rescuing a young lady from drowning in his lake, and was buried in the churchyard at Great Stanmore, to the east.

In central London Gilbert is commemorated by a bas-relief plaque on the wall of the Victoria Embankment near Charing Cross Pier and Embankment Underground Station (Northern, Bakerloo, Circle and District Lines). Across the road the Victoria Embankment Gardens have a statue of Sir Arthur Sullivan (1842–1900). By the Savoy Hotel on the Strand to the north is the Savoy Theatre, opened by Richard D'Oyly Carte in 1881, where Gilbert and Sullivan's operas from *Iolanthe* onwards were first staged. On the north side of the Strand are Southampton Street, where Gilbert was born, and (by the junction with Aldwych) Wellington Street, where the Gilbert and Sullivan pub has a collection of memorabilia.

George Gissing

b. Wakefield, West Yorkshire, 1857; d. St-Jean-de-Luz, France, 1903. *Workers in the Dawn* (1880); *The Unclassed* (1884); *Isabel Clarendon* (1886); *Demos* (1886); *Thyrza* (1887); *A Life's Morning* (1888); *The Nether World* (1889); *The Emancipated* (1890); *New Grub Street* (1891); *Denzil Quarrier* (1892); *Born in Exile* (1892); *The Odd Women* (1893); *In the Year of Jubilee* (1894); *Eve's Ransom* (1895); *The Paying Guest* (1895); *Sleeping Fires* (1895); *The Whirlpool* (1897); *The Town Traveller* (1898); *Charles Dickens: A Critical Study* (1898); *The Crown of Life* (1899); *By the Ionian Sea* (1901); *Our Friend the Charlatan* (1901); *The Private Papers of Henry Ryecroft* (1903); *Veranilda* (1904); *Will Warburton* (1905).

Gissing's early years were spent in Northern England. At Wakefield, 8 miles south of Leeds, his birthplace is marked by a tablet on No. 30 Westgate in the market place, where his father kept a chemist's shop. At the age of fourteen, after his father's death, he was sent to school in Alderley Edge, 12 miles south of Manchester. Academic promise won Gissing a place at Owens College, founded in 1851 and later to grow into the Victoria University of Manchester. His student days spanned the move from the College's old building on Quay Street, west of St Peter's Square and now the County Court, to the first of Alfred Waterhouse's new university buildings, the west wing of 1873, in Oxford Road a mile SE of St Peter's Square. His career ended in disgrace when he was caught stealing from fellow students: he was stripped of his prizes and distinctions, and sentenced to a month's imprisonment.

Prison was followed by a spell as a clerk in Liverpool and a visit to America before, in 1878, Gissing arrived in London to occupy the first of a series of shabby, fugitive lodgings. His experiences are powerfully evoked in his fiction, where London becomes a city of struggling writers and 'odd women' leading lives of quiet desperation amid the trappings of modern commerce and advertising. It is a compelling achievement, too little noticed until recently, which creates an interesting link between the London of Dickens (q.v.) and the London of George Orwell (q.v.).

In 1879–80, after his disastrous first marriage to Nell Harrison, he was lodging at No. 22 Colville Place, which is reached by following Goodge Street west from Tottenham Court Road and turning left into Charlotte Street. The house does not survive but the alley retains much of its atmosphere. In the quasi-autobiographical *Private Papers of Henry Ryecroft* he remembered this gloomy period:

> I see that alley hidden on the west side of Tottenham Court Road, where after living in a back bedroom on the top floor, I had to exchange for the front cellar; there was a difference, if I remember rightly, of sixpence a week, and sixpence, in those days, was a very great consideration—why, it meant a couple of meals ... Here I lived; here I *wrote*. Yes, 'literary work' was done at that filthy deal table, on which, by the by, lay my Homer, my Shakespeare, and the few other books I then possessed. At night, as I lay in bed, I used to hear the tramp, tramp of a *posse* of policemen who passed along the alley on their way to relieve guard; their heavy feet sometimes sounded on the grating above my window. ('Spring', Ch. 10)

In *Workers in the Dawn*, which belongs to these years, Mr Tollady has his printing shop on Charlotte Place, the next alley to run south from Goodge Street after we pass the junction with Charlotte Street.

Gissing, of course, spent much of his time in the British Museum and Library, east of Tottenham Court Road and reached via Great Russell Street. Marian Yule is one of several characters in *New Grub Street* who work in the domed, circular Reading Room:

> The fog grew thicker; she looked up at the windows beneath the dome and saw that they were a dusky yellow. Then her eye discerned an official walking along the upper gallery, and in pursuance of her grotesque humour, her mocking misery, she likened him to a black, lost soul, doomed to wander in an eternity of vain research among endless shelves. Or again, the readers who sat here at these radiating lines of desks, what were they but helpless flies caught in a huge web, its nucleus the great circle of the Catalogue? Darker, darker. From the towering wall of volumes seemed to emanate visible motes, intensifying the obscurity; in a moment the book-lined circumference of the room would be but a featureless prison-limit. (Ch. 8)

Two later London addresses are worth noting. In 1883, freed from Nell Harrison, Gissing lived at No. 33 Oakley Gardens in Chelsea, now marked by a plaque. The tiny square is found by following Oakley Street north from Albert Bridge and then taking a right on Phene Street. He made a longer stay in Marylebone (1884–91) at No. 7K Cornwall Terrace Mansions, between Baker Street Underground Station (Bakerloo, Metropolitan, Circle and Jubilee Lines) and Regent's Park.

By the mid-1890s Gissing had won himself a reputation that relieved the worst of his poverty. In July 1895 he was a guest at a literary dinner of the Omar Khayyám Club at the Burford Bridge Hotel in Surrey, near the foot of Box Hill some 1½ miles north of Dorking of A24. George Meredith (q.v.), who lived nearby, and Thomas Hardy (q.v.) also attended and press reports bracketed the three writers together. Gissing later moved to Dorking itself, living from 1898 to 1899 at No. 7 Clifton Terrace, separated from his second wife but unable to get a divorce. It was here that he met Gabrielle Fleury, with whom he spent his last years in France.

British Library and British Museum, Great Russell Street, Bloomsbury, London WC1: for Library phone (01) 636 1544; for Museum phone (01) 636 1555. The British Library is scheduled to move to Euston Road in 1991/92; at the time of writing there are guided tours of the Reading Room, not otherwise open to casual visitors.

Oliver Goldsmith

b. Pallas, Longford, or Elphin, Roscommon, 1730?; d. London, 1774. *An Enquiry into the Present State of Polite Learning in Europe* (1759); *The Bee* (1759); *The Citizen of the World* (1762); *The Life of Richard Nash, Esq* (1762); *An History of England in a Series of Letters from a Nobleman to His Son* (1764); *The Traveller: or, A Prospect of Society* (1764); *The Vicar of Wakefield* (1766); *The Good-Natur'd Man* (1768); *The Deserted Village* (1770); *She Stoops to Conquer: or, The Mistakes of a Night* (1773); *The Haunch of Venison* (1776).

Very little survives to remind the tourist of Goldsmith's early years in Ireland. 'Sweet Auburn', the scene of his most successful poem, *The Deserted Village*, is identified as Lissoy, Westmeath, off N55 8 miles NE of Athlone and in the region where he spent his childhood. Trinity College, Dublin, which he attended in the humiliating capacity of sizar (or poor student), has a statue (1863) outside its main front on College Green.

He completed his training as a doctor at Edinburgh University. Its mean huddle of buildings on Chambers Street, sometimes mistaken by strangers for almshouses, was replaced by Robert Adam's fine Old College of 1789.

After his arrival in England (1756) Goldsmith's life and career is rather better commemorated. He visited his patron Robert Nugent, later Lord Clare, at Gosfield Hall, between Braintree and Halstead in Essex. The Hall's exterior is a remarkable medley of different periods but the interior has some fine 18C state rooms. Goldsmith was also a guest at Lord Clare's house in Bath, No. 11 North Parade, though with his ungainly appearance and notorious tendency to social blunders he must surely have cut a strange figure in that fashionable city. He did, however, write a biography of Beau Nash (1674-1761), Master of Ceremonies and arbiter of social etiquette at Bath. Goldsmith's posthumously published poem *The Haunch of Venison* is addressed to his patron.

An unproved, tantalising tradition connects Goldsmith's best-known character (in *She Stoops to Conquer*) with the Anthony Lumpkin buried in the church at Leverington, NW of Wisbech in Cambridgeshire.

Most of Goldsmith's working life was spent in London. Thanks to the help of a kindly publisher, John Newbery, he lived (1764–67) at Canonbury Tower, facing Canonbury Place SE of Highbury and Islington Station (British Rail and Victoria Underground Line). The fine building is now part of the Tower Theatre.

His usual haunts were in the City near Fleet Street. Like so many other literary men of his age he is supposed to have frequented the Cheshire Cheese on Wine Office Court. His lodgings at No. 6 nearby have gone, though Nos 1–3, apparently of the same period, still stand. In 1762 Dr Johnson (q.v.) found him here on the verge of financial ruin and despair—disasters Johnson sensibly averted by selling the manuscript of *The Vicar of Wakefield* to a publisher. From 1767 until his death Goldsmith lived at No. 2 (demolished) Brick Court off Middle Temple Lane, where his loudly sociable habits irritated his neighbour, the legal historian William Blackstone. A stone in the raised part of the churchyard north of the Temple Church marks the approximate site of his grave.

Poets' Corner (fee) in Westminster Abbey has a monument of 1776 by Joseph Nollekens with a Latin epitaph by Johnson, who stuck to his choice of language despite a good-humoured protest from fellow members of The Club:

> But if we might venture to express our wishes, they would lead us to request, that he would write the Epitaph in English rather than in Latin. As we think that the Memory of so eminent an English Writer ought to be perpetuated in the Language to which his Works are likely to be so lasting an Ornament, Which we also know to have been the opinion of the late Doctor himself.

In fact, Johnson also paid a magnificent vernacular tribute to Goldsmith in a letter to Bennet Langton: 'let not his frailties be remembered; he was a very great man'.

Gosfield Hall, Gosfield, near Halstead, Essex: phone Halstead (0787) 472914.

Canonbury Tower, 30 Canonbury Place, Canonbury, London N1: tours for parties by prior arrangement; phone the Warden, Canonbury Tower Trust, (01) 359 4900.

John Gower

b. place unknown, 1330?; d. London, 1408. *Speculum Meditantis* (n.d.); *Vox Clamantis* (n.d.); *Confessio Amantis* (n.d.).

The obscurity that has overtaken the life and writings of Gower, poet and near-contemporary of Chaucer (q.v.), is more than compensated for by the survival of his splendid, well restored **tomb in the north aisle of Southwark Cathedral (at the south end of London Bridge). Wearing Henry IV's emblem of the swan on the collar round his neck, his effigy rests on copies of his three main works, beneath an arched canopy. The inscription, more charitable than posterity, remembers him as 'Angl. poeta celeberrimus'. Gower was a benefactor of the Augustinian Priory of St Mary Overie, of which the Cathedral was then part, and may have been living there at the time of his death.

Thomas Gray

b. London, 1716; d. Cambridge, 1771. *Ode on a Distant Prospect of Eton College* (1747); *Elegy Written in a Country Churchyard* (1751); *The Progress of Poesy* (1757); *The Bard* (1757).

Gray's connection with Cambridge spanned his entire adult life. He entered Peterhouse as an undergraduate in 1734 and left without taking a degree in 1738. After a continental tour in the company of Horace Walpole (q.v.), later perhaps the most vocal advocate of Gray's literary talent, he returned to his old college as a fellow commoner studying civil law. The second floor rooms he occupied in the Fellows' Building overlook Trumpington Street and the churchyard of St Mary the Less (or Little St Mary).

A man of quiet and finicky temperament ('dull in company, dull in his closet, dull everywhere', according to Dr Johnson [q.v.]), he pursued the noiseless tenor of his way far from the ignoble strife of social and academic politics. The only serious interruption of its calm occurred in 1756 and resulted from a morbid fear of fire that had led him to equip his room with a rope ladder and his windows with iron bars (still visible from Trumpington Street). Such nervous precautions invited an undergraduate practical joke:

> The other morning Lord Percival and some Petrenchians [undergraduates of Peterhouse], going a hunting, were determined to have a little sport before they set out, and thought it would be no bad diversion to make Gray bolt, as they called it, so ordered their man Joe Draper to roar out fire. A delicate white nightcap is said to have appeared at the window; but finding the mistake, retired to the couch. The young fellows, had he descended, were determined, they said, to have whipped the butterfly up again.

This contemporary account by the Reverend John Sharp of Corpus Christi is undoubtedly more accurate than later embellished versions which have the poet climbing down his rope and landing in a tub of water. But even the modest actuality of the incident greatly distressed him and, when the Master of Peterhouse failed to take his complaint seriously, Gray moved across Trumpington Street to Pembroke. 'This may be look'd upon as a sort of Aera in a life so barren of events as mine', he wrote to a friend.

Save for a brief period in London (1759–61) Gray remained at Pembroke for the rest of his life, quietly enjoying the substantial reputation his poetry had won, penning the letters that distinguish him even in an age of great correspondents, and assuming the Regius Professorship of Modern History in 1768. His rooms were in Ivy Court (or Second Court) above what is now the Senior Parlour on I staircase of the Hitcham Building.

Though his connection with Cambridge was the most enduring of Gray's life, the most poignant is to be found at Stoke Poges, north of A4 and Slough in Buckinghamshire. His mother retired from London to Stoke after the death of her husband in 1741, living at West End House (now Stoke Court) with her two sisters. In the course of his many visits over the years Gray formed the friendship with Viscountess Cobham and Miss Speed celebrated in the comic poem 'A Long Story' and wrote the *Ode on a Distant Prospect of Eton College* (his old school, south of A4 and M4). Most importantly, it was at Stoke Poges that he began and finished his *Elegy Written in a Country Churchyard*, that finely measured reflection on death on which his fame still depends. The *churchyard (near junction of B416 and B473), where Gray was buried, has a monument of 1799 (NT) bearing quotations from his poem. The grave of his mother (d. 1753) near the east wall of the church carries an epitaph by Gray that remembers her as 'the careful mother of many children, one of whom alone had the misfortune to survive her'.

Gray's travels in England and Scotland helped encourage the Picturesque appreciation of nature, approached in the spirit of a refined connoisseur and viewed through the reflected medium of a Claude glass. When they were published after his death, the letters he had written to Thomas Warton during a second visit to the Lake District in 1769 proved especially influential in making the region popular with visitors. At Grasmere (later, of course, to be Wordsworth's home) Gray found a vision of pastoral innocence, soon to be despoiled: 'Not a single red tile, no flaring gentleman's house, or garden-walls, break in upon the repose of this little unsuspected paradise; but all is peace, rusticity, and happy poverty in its neatest most becoming attire'. With a little judicious heightening of the landscape and the emotions, the journey through the Jaws of Borrowdale, south of Derwentwater, afforded a pleasantly frightening brush with the Sublime:

The rocks at the top deep-cloven perpendicularly by the rains, hanging loose and nodding forwards, seem just starting from their base in shivers. The whole way down, and the road on both sides is strewed with piles of the fragments strangely thrown across each other, and of a dreadful bulk; the place reminds me of those passes in the Alps, where the guides tell you to move on with speed, and say nothing, lest the agitation of the air should loosen the snows above, and bring down a mass that would overwhelm a caravan.

Eton College, Windsor, Berkshire: School Yard, College Chapel, Cloister Court and Museum of Eton Life open; also guided tours; phone (0753) 863593.

Sir Fulke Greville, Lord Brooke

b. Beauchamp Court, Warwickshire, 1554; d. London, 1628. *The Tragedy of Mustapha* (1609); *Certaine Learned and Elegant Workes Written in His Youth and Familiar Exercise with Sir Philip Sidney* (1633); *The Life of the Renowned Sir Philip Sidney* (1652).

Although Sir Fulke Greville's rather slender literary reputation today depends more on his Senecan closet drama *Mustapha* than the sometimes laboured poetry he wrote in imitation of Sir Philip Sidney (q.v.), it is in fact that friendship with Sidney which provides a major theme in his life and its surviving reminders. Greville was an exact contemporary of the better known poet at Shrewsbury School, Shropshire; now a Library, the School's old buildings stand on Castle Gates opposite the Castle. After studying at Jesus College, Cambridge, Greville again joined Sidney at court in 1577.

Of the several grants of land and property that rewarded his services to Queen Elizabeth and King James the most important was Warwick Castle, which he repaired and embellished after acquiring it in 1604. He died in London–stabbed by a servant whom he had slighted in his will–and was buried at the church of St Mary, in Warwick to the north of the Castle. His oversize black and white marble monument stands in the chapter house, bearing this inscription: 'Fulke Greville, servant to Queen Elizabeth, councillor to King James, and friend to Sir Philip Sidney. Trophaeum Peccati'.

Shrewsbury Library, Castle Gates, Shrewsbury, Shropshire: phone (0743) 241487.

Warwick Castle, Warwick: phone (0926) 495421.

R.S. Hawker

b. Plymouth, Devon, 1803; d. Plymouth, 1875. *Records of the Western Shore* (1832); *Ecclesia* (1840); *Reeds Shaken in the Wind* (1843); *Echoes from Old Cornwall* (1846); *The Quest of the Sangraal: Chant the First* (1864); *Cornish Ballads and Other Poems* (1869).

This eccentric Victorian poet and clergyman is usually remembered, when he is remembered at all, for 'The Song of the Western Men' (1825) and particularly for the rousing lines from its second stanza:

And shall Trelawny die?
Here's twenty thousand Cornish men
Will know the reason why!

Most of his working life was spent as vicar (1834–75) of the scattered parish of *Morwenstow near Bude on the north Cornish coast. Bounded by cliffs on one side and bleak moorland on the other, the village is reached from A39 via unclassified roads. If it seems remote to the modern visitor we have Hawker's reminder, in a letter of 1862, of its state in the 19C: 'Did you ever hear that for every 100 miles you live from London, you must reckon yourself a century back from your own date? We, therefore, who are 250 miles off, are now in the year 1610 in all that relates to agriculture and civilisation'.

The most prominent memorial to his years at Morwenstow is the Gothic vicarage built to his own design in 1837. Its chimneys are shaped in imitation of church towers, while the one over the kitchen is modelled after his mother's tomb. Over the front door he inscribed this verse:

A House, a Glebe, a Pound a Day,
A pleasant Place to Watch and Pray.
Be true to Church—Be kind to poor,
O Minister, for ever more.

When Tennyson (q.v.) dined here in 1848 Hawker was struck by the oddity of his famous hat and cloak, a curious reaction from a man who usually dressed in brimless hat, purple cassock and fisherman's jersey. He helped another visitor, Charles Kingsley (q.v.), with the topography of *Westward Ho!*, though he liked neither the novelist nor the novel.

Nearby is the church that Hawker restored—he is said to have destroyed one private pew with an axe himself—but did not take pains to keep clean. A visitor noted with distaste: 'The church floor was strewn with sweet-smelling herbs,—in fact carpeted with them, which however caused it to be always dirty. In fact *dirt* was over everything, vestry and pulpit very dirty. He said his cat always went with him to church, and sometimes into the pulpit'. There is now a window in Hawker's memory. In the churchyard is the grave of his first wife, Charlotte (d. 1863), and the figurehead from the ship *Caledonia*, a reminder of how many drowned sailors Hawker buried. On Vicarage Cliff (NT) to the west is the little hut he built from driftwood and used as an outdoor study.

In the last year of his life Hawker returned to his native Plymouth on the south Devon coast. He was received into the Roman Catholic Church on his deathbed. His grave in the Cemetery off Ford Park Road bears an epitaph from his most ambitious poem, *The Quest of the Sangraal*: 'I would not be forgotten'.

George Herbert

b. Montgomery, Powys, 1593; d. Bemerton, Wiltshire, 1633. *The Temple* (1633).

The castle of Montgomery in Wales (formerly the county town of Montgomeryshire) where George Herbert was born is now ruined, but the local church contains the fine tomb of his father, Sir Richard Herbert (d. 1600). The burial of his mother, who became Lady Margaret Danvers, is described under the entry for John Donne, who preached the funeral sermon.

Herbert's admission to Trinity College, Cambridge, in 1609 began a connection with the university that continued with a College

Fellowship in 1616 and later with his appointment as Public Orator. His duties in the second post included delivering addresses in Great St Mary's church, opposite the Senate House on King's Parade. In 1626 Herbert also became prebend of **St Mary's in Leighton Bromswold, 9 miles west of Huntingdon via A604. He paid for repairs to the church and appears to have supervised them with great care, for the tower, spacious aisles and fine woodwork exude a dignified simplicity that is perfectly expressive of his sensibility. Of special note are the two pulpits, apparently a unique feature in an English parish church, embodying his belief in the equal importance of praying and preaching. At Little Gidding, 5 miles NE, his friend Nicholas Ferrar organised a religious community which also attracted the interest of Herbert's fellow poet and Cambridge don, Richard Crashaw, and whose fame has been revived in our own century by the work of T.S. Eliot (q.v.). It was Ferrar to whom Herbert entrusted the publication of his poems, *The Temple*, on his death. Ferrar's tomb (d. 1637) stands outside the church of St John the Evangelist, a much-restored little building that still manages to retain its character and atmosphere.

In 1630 Herbert was appointed rector of Bemerton in Wiltshire, then a distinct village but now absorbed into the suburbs of Salisbury. In the words of John Aubrey, he found the church of St Andrew 'a pittifull little chappell of ease'. His restoration of it was largely obliterated by the work of T.H. Wyatt in 1866 but Aubrey's complaint about the lack of a proper memorial ('He lyes in the chancell, under no large, nor yet very good, marble grave-stone, without any inscription') has been remedied by a plaque and the 19C east window. The 'very ruinous' Rectory which Herbert also needed to repair and whose garden gave him particular delight still stands and is to the south of the church.

Montgomery Castle, Montgomery, Powys: Cadw: Welsh Historic Monuments; phone headquarters in Cardiff, (0222) 465511.

Robert Herrick

b. London, 1592; d. Dean Prior, Devon, 1674. *Hesperides* (1648).

None of the London scenes connected with Herrick survives unaltered. The original Wood Street where he was born and nearby St Vedast's church where he was baptised, both off Cheapside, were destroyed in the fire of 1666; while St Anne Street (formerly Lane) between Great Peter and Great Smith Streets in Westminster, where he lived from 1647 to 1662, has been demolished and rebuilt. Cambridge, however, is more fortunate: Herrick entered St John's College in 1613 and moved, apparently for financial reasons, to Trinity Hall in 1616.

Herrick is best remembered at Dean Prior, a village on A38 south of Ashburton in Devon and near the picturesque scenery of the Dean Burn Valley. He acquired the living of St Mary's in 1630 and held it until his death except for the London interlude, when he had been deprived of his position because of Royalist sympathies. The rural setting seems appropriate to the often delicately pastoral character of the verses collected in *Hesperides*, yet the robust epigrams directed at neighbours and members of his congregation are reminders of Herrick's discontent with country life. There is a monument of 1857 in the church.

James Hogg

b. Ettrick, Borders, 1770; d. Altrive Lake, Borders, 1835. *The Mountain Bard* (1807); *The Forest Minstrel* (1810); *The Queen's Wake: A Legendary Poem* (1813); *The Private Memoirs and Confessions of a Justified Sinner* (1824); *Altrive Tales: Collected Among the Peasantry of Scotland and from Foreign Adventurers* (1832); *The Domestic Manners and Private Life of Sir Walter Scott* (1834).

Although he is now remembered as the author of a powerful exercise in psychological Gothic, *Confessions of a Justified Sinner*, Hogg was known in his own day as a poet and peasant bard, discovered by Sir Walter Scott (q.v.) in the course of his researches for *Minstrelsy of the Scottish Border* and achieving a fame like that of his fellow countryman Robert Burns (q.v.). He clung to a title 'the Ettrick Shepherd', proclaiming his humble origins and appeared under this name, though usually caricatured as a 'boozing buffoon', in *Noctes Ambrosianae*, the long-running series of articles by John Wilson ('Christopher North') in *Blackwood's Edinburgh Magazine*.

In Ettrick, a village on B7009 SW of Selkirk, the site of Hogg's birthplace is marked by a monument; he is buried in the churchyard. Altrive Lake, the farm granted to him rent free by the Duke of Buccleuch in 1815, and Mount Benger, the farm he acquired in 1821 with disastrous financial results, lay north of Ettrick in the valley of the Yarrow near the junction with A708. Hogg was a regular patron of Tibbie Shiel's Inn, now a hotel, off A708 near the southern end of St Mary's Loch. Nearby is a statue that depicts him seated with his dog. The occasion in 1814 when he showed Wordsworth (s.v. Lake Poets, Rte 14) the sights of the Yarrow is remembered in the latter's 'Extempore Effusion Upon the Death of James Hogg'.

Gerard Manley Hopkins

b. London, 1844; d. Dublin, 1889. *Poems* (edited by Robert Bridges; 1918).

After an unhappy but distinguished career at London's Highgate School, whose old buildings were replaced shortly after he left, Hopkins found a more congenial environment at Oxford. During his undergraduate years at Balliol College (1863–67) he was influenced both by Walter Pater (q.v.) and the Oxford Movement. As an undergraduate he dedicated two sonnets to Oxford and, when he returned in 1878–79 as curate of the Roman Catholic church of St Aloysius on Woodstock Road near its junction with St Giles, hailed it in 'Duns Scotus's Oxford' as a

> Towery city and branchy between towers;
> Cuckoo-echoing, bell-swarmèd, lark-charmèd, rook-racked, river-rounded.
> (lines 1–2)

Hopkins had been received into the Catholic faith by John Henry Newman in 1866, and after Oxford he spent six months in

Birmingham at the Oratory of St Philip Neri which Newman had founded in 1847. It lies on the Hagley Road in the suburb of Edgbaston. Instead of remaining with Newman's Benedictine order Hopkins chose to enter the Society of Jesus and passed the rest of his short life at a long succession of its foundations. 'Permanence with us', he told a friend, 'is ginger-bread permanence; cob-web, soapsud, and frost-feather permanence'.

He served his novitiate at Manresa House, a fine 18C building in south-west London's Roehampton, south of A205 (Richmond Road) between Roehampton Lane and Richmond Park. He returned several times before entering his tertianship in 1881. After Manresa House he went north to Stonyhurst College, first as a student in 1870–73 and later to teach Greek and Latin in 1882–84. The College, whose nucleus is Sir Richard Shireburn's Elizabethan mansion, lies 12 miles north of Blackburn in Lancashire. The surrounding landscape of Pendle Hill appealed greatly to Hopkins' love of nature. So, too, did the Vale of Clwyd in north Wales, where he studied at St Beuno's College, 1 mile north of Tremeirchion. 'Looking all around but most in looking far up the valley', he wrote in his journal a few weeks after he arrived in 1873, 'I felt an instress and charm in Wales'.

In these surroundings he turned again to the poetry he had abandoned on becoming a Jesuit, writing 'The Wreck of the Deutschland' at a hint from his rector. The well in the much-restored St Winifred's Chapel at Holywell, on A55 8 miles NE of St Beuno's and a traditional object of pilgrimage, suggested the idea for his incomplete tragedy 'St Winefred's Well'; his lyric, 'The Leaden Echo and the Golden Echo', is a fragment from this drama. Yet, though he continued to write until the end of his life, Hopkins pursued a lonely and unrecognised career as poet. His dedication to the Society of Jesus and his awareness of the radically innovative character of his work made him shrink from publication, and he was supported only by his correspondence with Robert Bridges and Richard Watson Dixon. Even his connection with Coventry Patmore (q.v.), whom he visited at Hastings, was the friendship more of priest and devout layman than of two fellow poets.

Not all Hopkins' subsequent postings were as congenial as St Beuno's, and his last appointment as Professor of Classics at University College, Dublin in 1884 was particularly trying. The years at Newman House, on the south side of St Stephen's Green, were 'hard wearying wasting wasted'; it was the period of his 'terrible' sonnets. To the young W.B. Yeats (q.v.), who met him in Dublin, he seemed only a 'querulous, sensitive scholar'. Hopkins died of typhoid and was buried in the Jesuit section of Prospect (or Glasnevin) Cemetery in the north of the city.

He is remembered by a plaque in Poets' Corner (fee) of Westminster Abbey and a window in the church at Haslemere (off A3 in Surrey), where his parents lived in their later years.

St Winifred's Chapel, Holywell, Clwyd: Cadw: Welsh Historic Monuments; phone headquarters in Cardiff, (0222) 465511.

A.E. Housman

b. Fockbury, Hereford and Worcester, 1859; d. Cambridge, 1936. *A Shropshire Lad* (1896); *Last Poems* (1922); *The Name and Nature of Poetry* (1933); *More Poems* (edited by Laurence Housman; 1936).

Housman spent his childhood in the Bromsgrove area south-west of Birmingham. He was born in the parish of Fockbury, 2 miles NW of Bromsgrove and immediately west of the M5, at Valley House, a Georgian farmhouse since renamed Housmans. After his mother 's death the family returned in 1872 to live at Clock House nearby. Housman himself was baptised and his mother buried at the early Victorian church in Catshill, 2 miles north of Bromsgrove. In Bromsgrove itself the Housmans lived from 1859 until 1872 at Perry Hall, now a hotel, on Kidderminster Road. The poet attended Bromsgrove School in its late 17C building with 19C additions on Worcester Road.

Housman entered St John's College, Oxford, in 1877. Despite his obvious brilliance as a classical scholar, he made a disappointing performance in his exams and succeeded in obtaining only a pass degree.

The failure overshadowed his life in London for the next few years. He did unglamorous work for the Patent Office in Southampton Buildings, which connects High Holborn and Chancery Lane. His own office was in the little Quality Court off Chancery Lane nearby. He continued classical studies in his spare time and in 1892 redeemed his earlier disgrace by being appointed Professor of Latin at University College, on Gower Street near the British Museum and Library. Since 1885 he had been living in Highgate at No. 17 North Road, a Georgian row of houses running north from Highgate High Street. It was here that he wrote *A Shropshire Lad*.

In 1911 Housman was elected to the Kennedy Chair of Latin at Cambridge and a fellowship at Trinity College. He lived in the Victorian Whewell's Court opposite the College's main buildings, occupying rooms in the tower by the Sidney Street entrance. He spent the remainder of his life here, striking undergraduates more as a retiring don than as a popular poet.

Fittingly, he was buried in the county that had been the subject of his most famous work. His grave lies near the north wall of the churchyard in the charming town of Ludlow, overlooking the Shropshire hills. Wenlock Edge, off B4368 11 miles to the north, is mentioned in the famous lyric 31 of *A Shropshire Lad*: 'On Wenlock Edge the wood's in trouble'. The comparison which the lyric draws between modern feelings and those of a Roman soldier 'When Uricon the city stood' was inspired by a visit to Wroxeter (further north, off A5 between Shrewsbury and Telford) while excavations were being carried out on the substantial remains of Viroconium, as it is usually called. Yet *A Shropshire Lad* is less local than its generous use of Shropshire place names would suggest. It grew from childhood memories of the hills that had formed 'our western horizon' when he was at Bromsgrove and from a generalised longing for the English countryside, not from intimate knowledge of Shropshire. Nor did Housman hesitate to take liberties with the real geography of the area: the vane on the church steeple at Hughley (off B4371 north of Wenlock Edge) is by no means the 'far-known sign' that lyric 61 proclaims, for the village lies in a valley.

Wroxeter Roman City, Wroxeter, Shropshire: English Heritage, standard opening; phone (074 375) 330.

Thomas Hughes

b. Uffington, Oxfordshire, 1822; d. Brighton, East Sussex, 1896. *Tom Brown's School Days, By an Old Boy* (1857); *The Scouring of the White Horse: or the Long Vacation Ramble of a London Clerk* (1859); *Tom Brown at Oxford* (1861).

Hughes was brought up in the beautiful Vale of the White Horse, then in Berkshire but now in Oxfordshire, and remained attached in imagination to the area throughout his life. At the village of Uffington (2 miles north of B4507 between Wantage and Swindon) the fine church where his grandfather was vicar now has a plaque in his memory. Tom Brown, his most famous creation, attends Uffington School in the delightful 17C building nearby. It is now the Tom Brown's School Museum, with exhibits of local archaeology, history and crafts as well as Hughes' life and work. The first chapter of *Tom Brown's School Days* is an enthusiastic travelogue of Hughes' native

The Vale of the White Horse: an illustration by Richard Doyle to Thomas Hughes' The Scourging of the White Horse

region, while *The Scouring of the White Horse* is less a novel than a collection of local legends. The White Horse itself is carved on the chalk downs that rise to the south of B4507 near the turning for Uffington. On the downs to the south-west, enjoying a fine view, is Uffington Castle: 'a magnificent Roman camp, and no mistake ... all as complete as it was twenty years after the strong old rogues left it' (*Tom Brown's School Days*, Ch. 1).

Yet in the popular mind Hughes is best remembered for his connection with the school at Rugby (5 miles west of M1 junction 18 and 12 miles east of Coventry). His career there (1834–41) lacked the academic distinction gained by his contemporaries Matthew Arnold and Arthur Hugh Clough (qq.v.), and his best-known novel dramatised a hearty, athletic ideal of public-school life that immediately found favour with Victorian readers. Hughes is commemorated with a statue by Brock, but otherwise the school's buildings bear the imprint of a later Victorian architect, William Butterfield. The chapel where Tom visited the grave of Dr Thomas Arnold in the last chapter of the novel has gone; a monument to the headmaster (1844) may be found in Butterfield's building of 1872.

Like so many old Rugbeians of his generation, Hughes was an undergraduate at Oriel College, Oxford (1841–45). *Tom Brown at Oxford*, in which Oriel becomes 'St Ambrose', lacks the power of its predecessor and has never enjoyed the same popularity.

After Oxford Hughes went to London to study the law and lived in Lincoln's Inn, off Chancery Lane in Holborn. His first lodging was on the north side of Lincoln's Inn Fields near Sir John Soane's Museum. After his marriage in 1848 he kept chambers at No. 3 Old Buildings, to the left of the Inn's main entrance from Chancery Lane. During these years he was an active Christian Socialist, first encountering its ideals in the sermons delivered by F.D. Maurice in Lincoln's Inn Chapel, opposite Old Buildings. The effect on his view of the city around him is shown by this passage of reminiscence:

> I passed daily, twice at least, through the horrible nests of squalor and vice which then stood on the site of the New Law Courts [G.E. Street's Gothic building of 1874–82 on the north side of the Strand]. I soon found that (with the exception of thieves and beggars) these nests were peopled by shop workers—poor men, women and children, who if their employers could have flogged them, would have been in a far worse case than any negro slave. I say that the competitive struggle for life had brought them to this pass; and yet the most approved teachers, in reviews and newspapers, which I had begun to read, and even in Parliament, were insisting on 'free competition' as a corollary to 'free trade', and a necessary pillar of industrial prosperity.

From 1859 to 1882 he lived at a succession of addresses in Park Street, which runs south from Oxford Street and parallel to Park Lane.

In later life his appointment as a circuit judge took him to Chester, where he is remembered by a tablet in the interesting Norman church of St John's, on the east side of the city centre near the Roman amphitheatre. The house he built for himself in 1885 and named, predictably, Uffington, stands further east in Dee Hills Park, overlooking the river Dee. Hughes wrote to a friend, the American poet James Russell Lowell:

> Out of the windows of my den I look right over the Cheshire vale to the Packforten hills on the East & the lordly castle of the Tollemaches perched on the spur; & over the gleaming Dee and green water meadows to the woods & spire of Eaton on the South; while to the west (which I must go out on to the stair-case to contemplate) lie Chester Castle & Cathedral with the Welsh

> Moels on the horizon—there is nothing more delightful in the way of an all round view anywhere that I know, & it don't seem to me that the democratic republic will have an easy task in remaking it all.

The Moels are the peaks of the Clwydian Hills which rise beyond Mold, 10 miles west of Chester. The 'lordly castle of the Tollemaches' is the 19C Peckforton Castle, masterpiece of the architect Anthony Salvin, on a red sandstone crag rising from the Cheshire Plain, 14 miles SE of Chester. On the adjoining hill stand the fine ruins of the medieval Beeston Castle.

Tom Brown's School Museum, Uffington, near Faringdon, Oxfordshire: phone Faringdon (0367) 82675.

Uffington Castle and White Horse, Uffington, near Faringdon, Oxfordshire: English Heritage, open at any reasonable time.

Beeston Castle, Beeston, Cheshire: English Heritage, standard opening; phone (0829) 260464.

Victor Hugo

b. Besançon, France, 1802; d. Paris, 1885. Works written in exile: *Histoire d'un Crime* (1852–77); *Les Châtiments* (1853); *Les Contemplations* (1856); *La Légende des Siècles* (1859–83); *Les Misérables* (1862); *William Shakespeare* (1864); *Les Chansons des Rues et des Bois* (1865); *Les Travailleurs de la Mer* (1866); *L'Homme Qui Rit* (1869).

Victor Hugo fled France in 1851 after the *coup d'état* which established the Second Empire and exalted Louis Napoleon to the rank of Emperor. He did not return until the fall of Napoleon III in 1870. Most of these years were spent on the Channel Islands. He brought his family and mistress, Juliette Drouet, to Jersey in 1853 and lived in the parish of St Clement's, SE of St Helier. An inscription on the rock called Le Rocher des Proscrits at nearby Le Dicq commemorates his exile. When he was expelled for attacking Queen Victoria's friendliness towards Napoleon III he took refuge on the neighbouring island of Guernsey. In 1856 he bought *Hauteville House, near the Castle Pier in the south of St Peter Port. Its generous proportions offered ideal scope to his lavish taste in furnishing, and the main rooms of Hauteville House today still preserve the sumptuous appearance he gave them. They are in contrast to his bedroom and the simple study overlooking the sea where he maintained a demanding regimen of work each day. Hugo's work at Hauteville included his most successful novel, *Les Misérables*, and *Les Travailleurs de la Mer*, set on Guernsey. There is a statue of Hugo near the Guernsey Museum and Art Gallery in Candie Gardens to the north.

Hauteville House, 38 rue de Hauteville, St Peter Port, Guernsey, Channel Islands: phone (0481) 21911.

Leigh Hunt

b. London, 1784; d. London, 1859. *The Descent of Liberty: A Mask* (1815); *The Story of Rimini* (1816); *Lord Byron and Some of His Contemporaries* (1828); *Sir Ralph Esher; or Adventures of a Gentleman of the Court of Charles II* (1832); *The Autobiography* (1850); *Table Talk* (1851).

Though he was a prolific and in his own day a controversial writer, Hunt is now usually remembered for his friendships with more famous contemporaries.

All the surviving buildings connected with him are in London. From 1816 to 1822 he lived at Hampstead in the Vale of Health, reached from East Heath Road, though perhaps not in the cottage that now bears his name. It was here that he introduced Keats, another Hampstead resident, and Shelley (qq.v.) to each other, but without conspicuous success. After his return from Italy—where he had visited Byron (q.v.) and been present at Shelley's cremation—he lived in Chelsea (1833–40) at No. 22 Upper Cheyne Row, which has a plaque. His *Autobiography* indulged in fond reminiscence of the house and its then rural surroundings:

> I know not whether the corner I speak of remains as quiet as it was. I am afraid not; for steamboats have carried vicissitude into Chelsea, and Belgravia threatens it with her mighty advent. But to complete my sense of repose and distance, the house was of that old-fashioned sort which I have always loved best, familiar to the eye of my parents, and associated with childhood. It had seats in the windows, a small third room on the first floor, of which I made a *sanctum*, into which no perturbation was to enter, except to calm itself with religious and cheerful thoughts (a room thus appropriated in a house appears to me an excellent thing); and there were a few lime trees in front, which, in their due season diffused a fragrance.

Carlyle (q.v.) was a neighbour on Cheyne Row and it was Mrs Carlyle's uncharacteristically warm greeting on one visit that prompted a well-known poem, 'Jenny Kissed Me'. Less happy was his friendship with Dickens (q.v.), who later caricatured him as the selfish Harold Skimpole in *Bleak House*.

In later life (1840–51) he lived at No. 32 of the charming Edwardes Square, south of Kensington High Street. His last years (1853–59) were spent in Hammersmith, to the west of Kensington. His home at No. 16 Rowan Road (then No. 7 Cornwall Road), off Hammersmith Road, is marked with a plaque.

Hunt was buried in Kensal Green Cemetery, on Harrow Road opposite Kensal Green Station (Bakerloo Line and British Rail). His tomb (No. 13650 in Square 121) lies near the canal and is marked by a quotation from his poem 'Abou-ben-Adhem'.

Aldous Huxley

b. Godalming, Surrey, 1894; d. Los Angeles, California, USA, 1963. *Limbo* (1920); *Crome Yellow* (1921); *Mortal Coils* (1922); *Antic Hay* (1923); *The Little Mexican, and Other Stories* (1924); *Those Barren Leaves* (1925); *Jesting Pilate: The Diary of a Journey* (1926); *Two or Three Graces* (1926); *Point Counter Point* (1928); *Vulgarity in Literature: Digressions from a Theme* (1930); *Brief Candles* (1930); *Brave New World* (1932); *Eyeless in Gaza* (1936); *After Many a Summer* (1939); *Grey Eminence: A Study in Religion and Politics* (1941); *The Art of Seeing* (1942); *Time Must Have a Stop* (1944); *The Perennial Philosophy* (1946); *Ape and Essence* (1948); *Themes and Variations* (1950); *The Devils of*

Loudon (1952); *The Doors of Perception* (1954); *The Genius and the Goddess* (1955); *Heaven and Hell* (1956); *Brave New World Revisited* (1958); *Island* (1962).

The novelist was sent to Eton College in 1908 but developed the eye disease, a violent inflammation of the cornea, from which he suffered for most of his life and was forced to leave abruptly in 1911. He returned, however, as a teacher in 1917–19.

Despite problems with his eyesight Huxley went up to Balliol College, Oxford, in 1913. The novelist L.P. Hartley was a contemporary and friend. Huxley gained a First in English and left, in his own phrase, 'crowned with the artificial roses of academic distinction'.

During his Oxford years he was first introduced by the critic Desmond MacCarthy to Garsington Manor (off B480 4 miles SE of the city), home of Lady Ottoline and Philip Morrell, and at this time a centre for the younger generation of writers and intellectuals. Huxley's descent from the distinguished scientist T.H. Huxley on his father's side and from Matthew Arnold (q.v.) on his mother's side made him a welcome guest and he quickly became an intimate of the Garsington circle, meeting T.S. Eliot, Virginia Woolf (qq.v.), Bertrand Russell, Clive Bell and Katherine Mansfield, among others. After graduating from Oxford in 1916 he went briefly to work on Philip Morrell's farm. His experiences gave him material for his first novel, in which Crome, the country house of the title, is clearly a satirical version of Garsington.

In London Huxley and his wife lived from 1917 to 1920 at No. 18 Hampstead Hill Gardens, connecting Rosslyn Hill and Pond Street south of the Heath. From 1934 until 1937 they were tenants on the ground floor of the Albany, the exclusive block of flats north of Piccadilly which had numbered Byron (q.v.) among its previous tenants. Huxley found its genteel atmosphere little to his taste, and the management allowed him to use his typewriter only after being assured that he would write just poetry on it. In fact, he was producing a rapid succession of novels and travel books, and interspersing his residence in London with tours abroad in the company of D.H. Lawrence (q.v.), among others. In 1937 he left permanently for California, where he ended his days.

In 1971 his ashes were returned to England and buried in his parents' grave at Compton, off A3 between Guildford and Godalming. The cemetery is NE of the village.

Eton College, Windsor, Berkshire: School Yard, College Chapel, Cloister Court and Museum of Eton Life open; also guided tours; phone (0753) 863593.

Garsington Manor, Garsington, near Oxford: gardens open twice a year under NGS.

Henry James

b. New York, USA, 1843; d. London, 1916. *Roderick Hudson* (1876); *The American* (1877); *The Europeans* (1878); *Daisy Miller* (1879); *Washington Square* (1881); *The Portrait of a Lady* (1881); *The Art of Fiction* (1885); *The Bostonians* (1886); *The Princess Casamassima* (1886); *The Reverberator* (1888); *The Aspern Papers* (1888); *The Tragic Muse* (1890); *The Lesson of the Master* (1892); *Terminations* (1895); *The Spoils of Poynton* (1897); *What Maisie Knew* (1898); *In the Cage* (1898); *The Turn of the Screw* (1898); *The Awkward Age* (1899); *The Sacred Fount* (1901); *The Wings of the Dove* (1902); *The Ambassadors* (1903); *The Golden Bowl* (1904); *English Hours* (1905); *Italian Hours* (1909); *The Ivory Tower* (1917).

Although he had several times visited England during his youth, James did not settle in London until 1876. An essay in *English Hours* later recorded his first impressions of 'the dreadful, delightful city' and his conclusion that 'for the real London-lover the mere immensity of the place is a large part of its savour'. His first lodging, where he remained until 1885, was at No. 3 Bolton Street, north of Piccadilly opposite Green Park. Of these crucial years when he established himself in London society and literary life he wrote in his journal: 'I have *lived* much there, felt much, thought much, learned much, produced much; the little shabby furnished apartment ought to be sacred to me. I came to London as a complete stranger, and today I know much too many people. *J'y suis absolumment comme chez moi*'. In 1886 he moved to Kensington and a much grander flat on the fourth floor of No. 34 De Vere Gardens, now marked with a plaque, south of Kensington High Street almost opposite the Palace Gate to

Henry James at Lamb House.

Kensington Gardens. He stayed here until 1896, taking slightly ironic pleasure in the conventional way he furnished his rooms: 'expectedness everywhere'. In 1887–89 Robert Browning (q.v.) was a neighbour at No. 29 and so became a friend.

James' last London home (1912–16) was at No. 21 Carlyle Mansions, at the junction of Lawrence Street and Cheyne Walk in Chelsea. After his death here the funeral service was held at Chelsea Old Church, on the corner of the Walk and Old Church Street, though his ashes were buried in the family cemetery at Cambridge, Massachusetts. The church has a memorial tablet. A memorial stone was recently added to Poets' Corner (fee) in Westminster Abbey.

A gloomy visit to George Eliot at Witley, Surrey, is described under the entry for that novelist.

For all his relish of London, James hankered after a quiet, picturesque corner of England where he could comfortably root himself. The need was magnificently answered by *Lamb House in the coastal town of Rye, 12 miles NE of Hastings in East Sussex. He first leased the Georgian house, found near the church at the top of West Street, in 1898 and used it as a summer residence for the rest of his life. Though the garden room where he did much of his writing in good weather was destroyed by a bomb during the Second World War, the grounds otherwise have all the typically English charm he evoked in *English Hours*:

> a dear old garden—a garden brown-walled, red-walled, rose-covered, … divided by the width of a quiet street of grass-grown cobbles from the house of its master, and possessed of a little old glass-fronted, panelled pavilion … There is not much room in the pavilion, but there is room for the hard-pressed table and the tilted chair—there is room for a novelist and his friends.

In London, James was always keenly aware of the spirit of Thackeray (q.v.). His residence on the Sussex coast made him particularly appreciative of his predecessor's last novel, whose connection with the area is celebrated by a fine essay in *English Hours*, 'Winchelsea, Rye and *Denis Duval*'.

Lamb House, West Street, Rye, East Sussex: NT; for opening arrangements phone NT Kent and East Sussex regional office, (0892) 890651.

Richard Jefferies

b. Coate, Wiltshire, 1848; d. Goring-by-Sea, West Sussex, 1887. *The Gamekeeper at Home: Sketches of Natural History and Rural Life* (1878); *Wild Life in a Southern County* (1879); *The Amateur Poacher* (1879); *Greene Ferne Farm* (1880); *Hodge and His Masters* (1880); *Round About a Great Estate* (1880); *Wood Magic: A Fable* (1880); *Bevis: The Story of a Boy* (1882); *Nature Near London* (1883); *The Story of My Heart: My Autobiography* (1883); *The Dewy Morn* (1884); *The Life of the Fields* (1884); *Red Deer* (1884); *After London: Or Wild England* (1885); *The Open Air* (1885); *Amaryllis at the Fair* (1887); *Field and Hedgerow: Being the Last Essays of Jefferies, Collected by His Widow* (1889).

Jefferies spent the first twenty-nine years of his short life in the region near Swindon (north of M4 in Wiltshire), countryside he described in *Wild Life in a Southern County*, the semi-autobiographical *Bevis* and the openly autobiographical *Story of My*

Heart among other works. In the village of Coate, south of Swindon on A345, his family home at Coate Farm is now the Richard Jefferies Museum. The farm is portrayed as 'Coombe Oaks' in *Amaryllis at the Fair*, where his parents also appear as the Idens. Coate itself is the subject of 'My Old Village' in *Field and Hedgerow*. Nearby lies Coate Water, a 72-acre artificial lake created in 1822 and one of his favourite haunts in boyhood and youth. A contemporary described his shy, solitary ways:

> Supplied with his books—whether on history or fable, on astrology or Euclid, it mattered not—he was wont to launch his boat, rigged by his own hands, and, having placed his gun and a scrap of food therein, to cruise about the neighbouring lake. Thus alone all day, he was thrown upon himself and his own resources. He got to learn the ways of fish, of birds, and of all the denizens of nature. Then he would read his books, and having shut them up after a while, he would lie back in his boat, and dream long wakeful dreams such as rarely visit lads of his few years.

By A345 2 miles south of Coate is Chiseldon, where he attended the parish church and was married in 1874.

From Chiseldon we may continue SW into the open downland that was Jefferies' special love. The main object of such a journey should be Barbury Castle, an Iron Age hill fort which gives magnificent views of the surrounding countryside. It can be reached by taking B4005 west and then following an unclassified road south (4 miles), but it is much better to walk directly from Chiseldon along the Ridgeway (3½ miles). The course of this prehistoric track is traced, as far as modern roads permit, by the Countryside Commission's Ridgeway Path (85 miles long). It follows the Icknield Way from Ivinghoe Beacon, near Tring in Buckinghamshire, through the Chilterns to cross the Thames at Goring; then it heads west along the Berkshire Downs and, beyond Barbury Castle, continues south across the Marlborough Downs to Overton Hill and the Vale of Pewsey. Of Jefferies' many references to the Ridgeway, his essay in *Wild Life in a Southern County* may be recommended as an introduction.

In 1877 he left the countryside of his childhood, though he continued to write about it until the end of his life. His connection with Wiltshire is commemorated by a bust in Salisbury Cathedral (40 miles south of Swindon via A345). He lived first near London and then, after the onset of illness in 1882, at a series of places in South-Eastern England. In 1885–86 he was at Crowborough (on A26 between Tunbridge Wells and Lewes); his home, The Downs, stands on the northern continuation of the High Street as London Road. From there he went to Goring-by-Sea, on the coast west of Worthing via A259. The house and street where he lived have both since been renamed after him; they can be found off Sea Lane as it runs south from A259 near St Mary's Church. He was buried in the Broadwater and Worthing Cemetery in the northern part of Worthing. W.H. Hudson (1841–1922), author of *Green Mansions* and another sensitive observer of nature, chose to be buried near him.

Richard Jefferies Museum, Coate, Swindon, Wiltshire: phone (0793) 26161, extension 3130.

Jerome K. Jerome

b. Walsall, West Midlands, 1859; d. Northampton, 1927. *On Stage and Off* (1885); *Idle Thoughts of an Idle Fellow* (1886); *Three Men in a Boat (To Say Nothing of the Dog)* (1889); *The Second Thoughts of an Idle Fellow* (1898); *Three Men on the Bummel* (1900); *The Observations of Henry* (1901); *Paul Kelver* (1902); *The Passing of the Third-Floor Back, and Other Stories* (1907); *My Life and Times* (1926).

In Walsall, NE of Birmingham, the early 19C town house where Jerome was born is now a museum devoted to his memory, with an exhibition about his life and work as well as period furnishings. *Paul Kelver*, the autobiographical novel which he himself thought his best book, reflects his early struggle after leaving school at the age of fourteen and his progress from railway clerk to actor and eventually to journalist.

The region we most readily associate with Jerome lies along the course of the Thames from London to Oxford, celebrated in his amiable compilation of anecdotes and reflections about city dwellers on holiday, *Three Men in a Boat*. In fact, he first conceived the book as a serious historical guide, and in its final form it still bears enough marks of its origin to make it a useful as well as a pleasant travellers' companion. Fittingly, Jerome wrote it at his flat overlooking the river, in Chelsea Gardens at the junction of Chelsea Bridge Road and Ebury Street.

The fictional journey of *Three Men in a Boat* begins at the bridge in Kingston-upon-Thames, south-west London. The sight of Hampton Court (2½ miles) prompts Harris to remember his embarrassing time in the maze (Ch. 6). Despite the fact that he 'revels in tombs, and graves, and epitaphs, and monumental inscriptions' (Ch. 7), he is not allowed the chance to see the elaborate 18C tomb of Mrs Thomas in the church at Hampton (4 miles). In Chapter 8 Jerome mentions the tombs and scolds' bridle in Walton church (7½ miles). After being joined at Weybridge by George, the party camps for the night near Runnymede (18 miles), and Jerome recreates the scene when Magna Carta was signed in Chapter 11. After lunching the next day at the popular Monkey Island (27½ miles), they pass Cliveden woods, part of the estate where Charles Barry's 19C mansion (later owned by the Astor family) stands: 'In its unbroken loveliness this is, perhaps, the sweetest stretch of the river' (Ch. 12). Marlow (37 miles) is 'one of the pleasantest river centres I know of' (Ch. 13), and so makes an appropriate resting place for the night. The town's connection with Shelley (q.v.) is noted and the Hoby monuments in Bisham church on the opposite bank recommended to the visitor. Medmenham Abbey (40 miles), a mansion built on the site of a monastery, provokes memories of the 18C 'Hell Fire Club'. Sonning (48 miles) is praised as 'the most fairy-like little nook on the whole river. It is more like a stage village than one built of bricks and mortar' (Ch. 14). On the other hand, 'One does not linger in the neighbourhood of Reading' (Ch. 16). In fact, though he describes a two-day rest at Streatley (Chs 16 and 17) and praises Dorchester in Chapter 18, Jerome deals briskly with the last stages of the journey to Oxford (91½ miles), reached in Chapter 19. When it begins to rain on the way back, the three friends abandon their boat for the comfort of a railway train.

To the modern tourist the chief interest of the Thameside region near Oxford is Ewelme (off B4009 2 miles NE of Wallingford and 12 miles SE of Oxford). Jerome is buried in the churchyard of this pretty Chiltern village.

Jerome K. Jerome Birthplace Museum, Belsize House, Bradford Street, Walsall, West Midlands: for information phone Walsall Museum and Art Gallery, Lichfield Street, (0922) 650000, extension 3124.

Hampton Court Palace, East Molesey, Surrey: DoE monument; phone (01) 977 8441.

Cliveden, Taplow, Maidenhead, Berkshire: NT; phone Burnham (06286) 5069.

Samuel Johnson

b. Lichfield, Staffordshire, 1709; d. London, 1784. *London* (1738); *The Life of Richard Savage* (1744); *The Vanity of Human Wishes, being the Tenth Satire of Juvenal Imitated* (1749); *Irene* (1749); *The Rambler* (1750–52); *A Dictionary of the English Language* (1755); *The Idler* (1758–60); *Rasselas, Prince of Abyssinia* (1759); *A Journey to the Western Islands of Scotland* (1775); *Lives of the English Poets* (1779–81).

Related works: James Boswell, *Journal of a Tour to the Hebrides with Samuel Johnson, LL.D.* (1785) and *The Life of Samuel Johnson, LL.D.* (1791).

•Lichfield, 16 miles north of Birmingham, is more than just the city of Johnson's birth, childhood and youth, though this fact alone would lend it great interest. Here he formed friendships whose influence lasted throughout his life and was maintained by long, frequent visits. Its inhabitants, he loyally declared, were 'the most sober, decent people in England—the genteelest, in proportion to their wealth, and spoke the purest English' (Boswell's *Life*, Aetat. 67). Lichfield today, though greatly expanded beyond the community of 3000 people Johnson knew, has preserved much of the atmosphere of his time and enough specific buildings associated with him to reward a walking tour.

It begins in the market place where Johnson is commemorated by Richard Cockle Lucas' statue of 1838 with bas-reliefs around its base depicting episodes from the subject's local life. These include the infant Johnson sitting on his father's shoulders to hear the Tory Dr Sacheverell preach in the Cathedral, a story repeated by Boswell in his *Life* (Aetat. 3) but unsubstantiated by modern research, and the adult Johnson doing penance at Uttoxeter market (see below). Percy Fitzgerald's statue of Boswell (1908) is nearby. St Mary's Church, where the Johnson family worshipped, is now a Heritage Centre.

Johnson's birthplace stands at the corner of Breadmarket Street. The tall, steep-roofed house was built in 1707 by Michael Johnson, from whom his son inherited a tendency to 'vile melancholy' (*Life* for 1709), and used by him as both home and bookshop. After Michael died and Johnson went to London, Johnson's mother, his step-daughter Lucy Porter, and a servant, Catherine Chambers, remained to run the business. The house is now the Samuel Johnson Birthplace Museum, rich in relics of Johnson, his relatives and his circle of friends in Lichfield. A plaque on the building next door marks the former Three Crowns Inn where Johnson and Boswell stayed on later visits.

From Market Street we follow St John Street south. Opposite St John's Hospital stood the Grammar School, a large oak-panelled room attended by Johnson from the age of seven to seventeen, as well as by his younger contemporary, the actor David Garrick. The

Unfinished oil painting of Samuel Johnson by James Barry (c 1777)

only part to survive is the 17C Headmaster's House (now Council offices), then inhabited by John Hunter, whom the writer remembered for the brutal efficiency with which he taught Latin: 'My master whipt me very well' (*Life*, Aetat. 10–16). By retracing our steps north on St John Street and continuing on Bird Street we find, on our left, the fine 18C Swan Inn where Johnson and the Thrales stayed in 1774 on their way to Wales (see below).

As we enter the Cathedral Close by turning right from Beacon Street we notice on our left a plaque marking the house of Dr Erasmus Darwin (1731–1802), scientist and grandfather of a more famous scientist. Johnson and the elder Darwin were acquainted but of sufficiently similar temperaments that Lichfield friends found it unwise to invite them both to the same gathering. On the north side of the Close is the splendid 17C Bishop's Palace, now the Cathedral Choir School. Its tenant in Johnson's youth was Gilbert Walmsley, Registrar of the Ecclesiastical Court of Lichfield and the first man to give serious recognition to his talents. The account of Edmund Smith in *Lives of the English Poets* turns aside from its subject to indulge in affectionate reminiscence of Walmsley: 'Such was his amplitude of learning and such his copiousness of communication that it may be doubted whether a day now passes in which I have not some advantage from his friendship'. Johnson also knew the Palace's later tenants, the Seward family, of whom the best remembered is Anna Seward (1747–1809), poetess and 'Swan of Lichfield'.

The Cathedral, where Johnson may or may not have heard Dr Sacheverell preach, has monuments to Erasmus Darwin (by the south transept), Anna Seward and Gilbert Walmsley (in the NW chapel near the font). Busts of Johnson and David Garrick by Westmacott are next to each other in the south transept.

We leave the Cathedral Close by the path leading east to St Chad's Church (1 mile). The route takes us past Johnson's Willow, beyond which lay the unsuccessful parchment works run by Michael Johnson. St Chad's is the burial place of Lucy Porter and Catherine Chambers; a plaque can be found on the north side of the chancel. Returning to the picturesque Dam Street, we head south towards the market. A plaque remembers the probable scene of Johnson's earliest education, Dame Oliver's School.

St Michael's Church, on a hill by the road to Burton upon Trent, has the graves of Johnson's parents and his brother, Nathaniel. The Latin epitaph he composed on a last visit to Lichfield just before his own death is by the chancel steps. At Edial Hall, 3 miles SW on A5190 to Burntwood, Johnson tried unsuccessfully to establish a school after his marriage. The attempt ended in 1737 when he left for London with Garrick, one of the few pupils he had been able to attract.

The area north of Lichfield extending into Derbyshire is rich in Johnsonian associations. Uttoxeter (22 miles north via A515 and A50) was the scene of a famous and moving episode, best described by Johnson himself as reported in Boswell's *Life*. Recalling his conduct as a child, he confessed:

> Once, indeed, ... I was disobedient; I refused to attend my father to Uttoxeter-market. Pride was the source of that refusal, and the remembrance of it was painful. A few years ago I desired to atone for this fault; I went to Uttoxeter in very bad weather, and stood for a considerable time bareheaded in the rain, on the spot where my father's stall used to stand. In contrition I stood, and I hope the penance was expiatory. (*Life*, Aetat. 75)

A replica of Lucas' bas-relief of the incident on the Lichfield statue now decorates the conduit in the market, though there is some reason to suppose that Michael Johnson kept his stall near the gate to the churchyard.

At Ashbourne, 10 miles north of A50 on A515, Johnson frequently visited Dr John Taylor, a fellow-pupil at Lichfield Grammar School who grew into a worldly Whig clergyman. His house, The Mansion, stands on Church Street opposite the Tudor Grammar School. During a visit of 1777 Boswell stayed at the Green Man and Black's Head, whose sign still straddles the road, and attended Sunday service with Johnson at the fine church of St Oswald, which he reported 'one of the largest and most luminous that I have seen in any town of the same size'.

Johnson greatly admired nearby Dovedale ('He that has seen Dovedale has no need to see the Highlands') and some have supposed it the original of the 'Happy Valley' at the beginning of *Rasselas*. During their visit of 1777 he took Boswell 4 miles NW from Ashbourne to Ilam Hall, which has been replaced by a Victorian building (now a youth hostel) though the fine grounds where the Manifold emerges from its subterranean course survive. Johnson was stubbornly sceptical of this natural curiosity, but both men took pleasure in the place's association with Congreve (q.v.).

The same visit of 1777 took Johnson, Boswell and Dr Taylor to Kedleston Hall, 3 miles north of Derby. Lord Scardsale's grand neo-classical mansion, completed by Robert Adam in 1765, aroused all Johnson's ambivalent feelings towards displays of wealth by the aristocracy. He decided that he thought better of the building than he had earlier done when he had remarked that 'it would do excellently for a town-hall', though he still insisted that the main hall was ill-lighted and 'of no use but for dancing in'. He reassured Dr Taylor that he would not dream of expressing such opinions to the owner, but would merely say: 'My Lord, this is the most *costly* room that I ever saw' (*Life*, Aetat. 68).

In Derby itself Johnson was married to Elizabeth ('Tetty') Porter, a widow some twenty years his senior, in 1735. Boswell's *Life* (Aetat. 26) tells the story of how Johnson turned their walk from Birmingham to Derby into a demonstration of the 'manly firmness' he intended to adopt towards his wife. St Werburgh's Church on Friargate, where the ceremony took place, is now greatly altered.

Aston Hall, a partly Jacobean house 2½ miles N of the city centre in Birmingham, has a Johnson Room with 18C panelling taken from the home of Johnson's friend Edmund Hector in Old Square. The Hall is now a branch of the Birmingham Museums and Art Gallery.

In 1764 he visited Thomas Percy, who published his influential *Reliques of Ancient English Poetry* the next year, at the Old Vicarage in the village of Easton Maudit, off A509 9 miles east of Northampton. A plaque on the front pew of the church commemorates his worship here.

A visit to Oxford completes the review of Johnson's connections with Central England. He entered Pembroke College in 1728, having second-floor rooms over the main gateway, and left without a degree in 1731 because of financial problems. He was, however, fond of his old college, revisiting it and proudly calling it 'a nest of singing birds' (*Life*, Aetat. 21), though the only other Pembroke writer of this period to be remembered is William Shenstone (q.v.), whom 'he would not allow ... to approach excellence as a poet'. The award of an MA in 1755 came just in time for him to place the initials after his name on the titlepage of his *Dictionary*. 'It is in truth doing ourselves more honour than him, to have such a work done by an Oxford hand', remarked one of the dons responsible. A Doctorate of Civil Law followed in 1775, though Oxford had been anticipated by Trinity College, Dublin in entitling Johnson to the 'Dr' by which the world came to know him but he himself rarely used.

Johnson's famous dictum that 'when a man is tired of London, he is tired of life' (*Life*, Aetat. 68) pays tribute in a characteristically emphatic manner to the central role that the city played in his life and he, indeed, came to play in the life of London. His poverty during the early years after his arrival in 1737 assured that familiarity with its variety which he later recommended to Boswell. Toward the end of his life he listed for his future biographer's benefit some thirteen addresses where he had lived, most of them near Fleet Street and the Strand, and several in the Inns of Court.

The only one to remain is *No. 17 Gough Square, a pleasant backwater reached from the north side of Fleet Street via Johnson's Court (not named after him, but another of his addresses). It was his home from 1749 to 1758, the years when he was working on his *Rambler* essays and the *Dictionary*. His household included the blind

Anna Williams, sometime poetess and housekeeper for much of his life, and Frank Barber, the black servant whom he educated. Tetty Johnson died here in 1752. Dr Johnson's House is now a museum. Its contents include manuscripts, relics of Johnson and his circle, and portraits—of which James Barry's oil sketch (c 1777) over the fireplace in the dining room is the most striking. At the top of the house is the garret where he and his six assistants laboured on the completion of the *Dictionary*.

St Clement Danes, in the middle of the Strand just beyond Temple Bar, was Johnson's parish church for many years. It has a statue by Percy Fitzgerald outside its east end.

Johnson also has the distinction of being remembered in both Westminster Abbey and St Paul's Cathedral. In Poets' Corner (fee) at the Abbey we find his grave with a bust by Nollekens, near his lifelong friend Garrick. St Paul's is less lucky. Beneath the dome is John Bacon's statue (1795) of an improbably athletic figure draped in a toga.

Nothing remains in either Southwark or Streatham to recall Johnson's long, significant intimacy with Hester Thrale and her husband. The only surviving memento of the association has found its way to Hampstead, where the summer house Johnson used at Thrale Place has been re-erected in the grounds of Kenwood House on Hampstead Lane.

Greenwich Park, in south-east London by the Thames, was a favourite retreat of Johnson's while he was composing *Irene*, the tragedy he had brought half-finished with him to London. He took Boswell to the Park in the early days of their acquaintance:

> He asked me, I suppose, by way of trying my disposition, 'Is not this very fine?' Having no exquisite relish of the beauties of Nature, and being more delighted with 'the busy hum of men', I answered, 'Yes, Sir; but not equal to Fleet-street'. JOHNSON. 'You are right, Sir'. (*Life*, Aetat. 54)

On the same occasion he also made a curious criticism of Wren's Greenwich Hospital (now the Royal Naval College), thinking that it 'was too magnificent for a place of charity, and that its parts were too much detached, to make one great whole'.

With the Thrales Johnson several times visited Brighton on the Sussex coast, in the days when it was still Brighthelmston and had not fully achieved the fashionable status it enjoyed after the Prince Regent had chosen to build his Pavilion here. He worshipped in the Thrale pew at the church of St Nicholas on Dyke Road, which leaves the town to the NW; there is a plaque on the north wall. From Brighton Johnson went to 'see how our ancestors lived' (*Life*, Aetat. 73) at the magnificent late 17C Petworth House (24 miles NW via A283) and at Cowdray House in Cowdray Park, Midhurst (6 miles further west via A272), now ruined but still impressive.

Langton Hall in Lincolnshire, where Johnson stayed with his friend Bennet Langton in 1764, has gone but his connection with the area is remembered at Tetford in the Wolds 5 miles NE of Horncastle. He addressed the Tetford Club at the pleasant White Hart Inn, which still has a fine oak settle from the period.

Even these fragmentary reminders of Johnson's travels outside London, together with his more important connections with Lichfield, go some way towards challenging Macaulay's famous judgement:

> He had studied, not the genus man, but the species Londoner. Nobody was ever so thoroughly conversant with all the shades of moral and intellectual

character which were to be seen from Islington to the Thames and from Hyde Park Corner to Mile-End Green. But his philosophy stopped at the first turnpike-gate.

The best rebuttal—or perhaps the most intriguing test—of Macaulay's opinion is the Scottish tour Johnson made with Boswell in autumn 1773: 'He always said, that he was not come to Scotland to see fine places, of which there were enough in England; but wild objects,–mountains,—waterfalls,—peculiar manners; in short, things which he had not seen before' (Boswell's *Journal*, 26 August). It would not be possible to describe the trip in full detail here nor, in fact, is it necessary since Johnson's own *Journey to the Western Islands* and Boswell's *Journal of a Tour to the Hebrides* provide far better accounts than any modern guidebook could hope to offer. Of these works, Johnson's is the more precisely topographical and Boswell's the more entertaining, for it enjoys the great advantage of having Johnson as well as Scotland for its subject.

'Scottifying the Palate' by Thomas Rowlandson in The Picturesque Beauties of Boswell *(1786).*
'I bought some speldings, *fish (generally whitings) salted and dried in a particular manner, being dipped in the sea and dried in the sun, and eaten by the Scots by way of a relish. He had never seen them, though they are sold in London. I insisted on* scottifying *his palate; but he was very reluctant. With difficulty I prevailed with him to let a bit of one of them lie in his mouth. He did not like it.'*
Entry for 18 August in Boswell's Journal of a Tour to the Hebrides

The main surviving points, at least, of their itinerary may briefly be noted. It began and ended in Edinburgh, where Boswell was able to exult in his *Journal* entry for 14 August: 'I now actually had him in Caledonia'. He entertained Johnson at his flat in James Court, off

Lawnmarket. In the course of touring the major sights of the capital Johnson was unpleasantly surprised by the dirty and neglected state of St Giles, then divided into four Presbyterian churches, on the High Street but Boswell's *Journal* (16 August) assured readers: 'It is now very elegantly fitted up'.

After crossing the Firth of Forth the pair travelled up the east coast to St Andrews (on A915, 48 miles NE of Edinburgh), site of Scotland's oldest university, which Johnson's *Journey* judged 'a place eminently adapted to study and education, being situated in a populous, yet a cheap country, and exposing the minds and manners of young men neither to the levity and dissoluteness of a capital city, nor to the gross luxury of a town of commerce'. Boswell (18 August) offers a pleasant account of an evening walk round the former buildings of St Leonard's College off Abbey Street, then a private house and now St Leonard's School.

From New Slains Castle, on Cruden Bay 22 miles north of Aberdeen, now an impressive ruin, they visited the Bullers of Buchan (2 miles north on A975 and A952), a dramatic rock chasm which (wrote Johnson) 'no man can see with indifference, who has either sense of danger or delight in rarity'.

The westward route they then followed included two places of special interest: the magnificent ruins of Elgin Cathedral and Cawdor Castle, successor to the building supposedly occupied by the historical Macbeth, on B9090 6 miles SW of Nairn.

From Glenelg on the west coast they crossed to the island of Skye in the Inner Hebrides. Their month's stay included visits to Flora MacDonald, who had helped Bonnie Prince Charlie escape after the defeat of the 1745 rebellion, at Kingsburgh (now rebuilt; off A856 near Loch Snizort Beag) and the Macleods of Dunvegan Castle (A850 on Loch Dunvegan). The 15C–19C castle now displays a portrait of Johnson, by Zoffany after Reynolds.

From the island of Mull to the south they reached Iona, with its relics of Britain's earliest Christianity. Johnson admitted that he was 'less eager' than his companion to make the pilgrimage and left it to Boswell to record his famous extempore praise: 'That man is little to be envied, whose patriotism would not gain force upon the plains of *Marathon*, or whose piety would not grow warmer among the ruins of *Iona*!' (19 October).

Returning to the mainland at Oban, Boswell and Johnson then continued south, visiting Inveraray Castle on the north shore of Loch Fyne. Johnson was 'much struck by the grandeur and elegance of this princely seat' (*Journal*, 25 October) and gratified by the cordial welcome he received from the Duke of Argyll, while Boswell found more than architecture to delight the eye: 'I shall never forget the impression made upon my fancy by some of the ladies' maids tripping about in neat morning dress'. The 18C building, altered since that time, is mainly notable for its collection of treasures and paintings.

Four miles NW of Dumbarton and on the southern tip of Loch Lomond they stopped at Cameron House, where Johnson gave advice on Smollett's epitaph to the writer's cousin; both the house and the epitaph are described under the entry for that author.

After an unmemorable visit to Glasgow they made their last stop before Edinburgh at Auchinleck, 12 miles SE of Kilmarnock on A76, the family home of Boswell. A clash between his father, the Whig and Presbyterian Lord Auchinleck, and Johnson, Tory and Anglican, was almost inevitable:

> They became exceedingly warm, and violent, and I was very much distressed by being present at such an altercation between two men, both of whom I reverenced; yet I durst not interfere. It would certainly be very unbecoming in me to exhibit my honoured father, and my respected friend, as intellectual gladiators, for the entertainment of the publick; and therefore I suppress what would, I dare say, make an interesting scene in this dramatick sketch. (6 November)

Boswell (d. 1795) and his wife are buried in the family mausoleum adjoining Auchinleck church, which is now a small museum.

Because it produced no comparable literary record Johnson's visit to north Wales the following summer (1774) with Hester Thrale and her husband is less well remembered. The first object of their journey was Tremeirchion, a village on B5429 overlooking the Vale of Clwyd. Mrs Thrale had inherited the family home of Bach-y-Graig here (now gone) and returned after her marriage to Gabriel Piozzi (1784), of which Johnson violently disapproved, to build the house Brynabella to the south. She is commemorated by a plaque in the north chancel of the church. From Tremeirchion Johnson visited Denbigh Castle, 4½ miles south via A543. Two other impressive castles were included in the route across Wales: the ruins of Beaumaris on south-east Anglesey, reached from the mainland by the Menai Bridge and A545, and the shell at Caernarfon on A487 and the south shore of the Menai Strait. The party's final destination was near Pwllheli, on A499 and the southern shore of the Lleyn Peninsula. Mrs Thrale was born at Bodvel Hall, 2 miles NW of the town on A497.

Samuel Johnson Birthplace Museum, Breadmarket Street, Lichfield, Staffordshire: phone (0543) 264972.

Headmaster's House and Old Grammar School (Lichfield District Council Offices), St John Street, Lichfield, Staffordshire: visitors by appointment; for further information phone Lichfield Tourist Information Centre, (0543) 252109.

Bishop's Palace (St Chad's Cathedral Choir School), Cathedral Close, Lichfield, Staffordshire: visits by appointment; for further information phone Lichfield Tourist Information Centre, (0543) 252109.

Edial Hall, near Lichfield, Staffordshire: visits by written appointment.

Ilam Park, Ilam, near Ashbourne, Derbyshire: NT; phone Thorpe Cloud (033 529) 245. Ilam Hall is a Youth Hostel and not open to visitors.

Kedleston Hall, near Derby: NT; phone Derby (0332) 842191.

Aston Hall, Aston Park, Trinity Road, Aston, Birmingham, West Midlands: phone (021) 327 0062.

Old Vicarage, Easton Maudit, Northamptonshire: visitors by written appointment.

Dr Johnson's House, 17 Gough Square, London EC4: phone (01) 353 3745.

Kenwood House, Hampstead Lane, Hampstead, London NW3: English Heritage, standard opening but open Mondays and New Year; phone (01) 348 1286.

Royal Naval College (Greenwich Hospital), King William Walk, Greenwich, London SE10: phone (01) 858 2154.

Petworth House, Petworth, West Sussex: NT; phone (0798) 42207.

Cowdray House, Cowdray Park, Midhurst, West Sussex: phone Cowdray Park Estate, (073 081) 2423.

Cawdor Castle, near Nairn, Highlands Region: phone (066 77) 615.

Dunvegan Castle, Isle of Skye, Highlands Region: phone (047 022) 206.

Inveraray Castle, Inveraray, Strathclyde Region: phone (0499) 2203.

Auchinleck Boswell Museum and Mausoleum, Church Hill, Auchinleck, Strathclyde Region: visitors by appointment; phone Cumnock (0290) 20757 or 26529.

Denbigh Castle, Denbigh, Clwyd: Cadw: Welsh Historic Monuments; phone (074571) 3979.

Beaumaris Castle, Beaumaris, Anglesey, Gwynedd: Cadw: Welsh Historic Monuments; phone (0248) 810361.

Caernarfon Castle, Caernarfon, Gwynedd: Cadw: Welsh Historic Monuments; phone (0286) 77617.

Ben Jonson

b. London, 1572; d. London, 1637. *Every Man out of His Humour* (1600); *Every Man in His Humour* (1601); *Cynthia's Revels* (1601); *Poetaster* (1602); *Sejanus His Fall* (1605); *Eastward Hoe* (with George Chapman and John Marston [qq.v.]; 1605); *Volpone: or The Fox* (1607); *The Alchemist* (1612); *Epicoene: or The Silent Woman* (1616); *The Forest* (1616); *Bartholomew Fair* (1631); *The Devil is an Ass* (1631); *The Underwood* (1640); *Timber: or Discoveries Made upon Men and Matter* (1640).

Very little survives in London to recall the memory of Jonson's lifetime residence or his long theatrical career, though some account of the areas connected with the Renaissance drama is offered under the entry for Shakespeare (Rte 1). He was educated at Westminster School, in Little Dean's Yard to the south of Westminster Abbey. A poem later celebrated his master, William Camden, as him 'to whom I owe/ All that I am in arts, all that I know'. His grave is marked by a slab in the north aisle of Westminster Abbey with the magnificently simple epitaph: 'O rare Ben Jonson'. Poets' Corner (fee) has a medallion commemorating him.

Most of Jonson's connections outside London are with the country houses where the spectacular entertainments, masques and antimasques of his later career were performed. The chief surviving places now open to the public may be listed briefly:

Belvoir Castle, Leicestershire, west of A1 near Grantham. Rebuilt since the performance of *The Masque of the Metamorphosed Gypsies* (1621). Phone (0476) 870262.

Kenilworth Castle, now ruined, north of Warwick. *The Masque of Owls* (1624). English Heritage, standard opening; phone (0926) 52078.

Althorp, 16–18C mansion 6 miles NW of Northampton, off A428. Entertainment in 1603 for Queen Anne to celebrate James I's accession to the throne. For opening arrangements phone Northampton Tourist Information Centre, (0604) 22677.

Bolsover Castle, on A632 7 miles NW of Mansfield, Nottinghamshire. *Love's Welcome* in the presence of Charles I in 1634, a grander version of the entertainment offered to the King the previous year at nearby Welbeck Abbey (now an Army Training School). Bolsover Castle is English Heritage, standard opening; phone (0246) 823349.

A more important connection links Jonson and *Penshurst Place (SW of Tonbridge in Kent), birthplace of Sir Philip Sidney (q.v.) and home of the Sidney family. In 'To Penshurst', published in *The Forest*, progenitor of a series of 17C poems about country houses, it is celebrated for its architectural modesty, hospitality to guests and benevolent relations with the community around. The poem concludes:

> Now, *Penshurst*, they that will proportion thee
> With other edifices, when they see
> Those proud, ambitious heaps, and nothing else,
> May say, their lords have built, but thy lord dwells.

Penshurst Place, Penshurst, Tonbridge, Kent: phone Penshurst (0892) 870307.

John Keats

b. London, 1795; d. Rome, 1821. *Poems* (1817); *Endymion: A Poetic Romance* (1818); *Lamia, Isabella, The Eve of St Agnes and Other Poems* (1820).

London still offers significant reminders of the poet's brief life. A plaque at No. 85 Moorgate near its junction with London Wall in the City marks the site of his birthplace, a livery stable run by his father. He was baptised at the early 18C church of St Botolph on Bishopsgate to the east. From 1815 he studied medicine at Guy's and St Thomas's Hospitals on the east side of Borough High Street in Southwark, reached by following London Bridge south over the river. Guy's of course, is vastly changed since then and St Thomas' buildings have virtually disappeared, but on St Thomas' Street—where Keats was lodging when he wrote 'On First Looking into Chapman's Homer'—we find a fascinating survival of the medical conditions he knew. The Chapter House of Southwark Cathedral contains the Old Operating Theatre of St Thomas'. It dates from 1821, was rediscovered in 1956 and has been carefully restored; the cramped stalls from which medical students like Keats could watch operations are of special interest. A further reminder of the poet's medical career is the charming 17C–18C Apothecaries Hall on Blackfriars Lane, north of Queen Victoria Street in Blackfriars. Keats took and passed his exam for an apothecary's licence here in 1816.

In 1817 he moved north to Hampstead, which still preserves some of the rural atmosphere that delighted him and is still the London borough most closely linked with his name. His first lodging was on Well Walk, the picturesque continuation of Flask Walk from Hampstead High Street, next to the pub at the present No. 30. Here he nursed his consumptive younger brother, Tom, who died in December 1818.

It was partly to escape the associations of Well Walk after Tom's death that Keats moved to what is now the major landmark for his admirers: the *Keats House in Keats Grove near the southern tip of the Heath and Hampstead Ponds. Wentworth Place, to use its original name, was built in 1815–16 by two friends of the poet, Charles Wentworth Dilke and Charles Armitage Brown, as a pair of semi-detached houses sharing the same garden. Keats came in December 1818 to share the eastern half with Brown. From April 1819 the western half was let to Mrs Brawne and her daughters; Fanny, the eldest, became Keats' fiancée in the autumn. Returning to his bedroom one evening in February 1820, he coughed blood into his handkerchief and told Brown: 'I know the colour of that blood; it is arterial blood. I cannot be deceived in that colour. That drop of blood is my death warrant. I must die'. He left Wentworth Place in September and died in Rome early the following year. The house today, restored in a rather harsh and clinical manner, displays a large collection of Keats relics. In the pleasant garden, where he heard the nightingale that suggested the famous 'Ode', we find a successor to the plum tree he knew. The public library next door has a collection of early Keats editions.

Keats was a frequent visitor to Leigh Hunt (q.v.) at his cottage in the Vale of Health, reached from East Heath Road. He first met

Keats in the sitting room of Wentworth Place, now Keats House, by Joseph Severn (1821)

Shelley (q.v.) here, though their host later recalled: 'Keats did not take to Shelley as kindly as Shelley did to him ... Keats, being a little too sensitive on the score of his origin, felt inclined to see in every man of birth a sort of natural enemy'. His meeting (1819) on Hampstead Heath with Coleridge, then living in Highgate, is described under the entry for the Lake Poets (Rte 3). Hampstead Parish Church on Church Row has a bust of the poet donated by his American admirers in 1894.

Westminster Abbey always regarded the Romantic poets with suspicion and its joint memorial to Keats and Shelley in Poets' Corner (fee) was not unveiled until 1954.

Although most of Keats' life was passed in London, his several tours outside the capital are worth noting. They occasionally cast light on his poetry, and they show the writer who praised Shakespeare and Homer in memorable sonnets as an ardent seeker of literary shrines.

His trip with Brown to the Lake District and Scotland in the summer of 1818—the trip from which he returned with the sore throat presaging his fatal illness—was a combination of demanding walking tour and literary pilgrimage. From Ambleside near the head of Windermere he walked to Dove Cottage, Rydal Mount and other scenes connected with Wordsworth; they are described in detail under the entry for the Lake Poets (Rte 12C). He was disgusted by the crowds of tourists and by local reminders of Wordsworth's Tory allegiances, but profoundly moved by Windermere itself:

> the two views we have had of it are of the most noble tenderness—they can never fade away—they make one forget the divisions of life; age, youth, poverty and riches; and refine one's sensual vision into a sort of north star which can never cease to be open lidded and stedfast over the wonders of the great Power.

The 'dismal cirque /Of Druid stones, upon a forlorn moor' which makes a brief appearance in *Hyperion* (Bk 2, lines 34–35) may have been suggested by the Castlerigg Stone Circle, 1½ miles east of Keswick.

In Scotland Keats went to Alloway, the Brig o' Doon and other sights described in connection with Robert Burns; his visit to the poet's grave in Dumfries prompted a rather undistinguished tribute in verse.

In November 1819 he stayed at the Burford Bridge Hotel in Surrey, near the foot of Box Hill some 1½ miles north of Dorking on A24. From here he wrote the famous letter to his Oxford friend, Benjamin Bailey, which declared:

> I am certain of nothing but of the holiness of the Heart's affections and the truth of Imagination—What the Imagination seizes as Beauty must be truth—whether it existed before or not—for I have the same Idea of all our Passions as of Love they are all in their sublime, creative of essential Beauty ...—The Imagination may be compared to Adam's dream—he awoke and found it truth.

During the winter of 1818–19 he went with Brown to Chichester in West Sussex. They stayed with Dilke's parents at No. 11 Eastgate Square (now marked with a plaque) by the junction of East Road and The Hornet. Keats began 'The Eve of St Agnes' during the visit and scholars have suggested that the poem's medieval setting owes something to his impressions of Chichester Cathedral and its precincts. He was particularly struck by Vicars Close, a narrow street of 15C house with 18C frontages, off Canon Lane south of the Cloisters.

In January 1819 he and Brown travelled west from Chichester to attend the reconsecration of the *chapel at Stansted Park, the estate of Lewis Way, an ardent campaigner for the conversion of the Jews. It lies in wooded countryside about 3 miles north of Emsworth on A27, and east of the little village of Rowlands Castle. Keats was not impressed by the ceremony, which made him 'begin to hate Parsons'. Yet the chapel's delightful Regency Gothic, and particularly the armorial glass of its nave, must surely have helped the rich descriptions in 'The Eve of St Agnes':

> A casement high and triple-arch'd there was,
> All garlanded with carven imag'ries
> Of fruits, and flowers, and bunches of knot-grass,
> And diamonded with panes of quaint device,
> Innumerable of stains and splendid dyes,
> As are the tiger-moth's deep-damask'd wings;
> And in the midst, 'mong thousand heraldries,
> And twilight saints, and dim emblazonings,
> A shielded scutcheon blush'd with blood of queens and kings.
> (stanza 24)

From Portsmouth, further W, we can cross to the Isle of Wight. In 1817 Keats visited Carisbrooke Castle in the centre of the island:

> I have not seen many specimens of Ruins—I dont think however I shall ever see one to surpass Carisbrooke Castle. The trench is o'ergrown with the smoothest turf, and the walls with ivy—The Keep within side is one Bower of ivy—a Colony of Jackdaws have been there many years—I dare say I have seen many a descendant of some old cawer who peeped through the Bars at Charles the first, when he was there in Confinement.

During the summer of 1819 he stayed at Shanklin on the south-eastern coast, writing 'Lamia', beginning the disastrous *Otho the Great* in the hope of making money and sketching the church in his spare time. His lodging was in Eglantine Cottage at the south end of the High Street:

> Our window looks over house tops and Cliffs onto the Sea, so that when the Ships sail past the Cottage chimneys you may take them for Weathercocks. We have Hill and Dale forest and Mead and plenty of Lobsters.

From the Isle of Wight he moved north to Winchester, where he spent the autumn months of 1819 just before his final departure from England and where he wrote his 'Ode to Autumn'. His lodging near the Cathedral does not survive, but the modern visitor can still find some of the atmosphere which led Keats to tell his younger sister that Winchester was 'the pleasantest Town I ever was in':

> There is a fine Cathedral which to me is always a sourse of amusement; part of it built 1400 years ago; and the more modern by a magnificent Man, you may have read of in our History, called William of Wickham [William of Wykeham]. The whole town is beautifully wooded—From the Hill at the eastern extremity you see a prospect of Streets, and old Buildings mixed up with Trees ... And what improves it all is, the fashionable inhabitants are all gone to Southampton.

Old Operating Theatre, Southwark Cathedral Chapter House, St Thomas' Street, Southwark, London SE1: phone (01) 407 7600, ext 2739.

Keats House, Keats Grove, Hampstead, London NW3: phone (01) 435 2062.

Castlerigg Stone Circle, near Keswick, Cumbria: English Heritage, open at any reasonable time.

Stansted Park, Rowlands Castle, West Sussex: phone Havant (0705) 412265.

Carisbrooke Castle, Newport, Isle of Wight: English Heritage, standard opening; phone (0983) 522107.

Charles and Henry Kingsley

Charles Kingsley: b. Holne, Devon, 1819; d. Eversley, Hampshire, 1875. *Alton Locke, Tailor and Poet: An Autobiography* (1850); *Yeast: A Problem* (1851); *Hypatia: or New Foes With an Old Face* (1853); *Westward Ho! or The Voyages and Adventures of Sir Amyas Leigh, Knight* (1855); *Two Years Ago* (1857); *The Water-Babies: A Fairy Tale for a Land-Baby* (1863); *The Roman and the Teuton* (1864); *Hereward the Wake: 'Last of the English'* (1866).
Henry Kingsley: b. Barnack, Cambridgeshire, 1830; d. Cuckfield, West Sussex, 1876. *The Recollections of Geoffrey Hamlyn* (1859); *Ravenshoe* (1861); *Austin Elliott* (1863); *The Hillyars and the Burtons: A Story of Two Families* (1865).

The most important place in Charles Kingsley's life was always Devon. He was born on the edge of Dartmoor at Holne, an attractive village where his father was curate, 2½ miles west of Ashburton. The rectory, then badly dilapidated, stands a few hundred yards west of the church. The family moved away from Holne when Charles was only six weeks old but renewed their connection with the county in 1831 when Rev. Kingsley was appointed curate of *Clovelly, on the north coast 10 miles west of Bideford. He became rector the following year and remained until 1836. In later years Kingsley returned to the home of his boyhood, finding both a relief from the pressures of his busy, combative adult life and a stimulus to his novelist's imagination. The adjoining coastline became the setting for *Westward Ho!*, his hugely patriotic and hugely popular novel about England at the time of the Armada; Clovelly itself reappeared as 'Aberalva' in *Two Years Ago*, which takes place during the Crimean War. Indeed, Kingsley may be said to have drawn his contemporaries' attention to the little village, ensuring it a popularity that continues today. If at all possible, Clovelly should be avoided during the summer months, especially the weekends, when its charm often disappears beneath the burden of visitors.

To the side of B3237, which leads to Clovelly's car park, lie the church, the rectory where the Kingsleys lived and the surviving wing of Clovelly Court. In the Kingsleys' time the owner of the Court was Sir James Hamlyn-Williams, patron of the living, responsible for Hobby Drive, which stretches along the cliff to the east offering fine walks and views. In *Westward Ho!* Will Cary lives at Clovelly Court (Ch. 5), while in *Two Years Ago* it becomes 'Pentalva Court', home of the morbid poet Elsley Vavasour, whom Tennyson (q.v.) mistakenly supposed to be a likeness of himself. In the church we find a memorial to Kingsley, a fine Jacobean pulpit carved with Will Cary's initials and later monuments to the Cary family. From the car park we walk down the cliff to the steep main street—too steep to admit traffic—flanked with neat fishermen's cottages. Kingsley lodged here on a visit in 1849. There is a magnificent view of Barnstaple or Bideford Bay.

The best way to explore the coastline, rich in scenery and points of interest from *Westward Ho!*, is by walking the coastal footpaths as Kingsley did. The following list is merely a summary and, for convenience's sake, locates places in relation to the nearest road accessible by car. Six miles west via A39, B3248 and an unclassified road we find the fine 14C church of Hartland parish at Stoke, where Kingsley preached. On the coast to the south lies Marsland Mouth, one of a series of dramatic coves Kingsley described in *Westward Ho!*: 'To landward, all richness, softness, and peace; to seaward, a waste and howling wilderness of rock and roller, barren to the fisherman, and hopeless to the shipwrecked mariner' (Ch. 6). Rose Salterne's moonlight bathing here is interrupted by Eustace Leigh and the Jesuits. To reach the Mouth we follow A39 south from the B3248 turning to Eastcott (6 miles) and then follow unclassified roads 2½ miles through Gooseham; a footpath (½ mile) finally brings us to the coast. From Eastcott, too, we may take unclassified roads to the parish of Morwenstow (4 miles) where Kingsley visited the eccentric poet-parson R.S. Hawker (q.v.). It was Hawker who helped Kingsley discover the countryside south of Morwenstow, though he did not approve the novelist's use of history or topography in *Westward Ho!*: 'The whole Book is an assumption—and *me judice* a failure'. The fine medieval manor of Tonacombe, on the cliff near the road leading to Coombe, became 'Chapel'. Hawker and Kingsley also went beyond Coombe to Stowe Barton (NT; 3½ miles from Morwenstow), where they inspected the site of Sir Richard Grenville's mansion, resurrected in the novel as a 'huge rambling building, half castle, half dwelling-house' (Ch. 7). From Stowe Barton we may regain A39 by following unclassified roads east through the Coombe Valley to Kilkampton (4 miles). The church's 'lofty tower' and 'monuments and offerings of five centuries of Grenvilles' are briefly noted in Chapter 7 of Kingsley's novel.

Kilkampton ends the journey west and south of Clovelly. The sites to the east are more simply described, for they are concentrated in Bideford. Kingsley's introduction of the town at the beginning of his book can hardly be bettered:

> All who have travelled through the delicious scenery of North Devon must needs know the little white town of Bideford, which slopes upwards from its broad tide-river paved with yellow sands, and many-arched old bridge where salmon wait for autumn floods, toward the pleasant upland in the west. Above the town the hills close in, cushioned with deep oak woods, through which juts here and there a crag of fern-fringed slate; below they lower, and open more and more in softly rounded knolls, and fertile squares of red and green, till they sink into the wide expanse of hazy flats, rich salt-marshes and rolling sandhills, where Torridge joins her sister Taw, and both together flow quietly toward the broad surges of the bar, and the everlasting thunder of the long Atlantic swell. (Ch. 1)

Near the junction with Kingsley Road on the Quay is a statue of the writer commemorating his connection with Bideford. Just south of the bridge stands the church of St Mary, scene of the thanksgiving service held after Amyas Leigh's return from his journey round the world (Ch. 2). It was substantially rebuilt in 1864. In East-the-Water at the other end of the bridge is the Royal Hotel, whose unremarkable façade conceals a merchant's house of 1688. Tradition maintains that Kingsley lodged here at the start of his 1854–55 stay in Bideford when *Westward Ho!* was written. Westward Ho!, 3 miles NW, is an unattractive resort developed in the 1870s and named after the novel.

From Bideford and, in summer, Ilfracombe steamers make the crossing to the tiny island of Lundy (NT) in the Bristol Channel. In Chapter 32 of *Westward Ho!* the Spanish galleon *Santa Catharina* is wrecked on the Shutter Rock off its south-west coast: 'a huge black fang ..., waiting for its prey' (Ch. 32).

Though the most important, Devon is far from being the only scene of Kingsley's life and writing. Part of his childhood (1824–30) was spent in the village of Barnack, then in Northamptonshire but now in Cambridgeshire, 4 miles SE of Stamford. Henry Kingsley, younger brother and less famous novelist, was baptised at the fine font in the church. The building has a striking Saxon tower and Charles' last novel, *Hereward the Wake*, returned to the Saxon history and legends of the nearby Fens. He followed tradition and located the opening scenes at Bourne, Hereward's reputed birthplace, 11 miles NE of Stamford. A major setting later in the book is Crowland Abbey, 14 miles SE of Bourne: 'a vast range of high-peaked buildings founded on piles of oak and alder driven into the fen' (Bk 2, Ch. 1). The Saxon foundation dedicated to St Guthlac has of course disappeared and the present remains date from the Norman period onwards. The Danish sacking of the Cathedral at Peterborough, to the south, is described in Bk 2, Ch. 7, while the fall of Ely, further SE, occurs in Bk 2, Ch. 14.

The Rev. Kingsley's last clerical appointment brought his children to London and St Luke's Church in Chelsea. The early Gothic Revival building of which he was rector from 1836 until his death stands on Sydney Street, north of King's Road. The old Rectory is at No. 56 Old

Church Street, west of and parallel to Sydney Street. The neighbourhood was remembered not by Charles but by Henry in his unjustly neglected novel *The Hillyars and the Burtons*. It contains some fine early episodes in Chelsea, especially All Saints (or Chelsea Old Church) by the Embankment, which St Luke's replaced as parish church:

> Four hundred years of memory ... are crowded into that dark old church, and the great flood of change beats round the walls, and shakes the door in vain, but never enters. The dead stand thick together there, as if to make a brave resistance to the moving world outside, which jars upon their slumber. (Vol. 1, Ch. 13)

From London Charles Kingsley went in 1838 to Cambridge, where he studied at Magdalene College. His lodging was at the top of C staircase in the First Court. His vigorous and earnest piety does not seem to have been in sympathy with the college's atmosphere, for Magdalene was then known as 'a favourite home for young men who are of the opinion, either from conjecture or experience, that other colleges are too strict for them'. In 1860–69 Kingsley was back in Cambridge as Regius Professor of Modern History, a surprising appointment given that he had neither the equipment nor the temperament of a scholar. In fact, he owed it to royal patronage and acted as tutor to the Prince of Wales, the future Edward VII, then in residence at Madingley Hall (now a study centre), 3½ miles west of the city. Kingsley's own Cambridge base during the early years of his Professorship was at No. 3 St Peter's Terrace, an elegant mid 19C row that stands back from Trumpington Street immediately south of the Fitzwilliam Museum.

Social contacts made during his years as Professor took him to Yorkshire and Monk Fryston Hall (now a hotel; 2 miles east of A1 on A63 towards Selby), the home of Richard Monckton Milnes, Lord Houghton, described under the entry for Swinburne (q.v.). Given their differences in character and views, it is fortunate that the poet and the novelist never coincided as guests. Another and more important Yorkshire connection was formed in 1858 when he visited the limestone country near Settle (36 miles NW of Harrogate via A59 and A65). Kingsley stayed at Tarn House on the north shore of Malham Tarn (NT; 5 miles NW of Settle via an unclassified road and footpath). Taking his cue from the building's curious combination of neo-classical with Italian Gothic, he made it into 'Harthover House' in his fantasy for children, *The Water-Babies*: 'built at ninety different times, and in nineteen different styles, ... as if somebody had built a whole street of houses of every imaginable shape, and then stirred them together with a spoon' (Ch. 1). 2½ miles south and near the unclassified road leading to Malham is Malham Cove, a natural amphitheatre of rock 'just like ill-made pavements with deep cracks between the stones and ledges' (Ch. 2), where a stream emerges from the subterranean course it has followed since the Tarn. It is here that Tom, the chimney-sweeper hero of Kingsley's story, enters his underwater world.

Despite his busy career as writer and the public preferments which fame brought him Kingsley always regarded himself as first and foremost a country clergyman. He fulfilled this role conscientiously for his entire adult life in the parish of Eversley, 8 miles SE of Reading on A327. The rectory and 18C church lie about a mile south of the main village on an unclassified road. He first came here as curate in 1842, immediately after leaving Cambridge and taking holy orders.

In 1844 he became rector when his predecessor fled with the parish funds rather than answer 'a formal charge of a most revolting nature' about his conduct with a local married woman. The battle to reform a parish where the reputation of the clergy had sunk so low brought him into conflict with the patron of the living, Sir John Cope, who lived in the Jacobean mansion at Bramshill House (now a police training college), 2½ miles west of the church. Kingsley is remembered in Eversley church and buried in its churchyard.

In Westminster Abbey, of which he was appointed a Canon in 1873, the Chapel of St George near the west entrance has a bust by Thomas Woolner.

The adult life of Henry Kingsley took a very different course from his brother's. His career at Worcester College, Oxford, was cut short in 1835. Although he apparently left of his own will Chapter 7 of his best novel, *Ravenshoe*, shows him familiar with the attitude adopted by Oxford colleges towards overly high-spirited undergraduates. He returned from Australia in 1858 without a fortune but with the partly completed manuscript of *Geoffrey Hamlyn* and with a stock of experience that served him in later novels. His final years were spent in Cuckfield (16 miles N of Brighton in West Sussex via A23 and A272), where he is buried in the churchyard.

Rudyard Kipling

b. Bombay, India, 1865; d. London, 1936. *Departmental Ditties and Other Verses* (1886); *Plain Tales from the Hills* (1888); *Soldiers Three* (1888); *The Story of the Gadsbys* (1888); *In Black and White* (1888); *Under the Deodars* (1888); *The Phantom Rickshaw and Other Tales* (1888); *Wee Willie Winkie and Other Tales* (1888); *Departmental Ditties, Barrack-Room Ballads and Other Verses* (1890); *The Courting of Dinah Shadd and Other Stories* (1890); *The Light That Failed* (1890); *American Notes* (1891); *Life's Handicap: Being Stories of Mine Own People* (1891); *Many Inventions* (1893); *The Jungle Book* (1894); *The Second Jungle Book* (1895); *The Seven Seas* (1896); *'Captains Courageous': A Story of the Grand Banks* (1897); *The Day's Work* (1898); *Stalky & Co.* (1899); *Kim* (1901); *Just So Stories for Little Children* (1902); *Puck of Pook's Hill* (1906); *Rewards and Fairies* (1910); *Something of Myself* (unfinished; 1937).

Like most sons of Anglo-Indian parents, Kipling was sent back to England for his schooling. He attended the United Services College at Westward Ho!, the dreary north Devon coastal resort near Bideford named after the novel by Charles Kingsley (q.v.). Even if the story of Kipling's miserable childhood has sometimes been exaggerated, the college was still not a fortunate choice. Its most useful consequence was *Stalky & Co.*, a book that describes schoolboys with a realism that shocked contemporaries used to the work of Thomas Hughes (q.v.).

After leaving the United Services College Kipling did not return to England until 1889, when his Indian stories and verses were already beginning to attract the attention of the literary world. He quickly confirmed his reputation. His lodgings in London were at No. 43 Villiers Street, south of the Strand near Charing Cross, now marked by a plaque.

After his marriage to Caroline Balestier in 1892 Kipling spent several years in her native America. They returned in 1896 to live in South-Western England, moving the next year to Rottingdean, a charming little village on the Sussex Downs 4 miles east of Brighton.

At first they stayed at North End House, the summer home of his uncle, the painter Edward Burne-Jones. Here Kipling wrote 'Recessional', the poem that typified his role as poet of the Empire. Later in 1897 the Kiplings moved across the green to The Elms. Rottingdean Grange, an art gallery and museum, has a collection of letters, books and paintings relating to Kipling.

'What should they know of England who only England know?' Kipling asked. His Rottingdean years were spent getting to know England itself properly for the first time, and in particular they were spent exploring Sussex in an early steam-driven motor car. When they decided that Rottingdean was becoming 'too populated', the main purpose of the Kiplings' drives was to find a more suitable home. In 1902 they bought *Bateman's, a 17C ironmaster's house in the village of Burwash, on A265 27 miles NE of Brighton and near the Kent border. He wrote enthusiastically to a friend:

> Behold us lawful owners of a grey stone lichened house—A.D. 1634 over the door—beamed, panelled, with old oak staircase, and all untouched and unfaked. Heaven looked after it in the dissolute times of mid-Victorian restoration and caused the vicar to send his bailiff to live in it for 40 years, and he lived in peaceful filth and left everything as he found it.
>
> It is a good and peaceable place standing in terraced lawns nigh to a walled garden of old red brick, and two fat-headed oasthouses with red brick stomachs, and an aged silver-grey dovecot on top. There is what they call a river at the bottom of the lawn. It appears on all maps and that, except after very heavy rains, is the only place where it puts in any appearance ... Its name is the Dudwell, and it is quite ten feet wide.

Between the river and Burwash Common on A265 is the countryside of *Puck of Pook's Hill*, the book most completely expressive of his love for Sussex. Kipling lived at Bateman's until death and, when his widow died in 1939, the house was bequeathed to the National Trust.

Kipling unveiled the First World War memorial in Burwash, remarking that it 'occupied the very place it should do, right in the centre of the church approach—for surely it was a small thing that as they approached the House of God, they should pause awhile and remember the sacrifice'. The church and the inn opposite appear in 'Hal o' the Draft' in *Puck of Pook's Hill*.

Kipling died at the Middlesex Hospital in London and was given a grand funeral in Poets' Corner (fee) of Westminster Abbey.

Osborne House, Queen Victoria's residence at East Cowes on the Isle of Wight, has the splendid Durbar Room designed in the Indian style by Kipling's father, John Lockwood Kipling. Mrs Elsie Bambridge, Kipling's daughter, lived for many years at Wimpole Hall, the finest 18C mansion in Cambridgeshire. It stands 8 miles SW of Cambridge off A603.

Grange Art Gallery and Museum, The Green, Rottingdean, East Sussex: phone (0273) 301004.

Bateman's, Burwash, East Sussex: NT; phone (0435) 882302.

Osborne House, East Cowes, Isle of Wight: English Heritage; phone (0983) 200022.

Wimpole Hall, in Cambridgeshire, though its postal address is Arrington, Royston, Hertfordshire: NT; phone Cambridge (0223) 207257.

William Langland

b. place uncertain, 1330?; d. place unknown, 1386? *The Vision Concerning Piers the Plowman* (n.d.).

Although *Piers Plowman* is cast in the form of an autobiographical dream-vision and contains topographical references (most notably to Cornhill in London), the facts of the poet's life remain obscure. Examination of the poem's dialect agrees with its author's own reference to the Malvern Hills. The claim of Cleobury Mortimer, on A4117 11 miles east of Ludlow in Shropshire, to be his birthplace is advanced by an inscription in the church porch and, inside the church, by an east window of 1875 depicting scenes from the poem. Rival and more plausible claims have been made on behalf on Ledbury (16 miles SW of Worcester on A449), strengthened by the presence of a large field still called Longland or the Longlands nearby. Langland may have been educated at the Priory of Great Malvern, whose fine church survives.

Philip Larkin

b. Coventry, West Midlands, 1922; d. Kingston-upon-Hull, Humberside, 1985. *The North Ship* (1945); *Jill* (1946; revised 1964); *A Girl in Winter* (1947); *XX Poems* (1951); *The Less Deceived* (1955); *The Whitsun Weddings* (1964); *All What Jazz: A Record Diary 1961–68* (1970); *High Windows* (1974); *Required Writing: Miscellaneous Pieces 1955–1982* (1983); *Collected Poems* (1988).

Refusing the usual clichés about the signs of precocious talent poets display in childhood, Larkin's poem 'I Remember, I Remember' presents Coventry and his early life there as an undistinguished blank: 'Nothing, like something, happens anywhere'. 'Dockery and Son' looks back on his time at St John's College, Oxford, which he entered in 1940, with the same studious lack of sentimentality—though here, as in so much of Larkin's later verse, the melancholy which always underlies his wit has become more palpable. A more immediate product of his undergraduate years was his first novel, *Jill*, set in wartime Oxford, and his friendship with Kingsley Amis, a contemporary at St John's, who later testified that he used Larkin as model for the hero of *Lucky Jim*.

After Oxford Larkin made a career as a librarian, starting at Wellington, east of Shrewsbury in Shropshire and now on the edge of the new town of Telford. It gave him the drab provincial setting for his second (and only other completed) novel, *A Girl in Winter*. After working at University College, Leicester, and Queen's University, Belfast, Larkin began his long connection with the Brynmor Jones Library at the University of Hull in 1955. 'Here' (in his collection, *The Whitsun Weddings*) celebrates the sense of congeniality he felt with this unromantic and unfashionable city:

> Here domes and statues, spires and cranes cluster
> Beside grain-scattered streets, barge-crowded water,
> And residents from raw estates ...

The bleak, flat countryside of the Holderness peninsula answered his own temperament: 'Loneliness clarifies'.

'Church Going', probably the poem which did most to make Larkin famous, is deliberately unspecific in its location. 'An Arundel Tomb' finds a similar expression of secular humanist values in the monument of Richard Fitzalan, the 14th or 15th Earl (d. 1376 or 1397), who lies holding hands with his wife, in the north aisle of Chichester Cathedral:

> The stone fidelity
> They hardly meant has come to be
> Their final blazon, and to prove
> Our almost-instinct almost true:
> What will survive of us is love.

D.H. Lawrence

b. Eastwood, Nottinghamshire, 1885; d. Vence, France, 1930. *The White Peacock* (1911); *The Trespasser* (1912); *Love Poems, and Others* (1913); *Sons and Lovers* (1913); *The Widowing of Mrs Holroyd* (1914); *The Prussian Officer, and Other Stories* (1914); *The Rainbow* (1915); *Twilight in Italy* (1916); *Amores: Poems* (1916); *Look! We Have Come Through!* (1917); *New Poems* (1918); *Bay: A Book of Poems* (1919); *Touch and Go* (1920); *Women in Love* (1920); *The Lost Girl* (1920); *Movements in European History* (as 'Lawrence H. Davison'; 1921); *Psychoanalysis and the Unconscious* (1921); *Sea and Sardinia* (1921); *Aaron's Rod* (1922); *Fantasia of the Unconscious* (1922); *England, My England, and Other Stories* (1922); *The Ladybird, The Fox, The Captain's Doll* (1923); *Studies in Classic American Literature* (1923); *Kangaroo* (1923); *Birds, Beasts and Flowers: Poems* (1923); *The Boy in the Bush* (with M.L. Skinner; 1924); *St Mawr, Together with The Princess* (1925); *Reflections on the Death of a Porcupine, and Other Essays* (1925); *The Plumed Serpent* (1926); *David* (1926); *Mornings in Mexico* (1927); *The Woman Who Rode Away, and Other Stories* (1928); *Lady Chatterley's Lover* (privately printed, 1928; expurgated edition, 1932; unexpurgated edition, 1960); *Collected Poems* (1928); *Pansies: Poems* (1929); *A Propos of Lady Chatterley's Lover* (1930); *The Virgin and The Gypsy* (1930); *Love Among the Haystacks, and Other Pieces* (1930); *Apocalypse* (1931); *Etruscan Places* (1932); *Phoenix: The Posthumous Papers* (edited by Edward D. McDonald; 1936); *Phoenix II: Uncollected, Unpublished and Other Prose Works* (edited by Warren Roberts and Harry T. Moore; 1968); *Mr Noon* (1984).

One could not hope to better Lawrence's own description of his native corner of Central England and his hometown, *Eastwood, as he remembered them from boyhood: 'a mining village of some three thousand souls, about eight miles from Nottingham, and one mile from the small stream, the Erewash, which divides Nottinghamshire from Derbyshire. It is hilly country, looking west towards Crich and towards Matlock, sixteen miles away, and east and north-east towards Mansfield and the Sherwood Forest district. To me it seemed, and still seems, an extremely beautiful countryside, just between the red sandstone and the oak-trees of Nottingham, and the cold limestone, the ash-trees, the stone fences of Derbyshire. To me, as a child and a young man, it was still the old England of the forest and the agricultural past; there were no motor-cars, the mines were, in a sense, an accident in the landscape, and Robin Hood and his merry men were not very far away' ('Nottingham and the Mining Countryside', *Phoenix*). On his last visit, made in 1926, he found disconcerting physical changes and depressing social ones in Eastwood but he also renewed a sense of kinship, however anguished:

> I feel I hardly know any more the people I come from, the colliers of the Erewash valley district. They are changed, and I suppose I am changed. I find it so much easier to live in Italy. And they have got a new kind of shallow consciousness, all newspaper and cinema, which I am not in touch with. At

> the same time, they have, I think, an underneath ache and heaviness very much like my own. It must be so, because when I see them, I feel it so strongly.
>
> They are the only people who move me strongly, and with whom I feel myself connected in deeper destiny. It is they who are, in some peculiar way, 'home' to me. I shrink away from them, and I have an acute nostalgia for them. ('Return to Bestwood', *Phoenix II*)

Modern Eastwood shows the effect of further change—its population has quadrupled since Lawrence's day—but has at last recovered from its previous attitude of embarrassed neglect towards its native son. The visitor will now find Lawrence conspicuously remembered, and the town thoroughly deserves a walking tour.

The obvious place to start is at the Library on Eastwood's main street, Nottingham Road. The collection includes books by Lawrence and the headstone, decorated with a phoenix, from his grave at Vence; his body was later removed, cremated and reburied at the New Mexican ranch where he had lived with Frieda in the 1920s. From the Library we walk west along Nottingham Road and turn left for Queen's Square. Bromley House, on its western side, was the home of Lawrence's relatives after the death of his mother. From the same side of the square we can quickly reach Alexander Street, which leads back towards Nottingham Road. Before this, however, we take a left on Devonshire Drive. The second house on the right was the home of W.E. Hopkin, friend and mentor to Lawrence when he was in his teens. Lawrence attended Hopkin's Friday and Saturday night gatherings, and seems to have had the house in mind as the final home of Will and Anna Brangwen in *The Rainbow*. We may thus think of it as the setting for the opening chapter of *Women in Love*.

Returning to Nottingham Road we continue west and find, on our right, the entrance to Victoria Street. No. 8A is now the Lawrence Birthplace Museum, its interior carefully recreating a Victorian atmosphere. Arthur and Lydia Lawrence moved here in the 1880s shortly before the birth of their fourth child, the writer. The little house's shopfront is a reminder of Mrs Lawrence's brief and unsuccessful venture into the haberdashery business, one sign of her determination to cling to middle-class respectability in reaction against the working-class culture of her collier husband.

From the birthplace we return to Nottingham Road, which is followed a short way right to the Market Place. To the south on Church Street we find the parish church of St Mary's and, beyond, the Lawrence family grave with an inscription mentioning the writer. North of the Market Place on the right-hand side of Mansfield Road stand the former offices of Arthur Lawrence's employers, Barber, Walker & Co. Readers of *Sons and Lovers* will remember the scene in Chapter 4 when the young Paul Morel is sent to the 'new, red-brick building, almost like a mansion' to collect his father's wages.

Brinsley Colliery, where Mr Lawrence worked, lay further north off the Mansfield Road but we now turn right on Greenhills Road. To our right, and opposite the cricket ground, is the development known as The Breach, 'The Bottoms' of *Sons and Lovers*: 'blocks of miners' dwellings ... like the dots on a blank-six domino' (Ch. 1). The end-of-terrace house where the Lawrences lived from 1887 to 1891 is now No. 28 Garden Road. Though Lawrence's description in *Sons and Lovers* goes on to note that the house was 'substantial and very decent' Mrs Lawrence hated it, and it became the scene of the marital conflict fictionalised in the early episodes of *Sons and Lovers*.

It is now furnished as described in the novel, with a display of mining social history.

From the east end of Garden Road we walk right on Lynncroft and take another right on Walker Street. No. 8 (then No. 3) on the left after the junction with Percy Street was the Lawrence family home when they left Garden Road. Lawrence nicknamed it 'Bleak House' because of its high, exposed situation but in 'Return to Bestwood' described the view with relish:

> one looks across at the amphitheatre of hills which I still find beautiful, though there are new patches of reddish houses, and a darkening of smoke. Crich is still on the sky line to the west, and the woods of Annesley to the north, and Coney Grey Farm still lies in front. And there is still a certain glamour about the country-side.

Behind the house and reached from Three Tuns Road is the pub which Arthur Lawrence used as his local and which appears in *Sons and Lovers* as 'The Moon and Stars'.

We now retrace our steps along Walker Street back to Lynncroft, which is followed to the right. No. 97, on the right-hand side near the end, was the family home from 1902 onwards, and appears as Aaron Sisson's home in *Aaron's Rod*. Mrs Lawrence died of cancer here in 1910, living just long enough to hold an advance copy of her son's first novel, *The White Peacock*, in her hands. From Lynncroft, Dovecote Road leads left to the junction with Mill Road, where we find Beauvale School, the former Board School which Lawrence attended for five not very happy years. He left in 1898 to take up a scholarship at Nottingham High School.

The surrounding countryside is richly associated with Lawrence. Of the nearby places to visit, Underwood (2 miles) is reached by following Dovecote Road and then branching left on B600. To the right we pass the village of Greasley, from which New Road leads north to the ruins of Beauvale Priory, scene of the short story 'A Fragment of Stained Glass'. Also to the right of B600 we see Moorgreen Reservoir, the 'Nethermere' of *Sons and Lovers* and, most memorably, the 'Willey Water' where the drowning takes place in *Women in Love* (Ch. 14). B600 joins A608, which is followed briefly north to the turning for Felley Mill Lane on the right. South of the lane lies Haggs Farm, home of Lawrence's friend Jessie Chambers. It appears in *Sons and Lovers* as 'Willey Farm' and Lawrence's relations with Jessie Chambers are used as the basis for Paul's romance with Miriam.

The village of Cossall (off A6096 4 miles SE of Eastwood) is the 'Cossethay' of *The White Peacock* and *The Rainbow*. Church Cottage was the home of Alfred Burrows and his daughter Louisa, to whom Lawrence was briefly engaged. Burrows' interest in woodcarving, represented in the rebuilt Victorian church, left its mark on the portrait of Will Brangwen in *The Rainbow*. Marsh Farm, which stood near the canal bridge, has gone.

Over the Derbyshire border NW of Eastwood, two places are of particular note. Wingfield Manor, a ruined 15C manor house where Mary Queen of Scots was imprisoned, is visited by Paul and Miriam in *Sons and Lovers* (Ch. 7). It lies 6 miles SE of Matlock, near the village of South Wingfield and south of B5035. Middleton (on B5023 4½ miles SW of Matlock) was Lawrence's home in 1918–19, shortly before he quitted England for good. At Mountain Cottage, with magnificent views of the Via Gellia, he worked on the book that became *Studies in Classic American Literature*.

East of Lawrence's hometown three widely dispersed places demand a visit. Nottingham, of course, was well known to him as the urban centre nearest Eastwood. The High School he attended from 1898 to 1901, its Victorian buildings since greatly enlarged, can be found on Arboretum Street north of the Arboretum. On Shakespeare Street to the south are the former buildings of University College, now housing a polytechnic. Lawrence studied for his Teacher's Certificate here in 1906–08 and in Chapter 15 of *The Rainbow* he endowed Ursula Brangwen with some of his own reactions to the place. She moves from initial delight with the college ('Its rather pretty, plaything, Gothic form was almost a style in the dirty, industrial town') to disillusionment: 'the whole thing seemed sham, spurious; spurious Gothic arches, spurious peace, spurious Latinity, spurious dignity of France, spurious naïveté of Chaucer'. Southwell (on A612 12 miles NE of Nottingham) appears in Chapter 23 of *Women in Love*, when Ursula and Birkin view what Lawrence uncharitably calls its 'rigid, sombre, ugly cathedral' before having tea in the nearby Saracen's Head. *Lincoln Cathedral (A46, 23 miles NE of Southwell) is memorably evoked in *The Rainbow*. The description of Will and Anna's visit in Chapter 7 has an important place in the tradition of writing about Gothic architecture which stems from Ruskin (q.v.).

Elsewhere in England we can find reminders of the unsettled years between 1908, when Lawrence left the region of his birth, and 1919, when he and his wife Frieda finally left the country for a widening circle of travel that embraced the Continent, Australia, America and Mexico. His first teaching post (1908–12) was at Croydon in south London. The Davidson School, then newly opened, stands on Davidson Road as it leads north from Lower Addiscombe Road (A222), following the route of the railway line between East Croydon and Norwood Junction (British Rail). For portraits of Lawrence's fellow teachers we should turn to his second novel, *The Trespasser*. His Croydon lodgings were at No. 12 Colworth Road, south of Lower Addiscombe Road near Bingham Road station (British Rail). In 1915, the bitter period that saw the prosecution of *The Rainbow*, he returned to live in London. The Hampstead lodgings he shared with Frieda were at No. 1 Byron Villas, in The Vale of Health near North End Way, and are now marked by a plaque.

1915, too, saw Lawrence's first visit to Lady Ottoline and Philip Morrell at Garsington Manor (off B480 4 miles SE of Oxford). It was inevitable that he should at some point have come to this gathering place for the hopeful, promising or distinguished writers of his generation, and appropriate that he should have come during the First World War, when Garsington served as a centre for the disaffected. Yet it is surprising that Garsington, with its elegant and mildly aristocratic tone, should have played so important a part in Lawrence's development. With a fellow guest, Bertrand Russell, he formed an energetic if short-lived friendship and with Lady Ottoline herself an intimate and confidential friendship superbly captured in his letters during the years that followed. The conversations in *Women in Love* owe much to the intellectual atmosphere of Garsington and in the character of Hermione Roddice we may detect a sharp, though not entirely dismissive, portrait of its hostess.

That novel was finished in Cornwall, where Lawrence went from Hampstead in early 1916. He and Frieda first stayed with J.D. Beresford at St Merryn, 2 miles west of Padstow on the Camel estuary. At the end of February they moved SW to Zennor (on B3306

4 miles west of St Ives) where they rented Higher Tregerthen, a cottage by the coast NE of the village. Lawrence, whose mind was much occupied by schemes for removing himself from the decadence of Europe and the horrors of the First World War, at first believed that he had made a significant step in that direction. He told Katherine Mansfield, who visited him with John Middleton Murry, in a letter:

> I love being here in Cornwall—so peaceful, so far off from the world. But the world has disappeared for ever—there is no more world any more: only here, and a fine thin air which nobody and nothing pollutes.

But the world does not leave Utopian writers to their own devices, and the Lawrences' stay turned into a nightmarish version of Wordsworth and Coleridge's stay at Nether Stowey (s.v. Lake Poets, Rte 5). First Lawrence had to undergo 'the loathsome performance' of medical examination—and rejection—by the Army. Then local suspicion was aroused by the fact that Frieda was German and by a light accidentally shining in a window that overlooked a bay where German submarines prowled. In October 1917 the police came, searched the house and ordered Lawrence to leave Cornwall. He reported, rather mildly, to Lady Cynthia Asquith that the behaviour of the authorities was 'very sickening, and makes me very weary' but Frieda afterwards said that his Cornish experience changed something in him permanently. He was to remain in England for another two years, but faith in his native land had been extinguished.

Eastwood Library, Wellington Place, Nottingham Road, Eastwood, Nottinghamshire: phone (0773) 712209.

D.H. Lawrence Birthplace Museum, 8a Victoria Street, Eastwood, Nottinghamshire: phone (0773) 763312.

28 Garden Road, Eastwood, Nottinghamshire: visitors by appointment with Mrs Jessie Wright, 65 Garden Road, Eastwood, Nottingham NG16 3FY or Mr K. Roberts, 44 Rathmore Road, Oxton, Birkenhead, Mersyside; phone (0773) 719786 or (051) 653 8710 respectively.

Garsington Manor, Garsington, near Oxford: gardens open twice a year under NGS.

T.E. Lawrence

b. Tremadog, Gwynedd, 1888; d. Bovington, Dorset, 1935. *The Seven Pillars of Wisdom* (privately printed, 1926; publicly issued, 1935); *Revolt in the Desert* (1927); *Crusader Castles* (1936); *The Mint: Notes Made in the RAF Depot Between August and December 1922, and at Cadet College in 1925 by 352087 A/C Ross* (privately printed, 1936; publicly issued, 1955).

The soldier, scholar and writer was born at Tremadog, a 19C town developed by W.A. Madocks, near Porthmadog and the coast south of Snowdon. His birthplace, Woodlands, is marked by a plaque.

Lawrence's mother and father were not married (she was the governess for whom he had deserted wife and children) and their embarrassment about this irregular liaison made Lawrence's early childhood itinerant. By the time he was eight his parents had finally settled in Oxford and in 1907 he entered Jesus College with an Exhibition in History. During his undergraduate years he abandoned his interest in medieval culture, inspired by the example of William Morris (q.v.), in favour of Middle Eastern archaeology. An expedition to Syria in 1909 resulted in the thesis that gained him a First, later published as *Crusader Castles*. After the First World War he returned to Oxford a national celebrity, one of the few romantic legends to have emerged from an unromantic war. He took up a Fellowship at All Souls in 1919 and worked on the book which, after much rewriting, became *The Seven Pillars of Wisdom*.

Always made uneasy by his reputation as 'Lawrence of Arabia', he spent much of his subsequent life in an attempt to retire from publicity. In 1922 he joined the RAF as an aircraftsman under the name 'John Hume Ross' but was forced to leave the next year when the press discovered his identity. As 'T.E. Shaw' he joined the Tank Corps and was posted to Bovington Camp, north of A352 between Wareham and Dorchester in south Dorset. He was a frequent and welcome visitor to Thomas Hardy (q.v.) at Max Gate. The little cottage of *Clouds Hill, on an unclassified road north of the camp, became an important refuge from the Army life he hated. Lawrence repaired the building and spent his evenings here writing. It remained his closest approach to a real home in the unsettled years that followed, when he left the Army to rejoin the RAF. After being discharged in 1935 he returned here with plans to start a small printing press. Clouds Hill is still, as E.M. Forster (q.v.) said, 'the real framework, the place which his spirit will never cease to haunt'.

A few months after his discharge Lawrence died in a motorcycle accident on the road between Clouds Hill and Bovington Camp, and he was buried in the cemetery opposite the church at Moreton, west of the camp. His friend Winston Churchill attended the funeral and mourned a man whom he had hoped would 'quit his retirement and take a commanding part in facing the dangers which now threaten the country'. St Martin's church at Wareham has an effigy of Lawrence in Arab costume by Eric Kennington.

The same artist was responsible for the bust in the crypt (fee) of St Paul's Cathedral in London.

Clouds Hill, Wareham, Dorset: NT; for opening arrangements phone NT Wessex regional office at Stourton in Wiltshire, (0747) 840224.

Edward Lear

b. London, 1812; d. San Remo, Italy, 1888. *A Book of Nonsense* (1846; enlarged editions, 1861 and 1863); *Illustrated Excursions in Italy* (1846); *Journal of a Landscape Painter in Albania, Illyria, etc.* (1851); *Journal of a Landscape Painter in Southern Calabria and the Kingdom of Naples* (1852); *A Book of Nonsense and More Nonsense* (1862); *Journal of a Landscape Painter in Corsica* (1870); *Nonsense Songs, Stories, Botany and Alphabets* (1871); *More Nonsense, Pictures, Rhymes, Botany, etc.* (1872); *Laughable Lyrics: A Fresh Book of Nonsense Poems, Songs, Botany, Music, etc.* (1877).

Lear's most memorable contribution to literary topography, of course, was to people the English landscape with figures like the 'imprudent old person of Slough', the 'romantic old person of Putney' and the 'uncommon old man of Blackheath'. By comparison to this surreal abundance his real connections with English places are few and inexpressive.

In 1831 he took rooms on Albany Street in London, so that he could draw life studies of the parrots at the Zoological Gardens in Regent's Park. The Zoological Society of London had been founded a few years before by Sir Stamford Raffles and Sir Humphry Davy and its

Gardens, with the birds and animals housed in buildings by Decimus Burton, did not open to the general public until 1847.

Between 1832 and 1837 he stayed at Knowsley Hall, east of Liverpool, drawing the animals in the Earl of Derby's menagerie. The nonsense verses and sketches for which he became famous started as a means of entertaining the children in the household, whose company he seems to have preferred to the 'uniformly apathetic tone' of adult society at Knowsley. The Hall is not open to the public but its grounds, which contain a Safari Park, are.

After the work at Knowsley was finished he mainly lived abroad, leaving a record of his travels in books and landscape paintings. Return visits to England several times took him to the Isle of Wight. In the summer of 1846 he acted as drawing master to the young Queen Victoria at Osborne House, 1 mile SE of East Cowes. Her diary records that he taught 'remarkably well'. He was also a guest of Tennyson (q.v.) at Farringford near Freshwater on the western tip of the island.

During visits to London in 1857–59 he stayed just north of Marble Arch at No. 30 Seymour Street (reached via Great Cumberland Place; then No. 16 Upper Seymour Street and now marked with a plaque). His letters from this address are headed 'Hupper Seemore Street'.

London Zoo (Gardens of the Zoological Society of London), Regent's Park, London, NW1: phone (01) 722 3333.

Knowsley Safari Park, Prescot, Merseyside: phone Liverpool (051) 430 9009.

Osborne House, East Cowes, Isle of Wight: English Heritage; phone (0983) 200022.

Sheridan Le Fanu

b. Dublin, 1814; d. Dublin, 1873. *The Cock and the Anchor: Being a Chronicle of Old Dublin City* (1845); *Ghost Stories and Tales of Mystery* (1851); *The House by the Churchyard* (1863); *Wylder's Hand* (1864); *Uncle Silas: A Tale of Bartram-Haugh* (1864); *In A Glass Darkly* (1872).

Sheridan Le Fanu spent his whole life in Dublin. The supernatural tales and novels for which he is remembered belong to the years of seclusion after his wife's death in 1850, when he was living at No. 70 (then No. 18) Merrion Square, SE of Trinity College (where he had been a student). *The House by the Churchyard* is set in Chapelizod, west of Dublin. Le Fanu is buried in Mount Jerome Cemetery for Protestants in the suburb of Harold's Cross, about 2 miles south of the city centre.

Matthew Gregory ('Monk') Lewis

b. London, 1775; d. at sea, 1818. *Ambrosio: or The Monk* (1796); *The Castle Spectre* (1798).

For a man whose writing has much to do with the horrors of the charnel house, 'Monk' Lewis still managed to spend his life at a succession of unimpeachably respectable places. From the age of eight to fifteen he attended London's Westminster School, in Little Dean's Yard to the south of Westminster Abbey. During the years 1790–94 he studied at Christ Church, Oxford, though without great application and with frequent Continental interludes. In 1809 he bought—for 600 guineas—London chambers in the exclusive Albany, north of Piccadilly. Byron (q.v.), also a resident of the Albany, noted contemptuously that Lewis had 'looking-glass panels to his book-cases'.

Like many literary men of the time he was a guest, if not always a welcome one, at Holland House in Holland Park, where only the grounds and east wing of the original Tudor mansion now remain. After their first meeting in 1797 the fashionable Lady Holland reported: 'He is little in person, rather ugly and shortsighted; upon the whole not engaging, though better than I expected'. The two never agreed. Toward the end of one quarrel Lewis protested at her rudeness to him: 'She replied that when people forc'd themselves into a House against the will of its owners, they must take the consequence. He said he would remain no longer: she, the sooner he went the better'.

He found more romantic surroundings and less stormy hospitality at the Duke of Argyll's seat, Inveraray Castle, on the north shore of Loch Fyne in Strathclyde Region. When he met Sir Walter Scott (q.v.) here in 1798 he paid flattering attention to his poetry, then unknown. The castle is notable for its sumptuous interiors and collection of art.

Lewis was buried at sea after dying of fever on the way back from his Jamaican plantations.

Inveraray Castle, Inveraray, Strathclyde Region: phone (0499) 2203.

Richard Lovelace

b. London, 1618; d. London, 1658. Cavalier poet.

Of Lovelace's life there are only scanty topographical reminders. In the City of London the fine 16C–18C buildings formerly used by his old school, Charterhouse, survive on Charterhouse Square near the Central Meat Market. In Westminster Abbey Gatehouse, where he was imprisoned because of his Royalist sympathies in 1642, he wrote perhaps his best known poem, 'To Althea, from Prison', whose last stanza begins: 'Stone Walls doe not a Prison make,/ Nor Iron bars a Cage'. The poem remains while the stone walls, which stood near the main entrance to the Abbey, do not. This 'handsome man, but prowd', as John Aubrey described him, spent his impoverished last years on Shoe Lane (formerly Gunpowder Alley) leading north from Fleet Street, and on Rose Street off Long Acre and north of the Strand ('in a cellar', specifies Aubrey with a typically colourful flourish). He was buried in the church preceding Wren's St Bride's, on the south side of Fleet Street.

Lovelace inherited land in Kent, part of a patrimony spent on the Royalist cause, and lived for a time in Canterbury at Greyfriars. Originally part of England's first Franciscan Friary, it is pleasantly situated in a garden by the river, off Stour Street.

Charterhouse, Charterhouse Square, London EC1: guided tours in summer; phone (01) 253 9503.

Greyfriars, Stour Street, Canterbury, Kent: phone (0227) 61954.

John Lydgate

b. Lidgate, Suffolk, 1370?; d. place uncertain, 1450? Poet.

This prolific but largely neglected writer, self-proclaimed disciple and on occasion imitator of Chaucer (q.v.), derived his name from the small village of his birth, on B1085 7 miles SE of Newmarket in Suffolk. The Tudor half-timbered Suffolk House on the village street stands on the site of an earlier building in which he may have been born. The small 15C brass of a priest (head replaced) in the church of St Mary is said to represent him. His education and admission into holy orders associated him with the Abbey at Bury St Edmunds (to the NE), which enjoys a rival claim to Lidgate as his final resting place. In *The Worthies of England* (1662) the antiquary Thomas Fuller, though vague about the location of Lydgate's grave, quotes his Latin epitaph and renders it into English:

> Dead in this world, living above the sky,
> Intombed within this urn doth Lydgate lie,
> In former time famed for his poetry,
> All over England.

At Long Melford, 13 miles south of Bury St Edmunds via A134, the magnificent *Clopton Chantry of the church has its ceiling decorated with verses ascribed to Lydgate.

Bury St Edmunds Abbey, Suffolk: English Heritage, but located in a public park open most daylight hours.

John Lyly

b. place unknown in Kent, 1554?; d. London, 1606. *Euphues: The Anatomy of Wit* (1578); *Euphues and His England* (1580); *Alexander and Campaspe* (1584); *Endimion* (1591).

Lyly was educated at Magdalen College, Oxford. He also received an MA from Cambridge in 1579, though it is not known to which college he was attached, and later paid tribute to both universities in the courtly, balanced language that gave the word 'euphuism' to the history of English prose style:

> I meane not in the way of controuersie to preferre any for the better in Englande, but both for the best in the world, sauing this, that Colledges in *Oxenford* are much more stately for the building, and *Cambridge* much more sumptuous for the houses in the towne, but the learning neither lyeth in the free stones of the one, nor the fine streates of the other, for out of them both do dayly proceede men of great wisedome, to rule in the common welth, of learning to instruct the common people, of all singuler kinde of professions to do good to all. (*Euphues and His England*)

He was buried in the City of London at St Bartholomew the Less. The church, which has a 15C tower and a 19C octagonal addition of considerable charm, stands in the precincts of St Bartholomew's Hospital, north of Newgate Street.

Edward Bulwer-Lytton, first Baron Lytton

b. London, 1803; d. Torquay, Devon, 1873. *Falkland* (1827); *Pelham: or The Adventures of a Gentleman* (1828); *The Disowned* (1828); *Devereux* (1829); *Paul Clifford* (1830); *Eugene Aram* (1832); *England and the English* (1833); *Godolphin* (1833); *The Last Days of Pompeii* (1834); *The Pilgrims of the Rhine* (1834); *Rienzi: The Last of the Roman Tribunes* (1835); *Ernest Maltravers* (1837); *Money: A Comedy* (1840); *Zanoni* (1842); *The Last of the Barons* (1843); *Harold: The Last of the Saxons* (1848); *The Caxtons: A Family Picture* (1849); *'My Novel' by Pisistratus Caxton: or Varieties in English Life* (1853); *What Will He Do with It?* (1858); *The Coming Race* (1871); *Kenelm Chillingly: His Adventures and Opinions* (1873).

The list above provides only a partial record of the long and industrious career that earned Lytton a place among the most popular novelists of his age. His most important memorial is Knebworth House in Hertfordshire, west of A1(M) and reached from junction 7 near Stevenage. During Lytton's childhood his widowed mother altered the Tudor mansion by pulling down three of its wings and Gothicising the fourth. Lytton further elaborated its appearance after he inherited Knebworth in 1843. Externally, the result is not one of the century's happiest exercises in medievalism, though the *State Drawing Room inside is a spirited example of Victorian Gothic. Dickens (q.v., Rte 15) used the largely 17C Banqueting Hall for amateur theatricals in 1850 and Swinburne (q.v.) was a guest in 1866. Lytton's study preserves some personal memorabilia.

In London the novelist lived at No. 36 Hertford Street, near the southern end of Park Lane, from 1829 until 1835. These were the years of his marriage to the unstable and eccentric Rosina; their son, who published poetry under the pseudonym of 'Owen Meredith', was born here in 1831. After he separated from his wife Lytton kept an apartment in the secluded and exclusive Albany, north of Piccadilly and a fitting address for a writer who had to some extent modelled himself on Byron (q.v.). He apparently owed the honour of burial in Westminster Abbey more to his ancestry and political career than to his literary achievements, for he lies not in Poets' Corner but in the Chapel of Saints Edmund and Thomas the Martyr on the south side of the ambulatory (fee).

Knebworth House, Knebworth, Hertfordshire: phone Stevenage (0438) 812661.

Christopher Marlowe

b. Canterbury, Kent, 1564; d. London, 1593. *Tamburlaine the Great* (1590); *The Massacre at Paris* (1593/94); *The Tragedie of Dido, Queen of Carthage* (with Thomas Nashe [q.v.]; 1594); *Edward II* (1594); *Hero and Leander* (completed by George Chapman [q.v.]; 1598); *The Tragical History of Doctor Faustus* (1604); *The Jew of Malta* (1633).

A profitable walking tour of Canterbury, the city of Marlowe's birth and education, begins near the southern end of St George's Street at the church of St George the Martyr, where he was baptised in February 1564. The building suffered heavy bomb damage during the Second World War and only the shell of its tower remains. The same war-time raid destroyed the dramatist's reputed birthplace on the corner of St George's Street and St George's Lane nearby. We then follow St George's Street NW until, shortly after it becomes Parade Street, a right turn on Mercery Lane leads via Christ Church Gate to the Cathedral, where Marlowe regularly attended services during his schooldays. Of particular interest is the tomb in the Lady Chapel of Dean John Boys (1571–1625), Marlowe's fellow student at the King's School and Corpus Christi. An extreme example of Jacobean realism, it shows Boys looking towards the altar and seated by a table with an open book; the sides and back of the monument are carved to represent bookcases. The NW transept of the Cathedral gives access to the Cloister where, in the NE corner, the modern Chapter Library contains a collection including Renaissance editions of books Marlowe knew as well as the octagonal base of the Early English font from St George. By following the passage between the Chapter House and the Library and continuing through the Infirmary Cloister we reach the buildings of the King's School, where Marlowe was a pupil. The Norman exterior staircase in the NW corner of Green Court is worth special attention.

As an addition to this tour the visitor may take Rose Lane, which runs from the junction of Parade Street and St George's Street, becomes Marlowe Avenue and leads to the gardens of the Dane John. They contain a late 19C memorial to the dramatist in the form of a statue, the Muse of Poetry, by Onslow Ford.

At Hackington, immediately north of the city and reached via St Peter's Lane, The Causeway and St Stephen's Pathway, the church of St Stephen has a striking monument to Sir Roger Manwood (d. 1592), Marlowe's earliest patron and subject of an elegy. It combines a waist-high coloured bust of Sir Roger with a skeleton.

Marlowe entered Corpus Christi College, Cambridge, in 1581, receiving his BA in 1583 and MA in 1587. The 14C *Old Court, the oldest in Cambridge and then the only court of the College, has a plaque on its north side commemorating his residence there. A portrait of 1585 almost certainly depicting Marlowe hangs in the Hall; it bears a motto entirely appropriate to his life, 'Quod me nutruit me destruit' ('What nourishes me destroys me').

Central London retains nothing to remind the visitor of Marlowe's short but highly successful career as a dramatist, though some account of the areas connected with the Renaissance theatre may be found under the entry for Shakespeare (Rte 1). The only place to attract the visitor is in SE London at Deptford, where Marlowe met his early, violent death as the result of either a drunken quarrel or the political intrigues in which he was undoubtedly involved. He was buried at the old parish church of St Nicholas, off the High Street, in a spot which tradition places near the north wall of the 15C tower. The interior, badly damaged by war-time bombing, has a modern tablet replacing an older one in his memory. Its inscription concludes by quoting from the epilogue to his best-known play, *Dr Faustus*: 'Cut is the branch that might have grown full straight'.

John Marston

b. Coventry, West Midlands?, 1575; d. London, 1634. *The Metamorphosis of Pigmalion's Image and Certain Satyres* (1598); *The Scourge of Villanie* (1598); *Antonio's Revenge* (with John Webster; 1602); *The Malcontent* (1604); *Eastward Hoe!* (with George Chapman and Ben Jonson [qq.v.]; 1605); *The Dutch Courtesan* (1605).

Marston was educated at Brasenose College, Oxford, between 1591 or 1592 and 1594. He may have lived in Oxford again sometime between 1606 and 1609; he was certainly ordained deacon in the latter year at the pleasant village of Stanton Harcourt, 5 miles west of the city.

The intervening period, when Marston gained his often controversial reputation as satirist and dramatist, was spent in London. He was closely connected with that fertile breeding ground of Renaissance literary talent, the Middle Temple, which lies between Fleet Street and the Victoria Embankment. His father was Reader there and he himself was in residence by 1595, though he appears to have shown no very strong interest in the law. He was buried in the Temple Church, one of England's few remaining round churches, but his gravestone, marked by the inscription 'Oblivioni Sacrum', has since vanished.

Between 1616 and 1631 he was rector of Christchurch, Dorset, on the coast east of Bournemouth and notable for its lovely Priory Church.

Andrew Marvell

b. Winestead, Humberside, 1621; d. London, 1678. Metaphysical poet.

Marvell was born at the Old Rectory (since rebuilt) in Winestead, on the Holderness peninsula SE of Kingston upon Hull on A1033. His family moved to Hull in 1624 when his father became vicar of Holy Trinity, a handsome, partly brick church by the old Market Place. The poet himself was educated at the Old Grammar School south of Holy Trinity; the 16C building has been restored as a Heritage Centre. He was MP for Hull from 1659 until his death.

Between 1650 and 1652 Marvell was tutor to Mary, daughter of General Fairfax at Nun Appleton House in Appleton Roebuck, 7 miles south of York. To this period and place belong several of his best poems, 'The Mower', 'The Garden' and, of course, 'Upon Appleton House', a work whose importance to the tradition of country house poetry makes the subsequent rebuilding of Nun Appleton all the more regrettable. A better relic of the period is at Bilbrough, by the A64 3 miles NW: the magnificent tomb of General Fairfax (d. 1671) in the Victorian church of St James. Marvell's own familiarity with the area is shown by his 'Upon the Hill and Grove at Bill-borow'.

He was buried in London at an earlier church on the site of St Giles in the Fields, on St Giles High Street, near St Giles Circus. The present church, dating from the early 18C, has a memorial tablet in the north aisle.

John Masefield

b. Ledbury, Hereford and Worcester, 1878; d. Clifton Hampden, Oxfordshire, 1967. *Salt-Water Ballads* (1902); *Ballads* (1903); *The Tragedy of Nan and Other Plays* (1909); *The Tragedy of Pompey the Great* (1910); *Ballads and Poems* (1910); *Lost Endeavour* (1910); *The Everlasting Mercy* (1911); *The Widow in the Bye Street* (1912); *Good Friday: A Dramatic Poem* (1916); *Reynard the Fox: or The Ghost Heath Run* (1919); *Sard Harker* (1924); *The Trial of Jesus* (1926); *The Midnight Folk* (1927); *The Coming of Christ* (1928); *The Bird of Dawning* (1933); *The Box of Delights* (1933); *So Long to Learn* (1952); *Grace before Ploughing* (1966).

Masefield spent his childhood in Ledbury, on A449 8 miles SW of Great Malvern. His birthplace, The Knapp, is a big Victorian house in the north of the little town. Local tales and the beautiful surrounding countryside of the Malvern Hills appear frequently in his verse, especially *The Everlasting Mercy, The Widow in the Bye Street* and the Chaucerian *Reynard the Fox*.

He enrolled as a sea cadet at the age of thirteen, later deserting the merchant service for a roving life, before arriving in London in 1897 to start his career as journalist and writer. In 1912 he and his wife went to live in Hampstead at No. 13 Well Walk, the picturesque street reached from the top of Hampstead High Street via Flask Walk. In these years, when his poetry was first attracting notice, he was an intimate of Yeats (q.v.), visiting the Irish poet at his London home in Woburn Walk and at Lady Gregory's estate in Ireland. Masefield was one of many writers to carve his initials on the famous Autograph Tree in the grounds of Coole Park, described in the entry for Yeats.

In later life Masefield left London to be near countryside reminiscent of the scenes of his childhood. His writing celebrated England as 'A land of downs inestimably fair,/ With cornfields, apple-orchards, fruits and spires' ('On England', lines 10–11). From 1919 until 1933 he lived at Boar's Hill, beyond A34 SW of Oxford. His house, Hill Crest, has since been renamed Masefield House. From 1939 until his death he lived in Clifton Hampden, a village on A415 8 miles south of the city. His home, Burcote Brook, burned down shortly after his death and the Masefield Leonard Cheshire Home for the disabled now stands on its site.

Masefield, who had been Poet Laureate since 1930, was buried in Poets' Corner (fee) of Westminster Abbey.

Philip Massinger

b. Salisbury, Wiltshire, 1583; d. London, 1640. *A New Way to Pay Old Debts* (1633); *The City Madam* (1658).

The dramatist was baptised in Salisbury at the 15C church of St Thomas, north of the Cathedral and near the junction of High Street, Bridge Street and Silver Street. His father was confidential servant to the second Earl of Pembroke and so Massinger was probably brought up at the fine mansion of Wilton House, west of Salisbury. He studied at St Alban Hall, later incorporated into Merton College, Oxford, between 1602 and 1606, when he left without taking a degree. He was buried in London at Southwark Cathedral (then St Saviour's), immediately south of London Bridge and at the head of Borough

High Street, supposedly in the same grave as another dramatist, John Fletcher (q.v.).

Wilton House, Wilton, near Salisbury, Wiltshire: phone Salisbury (0722) 743115.

Charles Robert Maturin

b. Dublin, 1782; d. Dublin, 1824. *Bertram: or the Castle of St Aldobrand* (1816); *Women: or Pour et Contre* (1818); *Melmoth the Wanderer* (1820); *The Albigenses* (1824); *Five Sermons on the Errors of the Roman Catholic Church* (1824).

Except for a brief period in London when his Gothic tragedy *Bertram* succeeded at Drury Lane and its successors flopped, Maturin's life belonged almost wholly to Dublin. He studied at Trinity College (1795–1800) and later supplemented his income as curate of St Peter's by running a school at his home, No. 37 York Street, west of St Stephen's Green.

W. Somerset Maugham

b. Paris, 1874; d. Cap Ferrat, France, 1965. *Liza of Lambeth* (1897); *A Man of Honour* (1903); *Lady Frederick* (1912); *Jack Straw* (1912); *Of Human Bondage* (1915); *The Moon and Sixpence* (1919); *The Trembling of a Leaf* (1921); *The Circle* (1921); *Caesar's Wife* (1922); *East of Suez* (1922); *On a Chinese Screen* (1922); *Our Betters* (1923); *Home and Beauty* (1923); *The Painted Veil* (1925); *The Constant Wife* (1927); *The Letter* (1927); *The Sacred Flame* (1928); *Ashenden: or The British Agent* (1928); *Cakes and Ale* (1930); *Six Stories in the First Person Singular* (1931); *The Narrow Corner* (1932); *For Services Rendered* (1932); *The Summing Up* (1938); *The Razor's Edge* (1944); *A Writer's Notebook* (1949); *Looking Back* (1962).

Most of Maugham's long life was spent abroad, from his birth in Paris at the British Embassy (where his father was a solicitor) to his later years in the south of France. When his father died in 1884 he was sent back to England and to the King's School in the precincts of the cathedral at Canterbury. Early scenes at 'The King's School, Tercanbury' in *Of Human Bondage* suggest that his schooldays were unhappy, an impression confirmed by his description of the masters as 'frightening bullies' in *Summing Up* (Ch. 18). Yet in old age Maugham made substantial benefactions to the King's School and returned in 1961 for the opening of new buildings which include the Maugham Library. He donated the manuscripts of *Liza of Lambeth* and *Catalina*, his first and last novels, as well as copies of books from his collection. Maugham's ashes were buried in the garden outside the library.

Liza of Lambeth, the harshly realistic product of his observation of slum life while a medical student, was written in his London lodgings at No. 11 Vincent Square (off Vauxhall Bridge Road). A plaque now distinguishes No. 6 Chesterfield Street (off Curzon Street near Park Lane), the house he bought in 1909 when his plays first became hits on the London stage.

George Meredith

b. Portsmouth, Hampshire, 1828; d. Box Hill, Surrey, 1909. *Poems* (1851); *The Shaving of Shagpat: An Arabian Entertainment* (1856); *Farina: A Legend of Cologne* (1857); *The Ordeal of Richard Feverel: A History of Father and Son* (1859); *Evan Harrington; or He Would Be a Gentleman* (1860); *Modern Love and Poems of the English Roadside* (1862); *Emilia in England* (1864); *Rhoda Fleming: A Story* (1865); *Vittoria* (1867); *The Adventures of Harry Richmond* (1871); *Beauchamp's Career* (1876); *The Egoist: A Comedy in Narrative* (1879); *The Tragic Comedians: A Study in a Well-Known Story* (1880); *Poems and Lyrics of the Joy of Earth* (1883); *Diana of the Crossways* (1885); *One of Our Conquerors* (1891); *Lord Ormont and His Aminta: A Novel* (1894); *The Amazing Marriage* (1895); *On the Idea of Comedy and the Uses of the Comic Spirit* (1897).

Perhaps out of embarrassment at coming from a family of well-to-do tailors, Meredith was vague in later life about his birthplace, describing it as 'near Petersfield' and making one obituary writer suppose it to be Winchester. But it was Portsmouth, which appears—together with portraits of several relatives—as the 'prosperous town' (Ch. 1) of 'Lymport' in *Evan Harrington*. The novel is the best memorial to the writer's early years, for his birthplace on the High Street in Old Portsmouth has gone and all that survives is St Thomas, the church of his baptism, now incorporated into the Cathedral nearby.

Though never really a Londoner, Meredith had connections with London for most of his life. He was married in 1849 to Mary Ellen Peacock, daughter of the novelist, at St George's, Hanover Square, SW of Oxford Circus. He later lived in Chelsea. In 1858–59, when he was writing his first major novel, *The Ordeal of Richard Feverel*, he lodged at No. 8 Hobury Street, which runs north of King's Road between its junctions with Beaufort Street and Edith Grove. In 1862 he took as his London *pied à terre* a room in Tudor House on Cheyne Walk, the home of Dante Gabriel Rossetti (q.v.). The poet-painter's easygoing domestic habits were not to Meredith's taste and stories about the immediate cause of his departure abound. It is said that his fellow lodger Swinburne (q.v.) threw a poached egg at him for criticising Victor Hugo (q.v.), that Rossetti flung a cup of tea in his face during a quarrel over breakfast, and that Meredith took exception to the presence in the house of Fanny Cornforth, Rossetti's model and mistress.

Meredith's real homeland was in Surrey. After living in Weybridge he and his wife went in 1853 to join her father, Thomas Love Peacock (q.v.), at Lower Halliford, now part of Shepperton, on the opposite bank of the Thames. The older writer's house, Elmbank, stands at the head of Walton Lane. When the arrangement proved unsatisfactory Meredith and his wife moved to Vine Cottage nearby on Russell Road. These were the years of *The Shaving of Shagpat* but also of the marital problems later recorded in his sonnet cycle, *Modern Love*. The marriage and Meredith's stay at Vine Cottage ended in 1858, when Mary Ellen went to the Continent with the Pre-Raphaelite painter Henry Wallis. She died in 1861 and was buried in Shepperton churchyard. Shepperton Lock, reached via Ferry Lane from Chertsey Road, is made the meeting place of the hero and Lucy Desborough in *The Ordeal of Richard Feverel*.

Meredith remarried in 1864 in the church at Mickleham, off A24 between Dorking and Leatherhead. And in 1867 he moved to Flint Cottage, a little above Burford Bridge on Box Hill; the garden chalet where he wrote and sometimes slept was added in 1876. Flint Cottage remained his home for the rest of his long life and, when he achieved his position as a grand old man of English letters, it became a place of pilgrimage for distinguished contemporaries and aspiring younger writers. Visits from Robert Louis Stevenson (q.v.) were particularly important. Meredith's love of nature made him relish the splendid scenery of Box Hill (NT): 'I am every morning at the top of Box Hill—as its flower, its bird, its prophet. I drop down the moon on one side, I draw up the sun on t'other. I breathe fine air. I shout ha ha to the gates of the world. Then I descend and know myself a donkey for doing it'. He also took pleasure in the area's literary associations with Jane Austen, Fanny Burney and Keats (qq.v.) and added some of his own: Box Hill is the countryside of his masterpiece, *The Egoist*, and *Diana of the Crossways* makes use of Crossways Farm, to the left of A25 4 miles west of Dorking and near the village of Wotton. Meredith was buried in Dorking cemetery after Westminster Abbey refused him a place because of his attacks on conventional religion. The snub caused Hardy (q.v.) to wonder if the Abbey might not need a 'heathen annexe'.

In his later years Meredith had been a visitor to Eastern England. The sea by the esplanade at Felixstowe, 12 miles SE of Ipswich, is the scene for Matie and Browny's swim in *Lord Ormont and His Aminta*. He stayed several times in the quiet coastal town of Aldeburgh to the north: 'a place without charm, like Crabbe's poetry; only grandeur of Sea'.

John Milton

b. London, 1608; d. London, 1674. *On the Morning of Christ's Nativity* (1629); *L'Allegro* (1632); *Il Penseroso* (1632); *Comus* (1637); *Lycidas* (1638); *The Doctrine and Discipline of Divorce* (1643); *Of Education* (1644); *Areopagitica* (1644); *Paradise Lost* (1667); *Paradise Regained* (1671); *Samson Agonistes* (1671).

The many architectural records of Milton's near-lifetime residence in London have been obliterated. His birthplace in Bread Street off Cheapside (already a tourist attraction during his own life, according to John Aubrey) was swept away by the Great Fire, together with the old buildings of St Paul's School, which he attended from 1620 or 1621 until 1624, and the other City houses associated with later periods of his life. The process of destruction has continued with the disappearance of his various residences in the Westminster area during the Commonwealth and his tenure as Secretary for Foreign Tongues to Cromwell's Council of State (1649–59).

St Margaret's, Westminster (near the Abbey) has a memorial window of 1888 at the west end of its north aisle, with verses by the American poet John Greenleaf Whittier. The address given by Matthew Arnold (q.v.) at its unveiling was later published in the Second Series of his *Essays in Criticism*. The common tradition that Milton married his second wife, Katherine Woodcock, here in 1656 may well be mistaken; the ceremony was a civil one and probably took place at the Guildhall in the City. Katherine, however, was buried in the church in 1658 with her infant daughter. In Poets' Corner (fee) of Westminster Abbey itself there is a bust to Milton, though his views on politics and religion delayed its erection until some sixty years after his death. He was buried in the same grave as his father at St Giles without Cripplegate, a much damaged and much restored medieval church in the modern Barbican; a memorial can be found at the west end of the south aisle. In 1790 the antiquary Philip Neve described the opening of what was taken to be the poet's coffin, a proceeding that was more desecration than exhumation. A local publican took some of the corpse's teeth and a pawnbroker the hair, while the gravedigger charged sixpence for a sight of the plundered remains. William Cowper (q.v.) wrote a poem in protest, 'On the Late Indecent Liberties Taken with the Remains of Milton'.

Cambridge, where Milton studied at Christ's College, has happier memories to offer. Tradition points to N staircase in the College's First Court as the site of his undergraduate rooms. The identification was accepted by Wordsworth (s.v. Lake Poets, Rte 10) and *The Prelude* (Bk 3, lines 239–321) records a visit of homage in 1787, when he was an undergraduate at St John's, during which he succumbed to 'the weakness of that hour' and became uncharacteristically drunk with wine. A pleasant but unsupported story has it that Milton planted the mulberry tree at the far end of the lovely Fellows' Garden.

His first major poem, 'On the Morning of Christ's Nativity', was written during his Cambridge years but two lesser poems belonging to the same period, 'On the University Carrier' and 'Another on the Same', have more precise local associations. They are comic epitaphs to the local celebrity Thomas Hobson, who died in 1631 after having acted as London–Cambridge coachman and letter carrier for many years. Hobson is also remembered in the phrase 'Hobson's choice', from his habit of insisting that customers take the horse nearest the door of his livery stable or settle for no horse at all. He was buried at St Bene't's Church, the oldest in Cambridge, on Bene't Street near King's Parade.

Il Penseroso, written after Milton had left the university, remembers its atmosphere with a grave dedication that sorts ill with the traditional stories of his being badly treated as a student at Christ's:

> But let my due feet never fail
> To walk the studious Cloysters pale,
> And love the high embowed Roof,
> With antick Pillars massy proof,
> And storied Windows richly dight,
> Casting a dimm religious light.
> (lines 155–160)

In *Lycidas*, an elegy for his fellow undergraduate Edward King who drowned in 1637, the University appears personified as Camus, god of the river Cam: 'His mantle hairy, and his bonnet sedge,/ Inwraught with figures dim …' (lines 104–105).

Milton wrote these poems at the family home in Horton, a village west of London between Heathrow and Windsor, where he lived from 1632 until 1640. The church contains the tomb slab of his mother Sarah (d. 1637) in the chancel and a memorial window to Milton.

Comus was first performed on 29 September 1634 in the Great Hall, now partly ruined and roofless, of *Ludlow Castle, Shropshire. The occasion marked the appointment of the Earl of Bridgewater as Lord President of Wales, as the masque's opening speech makes clear:

And all this tract that fronts the falling sun
A noble peer of mickle trust and power
Had in his charge, with temper'd aw to guide
An old and haughty nation proud in Arms.
(lines 30–34)

Henry Lawes, music tutor to the family, provided the music and acted as producer, as well as playing the part of Thyrsis, who speaks the lines just quoted. The Lady, whose survival of danger enacts virtue's triumphant resistance to evil, was played by the Earl's fifteen-year-old daughter, Lady Alice Egerton; her two younger brothers were also in the cast.

At Tewkesbury Abbey (on A38 between Worcester and Gloucester) the old organ south of the choir stalls is known as the 'Milton Organ' because the poet is believed to have played it when it was in Hampton Court Palace during the Commonwealth.

In 1665 plague forced Milton and his family to flee London for Chalfont St Giles in Buckinghamshire (off A413 west of Rickmansworth). In the *'pretty box' at the end of the main street where the local Quaker Thomas Ellwood arranged accommodation for him, Milton finished *Paradise Lost* and began *Paradise Regained*—a poem that Ellwood naively attributed to his own suggestion. The small building, the only surviving house Milton lived in, is now a museum and library; its collection includes first and rare editions of his poetry. Ellwood (d. 1713) is buried at Jordans, about 2 miles south, in the graveyard of the Quaker meeting house built in 1688; nearby is Old Jordans, the 17C farmhouse (now a guesthouse of the Society of Friends) used before the meeting house was built.

City of London Guildhall, Guildhall Yard, off Gresham Street, London EC2: phone (01) 606 3030, and ask for the Keeper's Office.

Ludlow Castle, Ludlow, Shropshire: phone (0584) 3947.

Milton's Cottage, 21 Deanway, Chalfont St Giles, Buckinghamshire: phone (02407) 2313.

Hannah More

b. Bristol, Avon, 1745; d. Bristol, 1833. *The Search for Happiness* (1773); *Thoughts on the Importance of the Manners of the Great* (1788); *Village Politics* (1793); *Cheap Repository Tracts* (with Sarah More; 1795–98); *Coelebs in Search of a Wife* (1809).

It is convenient to begin by considering Hannah More's connections with London, since they belong to a distinct phase of her long career. On her visits from 1774 onwards she enjoyed great success in intellectual circles, winning the friendship of Sir Joshua Reynolds and Dr Johnson (q.v.), who regretted that she had not married her fellow Bristolian, Thomas Chatterton (q.v.), 'that posterity might have seen a propagation of poets'. David Garrick encouraged her playwriting career, today mercifully forgotten, and in 1776 she paid the first of several visits to Garrick's Villa (now flats), which Robert Adam had just finished modernising, on Hampton Court Road west of the Palace. Garrick's Temple to Shakespeare survives nearby; see Shakespeare, Rte 4. Hannah More was also a guest of Horace Walpole (q.v.) at Strawberry Hill in Twickenham.

Most of her life was spent in Bristol and its surrounding area. The city preserves few reminders of her presence there. The Trinity

Street school she ran with her four sisters does not survive, though the probable site of its successor at No. 43 Park Street, which runs NW of College Green, is marked by a plaque. South-east of the centre, the magnificent church of St Mary Redcliffe preserves her epitaph on Mrs Patience Little, greatly admired by Edmund Burke on one of his infrequent visits to his constituency.

After selling their school the sisters bought a house at No. 76 Great Pulteney Street in Bath, which they used as a winter residence from 1790 until 1802. Hannah, however, thought the fashionable centre a 'foolish frivolous place'.

That judgement is a reminder of the Evangelical turn of mind for which she is chiefly remembered and which led to her later career as educator, pamphleteer and author of improving tracts. These years were largely spent SW of Bristol near the Mendip Hills. She moved in 1784 to Cowslip Green, a small village about 10 miles SW of Bristol on A38, where the house praised by Walpole as 'first cousin at least to Strawberry Hill' is now Brook Lodge. When William Wilberforce visited in 1789 he was taken over the Mendips to the Cheddar Gorge and ts caves, but was struck more by the depressed condition of the local poor than by the scenery. Miss More and her sisters were inspired to begin a school, now the Hannah More Cottage, at Cheddar on the southern edge of the Hills. Their experiment in education grew to some twelve schools in the area before it became enmired in the so-called Blagdon Controversy (1800–03), which forced her to defend herself against the charge of Methodism.

In 1802 she moved to Barley Wood (now greatly altered), about half a mile NE of Wrington off A38. Her visitors included Coleridge (s.v. Lake Poets, Rte 5) and Thomas De Quincey, representatives of a younger generation unsympathetic to her Tory piety. Rather surprisingly, the poet Wordsworth 'made a conquest of Holy Hannah', as De Quincey irreverently put it. In 1828 problems with dishonest and unruly servants forced Miss More to retire to Bristol, but she was buried with her sisters in Wrington churchyard.

Garrick's Temple of Shakespeare, Hampton: open by appointment only; phone the Curator, Orleans House Gallery, Twickenham, (01) 892 0221.

William Morris

b. London, 1834; d. London, 1896. *The Defence of Guinevere and Other Poems* (1858); *The Life and Death of Jason* (1867); *The Earthly Paradise* (1868–70); *The Story of Sigurd the Volsung, and the Fall of the Niblungs* (1877); *Art and Socialism: A Lecture* (1884); *A Dream of John Ball and A King's Lesson* (1888); *News from Nowhere: or An Epoch of Rest* (1891); *The Wood Beyond the World* (1894); *The Well at the World's End* (1896); *How I Became a Socialist* (1896).

William Morris, who did so much to stimulate his countrymen's awareness of their environment in an age of mass production, rapid urban expansion and misguided restoration of Gothic buildings, deserves to be remembered by the modern traveller. The various places where he lived and worked, too scattered to be organised into a single tour, together form a powerful reminder of both his taste and the influence it has exercised on our own.

It is true that Walthamstow, where he was born and grew up, has changed in exactly the ways he deplored, its transformation from an Essex village into a suburb of NE London being now complete.

Morris himself lived to mourn it as 'once a pleasant place enough, but now terribly cocknified and choked up by the jerry builder'. Yet Walthamstow has one rewarding memorial. The Water House, his childhood home from 1848 to 1856, has been converted into The *William Morris Gallery. It lies in Lloyd Park on Forest Road (A503), which runs west from A104 just south of its junction with the North Circular Road (A406). The collection offers a useful introduction to Morris' life and work. Its contents include: designs by Morris, Edward Burne-Jones and Rossetti (q.v.) for Morris and Co.; specimens of the firm's work in various media (tiles, stained glass and wallpaper); Morris furniture; books printed at the Kelmscott Press; and a rotating exhibition of Pre-Raphaelite and later paintings from the gift of the artist Sir Frank Brangwyn.

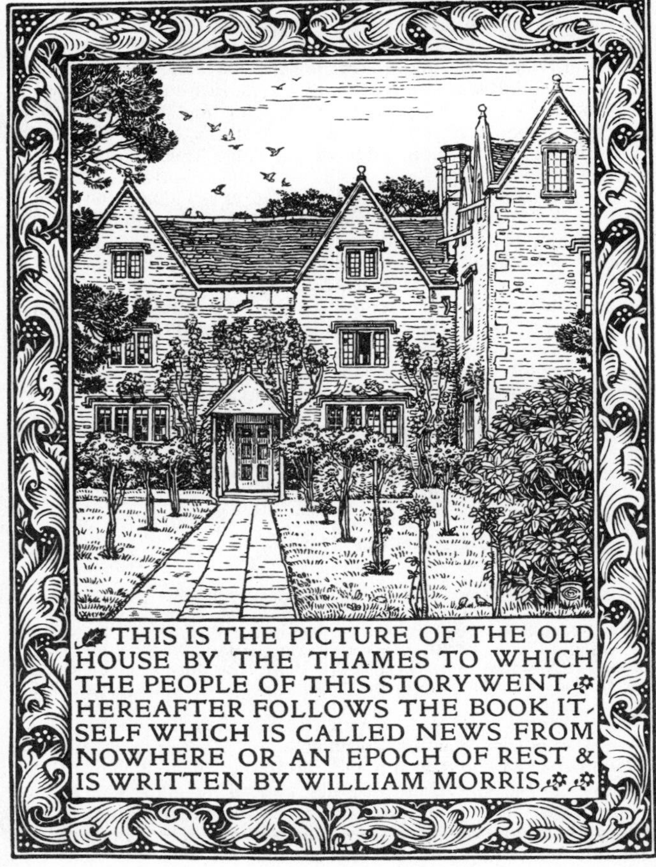

THIS IS THE PICTURE OF THE OLD
HOUSE BY THE THAMES TO WHICH
THE PEOPLE OF THIS STORY WENT
HEREAFTER FOLLOWS THE BOOK IT-
SELF WHICH IS CALLED NEWS FROM
NOWHERE OR AN EPOCH OF REST &
IS WRITTEN BY WILLIAM MORRIS

Kelmscott Manor: an illustration by William Morris to the Kelmscott Press edition of News from Nowhere

To discover the scenes that stimulated Morris' childhood imagination we need to travel north from Walthamstow into Epping Forest. By following A104 3 miles beyond its junction with the North Circular Road and then turning left on Rangers Road (A1069) for a further 2½ miles, we reach on our right Queen Elizabeth's Hunting Lodge (now the Epping Forest Museum). Morris's lecture on 'The Lesser Arts of Life' (1882) recalled 'the impression of romance' this fine half-timbered building made upon him. Waltham Abbey, another childhood haunt, lies further north. We follow A104 from the turning for Rangers Road to the Wake Arms roundabout at 8½ miles and take A121 west for 3 miles. The fine early Norman building has a Victorian extension with a window by Burne-Jones.

Marlborough College in Wiltshire, to which Morris was sent in 1848, proved a fortunate choice. The public school's lack of regimentation or emphasis on athletics allowed him the time to explore the surrounding countryside. He came to know Savernake Forest, SE of Marlborough between the A4 and A346, and the magnificent stone circles at Avebury, 7 miles west of Marlborough via A4 and A361.

When Morris entered Exeter College, Oxford, in 1853 he found the university in a crucial period of change. Its appearance was still powerfully reminiscent of the medieval city we glimpse in *The Dream of John Ball*: 'A vision of grey-roofed houses and a long winding street and the sound of many bells' (Ch. 2). Yet the present largely Victorian look of his own college was already being set by Sir Gilbert Scott's massive and gloomy Chapel (1854–60), very much the sort of exercise in Victorian Gothic from which Morris' subtler appreciation of Gothic would help to liberate English architecture. The Chapel now has a tapestry, 'The Adoration of the Magi', designed by Burne-Jones and made by Morris. Burne-Jones' undergraduate years at Exeter coincided with Morris' own, so beginning their lifelong friendship and artistic collaboration. In their first year they had rooms overlooking the small but very pleasant Fellows' Garden.

Morris revisited Oxford in 1857 with Rossetti and Burne-Jones to decorate the Oxford Union building on St Michael's Street with frescoes depicting Arthurian romance. Their work quickly faded from the unprepared walls, and the most permanent legacy of what Rossetti called 'The Jovial Campaign' was Morris' meeting with Jane Burden, whose heavy enigmatic beauty appears in so many Pre-Raphaelite paintings. They were married in 1859 at St Michael at the North Gate on Cornmarket Street, a little medieval church then just restored by G.E. Street (for whom Morris worked) and now restored again after a fire in 1953.

In November 1856 Morris and Burne-Jones took over Rossetti's old rooms in London at No. 17 Red Lion Square, south of Theobald's Road near its junction with Southampton Row. The house, on the south side of the square, is now marked with a plaque. Morris' career as an interior designer began informally when he furnished the lodging to his own taste with the aid of a local carpenter—'rather doing the magnificent', as Rossetti commented. It began formally with the creation of Morris and Co. in 1861, first housed at No. 7 nearby. Here Morris used to greet his customers in a round hat and workman's blouse that hardly suggested the gentleman, often treating their tastes and specifications with a contempt that hardly suggested the tradesman.

To gain some idea of the interiors Morris created we need to visit the Victoria and Albert Museum at the junction of Exhibition Road and Cromwell Road in South Kensington. Its *Green Dining Room or Morris Room, off Room 13 on the ground floor, was commissioned from the firm in 1866—a surprisingly early date which says much for the Museum's foresight. The panels depicting the seasons (by Burne-Jones) are especially fine. On the upper first floor Room 119 has wallpaper, carpet and tiles by Morris, as well as a wardrobe designed by Philip Webb and decorated by Burne-Jones for Morris' wedding present.

In 1860 Morris collaborated with Philip Webb in building a new home, The *Red House, at what is now Bexleyheath in SE London. The result—L-shaped, with a distinctive high-pitched roof of red tiles and deeply recessed Gothic porches—embodies a revealing paradox. Its contours look lovingly back to the simplicity of domestic Gothic, while its red brick proclaims brashness and experimentation. The Red House is reached from A2 (Rochester Way) by taking A221 (Danson Road) north and then turning right on Bean Road, which quickly leads to Red House Lane.

Morris left The Red House in 1865. Another epoch in his life, more mellow in its nostalgia for the past, was announced by a letter of 1871 to his business partner, Faulkner: 'I have been looking about for a house for the wife and kids, and whither do you guess my eye is turned now? Kelmscott, a little village about two miles above Radcot Bridge—a heaven on earth; an old stone Elizabethan house ..., and such a garden! close down by the river, a boathouse and all things handy'. *Kelmscott Manor lies by the Thames north of Swindon and is best reached from Lechlade. Morris' daughter left it to Oxford University in 1939 and it is now owned by the Society of Antiquaries.

Although his choice of the house, which fully deserves his first enthusiastic praise, announced Morris' belief in the quieter values of a pre-industrial age, his early years at Kelmscott were not entirely peaceful. Rossetti came for a series of extended visits meant to restore the health and peace of mind which his habit of combining chloral and whisky had damaged, but his presence soon created problems. He himself was no countryman and no lover of draughty houses, however picturesque, while Morris disliked the dogs which he insisted on bringing. Rossetti's love for Jane Morris stirred deeper tensions, though the question of its fulfilment—or of Morris' attitude to that eventuality—remains a puzzle to scholars. After the final break with Rossetti in 1875 Morris continued to use the Manor as his country home until his death, making it the subject of his essay, 'Gossip About an Old House on the Upper Thames', and the destination of the narrator's journey in *News from Nowhere* (Ch. 31).

He died in London but was buried at Kelmscott. The ceremony was appropriately simple and free from the commercial paraphernalia that often marred Victorian funerals, his body being brought to the church on a hay cart escorted by four countrymen. It was, remarked W.R. Lethaby, 'the only funeral I have ever seen that did not make me ashamed to have to be buried'. The gravestone in the local Cotswold style was designed by Philip Webb.

Nearby at Great Coxwell (8 miles SE of Lechlade) stands the magnificent 13C Tithe Barn which perfectly exemplifies the architectural values Morris admired and advocated. It is, as he said, 'unapproachable in its dignity, as beautiful as a cathedral, yet with no ostentation of the builder's art'. Further west in the Cotswolds (a region which Morris loved), he was several times a guest of Cormell Price, a friend from Oxford days, at Broadway Tower, on the hill outside the large village of Broadway (on A44 between Stow-on-the-Wold and Evesham). The Tower, a folly built by the Earl of Coventry in 1800, now contains exhibitions devoted to Morris and the Cotswold wool trade; the top floor and roof give a wide view. In September 1876 Morris came by way of Burford, on A361 9 miles north of Lechlade: G.E. Street's restoration of the lovely parish church prompted him to write a letter from Broadway Tower proposing the formation of the Society for the Protection of Ancient Buildings. His plan was given final impetus by the news, in the following spring, that Sir Gilbert Scott was to restore the lovely abbey church at Tewkesbury.

It is understandable that Morris should have felt the need for a London base in his later years, the period of his Socialist campaigning and of the Kelmscott Press (founded in 1890). It is understandable, too, that he should have chosen Hammersmith by the Thames in SW London and remote from the fashionable West End. Yet No. 26 Upper Mall, bought from the novelist George MacDonald in 1878 and renamed Kelmscott House, is a surprising addition to the list of homes that had begun with The Red House and continued with Kelmscott Manor. The plain late eighteenth-century building hardly agrees with his taste and this, perhaps, is why the narrator of his futuristic and Utopian fantasy *News from Nowhere* finds it has been replaced by a house of more Gothic appearance:

> It was a longish building with its gable end turned away from the road, and long traceried windows coming rather low down set in the wall that faced us. It was very handsomely built of red brick with a lead roof; and high up above the windows there ran a frieze of figure subjects in baked clay, very well executed, and designed with a force and directness which I had never noticed in modern work before. (Ch. 3)

Yeats (q.v.)—like several members of the rising literary generation, a frequent visitor in the late 1880s and 1890s—concluded that Morris 'was an ageing man content at last to gather beautiful things rather than to arrange a beautiful house'. Kelmscott House is now owned by the William Morris Society. The Kelmscott Press was located first at No. 16 and then at No. 14 on the same street.

William Morris Gallery, Water House, Lloyd Park, Forest Road, Walthamstow, London E17: phone (01) 527 5544, extension 4390.

Epping Forest Museum (Queen Elizabeth's Hunting Lodge), Rangers Road, Chingford, London E4: phone (01) 529 6681.

Avebury Stone Circles, Avebury, Wiltshire: English Heritage, open at any reasonable time.

Victoria and Albert Museum, Cromwell Road, South Kensington, London SW7: phone (01) 938 8500; recorded information (01) 938 8441.

The Red House, Red House Lane, Bexleyheath, London: visitors by written appointment (enclosing stamped self-addressed envelope).

Kelmscott Manor, Kelmscott, near Lechlade, Gloucestershire: visitors by written appointment with the Honorary Curator.

The Great Barn, Great Coxwell, Faringdon, Oxfordshire: NT; open at any reasonable time.

Broadway Tower, Broadway, Hereford and Worcester: phone (0386) 852390.

Thomas Nashe (or Nash)

b. Lowestoft, Suffolk, 1567; d. place unknown, 1601?. *Pierce Pennilesse His Supplication to the Divell* (1592); *Strange Newes, of the Intercepting Certaine Letters* (1593); *Christs Tears over Jerusalem* (1593); *The Terrors of the Night* (1594); *The Tragedie of Dido, Queen of Carthage* (with Christopher Marlowe [q.v.]; 1594); *The Unfortunate Traveller: or The Life of Jacke Wilton* (1594); *Have with You to Saffron-Walden: or Gabriell Harveys Hunt is up* (1596); *Nashes Lenten Stuffe* (1599); *Summers Last Will and Testament* (1600).

London today can boast nothing by which to remember the adult life and career of Thomas Nashe, pamphleteer, playwright, poet and, in *The Unfortunate Traveller*, proto-novelist.

Eastern England has fared a little better. He was born at Lowestoft on the Suffolk coast, being baptised in the parish church of St Margaret on the NW edge of the town. In 1573 his father became rector at West Harling, Norfolk, on the heath east of Thetford. The small and remote village church of All Saints is best reached by taking the A11 north from Thetford, turning right for East Harling and Middle Harling, and then following progressively minor roads. The seaside town of Great Yarmouth, 10 miles north of Lowestoft, has changed greatly since the winter of 1597–98 when Nashe stayed there to avoid the fracas caused by *The Isle of Dogs*, a play written in collaboration with Ben Jonson (q.v.) but now lost. A vigorous satirical description of the town, as well as a whimsical extravaganza in praise of its local herring, appears in *Lenten Stuffe*.

Between 1582 and 1586 he was an undergraduate at St John's College, Cambridge, apparently remaining in the city for some time after his graduation. His preface to *Menaphon* (1590) by Robert Greene speaks of his old college in terms of the highest respect as

> an university within itself, shining so far above all other houses, halls and hospitals whatsoever, that no college in the town was able to compare with the tithe of her students; having (as I have heard grave men of credit report) more candles lit in it every winter morning before four of the clock than the four-of-the-clock bell gave strokes.

A pamphlet entitled *The Trimming of Thomas Nashe Gentleman* (1597) and sometimes attributed to Gabriel Harvey, with whom Nashe engaged in a prolonged literary feud, offers a very different but probably untrustworthy account of his relations with Cambridge:

> (being distracted of his wits) he fell into diuers misdemeanors ... As namely in his fresh-time how he flourished in all impudencie toward Schollers, and abuse to the Townsmen; insomuch, that to this daye the Townes-men call euerie vntoward Scholler of whome there is great hope, *a verie Nashe*.

(A fellow of Pembroke College, Harvey came from Saffron Walden, 15 miles SE of Cambridge, where the museum has some fragments of his family home among its interesting display of local history.)

Nashe's connection with Sir George Carey or Carew, unique in a literary career otherwise lacking friends and patrons among the great, took him to the Isle of Wight for the winter of 1593–94. He stayed at Carisbrooke Castle, held by Sir George in his capacity as Captain General of the Isle.

Saffron Walden Museum, Museum Street, Saffron Walden, Essex: phone (0799) 22494).

Carisbrooke Castle, Newport, Isle of Wight: English Heritage, standard opening; phone (0983) 522107.

Sean O'Casey

b. Dublin, 1880; d. Torbay, Devon, 1964. *The Shadow of a Gunman* (1925); *Juno and the Paycock* (1925); *The Plough and the Stars* (1926); *The Silver Tassie* (1928); *Within the Gates* (1933); *I Knock at the Door* (1939); *The Star Turns Red* (1940); *Pictures in the Hallway* (1942); *Red Roses For Me* (1942); *Drums Under the Windows* (1945); *Oak Leaves and Lavender* (1946); *Inishfallen, Fare Thee Well* (1949); *Cock-a-Doodle Dandy* (1949); *Rose and Crown* (1952); *Sunset and Evening Star* (1954); *The Bishop's Bonfire* (1955); *The Green Crow* (1956); *The Drums of Father Ned* (1960); *Behind the Green Curtains* (1961).

A plaque now marks the site of No. 85 Upper Dorset Street (north of Grattan Bridge and Capel Street) in Dublin where O'Casey was born, thirteenth child of a poor Protestant family. An eye disease restricted his schooling and he went to work as a labourer. He was still doing manual work in the early 1920s when his plays were first performed at the Abbey Theatre. (The original theatre on Lower Abbey Street near the Custom House has been replaced by a modern building.) O'Casey's ironic view of Irish Nationalism in *The Plough and the Stars* caused a furore like that which had greeted the plays of Synge (q.v.) in the same theatre and, as on the earlier occasion, Yeats (q.v.) spoke out strongly in defence. Friendship with the older poet, then the most powerful figure in his country's letters, made O'Casey a visitor to Lady Gregory at Coole Park. His initials are among those carved on the Autograph Tree in the grounds, described in the entry for Yeats.

O'Casey first came to England in 1926. His decision to remain in exile was encouraged by his public quarrel with Yeats after the Abbey Theatre rejected *The Silver Tassie*. The increasingly experimental direction his writing took found little favour with audiences in the commercial theatre but O'Casey played a vigorous, combative role in English literary life to the end of his days. In 1938 he moved from London to the pleasant town of Totnes (on A385 and A381 in south Devon), living at Tingrith on Ashburton Road and sending his children to school at Dartington Hall, 2 miles north. In 1954 he moved to Torquay (on the coast 9 miles NE of Totnes), where he had a flat in Villa Rosa at No. 40 Trumlands Road, St Marychurch, near the Teignmouth road.

He died in a Torbay clinic. His ashes were scattered in the Garden of Remembrance at the Golders Green Crematorium, off Finchley Road in NW London.

'George Orwell' (pseudonym of Eric Blair)

b. Motihari, India, 1903; d. London, 1950. *Down and Out in Paris and London* (1933); *Burmese Days* (1934); *A Clergyman's Daughter* (1935); *Keep the Aspidistra Flying* (1936); *The Road to Wigan Pier* (1937); *Homage to Catalonia* (1938); *Coming Up for Air* (1939); *Inside the Whale, and Other Essays* (1940); *The Lion and the Unicorn: Socialism and the English Genius* (1941); *Animal Farm: A Fairy Story* (1945); *Critical Essays* (1946); *James Burnham and the Managerial Revolution* (1946); *The English People* (1947); *Politics and the English Language* (1947); *Nineteen Eighty-Four* (1949); *Shooting an Elephant, and Other Essays* (1950); *England, Your England, and Other Essays* (1953).

In infancy George Orwell was brought home from India, where his father was a Civil Servant, to Henley-on-Thames (on A423 and A4155 west of London) which he later made the 'Lower Binfield' of *Coming Up for Air*. He was educated at nearby Eton College (south of M4), though he recalled: 'I did no work there and learned very little, and I don't feel that Eton has been much of a formative influence in my life'. It was left to his friend and contemporary Cyril Connolly to describe the school's life during this period in *The Enemies of Promise*, while Orwell reserved his energies for 'Such, Such Were the Joys', an attack on the Eastbourne preparatory school (now vanished) he had earlier attended. For much of his youth and early manhood his parent's home, to which he periodically returned after his tramping expeditions, was the genteel Suffolk coastal resort of Southwold. Their house was No. 31 High Street.

In 1934, just after the publication of his first book, Orwell went to work and lodge at Booklovers' Corner in London's Hampstead. The building (now a café) stands at the corner of Pond Street and South End Road, south of Hampstead Heath and Parliament Hill. His impressions of the area, to which he returned towards the end of the Second World War, appear in *Keep the Aspidistra Flying*.

In 1936 Orwell made the journey to the depressed industrial north recorded in *The Road to Wigan Pier*. At Wigan, in the Lancashire cotton district NW of Manchester, the old joke about the pier has been given permanent form in the name of the museum complex by the canal, dealing with the town's industrial history.

Two rural interludes played an important part in Orwell's life. The first (1936–40) was at Wallington, 4 miles east of Baldock and A1 in Hertfordshire. He came to the village after his journey to Wigan, married his first wife Eileen in the parish church and set out from Wallington to join the Spanish Civil War. In 1946 he chose a far more isolated home on the northern end of Jura, south of Mull in the Inner Hebrides. *Nineteen Eighty-Four*, his last and most famous novel, was written here.

Though never a regular churchgoer, Orwell wished to lie in a churchyard—a final expression, perhaps, of that yearning for traditional Englishness which permeates his writing. The intervention of his friend David Astor made it possible for him to be buried at All Saints in Sutton Courtenay, a charming village 2 miles SW of Abingdon in Oxfordshire.

Eton College, Windsor, Berkshire: School Yard, College Chapel, Cloister Court and Museum of Eton Life open; also guided tours; phone (0753) 863593.

Wigan Pier, Wigan, Greater Manchester; phone (0942) 323666.

Thomas Otway

b. Trotton, West Sussex, 1652; d. London, 1685. *Don Carlos* (1676); *The Orphan* (1680); *Venice Preserv'd* (1682).

Otway's father was curate of Trotton, a small village off A272 3 miles west of Midhurst; an 18C tablet in the church commemorates the writer's birth. Shortly afterwards the family moved to Woolbedding, NW of Midhurst, where the father became rector. Otway was educated at Winchester College and Christ Church, Oxford. After a career in London as a dramatist, usually remembered for his tragedy *Venice Preserv'd*, he died in obscure circumstances—'in an alehouse unlamented', according to one contemporary. He was buried at St Clement Danes in the Strand, a Wren church completed only a few years before.

Winchester College, College Street, Winchester, Hampshire: phone the Bursar, (0962) 64242.

Walter Pater

b. London, 1839; d. Oxford, 1894. *Studies in the History of the Renaissance* (1873); *Marius the Epicurean: His Sensations and Ideas* (1885); *Imaginary Portraits* (1887); *Appreciations, With An Essay on Style* (1889); *Plato and Platonism* (1893); *Greek Studies* (1895); *Miscellaneous Studies* (1895).

Pater's entire adult life was spent in Oxford. He was an undergraduate at The Queen's College (1858–62) and became a Fellow of Brasenose College in 1864. Though he lived with his sisters first on Bradmore Road and later on St Giles, the true centre of his world was his rooms in the College's Old Quad on staircase No. 7. His friends in Oxford included Lewis Carroll (q.v.), but Pater remained modest and reclusive even when his work, with its stress on 'aesthetic' values, was exercising a strong influence over the writers of the 1880s and 1890s. The ante-chapel in Chapel Quad has a medallion showing him surrounded by Plato, Dante, Michelangelo and Leonardo da Vinci. He is buried in the cemetery of St Cross, reached from the High via Longwall and Saint Cross Road.

'Emerald Uthwart', an 'imaginary portrait' posthumously collected in *Miscellaneous Studies*, includes a lightly fictionalised reminiscence of his schooldays at the King's School, Canterbury. Among other things Pater remembers attending services in the Cathedral nearby:

> On Saturday half-holidays the scholars are taken to church in their surplices, across the court, under the lime-trees; emerge at last up the dark winding passages into the melodious, mellow-lighted space, always three days behind the temperature outside, so thick are the walls;—how warm and nice! how cool and nice! The choir, to which they glide in order to their places below the clergy, seems conspicuously cold and sad. But the empty chapels lying beyond it all about into the distance are a trap on sunny mornings for the clouds of yellow effulgence. The Angel Steeple [ie. the central tower, Bell Harry] is a lantern within, and sheds down a flood of the like just beyond the gates. You can peep up into it where you sit, if you dare to gaze about you. If at home there had been nothing great, here, to boyish sense, one seems diminished to nothing at all, amid the grand waves, wave upon wave, of patiently-wrought stone; the daring height, the daring severity, of the innumerable, long, upward, ruled lines, rigidly bent just at last, in due place, into the reserved grace of the perfect Gothic arch; the peculiar daylight which seemed to come from further than the light outside.

Coventry Patmore

b. London, 1823; d. Lymington, Hampshire, 1896. *The Angel in the House* (1854–63); *The Unknown Eros and Other Odes* (1877); *The Rod, the Root and the Flower* (1895).

Patmore's marriage to Emily Andrews—the subject of his best known poem, *The Angel in the House*—took place in 1847 at Hampstead

Parish Church. St John's, an 18C building that now conspicuously remembers its connection with Keats (q.v.), stands at the end of Church Row. Their married life was mainly spent in Hampstead and adjoining Highgate.

After Emily's death in 1862 Patmore lodged at No. 14 Percy Street (now marked with a plaque), which runs west from Tottenham Court Road. Visitors included Tennyson (q.v.) and various members of the Pre-Raphaelite group of painters with whom Patmore was associated. Percy Street was conveniently near the British Museum, reached from Tottenham Court Road via Great Russell Street, where he worked in the printed books department. His appointment by the Museum in the winter of 1846–47 had coincided with the completion of Robert Smirke's distinctive façade of columns. During his time there the domed Reading Room was added, built by Sydney Smirke to a plan by Patmore's superior, Sir Anthony Panizzi.

In 1864 Patmore took leave from his work to visit Rome, where he was converted to Catholicism and met his second wife, Marianne. They were married in London at the recently completed St Mary of the Angels on Moorhouse Road in Bayswater. It is reached from Westbourne Park Station (British Rail and Metropolitan Line) by taking Great Western Road south to Westbourne Park Road, which is followed to the left; we then make a right turn on to Chepstow Road and a second right on Artesian Road.

His second wife's fortune relieved Patmore from the need to return to his job at the British Museum. After several years spent enjoying the role of country gentleman he fulfilled a childhood ambition by moving to Hastings on the Sussex coast in 1875. His home was Old Hastings House (then The Mansion House), a fine Queen Anne building on the High Street of the old town. Among his visitors was Gerard Manley Hopkins (q.v.), with whom he corresponded freely, though the two poets rarely met. After Marianne's death in 1880 Patmore endowed the Roman Catholic church of St Mary Star of the Sea, also on the High Street. It was designed by his friend and future biographer, Basil Champneys.

In 1891 Patmore, already married a third time, was compelled to leave Hastings for Lymington. His last years passed in relative obscurity, though he formed a close friendship with Alice Meynell. Visits to her Bayswater home at No. 47 Palace Court (which runs north from Bayswater Road near its continuation as Notting Hill Gate) brought him into contact with her *protégé*, the poet Francis Thompson (q.v.).

British Library and British Museum, Great Russell Street, Bloomsbury, London WC1: for Library phone (01) 636 1544; for Museum phone (01) 636 1555. The British Library is scheduled to move to Euston Road in 1991/92; at the time of writing there are guided tours of the Reading Room, not otherwise open to casual visitors.

Thomas Love Peacock

b. Weymouth, Dorset, 1785; d. Lower Halliford, Surrey, 1866. *The Genius of the Thames* (1810); *The Philosophy of Melancholy* (1812); *Sir Hornbrook, or Childe Launcelot's Expedition: A Grammatico-Allegorical Ballad* (1813); *Sir Proteus: A Satirical Ballad* (1814); *Headlong Hall* (1816); *Melincourt* (1817); *Nightmare Abbey* (1818); *The Four Ages of Poetry* (1820); *Maid Marian* (1822); *The Misfortunes of Elphin* (1829); *Crotchet Castle* (1831); *Gryll Grange* (1860).

Although he was born on the Dorset coast Peacock spent most of his life by the banks of the Thames west of London, the stretch of countryside celebrated in his most ambitious early poem. It was an appropriately peaceful setting for a gentle poet and elegantly precise satirist, 'an idly inclined man ... professedly so in the summer'.

We cannot be sure when he first came to live at Marlow, on A404 between Slough and Reading, but he played host to Shelley (q.v.) at his house on West Street in 1816. The friendship was strengthened when, in 1817, Shelley bought Albion House on the same street, and the two writers together explored 'woody Marlow's winding vale' (*The Genius of the Thames*, Part 2, Stanza 24). They walked in Bisham Woods, over Marlow Bridge and south of A404, and boated up the Thames from Old Windsor to Lechlade, at the junction of A417 and A361 10 miles NE of Swindon. Mr Crotchet's guests follow the same route as the first leg of their journey to Wales, begun in Chapter 9 of *Crotchet Castle*.

In 1823 Peacock moved to Lower Halliford, which remained his home until death; the little village has now been absorbed into Shepperton, between Chertsey and Sunbury. Elmbank, the house he converted from two cottages, stands at the head of Walton Lane with its garden reaching down to the river. George Meredith (q.v.) joined the household briefly in 1853 after his marriage to Peacock's daughter, Mary, but the arrangement was not a happy one, as the rather malicious portrait of Peacock as Dr Middleton in *The Egoist* testifies. The young couple moved to Vine Cottage on Russell Road nearby.

The ruins of the 13C Newark Priory (13 miles south off A3 near Ripley) are associated with both Peacock's youth and his old age. He came here with Fanny Falkner during their mysteriously short-lived engagement in 1807 and returned in 1842, fondly remembering her

> Who, on that long-past August day,
> Beheld with me these ruins gray.
> ('Newark Abbey', lines 23–24)

Endlessly expounding their theories over country-house dinner tables or on picturesque excursions, the characters in Peacock's novels invite identification with the author's famous friends and contemporaries, notably Shelley, Byron and Coleridge in *Nightmare Abbey*. The settings of the novels—north Wales (*Headlong Hall*), the Lake District (*Melincourt*), the Lincolnshire coast (*Nightmare Abbey*), the New Forest (*Gryll Grange*)—are more elusive, though Peacock's special fondness for Welsh scenery shines through. In *Headlong Hall* (Ch. 7), which places Squire Headlong's country house near Llanberis in the shadow of Snowdon, the guests make an instructive excursion to the model town then recently developed by W.A. Madocks at Tremadog, near Porthmadog.

Samuel Pepys

b. London, 1633; d. London, 1703. Diarist.

Although he was born in London Pepys came from a family whose real roots were in Eastern England. This is now the region where he is best remembered. He apparently attended the *grammar school at

Huntingdon, east of A1 and now in Cambridgeshire, in 1644–45 or a little earlier. The charming little building, once part of a medieval Hospital of St John, has now been renamed the Cromwell Museum in honour of another famous pupil, whom Pepys admired; it stands on the High Street side of the Market Square. While being educated here he presumably lived with his uncle Robert in Brampton, 2 miles west of Huntingdon. Pepys House, a late 16C building by A604 near the roundabout leading to the village, was inherited by Pepys' father, who retired to it in 1661, and by Pepys himself in 1680.

Of all the scenes in the diarist's life Magdalene College, Cambridge, is, as his biographer Richard Ollard reminds us, 'the one that we can most nearly share with him'. Pepys entered the college in 1651, when he moved from Trinity Hall, and received his BA in 1653. Little is known about his undergraduate years except that he was formally admonished for being 'scandalously overseene in drink'. He frequently returned to Magdalene, usually in the course of visits to Brampton, as on the occasion when he went 'into the Buttery as a stranger and there drank my bellyful of their beer, which pleased me as the best I ever drank' (diary entry for 25 May 1668). His magnificent library was left to his nephew John Jackson for life and to Magdalene in 1726; in 1742 the college housed it in the eclectic 17C building that forms one side of Second Court. The *Pepys Library is notable for the original bookcases from Pepys' home in London, the manuscript of his diary and the manuscript translation of Ovid's *Metamorphoses* made for Caxton. Pepys bought the first part and the second part was acquired by Magdalene in 1966.

Elsewhere in Cambridge, Pepys attended service at the little church of St Botolph on Trumpington Street on 26 February 1660. In 1668 he walked to the fine church of St Andrew south of the High Street in Chesterton, NE of the city, 'and saw the place I used to sit in' (entry for 25 May). Further abroad, he visited relatives at Impington (2 miles north via B1049). Pepys' diary for 4 August 1661 records that he attended Sunday service with his great-uncle Talbot at the church of St Andrew: 'And at our coming in, the country-people all rise, with so much reverence. And when the parson begins, he begins "Right Worshipfull and dearly beloved" to us'.

Pepys was naturally familiar with the major sights on the various routes between London and Eastern England. He called several times at Audley End, 13 miles south of Cambridge east of B1383, before the mansion was altered by Vanbrugh (q.v.). His diary for 17 February 1660 describes how

> the housekeeper showed us all the house; in which the stateliness of the ceilings, chimney-pieces, and form of the whole was exceedingly worth seeing. He took us into the cellar, where we drank most admirable drink, a health to the King. Here I played on my Flagelette, there being an excellent Echo.

A later visit left him disappointed: 'Perticularly, the ceilings are not so good as I alway took them to be' (entry for 8 October 1667). At Baldock, by A1 and 20 miles SW of Cambridge via A10 and A505, he found the church of St Mary Virgin 'very handsome' (entry for 6 August 1661). The next day he reported a visit to Hatfield House: 'we bayted and walked into the great House through all the Courts; and I would fain have stolen a pretty dog that followed me, but I could not, which troubled me'. The Elizabethan mansion is 17 miles south of Baldock via A1.

If Eastern England is still rich in landmarks reminiscent of Pepys, London has changed too greatly to offer more than a scattered handful of places to visit. He was married in 1655 at St Margaret's next to Westminster Abbey. Axe Yard nearby, where he was living when he began his diary in 1660, has long since been swept from the map; it lay south of Downing Street off Whitehall. In Whitehall itself he witnessed the execution of Charles I outside Inigo Jones' splendid Banqueting House in 1649. At Charing Cross he saw 'the first blood shed in revenge for the blood of the King' with the execution of the regicide Thomas Harrison (who looked, Pepys reported in his diary for 13 October 1660, 'as cheerful as any man could do in that condition'). Two of Pepys' later addresses survive on Buckingham Street, south of the Strand near Charing Cross. The street and its neighbours were built on the site of York House, the Duke of Buckingham's mansion, in 1672. Pepys lived at No. 12 (1679–88) and then at No. 14 (1688–1700), now rebuilt.

The most expressive reminders of Pepys are in the City. In Fleet Street, eastern continuation of the Strand, the 17C Prince Henry's Room has a small display of portraits, prints and manuscripts assembled by the Samuel Pepys Club. The medieval church preceding Wren's St Bride's was the scene of Pepys' baptism in 1633; his father was a tailor in nearby Salisbury Court. In 1679 he fell under suspicion of complicity in the Popish Plot and was detained in the Tower of London, where his friend and fellow diarist John Evelyn (q.v.) visited him. From the brick tower of All Hallows by the Tower he watched the progress of the Great Fire in 1666. On Hart Street to the north we find St Olave's, a church which survived the fire, though it did need substantial restoration after bomb damage in the Second World War. Pepys worshipped here when he was living on adjacent Seething Lane and working as Secretary to the Admiralty, which stood on Hart Street's eastern extension, Crutched Friars. He and his wife Elizabeth (d. 1669) were buried beneath the high altar. Pepys' charming *memorial to Elizabeth on the north side of the chancel was complemented in 1883 by a memorial to himself on the south wall of the nave.

At Deptford in SE London Pepys paid regular visits to the Royal Naval Dockyard, closed in the 19C, and was Evelyn's guest at Sayes Court.

Cromwell Museum, Grammar School Walk, Huntingdon, Cambridgeshire: phone (0480) 425830.

Pepys House, Brampton, near Huntingdon, Cambridgeshire: visitors by written appointment.

Pepys Library, Magdalene College, Cambridge: phone the Porters' Lodge (0223) 332100.

Audley End, Saffron Walden, Essex: English Heritage; phone (0799) 22399.

Hatfield House, Hatfield, Hertfordshire: phone (070 72) 62823 or 65159.

Prince Henry's Room, 17 Fleet Street, London EC4: phone (01) 353 7323.

Tower of London, Tower Hill, London EC3: DoE monument; phone (01) 709 0765.

Alexander Pope

b. London, 1688; d. London, 1744. *An Essay in Criticism* (1711); *Windsor-Forest* (1713); *The Rape of the Lock* (1714); *The Iliad of Homer* (1715–20); *The Odyssey of Homer* (1725–26); *The Dunciad* (1728–43); *Moral Essays* (1731–35); *An Essay on Man* (1733–34); *Imitations of Horace* (1733–38); *Epistle from Mr Pope, to Dr Arbuthnot* (1735).

Scenes associated with an early period of Pope's life may be found at Chiswick in west London. From 1716–18 he lived with his parents on Mawson Row (then Mawson's New Buildings), a group of early 18C houses on Chiswick Lane South leading from the delightful Mall. His home is now the Fox and Hounds pub. One of his reasons for choosing the area was the desire to be near *Chiswick House, estate of his friend and patron, Richard Boyle, third Earl of Burlington, to whom the fourth of his *Moral Essays* is dedicated. In these years the house was a Jacobean building, finally demolished in the late 18C. The present Palladian mansion, where Pope was a frequent guest, was begun in the 1720s. It has recently been stripped of James Wyatt's additions and so has fared rather better than the peer's town residence, Burlington House in Piccadilly, which is encrusted with the work of later architects. The rich interior of Chiswick House includes *trompe l'oeil* paintings of Hercules, Venus and Apollo from Pope's Villa at Twickenham in the Summer Parlour, and portraits of Pope by William Kent (1685–1748) in the Blue Velvet Room and the Bedchamber. Of particular interest are Kent's *gardens, where the formal style begins to give way to the new taste for the Picturesque.

Pope is in fact the supreme example of an 18C poet whose life and writings are everywhere linked to the age's taste in architecture and, particularly, landscape gardening. This makes the loss of the Villa at Twickenham, SW of Chiswick, where he lived from 1719 until his death, all the more saddening. The modest house and its plot of land on Crossdeep overlooking the Thames were an endless delight to him; the final form they assumed was a creation as important as any of his poems during these years. Indeed, it is to the poetry that we turn for an account and justification of the principles which dictated the Picturesque laying-out of his garden:

> To build, to plant, whatever you intend,
> To rear the Column, or the Arch to bend,
> To swell the Terras, or to sink the Grot;
> In all, let Nature never be forgot.
> But treat the Goddess like a modest fair,
> Nor over-dress, nor leave her wholly bare;
> Let not each beauty ev'rywhere be spy'd,
> Where half the skill is decently to hide.
> He gains all points, who pleasingly confounds,
> Surprizes, varies, and conceals the Bounds.
> (*Moral Essays*, Epistle 4, lines 47–56)

The poem has proved more durable than the garden. John Serle, Pope's gardener, published a description the year after the poet's death but by 1760 Horace Walpole (q.v.) was writing to Horace Mann in horror at the changes wrought by Sir William Stanhope, brother to Lord Chesterfield and new owner of the property:

> it was a little bit of ground of five acres, enclosed with three lanes and seeing nothing. Pope had twisted and twirled and harmonized this, till it appeared two or three sweet little lawns opening and opening beyond one another, and the whole surrounded with thick impenetrable woods. Sir William has hacked and hewed these groves, wriggled a winding gravel walk through them with

an edging of shrubs, in what they call the modern taste, and in short, has desired the three lanes to walk in again.

The Villa itself has been replaced by a Victorian neo-Tudor building, now a school, St Catherine's College. The only surviving fragment of Pope's achievement is his famous Grotto. Really a passage beneath the road connecting the house and its riverside gardens, it quickly transcended this simple function and became a favourite retreat of Pope's 'from which', Dr Johnson (q.v.) observed disapprovingly, 'he endeavoured to persuade his friends and himself that cares and passions could be excluded'. A *camera obscura* reflected the outside world on to walls lined with minerals:

Thou who shalt stop, where *Thames*' translucent Wave
Shines a broad Mirrour thro' the shadowy Cave;
Where lingering Drops from Mineral Roofs distill,
And pointed Crystals break the sparkling Rill,
Unpolish'd Gemms no Ray on Pride bestow,
And latent Metals innocently glow:
Approach. Great NATURE studiously behold!
('Verses on a Grotto by the River Thames at Twickenham')

Pope in his grotto at Twickenham by William Kent or Dorothy Boyle, Lady Burlington

North of Crossdeep and in the centre of Twickenham's original village we find the parish church of St Mary. Pope's parents, his nurse Mary Beach (her tablet is on the outside wall), and the poet himself were all buried here. A monument erected by Pope's *protégé*, William Warburton, remembers him in his own words as 'one who would not be buried in Westminster Abbey'.

In the park NE of St Mary's is *Marble Hill House. This fine Palladian building was in Pope's time the home of Mrs Howard (later Lady Suffolk), mistress to George II, celebrated in 'On a Certain Lady at Court' as 'a Reasonable Woman,/ Handsome and witty, yet a Friend' but also, perhaps, portrayed as the heartless Cloe in the second of the *Moral Essays*. The grounds of Marble Hill were laid out by Charles Bridgeman, with Pope and later Horace Walpole advising.

Marble Hill House, home of Henrietta Howard, later Countess of Suffolk, friend of Gay and Walpole as well as Pope. From Colen Campbell's Vitruvius Britannicus *(1717–25)*

In Central England, and especially in a wide radius of Oxford, we may visit a rich list of places connected with Pope's life, reminding us both of people mentioned in his poems and of his taste in landscape gardening.

At Mapledurham House, off A4074 24 miles SE of Oxford and on the fringes of Reading, Pope visited his friends, the Blount sisters, in their Elizabethan manor and the charming village where it is set. His poem, 'Epistle to Miss Blount, on her leaving the Town, after the

Coronation', addressed to his special friend Martha, gives a playfully cynical account of the life she led in the country: 'Old fashion'd halls, dull aunts, and croaking rooks' (line 13).

Inevitably, Pope also knew Stowe, 20 miles NE of Oxford and near Buckingham, where Richard Temple, Viscount Cobham, had his house (now a public school) in *grounds that remain perhaps the most complete demonstration of 18C taste in landscaping. The temples are by Vanbrugh (q.v.), Gibbs and Kent, while the gardens were begun by Bridgeman and continued by Kent, with final additions by 'Capability' Brown. Pope's admiration is expressed in the fourth of his *Moral Essays*:

> Still follow Sense, of ev'ry Art the Soul,
> Parts answ'ring Parts, shall slide into a whole,
> Spontaneous beauties all around advance,
> Start ev'n from Difficulty, strike from Chance;
> Nature shall join you, Time shall make it grow
> A Wonder to work at—perhaps a STOW.
> (lines 65–67)

Rousham Park, east of A423 12 miles north from Oxford, preserves mementoes of Pope's friendship with the Dormer family. In a letter of 1728 he praised the **grounds through which the Cherwell runs, laid out by Kent, as 'the prettiest place for water-falls, jetts, ponds inclosed with beautiful scenes of green and hanging woods, that ever I saw'. With Chiswick House, they offer probably the best surviving reminder of the type of effect Pope himself created in his vanished garden at Twickenham.

Further north on A423 at Adderbury, 20 miles from Oxford, is the house that once belonged to John Wilmot, Earl of Rochester, described in more detail under the entry for the Restoration poet. In 1739 Pope wrote a poem complimenting Adderbury's then owner, the Duke of Argyll, and recording the disappointing results of sleeping in Rochester's bed:

> With no poetick ardors fir'd,
> I press the bed where *Wilmot* lay:
> That here he lov'd, or here expir'd
> Begets no numbers grave or gay.

At the pleasant village of Stanton Harcourt (on B4449 9 miles west of Oxford) Pope stayed for the autumn of 1718 as a guest of Lord Harcourt, frequently host to writers of the period. The poet was clearly charmed by the 15C half-ruined manor house where he was accommodated:

> A Stranger would be grievously disappointed, who should ever think to get into this house the right way. One would expect, after entring thro the Porch, to be let into the Hall: Alas nothing less—you find yourself in a Brewhouse. From the Parlour you step into the Drawing-room, but opening the iron-nailed door, you are convinced by a flight of birds about your ears & a cloud of dust in your eyes, that 'tis the Pigeon-house.

Most of the building was demolished in 1750 and only a few fragments survive. The most interesting are the kitchen and *Pope's Tower, by the church, where he worked on his translation of Homer's *Iliad*. There is a lovely view from the top.

The poet's delight in the decrepit irregularity of his surroundings at Stanton Harcourt has been cited as evidence of the romantic side to his otherwise Augustan sensibility. So has his interest in John Hewet and Sarah Drew, a local pair of devoted lovers killed by lightning during his stay, an interest shared by his friend and companion, John Gay (q.v.). Pope wrote the epitaph for their tomb in the churchyard and gave several accounts of their death in letters to friends. This is the version he sent to Martha Blount:

> Sarah frighted, & out of breath, sunk down on a heap of Wheatsheaves; & John, who never separated from her, rak'd two or three heapes together, to protect her, & sate down by her. Immediately there was heard so loud a crack that Heaven seemd burst asunder: every one was sollicitous for the safety of his next neighbor, & called to one another. Those who were nearest our Lovers hearing no Answer, stept to the Sheaves. They first spy'd a little Smoke, and then saw this faithful Pair, John with one Arm about her neck, & the other extended over her face, as to shield her from the Lightning; both stiff & cold in this tender posture: no mark or blemish on the Bodies; except the left Eyebrow of Sarah a little sing'd and a small Spot between her Breasts.

The age's reaction to such events was not uniformly sentimental. Lady Mary Wortley Montagu, to whom Pope also related the episode, answered in verse:

> Who knows if 'twas not kindly done?
> For had they seen the next year's sun,
> A beaten wife and cuckold swain
> Had jointly curs'd the marriage chain;
> Now they are happy in their doom,
> FOR POPE HAS WROTE UPON THEIR TOMB.

Pope himself privately composed an epitaph of rather different character from the public one to which Lady Mary referred:

> Here lye two poor Lovers, who had the mishap
> Tho very chaste people, to die of a Clap.

He visited *Cirencester Park in Gloucestershire several times, returning to assist and admire Lord Bathurst's ambitious transformation of his estate. His admiration of the peer's use of riches was expressed by the dedication of his third *Moral Essay* and by a famous couplet in the fourth, where Bathurst's name is linked with Burlington's:

> Who then shall grace, or who improve the Soil?
> Who plants like BATHURST, or who builds like BOYLE.
> (lines 177–178)

Pope's Seat, a rusticated stone temple in the neo-classical manner, recalls his connection with the place. The 'pleasant prospect' of the popular Cotswold village of Bibury (8 miles NE of Cirencester on A433), viewed on a visit to Bathurst, remained in his memory.

Like other famous literary men he also came to *Prior Park, at Combe Down 1 mile SE of Bath and reached from the south of the city via Claverton Street and Prior Park Road. John Wood the Elder built the grand Palladian mansion for Ralph Allen (1693–1764), the celebrated 'Man of Bath', and Pope headed the list of writers who paid tribute to Allen as the model of that benevolent philanthropy which the age so admired:

> Let humble ALLEN, with an awkward Shame,
> Do good by Stealth, and blush to find it Fame.
> ('Epilogue to the Satires', Dialogue 1, lines 135–136)

Few of Pope's friendships, however, kept an entirely even course. His final visit in 1742, when he was accompanied by Martha Blount, led to a lasting coldness between the two men. Now a Roman Catholic school, Prior Park is greatly reduced from its former glory inside, but its exterior and grounds remain magnificent. The Palladian Bridge is particularly notable.

Chiswick House, Burlington Lane, London W4: English Heritage, standard opening; phone (01) 995 0508.

Pope's Grotto, Pope's Villa (St Catherine's College), Twickenham, Middlesex: visitors by appointment; phone (01) 892 5633.

Marble Hill House, Richmond Road, Twickenham, Middlesex: English Heritage; phone London (01) 892 5115.

Mapledurham House, Mapledurham, near Reading, Oxfordshire: phone Reading (0734) 723350 or 723277.

Stowe (Stowe School), near Buckingham: grounds, garden buildings and main state rooms open, usually during the Easter and summer holidays; phone Buckingham (0280) 813650.

Rousham House, Steeple Aston, Oxfordshire: phone (0869) 47110.

Stanton Harcourt Manor, Stanton Harcourt, Oxfordshire: phone Oxford (0865) 881928.

Cirencester Park, Cirencester, Gloucestershire: phone (0285) 653135 or 654242.

Prior Park (Prior Park College), Combe Down, near Bath, Avon: grounds and chapel open; phone Bath (0225) 835353.

Beatrix Potter

b. London, 1866; d. Near Sawrey, Cumbria, 1943. *The Tale of Peter Rabbit* (1900); *The Tailor of Gloucester* (1902); *The Tale of Squirrel Nutkin* (1903); *The Tale of Benjamin Bunny* (1904); *The Tale of Two Bad Mice* (1904); *The Tale of Mrs Tiggy-Winkle* (1905); *The Tale of Jeremy Fisher* (1906); *The Story of a Fierce Bad Rabbit* (1906); *The Story of Miss Moppet* (1906); *The Tale of Tom Kitten* (1907); *The Tale of Jemima Puddle-Duck* (1908); *The Roly-Poly Pudding* (1908; republished as *The Tale of Samuel Whiskers*, 1926); *The Tale of the Flopsy Bunnies* (1909); *Ginger and Pickles* (1909); *The Tale of Mrs Tittlemouse* (1910); *The Tale of Timmy Tiptoes* (1911); *The Tale of Mr Tod* (1912); *The Tale of Pigling Bland* (1913); *Appley Dapply's Nursery Rhymes* (1922); *The Fairy Caravan* (1929); *The Tale of Little Pig Robinson* (1930).

No. 2 Bolton Gardens, just north of the Old Brompton Road in South Kensington, was destroyed by a bomb in the Second World War. The disappearance of this 'unloved birthplace' where she had remained with her parents until middle age caused Beatrix Potter little regret, for her life there had been enclosed and isolated. Her only outlets were the journals she wrote in code (deciphered by Leslie Linder and published in 1966), the letters to children that grew into published stories and her drawing. The search for objects and specimens for her delicate, precise sketches took her to the Natural History Museum and the Victoria and Albert Museum, both in the Cromwell Road to the north. The coat in *The Tailor of Gloucester* required special study of the Victoria and Albert Museum embroidery collection. On Kensington Church Street, near its junction with Kensington High Street, is the 19C church of St Mary Abbots where she married William Heelis, a solicitor from the Lake District, in 1913.

The marriage effectively brought her career as children's writer to an end. It also completed her escape from her parents' restrictive way of life and made her attachment to the Lake District permanent. She

Beatrix Potter by D. Banner

had first visited the area for holidays in childhood. On several occasions her parents rented the 19C Wray Castle (now a training college for Merchant Navy cadets) on the western shore of Windermere. In 1905 she bought the 17C *Hill Top Farm, in the little village of Near Sawrey 2 miles SE of Hawkshead, lavishing care and money on it during the following years. Several of her most popular children's stories were written here, and the farmhouse appears in her illustrations for *Tom Kitten* and, with other parts of the village (like the Tower Bank Arms), in *Jemima Puddle-Duck*. On her death she bequeathed it to the National Trust, together with some four thousand acres of land in the Lake District. Now one of the most popular attractions in the region, the little house gets very crowded in summer. Beatrix Potter's married life was spent at Castle Farm nearby, taking an active interest in farming and conservation, and regarding the arrival of tourists attracted by the fame of her books with some surprise. She found the English visitors 'very inquisitive and completely uninteresting. However it happens, the class of Americans who take the trouble to call, are quite different'. William Heelis' office in Hawkshead is now a National Trust shop and information centre, with a display of Beatrix Potter's watercolours and drawings.

Elsewhere in the Lake District, St Herbert's Island in Derwentwater provided the model for the 'Owl Island' of *Squirrel Nutkin*. The lake appeared again in the illustrations to *Mrs Tiggy-Winkle*.

In Gloucester the house she used in *The Tailor of Gloucester* stands on College Court, leading from Westgate Street to the Cathedral Close. It is now a shop and Beatrix Potter Centre.

Natural History Museum, Cromwell Road, South Kensington, London SW7: phone (01) 938 9388.

Victoria and Albert Museum, Cromwell Road, South Kensington, London SW7: phone (01) 938 8500; recorded information (01) 938 8441.

Hill Top, Near Sawrey, Cumbria: NT; phone Hawkshead (096 66) 269053.

John Cowper, Llewelyn and T.F. Powys

John Cowper Powys: b. Shirley, Derbyshire, 1872; d. Blaenau Ffestiniog, Gwynedd, 1963. *Wood and Stone: A Romance* (1915); *Rodmoor: A Romance* (1916); *Ducdame* (1925); *Wolf Solent* (1929); *A Glastonbury Romance* (1932); *Autobiography* (1934); *Weymouth Sands* (1934); *Maiden Castle* (1936); *Morwyn: Or The Vengeance of God* (1937); *Owen Glendower: An Historical Novel* (1940); *Porius: A Romance of the Dark Ages* (1951); *The Inmates* (1952); *Atlantis* (1954); *The Brazen Head* (1956); *All or Nothing* (1960).

Llewelyn Powys: b. Dorchester, Dorset, 1884; d. Davos Platz, Switzerland, 1939. *Ebony and Ivory* (1923); *Black Laughter* (1924); *Skin for Skin* (1925); *Henry Hudson* (1927); *Apples Be Ripe* (1930); *Impassioned Clay* (1931); *Earth's Memories* (1934); *Dorset Essays* (1935); *Love and Death* (1939).

T.F. Powys: b. Shirley, Derbyshire, 1875; d. Mappowder, Dorset, 1953. *The Left Leg* (1923); *Black Bryony* (1923); *Mr Tasker's Gods* (1924); *Mark Only* (1924); *Innocent Birds* (1926); *Mr Weston's Good Wine* (1927); *Unclay* (1931); *Bottle's Path* (1946).

John Cowper and T.F. Powys, the elder of the three literary brothers, were born at Shirley, off A52 4 miles SE of Ashbourne in Derbyshire. Neither the village nor the county subsequently played an important part in the life of a family which, despite the far-flung travels of its various members, was rooted in Somerset and Dorset.

Montacute, 4 miles west of Yeovil on A3088, is an important shrine for the Powys' readers. Rev. Charles Francis Powys brought his family to the village in 1885 and remained until his death in 1923. Montacute may not be the 'King's Barton' of *Wolf Solent* but Mr Urquhart's residence in the novel owes something to John Cowper's childhood memories of its wonderful Elizabethan mansion, Montacute House. His first novel, *Wood and Stone*, describes the village as 'Nevilton' and nearby Ham Hill, to the west, as 'Leo's Hill'. Sherborne, on A30 beyond Yeovil to the east of Montacute, is the 'Ramsgard' of *Wolf Solent*. John Cowper and Llewelyn attended its public school, while another brother, Littleton Charles, became headmaster of Sherborne Preparatory School. Ilchester, on A303 and A37 4 miles north of Montacute, was the birthplace of Roger Bacon, the medieval philosopher who inspired the necromantic legends recalled in *The Brazen Head*. The historic town of Glastonbury, 11 miles north of Ilchester via B3151 and A39, is the setting for another of John Cowper's works.

Dorchester and its surrounding countryside are also deeply connected with the Powys family. They lived in the county town from 1879 to 1885, when Rev. Charles was curate of the fine church of St Peter's. Llewelyn was born during these years and, like his brothers, was taken to tea with the elderly William Barnes (q.v.). The town is the setting for much of *Maiden Castle*, the novel which takes its title from the prehistoric fort some 2½ miles SW. Weymouth, on the coast 8½ miles south, gives its name to another of John Cowper's novels.

Of particular importance is the little village of East Chaldon or, more picturesquely, Chaldon Herring, some 8 miles SE via A352 and an unclassified road leading towards the coast. Though both John Cowper and Llewelyn lived here, it is mainly associated with T.F. Powys, who came in 1905 and stayed until 1940. His home was Beth Car, a brick house built by Henry Hardy, brother of Thomas Hardy (q.v.). East Chaldon is thus the model for the village that appears so often and under various names in his novels and stories, most memorably as the 'Folly Down' of *Mr Weston's Good Wine*. On the cliff top to the south is a stone memorial to Llewelyn, who died in Switzerland.

T.F. Powys left East Chaldon for another Dorset village, Mappowder (east of B3143), where he is buried in the churchyard. John Cowper spent his last years at Blaenau Ffestiniog in Wales, a country that exerted an obvious influence over his work, but his ashes were scattered in the Channel off Chesil Bank near Abbotsbury (on B3157 8 miles NW of Weymouth).

In their youth John Cowper and Llewelyn followed the family tradition and attended Corpus Christi College, Cambridge, though John Cowper was speaking for both of them when he remarked that the university 'had not the least influence upon my taste, my intelligence, my philosophy or my character'.

Montacute House, Montacute, Somerset: NT; phone Martock (0935) 823289.

Maiden Castle, near Dorchester: English Heritage, open at any reasonable time.

Matthew Prior

b. Wimborne, Dorset, 1664; d. Wimpole Hall, Cambridgeshire, 1721. *Carmen Seculare* (1700); *Solomon on the Vanity of the World* (1718); *Down-Hall: A Ballad* (1723).

After attending London's Westminster School in Little Dean's Yard to the south of Westminster Abbey, Prior studied at St John's College, Cambridge (1683–86). His rooms were apparently in the handsome late 16C Second Court. Although he went on to enjoy a career as diplomat in London and elsewhere, Prior maintained his connection with St John's and left part of his library to the College in his will. The other surviving places associated with his life are all within convenient reach of Cambridge.

In 1688–89 he was tutor to the Earl of Exeter's son at the fine Renaissance mansion of Burghley House near Stamford, Lincolnshire. His 'Epistle to Fleetwood Shepherd, Esq.', an early example of the Horatian style he aspired to in his poetry, gives a light-hearted account of his recreations there:

Sometimes I climb my Mare, and kick her
To bottl'd ale, and neighb'ring vicar;
Sometimes at STAMFORD take a quart ...

In 1719 a gift of £4000 from Edward Harley, Earl of Oxford, made it possible for Prior to buy a country house in Essex, Down Hall, which he improved and landscaped as well as making the subject of a pleasantly ironic poem. Down Hall has been replaced by a 19C building and Prior is better remembered at the Earl of Oxford's country seat, Wimpole Hall, 8 miles SW of Cambridge via A603. The 17C mansion was then being extended by James Gibbs. Prior was a frequent guest and died during a visit to Wimpole in 1721.

He was buried near his old school, in Poets' Corner (fee) of Westminster Abbey, the grave being at his request near that of Spenser (q.v.). His will made provison for the striking monument, though he had earlier offered a humbler memorial to himself in 'Epitaph Extempore':

Nobles and Heralds, by your leave,
    Here lies what once was Matthew Prior;
The son of Adam and Eve,
    Can Bourbon or Nassau claim higher?

Burghley House, Stamford, Lincolnshire: phone (0780) 52451.

Wimpole Hall, in Cambridgeshire, though its postal address is Arrington, Royston, Hertfordshire: NT; phone Cambridge (0223) 207257.

Sir Walter Ralegh

b. near Budleigh Salterton, Devon, 1552?; d. London, 1618. Poet and author of *The History of the World* (1614).

Hayes Barton, the E-shaped Tudor farmhouse that was Ralegh's birthplace, lies among wooded scenery north of the Devon coastal resort of Budleigh Salterton and west of East Budleigh.

After attending Oriel College, Oxford, Ralegh embarked on the adventurous career which elevated him from relative obscurity to a position as favourite at Queen Elizabeth's court and to fame as one of the best travelled figures of his age.

During his stay in Ireland he took part in the 1580 massacre of the Spanish garrison at Fort del Oro, near the harbour town of Smerwick, County Kerry, on the picturesque Dingle peninsula. In 1586 he acquired an estate including Youghal, a fishing town 40 miles east of Cork on N25. The tradition that he lived at Myrtle Grove, to the north of St Mary's Church, should be regarded sceptically. Better documented is his visit in 1589 to a neighbouring poet, Edmund Spenser, which is described under the entry for that author. In 1589 he was also granted the Castle at Lismore, north of Youghal, which remained in his possession until 1602. The 12C building, with good views of the River Blackwater, was rebuilt and remodelled in the 19C; it has a pleasant garden with an attractive Yew Walk.

In 1592 Ralegh acquired property at Sherborne in Dorset. After attempting to renovate the 12C Castle, which lies to the south of the town and its River Yeo, he built himself a new house in 1594, calling it The Lodge. The original castle was damaged during the Civil War, though its Norman gatehouse and keep still stand, while Ralegh's addition was much altered by 19C interiors in the Jacobean style.

In 1603 he was arraigned at Winchester on slender charges of involvement in a plot against James I. His hearing took place in the magnificent Great Hall of the Norman castle, near West Gate and the west end of the High Street. As a result he was committed for the second time in his life to the Tower of London. His first stay in 1592 had arisen from allegations of a liaison with Elizabeth Throgmorton, maid of honour to Queen Elizabeth, and had occasioned a poem, 'As You Come from the Holy Land', flattering his sovereign. His second and far longer period of imprisonment was spent in the Bloody Tower and is remembered by the naming of Ralegh's Walk nearby. He passed the time writing the ambitious *History of the World*.

He secured his release in 1616 by his plan for the Orinoco expedition in search of gold and silver but was arrested again on his return to England after its failure. He was probably held in the vanished gatehouse outside the main entrance to Westminster Abbey, though tradition points to a small cell in the White Tower at the Tower of London. His execution took place in 1618 at Old Palace Yard, the space of land between the Abbey and the Palace of Westminster now largely occupied by the car park. He was apparently buried at nearby St Margaret's, Westminster, where a window of 1882 with an inscription by the American poet James Russell Lowell commemorates him. A statue (1959) stands on the lawn in front of the Ministry of Defence in Whitehall.

Lismore Castle, Lismore, County Waterford, Republic of Ireland: only gardens open; phone Dungarvan (058) 54424.

Sherborne Old Castle, Sherborne, Dorset: English Heritage, standard opening; phone (0935) 812730.

Sherborne Castle, Sherborne, Dorset: phone (0935) 813182.

Great Hall and Round Table, off High Street, Winchester, Hampshire: phone (0962) 841841, extension 366.

Tower of London, Tower Hill, London EC3: DoE monument; phone (01) 709 0765.

Samuel Richardson

b. Mackworth, Derbyshire?, 1689; d. London, 1761. *Pamela: or Virtue Rewarded* (1740–41); *Clarissa Harlowe* (1747–48); *The History of Sir Charles Grandison* (1753–54).

'I know nothing of Situations of Places, Distances, Contiguities', confessed Richardson when he was preparing a revised edition of *A Tour through the Whole Island of Great Britain* by his fellow novelist, Defoe (q.v.). There can, in fact, have been few English writers who travelled less than he did.

During visits to Bath in the 1740s he dined with the philanthropist Ralph Allen at Prior Park, the magnificent Palladian mansion built by John Wood the elder at Combe Down, 1 mile SE of the city. Richardson accepted the invitation with a certain naive complacency as evidence of the position his writing had won him: 'Twenty years ago I was the most obscure man in Great Britain, and now I am admitted to the company of the first characters in the kingdom'. Somewhat diminished from its former glory, Prior Park is now a Roman Catholic school.

In London, *Clarissa* may be remembered by a visit to the charming

Flask Walk off Hampstead High Street. Richardson's heroine took refuge here, lodging with a Mrs Moore, but was soon discovered by Lovelace and again harassed by his attentions. Mrs Barbauld, editor of the novelist's correspondence, tells of a Frenchman who visited Hampstead in search of the exact house on Flask Walk 'and was surprised at the ignorance or indifference of the inhabitants on that subject'. She concludes that 'constant residence soon destroys all sensibility to objects of local enthusiasm'.

Richardson was buried at St Bride's off the south side of Fleet Street. His coffin is preserved in the interesting Crypt Museum, which also has a display about the church's connection with the printing trade. Richardson's own print shops in Fleet Street and Salisbury Court nearby, like his later homes in Fulham, have long since vanished.

Prior Park (Prior Park College), Combe Down, near Bath, Avon: grounds and chapel open; phone Bath (0225) 835353.

St Bride's Crypt Museum, St Bride's Church, Fleet Street, London EC4: phone (01) 353 1301.

John Wilmot, Earl of Rochester

b. Ditchley, Oxfordshire, 1647; d. Woodstock, Oxfordshire, 1680. *A Satire Against Mankind* (1675).

Much of Rochester's short and dissolute life, during which he nevertheless maintained a reputation as satirist and wit, was spent at court, where he was a special favourite of Charles II. But his deepest connections are with Oxfordshire, of which the following tour may be recommended.

It begins in Oxford, where Rochester attended Wadham College as a fellow commoner from 1660 to 1661. The College still has the four silver pint pots he presented. The traveller may then take A423 north to Adderbury (19 miles) where Rochester lived after his marriage in 1667 at Adderbury House, east of The Green. Pope (q.v.) came here in 1739 and left a permanent reminder of his visit in the poem, 'On Lying in the Earl of Rochester's Bed at Atterbury'. More fruitfully, A34 leads NW from Oxford to Woodstock (9 miles). The High Lodge that Rochester occupied from 1674 after his appointment as Keeper of Woodstock Park was later assimilated into the grounds of Blenheim Palace. It was remodelled in the Gothic style in the 18C. Rochester here acquired a reputation for scandalous living but also underwent the death-bed conversion recorded by Bishop Burnet. To the left of A34 at Over Kiddington (4 miles beyond Woodstock) lies Ditchley Park, Rochester's birthplace. A print of the 'low antient timber house, with a pretty bowling greene' (as the diarist John Evelyn [q.v.] described it) is displayed in the present building, which is by James Gibbs and dates from the 1720s. At the nearby village of Spelsbury on B4026 (15 miles) Rochester is buried in the churchyard in an unmarked family vault. From Spelsbury the tourist may continue SW via Charlbury to the charming Cotswold town of Burford (23 miles) at the junction of A361 and A40. Rochester attended the Grammar School in Church Lane; traces of the original 16C building have survived despite Victorian alteration.

Two surviving sites in London together give an apt indication of

Rochester's life there. He was briefly detained in the Tower of London for a few days of 1665 on a charge of abducting the heiress Elizabeth Malet, whom he subsequently married. In 1675 or 1676, again apparently in disgrace, he posed as a quack doctor and set up a stall on nearby Tower Hill.

Blenheim Palace, Woodstock, Oxfordshire: phone (0993) 811325.

Ditchley Park, Enstone, Oxfordshire: visitors by appointment; phone (060 872) 346.

Tower of London, Tower Hill, London EC3: DoE monument; phone (01) 709 0765.

Dante Gabriel Rossetti

b. London, 1828; d. Birchington, Kent, 1882. *Poems* (includes 'The House of Life'; 1870); *Ballads and Sonnets* (includes expanded version of 'The House of Life'; 1881).

A plaque at No. 17 Red Lion Square in London, south of Theobald's Road near its junction with Southampton Row, marks the lodgings Rossetti briefly shared with the artist Walter Deverell in 1851. It was Deverell who first discovered Lizzie Siddal and introduced her to the Pre-Raphaelite Brotherhood; she became Rossetti's favourite model and later his mistress. The lodgings were later occupied by William Morris (q.v.) and Edward Burne-Jones.

In the 1850s Rossetti and Lizzie Siddal visited Hastings on the Sussex coast. They returned in 1860 to be married in the church of St Clement's at the south end of the High Street. It was far from being a romantic occasion: the couple had known each other for ten, not always happy, years, while she was already gravely ill from tuberculosis and he approached marriage in a spirit of reluctant obligation.

On her death in 1862—not from tuberculosis but from an overdose of laudanum, whether accidental or deliberate—she was buried in the Rossetti family plot at Highgate Cemetery in London, where Rossetti's sister Christina (1830–94), author of *Goblin Market*, his brother William Michael (1829–1919) and his father Gabriele (1783–1854) also lie. Rossetti originally placed the manuscript of a number of his poems in his wife's coffin, but in 1869 arranged to have them exhumed for publication. The cemetery is entered from Swains Lane, south of Highgate Underground Station (Northern Line); the Rossetti plot lies on the far side of the oval walk in the western half.

The widowed Rossetti moved to Tudor House (or the Queen's House), No. 16 Cheyne Walk by the Chelsea Embankment. Except for an important and stormy period at Kelmscott Manor (described under the entry for William Morris) the 18C building remained his home almost until death. Its survival more than compensates for the disappearance of his earlier London homes. In the first year of his tenancy George Meredith and Swinburne (qq.v.) were lodgers but the arrangement proved fragile. Swinburne was in the habit of sliding naked down the banisters when drunk, which happened quite often; this and other manifestations of domestic chaos were offensive to Meredith. Rossetti himself indulged a passion for filling the house with china and bric-à-brac, and its garden with a progressively exotic menagerie of animals: peacocks, armadillos, gazelles, kangaroos, salamanders, wombats and an Indian bull which took his

Rossetti reading to Theodore Watts-Dunton (Swinburne's friend and companion) in the parlour at Tudor House, by H.T. Dunn (1882)

fancy, he said, because it had eyes like Jane Morris. He even toyed with the idea of keeping an elephant to clean his windows and, by arousing the curiosity of passers-by, attract buyers for his paintings. Ruskin (q.v.) was undoubtedly wise not to pursue his plan of joining the household, though he was a visitor to Cheyne Walk.

In the shrubbery between the Walk and the Embankment is a drinking fountain surmounted by a bronze medallion of Rossetti, designed by his friend Ford Madox Brown. It was unveiled in 1887 by the painter William Holman Hunt, whose speech on that occasion showed his lingering resentment at the greater publicity Rossetti's role in the Pre-Raphaelite Brotherhood had received.

In early 1882, his health badly damaged by chloral addiction, Rossetti was taken by the young novelist Hall Caine to convalesce at Birchington, on A28 3 miles SW of Margate by the Kent coast. Although the ugly little bungalow where he died on Easter Sunday has been demolished, Birchington is otherwise rich in memorials. The opening stanzas of Christina's poem, 'Birchington Churchyard', describe the scene of his burial:

A lowly hill which overlooks a flat,
    Half sea, half country-side;
A flat-shored sea of low-voiced creeping tide
    Over a chalky weedy mat.

A hill of hillocks, flowery and kept green
    Round crosses raised for hope,
With many-tinted sunsets where the slope
    Faces the lingering western sheen.

The south aisle of the church has a window of 1884 by Frederic James Shields. Its left light was intended to carry an adaptation of Rossetti's 'Magdalene at the Door of Simon' but the local vicar objected that the picture was unlikely 'to inspire devotional thoughts and feelings, and ... in some cases it might rather do the reverse'. Shields made a copy of Rossetti's 'Passover in the Holy Family' instead. Outside the south door is a *Celtic cross by Ford Madox Brown, its surface elaborately carved with symbolic motifs that repay study. Among them we note an Assyrian bull, reminiscent of 'The Burden of Nineveh', and a curious wedding ceremony in which the priest is blindfolded and the groom carries a book—perhaps the poems Rossetti had originally buried with Lizzie Siddal.

Highgate Cemetery, Swains Lane, Highgate, London N6: tours of Western Cemetery; phone (01) 340 1834.

John Ruskin

b. London, 1819; d. Coniston, Cumbria, 1900. *Modern Painters* (1843–60); *The Seven Lamps of Architecture* (1849); *The Stones of Venice* (1851–53); *The Elements of Drawing* (1857); *The Political Economy of Art* (1857); *The Two Paths* (1859); *The Elements of Perspective* (1859); *Unto This Last* (1862); *Essays on Political Economy* (1862–63; retitled *Munera Pulveris*, 1872); *Sesame and Lilies* (1865); *The Ethics of the Dust* (1866); *The Crown of Wild Olive* (1866); *Time and Tide, by Weare and Tyne* (1867); *The Queen of the Air* (1869); *Lectures on Art* (1870); *Fors Clavigera* (1871–78); *Mornings in Florence* (1876–77); *St Mark's Rest* (1884); *Praeterita* (unfinished; 1886–89).

We associate Ruskin's name less readily with Britain than with the Continent—with the landscape of the Alps and the architecture of Venice. In large measure this is perfectly just, and Ruskin himself could on occasion find it necessary to excuse an apparent neglect of his native land and culture. In the Preface to *The Seven Lamps of Architecture* he wrote, perhaps a little lamely: 'I could have wished to have given more examples from our early English Gothic; but I have always found it impossible to work in the cold interior of our cathedrals'. Yet his British roots, admittedly less conspicuous than his joyous, repeated discovery of Switzerland and Italy, still go deep. His life and works bear witness to the importance of his Scottish heritage, his connections with Oxford and, above all, his abiding love of the Lake District.

All of Ruskin's London homes have vanished. The Georgian terrace house at No. 54 Hunter Street, Brunswick Square, where he was born, was demolished in 1969. His two homes in the Camberwell area, then a newly fashionable and pleasantly rural suburb appropriate to a rising business family like the Ruskins, have suffered the same fate. Ruskin's idyllic account of No. 28 Herne Hill, the semi-detached villa where his family lived from 1823 to 1842, makes its disappearance (in 1906) and the radical changes that have since overtaken its neighbourhood all the more regrettable. According to *Praeterita* the house

> commanded, in those comparatively smokeless days, a very notable view from its garret windows, of the Norwood hills on one side, and the winter sunrise over them; and of the valleys of the Thames on the other, with Windsor telescopically clear in the distance, and Harrow, conspicuous always in fine weather to open vision against the summer sunset. It had front and

Ruskin's sketch of his childhood home on Herne Hill

> back garden in sufficient proportion to its size; the front, richly set with old evergreens, and well-grown lilac and laburnum; the back, seventy yards long by twenty wide, renowned all over the hill for its pears and apples, which had been chosen with extreme care by our predecessor … and possessing also a strong old mulberry tree, a tall white-heart cherry tree, a black Kentish one, and an almost unbroken hedge, all round, of alternate gooseberry and currant bush; decked, in due season, (for the ground was wholly beneficent) with magical spendour of abundant fruit: fresh green, soft amber, and rough-bristled crimson bending the spinous branches; clustered pearl and pendant ruby joyfully discoverable under the large leaves that looked like vine. (Vol. 1, Ch. 2)

The house remained in the family's possession after they moved and Ruskin sometimes used it in later years: the passage just quoted was written in his old nursery. The move in 1842 took him and his parents only a short distance north to a larger villa, No. 163 Denmark Hill, where he remained until 1872, the year after his mother's death. *Modern Painters* and *The Stones of Venice* were written in it, for he retained his study even during 1852–54, the period of his marriage when he and his wife lived at No. 30 Herne Hill, next door to his old home. No. 163 was demolished in 1947 but Ruskin's connection with the area is commemorated by Ruskin Park almost opposite the site.

Several London houses where he was a visitor do survive. His close and admiring friendship with Thomas Carlyle (q.v.) brought him frequently to Carlyle's House in Cheyne Row, Chelsea. Dante

Gabriel Rossetti (q.v.), whose Pre-Raphaelite paintings he championed, lived at Tudor House, No. 16 Cheyne Walk nearby from 1862 to 1882. Ruskin even debated lodging with Rossetti but rejected the idea, a wise decision given the contrast between his own finicky temperament and the painter-poet's domestic habits. George MacDonald—novelist, poet and Ruskin's adviser during the emotional turmoil of his middle life—lived from 1868 to 1878 at Kelmscott House (then The Retreat), No. 26 Upper Mall, close to the river in Hammersmith. The house later belonged to William Morris (q.v.).

The Ruskins' Scottish ancestry ensured that he made several childhood visits to 'the good town of Perth', as he remembers it in *Praeterita* (Vol. 1, Ch. 3). Bridgend, his aunt and uncle's home, has gone but No. 10 Rose Terrace on the SW edge of North Inch, where his aunt lived after her husband's death, remains. Ruskin returned to Perth in 1848 to marry Euphemia Gray at her home, Bowerswell, east of the Tay and reached by following the Bowerswell Road towards Kinnoull Hill. His parents did not attend the ceremony, perhaps because the house (formerly owned by the Ruskin family) held unpleasant memories of the suicide of Ruskin's paternal grandfather in 1818. Bowerswell is now an old peoples' home.

Ruskin returned to Scotland in 1853 with Effie, his *protégé* the Pre-Raphaelite painter John Everett Millais and Millais' brother William. The party stayed at remote Glen Finglas, north of The Trossachs in Scotland, where Millais began his famous portrait of Ruskin posed against suitably wild scenery.

On his way north in 1853 Ruskin stayed with his close friend Lady Pauline Trevelyan at the 17C family home of the Trevelyans, *Wallington, 12 miles west of Morpeth in Northumberland. Ruskin's unfinished contribution to William Bell Scott's decoration of the central hall, made on a later visit in 1857, can still be seen. On this occasion he first met Swinburne (q.v.), a man whose morals he deplored but whose poetry he greatly admired. The village of Ford, also in Northumberland (12 miles SW of Berwick-upon-Tweed), was improved on Ruskinian principles by his friend and drawing pupil Louisa, Marchioness of Waterford, of Ford Castle. She painted the murals of biblical scenes in the school.

From the late 1850s onwards much of Ruskin's energy was devoted to his attack on industrialism and to the plight of those 'miserable and abysmal places' the northern cities. The *Ruskin Gallery in Sheffield is a superb monument to his concern. Originally opened by the Guild of St George under his guidance in 1875 and reopened in 1985, at a different location and with some imaginative additions, it displays a remarkable collection intended to stimulate the minds and imaginations of working people: a library, geological specimens, watercolours, manuscripts, plaster casts of architectural details, photographs and prints.

In the years following the annulment of his marriage to Effie (who quickly married Millais) and the years of his unhappy attachment to Rose La Touche, Ruskin formed a close friendship with Lord and Lady Mount-Temple. He was a frequent guest at their home, Broadlands, off A31 south of Romsey in Hampshire, and stayed here while recovering from the shock of Rose La Touche's death in 1875. Broadlands had been the home of Lord Palmerston and later became the home of Lord Mountbatten.

Ruskin's connection with Oxford was renewed in 1869 with his appointment as the first Slade Professor of Art, a post he held until 1878 and again, though with unhappy results, from 1883 to 1885. The

Study by Ruskin of gneiss rock at Glen Finglas (1853)

connection had begun in 1837, when he entered Christ Church as a gentleman commoner, being treated by the young aristocrats who enjoyed that exclusive undergraduate status as 'a good-humoured inoffensive little cur' (*Praeterita*, Vol. 1, Ch. 11) and graduating in 1842 after delays caused by illness. During this period his over-protective mother took lodgings in the High Street. The neo-classical architecture of Peckwater Quad, where he had rooms, was not to his taste, though he could praise the chapel (Oxford Cathedral) for being, despite crudities, 'true, and of its time—not an accursed sham of architect's job' (Vol. 1, Ch. 11). The college's magnificent Tudor hall made him uncomfortable, but for social rather than aesthetic reasons: 'in Cardinal Wolsey's dining-room, I was, in all sorts of ways at once, less than myself, and in all sorts of wrong places at once, out of my place' (Vol. 1, Ch. 11). His interest in Oxford was rekindled by the building in 1855–60 of the *University Museum (originally the Oxford Museum of Natural History) on Parks Road opposite Keble College. Before he came disillusioned with the progress of the work, he enthusiastically approved the Gothic design by Benjamin Woodward, lectured the workmen employed on the project and even, according to tradition, built a brick column that afterwards needed discreet relaying.

In the later years of his professorial appointment Ruskin had rooms in Corpus Christi College, but in early 1871 he lodged at the Crown and Thistle on Bridge Street in Abingdon, south of Oxford. His route into the university allowed him to admire 'the wild hyacinths opening flakes of blue fire in Bagley Wood' (*Fors Clavigera*, Letter 6) and also inspired his famous road-building experiment of 1874. Noticing that the lack of a proper road forced carts to cross and so to damage the village green at North (or Ferry) Hinksey, he tooks lessons in stone-breaking and recruited a working party of undergraduates, including Oscar Wilde (q.v.), to make good the deficiency. The scheme provoked much laughter, both locally and nationally, and Ruskin himself later admitted that the road his pupils constructed was 'about the worst in the three kingdoms'.

The 1870s also reaffirmed the deep and loving connections with the Lake District which had begun with tours in childhood. *Friar's Crag (NT, with a memorial to Ruskin) on the NE shore of Derwentwater had left the most lasting impression:

> The first thing which I remember, as an event in life, was being taken by my nurse to the brow of Friar's Crag on Derwent Water; the intense joy, mingled with awe, that I had in looking through the hollows in the mossy roots, over the crag, into the dark lake, has associated itself more or less with all twining roots of trees ever since. (*Modern Painters*, Vol. 3, Ch. 17)

In 1871 he bought, unseen, the house and estate of Brantwood on the eastern shore of Coniston Water. He lived there first during his Oxford vacations and then permanently, under the care of his cousin Joan Severn, as he sank into old age and engulfing insanity. Badly dilapidated when he bought it, Brantwood is not of architectural interest, though the turret which he added and the lovely *grounds which he laid out, enjoy superb views of the lake and Coniston Old Man (2631ft). Most of the superb art collection which he assembled here was dispersed by the Severns after his death, though the house still has works by Burne-Jones, Samuel Prout and William Henry ('Bird's Nest') Hunt, as well as many paintings and drawings by Ruskin himself, together with personal relics and furniture he transported from Denmark Hill. *The Jumping Jenny*, the boat he designed, and the harbour he constructed for it are also noteworthy.

In the nearby village of Coniston the Ruskin Museum, opened the year after his death, has paintings, drawings, manuscripts, geological specimens from his collection and other relics from Brantwood. Ruskin's grave in the NE corner of the churchyard is marked by a monument, the work of his disciple R.G. Collingwood, featuring emblems of his life and work—most notably a figure of St George on the side facing the Old Man and, on one edge, wild roses in remembrance of Rose La Touche.

Ruskin is also commemorated in Poets' Corner (fee) of Westminster Abbey, suitably close to the tablet honouring a favourite author, Sir Walter Scott (q.v.).

Though not directly connected with Ruskin in his lifetime, one final location should be mentioned. At Bembridge School, on the eastern tip of the Isle of Wight, the Ruskin Galleries house a major collection of manuscripts, drawings and private papers assembled by the school's founder, John Howard Whitehouse.

Carlyle's House, 24 Cheyne Row, Chelsea, London SW3: NT; phone (01) 352 7087.

Wallington, Cambo, Morpeth, Northumberland: NT; phone Scots Gap (067 074) 283.

Ruskin Gallery, 101 Norfolk Street, Sheffield, South Yorkshire: phone (0742) 734781.

Broadlands, Romsey, Hampshire: phone (0794) 516878.

University Museum, Parks Road, Oxford: phone (0865) 272950.

Brantwood, Coniston, Cumbria: phone (0966) 41396.

Ruskin Museum, The Institute, Yewdale Road, Coniston, Cumbria: phone (053 94) 41387.

Ruskin Galleries, Bembridge School, near Bembridge, Isle of Wight: visitors by appointment with the Curator; phone (0893) 872101.

Sir Walter Scott

b. Edinburgh, 1771; d. Abbotsford, Borders Region, 1832. *The Eve of Saint John: A Border Ballad* (1800); *Minstrelsy of the Scottish Border* (1802); *The Lay of the Last Minstrel* (1805); *Ballads and Lyrical Pieces* (1806); *Marmion: A Tale of Flodden Field* (1808); *The Lady of the Lake* (1810); *English Minstrelsy* (1810); *The Vision of Don Roderick* (1811); *Rokeby* (1813); *The Bridal of Triermain: or The Vale of St John, in Three Cantos* (1813); *Waverley: or 'Tis Sixty Years Since* (1814); *Guy Mannering: or The Astrologer* (1815); *The Lord of the Isles* (1815); *The Field of Waterloo* (1815); *The Antiquary* (1816); *Tales of My Landlord, Collected and Arranged by Jedediah Cleishbotham* (*The Black Dwarf* and *Old Mortality*; 1816); *Harold the Dauntless* (1817); *Rob Roy* (1818); *Tales of My Landlord: Second Series* (*The Heart of Midlothian*; 1818); *Tales of My Landlord: Third Series* (*The Bride of Lammermoor* and *A Legend of Montrose*; 1819); *Ivanhoe* (1820); *The Monastery* (1820); *The Abbot* (1820); *Kenilworth* (1821); *The Pirate* (1822); *The Fortunes of Nigel* (1822); *Halidon Hill: A Dramatic Sketch* (1822); *Peveril of the Peak* (1822); *Quentin Durward* (1823); *St Ronan's Well* (1824); *Redgauntlet: A Tale of the Eighteenth Century* (1824); *Tales of the Crusaders* (*The Betrothed* and *The Talisman*; 1825); *Woodstock: or The Cavalier* (1826); *Chronicles of the Canongate* (*The Highland Widow*, *The Two Drovers* and *The Surgeon's Daughter*; 1827); *Tales of a Grandfather: Being Stories Taken from Scottish History* (1828; second series, 1829; third series, 1830; fourth series, 1831); *Chronicles of the Canongate: Second Series* (*The Fair Maid of Perth*; 1828); *Anne of Geierstein: or The Maiden of the Mist* (1829); *Letters on Demonology and Witchcraft* (1830); *Tales of My Landlord: Fourth Series* (*Count Robert of Paris* and *Castle Dangerous*; 1832).

Today, when Scott's poetry is usually forgotten and most of his novels are on their way to oblivion, it is hard to appreciate the reputation he once enjoyed. Although he modestly described himself as being beaten out of the field of poetry by Byron (q.v.) and generously praised Jane Austen (q.v.) for her delineation of ordinary life, he effortlessly outdistanced both these writers in his appeal to the reading public of his day. Scott's day, in fact, was a long one: to Dickens and George Eliot (qq.v.) he was still the acknowledged master of the genre in which they worked. If his popularity has faded, it has left its lasting influence. Scott wrote at a time when the fashion for wild landscape and for picturesque evidence of the medieval past was in the ascendant, and he gave this taste a local form and shape. His poems and novels sent people out to look at abbeys and views, castles and waterfalls, adding items to a tourist map we still in large part observe even when we forget the name of Scott. Perhaps the most striking aspect of his achievement was in changing the English attitude to Scotland. Scottish landscape had long been regarded as merely barren and its culture as suspect, attitudes which Bonnie Prince Charlie's rebellion not only intensified but promoted to official doctrine. Living when time had begun to lend the events of 1745 a romantic charm, Scott could make his country's history fashionable—a triumph neatly epitomised by his success in persuading George IV to wear the once forbidden tartan during his visit to Scotland.

The Old Tolbooth Prison, Edinburgh: an illustration to the edition of The Heart of Midlothian *published by A & C Black in 1860*

**Edinburgh was the city not only of Scott's birth but also of his working life as advocate and author. The obvious place to start a walking tour is the Scott Monument (1840–44, by George Kemp) on the south side of Princes Street. The novelist sits with his dog Maida beside him under a Gothic canopy and spire; historical figures and characters from his novels are depicted in the niches. Our first excursion takes us north into the Georgian New Town, still being developed during Scott's lifetime. We begin by walking west along Princes Street, turn right into Hanover Street and then take a left on George Street, where Scott lived at No. 107 soon after his marriage in 1797. On its south side is the 18C Music Hall where, at a banquet in 1827, Scott first emerged from his technical anonymity as 'The Great Unknown' and publicly acknowledged the 'Waverley' novels as his own. On that occasion he modestly echoed Macbeth's words:

> I am afraid to think what I have done;
> Look on't again I dare not.

George Street leads west to Castle Street, where he lived at No. 10 and No. 39, the latter being his home from 1802 until his financial crash in 1826. These were the years when the steady stream of poetry and novels issuing from his pen made him the most prominent figure in Edinburgh's—indeed, in Scotland's—literary life. Visitors to Castle Street included the peasant poet James Hogg (q.v.), who astonished the company by stretching full length on the sofa in imitation of Scott's wife, and George Crabbe (q.v.). Crabbe's stay in 1822 coincided awkwardly with the arrival of George IV in Edinburgh, an event that gave Scott particular pride. He returned hurriedly after greeting his sovereign with the glass from which the King had drunk stowed safely in his formal clothes:

> The royal gift was forgotten—the ample skirt of the coat within which it had been packed, and which he had hitherto held cautiously in front of his person, slipped back to its more usual position—he sat down beside Crabbe, and the glass was crushed to atoms. His scream and gesture made his wife conclude that he had sat down on a pair of scissors, or the like; but very little harm had been done except the breaking of the glass, of which alone he had been thinking.

From the north end of Castle Street we turn right on Queen Street. The Scottish National Portrait Gallery, next to the Queen Street branch of the Royal Museum of Scotland, contains portraits of Scott by *Raeburn and Andrew Geddes. The early 19C church of St Paul and St George, in Queen Street's eastern continuation as York Place, preserves the writer's customary pew. From here we can return directly to Princes Street on Leith Street, but a more interesting route goes south from York Place on St Andrew Street, cuts across St Andrew Square and completes the walk on St David Street.

The second part of our walking tour leads south from Princes Street into the Old Town. The Mound, almost opposite Hanover Street, quickly brings us to Lady Stair's House, a much restored 17C building which is now a museum devoted to Robert Burns and Robert Louis Stevenson (qq.v.) as well as Scott. From the museum Lawnmarket and Castle Hill, part of Edinburgh's Royal Mile, lead to the Castle. Always patriotic and always fascinated by his country's history, Scott instigated the search for the traditional Scottish Regalia (or 'Honours of Scotland')—including the crown, sceptre and sword—which had been forgotten since the Act of Union in 1707. They were discovered in 1818 and are now on display in the Crown Room. Mons Meg, the historic cannon exhibited in the dungeons (or French Prison) below the Old Parliament Hall, was returned from the Tower of London as a result of Scott's request to George IV during his royal visit in 1822. Its history is described in a note to Chapter 27 of *Rob Roy*.

We now return along Castle Hill and Lawnmarket, and take George IV Bridge to the right. Chambers Street, on the left, occupies the site of College Wynd, the street where Scott was born. The birthplace was demolished during his lifetime. The Old College of Edinburgh University at the end of Chambers Street was begun by Robert Adam in 1789 to replace the much humbler buildings Scott attended (1783–85). At the southern end of George IV Bridge is the church of the 17C Covenanters, Greyfriars Kirk. The writer's father, also Walter, is buried in its churchyard. Further south is George Square, a handsome 18C addition to the city whose dignity has been lessened by the university buildings which now occupy two of its sides. No. 25 was Scott's home from infancy, when his family moved from College Wynd, until his marriage in 1797.

From George Square we return north to the junction with Lawnmarket, and follow High Street eastwards. On the right we find Parliament Square, dominated by St Giles. In the western part of the square an arrangement of cobblestones marks the site of the old Tolbooth Prison, demolished in 1817, which gave its name to *The Heart of Midlothian*. The novel begins with an account of the Porteous Riots (1736) here. The south side of the square is occupied by Parliament House, a 17C building whose exterior was disguised by the addition of an Italianate façade in the early 19C. As headquarters of the Court of Session and the High Court it was familiar to Scott during his years as an attorney.

On Canongate, the eastern continuation of the High Street, we find the 17C Huntly House, now home of the City Museum, whose collection includes Scott relics. The tour ends at Holyrood Palace (formally the Palace of Holyrood House), whose double connection with Scott neatly illustrates the two aspects of his temperament. The fact that the Young Pretender, Princes Charles Edward Stuart, held court here in 1745 stirred his imagination and he recreated the scene in Chapter 43 of *Waverley*. But for all his attraction to Jacobitism, he was both a political realist and a loyal Hanoverian, and he proudly attended the state occasions in the Palace during George IV's Edinburgh visit. The King, who had made Scott a baronet in 1818, regarded him as 'the man in Scotland I most wish to see'.

Although Edinburgh was the scene of Scott's professional life, his heart lay in the Border Country he came to love in childhood and chose for home in middle age. The chief interest and the obvious starting point of a tour is his country estate at *Abbotsford, near Galashiels 29 miles SE of Edinburgh via A7. He bought the modest farm, set among fine countryside by his beloved Tweed, in 1811 and renamed it Abbotsford because the monks from Melrose Abbey used to cross the river here. In the years that followed he enlarged the estate and had, by 1822, demolished the original farmhouse to create the present splendid mansion. In a letter of 1824 he could, with justice, say of his achievement what Augustus had said of Rome: he had found it brick and left it marble. Abbotsford satisfied Scott's ambition of becoming a laird, the founder of a dynasty, and the life he led there smacked more of the country gentleman than the relentlessly busy novelist. Writing was reserved for the early morning and it is said that his sons took some time to realise their father was a successful author as well as landed proprietor. When Scott's finances crashed in 1826 he offered Abbotsford to his creditors but they refused it. He spent his last years struggling to fulfil the famous promise that his right hand would work off his debts. In 1831, suffering from gall stones and the effect of several strokes, he embarked on a Mediterranean cruise but returned to die at Abbotsford the following year.

Abbotsford and its contents have been remarkably well preserved, allowing the visitor to appreciate the expressive statement that the house embodied—a statement of taste as well as wealth and gentility. The 'Waverley' novels probably did more than any other single force to encourage nostalgia for the Middle Ages, and Scott chose to build in the medieval style later known as 'Scottish Baronial'. The interior is lavishly filled with armour and heraldic devices. Yet the fanciful pinnacles and Gothic corridors were discreetly combined with the modern conveniences that appealed to an Edinburgh lawyer who believed in rational progress. There is a steam central heating system, and the servants' bells work by air compression. The contents of Abbotsford remind us that Scott was also an indefatigable collector of souvenirs and mementoes: Napoleon's cloak clasp, Rob Roy's purse and sword, Burns' tumbler and a lock of the Young Pretender's hair are on display. The library has a fine portrait of Scott by Raeburn and a bust by Chantrey.

From Abbotsford we may explore the surrounding Border Country in two tours. The first (65 miles) begins by taking A6091 east to *Melrose Abbey, notable for its delicate stone carving. *The Lay of the Last Minstrel* praises its lovely east window:

The Moon on the east oriel shone
Through slender shafts of stately stone,
    By foliaged tracery combined;
Thou would'st have thought some fairy's hand
'Twixt poplars straight the osier wand
In many a freakish knot, had twined;
Then framed a spell, when the work was done,
And changed the willow wreathes to stone.
(Canto 1, stanza 11)

Scott was in the habit of showing it to his guests, like Wordsworth and his sister Dorothy, who came in 1803 (s.v. Lake Poets, Rte 14). We then continue SE, joining A68, to St Boswells, where we follow B6404 and then take a left on B6356 for *Dryburgh Abbey, beautifully sited in a loop of the Tweed. Scott is buried in the Abbey Church. 2 miles north on B6356 is *Scott's View, a lovely panorama of the Tweed and the Eildon Hills, where it is said that the horses pulling his hearse stopped out of habit.

From here we return south to B6404, which is followed to the junction with B6397, where a left turn brings us to Smailholm (8 miles). As an infant Scott was brought here to his grandfather's farm, Sandyknowe, and he later remembered the attempts made to cure the lameness that poliomyelitis had caused:

some one had recommended that so often as a sheep was killed for the use of the family, I should be stripped, and swathed up in the skin warm as it was flayed from the carcass of the animal. In this Tartar-like habilment I well remember lying upon the floor of the little parlour in the farmhouse, while my grandfather, a venerable old man with white hair, used every excitement to make me try to crawl.

Robert Scott's land included a charming 16C Border tower perched on a little hill by a small loch, and in the introduction to Canto 3 of *Marmion* Scott looked back on the days when he had

        thought that shatter'd tower
The mightiest work of human power;
And marvell'd as the aged hind
With some strange tale bewitch'd my mind,
Of forayers, who, with headlong force,
Down from that strength had spurr'd their horse,
Their southern rapine to renew,
Far in the distant Cheviots blue,
And home returning, fill'd the hall
With revels, wassel-rout, and brawl.
(lines 176–185)

From Smailholm we return SE, joining A6089 to Kelso (5 miles). Scott first came to this charming little town by the confluence of the

Teviot and the Tweed in 1783, when he briefly attended the grammar school and met James Ballantyne, later to be printer of his first books and his partner in business. Scott returned to Kelso in 1785, when he was eighteen, to stay with his uncle, Captain Robert Scott.

10 miles SW of Kelso via A698 and A68 is Jedburgh, where he made his first appearance as an advocate in 1793, the year after he had been admitted to the Bar. In 1803 he visited Wordsworth and his sister Dorothy at their lodging, No. 5 Abbey Close, and read them his *Lay of the Last Minstrel* (s.v. Lake Poets, Rte 14).

Further SW (via A68, A6088 and B6357) lies Liddesdale, the lovely region that Scott toured in the 1790s, collecting ballads for his *Minstrelsy of the Scottish Border*, the work that first brought him to public attention. Among the sights he visited is the romantic Hermitage Castle, 13C–14C stronghold of the Soulis family. We reach it by turning north from B6357 on B6399, a journey of 28 miles from Jedburgh.

The second tour from Abbotsford, some 75 miles in all, begins by taking A7 south to Selkirk (4 miles). Scott knew the town well from his duties as Sheriff of Selkirkshire, a post he held from 1800 until his death. A statue stands in the Market Place outside the former Court House, now the Town Hall. Bowhill, 2 miles west via A708 near the confluence of the Ettrick and the Yarrow, was the home of the Scotts of Buccleuch, whom Scott regarded as the head of his clan. The present building was begun in 1795 by the third Duke, to whom *Minstrelsy of the Scottish Border* was dedicated. Scott knew it well—his horse would turn up the avenue by habit—and it has relics of him as well as a fine art collection. Nearby Newark Castle, seen across the valley, is the setting for *The Lay of the Last Minstrel*. Wordsworth (s.v. Lake Poets, Rte 14) walked among the ruins with Scott in 1831. 'Yarrow Revisited' records Wordsworth's last impression of his friend, then obviously exhausted and near death.

A708 continues SE into the lovely valley of the Yarrow, associated like its sister valley of the Ettrick, with Scott's *protégé*, James Hogg. Like Hogg, Scott was a patron of Tibbie Shiel's Inn at the southern end of St Mary's Loch (8 miles). A708 then descends to Moffat, where we take A701 north and branch right up the Tweed valley via B712 to A72 (42 miles). Four miles east we find Neidpath Castle, home of the notorious fourth Duke of Queensberry, whom Scott visited. South of A72 8 miles further east is Traquair, claimed as the oldest continuously inhabited house in Scotland and as the original of 'Tully-Veolan', the seat of the Baron of Bradwardine in *Waverley* (Chs 8 and 9). The journey, which is now leading us back towards Abbotsford, is completed by a glimpse of Ashietiel, the house Scott rented from 1804 to 1812. It lies on the south bank of the Tweed about 7 miles east of Traquair.

Although Scott's name is most indelibly stamped on the Border Country near Abbotsford, his use of The Trossachs as setting for *The Lady of the Lake* and his romantic tale of the 18C outlaw Rob Roy MacGregor played a vital role in attracting tourists to the region. Its lochs and wooded countryside were already to the Romantic taste—Wordsworth and Coleridge had come on a walking tour in 1803 (s.v. Lake Poets, Rte 15)—but later visitors, like Ruskin (q.v.), saw them through Scott's eyes. A tour of the area may begin at Aberfoyle (off A81 27 miles north of Glasgow), where the name of the hotel recalls that in Scott's novel Bailie Nichol Jarvie met Rob Roy here (Chs 28–30). The waterfall at Ledard near the northern shore of Loch Ard (off B829 4 miles west of Aberfoyle) suggested the setting for Flora

MacIvor's harp-playing in *Waverley* (Ch. 22). Scott later regretted the theatricality of the episode but defended the beauty of the waterfall: 'It is upon a small scale, but otherwise one of the most exquisite cascades it is possible to behold'. A821 leads north from Aberfoyle into The Trossachs (5 miles), the gorge whose name means 'bristly country' separating Loch Katrine and Loch Achray. In *Rob Roy* Francis Osbaldistone describes his first view of this area:

Loch Katrine, engraved from a sketch by Thomas Allom in William Beattie's Scotland Illustrated *(1838)*

> Our route, though leading towards the lake, had hitherto been so much shaded by wood, that we only from time to time obtained a glimpse of that beautiful sheet of water. But the road now suddenly emerged from the forest ground, and, winding close by the margin of the loch, afforded us a full view of its spacious mirror, which now, the breeze having totally subsided, reflected in still magnificence the high dark heathy mountains, huge grey rocks, and shaggy banks by which it is encircled. The hills now sunk on its margin so closely, and were so broken and precipitous, as to afford no passage except just upon the narrow line of the track which we occupied, and which was overhung with rocks ... Add to this, that, as the road winded round every promontory and bay which indented the lake, there was rarely a possibility of seeing a hundred yards before us. (Ch. 30)

•Loch Katrine is best seen from a cruise on the suitably named *Sir Walter Scott*, which in summer makes the journey several times each day from the pier to Stronachlachar on the western shore. Ellen's Isle, named after the heroine of *The Lady of the Lake*, can also be seen by taking the road one mile north from the car park and pier to the Silver Strand (no cars). A821 east to Callander (8 miles) gives a fine journey along the northern shores of Loch Achray and Loch Venachar.

Two other places in Scotland demand mention. Glasgow, beating Edinburgh to the honour by several years, was in 1837 the first city to erect a statue of Scott. In George Square the figure by John Greenshields stands on top of a column originally intended for George III. Perth, by the Firth of Tay on the east coast, is proud of Scott's treatment of its history in *The Fair Maid of Perth*. North Inch, the 100-acre park by the Tay, was the scene of the Clan Combat of 1396 described in the novel (Ch. 34). The Fair Maid's House on Blackfriars Wynd is a rebuilt version of the one occupied by Simon Glover and his daughter Catharine.

Neither Scott's life nor the antiquarian interests so richly expressed in his fiction was by any means confined to Scotland. The English places associated with his name may briefly be listed region by region, proceeding from north to south.

In Northern England there are two important landmarks near his beloved Border Country. Norham Castle, once the stronghold of the Bishop Princes of Durham, is the setting for the first Canto of *Marmion*. It lies off A698 7 miles SW of Berwick-upon-Tweed. The second Canto of *Marmion* takes place in the ruined 11C Benedictine Priory at Lindisfarne, or Holy Island: 'A solemn, huge, and dark-red pile,/ Placed on the margin of the isle' (stanza 9). The island is reached by the causeway from Beal (near A1 8 miles south of Berwick-upon-Tweed).

In 1809 and 1812 Scott visited his friend J.B.S. Morritt at Rokeby Park near Greta Bridge, on A66 9 miles NW of Scotch Corner and the A1. The house is a Palladian mansion built for himself by the amateur architect Sir Thomas Robinson in 1735. The park and surrounding landscape appear in *Rokeby*, Scott's poem set during the Civil War; the subject of the lovely song 'Brignall Banks' lies about 2 miles SW.

Scott's life connected him with the Lake District in several ways. Carlisle (off M6) was the scene of his courtship and marriage. His wife, Charlotte Charpentier, lodged at No. 81 Castle Street and the couple were married in Carlisle Cathedral on Christmas Eve 1797. In *Waverley* (Ch. 49) the hero visits the Jacobite rebel Fergus MacIvor when he is imprisoned in the Norman keep of the Castle. Further south, Scott was a guest of both Wordsworth and Southey (s.v. Lake Poets, Rtes 12A and 12C). The lovely Vale of St John, SE of Keswick, is setting for *The Bridal of Triermain*. The poem describes the legends connected with the Castle Rock, whose

crags so rudely piled,
At distance seen, resemblance wild
To a rough fortress bore.
(Canto 3, stanza 4)

Scott's 'Helvellyn', like Wordsworth's 'Fidelity', was inspired by the death of Charles Gough on Helvellyn, reached from the western shore of Ullswater (see Lake Poets, Rte 12B). In 1825 his friend John Wilson, better remembered as 'Christopher North' of *Blackwood's Edinburgh Magazine*, honoured his fifty-fourth birthday with a regatta on Windermere. Scott watched it from Storrs Point, on the eastern shore 2 miles south of Bowness-on-Windermere.

The Isle of Man, off the west coast of Cumbria but nowadays reached from Heysham, Fleetwood or Liverpool, appears in one of his late novels, *Peveril of the Peak*. Peel Castle on its west coast is introduced as 'one of those singular monuments of antiquity with which this singular and interesting island abounds' (Vol. 3, Ch. 3). Julian Peveril and Fenella escape by boat from Fenella's Tower in Volume 3, Chapter 7.

Yorkshire is the setting for much of *Ivanhoe*, Scott's first and probably his most successful English historical novel. 'Templestowe', where Sir Brian-de-Bois-Guilbert holds Rebecca captive, is based on the earlier house on the site of the 17C Temple Newsam, near the River Aire east of Leeds. *Conisbrough Castle, home of Rowena's intended husband Athelstane, survives and its superb keep is quite as magnificent as Scott suggests, even if he wrongly insisted on its being Saxon rather than Norman:

> There are few more beautiful or striking scenes in England than are presented by the vicinity of this ancient Saxon fortress. The soft and gentle river Don sweeps through an amphitheatre, in which cultivation is richly blended with woodland, and on a mount, ascending from the river, well defended by walls and ditches, rises this ancient edifice, which, as its Saxon name implies, was, previous to the Conquest, a royal residence of the kings of England. The outer walls have probably been added by the Normans, but the inner keep bears token of very great antiquity. It is situated on a mount at one angle of the inner court, and forms a complete circle of perhaps twenty-five feet in diameter. The wall is of immense thickness, and is propped or defended by six huge external buttresses which project from the circle, and rise up against the sides of the tower as if to strengthen or to support it. These massive buttresses are solid when they arise from the foundation, and a good way higher up; but are hollowed out towards the top, and terminate in a sort of turrets communicating with the interior of the keep itself. The distant appearance of this huge building, with these singular accompaniments, is as interesting to the lovers of the picturesque, as the interior of the castle is to the eager antiquary. (Ch. 41)

The Castle is on A630 5 miles SW of Doncaster and A1.

The most memorable episode of *Ivanhoe* takes place in Central England. Prince John's tournament (Chs 7–13) is held on the field 1 mile north of Ashby-de-la-Zouch, on A50 between Leicester and Burton upon Trent. Scott, however, is careful to point out that the castle where Prince John holds his festival after the tournament is 'not the same building of which the stately ruins still interest the traveller' (Ch. 14).

The rest of Central England is the territory of *Kenilworth* and *Woodstock*, novels whose 19C popularity vied even with Shakespeare's reputation in attracting visitors to the area. In Kenilworth itself (on A452 and A46 between Coventry and Royal Leamington Spa) Scott stayed at the King's Arms Hotel, where his room is still pointed out. His novel recreated the splendour of the Castle in the time of Queen Elizabeth, most notably by its description of the revels in Chapter 35. The same novel made adroit use of the legend which associated Charlecote Park, outside Stratford-upon-Avon, with Shakespeare (q.v., Rte 7). *Woodstock* takes as its scene the vanished royal manor (built by Henry I) on A34 30 miles SE of Stratford and 8 miles NW of Oxford. Its deer park was assimilated into the grounds of Blenheim Palace. The legends connected with Wayland's Smithy, the striking dolmen in the Vale of the White Horse (off B4507 4 miles west of Wantage), are adapted to help the plot of *Kenilworth* (see especially Chs 9–11).

Scott first saw London at the age of four and, returning some twenty-five years later, was surprised to discover how accurate his memory of Westminster Abbey had been. Fittingly, he is now honoured by a prominent memorial in Poets' Corner (fee).

Scottish National Portrait Gallery, 1 Queen Street, Edinburgh: phone (031) 556 8921.

Lady Stair's House, Lady Stair's Close, Lawnmarket, Edinburgh: phone (031) 225 2424, extension 6593.

Edinburgh Castle: Historic Buildings and Monuments, Scottish Development Department; phone the enquiry desk in Edinburgh, (031) 244 3101.

Huntly House Museum, 142 Canongate, Edinburgh: phone (031) 225 2424, extension 6689.

Palace of Holyroodhouse, Royal Mile, Edinburgh: phone (031) 556 7371.

Abbotsford House, Melrose, Borders Region: phone (0896) 2043.

Melrose Abbey, Melrose, Borders Region: Historic Buildings and Monuments, Scottish Development Department; phone the enquiry desk in Edinburgh, (031) 244 3101.

Dryburgh Abbey, near St Boswells, Borders Region: Historic Buildings and Monuments, Scottish Development Department; phone the enquiry desk in Edinburgh, (031) 244 3101.

Smailholm Tower, near Smailholm, Borders Region: Historic Buildings and Monuments, Scottish Development Department; phone the enquiry desk in Edinburgh, (031) 244 3101.

Hermitage Castle, Liddesdale, Borders Region: Historic Buildings and Monuments, Scottish Development Department; phone the enquiry desk in Edinburgh, (031) 244 3101.

Bowhill, near Selkirk, Borders Region: phone (0750) 20732.

Newark Castle, near Bowhill, Selkirk, Borders Region: key available from the Buccleuch Estates, Bowhill; visitors are advised to phone in advance, (0750) 20753.

Neidpath Castle, Peebles, Borders Region: phone Aberlady (087 57) 201.

Traquair, Innerleithen, Borders Region: phone (0896) 830323.

Norham Castle: Norham, Northumberland: English Heritage, standard opening; phone (029 982) 329.

Lindisfarne Priory, Lindisfarne (Holy Island), Northumberland: English Heritage, standard opening; phone (028 989) 200.

Rokeby Park, Greta Bridge, near Barnard Castle, County Durham: phone Barnard Castle (10833) 37334.

Carlisle Castle, Carlisle, Cumbria: English Heritage, standard opening; phone (0228) 31777.

Peel Castle, Peel, Isle of Man: phone Peel Tourist Information Centre, (062 484) 2341.

Temple Newsam, Leeds, West Yorkshire: phone (0532) 647321.

Conisbrough Castle, Conisbrough, South Yorkshire: English Heritage, standard opening; phone (070 986) 3329.

Ashby-de-la-Zouch Castle, Ashby-de-la-Zouch, Leicestershire: English Heritage, standard opening; phone (0530) 413343.

Kenilworth Castle, Kenilworth, Warwickshire: English Heritage, standard opening; phone (0926) 52078.

Charlecote Park, Wellesbourne, near Stratford-upon-Avon, Warwickshire: NT; phone (0789) 840277.

Blenheim Palace, Woodstock, Oxfordshire: phone (0993) 811325.

Wayland's Smithy, near Ashbury, Oxfordshire: English Heritage, open at any reasonable time.

George Bernard Shaw

b. Dublin, 1856; d. Ayot St Lawrence, Hertfordshire, 1950. *Cashel Byron's Profession* (1886); *An Unsocial Socialist* (1887); *The Quintessence of Ibsenism* (1891; revised, 1913); *Widowers' Houses* (1893); *The Perfect Wagnerite* (1898); *Arms and the Man* (1898); *Candida* (1898); *Mrs Warren's Profession* (1898); *You Never Can Tell* (1898); *The Devil's Disciple* (1901); *Caesar and Cleopatra* (1901); *Man and Superman* (1903); *John Bull's Other Island* (1907); *Major Barbara* (1907); *The Doctor's Dilemma* (1908); *Misalliance* (1911); *Androcles and the Lion* (1912); *Pygmalion* (1913); *Heartbreak House* (1919); *Back to Methusaleh* (1921); *Saint Joan* (1924); *The Intelligent Woman's Guide to Socialism and Capitalism* (1928); *The Apple Cart* (1929); *The Adventures of the Black Girl in Search of Her God* (1932); *Too True To Be Good* (1934).

Shaw's birthplace in Dublin at No. 33 (then No. 3) Synge Street, SW of St Stephen's Green, is marked with a plaque. His childhood in this modest house was quietly unhappy, overshadowed by his father's habitual drunkenness and his mother's cold, unloving manner. The dreariness of his circumstances was partly relieved after 1866, when the family was able to take a Torca Cottage on the coast at Dalkey, SE of the city, with its fine views of Dublin Bay. Shaw retained enough affection for his native city to bequeath one third of his estate to the National Gallery of Ireland, on Merrion Square (West); there is a statue of him by the entrance.

In 1872 his mother took her two daughters to London, leaving her husband and son behind. After working for an estate agent, Shaw followed her in 1876. From 1887 until his marriage in 1898 they lived together at No. 29 Fitzroy Square, south of Euston Road west of its junction with Tottenham Court Road, and now marked with a plaque. His own description of himself (in *Sixteen Self-Sketches*) as sponging ruthlessly off his mother during these years is a characteristic exaggeration, but the account of his long disheartening struggle to make his way as a writer is not. After his failure as a novelist he turned to reviewing art, music and, eventually, drama; it was not until the 1890s, when he was in his forties, that he began to be recognised as a playwright. The most important scene of his success is the Royal Court Theatre in Sloane Square, Chelsea (between Knightsbridge and the King's Road). His connection with the Royal Court and its adventurous manager, Harley Granville-Barker, began with the production of *Candida* in 1904. In the years that followed Shaw was a close friend of the actress Mrs Patrick Campbell, the first Eliza Doolittle, whose home was at No. 33 Kensington Square (south of Kensington High Street via Young Street).

By this time he had cured the shyness from which he suffered in youth, to become an effective speaker and campaigner on behalf of Socialism. His friends in the Fabian Society included H.G. Wells (q.v.) as well as Beatrice and Sidney Webb. The interest in politics can be traced back to visits to William Morris (q.v.) at his house in Hammersmith.

After his marriage to Charlotte Payne-Townshend, Shaw lived at Adelphi Terrace (between the Strand and Victoria Embankment Gardens), an address favoured by several literary men of his generation. James Barrie (q.v.) was a neighbour but never an intimate friend.

The Shaws kept their London flat but after 1906 made their main home in Hertfordshire at Ayot St Lawrence (near A1 4 miles NW of Welwyn Garden City). Shaw's Corner is hardly an attractive house but it is impeccably respectable. It reminds the visitor of that streak of conventionality, even Puritanism, which underlay his flamboyantly eccentric views about diet, dress and medicine—about, indeed, any subject on which the Press cared to ask his opinion. On his death in 1950 his ashes were scattered in the garden and the house itself bequeathed to the National Trust. It remains virtually unaltered since his day, its atmosphere still bespeaking the organised regime which Charlotte imposed on her husband's rather disorderly habits. In the garden is the summerhouse where Shaw did much of his writing, safe from the possibility of interruption by visitors.

Shaw became a friend of Sir Edward Elgar through his involvement in the Malvern Festival, which Barry Jackson established in 1929 as a showcase for Shaw's work. The festival is still held each year, in late May–early June at Great Malvern in the hills west of Worcester, with Shaw's plays and Elgar's music taking a prominent place in the programme.

National Gallery of Ireland, Merrion Square (West), Dublin: phone (01) 615133.

Shaw's Corner, Ayot St Lawrence, near Welwyn, Hertfordshire: NT; phone Stevenage (0438) 820307.

Percy Bysshe Shelley

b. Field Place, West Sussex, 1792; d. Gulf of Spezia, Italy, 1822. *Original Poetry by Victor and Cazire* (with Elizabeth Shelley; 1810); *The Necessity of Atheism* (with Thomas Jefferson Hogg; 1811); *A Poetical Essay on the Existing State of Things* (1811); *An Address to the Irish People* (1812); *Declaration of Rights* (1812); *The Devil's Walk: A Ballad* (1812); *Queen Mab: A Philosophical Poem, with Notes* (1813); *A Refutation of Deism, In a Dialogue* (1814); *Alastor: or The Spirit of Solitude, and Other Poems* (1816); *A Proposal for Putting Reform to the Vote Throughout the Kingdom, by the Hermit of Marlow* (1817); *An Address to The People on the Death of Princess Charlotte, by the Hermit of Marlow* (1817); *History of a Six Weeks' Tour Through a Part of France, Switzerland, Germany and Holland* (with Mary Wollstonecraft Shelley; 1817); *The Revolt of Islam: A Poem in Twelve Cantos* (originally called *Laon and Cythna*; 1818); *Rosalind and Helen: A Modern Eclogue; with Other Poems* (1819); *The Cenci: A Tragedy in Five Acts* (1819); *Prometheus Unbound: A Lyrical Drama in Four Acts, with Other Poems* (1820); *Oedipus Tyrannus or Swellfoot the Tyrant: A Tragedy in Two Acts* (1820); *Epipsychidion* (1821); *Adonais: An Elegy on the Death of John Keats* (1821); *Hellas: A Lyrical Drama* (1822); *The Mask of Anarchy* (1832); *Defence of Poetry* (1840); *A Philosophical View of Reform* (1920).

Field Place, where Shelley was born, is a modest country house near Broadbridge Heath, NW of Horsham in West Sussex. Here the poet and his sister Elizabeth wrote the youthful verses for which they adopted the pseudonyms 'Victor' and 'Cazire'. His youthful radicalism and marriage to Harriet Westbrook alienated Shelley from his father, Sir Timothy, and he was refused admission to the house in 1815 when he arrived for the reading of his grandfather's will. He spent the afternoon in the grounds reading Milton's *Comus*.

During his years at Eton College (1804–10) Shelley's opinions and his love of explosive chemical experiments earned him the nicknames of 'Mad Shelley' and 'Atheist Shelley' from his fellow pupils. The school is west of London and most easily reached from Junction 6 of M4.

Shelley's undergraduate career at University College, Oxford, continued the pattern he had established at Eton and so was brief but spectacular. Shortly after his entrance in October 1810 he sent copies of his anonymous pamphlet, *The Necessity of Atheism*, to the heads of the Colleges. Questioned about its authorship, he refused to answer and was expelled in March 1811. Thomas Jefferson Hogg, fellow student, fellow radical and co-author, suffered the same fate. The modern visitor to the College can find a memorial of 1893, originally intended for the Protestant Cemetery in Rome, by following a passage from the NW corner of Front Quad. The dome is by Basil Champneys and the effigy of the drowned poet by Onslow Ford.

After Oxford Shelley's life was restless and mobile; many of the places he visited preserve no trace of his brief residence. He first met Harriet Westbrook in London in 1811, when he was lodging at No. 15 Poland Street, south of Oxford Street. He returned to the area in 1814 to resolemnise their Scottish marriage at St George's, Hanover Square, SW of Oxford Circus. The ceremony made their marriage legally binding but no more successful, for he left her less than a month afterwards. The curious and unhappy story ended in Hyde Park to the SW, where Harriet drowned herself in the Serpentine some two years later.

In London Shelley also met his second wife Mary, daughter of the radical philosopher William Godwin and the feminist Mary Wollstonecraft. The couple declared their love for each other in June 1814, beside her mother's grave in the churchyard of St Pancras Old Church, on Pancras Road north of the railway station. Mary Wollstonecraft's remains were later transferred to Bournemouth (see below) and the churchyard is now a public garden. Mary Shelley returned to London in the long years of her widowhood, and died at No. 24 Chester Square, near Eaton Square in Belgravia.

In Hampstead Shelley visited Leigh Hunt (q.v.) at his cottage in the Vale of Health, reached from East Heath Road. His host introduced him to Keats (q.v.), but the two poets never became close friends and Keats later declined an invitation to stay with Shelley.

In the winter of 1811–12 he took Harriet Westbrook to Keswick in the Lake District, renting what is now known as Shelley's Cottage on Chestnut Hill. He wrote enthusiastically of his surroundings:

> Oh! how you will delight in this scenery. The mountains are now capped with snow. The lake [Derwentwater] as I see it here is glassy and calm. Snow vapours tinted by the loveliest refractions pass far below the summit of these gigantic rocks. The scene even in winter is inexpressibly lovely. The clouds assume shapes which seem peculiar to these regions … Oh! give me a little cottage in *that* scene, let all live in peaceful little houses, let temples and palaces rot with their perishing masters.

He had been drawn to the area by the presence of the Lake Poets (q.v., Rte 12A) but Coleridge was absent and Wordsworth oblivious of his existence, so he met only Southey, then living at nearby Greta Hall. The older writer's radicalism had waned with the years and he was made uncomfortable by the presence of a youth who 'acts upon me as my own ghost would do'.

Shelley's relations with Thomas Love Peacock (q.v.) were considerably warmer, despite the portrait of Scythrop Glowry in *Nightmare Abbey*. In 1816 he visited Peacock at Marlow, on A404 between Slough and Reading. In 1817–18 he bought Albion House (now divided but marked with a plaque) on West Street; it was here that Mary Shelley wrote *Frankenstein* while he wrote *The Revolt of Islam* and pamphlets as 'The Hermit of Marlow'. His favourite walk was to

Bisham Woods, over Marlow Bridge and south of A404. He also went with Peacock on a boating expedition up the Thames from Old Windsor to Lechlade, at the junction of A417 and A361 10 miles NE of Swindon. The occasion is remembered in the fine poem, 'A Summer Evening Churchyard', quoted on a plaque on the churchyard wall.

When Shelley left Marlow he went abroad to an equally itinerant life and an early death by drowning. His body was cremated on the beach at Viareggio by a party that included Byron (q.v.), Leigh Hunt and that strange adventurer Edward Trelawny, who later wrote unreliable memoirs of both Byron and Shelley. The ashes were buried in the Protestant Cemetery at Rome with an epitaph by Hunt, but before the funeral pyre had burnt down Trelawny snatched what he declared to be Shelley's heart from the flames, though it is more likely to have been his liver. The heart (or liver) was returned to Mary Shelley and finally buried with her at St Peter's Church, Bournemouth, on the south coast. The graves of Godwin and Mary Wollstonecraft, removed from St Pancras Old Church, also lie here. The fine Priory Church at Christchurch, 8 miles east of Bournemouth on A337, has a monument to Shelley (1854) originally intended for St Peter's. The presence of these memorials in an area otherwise unconnected with the poet is explained by the fact that his son, Sir Percy Florence Shelley, spent much of his life at Boscombe Manor, between central Bournemouth and Christchurch. The building, now occupied by the Bournemouth and Poole College of Art, contains a museum of letters, pictures, costumes and other memorabilia of Shelley and his circle. The collection was started by Miss Margaret Brown and housed until 1978 in Shelley's last home, Casa Magni, on the bay of Lerici.

Westminster Abbey has been slow and grudging in its recognition of the Romantic poets. The present memorial to Shelley and Keats in Poets' Corner (fee) was not erected until 1954.

Eton College, Windsor, Berkshire: School Yard, College Chapel, Cloister Court and Museum of Eton Life open; also guided tours; phone (0753) 863593.

Casa Magni Shelley Museum, Bournemouth and Poole College of Art, Boscombe Manor, Beechwood Avenue, Boscombe, Bournemouth, Dorset; phone Russell-Cotes Art Gallery and Museum, Bournemouth, (0202) 21009.

William Shenstone

b. Halesowen, West Midlands, 1714; d. Halesowen, 1763. *Poems upon Various Occasions* (1737); *The Judgement of Hercules* (1741); *The School-Mistress* (1742).

Though he left Oxford without taking a degree, Shenstone's residence at Pembroke College helped that institution's claim to be a 'nest of singing birds' of which his near-contemporary, Dr Johnson (q.v.), liked to boast.

In his youth Shenstone spent time in London and the fashionable spas but in 1745 he retired more or less permanently to The Leasowes, the small estate where he had been born, at Halesowen, SW of Birmingham. Here he devoted himself to writing poetic trifles and, mainly, to laying out his gardens in the Picturesque manner. His achievement managed to provoke chilly admiration from a man as indifferent to natural beauties as Dr Johnson:

> Now was excited his delight in rural pleasures, and his ambition of rural elegance: he began from this time to point his prospects, to diversify his surfaces, to entangle his walks, and to wind his waters; which he did with such judgment and such fancy, as made his little domain the envy of the great and the admiration of the skilful; a place to be visited by travellers and copied by designers.

Shenstone's estate has since vanished beneath a park and golf course to the east of the town centre, though a fragment of the ruined Priory he incorporated into his effects remains. He was buried in the parish church and is commemorated by a large urn of 1771 with an inscription by his friend Richard Graves, author of *The Spiritual Quixote*.

At Hagley Hall (5 miles SW on A456), where Shenstone was frequently a guest of Lord Lyttelton, we can find surviving examples of the poet's taste. The rather plain house itself is by Sanderson Miller but the delightfully contrived *park, cunningly dotted with garden buildings, was laid out with Shenstone's help. He met James Thomson (q.v.) here in 1743.

The legend connected with Shenstone's poem 'Written at an Inn At Henley', probably dating from 1750, illustrates the pitfalls awaiting the literary topographer. Boswell's *Life* for 1776 tells how Johnson, relaxing in an unnamed inn after a visit to Blenheim Palace, quoted the last stanza with approval:

> Whoe'er has travell'd life's dull round,
> Where'er his stages may have been,
> May sigh to think he still has found
> The warmest welcome at an Inn.

Boswell adds: 'We happened to lie this night at the inn at Henley, where Shenstone wrote these lines'. Tradition and the guidebooks following in its wake have presumed this to be the 15C Red Lion at Henley-on-Thames, on A423 24 miles SE of Oxford, an inn which later equipped itself with rooms named after all three writers and a replica of the stanza scratched on one of its windows. Yet Boswell's account makes it clear that their overnight stop was between Stratford-upon-Avon and Birmingham, which they were able to reach by nine the next morning, and hence that the town must be Henley-in-Arden, Warwickshire, 6 miles NW of Stratford on A34, where the White Swan would seem a likely candidate. The objection is that Shenstone, a frequent guest of Lady Luxborough at The Barrels nearby, would have had little need to celebrate the hospitality of local inns. In fact, Richard Graves' *Recollections* (1788), based on personal knowledge of Shenstone and partly intended to correct the portrait Johnson gave in *Lives of the Poets*, states unequivocally that the poem was written in a 'summer house'—unnamed and unidentifiable—at Edge Hill, 6 miles north of Banbury, Oxfordshire. The misleading title may well have been supplied not by the poet but by his publisher, Dodsley.

Hagley Hall, near Stourbridge, West Midlands: phone (0562) 882408.

Richard Brinsley Sheridan

b. Dublin, 1751; d. London, 1816. *The Rivals* (1775); *The Duenna* (1775); *The School for Scandal* (1780); *A Trip to Scarborough* (1781); *The Critic* (1781); *St Patrick's Day: or The Scheming Lieutenant* (1788).

Sheridan was born at No. 12 Upper Dorset Street, now marked by a plaque, in an undistinguished part of north Dublin, and baptised at St Mary's, St Mary Street, off Capel Street to the south.

His father's declining fortunes as actor and manager brought him to Bath in 1770, where he organised 'Attic Entertainments'. The family lodged at No. 9 New King Street (with a tablet), south of the fashionable Royal Crescent and in a distinctly less fashionable quarter. In 1772 Sheridan became involved in a romance with the beautiful singer Eliza Linley and a train of melodramatic events that were transmuted into the comedy of his first success, *The Rivals*. In order to protect Eliza from the attentions of another suitor, a Major Mathews, he eloped with her to France from her lodgings at No. 11 Royal Crescent; on his return he found himself embroiled in local scandal, family disagreements and two abortive duels with the quarrelsome Major.

The couple were eventually married in 1773 at Marylebone Parish Church in London. Its site near the north end of Marylebone High Street is now a Garden of Rest. The couple lived nearby at No. 22 Orchard Street, the southern continuation of Baker Street to its junction with Oxford Street. Two of Sheridan's later London addresses are worth noting: No. 10 Hertford Street (tablet), which leads from near the south end of Park Lane by the Hilton Hotel, acquired in 1795 on the death of General Burgoyne; and the home of his last years, No. 14 Savile Row (tablet), running parallel with Regent Street. Two other sites recall the twin directions of Sheridan's career after his playwriting days were over. As theatrical manager he built a new Theatre Royal, Drury Lane in Covent Garden. Its destruction by fire in 1809 robbed London of a major landmark but provoked a typical witticism from Sheridan. Watching the blaze from a nearby coffee house he remarked: 'A man may surely take a glass of wine by his own fireside'. As Whig politician, notably active in the impeachment of Warren Hastings, he frequented Brooks's Club on St James's Street.

Sheridan was MP for Stafford. His residence, Chetwynd House in Greengate Street, is now the Post Office.

Despite the reduced and unhappy circumstances of his last years—caused by the loss of his theatre, the difficulties of the Whig faction to which he had adhered and by his excessive drinking—Sheridan received a public funeral at Westminster Abbey. He was buried in Poets' Corner (fee) and not, as he would have preferred, near the grave of his old political ally, Charles James Fox, at the west end of the north aisle.

Sir Philip Sidney

b. Penshurst Place, Kent, 1554; d. Zutphen, Holland, 1586. *Arcadia* (1590); *Astrophel and Stella* (1591); *An Apologie for Poetrie* (also titled *The Defence of Poesie*); 1595.

Sir Philip Sidney, whom contemporaries and later generations praised as the pattern of the Renaissance courtier, was born at **Penshurst Place, SW of Tonbridge in Kent. Later celebrated in a famous poem by Ben Jonson (q.v.), the house remains a magnificent example of a medieval mansion lightly refurbished in the Elizabethan manner. The 14C hall is particularly notable. Penshurst's collection includes portraits of the poet and parts of his armour.

Sidney was educated at Shrewsbury, county town of Shropshire, in the old buildings of the School (now a Library) on Castle Gates opposite the Castle. A statue, erected in 1923 as a First World War Memorial, stands outside the School's present buildings (1882) near the south bank of the River Severn. Because of his father's position as President of the Court of the Marches he also stayed at Ludlow Castle to the south. The tomb of his sister Ambrosia (d. 1580) is in the parish church.

In 1568 he entered Christ Church, Oxford. Family connections with the Earl of Leicester made him a visitor to Kenilworth Castle, now ruined but then a centre of aristocratic life, on A452 north of Oxford and Warwick.

His charm, learning and favourable position at court assured Sidney's familiarity with other great houses. In 1578 he received a deputation of university dons at Audley End, Essex, to the south of Cambridge; it included Gabriel Harvey, fellow member of the Areopagus, a group committed to introducing classical principles into English literature. More important were Sidney's visits to his sister Mary Herbert, Countess of Pembroke, at the splendid Renaissance mansion of *Wilton House, west of Salisbury in Wiltshire. He began the *Arcadia* at Wilton during a brief period of disgrace from the court in 1580. Its Single Cube Room has wall paintings by Thomas de Critz illustrating scenes from the prose romance.

After his death at the battle of Zutphen, Sidney's body was returned to London and buried in old St Paul's Cathedral.

Penshurst Place, Penshurst, Tonbridge, Kent: phone Penshurst (0892) 870307.

Shrewsbury Library, Castle Gates, Shrewsbury, Shropshire: phone (0743) 241487.

Ludlow Castle, Ludlow, Shropshire: phone (0584) 3947.

Kenilworth Castle, Kenilworth, Warwickshire: English Heritage, standard opening; phone (0926) 52078.

Audley End, Saffron Walden, Essex: English Heritage; phone (0799) 22399.

Wilton House, Wilton, near Salisbury, Wiltshire: phone Salisbury (0722) 743115.

Christopher Smart

b. Shipbourne, Kent, 1722; d. London, 1771. *Poems on Several Occasions* (1752); *A Song to David* (1763); *Jubilate Agno* (edited as *Rejoice in the Lamb* by William Force Stead; 1939).

The Kentish scenes of Smart's childhood in the villages of Shipbourne (on A227 4 miles north of Tonbridge) and East Barming (on A26 2 miles SW of Maidstone) are evoked in his poem 'The Hop-Garden'.

After his father's death in 1733 the family moved to Durham, where Smart attended the Grammar School in 17C buildings on Palace Green now used by the University Music School. He became a frequent guest of the Vane family, whom his father had served as steward, at Raby Castle (near Staindrop 20 miles SW of the city). At this fine 14C building, not yet reconstructed and modernised, he mixed on terms of apparent equality with the Vane children and fell in love with Anne, later remembered in *Jubilate Agno*.

In 1739 he entered Pembroke College (then Pembroke Hall), Cambridge, thanks to the generosity of Henrietta, Duchess of Cleveland and wife to Lord Barnard of Raby. Smart's academic career was distinguished: he rose from the humble position of sizar (or poor student) to Scholar of the University in 1742 and to Fellow of Pembroke in 1745, writing prize-winning poems as he went. Yet it was also marred by extravagance, as a 1747 letter by the poet Gray (q.v.), then at Peterhouse, vividly testifies:

> your mention of Mr Vane, reminds me of poor Smart (not that I, or any other Mortal, pity him) about three weeks ago he was arrested here at the Suit of a Taylor in London for a Debt of about 50£ of three Years standing. the College had about 28£ due to him in their Hands, the rest (to hinder him from going to the Castle, for he could not raise a Shilling) Brown, May & Peele, lent him upon his Note. upon this he remain'd confined to his Room, lest his Creditors here should snap him; & the Fellows went round to make out a List of his Debts, wch amount in Cambridge to above 350£. that they might come the readier to some Composition, he was advised to go off in the Night, & lie hid somewhere or other.

His friend Charles Burney, father of the novelist Fanny Burney (q.v.), offered a clue to at least one cause of Smart's difficulties: 'he ruined himself by returning the tavern treats of strangers who had invited him as a wit and an extraordinary personage'.

Although he maintained a formal connection with Pembroke until 1755, Smart went to London in 1749 to make his way as a professional author. The circumstances of his wedding in 1752 to Anna Maria (Nancy) Carnan are obscure, perhaps because it violated the conditions of his Fellowship, but it may have taken place at St Bride's on the south side of Fleet Street. It is certain, however, that he and his wife went to live at Canonbury Tower, facing Canonbury Place SE of Highbury and Islington Station (British Rail and Victoria Line). The fine 16C building, now headquarters of the Tower Theatre, was rented out as apartments; its tenants included Smart's father-in-law, the publisher John Newbery, who was also responsible for bringing Oliver Goldsmith (q.v.) to live here.

In 1756 Smart suffered his first attack of religious mania, which took the form of literal obedience to the Biblical injunction that he should pray without ceasing. His friend Dr Johnson (q.v.) regarded these symptoms with gruff compassion ('I'd as lief pray with Kit Smart as anyone else. Another charge was that he did not love clean linen; and I have no passion for it') but their recurrence consigned the poet to asylums and, finally, debtors' prison. Such places have long since vanished from the map of London and the best memorial to Smart's later years of suffering is his religious poetry, especially *A Song to David*.

Raby Castle, Staindrop, County Durham: phone (0833) 60202.

Canonbury Tower, 30 Canonbury Place, Canonbury, London N1: tours for parties by prior arrangement; phone the Warden, Canonbury Tower Trust, (01) 359 4900.

Tobias Smollett

b. Dalquharn, Strathclyde, 1721; d. Livorno, Italy, 1771. *The Life and Adventures of Roderick Random* (1748); *The Adventures of Peregrine Pickle* (1751); *The Adventures of Ferdinand Count Fathom* (1753); *The Adventures of Sir Launcelot Greaves* (1762); *Travels through France and Italy* (1766); *The Expedition of Humphry Clinker* (1771).

Smollett's birthplace, Dalquharn House, no longer stands but his family has left traces of its presence in the area where they had long been rooted and were of some importance. In 1763 his cousin James bought Cameron House, 4 miles NW of Dumbarton, 'ready-built rather than be at the trouble of repairing his own family-house of Bonhill, which stands two miles from hence on the Leven'. The writer came here on a visit in 1766 and described it in his epistolary novel, *Humphry Clinker*, a book that never misses an opportunity to praise his native land:

> We have fixed our head-quarters at Cameron, a very neat country-house belonging to commissary Smollett, where we found every sort of accommodation we could desire—It is situated like a Druid's temple, in a grove of oak, close by the side of Lough Lomond, which is a surprising body of pure transparent water, unfathomably deep in many places, six or seven miles broad, four and twenty miles in length, displaying above twenty green islands, covered with wood; some of them cultivated for corn, and many of them stocked with red deer. (Letter by Jeremy Melford, 3 September)

Cameron House was largely rebuilt in the 19C.

It was James Smollett who erected the monument to his famous relative at Renton (2 miles south). Consulted on the matter, Dr Johnson (q.v.) voiced his customary preference for a Latin tribute ('An English inscription would be a disgrace to Dr Smollett') and revised the proposed text. Not all his suggestions were adopted, and when Dorothy Wordsworth visited the spot in 1803 with her brother and Coleridge (s.v. Lake Poets, Rte 15) she noted: 'The Latin is miserably bad—as Coleridge said, such as poor Smollett, who was an excellent scholar, would have been ashamed of'.

The same Scottish trip of 1766, Smollett's last, took him to Edinburgh and so helped the eulogies of that city which appear in the August letters of *Humphry Clinker*. No. 22 John Street, off Canongate, where he stayed with his mother and sister, is marked with a plaque.

Most of his working life was spent in London. On his return from several years aboard ship as a surgeon's mate in the mid 1740s he set up medical practice in Downing Street off Whitehall. From 1750 to 1762, the years when he made his combative, sometimes ill-tempered way as a journalist and wrote the novels that established his reputation, he lived in part of a house at No. 16 Lawrence Street, off Cheyne Walk in Chelsea, where the famous Chelsea China Factory was active from about 1740 to 1784.

Yet it was *Humphry Clinker*, written during his retirement in Italy (1769–71), which most vividly and completely reflected Smollett's familiarity with Britain. Its Scottish references have already been noted but the English section of the itinerary followed by Matthew Bramble and his party deserves summary.

Their first major stop is at Bristol, where the Georgian architecture of Clifton and Hotwells, to the west of the city, still reminds visitors of the fashionable status enjoyed by the area. At Bath, which Smollett himself visited many times during the season, Mr Bramble first lodges in South Parade but is driven to Milsom Street by the noise of a fellow guest's French horns. He is sceptical of Bath's waters, contemptuous of the local society and grudging at best in his praise for John Wood the elder's famous Circus, then only recently completed:

> The Circus is a pretty bauble; contrived for shew, and looks like Vespasian's amphitheatre turned outside in. If we consider it in point of magnificence, the great number of small doors belonging to the separate houses, the inconsiderable height of the different orders, the affected ornaments of the architrave, which are both childish and misplaced, and the areas projecting into the street, surrounded with iron rails, destroy a good part of its effect upon the eye; and perhaps, we shall find it still more defective, if we view it in the light of convenience. The figure of each separate dwelling house, being the segment of a circle, must spoil the symmetry of the rooms, by contracting them towards the street windows, and leaving a larger sweep in the space behind. (Letter of 23 April)

'The same artist', he gloomily adds, 'who planned the Circus, has likewise projected a Crescent; when that is finished, we shall probably have a Star; and those who are living thirty years hence, may, perhaps, see all the signs of the Zodiac exhibited in the architecture at Bath'. The Royal Crescent (1769), by the younger and not the elder Wood, stands in magnificent rebuttal of this cynicism.

In their progress north the party visits the then fashionable spa of Harrogate, 8 miles west of A1 in North Yorkshire, now more redolent of the 19C than the 18C. At York Mr Bramble indulges the prejudices of his age and generation in an exaggerated form. He is unimpressed by the Minster:

> The external appearance of an old cathedral cannot be but displeasing to the eye of every man, who has any idea of propriety of proportion, even though he may be ignorant of architecture as a science; and the long slender spire puts one in mind of a criminal impaled, with a sharp stake rising up through his shoulder.

Praise is reserved instead for the Assembly Rooms on Blake Street, a pioneering piece of Palladianism designed by Richard Boyle, third Earl of Burlington, which displays 'nothing of this Arabic architecture ... and might be converted into an elegant place of worship' (Letter of 4 July).

At Scarborough on the North Yorkshire coast they join in the recent fashion for sea-bathing until Mr Bramble's embarrassing experience on the beach cuts the stay short. Though the town is, of course, greatly changed the visitor can still recognise its main features from Jeremy Melford's description:

> Scarborough, though a paltry town, is romantic from its situation along a cliff that overhangs the sea. The harbour is formed by a small elbow of land that

runs out as a natural mole, directly opposite to the town; and on that side is the castle, which stands very high, of considerable extent, and before the invention of gun-powder, was counted impregnable. (Letter of 1 July)

In Durham, much less damaged by time than Scarborough, the party is joined by the eccentric Lismahago and Mr Bramble is given a final opportunity to express his distaste for the medieval:

The city of Durham appears like a confused heap of stones and brick, accumulated so as to cover a mountain, round which a river winds its brawling course. The streets are generally narrow, dark, and unpleasant, and many of them almost impassible in consequence of their declivity. The cathedral is a huge gloomy pile; but the clergy are well lodged. (Letter of 15 July)

Assembly Rooms, Blake Street, York: open except when in use for public functions; for opening arrangements phone York Tourist Information Centre, (0904) 21756 or 21757.

Edmund Spenser

b. London, 1552?; d. London, 1599. *The Shepheardes Calender* (1579); *The Faerie Queene* (unfinished; 1590–96); *Amoretti* (1595); *Epithalamion* (1595); *Colin Clouts Come Home Againe* (1595); *Prothalamion* (1596).

Disappointingly little remains by which the traveller can remember Spenser. The only record of the London scenes of his birth and childhood is his own tribute in the *Prothalamion* to 'mery London, my most kyndly Nurse,/ That to me gaue this Lifes first natiue sourse' (stanza 8). His education at Pembroke College (then Hall), Cambridge, between 1569 and 1576 was marked by a similar tribute in *The Faerie Queene*: 'My mother Cambridge .../ With many a gentle Muse, and many a learned wit' (Bk 4, Canto 11, stanza 34).

Spenser's appointment in 1580 as secretary to Lord Grey de Wilton, Lord President of Ireland, and his subsequent posts in Irish public life made that country his home until just before his death. In 1580 he apparently witnessed the English massacre of the Spanish garrison at Fort del Oro near the harbour town of Smerwick, County Kerry, on the Dingle Peninsula. He profited several times from the 'plantation' scheme that deprived disaffected Irish landowners of their property, most importantly in 1586 when he acquired an estate including Kilcolman Castle, 3 miles north of Doneraile, which lies to the east of N20 between Limerick and Cork. He settled there in 1588 and wrote substantial parts of his epic allegory, *The Faerie Queene*, during his residence. Sir Walter Ralegh (q.v.) came as a visitor in 1589 from his estate at Youghal, a fishing town on the south coast to the east of Cork. Both this occasion and Spenser's trip to England the following year are described in *Colin Clouts Come Home Againe*. Kilcolman Castle and the house Spenser had added to it were destroyed in Tyrone's rebellion of 1598. Today the area is a wildfowl refuge and only the ruined tower and bailey survive, difficult of access. The surrounding countryside, however, is notable for both its intrinsic beauty and the contributions it may have made to the pastoral aspects of *The Faerie Queene*, especially in Book 4 (where, in Canto 11, stanza 41, the local river Awbeg is referred to as 'Mulla mine') and Book 6.

Spenser's marriage in 1594 to Elizabeth Boyle, wooed in his *Amoretti*, probably took place in the medieval cathedral which stood on the site of William Burges' 19C St Finbarr's Cathedral in Cork.

After the loss of his Irish home Spenser returned to London, though perhaps not in the condition of miserable poverty that earlier commentators believed. He was buried at the expense of the Earl of Essex near the tomb of Chaucer (q.v.) in what is now Poets' Corner (fee) of Westminster Abbey. William Camden described the funeral: 'His hearse was attended by the gentlemen of his faculty, who cast into his tomb some funeral elegies, and the pens they were wrote with'. In 1620 Lady Anne Clifford (see the entry for Samuel Daniel) commissioned a *monument by Nicholas Stone, notable for its description of Spenser as 'the prince of poets in his tyme' and for its inaccuracy about the dates of his life. The monument was corrected and repaired in 1778.

Sir Richard Steele

b. Dublin, 1672; d. Carmarthen, Dyfed, 1729. *The Christian Hero* (1701); contributions to *The Tatler* (1709–11); contributions to *The Spectator* (1711–12); *The Englishman* (1713–14); *The Conscious Lovers* (1722).

Like so many 18C writers of Irish birth, Steele was quick to declare himself an Englishman. He was educated at Charterhouse in the City of London, where he struck up the friendship with Joseph Addison (q.v.) that led to their collaboration on *The Tatler* and *The Spectator*. Though the school moved to Godalming, Surrey in 1872 its fine 16C–18C buildings survive on Charterhouse Square near the Central Meat Market.

From Charterhouse Steele went to Oxford, studying at Christ Church (1690) before transferring to Merton College, which he left in 1694 without taking a degree in order to join the army. Despite this premature departure he paid Oxford and Merton frequent tributes in later life, including this account of the characteristic sensations of a former undergraduate revisiting his old college:

> The sight ... filled my heart with unspeakable joy. Methought I grew younger the moment I stepped within the gate, and upon my entering the hall in which I had so often disputed, I found my logic come afresh into my head, and that I could have formed syllogisms in figures whose very names I had not once thought of for several years before. The libraries, quadrangles, and grove, all renewed in my mind, an hundred little pleasant stories and innocent amusements, though in the last place I could not help observing with some regret the loss of a tree, under whose shade I had often improved my acquaintance with Horace. (*The Englishman*, No. 34, 1713)

The only surviving reminder of Steele's adult life in London, where he was soldier, dramatist, pamphleteer and politician as well as essayist, has its own special interest. It is the simple gravestone of his second wife, Mary (d. 1718), the 'dear Prue' of his letters and imperious governess of his own somewhat unregulated habits, in the middle of the south transept of Westminster Abbey. The restrained, factual inscription that Steele composed in her memory is in marked contrast to the romantic enthusiasm with which he elsewhere spoke of Lady Steele.

He retired in 1724 to his wife's estate at Llangumnor, east of Carmarthen on the south coast of Wales, where he is remembered in the parish church on the hilltop. Shortly before his death he moved into Carmarthen itself and was buried in St Peter's Church, which has a stone tablet in his memory.

Charterhouse, Charterhouse Square, London EC1: guided tours in summer; phone (01) 253 9503.

Laurence Sterne

b. Clonmel, Tipperary, 1713; d. London, 1768. *The Life and Opinions of Tristram Shandy, Gentleman* (1759–67); *The Sermons of Mr Yorick* (1760–69); *A Sentimental Journey through France and Italy* (1768); *Letters from Yorick to Eliza* (1773).

Sterne entered Jesus College, Cambridge, where his great-grandfather Archbishop Sterne of York had been Master, as a sizar (or poor student) in 1733. Tradition remembers him reading Rabelais with John Hall, afterwards John Hall-Stevenson, under a walnut tree that grew in the First Court; he himself remembered the College by sending his most famous creation, Tristram Shandy, to it in Volume 1, Chapter 19 of the novel. A portrait by Allan Ramsay believed to represent the novelist hangs in the Hall.

After receiving his BA in 1737 Sterne embarked on a clerical career, more through necessity than vocation. He held his first curacy at the 15C church of All Saints in St Ives, 17 miles NW of Cambridge.

The following year he began an association with York and its surrounding area that lasted for the rest of his life, though after the fame of *Tristram Shandy* he frequently travelled to more fashionable parts of England and the Continent. The city's social life appealed to his taste for coffee houses and female company, while a steady flow of minor ecclesiastical appointments was ensured by his family connections with the Minster, where his uncle, Dr Jacques Sterne, was Canon Residentiary and Precentor. Dr Sterne lived at Gray's Court, by the Treasurer's House east of the Minster. Sterne himself delivered sermons at St Michael-le-Belfrey, immediately south of the Minster, and in the Minster, which was also the scene of his wedding to Elizabeth Lumley in 1741. Before her marriage Miss Lumley lodged on College Street (then Little Alice Lane), which runs east from Minster Yard. The church of Holy Trinity on Micklegate, west of the river, has a memorial to Sterne's friend Dr John Burton (d. 1771), identified as the original of Dr Slop in *Tristram Shandy*.

From 1738 to 1759 Sterne was rector of Sutton-on-the-Forest, 8 miles north of York on B1363, where he was rector of All Hallows. Except for its tower the church of All Hallows was heavily restored by the Victorians but its 18C pulpit, the one from which Sterne must surely have preached, still survives. A dedicated pluralist in an age of pluralists, he further acquired the living of Stillington, 3 miles further north, in 1744; his little church of St Nicholas is another victim of 19C restoration. If an anecdote told by the local squire is to be believed, he bore his pastoral responsibilities lightly: 'going over the fields on a Sunday to preach at Stillington, it happened that his pointer dog sprung a covey of partridge, when he went directly home for his gun and left his flock that was waiting for him in the church in the lurch'. His occupations were painting, music, unsuccessful attempts at farming and, according to contemporary rumour, infidelities that led to his wife's temporary insanity as well as a series of separations. In his wife's absence he turned to literary composition, writing the first two volumes of *Tristram Shandy* in his Sutton parsonage. The parsonage burned down in 1765, apparently through the carelessness of the unlicensed curate in whose care Sterne had by that time left his living. It was rebuilt only after Sterne's death.

In 1760 he was granted the living of Coxwold (18 miles north of York, east of A19), a picturesque village whose hilly situation suited his delicate health better than the low-lying Sutton. 'O 'tis a delicious retreat!' he exclaimed in a letter, 'both from its beauty, & air of Solitude; & so sweetly does every thing abt it invite yr mind to rest its Labours—and be at peace with itself & the world'. The *house he rented at £12 per year and inevitably named Shandy Hall is a charming building of c 1450 at the west end of the village. Sterne's income from his writing allowed him to make substantial improvements to it, including the installation of fireplaces in the Adam style. To the right of the main hallway is his study, the 'Philosophical Hut' where he wrote the later volumes of *Tristram Shandy* and the *Letters from Yorick to Eliza*, sentimental record of his attachment to Mrs Elizabeth Draper. Shandy Hall is now owned by the Laurence Sterne Trust.

The church of St Michael, with a striking octagonal tower, preserves the pulpit from which Sterne preached. His remains now lie just outside the south wall, after suffering misadventures grotesquely appropriate to a man who had called himself Parson Yorick. Sterne's funeral service was held at St George's, Hanover Square, his body being buried in the church's graveyard in Paddington. Bodysnatchers stole it and anatomists dissected it, apparently at the medical school in Cambridge, before his skeleton was recognised and returned to Paddington for reburial. On reopening the grave in 1969, shortly before the burial ground was turned into a building site, investigators discovered a litter of bones which included a skull matching the bust of Sterne by Joseph Nollekens, but with the top sawn off. The remains were given their third and presumably final burial at Coxwold.

Sterne visited the patron of his living, Lord Fauconberg, at Newburgh Priory, SE of the village. Towards the end of his life he sometimes took 'a delicious Walk of Romance' to the ruins of Byland Abbey to the NE where he liked to indulge in the prospect of reunion with Mrs Draper.

Shandy Hall, Coxwold, North Yorkshire: phone (034 76) 465.

Newburgh Priory, Coxwold, North Yorkshire: phone (034'76) 435.

Byland Abbey, near Coxwold, North Yorkshire: English Heritage, standard opening; phone (034 76) 614.

Robert Louis Stevenson

b. Edinburgh, 1850; d. Vailima, Samoa, 1894. *An Inland Voyage* (1878); *Edinburgh: Picturesque Notes* (1879); *Travels With a Donkey in the Cévennes* (1879); *Deacon Brodie: or The Double Life* (with W.E. Henley; 1880); *Virginibus Puerisque and Other Papers* (1881); *Familiar Studies of Men and Books* (1882); *New Arabian Nights* (1882); *Treasure Island* (1883); *A Child's Garden of Verses* (1885); *More New Arabian Nights: The Dynamiter* (1885); *Prince Otto: A Romance* (1885); *The Strange Case of Dr Jekyll and Mr Hyde* (1886); *Kidnapped: Being Memoirs of the Adventures of David Balfour in the Year 1751* (1886); *The Black Arrow: A Tale of Two Roses* (1888); *The Master of Ballantrae: A Winter's Tale* (1889); *The Wrong Box* (with Lloyd Osbourne; 1889); *The Wrecker* (with Lloyd Osbourne; 1892); *Island Nights Entertainments* (1893); *Catriona: A Sequel to Kidnapped* (1893); *The Ebb-Tide: A Trio and a Quartette* (1894); *The Body-Snatcher* (1895); *Weir of Hermiston: An Unfinished Romance* (1896); *St Ives: Being the Adventures of a French Prisoner in England* (finished by Sir Arthur Quiller-Couch; 1897).

Although posterity chose to construct a romanticised image of Robert Louis Stevenson from his final years in the South Seas, he was in fact a native of Edinburgh and never managed—nor, indeed, wished—to escape entirely from the city's shaping influence. As his friend W.E. Henley concluded in a sonnet, Stevenson's temperament embraced not only 'a deal of Ariel, just a streak of Puck,/ Much Antony, of Hamlet most of all' but also 'something of the Shorter Catechist'. Edinburgh today is still the best place to remember him. He was born into a famous and prosperous family of engineers at No. 8 Howard Place, near Inverleith Row and the Royal Botanic Garden just north of the Leith. For most of his childhood and youth, until he left the city in 1879, he lived in the New Town, the Georgian development whose beauty he rightly defended against contemporary criticism in his second book. The family home was at No. 17 Heriot Row, the wide and elegant street which forms the north side of Queen Street Gardens. The main landmark in the Old Town is Lady Stair's House, just off Lawnmarket, a restored 17C building which now houses a collection devoted to Stevenson, Burns and Sir Walter Scott (qq.v.). Brodie's Close, opposite, is named after the notorious 18C resident who was both town councillor and thief. His exploits suggested the play Stevenson wrote in collaboration with Henley and lie behind his far more serious study of the double life, *The Strange Case of Dr Jekyll and Mr Hyde*. The Castle nearby is the setting for the opening chapters of *St Ives*, a late work left incomplete at Stevenson's death. He is remembered by a plaque in St Giles Cathedral.

In *St Ives* Flora Gilchrist lives at Swanston Cottage, the Stevenson family's second home from 1867. Swanston, a neat little village now technically incorporated into the city, lies about 4 miles south and is reached by following A702, turning right on A720 (Oxgangs Road) and then taking a left on Swanston Road. The cottage is to the right, near the golf course. The Pentland Hills which rise SW of the village were well known to Stevenson and are praised in the last chapter of *Edinburgh: Picturesque Notes*.

In his youth Stevenson's delicate health forced him to study the law rather than follow the family tradition of engineering. In adult life it forced him to travel ever further from his country's uncongenial climate. In 1881, however, he did make a significant Scottish tour with his mother, his American wife and his stepson, Lloyd Osbourne. In June and July they stayed among the mountainous scenery of central Scotland at Moulin, a village on A924 north of Pitlochry. Stevenson wrote his fine short story 'Thrawn Janet' at Kinnaird Cottage. In August and September the party was at Braemar (on A93 NE of Pitlochry), staying in a cottage on Glenshee Road near what was then the church but is now the Invercauld Festival Theatre. During this visit Stevenson began *Treasure Island*, a story that neither he nor his wife regarded very seriously but which quickly became and has remained his most popular work.

South of the border Stevenson twice stayed in Surrey at the Burford Bridge Hotel, 1½ miles north of Dorking on A24. During both visits (1878 and 1879) he met George Meredith (q.v.), who lived at Flint Cottage on Box Hill nearby. On the second occasion Meredith read him parts of *The Egoist* and, when Stevenson exclaimed that the character of Sir Willoughby Patterne must have been modelled on himself, made his famous reply: 'I've taken him from all of us, but principally from myself'. However, 'Owen Woodseer' in Meredith's *The Amazing Marriage* (1895) is certainly a portrait of Stevenson, intended as a tribute to the younger writer's slightly fey, Bohemian charm.

Stevenson's last years in Britain (1884–87), when he was virtually a housebound invalid, were spent on the south coast at Bournemouth. From 1885 his home here was Skerryvore, a house bought for him by his father and named 'in commemoration of the most beautiful and difficult of all the lighthouses erected by the family'. It no longer stands but its site on Alum Chine Road, south of Poole Road in Westbourne, is now a memorial garden.

Lady Stair's House, Lady Stair's Close, Lawnmarket, Edinburgh: phone (031) 225 2424, extension 6593.

Edinburgh Castle: Historic Buildings and Monuments, Scottish Development Department; phone the enquiry desk in Edinburgh, (031) 244 3101.

Bram Stoker

b. Dublin, 1847; d. London, 1912. *The Duties of Clerks of Petty Sessions of Ireland* (1878); *Under the Sunset* (1881); *The Gombeen Man* (1890); *The Watter's Mou'* (1895); *Dracula* (1897); *The Mystery of the Sea* (1902); *The Jewel of Seven Stars* (1904); *Personal Reminiscences of Henry Irving* (1906); *The Gates of Life* (1908); *Lady Athlyne* (1908); *The Lady of the Shroud* (1909); *Famous Impostors* (1909); *The Lair of the White Worm* (1911).

Stoker was educated at Trinity College, Dublin, before coming to England in 1878 as acting manager to Sir Henry Irving. During the years of his prosperity he lived in Chelsea, first on Cheyne Walk by the river and later at No. 4 Durham Place, off Ormonde Gate behind the Royal Hospital. Just round the corner is Tite Street and the home of Oscar Wilde (q.v.), whose parents Stoker knew during his youth in Dublin.

The popularity of *Dracula* now attracts tourists to Transylvania, a region Stoker never visited, but most of his novel is set closer to home. The Westenra family live in Hampstead and the undead Lucy Westenra makes her nocturnal appearances on Hampstead Heath. She had been buried nearby in 'the tomb of her kin, a lordly death-house in a lonely churchyard, away from teeming London; where the air is fresh, and the sun rises over Hampstead Hill, and where wild flowers grow of their own accord' (Ch. 13, 'Dr Seward's Diary'). We may be tempted to identify the spot with Highgate Cemetery, whose western part has catacombs and mausoleums entirely appropriate to Stoker's Gothic effects, especially the scene (Ch. 16) when Van Helsing and his helpers confront the vampire Lucy as she returns to her grave.

Count Dracula makes his landfall in England on the North Yorkshire coast at the old whaling port of *Whitby. The dramatic storm heralding his arrival is described in Chapter 7. He claims Lucy as his victim in the churchyard of St Mary, a splendidly atmospheric spot which lies between the Abbey and the town and enjoys a fine view of the harbour. The Westenra family (and perhaps Stoker himself on his holiday visits) lodged at East Crescent, part of the 19C resort developed on the opposite cliff.

Stoker began the novel in 1895 at another of his favourite holiday retreats, Cruden Bay, on the east coast of Scotland 24 miles north of Aberdeen. New Slains Castle, which overlooks this dramatic stretch of coastline from the north, may well have shaped his conception of Castle Dracula. The area is also the setting for several other works: *The Watter's Mou'*, *The Mystery of the Sea* and the short story 'Crooken Sands'.

Highgate Cemetery, Swains Lane, Highgate, London N6: Eastern Cemetery open during daylight hours; tours of Western Cemetery; phone (01) 340 1834.

Henry Howard, Earl of Surrey

b. Kenninghall, Norfolk?, 1517?; d. London, 1547. Poet.

The only surviving places to remind us of Surrey, sonneteer and near-contemporary of Sir Thomas Wyatt (q.v.) to whom he wrote an elegy, are connected with the unhappy close of his life. In 1547 he was indicted for treason in the Great Hall of London's Guildhall. The charge apparently owed more to his enemies' political power and to his own quarrelsome disposition than to evidence of any substance. After being committed to the Tower of London and executed on Tower Hill, he was buried at the nearby church of All Hallows by the Tower (substantially rebuilt after bomb damage in the Second World War).

His body was later reinterred at St Michael in Framlingham, off A1120 between Stowmarket and the coast in Suffolk. His monument of 1614 stands among several fine Renaissance memorials to other members of the family of the Dukes of Norfolk.

City of London Guildhall, Guildhall Yard, off Gresham Street, London EC2: phone (01) 606 3030, and ask for the Keeper's Office.

Tower of London, Tower Hill, London EC3: DoE monument; phone (01) 709 0765.

Jonathan Swift

b. Dublin, 1667; d. Dublin, 1745. *A Tale of a Tub* (1704); *The Battle of the Books* (1704); *A Meditation upon a Broom-Stick* (1710); *An Argument against Abolishing Christianity* (1711); *The Conduct of the Allies* (1711); *The Drapier's Letters* (1724); *Cadenus and Vanessa* (1726); *Travels in Several Remote Nations of the World. In Four Parts. By Lemuel Gulliver* (ie. *Gulliver's Travels*; 1726); *A Modest Proposal for Preventing the Children of the Poor from being a Burden to their Parents or Country* (1729); *A Beautiful Young Nymph Going to Bed* (1734); *Strephon and Chloe* (1734); *Verses on the Death of Dr Swift, Written by Himself* (1739); *Directions to Servants* (1745).

Swift's life was divided between two countries: Ireland, 'where there is nothing I shall be sorry to lose' (or so he claimed in a letter written when he was sixty-two), whose ecclesiastical and political affairs absorbed much of his energies; and England, where the disappointment of his youthful hopes for advancement was counterbalanced by his later acceptance in literary society. He himself encouraged doubts as to his country of origin, to the annoyance of Johnson (q.v.) in his *Lives of the English Poets*:

> During his life the place of his birth was undetermined. He was contented to be called an Irishman by the Irish; but would occasionally call himself an Englishman. The question may, without much regret, be left in the obscurity in which he delighted to involve it.

In fact, Swift was an Irishman, and it is most convenient to begin by considering his connections with that country.

From the age of six he attended Kilkenny College in the county town of Kilkenny, beginning there a life-long friendship with his near-contemporary, Congreve (q.v.). The present buildings of the College stand on the north bank of the Nore near St John's Bridge; its former buildings were in the Close of St Mary's Cathedral.

Swift entered Trinity College, Dublin, when he was fourteen—an early age though not so unusual as one might think. His connection with the College is best remembered by Roubiliac's fine *bust in the Old Library. The various legends of his poor academic performance and bad behaviour, encouraged by his own references in old age to his 'dullness and insufficiency' as an undergraduate, are not fully supported by the College records.

After several years of frustrated clerical ambition he was appointed Dean of St Patrick's Cathedral in 1714. The position earned him the universal title, 'Dean Swift', and he held it until his death. His house in Deanery Garden does not survive but the *Cathedral itself is rich

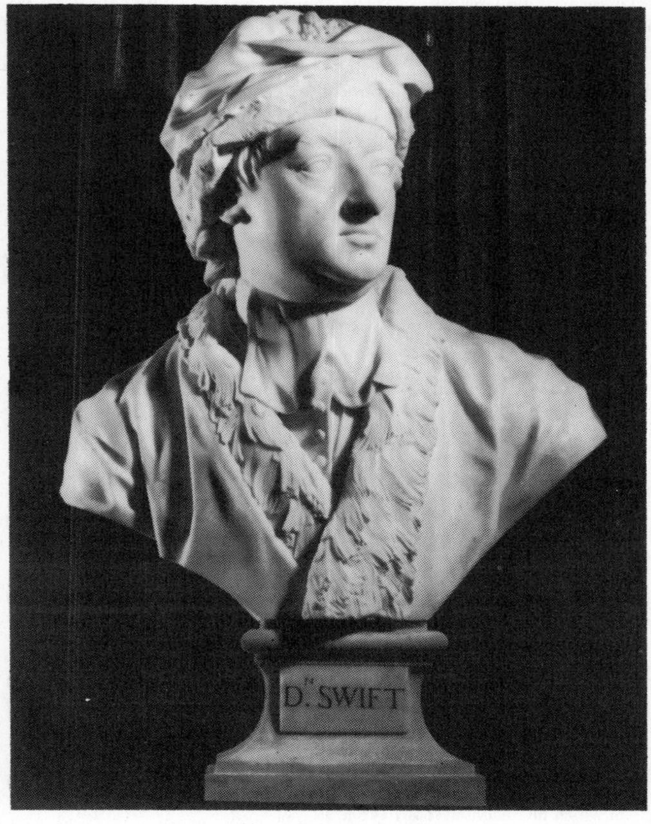

Bust of Swift by Louis François Roubiliac, in the Old Library of Trinity College, Dublin

in reminders. On entering we find, near the foot of the second column from the west end of the nave, brass tablets commemorating him and Esther Johnson, recipient of the letters later collected as *Journal to Stella*, constant companion and possibly wife by a secret marriage. Swift's diary for 30 January 1728 contained this entry:

> This is the night of her funeral which my sickness will not suffer me to attend. It is now nine at night, and I am removed into another apartment that I may not see the light in the church, which is just over against the window of my bed-chamber.

The tablets do not necessarily mark the exact places where Swift and Stella were buried, for they have been moved over the years in obedience to the differing opinions of successive Deans about the real relationship between the couple. A bust by Patrick Cunningham (1775) stands by the door leading to the Vestiaries nearby. Above is the tablet with Swift's Latin epitaph on himself, famous for its inscription of his eventual destination as 'Ubi saeva Indignatio/ Ulterius/ Cor lacerare nequit'. Another poet, Yeats (q.v.), has offered a fine free translation of the text:

> Swift has sailed into his rest;
> Savage indignation there
> Cannot lacerate his breast.
> Imitate him, if you dare,
> World-besotted traveller; he
> Served human liberty.

Swift's epitaph on Stella is at the other side of the doorway.

The north transept contains the pulpit from which he preached, while in a corner of the south transept we find, above the monument to Lady Doneraile, a memorial to his servant, McGee. The north choir aisle has a tablet to Frederick Herman, Duke of Schomberg, who died at the Battle of the Boyne (1690). In 1729 Swift wrote to the Duke's grand-daughter urging the propriety of a memorial but received no reply. The project went ahead at the expense of the Dean and Chapter, and Swift himself wrote the inscription with its reference to the ingratitude of Schomberg's descendants.

Shortly to the east of the Cathedral is the handsome early 18C Marsh's Library, the first public library in Dublin, of which Swift was a governor. It preserves his annotated copy of Clarendon's *History of the Great Rebellion*.

Swift was thoroughly familiar with Dublin Castle, having been born at No. 7 Hooey Court (gone) within its shadow. In 1724, after having spent several futile hours waiting for an interview with Lord Carteret there, he is reputed to have left two lines on a card:

> My very good Lord, it's a very hard task
> To wait so long and have nothing to ask.

Swift is among the many famous Irishmen whose heads are carved on the outside of the 19C Gothic Chapel.

By following James Street to the west of Dublin we reach the 18C buildings of St Patrick's Hospital (or Swift's Hospital), founded by a bequest in Swift's will and opened in 1757. It is now a psychiatric centre.

Little survives to commemorate the livings outside Dublin which Swift had held before he became Dean of St Patrick's. After his ordination in 1694 he had been appointed to the small prebend of Kilroot, on the coast between Carrickfergus and Whitehead. The church is now ruined and the house where he wrote *A Tale of a Tub* has been demolished. In 1699 he had become incumbent of the village of Laracor, on the Knightsbrook river near Trim, 27 miles NW of Dublin. The church where he preached to a congregation of a dozen and the house where Esther Johnson lived with her friend Mrs Dingley from 1701 have both been altered beyond recognition, though not all of the quiet scenery which Swift enjoyed in his walks. Both Swift and Esther Johnson were briefly the owners of Talbot's Castle, a medieval building now modernised, in Trim itself.

After the death of Esther Vanromigh ('Vanessa') in 1723 Swift made an extended tour through the south of Ireland. While staying at Unionhall or Castletownshead, both on the coast road south of Cork, he wrote 'Carberiae Rupes', a Latin poem about the wild scenery of the district; it was translated into English by William Dunkin.

Swift's connection with England began with childhood visits to his widowed mother, from whom he was separated for several years at a time. It was strengthened by his stay at Moor Park, near Farnham off A31 in Surrey. He served as secretary to Sir William Temple from 1689 or 1690 until that gentleman's death in 1699, with an interlude in Ireland (1694–96) after his ordination, editing Sir William's papers and becoming increasingly frustrated that the position did not lead to the advancement he had anticipated. It was here he first met Esther Johnson, daughter of the housekeeper. Moor Park, greatly changed and now a College of Adult Christian Education, lies 2 miles SE of the town near the ruins of Waverley Abbey.

In June–August 1714 he stayed with a friend from his Moor Park days, Rev. John Geree, at the village of Letcombe Bassett, on the Downs 2½ miles SW of Wantage. As he explains in his poem, 'The Author Upon Himself', he was seeking refuge from the political fighting between Oxford and Bolingbroke which accompanied the closing months of Queen Anne's reign:

By Faction tir'd, with Grief he waits a while,
His great contending Friends to reconcile,
Performs what Friendship, Justice, Truth require:
What could he more, but decently retire?
(lines 71–74)

His rural peace was disturbed by an unexpected and injudiciously public visit from Esther Vanromigh; Swift included 'the Berkshire Surprise' among the subtitles he originally planned for *Cadenus and Vanessa*, the poem that tells the story of their attachment. The house where Swift stayed no longer stands but Geree's church of St Michael survives.

Swift's closest friendships in England were with Pope and Gay (qq.v.), though *Verses on the Death of Dr Swift* prophesied cynically: 'Poor POPE will grieve a Month; and GAY/ A week' (lines 207–208). His most important visits to them took place in 1726, when he arrived with the manuscript of *Gulliver's Travels*, and in 1727, when he stayed at Pope's Villa in Twickenham and travelled with him to Lord Bathurst's estate at Cirencester, both described under the entry for his friend.

Old Library, Trinity College, Dublin: phone (01) 772941.

Archbishop Marsh's Library, St Patrick's Close, Dublin: phone (01) 543511.

Dublin Castle, Castle Street, Dublin: phone (01) 777129.

Algernon Charles Swinburne

b. London, 1837; d. London, 1909. *Atalanta in Calydon* (1865); *Poems and Ballads* (1866); *A Song of Italy* (1867); *An Appeal to England* (1867); *Songs Before Sunrise* (1871); *Bothwell* (1874); *Poems and Ballads: Second Series* (1878); *Mary Stuart* (1881); *Tristram of Lyonesse and Other Poems* (1882); *A Century of Roundels* (1883); *Poems and Ballads: Third Series* (1889); *Love's Cross Currents: A Year's Letters* (1901); *Lesbia Brandon* (edited by R. Hughes; 1952).

Though born in London, Swinburne divided his childhood between the countryside of South-Eastern and Northern England. His parents lived on the Isle of Wight at Bonchurch, a village beneath the downs on the south coast 1 mile east of Ventnor. Their home, East Dene, is now a hostel. When Dickens (q.v., Rte 13) came for a holiday in 1849 his attention was caught by 'the golden-haired lad of the Swinburnes'. His parents' connection with Bonchurch ended in the 1860s but the poet, like his father and sisters, is buried in its newer churchyard.

Always eager to prove a physical courage that his small stature might have seemed to belie, Swinburne undertook in 1851 the remarkable feat of climbing Culver Cliff, which rises some 254ft from the sea 8 miles NE of Bonchurch near the island's eastern tip. In 1857, and presumably in tamer mood, he called on Tennyson (q.v.) at Farringford near Freshwater on the western end of the Isle. The Poet Laureate invited him to dinner, treated him to the inevitable reading of *Maud* and reported favourably in a letter to a friend: 'what I particularly admired in him was that he did not press upon me any verses of his own'.

Throughout his early years Swinburne paid frequent visits to his grandfather at Capheaton, the family home in Northumberland, a fine 17C building off A696 18 miles NW of Newcastle upon Tyne. He was greatly impressed and influenced by the eccentric Sir John: 'It was said that the two maddest things in the North country were his horse and himself; I don't think his horse can have been the madder'. The bleak moors and coasts of Northumberland, too, left a lasting mark on his sensibility:

> Between our eastward and our westward sea
> The narrowing strand
> Clasps the noblest shore fame holds in fee
> Even here where English birth seals all men free—
> Northumberland.
> ('Northumberland', lines 1–5)

He was also a guest of Lady Pauline Trevelyan at Wallington, 3 miles north of Capheaton via B6342. It was here that he first met Ruskin (q.v.), apparently in 1857 when the critic came to assist the artist William Bell Scott in redecorating the house.

In fact, the young Swinburne made a habit of meeting the great, for in 1849 his parents had taken him to visit Wordsworth at Rydal Mount in the Lake District (s.v. Lake Poets, Rte 12C). It is reported that the elderly Wordsworth, who died only six months later, recommended his poetry on the grounds that 'there was nothing in his writings that would do the boy harm, and there were some things which might do him good'.

In 1849 Swinburne entered Eton College, south of M4 near Windsor. Lord Redesdale's famous description of his new schoolfellow shows that the future poet's highly distinctive appearance was

'At the Pines', by Max Beerbohm (q.v.). The elderly Swinburne (left) with Theodore Watts-Duncan, the companion of his Putney years

by then already established: 'He was strangely tiny. His limbs were small and delicate; and his sloping shoulders looked far too weak to carry his great head, the size of which was exaggerated by the touzled mass of red hair standing almost at right angles to it'. He was soon called 'Mad Swinburne', a nickname that echoed the one bestowed by the same school on Shelley (q.v.), a poet he much admired and emulated. A late work, 'Eton: An Ode', praised his old school in the stately language appropriate to public verse, but the writings he did not choose to make public suggest that its most permanent legacy was a lifelong obsession with flagellation.

Swinburne's career at Balliol College, Oxford, which began in 1856, was both distinguished and controversial. Its most important result, perhaps, was the friendship with William Morris, Rossetti (qq.v.) and the painter Edward Burne-Jones formed during their visit to the university for 'The Jovial Campaign' to decorate the Oxford Union building in 1857; this is briefly noted under the entry for Morris. Otherwise, Swinburne devoted more time to writing poetry than the authorities judged prudent. This—together with his republicanism, agnosticism, and complaints from the landlady of his lodgings in Broad Street about irregular behaviour—made Benjamin Jowett fear that his college would send him down and so 'make Balliol as ridiculous as University had made itself about Shelley'. In the event, Swinburne was apparently advised to leave without taking a degree, which he did in 1860.

A selection of the places Swinburne visited during the next decade indicates the range of his friendships, interests and activities. In 1864 he toured Cornwall with the landscape painter Inchbold. The ruined Tintagel Castle on the north coast 4 miles SW of Boscastle is described in a letter to his cousin Mary Gordon: 'The outer half of the castle, on the headland beyond the isthmus is on the very edge (and partly over the edge and on the slant) of the cliff; and has indescribable views of the double bay, broken cliffs, and outer sea'. The trip influenced *Tristram of Lyonesse* and is remembered in a poem of 1888, 'In Memory of John William Inchbold'.

Swinburne became a *protégé* and close friend of Richard Monckton Milnes (Lord Houghton), politician, biographer of Keats (q.v.) and book collector whose library contained many volumes of erotica. He was several times a guest at Milnes' country house, Monk Fryston Hall in North Yorkshire, 2 miles east of A1 on A63 towards Selby. The Hall is now a hotel that preserves much of its former character. In 1861 the poet met Richard Burton, explorer and translator of *The Arabian Nights*, here. The following year he struck a fellow guest as 'a cross between the devil and the Duke of Argyll'. Henry Adams, the American writer who was then acting as Milnes' private secretary, remembered Swinburne in his *Education* as

> a tropical bird, high-crested, long-beaked, quick-moving, with a rapid utterance and screams of humour quite unlike any English lark or nightingale. One could hardly call him a crimson macaw among owls, and yet no ordinary contrast availed.

Another powerful literary friend was the novelist Edward Bulwer-Lytton (s.v. Lytton), who wrote to Swinburne expressing admiration for *Atalanta in Calydon*. In the summer of 1866, when the controversy stirred up by the publication of *Poems and Ballads* was at its height, Swinburne stayed at Knebworth House, the 16C mansion Lytton had extravagantly enlarged.

During these years, when his fame and notoriety grew in equal proportions, Swinburne was living in London. In 1862 he went to lodge with Rossetti at Tudor House, No. 16 Cheyne Walk, by the Chelsea Embankment. The ensuing domestic chaos quickly drove away George Meredith (q.v.), a fellow tenant, and Swinburne's outrageous, frequently drunken behaviour appears to have been too much even for a man of Rossetti's easy-going habits. In 1865–70 Swinburne was at No. 22 Dorset Street, west of Baker Street just south of its junction with Marylebone Road. By 1872 he was at No. 3 Great James Street, which runs north from Theobald's Road near Gray's Inn Gardens and Gray's Inn Road. At a later date he moved a few streets north to Guilford Street.

This mobility may in part have been designed to escape the watchful eye of his family, who had joined his friends in concern about his heavy drinking. By 1879 the problem had reached a point where it justified fears for his health, if not his life, and demanded a drastic remedy. This appeared in the surprising form of Theodore Watts (later Watts-Dunton), a solicitor of literary tastes. With the approval of Swinburne's family he took the poet firmly in hand and removed him to Putney in south-west London. No. 2 The Pines, the house he rented on Putney Hill, still stands (though its number has been altered to 11) and is only a few minutes' walk from Putney Station (British Rail).

To contemporaries the suburb, then newly developed and still remote from London, seemed a strange, even comic destination for a fiery poet and No. 2 The Pines an inappropriately bourgeois address for an admirer of Mazzini and De Sade. Yet Swinburne remained there for the rest of his life, settling into a quiet and apparently contented routine: admiring the children in their baby carriages during his morning walk on nearby Putney Heath, confining himself to a single bottle of beer over lunch, and devoting afternoons to energetic but uninspired composition. He rarely went into central London or, indeed, left Putney at all. Visitors regarded his transformation with surprise tinged by disappointment. G.K. Chesterton (q.v.) came and found not the 'Anti-Christ in purple' he had expected but 'a very well-read Victorian old maid'. The atmosphere of the house and of Swinburne's later years was deftly caught by the young Max Beerbohm (q.v.) in his essay, 'No. 2 The Pines'.

Wallington, Cambo, Morpeth, Northumberland: NT; phone Scots Gap (067 074) 283.

Rydal Mount, Ambleside, Cumbria: phone (05394) 33002.

Eton College, Windsor, Berkshire: School Yard, College Chapel, Cloister Court and Museum of Eton Life open; also guided tours; phone (0753) 863593.

Tintagel Castle, Tintagel, Cornwall: English Heritage, standard opening; phone Camelford (0840) 770328.

Knebworth House, Knebworth, Hertfordshire: phone Stevenage (0438) 812661.

John Millington Synge

b. Dublin, 1871; d. Dublin, 1909. *In the Shadow of the Glen* (1905); *Riders to the Sea* (1905); *The Well of the Saints* (1905); *The Playboy of the Western World* (1907); *The Aran Islands* (1907); *The Tinker's Wedding* (1907); *Deirdre of the Sorrows* (1910).

Synge was born at No. 2 Newtown Villas, a substantial semi-detached house in the southern Dublin suburb of Rathfarnham. After his father died the following year his mother moved the family north to the suburb of Rathgar and a house at No. 4 Orwell Park, immediately north of the River Dodder.

The Synges were affluent and pious members of the Protestant

Ascendancy and as a child, at a time when protests against landlordism were at their height, he was frequently taken to the family estates in County Wicklow, south of Dublin. He several times stayed with his mother in the little coastal resort of Greystones (on L29 4½ miles south of Bray) and visited his grandfather, Francis Synge, at Glenmore Castle in the romantic Devil's Glen west of Ashford (9 miles south of Greystones on N11). The building later fell into ruins but has been partly rebuilt. The Glenmalur valley near Rathdrum, further south, is the setting for *In the Shadow of the Glen*.

In 1888, already starting to reject the family's politics and religion, Synge entered Trinity College, Dublin. He was later to insist that his education here made little impression on him. The Manuscript Room in the Old Library has manuscripts of his works.

After graduating in 1892 Synge spent several years on the Continent studying music and writing in a desultory fashion until a

'Thatching' by Jack B. Yeats from Synge's The Aran Islands *(1907)*

momentous meeting with Yeats (q.v.) in Paris in 1896. Afire with enthusiasm for the Irish literary revival and with the belief that artists should deal with Irish subjects, the older writer advised him to study folk life on the Aran Islands, and Synge's obedience to this suggestion helped him at last to find his literary voice. His visits each summer from 1898 to 1902 led not only to a fine prose account of the islands but also to the mastery of folk idiom that distinguishes his plays.

The little group of three islands lies in the Galway Bay some 30 miles SW of Galway, from which it can be reached by steamer or by air. The modern visitor can still find much to recognise from Synge's descriptions. Fishing remains an important means of livelihood, and the islanders still sometimes wear 'pampooties', the locally made cowhide shoes which Synge, always a stickler for authentic detail, made the original cast of *Riders to the Sea* wear. That play comes directly from his experience of Inishmaan, the central island in the group, where he spent much time strolling round the impressive ruins of Dún Conor, one of the many ancient fortifications which dot the landscape.

By the time Synge's plays were achieving success and causing controversy in Dublin's Abbey Theatre (see entry for Yeats), Synge was already suffering from Hodgkin's disease. He died in Dublin at No. 130 Northumberland Road (reached by following Lower Mount Street SE from Merrion Square) and was buried at Mount Jerome Cemetery in the suburb of Harold's Cross.

Manuscript Room, Old Library, Trinity College, Dublin: phone (01) 772941.

Alfred Lord Tennyson

b. Somersby, Lincolnshire, 1809; d. Haslemere, Surrey, 1892. *Poems by Two Brothers* (with contributions by Charles and Frederick Tennyson; 1827); *Poems, Chiefly Lyrical* (includes 'The Kraken', 'Mariana'; 1830); *Poems* (Includes 'The Lady of Shalott', 'The Palace of Art', 'The Lotos-Eaters'; 1833); *Poems* (includes 'Ulysses', 'Break, Break, Break', 'Morte d'Arthur', 'Locksley Hall'; 1842); *The Princess* (1847); *In Memoriam A.H.H.* (1850); *Maud, and Other Poems* (1855); *Idylls of the King* (1859); *Enoch Arden and Other Poems* (1864); *Ballads and Other Poems* (1880); *Tiresias and Other Poems* (1885); *Demeter and Other Poems* (1889).

Of the poet's various connections with Eastern England by far the deepest are in Lincolnshire, where the Tennyson family originated and where he himself spent his childhood, youth and much of his early adulthood. The county town of Lincoln makes a convenient starting point for a tour. Outside the east end of the Cathedral, between the chapter house and Priory Gate, stands a statue of 1905 by G.F. Watts which shows him, with his dog by his side, wearing the characteristic broad-brimmed hat and flowing cloak. The Usher Art Gallery on Deansgate south of the Cathedral contains a collection of personal memorabilia.

By heading east via Horncastle and branching north on country roads we enter the Wolds, an area still virtually as remote and rural as it was in Tennyson's day. He was born in the small village of Somersby, at Somersby House (formerly the Rectory) opposite the church, and passed a childhood, youth and early poetic career there overshadowed by family difficulties in the form of his father's poverty, epilepsy, alcoholism and opium addiction. Rev. George Clayton Tennyson (d. 1831) was rector of the small church and is buried outside its door; a bust of the poet is inside. Holywell Wood behind the Rectory was a favourite walk of Tennyson and his brothers. The neighbouring village of Bag Enderby, of which Tennyson's father also held the living, has a Perpendicular church of extreme and touching simplicity. Harrington Hall, further east, was the home of Rosa Baring, with whom Tennyson fell in love in the 1830s. Its walled garden is identified with 'high Hall-garden' of *Maud* (section 12).

In the small town of Tetford, a useful centre for tours of the Wolds, is the White Hart Inn where Tennyson was a customer; the oak settle he reputedly used is displayed in the bar. At Louth, a market town further north distinguished by the magnificent spire of its church, Tennyson attended the Old Grammar School (rebuilt) on Westgate from 1816 to 1820, upholding the time-honoured tradition by which poets dislike their schooldays and find their masters brutally insensitive. A day scholar, he lodged with his grandmother in the same street. His first volume of poetry was issued by a bookseller in the Market Place.

Near the village of Tealby, west of Louth and near Market Rasen, stood the now-demolished Bayons Manor, home of the poet's grandfather, always on bad terms with the Somersby family. His heir Charles Tennyson d'Eyncourt added to the house, originally just a small Regency building, in the same spirit that led him to extend the family name. His achievement provoked a contemptuous passage in *Maud*:

> Seeing his gewgaw castle shine,
> New as his title, built last year,
> There amid perky larches and pine,
> And over the sullen-purple moor
> (Look at it) pricking a cockney ear.
> (lines 347–351)

Suitably elaborate monuments to his branch of the Tennysons may be found in the chancel of Tealby church. The florid inscription honouring his grandfather, George, provoked another outburst from the poet, this time in 'Locksley Hall Sixty Years After' (1886):

> Gone the tyrant of my youth, and mute below the chancel stones,
> All his virtues—I forgive them—black in white above his bones.
> (lines 43–44)

'Locksley Hall, that in the distance overlooks the sandy tracts' (*Locksley Hall*, line 5) has been identified with the manor house at Saltfleet on the Lincolnshire coast east of Louth, though a more likely candidate is the house so named at North Somercotes, a few miles north.

Tennyson's connections with Eastern England were extended by his studies (1827–31) at Trinity College, Cambridge. During his undergraduate years he was elected to the exclusive society of the Apostles and won the Lord Chancellor's medal for his poem 'Timbuctoo' (1829). Of special importance was his close friendship with Arthur Henry Hallam, whose early death in 1833 led to the great elegiac sequence *In Memoriam*. No. 87 deals with a later visit to Cambridge that evoked memories of his dead friend. Tennyson is commemorated at Trinity by Thomas Woolner's good bust in the Library and Sir Hamo Thornycroft's statue of 1909 in the ante-chapel, which, according to one observer, makes him look like 'the prima donna's noble father in Victorian opera'.

Hallam had rooms in New Court while Tennyson himself lodged first in Rose Crescent, off Trinity Street, and then at the King's Parade end of Trumpington Street, in No. 57, whose bricked-over doorway is still clearly distinguishable between the neighbouring houses. The neo-classical building immediately opposite, now part of St Catharine's College, was once the Bull Hotel, from which Tennyson departed Cambridge in 1831.

He was a frequent guest at the Hallams' London home, No. 67 Wimpole Street, which runs south from Marylebone Road as an extension of Devonshire Place. This is the scene of the finely tuned seventh lyric of *In Memoriam*:

Dark house, by which once more I stand
Here in the long unlovely street ...

Hallam's body was returned from Vienna, where he had died, to be buried at Clevedon on the Severn estuary west of Bristol:

The Danube to the Severn gave
The darkened heart that beat no more;
They laid him by the pleasant shore,
And in the hearing of the wave.

There twice a day the Severn fills;
The salt sea-water passes by,
And hushes half the babbling Wye,
And makes a silence in the hills.
(*In Memoriam*, lyric 19)

Hallam is remembered by a tablet in the parish church of St Andrew, which Tennyson visited on his honeymoon in 1850.

Hallam's death in 1833 and the Tennyson family's move from Somersby in 1837 made the years that followed disturbed and restless: Tennyson became a traveller and a visitor to other men's houses. London connections are represented by: No. 14 Percy Street, off Tottenham Court Road, home of the poet Coventry Patmore (q.v.) and now marked by a plaque; Carlyle's House in Cheyne Row, Chelsea, described under that author; and the Star and Garter Inn, Richmond (for which see Dickens, Rte 7). His friendship with three other famous contemporaries is best remembered by a later occasion, in 1855, when he read *Maud* to an assembled company at the Brownings' lodging in Dorset Street, near Wimpole Street, and was covertly sketched by Dante Gabriel Rossetti (q.v.): see the entry for Robert and Elizabeth Barrett Browning. A London inn, the Cock Tavern, is celebrated in 'Will Waterproof's Lyrical Monologue' (1842), one of his rare ventures into light verse; relics of the building are preserved in the present inn of that name on the south side of Fleet Street near Temple Bar Memorial.

In 1835 he visited James Spedding at Mirehouse, Spedding's country house on the eastern shore of Bassenthwaite Lake in the Lake District. The lakeside view near the little, partly Norman church of St Bega is said to have inspired the setting for the closing scene of *Idylls of the King*, when Sir Bedivere carries the wounded Arthur

to a chapel nigh the field,
A broken chancel with a broken cross,
That stood on a dark strait of barren land:
On one side lay the Ocean, and on one
Lay a great water, and the moon was full.
('The Passing of Arthur', lines 176–180)

The long gestation of his Arthurian cycle owes something, too, to the visit he paid in 1848 to the ruins of Tintagel Castle near Boscastle on the north coast of Cornwall. The same trip also took him to the village of Morwenstow, north of Bude, where he met the eccentric poet-clergyman R.S. Hawker (q.v.).

Tennyson's appointment as Poet Laureate on the death of Wordsworth in 1850 and his marriage the same year to Emily Sellwood, whom he had met in Somersby, marked the beginning of a more settled life. From 1851 to 1853 they lived at Chapel House on Montpelier Row, a superb terrace of early 18C houses on the edge of Marble Hill Park in Twickenham.

From 1853 onwards his life centred on South-Eastern England. In that year he moved, first as tenant and later as owner, to Farringford near Freshwater on the western end of the Isle of Wight. The location answered his need for seclusion, while the house, originally built in 1806 but later enlarged, appealed to his love of the Gothic style: 'It is like blank verse. It will suit the humblest cottage and the grandest cathedral'. Literary friends who came to stay included William Allingham, Francis Turner Palgrave (editor of *The Golden Treasury*), Edward Lear (q.v.) and Edward FitzGerald (q.v.), whom Tennyson visited at Woodbridge in Suffolk. The young Swinburne (q.v.), who called uninvited in 1857, recommended himself by not attempting to press any of his own poetry on the Laureate. Among the public men who paid visits were Prince Albert and, in 1864, Garibaldi, who planted a tree which still stands outside the house. Farringford is now a hotel.

Emily Tennyson, who outlived her husband until 1896, is buried in the churchyard at Freshwater and there is, inevitably, a memorial to him in the church. Tennyson Down (NT) on the southern shore between Easton and The Needles is named to commemorate a favourite walk and has a striking monument. 'Crossing the Bar' was written on a voyage across the Solent between the Isle of Wight and the mainland.

Tennyson acquired a second and larger establishment with the building (1868–69) of Aldworth on Blackdown Hill (NT; 919ft) south of Haslemere, Surrey, and reached from the town via Tennyson's Lane (NT). It was designed by his friend, the architect James Knowles, who refused a fee on the grounds that his pleasure in Tennyson's poetry was sufficient reward. Of the result—eclectically Gothic with the French style predominating, deliberately grand and at odds with its natural setting—Tennyson's modern biographer has remarked: 'It may not look like a poet's home, but it could not be a more suitable seat for a Poet Laureate'. To Aldworth came visitors like Carlyle (q.v.), who could not be lured as far as the Isle of Wight, and Gladstone, who like Tennyson had been a close friend of Hallam.

Tennyson's funeral was held in Westminster Abbey, though several friends found the occasion hollow and disappointing, and he is honoured by a memorial in Poets' Corner (fee). In 1875 he had written the inscription for the monument to the Arctic explorer Sir John Franklin (d. 1847) in the Chapel of St John the Evangelist in the north transept. He considered it his best epitaph.

Usher Gallery, Lindum Road, Lincoln: phone (0522) 27980.

Harrington Hall, Harrington, Spilsby, Lincolnshire: future opening arrangements uncertain at time of writing; phone Spilsby Tourist Information Centre, (0790) 52301.

Trinity College Library, Cambridge: phone the Porters' Lodge, (0223) 338400.

Carlyle's House, 24 Cheyne Row, Chelsea, London SW3: NT; phone (01) 352 7087.

Mirehouse, near Keswick, Cumbria: phone Keswick (076 87) 72287.

Tintagel Castle, Tintagel, Cornwall: English Heritage, standard opening; phone Camelford (0840) 770328.

William Makepeace Thackeray

b. Calcutta, India, 1811; d. London, 1863. *The Yellowplush Papers* (1838); *The Paris Sketch Book, by Mr Titmarsh* (1840); *The Irish Sketch Book, by Mr M.A. Titmarsh* (1843); *The Luck of Barry Lyndon: A Romance of the Last Century. By Fitz-Boodle* (1844; revised 1856); *Notes of a Journey from Cornhill to Grand Cairo* (1846); *The Book of Snobs* (1848); *Vanity Fair: A Novel Without a Hero* (1848); *The History of Pendennis: His Fortunes and Misfortunes, His Friends and His Greatest Enemy* (1849–50); *The History of Henry Esmond, Esq. a Colonel in the Service of Her Majesty Q. Anne, Written by Himself* (1852); *The English Humourists of the Eighteenth Century* (1853); *The Newcomes: Memoirs of a Most Respectable Family, Edited by Arthur Pendennis Esqre* (1854–55); *The Virginians: A Tale of the Last Century* (1858–59); *The Four Georges: Sketches of Manners, Morals, Court and Town Life* (1860); *Lovel the Widower* (1861); *The Adventures of Philip on His Way Through the World* (1862); *Roundabout Papers* (1863); *Denis Duval* (unfinished; 1867).

When he first arrived from India in 1817 Thackeray was sent to Dr Turner's Academy at Chiswick in SW London, a borough whose connections with genteel education he later immortalised in the opening chapter of *Vanity Fair*. Miss Pinkerton's establishment in the novel has been identified as Walpole House on the delightful 18C Chiswick Mall.

We do not know if Thackeray shared Becky Sharp's sentiments — 'thank God, I'm out of Chiswick' (Ch. 2)—but he did leave Dr Turner's Academy slightly earlier than expected and was certainly ill-prepared for the rigours of *Charterhouse. The school was then still in its fine old buildings on Charterhouse Square near the Central Meat Market in the City. The novelist quickly showed himself indifferent to sport and given to reading novels, especially the 'Waverley' novels of Sir Walter Scott (q.v.). These do not appear to have been happy years, for his later memories centred on the brutality of public school life: his schoolmasters bear names like 'Birch' and 'Swishtail' while Charterhouse itself is nicknamed 'Slaughterhouse'. A certain mellowing is apparent in *The Newcomes*, where the school wears the transparent disguise of 'Grey Friars'. The aged and broken Colonel Newcome is received as a Poor Brother in Chapter 76 (which includes a description of Founder's Day at the school) and dies here in the final chapter:

> At the usual evening hour the chapel bell began to toll, and Thomas Newcome's hands outside the bed feebly beat time. And just as the last bell struck, a peculiar sweet smile shone over his face, and he lifted up his head a little, and quickly said 'Adsum!' and fell back. It was the word we used at school, when names were called; and lo, he whose heart was as that of a little child, had answered to his name, and stood in the presence of the Master.

Pensioners' Hall Charterhouse: an engraving by Thomas Shepherd in James Elmes' London and its Environs in the Nineteenth Century *(1829)*

Thackeray spent holidays with his mother and stepfather, Major Carmichael-Smyth, at their Devon home, Larkbeare, near Ottery St Mary, a mile south of A30 between Honiton and Exeter. His description of 'Clavering St Mary' in *Pendennis*, his most autobiographical novel, shows that mixture of sentiment and irony which is Thackeray's most distinctive trait:

> Looking at the little old town of Clavering St Mary from the old London road as it runs by the lodge at Fairoaks [Larkbeare], and seeing the rapid and shining Brawl [the Otter] winding down and skirting the woods of Clavering Park [Escot Lodge], and the ancient church tower and peaked roofs of the houses rising up amongst trees and old walls, behind which swells a fair background of sunshiny hills that stretch from Clavering westwards towards the sea—the place appears to be so cheery and comfortable that many a traveller's heart must have yearned towards it from the coach-top, and he must have thought that it was in such a calm and friendly nook he would like to shelter at the end of life's struggle ... Like Constantinople seen from the Bosphorus; like Mrs Rougemont viewed in her box from the opposite side of the house; like many an object which we pursue in life, and admire before we have attained it; Clavering is rather prettier at a distance than it is on closer acquaintance. The town so cheerful of aspect a few furlongs off, looks very blank and dreary. (Ch. 15)

The lovely collegiate Church of St Mary, rebuilt in 1337–42 by Bishop Grandison, is remembered less cynically for 'its grey towers, of which the sun illuminates the delicate carving; deepening the shadows of the huge buttresses, and gilding the glittering windows and flaming vanes' (Ch. 15). In the same book the quiet coastal resort of Sidmouth, 5 miles south, appears as 'Baymouth' and Exeter as 'Chatteris', the city treated to an exhibition of Miss Fotheringay's dramatic talents; she lodges with Captain Costigan near the Cathedral Close.

Though the Carmichael-Smyths did not long remain in Devon Thackeray kept his connections with South-Western England in later years. In 1848 he stayed with the Elton family at Clevedon Court on B3130 12 miles west of Bristol. The visit confirmed his unfulfilled romantic attachment to their daughter, Mrs Brookfield. The building itself, 14C with Elizabethan alterations, is generally identified with the 'Castlewood' of *Henry Esmond*, though the novel places it in Hampshire.

When he entered Trinity College, Cambridge, in February 1829 he was given ground-floor rooms between the main gatehouse and Chapel in Great Court, and wrote to his mother: 'Men will say some day, that Newton and Thackeray kept near one another!' He gave the same rooms to his hero Henry Esmond (Bk 1, Ch. 10), but his own Trinity career more closely resembled the misadventures of Pendennis, whom he made a student of 'St Boniface, Oxbridge' (Ch. 18ff). The love of novel-reading continued but to this blameless pastime he added a fondness for wine parties and gambling. Discouraged by poor exam results and with part of his patrimony wasted, he left in the spring of 1830. His fellow undergraduate Edward FitzGerald (q.v.) remained a lifelong friend.

From Cambridge Thackeray went to London and settled thoroughly into the life of a 'cockney', to use his own term for the urban spirit that pervades his fiction, whether it deals with elegant West End houses and clubs or with dubiously Bohemian quarters. In 1831 he entered the Middle Temple, south of Fleet Street near its junction with the Strand; his lodgings were at No. 1 Hare Court, off Inner Temple Lane. Though he never seriously applied himself to the study of law, he developed a lasting taste for the 18C literary associations of the Temple:

> I don't know whether the student of law permits himself the refreshment of enthusiasm, or indulges in poetical reminiscences as he passes by historical chambers ... but the man of letters can't but love the place which has been inhabited by so many of his brethren, or peopled by their creations as real to us at this day as the authors whose children they were—and Sir Roger de Coverley walking in the Temple Garden, and discoursing with Mr Spectator about the beauties in hoops and patches who are sauntering over the grass, is just as lively a figure to me as old Samuel Johnson rolling through the fog with the Scotch gentleman at his heels on their way to Dr Goldsmith's chambers in Brick Court; or Harry Fielding, with inked ruffles and a wet towel round his head, dashing off articles at Midnight for the *Covent Garden Journal*, while the printer's boy is asleep in the passage. (*Pendennis*, Ch. 29)

In 1838, after his marriage to Isabella Shawe, Thackeray settled in Bloomsbury at No. 13 Coram Street (then Great Coram Street), off Woburn Place. His domestic happiness was soon destroyed by his wife's mental breakdown in 1840. He left his two daughters in the care of his mother and travelled with Isabella on the Continent, before surrendering her permanently into professional hands. He returned only briefly to Coram Street before the lease expired in 1843 and lived a bachelor life for the next few years.

It was not until 1846 that he was again able to provide a home for his children. In that year he began his long association with Kensington by moving into No. 13 Young Street (now marked with a plaque), south of Kensington High Street near the SW corner of Kensington Gardens. *Vanity Fair* was written here, and in 1850 Charlotte Brontë (q.v.), a great admirer of the novel, was entertained to a memorably unsuccessful dinner. In 1854 he moved SE to the more fashionable Brompton. Although pleased by his 'neat new house' at No. 36 Onslow Square (marked with a plaque) Thackeray was never entirely at home in the neighbourhood.

It comes as no surprise, then, that he should have moved back to Kensington in 1861; yet the importance, elegance and expressiveness of the home he built for himself are a pleasant shock to the literary pilgrim. *No. 2 Palace Green, facing Kensington Gardens off Kensington High Street, is convincing evidence of the affluence his writing had at last won him—a gesture to show the world that his years of labour in Fleet Street had been rewarded. He acknowledged that the house was paid for by his salary as editor of the *Cornhill Magazine* and joked that it should have the emblem of the wheatsheaf at its door. As the cost rose to £8000 he ruefully agreed with the suggestion it should be called 'Vanity Fair House'. Yet the Palace Green home was more than just an announcement of the social position he had achieved. Thackeray chose to build in the Queen Anne style—and did so with immaculate taste—long before it was being generally revived by the Victorians. The house embodies that mild unease with mid-nineteenth-century culture and that sneaking preference for the eighteenth century and the Regency which we also find in his writings. The building has had a chequered history since Thackeray's time, becoming at one point the home of the Bravo family, whose son Charles Bravo died mysteriously of poisoning at Balham Priory in 1876. It now belongs to the Israeli Embassy.

Thackeray's use of several locations in South-Eastern England further reminds us of his love for the eighteenth century and the Regency. In Chapter 24 of *The Virginians* Harry Warrington visits the future General Wolfe at his home, now Quebec House, in Westerham near Sevenoaks. (In fact, Wolfe did not live in the house after the age of eleven). Thackeray's last novel, *Denis Duval*, again retreats into the eighteenth century and is set in the picturesque little towns of Winchelsea and Rye, east of Hastings. Its hero attends the 17C Peacocke's School in Rye's High Street. Henry James (q.v.), who lived in Rye, included a finely appreciative essay, 'Winchelsea, Rye and *Denis Duval*', in his *English Hours*. Brighton during the Regency is deftly conjured up in *Vanity Fair*, where Thackeray hails the fashionable resort as 'a clean Naples with genteel lazzaroni ... Brighton, that always looks so brisk, gay, and gaudy, like a harlequin's jacket ... Brighton, which used to be seven hours distant from London at the time of our story; which is now only a hundred minutes off; and which may approach who knows how much nearer' (Ch. 22).

Thackeray died at Palace Green with *Denis Duval* unfinished and his projected history of Queen Anne's reign unattempted. The offer of a grave near Oliver Goldsmith (q.v.) in the Temple Church was declined and he was buried in Kensal Green Cemetery, opposite Kensal Green Station (British Rail and Bakerloo Underground Line). His grave is No. 18177 in square 36 between South Avenue and the canal. Its simplicity and modest position prompted Richard Monckton Milnes, Lord Houghton, a friend since their days at Trinity College, to write:

> But, may be, he—who could so draw
> The hidden great—the humble wise,
> Yielding with them to God's good law
> Makes the Pantheon where he lies.

Some were surprised that the question of a funeral in Westminster Abbey had not been raised, and Shirley Brooks, a friend from *Punch*, started a subscription for a bust to be placed in Poets' Corner (fee). It was designed by Baron Carlo Marochetti, Thackeray's old neighbour in Young Street.

Charterhouse, Charterhouse Square, London EC1: guided tours in summer; phone (01) 253 9503.

Clevedon Court, Clevedon, Avon: NT; phone (0272) 872257.

Quebec House, Westerham, Kent: NT; phone (0959) 62206.

Dylan Thomas

b. Swansea, West Glamorgan, 1914; d. New York, USA, 1953. *18 Poems* (1934); *Twenty-Five Poems* (1936); *The Map of Love: Verse and Prose* (1939); *Portrait of the Artist as a Young Dog* (1940); *New Poems* (1943); *Deaths and Entrances: Poems* (1946); *Twenty-Six Poems* (1950); *In Country Sleep and Other Poems* (1952); *Collected Poems 1934–1952* (1952); *The Doctor and the Devils* (1953); *Under Milk Wood: A Play for Voices* (1954); *Quite Early One Morning: Broadcasts* (1954); *Adventures in the Skin Trade and Other Stories* (1955); *A Prospect of the Sea and Other Stories and Prose Writings* (edited by Daniel Jones; 1955); *The Beach of Falesá: Based on a Story by R.L. Stevenson* (1963).

For Dylan Thomas Wales was the magic territory of childhood, the culture that shaped his gifts, the narrow province from which he needed to escape and, always, the place where he could do his best writing. His family home is in the western part of Swansea, the Uplands, at No. 5 Cwmdonkin Drive, a street that proclaims its Edwardian respectability. Here, after leaving school and abandoning his job as a local reporter, Thomas first dedicated himself to poetry. Cwmdonkin Park, to the west, where he used to play as a child, now has a memorial.

In adult life his connection with Wales centred on the pleasant little town of Laugharne, on the coast and A4066 SW of Carmarthen. He first came in 1938 as a guest of the novelist Richard Hughes, returning later to rent Sea View near the town centre and finally, for the last years of his life, to live by the sea in the Boat House, beyond Cliff Road. He is buried in the churchyard. Several Welsh Towns have claimed themselves as the original of 'Llaregyb', the setting for *Under Milk Wood*, but it is certain that the radio play could not have been conceived without the influence and example of Laugharne.

Thomas' life in London—and, at the end, in America—made the need for such a retreat the more urgent. He first went to London in 1934, frequenting 'Fitzrovia' (north of Oxford Street and west of Tottenham Court Road) and later, when he was connected with the BBC, the area round Broadcasting House in Langham Place (north of Oxford Circus). In 1982 a memorial was added to Poets' Corner (fee) in Westminster Abbey.

Edward Thomas

b. London, 1878; d. Arras, France, 1917. *The Woodland Life* (1897); *Horae Solitariae* (1902); *Oxford* (1903); *Rose Acre Papers* (1904); *Beautiful Wales* (1905); *The Heart of England* (1906); *Richard Jefferies* (1909); *The South Country* (1909); *Windsor Castle* (1910); *The Isle of Wight* (1911); *Light and Twilight* (1911); *Algernon Charles Swinburne* (1912); *George Borrow* (1912); *The Icknield Way* (1913); *The Country* (1913); *The Happy-Go-Lucky Morgans* (1913); *Walter Pater* (1913); *In Pursuit of Spring* (1914); *Four-and-Twenty Blackbirds* (1915); *Keats* (1916); *A Literary Pilgrim in England* (1917); *Poems* (1917); *Last Poems* (1918).

Son of a railway clerk, Thomas went to Oxford as a non-collegiate student in 1897 and entered Lincoln College the next year. His rooms were in the Front Quad above those once occupied by John Wesley.

Thomas' first book had appeared the year he began his studies. After university he supported himself, with determination but often with great difficulty, by a stream of books ranging from the merest hackwork to writings on nature and topography that place him in the tradition of Richard Jefferies and George Borrow (qq.v.). The headnote above gives only a sample for, as Thomas himself remarked to a friend, if 'they put a list of books on my tombstone I shall want one as big as one of the stones at Stonehenge'.

The same love of nature that characterises his best work governed his choice of homes. In 1901–04 he lived in Kent at Bearsted, now virtually assimilated into its western neighbour, Maidstone. Above the village rise the North Downs where he delighted to walk. He then moved west to Else's Farm in Sevenoaks Weald, 4 miles south of Sevenoaks. Thomas brought W.H. Davies to the village and, despite his own poverty, helped support Davies while he began the *Autobiography of a Super-Tramp* (1908). From 1906 onwards he lived in the area round Petersfield (on A3 in Hampshire) to be near Bedales school, where he sent his son. Of his homes here the most interesting is the last: Yewtree Cottage, a cheap semi-detached workman's dwelling near the church in Steep (2 miles north of Petersfield). There is a memorial stone on the hill opposite.

In 1914 he visited the American poet Robert Frost, then staying in the village of Dymock (4 miles south of Ledbury in Hereford and Worcester). In his walks on the nearby Malvern Hills with Frost that summer, Thomas first saw how his precise, unsentimental vision of nature could be recorded in deceptively simple verse. It is, of course, for his career as a poet—cut short by his death in the First World War—that he is now chiefly remembered.

Francis Thompson

b. Preston, Lancashire, 1859; d. London, 1907. *Poems* (includes 'The Hound of Heaven'; 1893); *Sister Songs* (1895); *New Poems* (1897); *Health and Holiness* (1905).

The poet's strange and haunted life began among distinctly mundane surroundings at Preston in Lancashire. His birthplace at No. 7 Winckley Street, south of Fishergate near St George's Shopping Centre, is marked with a plaque. When he was still a child his family moved to Ashton-under-Lyne, 6 miles east of Manchester. Their home, which his father also used as surgery for his practice in homeopathic medicine and made a gathering place for the local Catholic clergy, was at No. 226 Stamford Street, the main thoroughfare which runs NE from Chester Square. In 1870 Thompson was sent to Ushaw College, 4 miles west of Durham. The College's most interesting feature, the chapel designed by Pugin in 1840, was rebuilt on a larger scale in 1885 after Thompson had left. At the age of seventeen he returned to Manchester and entered Owens College, now the University of Manchester, in Oxford Road a mile SE of St Peter's Square. He spent six unsuccessful years here as a medical student, failing his exams three times.

In 1885 he abandoned medicine, broke permanently with his father and came to London. He quickly sank into destitution and opium addiction. From this state he was rescued in 1888 by Wilfrid Meynell, editor of *Merry England*, to whom he had submitted several poems written on ragged scraps of paper. Meynell and his wife Alice, poet, essayist and critic, became Thompson's unofficial guardians, not merely establishing his reputation as a poet but making possible the circumstances under which most of his verse was written. He was a regular visitor to their home at No. 47 Palace Court, which runs north from Bayswater Road near its continuation as Notting Hill Gate. Here he met Coventry Patmore (q.v.), a poet of an older generation and by then almost a forgotten figure.

Thompson's life in London was relieved by retreats into the country, though neither they nor the Meynells' good offices permanently saved him from opium. In 1889 he stayed at a monastery in Storrington, a large West Sussex village 8 miles NW of Worthing. His 'Ode to the Setting Sun' and much of his most famous poem, 'The Hound of Heaven', were written while walking on Kithurst Hill south of Storrington and A283. In 1892–96 he lived with the Roman Catholic community at Pantasaph near the Dee estuary and the North Wales coast. It lies 2 miles west of Holywell and is reached via A55 and an unclassified road leading south.

Thompson was buried in London at St Mary's, the Roman Catholic annexe to Kensal Green Cemetery, opposite Kensal Green Station (British Rail and Bakerloo Underground Line). His gravestone bears the epitaph 'Look for me in the nurseries of Heaven'.

James Thomson

b. Ednam, Borders Region, 1700; d. London, 1748. *The Seasons* (1726–30; revised edition 1744); *Liberty* (1735–36); *The Castle of Indolence* (1748).

Thomson was born in the former manse at the village of Ednam, 2 miles north of Kelso on B6461. At nearby Ferneyhill there is an obelisk commemorating him, erected by David Stewart, Earl of Buchan, in 1819. The enthusiastic peer had opened his campaign on behalf of the poet's memory by holding an anniversary ceremony on the spot in 1791, an occasion to which Robert Burns (q.v.) contributed a poem. Thomson went to school at Jedburgh, on A68 11 miles south of Kelso, attending classes in the aisle of the splendid Abbey church. The rugged and impressive landscape of surrounding *Teviotdale contributed greatly to that new feeling for nature which he introduced into 18C poetry; its influence is particularly apparent in the 'Winter' section of *The Seasons*.

After studying at Edinburgh University, Thomson came permanently to England in 1725. The popularity of his verse and his own fluency in finding aristocratic patrons and friends made him a frequent visitor to country houses. In 1727 he stayed for the first time with the literary-minded Countess of Hertford at Castle House in Marlborough, Wiltshire. The house is now part of Marlborough College. It is hard to credit Dr Johnson (q.v.) when he reports that Thomson 'took more delight in carousing with Lord Hertford and his friends than assisting her Ladyship's poetical operations', for the poet was writing 'Spring' during his visit. As a guest of the Talbot family he found the 17C Ashdown House (off B4000 10 miles east of Swindon) a 'little solitary island, in the midst of a vast verdant ocean'. At Cliveden (by the Thames NE of Maidenhead) a 19C mansion has replaced the 17C building where Thomson's *Masque of Alfred*, with music by Dr Thomas Arne, was first performed in 1740. The occasion would hardly deserve remembering were it not for the inclusion of 'Rule Britannia' among the songs.

Two country houses are of special importance, for they remind the visitor of the close connection between Thomson's poetry and 18C landscape gardening, and of the appropriateness that made William Kent an illustrator of *The Seasons*. The magnificent grounds of *Stowe, to which Kent contributed, are praised in the revised version of 'Autumn':

Oh! lead me to the wide extended walks,
The fair majestic paradise of Stowe!
Not Persian Cyrus on Ionia's shore
E'er saw such sylvan scenes, such various art
By genius fired, such ardent genius tamed
By cool judicious art, that in the strife
All-beauteous Nature fears to be outdone.
(lines 1041–1047)

Now a public school, Stowe is 2 miles NW of Buckingham. *Hagley Hall (on A456 between Birmingham and Kidderminster) receives a tribute in 'Spring':

There among the dale
With woods o'erhung, and shagged with mossy rocks
Whence on each hand the gushing waters play,
And down the rough cascade white-dashing fall
Or gleam in lengthened vista through the trees,
You silent steal; or sit beneath the shade
Of solemn oaks, that tuft the swelling mounts
Thrown graceful round by Nature's careless hand,
And pensive listen to the various voice
Of rural peace.
(lines 909–918)

At Hagley Thomson met the poet Shenstone (q.v.) and revised *The Seasons*, accepting suggestions from his host, Lord Lyttelton.

The same appreciation of landscape led Thomson from central to south-west London, then a series of outlying but fashionable villages. In Hammersmith he frequented the Dove Inn (still a pub) at No. 19 Upper Mall by the river. From 1736 he lived in Richmond, celebrating the view from its Hill in 'Summer' (lines 1408–1445). The Royal Hospital on Kew Foot Road, near the Old Deer Park at the southern end of Kew Road, now incorporates the house where he lived from 1739 until his death. It was here that he received visits from Pope (q.v.) and William Collins (q.v.), and cultivated the habit he made the subject of his last poem, *The Castle of Indolence*. Charles Burney, father of the novelist (q.v.), 'one day at two o'clock in the afternoon, found him in bed, with the curtains closed and the windows shut' and was told: 'Why, Mon, I had not motive to rise'. Thomson found his final rest at the church of St Mary Magdalen between Paradise Road and George Street, where he is commemorated by a tablet of 1792, another fruit of Lord Buchan's admiration for his work.

Poets' Corner (fee) in Westminster Abbey has a memorial of 1762.

Jedburgh Abbey, Jedburgh, Borders Region: Historic Buildings and Monuments, Scottish Development Department; phone the enquiry desk in Edinburgh, (031) 244 3101.

Ashdown House, Lambourn, Newbury, Berkshire: NT; only hall, staircase, roof and grounds open; for opening arrangements phone NT Thames and Chilterns regional office at High Wycombe in Buckinghamshire, (0494) 28051.

Cliveden, Taplow, Maidenhead, Berkshire: NT; phone Burnham (06286) 5069.

Stowe (Stowe School), near Buckingham: grounds, garden buildings and main state rooms open, usually during the Easter and summer holidays; phone Buckingham (0280) 813650.

Hagley Hall, near Stourbridge, West Midlands: phone (0562) 882408.

Thomas Traherne

b. Hereford, 1637?; d. London, 1674. Metaphysical poet.

Traherne was educated at Brasenose College, Oxford, and apparently continued to live in the city for most of his life, despite holding a living at the village of Credenhill near his hometown in Hereford and Worcester. He is remembered by a tablet in the church. Traherne's appointment as chaplain to the Lord Keeper, Sir Orlando Bridgeman, brought him to Teddington in south-west London in 1672. From that year until his death he served as rector of St Mary, on Ferry Road near Teddington Lock, and is buried in the small brick church; it also contains a monument of 1674 to Bridgeman. Traherne's *Centuries of Meditation*, upon which his reputation as a devotional poet depends, was not discovered and published until 1908.

Anthony Trollope

b. London, 1815; d. London, 1882. *The Macdermotts of Ballycloran* (1847); *The Kellys and the O'Kellys, or Landlords and Tenants: A Tale of Irish Life* (1848); *The Warden* (1855); *Barchester Towers* (1857); *The Three Clerks* (1858); *Doctor Thorne* (1858); *The Bertrams* (1859); *Framley Parsonage* (1861); *Orley Farm* (1862); *North America* (1862); *The Small House at Allington* (1864); *Can You Forgive Her?* (1864); *The Belton Estate* (1866); *The Claverings* (1867); *The Last Chronicle of Barset* (1867); *Phineas Finn: The Irish Member* (1869); *He Knew He Was Right* (1869); *The Vicar of Bullhampton* (1870); *Sir Harry Hotspur of Humblethwaite* (1871); *The Eustace Diamonds* (1872); *Australia and New Zealand* (1873); *Phineas Redux* (1874); *The Way We Live Now* (1875); *The Prime Minister* (1876); *The American Senator* (1877); *Is He Popenjoy?* (1878); *The Duke's Children* (1880); *Dr Wortle's School* (1881); *Ayala's Angels* (1881); *Mr Scarborough's Family* (1883); *An Autobiography* (1883).

The novelist spent most of his childhood in a succession of homes at Harrow in north-west London, where his father made a characteristically ill-planned and unsuccessful attempt to establish himself as a farmer. He was sent as a dayboy to the famous public school at Harrow on the Hill. Poor and shabbily dressed, Trollope was uncomfortable among his affluent fellow pupils and his *Autobiography* remembers the walk between home and school as 'a daily purgatory' (Ch. 1).

He was no happier when his education at Harrow was interrupted by a brief spell (1825–27) at another famous school, Winchester College. If anything, the experience was more miserable since

Trollope's father, then embarked on an equally unsuccessful attempt to run a general store in America, was unable to pay his son's bills and the local tradesmen withdrew their credit:

> My schoolfellows of course knew that it was so, and I became a Pariah. It is the nature of boys to be cruel. I have sometimes doubted whether among each other they do usually suffer much, one from the other's cruelty; but I suffered horribly! I could make no stand against it. I had no friend to whom I could pour out my sorrows. I was big, and awkward, and ugly, and, I have no doubt, skulked about in a most unattractive manner. Of course I was ill-dressed and dirty. But, ah! how well I remember all the agonies of my young heart; how I considered whether I should always be alone; whether I could not find my way up to the top of that college tower, and from thence put an end to everything? (*Autobiography*, Ch. 1)

Despite these unhappy memories, obviously still fresh in old age, Trollope made use of Winchester at least once in his fiction. The conflict over 'Hiram's Hospital' in *The Warden* clearly derives from a legal dispute, eventually settled in 1857, involving the city's medieval *Hospital of St Cross. The Hospital stands on St Cross Road south of the centre. Its church is particularly notable.

This link between Winchester and *The Warden* has prompted speculation that the city might be the original of 'Barchester', centre of the 'Barsetshire' novels. Indeed, identifying 'Barchester' used to be a favourite pastime, and a source of much friendly rivalry, among clerics attached to various English cathedrals. Trollope may have seemed to encourage this by speaking of 'Barsetshire' in language that Hardy (q.v.) might have used about 'Wessex':

> I had it all in my mind,—its roads and railroads, its towns and parishes, its members of Parliament, and the different hunts which rode over it. I knew all the great lords and their castles, the squires and their parks, the rectors and their churches ... Throughout these stories there has been no name given to a fictitious site which does not represent to me a spot of which I know all the accessories, as though I had lived and wandered there. (*Autobiography*, Ch. 8)

Yet Trollope's familiarity with 'Barsetshire' was limited to his mind. Unlike Hardy, he never suggested that it had any existence outside the pages of his novels. The furthest he would go was this reference to a visit to Salisbury, apparently made in 1851: 'whilst wandering there on a mid-summer evening round the purlieus of the cathedral I conceived the story of *The Warden*'. He added: 'I stood for an hour on the little bridge in Salisbury, and had made out to my own satisfaction the spot on which Hiram's Hospital should stand' (*Autobiography*, Ch. 5). The bridge is presumably Harnham Bridge, south of the Cathedral Close. St Nicholas' Hospital stands nearby but the visitor will look in vain for any further warrant to give a local habitation and a name to Trollope's invention.

Trollope went to Salisbury in the course of his work for the Post Office, a job that took him to Ireland for most of the 1840s and 1850s. He was a guest of Sir William Henry Gregory at Coole Park by N18 north of Gort in Galway. The house itself, closely associated with Yeats (q.v.) and his circle, has been demolished but the grounds where Trollope indulged his passion for fox-hunting remain. In 1854–59 he lived SE of Dublin in the suburb of Donnybrook. His home, No. 5 Seaview Terrace, is reached by turning left from the main road between Dublin and Bray on to Ailesbury Road.

From 1859 to 1871 he lived at Waltham House in Waltham Cross, on the northern fringe of London. From 1872 to 1880, when he had abandoned 'Barsetshire' for his novels of political life, he lived in

London at No. 39 Montagu Square, now marked with a plaque, north of Marble Arch. He then moved to the village of South Harting, on B2141 11 miles NW of Chichester in West Sussex, where his home survives as Northend House. He died in London at a house on the site of No. 34 Welbeck Street, leading north from Wigmore Street, and, like so many eminent Victorians, was buried in Kensal Green Cemetery, opposite Kensal Green Station (British Rail and Bakerloo Underground Line). His grave is No. 28529 in square 138, SW of the church.

Harrow School, Harrow on the Hill, Middlesex: guided tours; phone (01) 422 2303.

Winchester College, College Street, Winchester, Hampshire: phone the Bursar, (0962) 64242.

Hospital of St Cross, St Cross Road, Winchester, Hampshire: phone (0962) 51375.

Sir John Vanbrugh

b. London, 1664; d. London, 1726. *The Relapse* (1697); *The Provok'd Wife* (1697).

After his early success as author of elegant comedy Vanbrugh, in Swift's ironic phrase, 'without thought or lecture/... hugely turn'd to architecture'. Apparently without formal training but with the technical assistance of Nicholas Hawksmoor he raised the English Baroque style to a new scale and a new pitch of grandeur. Walpole's reaction to Castle Howard sums up admiration for his achievement:

> Nobody had informed me that I should see at once a palace, a town, a fortified city, temples on high places, woods worthy of being each a metropolis of the Druids, the noblest lawn in the world fenced by half the horizon, and a mausoleum that would tempt one to be buried alive; in short I have seen gigantic palaces before, but never a sublime one.

His chief works, mostly too well known to require special commentary, may be listed briefly, with their arrangements for opening to the public:

Castle Howard, 17 miles NE of York. Begun in 1701 for the Earl of Carlisle. Phone (065 384) 333.

Blenheim Palace, Woodstock, 8 miles NW of Oxford. Begun in 1705 for the Duke of Marlborough. Phone (0993) 811325.

Seaton Delaval Hall, Seaton Sluice, near Whitley Bay, 11 miles NE of Newcastle upon Tyne. 1720–28, for Admiral George Delaval. Badly damaged by fire in 1822. Phone Tyneside (091) 2373040 or 2371493.

Audley End, Saffron Walden, 11 miles south of Cambridge. In 1721–22 Vanbrugh performed what one of his biographers has called 'the least creditable of all his undertakings', the reduction of the Jacobean mansion to its present sadly diminished proportions. English Heritage; phone (0799) 22399.

Stowe (Stowe School), 2 miles NW of Buckingham. In 1710 Sir Richard Temple (later Viscount Cobham) began to enlarge his house and landscape its grounds, eventually creating a magnificent essay in 18C taste that includes work by Kent and Gibbs as well as Vanbrugh. Vanbrugh may have had a hand in alterations to the house but his main surviving contributions are to the garden buildings: the Lake Pavilions on the SE side of the Octagon Lake, unfortunately altered in 1770; the Rotonda on the main lawn south of the house, with unhappy alterations to its dome made later in the 18C; and the Bourbon Tower, outside the grounds to the NE, an early example of medievalism. Grounds, garden buildings and main state rooms open, usually during the Easter and summer holidays; phone Buckingham (0280) 813650.

Of the several houses he built and occupied in London only one survives: Vanbrugh Castle, on Maze Hill in Greenwich. The present name replaces his own more whimsical choice, the Bastille, recalling the prison where he had the misfortune to spend some eighteen months during a youthful visit to the Continent.

Vanbrugh is buried in the City of London at St Stephen's, Walbrook, immediately south of the Mansion House and Bank Underground Station (Central and Northern Lines), a church by his most famous contemporary in architecture, Wren.

Edmund Waller

b. Coleshill, Buckinghamshire, 1606; d. Beaconsfield, Buckinghamshire, 1687. *Poems* (1645); *Divine Poems* (1685).

The manor house at Coleshill, off A404 6 miles NE of High Wycombe, where Waller was born does not survive but the parish church of Amersham, 2 miles further north, where he was baptised can still be visited. The Waller family later moved to Beaconsfield, 4 miles south, the poet's home for the rest of his life except his years of exile on the Continent. His house, Hall Barn, has since been rebuilt but his grave survives in the parish churchyard.

In 1620 Waller entered King's College, Cambridge, where he left no mark and apparently took no degree.

In London he married Anne Bankes at St Margaret's, Westminster, near the Abbey, in 1631. A less happy period of his life is recalled by the Tower of London, where he was imprisoned in 1643–44 for his part in a plot to secure the City of London for the King. He was banished from England, escaping a heavier penalty only by abject displays of remorse and perhaps by betrayal of his confederates. After his return (c. 1652) he behaved more prudently and wrote a panegyric to Oliver Cromwell.

Waller is also one of the impressive list of writers connected with Penshurst Place, SW of Tonbridge in Kent. In the 1630s he addressed a series of poems to Lady Dorothy Sidney ('Sacharissa') which compliment her in extravagant conceits and invoke the memory of Sir Philip Sidney (q.v.).

Tower of London, Tower Hill, London EC3: DoE monument; phone (01) 709 0765.

Penshurst Place, Penshurst, Tonbridge, Kent: phone Penshurst (0892) 870307.

Horace Walpole

b. London, 1717; d. London, 1797. *Aedes Walpolianae* (1748); *A Catalogue of the Royal and Noble Authors of England* (1758); *Fugitive Pieces in Verse and Prose* (1758); *Anecdotes of Painting in England* (1762–65); *The Castle of Otranto: A Gothic Story* (1765); *Historic Doubts on the Life and Reign of King Richard the Third* (1768); *The Mysterious Mother* (1768); *A Description of the Villa of Mr Horace Walpole ... at Strawberry-Hill near Twickenham, Middlesex* (1784).

Walpole was born at No. 22 Arlington Street, south of Piccadilly, the London residence of his father, Sir Robert, Prime Minister to George I and George II. It is now marked by a plaque. No. 5 opposite, bought by the father in 1742 and inherited by the son in 1745, has been demolished—a fate also suffered by Horace's later town house on the east side of Mayfair's much vandalised Berkeley Square.

From 1735 to 1739 Walpole studied at King's College, Cambridge, but was in residence only intermittently. Unlike his father, who had contributed largely to the Fellows' Building of 1724 by James Gibbs, he left no interesting trace of his presence there. The Great Court of Trinity College, however, enjoys an intriguing connection with his only novel. Revisiting Cambridge more than a decade after writing *The Castle of Otranto* Walpole realised that for its Gothic setting he had unconsciously drawn on memories of one of the colleges. The

The Cabinet of Strawberry Hill, in A Description of the Villa of Mr Horace Walpole ... at Strawberry Hill near Twickenham, Middlesex *(1784)*

letter to Madame du Deffand (27 January 1775) explaining this curious fact does not name the spot but, with its gatehouses, towers, chapel and hall with oriel window, only Great Court fully matches the scattered hints offered by the novel.

During his undergraduate years and again in 1743–45 Walpole passed summers at *Houghton Hall, 16 miles NE of King's Lynn in Norfolk, the Palladian mansion built by his father in 1722–31. He did not find county society congenial:

> Only imagine that I here every day see men, who are mountains of roast beef, and only seem just roughly hewn out into the outlines of human form, like the giant-rock at Pratolino! I shudder when I see them brandish their knives in act to carve, and look at them as savages that devour one another. I should not stare at all more than I do, if yonder Alderman at the lower end of the table was to stick his fork into his neighbour's jolly cheek, and cut a brave slice of brown and fat.

Characteristically, he took refuge in writing *Aedes Walpolianae* (1747), a descriptive catalogue of the many fine paintings his father had gathered. Their sale and dispersal in 1779, made necessary by the dissolute ways of Lord Orford, was a lasting source of grief to him. Like his father, Walpole is buried in the church, now largely Victorian, that stands in the park.

At *Strawberry Hill Walpole found a house more suited to his taste than the provincial grandeurs of Houghton and devoted much of his life to making it perhaps the most self-expressive environment any English writer has ever created. Well preserved despite Walpole's own fears for its fragility and its fate after his death, Strawberry Hill still stands as his best monument. It is situated in Twickenham, today thoroughly assimilated into south-west London, between Strawberry Hill Station (British Rail) and the Thames; it now houses St Mary's Training College.

When Walpole first rented Chopped-Straw Hall (as it was then known) it was a coachman's cottage whose chief attraction lay in its modesty and its rural but not remote location:

> It is a little plaything-house … and is the prettiest bauble you ever saw. It is set in enamelled meadows, with filigree hedges:
>
> A small Euphrates through the piece is roll'd,
> And little finches wave their wings in gold.
>
> Two delightful roads, that you would call dusty, supply me continually with coaches and chaises: barges as solemn as Barons of the Exchequer move under my window; Richmond Hill and Ham Walks bound my prospect; but, thank God! the Thames is between me and the Duchess of Queensbury. Dowagers as plenty as flounders inhabit all around, and Pope's ghost is just now skimming under the window by a most poetical moonlight. I have about land enough to keep such a farm as Noah's, when he set up in the ark with a pair of each kind; but my cottage is rather cleaner than I believe his was after they had been cooped up together forty days.

After buying the property in 1749 he began, with the aid of various architectural 'Committees of Taste', to transform it into 'a little Gothic castle'. The full story, told by running commentary in his letters and more formally in his *Description of Strawberry Hill*, can only be summarised here. By 1753 the original exterior had been decorated with battlements and the interior remodelled, most successfully in the charming Staircase Hall. In the course of the next twenty years there followed Library, Great Parlour, Holbein Chamber, Cloister, Gallery, and Chapel, until the building's original size had been more than doubled and its outlines rendered pleasingly asymmetrical.

In Walpole's lifetime Strawberry Hill became an object of curiosity to a steady flow of visitors. He even needed to print a list of regulations: advance notice was required, parties were limited to four people, and children were not admitted. Contemporaries sometimes reacted with amusement, derision or bewilderment, as in the case of the Frenchman who first removed and then replaced his hat in the unconsecrated chapel where the owner housed his cabinet of secular curiosities. And so began the long history of misunderstanding from which Strawberry Hill can still suffer today. Walpole has been credited with beginning a Gothic revival that was already underway before he ever added a battlement. He has been accused of gimcrack inaccuracy in his use of Gothic motifs, whereas in fact the details of Strawberry Hill constitute a jackdaw history of English ecclesiastical architecture. And he is sometimes supposed to have created an effect of Gothic gloom suitable to the author of *The Castle of Otranto*. Though he may at times have strived to achieve this note, it was always relieved by the Rococo aspect of his sensibility, the use of very un-Gothic materials and by an eclectic assembly of *objets d'art* (unfortunately later dispersed). However much Strawberry Hill may have grown in size and elaborateness it never entirely ceased to be the 'little plaything-house' its creator had first rented.

Like Pope (q.v.) before him, Walpole was both a frequent visitor to Marble Hill House nearby and an unofficial adviser to Mrs Howard (later Lady Suffolk), mistress to George II, in the laying out of her garden.

Houghton Hall, Houghton, Norfolk: phone East Rudham (048 522) 569.

Strawberry Hill (St Mary's Training College), Waldegrave Road, Twickenham, Middlesex: visits by prior arrangement; phone (01) 892 0051.

Marble Hill House, Richmond Road, Twickenham, Middlesex: English Heritage; phone London (01) 892 5115.

Evelyn Waugh

b. London, 1903; d. Combe Florey, Somerset, 1966. *PRB: An Essay on the Pre-Raphaelite Brotherhood 1847–1854* (1926); *Decline and Fall* (1928); *Rossetti: His Life and Works* (1928); *Vile Bodies* (1930); *Black Mischief* (1932); *A Handful of Dust* (1934); *Edmund Campion* (1935); *Waugh in Abyssinia* (1936); *Scoop* (1938); *Put Out More Flags* (1942); *Work Suspended* (1942); *Brideshead Revisited: The Sacred and Profane Memories of Captain Charles Ryder* (1945); *When the Going Was Good* (1946); *Scott-King's Modern Europe* (1947); *The Loved One* (1948); *Helena* (1950); *Men At Arms* (1952); *Love Among the Ruins* (1953); *Officers and Gentlemen* (1955); *The Ordeal of Gilbert Pinfold* (1957); *The Life of Ronald Knox* (1959); *Unconditional Surrender* (1961); *A Little Learning* (1964).

Waugh was born in Hampstead at No. 11 Hillfield Road (west of Finchley Road near Westfield College). In the normal course of events he would have followed his older brother's footsteps and gone to Sherborne School in Dorset but the appearance of Alec Waugh's novel *Loom of Youth*, highly critical of public school life, made a different choice expedient. So Waugh was educated at Lancing College (7½ miles west of Brighton via A27). *A Little Learning*, his own account of his early life, shows little fondness for the school except for the fine, massive Victorian chapel which dominates its architecture.

He himself was acutely conscious that Hertford College was not then among the more prestigious institutions in Oxford and that he accepted a scholarship there mainly because of his father's strained finances. 'I have to make a noise', he told his contemporary Cyril Connolly, 'because I'm poor'. The legend of his flamboyantly drunken behaviour during his undergraduate years (1922–24) has no doubt grown in the telling, including his own telling, but his bad relations with his History tutor and equally bad Third are a matter of record. Waugh the novelist, however, possessed Oxford with a confidence that Waugh the undergraduate could not. His fictional portraits of the University range from the farcical 'Scone College', whose quad echoes to 'the sound of the English county families baying for broken glass', at the beginning of *Decline and Fall*, to the richly nostalgic account in *Brideshead Revisited*. This novel mourned an Oxford 'submerged now and obliterated, irrecoverable as Lyonesse, so quickly have the waters come flooding in' (Part 1, Ch. 1).

Television has identified Brideshead Castle, which the novel locates in Wiltshire, with Castle Howard (off A64 17 miles NE of York). Waugh, in fact, did pay a visit in 1937 and Vanbrugh's Baroque splendours (particularly the domed Hall) may well have contributed to the fictional country house. However, Castle Howard's current popularity with visitors is in striking contrast to the picture of aristocratic decline offered by the novel. Waugh himself lived long enough to note 'the present cult of country houses' in a 1959 preface to the novel and to suggest with prophetic irony: 'Brideshead today would be open to trippers, its treasures rearranged by expert hands and the fabric better maintained than it was by Lord Marchmain'.

His passionate attachment to the old order of society made it fitting that he should acquire a country house for himself as soon as the success of his writing permitted such an elevation. In 1937 he bought Piers Court in Stinchcombe, on B4060 12 miles SW of Stroud and near the western edge of the Cotswolds. In 1957, defying the era of austerity, he moved to the larger and grander manor at Combe Florey in Somerset (on the edge of the Quantock Hills, off A358 8 miles NW of Taunton). These surroundings allowed him to indulge his taste for Victorian interior decoration, and he celebrated his arrival at Combe Florey by commissioning the famous factory in Wilton to reproduce a prize-winning carpet from the Great Exhibition of 1851.

Castle Howard, near York: phone (065 384) 333.

H.G. Wells

b. London, 1866; d. London, 1946. *The Time Machine* (1895); *The Island of Dr Moreau* (1896); *The Invisible Man: A Grotesque Romance* (1897); *The War of the Worlds* (1898); *When the Sleeper Wakes: A Story of Years to Come* (1899); *Love and Mr Lewisham* (1900); *The First Men in the Moon* (1901); *The Discovery of the Future* (1902); *Mankind in the Making* (1903); *A Modern Utopia* (1905); *Kipps: The Story of a Simple Soul* (1905); *The War in the Air, and Particularly How Mr Bert Smallways Fared While It Lasted* (1908); *Tono-Bungay* (1909); *Ann Veronica* (1909); *The History of Mr Polly* (1910); *The New Machiavelli* (1911); *Marriage* (1912); *Bealby: A Holiday* (1915); *Boon* (1915); *Mr Britling Sees It Through* (1916); *The Outline of History* (1920); *Russia in the Shadows* (1920); *The Salvaging of Civilisation* (1921); *A Short History of the World* (1922); *Men Like Gods* (1923); *A Year of Prophesying* (1924); *The World of William Clissold* (1926); *The Way to World Peace* (1930); *The Autocracy of Mr*

Parham (1930); *The Science of Life: A Summary of Contemporary Knowledge About Life and Its Possibilities* (1930); *The Work, Wealth and Happiness of Mankind* (1932); *The Bulpington of Blup* (1933); *The Shape of Things to Come* (1933); *Experiment in Autobiography: Discoveries and Conclusions of a Very Ordinary Brain—Since 1866* (1934); *The Fate of Homo Sapiens* (1939); *The Outlook for Homo Sapiens* (1942); *Mind at the End of Its Tether* (1945).

Not all the scenes of Wells' insecure and unhappy childhood, a rich trove of experience mined by his best novels, survive. At Bromley, then a separate town but now absorbed into south-east London, a plaque in the High Street (A21) marks the site of Atlas House, a grand name for the modest building where he was born and his father ran a china shop. The draper's premises in Windsor and Portsmouth where he was sent to work after the failure of the family business have gone.

The most interesting reminder of his early years is *Uppark in West Sussex (on B2146 6 miles SE of Petersfield), a charming country house built in the reign of William and Mary. Wells' mother had been in service with the Featherstonhaugh family here before her marriage and she returned as housekeeper in 1880 when the Bromley shop failed. So Uppark became Wells' intermittent home, and he was allowed the run of its library. It appears in *Tono-Bungay* as 'Bladesover House', which seems to the young hero 'a closed and complete social system' (Ch. 1). Chapter 2 of the novel gives a lightly fictionalised account of the famous episode in 1883 when Wells ran away from Portsmouth and returned unexpectedly home. The result of this rebellion against his fate as a draper's assistant was that he was sent to school in Midhurst (12 miles NE of Uppark), the 'Wimblehurst' of *Tono-Bungay*.

In 1884 Wells' success at Midhurst won him a place in London at the Normal School of Science (now Imperial College) on Exhibition Road in Kensington. His teacher, T.H. Huxley, had considerable influence over his later scientific writings. Another aspect of Wells' intellectual development, his Socialism, was represented by visits to William Morris (q.v.) at his Hammersmith home.

Despite his early promise Wells left the Normal School without distinguishing himself and, like so many young writers, was condemned to spend the next few years following a desultory career as a schoolmaster. In 1898, already on the way to success in the literary world, he went to live at Sandgate, west of Folkestone on the Kent coast. In 1900 he was able to exchange his rented home for Spade House, designed for him by C.F. Voysey, on Radnor Cliff Crescent. Here he wrote several of his most famous novels, including *Kipps*, whose final chapters reflect the problems Wells had encountered in building a house of his own. During these years he was frequently in contact with Conrad and Henry James (qq.v.), who both lived nearby.

Wells' life at Spade House epitomised the affluent, domesticated comfort to which writers of his generation aspired, but he was destined never to be content as either successful novelist or family man. In 1909 he abandoned Sandgate for London and bought No. 17 Church Row, one of the pleasant Georgian houses near St John's church in Hampstead. Finding it too cramped he moved back to the country in 1912, buying The Glebe, a Georgian house near the church in the village of Little Easton (off B184 6 miles south of Thaxted in Essex).

Little Easton was his main home until 1930, when he returned to London and a flat in Chiltern Court Mansions, south of Regent's Park at the junction of Marylebone Road and Baker Street. Arnold Bennett (q.v.), long a close friend and now a neighbour at Chiltern Court, died only a few months after Wells' arrival. In 1937 he moved a short distance north to his last home at No. 13 Hanover Terrace (now marked with a plaque), a fine street by Nash between Regent's Park and Baker Street's northern continuation as Park Road.

Uppark, South Harting, Petersfield, Hampshire: NT; phone Harting (073 085) 317 or 458.

Gilbert White

b. Selborne, Hampshire, 1720; d. Selborne, 1793. *The Natural History and Antiquities of Selborne, in the County of Southampton* (1789); *A Naturalist's Calendar With Observations in Various Branches of Natural History; Extracted from the Papers of the Late Rev. Gilbert White, M.A.* (1795).

'The parish of Selborne lies in the extreme eastern corner of the county of Hampshire, bordering on the county of Sussex, and not far from the county of Surrey; is about fifty miles south-west of London, in latitude 51, and near midway between the towns of Alton and Petersfield'. In these precise terms White's classic work introduced the village where he was born, spent most of his life and died. The very nature of his achievement, rooted in the gentle, vivid observation that comes from long familiarity, has attracted visitors to *Selborne ever since the book enjoyed its first success. They have rarely been disappointed. William Cobbett (q.v.) came in the course of his *Rural Rides* and found the village 'precisely what it is described by Mr White ... Nothing can surpass in beauty these dells and hillocks and hangers, which last are so steep that it is impossible to ascend them, except by means of a serpentine path' (entry for 7 August 1823).

In Selborne today White's home, The Wakes, is a museum dedicated jointly to his memory and that of Captain Oates, the Antarctic explorer. It contains two rooms furnished in the 18C style, as well as personal relics, editions of White's work, and displays about his life and achievement. The garden still has the ha-ha (or sunken wall) he built and his sundial. They face west towards The Hanger, a wooded hill offering fine views. White's very simple grave can be found in the churchyard north of the chancel; nearby is the ancient yew whose annual growth he measured. Inside the church, where White served as curate in 1757–59 and again from 1784 until his death, is a memorial window contributed by the Gilbert White Fellowship in 1920 and monuments to other members of his family.

Although Selborne is rich enough to satisfy the interest of most lovers of White's work, his connection with Oriel College, Oxford, should not be forgotten. He studied here as an undergraduate (1740–43) and remained as a Fellow for an additional probationary year. The poet William Collins (q.v.) was among his contemporaries.

Oates Memorial Museum and Gilbert White Museum, The Wakes, Selborne, near Alton, Hampshire: phone (042 050) 275.

Oscar Wilde

b. Dublin, 1854; d. Paris, France, 1900. *Poems* (1881); *The Happy Prince and Other Tales* (1888); *The Picture of Dorian Gray* (1891); *Intentions* (1891); *Lord Arthur Savile's Crime, and Other Stories* (1891); *Lady Windermere's Fan: A Play About a Good Woman* (1893); *A Woman of No Importance* (1894); *An Ideal Husband* (1899); *The Importance of Being Earnest: A Trivial Comedy for Serious People* (1899); *The Soul of Man under Socialism* (1895); *Salomé: Drame en un Acte* (1893); *The Ballad of Reading Gaol, By C.3.3.* (1898); *De Profundis* (1905).

Wilde was educated in Enniskillen, the county town of Fermanagh, at the Portora Royal School. His childhood and youth otherwise belonged to Dublin, where his father was a distinguished eye and ear surgeon and his mother, Lady 'Speranza' Wilde, a well-known advocate of Irish nationalism. He was born just east of Trinity College at No. 21 Westland Row, now marked with a plaque; the family later moved a few streets south to No. 1 Merrion Square. Wilde continued to live here during the first year of his studies at Trinity College but later moved into the college quadrangle known as Botany Bay. Edward Carson, whose savage cross-examination helped bring about Wilde's downfall in court, was a contemporary at Trinity but never a close friend.

In 1874 Wilde's academic success won him a Classical Demyship (or scholarship) at Magdalen College, Oxford. His lodgings were first in Chaplain's Quad, then in Cloister Quadrangle and, for his last two years, on Kitchen staircase overlooking the river and Magdalen Bridge. He was 'the happiest man in the world', attending lectures by Walter Pater (q.v.), helping Ruskin (q.v.) in the famous road-building experiment at North Hinksey, and winning the Newdigate Prize for Poetry. By the time he left he had become the most conspicuous member of a cult which rejected Victorian moral earnestness and cultivated exquisite style. His rooms at Magdalen were famous for their blue china and sumptuous furnishings.

In London his fame quickly grew, aided by the fun Gilbert (q.v.) and Sullivan poked at the Aesthetes in *Patience*. Despite the legend, he never walked down Piccadilly with a poppy or a lily in his medieval hand as Bunthorne sings of doing in the opera. Anyone could do that, he liked to point out: 'The difficult thing to achieve was to make people think that I had done it'. A favourite gathering place for Wilde and his circle was the Café Royal on Regent Street north of Piccadilly Circus. Here he dined with Frank Harris, Aubrey Beardsley, Richard Le Gallienne, Lionel Johnson, Lord Alfred Douglas and Max Beerbohm (q.v.) among others.

After his marriage to Constance Lloyd in 1884 he moved to No. 34 Tite Street, west of the Royal Hospital in Chelsea. Edward William Godwin, the architect responsible for Whistler's White House (now demolished) on the same street, was hired to make expensive alterations. Both the decor and the host greatly impressed Yeats (q.v.) when he came for Christmas dinner in 1888:

> He had a white dining room, the first I had seen, chairs, walls, cushions all white, but in the middle of the table a red cloth table-centre with a red terracotta statue and above it a red hanging lamp. I have never and shall never meet conversation that could match his. Perplexed by my own shapelessness, my lack of self-possession and of easy courtesy, I was astonished by this scholar who as a man of the world was so perfect.

The house is now marked by a plaque that remembers Wilde rather inadequately as 'wit and dramatist'.

No. 34 Tite Street saw both the height of Wilde's success and the disaster that followed, for it was sold up by bailiffs during his trials in 1895. The two main scenes of Wilde's humiliation and suffering do not survive: the Old Bailey, where he was sentenced to two years' hard labour for committing 'indecent acts', and Reading Jail, where he served most of the sentence, have both been rebuilt. However, the visitor to London can still see the Cadogan Hotel (on Sloane Street by Cadogan Place in Chelsea), where Wilde was arrested, and the outsides of Pentonville Prison, on the Caledonian Road north of King's Cross, and Wandsworth Prison, west of Wandsworth Common. Wilde began and ended his sentence at Pentonville. After his release in 1897 he lived on the Continent, adopting the name 'Sebastian Melmoth' in oblique allusion to his ancestor, Charles Maturin (q.v.).

Virginia Woolf

b. London, 1882; d. Rodmell, East Sussex, 1941. *The Voyage Out* (1915); *Night and Day* (1919); *Jacob's Room* (1922); *Mrs Dalloway* (1925); *The Common Reader* (1925); *To the Lighthouse* (1927); *Orlando: A Biography* (1928); *A Room of One's Own* (1929); *The Waves* (1931); *The Common Reader: Second Series*(1932); *Flush: A Biography* (1933); *The Years* (1937); *Three Guineas* (1938); *Roger Fry: A Biography* (1940); *Between the Acts* (1941); *The Death of the Moth, and Other Essays* (1942); *A Haunted House, and Other Short Stories* (1943); *The Moment, and Other Essays* (1947); *The Captain's Death Bed, and Other Essays* (1950); *Granite and Rainbow: Essays* (1958).

A plaque now marks No. 22 Hyde Park Gate (west of the Royal Albert Hall), the London home of Sir Leslie Stephen after his second marriage, to Julia Duckworth, in 1878. Vanessa, Thoby, Virginia and Adrian Stephen were all born here and brought up in the top-floor nursery. Julia died in 1895 and, after several years of gloomy, distracted bereavement like Mr Ramsay's in *To the Lighthouse*, Sir Leslie followed in 1904.

It was then that the Stephen children decided to leave Kensington for Bloomsbury, the then unfashionable and not quite respectable area round the British Museum. Their first home (from 1904) was at No. 46 Gordon Square, east of Gower Street and University College. In the various Cambridge friends of Thoby and Adrian who came to visit was the nucleus of the famous 'Bloomsbury circle': the artist Clive Bell (who married Vanessa), Leonard Woolf (later, of course, Virginia's husband), Lytton Strachey, and two young men of whom great things were expected, Saxon Sydney-Turner and Desmond MacCarthy. After Clive's marriage to Vanessa and the death of Thoby, Virginia and Adrian went in 1907 to live at No. 29 Fitzroy Square, west of Tottenham Court Road, a house once occupied by Bernard Shaw (q.v.). It is some indication of the neighbourhood's reputation in those days that Virginia thought it necessary to consult the police about safety before making the move. In later years—when the Bloomsbury group had expanded to include the economist Maynard Keynes, the artists Roger Fry and Duncan Grant, and had made friendly contact with E.M. Forster (q.v.)—Virginia lived at several other Bloomsbury addresses, now gone or drastically altered:

in Brunswick Square (1911–12), Tavistock Square (1924–39) and Mecklenburgh Square (1939–40).

These last two places also served as headquarters of the Hogarth Press, a venture begun in the early days of her marriage to Leonard and begun not in Bloomsbury but in the west of London at Richmond. The name was taken from its first home, Hogarth House in Paradise Road, between the Park and Richmond Station (British Rail and District Underground Line). Here she and Leonard published her own early work, as well as *The Waste Land* by their friend T.S. Eliot (q.v.).

A large part, then, of Virginia Woolf's life and sensibility was urban: *Mrs Dalloway* is obvious testimony to her rich absorption in the moods of city life. Yet 'Bloomsbury' also had its intermittently rural aspect: a summer and weekend life of picnics and dog-walking and adultery. Her own taste for the country had begun with childhood visits to Talland House (now flats) overlooking the bay at St Ives on the north Cornish coast. Sir Leslie Stephen abandoned the house after his wife's death but Virginia returned to Cornwall throughout her life. *To the Lighthouse*, nominally set in the Hebrides but Cornish in its flora and fauna, is the result of this association and of the adult contemplation of her parents it provoked.

Her connection with Sussex was equally important. In 1916 she found •Charleston Farmhouse, off A27 6 miles east of Lewes, as a country retreat for her sister Vanessa. The decoration which Vanessa, Duncan Grant and other artists added to it over the years make it the most striking example of Bloomsbury taste to survive. More work by the circle can be seen in the nearby parish church of Berwick, where the wall paintings include a Crucifixion (1942–43) by Duncan Grant. The charming little Monk's House in the village of Rodmell, between Lewes and Newhaven, was the Woolfs' home from 1919. She drowned herself in the nearby Ouse in March 1941, and her ashes were buried in the garden. Leonard Woolf kept the house until his death in 1969.

For much of her life Virginia Woolf felt herself at a disadvantage because, unlike her brothers, she had not been sent to university. In 1928 she went some way toward making the score even by lecturing the students of Newnham and Girton Colleges in Cambridge on the need to have a room of their own. Earlier she had visited Rupert Brooke (q.v.) in nearby Grantchester. In larger terms, she never lacked the *entrée* to the literary society of her day, calling on her father's old friend Thomas Hardy (q.v., Rte 5) at Max Gate and, like virtually all the writers of her generation, visiting Lady Ottoline and Philip Morrell at Garsington Manor (off B480 4 miles SE of Oxford). Her friendship with Vita Sackville-West took her to •Knole, the splendid Elizabethan mansion outside Sevenoaks in Kent. *Orlando* is an affectionate tribute to both Vita and the house. The lovely •Sissinghurst Castle, where Vita lived with her husband Sir Harold Nicolson, lies off A262 in Kent, 2 miles NE of Cranbrook and 1 mile east of Sissinghurst village.

Charleston Farmhouse, Firle, near Lewes, East Sussex: phone Ripe (032 183) 265

Monk's House, Rodmell, near Lewes, East Sussex: NT; for opening arrangements phone NT Kent and East Sussex regional office, (0892) 890651

Garsington Manor, Garsington, near Oxford: gardens open twice a year under NGS

Knole, Sevenoaks, Kent: NT; phone (0732) 450608. Park open all year to walkers.

Sissinghurst Castle and Garden, Sissinghurst, near Cranbrook, Kent: NT; phone Cranbrook (0580) 712850

Sir Thomas Wyatt

b. Allington, Kent, 1503; d. Sherborne, Dorset, 1542. Poet.

Quite as much as the very real distinction of his poetry, Wyatt's position as court favourite, his appointment to various diplomatic missions and his sometimes unhappy involvement in the political turmoil of the early Tudor period ensured that his life was well documented and spent in public places that have survived.

He was born at *Allington Castle, on the northern outskirts of Maidstone in Kent, returning there periodically in adult life—most notably the time somewhere between 1536 and 1540 when his unjustly neglected satires and *Penitential Psalms* were written. His father, Sir Henry Wyatt, had acquired the late 13C building in 1492 and many of the alterations to it date from his ownership. The visitor today, however, is less aware of them than of the restrained and scholarly repairs carried out by a later owner, Sir Maurice Conway, who rescued the castle from near-ruin between 1905 and 1929. It is now owned by the Carmelites.

In 1536 charges of complicity in Anne Boleyn's adultery made Wyatt a prisoner in the Tower of London. His relationship with Henry's wife, whose exact nature still remains unclear, had prompted the fine sonnet, 'Who so list to hount, I know where is an hynde'. His sojourn in the Tower provoked a poem complaining of his unjust imprisonment. ('Who list his welthe and eas Retayne/ Hym selffe let hym vnknowne contayne') and an elegy for Anne Boleyn's lovers, whose execution he witnessed, 'In mornyng wyse syns daylye I increase'. Another execution on Tower Hill, this time of his friend and patron Thomas Cromwell in 1540, led to another poem ('The piller pearisht is whearto I lent,/ The strongest staye of myne vnquiet mynde') and a second term of imprisonment in the Tower (1540–41).

Wyatt died the following year at Sherborne in Dorset, in the course of a diplomatic mission that was taking him to Falmouth. His grave in the fine Abbey Church is without proper memorial. A small tablet in the north transept marks a possible site, but it is equally reasonable to suppose that he may rest in the nearby Wykeham Chapel where his friend Sir John Horsey (d. 1546) and other members of the Horsey family are buried.

Allington Castle, near Maidstone, Kent: phone (0622) 54080.

Tower of London, Tower Hill, London EC3: DoE monument; phone (01) 709 0765.

William Butler Yeats

b. Dublin, 1865; d. Roquebrune, France, 1939. *The Wanderings of Oisin and Other Poems* (1889); *The Countess Cathleen and Various Legends and Lyrics* (1892); *The Celtic Twilight: Men and Women, Dhouls and Fairies* (1893); *The Land of Heart's Desire* (1894); *The Secret Rose* (1897); *The Wind Among the Reeds* (1899); *The Shadowy Waters* (1900); *Cathleen ni Houlihan* (1902); *In the Seven Woods: Being Poems Chiefly of the Irish Heroic Age* (1903); *Deirdre* (1907); *The Green Helmet and Other Poems* (1910); *Responsibilities and Other Poems* (1916); *Easter 1916* (1916); *The Wild Swans at Coole, Other Verses and a Play* (1917); *Two Plays For Dancers* (1919); *Michael Robartes and the Dancer* (1920); *The Player Queen* (1922); *The Cat and the Moon and Certain Poems* (1924); *A Vision* (1925); *The Tower* (1928); *Sophocles' King Oedipus: A Version For the Modern Stage* (1928); *Words For Music Perhaps and Other Poems* (1932); *The Winding Stair and Other Poems* (1933); *The Autobiography of Yeats* (1938); *Last Poems and Two Plays* (1939).

Like Swift (q.v.), whom he admired, Yeats divided his life between Ireland and England. In childhood he moved from Dublin to London and back as his father, Jack Butler Yeats, built a minor reputation in both cities as a portrait painter and artist in the Pre-Raphaelite tradition. Once his own poetic reputation was established, Yeats played a leading role in both the Irish literary revival and the various English movements which bridged the gap between Pre-Raphaelitism and Modernism.

His connection with England is best described first. In London his earliest homes were at No. 23 Fitzroy Road (off Regent's Park Road north of the Park and east of Primrose Hill) where he lived from 1867 to 1874, and at No. 14 Edith Villas (by the junction of West Cromwell Road and North End in Earl's Court) where the family stayed until 1876. Yeats was sent to school in Hammersmith at the Godolphin School in Iffley Road, reached from Hammersmith Underground Station (Metropolitan, Piccadilly and District Lines) by taking Beadon and Glenthorne Roads from Hammersmith Broadway and then turning right. 'Reveries Over Childhood and Youth' (later included in his *Autobiography*) remembers his painful shyness and sense of estrangement from his English fellow pupils.

From 1876 until 1880 the Yeats family lived at the most interesting of their London homes: No. 8 Woodstock Road in Bedford Park, above Chiswick High Road in north Chiswick. Begun by Norman Shaw in 1875, Bedford Park was England's earliest experiment in creating a planned garden suburb, noted for its tree-lined avenues, the quaint variety of its architecture and the artiness of its inhabitants. 'Reveries Over Childhood and Youth' vividly describes the 'romantic excitement' of moving there:

> We were to see De Morgan tiles, peacock-blue doors and the pomegranate pattern and the tulip pattern of Morris, and to discover that we had always hated doors painted with imitation grain, the roses of mid-Victoria, and tiles covered with geometrical patterns that seemed to have been shaken out of a muddy kaleidoscope. We went to live in a house like those we had seen in pictures and even met people dressed like people in the story-books. The streets were not straight and dull ... but wound about where there was a big tree or for the mere pleasure of winding, and there were wood palings instead of iron railings. The newness of everything, the empty houses where we played at hide-and-seek, and the strangeness of it all, made us feel that we were living among toys. We could imagine people living happy lives as we thought people did long ago when the poor were picturesque and the master of a house could tell of strange adventures over the sea. (Part 8)

On his return to London from Dublin in 1887 Yeats quickly began to move in the literary circles for which such a childhood had prepared him. He visited William Morris (q.v.) at his home in Hammersmith and Oscar Wilde (q.v.) in Tite Street. In 1891 he formed the Rhymers' Club, whose meeting place was the Cheshire Cheese, on the north side of Fleet Street by Wine Office Court. Regular attendants included Lionel Johnson, Ernest Dowson, Arthur Symons, Richard Le Gallienne, and John Davidson. They would dine in the restaurant downstairs before adjourning upstairs to read their poetry to each other. One evening Yeats surveyed the company and remarked: 'None of us can say who will succeed or even who has or has not talent. The only thing certain about us is that we are too many'. From 1895 until 1919 he lived at No. 5 Woburn Walk (then Woburn Buildings, now marked with a plaque), a charming little street of 18C shopfronts running east of Upper Woburn Place just before it joins the Euston Road. Here, in a living room which his friend Lady Gregory (see below) had helped to decorate, Yeats continued to hold literary gatherings, bringing Ezra Pound and John

Caricature of Yeats by Edmund Dulac (1915)

Masefield (q.v.) among others to Monday evening meetings where he distributed 'cigarettes and Chianti, and laid down the law about poetry'.

When he left Woburn Walk in 1919 Yeats lived for two years in Oxford. Like so many literary men of the age, he was a guest of Lady Ottoline and Philip Morrell at Garsington Manor, off B480 4 miles SE of the city. Yeats' life in Ireland began and ended in Dublin and its environs. He was born in Sandymount, a south-eastern suburb of the city, at Georgeville, a large semi-detached house on Sandymount Avenue (which runs NE from Merrion Road near the buildings of the Royal Dublin Society). On their return from England in 1880 the Yeats family lived first at Howth, on the coast NE of the city, and then in the southern suburb of Harold's Cross.

His passionate involvement in the Irish literary revival was epitomised by his work for the Abbey Theatre (founded in 1904) where, as producer and manager, he showed selfless determination in bringing the controversial plays of Synge (q.v.) before the public. The original theatre, near the Custom House on Lower Abbey Street in north Dublin, burnt down in the 1950s and the present building dates from 1966. From 1922, when he left the Oxford area and severed his long connection with England, until 1928 Yeats lived at No. 82 Merrion Square (NE of St Stephen's Green), a fine Georgian house which he made a meeting place for writers as he had earlier made Woburn Walk in London. It is now marked with a plaque. He left Merrion Square for a smaller house at No. 42 Fitzwilliam Square to the south, where he remained until 1932. The gardens of St Stephen's Green, to the west, have a memorial by Henry Moore.

On the whole, Yeats' connection with rural Ireland is better commemorated than his life in Dublin. Particularly rich is the area round Gort, on the west coast SE of Galway. Off N18 2½ miles NW lay Coole Park, home of Lady Augusta Gregory (1859–1932) from 1880 until her death. Yeats first met her in 1896 and their friendship was strengthened by common involvement in the Irish theatre during the years that followed. When she died he wrote: 'I cannot realise the world without her. She has been to me mother, friend, sister and brother'. His first visit to Coole Park in 1897 is finely remembered in 'The Wild Swans at Coole', and the house recurs throughout his poetry of the 1920s, embodying the traditional, aristocratic order to which he turned as a value in an age of civil discontent and anarchy:

> Great works constructed there in nature's spite
> For scholars and for poets after us,
> Thoughts long knitted into a single thought,
> A dance-like glory that those walls begot.
> ('Coole Park 1929', lines 5–8)

As Yeats himself prophesied, the house itself has gone: it was bought by the Free State Government in 1934 and demolished in 1941. All that remains is the grounds, the lake where Yeats counted the swans and the famous Autograph Tree, a copper beech carved with the initials of Yeats and other writers and artists connected with the Irish literary revival.

Nearby is **Thoor Ballylee, 3 miles NE of Gort off N66 to Loughrea. The Norman tower and the cottages that huddle at its base had originally been part of the Gregory estate before they were acquired by the Congested Districts Board. Yeats bought the buildings for £35 in 1916 and lived there intermittently until 1929, when the damp location and the cost of repairs no longer made it a practicable home. His lines, 'To Be Carved On A Stone at Thoor Ballylee', record the work he put into restoration:

I, the poet William Yeats,
With old mill boards and sea-green slates,
And smithy work from the Gort forge,
Restored this tower for my wife George;
And may these characteristics remain
When all is ruin once again.

The poem has now been carved on the tower, which has been rescued from the fate he foresaw. Inside the collection includes editions of his work and the oak furniture he installed, so large that it was built on the spot and could not be removed. Yet Thoor Ballylee is of interest as more than an unusually picturesque and well-preserved writer's house. Yeats' choice of it as home, like his admiration for Coole Park, expressed respect for the past and its traditional order in which art could flourish:

I declare this tower is my symbol; I declare
This winding, gyring, spiring treadmill of a stair is my ancestral stair.
('Blood and the Moon', Section 2, lines 5–6)

The symbol is explored in some of his finest poems.

If Coole Park and Thoor Ballylee stand for the values that Yeats espoused in middle age, Sligo and its surrounding countryside embody the Irish traditions he inherited in childhood and which, as folklore, legend and superstition, nourished his imagination throughout his life. In Sligo itself (on the coast west of Enniskillen via N16) he paid childhood visits to his maternal grandparents, the Pollexfens. The County Library on Stephen Street north of the river has a *collection of Yeats family portraits by his father and his brother Jack. The adjacent Museum has a collection of Yeatsiana.

The splendid countryside nearby, full of intrinsic interest, is also rich in reminders of the poet. 3 miles SW of Sligo and visible from the town is Knocknarea (1083ft), surmounted by a cairn, Misgaun Meaghbh or Miosgán Meva, monument to Maeva, Queen of Connacht (the 'Queen Mab' of English folklore). Yeats' early hero, Oisin, included in his wanderings this 'cairn-heaped grassy hill/ Where passionate Maeve is stony-still' (Bk 1, Lines 17–18). Yeats returned to the subject in 'The Old Age of Queen Maeve' (1903). Immediately SE of Sligo is the beautiful *Lough Gill. Among the many islands that dot the surface of the lake is Innisfree (near the SE bank), made famous as a picturesque refuge from the world in an early poem. Near Aghamore Bay at the east end of the lake is the Dooney Rock, where Yeats' fiddler made 'Folk dance like a wave of the sea' (line 2). Four miles north of Sligo on N15 we find Drumcliff and the Protestant church of which Yeats' grandfather was rector. Though Yeats died and was buried on the French Riviera, his remains were reburied here in 1948 in a grave just north of the porch. The location and the epitaph now inscribed on his tomb obey the instructions in the final stanza of 'Under Ben Bulben':

Under bare Ben Bulben's head
In Drumcliff churchyard Yeats is laid.
An ancestor was rector there
Long years ago, a church stands near,
By the road an ancient cross.
No marble, no conventional phrase;

On limestone quarried near the spot
By his command these words are cut:
Cast a cold eye
On life, on death.
Horseman, pass by!

Ben Bulben (1730ft), which offers a magnificent view from the top, rises north of the village.

Garsington Manor, Garsington, near Oxford: gardens open twice a year under NGS.

Thoor Ballylee, Gort, County Galway, Republic of Ireland: phone (091) 31436.

Sligo County Library and Museum, Stephen Street, Sligo, County Sligo, Republic of Ireland: phone (071) 2212.

Charlotte Yonge

b. Otterbourne, Hampshire, 1823; d. Otterbourne, 1901. *The Heir of Redclyffe* (1853); *Heartsease: or The Brother's Wife* (1854); *The Little Duke: or Richard the Fearless* (1854); *The Daisy Chain* (1856); *Dynevor Terrace: or The Clue of Life* (1857); *Hopes and Fears: or Scenes from the Life of a Spinster* (1860); *A Book of Golden Deeds of All Times and All Lands* (1864); *The Trial: More Links of the Daisy Chain* (1864); *The Clever Woman of the Family* (1865); *The Dove in the Eagle's Nest* (1866); *The Chaplet of Pearls: or The White and Black Ribaumont* (1868); *A Book of Worthies, Gathered from the Old Histories and Now Written Out Anew* (1869); *The Pillars of the House: Under Wode, Under Rode* (1873); *Magnum Bonum: or Mother Carey's Brood* (1879); *John Keble's Parishes: A History of Hursley and Otterbourne* (1898).

Charlotte Yonge spent all her long, quiet and industrious life in Otterbourne, by A33 5 miles south of Winchester. Her home, Elderfield, stands opposite the school and the church of St Matthew. These were built in 1837–39 and, though a local architect was employed, Charlotte Yonge confirms in *John Keble's Parishes* that the blue-brick church was designed mainly by her father, squire of the village and patron of the living, 'who started with merely the power of military drawing (acquired before he was sixteen years old) and a great admiration for York Cathedral [sic]' (Ch. 9). The apse was added in 1875 by T.S. Wyatt and paid for by Miss Yonge. She is buried in the churchyard at the foot of the memorial cross to Keble, who held the living.

The location of her grave acknowledges the influence that Keble's High Church views exercised over her voluminous writings. He was appointed vicar of Hursley in 1836, when he was already leader of the Oxford Movement, and remained there until his death in 1866. The village, 2 miles NW on A3090 beyond its junction with A31, still has the church he built in 1846–48, paid for by the royalties from his popular sequence of religious poems, *The Christian Year* (1827). The stained glass windows, whose design was supervised by William Butterfield, are noteworthy. Keble himself is buried in the churchyard.

INDEX TO LONDON

The region covered by this index extends slightly beyond the formal boundaries of Greater London to include a few sights often visited from the city—Eton College and Windsor Castle, for example. They also appear in the general index to places outside London.

INDEX TO PLACES OUTSIDE LONDON

The Index includes a handful of places formerly in the Home Counties but now in Greater London, whose boundaries are wide and sometimes mysterious to the casual tourist. These places are also listed in the index to London.

The following abbreviations are used to distinguish between places of the same name or confusingly similar names:

Beds	Bedfordshire	Lancs	Lancashire
Berks	Berkshire	Norf	Norfolk
Cambs	Cambridgeshire	Northants	Northamptonshire
Corn	Cornwall	Nthb	Northumberland
Derbys	Derbyshire	Oxon	Oxfordshire
Dor	Dorset	Salop	Shropshire
Glos	Gloucestershire	Som	Somerset
Hants	Hampshire	Staffs	Staffordshire
Herts	Hertfordshire	Susx	Sussex
IoM	Isle of Man	Warw	Warwickshire

Maps

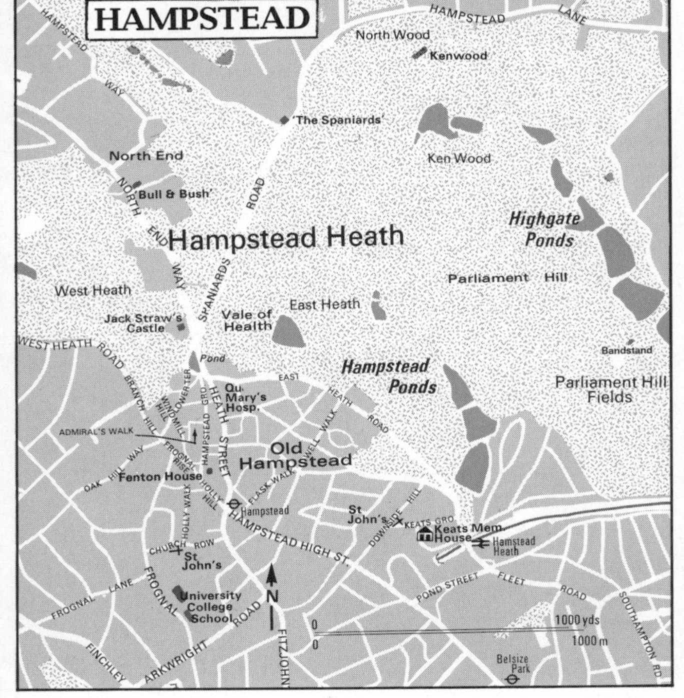

HAMPSTEAD
HAMPSTEAD LANE
North Wood
Kenwood
HAMPSTEAD WAY
'The Spaniards'
North End
Ken Wood
NORTH END WAY
'Bull & Bush'
ROAD
SPANIARDS
Hampstead Heath
Highgate Ponds
Parliament Hill
West Heath
East Heath
Jack Straw's Castle
Vale of Health
WEST HEATH ROAD
Pond
Bandstand
Hampstead Ponds
EAST HEATH ROAD
Parliament Hill Fields
Qu. Mary's Hosp.
BRANCH HILL
WINDMILL HILL
LOWER TER
HAMPSTEAD GRO.
HEATH STREET
WELL WALK
ADMIRAL'S WALK
Old Hampstead
OAK HILL WAY
FROGNAL RISE
Fenton House
FLASK WALK
HOLLY HILL
HOLLY WALK
Hampstead
St John's
DOWNSIDE HILL
KEATS GRO.
Keats Mem. House
Hamstead Heath
HAMPSTEAD HIGH ST.
CHURCH ROW
St John's
FROGNAL LANE
FROGNAL
University College School
N
ROAD
POND STREET
FLEET ROAD
SOUTHAMPTON RD
0
0
1000 yds
1000 m
FINCHLEY
ARKWRIGHT
FITZJOHN
Belsize Park

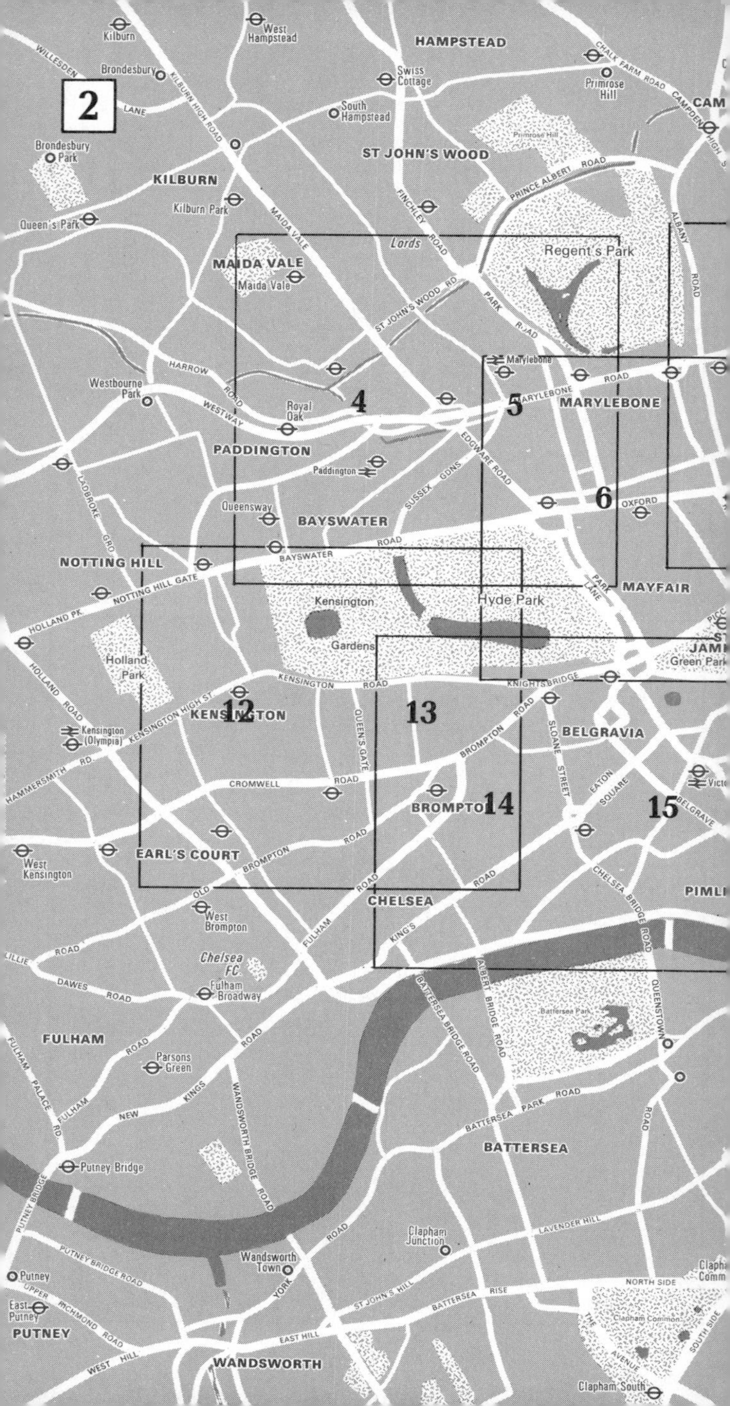
2
HAMPSTEAD
West Hampstead
Kilburn
Brondesbury
WILLESDEN LANE
KILBURN HIGH ROAD
Swiss Cottage
South Hampstead
CHALK FARM ROAD
Primrose Hill
CAMDEN HIGH ST
Brondesbury Park
ST JOHN'S WOOD
Primrose Hill
KILBURN
PRINCE ALBERT ROAD
Kilburn Park
Queen's Park
MAIDA VALE
FINCHLEY ROAD
ALBANY ROAD
Lords
Regent's Park
MAIDA VALE
Maida Vale
ST JOHN'S WOOD RD
PARK ROAD
HARROW ROAD
Marylebone
Westbourne Park
4
5
MARYLEBONE ROAD
MARYLEBONE
WESTWAY
Royal Oak
PADDINGTON
EDGWARE ROAD
Paddington
SUSSEX GDNS
6
OXFORD
LADBROKE GRO
Queensway
BAYSWATER
BAYSWATER ROAD
NOTTING HILL
NOTTING HILL GATE
Kensington
Hyde Park
PARK LANE
MAYFAIR
HOLLAND PK
Gardens
Green Park
Holland Park
HOLLAND ROAD
KENSINGTON ROAD
KNIGHTSBRIDGE
12
KENSINGTON
13
KENSINGTON HIGH ST
QUEEN'S GATE
BROMPTON ROAD
SLOANE STREET
BELGRAVIA
Kensington (Olympia)
HAMMERSMITH RD.
CROMWELL ROAD
EATON SQUARE
BROMPTON
14
15
BELGRAVE
EARL'S COURT
BROMPTON ROAD
West Kensington
OLD
ROAD
FULHAM ROAD
CHELSEA
CHELSEA BRIDGE ROAD
West Brompton
KING'S
LILLIE ROAD
Chelsea F.C.
ALBERT BRIDGE ROAD
BATTERSEA BRIDGE ROAD
QUEENSTOWN ROAD
DAWES ROAD
Fulham Broadway
Battersea Park
FULHAM
ROAD
Parsons Green
FULHAM PALACE RD.
NEW KINGS ROAD
WANDSWORTH BRIDGE ROAD
BATTERSEA PARK ROAD
BATTERSEA
Putney Bridge
PUTNEY BRIDGE
Clapham Junction
LAVENDER HILL
PUTNEY BRIDGE ROAD
Wandsworth Town
YORK ROAD
Putney
NORTH SIDE
UPPER RICHMOND ROAD
East Putney
ST JOHN'S HILL
BATTERSEA RISE
Clapham Common
THE AVENUE
SOUTH SIDE
PUTNEY
EAST HILL
WEST HILL
WANDSWORTH
Clapham South

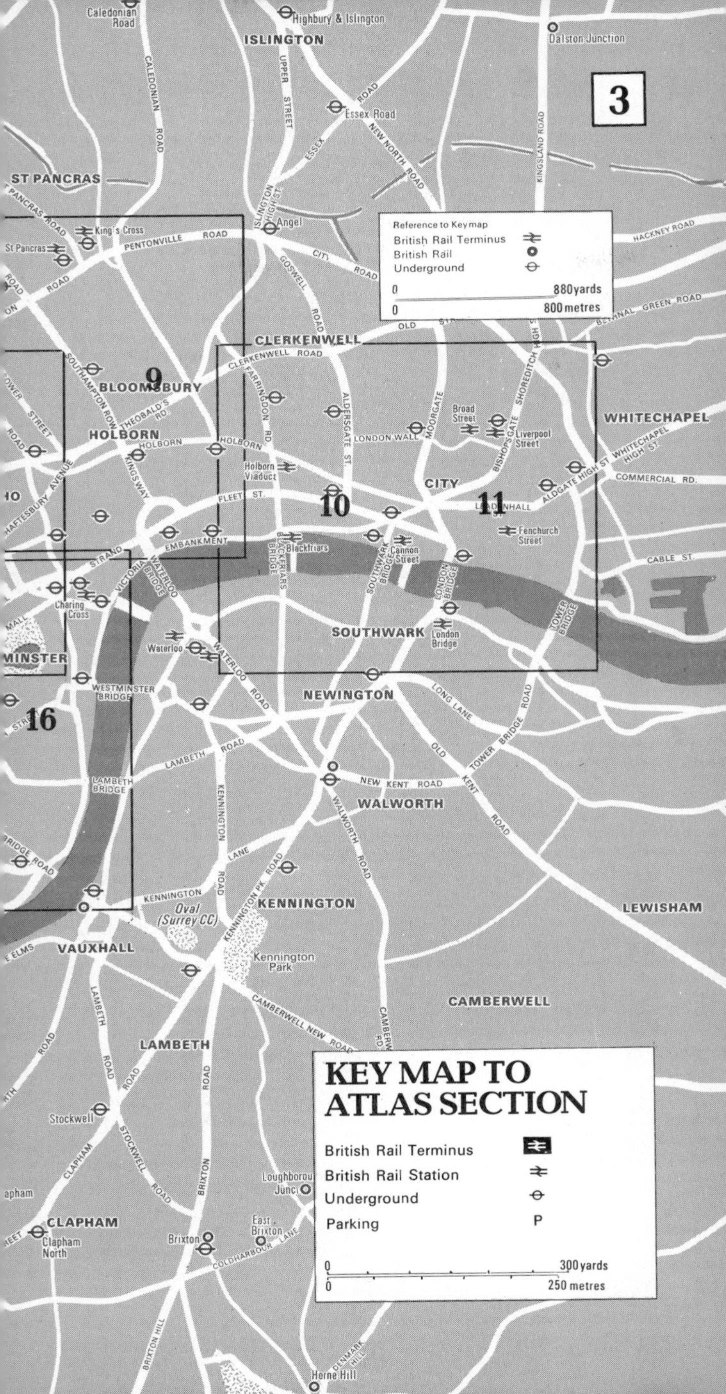

3
KEY MAP TO ATLAS SECTION
British Rail Terminus
British Rail Station
Underground
Parking
P
0
300 yards
0
250 metres
Reference to Keymap
British Rail Terminus
British Rail
Underground
0
880 yards
0
800 metres
9
10
11
16
ISLINGTON
ST PANCRAS
CLERKENWELL
BLOOMSBURY
HOLBORN
CITY
WHITECHAPEL
SOUTHWARK
NEWINGTON
WALWORTH
KENNINGTON
VAUXHALL
LAMBETH
CAMBERWELL
LEWISHAM
CLAPHAM
Caledonian Road
Highbury & Islington
Dalston Junction
Essex Road
Angel
King's Cross
St Pancras
Broad Street
Liverpool Street
Holborn Viaduct
Blackfriars
Cannon Street
Fenchurch Street
Charing Cross
Waterloo
London Bridge
Oval (Surrey CC)
Kennington Park
Stockwell
Loughborough Junct.
East Brixton
Brixton
Clapham North
Herne Hill

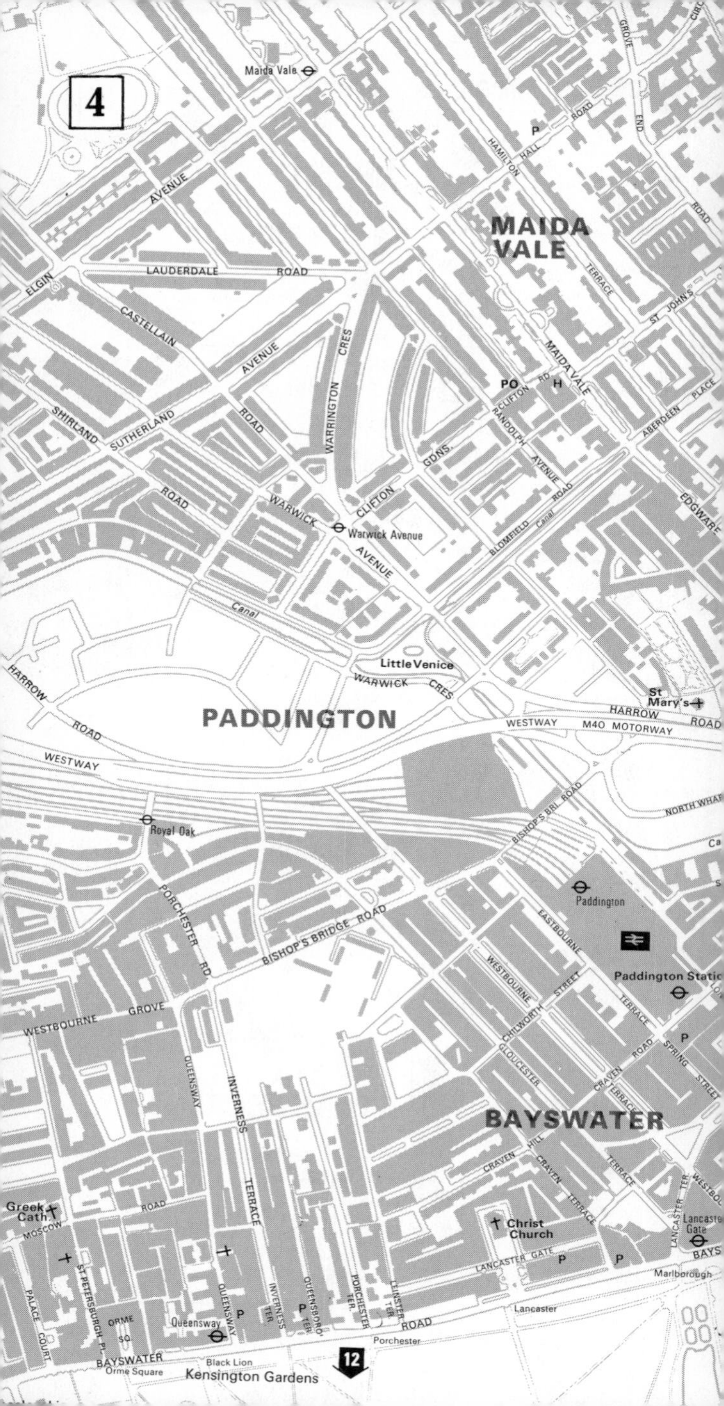
4
Maida Vale
MAIDA VALE
PADDINGTON
BAYSWATER
AVENUE
LAUDERDALE ROAD
ELGIN
CASTELLAIN
AVENUE
HAMILTON
HALL ROAD
GROVE END
ROAD
TERRACE
ST JOHN'S
MAIDA VALE
CLIFTON RD
RANDOLPH AVENUE
ABERDEEN PLACE
WARRINGTON CRES
SHIRLAND
SUTHERLAND
ROAD
ROAD
GDNS.
CLIFTON
WARWICK
Warwick Avenue
AVENUE
BLOMFIELD ROAD
Canal
EDGWARE
Canal
Little Venice
WARWICK CRES
HARROW
ROAD
St Mary's
HARROW ROAD
WESTWAY
M40 MOTORWAY
WESTWAY
NORTH WHARF
BISHOP'S BRI ROAD
Royal Oak
PORCHESTER RD.
BISHOP'S BRIDGE ROAD
Paddington
EASTBOURNE
WESTBOURNE
TERRACE
Paddington Station
CHILWORTH STREET
WESTBOURNE GROVE
QUEENSWAY
INVERNESS TERRACE
GLOUCESTER TERRACE
CRAVEN ROAD
SPRING STREET
CRAVEN HILL
CRAVEN TERRACE
TERRACE
LANCASTER TER.
WESTBOURNE
Lancaster Gate
Greek Cath.
MOSCOW ROAD
Christ Church
LANCASTER GATE
Marlborough
ST PETERSBURGH PL.
PALACE COURT
ORME SQ.
QUEENSWAY
INVERNESS TER.
QUEENSBORO' TER.
PORCHESTER TER.
LEINSTER TER.
ROAD
Lancaster
Queensway
Porchester
BAYSWATER
Black Lion
Orme Square
Kensington Gardens
12

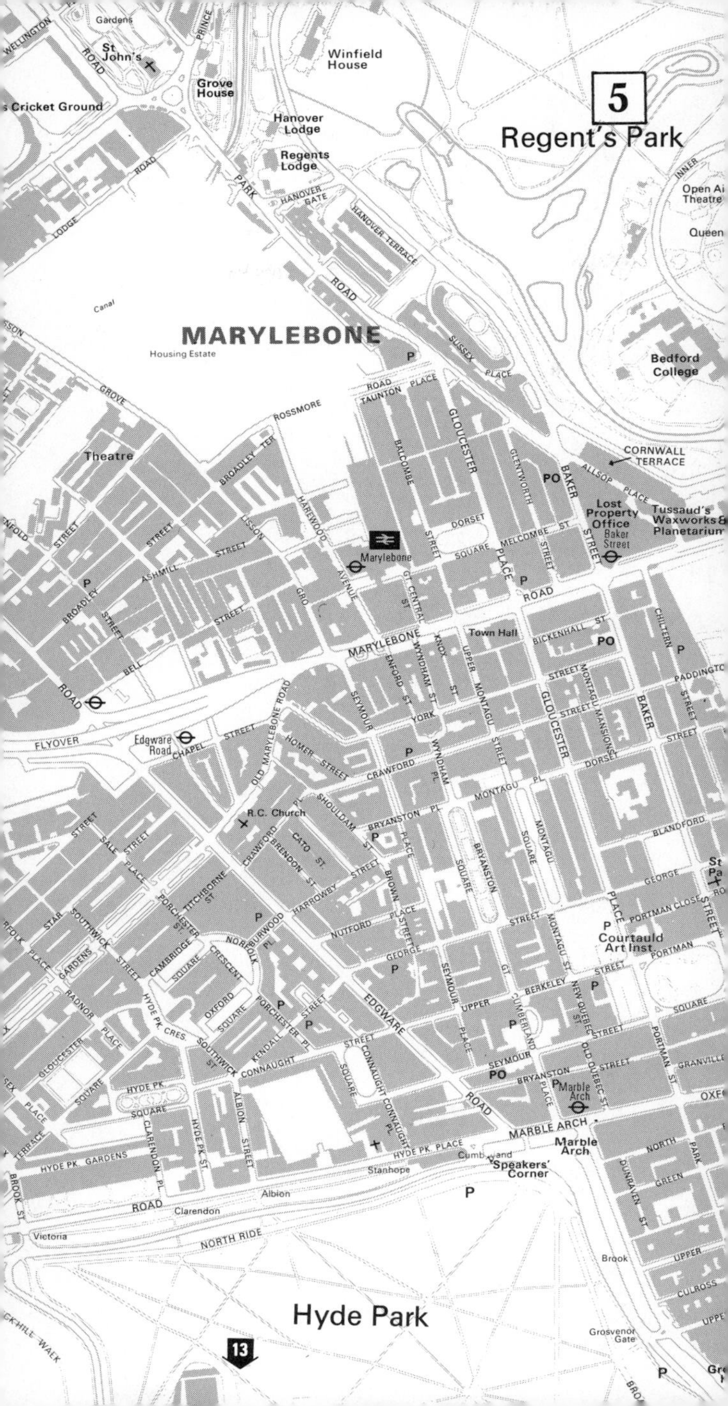

5
Regent's Park
MARYLEBONE
Housing Estate
Canal
Winfield House
Grove House
Hanover Lodge
Regents Lodge
St John's
Cricket Ground
Gardens
WELLINGTON ROAD
PRINCE
PARK ROAD
HANOVER GATE
HANOVER TERRACE
LODGE ROAD
SUSSEX PLACE
INNER
Open Ai
Theatre
Queen
Bedford College
CORNWALL TERRACE
ALLSOP PLACE
Lost Property Office
Tussaud's Waxworks & Planetarium
Baker Street
Marylebone
Town Hall
Theatre
GROVE
ROSSMORE ROAD
TAUNTON PLACE
BALCOMBE STREET
GLOUCESTER PLACE
GLENTWORTH STREET
BAKER STREET
DORSET SQUARE
MELCOMBE ST
BROADLEY TER
HAREWOOD AVENUE
LISSON STREET
ASHMILL STREET
BROADLEY STREET
BELL STREET
GT. CENTRAL ST
MARYLEBONE ROAD
BICKENHALL ST
CHILTERN
PADDINGTON STREET
ENFORD ST
WYNDHAM ST
KNOX ST
UPPER MONTAGU STREET
SEYMOUR PLACE
YORK STREET
MONTAGU MANSIONS
DORSET STREET
FLYOVER
Edgware Road
CHAPEL STREET
OLD MARYLEBONE ROAD
HOMER STREET
CRAWFORD STREET
WYNDHAM PL
MONTAGU PL
R.C. Church
SHOULDHAM ST
BRYANSTON PL
BRYANSTON SQUARE
MONTAGU SQUARE
BLANDFORD
CATO ST
BRENDON ST
HARROWBY STREET
BROWN STREET
GEORGE STREET
PORTMAN CLOSE
Courtauld Art Inst
PORTMAN SQUARE
SALE PLACE
TITCHBORNE ST
PORCHESTER PL
SOUTHWICK STREET
STAR STREET
NORFOLK CRESCENT
BURWOOD PL
NUTFORD PLACE
CAMBRIDGE SQUARE
SUSSEX GARDENS
RADNOR PLACE
OXFORD SQUARE
HYDE PK. CRES.
KENDALL
SOUTHWICK ST
CONNAUGHT STREET
CONNAUGHT SQUARE
CONNAUGHT PL
EDGWARE ROAD
UPPER BERKELEY STREET
GT CUMBERLAND PLACE
MONTAGU ST
NEW QUEBEC ST
OLD QUEBEC ST
SEYMOUR STREET
BRYANSTON STREET
PORTMAN ST
GRANVILLE
Marble Arch
MARBLE ARCH
GLOUCESTER SQUARE
HYDE PK. SQUARE
CLARENDON PL
HYDE PK. ST
ALBION STREET
HYDE PK. GARDENS
HYDE PK. PLACE
Cumberland
Stanhope
Speakers' Corner
Albion
Clarendon
Victoria
BROOK ST
NORTH RIDE
NORTH ROW
PARK
GREEN
DUNRAVEN ST
UPPER
CULROSS
Brook
Grosvenor Gate
Hyde Park
13
PO
P

6
Regent's Park
Cornwall Terrace
Royal Academy of Music
Lost Property Office
Tussaud's Waxworks & Planetarium
St Marylebone
Baker Street
Marylebone
Town Hall
PO
P
St James's (RC.)
St Paul's
Wallace Collection
Courtauld Art Inst
Marble Arch
Speakers' Corner
St Mark's
American Embassy
Grosvenor House
Grosvenor Chapel
Dorchester
MAYFAI
Hilton Hotel
Hyde Park
Serpentine
14
Cafe
Achilles
Apsley House Mus
Albert Gate
Hyde Park Corner
Royal Artillery Mem.
Wellington Arch
Rotten Row
Hyde Pk. Corner
Carriage Road
Underpass
Broad Walk
Park Lane
Lover's Walk
Grosvenor Gate
Brook Gate
Cumberland Gate
Stanhope
Albion
Pol. Sta.
Ranger's Lodge
Curzon
Oxford Street
Edgware Road
Baker Street
Gloucester Place
Marylebone Road
Wigmore Street
Portman Square
Grosvenor Square
North Audley Street
South Audley Street
Upper Brook Street
Upper Grosvenor Street
Mount Street
Bryanston Square
Montagu Square
Manchester Square
Seymour Place
Marble Arch
Bond Street

SPCK
Holy Trinity
Great Portland Street
University College Hospital
8
University Church of Christ
Nat. Cent. Lib.
Courtauld Inst. Gallery
Christ Church
7
Royal Academy of Dramatic Art (RADA)
University of London
Post Office Tower
RIBA
Whitefield Mem Ch
Goodge Street
Central Synagogue
Building Centre
Middlesex Hospital
BBC
All Soul's
YMCA & YWCA
All Saints
Tottenham Court Road
St Giles Circus
Polytechnic Inst.
Prot. Ch (French)
St Giles in the Fields
St Patrick's
Oxford Circus
SOHO
Hanover Square
Cambridge Circus
Palace
St Anne's
St George's
Sotheby's
Piccadilly Circus
Ref Library
Roy. Inst. of Gt Britain
Mus of Mankind
Arcade
Royal Academy of Arts
Design Centre
Burlington House
St James's
Haymarket
Her Majesty's
New Zealand Ho
Lansdowne House
Mayfair Th.
London Library
White's Club
Athenaeum
Travellers
Reform
Ritz Hotel
Brooks's Club
Boodle's
Economist
Jun Carlton Club
Army & Navy Club
Royal Automobile Club
D. of York's Column
Green Park
Naval & Military Club
ST JAMES'S
Oxford & Cambridge Club
Queen's Chapel
16
Bridgewater House
Char
St James's Palace
York Ho
Clarence House
Marlborough House
15
Green Park
Lancaster House
16
St James Park
Qu. Victoria
OXFORD STREET
REGENT STREET
PICCADILLY
THE MALL

8
CAMDEN
ST PANCRAS
SOHO
16
Euston Station
Euston
St Pancras
Friends' House
Wellcome Museum
Euston Square
Jewish Museum
Inst. of Archaeology
University College
University College Hospital
University Church of Christ
Nat. Cent. Lib.
Courtauld Inst. Gallery
Birkbeck College
Royal Academy of Dramatic Art (RADA)
Elizabeth G. Anderson Hospital
Royal College of Physicians
SPCK
Holy Trinity
Great Portland Street
Warren Street
Post Office Tower
Whitefield Mem Ch
Goodge Street
Building Centre
RIBA
Central Synagogue
Middlesex Hospital
BBC
All Soul's
All Saints
Polytechnic Inst.
YMCA& YWCA
Tottenham Court Road
ST GILES CIRCUS
Prot. Ch (French)
St Patrick's
St Peter's
OXFORD CIRCUS
Oxford Circus
St Anne's
St George's
Sotheby's
Piccadilly Circus
PICCADILLY CIRCUS
Roy. Inst. of Gt Britain
Design Centre
PO
P
HAMPSTEAD ROAD
EVERSHOLT
CARDINGTON STREET
MELTON STREET
GOWER STREET
EUSTON ROAD
EUSTON SQUARE
ALBANY STREET
ROBERT STREET
CLARENCE GARDENS
MUNSTER SQUARE
DRUMMOND
LONGFORD ST
OSNABURGH STREET
PARK SQ. EAST
WARREN STREET
WHITFIELD
GRAFTON WAY
FITZROY SQUARE
TOTTENHAM COURT ROAD
TORRINGTON
CHENIES STREET
ALFRED PLACE
STORE STREET
BEDFORD SQUARE
GOODGE STREET
CHARLOTTE STREET
CLEVELAND STREET
GT PORTLAND STREET
BOLSOVER STREET
CARBURTON ST
CLIPSTONE STREET
PORTLAND PLACE
NEW CAVENDISH STREET
DUCHESS STREET
LANGHAM PLACE
RIDING HOUSE STREET
MORTIMER STREET
WELLS STREET
BERNERS STREET
NEWMAN STREET
RATHBONE PLACE
PERCY ST
CAVENDISH SQUARE
MARGARET STREET
EASTCASTLE STREET
OXFORD STREET
REGENT STREET
HANOVER SQUARE
NEW BOND STREET
GT MARLBOROUGH STREET
CARNABY STREET
BROADWICK ST
POLAND STREET
BERWICK STREET
WARDOUR STREET
DEAN STREET
FRITH STREET
GREEK STREET
SOHO SQUARE
CHARING CROSS
OLD COMPTON STREET
SHAFTESBURY AVENUE
GOLDEN SQUARE
GLASSHOUSE STREET
COVENTRY STREET
LEICESTER SQUARE
SAVILE ROW
OLD BURLINGTON ST
CONDUIT STREET
BRUTON PLACE
VIGO ST

ISLINGTON
9
BLOOMSBURY
HOLBORN
GILES
Royal Free Hospital
GPO Mount Pleasant Sorting Office
Coram Found
Coram Fields
London House
Dickens's House
Housing Estate
Childrens' Hospital
National Hospital
Gray's Inn
Conway Hall
Cochrane Th.
Sir John Soane's Museum
Lincoln's Inn
Powis Ho.
Lindsey House
Land Regist.
Public Record Office
Royal College of Surgeons
Royal Courts of Justice
Winter Gardens Centre
Freemasons' Hall
LSE
Royal Opera House
Floral Hall
Fortune
Theatre Royal
Aldwych
Australia House
Bush House
St Clement Danes
Temple Bar
Temple Church
Temple Hall
St Mary -le-Strand
King's College
India House
Somerset House
Covent Garden
St Paul's
Savoy Hotel
Royal Society of Arts
Sadler's Wells
Waterloo Bridge
Pol. Sta.
'Discovery'
'Wellington'
Thames
King's Reach
Temple Gar
Chancery Lane
Staple Inn
Holborn
Russell Square
Covent Garden
Temple
King's Cross St Pancras
Museum
St George's
Osp. Ital.
Town Hall
Met. Wa Board
St Georges Gardens
PERCY CIRCUS
PENTONVILLE ROAD
KING'S CROSS ROAD
GRAY'S INN ROAD
FARRINGDON ROAD
THEOBALD'S ROAD
HIGH HOLBORN
KINGSWAY
ALDWYCH
STRAND
VICTORIA EMBANKMENT
LINCOLN'S INN FIELDS
CLERKENWELL ROAD
ROSEBERY AVENUE

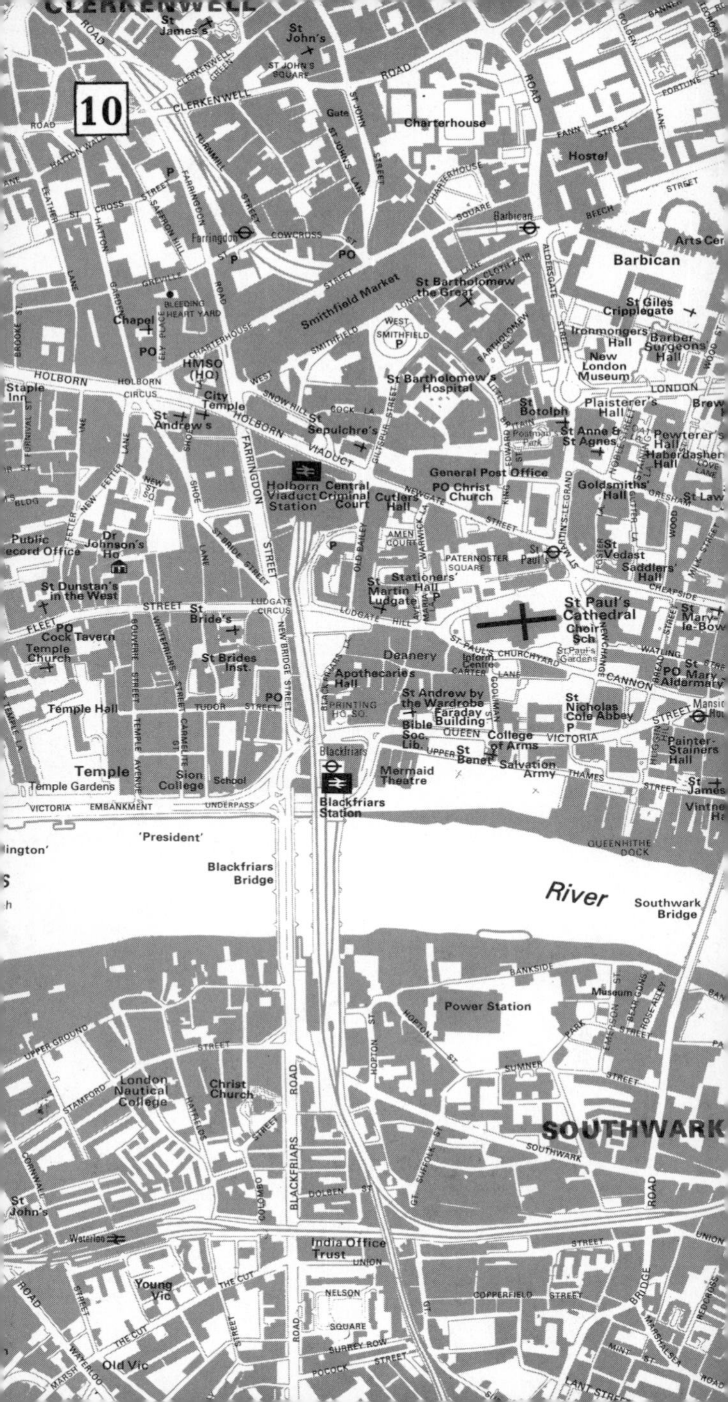

CLERKENWELL
10
St James's
St John's
St John's Square
Charterhouse
Hostel
Barbican
Arts Centre
Farringdon
Smithfield Market
St Bartholomew the Great
St Giles Cripplegate
Ironmongers' Hall
Barber Surgeons' Hall
New London Museum
West Smithfield
Chapel
Bleeding Heart Yard
HMSO (HQ)
Holborn Circus
City Temple
St Andrew's
Staple Inn
St Bartholomew's Hospital
St Botolph
Plaisterer's Hall
St Sepulchre's
Postman's Park
St Anne & St Agnes
Pewterer's Hall
Haberdashers' Hall
General Post Office
Goldsmiths' Hall
Holborn Viaduct Station
Central Criminal Court
Cutlers' Hall
PO Christ Church
Public Record Office
Dr Johnson's Ho
Amen Court
Paternoster Square
St Paul's
St Vedast
Saddlers' Hall
Stationers' Hall
St Martin Ludgate
Ludgate Circus
St Dunstan's in the West
St Bride's
St Paul's Cathedral
Choir Sch
St Mary-le-Bow
Cock Tavern
Temple Church
Deanery
Inform. Centre
St Paul's Gardens
St Brides Inst.
Apothecaries Hall
St Mary Aldermary
Temple Hall
Printing Ho Sq.
St Andrew by the Wardrobe
Faraday Building
St Nicholas Cole Abbey
Bible Soc. Lib.
College of Arms
Painter-Stainers Hall
St Benet
Salvation Army
Mermaid Theatre
Temple
Temple Gardens
Sion College
School
Blackfriars
Blackfriars Station
St James
Vintners Hall
'President'
Blackfriars Bridge
Queenhithe Dock
River
Southwark Bridge
Museum
Power Station
London Nautical College
Christ Church
SOUTHWARK
St John's
Waterloo
India Office Trust
Young Vic
Nelson Square
Old Vic

11
Bunhill Fields
Armoury House (HAC. HQ)
Playing Field
Artillery Ground
Goods Station
Flower Market
Spitalfields Market
Christ Church
Bishopsgate Inst.
Moorgate
Liverpool St. Station
Broad St. Station
All Hallows on the Wall
St Botolph
Girdlers Hall
Armourer's Hall
Carpenters' Hall
CITY
Dutch Ch
Drapers Hall
St Ethelburga
St Helen's
St Margaret
Stock Exchange
Bank of England
Merchant Taylors Hall
Baltic Exchange
St Andrew Undershaft
Span. & Port. Synag
St Botolph Aldgate
St Katherine Cree
Grocers Hall
Royal Exchange
Bank
Mansion House
St Michael's
St Peter's
Lloyd's
St Mary Woolnoth
St Edmund
Lombard Bank
Leadenhall Market
Barclays (HQ)
Lloyd's Register
Inst.of Marine Eng.
Fenchurch Street Station
St Stephen
Founders Hall
St Mary Abchurch
St Clement Eastcheap
Bank of China
Cannon Street
Cannon Street Station
Clothworkers Hall
Tower
St Olave
St Margaret Pattens
Trinity House
Monument
St Mary-at-Hill
Corn Exchange
Tower Hill
Trinity Sq Gardens
Mem.
Fishmongers Hall
St Magnus the Martyr
Bakers' Hall
All Hallows
Billingsgate Market
Custom House
Tower of London
Thames
London Bridge
PIER
HMS Belfast
Tower Bridge
London Pool
Southwark Cathedral
St Saviour's
Borough Market
St Thomas's
London Bridge Station
Guy's Hospital
George Inn
TALBOT YARD

12
4
Hill Gate
Queensway
Bayswater
Orme Square
Black Lion
Czechoslovakia Centre
London Museum
Kensington Palace
School
Qu. Elizabeth College
Town Hall
Library
St Mary Abbots
High Street Kensington
KENSINGTON
Commonwealth Institute
R.C. Church
West London Air Terminal
EARL'S COURT
Earl's Court
NOTTING HILL GATE
KENSINGTON HIGH STREET
CROMWELL ROAD
BROMPTON

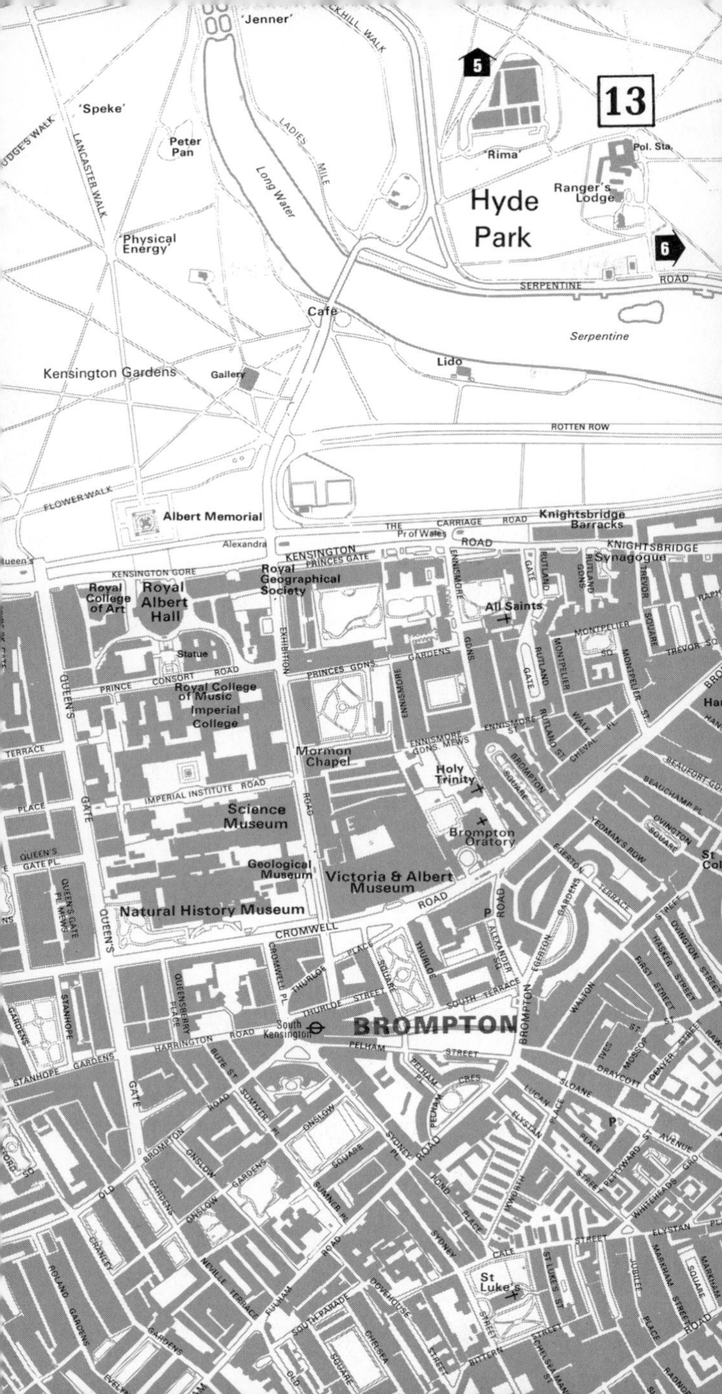
13
5
6
'Jenner'
'Speke'
Peter Pan
LANCASTER WALK
LADIES MILE
Long Water
'Rima'
Pol. Sta.
Ranger's Lodge
Hyde Park
'Physical Energy'
SERPENTINE ROAD
Serpentine
Cafe
Lido
Kensington Gardens
Gallery
ROTTEN ROW
FLOWER WALK
Albert Memorial
Knightsbridge Barracks
THE CARRIAGE ROAD
Pr of Wales
Alexandra
KENSINGTON ROAD
PRINCES GATE
KNIGHTSBRIDGE
Synagogue
KENSINGTON GORE
Royal Geographical Society
Royal College of Art
Royal Albert Hall
EXHIBITION ROAD
ENNISMORE GARDENS
RUTLAND GATE
RUTLAND GDNS
TREVOR SQUARE
All Saints
MONTPELIER SQ
TREVOR SQUARE
Statue
PRINCE CONSORT ROAD
Royal College of Music
Imperial College
PRINCES GDNS
QUEEN'S GATE
ENNISMORE ST
RUTLAND ST
MONTPELIER WALK
MONTPELIER ST
CHEVAL PL
ENNISMORE GDNS. MEWS
Mormon Chapel
Holy Trinity
BROMPTON SQUARE
BEAUFORT GDNS
BEAUCHAMP PL
IMPERIAL INSTITUTE ROAD
Science Museum
Brompton Oratory
YEOMAN'S ROW
OVINGTON SQUARE
QUEEN'S GATE PL
Geological Museum
Victoria & Albert Museum
EGERTON TERRACE
EGERTON GARDENS
QUEEN'S GATE PL MEWS
Natural History Museum
CROMWELL ROAD
ALEXANDER SQ
OVINGTON STREET
HASKER STREET
FIRST STREET
CROMWELL PL
THURLOE PLACE
THURLOE SQUARE
THURLOE STREET
SOUTH TERRACE
QUEENSBERRY PLACE
STANHOPE GARDENS
WALTON ST
South Kensington
BROMPTON
BROMPTON ROAD
HARRINGTON ROAD
PELHAM STREET
IVES ST
MOSSOP ST
DENYER ST
DRAYCOTT AVENUE
BUTE ST
PELHAM PL
PELHAM CRES
SLOANE AVENUE
LUCAN PLACE
ELYSTAN PLACE
SUMNER PL
ONSLOW SQUARE
ONSLOW GARDENS
OLD BROMPTON ROAD
SYDNEY PL
PELHAM ROAD
PETYWARD ST
WHITEHEADS GRO
OND PLACE
IXWORTH PLACE
ELYSTAN STREET
CALE STREET
NEVILLE TERRACE
CRANLEY GARDENS
ROLAND GARDENS
SYDNEY STREET
St Luke's
ST LUKE'S ST
JUBILEE PLACE
MARKHAM SQUARE
MARKHAM STREET
FULHAM ROAD
DOVEHOUSE STREET
SOUTH PARADE
CHELSEA SQUARE
BRITTEN STREET
SCHELSEA MANOR STREET
KING'S ROAD

14
Serpentine
Cafe
Lido
Gallery
ROTTEN ROW
Memorial
Alexandra
'Pan' Edinburgh
Bowater House
Knightsbridge Barracks
THE CARRIAGE ROAD
Prof Wales
KENSINGTON ROAD
KNIGHTSBRIDGE
Knightsbridge
PRINCES GATE
Synagogue
Royal Geographical Society
All Saints
EXHIBITION ROAD
PRINCES GDNS
Royal College of Music
Imperial College
Mormon Chapel
Holy Trinity
Brompton Oratory
BROMPTON ROAD
Harrods
TREVOR SQ
HANS CRESCENT
HANS PLACE
BEAUFORT GDNS
BEAUCHAMP PL
St Colomba
Science Museum
Geological Museum
Victoria & Albert Museum
History Museum
CROMWELL ROAD
THURLOE SQUARE
THURLOE STREET
South Kensington
BROMPTON
PELHAM STREET
CADOGAN SQUARE
SLOANE STREET
SLOANE AVENUE
ONSLOW SQUARE
FULHAM ROAD
St Luke's
KING'S ROAD
Chelsea Town Hall
ROYAL AVENUE
ST LEONARD'S TER
D. of York
National Army Museum
CHELSEA
Chelsea Physic Garden
Carlyle's House
CHEYNE WALK
CADOGAN PIER
Crosby

15
6
7
Achilles
Curzon
Apsley House Mus.
Lancaster House
Green Park
Hyde Pk. Corner
Underpass
Hyde Park Corner
Royal Artillery Mem.
Wellington Arch
St George's Hospital
The Horse Ride
Constitution Hill
Qu. Victoria Mem.
Buckingham Palace Gardens
Buckingham Palace
Queen's Gallery
Buckingham Gate
St Paul's
Grosvenor Crescent
Grosvenor Place
Belgrave Square
Halkin St
Chapel Street
Chester Street
Wilton Crescent
Wilton Place
Royal Mews
Westminster Theatre
Palace Street
Catherine Pl
Wilfred Street
Castle
Stag Place
PO
St Peter's
Lower Grosvenor Pl
Hobart Place
Grosvenor Gdns
Victoria Sq.
Buckingham Palace Road
Warwick Row
Bressenden Place
Victoria St
Ashley Place
Carlisle Place
Morpeth Terrace
Westminster Cathedral
Chesham Place
Chesham Street
Lowndes Place
Belgrave Place
Eaton Place
Eaton Square
Lyall Street
Lower Belgrave Street
Eccleston Street
Chester Square
Elizabeth Street
Victoria
Victoria Station
Vauxhall Bridge Road
Eaton Pl
Kings Road
St Michael's
Eccleston Bridge
BELGRAVIA
Eaton Gate
Cliveden Pl
South Eaton Place
Ebury Street
Gillingham Street
Guildhouse Street
Belgrave Road
Royal Court Th.
Sloane Square
Bourne Street
Chester Terrace
Victoria Coach Station
Elizabeth Bridge
Eccleston Square
Semley Place
Ebury Sq.
Cundy St
Buckingham Palace Road
BOAC Terminal
Hugh Street
Warwick Way
Warwick Square
Denbigh Street
Holbein Place
Sloane Gardens
Graham Street
Passmore St
Cambridge Street
George's Street
Holbein Mews
Pimlico Road
St Barnabas
Ranelagh Road
Ebury Bridge
Alderney Street
Winchester Street
Clarendon Street
Cumberland Street
Sussex Street
Gloucester Street
Charlwood Street
Drive
Chelsea Bridge Road
Sutherland Street
Westmoreland Terr
Lupus Street
Chelsea Barracks
Ebury Bridge Road
Grosvenor Canal
Ranelagh Gardens
Hospital
Gardens
Chelsea Embankment
River Thames
Chelsea Bridge

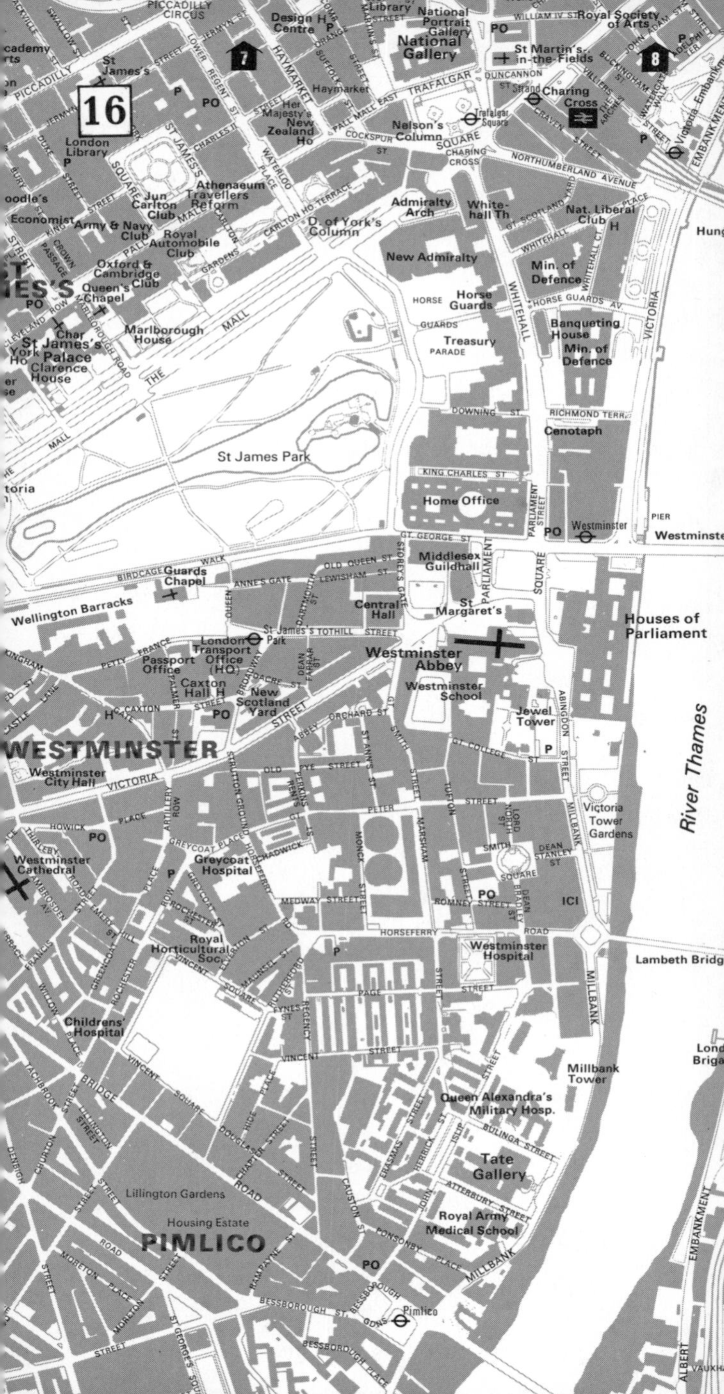

16
7
8
PICCADILLY CIRCUS
PICCADILLY
St James's
Design Centre
Library
National Portrait Gallery
National Gallery
Royal Society of Arts
St Martin's-in-the-Fields
HAYMARKET
Haymarket
Her Majesty's
New Zealand Ho
TRAFALGAR SQUARE
Nelson's Column
Trafalgar Square
Charing Cross
Strand
DUNCANNON ST
WILLIAM IV ST
ADELPHI TER
JOHN ADAM ST
BUCKINGHAM ST
VILLIERS ST
THE ARCHES
WATERGATE WALK
VICTORIA EMBANKMENT
Victoria Embankment
CRAVEN ST
NORTHUMBERLAND AVENUE
CHARING CROSS
COCKSPUR ST
PALL MALL EAST
London Library
JERMYN ST
LOWER REGENT ST
ST JAMES'S SQUARE
CHARLES II ST
WATERLOO PLACE
Athenaeum
Travellers
Reform
Jun Carlton Club
Army & Navy Club
Royal Automobile Club
Economist
Oxford & Cambridge Club
Queen's Chapel
Marlborough House
St James's Palace
Clarence House
York Ho
PALL MALL
CARLTON GARDENS
CARLTON HO TERRACE
D. of York's Column
Admiralty Arch
New Admiralty
Whitehall Th
Nat. Liberal Club
GT SCOTLAND YARD
WHITEHALL PLACE
WHITEHALL CT
Min. of Defence
Horse Guards
HORSE GUARDS AV.
HORSE GUARDS PARADE
Treasury
WHITEHALL
Banqueting House
Min. of Defence
VICTORIA
THE MALL
MARLBOROUGH ROAD
CLEVELAND ROW
St James Park
DOWNING ST
RICHMOND TERR.
Cenotaph
KING CHARLES ST
Home Office
PARLIAMENT STREET
Westminster
PIER
GT. GEORGE ST
BIRDCAGE WALK
Guards Chapel
Wellington Barracks
OLD QUEEN ST
LEWISHAM ST
STOREY'S GATE
Middlesex Guildhall
PARLIAMENT SQUARE
ANNE'S GATE
QUEEN
DARTMOUTH ST
Central Hall
St Margaret's
Houses of Parliament
Hung
St James's Park
TOTHILL STREET
London Transport Office (HQ)
Passport Office
PETTY FRANCE
Caxton Hall
CAXTON ST
BROADWAY
New Scotland Yard
DEAN FARRAR ST
Westminster Abbey
Westminster School
Jewel Tower
ABINGDON STREET
GT COLLEGE ST
ORCHARD ST
WESTMINSTER
Westminster City Hall
VICTORIA STREET
River Thames
Victoria Tower Gardens
MILLBANK
PETER STREET
TUFTON ST
MARSHAM STREET
LORD NORTH ST
SMITH SQUARE
DEAN STANLEY ST
DEAN BRADLEY ST
ICI
ROMNEY STREET
PO
P
H
Westminster Cathedral
Greycoat Hospital
GREYCOAT PLACE
ARTILLERY ROW
MEDWAY STREET
MONCK STREET
HORSEFERRY ROAD
Lambeth Bridge
Royal Horticultural Soc
VINCENT SQUARE
Westminster Hospital
PAGE STREET
Childrens' Hospital
Millbank Tower
Queen Alexandra's Military Hosp.
BULINGA STREET
Tate Gallery
ATTERBURY STREET
Royal Army Medical School
Lillington Gardens
Housing Estate
PIMLICO
VAUXHALL BRIDGE ROAD
TACHBROOK STREET
CHURTON ST
LILLINGTON STREET
MORETON PLACE
BESSBOROUGH ST
BESSBOROUGH GDNS
BESSBOROUGH PLACE
Pimlico
PONSONBY PLACE
CAUSTON ST
JOHN ISLIP
ERASMUS
HERRICK
RAMPAYNE ST
ST GEORGE'S SQUARE
ALBERT EMBANKMENT
Lond Briga

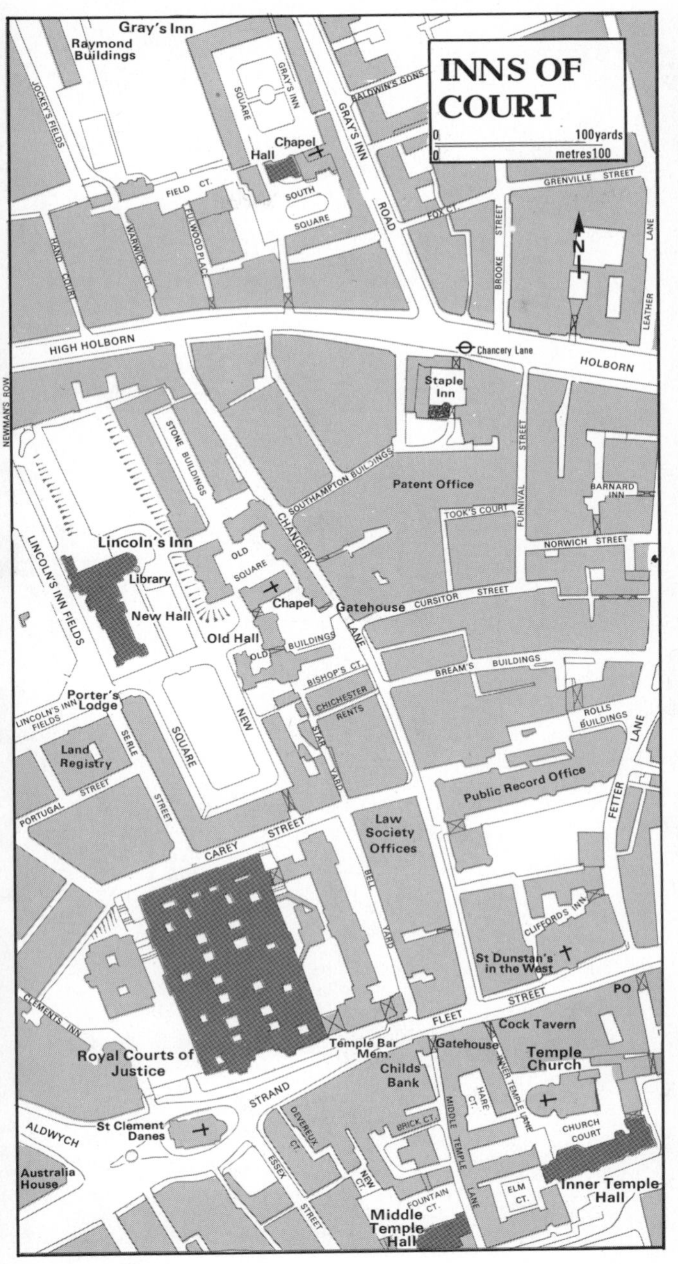

INNS OF COURT
0 100yards
0 metres100
Gray's Inn
Raymond Buildings
JOCKEY'S FIELDS
GRAY'S INN SQUARE
BALDWIN'S GDNS
GRAY'S INN ROAD
Chapel
Hall
FIELD CT.
SOUTH SQUARE
GRENVILLE STREET
FOX CT
BROOKE STREET
LEATHER LANE
HAND COURT
WARWICK CT.
FULWOOD PLACE
HIGH HOLBORN
Chancery Lane
HOLBORN
NEWMAN'S ROW
Staple Inn
STONE BUILDINGS
SOUTHAMPTON BUILDINGS
Patent Office
FURNIVAL STREET
BARNARD INN
TOOK'S COURT
NORWICH STREET
LINCOLN'S INN FIELDS
Lincoln's Inn
Library
New Hall
OLD SQUARE
Chapel
CHANCERY LANE
Gatehouse
CURSITOR STREET
Old Hall
OLD BUILDINGS
BISHOP'S CT.
BREAM'S BUILDINGS
CHICHESTER RENTS
Porter's Lodge
LINCOLN'S INN FIELDS
NEW SQUARE
ROLLS BUILDINGS
SERLE STREET
STAR YARD
FETTER LANE
Land Registry
Public Record Office
PORTUGAL STREET
Law Society Offices
CAREY STREET
BELL YARD
CLIFFORD'S INN
St Dunstan's in the West
PO
CLEMENTS INN
FLEET STREET
Cock Tavern
Royal Courts of Justice
Temple Bar Mem.
Gatehouse
Temple Church
Childs Bank
INNER TEMPLE LANE
HARE CT.
STRAND
DEVEREUX CT.
BRICK CT.
MIDDLE TEMPLE LANE
CHURCH COURT
St Clement Danes
ALDWYCH
ESSEX STREET
NEW CT.
ELM CT.
Australia House
FOUNTAIN CT.
Inner Temple Hall
Middle Temple Hall

MADINGLEY ROAD
Lucy Cavendish College
LADY MARGARET ROAD
Westminster College
St. Peter
Kettle's Yard Art Gallery
Folk Museum
HONEY HILL
STREET
NORTHAMPTON
Merton Hall
Sch. of Pythagoras
Wolfson Court (Girton College)
CLARKSON ROAD
Footpath
New Cou
GRANGE ROAD
QUEEN'S ROAD
FB
Wren Library
THE AVENUE
Footpath
Bin Brook
Trinity College Hostel
ADAMS ROAD
GARRET HOST
BURRELL'S WALK
Footpath
Robinson College
University Library
Clare Memorial Court
Clare Bridge
River Cam
King's Bridge
HERSCHEL ROAD
Clare Hall
Rugby Ground
WEST ROAD
Cripps Ct (Selwyn College)
CRANMER ROAD
History Faculty
Arts Faculties
SILVER
Selwyn College
Darwin College
Leckhampton House
SIDGWICK AVENUE
Ridley Hall
RIDLEY HALL ROAD
Newnham College
NEWNHAM WALK
SELWYN GARDENS
MALTING LANE
CHURCH RATE WALK
NEWNHAM ROAD
0 yards 100 200
0 metres 100 200
N
Car Parks
Covered
Open
SUMMERFIELD

CAMBRIDGE
Midsummer Common
Jesus College
Wesley Ho.
Cambridge Union
ADC Theatre
Holy Sepulchre
St. Clement's
Westcott House
All Saints
Sidney Sussex College
Whewell's Ct
Christ's College
Bus Sta.
Holy Trinity
St Andrew the Great
Emmanuel College
Guildhall
Arts Theatre
St Bene't
New Museums
Corpus Christi College
St Botolph's
Senate House
St Mary the Great
St Edward's
Museum of Geology
Mus. of Anthropology & Archaeology
Downing Site
University Arms Hotel
Parker's Piece
Pembroke College
St Mary the Less
Peterhouse
Downing College
Addenbrooke's Hospital
Fitzwilliam Museum
Engineering Labs.
Hobson's Conduit
Scott Polar Research Inst. (Mus.)
Railway Sta.
Fenner's
GPO
LION YARD
FOUR LAMPS
A45
A604
A603
KING STREET
JESUS LANE
SIDNEY STREET
ST ANDREW'S STREET
REGENT STREET
TRUMPINGTON STREET
TENNIS COURT ROAD
LENSFIELD ROAD
FEN CAUSEWAY
DOWNING STREET
PEMBROKE STREET
EMMANUEL ROAD
PARKER STREET
PARK TERRACE
MARKET STREET
PETTY CURY
KING'S PARADE
BRIDGE STREET
ST JOHN'S STREET
TRINITY STREET
SAXON STREET
UNION ROAD

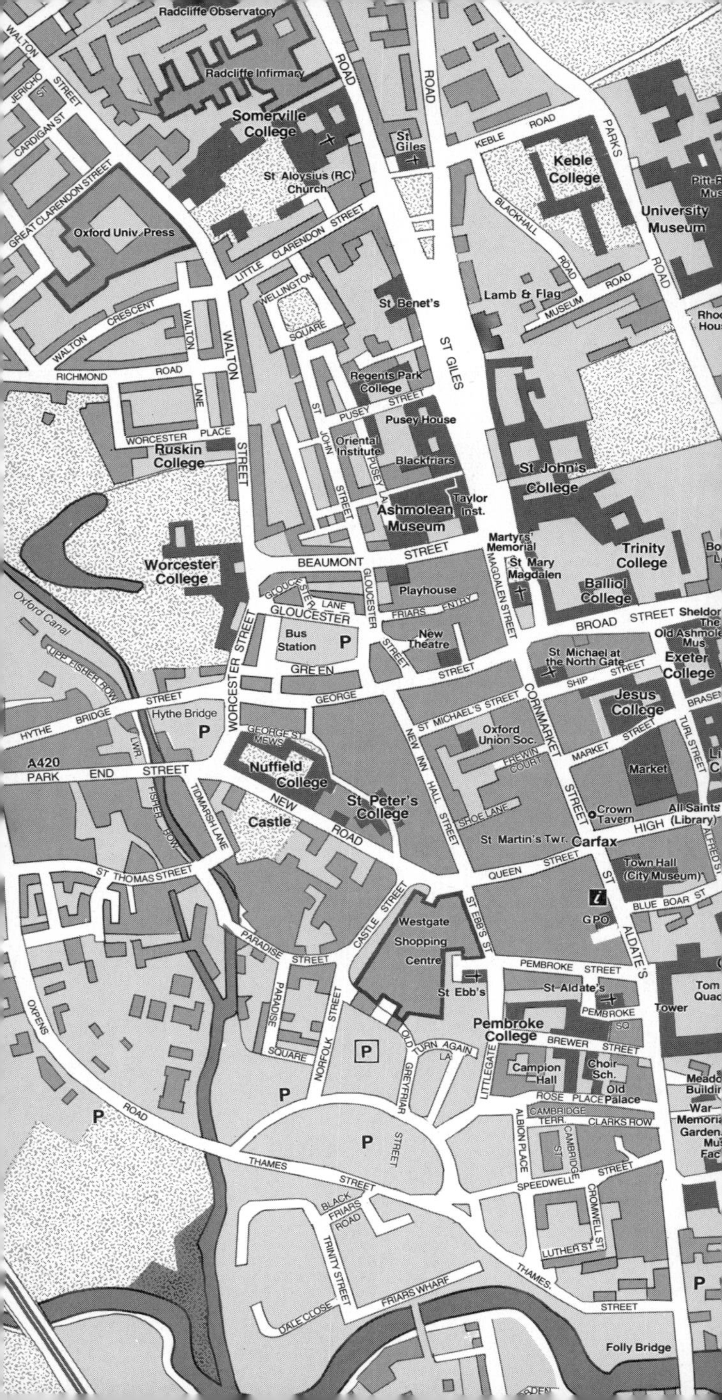
Radcliffe Observatory
Radcliffe Infirmary
Somerville College
St Giles
St Aloysius (RC) Church
Keble College
University Museum
Oxford Univ. Press
St Benet's
Lamb & Flag
Regents Park College
Pusey House
Oriental Institute
Blackfriars
Ruskin College
St John's College
Taylor Inst.
Ashmolean Museum
Worcester College
Martyrs' Memorial
St Mary Magdalen
Trinity College
Balliol College
Playhouse
Bus Station
New Theatre
Old Ashmolean Mus.
St Michael at the North Gate
Exeter College
Jesus College
Hythe Bridge
Oxford Union Soc.
Nuffield College
Market
St Peter's College
Castle
Crown Tavern
All Saints (Library)
St Martin's Twr.
Carfax
Town Hall (City Museum)
GPO
Westgate Shopping Centre
St Ebb's
St Aldate's
Tower
Pembroke College
Campion Hall
Choir Sch.
Old Palace
War Memorial Garden
Folly Bridge
Oxford Canal
A420
WALTON STREET
JERICHO ST
CARDIGAN ST
GREAT CLARENDON STREET
LITTLE CLARENDON STREET
WELLINGTON SQUARE
WALTON CRESCENT
RICHMOND ROAD
WALTON LANE
WORCESTER PLACE
ST JOHN STREET
PUSEY STREET
PUSEY LA
ST GILES
KEBLE ROAD
PARKS ROAD
BLACKHALL ROAD
MUSEUM ROAD
BEAUMONT STREET
GLOUCESTER STREET
GLOUCESTER LANE
FRIARS ENTRY
MAGDALEN STREET
BROAD STREET
WORCESTER STREET
GREEN STREET
GEORGE STREET
GEORGE ST MEWS
HYTHE BRIDGE STREET
UPP FISHER ROW
SHIP STREET
CORNMARKET STREET
ST MICHAEL'S STREET
NEW INN HALL STREET
FREWIN COURT
MARKET STREET
TURL STREET
PARK END STREET
LWR. FISHER ROW
TIDMARSH LANE
NEW ROAD
SHOE LANE
HIGH
ALFRED ST
QUEEN STREET
ST THOMAS STREET
CASTLE STREET
ST EBB'S ST
BLUE BOAR ST
ST ALDATE'S
PARADISE STREET
PARADISE SQUARE
NORFOLK STREET
PEMBROKE STREET
PEMBROKE SQ
OLD GREYFRIARS STREET
TURN AGAIN LA
LITTLEGATE
BREWER STREET
ROSE PLACE
CAMBRIDGE TERR.
CLARKS ROW
ALBION PLACE
CAMBRIDGE ST
OXPENS ROAD
THAMES STREET
SPEEDWELL STREET
CROMWELL ST
LUTHER ST
BLACK FRIARS ROAD
TRINITY STREET
FRIARS WHARF
DALE CLOSE
P

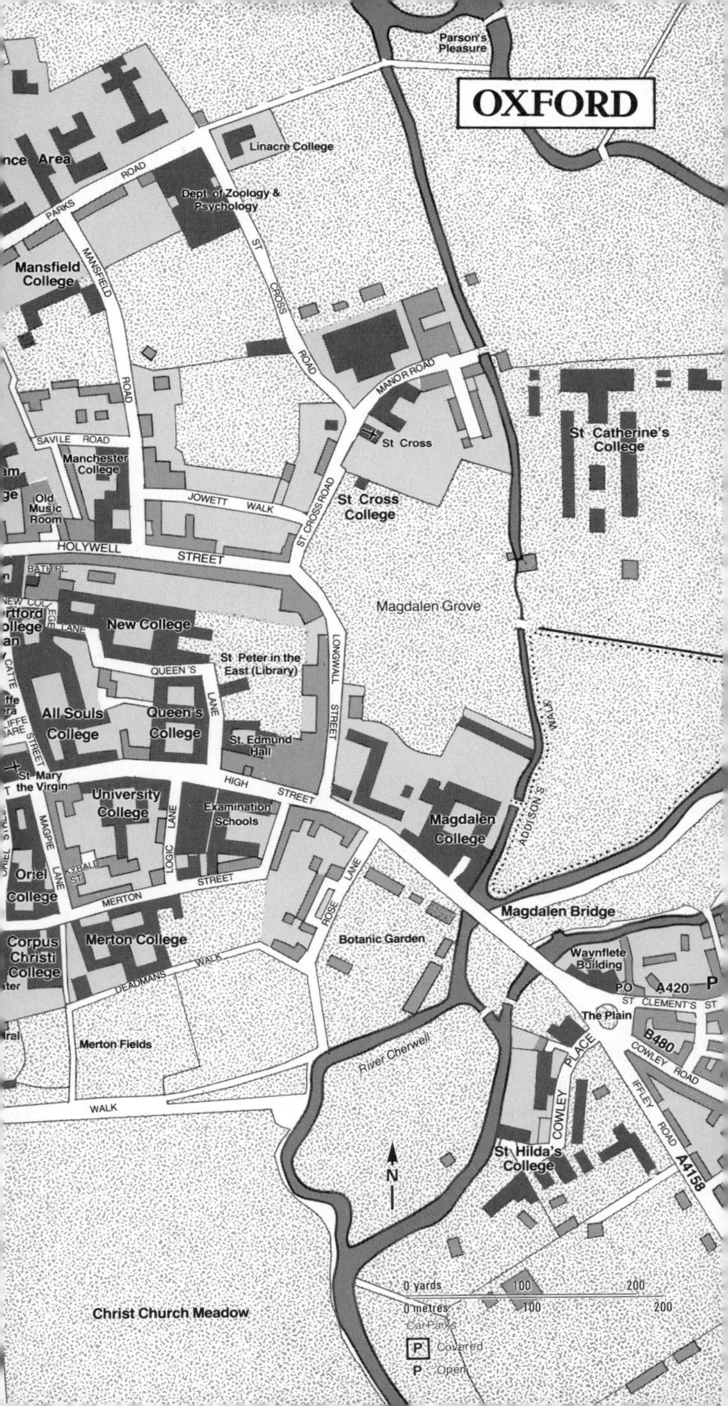
OXFORD
Parson's Pleasure
Linacre College
Dept. of Zoology & Psychology
PARKS ROAD
Mansfield College
MANSFIELD ROAD
ST CROSS ROAD
MANOR ROAD
St Cross
St Catherine's College
SAVILE ROAD
Manchester College
Old Music Room
JOWETT WALK
St Cross College
HOLYWELL STREET
BATH PL.
Magdalen Grove
New College
St Peter in the East (Library)
QUEEN'S LANE
LONGWALL STREET
All Souls College
Queen's College
St. Edmund Hall
ADDISON'S WALK
St Mary the Virgin
HIGH STREET
University College
Examination Schools
Magdalen College
MAGPIE LANE
LOGIC LANE
KYBALD ST
MERTON STREET
ROSE LANE
Oriel College
Magdalen Bridge
Corpus Christi College
Merton College
Botanic Garden
Waynflete Building
PO
A420
ST CLEMENT'S ST
The Plain
B480
COWLEY ROAD
DEADMANS WALK
Merton Fields
River Cherwell
COWLEY PLACE
IFFLEY ROAD
WALK
N
St Hilda's College
A4158
0 yards
100
200
0 metres
100
200
Christ Church Meadow
Car Parks
Covered
Open

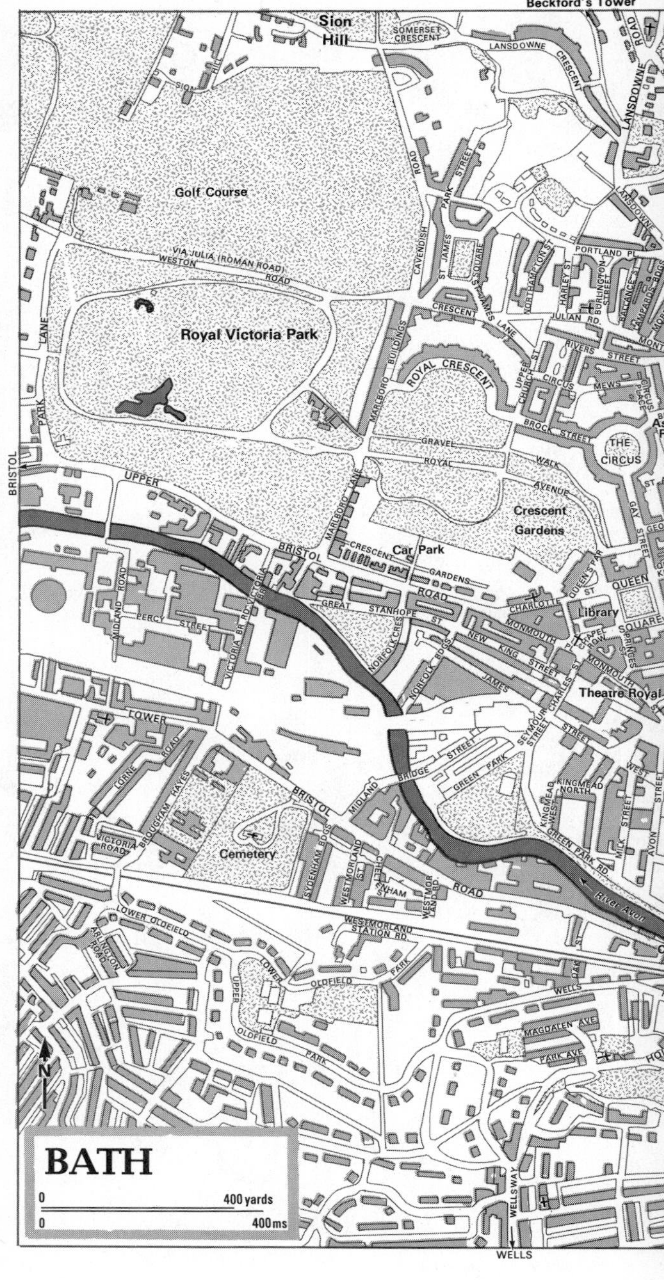

Beckford's Tower
Sion Hill
Golf Course
Royal Victoria Park
Royal Crescent
The Circus
Crescent Gardens
Car Park
Library
Queen Square
Theatre Royal
Cemetery
River Avon
Bristol
Wells
BATH
0 400 yards
0 400 ms

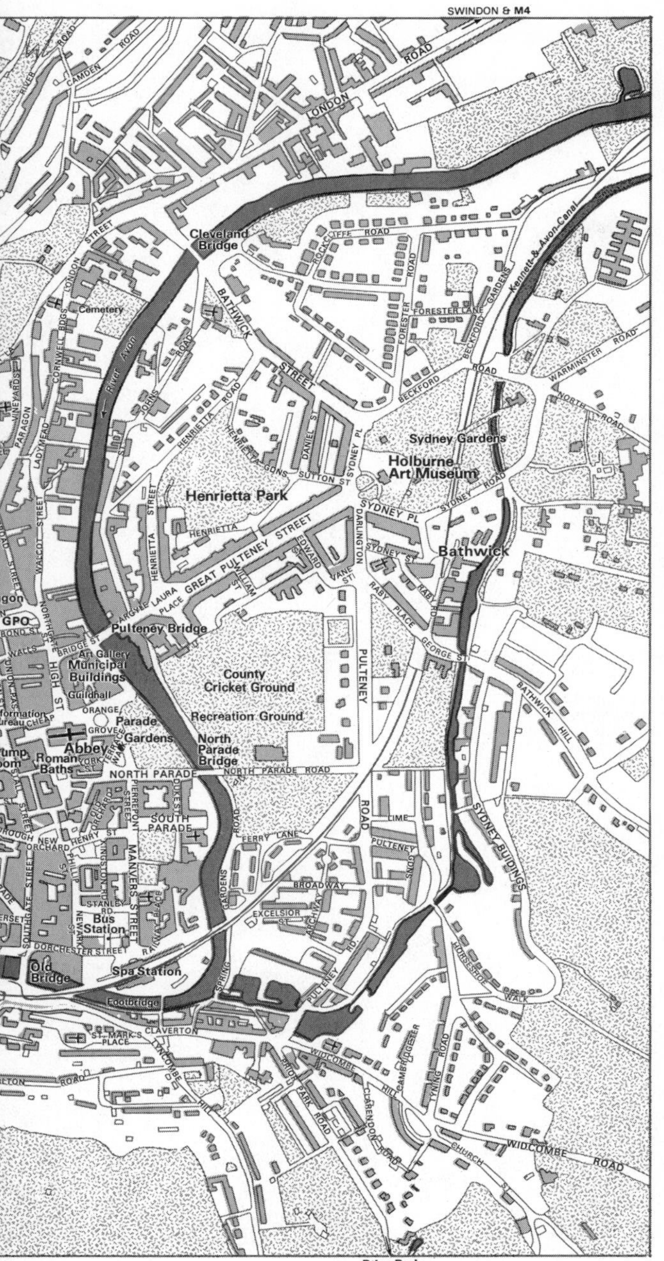

SWINDON & M4
Cleveland Bridge
Cemetery
River Avon
Kennett & Avon Canal
Sydney Gardens
Holburne Art Museum
Henrietta Park
Bathwick
GPO
Pulteney Bridge
Art Gallery
Municipal Buildings
Guildhall
County Cricket Ground
Recreation Ground
Parade Gardens
North Parade Bridge
Abbey
Roman Baths
NORTH PARADE
SOUTH PARADE
Bus Station
Old Bridge
Spa Station
Footbridge
Prior Park

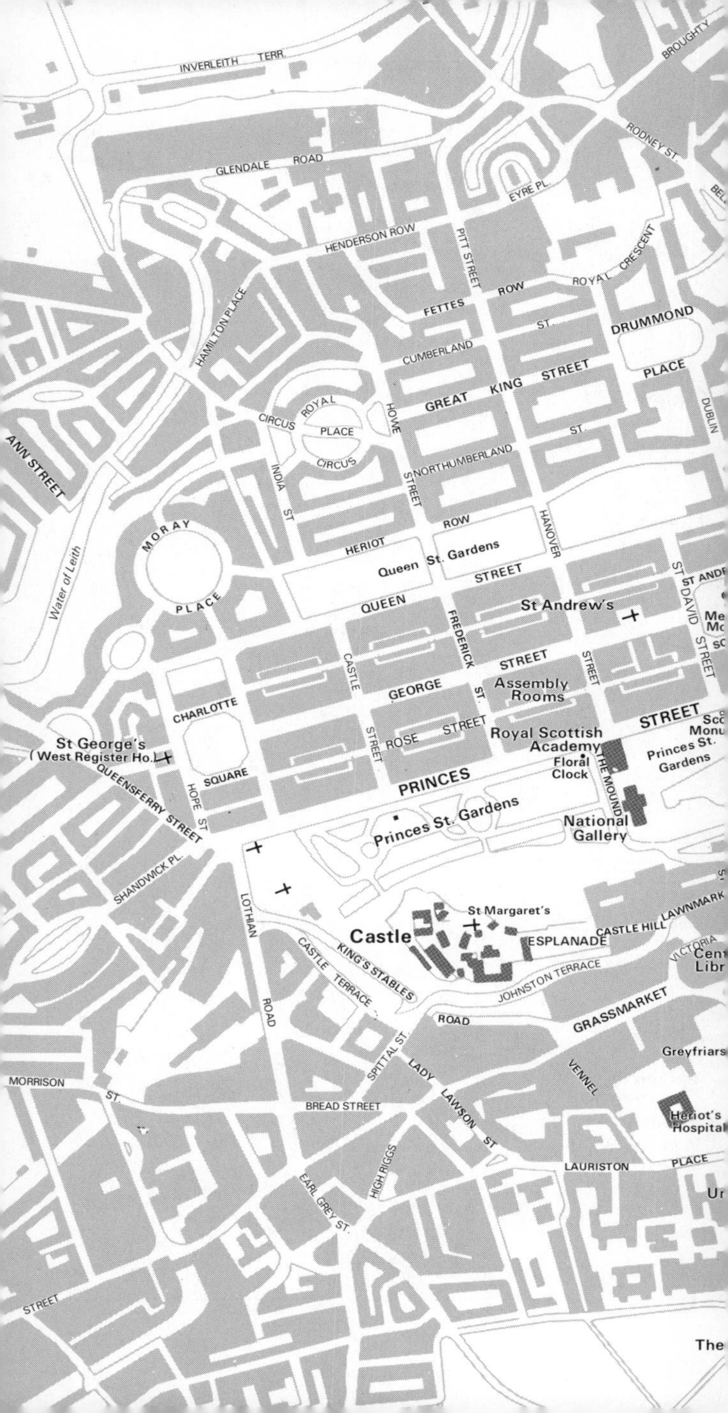
INVERLEITH TERR.
BROUGHTY
RODNEY ST.
GLENDALE ROAD
EYRE PL.
HENDERSON ROW
PITT STREET
ROYAL CRESCENT
FETTES ROW
ST.
DRUMMOND PLACE
CUMBERLAND ST.
HAMILTON PLACE
GREAT KING STREET
ROYAL CIRCUS
PLACE
CIRCUS
HOWE STREET
DUBLIN
ANN STREET
INDIA ST
NORTHUMBERLAND ST.
MORAY PLACE
HERIOT ROW
HANOVER STREET
Water of Leith
Queen St. Gardens
QUEEN STREET
ST ANDREW
St Andrew's
ST DAVID STREET
FREDERICK ST.
CASTLE STREET
GEORGE STREET
Assembly Rooms
CHARLOTTE SQUARE
ROSE STREET
Royal Scottish Academy
St George's
(West Register Ho.)
Floral Clock
THE MOUND
Princes St. Gardens
QUEENSFERRY STREET
HOPE ST
PRINCES STREET
National Gallery
SHANDWICK PL.
LOTHIAN ROAD
St Margaret's
LAWNMARKET
Castle
CASTLE HILL
CASTLE TERRACE
KING'S STABLES
ESPLANADE
VICTORIA
JOHNSTON TERRACE
GRASSMARKET
ROAD
Greyfriars
VENNEL
SPITTAL ST.
LADY LAWSON ST
MORRISON ST.
BREAD STREET
Heriot's Hospital
LAURISTON PLACE
HIGH RIGGS
EARL GREY ST.
STREET
The

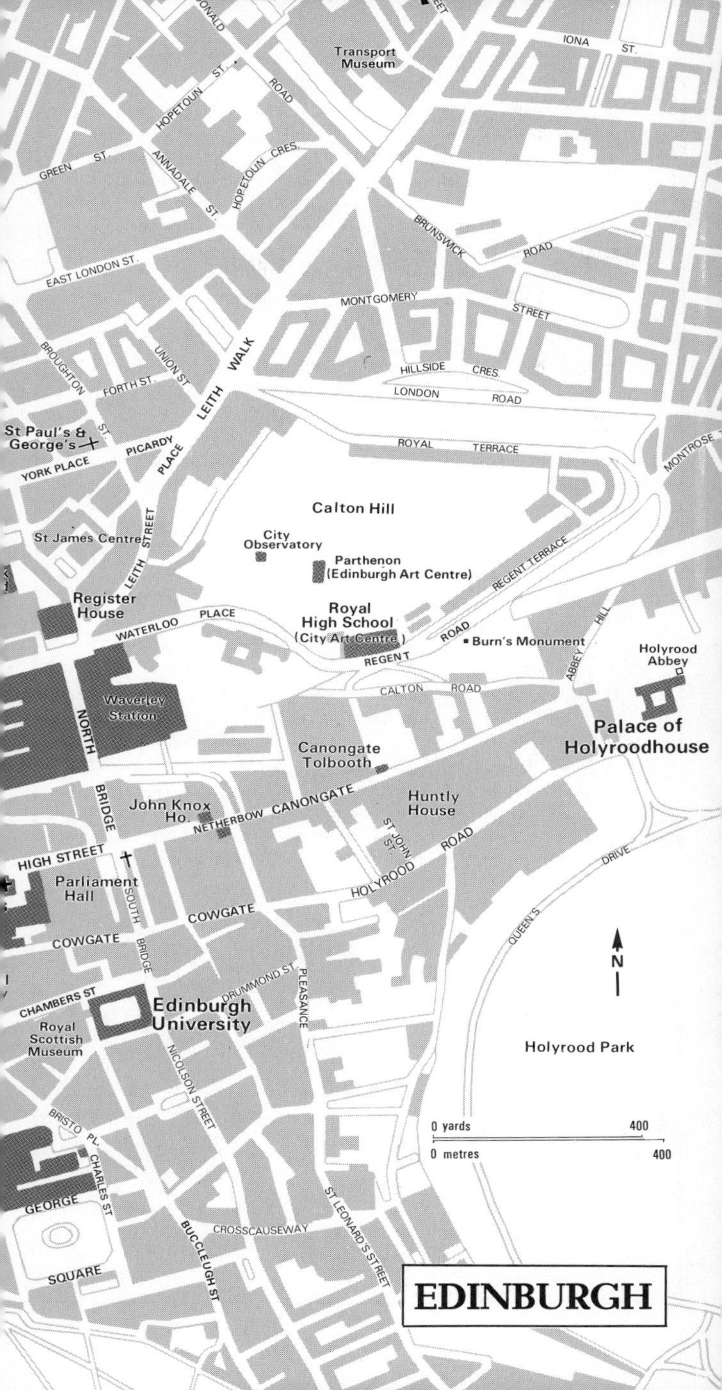
EDINBURGH
Transport Museum
IONA ST.
HOPETOUN ST.
ROAD
HOPETOUN CRES.
GREEN ST.
ANNADALE ST.
BRUNSWICK ROAD
EAST LONDON ST.
MONTGOMERY STREET
BROUGHTON ST.
UNION ST.
FORTH ST.
LEITH WALK
HILLSIDE CRES.
LONDON ROAD
St Paul's & George's
PICARDY PLACE
YORK PLACE
ROYAL TERRACE
MONTROSE
Calton Hill
City Observatory
Parthenon (Edinburgh Art Centre)
St James Centre
LEITH STREET
REGENT TERRACE
Register House
WATERLOO PLACE
Royal High School (City Art Centre)
REGENT ROAD
Burn's Monument
ABBEY HILL
Holyrood Abbey
CALTON ROAD
Waverley Station
NORTH BRIDGE
Palace of Holyroodhouse
Canongate Tolbooth
John Knox Ho.
NETHERBOW CANONGATE
Huntly House
ST JOHN ST.
HOLYROOD ROAD
HIGH STREET
Parliament Hall
SOUTH BRIDGE
COWGATE
DRIVE
QUEEN'S
N
DRUMMOND ST.
PLEASANCE
CHAMBERS ST
Edinburgh University
Royal Scottish Museum
NICOLSON STREET
Holyrood Park
BRISTO PL.
CHARLES ST
0 yards 400
0 metres 400
GEORGE SQUARE
CROSSCAUSEWAY
ST LEONARD'S STREET
BUCCLEUGH ST

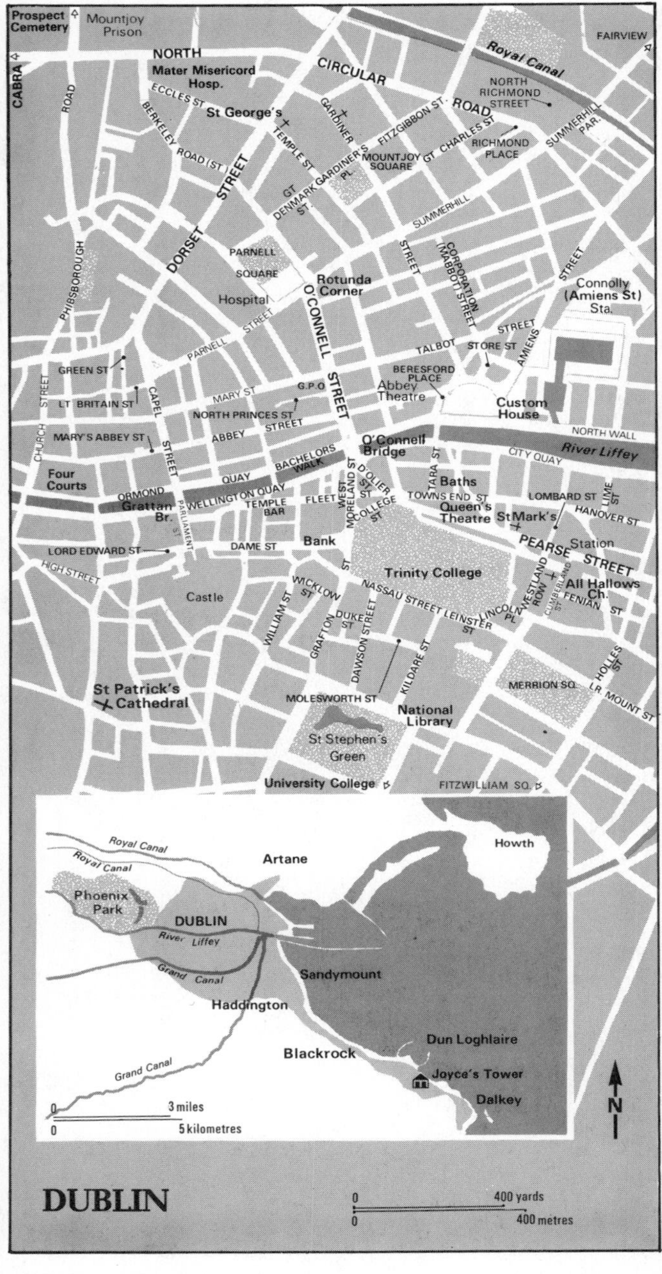

Prospect Cemetery
Mountjoy Prison
FAIRVIEW
NORTH CIRCULAR ROAD
Royal Canal
CABRA ROAD
Mater Misericord Hosp.
ECCLES ST
NORTH RICHMOND STREET
BERKELEY ROAD (ST.)
St George's
GARDINER
TEMPLE ST
FITZGIBBON ST.
GT CHARLES ST
RICHMOND PLACE
SUMMERHILL PAR.
MOUNTJOY SQUARE
GARDINER'S PL.
GT DENMARK ST.
DORSET STREET
SUMMERHILL
PHIBSBOROUGH
PARNELL SQUARE
Rotunda Corner
Hospital
STREET
CORPORATION (MABBOT) STREET
Connolly (Amiens St) Sta.
PARNELL STREET
O'CONNELL STREET
TALBOT STREET
STORE ST
AMIENS
GREEN ST
BERESFORD PLACE
Abbey Theatre
Custom House
LT BRITAIN ST
CAPEL STREET
MARY ST
G.P.O.
NORTH PRINCES ST
CHURCH STREET
MARY'S ABBEY ST
ABBEY STREET
NORTH WALL
River Liffey
O'Connell Bridge
CITY QUAY
BACHELORS WALK
QUAY
Four Courts
ORMOND
Grattan Br.
WELLINGTON QUAY
TEMPLE BAR
FLEET
WEST MORELAND ST
D'OLIER ST
COLLEGE ST
TARA ST
Baths
TOWNS END ST
LOMBARD ST
LIME ST
Queen's Theatre
St Mark's
HANOVER ST
PARLIAMENT ST
LORD EDWARD ST
DAME ST
Bank
PEARSE STREET
Station
HIGH STREET
Trinity College
Castle
WICKLOW ST
NASSAU STREET
LEINSTER ST
LINCOLN PL
WESTLAND ROW
CUMBERLAND ST
All Hallows Ch.
FENIAN ST
WILLIAM ST
GRAFTON ST
DUKE ST
DAWSON STREET
KILDARE ST
HOLLES ST
MERRION SQ.
LR. MOUNT ST
St Patrick's Cathedral
MOLESWORTH ST
National Library
St Stephen's Green
University College
FITZWILLIAM SQ.
Royal Canal
Royal Canal
Artane
Howth
Phoenix Park
DUBLIN
River Liffey
Grand Canal
Sandymount
Haddington
Dun Loghlaire
Blackrock
Joyce's Tower
Grand Canal
Dalkey
0 3 miles
0 5 kilometres
N
DUBLIN
0 400 yards
0 400 metres

Great Britain & Ireland

Kirkoswald
Girvan
STRATHCLYDE
A77
A713
A76
A74
A7
BORDERS
Hermitage
DUMFRIES AND GALLOWAY
Ecclefechan
Dumfries
Annan
A75
Castle Douglas
A75
Carlisle
M6
A596
Penrith
Workington
A66
Cockermouth
Keswick
Lake District
Whitehaven
A591
Grasmere
CUMBRIA
Rydal Mount
Windermere
Brantwood
Near Sawrey
Kendal
A595
Isle of Man
Peel
A1
Douglas
A590
Barrow-in-Furness
Lancaster
LEGEND
Town Populations
Over 500,000
100,000 - 500,000
Under 100,000
Writer's house open to the public
Clitheroe
LANCASHIRE
M55
Preston
A59
M61
M58
Wigan
LIVERPOOL
MERSEYSIDE
M53
Anglesey
Holyhead
Beaumaris
Conwy
Colwyn Bay
A55
Holywell
M56
Northwich
A5
Bangor
Denbigh
Chester
Caernarfon
Llanberis
Snowdon
Betws-y-coed
CLWYD
CHESHIRE
A41
GWYNEDD
A487
Beddgelert
A483
Wrexham
Nantwich
Tremadog
A5
Llangollen
Porthmadog
Pwllheli
A495
A41
A470
A53
Oswestry
A494
SHROPSHIRE
Dolgellau
A458
A5
Shrewsbury
POWYS
A483
Machynlleth
Montgomery
A49
A487
Newtown

NORTH ENGLAND
Scale 1 : 1 700 000
0 10 20 30 40 50 km
0 10 20 30
Berwick-upon-Tweed
Lindisfar
Norham Castle
A697
A1
Alnw
NORTHUMBERLAND
Wallington
Kirkharle
Belsay
Newcastle upon Tyne
TYNE AND WEAR
Durham
Bishop Auckland
CO DURHAM
CLEVELAND
Barnard Castle
Greta Bridge
Bowes
Darlington
Whitby
NORTH YORKSHIRE
Northallerton
Wensleydale
Rievaulx
Scarborough
Thirsk
Helmsley
Coxwold
Ripon
Castle Howard
Malham Tarn
Harrogate
York
Keighley
Haworth
LEEDS
Selby
HUMBERSIDE
Bradford
Kingston upon Hull
Halifax
WEST YORKSHIRE
Wakefield
Rochdale
Huddersfield
Scunthorpe
Barnsley
Conisbrough
Doncaster
SOUTH YORKSHIRE
MANCHESTER
SHEFFIELD
Gainsborough
Louth
Hathersage
Tetford
Somersby
Chesterfield
Bakewell
Lincoln
Horncastle
DERBYSHIRE
NOTTINGHAMSHIRE
Skegness
Matlock
Mansfield
Peak District
LINCOLNSHIRE
Southwell
Stoke-on-Trent
Newstead Abbey
Eastwood
Boston
Dovedale
Hucknall
Ashbourne
Nottingham
STAFFORDSHIRE
Grantham
Derby
Uttoxeter
Burton upon Trent
Stafford
Loughborough
Ashby-de-la-Zouch
Cannock
Lichfield
Wisbech
Leicester
Northborough
Stamford
Wolverhampton
Helpston
LEICESTERSHIRE
WEST MIDLANDS
Walsall
Hinckley
Peterborough
Nuneaton
BIRMINGHAM
Corby
Rockingham Castle
CAMBRIDGESHIRE
A1
A696
A68
A1(M)
A19
A66
A171
A170
A64
A19
A165
A163
A64
A19
A1
M62
M62
A15
M18
M180
A628
A46
A631
A15
A16
A6
A537
A158
A1
M1
A53
A46
A6
A17
A15
A606
A46
A16
A17
A1
A38
A606
A5
A47
A15
A47
M6
M69
A6
M1

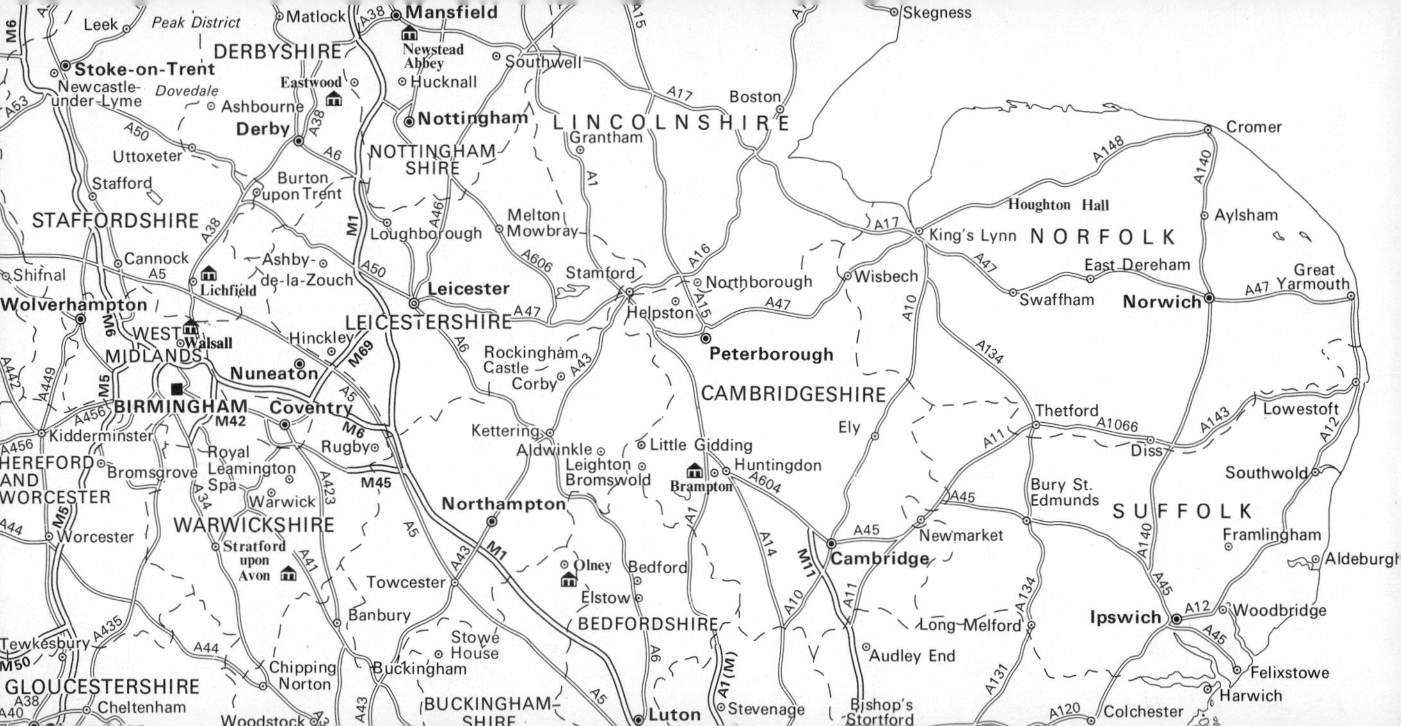

Leek
Peak District
Matlock
Mansfield
Skegness
DERBYSHIRE
Newstead Abbey
Southwell
Stoke-on-Trent
Newcastle-under-Lyme
Dovedale
Eastwood
Hucknall
Ashbourne
Derby
Nottingham
LINCOLNSHIRE
Boston
Grantham
Cromer
NOTTINGHAMSHIRE
Uttoxeter
Stafford
Burton upon Trent
Melton Mowbray
Houghton Hall
Aylsham
STAFFORDSHIRE
Loughborough
King's Lynn
NORFOLK
Cannock
Ashby-de-la-Zouch
Stamford
East Dereham
Great Yarmouth
Shifnal
Lichfield
Leicester
Northborough
Wisbech
Swaffham
Norwich
Wolverhampton
Helpston
LEICESTERSHIRE
WEST MIDLANDS
Walsall
Hinckley
Peterborough
Rockingham Castle
Corby
Nuneaton
BIRMINGHAM
Coventry
CAMBRIDGESHIRE
Thetford
Lowestoft
Kettering
Ely
Kidderminster
Rugby
Aldwinkle
Little Gidding
Diss
HEREFORD AND WORCESTER
Bromsgrove
Royal Leamington Spa
Leighton Bromswold
Huntingdon
Southwold
Brampton
Warwick
Bury St. Edmunds
SUFFOLK
Northampton
WARWICKSHIRE
Worcester
Newmarket
Framlingham
Stratford upon Avon
Olney
Bedford
Cambridge
Aldeburgh
Towcester
Elstow
Ipswich
Woodbridge
Banbury
BEDFORDSHIRE
Long Melford
Tewkesbury
Stowe House
Audley End
Chipping Norton
Buckingham
Felixstowe
GLOUCESTERSHIRE
Harwich
Cheltenham
BUCKINGHAMSHIRE
Stevenage
Bishop's Stortford
Woodstock
Luton
Colchester
M6
A53
A50
A38
A6
A46
A17
A15
A1
A148
A140
M1
A606
A16
A47
A5
A50
M69
M6
M5
A442
A449
A456
M42
A43
A10
A134
A143
A12
A11
A1066
A45
A44
A34
A423
M45
A604
A14
M11
A41
A435
A131
A120
M50
A40
A1(M)

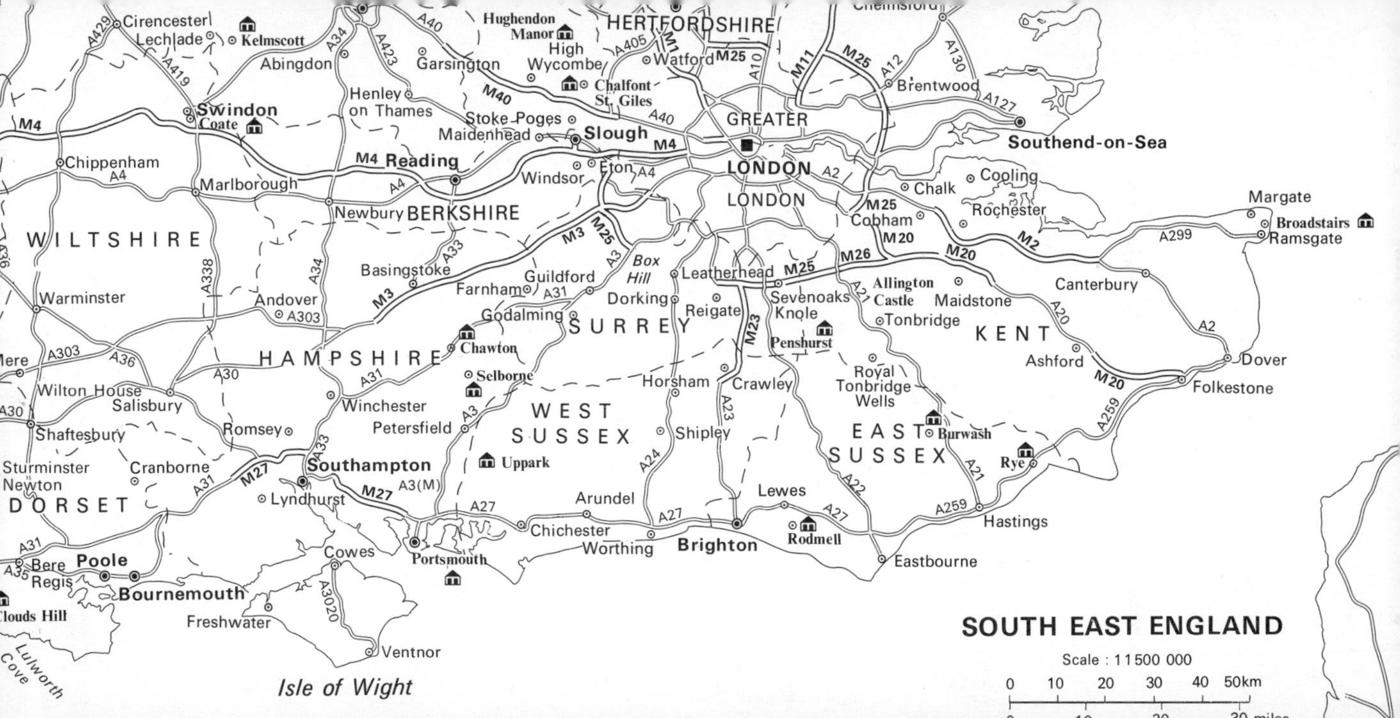

SOUTH EAST ENGLAND
Scale : 1 1 500 000
0 10 20 30 40 50km
30 miles
HERTFORDSHIRE
GREATER LONDON
BERKSHIRE
WILTSHIRE
HAMPSHIRE
SURREY
KENT
WEST SUSSEX
EAST SUSSEX
DORSET
Isle of Wight
LONDON
Cirencester
Lechlade
Kelmscott
Abingdon
Garsington
Hughendon Manor
High Wycombe
Watford
Chalfont St. Giles
Brentwood
Southend-on-Sea
Swindon
Coate
Henley on Thames
Stoke Poges
Maidenhead
Slough
Reading
Chippenham
Marlborough
Newbury
Windsor
Eton
Chalk
Cooling
Rochester
Cobham
Margate
Broadstairs
Ramsgate
Basingstoke
Guildford
Box Hill
Farnham
Leatherhead
Dorking
Reigate
Sevenoaks
Knole
Allington Castle
Maidstone
Tonbridge
Canterbury
Warminster
Andover
Godalming
Penshurst
Chawton
Selborne
Royal Tonbridge Wells
Ashford
Dover
Folkestone
Horsham
Crawley
Wilton House
Salisbury
Winchester
Petersfield
Shipley
Burwash
Shaftesbury
Romsey
Uppark
Rye
Sturminster Newton
Cranborne
Southampton
Lyndhurst
Arundel
Lewes
Rodmell
Hastings
Chichester
Worthing
Brighton
Eastbourne
Cowes
Portsmouth
Bere Regis
Poole
Bournemouth
Clouds Hill
Freshwater
Ventnor
Lulworth Cove
M4
M40
M1
M25
M11
M3
M2
M20
M26
M23
M27
A3(M)
A429
A419
A34
A423
A40
A405
A10
A12
A130
A127
A4
A2
A299
A33
A3
A31
A21
A20
A338
A303
A36
A30
A24
A23
A22
A27
A259
A35
A3020

Machynlleth
Montgomery
Newtown
Shifnal
Wolverhampton
WEST MIDLANDS
BIRMINGHAM
SHROPSHIRE
Aberystwyth
Devil's Bridge
Hagley
Ludlow
Kidderminster
Bromsgrove
Llandrindod Wells
Leominster
Worcester
Cardigan
HEREFORD AND WORCESTER
Malvern Hills
Great Malvern
POWYS
DYFED
Fishguard
Llandovery
Hereford
Ledbury
Tewkesbury
Brecon
Ross-on-Wye
Carmarthen
Haverfordwest
Milford Haven
Grongar Hill
Goodrich
Cheltenham
Gloucester
Laugharne
Monmouth
Abergavenny
Pembroke
Llanelli
WEST GLAMORGAN
Merthyr Tydfil
GLOUCESTERSHIRE
Bibury
Tintern Abbey
Cirencester
Neath
MID GLAMORGAN
GWENT
Swansea
Port Talbot
Chepstow
Newport
Porthcawl
SOUTH GLAMORGAN
Cardiff
Clevedon
Bristol
Chippenham
AVON
Weston-Super-
A470
A487
A44
A483
A49
A442
A456
A449
A435
M5
A484
A40
A465
M50
A477
A48
A470
A449
A46
A419
M4
A429
M32
A370
A4

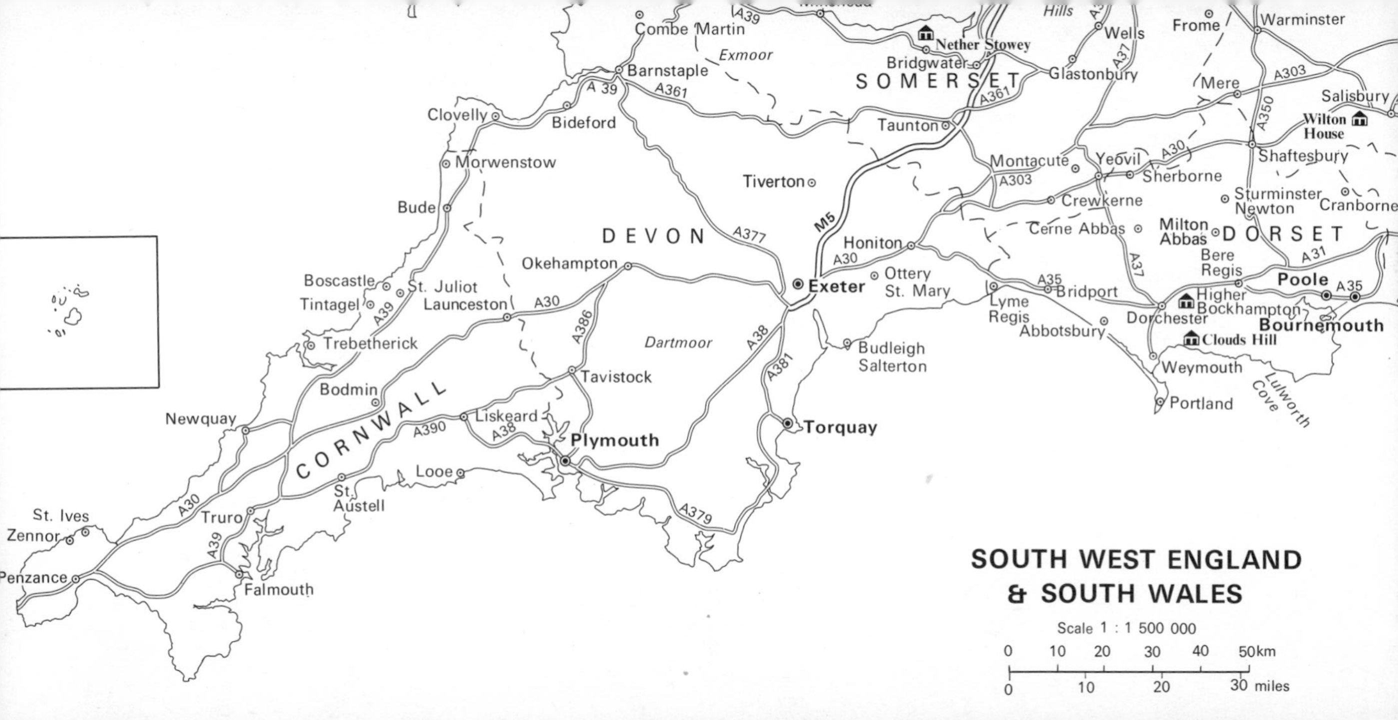
SOUTH WEST ENGLAND
& SOUTH WALES
Scale 1 : 1 500 000
0 10 20 30 40 50km
0 10 20 30 miles
CORNWALL
DEVON
SOMERSET
DORSET
Exmoor
Dartmoor
Hills
Combe Martin
Barnstaple
Bideford
Clovelly
Morwenstow
Bude
Boscastle
Tintagel
St. Juliot
Launceston
Trebetherick
Bodmin
Newquay
St. Ives
Zennor
Penzance
Truro
Falmouth
St. Austell
Looe
Liskeard
Plymouth
Tavistock
Okehampton
Tiverton
Exeter
Honiton
Ottery St. Mary
Budleigh Salterton
Torquay
Taunton
Bridgwater
Nether Stowey
Glastonbury
Wells
Frome
Warminster
Mere
Salisbury
Wilton House
Shaftesbury
Montacute
Yeovil
Sherborne
Crewkerne
Cerne Abbas
Milton Abbas
Sturminster Newton
Cranborne
Bere Regis
Lyme Regis
Bridport
Abbotsbury
Dorchester
Higher Bockhampton
Clouds Hill
Weymouth
Portland
Lulworth Cove
Poole
Bournemouth
M5
A30
A35
A37
A38
A39
A303
A350
A361
A377
A379
A381
A386
A390
A31

Stornoway
A859
Lewis
Amhuinnsuid
Hebrides
Western Islands
Harris
Outer
North Uist
South Uist
Dunvegan
Kingsburgh
A850
A863
Skye
Rum
Eigg
Hebrides
Mallaig
A830
Fort William
Kyle of Lochalsh
Glenelg
A87
A890
A832
A835
Ullapool
A837
A838
A836
Thurso
A882
A9
Wick
Lairg
Alness
Cromarty
Fortrose
Nairn
Cawdor
Inverness
HIGHLAND
A82
A86
Newtonmore
A95
Forres
Elgin
Huntly
GRAMPIAN
A98
Fraserburgh
A92
Peterhead
Cruden Bay
Ellon
A96
Aberdeen
A93
Ballater
Braemar
Stonehaven
A94

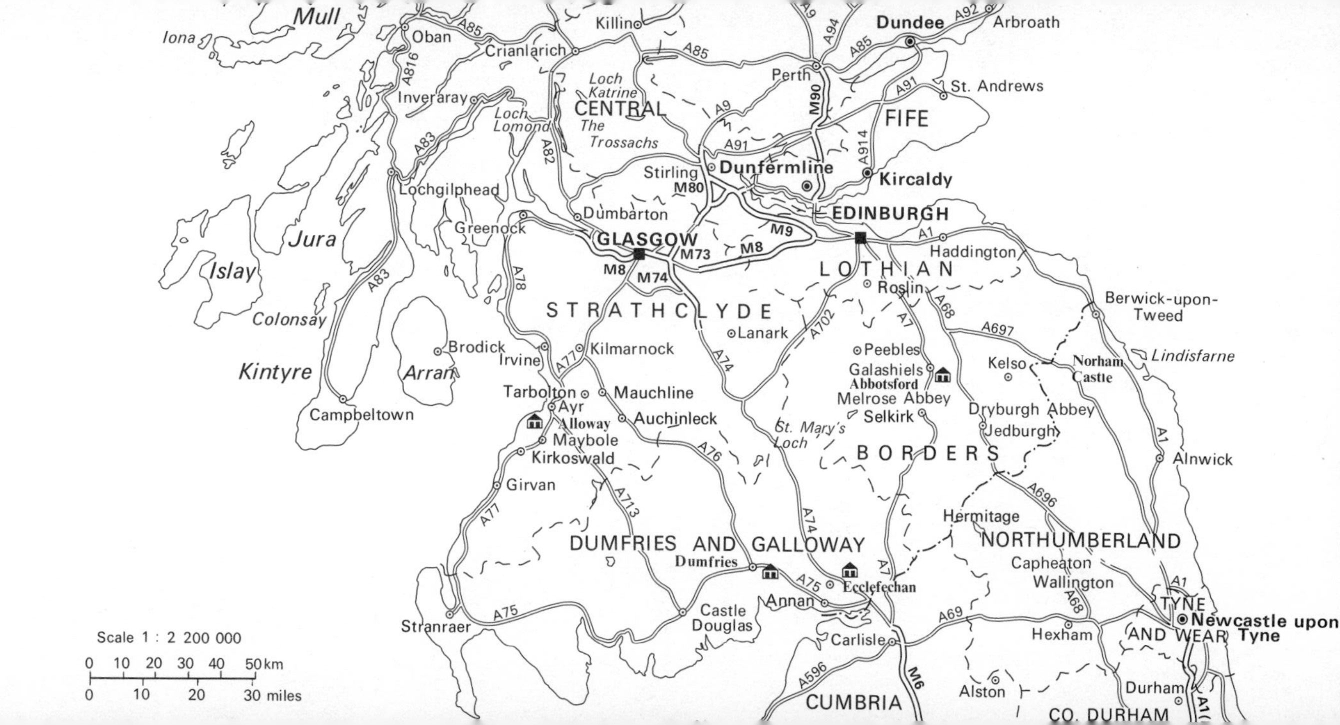

Mull
Iona
Oban
Crianlarich
Killin
Dundee
Arbroath
Perth
St. Andrews
Loch Katrine
CENTRAL
The Trossachs
Loch Lomond
Inveraray
FIFE
Stirling
Dunfermline
Kircaldy
EDINBURGH
Lochgilphead
Dumbarton
Greenock
GLASGOW
Haddington
LOTHIAN
Roslin
Jura
Islay
Colonsay
Kintyre
STRATHCLYDE
Lanark
Berwick-upon-Tweed
Lindisfarne
Brodick
Arran
Irvine
Kilmarnock
Peebles
Galashiels
Abbotsford
Kelso
Norham Castle
Tarbolton
Mauchline
Ayr
Alloway
Auchinleck
Maybole
Kirkoswald
Campbeltown
Melrose Abbey
Selkirk
St. Mary's Loch
Dryburgh Abbey
Jedburgh
BORDERS
Alnwick
Girvan
Hermitage
DUMFRIES AND GALLOWAY
Dumfries
NORTHUMBERLAND
Capheaton
Wallington
Ecclefechan
Annan
Castle Douglas
Stranraer
Carlisle
Hexham
TYNE AND WEAR
Newcastle upon Tyne
Alston
Durham
CUMBRIA
CO. DURHAM
A85
A816
A83
A82
A9
A94
A92
A91
A914
M90
M80
M9
M8
M73
M74
A1
A68
A697
A7
A702
A74
A78
A77
A76
A713
A75
A696
A69
A596
M6
Scale 1 : 2 200 000
0 10 20 30 40 50 km
0 10 20 30 miles

Scale 1 : 2 200 000
0 10 20 30 40 50km
0 10 20 30miles
Kintyre
Campbeltown
Brodick
Arran
Gweedorn
Letterkenny
DONEGAL
Donegal
Londonderry
LONDONDERRY
Coleraine
Strabane
Ballymena
ANTRIM
Larne
TYRONE
Cookstown
Omagh
Carrickfergus
Belfast
Bangor
Newtownards
Dungannon
Drumcliff
Sligo
Lough Gill
Enniskillen
FERMANAGH
Portadown
Armagh
ARMAGH
DOWN
Downpatrick
Ballina
SLIGO
Monaghar
MONAGHAN
Newry
Newcastle
Castlebar
Boyle
LEITRIM
Cavan
Dundalk
MAYO
ROSCOMMON
CAVAN
Claremorris
Longford
Edgeworthstown
LONG-
FORD
Drogheda
A2
A26
A29
A5
A6
N15
M2
A8
A32
A4
M1
A3
A1
A7
N16
N59
N4
N17
N55
N2
N5
N3
N60
N1
N61

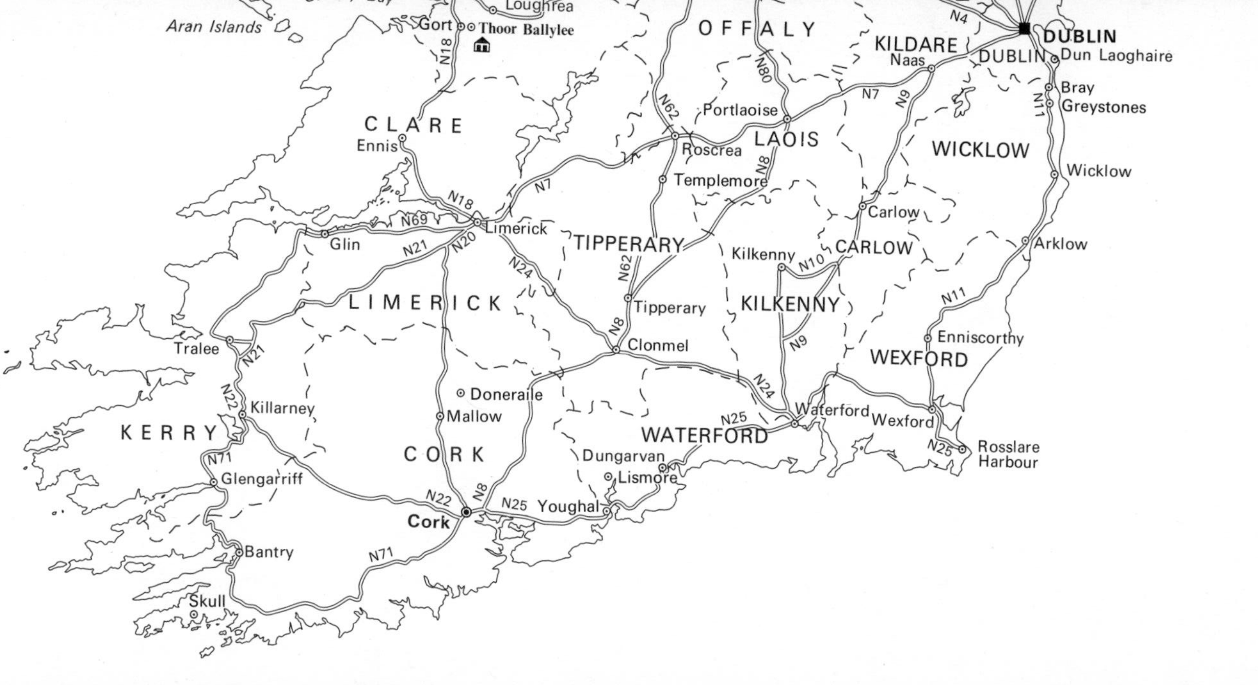

Aran Islands
Loughrea
Gort
Thoor Ballylee
N18
CLARE
Ennis
N69
N18
Limerick
Glin
N21
N20
N7
OFFALY
N80
N62
Portlaoise
LAOIS
Roscrea
Templemore
N8
TIPPERARY
N62
Tipperary
N24
N8
Clonmel
KILDARE
Naas
N4
N7
N9
DUBLIN
DUBLIN
Dun Laoghaire
Bray
Greystones
N11
WICKLOW
Wicklow
Carlow
CARLOW
Arklow
Kilkenny
N10
KILKENNY
N9
N11
Enniscorthy
WEXFORD
Wexford
Rosslare
Harbour
N25
N24
Waterford
N25
WATERFORD
Dungarvan
Lismore
Youghal
N25
LIMERICK
Tralee
N21
N22
Killarney
KERRY
N71
Glengarriff
Doneraile
Mallow
CORK
N22
N8
Cork
N71
Bantry
Skull